Night Sky and Red Crystal

Clare Francis is the author of five internationally best-selling thrillers, *Night Sky*, *Red Crystal*, *Wolf Winter*, *Requiem* and *Deceit*. She has also written three non-fiction books about her voyages across the oceans of the world.

Clare Francis

NIGHT SKY

AND

RED CRYSTAL

PAN BOOKS
IN ASSOCIATION WITH WILLIAM HEINEMANN

Night Sky first published 1983 by William Heinemann Ltd
and first published by Pan Books Ltd 1984 in association with
William Heinemann Ltd.

Red Crystal first published 1985 by William Heinemann Ltd
and first published by Pan Books Ltd 1986 in association with
William Heinemann Ltd.

This combined edition published 1994 by Pan Books
a division of Macmillan General Books
Cavaye Place, London SW10 9PG
and Basingstoke
in association with William Heinemann Ltd

Associated companies throughout the world

ISBN 0 330 34153 7

1 3 5 7 9 8 6 4 2

A CIP catalogue record for this book is available from
the British Library

Printed and bound in Great Britain by
Cox & Wyman Ltd, Reading, Berkshire

Night Sky

For my son, Thomas

ACKNOWLEDGEMENTS: My thanks to David Birkin, who navigated motor gunboats on clandestine missions during the war, and who let me study his collection of original charts and log books; to David Beaty and Tony Spooner, who flew Wellingtons and Liberators on U-boat hunting operations and were kind enough to provide me with much useful information; to Patrick Beesly for his help on the U-boat tracking techniques used by the Admiralty during the war; and to Robin Coventry and Sir Brooks Richards for their long and informative letters.

Contents

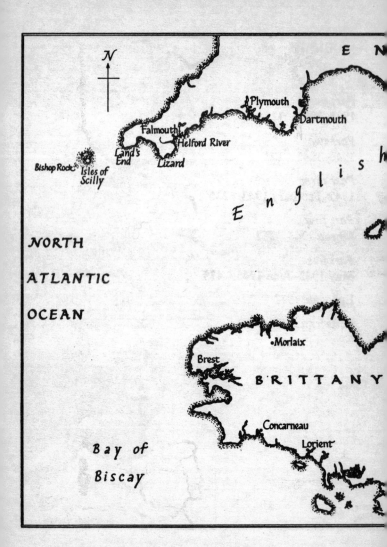

Part one
1935–1939

1

He was in a tiny dark cupboard, the door locked, the air foul and hot. Outside he could hear voices, sometimes loud and coarse, sometimes low and secretive. He tried to call out but he could make no sound. His body would not move, though nothing held it down. At some point he must have wet the bed, for the sheet underneath him was damp. Then his stomach heaved and without warning a thick trail of vomit streamed out, covering the pillow, clogging his hair. He was desperate to clean up the mess, but there was no water, no cloth, so he tried to mop it up with a corner of the sheet, wretched with the knowledge that this too was a mistake.

He lay back on the bed, shivering despite the heat. Tears of misery rolled down his cheeks and he cried a single '*Maman!*' Then he remembered that he was not allowed to call out, that he must stay silent. The loneliness enveloped him; he wanted to close his eyes and sleep for ever.

There were voices again now: his mother's, steady and light, and a man's, low and furtive. The voices droned on, then rose to a higher pitch. There was a scream, then silence. Suddenly he was in a room and he saw his mother lying motionless on a bed. She was held down by the man, her arms twisted behind her, unable to move. Then she looked up at the man, her lips open, her teeth bared. She did not cry out; instead she smiled. His mother and the man moved in a strange way he did not understand. Then the picture faded.

He was in the cupboard again, unable to breathe, suffocating with the heat. He could hear voices still, but they were more distant now. The despair pressed in on him, crushing and hopeless. But this time he did not cry: he was learning how not to cry. He felt as if he had been alone all his life.

Paul Vasson woke with a start. For an instant he couldn't remember where he was. Then he recognised the familiar outlines of the shabby room and, exhaling slowly, sank back onto the pillow. The voices from the dream murmured on. He listened and realised that they were floating up from the street outside. One, with a thick Provençal accent, he recognised as that of the old concierge next door. He closed his eyes and tried to sleep again. But it was no use. He had been dozing fitfully for less than half an hour and now he was wide awake.

He sat up and swung his legs to the floor. His mouth felt dry, his stomach unsteady. It was the fear. And worse than he'd imagined:

stabbing, cold, dragging him down. The nightmare hadn't helped either. The dream was always the same: the small room, the locked door, the suffocating heat. And such detail – so vivid. He remembered the shame of discovery and how, when his mother opened the door, he had wept even before she struck him. Later she had washed and dressed him in clean clothes and then – then she had given him a brief kiss on top of the head.

Or had that one startling kiss happened some other time?

He got up suddenly and, groping for the shutters, let in a small shaft of warm afternoon sunlight. He never let in too much light: it showed up the shabby furniture and the peeling paintwork.

He wondered what the time was – probably about four. Still too early to go out. He picked up *La Dépêche du Midi* from the floor and flopped back on to the bed. The headlines didn't interest him: half a million unemployed; France protesting against something called the Anglo-German Naval Treaty; increasing numbers of Jewish refugees arriving in France from Germany.

He skipped to the sports pages but couldn't concentrate and threw the newspaper back on to the floor.

God, he was nervous.

He stood up abruptly and walked naked across the room. Taking a clean towel from the dresser, he wrapped it round his waist and poured some water into a tin bowl that stood on the only table. He splashed his face and looked into the small mirror above. Usually he avoided mirrors, they made him uneasy, but today he wanted to be sure he looked normal, *ordinary*. The thin face stared back at him, the eyes small and dark. And frightened. Mustn't show the fear. Dear Lord.

Picking up a razor, he scraped at the soft stubble that sprouted unevenly on his chin. After a while he dropped his hand and, staring into the mirror, swore quietly. His skin, always sallow, had developed a yellow-grey tinge. He shivered and felt his stomach twist with griping pain. He realised with disgust that he must get to the WC and quickly.

He hurried out of the room and made for a door at the far side of the landing. He went in and almost retched. A foul stench rose from the pan and he saw that it was blocked. There was another WC two floors down, but there wasn't enough time. He crouched miserably on the seat, muttering, 'Dear Mother of God!'

The spasms faded at last and, his bowels empty, Vasson got to his feet and stepped quickly on to the landing, gasping for fresh air. He stood for a moment, listening. The house was quiet. Faint street sounds drifted up the stairwell and the murmur of snores floated across the landing. Most of the women were asleep or out, though some might have customers. No-one had seen him.

He went back into his room and was sure of one thing – he would go ahead with what had to be done. There was no going back, no giving up, not if he was to get out of this terrible place.

And he had to get out.

It wasn't just the filth and the disgusting women, it was the humiliation. The *Patron* had put him in charge of this house on purpose, just to humiliate him, he was certain of that. Any cheap *mac* in the *quartier* could have done the job. The women were old, worn-out and pathetic, their only customers drunks or perverts. He loathed the sight of them. The job was an insult.

At first Vasson had thought that the job was a testing ground, that after a short time the *Patron* would ask him into the Business itself. But after six months he realised the move would never come. The *Patron* was purposely excluding him from the real action, purposely keeping him here in this hole. Treating him like rubbish. A very stupid man.

He dressed carefully, choosing old but freshly ironed cotton trousers and a cool white shirt. He hesitated over the choice of shoes: his old ones were badly worn now, while the new ones hidden in their box were tantalisingly smart. They were two-tone black and white in softest Moroccan leather and very expensive. But too risky, he finally decided. The most junior of house-minders did not have money for things like that.

He leant down and unlocked the bottom drawer of the old *commode*. He went through the contents carefully: new suit in pale blue linen, white silk shirt, tie, cotton socks, and a wallet, including identity card, driving licence and seven thousand francs in large notes. He was particularly pleased with the suit: it had been a real bargain. At first Goldrich, the tailor, had pressed him for the full price but Vasson had soon worn him down. Belonging to an organisation did have one advantage: people didn't argue with you. Anyway, Goldrich was a Jew and Jews could always afford to reduce their prices.

The identity papers had taken a lot of finding. But, as Vasson kept reminding himself, they were almost untraceable and therefore worth every bit of the effort. He had gone to Lyons, though it had meant a tedious two-hour train journey. But the further from Marseilles the better. Even if the worst came to the worst and they thought of checking up, Lyons was an unlikely place to go for documents. Anyway, they wouldn't find anything: Vasson had avoided going to the local dealer – even if one existed, which he doubted. Instead he

15

had watched outside the Collège des Sciences Physiques in the Rue de la Trinité until, after two long days, he had finally seen a student who bore a resemblance to himself. The youth's height and colouring were right and Vasson judged his age to be about twenty-one or twenty-two. Vasson himself was twenty-three, but he never thought of himself as young. He had never felt young, even when he was a child.

He had followed the youth back to a tall ugly house on the edge of the town and seen a light come on in a top left hand window. Vasson had been sick at the thought of what he might have to do next: he loathed the idea of physical violence. But there was little possibility of the student leaving his wallet and identity card lying around in the daytime. Vasson would have to take them while the boy slept, although the risk of discovery – and of having to defend himself – was appalling.

As it was, the whole thing had been ridiculously easy. The side door of the house had been open and then, astonishingly, the student's door too. Vasson's heart had hammered so loudly that the *tête de con* must surely hear, but no, he slept on and it had taken only minutes for Vasson to find the wallet lying casually on a side table. He had crept out, sick with excitement, and vomited in the alleyway beside the house.

The wallet contained an identity card in the name of Jean-Marie Biolet, aged twenty-two, resident of 17, Rue Madeleine in the town of St Etienne. Vasson had been rather disappointed in the photograph: the likeness was not as good as he'd hoped. But a change of hairstyle and some glasses would hide the differences. The driving licence was a real bonus though, and more than made up for the photograph.

Vasson was immensely pleased with the result of his three-day excursion. He could easily have bought an identity card on the Marseilles market, but that would have been stupid: once the pressure was on, someone, somewhere, would have talked. As it was the card in the name of Jean-Marie Biolet could never be linked to Vasson. The knowledge gave him deep satisfaction. The identity would mean a complete break with the past. After today Paul Vasson, born in the Old Quarter of Marseilles, would cease to exist. The thought gave him a curious thrill.

Vasson examined the last item in the drawer: a leather money-belt. The remaining two hundred thousand francs should fit into the neat pouches, but he couldn't be sure until he actually got hold of the money and tried it in place. He'd asked for large notes, as large as possible, but they would still take up a lot of space. He would have to worry about that when the time came.

Vasson locked the drawer again and looked round the room. He picked up his washing things and put them into a hold-all with his raincoat and felt hat. He would leave the rest of his possessions; they would be no loss, no loss at all.

His eye caught a magazine cutting pinned to the wall above the bed and he took it down. It was an advertisement showing a stylised drawing of a car. Vasson examined it closely as he had a hundred times before. It was a D8SS Delage. The most beautiful, *perfect*, thing in the world.

He had often imagined what it must be like to drive such a thing, to feel it round your body: the leather seats, the throb of the 4-litre engine accelerating to over 160 kilometres an hour, and the shiny newness of the long, smooth body, as sleek as a cat's.

He folded the cutting and put it in his wallet. Soon – by tonight – he would have enough money to buy a D8SS. The thought made him sick with excitement and he almost giggled.

The air was very still, the cooling wind that sometimes wafted up from the harbour had died away and the atmosphere in the room was stifling. It was still a bit early to meet Jojo, but suddenly Vasson had to leave, to get going before he started thinking too much. Thinking was all right when he was making plans: he liked planning. But it was no good now – he kept thinking about what might go wrong.

Anyway it was too late now.

And then he remembered with a jolt that it really *was* too late.

He ran quickly down the stairs and out into the cobbled street, blinking at the harsh afternoon light. The Old Quarter was crowded and he had to push his way through knots of people meandering along the hot narrow alleys. A couple of Arabs walked towards him, their arms around each other, and Vasson cursed as he was forced to step round them. One of the Arabs laughed and brushed his lips across the other's bearded cheek. Bare-footed children were playing in the doorways while their mothers hung washing between the tall crumbling houses and leaned over the latticed balconies, shouting at one another.

Vasson regarded the scene with distaste: it had not changed since he had been a child here twenty years before. The people lived like pigs, squashed together. They had no will to change, no drive to escape. They were happy to exist like this all their wretched lives.

A child came pelting out of a doorway, shouting with laughter, and ran straight under Vasson's feet so that he almost tripped. He swore loudly. The child swerved quickly away and scampered down an alleyway, its feet flying. Vasson watched it angrily, half determined to chase after it. Suddenly the small figure lurched and fell forward onto the cobblestones, its limbs sprawled.

Vasson felt glad: it served the little devil right. The child did not move. Vasson wandered up the alley and looked down at it. He prodded its ribs with his foot. The child slowly lifted its head and turned towards him, its bleeding face crumpled with misery. Vasson stood and watched. The child lowered its head again and began to cry noisily.

There was something despairing about the sobbing shoulders. Tentatively Vasson reached down and touched the child. The child seemed not to notice. He grasped the small body and lifted it to its feet, holding it at arms' length. It was a strange sensation, to be holding a child. He patted the child's cheek rather brusquely. 'All right?'

The child did not answer but continued to cry. Vasson went on one knee and, very slowly, pulled the child towards him, putting an arm round the narrow shoulders. He felt the child stiffen. 'Don't touch me, you bastard!' The small face, so close to his, was ugly with contempt. Vasson got hastily to his feet and choked back his anger. The child ran off, screaming obscenities.

Vasson strode furiously back into the street. The bloody child had tricked him, made a fool of him. Children were no different from anyone else, he thought bitterly; they were out to get you, like the rest.

He turned on to the quay and hurried along the harbour, but went past the street where Jojo lived. Only when he felt calmer did he go back and walk up to Jojo's. He was still half an hour early. He paused, wondering whether to wait in the street or go straight up to the apartment.

It was the thought of Jojo's woman that made him hesitate.

She was a bitch, first class. She made Vasson feel uneasy. She was crafty, clever, like a cat, and, when she wanted to she could make people feel small – especially men who didn't go for her. Not that there were many of those. She was beautiful in a flashy grotesquely physical sort of way and men made fools of themselves over her. Vasson always went out of his way to avoid her.

Also, she was a whore.

For several minutes Vasson leant against the wall, full of indecision, angry he should be nervous of the wretched woman.

But suddenly he made up his mind and strode into the building, thinking: Christ, what the hell am I worrying about?

Today Jojo's woman was going to be the very least of his problems.

*

Solange lay on the bed and drew heavily on her cigarette. She noticed that her hands were shaking. She wasn't surprised: she'd never been so angry in her life. Her temper was, she knew, appalling. But it wasn't her fault, it was just the way she was made. It was the mixed blood or something. She liked to think she had some of the gentle qualities of her Cambodian mother, but her father seemed to come out in her every time. He had been half-French, half-Martinican, and his favourite sport was fighting. He'd died in a bar brawl.

Jojo had finally gone too far. She loved him most of the time but at other times she could kill him. This afternoon was one of the times when she could positively strangle him. Why, oh why couldn't he get going and actually *do* something? All he did was talk – and even then he backtracked.

There were sounds from the tiny kitchen and she guessed that Jojo was making some of his beloved black treacly coffee. She considered whether to go in and have it out with him again but she knew it would end the same way as before, with her throwing something. Just half an hour ago it had been an ashtray – the shards were still lying on the floor – but as usual Jojo had ignored her.

The row had been about the same old subject: their future.

They had discussed their plans more times than she could count. At first Solange had loved going over the details, it really used to cheer her up. The idea was simple: as soon as they had saved enough money they were going to take an apartment off La Canebière. Something really smart with large rooms and a beautiful bathroom, and live there together, just the two of them. During the day Solange would see her high-class punters, but strictly by appointment; she would have a maid-cum-secretary, dressed in elegant black, to answer the door and the telephone. Then Jojo and she would have the evenings all to themselves, they would walk down La Canebière and look at all the smart shops and visit the top restaurants, like that La Babayette place where the waiters wore stiff collars and the *crêpes* were *flambéed* at the table.

It was all going to be wonderful. She just *knew* their new life would be a success.

Solange had saved nearly all the money, even though it had meant taking on punters she could normally have turned over to someone else.

Then Jojo had got cold feet. He had started to mutter about the problems, always the problems. Solange had the unpleasant feeling he was just frightened, nervous of the *Patron* and how the old man would feel about it. To hell with it – girls had left the *Patron*'s establishments before and nothing had happened. Jojo was just a goddam coward.

It was more than she could bear to think of staying on at the Red House. It was a dead-end job: the decent punters didn't dare be seen round the place too often because of its reputation, though they all said they would love to visit her more often. And those who *did* come regularly were rubbish: no finesse, no style at all. Solange admired style.

She deserved better, everyone said so. But she couldn't get out on her own, she had no illusions about that. She needed Jojo to protect her, and she needed him *now*, damn it.

Jojo appeared in the kitchen doorway and she could see that he was still sore with her. He was avoiding her eyes and shuffling his feet like a spoilt child. Suddenly she didn't have the energy to yell at him any more. Her frustration and rage began to evaporate. She went towards him and hugged his back. 'I'm sorry.'

Jojo pulled a face. He enjoyed being a martyr and Solange knew she would have to cajole him into forgiving her, a process which could take two days or more. She thought: The bastard, how he's putting it on. But at the same time she knew she would play the role of repentant sinner to the full, as she always did.

She sighed. 'Am I forgiven?'

Jojo stared out of the window and shrugged, but she could see he was softening.

She smiled brightly. 'Let's go out for a drink. Come on. I'll buy!'

He moved away and she spotted a sheepish look in his eye. She thought: He's feeling guilty about something, he's got something to hide.

He murmured, 'I've got to go out. Vasson's arriving in a while and we're . . . going on a job.'

Solange froze. She knew exactly what that meant. It meant they were going to deliver a consignment for the *Patron*. The anger came surging back. 'You're mad, bloody mad! You . . . You realise that you could go down for *years* if you're caught. And it'll be *you* who gets caught, not the *Patron*! He should do his own dirty work.' Jojo started to move hurriedly round the small apartment, collecting clothing. She followed him, shouting, 'How do you think he gets so rich, eh? I'll tell you – by getting fools like you to move all the stuff around for him. And I suppose it's the hard stuff, *noire*! . . . Eh? Jesus!'

He turned on her. 'Shut up! Do you want everyone to hear?'

In the fraction of silence that followed, she heard a shuffling sound at the apartment door and stared at Jojo, horrified. He had heard it too and reached the door in two strides. He flung it open and she saw him relax. 'Oh, it's you. Come in, for Christ's sake.'

Vasson came through the door and Solange glanced at him furiously. She turned to Jojo, catching his arm as he walked back into the room. She heard herself shouting again. 'You have no brains, none of you. No *idea*! You think you're so clever!' She threw her hands up in a gesture of despair, 'You're mad!'

Jojo turned slowly to face her. He spoke deliberately, his eyes cold. 'Shut up, you nagging cow. You talk crap. Stick to what you're good at.'

Solange stared, aghast. He had never talked to her like that before. He'd always treated her with respect. Suddenly she realised why he'd said it: to impress Vasson. She glared at Vasson with distaste. She didn't like him at the best of times. He was a real little creep, always trying to muscle in. Some people were fooled by his polished airs and his educated accent – the Jesuits had schooled him, so they said – but not she. She had his measure: she recognised him for the shifty little rat he was.

There was something else about him too, though she couldn't quite put her finger on it; something not quite right, something that made her hackles rise.

She stared at Vasson and saw that he was looking uncomfortable. She thought: Good.

She pulled her mind back to the problem: something had to be done to persuade Jojo to drop this mad idea. She hated pleading with him in front of Vasson, but there was no other way. She whispered gently to him, '*Please*, Jojo. Don't go, don't get mixed up in that side of the business. The *Patron*'s just using you, don't you see that?'

Jojo frowned. 'Look, I do as I'm told and then I have a quiet life, okay? Anyway, it's extra money.' He turned to Vasson and said, 'I'll be with you in a minute.' He pulled off his shirt and, taking a towel, disappeared into the kitchen.

Solange yelled 'You're bloody mad' at the closed door, then groaned with exasperation. There was no getting through to the stupid idiot. He would end up in prison for years and she would be stuck in this tomb for ever. She thought: God, what a bloody mess.

She looked at Vasson. He was sitting on a small chair in the corner, lighting a cigarette and pretending not to listen but hearing everything. Solange hesitated. She hated the idea of asking him anything, far less a favour. But – it might just work. She pulled up another chair and sat beside him. 'Look, what do you think about this? I mean, you must agree that it's mad. If you're caught you'll take the time, not the *Patron*.'

He looked down at the floor and for a moment she thought he wouldn't answer. Then his dark eyes darted up to her face, and she was surprised by the intensity of his stare. He said, 'I just do as I'm told, like Jojo.' He smiled, but Solange noticed that his eyes were cold. He went on, 'You see, I'm a new boy around here, and I've got to stay on the right side of the *Patron*, otherwise I'm out.'

His eyes held hers, still smiling. So he was trying some charm on her, was he? Right, if that was the game, she could play it too.

She moved still nearer and put her hand on his leg. 'You're an intelligent man. You can see it's far too risky.' She gave him a long intense look from under her lashes. It was her favourite weapon and it usually did the trick. But almost immediately she saw that she had made a mistake. A look of alarm had come into his eyes, a look almost of . . . for a moment she was puzzled, then she had it: it was *revulsion*. She thought: Ah, so that's it, that's what I couldn't pin down: you're a woman-hater.

She withdrew her hand and stared at him. His smile had vanished and he was watching her coldly. Eventually he said, 'Nothing's risky if you're careful enough. Jojo was right, you should keep to your work and mind your own business.' He had put a small but unmistakable tone of insolence into the word 'work'.

Solange gritted her teeth. He had humiliated her and she thought: One round to you, but not the last!

Jojo came into the room and Solange moved away. One glance at Jojo and she knew he wasn't going to listen to any more arguments. She sat down on her favourite piece of furniture, a little pink *chaise longue*, and thought: To hell with him.

Jojo planted a kiss on her cheek, and said: 'See you later. Don't know when.'

Solange did not reply, but sat stiffly on the *chaise* staring out of the window. She felt the dull ache of anxiety in her heart and she knew she wouldn't stop worrying until Jojo was safely back.

Vasson watched Jojo striding ahead of him and wondered why he was in such a hurry. God forbid that the pick-up was going to be early. That would ruin everything. He had told the Algerian that it would be at ten, and everything had been arranged accordingly. Damn, he would have to make sure.

He put in a couple of loping strides and came up beside Jojo. 'What's the hurry? We've got hours yet. It's only six, you know.'

'Eh?' Jojo slowed up and looked around him, as if realising for the first time where he was. 'Oh. Sorry. I was . . . still thinking . . . you know.'

Vasson was relieved. It was the woman who was on Jojo's mind, not the pick-up. He shivered at the memory of the woman, with her roving hands and her large open mouth. She had no idea of how disgusting she was: the foreign brownish skin was somehow greasy and unclean.

But at least she'd got Jojo in a state and not thinking straight, which should make things easier. He wondered what to ask first. Best to make sure about the time. He said casually, 'It is still on for ten, isn't it?'

'What? . . . Oh, yes, yes. There's no change.'

Vasson gave Jojo a sidelong glance. He was frowning, his eyes on the paving in front of his feet. Vasson decided that some sympathy, some intimate conversation, was needed before it was safe to go on. He touched Jojo's arm and said, 'Look, I'm sure it'll all be all right when you get back. She'll have forgotten why she was angry.'

Gratitude flashed across Jojo's face and Vasson saw that he had been right to bring up the subject. Jojo shook his head. 'Honestly . . . I don't know why she has it in for me sometimes. It's a mystery to me. Trouble is . . .' He looked across with an expression that Vasson couldn't fathom. 'I like having her around.'

They turned a corner and Vasson had to drop behind Jojo to pass two black-scarved women talking in the middle of the street. He considered whether to ask the big question now or leave it till later. Jojo might refuse to answer in such a public place. It might be better to wait until they'd had a couple of pastis and Jojo was more relaxed. On the other hand time would be getting short by then and the right moment might not come up again. Vasson prided himself on judging the right moment.

Suddenly he decided that this was the best moment he would get. It was only fear, he realised, that had held him back.

He came up beside Jojo again, his heart thumping loudly. He swallowed and, leaning towards Jojo, said, 'Look, I've got a bit of a woman problem too. I want to see this girl tonight. She's really hot stuff . . . But, well, she can't get off work until nine and . . . it would mean a lot to see her for just half an hour or so. Is there any chance that I can meet you *there*?'

Jojo looked at him sharply. Vasson put on a rueful, sheepish expression and laughed. 'I know it's stupid, but I'm really mad about her and there's this other guy hanging about. If I don't get to see her tonight, he'll be there like a shot.' He sighed. 'He's got the lot: money, a car, flash clothes. My only hope is to see her and tell her . . .' He trailed off and tried to look lovelorn.

They turned on to the quay and up a small road beside a fish warehouse. This was where the car was kept. Jojo still hadn't answered and Vasson glanced across at him, trying to read his face.

Jojo paused to unlock the garage door. He was frowning. 'I'd have to tell you where the pick-up was and you know the *Patron*'s rules about that.'

Vasson nodded and stroked his chin. 'Yes, of course. I hadn't thought of that.'

Jojo backed the car out. Vasson closed the garage door and got into the passenger seat. The Citroën set off towards the quay, bumping gently over the cobbles.

Jojo lit a cigarette one-handed and said brightly, 'Well, where's it to be? Hamid's? Or shall we go to that new bar just off the Rue Caisserie? There's a place next door that does a really good *cous-cous*.'

Vasson thought: Shit! He's not going to buy it. That meant that Vasson would have to contact the Algerian to arrange a tail and then stay with Jojo all evening, right up until the end. He didn't like that idea at all: it would mean slipping away at the very last moment which would be risky, horribly risky. He felt angry. Christ, he didn't ask much. Just a little confidence, and Jojo, who was meant to be his friend, wasn't even going to give him that!

Jojo was waiting for an answer. Vasson shrugged and said in a tight voice: 'I don't care where the hell we go.'

'Oh, for God's sake, it's that bad, is it? This girl, I mean.'

'Yes, it is.'

Jojo sighed deeply. Eventually he said, 'Okay, okay, you win. But if it ever gets back to the *Patron* that I told you *where* to go, I'll kill you. He's really nervous at the moment. There's a lot of pressure, as you know.'

'Oh?'

'The Algerian. He's trying to move in again. You must have heard.'

'Ah. No, I hadn't.' Vasson enjoyed lying, mainly because he found it so easy. The best thing in the world was to carry a lie through all the way, to build on it, to refine it. He really liked that; it gave him a lot of satisfaction.

Vasson appeared to consider, then said, 'Well, of course, there's no way the *Patron* is going to find out, but ... if you really think there's a problem?

'No, go on. See her. Just don't let me down, that's all. *Be* there, and on time.'

They stopped at a junction. Jojo turned and said softly, 'Okay, the place is a small store off the Quai de la Rive Neuve. Behind the big warehouse, L'Entrepôt du Midi. It's got Laborde et Fils over the main door. It's in the same street as that night club, La Ronde.'

'Okay, and thanks. Thanks a lot. I'll remember the favour.' Vasson smiled warmly. He really *was* pleased. Jojo had done him the biggest favour of his life.

'Where to, then?'

'Hamid's. I don't like that new place.' Vasson didn't like the new place because there was only one telephone and it was on the bar itself.

Hamid's was already crowded and the air was thick with smoke and the smell of herbal tobacco. The two men squeezed in at the far end of the counter and ordered Pernod. Vasson didn't attempt to keep the look of triumph off his face. After all, he had every reason to be happy: he was in love, wasn't he?

There was only the phone call left now, and that would be easy. He waited for Jojo to order another round, then made a show of looking at his watch. 'Look I can get her on the telephone at work now. It'll save me having to go round to meet her.'

Jojo stirred the water into his Pernod. 'Where does she work?'

'La Belle Epoque. It's a dress shop off La Canebière. Very classy.'

'What's her name?'

'Marie-Hélène. Hey, why all the questions? You're not thinking of pinching her, are you?' He gave Jojo a friendly dig in the ribs and leered at him, thinking: This inquisition has got to stop.

Jojo smiled and said, 'No, I've got enough trouble with Solange. She doesn't give me enough time for other women. Anyway, I'm not an educated type like you. I'm not into classy pieces who work in dress shops.'

Vasson took out his wallet and put some money on the bar. 'Here. Have another while I'm phoning.' A drink would keep Jojo busy.

Jojo caught his arm. 'What's that you have there?' He was peering at Vasson's still-open wallet.

Vasson's heart missed a beat and he thought: God, what the hell's he spotted?

Jojo smiled and, taking the wallet, pulled out the newspaper cutting of the Delage. 'That car again, eh? What with girls from La Canebière and cars like this . . .' He shook his head and flicked the picture with his finger. 'You have expensive tastes. Very expensive.'

Vasson shrugged and smiled casually. 'No harm in dreaming, is there?'

'None at all.' Jojo replaced the cutting and handed the wallet back to Vasson. 'No harm at all. Just as long as you don't try to get it the easy way.' He grinned broadly to soften the words, but Vasson thought: Goddam you, you're treating me like a child too.

He said lightly, 'I know there's no easy way.'

He pocketed the wallet and, moving quickly down the bar, went through a door into the back. Hamid was there. Vasson asked, 'Mind if I use the telephone?'

Hamid looked up. He was a Tunisian Arab who, after twenty years in Marseilles, still wore a jellabah. He indicated the telephone on the desk, 'Salam, my friend. Please, please.'

'It's a private call. Do you mind?'

The old man smiled. 'Of course, of course.' He disappeared into the bar and closed the connecting door.

Vasson thought carefully. There was a second extension in the bar itself, but he would know immediately if anyone listened in because of the noise. It was possible there was another extension upstairs, but doubtful. Hamid was a careful businessman. He wouldn't spend money on luxuries like that.

He raised the receiver and asked for the number he'd been given. There was a long silence and for a moment Vasson was worried in case he'd memorised the wrong number. But then there was a voice on the line, 'Yes?'

'It's me.'

'Have you any news?'

'Yes, ten tonight, at a warehouse named Laborde et Fils, behind L'Entrepôt du Midi, on the other side of the harbour.'

'Got it.'

'And the other address?'

'When you deliver what you owe me.'

There was a silence. 'All right. A briefcase will be delivered to you at the corner of Rue Caisserie and Rue Roger at exactly ten-thirty. Make sure you have that address written on a piece of paper ready to hand to the driver. Goodbye.'

Vasson replaced the receiver. He moved round to the other side of the desk and found a pencil and a piece of clean paper under the piles of till receipts. In block capitals he carefully wrote the address of the heroin processing laboratory that the *Patron* maintained in a quiet suburb on the south side of the city, beyond the hill of Notre-Dame de la Garde. He had delivered some stuff there once. They had told him it was only a safe house, but he had checked on it. He had gone back and watched the place: two men arrived at eight and left at four on the first day. And the second day. And the third. Regular little workers, they were.

He had followed one home. A garrulous neighbour had informed him that the worker was a chemist who used to work for a big pharmaceutical company somewhere. No one was sure where he worked now. Vasson hadn't bothered to check on the second worker: he knew he'd found the laboratory.

He put the piece of paper in his back pocket and went through into the bar. Jojo had obviously been watching the door: as Vasson looked round he found the other man staring at him. Vasson smiled and waved. But something else was expected. Of course: he smacked his hand in the crook of his elbow in the age-old obscene gesture.

Jojo laughed and shouted, 'Lucky devil!'

Yes, thought Vasson, how right you are.

Vasson peered up and down both streets again. Occasionally the headlights of a car came sweeping up the Rue Caisserie, but none of them slowed down. He felt sure it must be after ten-thirty, but without a watch he couldn't be positive. He had left Hamid's just before nine and gone to a strange bar in the north of the Quarter until just before ten. Since then he'd been walking the streets for at least half an hour. He decided a watch was one of the first things he was going to buy with the money. He rather liked the new metal Rolexes: smart yet practical.

He'd never had real money before, but he knew exactly what he was going to do with it. There would be a small rented apartment in the 18th Arrondissement, a D8SS Delage – though he probably wouldn't be able to afford a new one – and a nice little business. A club probably, with high-class girls and some expensive décor. But whatever the business, he would work hard at it and it would be a success. He couldn't understand people who spent wildly instead of investing for the future. There was no way he was going to be caught in *that* trap. Apart from the Delage which would have to be bought for cash, he was going to invest every penny.

There was still no sign of a car. Vasson began to feel nervous. They must come soon; they needed that address.

Suddenly a terrible thought came to him. Suppose . . . suppose they had got the address out of Jojo . . .

He felt sick and groaned. *Of course.* Why hadn't he thought of it before? If Jojo had talked . . . then they wouldn't turn up in a million years. *And they wouldn't bring the money.*

Oh God, please don't let it be true, please.

He leant back against the wall and stared through the darkness at the building opposite. The thought of not having the money was so appalling that he couldn't imagine it. The money was everything . . .

He stayed immobile against the wall, as if by freezing his body he could postpone the moment of truth.

The time must be at least a quarter to eleven.

There was a sudden flash of light and he looked up. A long low car was sliding into the kerb. He stared at it uncomprehendingly.

A car . . . *The car* . . .

Oh dear God, thank you, *thank you*. He stepped forward, half-chuckling, half-crying.

The rear door opened and a voice called, 'Get in!'

Vasson stood by the open door. 'No, I'd rather not.' Through his elation he thought: I'm not going to be caught by that old trick.

The voice said, 'I thought you'd want to count the money.'

Vasson considered. They were right, of course. But it was still too risky to get in; he would take a quick look at the cash and he'd soon know if there was a lot missing. 'No, just hand it over.'

'You have the address ready?'

An old attaché case appeared from inside the car and Vasson crouched on the pavement to open it. In the dim light of the street lamp he saw piles of clean new bank notes. 'They're new! I asked for old!'

'They're straight out of the bank. Clean as a whistle.'

'But how do I know they're not hot?'

'They're not pinched, if that's what you mean.'

Vasson cursed, but he knew he was beaten. He'd have to accept the new notes and like it. He thrust the piece of paper into the car and a hand reached out to close the door. Vasson leapt for the door and held it open. 'Stop! You promised! You promised to tell me what happened.' He clung on to the door. No-one was going to close it until he had an answer.

There was a pause, then the voice said, 'Okay, okay. We gave the news of the pick-up to our friends at the commissariat.'

'Why? Why *them*?'

'We owe them a favour. Anyway we want them to get the odd conviction; it keeps everyone happy.'

So, it was prison for Jojo. He'd got off lightly then. Vasson was glad: he'd quite liked the guy.

The voice had fallen silent. Vasson prompted, 'Well? What about the *Patron*?'

'We've already dealt with him. He had . . . a little accident, about half an hour ago. And the laboratory, the technicians – we'll be taking them over ourselves.' There was a pause, then the voice said mockingly, 'Does all this meet with your satisfaction?'

Vasson ignored the sarcasm and grinned, 'Oh yes, oh yes!'

28

The car revved up. 'You won't be staying around, will you? The Algerian doesn't think it'll be very healthy for you.'

'Don't worry, I'm going on a long trip. To Algeria.'

As the car drove off, Vasson laughed. To Algeria. He liked that. Very neat.

He walked rapidly, the attaché case swinging in his hand. God, what a coup! What a strike! Perfect – the whole thing had gone perfectly.

And it felt so good! *Sweet* – yes! That's how it felt.

He had only one regret: that he hadn't been able to see the *Patron*'s expression when he realised he'd been outmanoeuvred. The bastard, that would teach him.

Vasson paused near the house. The place seemed quiet. If possible he wanted to get to his room without meeting any of the girls.

He crept up to the doorway and into the hall. No-one. He ran lightly up the stairs to the landing outside his room. He put his ear to the door and listened carefully.

There was no sound; nothing to worry about. Everything was going to be all right.

He put the key into the lock and in that instant he knew that it had all gone dreadfully wrong.

The door was already unlocked.

As it swung open he saw the bottom drawer gaping at him. The lock had been broken. He stared stupidly at it until a slight movement caught his eye.

There was someone in the room.

It was Jojo's woman.

She was staring at him, her eyes wide and angry.

For a moment neither of them moved. Vasson noticed that the woman was panting heavily. Slowly he looked round the room and understood why. The bitch had been through the place. Magazines spilled off the shelves; his new suit lay in a crumpled ball on the floor. The beautiful white silk shirt hung off the side of the bed, a smear of dirt showing grey on its sleeve.

He thought: God, why did she have to *spoil* everything? Why couldn't she have left me *alone*?

Then he saw the money. The thirty thousand francs advance payment lay neatly stacked on top of the chest. Next to it were some papers.

Oh God. The papers.

He closed the door slowly behind him and faced her. 'Why? Why did you come here?'

'You bastard! You shopped Jojo! You bastard!' She started to scream at him.

Vasson thought: Damn, damn. He had to think clearly but it was impossible while she was still yelling. 'Shut up!' he shouted.

Her mouth closed in surprise.

Quickly he said, 'What gave you that idea? That I shopped Jojo?'

'Oh, I *know* you did! My friend told me, my *Inspector* friend.'

'Impossible.'

'Oh he didn't *say* it was you.' She was beginning to scream again. 'But as soon as he told me someone had, I knew it *had* to be you. And what do I find, eh? *All this!*' She picked up the money and shook it at him.

He thought: Perhaps she hasn't seen the papers, perhaps it's all right after all. But then he realised she *must* have, when she took them out of the drawer.

She had seen the papers.

She knew his new name.

He took a step forward and said quietly, 'Give me the money.' She started to move to one side and he saw her glance at the door. God, she was stupid. He took a step sideways and cut her off.

She stared at him defiantly. 'You bastard, take your bloody money!' She threw the notes at him and they fluttered down to the floor.

She's done it again, he thought. Dirtied everything unnecessarily, spoilt it all.

He reached for her and saw the fear leap into her eyes. He would have to be quick otherwise she'd scream. He grabbed at her but she pulled free and ran for the door. Even before she got to it, he knew he would be able to catch her and he felt a surge of power. She was grappling with the handle. He came up behind her and got a hand round first one arm then the other. Then he thought: God, what do I do next?

She was kicking backwards at him and he pulled her closer so that her legs would lose their momentum. She started to yell and he suddenly realised what he would have to do. He put an arm round her throat and as her hand shot up to pull it away, he raised his other arm. After that it was a simple matter to slide his hands on to her neck.

He squeezed and the yelling stopped. Her breathing changed to a series of loud agonising rasps. It was too noisy: he would have to squeeze harder. The noise changed to a gurgle and he thought: That's better. Then she started to fight, writhing her body from side to side

30

and kicking her legs again. It occurred to him that it would be much easier on the floor.

He twisted her round and started to push her down. At the sight of his face she went for his eyes and he felt her nails digging into his skin. Panicking he squeezed harder and she grasped desperately at his hands again. Her eyes began to pop and he stared at them, amazed at the enormous size of the human eye.

He wondered how much longer it would take. He was running out of strength. It was much more difficult than he'd thought: she was so strong. He looked down at her. She was purple now and her tongue was protruding from her mouth. The sight was disgusting and he closed his eyes.

At last he looked again. Her eyes were staring blankly and the obscene tongue was hanging swollen from the mouth. Tentatively he let go. The head lolled back. The body lay still.

He backed away on hands and knees and crouched, crying quietly. God, what a stupid bitch. Why couldn't she leave well enough alone?

His stomach heaved and he lurched to the basin to throw up. Afterwards he dipped a cloth in the water jug and washed his face for a long time.

Eventually he realised it was late. The last night train left in half an hour. He picked up his crumpled clothes from the floor and began to change. By facing towards the basin all the time he could avoid looking at the body. When he had changed he picked the money up from the floor, leaving only one note which was protruding from under the woman's head. He packed the money into the money belt along with the notes from the attaché case. The new identity papers went into his jacket pocket.

At last he was ready. The clothes didn't look too bad, though the shirt was dreadfully creased. He would have it dry-cleaned when he got to Paris.

He looked in the mirror. He looked just the same but he didn't feel it. He would never *feel* the same again. That woman had tainted him with her dirt. It must never happen again. He would make sure of that.

Thank God at least for the money, the sweet, beautiful money. That made him feel clean again.

2

It was a clear, cloudless September day. In Plymouth Sound anchored warships were silhouetted black against the sparkling sea and twelve miles away, on the horizon, the tall Eddystone Lighthouse was clearly visible, a dark needle against the pale blue sky. A fresh south-westerly breeze was blowing in from the sea and on the exposed height of Plymouth Hoe it was rather cold. Only a handful of people were braving a stroll along the historic pathways where, according to popular legend, Drake had played his game of bowls.

Julie Lescaux sat on a bench and stared out beyond the breakwater to the wide English Channel. She thought: I could always kill myself.

But she knew she wouldn't. She hadn't the nerve to do something like that. Even at school she'd never had the nerve to do anything daring or risky. When some of the other girls had dressed up to look eighteen and gone dancing in the city, she'd ducked out. They'd called her a goody-goody. And they were right: she had always been – well, anxious to do the right thing.

Julie thought: If only they knew the truth.

It was strange how life changed – and so quickly, without warning. She'd always thought of herself as an ordinary sort of person who would always have an ordinary life. Well, perhaps ordinary sounded a bit dull. Average was better.

Yes, she thought: That's what I am – average.

And yet it was she who was going to be different from all the others. She, the goody-goody. Bad things were half-expected of girls like Maggie Phillips, who had begun pencilling her eyebrows and wearing high heels at sixteen; Maggie who had lots of boyfriends and was considered 'flighty'.

But it hadn't happened to Maggie; it had happened to Julie.

Julie could imagine what people would say. They would use all the stock phrases, all the old clichés.

But there was no way round it. No way round the bald facts.

She was just nineteen and pregnant.

She had got into trouble.

She had been 'easy'.

She had ruined her life.

She tried to imagine what it was like, to have people whispering and sniggering about you, talking behind your back and pointing you out. It would be terrible, she knew, not just for her, but for Mother. Mother would find it unbearable, worse than anything else that could possibly happen. Her mother believed in respect and being able to hold your head up. She set great store by what people thought.

It would be like stabbing her in the back.

Unless Julie got married. But she knew there was no chance of that, none at all.

Her mother . . . Julie had no idea how she was going to tell her. Whichever way she did it, her mother would die of shame and anger and bitterness. She would accuse Julie of ingratitude and disloyalty and selfishness and say she had ruined both their lives. Julie could hear her very words.

The only thing worse would be another interview with Doctor Hargreaves. Julie shrank at the memory. It had been deeply humiliating, much worse than she'd ever imagined. He had called her shameless and ungrateful. He'd asked her why she'd gone and thrown herself at the first man who'd asked.

She hadn't replied. She'd thought: Perhaps he's right. Perhaps I am shameless, ungrateful.

In the end he had told her he would keep her as a patient, but only out of loyalty to her mother. Then he said – and the words had taken Julie by surprise – that the baby would need to be adopted and that he would arrange it.

She hadn't thought about what would happen to the baby. How strange! The whole fuss was about having a baby, and she hadn't thought about the actual baby, the object of it all. A baby . . . She knew nothing about babies, she'd never even held one. Did she want a baby? Would she love it? She had no idea.

A gust of wind blew across the Hoe and lifted the hem of her frock. She pushed the skirt down again and pulled her coat round her knees. When she looked up she was aware that someone was staring at her. It was a sailor walking slowly towards her. Julie looked quickly away and waited nervously for him to pass.

For an awful moment she thought he was going to stop and try to pick her up. But, after pausing for a moment, he suddenly quickened his step and walked away.

Julie relaxed and sat back on the bench. It would have been surprising if he had tried to pick her up. She rarely had trouble of that kind. She supposed it was because she didn't look the type. She was wearing the white gloves her mother insisted she wore, and a frock at least two inches longer than the current calf-length fashion; not exactly the outfit for a scarlet woman. She didn't *look* easy, *even if she was*. Julie groaned and shut her eyes tightly.

She stood up and began to walk slowly along the Hoe.

Easy . . .

But she hadn't been 'easy', far from it. It had only happened twice, and then after days of argument and fierce persuasion. Even when she'd agreed to it, she'd had terrible doubts. She had realised that there should be much more love and tenderness and caring. But Bill had been very clever. He had swept away all her arguments and told her she was being too romantic and that life wasn't like that. He had made her feel very gauche and silly. His favourite word for her was 'immature'. He told her that all the other officers slept with their girlfriends and no-one thought anything of it. He had made her feel like the odd one out. Yes, he had been very clever.

She had held out for a long time, then he had threatened to take another girl to the Summer Ball. It was Mother who had been horrified at the thought of Julie not going. The Summer Ball was the social event of the season. She had forced Julie to write to Bill and make it up.

So she had gone to the Ball and drunk gin, which she had only tried once before, and then wine, which she wasn't used to either. Afterwards Bill had driven her up on to the moors and it had happened for the first time.

It was brief and painful and Julie had wept. He had promised her it would be better the next time. But if anything it had been worse. On the second occasion they had driven on to a remote headland. But this time he didn't say a word, he didn't even kiss her, he just grabbed her and pulled at her clothing. Then he lay on her and hurt her again, except that it lasted much longer and she hated it even more than the first time.

Afterwards she had felt miserable and unclean. It had been so beastly, so ugly. If that was love then she didn't want anything more to do with it. One thing she knew straight away: she would never let Bill do it again.

She had felt wretched for weeks. Her mother had put her unhappiness down to being in love. Poor Mother! She still thought that Bill was marvellous. Bill was everything she wanted for Julie: he was well-spoken, dashing and a gentleman. Mother had never let Julie go out with anyone she considered common. Julie was not allowed to go to the Golden Dance Hall to meet the non-commissioned ranks like the rest of her school friends did.

The idea of Bill being a gentleman made Julie smile grimly. She had used the risk of pregnancy as a reason for not giving in to him, but he had swept that aside as he swept everything else aside. Nothing, he had assured her, would happen; he would take care of that. A real gentleman, Julie thought bitterly.

A small sailing craft had appeared by Drake's Island and was heading out into the wide expanse of the sound. She thought how pretty it looked, with its white sails and gay red hull. It was skimming over the waves, fast as the wind.

She walked on and for no particular reason thought of her father. Perhaps it was the boat that reminded her.

She remembered his dear gruff voice. He had died when she was twelve and it had broken her heart. She still missed him dreadfully.

Her father would have understood about this. He would have listened and sighed and looked at her with love in his eyes and taken her in his arms and said: Juliette, my Juliette. He would have understood. He would have protected her and found a way for her to survive it all.

Perhaps he would have taken her away . . . Julie stopped abruptly. She hadn't thought of that. That would be an answer. To go away. But where? She had only a few pounds saved. As a junior secretary she earned just fifteen shillings a week and it was hard to save on that. Anyway, she couldn't stay in her present job: she'd have to leave Plymouth and go to a new area and find a new job, and that wouldn't be easy. And then what? She had few relatives to go to. There was only Aunt Beryl at Ramsgate, and she – well, she was like her mother.

She had never met her father's family in Brittany; her mother had always discouraged any contact with them.

Julie walked down the long flight of steps into Grand Parade and wondered if it was five o'clock yet. She usually went out on Saturday afternoons, either to meet some of the girls for tea at the tea house, or in the old days, to go out for a drive with Bill. She always promised to be back by five-thirty.

Today she had told her mother she was going into town, but nothing more. Her mother had been suspicious and as soon as Julie got back to the house there would be questions. Then the truth would have to come out, and nothing would ever be the same again.

Julie turned into West Street and walked down the hill towards Radley Terrace and her home at Number 34.

As she drew near the bottom of the hill two women came round the corner, walking arm-in-arm. One of them was Maggie Phillips. Julie's first thought was to turn round and get away, but she realised that Maggie had seen her and was waving. It was too late. She made herself walk on.

'Hello, Julie! Well, it's a long time since we saw you round these parts.' Maggie gave a dazzling smile between vermilion lips. She modelled herself on Joan Crawford, down to the padded shoulders and the peep-toe shoes. 'We thought you'd got too grand for us.'

Julie felt herself blushing. 'No, I – I haven't been doing anything special.'

Maggie looked at her enquiringly and said, not unkindly, 'Oh, it's like that is it? No more boyfriend, eh? Oh well, there'll be others.'

Julie gave her a thin smile and nodded.

'What about coming to the Golden tonight then? Joan and I are going, and maybe Phyllis. It'll be fun – they've got a really good American-style band tonight.'

'Thanks . . . it's kind of you but I can't. I . . .'

'Oh come on. It'll be good fun. We'll get a table and sit all demure and ladylike on the side.' She giggled.

Julie shook her head. 'Really, my mother's not keen . . .'

'Your mother doesn't own you, does she? Break loose, my girl, that's what I say! What about next Friday then? Joan and I are going to the Rialto with two nice Navy lads. They can bring along one of their mates. Go on, say you will. It's the new Gable-Crawford movie!'

Julie felt worn down and heard herself say, 'Oh, all right.'

'We'll meet you outside for the early house then. Byeee!'

Julie walked quickly away. She could have kicked herself. Why had she agreed to go to the pictures? She didn't want to go anywhere with anyone, let alone a group of strangers. Why did she always agree to things she later regretted?

She paused at the corner of the street and thought: Yes, that's the problem. I agree to things I don't really want to do. Why? Why *had* she agreed to Maggie's suggestion? To avoid unpleasantness perhaps. But no, there was more to it than that. She had wanted to *please* Maggie. That was the key: she had been anxious to please. Just as she always tried to please her mother. And her employer. *And* Bill. She hated to remember it now, but she had tried to please *him* too.

Julie thought: What a revelation. I live to please other people. And look where it's got me! Into the oldest trap in the world.

As she approached the house she found she was dangerously near to tears. She turned and walked quickly away from the house until she felt more composed. Then she blew her nose and retraced her steps.

It would be time for tea at Number 34, and she mustn't be late.

Julie leant back against the chair and wondered how much longer it would be before she could get to bed. She was desperately tired. The emotion and tears of the last few hours had left her feeling drained and now a small ache at the back of her neck was threatening to become a full-blown headache.

Anyway there was nothing new to say, nothing that hadn't been said already.

Julie rubbed her neck and turned to look out of the window into the twilight. The road outside was lit by the soft glow of the street lamps which cast a pale light into the small front room. Normally Mother would have the curtains drawn and the lamps lit by now. But the ritual had been forgotten and the room seemed eerie and unreal in the gloomy darkness.

There was a loud sniffle and Julie looked back at her mother.

Mrs Lescaux was sitting on a low stool, rocking back and forth. Now and then her body shook with a great sob and her breath came in long shuddering gasps. At other times she moaned and shook her head and put a large wet handkerchief to her eyes.

Julie sighed and wondered what she could say that would help. But there was nothing . . .

Mrs Lescaux blew her nose loudly and raised her head. 'How can you be *sure* he doesn't love you, that's what I want to know.'

'I just know, Mum.' They had been over that one half a dozen times already.

'Well *how* do you know?'

Julie closed her eyes. 'I told you, he's been avoiding me. And . . .'

Mother said impatiently, 'Yes?'

'Well, I saw him with another girl. She seemed much more his sort.'

Mrs Lescaux got wearily to her feet and moved to a chair nearer the window. Julie saw that her eyes were red-rimmed and bloated, and her face mottled with angry red patches. She had never seen her mother look anything but neat and composed before, and it made her feel terrible.

Mother said, 'What do you mean by that? More his sort?'

'I mean . . . she was more his class, Mother.'

'I don't see what that's got to do with it! You're as good as anyone else. As good as *anyone*. No!' She shook her head vehemently. 'That can't have anything to do with it!'

Julie thought that class probably had a lot to do with it, but it was best not to say so. Instead she nodded and said, 'Well, maybe I'm wrong, maybe that didn't make any difference. But the fact is he doesn't love me, Mother.'

'But you can't be sure of that! Perhaps he just never *told* you . . . Anyway, love can grow. Take it from me.'

Julie thought: Oh God, how do I make her understand? She said gently, 'Mother, please believe me when I tell you this. He doesn't love me.'

He had come to the house for tea a couple of times and Mother had gone to a lot of trouble, making cakes and sandwiches and laying everything out properly. But though he had been polite enough, she had sensed a mocking edge to his comments when he thanked her for the tea or admired the china or enquired about her mother's health. Now Julie could see that he must have thought it all rather quaint, the tea parties with the lace doilies, and Mother's refined manner, and the polite conversation.

If I'm right, Julie thought, then I'd rather die than let him know I'm in trouble.

Mrs Lescaux cleared her throat again. 'You must try once more, try to *tell* him at least. He might well ask you to marry him. How can you be certain he won't?'

'Oh, I'm certain, please believe me.'

'I've a good mind to tell him myself. Or his commanding officer. He'll probably be *ordered* to marry you.'

Julie felt a surge of anger. 'Mother, if you so much as *think* about doing such a thing I shall never speak to you again!'

'Well! That's a fine way to speak to your own mother! There's a daughter's loyalty for you!' She started sobbing again. 'And after the way you've treated *me*! Bringing such shame on me, such shame!'

'Oh Mother, please don't start all over again. I told you, I'll go away. No-one will ever know.'

'Go away! On what! Where will you go?' Mother shouted angrily.

It was a good question. 'I'm not sure yet. But it would be the best thing, Mum. At least that way no-one will know, and . . . And you can make up some story about me getting a job somewhere else . . .'

Mrs Lescaux dabbed at her eyes again and shook her head. 'Well, if there's no other way . . . But—' She threw her head back, looked up at the ceiling and closed her eyes in a gesture of suffering. 'But . . . goodness knows where the money's to come from. It'll cost, mark my words. I can't send you to Aunt Beryl's, I just couldn't face that. That means a boarding house – dreadfully expensive. And you wouldn't be able to find work, not in your condition!'

'I could go to Brittany.'

'What –?'

'Well, it's out of the way, isn't it? And Dad's people would probably take me in. For a while at least.'

'No –!' Mrs Lescaux looked horrified. 'You've never met them. You don't understand. They're not like us. They're . . .' She sighed with exasperation. 'They're . . . farmworkers . . . fishermen, that sort of thing . . .'

Julie remembered her loving kindly father and thought that,

surely, his family couldn't be so different from him. He'd come to Plymouth on a French frigate before the Great War and met Mother at a tea dance in the town. Later he had returned and they had married. He'd worked at the fish market, eventually rising to foreman and wearing a suit that always looked uncomfortable on him. To please Mother, he'd never spoken French or talked about his family – at least within earshot.

With Julie it was different. At bedtime he spoke to her in French, telling her stories about the mythical sea creatures of Breton legend; talking about his family, his childhood and Brittany itself. Sometimes he even spoke Breton, the strange harsh language which was his native tongue.

He had been a good father and she had loved him with all her heart.

'No,' her mother said decisively, 'you can't go there. They wouldn't be very understanding, you know! You must go somewhere else. You could be back four or five weeks after the – event. They might even give you your job back.' She sniffed again. 'Oh, what a muddle, what a muddle!'

Julie frowned. 'Mother, I don't think I could come back. You see – there'd be the baby.'

'What are you talking about? You won't even see it. It'll be taken away straight after the – after the *event*.'

'But I'm not sure . . .' A vivid picture came into Julie's mind, of a tiny baby lying in her arms. The baby was looking uncertain and frightened; it was crying and reaching out for her, for *her*. She hated the thought of someone taking it away and sending it to a strange, anonymous place that she'd never be allowed to see or to know about, a place where – God forbid – it might not be loved. She said, 'Suppose I wanted to keep the baby . . .'

Mrs Lescaux snorted. 'Don't be so silly! It's out of the question! All the girls who – who have this problem have their babies adopted. It's quite normal.'

Julie shook her head. 'But I think I might want to keep the baby very much. I'd never forgive myself if I gave it away.'

'Now I've heard everything! How selfish can you get! First you get yourself into trouble, then you want to ruin *my* life as well as your own! Really! You young people just don't *care*!'

'Please don't shout, Mother.'

'I'm not shouting!' Mrs Lescaux closed her eyes and blew her nose again. Then she said, more quietly, 'The only way to keep the baby is to marry, don't you understand that!'

Julie felt sick. They were going in circles, nowhere, in circles.

'At least *try* to see him once more. Do just that for me, just that one thing. Is that too much to ask?'

'But I won't tell him. I won't tell him.'

Mrs Lescaux shook her head in exasperation. 'All right, all right. But at least see if he still cares for you. Please, I'm asking you this one thing. *Please.*'

Julie stared angrily at her hands. She hated the thought of trying to see him again. It would be humiliating and shaming and it wouldn't help, she knew it wouldn't. Anyway, what excuse could she find for visiting him? She would rather die than just turn up and ask to see him; he would think that she still liked him, that she was still prepared to go off in the car with him ... The thought made her shudder. 'Mother, I can't just go and see him, not like that, he'll think I have no pride.'

'Well, you didn't, did you –' Mrs Lescaux bit her lip.

Julie stared at her mother and the tears came again. She had cried so much she didn't think she could manage any more. But the tears came nevertheless, rolling effortlessly down her cheeks. She suddenly thought: I can't face any more.

She was tired of crying, tired of arguing. Her head throbbed and her throat ached. All she wanted to do was sleep. She would do anything for that, and for the privacy of her own room.

Wearily she said, 'All right, Mother, you win. I'll try to see him tomorrow.'

The bus lurched into bottom gear and began to climb slowly up the hill behind Millbay Docks. It was only a mile or two to the Naval Dockyard, a journey which would take fifteen minutes at the most. Julie felt a rising panic. She had found only the flimsiest of excuses for going to see Bill and she had the unpleasant feeling that he would see straight through it.

But it was the only pretext she had and it would have to do.

Back in the early summer Bill had taken her to a party aboard a small sailing boat moored in a creek near the dockyard. Late in the evening a few people started to sing sea ballads and everyone stopped to listen. Some of the ballads were mournful, about the cruelty of the sea and the separation of lovers. Julie had been rather taken by them. The evening had been still and utterly peaceful and, though the lights of Plymouth were brightly reflected in the calm water, the city seemed very far away. Julie had looked out beyond Drake's Island, to where the water was dark and cold, and she'd thought how romantic it all was. The sea, so vast and cruel, which asked so much of the noble men who sailed on it ... And the songs, they were so lovely, so sad, with their tales of brave sailors who withstood so much only to drown in the icy water.

Afterwards she told Bill how much she'd loved the songs. Two days later he thrust a book in her hand. It was a pocket edition of *Naval Songs and Ballads*. It was the only present he'd ever given her.

And now she was taking it back.

It was the only excuse she could find for seeing him again.

He would think it strange that she was returning a gift, but she was going to pretend it had been a loan. Then she could thank him for letting her keep it for so long and apologise for not returning it sooner. He wouldn't be fooled for a moment, of course – he had told her it was a gift at the time – but it was the best she could do. And when they met it would at least give her something to talk about.

If they met. He might not be there at all. With a bit of luck he would be out for the day, driving up on to the moors with his new girlfriend for a quiet Sunday lunch.

One thing at least, she hadn't dressed up for him. If he *was* there she didn't want him to think she had spent a lot of time over her appearance. There were no white gloves today, nor a hat. She was wearing a plain blue summer frock with an off-white linen coat. Her long dark hair was drawn back from her face by two combs, but otherwise it was loose and unpinned. It looked as if she were going out on an errand, and that was exactly the impression she wanted to make.

The bus trundled past the main gates of the dockyard and came to a noisy halt in the next street. Julie got out and walked towards the gates of HMS Drake, the shore establishment attached to the dockyard. She was dreading the next part. She would have to ask for him at the gate and admit that no, she wasn't expected, and the men on the gate would look at her knowingly, and smile at each other. She thought: Still more humiliation. It never ends.

She approached the gatehouse and saw that there were three sentries on duty. As she came towards them they turned to stare at her and two of them exchanged glances. She thought: Oh God, this is going to be even worse than I thought.

Suddenly there was a burst of noise.

Julie jumped with fright and spun round. It was the roar of a car engine. The car itself, a vivid blue Austin 7, rattled past and ground to a halt beside the sentries. A young man was leaning out of the window waving a pass in his hand.

Julie stood stock still and tried to regain her breath. She was shaking with fright.

The young man was looking back at her with a rueful expression. Then his head disappeared into the car and the door was flung open. He leapt out and said, 'I'm terribly sorry, I didn't mean to startle you. I came round the corner rather fast, I'm afraid.' He grinned at her, then looked serious again. 'I say, you're really shaken. I'm so sorry. What an idiot I am.'

Julie shook her head. 'I'm fine. It was rather a shock, that's all.'

'You're sure you're all right then?' He peered at her solicitously and put a hand on her elbow.

'Yes, really.'

'Well . . . if you're sure.' He glanced at the sentries. 'Are you being looked after? I mean, can I find anyone for you?'

'No, no, I . . .' Julie paused and looked carefully at the young man. He was vaguely familiar and she realised she must have met him before at some time. He was dressed in a large shapeless sweater and baggy rust-coloured trousers, and on his head was an old black cap speckled with paint. He looked rather roguish, like a pirate.

He was smiling at her; there was no doubt he was very charming, but Julie wondered if it wasn't laid on. Bill had been charming too, but that had meant nothing, nothing at all.

He was waiting for an answer and she said, 'I was hoping to see a friend, but I think I've missed him . . .' It sounded weak and she trailed off.

'Oh, it's impossible to find anyone on a Sunday. But if you want me to ask . . . ?'

She took another look at him. He was watching her intently, waiting for her reply, his eyes friendly and enquiring. Maybe she'd been wrong: maybe he was everything he seemed, and wasn't the sort to make fun of her. She decided to trust him after all: it would be a lot less embarrassing if he asked about Bill rather than the sentries.

She said, 'Well, perhaps you could ask if Bill Crozier is around.' She looked down, a little flustered, then remembered the book and fumbled in her handbag. 'I wanted to return something he lent me.' She held the book up as if it were a trophy.

'No problem.' He smiled and she noticed the eyes again. 'Look, why don't you hop in the car and we'll go and ask in the wardroom. Someone there might know.'

She nodded and after he had spoken to the sentries they got into the car and drove slowly into the establishment. He laughed. 'We're not allowed to drive fast in here, so you're safe!'

She smiled politely and looked out of the window at the barrack-like buildings.

He negotiated the car round a sharp corner and she could feel him

42

looking at her. He said, 'Didn't you come to that party on my boat? The one where we had the singsong?'

She looked at him blankly. 'Oh, was it your boat? I didn't know.'

'Yes, *Dancer*'s her name.' He laughed again. 'Oh, and my name's Richard Ashley. We were probably introduced, but there were so many people there ...'

'I'm Juliette Lescaux.'

'Of course!' He lifted both hands off the wheel in an expansive gesture. 'I remember the French name now. *Are* you French in fact?'

Julie thought: God, he knows my name. Perhaps I'm infamous already. Perhaps Bill has been talking about me ... She glanced across at the young man but his expression hadn't changed, it was still interested and amused. No, she thought, I'm being stupid: he really did remember my name because it's French.

She said, 'Half. I'm half French. My father came from Brittany.'

'Ah, what a fantastic place to come from. I sailed over there last year and had the most wonderful time. The locals were so amazed to see old *Dancer* and me all alone that they couldn't do enough for us.'

Julie looked at him curiously. 'You sailed the boat alone?'

'Oh yes, always do if I can. Nothing to compare with it.'

Julie didn't reply immediately: she was thinking of what would happen if Bill was at the mess. She dragged her mind back to what Richard Ashley had said. 'Isn't it risky, alone? I mean what happens in a storm?' They drew up outside the wardroom. Julie regarded it with horror.

'In a storm?' Ashley was considering her question. 'Oh, I just shorten sail and go below for a sleep.' Leaving the engine running, he got out of the car and stuck his head back through the window. 'Unless I'm about to bump into the land. Then I sail like hell!' He grinned. 'Won't be a tick.' She watched him walk to the door and disappear into the building.

Julie sat still, thankful for the safety of the little blue car. She began to pray that Bill wouldn't be there. The last time they'd met, Bill had made it plain that he didn't want to see her again. Well, he hadn't actually *said* so, not in so many words, but she'd known by the long silences and the way he'd avoided her eyes. Julie put her hands over her face and thought: Please God, don't let him be there.

The door to the wardroom opened and Julie's heart went into her mouth. Richard Ashley came out and closed the door behind him. He was alone. Julie closed her eyes with relief.

Richard slid back into the driver's seat. 'Sorry, no luck, no-one seems to know where he is. But he *is* expected back fairly early this evening.'

'Oh.' Julie wondered what to do next. She didn't want to go home, not yet.

'I say . . .' Richard's face was alight with enthusiasm. 'What about coming down to *Dancer*. I'm doing a bit of work on her today. I could do with someone to help . . . I mean with the sandwich-making and all that. Everything's on board: cheese, bread, you name it. It would be much more fun than working on my own. Then I could bring you back here later.'

'Oh –' The question took Julie by surprise. She had no desire to go home, but on the other hand she didn't know this man . . . she wasn't sure she wanted to spend an afternoon with him. Anyway she wasn't dressed for a boat. She looked down at her flimsy frock and stockinged legs. Climbing about in boats would ruin her stockings and probably dirty her frock too.

Richard followed her look. 'Oh don't worry about your clothes. As long as you don't mind taking your shoes off then the heels won't damage the deck.'

For a moment she looked at him in amazement, wondering how a boat's deck could be so important, then she saw the funny side of it and smiled a little. He looked at her, puzzled, then understanding flashed into his eyes and he laughed. He said, 'You'll have to forgive me. You see, *Dancer's* the love of my life and, like all good women, she has to be pampered!' Still laughing, he let in the clutch and the car moved off.

They stopped for a moment outside another building while he collected some things from his quarters and then they were through the gates and heading towards the Tamar River. Julie realised they were on their way to the boat, though she hadn't actually said she would go. But she was glad. Why not? She had nothing better to do.

They left the main road and started slowly down a rough lane towards the water. As the car bumped and swayed along, Julie asked: 'How did you manage to find this amazing colour?'

'Sorry?'

The little car was noisy and Julie raised her voice. 'The car, why is it such a bright blue?'

'Ah! What colour is every *other* Austin 7 in the world?'

'Black. Or sometimes grey. Or a sort of beige.'

'Exactly! Very dreary. That's why I decided to paint this one blue!' He laughed again. He seemed to laugh most of the time, and Julie found herself smiling too.

She decided she was glad she had come.

The afternoon was warm and Julie lay on the foredeck with her face

44

towards the sun. She had taken her stockings and shoes off in the car and left them on the back seat with her coat. Richard had lent her a waterproof jacket to put round her shoulders in the small rowing boat and then, when they arrived on board *Dancer*, he had found her a sweater. The sweater was enormous and she probably looked extraordinary in it, but she didn't mind. Somehow it didn't seem very important.

She had done very little all day and it had been wonderful. She had made the sandwiches and boiled up the kettle for a cup of tea. Then she had lain down here and let herself be lulled by the lapping of the water and the gentle movements of the boat.

Eventually she drifted off into a pleasant dreamless sleep, very different from the long, troubled nights of the previous week. Only the occasional noise of hammering or loud humming from the inside of the boat interrupted the stillness of the day.

When she awoke she guessed it was late afternoon, about four or five o'clock. She looked up and saw that Richard was sitting on top of the cabin roof with a mug of tea in his hand, watching her with amusement. He grinned. 'Have a nice sleep?'

'Oh, I'm sorry. I didn't mean to sleep so long. I just seemed to nod off.'

'Yes, it does that to you, the sea.' He put down the mug and said, 'Look, I've finished my carpentry. Well . . . I wouldn't say my carpentry was exactly *finished*, but it's as *done* as it ever will be – and it's still standing. So why don't we go for a short sail? Just into the sound and back. Won't take long.' He stood up and made a sweeping gesture with his arm. 'It'll blow the cobwebs away!'

Julie looked at him nervously. She had never been sailing before and the idea didn't appeal to her at all. Yachts looked very unstable – they always seemed to be on the point of tipping over. She also suspected that she was prone to seasickness. Once she and Mother had gone on a steamer trip to Fowey and Julie had felt very peculiar on the way back. Anyway, she knew absolutely nothing about sailing.

He was looking at her expectantly and she said, 'Thank you. It's awfully kind of you to offer but . . . well, I've never sailed before.'

'Then it's high time you did!'

'No, really, I . . . I get seasick.'

'Don't worry! Most people do – *especially* me. I'm always sick as a dog for the first day or two. But that's out at sea. It'll be fine in the sound, there's not a ripple, not a wave. Honestly, trust me!' He lent down and offered her his hand.

She stared up at him and thought: Yes, I do trust you, it's impossible not to. She took his hand and let him pull her up.

He pushed her gently in the direction of the cockpit and went forward to untie a rope.

She called, 'Where shall I sit? On the seat in the back here?'

He laughed. 'It's called the cockpit, and it's situated in something called the stern! This sharp end up here, this is called the bow. Yes, just sit there, next to the companionway.'

Julie sat down and gripped the piece of wood that ran round the cockpit. She watched him pull up the sails and arrange the ropes. Then he threw a chain off the front of the boat and she realised they were off. For a moment everything flapped and there was the most terrible din. Then he ran back to the cockpit and pulled some more ropes. Suddenly the sails stopped flapping and *Dancer* leapt forward.

For a while the yacht skimmed along quite steadily and Julie began to relax a little. Then the little boat shuddered and the next moment it was tipping over. Julie gripped the side and felt a touch of fear. It seemed to her that there was nothing to stop the boat from going all the way over and turning upside down.

She looked back anxiously and saw that Richard was steering the boat quite happily. He said, 'Isn't this wonderful! There's nothing like a good sail! It's a wonderful day for it, too. A really nice breeze.'

Julie looked towards the bow again. It seemed to her that there was altogether too much wind. The boat was still leaning over at a sharp angle and showed no signs of coming upright again. Julie found it impossible to believe that everything was all right, though Richard obviously thought so. She could not rid herself of the feeling that something unexpected and frightening would happen at any moment.

Dancer sped past Drake's Island and into the open sound. Small wavelets rushed at the boat and *Dancer*'s bow pushed a curtain of fine spray up into the air and back into the cockpit. Julie shivered slightly and wondered how much further they would go. Then Richard leaned forward and loosened some ropes. The boat changed direction and gradually came upright again. Immediately the motion was easier and the waves, instead of rushing at the boat, seemed to be travelling with it.

'That's better, eh? No point in getting wet.' He looked at her with a funny mock frown, and she realised he had changed course for her, to make the sail more enjoyable.

'Thanks. It's better like this.'

'Oh yes, it's always better going with the wind. I only wish the wind always blew from behind. But it never does. Quite the opposite, in fact.' He cast his eyes skyward. 'Sometimes I think there's a heavenly conspiracy to make sure it always comes from ahead.'

'Do you really get seasick?'

'Most certainly. There are two stages to seasickness, so they say, one when you want to die, and the second when you're frightened you're not going to. Well, I go through both! The only remedy is to keep busy, stay on deck as much as possible – and remember it can't last for ever.'

'And do you often go far? To places like Brittany?'

'Whenever I have the time I do. This summer I went to the Scillies. Now the Scillies! They're the most wonderful islands in the world. I spent a whole fortnight there and, you wouldn't believe it, but I anchored at a different place every night. Most of the islands are uninhabited. You can walk all day and see nothing but birds.' He said blissfully, 'At one point I didn't see another living soul for four whole days.'

Julie thought: What a strange one you are. All that laughter and charm and you like being on your own.

He went on, 'The Scillies are covered in wrecks, you know, literally hundreds of them. Not surprising really, when you consider where they are, stuck miles out into the sea, just there in the entrance to the English Channel. And they're low, of course; ships can't see them until they're almost on top of them. Not a good place to find yourself in bad weather.' He laughed as if such danger were a great joke and Julie suspected that he would like nothing better than to be sailing off the Isles of Scilly in a storm.

He started to tell her some stories about the Scillies; about the famous wrecks and the people who lived there and the beautiful scenery. As he talked Julie found herself watching him. He was attractive, there was no doubt about that, but not in an obvious way. He wasn't good-looking as Bill had been, and he would probably put on weight when he was older. But those eyes did light up his face. He reminded her of a teddy bear, kind and safe and – yes, cuddly.

She decided that her first impression had been wrong. His charm was not laid on, it was perfectly natural; it stemmed from his enormous enthusiasm for everything he did.

She looked at him and thought: I could have liked you a lot. *Could have* – she had used the past tense automatically. There would be no boyfriends now: that was all over.

Anyway, he probably wasn't interested. Why should he be? There was nothing special about her; Bill had made that quite plain at their last meeting. Besides – how stupid of her not to think of it – he probably had a girlfriend already.

Dancer was sailing quietly into the Cattewater, the creek that leads to the Barbican – the oldest part of the city – and to the fishing harbour. Julie was quite enjoying herself now that there were no waves and hardly any wind.

Richard said, 'Well, best not get into the harbour itself. We'll probably meet a fishing boat coming out. I'll gybe her round and we'll head back to the mooring.'

Julie nodded, not having the slightest idea of what gybing involved. The next moment he shouted, 'Mind your head,' and there was a great crash. For a second Julie thought the mast had come down, but then she saw that it was the noise of the sail changing sides. She laughed and put her hand to her chest. 'You might have warned me!'

'Sorry, I forgot you didn't know about sailing. Listen. I'll explain a few of the basics. It's really quite simple. You see, there are just three things to remember. First, always know where the wind's coming from. Second, pull the sail in just enough to stop it flapping. And three, always try to avoid gybing!'

Julie found herself laughing with him. 'Then how do you turn round?'

'Ah, you turn *into* the wind. That's called tacking.'

She shook her head. 'I'm afraid it's all beyond me. In future I'll leave the sailing to you.'

He didn't say anything but stared at her, searching her eyes. She glanced quickly away, angry with herself. He had taken her remark as an indication of interest; he had thought she was staking a claim. Well, she'd have to make it quite clear that she hadn't meant anything of the sort. What a pity. The day had been going so well.

He was talking again and she saw that he was serious now. 'Sailing is a wonderful freedom, you know. You can just set off for who-knows-where whenever you please. I keep *Dancer* stocked up with food and water all the time. Then I can go whenever I have the time.'

'Isn't it enough to be in the Navy?'

'Oh no, it's not the same at all. Being at sea with three hundred other people in a tin ship is ... well, it's my job. I enjoy it, but it doesn't compare with setting off on your own. I love the excitement, you see, and the challenge of making for a new place, and exploring it. There's nothing like it.'

'But why on your own?'

He thought for a moment. 'Well, I don't always go on my own. I often sail with my father – *Dancer*'s really his boat, not mine. But half the trouble is I haven't met a crew who wants to do the same kind of sailing as I do. So ... there's no other solution. You see, I believe you've got to go out and do what you want to do.'

Julie stared at him. She admired him for his certainty and his self-assurance. It must be wonderful to be so sure of what you wanted and to have such confidence in your ability to succeed. But most of all she admired him for his ability to make his own decisions. She thought: Why can't I be like that? Why am I so bad at deciding? It was easier when you were a man, of course; somehow men had fewer people to consider. But all the same, she should be able to do it, to decide things for the best.

As they sailed back across the open sound the wind increased again and *Dancer* pulled away, cleaving a straight path through the waves. Julie stared ahead, trying to enjoy herself but feeling the unhappiness closing in on her again. The day was almost over. Soon she would have to decide whether to return to the wardroom and risk the dreadful humiliation of seeing Bill, or give up and go home to face her mother. What a choice!

Dancer drifted slowly into the creek and Richard Ashley sprinted forward to lower the sails. As soon as he'd finished he ran back and pushed the tiller hard over so that *Dancer* turned in a neat semicircle. Then he picked up a boathook and, running forward again, used it to fish a bright red buoy out of the water. He was breathing hard. He called back, 'You see, nothing to it! You could learn in no time!'

She smiled. Sailing was as much a mystery to her as it had been at the beginning of the day. The only thing she *could* say was that the experience had been less unpleasant than she'd thought. But the sea still terrified her. She decided she had no desire to try it again.

By the time they got back to the bright blue car it was six o'clock. On the journey back to the officers' quarters Julie hardly spoke. Then he asked, 'Well, what do you want to do? Shall we see if Bill's there? Or do you want to give me the book to pass on?'

'I . . . I don't know.'

'Well, shall we see if he's there then?'

Julie was frozen with indecision. Whatever she did would be wrong. And now there was the added complication of this man – he must have guessed what the situation with Bill was: boy gives girl brush-off, girl can't take hint. He must think she was cheap, to be chasing after a man like this.

Suddenly she made up her mind. 'No, I'll go straight home, thanks. The book really isn't important. I can catch a bus outside the dock-yard.'

'No, I won't hear of it. The least I can do is to drive you home. Where do you live?'

She told him and leant her head back on the seat, happier than she had been for days. It was lovely to have made a decision, and now she had taken it she knew it was the right one. It would have been dreadful to go cap in hand to a man she didn't love and certainly didn't respect. Bill had made it plain that the affair was over. It was up to her now, to make the *best* of a bad situation.

She would go away and make a fresh start.

She glanced across at Richard Ashley. His face was set in lines of concentration as he negotiated the narrow streets of Plymouth. She was thankful to him. He was right about reaching out for things and leading your own life. If you didn't, it seemed to her that everyone else used you to lead theirs. Her mother meant well, but she had always pushed Julie into doing things *she* wanted her to do. And Bill, he had used her too.

Yes she would definitely go away.

But not to anywhere in England: here there was nowhere to go and no-one to help her. It would have to be France then. The thought was rather frightening. She had never met any of her father's immediate family. All she knew was that her grandparents must be very old by now – perhaps dead even – and that she had an uncle and an aunt. And possibly some cousins, though she wasn't sure about that either.

She would have to tell them she had been married, of course, and that it hadn't worked out. They probably wouldn't believe her, but it wouldn't matter as long as appearances were kept up. She would go out and buy a wedding ring. The thought gave her a curious thrill. She would call herself Mrs something – but not Crozier, that was for sure – no, it would be another name. She would have to think up a good one.

She would need a passport, she hadn't thought of that before. She wasn't sure, but she seemed to remember that when you were under twenty-one you had to have parental permission. That would lead to problems with Mother. Julie sighed at the thought of yet more battles ahead.

'Anything the matter?' He was looking at her, concern on his face.

Julie realised she must have sighed out loud. 'Oh no, nothing. I was just thinking, that's all.'

He nodded and looked back at the road.

The little car drew up outside Number 34 Radley Terrace. Julie had no doubt her mother would be peering through the curtains, but she didn't care. She turned to him. 'Thanks so much. It's been a lovely day. I can't tell you how much I enjoyed it.'

'It was *my* pleasure entirely!' He glanced down at his hands then said, 'Look, it would be super if you could come again some time. Would you like that? I could do with a first mate.'

'Oh, I . . . I'm very honoured to be asked. But, well . . . I'm going away soon, you see. Very soon.'

'Ah!'

He was taken by surprise, she could see that, and she tried to smooth the moment over. 'I'm going to live with my relatives in France for a while, to work there and learn the language. I've always wanted to go.'

'To Brittany?'

She nodded.

'Well, I hope you have a good time there. I'm sure you will. The Bretons are wonderful people.' He sounded disappointed and a little puzzled. He must think her devious for not having mentioned the trip before.

Julie wished she could explain about having to go, but there was no point in starting explanations she couldn't finish. It was best as it was.

She opened the door and said, 'Goodbye, and thank you again.'

He smiled at her and the kindness was back in his eyes. 'Bye. I hope it all goes well!'

What a nice man you are, she thought.

She closed the door and walked up the path. The sound of the noisy little engine faded down the road. She turned to wave, but the bright blue car was already out of sight round the corner.

She paused at the front door, the key in her hand, and thought: Brittany. Yes, I'll definitely go to Brittany.

It was easy to say now, surprisingly easy . . . but would she ever be able to go through with it?

She thought: I'm going to *have* to.

And she opened the door and went quickly into the house before she changed her mind.

3

The Bay of Lubeck is wide and open. On its southern shore lies the busy port of Travemunde and beyond that, some miles up the broad Trave River, is the city of Lubeck. On the north-western shore of the bay, some twenty miles from Travemunde and well away from prying eyes, is the small harbour of Pelzerhaken. It was here that the German Navy had built one of its principal research establishments, a group of low, ugly buildings surrounded by barbed wire.

On this September day a blustery north-easter was blowing in from the Arctic, bringing a cool foretaste of the winter ahead. Out in the wide bay short steep seas bowled in from the open Baltic, throwing angry white surf on the holiday beaches lining the shore. At the single wharf in Pelzerhaken Harbour the trials ship *Welle* tugged uneasily at her lines as the strong wind pulled at the mass of aerials and strange dish-shaped objects sprouting from her super-structure.

David Freymann shivered and pulled his jacket tighter round his neck. He felt the ship move slightly and hoped that, once they got under way, he wouldn't be seasick. He usually was, even in a rowing boat.

Ellen said he was stupid even to consider coming on this trip because he was bound to disgrace himself. She also said that the only reason he got seasick was because he was overweight and didn't take any exercise. Ellen had a way of implying that everything was somehow David's fault, but he didn't mind. In most ways she was a good wife and she wasn't having an easy time of it at the moment. She complained about being neglected and she was absolutely right. His work was taking up more and more time. He had tried to explain to her how important it was and how much it meant to him, but she didn't understand. That, he thought fondly, was women for you.

He realised with a shock that, come October, they would have been married fifteen years. On their anniversary it would be a good idea to spoil her a bit; he would take her out for a meal in Berlin, to a good restaurant on the Unter den Linden. Fifteen years: he could hardly believe it. Little Cecile must be almost eight. It was strange how the time flew so quickly, yet one remained young inside. He'd be forty-five this year, almost middle-aged.

Still, as long as you achieved something lasting, then age didn't really matter. He looked up at one of the dish-shaped objects above the *Welle*'s bridge. Now *there* was something lasting, something that really mattered. An achievement that any man would be proud of.

David walked across the deck to where Hans Rathenow was stand-ing. Hans had been David's colleague for a year now, ever since they had joined the new Gema Company together. Hans was a good sort: hard-working, straightforward and kind. David liked him a lot. There was a bond of fellowship and camaraderie between them which came from working on the same project. Together they had solved the problem of range measurement. It had been a hard one to crack but somehow David had known they would do it.

Hans inclined his head in the direction of the land. 'The brass are late.'

David laughed. 'That's their privilege.'

'How many are there going to be? Do you know?'

David shook his head.

'Well, I hope there aren't too many, otherwise we'll never be able to deal with all their questions.' Hans liked to have plenty of time to consider questions, so that his answers could be as precise and complete as possible.

The two men watched a lorry bump along the wharf and stop in front of a warehouse. Hans turned and said, 'By the way, have you heard the rumour about Telefunken?' David looked blank and Hans continued, 'Evidently, they're to be given a government contract like ours, but to develop a device for aircraft.'

'Oh.' David frowned and tried to hide his surprise. 'I thought *we* were to do the work on small devices. I . . . I've been working on the programme scheduling.'

'Yes.' Hans gave David a sympathetic glance. 'I know. And I know you are right in your approach. But I fear that Schmidt does not see it your way.'

David stared into the distance, and sighed. Schmidt, head of the research programme and recently appointed Chief Scientist of the Third Reich, had long been a thorn in his side.

David touched the other man's arm. 'I tell you something, my friend – not only am I sure that it is possible to develop small devices for aircraft, but I am certain those devices could be made incredibly powerful. Can you imagine what definition and detail could be achieved by using exceptionally short waves?'

Hans smiled kindly. 'Yes, but David, no valve exists which is remotely capable of such a thing. Where is your power to come from?'

'I have an idea; I believe it could work. It would take less than six months to prove either way. All I need is two people, a bit of space and some resources.' He ran a hand through his hair. 'But this new contract . . . Now Schmidt will have the perfect excuse to refuse me permission. And I've no doubt he *will* refuse.'

Hans nodded solemnly.

The wind gusted across the deck and David stamped his feet to ward off the cold. He said, 'I could offer my services to Telefunken, I suppose. Perhaps they might be prepared to follow my idea in spite of Schmidt.'

'I doubt it, I doubt it very much.' Hans paused, deep in thought. When he finally spoke, it was very quietly and David had to turn his head to hear. 'You must think very carefully about your position, David. I worry about you.'

'What do you mean? Schmidt cannot eat me, you know. He is

stupid and arrogant, certainly, but he knows my worth. He won't throw me out or anything. Why should he?'

'It is not Schmidt himself I worry about. It is the . . . the official policy.'

David began to understand. 'My friend, you mean I will be pushed out because I am Jewish?' He smiled and shook his head. 'First, I don't believe this silly campaign will go on. Second, they will never interfere with work like mine; it's too important. They aren't stupid, you know.'

'I hope you're right, but I think you're being too generous. I fear it will get worse, not better.'

David shrugged. The events of the last year had been . . . unfortunate, even – yes – deplorable. The Nuremburg decrees had been a shock. Most Jews had been deprived of their citizenship and inter-marriage with Aryans was now forbidden.

Too late for Ellen and me, David thought. They can't *un*marry us after all these years.

There were other things, of course. A number of Jews had been arrested and never seen again. But then the same was happening to others: leftists, intellectuals, trouble-makers. It wasn't *only* the Jews. It was just a question of keeping your nose clean. Keeping out of trouble.

David shook his head. 'No, Hans. I honestly don't think it'll get any worse.' He thought of adding: anyway, not for me. But it sounded too selfish and uncaring, and he kept silent.

A fleet of cars appeared at the end of the wharf and there was a flurry of activity around the ship as sailors stood to attention. The two men began to walk slowly along the deck towards the group already waiting at the top of the gangway. David could see that Hans was still frowning and he said softly, 'So the Jews are excluded from the professions, but that is nothing new. It was the same before the Great War. Anyway, I am more German than Jewish. I'm only half Jewish, in fact. I haven't been inside a synagogue for years, my wife is gentile, my daughter goes to a nice Christian school. I am no threat!'

'That's not the point,' Hans persisted. 'You are officially Jewish. You have your scientific status – *at present* – but you are not safe where you are. Why don't you think about working in this place?' He indicated the complex of stone buildings that made up the research establishment.

David stood still, astonished. 'Here? Why?'

'Haven't you heard? The Navy is refusing to throw Jews out of the service. Old Raeder is defying Hitler. As a naval scientist you would be safe. Hitler will never take on the whole Navy: he's too frightened of it.'

David walked on slowly, shaking his head. Hans meant well, there was no doubt about that, but come and work here? No, it was impossible. Very little original work was done in the establishment. He would die of frustration.

The two men joined the rest of the scientific and naval personnel standing silently in a knot by the rail.

David stroked down his windswept hair and watched the group which was making its way up the gangway. He recognised the well-known figure of Grand Admiral Raeder, Commander-in-Chief of the German Navy, but he was not certain about the others. He was no expert on rank or uniforms, but he guessed there were at least five other admirals in the group. Behind the Grand Admiral was Schmidt, looking as officious and self-satisfied as ever. David sighed inwardly. How simple life would be if the Schmidts of this world were not allowed to poke their noses into the *real* work. The problem with Schmidt was that he was not overblessed with brains. He had never been a good scientist, let alone a great one. Perhaps that was why he had grabbed an administrative job: it was the only thing he could do.

David stood back as Schmidt started to introduce the managers of the Gema Company to the naval officers. David thought how strange official protocol was, when the organisers came before the people who actually did the work. Still, as long as he was allowed to get on with his project, he didn't really mind who took the glory.

When it was David's turn to come forward he tried to concentrate on the name and rank of each man as he shook hands with him but, apart from Raeder, he managed to memorise only about half of them. After the introductions one name – Doenitz – stood out in his mind and he tried to think why. Then he remembered: it had just been announced that Doenitz was to command the new submarine arm of the Kriegsmarine.

U-boats: now there were vessels in need of a really small high-definition apparatus. If the opportunity arose it would be interesting to talk to Doenitz. David looked at the rings of Doenitz's sleeve to make sure that his rank was indeed no higher than that of captain. There was a chance, then, that David would be allowed to talk to him without Schmidt interrupting. Schmidt did not like anybody talking to really senior officers without him being present. He said it was a matter of protecting his scientists from outside interference, but David knew better. Schmidt just hated anything going on without his knowledge, particularly when a scientist had views which differed from his own.

The main group had moved off towards the bridge. Schmidt was pointing to the bowl apparatus and explaining the reason for its shape which differed considerably from that of the earlier prototypes. As Schmidt's voice droned on David felt the deck vibrate beneath his feet and saw that the *Welle* was beginning to move gently away from the wharf. The wind was coming in great gusts now; the sea outside must be very rough.

David began to wish he hadn't come. He'd always disliked physical discomfort – as a child he'd been hopeless at sport and rough games – and he had no doubt the *Welle* would toss and roll like a pig.

Schmidt's voice had ceased and everyone moved into the large chart room behind the wheelhouse. David followed and looked for a quiet corner to stand in, but Schmidt impatiently beckoned him forward and directed him to join some junior officers on the outside of the group. The group had formed a circle round a large metal cabinet bolted to the chart room floor. On the top of the cabinet was a circular screen which the senior officers were watching expectantly.

Schmidt cleared his throat and announced, 'It will take us a few moments to get to the open sea, where the device can best be demonstrated. We beg your indulgence, but we assure you that the wait will not be in vain. You will not be disappointed!'

David felt faintly embarrassed at Schmidt's manner. He was making it like a circus performance. The brass were intelligent men; they didn't go in for dramatics.

Suddenly there was a quiet voice at David's elbow. 'We have not met. My name is Fischer, Karl Fischer.' David turned to see a young officer with his hand outstretched.

'Ah, I'm Freymann, David Freymann.' He shook the hand, then said by way of explanation, 'I work on this project. My field is radio ranging.'

Fischer nodded. 'Well, it will be most interesting to see this device working. I had no idea anything like this was being developed. It is really most extraordinary.'

David smiled politely. 'And yourself, are you on the naval staff?'

'No, no.' Fischer shook his head, and David noticed how even and finely drawn were the younger man's features. The hair was blond, the eyes pale-blue: he supposed this was what the Nazis meant by Aryan. Then he thought: Why on earth did I think that? I'm getting as bad as Hans.

Fischer was saying, 'I have come here with Captain Doenitz. I'm with the First U-boat Flotilla at Kiel, in command of U-13.'

'Ah.' David did not know much about the new submarine arm.

'It is the first operational flotilla. It is a great honour to serve in it.'

'Indeed, indeed. It is wonderful that Germany has submarines again, after all these years.'

Fischer looked at the device humming quietly in the centre of the chart room. 'And this, will it be useful for submarines?'

'Well, at present – in this form – no. As you see the whole thing is too large. Really it is only suitable for use on ships – or on land, of course. It would never fit into submarines or, for that matter, aircraft.'

'I see, I see.' Fischer frowned in concentration. 'And what about being *detected* by such a thing. Could an enemy detect *us* easily? I am thinking particularly of when we are on the surface at night.'

David looked at Fischer with new respect. Here at least was someone who recognised the possibility of an enemy possessing this device, which was more than Schmidt did. He said, 'Well, yes, a surfaced submarine *could* be picked up. But it would be difficult. A submarine is so low in the water – and so much smaller than a ship, of course – that the conditions would have to be perfect for an enemy to see you. I mean, a calm sea and the range between three and five miles. But even if a ship did manage to detect you I imagine there would be plenty of time to dive and get away. A plane . . . now a plane would be a bit more tricky. If a plane managed to detect you it could be on top of you very quickly.'

'I thought you said it was impossible to construct a device small enough to fit in a plane.'

David shook his head. 'Ah, no. What I said was, *this* device is not suitable for planes. I did not say it was impossible to develop small devices. Quite the opposite.'

Fischer nodded slowly. 'After the demonstration, could we talk again? I know that Captain Doenitz would be most interested in what you have to say.'

'Of course.' David was pleased. It would be an honour to talk to Doenitz.

The *Welle* had begun to pitch gently and David realised they must have reached the open sea. He looked out through one of the chart room's large ports and saw rolling, white-topped waves. He tried to concentrate on the horizon: someone had told him it stopped you from feeling sick.

Schmidt was speaking again. 'As you know we have been working hard on the development of the DT device. Incidentally, I shall continue to call it by its cover name, the DT Apparatus, because secrecy is so important. Originally you may have heard it called the revolving turret device, but more properly it should be called a radio detection and ranging device, or radar for short.' He cleared his throat and paused. Ever theatrical, David thought. Well, perhaps it was justified. It was, after all, a special occasion.

'When we last demonstrated the device, we could not give you great range accuracy. And of course it is not much good if you don't know how far away your opponent is. But now . . .' Schmidt put a hand on the metal cabinet. 'I am glad to say that, by means of a revolutionary new concept, we can give you the range of your enemy to within about a quarter of a nautical mile.'

Schmidt's audience was silent and expectant. For a moment there was no sound except the hum of the device and the vibration of the ship's engines. Then the chief scientist continued, 'We have developed a *pulse* system which sends out a short but powerful radio signal in a single burst. It then waits for the signal to return before sending another. By measuring the time it takes for the signal to get to its target and return, we can measure range with a good degree of accuracy.'

Schmidt raised his voice. 'Furthermore, gentlemen, that range is now improved. You will be able to see land approximately ten miles away, other ships eight miles away, and aircraft as much as fifteen miles away.'

He stepped to one side. 'And now, gentlemen, I invite you to look at the screen, to see for yourselves.'

Admiral Raeder and the senior officers stepped forward and leant over the screen. Schmidt pointed to a piece of coast visible on the port side and then put his finger on to the screen. Comparisons were made and there was a great deal of nodding; the brass were obviously impressed. David felt pleased. Schmidt then ordered the aerial to be rotated and the group examined the echo of a ship which was just visible on the horizon. Raeder summoned more of his colleagues and Schmidt began his explanations afresh.

David was feeling sick. The trick of staring at the horizon had not worked at all. The *Welle* seemed to be rolling and pitching in every direction and each new movement took his stomach by surprise. He edged towards the door in case he had to make a sudden dash for the rail. He realised he should try to be unobtrusive, but he was fast getting to the stage where he didn't care.

Suddenly the sickness welled up. David pulled open the door and heaved over the rail. As soon as his stomach was empty he felt better. The fresh wind helped too; it seemed to blow the cobwebs out of his head. He concentrated on the horizon again. This time the trick seemed to work and the nausea passed. But he decided against going back into the chart room; he wouldn't last five minutes in there.

After a while he became mesmerised by the rise and fall of the waves. At one point he looked down to where the waves growled along the ship's side. But that was a mistake – it brought the nausea back – and he quickly looked up again. Then he tried closing his eyes and found that, despite the sharp wind, he was able to doze where he stood. The sensation was quite pleasant: he felt as if he were floating, gently suspended in water.

'Ahem.' Someone was clearing his throat. For a moment David hoped the sound might go away, but it was repeated. Reluctantly he opened his eyes and turned round.

It was Fischer. Beside him stood the tall, erect figure of Captain Doenitz.

Fischer said, 'Herr Freymann, may I introduce Captain Doenitz? The Captain would be most grateful if you would answer a few of his queries.'

David tried to wake himself up. He smiled thinly and said, 'Of course.'

The captain was frowning in concentration. He had a sharp face with thin lips and protruding ears. But most of all David noticed his eyes, which were small and penetrating, like those of a small animal.

Doenitz spoke slowly, choosing his words carefully. 'I have grasped the principles of the DT device. I understand how it can be used against aircraft and surface vessels *by* surface vessels. But I gather this device will never be suitable for submarines. Is that correct?'

David made an effort to concentrate. 'In its present form, no. It is too large and cumbersome.'

'Can it be made smaller?'

'It is possible, but it means using shorter wavelengths.'

'And this can be done?'

David nodded. 'Work on slightly shorter wavelengths is to start soon, I believe.'

'Slightly – ?'

David sighed and looked down. What was he to do? Tell the truth and suffer Schmidt's wrath, or toe the official line?

He brought his eyes back to Doenitz's face. The captain's expression was enquiring but anxious. The answer was obviously important to him.

David thought: Why not? This man deserves to know.

He said, 'Yes, only *slightly* shorter. Investigation into really short wavelengths is not being considered at present. There is a belief that such short wavelengths are impossible to generate – and that they

59

would be *less* efficient rather than *more* efficient. But . . .' David said firmly, 'this is only a belief. It is by no means proved.'

Doenitz was trying to absorb the information. 'But if it *was* possible,' he said slowly, 'it would be useful for us?'

'Not just useful, it would be *revolutionary*!' David talked rapidly, his sickness forgotten. 'You see, first, short waves would make the device very small indeed. It would be no more than the size of – of say a large suitcase standing on its end. Obviously it would fit easily inside a plane or a submarine. That would mean – well, you can imagine! For the Luftwaffe, it would mean they would be able to see enemy planes coming from miles away, even at night. For you, it would mean you could find your enemy and make your attack in the blackest of conditions!'

David always liked to understand the practical applications of his work. So few scientists did, and that, he believed, was a great mistake. It meant you were much slower to appreciate the shortcomings of your inventions – and slower, too, to *foresee* problems.

David paused before going on. So far he had stated facts that were generally accepted – although Schmidt would have a seizure if he knew David had mentioned them. But it was the next part – the most *important* part – that was really David's personal theory. And not only was the theory unproved, but Schmidt was bitterly opposed to it.

David hesitated, then said quickly, 'It would also be revolutionary for a second reason – though I must tell you immediately that I am almost alone in this belief.'

Doenitz nodded and David went on, 'I believe that a valve could be developed to give enormous power on short waves. This would mean that the device would be small *and* immensely powerful. It would give the most incredible definition . . .'

He was not explaining it properly. These men wanted to know what it meant in practical terms. He searched for the right words. 'It would *pick out* each individual object in a group of objects, almost like a photograph. This device here –' he indicated the cabinet in the chart room – 'is useful only for seeing objects against the *sky*, so to speak – for things standing out against a blank background, like an aircraft in the sky or a ship on the horizon. Even then it would be of limited use in a plane because when it is angled down to the land or the sea it cannot pick out individual targets. It gets too many echoes back from the sea or the land for the user to distinguish individual towns or buildings or ships out of the blur.'

David paused to make sure he had been understood. The two men nodded and he went on, 'Now a shortwave device . . . well, it could see like – like a pair of eyes. From the air it could look *downwards* and read the land like a map. It could pick out individual towns, rivers, lakes, and roads; it could identify individual bombing targets; it could see small objects floating on the surface of the sea; it could see a submarine sitting on the water. *Nothing* would be hidden from it.'

Doenitz stared at David in alarm. 'If this is true, it is . . . very important. But you say that there is doubt about this. You say some people believe such a device would be *less* efficient?'

David spoke carefully. 'There is a school of thought which believes it is impossible to develop the power. But personally I do not. I believe the necessary valve *can* be developed.'

'If there is the slightest chance of it, then –' Doenitz pursed his lips and looked out to sea.

'Of course I would have to do a lot of work on it. And I would need official support . . .'

Doenitz looked at him sharply. 'I have no say in scientific policy. However . . . I shall do what I can.'

David nodded and wondered how much longer he could survive without being sick again. He gave himself a minute, certainly no more. It had been all right while he'd been talking.

Doenitz fixed his dark, penetrating stare on to David and said, 'So a submarine would be particularly vulnerable to a shortwave device?'

'Yes.'

'Do we know if anybody else is working on it? The British, for instance?'

'I'm not sure. I can only say that, as a scientist, I have read nothing – I have heard nothing – to indicate that they have the secret.'

'If they did . . .'

David thought quickly. 'If they did then we could produce a warning device, a detector, to tell a vessel that radar was being operated against them.'

Doenitz's eyes lit up. 'Ah, so there *is* a defence.'

'Yes,' David agreed. 'But we can only develop a detector when we have developed our own technology. No technology, no detector.' David was forced to be brief; he had only a few seconds left.

'I understand. Thank you.' Doenitz inclined his head and for a moment David thought he would continue. But he turned and walked away.

David threw himself across the rail and heaved miserably. Though his stomach was empty, the convulsions went on for several minutes. When he finally looked round the two naval officers had gone.

David laid his head on his arm and closed his eyes. He no longer cared what he looked like; nor did he mind if people were laughing at him. He just wanted to die.

After several minutes he looked up. There was no sign of land. It seemed to him that they were still heading out to sea.

Hilf mir Gott! It was an expression his father often used. His father – dead, and thank God for that. He had been Jewish and proud of it.

'Freymann! Freymann!'

Without bothering to look up David knew it was Schmidt.

'Freymann, I am appalled!' The voice was angry, hissing like a snake. David waved a hand of acknowledgement. Nothing would make him raise his head again.

'I absolutely forbid you to speak to anyone else during this trip. You are absolutely not to be trusted. How dare you! How dare you give people the idea that we don't know what we're doing!' The voice spluttered for a moment, then continued, 'Your lunatic ideas! They are dangerous and stupid and . . . I will speak to you later. In the meantime keep away, just *keep away!*'

David waved a hand again. Schmidt's order suited him perfectly: no more talking and no more questions to answer. If no-one was going to believe him, there was no point anyway.

He was beginning to think Ellen was right: he should never have come.

Doenitz excused himself from a discussion on the use of radar in surface warfare and left the chart room. He chose to go out to the starboard side of the ship so as to avoid the scientist, Freymann, who was still wedged firmly against the port rail.

Doenitz walked slowly towards the afterdeck and wondered if there had been any truth in what the odd little man had said. The fellow had been so enthusiastic, so *sure*, that Doenitz had almost been convinced. But then he had talked to Schmidt and Schmidt had been adamant that Freymann was talking nonsense. In fact he had been so vehement Doenitz suspected that there was a great deal of animosity between the two men. Personal differences should not be allowed to interfere with people's judgement. Doenitz never allowed such things to happen among his men. Nor did he let himself be swayed by personal feelings. One's duty was to serve, and to serve to the utmost of one's ability.

But these scientists were different. They seemed to be incapable of working as a team. Still, Doenitz thought, one has to learn to live with these people, irksome though they may be, if one is to benefit from their extraordinary inventions.

He considered whether to bring up the subject of Freymann's theory with the Grand Admiral. But no, he decided, it would not be necessary. Schmidt had promised Doenitz that the theory would be investigated, and finally and conclusively proved or disproved either way.

Besides, Doenitz had more important things to worry about. For years Germany's strength had been severely curtailed by the humiliating Versailles Treaty, but now at last the Anglo-German Naval Agreement had been signed and Germany was allowed to build a navy again.

It was a race against time.

German U-boat development had never really stopped – it had been carried out secretly in Holland since 1922 – but it would be years, perhaps as many as ten years, before the Kriegsmarine – and particularly the U-boat Arm – would be powerful enough to take on the Royal Navy.

There was a tremendous amount of work to do. It wasn't just a question of building vessels but of development and training . . .

Doenitz had paused at the after rail, but now he turned and started to pace back along the deck. He looked up and saw the figure of Fischer waiting patiently a few yards away. The U-boat arm needed more men like Fischer, men who served with skill, optimism and enthusiasm.

He beckoned the younger man over and the two of them fell into step. Doenitz said, 'It has been an interesting day, hasn't it?'

'Yes, sir. Most fascinating. This device will obviously be very useful to us.'

'We will see. I don't always believe everything that these things are meant to do. When we've had a chance to try it *on exercise*, then I will believe it!'

'Will we have a fleet exercise soon?'

'In the spring, I expect. And then we will be able to display our tactics for the first time. It is very important that we show the High Command the effectiveness of the wolf pack. They must understand that our success depends on numbers.'

Fischer nodded thoughtfully. 'Yes, sir. I see. Greater numbers . . .' He looked at his new commanding officer with gratitude. 'Thank you for telling me. It makes me realise how important our training programme will be this winter.'

Doenitz nodded. His policy was always to tell his junior officers as much as possible. Above all else he valued trust and loyalty, and he believed that they grew not from aloofness, but from mutual openness and understanding of each other's problems. He intended to be fully

63

involved in the day-to-day activities of his men. Whenever possible he would meet boats when they returned from exercise, he would attend debriefings, he would hear about operational problems first-hand. He did not intend to lose touch with his men, ever.

There were certain things they could not be told, of course. It would be wrong to talk about the power struggles between the Navy and the Luftwaffe, which Goering, as Hitler's favourite, was already winning; it would be wrong too to say how worrying Hitler's ideas about warfare were. Hitler had made a friendly gesture to Britain, it was true, and that was the wisest thing to have done, but Doenitz wondered if Hitler appreciated that a war, if it came, would inevitably be fought against Britain. And the only way to beat Britain was to choke off her supplies, to sink all her merchant shipping, to make her slowly but surely starve.

For that they needed U-boats and lots of them.

Doenitz said, 'Yes, we have much to do this winter. As soon as the flotilla is up to strength, we will work up our tactics.' He looked towards Pelzerhaken which was coming up ahead as the *Welle* made for the shelter of the harbour once more. 'The wolf pack will revolutionise warfare at sea. Think of the number of ships that can be sunk by a group of U-boats hunting together; it will be three to four times the total that all U-boats could achieve on their own. Also, I believe that such tactics will take our enemies by surprise.'

Fischer frowned. He was wholeheartedly behind his new captain and just as anxious to prove that these new tactics would work. But he, like everyone else, had heard about the new British invention, Asdic, which used sound waves to detect submarines underwater. The British seemed to think their invention would mean the end of the submarine as an offensive weapon. Tentatively he asked, 'What about Asdic? The British are boasting about it. They seem very confident in it.'

Doenitz stopped and looked at Fischer. 'But it's only effective against *submerged* boats. When we attack, it will be at night on the *surface*. They will have no defence against that. Of course, after an attack they will come after us and then, once we are dived, they will use it against us. But even so, we only have their word for its effectiveness. It's like this radar here; I will believe it when I see it!'

The captain started pacing the deck again and Fischer had to stride out to keep up with him. Doenitz said with emphasis, 'In fact, Asdic has done us a good turn. It has made the British complacent. You know they have fewer submarines than the French? They think submarines will not be important. Well, if war comes, we will prove them wrong.'

'What about the small DT device the scientist was talking about? Will we be getting some for our boats?'

Doenitz shook his head. 'Apparently the little man suffers from over-optimism. He was talking about a really small device, but it seems this will not be possible. If we are lucky we will get something that might just fit into a U-boat. Even then I will want its effectiveness proved.'

Doenitz clasped his hands behind his back and wished the *Welle* would hurry back to her berth. He wanted to return to Kiel as soon as possible. There was so much to do and so little time to do it in.

Fischer went on, 'And the British – they don't have the DT device?'

'No, they don't.' Doenitz almost added: at least that's what we're told. Schmidt had better be right about that, otherwise – well, the consequences hardly bore thinking about.

'That's the main thing anyway,' Fischer said with a smile. 'At least we'll be free to make surprise attacks on the surface.'

'Yes.' And if we don't have that, thought Doenitz, we don't have anything. If, by any dreadful chance, the little scientist was right, if a device could be made to pick out a submarine on the surface in any weather, on the thickest of nights, then his wolf pack strategy would be in ruins.

His boats and his men would be desperately vulnerable.

Like sitting ducks.

The Hamburg-Berlin express lumbered slowly into Lehrter Bahnhof. The squeal of brakes and the hiss of escaping steam woke David up. He stretched his arms and nudged Hans, still snoring in the seat beside him. 'We're here.'

It was late, almost ten o'clock. David couldn't remember what time the last train to Hennigsdorf left, probably about eleven. He should have plenty of time to get to Stettiner Bahnhof and catch it.

Hans was looking at his watch and cursing. 'I must rush. My train leaves in half an hour!'

David followed him on to the platform and said, 'You go ahead. I'm going to see if I can get something to eat.'

Hans laughed. 'What, more?' Then waved and strode off.

David went into the station buffet and ordered bratwurst, sauerkraut, black bread and beer. He was amazed at how hungry he was, even after the substantial dinner he had eaten on the train. One good thing about seasickness – the *only* good thing – was that you felt marvellous afterwards.

Ellen said he ate too much, and she was right. But there would be nothing hot waiting for him when he got home; Ellen liked to eat early and have the kitchen tidied by the time she went to bed at ten.

She was a good wife, Ellen, but she did like her sleep. David had long since realised that she couldn't function without at least nine hours a night. He never disturbed her when he came in late and he always woke her in the mornings with a cup of lemon tea. On Sundays he did not wake her at all, and she often slept until ten or eleven. Then he would take Cecile for a walk, and they would have long talks about how trees grew, and why steam drove trains and what made lightning strike church steeples. She was a bright child and David was immensely proud of her. Her science reports were very good and David secretly hoped she might be a physicist or perhaps a biologist. He never said as much to Ellen, who thought science not only dull but extremely unsuitable for a girl.

It was ten-twenty and David hurriedly finished his meal. The last train might well leave before eleven and it would be stupid to miss it.

Outside the station he waited for a bus to Stettiner Bahnhof. But when none had appeared after five minutes he decided to walk. It would do him good. Anyway the station wasn't far, just ten minutes walk along Invalidenstrasse. He relaxed again. There was plenty of time. He needn't have worried.

Ellen said he didn't worry enough, and there was some truth in it. Yet he did worry about things that mattered, like Cecile and her education and her happiness. What he couldn't see any point in fretting about was money or the cost of living or politics or any of those things.

When David arrived at Stettiner Bahnhof he discovered he had ten minutes to spare. The last train for Hennigsdorf was due to leave at ten-fifty-five.

He sat on a bench to wait. Somehow he had known he would have plenty of time. He often got a feeling about things. He had a feeling about his shortwave research project. He just knew that somehow, somewhere, it would go ahead. It was just a question of waiting and putting his case before the right people. Whether his talk with Doenitz had helped or not he did not know, but it had certainly stirred things up a bit. Schmidt had been purple with anger. David smiled and thought: Well, it can't do any harm.

The Hennigsdorf train arrived and he got into an empty compartment. Eventually the train drew out and began its slow journey into the suburbs.

David watched the bright lights of the city pass by and considered his project. The more he thought about it, the more determined he was to get the thing off the ground. They all said the idea was impossible. They said that no valve could ever produce the sort of power he needed. True, nothing existed at the moment – but it *could*. It *would*. He would make one.

The train drew into Hennigsdorf and he got out, turning the matter of the valve over in his mind. He went out of the station and automatically turned left towards home. He walked with his head down, deep in thought. At present there were two kinds of valve, the klystron and the magnetron. If he could take the best qualities of both and combine them . . . keep the magnetron but use a closed resonator . . .

He was passing a shop and something in the window caught his eye. He looked up. It was a large notice pasted across the window. It said, simply: *Jude!*

David realised it was old Finstein's shoe shop. He stood staring at the window for a long time. He knew this happened in the centre of the city, but here, in Hennigsdorf? This place was so quiet, so safe. Everyone knew each other. Damn it, everyone knew old Finstein.

He walked slowly on, thinking of what Hans had said. He couldn't believe there was really a risk of losing his job. For others, well, he had to admit that it was not a good time to be in business or one of the professions. But the Jews had been through times like this before. As he'd said to Hans, there had been some unpleasantness before the Great War, but it had passed like these things always did. The new laws would make marriages like his and Ellen's illegal. Well, he repeated to himself, they couldn't *unmarry* two people who had been married fifteen years. As for Cecile, nothing would happen to her. She was a second generation *Mischlinge*, or mixed-blood. She counted as German. Nothing would ever happen to her or to Ellen. And as for making him leave – well, they were doing that to the poor and to the business people but they would never do that to him. They *needed* him; they knew it and he knew it. There was no more to be said.

He turned into the street where he lived and felt the familiar warmth of anticipation. Whenever he walked up the slight hill under the row of linden trees, he looked forward to the first sight of his small house, so neat and pretty. It gave him a peculiar thrill to think that this was his own small patch.

The house was dark, as he knew it would be, and he opened the door very quietly so as not to wake anybody. He checked that all the doors were locked and then climbed the stairs. He paused on the landing and crept towards the open door of the back bedroom. He looked in and saw Cecile's dark hair spread across the pillow.

He knelt beside the bed and caressed her hair.

He whispered the words he had always whispered, ever since she was a baby. 'I love you, *meine kleine Rosenknospe*, I love you.'

He thought: What a lucky man I am, to have so much – my work, my house, my family. And you, my *Liebling*, most of all, to have you.

And then he whispered out loud, 'I will love you and protect you always. Always.'

4

The tolling of a single bell echoed faintly over the city. Vasson thought: Is it really Sunday? He'd quite forgotten.

Mea culpa! Mea culpa! Lord forgive me, for I have sinned . . .

To hell with it. He hated Sundays.

It was a perfect August day, clear, sunny and not too hot. The sunlight was bright yellow, transforming the drab streets of the *dix-huitième* into brilliant ribbons of light. Vasson screwed up his eyes and walked slowly across the Place du Têrtre. A couple of artists sat doggedly at their easels, painting yet more bad pictures of the Sacré-Cœur. They were probably English or American like most of the so-called artists in this quarter. Vasson had heard that many were packing their bags and disappearing back to their own countries. Apparently the wealthy American tourists had already left their expensive hotels and crowded aboard the transatlantic liners in Cherbourg.

Let them go, Vasson thought. They're no loss to anyone. Life in Montmartre would be just the same without them.

He walked gently towards Pigalle – gently because his head ached and his eyes hurt and he had a stinking hangover. He should have stayed in bed.

On the street corners and in the cafés the news-vendors were doing a roaring trade. It seemed that all the residents of Montmartre wanted a newspaper today and when Vasson tried to buy *Turf*, the only paper he ever bought nowadays, he found it had sold out like all the rest. It was annoying. He was planning to bet on a big race at Longchamps and now he wouldn't be able to study the form.

The world had gone mad; everyone was behaving like a lot of frightened rabbits. So the Germans were going to swallow up the

Poles. So what? Vasson couldn't see how that affected France. Poland had nothing to do with France. At least it damned well *shouldn't*.

He emerged on to the Boulevard Rochechouart and walked the last few yards into Place Pigalle. The club was situated in a tiny street leading off the circus. In the harsh light of day the façade looked drab and slightly seedy, but in darkness, when the name was illuminated in scarlet and the doorway open to reveal the softly lit staircase, the effect was inviting and seductive.

Vasson went down the stairs into the darkness of the club, grateful to rest his eyes from the painful sunlight. The floor had been washed and the chairs were upturned on the tables. He walked round the edge of the room to the bar. Without a word the barman poured him a coffee and pushed it across the counter.

Vasson pulled a chair off the nearest table and sat down wearily. He cast a critical eye around the room. He had the feeling that the previous night's takings must have been high. The club had been crowded from ten onwards and most of the customers were big spenders. But . . . He sighed. There was so much room for improvement. The takings could be so much better, maybe even *double*, if only –

If only –

He knew exactly what made a successful club. He had analysed the ingredients countless times during the last four years.

There was the music. Now that was the one thing this club could boast about. Its music was much classier than you generally heard in the small intimate clubs. Instead of an accordion or solitary piano, there was a three-piece band, with piano, bass and drums. And the band was good. They played a few of the new-style swing numbers for those who wanted a wild dance, but for the rest of the time they stuck to slow romantic stuff. Perfect for getting the customers close to the girls and keen to spend their money.

The décor: now that could be much better. It was very out of date, all red plush and gilt. From the look of it nothing had been changed since 1910. Vasson would have liked to see mirrored walls, chromium furniture and a black linoleum floor, the kind of simple sophistication which was all the rage.

But the main problem was the girls. Some of them were distinctly rough-looking even in the near-total darkness of the club. Only the drunkest or blindest customers managed to find them attractive. They should be replaced, and straight away. It was stupid to economise on the girls' wages. Much better to pay more and get top class women who would not only attract the money but be highly skilled at extracting it.

He sighed. This club could be one of the best small places around, if not *the* best.

He downed his coffee and took the cup back to the bar. The barman was washing glasses. Vasson called, 'Hey, how *were* the takings last night? They must have been good.'

The barman eyed Vasson impassively. 'Good enough, I should think.'

'But I mean, a record or what?'

The barman stared and there was a hint of insolence in his expression. Vasson was irritated; the man was being less than co-operative. He said impatiently, 'Look, I need the information if I'm to run this place properly. That *is* what I'm meant to be doing, you know, running the place!' He knew he sounded peevish, but he couldn't help himself.

The barman smirked and shrugged his shoulders. Vasson wanted to hit him.

Suddenly there was a voice at Vasson's shoulder, so close that it made him jump. 'Yes, you run the club – but it's me that runs the money. And don't you forget it.'

Vasson flushed and turned round. It was Birelli. Birelli was small, fat and bad-tempered. He was wearing a flashy suit and expensive gold cufflinks. He looked every inch the proprietor of a small club.

Which was precisely what he was.

Birelli owned three clubs, and this was one of them.

Vasson said nothing. Birelli wanted a reaction and he bloody well wasn't going to get one.

Birelli took out a cigar and slowly lit it, his beady eyes watching Vasson through the clouds of smoke. Finally he said, 'While I'm the owner of this place, I will worry about the takings, and no-one else.' The little man exhaled and the stench of garlic hit Vasson's nostrils. Instinctively Vasson pulled back, but Birelli moved closer and said with emphasis, 'You would do better to mind your own business and stick to your job, such as it is. If you go on poking your nose into things that do not concern you, you'll be amazed at how quickly you'll be out in the street.'

Vasson shivered. He had the urge to crush the man's head against the wall. He wanted to chant obscenities at the pompous self-satisfied little pig, then beat him into pulp. And to think he had actually put up with this cheap little crook for more than six months. It was obscene!

Birelli was watching Vasson's reaction with satisfaction, and Vasson realised the little man knew exactly what was going through his mind.

70

Birelli drew breath and said, 'Furthermore, while we're on the subject of you and your incompetence, I'm tired of hearing about your grandiose ideas. They are idiotic rubbish; they're not worth anything. You have no idea what makes a club go. You can *spend* money, oh yes! But you have no idea what *makes* money. You think your ideas are so much better than anyone else's. Well, if you're so brilliant why aren't you a tycoon, eh? Why don't you own all the clubs in the area? Eh?'

Vasson gripped the side of the bar and waited. He wanted the heat to go out of his anger so that he could think clearly. He needed to be calm when he decided what to do next.

The coolness came over his body and then he knew.

Very slowly he reached forward. At first Birelli looked bemused, then realisation dawned and he turned white. As Vasson's hands closed round his neck, he screamed and tried to step backwards.

Vasson's hands closed rapidly round the fat neck and he began to shake the man, slowly at first, then rapidly so that the head snapped backwards and forwards like a puppet's. Then he lifted him by the neck, thrust him against a wall and started to smash his head against the hard surface of the red flock wallpaper.

Birelli had been screaming but now, as his head thudded dully into the wall, his breath came in long gasps. Blood began to smear the red flock and his eyes were round and staring like little white eggs.

Vasson found the movement of the head hypnotic as it snapped backwards and forwards; he wondered what it would take to make the head snap right off. He had got into a rhythm now and it was strangely satisfying. He wanted the rhythm and the feeling of satisfaction to continue.

Suddenly an arm encircled Vasson's neck and forced him to let go. Vasson felt an overwhelming disappointment and then, almost immediately, relief. He was sorry that the disgusting little man was going to escape lightly. On the other hand, he was glad he had been stopped. He had forgotten himself, and he didn't like doing that.

The armhold was vice-like and Vasson felt a moment of panic. He should have remembered about the barman. The man was large and powerful: he could hurt people.

Vasson tried to think. It would be a mistake to struggle; better to play dead. He made himself go limp and heard the barman grunt as his arm took the additional weight.

For a second Vasson thought nothing would happen, then there was a sickening blow to his kidney and he screamed.

After what seemed a long time the barman finally loosened his grip and let Vasson slide to the floor.

Vasson lay still for a moment then slid quickly under a table, out of reach. God, the pain! It was terrible, a great stabbing ache in his side. He felt sick.

He heard a sound and looked round. He could see the barman's feet advancing towards the table.

Vasson crouched lower and shouted, 'I've no argument with you, friend. How about laying off, eh?'

There was silence. Vasson crawled out on the other side of the table and got cautiously to his feet.

The barman was hovering, fists clenched. Vasson panted desperately, 'Look, be a good bloke and lay off. You've done me in the back and I'm in bloody agony. You've done your bit, *for Christ's sake.*'

For a moment the barman stared at him, then he hissed, 'Coward!'

Vasson didn't care what the man thought, just as long as there was no more fighting.

The barman advanced again. Vasson retreated quickly towards a wall.

Suddenly there was a loud groan. Both men stopped and looked across at the proprietor. He was slumped untidily on the floor, blood pouring from his head, his face sheet white. Vasson thought with satisfaction: Perhaps I did the sod some real damage after all.

The barman murmured angrily, 'You've half killed him!'

'No!' Vasson said hastily. 'He'll be all right. It's only superficial. Looks worse than it is. Really –' He let out a great moan of pain and clutched his back. The barman stared in surprise. Vasson groaned and started panting. 'God, my back! The *pain!*' The barman was impressed, just as Vasson had intended him to be.

The barman lowered his arms. He was still unhappy but it was obvious the fight was over. Vasson almost smiled with relief.

Birelli was groaning again and the barman shuffled over to take a look at him. Quickly Vasson straightened his jacket and tie and smoothed down his hair. He moved rapidly away from the barman, round the room to the stairway.

The barman spotted him and said, 'Oi! Hold on!'

Vasson poised himself on the bottom step and snapped, 'Just tell the ugly bastard that if he has any silly ideas about getting his own back, I'll tell the cops about the extra activities upstairs! Okay?'

The barman looked angry again and started to move towards him. Vasson sprinted up, three steps at a time, and ran into the street. He didn't stop running until he was across Pigalle and into Montmartre.

'Bastard! Bastard!' He kicked a wall angrily. He wished he'd finished Birelli off, squeezed his neck *tight* until he'd bloody choked! At the same time he hated himself for having lost control.

'God damn it!' He roared on up the street, bumping into people and forcing a woman off the pavement.

He came to a pavement café and threw himself disgustedly on to a chair. He stared blindly across the street still shaking with rage and humiliation.

Later, when the rage had subsided he walked on, more slowly this time, wondering what the hell he'd done to deserve his luck.

It had been four years now. Four years since the disaster.

Even now he could hardly bear to think about it. He could hardly bear to remember the smell of that lovely, sweet money.

Paris was just as he imagined it would be, except better.

For the first few days he stayed at a good hotel and strolled around, eating at different restaurants and watching the smart ice-cool Parisians as they ate and talked and did their business. He was cautious: he wanted to get a feel for the latest fashions before buying any clothes; and he wanted to be sure that he had found the right neighbourhood in which to rent an apartment. For the moment he was happy to watch and listen and relax; to savour the freedom that money brought. The money: it was like the feeling of hot sunshine on your skin, warm, sensuous, intoxicating.

When he felt ready he slowly began to acquire the trappings of a successful man. First he bought a few really good clothes and some gold cufflinks. Then he began to look for an apartment. It had to be fairly near Pigalle where the club would be, but not too near. Montmartre was impossibly vulgar, so it would have to be the *neuvième*.

It took several days to find what he wanted. The apartment was in a purpose-built block in a quiet street off the Rue de Clichy. It was in need of decoration, but it would do until he was properly established, and then he would go to an even better place in the *huitième*, somewhere off the Champs Elysées.

The only luxury he would allow himself at this stage was the car. He had wanted it so long that he couldn't bear the idea of waiting any longer. He decided, rashly, to have a new one after all. There was a showroom on the Champs Elysées which had Delages and Bugattis in the window. It gave him a curious thrill to walk in and ask for a D8SS, for immediate delivery. The manager himself came out of his office and showed him a car with Falaschi bodywork in green. He liked the body – very much. It was open, with sleek wings which flowed into the running boards and a long, long bonnet.

Perfect – except for the colour. He wanted red, ruby red, with black leather upholstery. The manager was downcast. That could take weeks, maybe months.

Vasson said he would wait for it.

The manager went to the telephone. He returned smiling. It would be only two weeks, after all.

Two weeks. Vasson rather enjoyed the idea of waiting. It would be a sort of sweet agony. It appealed to his sense of Christian guilt. Yes, he would wait for the red one.

He paid a deposit, in cash as usual.

The money was lasting well; the hotel, the month's advance rent for the apartment, the new clothes and the cufflinks had hardly made a dent in it. But the car would, of course. For the deposit he had to dip into the crisp new notes for the first time.

The two weeks passed surprisingly quickly. He busied himself looking at premises around Pigalle. It would take quite a while to set up the club: there were difficulties – permits, licences, access and so on. And he had to be careful; his new identity wouldn't bear detailed examination by the police. Everything must be in order; none of the paperwork must be forgotten. If anything the difficulties made him more determined.

Then at last the two weeks were up and he telephoned the showroom. Yes, the car was there, ready.

It was like Christmas, or a birthday except he'd never known what it was like to get presents before. His heart started to hammer with excitement as he walked along the Champs Elysées. He approached from the opposite side of the avenue, under the trees, and stopped at an intersection to cross the wide boulevard. He looked across at the showroom and frowned. He couldn't see a ruby red car anywhere, either in the window or on the wide pavement outside. He thought: Damn, it hasn't arrived after all.

He was just about to cross when he saw something that made him freeze. A man was leaning against a tree pretending to read a newspaper, but actually watching the showroom.

There was another further up the avenue, standing in a shop doorway, smoking a cigarette.

Oh God.

They were waiting for him.

Sweat started from his forehead and he went quite cold. For several moments he stood absolutely still.

The man in the doorway threw his cigarette away and looked up and down the avenue. Vasson turned quickly away and walked rapidly towards the Etoile. He came to one of the large pavement cafés and, going to the bar, asked to use the phone. He called the showroom and said he was delayed. Were they certain the car was absolutely ready? There was a slight hesitation, then they had assured him it was ready, there and waiting. He told them he wanted to drive it straight off and did they have it parked right outside? There was a moment's silence, then they told him yes, it was just outside, ready to go.

Vasson watched the showroom for ten minutes. There was no red Delage outside and none arrived while he waited. Instead there was plenty of activity among the men staked outside. A man came out of the showroom and spoke first to the man under the tree and then to the one in the doorway. There was a third Vasson hadn't spotted before, in another doorway on the other side of the showroom. After their discussions they looked more relaxed as if they had been told that the action was off for the moment.

Vasson turned away, sick at heart.

It must have been the money, it could only have been the *money*. The money must stink to high heaven.

He walked a long way, then went into a café and had a drink. It made him light-headed and he felt slightly hysterical. He had the dreadful desire to cry.

Later he sat in a daze, thinking, thinking hard. At last, late in the evening, he left the café and walked slowly towards the apartment.

He stayed in the apartment for three days, lying on the bed smoking or sometimes pacing up and down, thinking of a way to utilise the money.

There was no way. He had known that straight away, but it took him three days to face it. Then he wept.

He had been so naive it was incredible. How the Algerian must have laughed! How they all must have laughed! They'd probably been wondering how to get rid of that rotten money for years. The Algerian wouldn't have printed it himself, it wasn't his style, but he'd probably bought it cheap for an occasion like this . . .

At one point he thought of revenge, he thought of nailing the Algerian with the money, of doing a deal for perhaps half the two hundred thousand.

But he was frightened. If he went to Marseilles he knew the Algerian would kill him. He wouldn't get within a mile.

He tried to remember how lucky he was not to have been caught. And there was still some money from the down-payment: clean money. But it didn't help. He had been robbed and cheated, and it hurt like hell.

A week later he tried to shift some of the bad money with a bullion dealer. The dealer got the scent of the money even as it came out of the briefcase: Vasson saw it in his face. He made a quick exit before the dealer reached a telephone. It was no better at a small pawn-brokers: the old Jew handed the money back and yelled, 'Get this rubbish out of here!'

Vasson realised the money was well known. It must have been around for years.

Eventually, in desperation, Vasson sold the lot for three thousand francs to a *pied-noir* who hoped to offload it in Tangiers.

The good money lasted a year, spent carefully. There was no club, no car, no security.

He was back where he'd started.

Vasson strode up the steps and steeply-climbing streets that lead into the heart of Montmartre, and felt the sweat soaking his back. He walked faster again, pushing his body harder and harder to ease the pain in his kidney and the bitterness in his mouth.

Finally he turned into a small dark café and sat near the window. The group of men sitting at the counter glanced at him and resumed their conversation. They knew he never said hello. The waiter brought him a coffee.

He considered ordering a pastis; it might just revive him. He'd drunk enough the night before. He couldn't remember exactly how many. Twenty or more. The memory sickened him, not only because of the hangover but because the evening had cost him at least a hundred francs.

Raoul had talked him into going. Well, Raoul could damn well buy him a pastis.

He closed his eyes and tried to remember what it was like to feel well. It had been a long time since he'd felt really well; there had been too much drink and too many cigarettes. And now the kidney, which was still aching viciously.

Someone sat down at the table. Vasson opened half an eye and saw that it was Raoul. Vasson said, 'Buy me a drink, you *tête de con.*'

'Have you read the news? Have you read the news?' Raoul unfolded his newspaper and started to read avidly.

Vasson waited for a moment, then leant forward and took Raoul's wrist. 'Look, after last night you owe me a goddam drink!'

Raoul looked up impatiently. 'Oh for Christ's sake shut up, will you? I'm reading this.' He flicked his hand across the newspaper. 'This Polish thing... it means war, do you realise? We will be at war by the end of the week!'

Vasson controlled his annoyance. Raoul thought he knew so much about world affairs, but he couldn't even run a couple of girls at a profit. 'War? So, maybe there'll be a war. But it's not going to affect us.'

Raoul slowly lowered the newspaper and stared across the table. 'Listen, big-time operator, this is the end of it, as far as I'm concerned. If France is going to war, then I will be there fighting, and you can rot here, hatching your grand plans. Alone.'

Vasson regarded him with contempt. 'Then I'm sorry for you, because I'll be the richer.'

'That's what you've been saying for the last three years – and I'm still counting my *sous*.' Raoul stabbed a finger across the table. 'And so, for that matter, are you!'

Vasson flushed. They'd had an idea to open a club, but it had failed for the usual reason: lack of money. They'd tried to borrow some, even tried to extort some, but it had all come to nothing.

Vasson retorted, 'At least I try, which is more than you do.' Raoul was a lazy swine who'd be quite happy to sit around for ever, earning nothing and drinking himself stupid. Vasson added, 'None of your ideas are worth a sou.'

Raoul shrugged; he'd heard it all before. 'There's nothing wrong with my ideas. It's you! You just find problems that aren't there.'

Vasson gave a short laugh. He knew Raoul's ideas all right: bank robbery. The quickest way to get inside, short of stabbing a *flic* and waiting to be arrested. God!

Raoul bought two pastis and plonked them on the table. 'Look, the idea of setting up your stupid club would never have worked anyway. We're small-fry. We could never have set up a big place like that. Hundreds of women indeed! High-class décor!' He shook his head. 'Look, for a start our police contacts just weren't good enough. And then do you think the existing businesses would have made room for you without a fuss? I tell you it would never have worked.'

Vasson watched him coldly. He decided Raoul was simply a very stupid man.

Raoul said tolerantly, 'You know, you should use that learning of yours, and get a good job with prospects. You *do* have an education, don't you, eh? I mean you read books and all that. It's obvious that someone stuffed the knowledge in somewhere. Well, you should use it!'

Vasson stared out of the window. He loathed people referring to his past.

Raoul went on, 'Was it the priests? That gave you the learning, I mean? I knew a lad once who'd started life with nothing – on the scrapheap at five years old, he was – and the priests took him in and stuffed his head full of books and Latin and he ended up a professor, a *professor*! The nephew of my mum's best friend, he was. Very proud, his family, very proud.' He turned to Vasson. 'Was it the priests, then?'

'Shut up,' Vasson snapped.

He downed his pastis and stood up. Raoul looked up in surprise. 'Where are you off to?'

'Away. Somewhere. So I'll say goodbye. I hope you enjoy the army and getting killed. Should be fun.'

'Don't be like that.'

Vasson leant over the table. 'We'll see who's the clever one, and I tell you, it isn't going to be you!'

He strode out of the café and up the street, swearing under his breath. So Raoul wanted out. Fine! Let them all go to hell. He could manage very well on his own.

The room was at the back of a tall, dingy house in the Rue St Vincent. It cost him a few francs a week, so that, after meals and clothes, he could save about one hundred a week. When he had a job.

The idea was to save enough for a lease on a club premises. By any calculations it should take twenty years to buy even the most modest property. Even assuming he had a job. He grimaced: it was pathetic, laughable.

Wearily he climbed the dirty narrow stairs and opened the door of the room. It was dark inside. He felt his way across the window and opened the shutters. Even then there wasn't much light: the window gave onto a narrow opening between tall buildings.

The room was a mess. High-heeled shoes lay scattered on the floor and piles of skirts and dresses were draped over the two chairs. I'll have to get rid of her, Vasson thought. She was a brainless little country girl named Yvette, and she was cluttering up his life. It had been her idea to move in, not his. He should have kicked her out straight away.

He threw some cheap magazines off the bed and lay down. His head ached and his kidney was still hurting badly. He wondered if the damage was serious. Perhaps he should go and see a doctor, except that doctors cost money and he begrudged paying them.

He lit a cigarette and began to think.

No job. No prospects. He'd been through it before. There'd been four, maybe five, jobs in the last four years. The story was always the same: they wanted him to work like hell, but they offered him nothing in return. No real share of the action. No opportunity to change or improve things. And then – then came the disagreements. They always blamed him – *him*! – though the problems were their own stupid faults.

He felt cheated. Frustrated. Bitter.

Like he did now. Especially now. Because he hadn't managed to control himself and he'd half killed a man and that frightened him.

But it was the fault of the system. It was the system which was killing him. The fat kings ran the system and they had it sewn up. You didn't have a chance without weight and influence – and that meant money. And you couldn't get the money without the influence.

The system stank.

Christ, he thought, I just go round in bloody circles. And the circle always comes back to money.

Suddenly he was tired. He stubbed out his cigarette and closed his eyes. He liked sleep. He liked the blackness and the peace of it and the way it passed so much of the time.

The dream, when it came was vivid. He was back in Marseilles, in the Algerian's car. His arms were bound and he was lying on the floor. The Algerian was discussing how he would kill him. But Vasson didn't care because he had the money on the floor next to him. *He had the money*. He knew he'd be all right.

But then he was slipping, down the floor of the car, on to the road. Someone had opened the door. It was his mother. As he fell past her he called to her, but she looked past him at the Algerian and smiled.

There was darkness. He was in the cupboard again. He shouted and yelled, but the door was made of steel and so thick that no-one could hear. Finally, after time which seemed to have lasted for ever, the door was opened. He did not want to come out. But it was one of the priests and refusal was not allowed.

He asked for his mother.

'Your mother is a long way away, Paul.'

'But I want her.'

'Paul, your mother has not yet found the way to the true God. She is – searching for Him. While she searches, she cannot come to you.'

'Searching? Why is she searching?'

'Paul, your mother is a long way away . . .'

No, she was near, he knew she was near. Why did they lie to him? Why did they keep her away?

Maman, maman –

He awoke. Someone was there, in the room.

It was Yvette.

'You all right?' She teetered across to the bed on her high heels and put her heavily made-up face close to his. He closed his eyes in disgust.

'You were muttering away. I thought you were awake, talking to yourself! Sorry, did I actually wake you up?' She was using the little-girl-lost voice she usually kept for fat rich men. It annoyed him.

He said irritably, 'Get out. I want to sleep.'

'Oh, well, don't mind about me. I'll stay quiet as a mouse. You won't even know I'm here.' She began to stroke his forehead.

He brushed her hand away and reached for a cigarette.

'Let me get you a cold drink, eh?' she persisted.

'No. And I've something to tell you. I'm going away.'

She stared at him and then nodded. She wasn't surprised. 'Can I come too?' She knew it was risky to ask, he might fly off the handle like he sometimes did. But she wanted to go with him. She wanted to look after him.

He said, 'No.'

She kicked off her shoes and lay on the bed beside him. She knew exactly how far she could go before he got angry. She put an arm across his waist and moved her head against his.

'I'll miss you terribly.'

'Like hell.'

'I know I don't suit you . . . I mean I'm not attractive to you, and all that. But I'd look after you, you know that.'

Vasson sighed. The sex thing again. It was her only level of understanding. Everything began and ended with sex. She couldn't understand how repulsive she was to him, how he couldn't bear her to touch him.

He sat up suddenly and, pushing past her, stood up. 'I'm off tomorrow, so you'd better find somewhere else.'

'Where are you going?'

'I don't know.'

'What about this war then?'

He glanced at her impatiently. 'What about it?'

'Well, *that* might offer some opportunities, I mean for the two of us.' She was always trying to think of money-making ideas. They were always pathetic, just like her.

He didn't answer, but began to pack his suitcase.

She fluttered valiantly on. 'There'll be shortages, right? And a black-market. Bound to be. That's where the money'll be. In buying things up cheap. You've got enough saved to make a start. It'll be a real money-spinner, you'll see!'

Vasson paused and looked at her. 'And what do you think people will be short of?' he asked.

She thought for a moment, her pencilled eyebrows puckered in concentration At last she said, 'Oh, stockings, make-up, clothes, things like that . . . Oh and food I suppose. And I could think of lots more, I'm sure I could –'

Vasson stared out of the window. The silly girl might actually have something. Perhaps there *would* be a war, perhaps it would go on for some time, perhaps there would be plenty of money to be made.

He pushed the last few things into his suitcase. He said abruptly, 'I'm off then.'

'Oh, please . . . !' She started towards him, a pleading expression on her face.

He glanced at her, thinking again how repulsive she was, and turned away to open the door.

She yelled, 'You shit!' But he walked quickly down the stairs and by the time he reached the street he couldn't hear her any more.

He walked rapidly, needing to get away quickly. He thought: It's good to be free again. He would get another room, alone. He would start again.

He stopped for a coffee and a cigarette in a place he hadn't been to before. He thought about the girl's idea. There definitely might be something in it. Luxuries, food, what else had she said – stockings. Yes, and cigarettes would be short too.

A war might be rather a good thing after all.

5

The coast is wild and rugged and utterly beautiful. From its border with Normandy to the point where the land turns to face the open Atlantic the North Brittany coast measures little more than a hundred miles as the crow flies. But this means nothing. It is so indented with bays and deep estuaries that its true length is at least twice that distance. Most of this length is impenetrable to anything but the smallest craft – and then only in good weather – for the land is defended by a great barrier of natural hazards.

A thousand storms have shaped the jagged cliffs and eaten into the soft rock, leaving a dense fabric of reefs, islands and islets to seaward. Some of the dangers stand proud and high in the water: great stacks of rock rising like dragon's teeth, or larger islands which lie cowed and barren before the wind. But most of the perils lie near the surface: sharp reefs marked only by breaking water, or islets so low that they are almost invisible. These dangers reach out four, five, sometimes twelve miles from the land.

Then there are the tidal streams. They run very strong along these shores, ripping across rocks and reefs, tearing through the deep channels, and swinging into bays and inlets, making accurate landfall difficult even for the most careful of navigators.

The strongest winds come in winter, blowing storm force from the Atlantic. They send before them armies of waves which curve in towards the shore, gathering speed until they break on the myriad of rocks and islets in a cauldron of white foaming surf, then advance, still snapping and roaring, on to the fragile mainland itself.

This coast is no friend to the sailor. Only those familiar with its dangers dare approach it with impunity; strangers must rely on good charts and blind faith. At night the dangers are marked by the powerful lights of tall lighthouses; with the help of leading lights and channel buoys it is even possible for small fishing craft to navigate one or two of the estuaries in darkness. But for the most part this coast does not invite visitors; the great lighthouses serve to warn rather than welcome.

The wind blows the fine salt mist several miles inland, so that only the hardiest vegetation can grow there. There is gorse and heather and thin coarse grass, and the pastures, such as they are, support only a small number of cattle. Further inland there are market gardens and fields of wheat and richer pastures, but even here the land gives grudgingly and there is none of the lush abundance of Normandy or Picardy.

Like all wild, windswept places the land is rich with romantic legend. Except that in Brittany fact and fable are closely intertwined. The people who have inhabited this land for centuries are quite alien to their neighbours in the rest of France. Brittany is French by nationality, but not by race, language or culture. The proud, tough Bretons are not Gauls but Celts, and their closest links are with Cornwall, Wales, and Ireland, from whence they came centuries ago. The Breton language sounds harsh to the French ear and the names of the rocks and headlands are easier spoken by a Cornishman than a Frenchman: Beg an Fry, Mean Nevez, L'Aberwrac'h, Lizen Ven, Pen Ven. You would even be forgiven for thinking you were in Scotland when you hear their music, for they play not the accordion, but the plaintive, mournful bagpipes.

To the great nation of France, Brittany is something of a backwater, not sufficiently fertile or industrially developed to demand a great deal of attention. For the Bretons, proudly nationalistic and stubbornly independent, their subjugation to the mother country is tolerated with equanimity, and the benefits, if any, absorbed. The idea of freedom has long been forgotten – the land has been fought over often enough as it is – but the people remain independent in spirit.

The land is poor and in places infertile, but the Bretons find it sufficient for their needs; the way of life is simple and austere and not to the taste of the sophisticated French, but for the Bretons this is the only life they know. Many of them live off the sea, and the sea is the harshest life there is.

It was a pleasant day in August and the coast looked almost benign.

The sun had penetrated the morning mist at midday and now in the late afternoon the ragged headlands and narrow estuaries were lit in firm bold colours. The greeny purple of the sparse vegetation showed clearly against the grey and terracotta of the jagged rock formations. The sea itself was a pale grey-blue and unusually calm. There had been no gales for some days and only a slight swell washed around the walls of rock and on to the narrow pebble beaches.

Julie lifted her head and let the soft salt wind caress her face. For a few moments she stood quite still, listening to the gentle murmur of the surf far below, watching the waves ripple across the wideness of the sea. The cries of seabirds echoed faintly on the wind; occasionally one would fly high into the air and she followed it as it glided motionless on the breeze.

Julie closed her eyes, thinking; It's so beautiful and I love it all.

She opened her eyes and looked again. She loved it partly because it *was* beautiful and partly because she was happy here. She loved the peace and the loneliness of it; on a day like this you could walk for hours and never see a living soul. At first the remoteness had seemed strange and unsettling after the close warmth of the city. But slowly she began to appreciate the austerity and rugged beauty of the landscape. Now it seemed so familiar that she might have lived here all her life.

Standing on the headland it was difficult to believe that Plymouth and England lay just a hundred miles across the Channel. It seemed like a thousand. The small house in Radley Terrace belonged to another life, another *person.* That's what she had been then – another person.

Suddenly she remembered she should have counted to twenty by now. Peter must have been hiding for ages. She yelled, 'Twenty! I'm coming!'

She knew exactly where he would be. There were few places to hide on the windswept headland. The heather and gorse grew low and sparse, clinging to the stony soil around the rocky outcrops, and there were no trees. The only object capable of concealing a small boy was a large boulder which stood round and grey against the skyline. There was also a slight dip in the ground where someone could lie still and remain unseen, but Peter preferred a really solid hiding place, so it had to be the boulder.

But it was important to make a proper show of searching. She said in a loud voice, 'My, my! Where *can* he be?' then called, 'Peter, Peter, where are you?' At this point he often gave the game away by calling, 'Whoo-hoo!', a funny cry that always made her laugh. But he had got much cannier recently and had finally realised that keeping quiet was the smart thing to do.

Julie approached the boulder and waited. Sometimes Peter couldn't bear the suspense any longer and jumped out with a loud 'Boo!', but he was being patient today.

For a moment she thought she was mistaken and he wasn't there after all, but then she heard a small giggle. She crept silently up to the boulder and, running quickly round it, pounced on the small person crouching behind. With a shriek he tried to run away but her arms went round the little body and the two of them rolled on to the ground, yelling and giggling.

They wrestled and tickled each other until Julie cried, 'Enough, enough!' She rolled on to her back, panting hard. Peter plonked himself on her stomach and grinned triumphantly.

'I give up. You win, you horrible child!'

Peter bounced with delight, then chanted, 'Again, again. Please let's play it again!'

'In a minute. Give your poor old mum a chance to recover.'

He nodded gravely as he always did and, getting up, wandered off to examine some tiny blue flowers peeping up through the heather. He was always fascinated by tiny things.

He called, 'Mummy.'

'Yes, darling.'

'Shall I pick you some flowers?'

She smiled. 'That would be lovely.'

She watched him as he carefully bent down to search for the stems of the flowers. When he was younger he had yanked them off at the head but she had explained to him why it was better to pick them at the bottom and he had listened with his little head on one side, and then nodded. Now he set about doing the job properly, a frown of concentration on his forehead.

She smiled as she watched him. He was a small boy now, almost three and a half years old, but there was still a lot of the baby in him.

Most of the rounded chubbiness had gone and every one of the babyish creases, but he still had a lovely velvety skin, and when his little arms went round her neck and he hugged her tight she loved to feel its softness against her. He still needed plenty of hugs, thank goodness. She couldn't bear to think of him growing up and not wanting them any more. The two of them spent at least two hours a day just talking and reading. Julie looked forward to those hours: to the little body that wriggled into bed in the mornings and snuggled close; to the small fellow who needed a hug when he'd grazed his knee; and to the sleepy bedtime boy who wanted just one more story before falling asleep in her arms.

Her only regret – and it was a big one – was that she had to spend so many hours away from him, working. But that couldn't be helped: they couldn't survive without money.

Sometimes she wanted him to stay just the way he was now, not to grow up and drift away from her. At the same time she was fascinated by his development, the way he picked up new words and slotted them into one of his two vocabularies, French or English, and the way he thought things out for himself. The other night, when he'd been up late, he'd announced that, since the moon was nowhere to be seen, it must have forgotten to put its light on. She had been careful not to laugh – the logic was, after all, irrefutable – and she had nodded seriously instead.

Peter was striding towards her, lifting his feet high in the air to get across the carpet of springy heather. In his preoccupation he forgot to hold the bunch of flowers upright and a few of the tiny blooms were torn away by the ragged branches. When he arrived breathless beside her he looked at the flowers in surprise, puzzled that some should have so mysteriously disappeared. But apparently the loss was not too serious: he thrust his arm out and proudly announced, 'Here's a present, just for you!'

Julie thanked him and got to her feet. 'They're quite lovely,' she said. 'I'll put them in water when we get back.' She placed the flowers in a pocket of her cardigan and glanced at her watch.

It was getting on for four-thirty, time they went back for tea. They walked up to the path which led inland towards the village.

'Mummy, hide and seek again? You promised.'

Little demon. He never forgot.

They played two more games, first Julie hiding, then Peter, and then it really was time to head for home.

They climbed the narrow path which led upwards round the side of a rocky bluff and along the top of a steep cliff. Although the cliff was fenced at this point and the drop a safe distance away, Julie gripped Peter's hand more tightly. They came to a corner where the path led away from the cliff and paused.

Peter said, 'Look, a fishing boat!'

Julie turned and followed his gaze. A small boat was drifting gently a short distance from the shore, its tan sails hardly filling in the windless lee of the headland. Several rocks were plainly visible just above the surface on the seaward side of the vessel. Julie shook her head. The Bretons were known for their knowledge of this coast, but all the same . . .

She looked beyond the boat, towards the horizon. At night she could see the flash of a light from her bedroom window. Now, squinting her eyes against the sun, she could make out the form of the lighthouse itself. It was a tall grey and red structure standing stark and solitary in the middle of the sea. It marked a plateau of rocks lying just beneath the surface some miles offshore. She shivered slightly; the tower seemed lonely and somehow sad.

She turned away. 'Come on, darling.'

They climbed up to the top of the ridge and walked slowly towards the village, just visible through a dip in the land. Although the path was fairly level now, Peter was puffing and panting as he strived to match her step. Presently he began to hang back and Julie wasn't surprised when he said, 'Mummy, please carry me.'

She lifted him over her head and on to her shoulders.

She said, 'I don't promise to take you all the way. You're too heavy, young man!'

It was true: in five minutes or so her shoulders would ache and then she would have to put him down. A man could have done it easily. But there wasn't a man.

She hardly ever thought about Peter's father. It was as if he belonged to another world that had existed a long, long time ago. Her memory of him was completely neutral; she neither hated him nor cared about him. It was almost as if she had never really known him. The only thing she felt, possibly, was gratitude: he had after all given her Peter. But at the same time she never thought of Peter as belonging to him. Peter was hers and hers alone.

She'd adored her son from the start, and it surprised her. In the months before the birth she didn't have much time to think about how she'd feel; she was too busy sorting things out – difficulties mainly. It was only in the last few weeks that she realised she was about to give birth to a *person*, somebody who would rely on her for everything. It frightened her, but she was determined to do the right thing, to do her *best*.

Settling in Brittany had been far from easy. Looking back, she wondered how she'd stuck it out. In fact, at one point just after she arrived, she'd nearly given up and gone home to England.

The village was in full view now, a group of grey stone cottages standing out against the pastel grey-greens of the fields. Julie regarded it fondly. She was glad she hadn't given up and run away.

As soon as she'd decided on Brittany Julie had written to her uncle and aunt. She didn't know their full address, only the name of the village: Tregasnou. She asked if she could stay with them while she found somewhere to live.

The reply came in two weeks. It was short, stiff and impersonal: they would be expecting her and they had a spare room where she could stay.

The journey lasted three days. She took a ferry from Dover to Calais and then a train to Morlaix. She had to change three times and then wait two hours for a bus from Morlaix to Tregasnou. By the time she walked up the long hill to the small grey house, a heavy suitcase in each hand, she was exhausted.

The farmhouse was typically Breton; it was built of grey stone with a high, pitched roof and low eaves which came almost to the ground-floor windows. There were two small dormer windows in the roof where the upper rooms must be. Various outbuildings extended from the back of the house and, as she approached, Julie heard the sounds of animals stamping and shuffling in a barn somewhere.

The house was silent and, though it was almost dark, there was no light showing in the window.

Julie knocked on the door. There was no reply. She knocked again, louder. After a minute there was the flicker of a light as an inner door was opened. Finally the front door swung open and a large, rather fierce woman stood in the doorway.

Julie smiled and said in French, 'I'm Julie.'

Suddenly the woman smiled and nodded. She called something over her shoulder, then beckoned Julie in.

A small, squat man appeared from the back room and with a shy smile shook her hand. 'You are welcome, welcome. Please come in.'

She was shown to a chair by the kitchen range and offered coffee. Her uncle and aunt sat opposite, watching her and smiling politely. Julie realised they were nervous. They were sitting upright in their seats, their hands clasped in their laps, looking strangely uncomfortable. For several moments no-one could think of anything to say.

'It's kind of you to have me to stay,' Julie said at last.

Her uncle smiled. 'Not at all, not at all.'

Her aunt took a decisive breath and said, 'Well, let's make sure you're comfortable. First, have you had something to eat?'

'I had a sandwich on the train.'

'Perhaps you would like some soup?'

'Oh, thank you.' Julie smiled gratefully.

Her aunt got up and put a pan on the stove. She turned and started to speak again, quicker this time. Julie concentrated on what was being said, but to her chagrin, missed several key words. Before she could ask her aunt to repeat them her uncle was speaking and Julie realised with bitter disappointment that she could not understand all he was saying either. It was the accent, perhaps, or maybe her French was rustier than she thought.

At one point her relatives started to speak in Breton until, remembering Julie was there, they returned apologetically to French.

Julie suddenly felt depressed. She'd assumed that because her father came from this village she would have some bond with these people, some feeling of belonging. Instead she felt a complete stranger, a foreigner who knew and understood nothing.

And it was clear that her uncle and aunt found her equally strange. They'd probably never met an English person before – nor, for that matter, any kind of foreigner. She was beginning to realise just how remote the village was.

It was clear too that the farmer and his wife were not used to having guests. Julie had the feeling that she was upsetting the routine of the small household, and that they didn't really know what to do with her. When finally she said she was tired and they showed her to a tiny upstairs room, she knew they were relieved.

The next day started well. Julie tried hard to make conversation and offered to help her aunt with the chores. But soon she was depressed again. Her aunt was obviously uneasy about something and refused to let Julie help her with even the simplest tasks, while her uncle treated her with rigid politeness and exaggerated respect. The effect was rather chilling.

That evening it came to a head. They had finished supper and Tante Marie started to clear away the dishes. Julie got quickly to her feet and carried the cheese and butter towards the larder.

'No, no!' Tante Marie made her put the plates down. 'We can't have you doing these things.'

'But I must help, otherwise . . .' Julie struggled to find the right word. 'I will be a burden.'

Tante Marie looked crosser than ever. 'But you are a guest. You must not work!'

'But please . . . I feel I am imposing on you.'

'It is no imposition.' Tante Marie looked quite shocked.

'You are kind. But you must let me pay you, for my food and my bed, just until I can find a room to rent. I will look for one tomorrow.'

'A room?'

'Yes, a room to rent.'

'But – why?'

Julie stared at the older women. She began to wonder what they had understood from her letter.

'Well, I can't stay with you for ever.'

Her uncle and aunt exchanged glances. Her aunt sat down slowly. 'You mean, you're staying a long time?'

'Yes, I want to.' She laughed nervously.

Gently Tante Marie took her hand and patted it. Then Julie found it easy to explain everything they hadn't understood from the letter: how she wanted to stay in the village, how she was going to find a room, then a job ...

It was more difficult to talk about the baby, of course, particularly when she had to explain about the husband who was meant to have deserted her. But she did it, because they'd have to know some time and it might as well be now.

After she'd told them, she felt much better. At least everything was out in the open.

It was different then. In some strange way, her aunt and uncle were pleased. They insisted she stay with them. Terms for board and lodging were soon agreed. Everything was settled.

They went out of their way to make her feel at home. Her uncle prepared a room for her at the back of the house in the lower of two rooms which had once been used for storage; her aunt allowed her to help with the chores; and the formality of the evenings was replaced by what Julie realised was a well-established routine of occasional conversation interspersed with long silences.

But it was a long time before she did feel at home, partly because the way of life *was* so different and partly because she was lonely. The villagers did not take easily to strangers, let alone foreigners. And she had the unpleasant feeling they had heard the story about the disappearing husband and not believed it. Doubtless one or two of them were aware that she was entered on the Aliens Registration at Morlaix as Juliette Lescaux, not Juliette Howard, the name she had called herself when she arrived in France. She had chosen it after her favourite film actor, Leslie Howard, and then laughed at her stupidity: 'H' was the one letter the French could not pronounce.

Finding a job was the hardest part. There weren't many jobs around, even for those who spoke good French and weren't pregnant.

But she persevered. At last, when her money was beginning to run low, she was taken on as a secretary to a vegetable wholesaler in Morlaix. She suspected that the manager was tickled by her English accent, but whatever the reason, she wasn't going to turn the job down.

She was still there, three years and a baby later.

Peter was like a lead weight on her shoulders. She said, 'You're breaking my back. I'm going to chase you home!'

Peter giggled. 'I'll win! I'll win!'

She lowered Peter to the ground and the two of them ran down into the village and along the main street. Tregasnou was a small village, no more than a scattering of cottages built around a crossroads. There was one shop and a café. The shop sold bread brought in daily from the larger village of Plougat, as well as butter, cheese, simple provisions, and a rough local wine. For everything else you had to go into Plougat itself, or, for really special shopping expeditions, to Morlaix.

Because Julie worked in Morlaix she often delivered or collected items for her neighbours. She was pleased to do it because it helped her to get to know them. Not an easy thing by any means. At one stage she despaired of being accepted by them. But then she realised it was a mistake to be too interested in their customs or to be too curious about their lives. They distrusted that. It was better to show polite interest and then offer information about England and how things were done there. They respected national pride and liked to hear about foreign customs, if only to reassure themselves that, all things considered, their way of doing things was the best.

Julie thought some of their ways were quaint, others just out-of-date – it wasn't done for women to go into the café for instance – but she never commented on it. That was the way things had always been done around here, and she wasn't about to change them.

Now, on Sunday afternoon when almost everyone in the village took a stroll, it was impossible for her to get down the street without stopping for a chat. Most people made a pretence of talking to Peter and she realised it was mainly shyness which had held them back. Some were intractable – the old people mainly, who distrusted French-speaking people, let alone foreigners – but most treated her with kindness and warmth.

Peter was running ahead, his small legs flying in a funny wheeling motion which was peculiarly his own. Julie walked briskly after him, waving briefly at an old woman sitting in her doorway, and to a fisherman and his wife strolling towards her. Because it was a Sunday people were in their best clothes, black for the older women, simple printed cotton frocks for the younger. The men wore ill-fitting suits and shirts too tight at the neck so that they ran their fingers inside their collars. Julie smiled. The women loved dressing up, but how the men hated it!

Peter disappeared into the lane that formed one arm of the crossroads. When Julie turned the corner and looked up the hill she saw that the small figure had slowed down and was waiting for her. She caught up with him and bent to kiss him, then together they climbed slowly towards the small house which stood alone on the brow of the hill.

After a while Peter began to drag his feet and look unhappy. His breath came in short pants, like a small steam engine. Julie reached down and, taking his hand, squeezed it.

She said, 'Not far now.'

He gripped her hand tightly and looked up. 'Mummy, it *is* a tall hill, isn't it?'

She nodded and smiled. She thought: Why can't it always be like this? Why did Monday ever have to come?

Finally they reached the house. Julie pulled the latch and they entered the darkness of the front parlour. The room was simply furnished with a large darkwood table, six straight-backed chairs, and a dresser. The walls were covered with a traditional Breton wallpaper, a pattern of flowers on trelliswork, and were bare of pictures except for a cheap religious print framed in gilt. The ceiling was low and supported by heavy beams.

As they took their coats off there was a call from the kitchen and Tante Marie appeared. As soon as she saw Peter her round face broke into a smile.

She leaned down to pinch Peter's cheek. 'And how did you enjoy your walk, my hero?'

'Oh, we saw a boat, and I picked Mummy some flowers . . .'

Peter chattered on in his broken French, and Tante Marie listened studiously, exclaiming loudly at the amazing things that had happened, and sighing deeply at the list of creatures that had not, on this occasion, presented themselves for Peter's inspection. There had been no ants' nest this time, nor a nesting plover.

Julie sank gratefully into a chair by the old stove and watched Tante Marie's face as it went through all the necessary reactions from astonishment to amazed delight. Julie decided, not for the first time, that it had all turned out pretty well. Not only did the old woman love Peter, but she took trouble with him. During the day, while Julie was away, she taught him things, about why plants and flowers grew, and how things worked; and they drew pictures and built paper castles together.

The old woman straightened up and, going to the larder door, emerged with bread, cold meat and a dish of late strawberries. 'Here, a surprise!' She put them on the table and Peter wriggled up on to a chair, his little face glowing with delight.

Tante Marie sat down on the other side of the kitchen range and smiled as she watched Peter. 'I picked the strawberries this afternoon. We'll have a few more bowlfuls yet.'

When the old woman smiled her face was transformed. She was only about fifty, but she looked ten years older. Like many of the women in the village she made no effort with her appearance beyond neatness and cleanliness. Her grey-black hair was parted in the centre and scraped back into a bun at the nape of her neck. Her figure was full and round and it was a long time since she had made any attempt to lose weight. Now she thought it unimportant. Her clothes were simple to the point where she had two working dresses, which she wore alternate weeks, and one best dress. She hardly ever felt the cold and made no concession to the weather, except when there was snow on the ground, and then she wore a cardigan.

Her face was round and plain and red-cheeked. She thought life was too serious a business to smile about it. When her husband read from the newspaper she always tutted and shook her head: she thought the world mad and she viewed people's motives with distrust. The only important things, she believed, were the family, honest work and fear of God.

But with Peter she was different. With Peter she smiled a lot. She had never had children of her own.

Peter pushed the cold meat to one side and got down to the strawberries. Tante Marie turned to Julie and sighed. 'Your uncle is very worried. He thinks war will really come.'

Julie frowned. She really hadn't been following the news very carefully. Occasionally she glanced at her uncle's newspaper, or listened to a neighbour's wireless – there was none in her uncle's house – but her real passion was for books. In England she'd hardly read at all, it hadn't interested her. But in Brittany she'd started reading to fill the long evenings and improve her French. Now it was her greatest pleasure and she was rarely without a book in her hand.

People had talked about war, but she hadn't taken it seriously. Now she wished she'd read the papers more often.

'Do you think there'll be war?' Julie asked.

'I think people are selfish and cruel enough to do anything. Particularly the Germans.' Tante Marie had firm opinions about almost everything.

'But why? Why do the Germans want war?'

Tante Marie shrugged. 'You ask me? I wish I could tell you. The usual things, I suppose. Power and hate and jealousy.'

There was the sound of a door opening. Tante Marie inclined her head at the front parlour. 'Here's your uncle. Ask him. He's been down in the village talking about it most of the afternoon.'

The parlour door opened and Jean Cornou came in. He nodded a greeting.

Julie smiled up at her uncle. 'Hello. Did you have a good afternoon?'

He grunted and shook his head. He pulled up a chair and sat down, breathing heavily after his climb up the hill.

'The news is bad, bad.' He shook his head again.

Jean Cornou was short and square, with wide shoulders and muscular arms. He farmed the land around the house the only way he knew, and that was the old way, with little machinery and a lot of hard work and the help of a single farmhand. His face was uneven, open and kind. In his best clothes, which he wore now, his rough hands and face and muscular body looked oddly out of keeping with the dark three-piece suit and white shirt. The waistcoat was anyway too tight for him and his stomach bulged against the buttons.

He leant forward to take off his jacket, then unbuttoned his waistcoat and sighed deeply.

'The Germans look as though they are going to attack Poland. If they do there'll be a war. A war!' He snorted with disgust.

Julie frowned. 'But who . . . Which countries will fight?'

'Oh, Britain and France will fight Germany. Now that those filthy Russians have done the dirty and signed up with Germany, there'll be no stopping Hitler. Communists! They're not to be trusted. They've sold us down the river, just as I said they always would. Nothing but trouble, trouble. The great hope of France, they were meant to be. Yes, indeed. And what happens? They sell out at the first opportunity!'

Tante Marie shook her head and tutted quietly.

Peter had dropped a book on the floor and Julie automatically went to pick it up. Peter said, 'Mummy, read me a story!'

'Later, darling, I'm talking. Here, look at the pictures in this one. When you're finished I'll tell you a story. Promise.'

He nodded and started to turn the pages of the book. Julie stroked his head and returned to her chair.

She looked at Jean. 'So what'll happen? Will it last long? I mean, surely it'll be settled quickly?'

Her uncle shrugged. 'Who knows? With every country in Europe jostling for position, anything can happen. Who knows who will get involved and how far the fighting will spread? All I know is that, thanks to those spineless communists ganging up with Hitler, the cause of socialism has been set back fifty years. Everyone's anti-communist now – *and* anti-socialist. They put the two together, communist-socialist, socialist-communist! Everything that the working man has won in the last five years will be lost for ever, mark my words! We think of Hitler as a fascist – well, this Daladier government of ours is not far behind, not far at all! And speaking of communists, Michel was down at the café.'

Tante Marie glanced up from her knitting and they both looked at Julie. She blushed, mainly because they were expecting her to. Michel Le Goff was Tante Marie's nephew. He came to the house quite often. Julie enjoyed his visits; he was clever, well informed and politically argumentative. He was probably quite attractive too, if you cared to think about him that way. But she did not, not at the moment anyway. She hadn't closed her mind to the possibility of liking him, but she wasn't ready to encourage him yet. Perhaps she never would be. But until her mind was made up, she did wish people wouldn't pair them off.

Peter was fidgeting at the table. 'Mummy, I've finished. Read me a story now. Please. You promised!'

'Yes, of course, darling. And it's almost bedtime, too.'

She picked him up and carried him through the back door of the kitchen into the extension. There were two rooms, one on the ground floor and, at the top of some steep, narrow stairs, a small attic bedroom. Julie used the main room as a bed-sitting room, though she nearly always sat in the kitchen during the evenings. The room was simply furnished with a bed, a chest of drawers, and a chair. Soon after her arrival she had whitewashed the walls and hung a couple of colourful pictures to brighten the room up. Though she didn't like needlework, she had even made some gay curtains for the window.

On the chest of drawers there were several framed photographs of Peter, and one of her mother. When Julie thought of her mother, she sighed. She wrote to her mother regularly, every month or so, but she rarely got a reply. The few letters she did get were bitter and full of reproach, begging her to come back to England and live in Plymouth again. Her mother never missed an opportunity to make it clear that she felt abandoned and betrayed. 'Disloyal' and 'ungrateful' were her favourite expressions.

It was clear to Julie that her mother could not have read any of her replies, otherwise she would have understood. Julie had explained that she was happy here, that she enjoyed her work and she loved the people. But now, after so much time, Julie suspected that Mother did not want to understand. Mother hated the idea of Julie liking Father's people and living the kind of life Father had lived and which Mother had tried so hard to drag him away from. The suspicion made her sad but all the more determined not to go back. Life at the little house in Plymouth would suffocate her. Here at least she was free.

She undressed Peter and gave him a quick wash. As she dried him he wriggled away from her and dashed off round the room attempting as usual to evade capture, pyjamas and bed. Julie chased after him, roaring like a lion. At last she caught a flying arm and threw him giggling on to the bed.

Peter cried, 'Again!'

Julie put her head on one side and listened; there was the sound of a new voice from the kitchen. It was Michel's. She said firmly to Peter, 'No.'

Peter began to whine. 'If you don't, I'll cry.'

'And if you don't let me put these pyjamas on, there'll be big trouble.' She gave him a mock glare.

Peter's lower lip wobbled and he began to cry, though rather half-heartedly. He often cried when he was tired. She kissed him and felt the soft, cool arms encircle her neck. She put her arms round his small irate body and, taking him on her knee, began to rock him gently back and forth as she had when he was a baby.

After a while she felt a kiss on her ear and a small voice said, 'Story now?'

'Yes, we'll have *two* stories tonight.'

She read him three stories because he'd been a good boy and because she always read him one more than she said she would. Then she carried him up the narrow stairs to the attic bedroom. It was a small room, with one bed and a tiny window, but it was snug and Peter loved it because when he woke up in the night he could call down to her and, in the morning when he crawled into her bed, it wasn't far for him to come.

She gave him a last kiss and went down the stairs to the chest of drawers. She opened the top drawer and, taking out a small mirror, examined herself critically. She didn't like her face much. Its shape was all right – oval – and her skin was as clear as a bell, but the face seemed to her incredibly *ordinary*. Her best feature, she supposed, was her eyes, which were large and dark and fairly pretty – but she'd never dared pluck her eyebrows as the fashionable women did and so her eyes probably made little impression. Nose – all right but definitely nothing special. She sighed: really there was nothing very special about any of her.

Except her hair. That *was* something she was proud of. It was dark – dark *auburn*, they called it – and naturally curly where it met her shoulders. She never did much to it, usually parting it in the middle and holding it back with a comb at either side. She'd tried a fancy rolled style once or twice, but the hairdo seemed to detract from the hair itself and she'd let it down again.

She brushed it now until it shone, added a touch of lipstick, and stood back.

No, nothing special about her tonight. Anyway, it was only Michel.

But at least he was a man, and unmarried at that. And she didn't meet very many of those. She was beginning to think it would be a good idea for her to have a husband. She took a last look in the mirror and thought: I'm nearly twenty-four, I mustn't leave it too late. She smiled ruefully; some people would say she was already on the shelf.

She straightened her dress and walked into the kitchen.

Michel's voice was saying, 'But you have to understand, it's only political expediency – political *survival* – that's all!' Julie's heart sank a little as it always did when Michel and Jean started on politics.

Michel spotted her and, getting quickly to his feet, stared into her face. His gaze was hard and penetrating. Julie decided, not for the first time, that there was something altogether too earnest about Michel. After a moment he smiled quickly and stooped to kiss her on both cheeks.

He said apologetically, 'I'm defending myself again. Jean thinks my politics stink.' He shrugged slightly, and half smiled. But Julie knew that, behind the casual manner, he was deadly serious about his opinions. Michel nodded slightly and sat down to face Jean again, saying, 'Look, it's not something the Soviet Union wanted to do, but they had no choice, don't you see? We and the British, we offered them nothing, no guarantees, no treaties, just hot air . . .'

Julie listened quietly, trying to follow the arguments. There was something about the intensity of Michel's opinions which was rather unnerving. He spoke with an earnest fury that tolerated no opposition. It was a pity, she decided, because in most other ways he had a lot to recommend him.

He was dark, like many of the French: his hair was almost black and his eyes deep brown. He was pleasant looking, though he had a way of frowning which made him look severe. He dressed well, and Julie guessed his clothes cost a lot. She smiled to herself: only in

France could you find a communist who dressed like a capitalist. But then half the population were communist when it suited them. The rest of the time they were socialists, or Republicans, depending on their mood.

Michel worked in Morlaix, in an insurance office. She sometimes bumped into him when she was out shopping in her lunch hour and occasionally he would buy her a coffee. Then – when he was off the subject of politics – she enjoyed his company much more. He had a dry wit and an interesting way of describing everyday things. But she'd avoided seeing him in the evenings; that would imply there was more to their relationship than family friendship, and she didn't want that.

She concentrated again on the conversation. Michel was speaking forcefully, his fists clenched.

'The Soviet Union does not want war. So what's wrong with her manoeuvring to avoid it? If we had any sense that's what we'd be doing too instead of pledging support to Poland, which is undefendable anyway!'

Jean Cornou leaned forward in his chair and, picking up a poker, flipped open the door of the stove. He stabbed thoughtfully at the fire. 'But someone has to protect countries that need protecting. Your precious Russia, she doesn't care about anyone else at all. She may be avoiding war for herself, but not for everyone else!'

'Nonsense, war should be avoided at all costs. Who wants to fight? You? Me? Of course not! The end justifies the means!'

Julie said suddenly, 'There's nothing wrong with avoiding war – so long as it achieves real peace. If it just gives the bullies time to move into a stronger position, then it's no good, is it? That's what it's all about, it seems to me – bullying.' She added almost to herself, 'They should let the women run things, then we might have a bit of sensible government and people would be left to live in peace.'

Everyone was looking at her in surprise. She'd never spoken during a political argument before. There was a long silence and Julie dropped her eyes. She'd gone too far.

She added nervously, 'Anyway, why don't we talk about something else for a change. This subject is very depressing.'

Tante Marie put down her knitting. 'A good idea. I'll put some supper on the table. Michel, will you stay for a bit?'

There was no reply and Julie looked up. Michel was staring at her. 'A fine speech!'

There was a mocking note in his voice and she wasn't sure if he was laughing at her or not. She got up and helped Tante Marie to lay the table. As she passed Michel's chair he said, 'Really, it was a fine speech.'

He looked as though he meant it and she thought that maybe she'd misjudged him. She put her hand on his arm and smiled.

They sat down at the table and talked about the harvest and the fishing industry, the weather and the fruit crop.

Eventually Michel said, 'And what about your job, Julie? Are you happy there?'

'Yes, happy enough. It's quite interesting really. I've become something of an expert on vegetable prices.' She didn't add that she was often bored. But it was a job and it brought the money in. That was all that mattered.

'I only wish –' She paused. 'I only wish I had more spare time.'

Michel leant forward. 'You should ask for shorter hours!' The subject of long hours was one of his favourite subjects. He considered anything over a forty-hour week to be slave labour. 'The other way is to give up work altogether.'

Julie gave a short laugh. 'And how would I live then?'

He shot her a glance. 'You could find someone to support you.'

She felt herself blushing and looked furiously at the table. I walked straight into that one, she thought.

Michel was looking at her with a rather smug, self-satisfied expression. Suddenly she wanted to wipe the smirk right off his face.

She said crossly, 'I'm not interested in marrying just to find someone to support me. Women who do that are fools and the men who marry them even more stupid. When I find a man I want to marry, *then* I'll be happy to let him pay the bills!'

Michel looked at his hands and said quietly, 'But marriage is a practical arrangement. If you think it's made in heaven, well – then you are not as clever as I thought you were.'

He was warming up for an argument, Julie could see that. He would call it a discussion, but it would really be a sparring match. Michel always won those kind of arguments. He had a way of twisting words and turning logic until his opponent's opinions appeared ridiculous.

Suddenly Julie wanted to be on her own. She made an elaborate pantomine of looking at the clock over the mantelpiece. 'Goodness! Is that the time? I really must get to bed.'

She stood up and made herself smile. 'It was nice to see you Michel. Good night.' They kissed each other on both cheeks, and she saw that he was looking pleased with himself again. Damn him, she thought, why does he have to be so *satisfied* with himself?

Later, when she lay in bed, she went over the conversation again in her mind. Until now she'd thought Michel kind and thoughtful under his façade of cleverness and indifference. But now she was having second thoughts. He wasn't kind at all; he was conceited and intolerant. There was no question of letting their friendship develop; it would never work. She'd never be happy with a man who had to score off everyone as if the whole of life were a political debate. And she hated the way he was amused by almost everything she said, like a patronising father listening to a child.

No, whatever happened, she could never love Michel.

She thought of the alternatives – none – and wondered if she was being too fussy. A lot of women grabbed the first man who came their way and lived happily ever after. Or did they? One never knew.

All she wanted was someone kind, thoughtful and reasonable to look at. She smiled to herself. Not much! Just what everyone else was after too.

She turned over and tried to sleep. She remembered rather guiltily that she hadn't given another thought to this war. It was a very worrying thing. And yet it was difficult to be worried about an event which everyone must be working so hard to prevent. If it *did* happen it would, of course, be dreadful. But she couldn't help thinking how lucky it was that Peter and she lived so far from the German border, and that her uncle was too old to fight. The war, if it came, would hardly touch them at all. It was awful to think so selfishly, but one couldn't help it.

No: whatever happened, her little family would be safe.

It was a comforting thought and almost immediately she fell into a dreamless sleep.

6

David looked at the note on his desk. It read: Please report to the Director at your earliest convenience.

The message was innocent enough, but it gave David a twinge of uneasiness. In the past few days the laboratories had been rife with rumour. It was said that several projects were to be cancelled and that many more of the clerical and administrative staff would be liable for conscription. Already some seventy of the non-scientific personnel had been called up.

David took off his white coat and pulled on his jacket. Absent-mindedly he pushed his hair out of his eyes and looked at the note again. Best to get it over with, whatever it was. Automatically he checked his desk to make sure there were no confidential files lying around. He always did that; you could never be too careful.

The Director's office was on the third floor and David decided to walk up the stairs rather than use the lift: it would be good for him. He really wasn't as fit as he should be. He only wished he could find more time for exercise.

He arrived in the outer office breathing heavily and, when the secretary asked him to wait, he was glad of the chance to sit down for a moment. They'd never asked him to wait before. The Director usually made a point of not keeping the senior scientists waiting, and on minor matters he liked to come down to the laboratories rather than call them away from their work. Still, one shouldn't attach any undue importance to that. It probably meant nothing.

There had been other incidents, of course, and David was well aware that they *did* mean something. When a new steering committee had been set up within the Gema Company he and another scientist had been excluded from it. Both of them were Jewish. Shortly afterwards, for no apparent reason, he had been told that he would not be attending a demonstration of the new Wassermann early-warning radar system.

And then there were the small things: the way people avoided him, the way he seemed to be left off circulation lists of important documents. David knew that it all meant something and it left him apprehensive. But at the same time David trusted the Director. They had worked well together for a long time. The man had gone behind Schmidt's back and provided David with facilities and a decent budget for the Valve Development Project. The man knew the importance of science. And, David thought without vanity, he knows the value of a top-rate scientist.

Ten minutes later the secretary showed him into the Director's office. The Director was sitting behind his desk, busily reading some papers.

'Do be seated, please.'

David noticed that he didn't look up.

Eventually the Director shuffled the papers into an untidy pile and glanced quickly at David. 'Herr Freymann –' He looked out of the window, then down at the desk. 'I regret to tell you that due to a major policy decision all long-term research is to be cancelled. This has come from the highest level, you understand. It is out of my hands. In fact –' he met David's eyes '– the order came from the Fuehrer himself.'

'So the Valve Project is to go?'

'Yes.'

David wasn't entirely surprised. The project was, after all, a shot in the dark as far as Gema were concerned. Back in 1936 Schmidt had produced a document which 'proved' that short-wave radar was not only impossible to develop but not worth developing anyway. By supporting David for the last two years – albeit secretly – the Director had gone out on a limb. He couldn't be blamed for backing out now.

The Director cleared his throat. 'It's not as if you had achieved concrete results. I mean, the valve does not produce the required power, does it?'

David looked him straight in the eye and said, 'No, I'm afraid it appears not to.'

The other man nodded, relieved. 'Well, there we are then.' He picked up a paperweight and moved it nervously from hand to hand. 'There is also another problem and that is – this special scientific status. It appears that this special status is to go and . . . there is to be no widespread immunity from the draft.' He pursed his lips. 'Only those involved in work vital to our present needs are to be kept on.'

'You mean –' David frowned. He didn't understand.

The Director spoke rapidly. 'I mean that only those essential to the development of existing systems like the Freya and the Wassermann are to stay. All others are to go. Your work on the development of new systems is too futuristic and . . . and your contract is not to be renewed.'

'But it has two years to run. I can continue to work on *something*.'

The Director looked uncomfortable. 'No, it has been decided to let you go. Immediately.'

David stared at him and felt a tremor of fear. 'I am to go?'

'Yes, I am sorry, but these are my instructions. It is out of my hands. I have been *told*, you understand.'

David's throat was dry and he swallowed repeatedly. He was trying to understand, he wanted to understand . . . But all he could see was a great hole opening up in front of him. Without his scientific status, without protection, he would be completely vulnerable . . . open to dispossession and God only knew what else. He felt as if his feet were being knocked from under him.

The Director was examining the paperweight and looking unhappy. David said, 'Herr Director, we have known each other for a long time. You realise what this means for me? You know that without special status I am – I have no *protection*.'

'I am sorry. There is nothing I can do. I myself am most upset about this treatment we are getting. Science is obviously not very highly rated by those in authority. It is most unfair! Most unfair! Really – there is nothing I can do. I am sorry.'

The man was avoiding his eyes and David stared disbelievingly. The decision itself was bad enough, but this – this cold impersonal expression of regret, it was terrible. This man had been his colleague, his workmate . . .

'Herr Director, I realise that perhaps you cannot help me directly – work here – but you can help me in other ways –'

David thought rapidly. Without protection he and Ellen and Cecile would have to leave. There was no other choice, not if one wanted to work and live freely. What would he need? His passport was in order, thank God, complete with its red 'J'; Cecile was on Ellen's passport, so that was all right; but they would need emigration papers. Or what did they call them now? Deportation papers, that was it, deportation papers . . . David asked, 'Could you help me to get deportation papers? If I can't continue with my work it would be best to leave. I hear that one needs help to get these papers. Would you? Help, I mean?'

'I'm sorry, I really don't think I can help. If I could, believe me, I would. Now, if you'll excuse me . . .'

David sat frozen in the chair. He could hardly believe his ears. Perhaps the Director had not understood. It would only take a word from him, a telephone call, that was all.

'Please, all I ask is your backing. Just to leave. That's all I want to do. Really, it won't be much trouble.'

'Herr Freymann, I cannot help. It would not be *right* of me to interfere. It would not be appropriate, you understand. I try to keep out of politics – and such matters.' He stood up. 'I am sorry.'

David got unsteadily to his feet and opened the door.

'Oh, and –' There was a note of embarrassment in the Director's voice. 'I will need all your confidential papers. I will send my secretary to collect them shortly.'

David nodded and made his way back to his office. He walked again, but this time because he needed to be alone. He was stunned; he felt like a child who was being punished for something he hadn't done. Not only had he done nothing to be ashamed of, he had worked hard and with brilliant results. He couldn't believe that such achievements could be overlooked and ignored. It was incredible. He thought: How can they do this?

But even as he thought it, he knew they could – they *had*!

He felt tremendous anger, but not at them: at himself for being so ostrich-like. He had hidden behind his scientific status; he had believed he was important enough to escape this persecution. He shook his head. What a fool he had been, what a fool. He had made the mistake of thinking he was *different*. The sin of pride!

He closed the door of his office and sat heavily on his chair. Almost immediately there was a knock on the door and Hans came in.

'David, David. What can I say?'

'Nothing.'

'What will you do?'

'Oh, try to get out, I suppose. Except that it's probably too late for that.' He laughed bitterly.

'And your special research?'

David shook his head. 'Ended. I go, it goes. All for nothing.'

'But it was going well?'

There was a pause. David looked into Hans' eyes. 'Don't ask me, just don't ask me. It's better that way.'

There was a sound from the door and David jumped slightly. It was the Director's secretary. She was already in the room.

He thought: Now they're not even knocking before they come in. Without a word, he got up and unlocked his filing cabinet. He took out the batch of files marked with a red star and handed them to her. She nodded and left the room.

Hans asked, 'Your results?'

'Yes, everything.'

Hans sat down and put his head in his hands. 'Is there no end to their stupidity? Have you heard? Singers and entertainers are to escape conscription – apparently they are indispensable – but not scientists. Hitler has no idea, no idea!'

'No.'

Hans looked up. 'What will you do?'

'There's nothing I *can* do. I imagine they will confiscate my identity card and issue me with a new one – with the name Israel, just like everyone else. I mean,' he smiled ruefully, 'just like other *Jews.*'

And there'd be more, David knew: there'd be the star on his clothes, the declaration of his wealth and, shortly afterwards, the confiscation of all his belongings.

'Haven't you protected yourself?'

'Oh the house is in Ellen's name, and some of our savings. But I couldn't transfer everything. They stopped all that.'

'But Ellen. Your marriage is privileged, isn't it? I mean she's not Jewish, is she?'

'The special status of mixed marriages ended some time ago.'

'Oh, I didn't realise.'

'Nothing can save me, Hans. I have been a fool, a fool.' He felt himself near to tears, and turned his head away.

Hans said anxiously, 'I wish I could help.'

David shook his head. 'No, my friend, I don't think you can. My only hope is to buy some deportation papers. I hear they're very expensive, but . . . I might have enough money.'

'If there's anything I can do . . .'

For a moment David felt a glimmer of hope. 'Not unless you know an official? Someone with influence?'

Hans frowned. 'No, I'm sorry.'

Everyone seemed to be saying they were sorry today. Sorry but unable to help. At least Hans meant what he said; he was a good sort. But David made him leave: he couldn't bear to be pitied any more. Besides he wanted to be alone. Hans said he would look in again before the end of the day. But he didn't: they both knew there wasn't any point.

David sat in the chair for a long time, staring out of the window. No-one came to see him and eventually he heard people leaving for home. Finally everything was quiet. At seven he heard the night watchman closing doors and checking windows. He put on his reading light and spread some papers on his desk. When the watchman put his head round the door David was engrossed in his work.

The watchman wanted to know how long David expected to stay in the building. David replied that he would be gone by ten, and the watchman nodded and left.

As soon as he had gone. David got up and went to the door. He listened and, satisfied that the building was empty, walked quietly down the corridor to the first laboratory. He went straight to a small cabinet and tried the door. It was locked. He crossed to a desk and feeling behind a drawer found the spare set of keys the technicians kept there.

The key which fitted the cabinet was smaller than the rest and David found it immediately. He opened the door of the cabinet and took out the camera and rolls of film which he knew he would find there.

David went back to his office and opened the filing cabinet. His mouth was dry with excitement. The file he wanted was marked 'Corporate Structure'. The papers it normally contained were unclassified and uninteresting; it was a file people hardly ever bothered to look at, which was why David had chosen it.

He took out the file and laid the papers on the desk. He loaded the camera, checked the exposure and, putting the first page under the light, pressed the shutter.

At first he couldn't keep the camera still and realised it was because his hands were shaking. He sat down for a moment and tried to calm down. It was vital to get good pictures; it was the only hope.

He stood up again and this time he could see the page clearly through the viewfinder. The job took over an hour, because he took two pictures of each of the ten pages and checked the exposure every time.

He wound the film on to the take-up spool and took it out of the camera. He replaced the camera in the laboratory cabinet and then returned to his office. He picked up all the papers that he had photographed and, putting them in the waste paper basket, set fire to them.

It gave him a curious feeling, to watch the beautiful drawings and the results of the last two years' work crinkle up and blacken in front of his eyes. So much work! So much love! He felt a stab of uncertainty. It was such a final act, this burning. It meant there was no going back. But then there had been no going back the moment he had lied to the Director about the Valve Project. The Director had asked him if the valve was producing the necessary power and David had said it wasn't. There had been no point in telling the truth. The decision to cancel long-term research had been taken at the highest level. The truth wouldn't have saved his project – or himself.

Why had he concealed the truth all this time? He still wasn't sure. It was partly caution – he wanted to announce his results only when they were fully proven so that Schmidt couldn't tear them to ribbons. And it was partly – what? Foreboding, an uneasy feeling that he might after all be vulnerable to the Nazi campaign? Yes, that too. But also – and he was ashamed to admit it – also pride. He wanted to keep the glory for himself, to show them that they were wrong and that he had been right all along, and show them in a dramatic way, by demonstrating a short-wave radar itself. That was still a good way off yet, and he would have needed more resources and at least ten assistants. It would have been difficult to keep it quiet much longer . . .

Over the last few months he'd been falsifying the test results, only a little – but just enough to make the Director think the valve was not going to be a success. Only his assistant had seen the results, but he was young and easily persuaded that there were still immense problems to be solved.

But there were no immense problems. Once he had discovered the best way of combining the two types of valve, he was there. Within a few months he'd produced a valve which generated 500 watts on the very high frequency of 3,000 megacycles. Despite its immense power the valve could be made very small, just as he had predicted. The radar that could be developed from the valve would be very small too. And he had predicted that too.

He felt a glow of pride. He had been *right* and Schmidt *wrong*. It was a pity Schmidt would never know.

He tucked the spool into an inside pocket of his jacket and, wiping the sweat from his forehead, took a last look round the office.

This had been his second home, the place where he had come to do the work he loved, the place he associated with contentment and security and achievement. And he would never see it again.

Oh Dear Lord. He wiped the tears from his cheeks and, closing the door behind him, walked down the passage.

As he approached the main entrance he felt a stab of pain in his stomach. Heartburn, probably. He always got it when he was late for a meal. Then, as he emerged into the darkness, it occurred to him that it was not heartburn at all, but fear.

He looked over his shoulder and, pulling his hat down over his face, walked rapidly into the night.

The room was hot and stuffy and David found it difficult to stay awake. At about four he nodded off. A loud voice announced 'Next!' and David woke with a start. He looked rapidly around him. There were three people ahead of him and about fifty behind – there would be many more, perhaps a hundred, in the street. With a bit of luck he might get in today. Otherwise he would have to wait outside in the street all night until they reopened the office in the morning. He'd already been waiting three days.

He looked at the man ahead of him. He was well dressed and prosperous-looking; he'd probably been a jeweller or a clothing manufacturer before the crack-down. They would have confiscated his business by now. Looking at him, David guessed he'd been clever and hidden plenty of money and valuables. Otherwise he wouldn't have bothered to come here. Yes, he looked the clever sort. Not like me, David thought, with no money and no influence.

It was stupid to come here really. But he was doing it out of duty to Ellen and Cecile. He had to *try* to get the papers, he owed them that much at least.

It was five when he finally got into the *Gauleiter*'s office; David was the last before they closed for the day. A young man looked at his papers and asked, 'What are your means?'

David thought rapidly. Did they want to know what he was supposed to have or what he *actually* had? After confiscation you weren't meant to have much left.

He answered, 'Enough.'

'Are you sure?'

'Yes.'

The young man gave him a hard stare and waved him through to the next room. It was a long palatial office at the end of which was a large desk. Behind it sat a gross figure smoking a Bavarian pipe, and beside him a male assistant with a red ledger in front of him.

David stood in front of the desk. The large man was reading a newspaper. He took no notice of David.

Without looking up the assistant said, 'Deportation papers will cost you 250,000 marks. How do you intend to pay?'

David gulped. When he'd last heard they had been priced at 150,000 marks which he might have been able to borrow from Ellen's father. But this!

'Well?' The assistant was impatient. It had been a long day and he wanted to get home.

David thought: I must say something – anything – just in case. He said, 'I'll pay in cash – but it'll take a week.'

The assistant looked at the fat man. 'Herr Deputy Gauleiter, he wants a week to pay.'

'What?' The fat man looked irritated at being disturbed. 'No, no, no! Get him out! No money, no papers.'

It was all happening so fast. David tried to think. He said, 'Tomorrow then! Tomorrow!'

The assistant stared at him, then nodded briefly. He scribbled on a card and handed it across the desk. 'This will get you straight in here tomorrow. But if you do not have the money you will be arrested for wasting the Deputy Gauleiter's time.'

David went out into the street and leant against the wall. He was tired, so tired. He looked at the long line of waiting people, each wearing a star, each with a look of resignation on his face. Probably one in fifty could raise 250,000 marks. For some people it amounted to a lifetime's pay. For David it was about ten years' salary.

There was only one source he could get the money from: Ellen's father. But it would represent a vast amount of money to him, more than his life savings. David shook his head and began to walk. How much was he worth to his father-in-law? Not that much, never that much.

Why then had he bothered to go through that play-acting back there? It was a waste of time: he'd known it was no use the moment he'd heard the amount they wanted.

There was no point in going back, tomorrow or ever.

Suddenly David made up his mind and walked briskly away. He'd given them their chance; he'd tried to do things their way. Now they left him no choice.

He took a tram to the Tiergarten. On the south side of the park were some of the principal embassies in Berlin. He hadn't thought which embassy he would try first: perhaps the British, then the French. If he had no luck there he would try the Americans or one of the Scandinavian countries.

He got off at the end of Tiergartenstrasse and walked. In the park he could see a group of *Jungvolk* training for their initiation into the Hitler Youth. Some were running the compulsory sixty metres, others jumping the 2.75 metre long jump. Another group were sitting in a circle chanting the *Schwertworte*, the short version of the Nazi dogma which had to be learnt by heart. The children looked so sweet, sitting there in the sun in their neat uniforms, that David stopped to watch them for a moment.

As he neared the embassies he pulled his raincoat on. It wasn't raining but he wanted to hide the star stitched onto his jacket. They might stop him otherwise; they might prevent him from going in.

The first embassy was just visible through a thick screen of trees, an imposing white mansion set back from the road behind metal railings. David was fairly sure it was the United States Embassy. Perhaps he should try there first: in the last ten years the country had taken a lot of Jews in. Yet at the same time it was neutral – perhaps they wouldn't be interested in trading his information.

David strode on, still undecided. Suddenly he stopped and frowned. There was a group of people on the pavement, standing quietly, waiting. Between them and the gates of the mansion were stormtroopers. The troopers were facing the people, weapons held ready across their chests.

David walked slowly up. It was definitely the United States Embassy. The waiting people were Jewish. No-one was being allowed in. He asked one of the waiting men: no-one had been allowed in for weeks.

It was the same outside the French Embassy, and the British. Except that there were fewer people waiting.

He thought: I'm so stupid; of course they're not going to let people in. Of course!

The telephone, he should have used the telephone. He walked rapidly through the streets until he found a post office. He went up to the counter and asked for a booth. The girl behind the counter was young and quite pretty. She glanced up and then stared at him hard.

David thought: There's going to be trouble; she's going to make trouble. The girl blinked then asked, loudly and deliberately, for his identity papers. The other counter staff fell silent; people looked. David felt in his jacket pocket and passed over his papers. Quickly, he pulled open his raincoat: it was a serious offence to hide the star on his jacket. The girl looked at him triumphantly and said, 'Non-aryans are not permitted to use the telephones here.'

It was a new restriction David had never heard of. In fact he was certain that no such restriction existed. But there could be no argument: that was one thing he'd learnt during the last week.

They watched him as he turned and walked into the street. He heard the girl laughing as he closed the door, and the heat of humiliation burnt his cheeks. He shrank into the porch and leant against the cold stone. The tiredness hit him like a hammer. He hadn't slept properly for three days and now he felt sick with fatigue.

He looked at the time: it was nearly six. The embassy staff would have shut their offices by now anyway. It was too late to do anything more today. Another day gone and nothing achieved.

He thought: I'm tired, just tired.

He went to the station and took the train home. As he walked towards his house he passed the little shoe shop and looked in the window. The posters marked 'Jew!' had long since disappeared. Now there was one small notice discreetly placed among the shoes on display. It read: Under new management. David wondered what had happened to Finstein. No-one bothered to ask about their neighbours any more; it was better not to know.

When he came round the bend in the road the sight of the small cosy house no longer thrilled David. Instead it reminded him of his family and his responsibilities. He wanted to protect his family, to provide and care for them. If a man couldn't do that then he wasn't worth much.

As he opened the door he wondered if Ellen would be crying again. She had been crying almost continuously since he had lost his job. He couldn't blame her, of course; she had every reason to cry.

He called a hello and waited for Cecile to come bounding into the hall and give him a hug as she always did.

There was silence and he called again.

The kitchen door opened and Cecile came out. She was sobbing into a handkerchief. She didn't run up to him but hovered miserably by the door, shaking her head from side to side. 'Oh Daddy, Daddy!'

David stepped forward, his arms outstretched. 'My little rabbit, whatever is the matter?' Cecile had never cried before, not like this. She was usually so brave, so fearless.

Ellen appeared in the doorway behind her. 'It was no good, I suppose? You haven't got the papers?'

He shook his head. 'They wanted . . . too much.'

Ellen said firmly, 'Go upstairs, Cecile. I want to talk to your father.'

Cecile gave a sob and ran past him up the stairs. David looked at Ellen in bewilderment. She beckoned him into the living room.

'David, I have something to tell you.' She paused and started fiddling with a china dog on the mantelpiece. Eventually she said, 'Cecile and I are going away. I've been talking to my father and we've agreed that it's the only way.'

David looked at her blankly. 'What do you mean?'

Ellen took a breath and turned to face him. 'We want the best for Cecile, don't we? Well, there's only one way to be sure she doesn't suffer. And that's to get right away. I'm sorry, David, but I think it will be better if we . . .' She licked her lips nervously, '. . . if we live apart.'

'Live apart?'

'Yes, Cecile and I are going away, to a new place.'

'A new place? But . . . it'll be so difficult for Cecile . . . settling into a new school. And . . . at least everyone knows us here, accepts us . . .'

'Accepts us? Are you mad? Don't you realise what it's been like for me? And for *Cecile*? You have no idea what she's been through at school. They all *know* about you, they all know that Cecile is partly Jewish. They all taunt her, do you hear me, they *taunt her*!' Ellen was spitting at him, her eyes blazing.

David sank into a chair and murmured, 'Oh God, oh God.'

'I told you it was happening, but as usual you had your head in the clouds, where it always is. I told you last November when . . . when . . . those awful things happened, but you wouldn't listen!'

She was referring to Crystal Night, a major pogrom against the Jews; many synagogues, shops and flats had been destroyed.

David shook his head. 'But wherever you move to they'll still *know*. You'll still be my wife and you can't hide that.'

Ellen drew a deep breath. 'I am going to divorce you, David. I'm going to take a new name and make a fresh start. For Cecile, it's for Cecile. You must see . . . how important it is, for her sake.'

David was dumbfounded.

She couldn't be doing this to him. The idea of losing his little rabbit was almost more than he could bear. They sat in silence for a while. Then a terrible thought came into his mind. He trembled as he asked, 'When? When are you going?'

'Tonight. My father's coming to collect us in the car.'

David felt as if a vice were tightening around his heart. He gasped, 'Oh no, oh no. Not yet, please not yet.' Then he remembered the telephone call and how he would sell his invention. He looked up and said brightly, 'You *mustn't* go, not yet. I forgot to tell you. I've got to make a telephone call in the morning. There's a really good chance we'll get papers. Really! The best chance yet! I'll go to the post office first thing in the morning.'

Ellen moved impatiently towards the door. 'David, these schemes of yours . . .' She shook her head. 'Anyway, I don't want to live abroad. I want to stay here with my family.'

David cried bitterly, 'I'm your family too, remember!'

But she had gone.

Oh God! He tried to think, he tried to make himself think, but it was no good, he was just too tired. Hopelessness and despair overwhelmed him.

Dear Lord, what have I done? What have I done?

After a while he climbed the stairs to Cecile's room. He found her lying on the bed, crying silently. He went to her and touched her arm. She reached out to him and together they sat on the edge of the bed, their arms around each other, rocking gently.

David thought: Everything I want is here, my family, my daughter. Is it so very much to ask? What did I do that they should take it away from me?

Finally, after a long time, he said, 'My little rabbit, it's for the best, you know, your mother is right. You will be safer with a new name and a new place to live.' She started crying again and he said, 'I want you to be very brave. I want you to go away and to make a success of your life. And to forget about me.'

'I couldn't, Daddy, I couldn't.'

'But you must. I'm going to go abroad. I can't be a proper father to you when I'm away.'

'But you'll always be my Daddy.'

'Yes, yes, I'll always be your Daddy.' David hugged her tightly and wept quietly.

Then there were sounds from below and, without a word, Ellen came and took Cecile downstairs. David couldn't bring himself to watch them go. Instead he sat on Cecile's bed and put his head in his hands.

The silence pressed in on him and, when he couldn't bear it any longer, he lay down and put his arms over his head. Finally he fell asleep and dreamed that Cecile was dead.

When David woke it was dawn and he was very cold. For a while he

111

lay on the bed watching the thin, grey light illuminate the toys and gay pictures that decorated the neat, feminine room. The room looked cold and unused, as if Cecile had been gone a long time.

He sat up. His head ached viciously. Lack of sleep and food.

Mechanically, he got up and went into the bathroom to wash. In the main bedroom he found a clean shirt and his best suit, and put them on.

He went downstairs. The house was deathly quiet. Normally Cecile would be chattering away in the kitchen while Ellen made the breakfast. He decided to turn the wireless on as soon as he got into the kitchen.

But first he went into the dining room and, reaching up to the top of the dresser, felt for the black canister. As his fingers closed over it he felt a thrill of excitement. So much in such a small container!

But small though it was, it was still too large. It would be impossible to hide on his body. Any good search would soon discover it under his arm, or strapped to his leg. He opened the cannister and took out the roll of film. It was only half an inch high and an eighth of an inch in diameter.

He went into the kitchen and found a piece of greaseproof paper. He cut an oblong strip and rolled it round the film, then tied the ends with cotton.

David was pleased. It was small enough now to be hidden in his mouth. Or even in other places where people wouldn't look. Well, hopefully not.

Getting the film developed had been the most difficult part. The local photographic shop had been out of the question; they would have reported him straight away. There was a man at Gema whose hobby was developing and printing his own photographs, but it would have been far too dangerous to contact him. Then David remembered the processing laboratory which the Gema Company used for all its photographic work, and he went there. He went there straight away, before the laboratory knew he had been dismissed. He went there while he was still angry and had the nerve to ask them to process the film and transfer it onto the smallest possible negative. He said it was top secret, and they mustn't talk about it. His own daring had amazed him.

It was the strangeness of the request which made the laboratory carry out the work without question. The technicians were called in from the processing lab and everyone was so engrossed in deciding how the reduction could be done they didn't stop to query it. They didn't even notice the sweat on David's brow or the way his hands shook as he passed over the film.

Now David held the tiny packet in his hand and wondered where he should hide it for the moment. Best to be on the safe side. He took some surgical tape from the first aid box in the bathroom and stuck the roll on to the under side of his upper arm. It was not very satisfactory – if they were actually looking for a roll of film they would find it straight away – but it would have to do.

He found some bratwurst and black bread in the kitchen. There was a spoonful of coffee in a jar; he put it in a strainer and poured hot water over it. It tasted foul. He sat at the kitchen table and looked out at the small, neat garden. In the summer they always spent Sunday afternoons there, just the three of them. David turned on the wireless. The set was a new *Volksempfanger* People's Receiver; he had bought it as a present for Ellen's birthday.

David listened half-heartedly, thinking of Cecile. The announcements were always the same nowadays. People were exhorted to greater service and sacrifice for the Fatherland; they must unite against the enemies of Germany; the young men must be ready to serve in the cause of the Fatherland. Today the enemy seemed to be Poland who were even at this moment threatening the very security of the beloved Homeland. Poland? It had been Czechoslovakia for so long that David couldn't get used to all this talk about Poland. But perhaps Poland had been the enemy for some time; he hadn't been listening to the wireless very much recently.

The announcer turned to home news: today another great step had been taken in the eradication of the common enemy! The filthy Jews would no longer be permitted wireless sets. No longer would they be permitted to enjoy the fruits of their thieving and usury! Millions of honest, working Germans would now be free to listen in peace, in the knowledge that not a single conniving Jew was listening to their beloved programmes!

David froze with a piece of bread halfway to his mouth, and felt vaguely sick. He should have realised that this campaign was much, much worse than the ones before. And now it was almost too late. But not quite.

He washed up the breakfast things and went into the hall. It was eight-thirty. He looked at the telephone which stood on a small table beside the stairs. The embassy offices would be staffed by now; he should call as soon as possible. And yet – not from here. The operator might have instructions to report all calls made to embassies; she might listen in; *they* might listen in. No, he would go to the post office; that would be safer.

At the post office there was a queue for the telephones. David waited quietly. He did not mind waiting. The important thing was

113

not to attract attention or get in anyone's way. At one point a large woman came bustling in and, seeing the line of people, sighed loudly. Without a word David stood back and let her take his place. She started to say something but, seeing the star on his jacket, tightened her lips and turned away.

Eventually there was only one person ahead of him and no-one behind. David eyed the girl at the desk nervously. She looked all right but you could never tell. When his turn came she glanced up quickly and, without comment, directed him to a booth.

So far, so good.

He gave the operator the number of the British Embassy and waited, swallowing nervously. He hadn't really thought of what he would say. It was so difficult to know when you didn't even know who you'd be speaking to.

There were several loud clicks on the line and a woman's voice said in German, 'British Embassy.'

'Hello. I wish to speak to . . .' He thought: *Who?* '. . . to the attaché who deals with scientific matters.'

There was another click. A man's voice said, 'Yes?'

'I am a scientist,' David began lamely. 'I wish to emigrate. I –'

The voice interrupted, 'The immigration section of this embassy has closed. We are not dealing with any new applications.'

'But you don't understand, I . . . I have special information.' David hated to say such a thing over the telephone but he had the feeling the man would soon ring off.

'Who are you?'

David paused unhappily. 'I'd rather not say . . . it's too risky. Can't I meet someone? Or come to the embassy?'

'One moment please.'

David waited uneasily. He hadn't thought about the problems of making contact. It was horribly dangerous . . .

The voice said, 'It is regretted, but we cannot be of assistance.'

David felt his heart lurch. 'What do you mean? I have vital information, of great value!'

'We regret but, in view of the gravity of the international situation, it is impossible for us to become involved.'

David stared at the wall of the booth, the receiver forgotten in his hand.

The voice spoke again. 'Hello?'

'Yes.'

There was a pause as if the owner of the voice was considering what to say. 'We are not alone. Do you understand what I mean?'

'Yes.' David understood. The conversation was being listened to.

He replaced the receiver, and tried to think. He was confused; the certain knowledge that they were listening had been a shock. He hadn't been ready for that. He must think again.

Perhaps the Swedes? Yes, the good neutral Swedes. He found the number in the directory and gave it to the operator.

After a few seconds there was a reply. David was about to speak when there were two loud clicks. David froze, then slowly replaced the receiver.

He paid for the calls and left the post office.

He had to think: *he had to think*.

He walked into the street, his head down, his mind working. One thing was clear, absolutely clear: to try to contact an embassy would be suicide. He would never get near them. If he arranged a meeting the Gestapo would be there first. If he tried to deliver a message they would intercept it.

It was awful to give up the idea – but there was no choice. What else could he do?

What did that leave? He thought desperately, but there wasn't much. Only escape. Escape without papers, without help . . . He shook his head and strode on, head down, carefully avoiding other pedestrians.

The black jackboots were right in front of him before he saw them. He tried to step sideways but a second pair of boots blocked his way. David looked up and felt a stab of fear. Two young SS men were facing him; they were both smiling. David stepped quickly against the wall and tried to slide along it. The young men laughed and shouted. He felt a sharp blow on his head. He knew he had to run. They were coming for him again. He gathered his strength and made for a new gap between a uniformed body and the wall. He pushed through the gap, felt a blow on his shoulder, pushed again, and was through.

He ran. He ran as he used to do at school; fast, his chest out, his arms pumping. His lungs were bursting, they wouldn't draw enough air. His legs felt heavy as lead. He rounded a corner and staggered against a wall, his chest heaving, his head pounding.

He looked behind. There was no-one.

Thank God. Thank God.

How stupid! How stupid! Must be more careful, must be more careful.

He walked slowly on towards home, his heart still hammering, his breath still rasping in his throat. So unfit! So pathetically unfit!

Finally he neared the house and paused. The windows were dark, the front door closed as he had left it.

The house was quiet. The front door yielded easily to the key. He went in quickly and closed the door. The living room looked untouched, as neat and ordered as usual. He peered out of the window into the street. Nothing.

But there wasn't much time, he knew that now.

He sat for a moment so that his hands would stop shaking and thought: I'm too old for all this, too old and too tired.

Then he got up and looked through the bookcase until he found Cecile's World Atlas. He knelt on the carpet and studied the map of Europe. He would go west, that was certain; the east was trouble. That meant Switzerland or France or Belgium or Holland. Switzerland was out; they were too uncharitable and, even if you got over the border, it was rumoured that they sent you back again. Belgium or Holland; he wasn't sure about them. But France . . . France had taken lots of Jews, he knew that. And even if he couldn't stay there they would send him on somewhere else, he was sure of that.

France . . . he turned to a map which showed the Franco-German border more clearly. He stared at the long winding line and wondered where it would be best to cross. It would all be heavily militarised, of course, but it shouldn't be too difficult to get through, not if he was patient.

A long section of the border ran along the Rhine, so that was no good; the bridges would be heavily guarded and he couldn't swim. Where the border turned west then, towards Luxembourg. He put his finger on the Saar region. What was wrong with the map there? Of course! He sighed; the atlas was pre-1935 and didn't show the new border. In 1935 the Saar region had become German again. He didn't dare cross there; it would be hopeless if he didn't even know where the border was. That left the stretch to the east of Saarbrucken.

He looked at the railway lines. How far could he get without risking being picked up? Mannheim perhaps. Then what? It was sixty kilometres from Mannheim to the border. He made up his mind: although he was unfit, he would walk. He would *make* himself walk. He'd been quite a walker in his day. When he was a student he used to go hiking in the Bavarian Alps; he had covered twenty kilometres a day sometimes.

He would need food, money and equipment. He tore the page out of the atlas and put the book away. He stood up and tried to remember what there was in the house. Money: he had enough to buy his train ticket and a few meals, no more; but it should be sufficient. Anyway he would be taking as much food as possible. He went into the kitchen and looked in the cupboards. There were cans of sauerkraut, beef, and fruit. He decided to take them all. But he would need something to carry them in. Not a briefcase; people associated them with wealth and money, and he might be robbed. A shopping bag? Even that wasn't very safe nowadays. He looked round the kitchen. There was nothing else: the shopping bag would have to do. It was made of woven straw and should be fairly strong. He would make straps for it, to carry it on his back. He thought of the lovely rucksack he had in his bedroom, but that was out of the question; it was far too obvious.

He took a sharp knife from the kitchen drawer and wedged it into the bottom of the bag. What else? A small torch, some string, a can opener . . . But he mustn't take too much. He had a long way to walk.

Shoes, he would need good shoes, and some warm clothing. But again he mustn't take too much. A raincoat, a warm sweater . . .

Finally it was done. He tried to think of what he might have forgotten, but everything else of use was too heavy and bulky to be carried.

When should he go? It was a long journey to Mannheim – at least a day, even by express. It would be best to start first thing in the morning so that he could complete the rail journey in a single day and avoid arriving at Mannheim in the middle of the night, when they would pick him up more easily. He should leave first thing the next morning then. In the meantime he would rest and go over all the details.

He went to his room and lay on the bed. Occasionally he took out the map and had another look at it. Towards evening he made himself a hot meal of eggs and sausage and then went upstairs for a bath. He removed the package from under his arm and put it in the pocket of his jacket. He would fix it back on in the morning. After his bath he went straight to bed, his clothes for the morning ready folded beside him.

He didn't sleep immediately, but stared out of the window and watched the clouds darkening in the gathering dusk. He was really quite pleased with his preparations. Ellen had always accused him of never getting on with things. Well, she couldn't say that now. He had planned it all and he was going to go through with it. And when he got to France he would sell them his secret and buy himself a new life. One day he would send for them, Ellen and Cecile, and they would be proud of him. Yes, proud.

He fell asleep surprisingly easily and awoke only when a dog barked in the next door garden. He flicked on the light and looked at the time. It was five to twelve.

He went straight back to sleep and dreamed that Cecile was in the kitchen, laughing in the sunlight.

When the crash came he thought it was part of the dream, a plate dropped on the floor.

Then he was wide awake.

There was a moment of ear-splitting silence.

Then there was another crash and he heard a loud drumming noise. The noise got louder. It was the sound of people running up the stairs.

David sat up and started to get out of bed.

The door burst open and David knew it was too late. It was too late for everything. In that instant he knew that he would never see his little rabbit again.

There were two of them in the room. They grabbed him and dragged him on to the landing. He heard a dull thud and realised his head had crashed against the door frame. At the top of the stairs he was pushed. He fell forward, putting his arms out to break his fall. He came to a stop halfway down. He got slowly to his knees, holding onto the banisters while he caught his breath.

When the kick came it took him entirely by surprise. He couldn't understand why the hall was rushing up towards him. He put his arms out in front of him, but he knew he was going too fast, too fast. There was a sickening crunch, he felt his head snap round and he thought: They've killed me!

Then he was being pulled to his feet and a terrible pain shot through his shoulder. He cried out. But they were dragging him again, pulling on his shoulder, and he nearly fainted with the pain. He could hear them talking, but it seemed a long, long way away.

They threw him down and, after a while, he opened his eyes. He was in the living room. All the lights in the house were blazing; they hurt his eyes. He could hear movements above and dull thuds and crashes; they were going from room to room. He thought: they're searching. He groaned: *Oh God*, they're searching for the *film*. It was sitting in his jacket pocket. They would find it straight away. *God, how could I have been so stupid?*

He sat up gently and leant against an armchair. The shoulder was agony, probably broken somewhere.

Boots drummed down the stairs and David felt his stomach turn. The footsteps went into the kitchen and there was a deafening sound of breaking china and glass. He waited, his heart hammering against his chest.

Finally they came in. David was surprised to see that they were quite young, only about twenty. There were three of them, not two. They had some of Ellen's jewellery and the nice piece of Meissen china she kept on the dressing table. David felt relief: perhaps that was all they'd been after.

'Up Jew! Now!'

David struggled to his feet. Although he had pyjamas on he felt naked and bare. Why hadn't he slept in his clothes? That would have been the sensible thing to do. *Oh God.*

Two of them came up to him and David felt his bowels turn to water. One said, 'Where's the gold, Jew?'

'I have no gold.' David saw this would not please them and added quickly, 'Only money. Upstairs in my wallet.'

'Where's the gold, Jew?'

'I have none.'

They punched him in the stomach first, then around the head. Then, when he was down, they kicked him.

Then they pulled him to his feet and told him they were going to break his fingers.

Through his swollen face David said, 'There's no gold, I promise.'

One of them grabbed his hand and David closed his eyes. He felt himself dirtying his trousers. Then he fainted.

They slapped his face until he came round.

One of them said, 'Put him in the truck.'

David knew he had to do or say something now, or it would be too late. 'Please, can I put my clothes on?'

There was no reply.

'Please, I've dirtied myself.'

The leader pulled a face of disgust and indicated he could go upstairs.

David clambered up the stairs to his room and went to his jacket. The film was still there. *Thank God.*

He started to pull his pyjamas off. He fumbled with the buttons, then tore at them. He was taking too long: they would come for him. He tried to hurry but his hands wouldn't stop shaking and his shoulder was agony.

He pulled on his shirt, some underpants, and started to climb into his trousers.

He heard clattering on the stairs again and pulled desperately at the trousers. As he fumbled with the buttons a young corporal came in and started to pull at his arm.

David yelled, 'My jacket! My jacket!'

The corporal stopped while David picked it up. God, David thought, I nearly lost it again. God!

He ran quickly down the stairs. He was learning, learning: if you didn't run you got pushed.

They were taking a last look round. David waited by the door, leaning against the wall. When they weren't looking he took the packet out of his pocket and slipped it into his mouth.

When they had taken all they wanted they took him out of the house and pushed him into the back of a truck. It drove off so fast that David had only a moment to look back at the house. It seemed so strange, its lights still blazing, its front door open. David almost shouted for them to stop so that he could go back and lock up. It was wrong to leave it like that, so vulnerable, so open.

But then he realised it didn't matter. What hadn't been smashed or stolen tonight would be taken the next morning anyway.

Part two
1940–1941

7

The waiting was the worst.

Vasson lay on his bed and listened to the approaching rumble of cannon and the occasional blast of a distant explosion. The cannon was German, he decided, and the explosions were French. The gallant French Army was presumably pausing long enough in its rapid retreat to destroy fuel dumps. About all they had managed to do, Vasson thought with contempt.

By afternoon he knew he was right about the fuel dumps. The sky over the city had turned black with the smoke of burning oil. It was as dark as night. Paris looked like a lost city: there were no lights, hardly any people and total blackness.

Then the rain came. It was a steady downpour and it fell in thick black droplets, streaking houses, pavements, and the odd passer-by with oily grime.

Vasson was annoyed. He had planned to go out for a pastis at about five – assuming somewhere would be open – but now he'd have to stay in or risk having his clothes ruined.

Several times during the afternoon he went downstairs to the front door and looked out. The streets were almost deserted, except for the occasional refugee making a last attempt at flight.

Vasson couldn't see any point in leaving the city. For days people had been packing up their belongings and setting out with nothing more than a few pathetic bundles tied on to bicycles or handcarts. They had no idea where they were going, nor where they would get food and shelter. It was madness. They would starve – or get shot. It was much better to stay in the city, Vasson decided. The Germans wouldn't eat everybody. Life would continue, one way or another.

The war had been going on for nine months now. In that time Vasson had been busy. As soon as war was declared he spent all his savings on stockings, petrol and car tyres. It was an enormous risk to spend every penny, yet it was hard to see how he could go wrong. He bought himself a cheap secondhand car and stored the stuff in a rented garage out in the suburbs at Clichy. As soon as things started to get short, he began to sell.

He sold slowly, carefully, realising only enough cash to buy new stock, when he could find it. He travelled to small towns, to the suburbs of northern cities and the outskirts of Paris. When the price was right he bought more stockings as well as perfume and lingerie.

He also bought more food: coffee and sugar mainly. The prices were high, but not half so high as the selling prices in central Paris.

It took him five months to double his stock; now he looked forward to the real pay-off. It wouldn't come for a while of course. He knew he'd have to be patient. It would take time for the occupation to take effect. But when rationing and severe shortages bit, he'd be ready to clean up.

The war was going to be a little gold mine, no doubt about it.

But the waiting was the worst.

It was a short night. The sounds of explosions and cannon fire continued until two in the morning. Then there was silence. For a long time Vasson did not sleep, but lay awake smoking and thinking about money. Finally, at about three, he dozed off. As the early summer dawn broke, the motorcycles came. They were far away, probably on one of the main boulevards, but the sound carried a long way on the still June air. Vasson was instantly awake. So they were here at last.

Later, at about six, he went to the front door and peered out, but the streets were deserted. The Germans wouldn't bother with Montmartre yet, he reasoned; they would tie up the city centre and the military posts first. He went back to bed and, at about seven, sank into a dreamless sleep.

He woke at midday. He got up straight away, washed thoroughly and dressed. He chose his best clothes, such as they were. It was silly to bother really, but he wanted to look good.

He left the rooming house and went towards the Etoile and the Champs Elysées, because if anything was happening it would be happening there. He walked because he wanted the exercise and because he wanted to see the Germans.

He saw his first German at Pigalle. There were six of them in an armoured car. They were looking relaxed and at ease. They know they've won, Vasson thought, they know there won't be any trouble. He watched them for five minutes. They laughed and joked and pointed at things which interested them. They watched the Parisians politely, but did not attempt to talk to them. It was just as Vasson had thought: they didn't want to stir up trouble, they just wanted life to go on as usual.

Most of the cafés were closed, some boarded up, but Vasson found one which was open and stopped for some breakfast. He had no trouble buying a coffee but there was no bread, so he ate biscuits instead. The proprietor and his wife were talking loudly as they served their customers. Death to the Germans! They would rather die, they said, than serve the filthy Boches. They would make the scum realise they weren't welcome here! Vasson thought: A month and they'll be serving the Germans happily at double their normal prices.

He walked on towards the Champs Elysées. When he arrived he found a large crowd was already lining the long boulevard. Everyone was waiting, but no-one knew what for. There was no information, but then that was nothing new: there had been no information for weeks. Vasson leant against a tree and lit a cigarette. People should welcome the Germans: they couldn't be any worse than the French Government. Not only had the Government left Paris without telling anyone, but they had left everything totally disorganised. There had been no call for resistance, no advice on what people should do, no organised evacuation. All they had done was put up posters telling people to 'keep calm'. The newspapers had been censored for weeks, so that no-one knew what was happening until they heard the fighting and saw the troops retreating. It was laughable!

The Germans could only be an improvement.

When they came, they came in style. In triumph. There were tanks, armoured cars, mounted troops, and ranks of field-grey infantry marching in precise formation. It was an incredible sight. Most of the people stared in silence, their faces angry or disbelieving; some shouted bitter comments. Vasson watched, his face impassive, and wondered how long it would be before the Germans emptied all the shops and set him up for life.

The first month was all brass bands, martial songs and jackboots. The Germans seemed to be everywhere, their music blaring out day and night in every part of the city. Posters appeared saying: TRUST THE GERMAN SOLDIERS. Strange new newspapers came on to the newsstands: *Aujourd'hui, La France du Travail*, their pages full of German propaganda. Even the long-established *Le Matin* and *Paris-Soir* weren't slow to be forced into line and before long they too came out with glowing pro-Nazi headlines. The swastika appeared over hundreds of buildings.

The first week was good for the retail trade – or so people believed. The Germans made straight for the shops and swept up all the lingerie, perfumes and stockings they could find. And paid for them. Motor coaches brought hundreds of soldiers up into Montmartre to see the sights – ostensibly the Sacré-Cœur, but really the nightclubs and the girls. The Parisians were pleasantly surprised.

By the end of the month there was chaos. The Germans had paid for everything in occupation money which was found to be worthless; the food disappeared from the markets to feed the German Army;

petrol suddenly disappeared from the filling stations; and, overnight, prices shot up.

Vasson began trading. He started by selling coffee and petrol to the French. He dealt only in francs, in cash. As soon as he had money he spent it again, increasing his stock.

A few weeks later it was time to start dealing with the Germans. They had an almost insatiable desire for stockings, lingerie and perfume. Now that they'd emptied the shops they were happy to buy on the black market. But Vasson needed a contact: someone in supplies, who would buy his luxuries in exchange for food or tyres or petrol – he wasn't prepared to deal in worthless German money.

It didn't take long to find his man, a quartermaster sergeant called Seiger. Vasson would have preferred to deal with an officer, to make the operation more permanent and above board, but right from the start Seiger and he understood each other perfectly. It was too good an opportunity to miss. By September Vasson had doubled his stock, rented a decent apartment, and bought himself two new suits.

This time Vasson was determined not to fall into any traps. He would go carefully, always consolidating, always spreading the risks. The best way to spread the risks was, he realised, to branch out into other businesses. He started looking for opportunities. The girls racket was no good: everyone was on to that one and anyway half the girls had developed a bad case of patriotism and wouldn't go with Germans. The clubs were no good either; they were still wrapped up too tight.

For a while he settled for dealing in a wider range of goods – more foods, more imported goods – but he still wasn't happy: if for some reason he was closed down he would have nothing to fall back on.

Then he stumbled on the answer, accidentally.

He'd been tipped off about a large quantity of lingerie in a warehouse in the southern suburbs. He'd never been to the place before, he didn't know who ran it, but that didn't matter. He'd discovered that, when offered cash on the spot, people were quite happy to do business with him. This one would be no exception.

But he was wrong. The warehouse was run by an old Jew called Goldberg, and Goldberg did not want to do business with him. Not on any terms, not at any price. He would not say why; instead he was belligerent and rude. He called Vasson a leech and a verminous parasite. He shut the door in his face.

Vasson went to Seiger; Seiger arranged a meeting with a smart young man in the black uniform of the SS; the smart young man took him to see a man in civilian clothes, someone by the name of Kloffer.

They met in an apartment in the Rue Lalo behind the elegant Avenue Foch.

Kloffer was different from the Germans Vasson had met before. He was quiet, cool and slim, like a snake. He hardly spoke while Vasson told him about the Jew with the warehouse full of lingerie. He merely nodded slightly and, when Vasson had finished, gave a small bow and left.

Kloffer left so quickly that there was no time to ask questions. Vasson was left in the air. He felt slightly cheated. Would they do anything? He wasn't sure. And, if they did, would they tell him?

After a few days Vasson could bear the uncertainty no longer. He drove to the Jew's warehouse to see if anything had happened. As he neared the place he felt a delicious sense of anticipation, as if he was about to be given a treat. He was not disappointed. The doors of the warehouse were open, the interior gaping and empty. The glass in the windows had exploded from the force of a fire which, from the scorch marks on the walls, must have raged for hours. Vasson was pleased; the Germans must have been impressed by what he told them. As for Goldberg, he'd deserved it. He hadn't listened.

Vasson expected to see Kloffer again, but he heard nothing. He was disappointed. He wanted to see Kloffer again, to talk about the raid, to go over the details and to remind Kloffer that it was he, Vasson, who had provided the information. He wanted his contribution to be recognised; yes, damn it, and properly acknowledged. But there was nothing.

During the rest of September and October the Germans dropped their softly-softly approach to the population: the honeymoon was over. There were arrests of communists, trade unionists and leftist-intellectuals; the bread ration was low, unemployment was high.

In November there was more trouble: a mass demonstration by students in the Champs Elysées on Armistice Day. The Germans arrested the ringleaders for left-wing activities.

Every week Vasson went to meet Seiger. They always met in a small bar near the Porte de Clichy. The place had two advantages for Vasson: no-one knew him there and it was near the rented garage where he kept his stock.

Early in December Vasson bought a batch of high-quality stockings off a little shopkeeper in the *vingtième*. He decided to offer them straight to Seiger. He would ask for cigarettes in return; cigarettes always sold well and at the moment they were fetching particularly high prices.

He walked into the bar feeling excited, as he always did. He enjoyed doing business. It was lovely and clean and *definite*. He liked thrashing out the terms with Seiger, playing the game they always played: hedging and evading, stating and overstating, until finally the bargain was struck. There was nothing like it.

But today there was no Seiger. He searched the small bar for the familiar uniform, but it was missing. How irritating! Vasson did not like arrangements to go wrong.

Vasson took another look round the bar. No, there was no Seiger. Instead – Vasson's heart gave a small thud – instead there was Kloffer. He was sitting alone at a table. He gave no sign that he had recognised Vasson. Vasson looked round again, wondering what to do. Should he go up to Kloffer and admit he knew him? Or should he ignore him? He decided it would be safer to ignore him. He went to the bar and sat down. The proprietor sniffed at him, 'Your friend not here today then?'

'No.'

The man sneered, 'Well, that's a loss, isn't it?'

Vasson ignored him. Another cheap patriot. He ordered a coffee, then changed his mind and asked for a pastis. He looked round at Kloffer. The German was sitting staring out of the window. Vasson downed his drink and, as he put the empty glass on the counter, he saw Kloffer get up and leave the bar. Vasson paid and followed the German out.

When Vasson reached the street he looked quickly up and down. Kloffer was disappearing round a corner to the left. Vasson walked quickly to the corner and rounded it. There was a black Citroën beside the kerb. Kloffer was waiting at the open rear door. There were two men in raincoats and fedora hats sitting in the front. They might as well have a sign on the side saying 'Gestapo'. Kloffer said, 'Get in.'

Vasson got in followed by Kloffer. The car sped south, towards the Etoile. Vasson asked nervously, 'May I ask where we're going?'

Kloffer stared straight ahead. For a moment Vasson thought he wouldn't answer, then he said, 'To my office.'

Vasson wondered where that would be. But he didn't ask. There was something about Kloffer's manner that discouraged questions.

The car rounded the Etoile and turned into the Avenue Foch. Vasson suddenly realised where they must be going and his mouth went dry. The Gestapo and the SS lived down here: the street was fast getting the pseudonym Avenue Boches. But why were they bringing him here? A nasty suspicion flashed through his mind and for a moment he thought: They're busting me, they're going to close me down. Then he decided not. If they were busting him they would

128

have got him at the garage and taken his stock and ransacked his apartment.

The car drove under the archway of number 82 and stopped. This was the lion's mouth. It was well-known: Gestapo Headquarters. Its two neighbours, numbers 84 and 86, were occupied by the SS.

Vasson followed Kloffer up the stairs to the third floor. When they finally entered a large room with deep carpets and a large empire-style desk, he felt calmer. It was difficult to believe that anything terrible could happen in these surroundings. Vasson looked at the luxurious décor and realised that Kloffer was important.

Kloffer took off his hat and coat and told Vasson to sit down. When they were both seated Kloffer stared straight at Vasson and asked, 'What is your name?'

Vasson almost let the surprise show on his face, but he covered it quickly and said, 'You know my name: it's Jean-Marie Biolet.'

'No, your real name.'

'That *is* my real name.'

A flicker of impatience crossed Kloffer's face. 'Come now, I know it is not.'

Vasson thought quickly: How? How did he know? It *must* be a guess. Vasson had *never* been taken in by the police, not once; no-one had checked his identity since he arrived in Paris.

It had to be a bluff.

'It's my real name,' Vasson repeated.

'We could get the prefecture to check it. Somehow I don't think your thumb print would match that on your identity card.'

Vasson shrugged. 'So check them. You'd be wasting your time. I am Jean-Marie Biolet and I come from St Etienne.' He added, 'Anyway, what does it matter? Either I can help you or I can't.'

Kloffer's sharp rat-like eyes fell to the pad on the desk in front of him. Vasson realised he wasn't going to press the matter. *Thank God*.

'Very well,' Kloffer said, 'I want someone. I think you can find him for me.'

Vasson felt the relief flooding over him. So that was all they wanted – a person. It was to be a job like the one he'd done on Goldberg. Find and identify. Simple. But he was puzzled. Who could it be? He didn't know anyone these people might want.

Kloffer continued, 'The person we want is a communist agitator by the name of Cohcn. He is a professor at the Sorbonne but has recently . . . gone to ground.'

'But I've never heard of Cohen, I don't know Cohen . . .'

'Exactly. You will be perfect for the job.'

Vasson began to understand. This was no Goldberg job. This wasn't a simple matter of pointing out an insignificant Jewish wholesaler, it was more, much more.

Vasson said stiffly, 'But why me?'

'Oh, come now. You will be excellent for the job. You have all the qualifications. You have already proved that.'

'But supposing I fail . . .?'

Kloffer looked impatient. 'Oh you won't do that. I have a feeling about you.' He stabbed a finger at Vasson. 'I have a feeling that you will be very good at the little tasks I ask you to do.'

'But . . . where would I start? How will I find him?'

Kloffer smiled thinly. 'We have some information. Cohen is a history professor at the Sorbonne. He is also the leader of a communist cell. We have detained most of them. Now I want Cohen himself. We picked up his girlfriend the other day, her name's Marie Boulevont. We released her but –' Kloffer cleared his throat and looked unhappy '– but we lost her. She was living at 56, Rue Brezin. Now she too has disappeared.'

In other words, Vasson thought, they've made a mess of it.

'We will give you a new name and student's papers and anything else that might be useful. Normally we would wait for someone to tell us where Cohen is, but in this case we want him in a hurry. As soon as possible. You understand?'

Vasson was trying to sort out his thoughts. He'd expected all kinds of things. But this . . . It would be difficult, and very dangerous. Political activists would not be kind if they caught him. Christ, they'd kill him without a second thought.

The money would have to be good, bloody good. Vasson looked up sharply: the German hadn't mentioned that.

Vasson said, 'I'd want good money for the job, in francs or gold, on delivery. What are you offering?'

Kloffer looked amused. 'Oh, a great deal. Freedom from arrest. Your little black market operation is, after all, totally illegal. It could get you into a lot of trouble. Also freedom from investigation into your background and your – what shall we say? – dubious identity.'

Vasson waited. Kloffer said, 'That is all.'

God! Kloffer was nothing but a cheap blackmailer. He might have known. The humiliation burnt Vasson's cheeks. He thought: No, you're bloody well not going to get away with it.

Vasson looked calmly down at his hands and said casually, 'No.'

'What do you mean?'

'I mean that I don't accept your terms. I have nothing to hide. You can close me down if you like.'

Kloffer stared across the desk.

Vasson glanced out of the window. 'Now if we were to come to a sensible arrangement I could do a first-class job . . .'

'Go on.'

'I mean that you could get any rat to do a mediocre job on those terms. But me? If I am paid a decent rate for the job, I will do it well. And *quickly*. If not . . .' he shrugged. 'If not, well, it would take you a lot longer to find your man, wouldn't it? Bust me if you wish – it really makes no difference.' Vasson stared him straight in the eye and thought how it would, of course, make a hell of a difference: it would put him right back in shit street without any money.

Kloffer put his fingertips together and touched his lips thoughtfully. 'How much would you require, Monsieur Biolet?'

'Fifty thousand francs.'

'Out of the question.'

'How much are you offering?'

'Ten.'

They settled on ten. Vasson didn't want to argue. He didn't want Kloffer to lose too much face, otherwise he'd bear a grudge. Anyway, Vasson thought, I'm bloody lucky to get anything at all. It would be silly to push his luck.

He could always ask for more next time.

He knew there *would* be a next time. The job was right up his street. He liked everything about it except the idea of getting caught: *that* terrified him. But the rest? Yes, very nice.

He liked the idea of a new identity, a new personality which, after the job, would disappear without trace. It was neat. A clean *out*, with no come-back. It was a challenge, too, something to get to grips with. It would give him a chance to show what he could do. He liked that.

And then there was the money, the lovely money.

The next day Vasson went back to the Avenue Foch, to an anonymous office on the ground floor, and collected a complete set of cards covering identity, student status, food ration, tobacco ration and military service, all of them in the name of Legrand. When Vasson saw the cards he went white with anger: the cards were hard, clean and unscuffed. They looked brand new, which was exactly what they were. He wondered if Kloffer was trying to nail him, or just being stupid. It was probably stupidity fuelled by the German passion for efficiency.

Another thing: there was no student enrolment card, which was necessary for the Sorbonne. Furthermore the card would be inspected frequently, so it would have to be genuine.

He went up to the third floor and told Kloffer what he wanted.

Kloffer was not pleased. 'What you ask is very difficult as well as unnecessary.'

'It's essential.'

Kloffer nodded curtly. It was agreed.

Vasson returned to the ground floor and settled down to wait because he didn't want to be seen going in and out of the building too often. Eventually, late in the afternoon, a sergeant called him into the ground floor office and passed him a new set of cards. The name was now Philippe Roche, and the student enrolment card was obviously genuine. Vasson guessed the other cards were genuine too: they were soiled and scuffed. He was uneasy again: suppose this Philippe Roche had been at the Sorbonne? Suppose Vasson bumped into someone who knew him?

Vasson looked up. 'Is this person known at the university?'

The sergeant smiled. 'No.'

'Did he ever go there?'

The sergeant eyed him lazily. 'No he never went there. He never started his course.'

Vasson nodded. He didn't want to know any more.

On the way back to Montmartre Vasson bought some slacks, two casual shirts, two sweaters and a donkey jacket from a cheap shop. Back in his room he crumpled and dirtied them a little, then changed, leaving all his own clothes behind. He packed a small bag containing his washing things and some pyjamas, then left. He went straight to the Left Bank and wandered around the bookstalls beside the river until he found some old textbooks on French history. At a stationery shop nearby he bought a couple of blank pads, some pencils and a pen. Finally he wandered into Montparnasse and found a room to rent.

Then he was ready.

He would start with the girl, the girl who was meant to be a special friend of Cohen's.

But first he spent a morning just walking round the Sorbonne and the Left Bank cafés, watching the students, listening to their conversation. It was fairly easy to gauge their mood: most of them were angry, either about the Armistice Parade arrests, or the disappearance of university staff, or the curbs on student activities. Some even spoke of countermeasures, of demonstrations and open defiance.

They were incredibly naive, Vasson decided. They talked openly, in public places, without realising the need for discretion. Beyond lowering their voices they had no sense of secrecy, no idea that informers might be listening. Vasson thought: This could be easier than I imagined.

In the afternoon he went to 56, Rue Brezin, the last known address of the girlfriend, Marie Boulevont. Now that Kloffer's watchers had gone, she might have returned. But she hadn't. The *concierge* hadn't seen her for weeks and didn't know where she'd moved to. Vasson wasn't surprised. The girl would have been stupid to return.

He would have to start from scratch then. In a strange way he didn't mind. It was more of a challenge that way.

The next morning he examined the mass of notice boards in the history department at the Sorbonne and decided to go to the lecture on Enlightened Despotism in the Eighteenth Century. It was well attended and he had a job getting in. The lecture was long and tedious. Vasson spent his time looking at the hundreds of faces around the hall. They all looked the same: like communists. Finally, when the lecture was over and everyone was crowding through the exits, he chose a group of five students who were talking heatedly. They looked as if they might be political types. He followed them to a café on the Boulevard St Germain.

He sat at an adjoining table and listened. They were still talking heatedly – about lectures clashing because of the appalling new timetable. Vasson waited impatiently. This group was a dead end, he could sense it. Damn. He would have to think of a surer way.

Then Vasson realised that their voices had dropped and only the occasional word was reaching him. One of them was saying how terrible something was and the others were agreeing. Vasson strained to hear.

'. . . he was arrested . . . that is certain . . .'

The voices dropped again and Vasson lost the reply. Then a third voice said, 'But it's terrible to sit and do nothing!'

How right you are, Vasson thought.

Impulsively he got up and stepped over to the students' table. 'I . . .' He hovered nervously. 'I saw you in the lecture . . . I'm a new student. May I . . .?' He indicated his chair and looked suitably uncertain.

One of the students nodded. Vasson stuttered 'Thanks' and drew up his chair. They made room for him and he sat down.

They stared at him expectantly. Vasson laughed nervously and said, 'It's hard to find your way around!'

They nodded and one, a boy with thick pebble glasses, said, 'We've been here a year and we still can't find our way round!'

Vasson smiled anxiously and said, 'Is there –' he searched for the words '– is there a lot of trouble in the university? I mean, what should one *know* about?' He peered round the table earnestly.

'Oh, just don't get involved in – well, anything political.'

Vasson nodded violently.

There was a silence. Vasson looked pensive. 'And . . . have there been many arrests?'

The boy with the pebble glasses sighed. 'Yes, students and staff. Efforts are made to discover what has happened to them but . . .' He trailed off and shrugged.

Vasson looked grave. 'I was assigned to Professor Cohen, but now I am to be in another group. Did he –? Was he . . . taken?'

Pebble-glasses shrugged. 'Nobody's sure what happened to him. It's thought he's in hiding, but I wouldn't know.'

Vasson stared at him and realised with disappointment that he was telling the truth.

It was worth one more shot. He said, 'Also I was given the name of a friend of his, by a friend of my family. But – well, it's very upsetting, because she too has been taken or –' He shook his head bitterly '– or disappeared. And I don't know what to tell this friend. It's all very tragic, very tragic.'

'Who's Cohen's friend?'

'Ah!' Vasson made a show of looking through his pockets as if for a scrap of paper which he couldn't find. By an effort of concentration he suddenly remembered the name. 'Er. Oh yes. Yes, it was Marie, Marie Boulevont. That was it!'

One asked, 'Marie Boulevont?'

Vasson stared vacantly into the distance and nodded slowly.

They were shaking their heads. Vasson stood up, still saying, 'Very sad, very sad.' He added brightly, 'Well, thank you for telling me the form. See you again soon!'

Damn.

He would have to find a better way. There was only one problem: he couldn't think of one.

Damn.

The next day he looked more carefully round the lecture room and chose a serious-looking student of about twenty-seven. He looked much more the type: thoughtful and politically committed. But the student went back to his rooms and stayed there all day. It was another dead end.

The following day was Friday. There was no major history lecture that day but a series of smaller seminars on specialist subjects. Vasson thought: What would a communist be studying? He decided on European History from 1860 to 1930, the period covering the Russian Revolution.

There were only thirty students in the seminar. Vasson looked casually round the room a couple of times, taking a careful look at each student. One, he noticed, was staring at him. He was about twenty-two, with short curly hair and glasses. His stare was intense and hard; he was summing Vasson up. When their eyes met the student looked away and a few seconds later Vasson saw him exchange an almost imperceptible glance with another student across the room. Vasson felt a quickening of the pulse. This one was clever and sophisticated enough, that was certain.

The seminar was about the decline of nineteenth century liberalism and was interminable. At one point the professor asked each student for a definition of liberalism. Vasson felt a moment of panic. He hadn't reckoned on that. But in the end it was easy, he just gave a garbled version of two earlier replies, defining it as freedom of the individual from excessive central control. As he spoke he was aware that Curly Head was watching him. When it came to Curly Head's turn his reply was clipped and informed; he was obviously a thinker. There was also a hint of intolerance and dogma in his speech. He even dared to differ with the professor on a point concerning 'old' liberalism versus 'new'.

Vasson stiffened: this one was a political animal.

At the end of the seminar, when they all got up, Vasson stood aside to let Curly Head pass. The student went by with his head averted. But Vasson thought: He knows I'm here, he knows it very well.

Vasson let Curly Head disappear down the corridor, then asked a student next to him, 'Who was the one going on about new liberalism?'

The student was in a hurry. He was irritated at being detained but answered, 'Eh? Oh, Laval.'

Vasson picked up Laval-Curly Head as he left the building. It was four, almost dusk. The student was heading south down the broad pavement of the Boulevard St Michel. He was walking fast, his thick woollen coat flapping out behind him, his head thrust forward. Vasson followed at a safe distance, his pace settling into a steady rhythm.

Quite suddenly Curly Head glanced over his shoulder and looked straight at Vasson. Vasson thought: He's on to me.

Curly Head hurried on. Vasson slowed his pace, walking more casually, and made a point of keeping his head down and his eyes on the pavement. At the next corner he turned down a side street, away from the main boulevard. When he guessed he was out of Curly

Head's view he crossed the street and doubled back at a run. At the corner he stopped and looked carefully round until he could see up the length of the boulevard. Curly Head was some way away, still walking fast. Vasson pulled his coat up round his ears and followed. After a few moments Curly Head looked back again, but Vasson stepped quickly behind another pedestrian. This time he was not seen.

Curly Head walked across the south side of the Jardin du Luxembourg and into the streets of Montparnasse. He looked behind him only once more, just before he turned into a small rooming house. Again, Vasson was certain he hadn't been seen. He took up station near the house, but on the same side of the street so that he couldn't be spotted from the windows. It was bitterly cold and after an hour it began to rain.

Vasson sheltered in a doorway and thought of going back to his own room. But he decided not: the wait wouldn't do him any harm.

By seven the feeling had gone in his feet. All he could think about was drinking hot soup and red wine in a warm bistro.

At almost eight Curly Head came out. It was so dark Vasson almost missed him. Curly Head seemed more relaxed than before and strolled along quite casually. He didn't go far; just to a café in the next street. Vasson peered through the window. The black-out curtains were too effective and he couldn't see anything. He went to the door. Here there was a slight crack between the frame and the black cardboard stuck to the inside of the window. Vasson put his eye to the crack and saw that Curly Head had joined a group of people at a table. Vasson thought he recognised two of them; one was the student who had exchanged the glance with Curly Head at the seminar; and the other, a girl, had been there too, sitting at the back.

Vasson walked away and looked for another café where he might get something to eat and warm up. But there was nowhere. In disgust he settled down to wait in a doorway opposite Curly Head's café.

It was a quarter to ten and very cold when they drifted out. It was too risky to follow Curly Head again and anyway there wasn't much point: he was probably going straight back to his rooms. Vasson decided on the girl instead; she might be an easier nut to crack. She didn't live far away. She went straight to a cheap rooming house, rather like the one Curly Head lived in. Nothing was likely to happen that night, Vasson decided. He noted the address and went back to his room to sleep.

He returned to the girl's place early, at seven. The girl wouldn't have gone out yet. He was right: she didn't emerge until midday. He followed her to the Boulevard St Germain. She went shopping.

Vasson began to wonder if this was going to be another dead end, but then she went into a glass-enclosed pavement café and sat at a table on her own. She started to read a book, looking up only to ask for a coffee. She did not look into the street. She obviously wasn't expecting anyone.

He went into the café and walked past her table, then doubled back and stooped down to look at her. 'Hello, aren't you – ? Haven't we met – ?'

She looked up at him curiously. She was plain, with thick black eyebrows, dark lanky hair and unattractive glasses. Definitely the intellectual type. Brainy but not clever, Vasson decided. She said, 'Sorry. I don't remember . . .'

Vasson shook his head and introduced himself. 'No, why should you remember? We only met briefly, ages ago. And then I saw you in the seminar yesterday. I've just switched courses, from geography.'

She squinted at him through her spectacles. 'Where did we meet first then?'

'Ah, well . . .' He looked carefully round the café. 'Perhaps it's best to say at mutual friends and leave it at that.'

She said nothing but licked her lips uncertainly.

Vasson dropped his voice. 'One can't be too careful.'

She nodded and frowned.

'I saw Laval in the seminar too, but I didn't contact him. Too dangerous. Anyway he may not remember me. Did he mention seeing me yesterday?'

She shook her head. 'No . . . He said nothing.'

Vasson nodded. 'Just as well.'

'Shall I mention seeing you? To Jean, I mean.'

Jean must be Laval. 'No, no. Best not to. I –' Vasson tried to look hunted. 'I have to be very careful . . .'

She said in a low voice, 'One cannot be too careful, that's for sure.'

'If only more precautions had been taken in the beginning.'

'Yes.'

A waiter came up and Vasson ordered coffee. He smiled brightly at the girl. 'I don't even know your name!'

For a moment she looked startled, then said quietly, 'Sophie.'

'What a beautiful name!' He thought: For such an ugly girl.

She was pleased. 'Oh. Thank you!'

Vasson looked down at the parcels beside her. 'Been shopping?'

'Yes. My allowance came through – I needed some clothes. There isn't much in the shops but . . .' She laughed and pushed some strands of greasy hair back from her forehead. 'I found a couple of things.'

God, she's plain, Vasson thought, plain and boring. But he felt he should let the conversation continue in the same vein. He bought her another coffee and they talked about her life, her family and the poor opportunities for women in publishing, where she hoped to get a job.

He listened attentively for twenty minutes, then decided the moment had come. He leant towards her and, looking deep into her eyes, said, 'I can't tell you how good it's been talking to you. I'd love to see you again. Can we meet later, for a bit of food? It would be fun.' He touched her hand.

'Oh. Yes. I – er – yes.' There was a blush on her cheeks.

Vasson hoped he wouldn't have to keep this up much longer.

The girl was flustered and confused. She was making a mess of gathering her belongings. Vasson picked a package off the floor and smiled at her. 'I can see I'm going to have to look after you!' Her face went scarlet and she looked down at the floor.

He suddenly looked serious. 'By the way, perhaps you can tell me –' He put his hand on her arm. 'I've been a bit out of touch. On purpose, of course. But –' he lowered his voice to a whisper '– I've been dying to know . . . Is Cohen all right, have you heard.'

Her eyes came straight up to his. She said immediately, 'He's all right. He's safe.'

Vasson made a show of beating his hand on his forehead. 'Thank God. Thank God for that!'

She started to pull on her coat while still in her seat and was soon struggling with a sleeve. Vasson jumped up to help her. When the coat was on he let his arm brush across her shoulders. Then he sat down again and put his face close to hers.

'We'll win in the end, you know. We *will* because we *must!*'

She nodded emphatically, her eyes shining up at him.

They stood up. Then he touched her arm and pulled her down into her chair again.

'One thing –' He frowned. 'I have reason to believe Marie may be in danger.'

She gasped. 'Marie . . .?'

He nodded.

The girl looked at him. 'Oh no! Why?'

'The word is that they're looking for her again. I don't know how to warn her.'

The girl said, 'Oh God. She was in a safe house, but now . . .' She trailed off unhappily.

'Now – ?'

'I'm not sure . . .'

'I looked for her at the Rue Brezin, but of course she hasn't been back there.'

'Oh no, she wouldn't go back there. The Boches have been watching it. It isn't safe. She's – Well, I *think* she may be at Su's place.' She used the expression *chez Su*.

'Su's.'

The girl nodded. 'Yes, Su's.' Obviously this Su was well known. Suzanne perhaps?

'Ah . . . Where do I find Su nowadays?'

The girl looked at him sharply and stared. A shiver ran up Vasson's spine. Something was wrong: he'd made a mistake.

She said, 'Surely . . . You must know . . .'

He tried again. 'I just haven't seen Su for some time . . . You know how it is . . .'

She said slowly, 'But you are acquainted with her?'

Vasson smiled. 'Of course.'

The girl's face went sheet white. She got up from the table and, grabbing her possessions, stumbled out. Vasson followed, cursing softly.

Su? Who the hell was Su?

When he got out of the café he soon spotted the girl, half-running, half-walking down the street. From time to time she twisted round and looked back. She didn't see Vasson. He guessed she was short-sighted.

She crossed the boulevard and hurried towards the Sorbonne. She passed the main university building and turned down a narrow back street. Vasson got to the corner and paused. He edged slowly along the last few inches of wall and peered cautiously round.

The girl was two yards away, coming straight towards him.

He yanked his head back and sprinted away. He dived into a recessed doorway and pressed his body against it, panting hard.

The girl came into his field of vision. She looked anxiously up and down the street, then turned on her heel and disappeared.

He left it five seconds and looked out. No-one. He approached the corner again and peered round.

She was walking away from him. She began to turn her head. He pulled back.

He looked again. She had gone.

He walked towards the spot where she had disappeared.

There were three doorways in the vicinity. One belonged to a dingy restaurant. He glanced at the name over the door.

It was called Chez Le Marechal Suchet.

Chez Su.

Vasson groaned inwardly. No wonder she was on to him. Every

student must know this place. Su was no lady; Su was a bloody *maréchal*.

He wondered what to do next. The girlfriend, Marie Boulevont, might be here. If she was, she'd have to come out some time. But most likely she'd go straight to ground. Damn! He'd really blown it.

He decided to wait. There was nothing else to do.

Half an hour later the girl poked her nose out of the door. She looked carefully up and down the street. Even from several yards away Vasson could see that her face was bright red. She'd probably been crying. She took a last look up the street and disappeared into the doorway. When she came out again there was another girl with her, someone older, prettier, more self-assured. She was carrying a small case. Marie Boulevont?

Yes, Vasson decided, Marie Boulevont.

At the end of the street the women stopped, spoke excitedly for a moment and split up. Vasson followed Marie.

She was clever. He almost lost her twice. At the Boulevard St Germain she took the Métro to the Étoile, then hopped on a bus just as it was leaving. Vasson was lucky to jump on another bus going in the same direction. She got off at Montparnasse, almost back where they'd started. Then she walked again, constantly looking over her shoulder. At one point she dived into a shop. Vasson took a guess and sprinted round the block to the back of the building. There was a tradesman's entrance. Just as he got there, the door opened and Marie came out.

Got you! Vasson thought.

Then she walked again, quickly. She doubled back once more, looked over her shoulder one last time and disappeared into a doorway beside an *épicerie*.

Vasson waited uncertainly. He had no idea what this place was. It might be a safe house she was going to use. It might just be a friend's place. There was no certainty Cohen was there.

After an hour she came out again. She was nervous. She looked up and down the street, then walked quickly off. She was empty-handed. That meant she had left her case inside. That meant she was coming back.

Vasson came to a decision. He walked in the opposite direction until he found a telephone. He called Kloffer.

He said, 'Just two men – and not with Gestapo written all over them.'

'What do you mean?' Kloffer replied.

'I mean choose fellows without leather coats and felt hats – people with *French* clothes for Christ's sake.'

Then he went back and waited. God, Kloffer's men were taking for ever. The girl would be back soon. Shit!

After ten minutes Vasson swore again, louder.

Finally he saw Kloffer's men. They still looked like Krauts. 'Come on!'

Vasson led the way angrily along the street and into the door Marie had come out of. The house was on five floors. Off each of the two landings there were three doors.

Vasson guessed at a front room. They knocked on the first door. There was no reply and one of the Germans opened it with his shoulder. Nothing. A door at the back of the house flew open and an old woman thrust her head out. Nothing there either. The old woman said the third room wasn't occupied.

They went to the next floor.

Cohen was in the front room.

Vasson knew it was him the moment the pale, narrow face appeared round the door. He was small, dark and insignificant looking. He came out quietly, with resignation. Vasson felt vaguely disappointed. The man hadn't even tried to escape.

Kloffer's men searched Cohen, then the room.

Vasson was impatient to go. 'Come on!'

The Germans went first, Cohen between them. Vasson hung back and followed them at a distance. In the next street was the inevitable black Citroën. Vasson sat uneasily in the front. He didn't like being seen with Kloffer's heavies. On the other hand he wanted to be there when Cohen was brought in. He wanted to see Kloffer's face.

There was no sound from Cohen in the back. Vasson half turned his head. 'You should always choose a room with another way out, you know. That was silly of you. The girl was stupid as well – she led me straight to you.' He shook his head. 'It was all too easy.'

There was silence. Vasson craned his head round until he could see the man's face. 'You weren't very clever, professor.'

Cohen was looking out of the window, his face white and expressionless.

Vasson stared for a moment then turned back, uneasy and vaguely angry. The sight of the man was disturbing. His silence was accusing. Vasson decided it had been a mistake to travel in the same car. The next time he would take care not to.

The driver glanced across at Vasson and, smiling, said, 'Don't worry. He won't be so quiet when we've started talking to him.'

Vasson shuddered and looked out of the window, wishing the journey would end quickly.

When the car finally arrived at 82, Avenue Foch, Vasson got out hurriedly and ran into the building without looking back. He didn't feel comfortable until he was shown into Kloffer's office.

The German had a faint smile on his face. 'Very good. Very good.'

Vasson relaxed. Kloffer was obviously more than satisfied with him. Immediately he wondered if he could double his price next time – perhaps even treble it.

There was only one loose end. The plain girl with glasses. She could identify him. That had been a silly slip, about Su's. He would have to be more careful in future.

He gave Kloffer her name and the address of her room. Then he pushed her out of his mind. He didn't want to know what Kloffer would do with her. It was none of his affair any more.

That night he returned to his apartment, burnt the student clothes, carefully hid the bundle of student identity papers, and assumed the name of Biolet again.

He went to bed content. All things considered it had gone pretty well really. Though it hadn't been as neat as it might have been – there had been a slip or two. He must be careful not to let that happen again, it might not be so easy to cover himself next time.

8

Julie took a last look round the small whitewashed room, picked up her bag and went through the kitchen into the front parlour. She saw that Tante Marie and Peter were already outside, standing by the waiting fish truck. As she came out of the house and closed the front door behind her she thought: I might never see this place again. It seemed all wrong, to be going. This was her home, her life, and she was abandoning it like a rat leaving a sinking ship.

Peter was in Tante Marie's arms, a frown of bewilderment on his face, his eyes fixed intently on the tears running down the old woman's cheeks. Julie could see that he still didn't understand why they were going. But then why should he? He was four years old: Germans and conquerors meant nothing to him.

Nor, for that matter, did the problems of having a British passport in a country occupied by an enemy power.

During the last few days Julie had tried to imagine what that might mean. At best the two of them might be deported back to England.

But Uncle Jean thought that unlikely; the Germans weren't that considerate, he said. So what *would* happen? Perhaps they would be interned or sent away; perhaps they'd be forced to work in camps; or worst of all, separated. Julie couldn't bear the idea of Peter being taken away from her and ill-treated or half-starved: it was unthinkable. It was her duty to get him away. That was what she was doing. Her duty.

Uncle Jean came round the front of the truck and, taking Julie's bag, threw it into the back. He turned to her and put his hands on her shoulders.

'Now Georges here will drive you to Morlaix. The boat you're going on is called *Fleur*. Make sure Georges takes you all the way to the boat and gets your bags on board for you. There's chaos everywhere, they say, so be sure to stick with him, eh?'

Julie nodded and Jean went on, 'It's a good boat, *Fleur*, it's one of the newest and biggest in Morlaix. It'll get you safely to England.' Then he embraced her with a ferocious loving hug which left Julie breathless and a little tearful.

Jean took Peter and handed him up into the cab. Julie and Tante Marie embraced and the old woman said, 'It's for the best, you know that. We'll be happy because we'll know you're safe.'

Julie nodded and got up into the cab. The engine coughed into life and they were off, bumping down the road, away from the little house. Peter jumped up and down, waving wildly, as if it were a day outing. Julie waved more slowly and, when the house and the two figures standing in front of it had disappeared from sight, she blew her nose and stared doggedly at the road ahead.

Peter craned his head to stare at her face. 'What's the matter, Mummy?'

'Oh, I'm just thinking.' She smiled briefly.

'When will we be coming home again?'

'Well, darling, as soon as the Germans have gone.'

Peter frowned and put his head on one side. 'When will that be, Mummy?'

Julie sighed, as much from the relentless questioning as the problem of finding an anwer. 'I honestly don't know, darling. It depends on lots of things . . . Perhaps it'll be a long time, a very long time.'

'They won't kill Uncle Jean and Tante Marie, will they?'

'No! Of course not! Only soldiers get killed.'

'They'll be all right, then?'

'Yes.' She gave him a reassuring hug, and wondered if the old couple *would* be all right. She knew she'd worry herself sick about

143

them. There were bound to be shortages and severe hardships. Already meat was on sale only three days a week; the *patisseries* were closed two days a week; petrol was rationed. And that was *before* the defeat. Under the Germans . . . It would be worse, much worse.

Still, Julie remembered, this was an independent, self-sufficient community. They should be able to manage. Tante Marie had told her about terrible droughts and unusually cold winters in the past when people had almost starved. Those hardest hit were helped by the others with donations of food. Then later, when things were better, the debts were repaid in kind and with interest.

This time there was one major difference, though. The shortages might go on for years . . .

As the lorry bumped gently through the soft greens and bright yellows of the lovely June countryside, Julie tried to imagine the Germans here, with their trucks, their tanks, their hard grey efficiency. They would take over everything; they would be able to bully anyone they chose.

They'd be here in just two days, so it was said. That was the incredible part. Julie didn't understand how it could happen: how Paris could fall so easily, almost without a murmur; how the Germans could sweep across the country in so short a time. But then she knew nothing about fighting. She just hadn't understood what was happening.

At the same time it was strange that no-one else had guessed what was happening either. There had been no warnings until the Germans were already inside the country, almost at Paris. Why hadn't the Government said something? Why had they avoided telling anyone? It seemed extraordinary.

The driver, Georges, said, 'There might be a delay when we get near the town. Evidently some of the roads are almost impassable in places.'

Julie looked at him questioningly.

'The people. Thousands of them. All on their way to Brest, to get on ships and get the hell out of here. Can't blame them either!'

They saw the first of them just before reaching the main Lannion-Morlaix road. There were people sitting in the hedgerows, resting and sleeping, while others foraged in the fields, pulling up vegetables and chewing on them, raw. Some waved to the fish truck and shouted, 'Any food?' Julie shook her head unhappily.

When they got to the junction itself there were many, many more people: women pushing prams piled high with bags and children; men striding along with heavy bundles on their backs; one family with a cage full of rabbits on the back of a bicycle. Again, there were cries of, 'Food? Some food? Anything to spare, friend?' Julie stared dismally out of the window. Every family, every child that she saw wrung her heart.

She murmured, 'I wish I could give them something.'

The driver shook his head. 'No. It's each man for himself. You have some food with you?'

She nodded.

'Well, my advice is, keep it! And guard it well. I think we'll all have to look after our possessions from now on!'

The truck slowed to a crawl as they came up behind a knot of people who stayed obstinately on the centre of the road. Julie guessed they were just too tired to step aside. Where had they come from? Paris? Even further? It must have taken them days to get this far. And where had they slept? Had they eaten?

It took half an hour to do the last three kilometres. The road leading to the quay was thronged with people. Most were standing in lines outside food shops, waiting silently, a look of resignation on their faces. At one corner there was an angry scene with groups of men pushing and shouting at each other. Two of them were trying to tear down a poster. Julie recognised the poster; it was one which had been pasted up all over the town. It read: WE WILL WIN BECAUSE WE'RE THE STRONGEST. As the fish truck passed, two men started to fight, their arms flailing in the air. Julie shuddered. 'Why are they fighting?'

Georges shrugged. 'Disgust at the Government, I should think. After all, we're not the strongest and we've lost, haven't we!'

At last the truck turned on to the quay and Georges said, 'This is it. The boat's just down there.' Julie gasped. The port was a mass of fishing boats. She had never seen so many in harbour, not even when a storm was blowing. Groups of refugees were standing on the quay, looking hopefully at one or two of the boats, but most were walking dispiritedly away.

Georges nodded at the boats. 'They can't take all this lot, so they're only taking servicemen and special cases.' He opened the door and added with contempt, 'That is, those boats which are going at all.'

Julie asked, 'Are you going?'

'Oh yes! I'll go and fight with the British, or anyone else for that matter. Well, I'm not going to stay here and say good day to the Germans, am I?'

Julie handed Peter down to Georges and said, 'No, I don't suppose you are.'

Georges shouted at a man on a nearby boat who nodded back, then

145

Georges led the way on to the deck of the boat nearest to the quay. They had to cross the decks and climb the bulwarks of four boats before Georges finally said, 'Here we are.'

Julie passed Peter over the last bulwark then climbed aboard herself. Carefully she checked that the two cases were all right and that she hadn't forgotten the small basket of food that Tante Marie had given her. The luggage and the food made her feel secure, as if nothing could happen to her and Peter while she had them.

Georges was leaving and Julie thanked him. Then someone – Julie supposed it was one of the crew – took her cases and told her to sit on deck. She sat on a hatch-cover with Peter on her knee and waited, watching the people on the quay, some queuing for bread outside a *boulangerie*, others staring at the boats. They're wishing they were here in my place, she thought. It made her feel guilty, mainly because she was so glad it *was* her and not them.

She wondered how long it would be before the boat left. She knew that the fishermen always left on the tide. Morlaix was quite a distance from the sea, up a winding river. At low tide the upper reaches of the river were too shallow, but at Morlaix there was a lock which kept a good depth of water in the basin. The lock opened only for a few hours around high water.

Fleur was a large boat, about eighty feet long; she would need the full height of the tide to get down the river, Julie guessed. Jean had arranged for Julie to come on this boat because she was larger and safer for a Channel crossing, and because he knew the men who had built her.

A truck drew up on the quay. Some soldiers, apparently wounded, were helped out. A group of fishermen were mustered and the wounded were carried or helped across the boats. Julie suddenly realised they were coming towards *Fleur*.

The soldiers were taken below to where Julie guessed there must be a small cabin. Now there were more people arriving. Like her, they were civilians. Most were carrying heavy luggage and wearing thick coats and jackets. Julie began to feel a little nervous. There were more than twenty passengers on the deck now but, she guessed, nowhere for them to shelter. The soldiers had the cabin and the small wheelhouse was clearly the crew's domain. Those on deck would have to stay on deck. If the weather turned bad, they would freeze . . .

She looked anxiously at Peter's coat. It was warm, but not water-proof. If it rained he would get soaked to the skin. And her own coat . . . She grimaced: such vanity! She had worn her best coat – a lightweight linen one – with a raincoat over it. She felt cold already.

One of the crew was passing. Julie touched his arm. 'Do I have time to get something from my luggage? Some warmer clothes?'

'Ah!' he shrugged. 'The bags are piled up in the hold. It'll be a job to get yours out now. Look, we're just leaving. If you're cold I'll find you something later. All right?'

Julie hesitated: she felt she should press the matter, but then it was too late, he was gone. The boat's engine throbbed into life and they were moving, first into the lock, and then down the long, narrow river through fields and tree-covered slopes towards the sea. A young man shouted, 'Vive la France Libre!' And everyone laughed and cheered.

A man sitting next to Julie grinned. 'We live to fight another day. Eh?'

Julie smiled back. Suddenly she felt happy; the laughter and cheerfulness were infectious. And he was right; by going to England they could at least *do* something to fight back.

After a while the river widened into the flat expanse of the estuary. The sky was overcast but the sun was making a brave attempt to shine through a patch of thinner cloud. Suddenly it succeeded and the land turned from a dark sombre grey to a paler shade of green. Over to the right, beyond the low hills, was Tregasnou. Already it seemed distant and remote.

But I'll be back, Julie thought. She hugged Peter and said, 'Everything's going to be all right, darling. Wait and see!'

As the boat emerged into the open sea a stiff wind began to blow across the deck and Julie pulled her coat more tightly about her. She looked around for somewhere sheltered to sit. The deck was long and exposed. The only place that might offer some protection was the side, next to the deep bulwarks. Julie was just about to move Peter across when the boat rolled and water splashed up through some sort of drain holes. Soon the part of the deck where she had planned to sit was drenched with water.

It would have to be somewhere else. The bow was high and flared, with a tiny triangle of decking. It might just offer a bit of protection. Anyway it was better than nothing. Holding tightly to Peter's hand, Julie made her way unsteadily forward. The boat rolled again and she made a grab for the rail. Her hand missed and she staggered sideways, falling over someone's leg and almost sitting on a man's lap. A voice said, 'Hey! Watch where you're going!'

Peter cried, 'Mummy, Mummy! I've bumped my knee.'

Julie gasped, 'Sorry', and got to her feet. Holding Peter firmly in one hand, she held tightly to the rail with the other, and started forward again. Holding on made the trip much easier and they got to the bow without further trouble.

In the bow there was a large winch which, Julie guessed, was for pulling up the anchor. Around it there were several coils of wide oily rope. Julie sat on the largest and pulled Peter down beside her.

Almost immediately he said, 'I'm cold, Mummy.'

'Well, come on to my lap then.' She undid her coat and raincoat and stretched them round Peter's body, hugging him to her.

It was definitely less windy up here, Julie decided. On the other hand the motion of the boat seemed worse – or maybe it was her imagination. The roll was the same, but now the deck was going up and down as well. She closed her eyes and tried not to think about it. Then the boat lurched and seemed to plunge into thin air. Julie felt her stomach take off and she reached down as if to hold it.

Peter said, 'Mummy, I feel funny.'

Oh God, Julie thought. She said calmly, 'Well, lie down darling, then you'll feel better.' She stretched him out across the coil of rope and laid his head on her lap. His face was sheet white and he burped slightly. He'll be sick in a second, Julie thought. She looked around for the nearest place to take him. The sides of the boat were too high here; she would have to take him several yards down the deck before they were low enough to hold his head over the water. Perhaps it wasn't so clever to have come up here after all.

She looked down at Peter again. His eyes were shut and his mouth slightly open: he was sound asleep. She relaxed and leant back against the rope. Thank goodness for that. It would be nice if she could sleep too . . .

The boat leapt again and Julie felt her stomach twist. She shivered and thought: Why didn't I get those clothes? She felt Peter's cheek and hands: he was cold too. What a fool she'd been! But it wasn't too late; she would go and fetch the extra clothes now.

It meant a trip to the wheelhouse to ask one of the crew. She looked down the deck: it suddenly seemed rather a long way, and the deck was treacherous with running water. It wouldn't be so bad if she didn't feel so tired . . .

The other passengers were lying across the top of the hold or draped over the rail being sick. One woman raised her head and vomited on the deck. The sight of it made Julie retch and she knew she couldn't make it down the deck, at least not quite yet. If only she could get her head down . . .

She lifted Peter's head and shifted her body until she was more or less lying on her side, then moved him until he was lying in the curve of her body. It was wonderful to lie down; she felt much better. And

148

the cold didn't seem to matter so much like this. She closed her eyes and thought: I'll definitely get the clothes in a minute.

A cry woke her and she looked up to see some of the passengers brushing spray off their clothes. The motion was worse than before and now and again the bow came down with a terrible shudder, as if the boat had hit something. The wind was reaching into the bow section now, whistling round, icy and chill against Julie's skin. She shivered again and wondered how much longer she dared leave it before she got the clothes. The longer she left it, the worse it would be. And yet she knew she would be sick if she got up, and she daren't leave Peter . . .

She thought: I'm just making excuses.

She made herself sit up. She tucked Peter into the coil of rope and, getting to her feet, started gingerly down the deck. The wind blew her hair into her eyes and then something cold and solid hit the back of her head. She gasped with the shock. Cold water seeped down her neck.

She got halfway to the wheelhouse and leant over the rail. A vague memory came to her, something someone had said about feeling seasick: first you want to die but then you're afraid you're not going to. Who'd said that? She couldn't remember. Whoever it was, he was right.

But afterwards, when her stomach was empty, she was surprised to find she felt much better, and she started down the deck with new determination. The crew member she had spoken to before was standing outside the wheelhouse. As she reached him he held out a helping hand and she grasped it gratefully.

She gasped, 'Thank you so much. It's a bit rough for me, I'm afraid.' She looked up at him, a smile on her face. He began to smile back, then his face froze and he stared past her at a point over her head, his mouth open.

Suddenly he was shouting, so loudly that Julie stared at him in amazement. Suddenly everyone was yelling and pointing and Julie turned to see what they were looking at.

It was a plane.

It was coming straight for them, low over the sea.

The yelling stopped and there was silence. Everyone was watching the plane. It came closer and closer, its grey outline getting darker, more solid. Julie felt her heart beating against her chest. It couldn't be, surely . . .

The plane tipped its wings and went off at an angle, then tipped the other way: it was circling round them. A voice yelled, 'It's German! It's a German!'

There was a crash; it was the wheelhouse door opening. A large, red-faced man came roaring out, shaking his fist at the plane. 'Bloody swine! Bloody swine!' Julie guessed it was the skipper.

'What should we do? What should we do?' someone said.

The skipper shouted, 'Nothing, that's what. Absolutely nothing!'

The plane straightened up and flew in the direction of Morlaix, waggling its wings. Then it turned back towards them. But it didn't circle again. Instead it came straight for the boat, passing so low over the masts that Julie thought it would hit them.

A passenger cried, 'Turn back! He's trying to tell us to turn back. Quick, otherwise he'll shoot us all!'

People started arguing and shouting. One man – a fairly well-dressed man in his fifties – got to his feet, lurched up to the skipper and ordered him to turn around. The skipper told him to do something unpleasant to himself and, when he'd finished, to mind his own business. The passenger started to yell at him, his voice shrieking above the sound of the wind and the waves. A couple of women screamed as the plane made another pass close over the masts.

Julie thought: They've all gone mad. It's a nightmare.

She watched the plane turn and head towards the boat again. The noise, when it came, was staccato but very faint, as if it didn't come from the plane at all. At first Julie didn't understand what the noise meant and she was puzzled to see everyone throwing themselves on to the deck. For a second she stood there against the rail, frozen with surprise. Then at last she realised: bullets. She dropped like a stone and crawled against the raised side of the hold.

She thought: Peter! and looked up along the deck to the bow. There was someone in her way and she craned her head up further.

He was sitting up, looking bemused. He was swinging his feet over the rope coil and putting them on the deck.

He was going to stand up.

Julie screamed, 'Peter! *Get down! Get down!*'

He was looking around, searching for her.

Then he stood up.

The plane swooped over in a roar of noise.

Julie got up and started to run.

She started well, keeping her balance as she ran up the deck. The boat rolled and she swerved sideways. There was a sharp blow to her ankle, and then pain. She got a grip on the rail and ran on. The bow sank into a wave with a thunderous roar and a sheet of spray came swooping across the boat. She saw it coming and wondered for an instant whether to duck. But then it had slapped into her and she gasped at the coldness of the water: it had gone straight through her clothes.

Another two strides and she reached Peter. She rolled into the coil of rope, pulling him down with her and sobbed with relief.

Peter pushed away from her and said crossly, 'Mummy, you're all wet! You're all wet!'

'Yes, darling.' She caught her breath then looked back along the deck, trying to gauge what was happening. She had a feeling they were turning: the wind was blowing differently, and the boat was not bumping so ferociously into the waves. Turning . . .

She listened for the plane, but there was nothing. She stood up quickly and looked around. Yes, they were definitely turning: the land was almost ahead of the boat now. They were going back towards Morlaix.

Julie knew she should be disappointed, but all she could feel was an overwhelming sense of relief; somehow nothing ashore could possibly be worse than staying out here on this awful boat, feeling like death and being fired at . . . All she wanted was to be warm, dry and safe again.

The sound of the plane's engine came softly over the water, a faint buzz gathering into a deep drone as it approached once more. Julie crouched down beside Peter. This time the plane did not fire, but swooped straight over the boat. Everyone froze where they lay, listening and watching, but it flew straight on, heading into the distance until, no more than a small black speck near the horizon, it was lost in the low grey cloud.

'And good riddance!' It was the skipper. He was smiling broadly and talking excitedly. As he spoke, a few people cheered and someone cried again, 'Vive la France Libre.' Some of the passengers still looked unhappy and a few were arguing. But then, Julie thought, there were bound to be some people who didn't like turning back. It was inevitable. Well, at least they weren't about to die out here, shot like rabbits or drowned. That was something to be grateful for.

The skipper strode into the wheelhouse and Julie sank back on to the rope coil. Her teeth were chattering so loudly she had to clench her jaws to stop the noise. She remembered the clothes again. She really should make the effort to get them, but her mind was frozen and numb. It was rather nice, the numbness, like a dream. Nothing seemed very important any more, nothing except sleeping and lying here . . .

The bow hit a wave and water splattered and sloshed over the deck. People complained again. Then there was another wave and, as the bow fell fast, down into the void, Julie felt herself and Peter almost lifted off the deck.

Suddenly Julie was awake. Why were they hitting waves again? What had happened? She staggered to her feet and looked for the land. It was *behind* them. They had turned again. They were heading back towards England.

No, Julie thought, it's the wrong thing to do. Wrong.

Suddenly she was angry and frightened. She swayed down the deck again and opened the wheelhouse door. The skipper was at the wheel, a cigarette clamped between his teeth.

Julie asked, 'Why? Why have we turned back?'

The skipper glanced at her. 'Because, dear lady, we are going to England. And no stupid Boches are going to make me change my mind! That's why.'

'But what if they come back? They'll shoot us.'

'Don't worry your head about that.'

'But I do – we must. People could get hurt.'

The skipper drew hard on his cigarette and looked at her through narrowed eyes. 'Look, we go on. And that's final. Now go back on deck.'

'But what does everyone else want? Aren't they worried too?'

'Look, lady, we go on, all right? You wanted to go to England, didn't you? Well, it's a bit late to change your mind. I can see the problem – you're wet, you're sick, and it all seems a bad idea now. Well, you ladies are never happy at sea, but I'm afraid you're just going to have to put up with it. We go on!' He shook his head knowingly. 'That plane won't come back again, I know it!'

For a moment Julie didn't trust herself to speak. His attitude was exasperating. How did he know the plane wouldn't come back? It seemed highly likely to Julie that it would come back and soon.

She made an effort to pull herself together and said, 'But suppose the plane *does* come back . . . What then?'

The skipper turned and shouted down into the small cabin below, 'Someone! Show this lady back on to the deck!'

Julie found herself shaking with anger and tiredness. She tried to calm herself. 'Don't worry, I'm going. But please, my son and I, we're wet and cold . . . do you have anything warm . . . ?' She trailed off.

'Here.' He passed her a jacket from a peg on the side of the wheelhouse. He looked at her pityingly and added, 'If it gets much worse we'll see if we can find your child a place in the cabin.'

Julie's anger melted away and she nodded with gratitude. 'Thank you.'

She wiped a hand over her face, put the jacket on and started the long awkward journey back to the bow. Halfway along the deck she waited a moment while spray flew across the boat, then, when the coast was clear, she set out on the last few yards. But before she reached the protection of the bow she felt the thud of the boat meeting a wave and a curtain of spray rose into the air in front of her. The water looked insubstantial but when it hit her it was like something solid, as if a powerful man had slapped her in the face. The force took her breath away and for a moment she almost lost her footing.

She gripped the rail more firmly and hurried into the shelter of the bow. The jacket had kept some of the water off her clothes but now an ice-cold river of seawater was streaming down her back. She said, 'Oh God!' and gritted her teeth as she lay down beside Peter and pulled him inside the jacket.

Despite the jacket she found herself shivering violently. Peter was still cold too; his skin was cool against her cheek. She found herself praying: Dear Lord, please let this end soon, please let it be over, please get us there *quickly*. But she knew it was hopeless; the journey had only just begun. They must be only ten or fifteen miles from the coast, and the English Channel was at least eighty – or was it a hundred miles wide? She couldn't remember. However far, it would take hours, all night and most of the next day at least. She couldn't even imagine that amount of time.

The plane came back half an hour later.

This time it did not bother to circle. It started firing straight away. The noise was much louder this time; the staccato rat-at-at of the bullets seemed to fill the boat. There were loud pings, too, and the sound of tearing wood. As the plane roared overhead someone screamed, a piercing and dreadful scream. It was a man; he was clutching his stomach, a look of horror on his face. Julie found herself staring: she had never heard a man screaming before.

Peter was sobbing, 'Mummy, mummy! What's happening?'

Julie hugged him tight, then something caught the corner of her eye. It was the plane. She could see it banking behind the boat, then levelling up. It was coming in for another run. It was heading straight for her. Straight for Peter.

She looked around desperately. There was nowhere to hide, nothing . . . Just the winch.

It might just be big enough.

She pulled Peter to his feet and yanked him across the deck. He tripped and the deadweight of his body pulled at her shoulder. He was crying now. She gripped him under the arms and swung him in behind the winch. She crouched in front of him and put her arms round him. She tried to make herself as narrow as possible. The winch base was about two feet wide: she had the feeling her shoulders must be sticking out . . .

As she put her head down the din started. This time it was deafening: the clanging of metal, the whistle and thud of the bullets. There was another scream and several shouts.

The seconds stretched out endlessly. She heard each bullet as it hissed and thudded around her. She waited for the one that would tear into her body.

It never came.

In a roar of engines the plane was overhead and gone again. And they were both alive. Julie whispered into Peter's hair, 'Oh my darling, my little darling. It's all right, it's all right.'

She looked at him, at his big round frightened eyes, and said, 'Now, stay here. Right here, do you understand? I'll be back in a moment.'

Peter screamed, 'No! Mummy, don't go! Don't go!'

But Julie was already on her feet. '*Stay there!*'

She ran down the deck and straight into the wheelhouse. When she opened the door she was almost sick. Two men were lying on the floor: one had a terrible red oozing mass of brains and bloody flesh instead of a face. The other was the skipper. His eyes were staring straight at her, sightless and also quite dead.

She gulped and forced her eyes up to the man at the wheel. He was staring at her, his mouth gaping and his eyes dazed.

Julie said firmly, 'Turn round! Turn towards the land!'

He stared back, his mouth moving noiselessly.

Julie drew breath and said again, 'Turn now or we'll all be dead!'

The buzz of the plane was getting louder again. Julie reached over and started to turn the wheel. The man's eyes suddenly focused and his hands fumbled at the wheel too.

The boat began to turn, but slowly, so slowly. The noise of the engines was getting much louder again.

Julie sobbed, 'Oh *please, please.*'

At last the boat was turning more quickly.

The plane roared over. There were no bullets this time.

They were going to be all right.

Julie waited to see that the helmsman was keeping the boat on course, then closed the wheelhouse door and walked quickly back to Peter.

They were going home.

Perhaps, Julie thought, we were never meant to go away at all.

The boat couldn't get up the river; it was low tide. Instead they picked up a mooring off a small fishing village at the top of the estuary, where it narrows into the Morlaix River. The dead were covered with canvas and left on board, the living were ferried ashore in a small rowing boat.

As they waited their turn for the boat Julie stood at the rail with Peter in her arms, looking at the quiet, golden land and thinking it was like a dream. There in the shelter of the river the air was warm and languid; a perfect summer day. The afternoon sun burned hot on her back, warming her slowly, deliciously. Like a dream. It was hard to imagine that the appalling boat trip belonged to the same day.

At last it was Julie and Peter's turn to go ashore. They squeezed in the back of the dinghy next to a young man. Julie recognised him: he was the one who had cried 'Vive la France Libre!' when they set out. Now there was no laughter in his face; he was silent, staring blankly into the distance ahead.

They landed at a stone slipway. When Julie stepped ashore and felt the solid stone beneath her feet she sighed with relief. The young man passed Peter across and Julie hugged him tightly to her. 'It's all over, darling. It's all over.'

The young man carried their baggage as far as the main road, then left. Julie sat Peter down on a grassy bank and stretched out beside him. For a moment she closed her eyes and let the sun warm her face. The relief of being on dry land was almost as great as the comfort of knowing they were safe. She reached for Peter's hand and said, 'I love you, darling.'

Peter rubbed his eyes. 'Mummy, I'm hungry and I want to go home.'

'Of course, sweetheart. We'll start with some food!'

Julie unpacked the food basket and they ate. She was surprised to find she was ravenous. The two of them consumed a whole section of sausage, a large slice of hard cheese, four chunks of bread, and two apples. It was wonderful to eat in peace and quiet, the land steady beneath one's feet, the wind no more than a slight breeze rustling in the trees.

While they ate Julie began to think. This village was the wrong side of the river for Tregasnou. To get home they would have to go all the way inland to Morlaix and then double back on the other side of the river. It was a long way. The alternative was to find someone to ferry them across the river. But the river was still very wide at this point. And the country on the other side was pretty remote; she wasn't sure if they'd be able to find any transport once they got there.

The thought of home was wonderful. More than anything she

wanted to return to the safety of the small grey house. Yet the problem of having a British passport remained. Peter would still be at risk. For his sake perhaps it was wrong to give up so easily. Perhaps she should make another attempt to get away. To Brest: that was where the ships were. Perhaps there'd be a place on one of them . . .

It was so difficult to decide. In her heart she wanted to stay, yet her main responsibility was to Peter.

She would think about what to do on the way to Morlaix, she suddenly decided. Morlaix was the way home *and* the way to Brest. Yes, she would make up her mind there.

One thing was soon clear: if they wanted to get into the town they would have to walk. While they had been eating only one car had come out of the village and, though Julie had stood up and waved, it hadn't stopped. There was a bus stop, but the next bus wasn't due for another two hours. If it came at all.

As soon as they finished eating Julie stood up. It was six in the evening; they must get to town before dark. The bags were a problem: she hadn't packed very much, but there was still too much to carry. She took the essential clothes and crammed them into one suitcase, leaving the other by the roadside. She wrapped the remaining food in some paper and put it in her raincoat pocket. Now she had one case, her handbag – and Peter.

She wondered how far a four-year-old could walk before he got tired. One thing was sure: it wouldn't be as far as Morlaix.

He was very good to begin with, marching well, his little arms swinging back and forth. Then, after twenty minutes, he began to flag. Their pace slowed. After another fifteen minutes Peter said, 'Mummy, please can we stop? I'm so tired.'

Julie smiled down at him. 'Of course, darling. We'll stop for a minute.' They sat at the roadside. When they started off again, Julie tried to make a game of it, pretending they were soldiers marching off to save Morlaix from ferocious bandits. It worked for a while, then Peter flagged again.

For a while Julie half carried, half pulled him along. Later she put him on her shoulders, though the extra weight made her arms and back shoot with pain, and she often had to stop and catch her breath. Her feet were agony and she cursed herself for wearing unsuitable shoes. But then hiking hadn't been part of the plan.

In the end it took three hours to do the twelve kilometres. The bus never came; Julie'd had a feeling it wouldn't.

When finally they arrived in Morlaix it was strangely quiet, the streets empty of people, the shops and restaurants shut and boarded. Only a few bars were open, their customers peering furtively out as if they were expecting the Germans at any second. Perhaps they are, thought Julie. She didn't honestly care. She sat on a bench near the port, her head back and her legs outstretched, and Peter cuddled against her side. She decided that whatever happened they would go no further tonight.

She thought of going to her employer's house. He lived on the edge of town, a ten minute walk away. Or there was a girl who worked in her office who had an apartment nearby. Or there was Michel.

Michel would know the best thing to do; she would go to Michel. She knew the building he lived in; it was five minutes away. She looked at Peter: he was asleep. She left him on the bench for a moment and looked for a place to leave the case. In the end she left it under a parked van. If anyone drove the van off, it was too bad.

She took Peter in her arms and walked. The rest on the bench had been a mistake: it had given her feet a chance to swell up and the blisters to weep. She stopped, kicked off her shoes and tucked them into the top of her handbag. It was a great improvement.

When she reached the apartment building the door was locked and a ring on the *concierge*'s bell produced no answer. There were individual bells for each apartment. Beside each bell was a number but no name. She didn't know which apartment was Michel's, so she pressed them all. At last a man opened the door. It wasn't Michel, but he let her in and told her which apartment she wanted.

When she reached the apartment door there was no answer to her knock, so with Peter fast asleep in her arms, she sat outside the door and waited.

He came back at eleven.

When he saw her, he stared.

She smiled stupidly at him and said, 'Thank you for coming back.'

When she first woke up she couldn't remember where she was. The room was dark and shuttered and she couldn't make out its features. Then she remembered and, hugging Peter's warm body closer to her, closed her eyes and slept again.

Later she was woken by someone opening the shutters. Brilliant sunshine streamed into the room and she screwed up her eyes against the light. She was lying on the sofa where she'd sat on her arrival the night before. She hadn't had the energy to move, though Michel had offered to take the sofa and give her his bed.

Now he was beside her, holding out a cup of coffee. He was frowning. 'I found your case all right.'

Julie exclaimed, 'Oh! I'd forgotten about it!' Then said hurriedly, 'Thank you.'

Michel nodded briefly. 'Now, there isn't much time, so we've got to hurry.'

Julie stared at him. 'What do you mean?'

'I mean that the Germans are almost here. They'll arrive some time today. At least that's my interpretation of the complete black-out on news. There's nothing on the wireless except people telling us to keep calm. That *must* mean we're for it!' He spoke with a bitter smile.

Peter was waking up, rubbing his eyes and looking round at the strange room.

Julie said, 'Then – should we go to Brest? Get on a ship?'

Michel laughed. 'Hah! There is nothing but good French chaos there.' He shook his head. 'A friend has just come back. He told me all about it. Evidently there are thousands of people at the port all trying to get on ships that do not exist. The military got away all right, then they started to let civilians on the few remaining ships. Some got away, but one large ship had a collision with a naval boat and sank. Right there, just outside Brest.' He lit a cigarette. 'Now? Well, there are no ships left, apparently. Just people trying to hide, running round in circles because there's nowhere to go. They also say that it's as black as night all day long. The fuel dumps at Maison Blanche were set on fire. It sounds like Dante's Inferno!'

Julie shivered. Thank God she hadn't gone there. She was fright-ened by crowds and disorder. That's what she'd hated most on the boat, the hysteria, the loss of control when the plane had fired on them.

She said calmly, 'Then I shall go home.'

'Yes. But first we have work to do –' He indicated that she should get to her feet. 'Comb your hair, change your dress. We're going out.'

He was so firm, so definite, that it never occurred to her to question him. Instead she looked at herself. She *did* look dreadful. Quickly she washed, tidied her hair and put on a clean dress. She changed Peter's shirt and trousers, gave him a *tartine* of bread and jam to chew on, and came back into the living room. 'We're ready.'

Michel stuffed his wallet into the back pocket of his trousers and led the way out. She followed, pulling Peter along with her. Michel walked fast and Julie had to pick Peter up and half-run to keep up with him. She was too breathless to ask where they were going.

They turned a corner, then another, until they came to some double doors set in a high stone wall. Michel took out a key and, unlocking the padlock, swung open one of the doors. He brought out a *vélo*.

He locked the door again and said, 'Hop on.'

The little motor coughed into life and they were off, Michel bicycling furiously to get up speed and Peter giggling with delight on Julie's lap.

In contrast to the night before, the streets were busy this morning, people hurrying everywhere with baskets and bags in their hands. There were long queues outside the *boulangeries* and the *charcuteries* again. After a few minutes they came into a square and stopped. Michel got off. He jerked his head in the direction of a large building and said briefly, 'We're going in there.' Julie recognised it immediately: it was the *Sous-Préfecture*.

She followed Michel in. Inside there was chaos: people were milling around, rushing from office to office, shouting, looking harassed. All the doors were open, showing empty desks and stacks of papers. Two women were going towards the main door carrying boxes. One said to Julie in amazement, 'These are all to be burnt! I ask you – burnt!' Michel lifted Peter into his arms and took Julie's hand. He led her up the stairs and along a corridor with numerous doors leading off it. He looked at the labels on the doors and finally said, 'Ha, here we are!'

The office was empty. Michel gave Peter to Julie, went straight in and started searching the drawers and filing cabinets. Julie stared in astonishment. 'Michel!' she exclaimed. 'Stop! Stop! What are you *doing*? Someone might come!'

There was an old safe sitting on the floor in the corner. Michel tried the handle. It was locked. He told Julie to wait and left the room. Julie sat down and tried to work out what was happening. Why had Michel brought her here? What was all this to do with her? In a moment Michel was back. With him was a woman. The woman went to the safe and opened it with a key from a large ring hanging on her belt. She nodded at Michel, said 'It's a pleasure', and left. She didn't even look at Julie.

Whatever was going on, the woman was in on it too. Julie took Peter off her knee and stood up. 'Michel, please tell me what's going on!'

Michel grunted, 'Here we are!' He took two cards off the top of a pile and passed them to Julie. 'Start to fill one in, will you? The second's just a spare. I must go and make sure your name vanishes from the Aliens Registration and appears on all the voting lists.'

Julie stared at the cards. They were identity cards. They were blank.

Michel was disappearing down the passage. Julie ran and called after him, 'Michel, I may be down under the name of Howard as well as Lescaux!'

He waved an acknowledgement and vanished into another doorway.

Shaking her head, Julie went back and sat at the desk. Suddenly she smiled. Peter looked up at her and asked, 'Happy Mummy?'

She grinned down at him. 'Yes, very happy Mummy!'

She looked at the blank card and thought carefully. After a moment she began to write in some of the details. She kept her name, Lescaux, and entered her father's name correctly. But instead of her mother's name she put 'Jeannette Lescaux'. For her mother's maiden name she put 'Leforge' because it was the first name that came into her head. Under the heading 'Name Before Marriage' she put nothing. To pretend to be married would complicate matters. She slipped the second identity card into her handbag.

She sat back and smiled at Peter. Then her eye caught the safe. It was still open, the pile of blank identity cards visible at the front of the shelf. On an impulse Julie reached in and took a batch off the top.

She stuffed them into her bag, her heart beating furiously. It was rather risky. But why *not* take them? They might be useful. She had never stolen anything in her life before.

Michel came back. He looked at her new card, nodded, and looked through the rubber stamps on the desk. He found the one he wanted, picked it up, inked it and stamped her new card. He then inked her thumb and pressed it on the space left for thumbprints. 'And again. Here.' He pressed her thumb on an official form. It was an application for an identity card.

Julie whispered. 'You're a magician!'

Michel shrugged, but Julie could see he was pleased.

'How on earth did you *do* it though? I mean, why did that woman open the safe for us?'

'Oh I told her the Germans would torture and kill you if we couldn't find you a proper identity.'

Julie shook her head. 'You're amazing!' And I mean that, she thought. She added, 'I owe you a debt of gratitude. I hope I can repay you one day.'

'It's nothing. Anyway –' he looked into her eyes '– it is an honour to do it for you.'

Julie blushed and stood up. Perhaps – perhaps she'd been wrong. Perhaps she had misjudged him and he was rather nice after all.

Her eye caught the rubber stamp. 'Are there two of those?'

'Why?'

'I want one, that's all.'

Michel looked at her in surprise. 'Good God, what for?'

'I don't know . . . just in case, I suppose.'

He handed her the stamp. 'Just don't get caught with it, that's all.'

They walked quickly down the passage and out of the building. By the *vélo* Michel asked, 'Can you drive one of these things?'

'I think so, but – what about you?'

'I have things to do. You drive back to Tregasnou. I'll deliver your suitcase and pick the machine up another time.' He glanced nervously round the square and Julie suddenly thought: He's going to stir up trouble somewhere. She said, 'Do be careful. You're not going to do anything silly are you?'

'My friends and I have got to make our plans, that's all.'

Julie looked at Michel with admiration: already he was making plans against the Germans, arranging meetings, doing something positive. She said, 'I won't ask what you're planning. But whatever you do, be careful. Don't risk your neck! And good luck!'

'What?' He looked at her in mild surprise.

'I mean, the Germans . . . they might catch you . . .' She trailed off, uncertain.

'Ha! I won't be going in for cheap heroics, if that's what you mean. I'm not going to risk my neck. Quite the opposite. I think the Germans and I might get on very well.'

Julie blinked. 'What do you mean?'

Michel leant over the bike until his face was close to hers. 'My dear, I'm with whoever rids us of the scum corrupting this country – the right-wing dictators who've robbed the working people of their rightful inheritance for more than a hundred years. I'm for whoever's against them!'

'But you're not going to work *with* the Germans?'

He shrugged. 'Who knows? It depends what there is to be gained.'

'But they're overrunning our country. They're – enemies!'

'Yes, but they won't stay for ever. And after the war – *after* – there'll be a chance to build a new state, a people's state. In fact, it's the best chance we've ever had to sweep the system clean!'

Julie got silently on to the *vélo*, lifting Peter up in front of her. Michel untied a piece of cord attached to the small luggage rack and gave it to Julie. 'Here, you'll need this to keep Peter on.' Julie took it and looped it round both her own and Peter's waists, then tied a knot.

Michel was saying, 'You shouldn't meet any Germans yet. But do watch out for planes. If you hear one, make for the ditch, and fast.' He took her face in his hands and without warning kissed her firmly on the lips.

Julie didn't move or respond. While he kissed her she stared at the

161

side of his head and his closed eyes and thought: Why did I ever think I might like this man?

Michel stood back and said, 'Juliette, keep yourself safe for me, won't you?'

Julie stared at the ground then looked up at him. She said, 'No!' and saw a look of surprise on Michel's face. 'Look, I owe you a big favour which I will try to repay one day. But while you . . . you play your dirty games, forget anything else. Especially friendship! How you can consider dealing with the Germans is . . . beyond me!'

He was annoyed. 'You just don't understand.'

'That's right, I don't. Goodbye, Michel.'

She pedalled slowly away, wobbling slightly as she got her balance. He was shouting. 'I'll send your suitcase over when I can.'

She didn't turn round but pedalled rapidly until the motor fired. Peter squealed with excitement. 'Mummy, we're going so fast!'

Julie didn't answer. She was thinking about Michel. How could he? How *could* he? Whatever one believed it must be wrong to actually *help* the enemy. That would mean helping to prolong the war. It might even mean helping to kill one's fellow countrymen. As she rode along she shook her head and muttered in disbelief. God only knew what Tante Marie would say when she heard . . .

The thought of Tante Marie and the small grey-stone house cheered her up. She bent slightly and briefly kissed Peter's head.

Peter's small voice came floating up. 'Mummy, are we going home?'

Julie said firmly, 'Oh yes, darling! We're going home.'

9

At last a tender came into sight, nosing its way round the end of the distant pier and heading towards the warship anchored in the middle of the large natural harbour. Although the harbour was well protected from the rolling Channel seas and long Atlantic swells, a blustery west wind was funnelling between the hills, creating an unpleasant little chop which made the tender roll slightly as it progressed steadily across the water.

Richard Ashley watched it approach and thought longingly of sleep. He'd snatched only a couple of catnaps in the last thirty-six hours and now he was dog-tired. It would be sensible to go back to his bunk and turn in. But he couldn't bring himself to do it. An evening's run ashore was not something to be given up lightly, not when you'd gone without leave for three weeks. And particularly when the leave was here in Falmouth.

The place had happy memories for him – of sailing here in *Dancer*, first, in the early days, with his father, then later with friends from Dartmouth. Once, though, he had come here alone. He'd been on passage to the Scillies, and Falmouth, being the most westerly port on the English mainland, had been the last stopping place before setting out on the final sixty miles of open sea. He remembered that holiday among the beautiful, bleak Scillies with especial fondness.

A group of ratings clustered at the rail, waiting impatiently for the tender. For them, Falmouth was just another port with another lot of pubs.

Not that pubs weren't a consideration for Ashley too. He enjoyed drinking. Just as he enjoyed the other opportunities ashore. In his wallet he had the telephone number of a girl he vaguely knew who lived not far away. He would take her out to dinner if she were free. It had been well over a month since he'd spent an evening with a girl.

A night out would cheer him up. Like everyone else in the ship he needed it. They'd had a rotten couple of months. After Dunkirk they'd started convoy work, escorting ships along the south coast and through the Dover Straits, fighting off increasingly heavy air attacks. By the end of July they were losing ships at an alarming rate and, when three destroyers were lost in the space of a few days, the Admiralty was forced to abandon day-time passages through the eastern half of the Channel. Now even the western Channel was difficult. On this last convoy, which had been westward bound, they had been attacked by Stukas south of the Isle of Wight and had lost a horrifying five ships before the attack had been driven off. It seemed to Ashley that, ever since Dunkirk, the Navy was being forced inexorably out of the Channel.

The tender was closer now, and turning in a long slow arc which would bring it neatly alongside the destroyer. Ashley put his face up to the blustery west wind and breathed deeply, willing himself to wake up.

'God, they're not letting you loose too, are they, Ashley?'

He turned and saw Blythe, the gunnery officer, also in best shore-going uniform.

Ashley smiled. 'Of course. Begged me to go actually.' He thought how trite and out of place the old jokes sounded now, yet one trotted them out as a matter of course, to maintain a feeling of normality.

Blythe said, 'Want to join forces? I thought of sampling the ale in a few of the local establishments.'

Ashley watched the tender bump alongside and considered. An evening with Blythe would be ruinous. The two of them had been out drinking together once before and ended up speechless and legless on the floor of a hotel ballroom in Weymouth. His hangover had lasted two days.

He chuckled at the memory. 'Just a quick one then. But I won't be able to stay long.'

'Aha!' Blythe gave him a steely glare. 'A woman, is it?'

Ashley grinned enigmatically and started down the gangway to where the tender was waiting, already crowded with the ratings who, anxious to start their precious leave, had swarmed aboard the moment it came alongside.

As the two men took their seats the boat drew away and Ashley turned to get a good view of the forward bulwarks, where a damage repair party was working on a series of dented, hole-peppered plates. A gunner had died up there during the last air attack. Although they'd been at war for a year, it was the first time Ashley had seen a man die at close quarters. The scene was still vivid in his mind.

He shook his head and muttered to Blythe in an undertone, 'You feel so damned ineffectual.' Blythe nodded; he knew exactly what Ashley meant. In company with another destroyer they had been trying to protect fourteen ships against a dozen or more enemy aircraft: an unpleasantly one-sided fight.

Ashley added, 'Let's hope the RAF have some more luck soon.' The Battle of Britain had been raging for a couple of months and still the bombers came, against convoys, against ports and military establishments and, increasingly now, against cities and civilian targets.

The tender buffeted its way up-wind towards the town nestling comfortably in the lee of a hill, its buildings rising haphazardly from the water's edge. Eventually they came to the small-boat moorings, where coastal patrol boats, oyster smacks and the occasional yacht lay swinging to the tide.

Suddenly Ashley peered ahead. An MFV – a motor fishing vessel – lay close under the town. She was painted dull grey and had obviously been requisitioned as an inshore patrol boat. Yet there was something unusual about her, something that didn't quite fit. For a moment he couldn't place what it was, but then, as the trawler came into full view, he had it.

The vessel was French. It was nothing definite, nothing you could tie down. But her lines and the long canoe stern definitely looked more Breton than Cornish. As the tender passed astern of her, Ashley saw someone come out of the deckhouse and saunter to the rail. He was wearing plain overalls and was bare-headed. A cigarette hung from his lower lip in the Gallic manner.

Ashley had seen French fishing boats in England before – everyone had. They had been appearing regularly since the fall of France in June, three months before. But this was the first time he had seen one under the white ensign. He wondered if the crewman on deck had been a French fisherman and, if so, how he liked Naval discipline. Not, he guessed, very much at all.

The tender came alongside a stone quay. Ashley was the first off, running up the steps two at a time and striding away across the cobblestones. Blythe was panting when he caught up with him. 'Gosh, what's the hurry, old man?'

'I spied a pub, Blythe, and I didn't want it to get away.' In truth he had been in a hurry to feel the land under his feet and he had run up the steps for the sheer pleasure of it. Like most people who loved the sea, he hated to spend too long on it and, after a few weeks, felt desperate for the land again.

Blythe laughed and followed Ashley up a narrow street and into the saloon bar of a pub with a low door and thick oak beams. Ashley knew immediately that it was the sort of pub he liked – old, rather dowdy and, most important of all, unpretentious. It would be very easy to stay here all evening and drink several pints too many. Instead, he had just one pint and went out to find the nearest telephone box.

He called his parents first, at their home in Hampshire. As always, his mother was light-hearted and gay. She considered it bad form to mention any anxieties she might have about her family, and always made a point of imparting only good or amusing news, usually about one of her many dogs. His father, now back in the Navy at a desk job after more than ten years' retirement, was more serious, and listened attentively to his son's news, limited though it was by the constraints of secrecy. When the conversation was over, Ashley put the telephone down with regret. He liked his parents very much.

Then he called the girl.

He'd met her twice, once at a party given by his sister and once when staying with an old schoolfriend. She was a good-looker in a cool English sort of way. She was the sort who liked riding and hunting and going to dances. She wasn't exactly a ball of fire, he remembered, and she certainly wouldn't offer him more than a kiss on the cheek – but she might be quite fun all the same.

She was at home when he called, and in her cool voice said that yes, she would like to come out to dinner very much. She would borrow her father's car and meet him in an hour.

He walked back to the pub to find that it had filled up considerably. He spotted Blythe at the bar, well into another drink, and made his way through the crowd towards him. Ashley felt far less tired now; he decided he was in the mood for a party. He slapped Blythe on the back and grinned. Blythe nodded briefly then returned to the discussion he was having with two men, one a balding, overweight civilian wearing the armband of the Auxiliary Fire Service, the other a silver-haired merchant navy officer. For a change, they were talking about the war.

With a sigh, Ashley settled down to listen. The AFS man was wagging his finger vehemently. 'They'll invade before the end of the month, mark my words. The bombing of London and the ports – that's just to soften us up, you know. As soon as they've knocked the RAF out of the sky, then they'll be on their way!'

Ashley interrupted brightly, 'Hello', and introduced himself to the two men. They shook hands.

Blythe resumed, 'But the Jerries won't be able to do that. Knock the RAF out of the sky, I mean.'

'But they will – they are!' the AFS man insisted. 'Oh, the BBC tell us it's all going all right, but you don't want to believe them, you know. They just tell us what they want us to believe.'

A professional pessimist, Ashley noted. He interrupted lightly, 'Now, old chap, that sort of talk isn't going to win the war, is it?'

'That's as may be, but we might as well face facts!'

Ashley smiled charmingly at him. 'Then what do you suggest we do to stop the Germans coming?'

'Ha! Not much we can do now. It's too damn late.' The AFS man tutted with contempt and took another sip from his drink.

The merchant seaman looked thoughtful and said, 'I still don't understand how France went under so quickly . . . I just don't understand even now.'

The AFS man dropped his glass to the bar with a bang. 'I'll tell you why – because the Frenchies aren't fighting men, that's why. In fact, they ran backwards the moment they saw the first German tank.'

Ashley felt the adrenalin pump into his blood. He said coolly, 'That's not true.'

'Well, they didn't put up much of a fight, did they?'

'Incorrect, old boy. They held Dunkirk while we got out. They fought all the way.'

The AFS man was determined to press on. 'But if they fought so

166

hard, how did the Jerries get from Paris to Brest in five days, eh?' He turned to Blythe and laughed. 'Seems mighty strange, doesn't it?'

Blythe looked nervously towards Ashley and muttered, 'Er, how about another drink . . . ?'

Ashley knew he should turn away and laugh it off, but he couldn't. After a moment's pause he said in a low voice, 'You're speaking about friends of mine.'

The AFS man shrugged a little. 'Well, facts are facts, and when the invasion comes it'll be no thanks to the French.'

'Nor, I'm sure, to you!'

'Now look here – !'

Blythe tugged at Ashley's sleeve. 'Er, how about another pub, Richard? Come on, it's just not worth it.'

Ashley looked into the AFS man's belligerent piglike eyes and knew Blythe was right. With an enormous effort he closed his mouth and, putting his drink on the bar, turned to leave.

At the last moment he couldn't resist a parting shot. He lent towards the man and whispered, 'When you're next fighting a fire, careful you don't get your hose up the wrong passage!' He turned and pushed his way quickly through the press of bodies to the cold freshness of the street.

He heard Blythe come up behind him and said half to himself, 'Slow strangulation for that one. I could cheerfully kill types like that.'

'I agree.'

'Murder by degrees.'

'Yes, but it's never worth it . . .'

Suddenly it all seemed rather ridiculous and Ashley laughed out loud. 'No, it could be the ruination of my brilliantly promising career!'

Blythe smiled with relief. 'Not to mention your prospects.'

Ashley chuckled. He could laugh now, but his future in the Navy had been a touchy point until the war. He'd blotted his copy book by answering an admiral back in something less than respectful terms. He knew Blythe had heard about it – everyone had – and now he enjoyed making a feature of it. It gave him the reputation of being rather a devil in the wardroom.

Blythe said cheerfully, 'How about going to another boozer? There's the Admiral Something-or-another up the hill.'

'No.' Ashley suddenly felt tired again. More drinking wouldn't help. 'I've other plans. I'll see you tomorrow.'

Blythe winked. 'Aha! Tender loving care, is it? Good luck!' With a quick wave, he walked off up the hill.

Ashley looked at the time. He still had half an hour before meeting the girl. He decided to wander down to the water, to rid himself of the last taste of the unpleasantness in the pub.

The moment he stepped back onto the quay he was glad he had come. The early evening sunlight had ripened into a warm yellowy gold, illuminating the soft purple-green Cornish hills with a mantle of vibrant colour. Looking across to Flushing, its small cottages gleaming white above the water's edge, and watching the small-craft catch the golden light as they swung quietly and obediently to their moorings, it was difficult to imagine losing all this to the Germans. More than that, it was unthinkable. And if, like the AFS man, one ever started to believe it, then that was the beginning of the end.

He thought again: Nasty little man. And determined to forget about him.

He walked idly along the length of the quay and paused. Jutting out from the maze of houses and workshops that lined the waterfront there were a number of quays and jetties, with harbour craft and fishing vessels tied alongside. Against one, he could just make out the masts and upperworks of what looked like a grey MFV.

Ashley stared for a moment, then, carefully gauging the distance, walked up to the main street and made his way along it until he guessed he was above the boat. Then, at the first alley, he cut down towards the water again.

It was the right quay. The MFV lay close against the wall beside a fuel pump.

He went closer. It was the French boat all right. He took a long look at her. She was in good condition, the grey paint bright and fresh on her sides and the sails clean and neatly furled. The original fishing gear had been left intact: on the main deck there were two large winches for hauling the nets and against the bulwarks on the afterdeck, two trawl boards.

There was no-one about. Ashley crouched on his heels and called down.

After a few moments a face appeared at the window of the deck-house. The face watched Ashley to see if he would go away and, seeing that he wasn't going to, emerged reluctantly on to the deck. It was the man Ashley had spotted from the tender. He was still wearing overalls and smoking. He raised his eyebrows.

Ashley smiled. 'Hello. Just wondered where the boat came from originally.'

There was a frown of puzzlement.

168

Ashley took a guess and, switching to his inadequate French, tried again.

'Ah!' the man nodded. 'Concarneau!'

Ashley smiled to himself; he'd been right about the boat then. Concarneau was on the south coast of Brittany and a well-known fishing harbour. Ashley had been there once. He said so and the Frenchman nodded slowly and smiled. Ashley wanted to say how hospitable the people had been and how much he'd enjoyed it, but his French wasn't up to it. Instead he said that the town was very nice.

He would have liked to know what the boat was doing nowadays but, since the beginning of the war, one didn't ask questions like that. Instead he asked, 'And where did you go to fish . . . er . . . before?'

'On the banks.'

'A long way?' Ashley gestured to show what he meant.

The man shrugged. 'Away four days or so.'

Someone else appeared from the deckhouse. An RNVR lieutenant, dressed in uniform jacket and battered cap. He smiled up at Ashley. 'Evening. What can we do for you?'

Ashley switched back to English with relief. 'Just interested to see a Concarneau boat after all this time.'

'Ah. You know Concarneau?' With surprise Ashley realised the lieutenant wasn't English; there was a slight accent that was almost but not quite American.

He replied, 'I've sailed around there.'

The lieutenant nodded politely. 'In a small boat?'

'A sloop. Smallish. Twenty-five feet overall.'

'Very nice. You cruised a lot?'

'Yes, most of Normandy and Brittany.'

There was a pause. The lieutenant asked, 'What ship now?'

'Destroyer. A bit more solid underfoot.'

The lieutenant smiled. Ashley stood up. 'Well, I must be going now.' He said to the fisherman, '*Au revoir! Bonne chance!*' And, waving to the lieutenant, turned to go.

'Hey, wait a moment.' The officer vanished behind the wall and, after a few seconds, appeared over the top of the ladder. 'Look, er, how about coming aboard for a drink this evening?'

Ashley looked at his watch. He was late already. 'Sorry, got to dash.'

'Perhaps later then?'

Ashley hesitated. 'Where do you come from?'

'I'm a French-Canadian, from Quebec. But then you speak French too, don't you?'

Ashley threw back his head and laughed. 'Exceptionally badly!'

The Canadian smiled but his eyes were serious. He asked for Ashley's name, then said, 'Try and drop by later. I'd like to show you the boat.'

'I'll do my best.' Ashley waved again and walked off, glancing briefly over the boat as he left.

When he was half way up the main street he stopped in his tracks. There was something wrong with that MFV.

He walked on, not quite certain what it was. It was only when he got to the hotel where he was due to meet the girl that it came to him. That boat was going to make a rotten patrol boat.

It had no guns.

The girl was beautiful, well-bred and boring. Ashley wouldn't have minded if she'd had a sense of humour, but if she had one, it was well hidden. Nor would he have minded if she'd been especially attractive. But she was too cool for that. Making love to her would be like embracing a cucumber – a distinctly one-sided experience.

He decided he must be getting more discerning in his old age. A few years ago he wouldn't have cared what a woman's conversation was like if she was as lovely as this one. But now he was more particular. He liked his women warm, attractive and – what? Funny, earthy, capable of laughter. And this one most definitely was not.

By nine the conversation was drifting aimlessly and Ashley found himself drinking too much. By ten he was bored and restless.

When she started talking about the problems of finding young men to come to the austerity dance that her father was giving for her in London, Ashley knew he had to get away. He made a show of looking at his watch and said he had to be back at his ship at eleven, which was not quite true.

The moment he'd seen her off he felt a wonderful relief. There was still a good hour before the last boat left, still time to have some fun. He sauntered down the dark main street, wondering whether to go in search of Blythe. Almost immediately he decided against it. He could drink with Blythe any time.

Instead he made his way down to the water again, going carefully because of the blackout. After a while he heard the sound of lapping water and knew he must be nearing the edge of the quay. The dark outlines of a vessel showed black against the night. It was the MFV, riding high on the top of the tide.

He called across. After a moment there was a sound and a voice challenged him. He recognised it as the Canadian's and said, 'It's Ashley. I've come to claim that drink!'

The Canadian said, 'I thought you might.'

Ashley climbed on board and followed the other man down the companionway. Once below, the Canadian led the way forward into a wardroom which must originally have been the fish hold – and quite recently, Ashley guessed; the place still reeked of fish. Now there were two wooden bunks, a centre table, and an oil lamp hanging from the deckhead.

'Very nice!'

'Not bad considering this was a working boat just a few months ago.' the Canadian put out his hand and smiled. 'My name's Laperrine, by the way. Have a drink.'

Ashley chose gin and sat down. 'Your crew . . .' he began, 'are they all French?'

'Only the one. The man you met. He – well, he knows his way around and was willing to sign on, so we took him. The rest are British, ex-fishermen mainly.'

'And –' Ashley paused, wondering whether his question would be considered too probing. But what the hell. The drink had made him reckless. He asked, 'Will you be patrolling this part of the coast?'

Laperrine sat down on the opposite side of the table. 'Here . . . and hereabouts. Tell me, have you been in destroyers long?'

Ashley wondered what lay behind the question. He replied, 'A couple of years. Before that I did a stint on torpedo boats.'

'You enjoyed that?'

Ashley nodded. 'Yes, very much. Fast, exciting stuff. But with war coming I thought I might not see a lot of action. So I transferred back to proper ships again. Not very popular with the brass!' He laughed.

Laperrine smiled. 'Well, the top speed of this thing is six knots. Not exactly fast and exciting.'

Ashley leant forward. 'But there are compensations?'

The Canadian smiled. 'I think so.'

An infinitessimal shudder of excitement went down Ashley's spine and the effects of the drink cleared from his brain. 'May I ask a leading question? Why don't you have any guns?'

'Ah . . . Well, we do.'

'But nothing mounted on deck.'

'No. We keep our weapons out of sight.'

The man was going to tell him more, Ashley was certain of it. Smiling, he pressed, 'Because – ?'

Laperrine paused, as if weighing him up. 'You must say nothing – And I only tell you because – well, I think you might be interested.'

He took a breath. 'We're going to the other side, to mingle with the fishing fleets off the west coast, to . . . exchange things.'

Ashley had guessed it would be something like that. He suppressed a smile of exhilaration. Then he remembered the grey paint. 'But – you can't go like this, surely.'

'Oh no. She'll look just like any other Concarneau trawler by the time we've finished with her.'

Ashley said quickly, 'Go on.'

'There's not much more to it really. We're only just setting up the operation. But we do need more people. To be exact, someone who would command another boat. You would be . . . ideal. You know the coast, you know the people and you speak French –'

'Not very well!'

'But you understand it?'

Ashley nodded confidently, as if it were entirely true, which it wasn't. His French was really quite poor. He asked, 'But what about the fishing fleets – surely they're kept under guard?'

'Yes, guard boats go out with the fleets, but the Concarneau trawlers are allowed out for as much as two to three days at a time. It should be easy to slip in amongst them at night.'

Yes, of course it would. Ashley could imagine it. Pretending to fish, closing with the other trawlers, passing arms, receiving information. He could see it all and the idea thrilled him.

He looked up at the Canadian. 'I wouldn't mind knowing more.'

Laperrine smiled because he had been right about Ashley, and because he could see the glint of excitement in the other man's eyes. 'Good. I'll tell the Department.'

They had another drink then Ashley got up to leave. 'By the way, where on earth are you going to take her, to get her repainted?

'Somewhere quiet, away from curious eyes. Our base is to be at Helford. We'll probably do it there.'

The Helford River was just south of Falmouth, a quiet, beautiful place, but overlooked by a couple of small villages and a number of large houses. Ashley thought: It won't be any good.

He shook his head. 'You should go somewhere more isolated. What about the Scillies? Somewhere like New Grimsby. No-one would ever see you there.'

Laperrine smiled and shook Ashley's hand. 'It sounds a good idea.'

It was late. Ashley had to hurry to catch the last boat back to the ship. As he walked briskly along the dark deserted streets he felt euphoric.

The whole thing was mad. Going over to the other side, masquerading as a working boat, mingling with the fleet under the noses of the

Germans. It was the stuff that boy's adventure books were made of, the sort of thing he had loved to read about as a child.

That, he realised, must be why the idea appealed to him so much. He had always suspected that, in some ways, he had never grown up.

He laughed out loud. What the hell did it matter?

He adored the idea, he couldn't resist it. He couldn't wait to be frightened out of his wits and exhilarated at the same time. It was what he'd been waiting for all his life.

10

David curled his body up into the foetal position and thought about a field full of flowers. Flowers got him off to sleep faster than anything else. Some days he didn't need to think of anything, he just fell asleep the moment he lay down on the wooden boards. But when he was in pain it was different. It was usually his stomach which gave him trouble; sometimes the pain was awful. But today it was his knee; heavy rain had made the quarry treacherous and he had fallen heavily, twisting his knee and splitting open the skin. So today he needed to think of something, and it was best to think of flowers.

The sounds of the hut did not bother him. The continuous moaning and sighing, the sounds of suffering, the coughing and rasping of breath did not touch him at all. His ears heard the sounds but his mind cut them out, because his mind did not want to hear them.

He lay still, concentrating on the flowers, ignoring the pain, waiting for the escape into unconsciousness. Sleep was the one thing he looked forward to: it was God-given, miraculous, a gift from heaven. He waited for a long time, and then the sleep came at last, drifting in like fog out of a valley.

His mind was closed to sounds – yet he heard. He heard the sudden clatter of a stick being run along the side of the hut. Everyone heard it. Even before the door of the hut was opened men were getting off the wooden bunks and standing up, their faces impassive, their eyes staring disinterestedly at a point on the opposite wall.

Automatically David climbed down from the flat wooden shelf that was called a bunk – it was the top tier of three – and stood in the passage that ran the length of the hut. He felt nothing, showed nothing. He concentrated on standing upright despite the pain in his knee.

Two of the *Prominente* marched in, beating their sticks loudly against the door until all three hundred men were standing silently. There was no moaning or sighing now; the *Prominente* beat you if you made too much noise.

'You will wait!'

So they waited. David stared at the wall opposite and thought of the flowers again. The field was very large and quite overgrown with tall grass. But rising from the grass were tall poppies, brilliant red and moving gently in the breeze. A stronger wind came rippling across the grass, turning the colour of the grass from green to yellow, and bowing the poppies' heads over, as if in shame ...

David liked to concentrate on a different picture each day. From the moment he reached the quarry in the morning until he lay down to sleep at night, his body crying for rest, he liked to develop a picture, to find each small detail and fit it in place, until the composition was complete.

Otherwise he did not bother to think at all. Thinking was a great mistake. Those who thought of their past, of things they had lost, of families they were unlikely to see again: those were the ones who suffered.

David had been in Dachau almost a year. Soon after his arrival he learnt that you survived only by living each moment as it came, second by second. It was important to question nothing, challenge nothing, desire nothing. If you desired such things as freedom, food, clean water, you simply went mad.

He also learnt not to get angry. He wasn't angry now at being disturbed from his sleep. Anger was pointless. You just lived each second, each minute as it came ...

They had taken him first to Sachsenhausen. After two days they put him on a train and transferred him here, to Dachau. They had been the worst, those first few days; afterwards everything had seemed almost bearable. On the train each truck was crammed tightly with people. There was no food or water. When finally the door of the truck was opened and David, blinking in the strong light, saw that some had died and were being piled at the side of the track, he began to realise that you must live each minute, second by second, without thought, without question.

The most difficult thing was understanding the system and the rules – understanding how to survive. Oddly, the SS were the easiest to deal with. They liked order, numbers that tallied and obedience. One could cope with that. On arrival there had been prisoner registration. They had waited, the two thousand Jews off the train, in a long line. They had been allowed to sit until it was their turn to stand and advance to the desk of one of the four clerks sitting in the middle of the central compound. Their names, professions, and the details of their parentage were all carefully typed on forms; they were issued with a number; then they passed on to delousing and uniform issue.

Order and numbers: one could cope with that.

It was the *Prominente*'s rules that were impossible because they had none. They had been hand-picked by Himmler, these *Prominente*, from jails across Germany. They were all serving long sentences, for violent crimes mostly. It was said that the majority had been here since 1933 when Himmler personally created this, his showpiece, his first concentration camp.

The *Prominente* had no rules. They kicked, beat, hacked . . . sometimes they pushed men off the highest point of the quarry and watched them fall to their deaths. If you worked too slowly they might shoot you – or they might drop a heavy stone on your foot, or club you, or beat you round the head. They loved their work, these men. They picked people at random. You never knew who would be next. *That* was their secret: there was no order, no pattern, just uncertainty and fear. You never knew what might happen. But if you were clever you learnt not to care. It might be you, it might be your neighbour. Some weeks before, two men – David had not known them – had stood together at the top of the quarry, embraced briefly, and jumped to their deaths. It had been their own choice. It seemed to David that the gesture was noble, something fine and clean in the stinking cesspit of the camp. Those men, by choosing to die, had placed themselves high, high above the contemptible creatures who ran the camp and dared to call themselves human beings.

David envied the two men their courage. It was a courage he lacked. But then he'd probably die soon anyway. If you didn't die at the quarry, dysentery or disease got you. David's bunk-mate had died of typhoid the day before; that's why there'd been room on the bunk for David to curl up.

David had probably caught the disease already. The thought didn't bother him too much. When it came to living or dying, he didn't care much either way.

The *Prominente* shouted, 'Attention!'

David made the effort to bring his heels together and stand straight. He reckoned he could stand another five minutes at the most. That should be enough.

Two SS officers came in. They wore the insignia of the Death Head battalion. One referred to a list clipped on to a board and said, 'Stand forward the following: Abraham, Freymann . . .'

David stepped forward. His heart was hammering hard against his ribs. Perhaps . . .?

Perhaps, dear God, this is the end.

An overwhelming regret came over him: a regret for everything that had been taken away from him – his beloved little rabbit, his home, his work. Everything he had ever cared about. *I loved it all so much.*

The other names had been read out – there were only five of them – and now the prisoners fell into line and followed the SS men out of the hut. The procession made its way quickly across the compound.

David tried to keep up, but the knee slowed him down. He began to lag behind. He suddenly thought: So what? If he was to die anyway, what difference did it make if it was now or five minutes later against a wall outside the compound?

The thought calmed him and he stopped trying to keep up.

He was getting used to the idea of dying. His first response had been emotional, the response of a man who had something to live for. But now, as he limped painfully along, he could see the rational side of it. There was nothing to live for. Death would, after all, be a merciful release – his stomach trouble was getting worse and sometimes he sicked up blood. A bleeding ulcer probably. The work at the quarry had been getting more difficult for him: he was breathless, weak and more prone to fall. Each day the effort of working, of pushing his body to do things it was no longer capable of doing, was more agonising.

One of the SS men had turned and was looking down the short line of walking men. He saw David, now ten yards behind. David thought: He'll probably club me.

But the SS man did not stride angrily towards him. Instead he waited.

David struggled on. When he came level with the soldier he braced his body for a blow. Three more steps and he was past. There was no blow. Through the corner of his eye David saw that the SS man was behind him, following slowly. He seemed quite happy. Good Lord, David thought, whatever next?

They passed through the main gates and approached a side compound surrounded by a single wire fence. There were three huts inside, all of them quite new and in good condition – raised off the ground and fitted with windows. They were like barracks, David realised. Why had they been brought here? For interrogation?

Surely not after all this time. Perhaps for notification of a transfer. But one was never *told* of such things . . .

David thought: Whatever it is, they won't kill us here.

They waited outside one of the huts. David counted the prisoners in the group. Yes, seven in all. He recognised one: Meyer. Meyer had also been a scientist, a very important one and director of a large laboratory. Meyer looked terrible. The skin of his face and chin hung in folds, and he had the stoop of an old man. The striped uniform bagged out from his emaciated body. He was no more than fifty-five; he looked seventy.

I must look just as old, thought David. He too had lost weight so fast that the skin around his body was loose and wrinkled.

'In!' It was one of the SS men.

They filed into the hut and looked about them. The inside was clean and well fitted, the wood bright and new and sweet-smelling. Along the sides of the hut were wide benches with chairs in front of them. There were also three desks, a filing cabinet, and several typewriters. An interrogation centre? An office? It could be anything.

'Be seated!'

The prisoners looked around in surprise. You were not usually asked to sit down. One prisoner sat on the floor. The SS sergeant snapped, 'On the seats! The seats!'

When they were sitting down, an officer came in, and behind him, a soldier carrying a heavy object under a cover. The object was placed on a bench.

The officer faced them, his body erect, his manner efficient. 'Under the direct orders of Reichsfuehrer-SS Himmler, this laboratory is to function forthwith! You, as prisoners of the Reich, are to serve in it to the fullest of your ability.'

David stared, dumbfounded. They were to *work* here! It was incredible. The significance of Meyer's presence suddenly dawned on him. Another top scientist . . . It must mean *scientific* work. Incredible!

The officer was saying, 'You will work on projects that will be assigned to you. Your first is here.' He indicated the object on the workbench. 'We have obtained a device from an enemy aircraft. You are to dismantle it, examine it and analyse your findings. We must know what it does, how it does it, and the way to produce it.'

David's heart lifted with hope. This was a genuine scientific project, requiring careful analysis . . . And by skilled scientists like him and Meyer. That meant they would be treated as special prisoners and not returned to the main camp.

Yet a part of him waited, listening carefully. Nobody who survived in this place ever believed what they were told. One must always wait and see. There could be a catch somewhere. There usually was.

The officer continued, 'Now, you are all qualified in this type of electronics, is that correct?'

Nobody was likely to admit they weren't, David thought wryly.

'Your leader will be –' he looked at his list '– Meyer. You will work under him. You will obey him. Is that understood?'

They stared blankly. No-one dared to speak.

'You will ask Sergeant Klammer for any equipment you may need. This project is of great importance. Herr Himmler himself is in personal control, you understand. You will work with all speed and concentration. You will produce results that will be of the highest excellence. Any questions?'

There was silence. Questions were not usually encouraged, they had got out of the habit of asking them. The officer nodded and was turning to leave, when a voice said, 'Yes, I have a question.'

David looked round nervously. It was Meyer. He was standing, looking straight at the officer. Silly old fool, David thought, why did he have to open his mouth! All eyes swivelled back to the officer. But there was no irritation on his face, no anger. Instead there was a slight pause and the officer said, 'Yes?'

Heads turned back to Meyer. The old man said, 'To work efficiently, we will need better quarters and better rations. I cannot have half my team down with disease and malnutrition.' His voice was steady and surprisingly clear.

David thought: My God! You amazing old man. What a nerve.

The eyes returned to the officer. He was nodding. 'Agreed.'

Just like that.

Then they were left alone to make a list of their technical requirements.

They sat in a group round Meyer and looked at each other, searching each other's faces for confirmation of what they couldn't yet believe. One man – his name was Richter – was sobbing violently, his head down on his knees, overcome by the improbability of it all.

David was still looking for the catch, and at last he had it. When they had analysed the device, when the work was done, suppose there were no more of these projects? What would happen then? They wouldn't be kept here. No, they would be taken back to the main camp, back to the quarry. It would be twice as bad, having to go back.

And yet . . . the work would take several weeks, maybe months . . .

And a month in this place was a very long time indeed. Long enough to start hoping that it would last for ever . . .

It didn't occur to David that there was anything wrong in wanting to work until Meyer said, 'Whether or not we feel it is *right* to be involved in this project, we have no choice –'

The moral aspects hadn't entered David's mind. Here in this camp matters of principle were irrelevant, ridiculous even. You didn't consider whether things were right or wrong: if you did you would die of outrage. Wrong –? The idea had never occurred to him. Did it bother him, that he would be aiding the Nazis against their enemies? Did it matter when Jews were fighting for their very survival?

The answer was very simple. It came to David when his clean new uniform was issued to him, when he was able to take his first real shower in a year, when he had his first decent meal in as many months, and when he saw the sleeping quarters – clean, fresh, with individual bunks and a flushing lavatory. Then everything was very simple. You knew what you had to do: you had to survive. If you refused to work, someone else would take your place. A single gesture of defiance would change nothing.

That night, as he lay on his clean, sweet-smelling bunk in the sleeping quarters, he wept a little. Mainly from relief, but also from pity, both for himself and for his fragile pathetic hopes for the future, rekindled after so long. He thought of Cecile and Ellen and tried to imagine what their lives were like without him. It was more than a year since he'd seen them.

When finally he fell asleep he dreamed that he invented a magical device which would win the war for Germany. Suddenly he was a hero, he was freed from the camp and given the Iron Cross with Oak Leaves. But when he looked at himself he discovered, with horror, that they had given him an SS uniform. He told them it was a mistake and tried to tear it off, but the black cloth was stuck to his skin and as he tore at it, his flesh came away in his hands . . .

He woke with a start, his heart beating wildly. He thought: Is what I'm doing so bad? But no, it couldn't be, it really couldn't be. What would be bad would be to give his secret away; the small package of microfilm: *that* would be unforgivable.

The next morning, after roll call, David asked to collect something from his old hut. It was a request that would have been inconceivable two days before, but now they let him go.

When he got to the hut it was empty; the able-bodied had left for the quarry and the night's sick had been taken to the infirmary, euphemism for the hut which housed the rank stench and hopelessness of death and disease.

When he was sure he was quite alone he went behind the door and, using an old metal food bowl, scraped at the hard earth floor. He didn't get the right spot at first and had to search over a wider circle until, at last, his hand closed over the small package. He pushed the earth back into the hollow and stamped it down. Then, wedging the package under his arm, he walked back to the special compound. He hid the package behind the lavatory cistern in the sleeping quarters.

Then he went to work.

It was some sort of radar jamming device, that was obvious. But determining how it worked, and which type of German radar transmitter it was designed to jam, took longer. They split the device into twenty units and each took some pieces to analyse.

After two weeks they were getting somewhere. The device seemed to be aimed at the Freya early-warning system, which worked on a frequency of 125 megacycles and was capable of detecting enemy planes at a distance of seventy-five miles. David knew all about it. He should do – the Freya had been developed by the Gema Company.

As he worked on his section of the device David began to wonder how the British had discovered the existence of Freya and its frequency. Freya was a large unit fixed to the ground, it was not something that could be captured or examined by spies. They must have more sophisticated detection equipment than anyone had thought. But then, David realised, he was out of touch . . . *everyone* here was. It was a year since long-term research had stopped, a year since scientists had been called up or sent away to camps.

But David's thoughts went further: if the British could detect radar, then they themselves must be capable of developing it . . . The conclusion was inescapable. He discussed it with Meyer.

The older man said briefly, 'Yes, I expect they have radar by now.'

'To stay ahead Germany should have continued her research, then,' David said.

'Yes, in this business to stand still is to fall behind.'

'But there is still some development going on?'

Meyer exclaimed, 'No! As far as I can gather, we're all they have. Ironic, isn't it?'

David turned to him, amazed. 'Surely they've kept some laboratories going?'

'Oh, very few. And nothing of importance. I asked for detailed reports of any work that had been going on while I – in my absence. They were not able to give me anything. I tell you, we are Germany's principle electronics development laboratory now.' And Meyer laughed drily, 'We're cheaper this way, you see. No salaries to pay.'

David stared at the bench. For the first time he began to appreciate the importance of what they were doing. He asked, 'What are we going to tell them? I mean, when we give them our findings?'

Meyer said simply, 'We're going to tell them what we've found. But –' he lowered his voice '– we are not going to draw their conclusions for them. Let them discover the hard way that the British have radar. I am not going to tell them. Nor are you.'

David shook his head. 'No, I won't tell them.'

The knowledge made David feel better. It was only a small act of omission, but at least it was something positive, some small act of defiance.

David looked up from his work again. 'By the way, who are we reporting to? Is it really Himmler?'

'I believe so. But copies also go to other departments, including the Chief Scientist's.'

'Who is –?'

Meyer looked at him in surprise. 'Why Schmidt, of course.'

Nothing changes, David thought. He wished it didn't matter to him that it was Schmidt, but it did. It made his stomach twist.

After a month they handed over their second stage results. David began to wonder how much longer they could spin out their work – another two weeks, four at the most. The lab had the air of permanence about it, yet it was impossible to believe that anything was permanent in Dachau . . .

The thought of returning to the main compound haunted him, as it haunted everyone. The seven of them were relatively healthy now. They had warmth and security. They had hope. It was terrifying, to have so much.

There were several other laboratories, David discovered, one was run by the SS Health Institute, another by the Luftwaffe Research Bureau. You didn't know what was done in them: you didn't ask such things in case the answer sickened you. These labs also seemed permanent, but you never knew about that either . . .

David remembered that Himmler had a passion for specialised knowledge: that explained all the different labs. Before the war Himmler had organised archaeological digs, to prove some obscure theory, David couldn't remember what exactly. Something about purely Germanic races being the forerunners of the Teutonic knights. The man was crazy. That he'd reached such high rank said a lot about the system.

A week later the workload was growing lighter and the scientists grew nervous. It would be difficult to spin things out much longer.

Then, like manna from heaven, another object was delivered to the laboratory. This time they all exchanged smiles.

Like the first device this object was to be taken apart and analysed. With delight David and Meyer realised that it was something quite new, something they could only guess at. It would take weeks to understand properly.

They had been reprieved.

Sergeant Klammer shouted, 'Assemble!'

David looked up from the bench and felt a jump of alarm. Sergeant Klammer never interrupted them when they were working. It must be something out of the ordinary.

Sergeant Klammer waited impatiently while they got up and gathered in a group in front of him.

When he spoke, it was with such emphasis that spit flew from his mouth. 'You will cease work for the time-being, and tidy the laboratory. Within an hour it must look perfect. Then you will prepare answers to any questions that might be put to you concerning your work. Is that clear?'

Meyer nodded. They were dismissed. When Klammer had gone they turned questioningly to Meyer.

Meyer shrugged. 'Don't ask me.'

David thought: It must be Himmler. It was the only person it could be. He had been to the camp before. It was his creation: he liked to take a personal interest in it.

When the preparations were done they waited. They were denied permission to collect their midday meal, so they went without. Nor were they permitted to carry out any work which might make the lab untidy.

By three in the afternoon David felt faint. His stomach had got used to having food regularly, and it didn't like going without. His ulcer started to throb dully: soon the throb would grow into an angry pain.

At four they were still waiting.

Finally Klammer burst in. 'Attention!'

They stood up and stared fixedly at the opposite wall. One tries to look anonymous, David thought: faceless but servile; unimportant yet valuable. You look like they want you to look.

There were voices and the noise of feet on the steps. A group of men entered the hut. David stared at the wall, but from the corner of his eye he saw the black uniforms of high-ranking SS officers.

The group advanced into the hut. Someone laughed loudly. David thought: They've just had a good lunch.

As they came into his field of vision, David took a surreptitious look. Most were senior officers: he did not know their faces. Except – yes, Himmler. He recognised him from photographs. He was small, with close-cropped hair and a weak chin. His eyes were pale and cool behind rimless spectacles. He looked harmless, like a bank clerk.

There were others, some in civilian clothes. David glanced at them. He saw a face he knew.

It was Schmidt.

Schmidt was hanging back in a corner, looking uncomfortable. He took an occasional look at his surroundings, at the bare walls and simple equipment, with slight distaste. David thought: Well might you look uncomfortable, my friend. Schmidt hadn't spotted him yet. David watched him, waiting for the moment when he would, but Schmidt was keeping his eyes away from the prisoners' faces. David felt vaguely disappointed.

Himmler was strolling down the room, nodding as pieces of the enemy devices were shown to him. Then he turned and searched for someone. His eyes fell on Schmidt and he smiled slightly. He beckoned the Chief Scientist towards him.

There was total silence.

'Herr Schmidt . . .' Himmler's voice was surprisingly soft, almost gentle. 'I trust you are pleased with what we have arranged here.'

Schmidt spoke in a near whisper. 'Yes, it seems most satisfactory.'

Himmler smiled benignly, like a kind schoolmaster. 'Well, I'm sure you will want to speak to some of the prisoners about their work. So please go ahead.'

Schmidt stared uncertainly.

Himmler made a small bow. 'Yes now, by all means. We are quite happy to wait.'

Schmidt looked unhappily around him, hoping for an escape. He focused on Meyer and stared hard. Then recognition sprang into his eyes and he relaxed visibly. David thought: Of course, he knows Meyer well. Schmidt went up to Meyer, and soon they were examining a cathode tube captured from a British bomber. A buzz of conversation sprang up around the room.

David wondered what had gone on there between Himmler and Schmidt. Perhaps Himmler was doing Schmidt a favour, and didn't want him to forget it. Perhaps Schmidt had been desperate for scientists and had been forced to ask the SS to provide them. You would think that the SS would be embarrassed to use Jews, the inferior race. But no: Himmler was obviously delighted with the laboratory. It was Schmidt who was uncomfortable here.

Schmidt was standing in front of him. 'Freymann . . .'

He was looking startled and David suddenly realised it was his physical appearance which Schmidt found so surprising.

Schmidt dragged his eyes down to the bench. 'And what have you been working on?'

David explained, as simply and briefly as possible. Schmidt seemed satisfied, and began to turn away. But then he paused and said, 'We looked into that shortwave radar idea again, that one you kept pressing. We established once and for all that it was not possible to develop it, nor indeed *wise*. It would be grossly inefficient.'

He was waiting for David to comment, but David stared past him and did not reply. He did not know what to say. Schmidt added irritably, 'It was a waste of time and money to research it. But of course, *you* knew best, didn't you?'

David said, 'Yes, it was a mistake. I see that now.'

The party began to leave, their boots shuffling across the wooden floor, their voices loud and raucous. Himmler was enjoying a joke with one of his junior officers, his lips pulled back in a pleasant smile. He had obviously enjoyed his day at Dachau.

As the door closed and silence fell, David sat down wearily on his chair. He felt terribly depressed.

To think he had worked willingly for these people. It made him feel ashamed. It had been vanity, really; wanting to show how brilliant he was, wanting to impress. Of course, he'd talked himself into believing he'd done it for the state and was working for a great common good which touched everyone equally. He'd separated the state – the people – from the Nazis. But he'd been quite wrong. The people, the state, the Nazis were all one. You only had to look at Schmidt to see that. How else could a scientist, a *thinking* man, visit this place and be untouched.

Vanity. It was leading him on even now. It was pricking him over the shortwave radar and that remark of Schmidt's. How he'd love to prove to Schmidt that he was wrong. How he'd love to show him!

Pure vanity.

Shaking his head, he got slowly to his feet and went back to work.

11

The staff car slowed to a crawl as it negotiated the wide streets of a town. The change of pace made Doenitz wake up and look out of the window.

His staff officer, a young man called Schneider, said from the front of the car, 'This is Morlaix, sir. We are approximately forty minutes from Brest.'

Doenitz nodded and stared at the monotonous procession of houses and shops. All French towns looked alike to him. He closed his eyes again. He often catnapped, particularly on long journeys. It helped to clarify his mind when he was working out difficult problems.

But, though he'd been over it time and time again, he could find no solution to his greatest problem: this early war with Britain.

When war was declared he'd had a meagre fifty-six U-boats of which only twenty or so were suitable for the Atlantic. Six months later he was down to a dangerously low total of thirty-two . . .

Only this miracle, the occupation of France, had saved the German war effort.

Doenitz stared out of the window at the Breton countryside and blessed the marvellous turn of fortune which had given him the long west coast of France and unlimited access to the Atlantic. It was everything he could have asked for. His boats no longer had to return to Germany round the north coast of Scotland and run the gauntlet of the shallow North Sea. Now they could reach their hunting grounds more safely and much, much quicker. Just three months after the occupation, Doenitz had transferred two flotillas to Lorient and a third here to Brest.

The car turned a corner and Doenitz glimpsed the sparkle of water in the distance. He looked at his watch. They must be nearing Brest.

Doenitz said to Schneider, 'Please give me the details of the programme.'

There was a rustling of papers and Schneider said, 'Sir. At 1230 there will be lunch in a restaurant adjacent to the dockyard. At 1430 we meet Herr Dorsch, the architect from the Todt Organisation, and tour the dockyard. At 1600 we have a general review meeting with the Naval Commander, Brest. Also you will wish to meet U-319 when it returns. The last ETA we received was 1530.'

Doenitz nodded. 'Very well.'

U-319 was commanded by Kapitanleutnant Fischer. Fischer was a good man. He had done especially well on this patrol. Doenitz remembered the brief radio signal received at HQ in Paris yesterday. It had reported six ships sunk. Six! And by one boat during a five-day patrol. It was remarkable. Yet many of the other boats were achieving great successes too. The average sinkings per U-boat per day were way up. September should be a record month, with at least fifty ships sunk.

Fischer already wore the decoration of the Iron Cross of the Knight's Cross, First Class. Doenitz would present him with the Oak Leaves this afternoon. In the U-boat Arm they did not wait for boards of senior officers to approve awards; decorations were given immediately, on the dockside, when emotions were running at their highest and the men could share the recipient's moment of glory.

The car was travelling along the edge of a wide estuary. The occasional farmhouse had given way to a string of small villas: they were coming into Brest.

Doenitz considered the rest of the day's programme: the planning session with the Todt Organisation man should be straightforward. It was a matter of discussing the construction of the necessary dockyard modifications. Work was already in progress. They were using Polish labour apparently, and Poles always worked hard.

The staff meeting would be the usual mixture of optimism and resignation. The staff did not bother – or maybe, Doenitz wondered, they did not dare – to ask for the one thing they knew he could not provide: more boats.

Only six new U-boats were being launched this month; in August it was a disastrous two. It had been the same in May, June, and July ... Not enough even to replace losses!

The High Command always told him it was a matter of resources – what they really meant was that everything was going into Goering's precious Luftwaffe.

They were descending into the dockyard area. The car swept in through some large stone gates and approached an ugly grey stone building over which flew the flag of the Third Reich and the ensign of the Kriegsmarine. Waiting on the steps of the building were the commander of the 1st U-boat Flotilla and his staff. An ordinary seaman was keeping a tight rein on the flotilla's mascot, a goat draped with the flotilla's insignia. Doenitz was pleased. Back in 1935 this flotilla had been the one and only U-boat flotilla, and Doenitz himself had been its commander. Doenitz remembered with pride that the men themselves had thought them up, the insignia and the mascot.

Immediately the greetings were over they went to the restaurant. The lunch was indifferent. Doenitz considered French food to be very overrated. The wine, however, was excellent, though he drank very little.

He cut the lunch short and they started the tour of the dockyard early. Brest was a well-developed port, as one would expect of one of France's major naval bases, and considerable repair facilities already existed. It was a question of making modifications, Dorsch explained. The larger drydocks needed to be adapted to take two U-boats at a time; also more engineering shops and welding facilities would have to be created.

'How long will the work take?' Doenitz asked.

'Eight weeks at the most.'

'Good.' Once the work was done another flotilla could be moved to Brest from Kiel. Doenitz wanted as many boats as possible here, where they would be most effective.

As the party walked slowly back towards the cars the distant drone of a plane sounded high in the sky. Everyone looked up.

'One of ours.'

Doenitz nodded. So it should be. Goering had promised air supremacy: he'd better deliver it otherwise here in port the U-boats would be totally vulnerable to air attack. Rumour had it that the air battle with Britain was not going so well.

He turned to the architect. 'Herr Dorsch, how long would it take to create sail-in bunkers for my boats? Ones that would be invulnerable to air attack?'

Dorsch was taken by surprise. 'Oh? Er, I would think – allowing for the fact that the roof would have to be massively thick – my goodness, yes, very thick indeed ... er, I would say, at least six months. All the concrete ... all the labour. How many boats would need to be protected at once?'

'Ten, twelve, more if it was possible.'

'It would be ... a massive project.'

'But possible?'

'Oh yes! Most certainly!'

Doenitz was pleased. If the air battle was lost then at least his boats would be safe in port.

That left one really vulnerable point: the run across the Bay of Biscay. It was here, in the approaches to his new French bases – Brest, Lorient, La Palice and St Nazaire – that his boats were most exposed to enemy air patrols. Rather than search the open Atlantic, it was easier for the British to wait for departing or returning boats in the Bay.

He made a mental note to ask at the staff meeting about the current state of enemy air activity. What the U-boats really needed was proper air cover. But they never got it, Goering saw to that.

Back at headquarters the flotilla commander, Korvettenkapitan Scheer, was waiting and the meeting began promptly.

The routine reports of successes, losses, and mechanical breakdowns were read out. The U-boat quotient – the average tonnage sunk per U-boat per day – was going up monthly. Everyone was pleased.

'But soon it will go up very much more,' Doenitz said. He explained that, as soon as another flotilla could be based on the French coast, they would have enough boats to reintroduce properly organised wolf pack tactics. The wolf pack would increase kills dramatically. Doenitz also promised first-class intelligence to help locate convoys.

Then they looked at the problems. Scheer, the flotilla commander, was most concerned about air attacks. The RAF had taken to carrying – and dropping – depth charges. And as Doenitz had foreseen, many of the attacks were being made in the Bay of Biscay.

'But the boats manage to dive in time?' Doenitz asked.

'Yes,' Scheer agreed, 'but sometimes it's closer than we'd like. In bad visibility the enemy never find us, of course. But in thin cloud they often see us first and, attacking from down-wind as they do, well . . . Our men neither hear them nor see them until it's almost too late. And with these depth charges . . .'

'But a good look-out solves the problem?'

'Well – yes,' admitted Scheer.

'That's the answer, then, isn't it?' Doenitz said a little impatiently. 'And as many boats as possible should sail at dusk to benefit from the cover of darkness. Any other suggestions?'

There was a short silence, then someone said, 'Any chance of getting the magic eye?'

A few U-boats had been fitted with a large and cumbersome radar device just before the war, but the results had been so poor the idea of having radar in U-boats had been dropped and the sets removed. Since then all research into small sets had ceased.

Doenitz replied, 'No. There will be no radar. Tests prove that sets small enough to fit into our boats would be impossible to develop.' He remembered the Chief Scientist's report: it had been quite definite.

There was a knock at the door and a junior officer came in and saluted. 'Sir, U-319 has entered port. Estimated arrival time is 1610.' Doenitz looked at his watch. Fifteen minutes. He smiled. 'Good! Let's get down there.' He got to his feet and led the way out of the room. He always loved meeting the boats and he tried to do so as often as possible. In the old days, when his HQ was attached to the U-boat base at Kiel, he could meet every boat at the end of every patrol. Now – well, it was impossible. His HQ was in Paris and his bases scattered around the coast of the European continent.

As he walked briskly towards the dock Doenitz called to Schneider, 'You have everything?'

The staff officer replied, 'Yes, Admiral.'

The small party arrived at the dockside. They still had ten minutes to wait. Doenitz sat on a bollard and gazed in silence across the wide expanse of Brest Harbour. He looked round only once, when the braying of the mascot interrupted his thoughts. He saw that, in addition to the band and the official guard of honour, at least a hundred officers and men had gathered. It was always the same: everyone always made the effort to come out and welcome a boat home. It was part of the remarkable loyalty and camaraderie that united his men. He never felt less than immensely proud of them . . .

Though there were some he couldn't help feeling especially proud of: his two sons, one already in the service, the other in S-boats.

Someone shouted and everyone looked up. The nose of U-319 appeared from behind a jetty. There was loud cheering from the assembled crowd. The band struck up the Kretschmermarch. Doenitz felt a lump in his throat. This occasion, this moment of emotion and relief and pride, never failed to move him. His men were the best in Germany, the best in the world. They deserved to return like this, in triumph, for they were the bravest of them all . . .

The crew lining U-319's deck cheered back, waving and shouting to the crowd on the dock. They were in high spirits: obviously everything had gone well. As the submarine manoeuvred alongside there was some cheerful banter between the crew and the crowd. Doenitz smiled; he encouraged informality at moments like this. He reflected that, because of his presence, the comments were probably quite subdued. He could see Fischer in the conning tower, his face lit by a wide grin. The goat brayed loudly and everyone laughed.

When the boat was secure and the gangway rigged, the chatter of voices died away, the band stopped playing and there was a hushed silence. Everyone had guessed what was to happen. The crew stood in line along the decks. Fischer appeared through a hatchway still in his U-boat uniform of plain blue overalls and soft white cap, took a last look at his boat, and walked down the gangway. Doenitz stood waiting at the end and, as Fischer stepped on to the dock, the two men faced each other, saluted and shook hands.

The crowd waited expectantly as Doenitz said a few words. Schneider then stepped forward, a small box in his hand, and opened it. Doenitz took out the simple iron cross with oak leaf on a long ribbon, and placed it round Fischer's neck. The two men saluted again, the band struck up a tune, and a great roar went up from the crowd. Scheer presented Fischer with a bouquet of flowers and the young U-boat commander, his face a picture of pride and joy, led Doenitz and Scheer aboard his boat to present his crew to their senior officers.

To complete the formalities Fischer then inspected and saluted the guard of honour.

Scheer was at Doenitz's elbow. 'Sir, would you like to attend the debriefing? Or would a copy of Fischer's report be sufficient?'

'I will attend if I may.'

'Of course, Admiral!'

The formal question had been asked. The reply given. But, Doenitz thought, if they hadn't asked me I would have invited myself anyway.

Fischer sat near the window, his yellow hair lit gold by the late afternoon sun. From time to time he glanced at the written log on his knee to remind himself of precise times or sequences of events. But for the most part he spoke from memory, his pale blue eyes fixed at a point high on the opposite wall, his mind back in the North Atlantic. He told first how, on their way to their designated patrol area, they had come across a small convoy, probably from the Mediterranean. They had sunk two of the ships before being chased off by a destroyer. They then continued to their patrol area.

Fischer went on, 'In company with U-253 and U-90 we arrived at the grid reference point at 0700 on the fifteenth. We fanned out and zigzagged in twenty mile legs, covering a corridor fifty miles wide across the expected path of the convoy. U-90 spotted them at 1900 hours, dead ahead. She reported the sighting to us by radio. I passed on the report to Command Headquarters. I then ordered U-253 to make her approach from the south and U-90 from the north. We ourselves would lay in wait dead ahead. At this stage it was impossible to gauge the speed of the convoy, or the pattern of its zigzag, but I ordered that there be no further communication between our boats until the action was completed, to lessen the risk of detection.'

Doenitz watched Fischer's abstracted face and was nostalgic for the time in 1915 when he himself had seen active service. Then he too had made reports like this: dispassionate, objective, but loaded with a multitude of things unsaid – fear, exhilaration, uncertainty. Would the convoy alter course at the last moment? Was it going faster than they had estimated? Which ship should they go for?

Fischer went on, 'We dived to periscope depth and manoeuvred to a position in front of the convoy and dead ahead of it. The convoy consisted of at least thirty ships, but it appeared to have a very small escort: we spotted only one frigate and three armed trawlers. Suddenly, as we waited, we saw the frigate detach herself from the convoy and steam away to the south. I thought she must have spotted U-253, but later I discovered that this was not in fact the case. We never found out why she dashed off in this way. We waited, keeping an eye on both the convoy and the frigate. At 2030 we spotted the frigate coming in to make a pass across the front of the convoy. Unfortunately, this pass would bring her very near to our position. I had a feeling the convoy was about to alter course and, though I had been planning to take us a bit further to the north, I had no choice but to dive. We stayed submerged for twelve minutes. We listened to the frigate pass then, using minimum speed, came to periscope depth again.'

Fischer paused, a look of exhilaration in his eyes. 'We could hardly believe it, but when we took a look around we discovered we had come up in the middle of the convoy!'

A ghost of a smile passed Doenitz's lips. It was indeed a remarkable stroke of luck! He could imagine the amazement and the excitement in the U-boat.

'There was a large tanker coming straight into the perfect target position. All we had to do was wait! However, since it was a very dark night and the convoy was well spread out, I decided to surface. There was a good chance of remaining unseen, and I wanted a more stable firing platform. We fired two torpedoes at the tanker. She went up straight away. We retreated so as not to be illuminated by the burning ship. Another ship came into target position. We got her with a single torpedo. Then we saw other ships on fire: U-253 and U-90 were obviously busy too. At this point the frigate came sniffing around so we went down to periscope depth, but she never found us. We continued to find targets in the centre of the convoy.'

Fischer looked down. 'We know to our certain knowledge that we sank four ships that night. We used only eight torpedoes.' There was a moment's silence. No-one liked the thought of ships being destroyed because men died, drowned or burnt alive.

'Finally, when the convoy had passed, we surfaced. Eventually we made radio contact with U-90 and U-253. They had scored four and six hits respectively. Thus we sunk approximately half the convoy.'

The senior officers exchanged glances of satisfaction. Doenitz nodded slowly. 'And so you were not detected by the enemy at any stage?' he asked.

'No, sir!' Fischer smiled. 'I don't think they had any *idea* of where we were. I believe that, when we're submerged, their Asdic can't distinguish the noise of our engines from those of the ships in the convoy. As long as we're sufficiently close to the ships, the Asdic won't pick us up.'

'I agree,' Doenitz said. 'Again, Kapitanleutnant Fischer, my congratulations on your fine achievement. At this rate, our tiny band of boats will win the war!'

They think I am just saying that, thought Doenitz, but it is absolutely true.

The debriefing was over. Doenitz poised himself to get out of his chair.

'Sir, perhaps I did not answer quite accurately just now.' It was Fischer.

Doenitz looked up sharply. 'Yes?'

'We did have an engagement with the enemy, but it was much later. Just sixty miles from Brest, visibility one mile, the lookout thought he heard an aircraft engine. Fortunately he was a man with exceptionally sharp ears. I must admit I did not hear it, though I was in the conning tower. I took no chances and ordered a crash dive. We were just in time. The last man down saw a Sunderland appear to the south. It was banking sharply towards us. When we were down we heard one bomb explode, but it was some way off. After that, nothing.' Fischer shrugged, 'It was a fluke. But it was lucky we had such an excellent lookout.'

'Yes. It was lucky.' Doenitz stood up. 'And it banked only when it saw you, this plane?'

'Yes, sir.'

'A fluke then.' Doenitz put out his hand. 'Goodbye, Fischer. And I look forward to hearing about your future patrols. May all of them be equally successful!' He leant forward and said in an undertone that no-one else could hear. 'It is a long time since the early days at Kiel, isn't it?'

Fischer grinned. 'Yes, sir.'

'A long time . . .' Doenitz turned away and strode out of the room.

12

The apartment was in a narrow street near the Porte d'Auteuil in the *seizieme*. It was small, plainly furnished, and in every way unremarkable. It was just what Vasson wanted. It was high time to move. He'd been in the other place six months, ever since the previous December when he'd started working for Kloffer. It had been too long. He moved in at noon and carefully unpacked the contents of two of his three suitcases. In the bedroom there was a single narrow wardrobe with just enough room for his suits. His shirts, casual trousers, pullovers and best underwear he folded carefully and placed in the drawers of a large chest in the corner. He put two mothballs in each of the drawers and another four in the wardrobe. He didn't want to get back and find all his best clothes peppered with holes.

He opened the third suitcase and checked the contents. One inexpensive badly-cut suit, three cotton shirts, three pairs of cheap casual trousers, socks, shoes, underwear – his working clothes.

He took out his wallet. Papers in the name of Lebrun, a hundred francs, and the special travel permit which he would destroy once he was over the border in Belgium. He looked again at the money: would it be enough? He couldn't think of anything he could possibly spend it on between now and the border. He had already paid six months' rent in advance and given the *concierge* a float to cover the electricity and any other bills that might turn up. No, he wouldn't need any more cash; anyway the less French money he had on him the better.

He looked at his watch. Three-thirty. Just time to go to Sèvres, then Clichy, and back by seven.

He shut the suitcase, placed it ready by the front door and left the apartment. He shouted a word to the *concierge* and went into the street. His car, a six-year-old Citroën, was three minutes' walk away. It was a habit, now, to leave his car at least two streets away from wherever he was living. Possessing a car was not so unusual, but having enough petrol to use it every day certainly was.

When he got to the car he went straight to the boot and unlocked it. The large leather grip was still there, as he knew it would be. It amused him to think of all the people who must have walked past the car in the last few hours without having the slightest inkling of what the vehicle contained.

He closed and locked the boot, and got into the car. Since the Occupation almost a year ago the traffic in Paris had thinned down considerably; the trip to Sèvres should take fifteen minutes at the most.

In fact he reached the Porte de Sèvres in five minutes and the Rue du Vieux Moulin in twelve.

Sèvres was a suburb on the south-west outskirts of the city. Vasson had chosen it because it was quiet, genteel, and, like everything else in his life nowadays, unremarkable. Rue du Vieux Moulin was a sleepy street of two-storey late nineteenth-century houses set back from the road in their own gardens. The villas, once impressive, now had the unmistakable air of decay, as if their once-affluent owners could no longer afford to keep them up.

Vasson drove the full length of the street to make sure that everything was quiet, parked in a nearby street, then, taking the leather grip from the boot, set off on foot for Number 22, Rue du Vieux Moulin.

A few moments later he wished that, for once, he had parked outside the house; the bag was heavy. But it was too late now.

He wondered if Madame Roche would be in. It didn't really matter either way: the old woman was incapable of a suspicious thought. You could go in with a mask over your face and blood on your hands and she wouldn't notice.

He reached the house at last and opened the gate in the low wall surrounding the austere garden, which was laid to gravel and shrubs. In the balmy air of the warm summer day, the house was quiet and most of the shutters drawn. The old woman was probably having a nap.

Vasson walked round to the side of the house where some steps led down to the semi-basement level. At the bottom of the steps was a door which he opened with a key. Inside, there was a passage with four rooms leading off it. The first, which must once have been a servant's room, was now a bed-sitter; the second was a primitive wash-room with a stone sink and lavatory; the other two were storage rooms.

Vasson went into the bed-sitting room, laid the leather bag on the bed, and listened for sounds from the upper floors. Still nothing. He crossed to the wardrobe and opened the door. He kept a spare set of clothes here, as well as two sets of papers which Kloffer didn't know about. The papers were strapped to the underside of a shelf at the bottom. They were still there.

He picked up the bag and, leaving the room, started down the passage towards the store rooms. It was dark and he had to feel his way along the wall. Finally he reached a door and, opening it, fumbled for the light switch.

The room was square and windowless except for four small ventilation grilles near the ceiling. Once it must have been stacked with wine but now only a few dusty bottles lay forgotten in an old rack. The room had an earthen floor which, because it kept the air cool, made it perfect for wine storage. The earthen floor also made the room perfect for storing articles like gold Louis and *demi-barres*.

Vasson locked the door and crossed the room. A wooden table straddled one corner. On it was some ancient photographic equipment: two developing trays, an enlarger, and five bottles of chemicals. Vasson had picked them up for a few francs in a pawnbroker's. Photography was what he was supposed to be doing when he locked himself in this room.

He moved the table and, taking a trowel from the leather bag, started to dig. He made a hole ten inches deep then, removing two small canvas sacks of coins and a solid bar from the bag, carefully buried them. He spent some time flattening the earth and beating it down with his feet before replacing the table.

That made two hundred thousand francs in gold. A tidy sum – but not enough, not enough by far.

It had taken months and months to wrest a decent wage out of Kloffer; even then it was in paper money and Vasson had been forced to go to the black market for gold. It had cost him dear. But gold it had to be; with inflation, paper money wouldn't be worth a *sou* in a couple of years. Then, in May, Vasson had finally persuaded Kloffer to pay him directly in gold. It didn't cost Kloffer anything – he and his friends were stealing vast quantities of the stuff – but it did save Vasson a lot of time and money.

He should have been paid in gold from the beginning, of course. It made him angry to remember how he'd had to beg, cajole and threaten to get what was, after all, only his due. He'd been shabbily treated, no doubt about that.

He replaced the trowel in the bag, closed the store-room door and went back to the bed-sitting room. He left six months' rent money on the bed with a note saying that he wouldn't be back for some time, and left. The old woman thought he was a commercial traveller.

The house was still quiet, the old woman probably on the point of getting up. It was the perfect place for a cache. But then it was bound to be: he'd taken a lot of time and trouble to find it.

The drive to Clichy took thirty minutes. The lock-up garage still had quite a lot of stuff in it – stockings, perfume and petrol – but there was just enough room for the car. He parked it and locked up carefully. As he walked towards the nearest boulevard he thought about the remaining stock and wondered whether it would be a good time to sell. But he couldn't make up his mind; he hadn't been following the market recently and he didn't know how prices were. What he *did* know was that new stock was almost impossible to come by; most of his old sources had dried up. Also ... what? He'd lost interest, that was what. The market bored him: it was too restricted and the profit too hard to come by. Besides, the big boys had moved in and begun to squeeze everyone out, just like they always did. Diversifying was the wisest thing he'd ever done.

He reached the Rue Jean Jaurès and looked for a *vélo-taxi*, but it was almost five-thirty, the rush hour, and the few that he saw were already occupied. He cursed and walked towards the nearest Métro at Porte de Clichy.

He hated the idea of taking the Métro: it was too – well, public.

Ever since the last operation he had kept away from crowds. He'd had a feeling, an indefinable but distinct feeling, that he was no longer safe. The project had been straightforward. He had bust a small escape line taking shot-down pilots from North-East France through Paris to Spain. The members of the line had been typically trusting and weak on security, but somewhere, somehow he'd disturbed something else. There was a loose end somewhere. He didn't exactly know what . . . But he was certain, absolutely sure, he was no longer safe. Someone was on to him. The word was out; it was time for him to go.

The Métro was even worse than he'd feared. He hated confined spaces and, after changing at St Lazare, the train was horribly crowded. The bodies pressed close against him and he shuddered with the beginnings of panic. He changed again at Miromesnil. The train was slightly less crowded this time, but he still had to stand. After a few moments he felt a tingling in his spine. It was a feeling he never ignored. Without moving his head he looked at the reflection of the other passengers in the window. A man behind him seemed to be staring at him. Vasson studied the face desperately. Did he know him? No. He was certain he didn't. He relaxed again. It was his nerves. He was imagining things. Christ, it really was time to get away.

He got back to the apartment in Auteuil at six-fifteen. He stripped off and washed the whole of his body. Washing always made him feel good. He lay on the bed, smoking thoughtfully, until six-fifty, then dressed. When the bell rang he picked up the suitcase, locked the apartment behind him, and slid the key under the *concierge*'s door.

A car was waiting at the kerb. It looked like a taxi, though Vasson knew it wasn't. Even the driver looked French. Vasson thought: Kloffer's learning at last.

Kloffer was sitting in the back, looking like a fat cat. Vasson sank on to the seat beside him. The car moved off and the German asked 'Any problems?'

'No.'

Vasson waited. Kloffer was here for a reason; he wasn't seeing Vasson off out of the kindness of his heart.

Eventually Kloffer said, 'This car will take you all the way to Brussels.'

'I thought –'

'We decided against the train. We don't want anyone to see you leave.'

Vasson shrugged. 'Very well.'

'I think you'll agree that it's wise . . .' Kloffer turned and looked at Vasson. 'Your old apartment – we caught someone waiting outside. He had a weapon. It seems he wanted to kill you.'

I knew it, Vasson thought.

Kloffer smiled. 'We don't want you dead when I've promised you to Brussels. They would think me *most* inefficient!' He giggled slightly.

Vasson was wondering where he'd gone wrong. He hated loose ends, he hated not knowing. He asked, 'Who was the man? The one who was waiting for me?'

'Oh, the brother of one of the girls we arrested last week.'

'Was he working on his own?'

'We don't know. He says nothing.'

Vasson cursed. That meant it would be unsafe for him to return . . . Not until he knew for sure. Damn. He said suddenly, 'I must know – whether he was on his own. Also if he had a description of me, and how he knew where I was living. Everything!'

'We will do our best.'

'You'd better. Otherwise –' *Otherwise I'm as good as dead.* 'Otherwise I won't come back here. You understand?'

'Indeed.' Kloffer looked quite happy about it. Vasson had the feeling that there was more to this Brussels trip than Kloffer was admitting to. Perhaps there was a deal. If so, Kloffer would never tell him the terms.

'Have you any more information about the Brussels operation?'

Kloffer shrugged. 'Not really. But apparently there is just the one organisation. It seems that they collect the airmen not only in Belgium but some in France too and send them all the way down to Spain. A long way – there must be hundreds of people involved. Yet we haven't succeeded in stopping them. Amazing. You'd think someone would talk!' He sniffed with irritation. 'Your operation against the Paris couriers – that was excellent while it lasted. But we have evidence that all the people we removed have been replaced. No, there's only one way to get these pests, and that is from Brussels. Otherwise we'll just go on wasting our time.'

'What's been tried so far?'

'I'm not sure – you must ask them. But I gather that attempts at infiltration have failed.' Kloffer looked pleased.

Ah, thought Vasson, so that's it. The Brussels people had failed; Kloffer was coming to the rescue with his own man. No wonder Kloffer wasn't shedding any tears. All the more glory for him.

They were approaching the Avenue Foch. Kloffer said to the driver, 'Drop me on the next corner.'

Vasson said, 'And the money? Are they clear about the method of payment? I want that agreed before I get there.'

'Yes, yes,' Kloffer said impatiently.

Gold was to be deposited in the Banque de Paris and the receipt slips sent to Brussels, poste restante. It was quite simple, Vasson thought, but you'd think I was asking for the bloody moon.

The car came to a halt and Kloffer opened the door. 'Goodbye. All success. I know that if anyone can do it, you can.'

Praise indeed. Kloffer was getting quite pleasant in his old age.

Kloffer got out of the car and leant in through the door. He was smiling, though Vasson noticed that his eyes were sharp as a cat's. Kloffer said softly, 'Oh, by the way, are you happy with your papers?'

He never usually enquired. Vasson was instantly suspicious. 'Yes, why?'

'I thought you might not like the name we chose.'

Vasson waited.

'Well, it's Paul Lebrun, isn't it? I thought you might not care for the Paul.' Kloffer grinned briefly and was gone. The car drew rapidly away and Vasson was thrown against the seat. He stared blindly ahead, unable to breathe, a vice around his heart.

Kloffer knew his name.

God!

He felt angry, then sick with fear.

Kloffer knew his name.

Kloffer must know that Vasson was wanted in Marseilles . . . Kloffer could blackmail him . . . Kloffer *was* blackmailing him?

Vasson tried to assimilate the awful fact into his brain, but it hurt, *it hurt.* And it was being vulnerable, the dreadful realisation that he could be pressurised – humiliated – that hurt the most.

Where had he gone wrong? How had Kloffer found out?

He didn't know, and he would never know unless Kloffer chose to tell him. And he was sure Kloffer *wouldn't* choose to tell him; instead the German would let the question fester in his mind. Yes, that was Kloffer's way.

He was sure of another thing too: the timing of Kloffer's little bombshell was carefully planned. The German wanted to remind Vasson who was in control; he wanted Vasson to come back afterwards, like a good boy.

Vasson shuddered with humiliation. To hell with Kloffer!

But even as he thought it he knew he had lost. Kloffer had him, just *there.*

As the car sped into the gathering darkness Vasson pressed his head into the corner, his face contorted with rage and bitterness, and thought: It's all so *unfair*. Why does it always happen to me? *Why me?*

At midnight the car stopped outside a cheap hotel. Vasson had no idea where he was, except that it was somewhere in Brussels. The driver said he'd been told to take Vasson there. The hotel wasn't expecting him. At first the proprietor said he had no rooms, then he decided he had one after all, but, being his best room, it would cost a bit extra. When Vasson saw the room he realised he'd been had again – the room was dreadful: depresssingly airless and none too clean. A single unshaded light hung from the ceiling. It was not his day.

For a few moments he sat on the bed and looked in despair at his surroundings. The room brought back memories of other squalid rooms: the ones in Montmartre, all shabby, all depressing; the ones in the Old Quarter, hot and claustrophobic; the bare cell at the Jesuit school, white and unspeakably barren; and – so long ago – that other room. *God* . . .

He undressed slowly and got into the bed. At least the sheets were clean.

Tomorrow he would spell it out to the Boches: no more cheap hotels, no more squalor. Lots of cash, lots of information, and no interference. In one way it was irritating to have to educate them, the way he'd educated Kloffer, but at the same time he was rather looking forward to it. It was a challenge, and he would win it, the way he'd won with Kloffer.

Except that Kloffer knew his name . . .

After a long time he fell asleep.

He was in the old lady's house in Sèvres, walking along the passage, when he saw that the door to the storeroom was open and the light on. There were voices inside. He tried to get to the door but he couldn't move. He looked down and saw he had weights on his feet. Then Kloffer came out. He was carrying the gold. Kloffer grinned and said, 'I knew it was here all the time! I knew! Goodbye! Goodbye!' Then Vasson's arms were grabbed from behind and he was dragged out. Kloffer called, 'They're going to cut off your head, isn't that interesting?'

They put him in a cell. It was like the one at the school: bare, soulless, destroying. Father Ignatius was leaning over him. 'Eternal Father, I confirm; Eternal Son, I confirm; Eternal Holy Spirit, I confirm. May the Lord forgive you, Paul, for you have sinned. Like your mother sinned.'

What had his mother done? What sin could be so terrible? He

heard himself ask, 'What sin? What sin?' and Father Ignatius shook his head gently and said, 'It is better that you do not ask, my son.' 'But why doesn't she come?' 'She doesn't choose to, Paul, and it's better that she doesn't.' 'But Father Francis told me she was dead.' 'Well, she is in a way, Paul.' 'I don't understand, I don't understand!' 'It is not for us to understand, my son, we must accept God's will – and with love in our hearts.'

I don't understand. I never have. Why doesn't she come to me? What has she done that is so terrible? Why did she beat me? *Why does she hate me so?*

I don't understand.

German efficiency was enough to drive anyone mad, with its rigid structures, its unyielding demands and its inevitable duplications. But it did mean everything got written down.

It was all there in the files. Every operation against the escape line which operated from Brussels. There was tons of it, much of it irrelevant, but Vasson wasn't complaining, although it took hours to sort out what was useful and what wasn't.

Generally, reports to be seen by senior officers were far too optimistic and evasive to be useful. Much better were the situation reports with limited circulation. Names, places, hypotheses, action to be taken . . . it was all there.

Gradually Vasson built up a picture. The airmen got themselves to a farm or whatever, presumably having buried their parachutes and any other evidence of where they had landed. The farmer harboured them, or quickly passed them on to someone who would. Then, as soon as could be arranged, they were picked up by the organisation proper. How were they transported? Impossible to say, but for the longer parts of the journey it was certainly by train. Several of the couriers arrested so far were young girls. Vasson could imagine them: innocent-looking, charming, pretty enough to distract if necessary. Yes, the system must work well.

The couriers were probably changed at Brussels and again at Paris and maybe a third time on the way down to the Spanish border. He wondered how careful they were: whether or not the couriers actually met and knew each other or whether they operated a cut-off system whereby the airmen were taken to a park bench by one courier and left there for ten minutes before the next came to pick them up.

He looked up the interrogation reports. Some of those arrested had talked, but they appeared to be small fry – collectors or minor couriers. None of them had known the names of the main couriers, those who must be in touch with the central organisers. Others hadn't talked even when they were about to die. Extraordinary how little value people put on their own lives.

The infiltration operations mounted so far had been amateurish – and that was putting it kindly. The SD had sent two of its men into the Belgian countryside dressed as Canadian airmen. They were found four days later, dead. It was no surprise to Vasson; the two men probably spoke English with a German accent and didn't know what maple syrup was. The line must have an interrogation centre somewhere, where airmen's credentials were checked. Well, even if they hadn't they certainly would now, after that little fiasco.

Another time a Belgian-born SD agent had infiltrated the line as a courier, had sprung his trap far too soon and managed to catch only two people. The agent had then run like hell out of Brussels and was never seen again. An amateur.

One operation had been quite successful, however. Twenty arrests were made. But Vasson couldn't find the details; the report was marked: Refer to Luftwaffe Intelligence. He must ask about that.

He looked at the current situation report: there appeared to be only two leads at present; a young girl, the sister of a girl in custody, plus an older woman whose address had been found in the apartment of a minor courier. Both women had gone to ground. Nothing about this surprised Vasson: the Gestapo had probably gone straight round to their homes in full view of all the neighbours and waited for them to return. Subtlety and patience were not the Germans' strong points.

He noted the names of all the suspects to date and took brief details of addresses, possible roles in the line, and probable leads. It didn't add up to much. In their usual blundering way the Germans had fouled up everything that might have been worth pursuing.

Vasson went back to Mueller's office. Mueller was his liaison man: quite senior, a colonel in the SD. For some reason Vasson didn't understand, here in Belgium escaping airmen came under the Nazi security service or Luftwaffe Intelligence, and not the secret police.

Mueller was pale and fat, rather like a large slug. He looked as though he had indigestion; from time to time he unhappily patted his obscene stomach which pressed relentlessly against the field grey cloth of his uniform. 'Well?' he asked impatiently. 'Have you seen everything you need to see?'

'I think so.' Vasson sat down, though he had not been invited to do so. Mueller would not object. Mueller, for all his arrogance and impatience, was not a problem: he was a realistic man. He wanted results and he'd made it clear he was prepared to pay for them. Vasson's anger at being put in the seedy hotel was forgotten when Mueller had agreed to all his requests.

Vasson said, 'But there is one thing. An operation involving Luft-waffe Intelligence. The report's not in the file.'

'Ah yes. That was a joint operation. Extremely successful. For a week or so we operated a loop in the escape line.'

'A loop?'

Mueller looked patronisingly at Vasson. 'Ah? You do not know? No, why should you. We invented the idea!' His fat face crinkled up in what Vasson realised was a smile. 'A loop is an extra link in the escape chain which the organisers do not realise is there and which we create to extract intelligence. We pretend we are Resistance interrogators who must check the bona fides of the airmen. We ask them to tell us everything about their units and operations so we can check the facts with London.' He shrugged. 'It works every time. During this last operation they told us everything . . . Most useful for the Luftwaffe and most useful for us too; we got several good descriptions of the people harbouring airmen. We made a number of arrests.'

Twenty to be precise. But, Vasson thought, they can never use that one again, not with this line anyway.

'One more thing,' Vasson said. 'Is the line in direct communication with Britain? Can they actually check the airmen's identities by radio?'

'We believe not. At one time we picked up clandestine radio transmissions from this area, but no longer . . . We must have got the operator.'

'So they have no contact . . .'

'But they have back-up from London; a department of the British Ministry of Defence, called MI9, sends them money regularly, and probably arms too. The British have a name for the line – they call it Meteor.'

'Meteor . . .'

Mueller sat upright and looked impatient again. 'Now! We have provided you with cash, we have provided you with information; what else do you require, may I ask?'

'A work permit in the name of Paul Lebrun. My occupation should be given as Engineer and the place of employment as some engin-eering works in, say Lyon. Then in brackets it should say: On second-ment duties to Wehrmacht.'

'You want to say you're working for the Wehrmacht?'

'That's right. I'll also need a special travel permit which allows me frequent journeys between my base in Lyon and the occupied territories.'

'That's all?'

'Yes.'

'Now!' Mueller said disparagingly, 'How exactly do you propose to bring off this amazing success that I am told you will achieve?'

'I don't know.'

Mueller's face showed uncertainty: he wasn't sure if Vasson was purposely misleading him or just being difficult. 'I suggest you inform me when you *do* have a plan.'

'Certainly. But for a few days I want to get to know the city and feel my way around.'

Mueller eyed him suspiciously. 'You will not start anything without informing me, will you, Lebrun?'

'No.'

As Vasson left, Mueller repeated, 'And you have no plan at all?'

Vasson shrugged. 'In good time. You didn't give me many leads ...'

Mueller nodded abruptly. 'Please report back in two days.'

Vasson hurried out, thinking: Like hell! He would report only when he was ready, and even then he wouldn't tell Mueller a damn thing about what he was doing. The Germans would only foul it up. Anyway he loved to have it all to himself; he hated to share it until the last possible moment.

His plan was the same as always: he had it all worked out. But this time it would take longer, he realised that; there were so many people involved, so many contacts to make. Yes, it would take time ... But he didn't mind; it added to the challenge and the excitement.

This one would be the best one yet, he felt it in his bones. This would be his greatest triumph.

13

Falmouth. At least it *should* be. Since the first invasion scare all the railway signs had been removed, so one had to use timetables and guesswork to decide your location. Smithe-Webb stepped off the train, sniffed the sharp, salty Cornish air and thought how wonderfully refreshing it was after the smoke and grime of London.

It *was* Falmouth: there was a naval staff car outside the station, waiting to take him to Helford. The major settled back in his seat and admired the rolling green countryside. He only wished he could get away from London more often. But his department of MI9 was based at the War Office in Whitehall and he hardly got away at all.

In his year at MI9 he'd heard a few whispers about Helford and the naval unit there – but nothing very definite. It was a clandestine outfit, and, although he'd guessed that they went over to what was known as the Other Side, he'd heard little else. He'd had few dealings with the Navy: almost all the Allied servicemen stranded in Europe – his customers, as he called them – were airmen and soldiers.

But since MI9 had asked for the Navy's help, Smithe-Webb had been finding out a bit more. The DDOD(I), the head of the Navy's Irregular Operations Division, had told him a bit about the Helford operations and, what was more important, had promised to help. He had, however, suggested that the major go down to Helford and talk to someone who knew the Other Side well, someone who could advise him on the practical problems his people were likely to meet. The inference was clear: the Navy could manage their end of the operation all right, but could MI9 control *theirs*?

Smithe-Webb took the point; that was why he was here.

After half an hour the road descended steeply towards the dull glint of water visible in the distance. They passed through a picturesque village and came to the banks of a wide river. The car stopped and Smithe-Webb got out. A launch with two ratings was waiting at the jetty and, as soon as he had climbed in, it set off towards a cluster of vessels moored in the main stream of the river. There was a large three-masted yacht which had a number of dinghies tied to it – some kind of mother ship perhaps; then, moored around it, four or five largish fishing boats. Most of them were painted regulation grey, but one had a strange combination of colours. Her superstructure and most of her topsides were grey, but her after end was bright scarlet with some kind of pattern on it. There were several men standing in a small boat, painting the scarlet with grey. The launch made a neat semi-circle and approached the many-coloured boat. As they drew near Smithe-Webb saw the shadow of a name on the stern. It read: *Marie-Claire. Brest.*

The launch came alongside and a rating threw a line to someone on deck. Smithe-Webb looked up and stared in amazement. The fellow was a sight: unshaven, dirty and dressed like a fisherman. If they were playing at pirates, Smithe-Webb thought, they certainly looked the part.

Smithe-Webb put a foot up on the rubbing strake and hoisted himself over the gunwale onto the deck. He looked expectantly at the piratical figure, but after making fast the launch's painter the fellow sauntered off down the deck.

Suddenly there was a voice from behind. 'Good morning!'

Smithe-Webb turned and was met by a pair of penetrating blue eyes and an outstretched hand. Like the other fellow, this chap looked a mess: his clothing was shabby and oil-stained, he had two days' growth of beard, and, if the major wasn't mistaken, his breath reeked of alcohol. Smithe-Webb asked uncertainly, 'Er – Lieutenant Ashley?'

'Yes, I'm Ashley. But, if it doesn't seem impolite, who on earth are you?'

Richard Ashley smiled ruefully. 'Sorry, didn't mean to be rude, but we've just got back and . . . we're not at our best. Come and have a cup of something. I'm not sure what we can offer you . . .'

'Not to worry,' said Smithe-Webb hastily. 'Don't want to put you out or anything.'

'No, no. Must find you something, This is after all a ship of His Majesty's Navy and traditions must be upheld . . .' He laughed and Smithe-Webb saw that, despite the smiling mouth, the face was strained and drawn.

Smithe-Webb followed Ashley down the deck. He noticed that two men were grafting a plank of wood into a gap in the gunwale and that the deckhouse was riddled with bullet holes. Ashley turned and caught his gaze. 'We were badly straffed. One dead and two wounded. We've never been caught like that before.' He led the way into the deckhouse and indicated that Smithe-Webb should take a seat. 'That's the problem with going down to the Bay: it's fine once you're there, looking like any other old fishing boat, but it's an awful long way there and back. We get some air cover on the way out, but . . .' He smiled thinly. '. . . well, it's awfully lonely on the way home.' He reached down into a locker and pulled out a bottle of cognac. 'Don't suppose you'd like a glass of this delicious brew?'

Smithe-Webb shook his head. 'A bit early for me.'

Ashley nodded. 'I'll order you a tea then – I think that's all we've got.' He opened the door and shouted down the deck. He came back in and smiled. 'For myself, I'm going to have a large one of these. One of the few perks of the job. The fishermen with whom we, shall we say, *trade*, they give us this stuff. And magic it is too!'

A minute later one of the crew brought the tea, which was dark brown and very sweet and had obviously been brewing for some time. Smithe-Webb gritted his teeth and took a sip. The tea was ghastly and he grimaced. Ashley was talking to the sailor about the repair work and didn't see.

Smithe-Webb took the opportunity to take a look at the lieutenant.

He reckoned the chap was somewhere in his late twenties, though he looked older, probably because of the tiredness. He was average-looking: of medium height, unremarkable features and, Smithe-Webb guessed, with a tendency to put on weight. But the blue eyes were extraordinary; you noticed them straight away. Another unusual thing was the way the man talked. His face was immensely alive and – what was the word? – magnetic. You couldn't take your eyes off him.

The sailor was asking a couple of questions. Like the rest of the crew he was fairly unkempt and Smithe-Webb noticed he had a strong foreign accent.

When the sailor had gone the major asked, 'Your crew, are they – RN?'

Ashley laughed. 'Most of them! The rest could be loosely described as on loan. Free French, ex-fishermen and very fine lads they are too.'

Ashley sat down, the brandy glass at his elbow, and lit a cigarette. 'I must apologise again for my rudeness. Quite honestly, I forgot you were coming. They did tell me, but you know how it is . . .!'

'Yes, I can imagine.'

'In this kind of operation, you ignore half the rules – and the other half don't apply. Orders never get written down . . . Besides which my memory is –' he laughed, '– not of the best!' Smithe-Webb felt sure it was perfectly adequate, but smiled nonetheless.

Ashley asked, 'So how can I be of help?'

Smithe-Webb said, 'Right. Perhaps I'd better tell you a bit about my department first. Basically, our job is to help our chaps to get out of Occupied Europe. Immediately after Dunkirk most of our customers were soldiers who got left behind after the evacuation. Quite a few made it back by getting help from the locals and making their way to neutral territory. Since then it's been mainly airmen, though we still get quite a few soldiers and even the odd sailor. Obviously it's pretty difficult for chaps to escape once the Germans have got them, but some do manage to get over the wire and our job is to try to make it easy for them once they're out. Having said that, by far the greatest number of our customers are evaders – men who've been shot down or whatever and have managed to keep *out* of German hands. We encourage the locals to look after them and get them back to us safely. Obviously I can't give you the details of how this is done . . .'

Ashley nodded. 'No, of course.'

'Our problem is that our present . . . er, methods . . . are under a lot of pressure, both from the Germans and from the sheer scale of the operations. The number of evading airmen is increasing and quite apart from not wanting to let our men fall into enemy hands, we *need* them. Those pilots are absolutely invaluable to the war effort. We have to get them back.' Without thinking Smithe-Webb sipped at the mug of tea and immediately choked.

'Bloody awful, isn't it?' Ashley smiled. 'But try and persuade Leading Seaman Evans to make it any other way and there'd be a mutiny. Change your mind and have a brandy?'

Smithe-Webb raised his eyebrows. 'No, really.' Ashley poured himself another drink and Smithe-Webb wondered if the fellow always drank like this. He brought his mind back to the matter in hand. 'So . . . we're trying to open up more routes. There's an idea under consideration which would involve your outfit. At this point we're having a good look at the plan to see if it's really on or not. And that's where you come in . . .'

'Yes, I'd heard something about it. Glad to help, of course. I've already picked up quite a few airmen. I never know when they're coming, mind, they just get bundled aboard. But there's never any problem.'

'Yes, indeed. But this would be more organised, and the numbers much greater. Also . . . we weren't thinking of the Bay . . . Rather, we were thinking of going straight across. To North Brittany.'

Ashley sat up. 'Ah! I see!'

'I was hoping you might be able to tell me what would be involved.'

Ashley frowned, but he was obviously excited by the idea. 'Well of course the whole thing would have to be organised differently. It'd be no good using these boats, for a start. MGBs would be much better.'

'Yes, that's what your department suggested.'

'We're getting two, did you know that?'

The major nodded.

'They'll make a lot of difference to your sort of operation. We can go in at night, really fast, do the job and then be out again before anyone knows we were there. In fact, it has already been tried once or twice.'

'Oh?'

'Dropping off the odd person with their luggage, that kind of thing. Not your department, of course?'

Smithe-Webb shook his head. 'No, one of the others. SOE, in all probability, sending in agents.'

'The only real problem has been to get the passengers from the boat to the shore in one piece and not half-drowned. Even in a fairly sheltered spot the surf can be pretty rough. But that's being looked at . . . Our chaps are trying to come up with a special surfboat.' He paused. 'But having said that, MGBs are definitely the answer. We could pick up ten, twenty, maybe even thirty men in a night.'

The major smiled. 'That would be excellent. But what about the North Brittany coast? Your CO thought it might be difficult . . .?'

'Oh, did he? Well, let's have a look, shall we?' He called out of the door. 'Evans! Get over to *Spray* and fetch me some charts, would you? North Brittany and English Channel.' He said to Smithe-Webb. 'We only carry three charts on this boat and they're French. Wouldn't do to be caught with a set of best Admiralty charts, would it?'

Ashley was enjoying himself, Smithe-Webb could see. The signs of strain had gone from his face. The major found himself liking the chap. He was a straightforward sort of person, which Smithe-Webb always admired, and he had a sort of easy charm that made you warm to him. Just as long as he knew what he was doing. Smithe-Webb had the feeling he did.

'Good Lord!' exclaimed Smithe-Webb softly. There were rocks everywhere. Unless he was reading it wrong the chart showed the coast to be completely impenetrable. Even the estuaries seemed littered with dangers. 'Good Lord!' he repeated.

'It's not as bad as it looks,' Ashley said slowly. 'Many of these rocks are covered except at dead low water. If one studies it carefully one can usually find a way through. Now, where roughly were you thinking of mounting your operation?'

Smithe-Webb put his finger on the coast north-east of Morlaix. 'Somewhere around here if possible.'

'Right, let's look at the large-scale chart.' He pulled out another chart and stared at it intently. 'Yes, there are several spots that are possible from my point of view. But we have to find a place that's good for your people too. Have they come up with any suggestions?'

'Not yet. Communications are a bit difficult at the moment.' Which meant he had no wireless operator there. Oh, that he had! It had taken long enough to persuade DDMI(P/W) that wireless operators were essential, then there'd been delays in finding volunteers and training them. After all, not everyone wanted to be a sitting duck for the Gestapo's wireless detectors.

'But you will be getting some local intelligence? On the siting of gun emplacements, and patrols and so on . . .?'

'Oh yes, in due course.'

'Right. Until then, let's assume that the main headlands are to be avoided. That would give us this cove here, and this bay . . .' He traced the coastline thoughtfully. 'No, not this one. The cliff's absolutely sheer at this point and there's no path . . .

Smithe-Webb looked up, astonished. 'How on earth do you know that?'

'I tried to climb it once!'

'Good God!' Smithe-Webb was impressed.

'Here . . . this cove here . . .' Ashley stabbed a finger at the chart. 'This would be ideal. The approach is reasonably straightforward, there'd be no problem anchoring, and I can't see the Germans having guns and sentries in the bay itself . . . Also there's decent access to the beach from the cliff, or so it would appear. I've never been there myself so I couldn't be sure.'

Smithe-Webb was staring in disbelief. It was too good to be true. The place was only a mile or two from Tregasnou. What a stroke of luck! But perhaps there were disadvantages he hadn't spotted. He asked, 'What do my people need to look for when they recce the place? What are the problems going to be?'

'Well, we'll only be able to operate on moonless nights so some sort of signalling arrangement will be essential – by shaded torch or whatever – so there really mustn't be any Germans anywhere near by. It would be useful to know exactly how bad the surf gets too . . . You can never tell whether one spot's going to be worse than another.' He paused and thought for a moment. 'Also your people will have to be prepared for some long waits on the beach; we could never give a definite time of arrival. Some nights we might not be able to turn up at all. You know – weather or engine failure or whatever. They'd have to be prepared for that . . . have contingency plans to hide all the passengers again, and so on. Oh, and we couldn't operate in high summer . . .'

'What?' Smithe-Webb frowned.

'No, I'm afraid not. The nights in mid-summer just wouldn't be long enough to get us over and back in time. From Dartmouth, where the MGBs will be based, it's a hundred miles. That's well over four hours even in a fast boat. Allowing one to two hours for approach and pick-up and four hours back, that's ten hours – call it twelve. We could probably operate as late as April with a bit of luck. In winter there's more bad weather, of course, but at least you can slow down and take it easy and know you have plenty of darkness to hide under.'

Ashley looked up at Smithe-Webb and smiled cheerfully. 'It's August now. By the time the thing is set up we'll be into autumn. So we'll have at least six months. We could get an awful lot of airmen out in that time! All it needs is reasonably good communications and some efficient organisation at your end.'

Smithe-Webb stared back at the chart and wished he could smile as cheerfully. Organisation was the one thing he couldn't guarantee. He hadn't mentioned that, and didn't intend to. No point in getting a sour note into the proceedings.

Richard Ashley said, 'The pick-up must be fast and well thought out – on both sides – otherwise . . .'

Smithe-Webb nodded. He had the message loud and clear. If there was a muck-up then everyone would get caught.

'. . . But I'm sure your people will be first class. The Bretons usually are.'

'They're good people,' Smithe-Webb agreed. He wasn't sure he could say the same for the Free French officer who was meant to be organising the line. Smithe-Webb hadn't liked the chap at all. But no point in fretting about it; they'd been forced to use him. The Free French had to be humoured and that was all there was to it. But, Smithe-Webb thought sadly, it was not the same as choosing your own man, not the same at all.

But on this side of the operation he might be able to get the man he wanted. He asked Ashley, 'Do you think you might be able to do the job yourself? You used to be on MGBs, didn't you? It would be tremendous from our point of view.'

Ashley stroked his chin. 'I was on torpedo boats actually, not gun boats. But . . . well, I *am* rather tempted. They say the new boats can do 30 knots. Very useful for getting out of trouble!' He smiled. 'Yes, I'd love to give it a go.'

He shot a glance at Smithe-Webb, and said mischievously, 'We could fix it between us. If you tell the Admiralty that you need me and then I volunteer, they can't refuse, can they?' Suddenly he laughed, his eyes sparkling with amusement, and Smithe-Webb had the feeling that few people refused Richard Ashley anything.

Smithe-Webb found himself smiling too. His feeling of optimism returned. If these MGBs could get there and back, then they were halfway there.

Ashley watched the launch heading back towards the jetty and wondered if he should have gone into the problems in more detail.

He walked slowly along the deck. God, he felt tired. He sat on the hatch coaming, and lighting a cigarette, inhaled deeply.

He tried to think, but the tiredness was clouding his brain. Or perhaps his mind was addled by the cigarettes and the brandy. Just as likely.

Problems . . . There'd certainly be a few. He'd made it sound easy and it wasn't. He should have told the major about the navigation problems: the tricky tides and the lack of navigation aids. He should have admitted that it would be bloody difficult to find the right place at all.

Then there was the weather: he should have spelt out the problems in more detail. Even in fairly rough conditions they might have to cancel operations; in gales they most certainly would.

Damn. He should have made the whole thing plainer.

Still ... they should be able to get across pretty often. A lot depended on the efficiency of the organisation on the other side, of course. The major had been a little evasive about that ...

Perhaps the escape line was brand new, or badly run or – perhaps it was a complete shambles. Yes, there was always that possibility, though he'd be surprised. The Bretons were a cool, determined, closely-knit people. He'd be surprised if they mucked things up.

Well, whatever the situation, he'd give it a go. It was a marvellous challenge.

Besides, he had been on the Bay run for over nine months now and it was getting to him. Pretending to be a fishing boat was too much like sitting waiting to be a target at the Germans' convenience. The boat had an engine, to be sure – but it produced only six knots. As much good as a wound-up elastic band. And then there was the small problem about being captured when disguised as a French fisherman. According to the powers-that-be all you had to do was to pop a Royal Navy Issue cap on your head, show your papers, and you'd be treated as a prisoner of war. Ashley wasn't so sure: he had the feeling the Germans would politely ignore the caps and line you up against a wall for target practice.

He thought back to the last trip ... It had gone wrong from the start. They'd gone to the Scillies as usual, to their secret anchorage, and turned the boat from a grey MFV into a Concarnean trawler, complete with bright orange paint and a few fancy patterns on the transom. But as soon as they'd left, the weather had turned bad and they'd had an uncomfortable trip. When they eventually got to the Bay it had taken far too long to make contact with the fleet, and a *Raumboot* had got suspicious and almost put a landing party aboard. Finally, on the way back, they'd been caught. Good and proper. In his mind's eye he saw it all again: everyone reaching for weapons, the low-flying plane, the bullets tearing into Jean-Pierre's body ... He shuddered.

Perhaps he was losing his nerve. He took out another cigarette and lit it. He looked at the hand holding the cigarette: its fingers were bright yellow with nicotine and shook slightly. Too many cigarettes. Too much booze. Definitely time for a change.

A tern called overhead and he looked up. He followed it as it soared towards the river mouth and the open sea. Any time now it would be flying south to its winter quarters on some Atlantic island. This summer there had been thousands of terns on Scilly.

The islands: that was the one thing he would miss.

Whenever they'd sailed to the secret anchorage in the north of the islands, to paint the fishing boat, he'd been happy.

The secret anchorage lay between two islands – Tresco and Bryher – in the small inlet known as New Grimsby Harbour. He had remembered coming there before the war – when was it? – '35? Some time then. The narrow inlet had been empty then, not a fishing boat or islanders' gig to be seen. He had anchored *Dancer* in the centre of the basin, and rowed across to Bryher and made a camp on the shore, and walked round the island and watched the incredible surf in Hell Bay and wondered what it would be like to be shipwrecked. In the evening he had made a fire and cooked a couple of mackerel and slept under a tarpaulin in the shelter of a rock. The dawn had been still and yellow and he had watched a cormorant diving into the cool depths of the secret harbour. Later an oystercatcher had appeared, its long yellow beak probing the stones uncovered by the falling tide. He had sat for a long time, quite motionless, not wanting anything to change, hoping it would be like that for ever.

He'd been twenty-one then, fresh out of Dartmouth, and greedy for everything, preferably all at once. Strange how everyone told you there was no going back, that the simplicity of your youth could never be recaptured; strange how right they were. But one day, when the world was sane again, he'd go back. One day, when there were no grey ships of war to ruin the quiet of that marvellous place, only *Dancer* tugging gently at her chain . . .

In the meantime he would miss the place.

He rubbed his eyes. His head ached terribly. He got wearily to his feet. He found himself reaching automatically for a cigarette and stopped in mid air. He must get fit. Soon he'd be running a proper ship again, crewed by the lads in blue. He was rather looking forward to it.

14

Julie drew the curtains over the tiny window and took a last look at the child in the bed. Peter was already fast asleep, his mouth slightly open, his breathing slow and steady. She pulled the covers up round his neck and kissed him softly on the cheek. He was such a big boy now, five and a half, and tall, oh so tall. She could hardly believe it – the time had gone so quickly. It seemed only yesterday that he was a baby.

She took a last look at him, then, picking up the flickering oil lamp, went down the steep staircase to her room. She paused and listened carefully. There was quite a wind; it was blowing round the house in long sighs. Outside, one of the cattle moved noisily against the side of the barn. Somewhere down in the village a dog was barking. Then, from almost overhead, a creaking noise. Julie stiffened, then relaxed as she recognised the sound of Peter settling more comfortably in his bed.

It was a habit now, listening. And not just for Peter – that was instinctive – but for other human sounds. The sounds of people arriving with messages or sometimes even 'parcels': foreign airmen with pale, frightened faces who were taken off into the night to some other more welcoming farmhouse. The comings and goings went on all the time now that autumn had come. She dreaded them; they made her horribly nervous. Yet – she had an awful urge to *know*. It was like being punished: the sooner you knew what was in store the easier it was to cope with.

And now she heard something. The sound of the back door opening. Someone had come then. Her heart sank. She opened the bedroom door and went quietly through into the kitchen. The figure of her uncle was leaning against the open doorway talking quietly and urgently to someone outside in the darkness.

Julie looked at the clock on the mantelpiece. It was eight o'clock.

They must have forgotten the time. They must have! She hovered uncertainly, wondering whether she should interrupt.

Now the person outside was speaking. The voice was louder, less secretive. Julie recognised it: the voice of the stranger, the *leader*, as he was meant to be. He was making no attempt to be discreet; he never did. But at this time of the evening Julie could hardly believe it. The man was mad ... or stupid! Worse, from the way he was talking, Julie had a feeling he wasn't going to stop.

The voice was saying, '. . . No, no, there is no problem there. I have

Gaston from Plouga in charge. I have given him orders to bring the ten parcels from Madame Lelouche's place. It is all organised, I assure you . . .'

Julie sighed with frustration. Surely Jean must realise the time and how dangerous it was . . . She looked at the clock again. It was two minutes past eight. She could bear it no longer. She came up beside her uncle and looked worriedly at the leader, waiting for a break in the conversation. But he continued to speak and Julie suddenly realised that he was doing it to impress her, to show her how important he was. She bit her lip with the effort of staying silent. Eventually the man said, 'Ah, Madame! Good evening. I am sorry to disturb the household . . .'

'Monsieur, . . . please, the soldiers will be back soon. You . . . your visits here put us in danger! Wouldn't it be possible to come back later? Please!'

The stranger smiled thinly. 'Madame, our business has to be properly planned! You obviously don't understand what is involved . . . And I assure you that there is no danger.'

Julie thought: This man is impossible, like a brick wall. 'Monsieur, surely the planning could be less – public!'

Jean shuffled uneasily and the stranger began to look annoyed. Julie couldn't help feeling glad; at least she was getting through to them. The stranger said coldly, 'Madame, you would do better to keep out of matters that do not concern you!'

Julie felt a surge of anger. 'Monsieur, they concern me directly – which you seem to forget at your convenience!'

Jean put a hand on Julie's shoulder and said gently, 'It's all right, he's just going. Really.'

'Not a moment too soon!' She turned and strode over to the stove. She began to stir the soup too quickly and immediately slopped some of the liquid over the side of the pan. There was a spitting and hissing as the soup hit the hotplate. Julie reached impatiently for a cloth and dabbed the remaining liquid off the stove. She was shaking with anger. She hated losing her temper. She knew she should try to calm down but while this dreadful man was still at the door she just couldn't. A pity Tante Marie was looking after Madame Gillet for the evening: she would have given him short shrift.

The burning soup was hissing loudly; Julie missed the sound of the front door opening and the steps crossing the front parlour. The rap on the parlour door made her jump so much that she jerked at the spoon and hot liquid spattered over her apron. She stared in horror as the door opened and the two familiar uniforms appeared. The two soldiers smiled politely at her as they always did, then looked

214

curiously past her to where her uncle and the leader stood at the open back door.

For a moment they were all frozen, like a tableau: Julie at the stove, the soldiers in the doorway and the two men at the open back door. Then Jean gave the Germans a slight nod, turned his back on them and said to the man, 'Well, I'll deliver that grain in the morning, then. But I've only four kilos to spare – and I'll have to charge you a good price for it!'

The man smiled. 'Fair enough. I know how it is – we must be commercial about this! Oh, and you won't forget the other matter?'

Julie realised with dismay that the leader was enjoying the scene. He was going to play it out! He thought he was being so clever. Julie thought: What conceit! And she had the feeling he was fooling no-one: the two soldiers looked distinctly suspicious. Julie clattered some plates and said rather too loudly, 'The soup is ready. Please go and sit down.'

The soldiers looked surprised: normally Julie never spoke to them. They shuffled back into the parlour and as soon as she heard them drawing up their chairs, she took in a tray with two bowls of soup and some bread on it. As she put the bowls on the table she heard the distant sound of the back door closing. The horrid man had gone. At last!

One of the soldiers started to speak to her, something about what a cold day it was. She ignored him as she usually did and he fell silent. Good. One might have to provide accommodation and two meals a day for them, but there was no law that said one had to speak to them. Julie left the room, closing the door firmly behind her.

Her uncle was standing by the stove. He made a wide expansive gesture with his hands, as if to say, What could I do?

Julie slumped into a chair and her uncle drew up another close beside her. They sat in silence until, finally, they heard the sound of chairs being scraped back in the parlour and the front door opening and closing again. The Germans had gone out for their customary drink. After a few minutes Julie spoke.

'That man . . .' She shook her head. 'He is a *danger*. I know it – everyone knows it.'

'Yes, but . . . Julie, please realise, we have to put up with him. He's the only contact we have, the only hope of getting all the parcels away.'

'Yes, but at what cost?'

The old man sighed. 'I know, I know. But you must understand that there are no less than thirty parcels waiting to be sent away. If we can't make contact with the British and have boats sent over, we'll be stuck with them. The longer these parcels are here, the greater the risk for those hiding them. And there are more arriving every day! We must, we *must*, keep that contact, otherwise what are we to do? Give them over to the Germans, eh? Wait until our houses are bulging with British airmen and pretend they're really French. Eh?'

Julie nodded wearily. She had to acknowledge the difficulty of passing the British off as local people. Quite apart from the language difference, they *looked* so alien. She said with a sigh, 'I do see the problem. But I can't understand why you should have to put up with that – that person. Surely the line could be run just with local people and perhaps one outside wireless operator. Surely!'

'Ah, but that's the problem. The only wireless operator is far away – in Paris, I think. And this fellow, he is the only person with contact. The British sent him over. What can we do?'

'Make him be quiet for a start!' Julie found herself getting angry again. 'Even I, a person who tries *not* to hear anything, even I know exactly who's in the organisation. I could give you a list right now! And if I know, then the whole village knows, not to mention the whole of the Côtes du Nord!'

'But who would talk? No Breton! Never!'

Julie laughed bitterly. 'I wish I had your faith in human nature!'

Then she sighed and patted her uncle's hand. He looked so old and worried that she hated to depress him.

The old man said softly, 'But we have to do something, don't we? We can't stand aside and just watch, can we?'

'I don't know. Sometimes I wonder if all these terrible risks are worth while.' She looked at her uncle and said simply, 'Anyway, look at me. I do nothing and *my* conscience is clear.' She looked away and patted his hand again. 'But I can see that you must do what you must. I don't blame you for that. Just . . . *do* try to keep it away from us, Jean, please. I worry so much about Peter . . .'

Jean nodded, and said thoughtfully, 'But Juliette, we don't hide parcels here. We agreed that. For *your* sake, and Peter's. So there is really very little risk for you. For me – ah, well, that doesn't matter. I'm an old man.'

Julie said heavily, 'Even then, they take hostages, don't they? And shoot them? Innocent women and children. Oh, the children!' She could hardly bear to think of it. There had been an incident in Morlaix, after a German had been shot. They had taken twenty women and children, lined them up and mown them down. Julie had heard the shots from her office. She had cried out and wept with rage and uselessness.

Jean said impatiently, 'That was the communists! Stupid fools.

216

They just kill Germans and never think of the consequences. *They're* the real dangers! I'll never help that lot of anarchists, never! And –' he wagged a finger '– I will never have another one of them in my house again. And that includes Michel –'

'I agree that their methods are – wrong. But they *are* on our side, uncle.'

'When it suits them! Ha!' Jean stood up, went to the mantelpiece and picked up his pipe which he tapped angrily against the chimney. 'They were on the German side at first, remember? Remember? Then, when the Germans did the dirty on Russia – which anyone of any brain could have seen coming – then they changed sides. Very convenient! Ha!'

He filled his pipe with a plug of tobacco and lit it in a cloud of smoke. Julie hoped he wouldn't regret it: the tobacco was his last until the beginning of the month.

The old man puffed more calmly at his pipe and said quietly, 'I'm sorry about Michel – but I feel rather strongly about the matter. I told him to his face. I told him he wasn't welcome here!'

Julie frowned. 'When?'

The old man stared at her. 'But . . . didn't you know? He's back.'

'What!'

'Yes, he's here, God rot his soul. I saw him in the village today. I thought your aunt had told you? Anyway, I told him that, with regret, he was not to set foot in this house again. I told him –'

Julie got to her feet. 'Where is he?'

The old man looked at her sharply and shrugged.

She went to the table and picked up her purse. 'I'm going down to the village – to see if I can find him.'

The old man said, 'God in heaven, why?'

'Because . . . Well . . .' It was difficult to think of a reason. Finally she said, 'He *is* one of the family . . . Maybe he needs help.'

And, she thought, because I want to see him anyway, I want to see him very much indeed. She said, 'I don't mean any disrespect, uncle, and I understand about not having him in the house, but –'

Jean raised his hand. 'Stop! Don't say any more. Talk to him if you must, but if you take my advice you won't be seen with him. And don't tell me what he's up to. I don't want to know!' He added automatically, 'And be careful down the lane. I never trust those soldiers.'

'I'll be careful.' She blew him a kiss and, pulling on her warmest coat, hurried out into the night.

It was very dark. The wind was howling in from the sea, tearing at the hedgerows and whistling through the occasional solitary pine, bent into a tortured shape by a hundred storms.

Julie shivered slightly and walked more quickly, her head bent low, her eyes on the dark road ahead.

Yes, she wanted to see Michel, she wanted to see him very much. She had been thinking about him increasingly in the last few months, hoping he'd come back . . .

The last two years had been lonely. When Peter was small and needed her so much she hadn't minded being on her own. But since he'd been at school and often went out to play with his friends the loneliness was awful, like a terrible weight, pressing down on her.

Sometimes she felt guilty at being lonely. She'd been so happy here, she'd adored the peace and tranquillity, she'd been so grateful for finding a home: in those early days she'd loved everything about it. She still did! And yet . . . the thought of staying here for ever, with only Peter and Jean and Tante Marie and her books for company, filled her with dread. She was twenty-five and the years were beginning to slip away. Twenty-five! Her chances of – why couldn't she say it? – *of finding a husband* were getting slimmer all the time. And she *did* want a husband, she knew that. Often she lay awake at night imagining what it would be like . . . Having someone to talk to and laugh with, having someone *there*. What she wanted more than anything was to *share* – her life, Peter, everything. When she imagined being married, the lovely feeling of warmth and tenderness, she wanted it very badly.

There was no mistaking the café in the darkness: light was leaking from its blacked-out windows in a dozen places and the sound of voices and laughter floated on the air. Julie approached slowly. If Michel wasn't here, then someone would probably know where he was.

She waited: there was no question of going in on her own. At last someone came out. It was an old man called Pierre, a cowherd from a nearby farm. He'd had several glasses too many. She gave him her message and directed him gently back into the café.

A few moments later the old man reappeared, nodded to her and went off into the night.

Then the door opened again and Michel was standing there.

Julie started to smile. 'Michel, how lovely to . . .' But he was looking behind him. Then, taking her arm, he pulled her quickly away from the café.

They walked briskly, in silence. Presently they came to a barn at the edge of the village. His voice whispered, 'In here!' Inside it was pitch dark. Julie could hear Michel tramping across a bed of straw to the far side. She put out her hands and felt her way forward. She tripped over a bale of straw, recovered, and bumped her shoulder against the side of what was probably a cart.

'All right?' His voice was close by.

'I think so.' She sat down carefully and heard him sit beside her. She asked gently, 'Are you in trouble? What's the matter?'

'Mmmm?' He laughed softly. 'No, I'm not in trouble. Well – no more than usual.'

'Then, why all this?'

'I just thought it would be better if you weren't seen with me, that's all.'

'Better for who?' But she knew what he meant.

'Why, better for you, of course! Your uncle doesn't want me in his house, half the village think my politics stink, the other half are prepared to argue with me over a glass of wine – but none of them would let his daughter be seen with me. Better for *you*!'

She asked, 'Where have you been all this time?'

'Oh, away.'

She could tell that he didn't want to say any more. But she ventured, 'You've been all right though? Safe, I mean?'

'Oh, yes. Don't worry your head about me. I always look after myself.'

'Michel, I must ask . . . You haven't been working with the Germans, have you? I couldn't bear that.'

'Good God, no!'

He sounded outraged and Julie said quickly, 'I mean, you did talk about it . . . In Morlaix. Don't you remember?'

'Ha! That was a long time ago. And I never worked with the Germans then anyway. Now? I can assure you that I kill them, blow them up and destroy them whenever I can. But the less said about that the better.'

'Yes, yes. I'm sorry. I didn't mean to . . .'

'Forget it.'

Julie peered through the darkness and said wistfully, 'I wish I could see your face.'

He laughed. 'It hasn't changed. Just older. Here, I'll have a cigarette. That'll shed some light. I've been longing for a smoke for hours, but I'm too mean to share any of my hard-earned cigarettes with the old fools back there. They think anyone from the town has plenty to spare.'

She heard him fumbling in his pockets, then there was a sudden blaze of light and he was drawing on a cigarette. She looked at his face and was slightly shocked. She'd forgotten how deep his frown was and how narrow his mouth. She'd forgotten, too, how bitter was his expression. She realised she'd forgotten a lot about him . . .

He was asking, 'And how have you been?'

'Oh. All right really. We have just about enough to eat. There's no help on the farm any more, so Jean has to keep it going by himself. Tante Marie and I help when we can . . . And Peter does too, of course.'

'Peter, he must be quite a young man by now.'

'Yes. Five and a half.'

'And he's well too?'

'Yes.' She didn't elaborate. His question had been polite but automatic. She had the feeling he wasn't really interested.

'Are you still working in that place at Morlaix?'

She nodded in the darkness. 'Yes, the same old place. Sometimes I think I'll be there when I'm sixty.'

'But your papers. They've stood up all right?'

'Oh yes!' She reached out and found his wrist. 'I can't tell you what a difference it's made. Knowing they're all right – genuine. It's given me peace of mind. I can't thank you enough!'

She fumbled for his hand, but there was no answering squeeze and his hand felt limp in hers. Blushing in the darkness, she withdrew. He asked, 'Did you ever use that stamp and those papers you pinched?'

She frowned. 'No. I still don't really know why I took them. It seemed a sort of safeguard at the time.'

'Well, hang on to them. You never know when they might come in useful. But for God's sake don't tell anyone about them and don't leave them lying around. Have you got them hidden?'

'Of course.' Julie felt a little hurt: did he really think she would leave them lying around? 'I've got them well hidden where no-one can find them. We've got two soldiers billeted on us, you know.'

'What!'

His voice was very sharp and she wondered why he was so surprised. She said quickly, 'Yes, lots of people have. It's nothing unusual.'

'But your uncle – he's involved with this escape line.'

Julie gulped and stared at the glow of Michel's cigarette, wondering what on earth she should say. Jean certainly wouldn't have told Michel about his involvement. How, then, did Michel know?

'Well?'

'I . . . I can't say. We don't talk about those sort of things.'

He sighed impatiently. 'Come on, Julie, don't be silly! I know all about it. I heard within five minutes of coming back to the area. My people in Morlaix not only know who works the line, but they know all the operational details.'

'Oh no –'

'It's common knowledge. Among my comrades, anyway.'

Julie felt her heart turn to ice. 'The Germans . . .' she whispered. 'Do they know?'

'I wouldn't be surprised. And what bothers me is that, when the trouble breaks as it surely will, the finger of blame will probably be pointed at me and my friends when in fact it's that lunatic who's running your line who should be shot. He's obviously never heard of the word "security". Where did they find him, eh?'

'London.'

'Ah, a Free French hero then?'

'Yes.'

Michel exclaimed, 'The sooner you're rid of him the better.'

'I know, I know. I hate the horrid little man. He's so conceited, you have no idea. Everyone – well, they go along with him because he's the only link with London.' She sighed deeply. 'I wish they could see what madness it is.'

'My only advice is to keep well out of it. Don't get involved! The work is best left to men and old ones at that, then it doesn't matter so much when they get shot.'

So practical – or callous, depending on how you looked at it. Julie stared into the darkness, trying to understand how one came to think like that.

She heard Michel stand up and saw the glow of the cigarette disappear as he stubbed it against the side of the cart. A couple of sparks floated down and Julie automatically reached out to catch them before they touched the straw.

He said, 'Come on! It's time we got back. We don't want Jean to think that I'm filling your head with revolution, do we?'

Julie thought: But we haven't even begun to talk . . . Then she remembered what she'd wanted to talk about. Suddenly it didn't seem very important any more.

She heard him move off towards the crack of grey light which marked the door. Julie got hurriedly to her feet and followed him, stumbling across the bundles of straw When she reached the door he had opened it and was waiting. In the faint grey illumination of the night she could just make out his features. They were severe and hard. Julie looked at him curiously, wondering how she could have forgotten how very serious he was and how very – unyielding.

He said, 'By the way, do they tell you when a boat's coming?'

'No. I never ask – and they never tell me. Why?'

'Well, just keep out of the way tomorrow night. According to my information, there's going to be an operation then. I'm sure the information's good. No moon, you see, and the country crawling with hidden airmen longing to get home. If it isn't tomorrow night then it must be soon after. But my friends say it'll be tomorrow – and they don't usually get these things wrong.'

Julie closed her eyes. Was there anything he didn't know? She said slowly, 'I'll . . . take Peter away for the night . . . Thanks for telling me.'

He took her arm and guided her out into the road. They walked in silence until they reached the crossroads at the centre of the village. People were coming out of the café. Instinctively they drew into the darkness at the side of the road and followed the wall round until they were in the lane and heading up the hill towards the house.

Julie didn't want him to come any further. She turned and whispered, 'Goodbye, Michel.' On an impulse she added passionately, 'Don't kill Germans if you can avoid it. They'll only take hostages again. Children . . . They take children, Michel.'

'Same soft-hearted Julie.' There was a trace of scorn in his voice and she felt hurt. How could he be so hard? And why did he have to make her feel foolish? He went on, 'Of course we do try to avoid killing Germans. But when it comes to blowing up something important, we have to do it, and that's all there is to it. Children suffer anyway, from bombing raids, starvation, lots of things. The destruction of a factory is more important than – many things. But it's nothing to how the Russian peasants are suffering . . . They're dying in their thousands!'

Julie could think of nothing to say. He added, 'Anyway, you'd do best not to think about such things. They'll happen whether you worry about them or not.'

Julie suddenly felt sad and tired. She said softly, 'Goodbye, Michel', and walked away. He hurried after her and took her arm. 'Julie, remember one thing – don't get involved!'

'Yes, you told me.'

'But you might get into trouble without realising it. You . . . don't know how they can drag you into these things.'

Anyone would think she was a seventeen-year-old straight out of school. She pulled in her breath and said tightly, 'I'll remember that.'

She walked away and this time he did not follow her. Despite the steepness of the hill she walked rapidly, hitting the road with her feet, pumping her legs in steady rhythm, climbing faster and faster until she realised she was almost home. But she didn't want to go into the house yet and she walked on towards the open cliffs and the low roar of the distant surf.

For a moment she almost continued past the end of the made-up road and onto the track which led through the fields to the open heathland. Then she remembered that there were patrols along the clifftop and they shot on sight. She stopped and leaned against a low wall and wrapped her arms tightly about her and sighed deeply.

She tried to separate her thoughts, to look at them coolly so that her anger would go away.

For one thing, it was obvious that he didn't care for her. He pretended to be concerned for her safety, but she couldn't help wondering why. There must be a reason. Because in every other way he was as cold as ice. No, he didn't care for her. The strange thing was, she didn't mind a bit now. In fact, she was rather glad because she realised she didn't care for *him* either. It was impossible to care for someone as hard and callous as that. She had forgotten just how cold he was . . .

There was something else, too. She hated to admit it, but her pride had been hurt. She had gone to meet him, imagining he would be glad to see her – and he had treated her like a child. He had humiliated her – very subtly but very definitely – and it made her shudder.

She was angry – but not with Michel, with herself. What a fool she'd been! She'd built up a picture of Michel that bore no resemblance to the person he really was. She'd imagined him as a husband, as a lover; she'd made him into what she wanted him to be. It was self-delusion. Puppy love!

It began to rain, the drops driven by the wind into a horizontal curtain of penetrating wetness. Julie pulled her coat more tightly about her and began to walk slowly back down the lane. She wasn't angry any more, just rather cross and sad.

One thing: she wouldn't be so stupid again.

The most important thing in her life was Peter. He was the only one who really mattered. Tomorrow night she would take him to stay in the village, in a safe house, away from everything. Then if anything went wrong . . . *neither* of them would get caught.

A floorboard creaked and Julie woke with a start. It had taken her an hour to get to sleep and now she was wide awake again. It was hopeless: she was as jumpy as a cat and she knew it would take just as long to get back to sleep again. Being in a strange bed was half the problem; Madame Boulet's house was only a short distance down the lane, in the centre of the village, but it might as well be a hundred miles away. Apart from anything else, the bed was lumpy.

She put out an arm and touched the sleeping figure beside her. That was another thing: though it was lovely to share a bed with Peter, she found it difficult to relax in case she should move in her sleep and disturb him. It was disconcerting, too, to hear the steady breathing and occasional sighs of someone sleeping beside you, even when that someone was your own child.

But what really made it impossible to sleep was knowing what was happening – out *there*, in the fields and down on the beach. Julie began to wonder how they got the airmen to the beach. Did they creep across the fields like shadows? Or did they walk brazenly along the roads? Whichever way, the risk was tremendous. Sometimes the Germans sent out extra patrols . . . And then how did the boat find the right beach? Did they signal? No, surely not . . .

She couldn't see how it could be done safely. There were too many things to go wrong.

Best to try to sleep. She closed her eyes and made a conscious effort to relax her body.

Suddenly there was a faint moan. Instantly she was tense and alert again. It had sounded like someone in terrible anguish, sighing . . . She listened, straining to pick up the slightest noise, but all she could hear was the roar of silence.

Then it came again. A slight moaning which began as a low murmur and grew into a whine.

Julie suddenly relaxed with a groan. What a nervous idiot she was becoming! It was the wind. Only the wind!

She closed her eyes again and tried to calm herself. The wind . . . It sounded so different here. At home it whistled or, sometimes, when it was really blowing, it howled like an animal in pain. But this moaning . . . it made her feel uneasy. She tried to guess how strong the wind was now. A gale at least. The sea would be rough then, and there would be large breakers on the beach. She tried to imagine what it must be like for the British boat, trying to get in towards the land. Perhaps enormous waves were breaking right over it . . .

There was a faint tapping on the door. Julie almost jumped out of her skin. She lay rigid.

The tapping came again, soft but insistent.

Julie got quickly out of bed, pulled the covers up over Peter, and dragged on her dressing gown. She tiptoed to the door and opened it.

Madame Boulet was standing there, her anxious face illuminated by the candle in her hand. Immediately Julie knew something was wrong. 'What is it?'

The older woman whispered, 'Come down. Please. Now.'

Julie tied her dressing-gown cord and, closing the door behind her,

224

followed Madame Boulet down the stairs. The hall was in darkness, but light was coming from the kitchen door which was slightly open. As they approached Julie could hear the low murmur of a man's voice.

The two women went in. Monsieur Boulet was sitting by the stove, fully dressed, his face solemn. Another man who Julie knew only vaguely was sitting opposite, talking urgently. When they saw the women they rose to their feet, anxiety on their faces. Julie thought: God, the Germans have found out. Everyone's been captured. Everyone's been killed!

Julie said, 'What is it? Please tell me!'

The second man said quickly, 'Nothing's happened! Not yet anyway. But we need your help, Madame.'

Julie let out a sigh of relief and sat down weakly on a chair. 'Thank God . . . I thought for a moment . . .' Then she remembered what the man had said. 'Help? How can I help?'

'Madame, believe me I would not ask . . . except that you are the only person . . . Madame, we need someone who speaks English. There is a young pilot. He is injured. We have done what we can for him but . . . Please come and talk to him. Otherwise – Otherwise we are all in trouble. Please, Madame.'

'I don't understand . . . What do I have to do?'

'Madame, please, I beg of you. It isn't far. Just at Roget's farm, up near the point. You will understand when we arrive. Please, we have no time . . .' He glanced at the clock on the mantelpiece. Julie saw that it was almost midnight. She looked back at the man. She remembered that he was a farmer from the next village, a nice man who usually smiled. Now, as he waited for her reply, his face was deathly serious.

They were all watching her, waiting for her to speak. Julie felt the beginnings of panic. How could she possibly decide at a moment's notice? It really wasn't fair!

Then she realised they must be desperate. For them to ask her something like this – and in the middle of the night – something must be very wrong. Perhaps this pilot had terrible injuries . . . Perhaps he needed help . . . And he was young, the man had said . . .

Julie said abruptly, 'I'll go and get dressed', because it was easier to say that than to refuse. She hurried from the room before she changed her mind.

In the darkness of the bedroom she found some clothes and started to pull them on, wondering what she was getting herself into.

She dropped a shoe which clattered to the floor. Peter turned over and moaned quietly. Julie found the shoe and put it on. She went over to the bed and, leaning down, put her face against the soft, gentle cheek.

She took a last look at him, murmured, 'I love you' and left the room.

The staircase was in total darkness and she had to feel her way down. When she reached the kitchen the lights were out and the back door already open. A blast of cold air came from the door, making her shiver. Someone helped her on with her coat and then she was outside, following the man as he led the way down the side of the house.

They turned a corner of the house and met the full force of the wind. It tore at Julie's coat and blew her hair across her eyes until she could hardly see. She pulled the coat back round her and held her hair back from her face and saw that they had reached the road.

In the blackness Julie could just make out the figure of the farmer as he strode off in the direction of Roget's farm. She followed quickly before she lost him in the murk. So they did use the roads on these night jaunts. Julie glanced nervously behind her. Sometimes she'd heard German trucks driving through the village in the middle of the night. If one came along now what would they do? Jump over the wall into a field, presumably. If there was time.

The farmer's pace was relentless and when they came to the steep hill which led up to the point Julie had to make an effort to keep up. She thought of asking him to slow down, but then she remembered what he'd said about there being no time and she pushed herself on, concentrating on each step, closing her mind to everything except the rhythm of her stride.

At one point she looked up and he was gone, melted into the pitch darkness ahead. But then he reappeared again, standing, waiting for her to catch up. He whispered, 'Nearly there', and set off again briskly. Julie made a final effort, pumping her legs, swinging her arms, and then at last they arrived. The black bulk of a building loomed up ahead and a low voice came out of the darkness. The farmer answered with a single word and then they entered the farm-house.

Someone took her arm and led her along a passage. Another door was opened and there was a sudden blaze of light. Julie blinked.

She found herself in what was obviously the front parlour. It was full of people. At least twenty. At first it was difficult to make out the faces, but then her eyes became accustomed to the light and she saw several people she knew, villagers and men from outlying farms. The rest – perhaps ten or twelve of them – were strangers, all young men, all slightly out of place despite their rough working clothes.

226

Everyone was staring at Julie, some with a kind of horror on their faces, some with hope and relief. No-one spoke. Julie cast around, looking for some kind of clue. She expected to see a figure on a stretcher, but there was none. Perhaps he was upstairs . . .

A villager glanced nervously towards the far end of the room, someone else did the same . . . Julie followed their eyes. And then she saw.

One of the young men was standing by the fireplace. He had a bandage round his head and a frightened look in his eyes.

In his hand was a gun. It was pointing at the other people in the room.

Suddenly Julie understood.

She had been brought here to get the gun out of his hand.

For a long time she stood quite still, looking at the young man, and wondering where to start. Finally she took a step forward and smiled at him. 'Hello, my name's Julie. Who are you?'

The young man stared at her, his face taut and uncertain. The gun waved slightly in his hand.

Julie thought: I must try something else. She took a breath and said brightly, 'There's obviously something the matter. Would you like to tell me about it?'

The young man blinked rapidly and tried to focus his eyes.

Suddenly he spoke, so loudly it made Julie jump. 'I know who you are! You're a spy too!' The voice was high-pitched and tense, the accent Welsh.

'A spy?' Julie laughed gently. 'Goodness gracious me no. I'm English!' In the pause that followed she realised that this may not appear very logical and added, 'No, you see I just happen to live here . . . among these good people and . . . They're trying to help you, you know, to get you home. You do realise that, don't you?'

'No! No! They're not to be trusted, they're not! They're spies! I saw one with a German!'

'But . . . if they were spies they would have handed you over to the Germans long ago, wouldn't they? They wouldn't have bothered to hide you for so long, would they? Not if they were going to give you up.' She smiled gently. 'Haven't they cared for you? Haven't they bandaged your head?'

'But I saw one talking to a Kraut!'

'Maybe the German asked him something. It would have looked odd if he hadn't replied, wouldn't it? We have to reply to the Germans, however much we hate it. I give you my solemn word that no-one here is on the Germans' side. I am telling you the truth, believe me.'

227

The young man frowned and clamped his lips together.

'Why don't I tell you all about myself and then you can tell me all about your family and your home. Eh? Wouldn't that be nice? Why don't we get rid of everyone else and talk, just the two of us?' She walked slowly across the room towards him. As she started to move, his eyes leapt with fear. But then they relaxed a little and followed her, searching her face, half hopeful, half uncertain. Julie felt a surge of confidence. She could see that he wanted to believe in her; he was only frightened.

Finally she stood in front of him. He did not move. She said, 'We'll tell the others to go away, shall we? And then we can talk.' She turned and signalled to one of the villagers for them to go. People started standing up and shuffling towards the door. He shouted, 'No, no! They must stay.'

Everyone stopped. Julie smiled and, reaching out, touched his hand, the one holding the gun. 'They only want to go down to the boat and get you people home. You want to get home too, don't you?'

He shook his head. 'Yes, yes . . . But . . .' He closed his eyes and said wearily, 'It's all so crazy.'

'I know, I know. You've had a tough time, I can see that. Poor old thing, poor old thing. I bet it's been terrible.'

'Yes, yes! Jesus Christ, Oh God . . .!' His voice cracked and Julie felt a moment of fear.

She said quickly, 'Remember your duty!'

'My duty?' The young man looked at her, puzzled, trying to understand.

'Yes. Your duty. It's quite clear, you know. You must get back to England. That is what they want you to do. And you know why? So that they can get you back home to your family. That's what they want you to do. They're not going to ask you to fight again, you know . . . not after all you've done. You can go home, back to where you belong. Back to your family. Really.' The young man's face cleared a little and Julie thought: I'm on the right track. She prompted gently, 'You have a family?'

He nodded slightly and for a moment she thought he would cry. He whispered, 'Mum . . . and Dad . . . And my sister, Susan.'

'And a girl? You have a girl?'

He looked at her as if his heart would break. 'Yes, yes . . .' His eyes filled with tears and he bowed his head and began to sob quietly. Slowly, Julie reached forward and removed the gun from his hand. She passed it to one of the men and then, reaching out, took the young pilot and cradled him in her arms. He clutched at her, his head on her shoulder, his tears warm on her neck.

She thought: But he's no more than a boy; just a boy. And they send children like this to war . . . what madness it all is. She patted his back and said, 'It's all right now. Everything's all right now.'

There was activity behind her: people were moving about and whispering. Someone touched her arm and breathed, 'We must go now or it will be too late. Will you bring him? Down to the beach?'

Julie hesitated. The beach . . . No-one ever went to the beach. It had barbed wire and patrols.

The young pilot clutched at her, still sobbing. She held his head to her shoulder and patted his back again. She looked at the man waiting beside her and nodded slowly. 'Yes, I'll bring him. Just tell me what to do.'

Julie felt the pilot stumble behind her. She held tightly to his hand and turned her head. She saw that he had regained his balance and was tentatively stepping forward again. She whispered, 'Are you all right?' but the wind tore her words away and he didn't hear. She asked again, louder.

He nodded, 'Yes, I'm okay.'

Julie squeezed his hand and said, 'Well done. Not far now!'

She peered down the path to where the man ahead of her had been. But there was no-one now, not even a shadow against the greys and blacks of the night mosaic. Julie drew in her breath and started forward again. The path was uneven and narrow, carved uncertainly into the side of the cliff and descending rapidly to the beach below. Sometimes, when a rock protruded, it disappeared altogether and Julie had to reach down with her foot until she found it again some distance below. She went forward carefully, leaning slightly inwards towards the cliff face, her leading hand feeling along the safe hardness of the solid rock. She tried not to think of what lay below.

At one point she stepped on a loose stone and almost lost her footing. She was wearing the wrong kind of shoes, of course: leather with a slight heel – horribly slippery. She should have brought canvas shoes. She also wished for the hundredth time that she'd worn a scarf: when the wind tore down the cliff it blew her hair across her face until she could hardly see.

The path seemed interminable. Behind, the pilot stumbled again; she gripped his hand again and turned to make sure that he had regained his balance.

Above the dull roar of the wind it was just possible to hear a low rumbling, like muffled thunder. As they went down it grew steadily louder. The sound of the surf. Julie's spirits rose: they must be very near the beach now.

Without warning the path suddenly fell sharply away beneath her feet. Julie felt down the slope with her foot, but there was nothing: no ledge, no rock, no sign of the path. She sat down, pulled the pilot down beside her and, letting go of his hand, levered herself over the edge. She felt a jolt of fear as she began to slide downwards, faster and faster. Then, just as she grabbed for a handhold, she saw the beach rushing up towards her. With a soft crunch, she landed on the pebbles.

She got to her feet and dusted her coat down. The young pilot hadn't appeared yet. She called up, 'It's all right. The beach is just here! Just slide down like I did!'

There was no reply. For a moment she thought she was going to have to climb back up again. Then she heard his voice, almost carried away by the wind. 'You sure?'

'Yes, yes. Just slide!'

There was a moment's pause, then a figure shot down and fell on to the pebbles beside her. Julie said, 'Well done.' She helped him up and, holding hands again, they started slowly down the beach.

Julie could just make out a line of pale grey that revealed the breaking surf and, to the left, a blackness, much inkier than the sky, which marked the high cliffs around the cove. But where were they meant to go? Where were the others? She stopped uncertainly and looked around, peering into the darkness.

'What's happening?' The pilot's voice sounded frightened again.

'It's all right. I'm just waiting for them to find us.'

She only wished they would.

As if in answer, a shadow, darker than the rest, emerged in front of them. A voice said, 'Here! Follow me!' Julie sighed with relief and, pulling the pilot behind her, followed the dark figure along the beach. They came to a finger of rock which protruded from the cliff. The rest of the group were waiting on one side of it, some of them sitting against the rock, their faces pale and indistinguishable in the gloom, others standing in groups of two or three. As Julie walked up she was surprised to hear the sounds of raised voices. With dismay she realised that there was a row going on.

The pilot pulled at her hand. 'What the hell's going on?'

It was a good question. But she said, 'Don't worry. It doesn't mean anything. They're just having a friendly argument.'

'Jesus . . . Can't they shut up, for Chrissake?'

Julie found a place against the rock and sat down with the pilot next to her. She listened anxiously as the angry voices continued. The pilot was right: it would be a good idea if they shut up. She wondered what on earth they could be arguing about. What could possibly be so important at a time like this? She peered at a man who sat down wearily on the other side of her. She thought she recognised him. She asked softly in French, 'Who's that?'

The reply came back, 'One of us.'

Julie whispered, 'Can you tell me what's happening?'

'Well, we're waiting for the boat but . . . it may be badly delayed by the weather.' He bent over towards her. 'In truth, it's doubtful it'll come at all . . .'

Julie's heart sank. The thought of having to look after her pilot for much longer filled her with despair. She imagined having to lead him up the cliff again. That was bad enough. But then what? Would they expect her to keep the young man with her? To hide him at the house? No, it was impossible! She said to the villager, 'What happens, then, if the boat doesn't come?'

'We all go home – with our guests, I suppose.'

'Do they go back to – where they were before?'

'I have no idea. You'll have to ask our leader.' There was contempt in his voice as he spoke the word 'leader', and Julie realised he disliked the man too. She asked, 'But why's everyone arguing?'

'Because the whole thing's a mess. No-one knows who's meant to be doing what. Virtually all our helpers are down here on the beach when some should still be up on the cliff. Half say the boat won't come, the other half want to wait. Our leader is telling all those who want to stay to go and all those who want to go to stay. Marvellous, isn't it?' The man spat with contempt.

Julie looked around. The mention of the dreadful man reminded her of Michel's warning. It had been quite clear. He'd said that the Germans probably knew all about this . . . If he was right and they did . . .

God.

She closed her eyes. She was terribly frightened, that was all. Just frightened. And yet . . . she couldn't shake off a terrible sense of foreboding. She was certain it was all going to go wrong. It was partly instinct and partly a feeling that nothing could go right while this leader was in charge . . .

Something had changed. Julie opened her eyes. It was the arguing – it had stopped. Instead everyone was staring out to sea. Involuntarily Julie squeezed the pilot's hand.

There was a sudden burst of activity. Orders were passed. Three men ran down the beach. Others came along the line and told the waiting passengers to be ready to move. Julie and her pilot stood up. A tall, lanky figure detached himself from Julie's group and started moving down the beach. A dark figure ran after him and pushed him back against the rock, saying in ragged English, 'Wait! When I say!'

Julie stared at the line of surf, straining her eyes to distinguish the shadows in the darkness. At first she thought she was mistaken, but then she saw it: the dark shape of a small boat coming through the surf, and then there were men jumping out, two or three of them, pulling the boat up the beach and blending with the men who had run down to meet them. Incredible. The boat had come in spite of the weather. It had not forgotten them after all.

Now four people were being led down the beach. Julie's pilot said plaintively, 'Why not me? What the hell's happening?'

He sounded tearful again and Julie said soothingly, 'It's all right. You'll be next. I expect the boat can't take everyone at once.'

The shape of the boat showed black against the whiteness of the surf and Julie realised it had been launched again. Dark figures climbed in, a curtain of water rose up as the boat met a wave, and then they were gone, vanished into the night.

Julie wondered how on earth the small boat found the large one in the darkness. She hadn't seen a single light.

It was twenty minutes before they returned. The pilot kept saying, 'Christ, they're not coming back! They're not coming back!' And Julie replied, 'Of course they are. Honestly, I promise they are, I promise.'

And then at last the boat was back and it was time for Julie's pilot to go. She started to say goodbye but one of the villagers hissed at her, 'No, you must come too. Now! Come!'

'What?' But he didn't reply and Julie found herself hand in hand with the pilot again, stumbling uneasily down the pebbles towards the water. As they approached the boat two men detached themselves from the waiting group and came towards them.

A man next to Julie said, 'She's here, over here.'

The two figures came up and a voice said, 'Hello, do you speak English?'

Julie laughed nervously. 'Yes.'

'Look, there's this walkie-talkie we'd like to give you. I was trying to explain how it worked. Do you think you could remember a few instructions?' His voice was very English and upper class: an officer.

'I'll try.' Julie made the effort to concentrate as he handed her the walkie-talkie, a small oblong object which was surprisingly light. The British officer spoke slowly and carefully, repeating everything twice. He spoke about frequencies, range, aerials, batteries, and procedures. Eventually he said, 'Do you think you've got all that?'

'Yes, I think so.'

'It's always best to explain it verbally, but it is all written down as well, on the plate on the side. Look, why don't you give it a go? Turn it on now and then you can listen to me talking to the MGB and get the idea. Okay?'

'Yes.'

The officer looked nervously round. 'Must go now! Bye!'

Julie had a ridiculous urge to ask him to stay for a while, but he was gone, striding towards the boat which was already being pushed down into the water. Julie looked for her pilot, but couldn't distinguish him among the group of people waiting round the boat. In case he could see her she raised her hand and waved goodbye before walking back up the beach.

When she reached the finger of rock she sat down and turned on the radio. There was a slight hissing and crackling. Then suddenly there was a voice which made her jump.

'Safely launched and on the way.'

'Roger.' The acknowledgement was so clear it sounded as though it had come from a few feet away. Julie listened, waiting for more. But there was nothing, just the hiss of the receiver.

A figure came up beside her and said, 'Come on! Time to go! Hurry!'

She got to her feet and reached for the button to switch the radio off.

Suddenly a voice crackled, 'Have run my distance but no visual yet.'

'Try further west.'

'Roger.'

Julie waited, mesmerised.

'Found a rock. Any ideas?'

There was a short silence. A new voice came on, stronger than the one before. 'Go north, Jimmy, you forgot the tide. And look out for more rocks on the way.'

'Roger.'

The man at Julie's elbow hissed, 'We *must* go. Come! Come!'

The radio had a strap. Julie hooked it over her shoulder and began to follow the man along the beach, back to the path. She left the radio on. It couldn't do any harm while they were down on the beach blanketed by the sound of the rumbling surf.

They were almost at the path when the radio crackled again

The strong voice said, 'Got you, Jimmy. Turn east, fifty yards.'

'Roger. Yes, visual now.'

There was a pause, then, 'Where the hell are you going, Number One?'

'Avoiding a rock, sir.'

The radio hissed, then, 'Well, try and avoid the scenic route, will you?'

Reluctantly Julie turned the radio off and handed it to the man who was waiting to push her up the slide, the steep slope immediately above the beach. Another villager was waiting on the path above, ready to pull her up.

Halfway up the slope Julie almost slipped and slid back on to the beach again, but then she managed to find a foothold and push herself up until she could reach the hand of the man above. Once on the path the climb was much easier than the descent had been. It felt safer, going up, and her shoes seemed to grip the stony surface better.

As she climbed she felt ridiculously happy. The mixture of fear and elation made her want to laugh. Then she remembered the awful row on the beach and the risks they had all taken and realised it was relief that had made her lightheaded.

As they reached the clifftop, she remembered too that there was still a long way to go. She didn't think about laughing again until they had crossed the heathland and reached the fields, and her uncle had emerged from the shadows and taken her arm and led her firmly back to the farmhouse: only then did she smile. She suddenly understood why men enjoyed danger so much. She'd never felt so alive in her life!

It took her until dawn to sleep. She heard the clank of the milking pails and the sound of Tante Marie leaving to fetch Peter from Madame Boulet's before she finally began to doze off.

She kept remembering the scene on the beach and the dark silhouette of the boat against the surf. There was something warm and comforting in the memory, in the sight of the boat and the sound of the voices on the radio. The voices made her feel nostalgic, almost homesick. It had been a long time since she'd heard an English voice.

She remembered her childhood: the school outings to the beach, the occasional walks along the Hoe, the lovely view over the Sound, the chatter of her school friends . . . Yes: carefree days. She rather missed them.

Then she remembered what had come after. Peter's father had had a crisp upper-class accent just like the voices of those officers on the radio. Suddenly the memories weren't warm and comforting any more.

It was stupid to think about home.

There was no going back. There never would be.

But, even as she fell asleep, the nostalgia remained.

Part three
1942–February 1943

Fischer felt his eyes begin to close and, blinking rapidly, pulled himself quickly upright. He moved to the other side of the conning tower and stared out into the murk.

Not far now. They were well into the Bay – or as it was called by the lads, the Black Pit. Fortunately it was living up to its name this morning: it was a filthy day. A south-westerly gale was blowing, it was overcast and visibility was down to no more than a mile. Perfect cover for a submarine.

The weather was also bitterly cold, but Fischer didn't mind that either: nothing could be as cold as the place they'd come from.

It had been one of the longest patrols they'd ever been on. They'd gone up almost as far as Greenland – a hundred miles short of it, to be precise. And then they'd waited. It was so cold that the boat had iced up every few hours. They'd had to half-submerge then, to get the guns underwater and melt the ice off them. Not that the seawater was exactly warm, but it was just above freezing and that was all that mattered.

The wind hadn't been kind either: it had blown a gale or more almost the whole time. Conditions below had been worse than normal, and that was saying something in a Type VIIC. The accommodation had been running with water, both from the terrible condensation and from the waves that inevitably slopped down the conning tower hatch. The men had put up with the damp and the discomfort with their usual good humour. The only time Fischer had heard rumblings of discontent was during a storm when, instead of diving to escape the pounding and rolling, he'd been forced to keep U-319 on the surface to watch for a convoy. A lot of the crew had got sick and after six hours few except Fischer cared whether they ever found any targets or not.

They didn't find the convoy that day. Somehow Fischer had known they wouldn't. But he'd been ordered to watch for it, so watch he did.

It was four days later when they eventually found a target. It was a small convoy – only ten ships and one tanker – and well escorted by two destroyers. Fischer made contact with the other U-boats in his pack and they closed in. It was a disappointing fight: Fischer had just lined U-319 up for the tanker when the destroyer suddenly came straight for them and they were forced to dive. The ship dropped a few depth charges and by the time Fischer had got U-319 away and surfaced the convoy had got well ahead. It took him two hours to manoeuvre back into position; even then he managed to fire only two torpedoes before the destroyer was on to him again. And what was worse, the torpedoes had missed – at least there had been no *sound* of an explosion. It was all very unsatisfactory.

They did manage to find another convoy and sink two small ships before they ran out of torpedoes. But two ships was a poor tally and Fischer couldn't decide whether he'd suffered from bad luck, poor intelligence, or a simple lack of convoys. How did one ever know?

One thing was certain though: targets were not as easy to come by nowadays. He remembered the autumn of 1940, The Happy Time, it was called, when it was easy to sink eight, maybe even ten ships on a single patrol. Now, in this January of 1942, nothing was easy.

There was always something that conspired against such achievements: the weather, the convoy escorts, Allied air cover, something . . .

Maybe the debriefing would shed some light. It wouldn't be long now . . .

Fischer glanced at his watch and saw that it was almost 0800. Time to get some sleep. He nodded to the second watch officer and climbed down to the attack room below.

The *Leitender* – the Chief – and two of the technicians were crouched round the periscope which was in the raised position despite the fact they were on the surface.

'Still having trouble, Chief?'

'Yes, Herr Kaleu. Hydraulics leaking somewhere. Haven't much chance of locating the fault before we get in, I'm afraid.'

Fischer nodded. There was always something. He asked, 'Can we raise it manually?'

'Oh, I can still give you hydraulic power, but a bit slower, that's all. I'll just have to keep topping up the oil. Don't worry, Herr Kaleu, you'll have your *Spargel*.'

Fischer smiled. *Spargel* meant asparagus; it was their nickname for the periscope. They had an abbreviation or nickname for most things – even himself. They called him Herr Kaleu, short for Kapitanleutnant. Emblems of authority were favourite targets: they had nicknamed the swastika *Wollhandkrabbe*, after a particularly unpleasant fresh-water crab.

Fischer removed his wet weather gear and climbed down into the control room, wondering if the periscope would ever get fixed properly. Half the repairs carried out in the dockyards never held up for very long and broke down at the worst possible moments. They were still having problems with one of the hydroplanes and that had been going on for three patrols now.

238

Fischer automatically glanced round the control room before making his way forward to what was politely called the commander's cabin. It was in fact nothing more than a tiny recess with a curtain across the front of it. Still, it was an awful lot better than his men got. Fischer had heard that the British submarines were quite luxurious, with one bunk to each man. Here on the Type VIIC most of the lower ranks slept where they could, in hammocks or on the floor or between the torpedoes. They were allowed hardly any possessions, just a clean set of underwear and a few odds and ends.

Fischer supposed the whole boat must stink by now, but they were all so used to the intertwined smells of lavatories, diesel and sweat that nobody noticed.

When Fischer reached his cabin he paused only to hang up his cap before lying down and closing his eyes.

He never had trouble getting to sleep and when he was dog-tired as he was now it was that much easier. And the sleep when it came was the sleep of the just: deep, untroubled and dreamless.

It seemed to Fischer he was awake a fraction of a second before the klaxon blared. By the time it was in full cry he was running. Three seconds after it sounded he was in the control room, just in time to see the first man tumbling down from the conning tower.

The diving procedure was well under way: the men were running forward to get their weight into the nose, the hydroplanes were fully angled; the boat was starting to tilt downwards as she began to submerge at full speed. He looked quickly round to see if any problems were developing in the control room. None. He looked up to see if all the men were down from the tower and the hatch closed. Not yet. He watched, trying to judge from the angle of dive exactly how long the men had before the hatch had to be closed, whether or not any remained on the wrong side.

The last man fell down, the hatch clanged shut.

Now they had to wait. Diving took between forty and sixty seconds. Even on a good day it was an awfully long time.

Even now it was only eight seconds since the klaxon had sounded.

There was an instant of silence. The men stared across the cramped control room, their eyes locked on each other's faces.

Then for the second time that night Fischer had the strange sensation that he knew what was coming a moment before it actually happened. It seemed to him that he grabbed at a rail and tensed his body a fraction of a second before the bomb actually exploded.

The roar blasted his ears and jarred his senses. He felt the boat thresh violently, like a rat shaken by an angry dog.

Then darkness. A faint glow of light. Smoke. And the acrid smell of white-hot electrics.

Fischer yelled, 'Damage control reports!'

Voices started screaming at him, 'No rudder control!'

'Fire in the afterends!'

Fischer shouted, 'Pressure tanks?'

'Pressure normal!'

'Pressure hull?'

'No leaks!'

There was a pause, then, 'Fire in afterends extinguished, Herr Kaleu!'

'Any further damage?'

An engineer appeared from aft. 'Herr Kaleu! Starboard shaft buckled. Port shaft bent.'

'How bent?'

He was a young sailor, no more than nineteen. He didn't have an answer. Then his face brightened and he said, 'Well it's still turning!'

'I want a full report from the Chief at his convenience!'

'Yes, Herr Kaleu!'

Fischer absorbed the information. No rudder, no shafts.

Christ, the bomb had blown the whole of the bloody back end off!

But the pressure hull was intact: that was the important thing. They were still diving. There was no loss of diving control. He looked at the depth indicator. 'Level off at twenty metres.'

'Yes, Herr Kaleu!'

What they lacked was steering. He looked at the compass bearing. It was veering round. They were turning slowly to port.

'Trim?'

'Stable.'

The turn wasn't too sharp then. Hope yet.

The Chief hurried into the control room. 'Starboard shaft unserviceable, Herr Kaleu. Port shaft just about serviceable. But I can't give you more than – say, a knot submerged and two surfaced. Even then the engine might not like it.'

Fischer nodded.

It was decision time. He knew immediately that there was only one decision he could make.

He turned to the First Watch Officer. 'We'll give it fifteen minutes, *Eins WO*, then we'll go to periscope depth and send a signal to Brest, asking for assistance. I'll dictate the message in just a moment. In the meantime . . .' He looked round until he saw the figure of the man who'd been on watch, the Second Watch Officer, standing in his dripping oilskins, his face sheet-white. '*Zwei WO*, I want an incident report. Now!'

'There was no warning, Herr Kaleu. It even came from the north-east, downwind, so we didn't hear it until it was almost on top of us. All of a sudden there it was, coming straight for us . . .'

'This is very important,' Fischer interrupted. 'Are you sure it was coming straight for us?'

'Yes! No doubt about that.'

Fischer nodded. 'Continue.'

The second officer gulped. 'I could see that it was a big plane, a bomber, and that it was close, awfully close. I knew that by the time we got to the guns it would be on top of us, so I ordered diving stations straight away . . .' He looked up anxiously.

If Fischer had been there he would have ordered the men to the guns, to get in at least one burst. On the other hand there had been so little time . . . He said quietly, 'I think there was nothing we could have done either way. At least the dive has protected us from a second attack.'

The young man looked relieved and continued, 'As I closed the hatch I reckon the plane was no more than, say, twenty metres away.'

'Tell me, was it still overcast and the visibility low?'

'Yes, Herr Kaleu. You were there, you saw what it was like . . .'

'Yes, yes,' Fischer said impatiently. 'I just wanted to know if it had changed suddenly . . .'

'Oh no. Just the same.'

'Thank you. That's all.'

The young officer left. For a while Fischer sat motionless on the seat, then he walked slowly back into the control room. A chart of the Bay of Biscay lay open on the tiny chart table. Fischer stared at it blankly.

Bad weather, overcast conditions, poor visibility . . . Perfect cover for a submarine.

Like hell!

The plane must have known they were there; it must have!

He stared at the chart as if it might explain it all. But there was no simple answer, he knew that. Nothing that fitted any of the known facts.

The plane had *known*! And U-319 had been just like a sitting duck. Intensely vulnerable. Unable to defend herself. It – changed everything.

Fischer murmured wearily, 'God in heaven!' Then, reaching for a pad and pencil, he started to draft a wireless signal.

*

Doenitz picked up the signal and read the last few lines again.
'... ENEMY CAME STRAIGHT IN TO ATTACK IN POOR VISIBILITY. IMPOSSIBLE THAT ENEMY HAD ADVANCE VISUAL SIGHTING. REPEAT IMPOSSIBLE. CONCLUDE ENEMY PINPOINTED US BY NON-VISUAL MEANS ...'

Non-visual means ...

Doenitz laid down the signal. This was the third time in a month. On three occasions boats had reported sudden unexpected attacks, on three occasions they had been caught unawares on the surface. He could believe that the first two boats might have had sleepy lookouts, he could believe that their commanders might have under-estimated the visibility ...

But U-319? Fischer? Impossible. Fischer would never conceal the facts. If Fischer said the visibility was poor, then it was.

Doenitz called through to his staff officer, 'Get me Herr Schmidt at the Reich Research Directorate in Berlin.'

While he waited for the call to go through, Doenitz reflected on his previous conversations with Herr Schmidt. There had been several in the last six months. On each occasion Doenitz had asked if there was any information about new British antisubmarine devices. Three times he had come right out and asked the vital question itself: Was it possible that the British planes had search radar? Schmidt had hedged round the answer. His favourite expressions were 'very unlikely', 'improbable', and 'our information suggests not'. The man always promised to look into the matter again, but Doenitz had the suspicion that nobody was looking into it at all.

Well, this time there could be no doubt. This time Herr Schmidt would be forced to admit that the British not only possessed a search device, but that it was extremely effective. He wondered how Herr Schmidt would try to explain the phenomenon.

And however he did explain it, he had better be able to suggest a countermeasure. Otherwise ... Doenitz sighed grimly. Otherwise the effectiveness of the fleet would be severely curtailed. He would have to order the boats to submerge as they crossed the Bay. And if the British extended their air patrols further out into the Atlantic, then the boats would have to stay dived for even longer.

That meant it would take them twice as long to reach their patrol area: most U-boats could travel at a top speed of only seven knots submerged, compared to seventeen on the surface. Worse, at some time during their submerged run across the Bay, the boats would have to surface – for air and to recharge their batteries. Then ... then they would be desperately vulnerable.

If too many boats were caught on the surface and lost, it would be disastrous. The U-boat Arm was still desperately short of operational craft: instead of the three hundred or so he'd hoped for, Doenitz still had only ninety, and that was after more than two years of war. As before, the building programme was disastrously short of target and now, as if to forestall any chance of improving the situation, the winter was so severe that the Baltic ports were iced up and trials of new boats and training of new personnel had come to a complete standstill.

For Doenitz the shortage was doubly frustrating because, against his and Raeder's advice, Hitler had personally ordered much of the fleet to be redeployed. There were twenty-three boats – far too many – in the Mediterranean, where the waters were shallow and dangerous. Now, in the latest madness, twenty-six boats had been ordered to defend Norway against a supposed Allied invasion which, from what Doenitz heard, was very far from certain. Using U-boats as sentries was a waste of time; they could achieve much more spectacular results by squeezing the supply lines dry. But OKW – the High Command – was unconvinced. Doenitz could only advise. What more could he do?

And now this! A new threat, a new problem.

The telephone rang. The staff officer announced Herr Schmidt and put him through. Doenitz kept the formalities to a minimum, then told Schmidt the facts. He continued, 'I am having a meeting here in Paris with the Navy Technical Branch tomorrow. It is essential that you or your representative be here, Herr Schmidt. This matter is of the gravest consequence.'

The voice at the other end of the line was conciliatory. 'Of course I will come myself, Herr Admiral. If I set off now I can be with you first thing in the morning. I will have one of my people with me. He will have all the available data . . .'

Doenitz replaced the receiver, puzzled. Schmidt hadn't sounded at all surprised. Far from it. It was as if he'd been expecting the call. And his tone had been odd, too: evasive yet positive, almost as if he had a solution ready to pull out of his hat . . .

Doenitz rubbed his forehead. The politics of dealing with section chiefs in Berlin always gave him a headache. Doubtless he would find out what Schmidt had up his sleeve when the man chose to tell him. Hopefully tomorrow.

In the meantime he must take the painful decision to protect his boats. Even though it would slow them down considerably, he must order his boats to cross the Bay submerged.

He called for his staff officer. 'Werner, take a directive to all flotillas, Operational Area West.'

*

'As it happens, we think we can tell you exactly what it is,' Schmidt said calmly. 'Although we will have to make further checks, of course.'

Doenitz said sharply, 'Yes?'

'Well, it appears that the British bombers are being fitted with a type of radar . . .'

Doenitz blinked. There was a deathly silence round the table. The technical staff stared at the Chief Scientist in horror.

Schmidt licked his lips nervously. '. . . a compact search radar.'

'Are you sure of this?' Doenitz asked.

'A detection station in Normandy picked up a signal from an airborne source. It was quite definitely an intermittent signal. That means it was rotating . . . A search radar.'

Doenitz frowned and said slowly, 'I always understood that radar could not be made small enough to fit into an aircraft.'

There was an awkward silence. Schmidt looked cross.

Doenitz sighed and asked quietly, 'What about the wavelength? Is it one we understand?'

'Oh yes!' Schmidt replied immediately. 'They are using a 1.5 metre wavelength similar to our own systems. It's nothing new.'

'So?'

'We can manufacture a radar detector. This would pick up signals from approaching aircraft and give your vessels good warning.'

'How good?'

Schmidt shrugged. 'Ten, maybe fifteen miles . . .'

Ten miles . . . It was adequate – *if* Schmidt was right.

Doenitz asked, 'But how soon could these be manufactured?'

'It would take a lot of development. The receiver itself wouldn't be too complex . . . But the aerial –' He shook his head. 'That would have to survive submergence . . . It would take time to develop . . .'

Doenitz leant forward in his chair. 'But we don't *have* time!'

Schmidt looked uncomfortable. At length he said, 'Well, perhaps a mobile aerial might be possible . . . But it would have to be assembled every time the U-boat surfaced and taken down again every time it dived. It wouldn't be ideal –'

'I don't care!' Doenitz interrupted. 'If it works we must have it! We have absolutely no choice.'

He gave the Chief Scientist a harsh look. 'I don't care what the thing looks like, Herr Schmidt, I don't care if it's made out of plywood – but I want that detector in sufficient quantity, and I want it *now*!'

16

They came for David one cold February morning.

There was no warning. Sergeant Klammer and a soldier just marched in and told David to pack his belongings and be ready in five minutes. Just David, no-one else.

David stared, shocked. 'Where am I going?'

Klammer shrugged; he didn't know.

When the two guards had gone David looked at Meyer in horror. The old man patted his arm and said, 'Remember, they're allowing you some belongings. That's a good sign!' The faces of the other scientists were apologetic, guilty even, because they were being allowed to stay. David didn't blame them; he would have felt the same himself.

Meyer helped him pack his belongings. It didn't take long – they fitted into a small bundle. Then the two men sat down to wait.

When the soldiers came back David turned to Meyer, wanting to say many things. But he muttered only 'Goodbye', and, unable to say any more, followed Klammer quickly out of the hut into the bitter morning cold.

There was thick snow on the ground and more was falling. The path was slippery underfoot and David had to walk carefully. Suddenly he stopped in utter panic. He'd forgotten the most important thing of all! He shouted at Klammer's back, 'Please! One moment!' Then, before Klammer could say anything, he hurried back to the hut.

Inside, Meyer looked round in surprise. David cried, 'My medicine! I forgot my medicine!' Meyer took his arm and together they searched for it. They found it on the windowsill above David's bunk. David grasped the bottle and praised God. Shaking slightly, he placed it in his bundle, carefully wrapped in some overalls.

'Nothing else you've forgotten?' Meyer asked kindly.

David tried to think, but his mind was in a jumble. Klammer arrived and barked, 'Hurry!' David whispered desperately to Meyer, 'I don't think so.' Then, wringing Meyer's hand once more, he stumbled out into the snow.

Klammer led the way to the main gates, where a soldier was waiting to take over. The soldier marched David up the road towards the railway station. David approached it with foreboding. He hadn't seen the place since his arrival all those months before and he'd forgotten how bleak it was. The solitary station building loomed dark against the stark whiteness of the snow, and the wind was howling across the desolate expanse of sidings.

There was only one train, a train made up of cattle trucks.

David's mouth went dry. He remembered the horror of the journey from Sachsenhausen, the stench, the cries, the dying people. He couldn't believe that he must go through it all over again.

He stumbled and fell in the snow. As he picked himself up, his stomach stabbed with pain. He started off again but staggered, unsteady on his feet. The attacks often affected him that way. He thought: I'll never survive another journey.

The soldier led the way down the train. The trucks stank of excrement and, it seemed to David, of human suffering too. He struggled on, his head bowed against the driving snow.

They approached the end of the train. Here there was a single carriage, painted dark grey with windows. The soldier indicated that David should get in. David's heart lifted slightly.

Inside the carriage there were compartments with plain wooden seats and overhead luggage racks. The soldier pushed him into one and closed and locked the door. It was very dark inside, but after a while David's eyes became accustomed to the faint glimmers of light that seeped in through the drawn blinds.

He couldn't believe his luck. There must be a catch somewhere.

After a couple of hours the train started. Almost immediately the door was flung open and the compartment flooded with light. David jumped slightly. It was the guard, coming to tell him that he had two minutes to go to the lavatory. Later they brought him a blanket, some food – sausage and dry bread – and a cup of water.

David relaxed. He was going to be all right after all.

Slowly he stretched out on the long wooden seat and pulled the blanket over him. He tried to think, to work out where they might be taking him. He remembered, too, everything he was leaving behind – his work, half-completed; the safe, comforting routine of his day; the warmth of companionship. He had got very fond of his colleagues; he would miss them dreadfully.

Finally the steady rhythm of the clicking wheels lulled him into an almost dreamless sleep. Only when the train suddenly stopped did he wake. It stopped many times through the afternoon and early night, sometimes for hours at a time.

Once David woke in the night and tried to guess what time it was. Probably about three or four. He rubbed his eyes and realised he was mistaken. It must be much later: a crack of thin grey light had appeared at the edge of the blind. It was dawn. He must have slept much longer than he'd thought.

The train was going very slowly now; the sound of the wheels had fallen to a lazy rhythmic click. There was a loud squeal of brakes. Perhaps they were approaching a station. If they were going north, then they might be at Nuremberg by now, or Leipzig.

He sat up from where he had been lying on the seat and put his eye to the crack in the blind. The blind was permanently drawn, the section of heavy black canvas fastened to the window frame with nails at three-inch intervals. But between two of the nails the fabric bagged slightly. By pulling at it with one's finger and pressing one's eye close to the gap, it was just possible to see out.

He saw several railway lines, sheds, some sidings: a largish town then, maybe even a city. The brakes squealed again and the train juddered as it slowed still further. There was a loud clattering and the carriage suddenly jerked to one side: they were crossing onto another line. More sheds; a marshalling area. They came up alongside a stationary line of cattle trucks.

Then they stopped.

Suddenly there was a loud clanging and shouting. Soldiers were pulling back the doors of the cattle trucks. Men came pouring out, jumping on to the ground, standing blinking in the sudden light. The men were poorly dressed and foreign-looking, thin but not starving.

The men were moving now, walking obediently across the tracks towards David's train. There was more clanging and the sound of large metal doors sliding; they were getting into David's train.

After an hour there was more shouting and from far away at the head of the train David could hear the locomotive panting in long deep gasps as it pulled on its heavy load. The clank of couplings sounded down the train and the carriage jerked forward. From beneath there was the low rumble of the wheels on metal tracks.

David sat up and returned to his vantage point. They were slipping through the sidings and crossing junctions again until he guessed they were back on the main line. A stationary goods train appeared on the next track. David peered at the words chalked on each truck, trying to read the destinations. He saw Mannheim, Frankfurt, Mannheim again . . . Cities in the west.

Then the train was on the main line, going straighter and faster. With excitement David saw that they were approaching a station. There were platforms, station buildings, and a name . . .

Mannheim.

Something stirred in his memory.

Of course, David remembered and smiled to himself. This was the place he had planned to make for in his great escape from Berlin.

This was the place he was going to reach without any trouble, by getting on a train and sitting quietly in a corner.

David shook his head slowly. What a child.

The train passed through several small stations, but the names flashed by too fast to read them.

After a while David dozed again, rocked by the motion of the train, and it was not until much later when the brakes squealed that he woke again.

It was Saarbrucken.

They were at the French border.

He sat for a long time, quite immobile, waiting. At last the train started moving again.

A small village. Name: Wendel. German name, German architecture.

Then a small town with a long name. He missed seeing it on his side of the train because they were going so fast. He had to stand up quickly to catch it from the corridor window.

Faulquemont.

French name. French architecture. French vehicles . . .!

Then he laughed. What a joke!

The Germans were taking him to France! They were taking him where he had wanted to go all those months ago.

He smiled for a long time. France . . .! What a joke! What a joke!

Suddenly he wasn't smiling any more. Pain came suddenly, without warning. It came in a great stab that took the breath out of him. He bent over and, clutching his stomach, reached for the precious bottle of medicine. He swigged a mouthful and waited for the soothing liquid to quench the burning in his belly.

Trembling, he lay down and, all euphoria gone, thought disconsolately: When all is said and done, France, Germany, it makes no difference, not if I'm dying.

And I started dying a long time ago.

After that David lost track of the hours. The pain dulled his brain and the darkness confused him, and he slept most of the time. Life became a dream, a nightmare of dim awareness.

Only when the guard slid the door open with a bang did David wake up, blinking at the sudden light. Usually the guard placed the food hastily on the floor and left, or waited impassively while David went to the lavatory. But one day he shouted, 'Out! Out! Come on!'

David tried to gather his wits. How long had he been in the train? Three days? Longer? He stumbled towards the door. It was a moment before he remembered his bundle; he'd left it on the seat.

He reached down, picked it up and followed the guard out of the door, bumping into the wall as he tried to find his balance.

He stepped down off the train. Sidings again. Warehouses and sheds. A large city. But very French, still very French.

The labourers were pouring out of the train too. David saw that many of them were staggering and falling. Those who didn't get up were kicked or beaten with rifle butts, then thrown against the side of the track to where the dead and dying already lay in a pathetic pile of ragged limbs.

He tore his eyes away and followed the guard across the tracks. Suddenly there was a *crack!* Then another: the sharp whine of bullets. David winced but made himself keep walking. Why look back? He knew what he would see. They were killing the weak, finishing off the dying. Why look back? It only broke your heart.

They came to a lorry. The guard indicated that David should get in the back. It was a high lorry and David had difficulty climbing up. The guard, a boy of about twenty, helped him up.

David scrambled in and the guard came in behind him. For a while David sat quietly, then asked, 'Where are we?'

The guard looked surprised at David's German. Then he snapped, 'No questions!'

David nodded. 'Just asking.'

There was a short silence, then the guard murmured, 'Brest.'

'Ah!' David exclaimed. He nodded as if he'd known all the time.

Brest: where was it? David had never been very good at geography. Brest . . . A port, surely, right on the west coast. So he'd reached the sea after all! The idea gave him pleasure.

The truck moved off. The sidings and marshalling yards gave way to warehouses and sheds, and then they were climbing a hill. David's eye was caught by the sparkle of light on water. He watched fascinated as a great natural harbour opened out before him, a wide expanse of water that seemed to be bounded by gently sloping woodland on every side.

Then the water was obscured by houses and they were skirting round the edge of the city, which appeared to be built on a small plateau overlooking the harbour. The houses disappeared again and, as the truck turned inland, David saw that there was a man-made harbour immediately below, with several warships at its quays. There were dry docks too. And a submarine, which was moving across the harbour, its wake a line of darker grey against the brilliant whites of the sparkling water.

The road dropped away and turned, and then they were down

almost at water level. They crossed over a small canal and rumbled through another commercial area before coming to a sudden halt.

Almost immediately the truck started off again and David realised they had passed through the gates of a defence establishment: there were several guards on the gate, as well as barracks and military vehicles. Most of the personnel were wearing naval uniform.

David relaxed a little: he liked the Navy. Though formal and correct, they always seemed straightforward and trustworthy. The officers were of the old school: proper gentlemen, many from the old families, and few real Nazis among them. It would be good to work here . . .

The truck stopped outside a squat brick building. The guard jumped out and indicated that David should follow.

Inside the building a girl showed him up to an office and ushered him in. When David looked back he saw that the guard had gone.

There was a German naval officer sitting behind a desk. He stood up, a thin, nervous-looking young man. 'I am Kapitanleutnant Geissler. Please be seated.'

David waited for the officer to sit down then lowered himself gingerly on to a chair and waited.

'Herr Freymann, we understand you are highly qualified in radio-electrics and that you have been working for some time on the design of radio ranging devices.'

David nodded, a little taken back by the 'Herr'. It was a long time since anyone had called him that.

The officer went on. 'There is a company here in Brest which we have appropriated to produce electronic and radio components for us. They are making one particular piece of equipment which has the highest priority. It is essential that this device is produced with all speed and in some quantity . . . The officer looked a little unhappy. 'However there have been problems . . . Problems of a technical nature. We wish you, Herr Freymann, to supervise the technical side of the operation.'

David nodded and waited for the rest.

'The device is needed to protect our U-boats from enemy attack.' The officer stood up and picked up a thin file from the top of a filing cabinet. 'I have the technical specifications here. If you could study them immediately – then I will take you over to the manufacturing unit and you can see the organisation for yourself.'

David frowned. Protecting U-boats, but from what exactly? He still felt woolly-headed from the journey. As he took the file and opened it, he tried desperately to clear his brain.

There were a few pages of written specifications and a fold-out plan. Both were headed: *Project Metox. Most Secret*. David started to read the first page of the specifications.

He blinked.

It was an anti-*radar* device.

His pulse quickened and his mind cleared. This meant that the British had radar, just as Meyer and he had guessed.

He looked again at the specification. It stated the necessity for the Metox device to pick up signals at maximum possible range, up to thirty nautical miles. The absolute minimum tolerable range was six miles. That seemed very precise . . .

David looked up and asked, 'Why this six miles? What is so special about six miles?'

The officer replied, 'Ah. You see, our U-boats must have plenty of warning. They need at least one minute to dive, and another thirty seconds to get below bombing depth!'

Bombing . . .? David stared with incomprehension. Bombing. 'You mean *aircraft* attack . . .?'

'Yes, indeed!' The young man exclaimed. 'These aircraft approach at over 200 knots, you must realise. We need warning of over five miles to give enough time . . .'

But David wasn't listening. The British had succeeded in putting radar in aircraft. That meant they had made it small enough. But *how*? How had they done it?

Rapidly he searched down the first page of the specifications and then flipped impatiently over to the second. Where on earth was it? There! At last!

The detection device was to cover the wavelengths 1.4 to 1.8 metres.

David stared, trying to understand.

The British radar wasn't short-wave after all. It was within a range of wavelengths Germany had been using for some time.

Nothing new at all.

David felt a mixture of relief and anxiety – relief that no-one had got to the short-wave idea before him and anxiety that perhaps he had got it wrong and it wasn't possible after all.

He dragged himself back to the rest of the specification and read through it, glancing at the large-scale drawing. It was all quite simple. Whoever had designed this detecting device had got the basic idea right. There was a simple aerial, which led to a radio receiver. When the receiver picked up a radar signal from an approaching plane it emitted a high-pitched warning signal. The main problem, David saw immediately, was to get the emitter to give off a strong signal whatever the range and frequency of the incoming radar waves. The receiver itself was relatively straightforward.

'What problems have you been having, then?' he asked.

The Kapitanleutnant breathed in with obvious annoyance. 'It is difficult to be precise. Most of the devices produced so far have had small but serious defects. We don't know why. We need you to tell us and to prevent it happening in the future.'

'I see. And the technicians at this factory, are they competent?'

'Apparently so.'

'And the components, where have they been manufactured?'

'Mainly in Germany, a few in France. They all appear to be up to standard, but . . .! There always seems to be something wrong with the finished sets. We need someone to make sure these faults are stamped out!'

David closed the file and stood up. 'I am ready then. At your convenience.'

It took two days at Goulvent, Pescard et Cie for David to realise that the Metox project was a shambles. Some of the components weren't up to standard, the assembly line was disorganised and the French personnel were less skilled than he'd been led to expect.

The problems could be solved, no doubt about that. As always, it was a question of identifying the trouble spots and eliminating them. But it would take time – rather a long time by present standards. From the moment he arrived David had run into an unexpected difficulty: he was virtually unable to communicate.

He was more than a little surprised when the factory personnel failed to understand more than a few words of his French. He spoke the language badly, admittedly, but not *that* badly. Of course, it would have helped if some of the French personnel had spoken German, but they didn't and that was that. To make matters worse, the anxious young Kapitanleutnant kept hanging over David's shoulder, listening to his hesitant questions and staring angrily at the French technicians when they shrugged or gave the briefest of replies.

Secretly, David was glad most of the replies were short because then at least he could understand them. When one of the French started a monologue delivered at high speed and great length his heart sank. There was absolutely no hope of following it, and he could almost believe they were doing it on purpose, just to confuse him.

For a man who loved to communicate precisely and economically the frustration was terrible. David felt as if he were foundering in cotton wool.

The evenings only served to make him more depressed. He was

escorted back to a cold bare room in some barracks within the dock-yard compound. The food, sent over from a naval canteen, was good, but otherwise David found the accommodation almost unbearable. He was not used to being on his own. The silence and the smallness of the room pressed in on him: for the first time in his life he could guess at the terror of solitary confinement. Before, he had always been with people, whether working, living, or suffering, and he missed them. He even missed Fengal, the most irascible of the team back at the laboratory! Even him, the old shark.

The situation was ironic, he had to admit. Never had he been safer – never had he felt so discontented. It was, of course, because they had given him back so much . . . He had got to expect things.

The answer was work. Work always made him happy.

He paced his room and decided on some priorities.

The first was easy: he would make a success of the project even if it killed him.

The second was not so easy: Kapitanleutnant Geissler had to go.

And while he was about it he might as well have a third: to ask for another billet, one nearer other prisoners, somewhere with a bit of company. The request would probably be refused, but it never did any harm to ask.

He took a scrap of paper from the table and rummaged for the pencil stub which he always kept in his small bundle along with his other treasures: an eraser, a small slide rule and a picture postcard of Berlin; all possessions he'd been allowed to acquire while in the camp laboratory.

Taking up the pencil he wrote a work list for the next day, itemising each action in his neat handwriting made necessarily larger by the bluntness of the pencil.

When he had finished he regarded the list critically. It was not much, but it did at least make him feel that he had started.

He went to sleep immediately and woke early, his mind already busy. He jumped out of bed, examined his job list, then waited impatiently to be picked up for work. When the van finally deposited him at the factory door, he went straight to his office. He got out two blueprints of the Metox device, one in German, the other in French and, by comparing them, made a careful crib of all the technical words he would need for his conversations with the French technicians.

Next came the more difficult part: the Kapitanleutnant.

Geissler arrived sharp at eight, as he always did. David forced a warm smile, offered him a chair, and then, his heart in his mouth, dived straight in. 'Herr Kapitanleutnant, may I ask you a great favour?'

Geissler looked a little suspicious. He murmured uncertainly, 'Ask.'

David smiled briefly, then put on a suitably serious expression. 'I need to get deeply into the operation here. I need to talk to the men – at length. I also ... have a need to do everything at my own pace ... In short, Herr Kapitanleutnant, I need to work on my own. Of course,' he added hastily, 'I will report to you regularly. Every day, if you wish! Every few hours, if you wish! But ...'

Geissler had got to his feet and was holding up his hand, as if stopping some imaginary traffic. David stood up uncertainly. The officer shook his head and David's heart sank. Then Geissler said, 'Say no more. I understand perfectly. If you feel you will get better results on your own, then your request is automatically granted!'

The officer clicked his heels and left. David sat down in surprise. It had been so easy! He rubbed his hands. He felt a surge of excitement similar to those he had felt when starting new projects in the old days.

Next, to battle with the French language. David picked up his files and left his office. He was careful to avoid the director, an effusive, overbearing man, and went in search of the chief technician, a man called Gallois. He found him in a corner of the main workshop, staring disconsolately at some components on the bench.

David mustered his best French and said, 'Good morning. May I have a word with you?'

Gallois looked up and then past David's shoulder. 'Ah! No lieutenant today!'

'No.'

The Frenchman raised his eyebrows. 'You are in charge, then?'

David wanted to say: Hardly. But he didn't know the word and settled for, 'No, *they* are always in charge.'

'Ah! So what can I do for you?'

'Could we talk, please, about the problems on the Metox?' David spoke slowly and distinctly.

'Certainly. I am at your service.'

David was rather pleased: the fellow seemed to have understood him. They began to walk towards the drawing office.

Suddenly the Frenchman asked, 'You are German?'

'Yes.'

There was short silence, then, 'And you work for the German Navy?'

'Work?' David laughed. 'I "work" for the people I must!'

'But – you are employed by them?'

David frowned. He didn't understand the verb. 'Employed?'

'Yes. You earn money?'

David smiled grimly. 'Ha! No! No, my friend. I am a prisoner.' A look of confusion came over Gallois' face. David added, 'A prisoner, just like . . .' he searched for the word for labourers '. . . the workers I saw on the train.'

Understanding came over the Frenchman's face. 'Ahhh,' he murmured.

The mention of the labourers reminded David. He stopped and faced Gallois. 'Why are they brought here? What work do they do, all those people?'

'They are Poles. They are building the U-boat pens. Great shelters of concrete to stop bombs . . .' He threw out his hands to demonstrate a massive explosion.

They walked on.

The Frenchman asked, 'Why are you a prisoner?'

'I'm Jewish.'

The Frenchman nodded. 'I see.' And walked on in silence.

When they were sitting with the plans spread out in front of them, the Frenchman asked, 'What happens if you cannot solve the problems? What if this Metox does not work very well?'

'Ah!' David snorted. He indicated with his head. 'Back there, I suppose, to where I came from. But don't worry. It won't happen. We will make the thing work . . .'

They began with the problem of the aerial connection, then went on to the placing of the valves, and the suitability of the proposed amplifier.

To David's surprise they managed to cover the three main problems within an hour, in each case arriving at agreement as to the necessary action to be taken. Strangely, David's French seemed to have improved dramatically. He was elated.

David folded the large-scale drawing and beamed at the Frenchman. 'A simple device, with simple problems. I knew we could sort it out!'

Gallois nodded slowly. 'Yes, one can always sort these things out . . .' He smiled ruefully.

David regarded him for a moment, then said impulsively, 'Tell me, was my French so awful – when I arrived?'

The Frenchman looked down. 'Awful?'

'Yes, you know . . . No-one seemed to understand me.'

'Oh, we never understand Germans very well.'

'Ah.' David frowned. Some confusing, unsettling thoughts drifted through his mind. 'The matters we've been discussing . . .' He paused and looked sideways at the Frenchman. 'The problems with the Metox . . . why was it you were unable to solve them before . . .?'

Gallois made a face. 'Ah! The Germans, they never provide the information and equipment we need . . . We've asked and asked . . .' He trailed off and shrugged.

David nodded slowly. 'Yes . . . quite . . .' He thought of asking why the Germans had not responded to these demands, but something about Gallois' manner did not invite any more questions.

'Well,' said David brightly. 'I am sure the project will be a great success!'

'Without doubt,' the Frenchman replied coolly.

David walked quickly back to his office, his mind already going through the letters he would have to write and telephone calls he would have to make, and realised with mild surprise that his stomach hadn't been hurting at all today. In fact he hadn't felt so well in months.

It was the challenge of the work. As he thought, it was just what he needed.

17

Motor Gunboat 309 had two outstanding characteristics: she was wet and she was as explosive as a bomb.

The south-westerly Force 6 was revealing the first of her attributes: her speed was reduced to thirteen knots and she was twisting and bucking like a wild horse. Every few seconds she dug her nose deep into a wave and chucked a wall of cold, very solid, water back along her 110-foot length, up and over the open bridge, drenching the four men who stood there peering into the impenetrable darkness.

There was a loud thud and a particularly large lump of sea flew up over the bows. Ashley ducked instinctively behind the reinforced glass screen. The water hit the bridge with a dull slap, showering spray in all directions. Ashley felt a rivulet of freezing water running down his back and reflected that things might be worse: an E-boat could at this minute be firing at them and igniting the perfect mixture of air and high-octane petrol in their fuel tanks. And what a lovely bang they would make, he thought. A nice big orange whooomph!

And the Jerries wouldn't have to worry about looking for survivors: there wouldn't be any. Instant cremation.

All things considered, he'd rather be wet.

As if reading his mind, Jones, the coxswain, shouted, 'When are we getting these new boats then, sir?'

'Ah, cox, when indeed? According to the Master Plan we already have them!'

'Yes, sir.'

'But according to the grapevine, it'll be some time at the end of the year.'

Jones blew the saltwater off his lips and exclaimed, 'About bleedin' time too, sir. This old girl's as wet as Glasgow on a Saturday night! If I'd wanted to be a submariner, I would have bleedin' well volunteered.'

Ashley smiled. 'On the other hand, Jones, a diesel-powered boat could be a real bore! A dry bridge, reliable engines, non-explosive fuel – there'd be no feeling of adventure. That first pint back in Dartmouth wouldn't taste the same at all!'

'Ha!' the coxswain retorted. 'After a ride on the Hamoaze ferry, lemonade tastes like bloody champagne to me, sir! But, you know, sir, I wouldn't mind about the weather, 'cept we've been having it all bleedin' winter. Not a break, 'ave we 'ad, not a single one.'

'No, cox,' Ashley admitted. 'We can't have been saying our prayers right.'

In fact, there had been breaks in the weather, but they had come during the full moon, or when 309's engines were out of action, or when there was no operation planned. Whenever an operation *had* been set up it had blown Force 5 or more. Nothing unusual for winter in the English Channel, but uncomfortable, wet and – for this kind of job – dangerously slow. A delay on the outward journey meant a late arrival, a nervous wait at the pick-up point, and a mad dash to get back across no-man's-land to British coastal waters before dawn.

Ashley peered at the luminous hands of his watch: it was already 2330 and, he guessed, another two to two-and-a-half-hours to the pinpoint. An 0200 arrival would give them only forty-five minutes – or an hour at the most – to make the pick-up. It would be horribly tight. In this wind it would take the beach party at least twenty minutes to reach the shore. Five minutes to sort out the passengers and get them loaded. On the way back they would have the wind behind them but it would still take, say, fifteen minutes. Horribly tight.

Worse, he had the unpleasant feeling the wind was freshening.

They'd had miserable luck all winter, one way and another. First they'd had an inexperienced navigator and, on one occasion, had waited at the wrong beach for over three hours. Then, a week or so later, the engines had started to play up. As the Chief, an inevitable Scot by the name of McFee, was always saying, 'Seawater and petrol don't mix.' He did his best with the three supercharged Hall Scott engines but even he couldn't make the damn things work when they weren't in the mood. Bad weather made them especially temperamental; 'Like a woman caught in the rain', the Chief said contemptuously. A week before, they'd packed up two miles off the Brittany coast, just as they were being opened up for the journey home. The Chief had managed to coax a couple of knots out of the starboard engine, just enough to get them out of sight of land before dawn. Eventually, water was found in the fuel system, was cleared, and they managed to get under way again, but not before getting a nasty fright from a patrolling E-boat.

Ever since, the engines had been giving trouble of some kind or another and they needed constant nursing to keep them going.

But at least they had got rid of the dodgy navigator: that was something. All they needed now was a break in the weather.

Ashley poked his head outside the screen: yes, he could swear the wind was increasing. The barometer was probably dropping through the floor. He reached for the voice pipe and called down, 'Macleod! How's the barometer?'

A voice came floating up, 'The *Jimmy*'s in sick bay, sir! Elliott here.'

'Sick bay!' Ashley sighed and said 'Bugger!' under his breath. He put his mouth to the pipe again. 'On my way!'

As Ashley climbed down the exposed bridge ladder he felt the MGB's bows dive into a wave and instinctively flattened himself against the side of the boat. The action avoided the worst of the water: instead of pouring down his neck the sheet of water slapped into his back. As he made his way aft he felt the wetness seeping through his oilskins into his clothes. So much for oilskins.

He reached the door, yanked it open, and climbed down into the relative peace of the accommodation. The sick bay was not as grand as it sounded: it was an ordinary bunk which happened to be situated next to the locker housing the medical stores. The First Lieutenant was lying on the bunk, his face white and his breathing irregular. Two seamen were taking off his boots and covering him with a blanket. There was an ominous black bucket on the floor beside him.

Ashley looked at one of the seamen. 'What's up?'

'Sick, sir. Chucking up and – the other, sir.'

Ashley went to the side of the bunk. 'Christ, Number One, couldn't

258

you have thought of something more original? Been overdoing the champagne and smoked salmon, eh?'

'Sorry, must have been something I ate.' The voice was soft with a gentle Canadian accent. 'I'll be all right in a moment, I'm sure. Once I've . . .' A look of disbelief came over the man's face and he suddenly threw himself over the bucket. Ashley looked away; the sight of vomit always made him retch.

When Macleod had sunk back onto the bunk Ashley turned back and said, 'I don't think you'll be fit for anything, Macleod. You'd best stay here.'

'No! I'll be okay. Really!'

'Stay here! That's an order. We'll manage without you. Very well, in fact. You'd be surprised!' He grinned.

Macleod smiled faintly and closed his eyes. The smile vanished from Ashley's face and he said quietly to one of the seamen, 'Keep an eye on him – temperature, pulse, everything. He looks bloody awful to me.'

He turned and made his way back to the deck, thinking: Damn!

The Canadian was his best man; very keen and very able. He must be really ill to have agreed to lie down; if he was capable of getting to his feet, he would. Ashley gritted his teeth. He'd have to find a replacement – Macleod was leader of the beach party. Macleod was the only one who spoke decent French.

Apart from himself there was only one other officer on the boat: the navigator, a man called Tusker. He was RN (Retired) and had bamboozled his way back into active service by nagging the Admiralty to death. Unlike the first navigator, Tusker was brilliant at his job. He'd got *309* through rocks and narrow channels into countless pick-up points, in filthy weather and without a decent navigation aid in sight.

There was only one problem: he was forty-five and had a gammy leg.

Ashley made his way forward again, gripping tightly on to the available handholds. The boat pitched sharply forwards and then, trembling and shivering, heaved herself up once more, ready for the next wave.

Ashley climbed into the small space optimistically called the chart room. It was a wooden structure built on to the deck just in front of the bridge. Tusker was crouching over the collapsible chart table – a simple device which, when the boat pounded heavily, often lived up to its name. As usual, Tusker was making careful calculations. He never stopped, from the moment they left until the moment they got back, reworking the tides, the course, the speed, and the ETA.

'How we doing, Tusker?'

'Ah, should reach Les Vaches at 0135, and drop anchor at 0200.' He always used Les Vaches, a large pair of odd-shaped rocks three miles off the beach, as a navigation point. He aimed the MGB straight for them and then, as he liked to point out, when they almost hit them they knew exactly where they were. He'd never failed to find them yet, despite a shortage of navigation aids. All there was to confirm the dead reckoning position was an echo sounder ticking away in the corner of the chart room.

Tusker wiped some drips off the transparent plastic chart cover and pointed at the chart. 'We crossed the Hurd Deep forty-five minutes ago. I hope to pick up the edge of the Plateau de Triagoz in just over an hour. That'll give us a good lead in. Unless of course we have to reduce speed still further . . .?'

'No, we must bash on, whatever the weather. Otherwise we'll be too late. We're cutting it a bit fine as it is.'

The two men braced themselves as *309*'s bows rose into the air and began to descend rapidly towards an approaching wave. There was a loud crash and the boat shuddered. Cascades of water thundered over the chart room, pouring down the windows and penetrating the cracks in the wood. Tusker methodically wiped the drips away and gazed down at the chart again. 'Whatever the revs say, I'd be surprised if we were doing thirteen knots in this sea.'

Ashley nodded. 'I've allowed a bit for the sea conditions, but I dare say you're right. I still want to press on, though. Once we reach the plateau we'll start to get in the lee of the land. Things should improve then.' He blew out his cheeks. 'By the way, Macleod's sick, so I'll be leading the beach party. That means you'll be in charge until I get back.'

Tusker's eyebrows shot up. 'I say, that's a bit irregular, isn't it? I mean, why not send Talbot or Eddington to the beach. They'd do the job all right.'

'No, I'd rather go myself,' Ashley said crisply. He didn't want a discussion. He was perfectly well aware that a commander shouldn't leave his ship, but this was a very small ship and the circumstances rather unusual. 'No, I'd prefer Talbot and Eddington to stay here. You'll want them if there's a fight. It's more important to leave the ship properly manned. Anyway . . .' He smiled breezily at Tusker, '. . . after all this time I want to have a look at this beach and meet some of our Breton friends.'

Tusker nodded reluctantly. 'As you say.'

'Now, this is the form. You are to wait until 0315, at the very latest, and then you are to leave, even if we haven't returned. Is that understood?'

The other man nodded.

'And if there's any sign of trouble, the usual rules apply – get out and as quickly as possible. Just because I'm ashore, don't try to be clever and wait around. Understood?'

'Understood.'

'Good!'

It was raining now, drumming against the window, mingling with the salt spray in a steady deluge of running water.

Ashley murmured, 'Christ! We're not going to see very much at this rate.'

'No, but it may not last. We've still got an hour before we need to start worrying about visibility.

Ashley sighed. 'I just wish that, for once, we'd have a bit of luck. It would make a pleasant bloody change!'

It was 0140. There was no sign of Les Vaches. Although the seas were much lower here in the shadow of the land and the boat was riding the waves more easily, the weather was still foul. Every few minutes heavy showers came through, obliterating the few precious yards of visibility, turning the already dark night into a wall of black.

Ashley stood at the side of the bridge, his teeth set, his eyes straining to penetrate the inky darkness. He tried to resist the temptation to call down to Tusker again, but failed. He reached for the voice pipe. 'Tusker! Any ideas?'

'Give it five minutes, then we can try turning east.'

'Five minutes is a hell of a long time!' Ashley knew he was sounding testy but, damn it, he was.

'Yes, five minutes should get us right up to Les Vaches,' came the calm response.

'I thought we were meant to be there already!'

'Well, allowing for losing some time in those seas . . .'

'Okay! Five minutes!'

He threw the pipe back into its socket and stared back into the darkness. He had four men on the bridge now, all of them looking – for anything: any sign, any indication of rocks, land, E-boats, anything. A hundred miles, they'd travelled, and now they were looking for two rocks in the middle of the sea. Ridiculous!

Nothing. Not even the customary smell of the land. Ashley thought: Tusker's finally blown it.

The rain stopped. Strange new shadows flickered across the pattern of the night. Ashley screwed up his eyes. It was almost impossible to know what you were seeing . . . But the visibility had definitely improved, no doubt about that.

'Sir! Port bow! I think I see something, sir!'

They all turned and stared, no-one speaking, an electric silence filling the bridge.

'Yes, sir.' It was the coxswain's voice, steady and firm. 'Just fine on the port bow, sir. A rock, I would say.'

Ashley looked again, and saw it this time. It was a large rock. One of two. Les Vaches.

Ashley breathed out slowly, his body sagging as the tension eased away. He called down the pipe, 'Well done, Tusker. Your rock's popped up on the port bow.'

Thank goodness it had. He always had a vision of getting the boat lost and steaming on to a barely submerged rock and the boat tearing her guts out . . . He tried not to think of such things, but on bad nights one couldn't help it . . .

Tusker took some bearings and they pressed on towards the land. Because the wind was offshore and would carry the sound of their engines away from the ears of German sentries, Richard decided to risk a fast approach. Time was ticking away. It was 0150.

At two miles they reduced speed to five knots, searching for the familiar landmarks, feeling their way in towards the anchorage. Finally they were on station, one mile offshore in the open arms of a wide, rocky bay, lying to their grass-rope anchor. It was 0215. Only one hour at the most.

The beach lay in a cove in the western arc of the bay, its sides guarded by a myriad of small rocks. The surfboat was already in the water, the two crew waiting at their oars which were muffled with heavy sacking.

Ashley jumped down and sat in the stern, a compass in his hand and the wireless on the seat beside him. At his feet was their new gadget, a hydrophone, which, when its sensor was dropped in the water, would pick up the sound of 309's echo sounder and guide them back to her. They would need it tonight.

The surfboat buffeted her way through the waves, the water hissing and slapping at her sides. Already the MGB was a shadow in the deeper darkness behind them.

Ashley looked at his watch. It was 0222.

He couldn't help thinking that for once they really were cutting it a bit fine.

The clock ticked loudly on the mantelpiece, syncopating with the gentle snores of Tante Marie, asleep in the chair on the opposite side of the hearth.

Julie stared at the book which lay open but unread on her lap and listened intently to the other sounds, the sounds of the night. A wind was blowing, quite a strong one, vibrating the windows and moaning softly around the buildings; and there was rain, coming in sudden squalls, drumming loudly on the outhouse roof, pit-patting against the glass.

She listened and almost imagined she heard the rumbling of the surf down in the cove and the scrunch of boats as they grounded on the pebbles. Almost imagined, too, that she heard the sound of footsteps as the guides led the passengers past the farmhouse down to the beach . . .

With a sigh, Julie returned to her book. Always imagining things!

But she stared at the pages, unseeing, and thought of the waiting men and the steep path to the beach and the dark cover again. She hadn't been back to the beach since that night, four months ago now. In one way she was sorry – she'd rather enjoyed it – but she was determined not to get involved too deeply. Her instincts still told her that it would all go wrong, that, sooner or later, it would end in disaster. And she couldn't bear the thought of being caught. Nothing could be worth that.

At the same time she couldn't help worrying. Especially tonight.

The night had a bad aura about it, an indefinable atmosphere of depression and doom. She couldn't say why, or in what way. At ten she had gone to bed and tried to sleep, but her feeling of despair had been so strong that she had come down to sit with Tante Marie and wait. Of course a man would laugh at the whole idea of *feeling* these things, but for her it was almost tangible.

Except that now, two hours later, she wasn't quite so certain as before. Perhaps nothing was going to happen after all. She rubbed her eyes. She was beginning to feel tired. It might be worth trying to go back to sleep again.

It was comfortable there by the stove. She rested her head against the chair-back and closed her eyes. She'd make the effort to go to bed in a moment.

Suddenly she stiffened.

There was a slight unidentifiable sound, something that hadn't been there before . . .

She stood up and, dousing the small oil lamp, went to the door and opened it.

The wind was sighing and rustling round the farmyard, a cow

263

shuffled restlessly in the barn, then . . . Yes, it was there! *Something* . . . Julie felt her blood run cold.

But what was it! *What*?

Machines? Men?

Whatever – it was something that shouldn't be there.

Quickly she closed the door, lit a candle and took it to her room. She found warm clothes: vest, woollen blouse, thick sweater, trousers, socks, sturdy shoes. Back in the kitchen she took a waterproof cowman's jacket from the back of the door and Jean's beret, pulling it low over her head and tucking her hair up inside the crown.

She touched Tante Marie's arm. The old woman woke with a start and looked at Julie in horror. She exclaimed, 'Where are you going? What's the matter?'

'Don't worry! I just have to get out, that's all. Just to listen . . . and watch for them.'

'Julie, don't go!' Tante Marie hissed. 'You don't know where the patrols are! You might stumble into one of them. Don't go, I tell you!'

Julie shook her head. 'I'll be careful . . . I just want to see that everything's all right. That's all. Don't worry.'

She turned quickly and went to the door. Waving briefly to the old woman, she stepped out into the night. She waited a moment to get her eyes accustomed to the darkness, then walked quietly round the side of the house to the road.

She paused and listened. Whatever that sound had been, it had gone. There was nothing now, only the rustling of the trees and the sigh of the wind.

But still, she had to go. She set off along the road, walking rapidly, her shoes making no sound on the hard surface. After five minutes she had made good progress: almost halfway up the hill that led to the open heathland. She walked steadily, her hands deep in her pockets, her mind locked on the necessity of reaching the clifftop. Once there she would wait and listen until she knew everyone was all right.

She stopped dead. There was that sound again.

It was a low whining, far off, back towards the village.

It was like the whining she'd heard in her imagination once: the whining of trucks. Trucks climbing.

Up the hill towards her.

She froze, still listening, unbelieving . . .

. . . the sound of trucks climbing. Oh God!

Then she ran, she ran fast and straight; she ran along the dark narrow lane, up and up, on and on, until the air rasped in her throat and the heavy shoes were like lead on her feet.

She ran with grim determination, absolutely certain that she must reach the clifftop: absolutely sure that she must get there before *them*.

She ran until her lungs were bursting and her heart was hammering in her ears.

And she didn't look back – she didn't dare. She just ran. Push, push . . . On, on . . . Think of nothing . . . Just trucks! Climbing! *Oh God, let me get there first*!

She was slowing. She panted, 'Come on! Come on!'

The heathland, at last. Now gorse reared up and pulled at her clothing; and the uneven ground rose and fell unexpectedly before her, jarring her legs, unbalancing her body. She stumbled and picked herself up again, still running.

It was dark, very dark. She tried to get her bearings. It was a long cliff and there were several paths, all leading down. Only one path was the right one. She looked ahead, trying to read the contours of the land. It all looked the same!

Now the effort was terrible. At every breath her lungs shot with pain and at every stride her legs flailed, less and less controllable, until she was half-running, half-staggering.

She sobbed, 'Come on! Come on!'

She tripped and fell. She put out her hands, too late. Her head hit the ground with a dull thud. For a moment she was dazed then she thought: *Get up*! She pulled herself up and staggered forward again.

Now at last there was something paler ahead. The wide expanse of the sea. Bordering it was the dark rim of the clifftop. Sobbing with relief she looked wildly to right and left. Which way?

Right. Yes: right.

She ran, looking desperately for familiar landmarks.

Then she saw a hillock, and a hollow . . . She was there. At the path.

She stopped, panting wildly. There was nobody. She called softly. Nobody. Perhaps the lookout was further along the cliff.

She hesitated for a moment, then set off, down the steep path towards the rumble of the surf. This time she took the path much faster, half-falling, half-running, stumbling against the larger rocks and scrabbling at the loose stone hill for handholds. A rock came up and knocked her chin and she heard her teeth close with a sharp snap. The warm, unfamiliar taste of blood filled her mouth.

The ground fell away: she had reached the slide at the bottom. She thought of jumping, but it was at least six feet and she was too tired. Wearily, she sat down and slid. The beach rushed up, she braced her legs. They gave way under her and she landed heavily on her side.

Slowly she got to her feet and staggered across the pebbles. She was so tired she'd almost forgotten why she had come. She called softly. Nothing. She called louder. Where were they? She thought: Oh God! Please let them be here. *Please!*

The finger of rock was deserted: no-one was waiting there. Down to the water then.

Suddenly, close by, there was a voice. Julie jumped and gave an involuntary cry. The voice repeated, 'St Brieuc!' It must be a password and she didn't know the response.

She was shaking violently. She cried, 'It's me, Julie Lescaux. I don't know the password. Please – I've come to warn you . . .'

'We can't go now! The surfboat's already on its way!'

There was a short silence, the men huddled in a nervous group, their faces hidden in the darkness. Then everyone spoke at once. One voice emerged high above the rest. Julie recognised it immediately: it was the leader. 'We must go now! Now! We must abandon the mission!' His voice was shrill, anguished. 'Come on! Let's go!'

Again, there were many voices. Julie realised with a shock that one of them was Jean's. Then there was a lone voice, a strong voice, someone who commanded, 'Stop!' And there was silence again. The strong voice went on, 'Those who want to go, go now! The rest of us stay and get our passengers away.' There were mutterings of agreement, then the leader was speaking again, louder, shriller, 'It's madness to stay! We must go now! Now!' The strong voice said, 'Go then!' Julie realised it was the voice of the man who'd sat next to her by the rock, that first time, a man she'd later realised to be a fisherman from a small cove in the next bay: a man called Gérard.

Now Gérard came close to her, saying, 'Here, Julie, the wireless! Try to make contact with them! Warn them!'

The hard oblong box was thrust into her hand. Julie grasped it. She walked unsteadily away and sat on a rock, trying to remember how it worked. Her body was still shaking with exhaustion and she fumbled clumsily with the knobs. She tried the on/off button. It was difficult to know if it was working: the surf was roaring and the wind whistling so loudly that she couldn't hear. She put the receiver part to her ear: there was a faint crackling. Now the aerial. She pulled it up, found the transmitting button, and pressed it. She called, 'Hello.' There was nothing. She tried again: still nothing.

She thought: I'm doing something wrong.

She peered at the various buttons and remembered something about two different frequencies. She found a sliding switch and pushed it the other way. She called again, 'Hello.'

The wireless crackled and, above the rumble of the surf, she heard a tinny voice, 'Bertie here, Please identify. Over.' Julie shivered with surprise.

Then she remembered that she was meant to say something: a password. But it was no good, she couldn't remember it. She pressed the transmitter and said, 'Beach here.' Now what? Information. She said hastily, 'You may be in danger. The Germans are searching the cliffs.'

The wireless crackled, 'Understood. But our party's arrived, hasn't it? Over.'

Julie was confused until she realised she was talking to the ship, not the boat. She looked quickly along the beach. Yes – he was right – something was happening. The men had gathered at the water's edge and a shape was showing dark against the whiteness of the breaking waves: the surfboat.

She pressed the transmitter. 'They're here. We'll get them off again as soon as possible.' She left her finger on the button but couldn't think of anything else to say. She released it, then pressed it again hurriedly and said, 'Over.' When she let go again the man on the ship was already speaking, '. . . short message when they leave. Out.'

Julie blinked and wondered whether to reply, but 'Out' probably meant that the man had signed off. She'd understood what he meant: they wanted to know when the surfboat left. Best not to talk again and confuse the matter. She switched off the wireless and, getting up, walked along the edge of the water towards the surfboat.

It was terribly windy: she had to lean her body forward in order to walk. The surf was very loud, too, and it was impossible to hear anything above the thunderous roar. Julie hoped someone was keeping a good lookout up on the clifftop . . .

As she approached the boat, she saw frantic activity: the men were dragging things out of it and removing the oars from the rowlocks. She saw with horror that one of the oars was broken. Most of the men went to one side of the boat and, with a heave, tipped it right over. Water poured out and Julie realised it must have been half full.

Suddenly the firm voice of Gérard was at her elbow again. 'Julie! Come!' His tone was urgent, authoritative. He led her past the men working on the boat to a figure who stood slightly apart from the rest.

Gérard pulled her in front of the figure and said, 'Please explain that the Germans are near!'

Julie realised it was one of the British crew. She said in English,

'We think the Germans are about! Searching the clifftop. They may know you're here. You must get away quickly, straight away!'

The figure stepped closer and she felt a strong hand grip her arm. 'Tell your friend, it's not just the oar that's broken – there's a hole in the boat too! We've got to find something to stuff in it, and quick!'

She translated quickly and turned back, saying, 'Yes, he understands that.'

The hand was still on her arm. 'And tell him we can only take six passengers. It's just too rough out there to risk any more.'

Again, Julie translated. Gérard nodded. The British officer said, 'Right! Let's get going!' The men were already at work: tearing a wool jacket in half to make a bung, sorting out passengers, cutting cord to whip together the two pieces of broken oar.

So little time! Julie stood, frozen with worry, willing them to finish.

But a moment later there was an exclamation. It came from someone standing a little way up the beach. There was something about the shout which made everyone stop and look up. The man was running frantically towards them, hissing, 'A light . . . A signal!'

Julie looked up at the cliff and felt a thud of fear.

There was a dim red light, blinking through the darkness.

A warning. Blood-red.

For a second there was silence, then Gérard's voice floated over the thundering surf. 'The boat! We must hide the boat! In the rocks on the point. Quick!' Everyone jerked into action, hauling on the boat, dragging it along the beach.

The British officer ran up to her and grabbed her arm. 'What in hell . . .?'

'The Germans! They're coming!'

'Christ!' He turned and shouted, 'Jenkins! Turner! Pick up your weapons! Get this boat hidden, then follow these men!'

The boat was halfway up the beach now. Her heart in her mouth, Julie ran as fast as she could over the slippery pebbles, following the rapidly moving shadows of the men as they fled across the beach to the rocks.

By the time she reached the point, the men had hidden the boat behind a large rock and were covering it with seaweed. As soon as the boat was camouflaged people moved quickly away towards the jumble of rocks and boulders that tumbled down from the headland above, and slid quietly into the shadows of the crevices.

Julie looked blindly around, panic rising in her throat. Where was Jean? And Gérard? She stumbled closer to the rocks, searching desperately. Then Jean was beside her, taking her arm, guiding her in towards the rocks. She cried, 'Oh Jean!'

'Julie, it'll be all right. All we have to do is keep quiet! Now, go in here. In here!' He pushed her into a crevice between two tall rocks. She settled herself on the stones and then realised Jean hadn't followed her. Where was he? Why hadn't he followed?

All around her there were clicking noises: Julie realised the men were checking their weapons. She felt sick. *Where* was Jean?

Suddenly he was back, pushing another figure towards her. With surprise she realised it was the British officer. She hissed, 'Jean! Jean! Where are you going?'

'I'll just be next door! Next rock!'

The officer had crawled in beside her and was tugging gently at the strap on her shoulder. She'd forgotten about the wireless.

'Sorry,' he whispered. 'But I must contact my boat. Our own set got wet.'

'Of course.' She felt a fool, for having panicked. She passed over the wireless and listened as he clicked the switches. There was a hum and he said, 'Bertie, Bertie, this is Alfie calling. Over.'

There was a silence, then he tried again. Still nothing. Julie felt for him. Suddenly she felt guilty. She should have thought of calling the ship herself as she came along the beach. The wireless probably would have worked then, out in the open. Stupid of her!

She started to say, 'I'm sorry, I . . .' But he said 'Shush!' and she bit her lip.

After another two minutes he called into the wireless again. Still there was nothing. She heard the click of switches again and realised he was putting the wireless down onto the ground. He sighed and said very quietly, 'I think that perhaps it just isn't my day.'

Then he leant closer to her and whispered, 'Sorry, I didn't mean to shut you up just then, but I thought I heard something . . .'

'That's all right.'

'You've been a great help. Thank you.'

Julie nodded briefly in the darkness, then turned her head to listen for sounds from the beach. She strained her ears but it was impossible to hear anything over the rumbling of the surf. Suddenly there was a scraping noise; the officer was moving forward. His figure became a silhouette against the paler black of the sky, a weapon just visible in his hand.

Tentatively Julie followed until she too could see down to the impenetrable darkness of the beach.

After a while, she realised quite a lot of time had passed. Half an hour, maybe more. And still there was nothing.

Perhaps they were going to be safe after all.

Suddenly she sensed the officer stiffen. He got up on one knee, then rose and walked forward until he was standing just clear of the rocks.

Then she heard a sound: the sound of an engine. Not a truck, not from the cliff. It was something more familiar. She tried to place it. It was the sound of an engine over water, like a fishing boat's but deeper, throatier . . .

She heard the Englishman say, 'Christ All Bloody Mighty!' Then he turned and crawled slowly back in beside her. She thought she heard him laugh; she must have misheard. But no, there it was again.

She whispered, 'What is it?'

He said bitterly, 'I think I've just missed my bloody boat!'

Ashley opened his eyes and frowned slightly. Hanging from the ceiling above him there was a model aeroplane made of cardboard and paper. He turned his head. On the walls there were a couple of bright paintings – one of a tractor, the other of a car – and two posters of Paris. A child's room. A rather small child at that: he looked down and saw that his feet were protruding from the end of the totally inadequate bed. It was the coldness of his toes which had woken him.

He looked at his watch: nine-thirty. GMT, that was: an hour later in France. He must have been asleep for three hours then.

They had waited in the rocks until five when a lookout had come to tell them that the Germans had gone. Then the Bretons had had a short conference to decide who was going to take charge of the airmen, and who Ashley and his crew. Ashley tried to understand what arrangements were being decided, but the men whispered in Breton or, once or twice, in heavily accented French, and he couldn't catch it. Then he'd searched for the girl and asked her and she had told him that his men were to be hidden in a safe house – she wouldn't tell him where – and he in another. He'd asked if he couldn't be hidden in the same house, and she'd said no, there wasn't room. She was quite abrupt.

'Well,' he said, 'just tell me who to follow.'

'Me. You're to be hidden in my house.'

He tried to see her face in the darkness. 'How very kind . . .'

'Hardly! There's nowhere else, that's all.'

She was cross, he could tell, though he couldn't guess why. Best not to say any more then. He'd followed her without a word, up a steep path to the top of the cliff and then across some heathland to a road. She'd started off at a cracking pace, up the cliff, but then slowed and at one point she staggered and almost fell. He'd reached for her arm, but, politely but firmly, she'd pulled away.

When they reached the back door of the house she'd told him to wait outside. Within a minute she was back, leading him into a warm room, very dark: a kitchen he guessed. Again he'd waited while she disappeared into a back room. This time it was several minutes before she returned. She guided him through a door and up some narrow steep stairs to an attic – this attic.

All she'd said before going was, 'Don't make a sound and don't put your face to the window! Oh, and your clothes, they're wet, I suppose? Leave them at the top of the stairs, just here!' And then she was gone.

Two thoughts had entered his mind before he fell asleep: the first, that someone had just been asleep in this bed, it was so warm, and the second, that the cross English-speaking lady was not very pleased to have him here, not very pleased at all.

Now, in the morning light that filtered through the one small window, he took another look round the child's room, pulled his feet in out of the cold and closed his eyes. He might as well go back to sleep again: he wasn't going anywhere – and certainly not without any clothes on.

Suddenly he was wide awake again. A door had closed in the room immediately beneath. Someone was climbing the stairs. He reached down to the floor and, picking up his gun, pointed it towards the top of the stairwell.

A head appeared, with dark, longish hair. The girl.

He relaxed and put the gun back on the floor.

She was carrying some bread and a mug of hot liquid, her head bent down, intent on preventing the liquid from spilling. She came up to the bed and, crouching down, placed the mug on the floor. The bread was more difficult: she thought of balancing it on top of the mug, but put it on the bed instead. Then she looked up at him.

He stared at her in astonishment.

He realised with a shock that he knew her.

But where on earth from? He couldn't think. He examined her face for clues: dark eyes – tired today, with grey shadows under them – neat features, a lovely mouth, and fabulous clear pale skin. Very attractive – lovely even. But *where* had he met her?

He realised he was staring: she had looked away, embarrassed, and had started to speak. '. . . we've found some clothes for you. I'll bring them up directly. It's best not to wear your other ones – they look far too Navy if you're seen. And you *must* take care not to be seen – we have soldiers billeted here.'

Ashley blinked in amazement. 'What?'

'Yes, two of them. They sleep in the main part of the house, at the front. They're up at six-thirty, out by seven and back at about eight

in the evening. For a meal. Then they usually go out for a drink –
until about ten.'

Ashley raised his eyebrows. 'It's a bit close for comfort, I must
say . . .'

'On the other hand,' the girl said, 'they wouldn't think of looking
for anyone in the same house, would they? I mean, you're probably
safer here than somewhere more isolated.'

He smiled. 'Yes, I hadn't thought of that.' He looked at her with
new admiration.

'Just as long as you're *not* seen.' She was looking at him sternly.
'I'm afraid that means not going out. And no noise, either. It's vital.
You do understand that, don't you?'

He sat up in bed and looked down at her. 'I understand that very
well – I understand the risk you're running. And I'm very grateful,
believe me.'

'Fine, well as long as you obey the rules there'll be no problems.'
She was so schoolmarmish that Ashley couldn't help hiding a smile.
She glanced up, saw his amusement, and flushed.

'Right,' she said tightly, getting to her feet. 'I'll get those clothes
then.' She brushed at her skirt with agitation.

He could see he had annoyed her. He said hurriedly, 'Thank you.
I'm really most grateful. And I'm really most sorry for the trouble
I've caused.'

She hesitated, searching his face. Then she nodded slightly. 'Don't
mind me. It's just been a long night and – they arrested some people.'

Ashley said, 'I'm so sorry.'

She went on, 'Three people, two local and one from – elsewhere.
It could have been worse, of course. We're grateful there weren't
more.'

Ashley thought for a moment. He said, 'Did these people know
about the beach, about our visits . . .?'

'Oh yes.'

'So –' He didn't know how to put it '– so the Germans might
extract the information from them.'

She hesitated. 'It's possible.'

'Then . . . that beach might be risky. Well,' he said brightly, 'there
must be other beaches near here! We'll arrange a pick-up as soon as
possible and get ourselves off your hands!'

She nodded briefly, then frowned. 'There's only one problem. One
of the men arrested was the leader – he was the one with access to
the wireless operator, somewhere near Paris. It'll take time to set up
another link, particularly if the wireless operator has to go into
hiding, or gets caught . . .'

Ashley sighed heavily. He didn't like the idea of being cooped up here for any length of time. All he wanted was to get back to his boat; he hated to think of the old tub being commanded by anyone else, even if it was Jimmy Macleod. He hated, too, the prospect of not being able to move around, of being a virtual prisoner. He looked around the room with dismay: it was tiny. What the hell was he going to do all day?

The girl had come closer. She said softly, 'I'm sorry. It's going to be rotten for you, stuck up here all day long. But I'll bring you some books – some English books. And I've got a cribbage board –' She shrugged. 'If you play, of course.'

He looked at her and grinned. 'Under the circumstances, I'll be glad of anything, anything at all!'

She smiled back and he thought how lovely she looked when she was happy.

Then, suddenly, he had it. Where he'd seen her before. Plymouth! He'd met her in Plymouth – the girl who'd come sailing with him that day! How extraordinary!

His stare had flustered her; she was turning to walk away.

'Wait a minute!' he exclaimed. 'D'you realise we've met before?'

Julie's heart sank. She'd known, from the moment she'd looked into his eyes, that she had met him before. It had taken her some minutes to fix the exact time and place. But then she'd remembered it all: the sunny afternoon, the boat, the sail round the harbour.

And now her heart sank because she wanted it forgotten and he had remembered.

She turned and said lightly, 'Oh yes?'

He smiled. 'Absolutely! You came sailing with me. Around Plymouth Sound.'

She inclined her head. 'Oh really?'

'Yes.' He looked rather surprised that she hadn't remembered. 'In *Dancer* – my 25-footer . . . Don't you remember?' He put on a half-hurt half-amused expression.

She nodded, as if it had just come back to her. 'Oh yes. I think I remember now. It was such a long time ago . . .'

'Yes, I suppose it was,' he laughed. His expression changed and he said, 'But what are you doing, living here?'

'My family – they live here. My uncle and aunt.'

'And the child, is that yours?'

Julie hesitated. She didn't want him to know anything about Peter, nothing at all. She said abruptly, 'Yes.'

'How old is he – or is it a she?'

Julie went cold. Now the questions – next the mathematics. It wouldn't take him long to work it out. She thought quickly and decided it might be all right if she took a few months off. 'Five. His name is Pierre. He's at school.' She wasn't lying about his name: ever since the Occupation she'd made sure he was known by the French version of his name.

'Well, I look forward to meeting him, if only to tell him I'm very sorry for pinching his bed. He wasn't too put out, I hope?'

'No.'

'Still, it must have been rotten going into a cold bed.' He smiled warmly. 'I look forward to meeting him.' She saw that he was about to ask another question and, indicating the mug on the floor, she said quickly, 'Your coffee's getting cold.'

He exclaimed, 'Oh!' And beat his hand against his head in an exaggerated gesture of stupidity. He looked at her, his eyes twinkling, and said, 'I promise to be a better guest in future!'

She smiled faintly and turned to go down the stairs.

He called softly, 'And your husband? Is he here?'

She paused at the first stair and, not looking at him, said, 'No, there's no husband.'

'Oh! I'm sorry. I –'

Julie immediately wished she hadn't said it. He would think she had a husband who was killed in the fighting. But it would be a mistake to explain further; it would mean telling less than the truth, and she hated lying. Instead she murmured, 'I'll go and get those clothes then.'

'Thanks. And one more thing!'

'Yes.'

'I'm sorry,' he said apologetically, 'but I've forgotten your name.'

'Julie.' Immediately she realised that this too had been a mistake. The less he knew about her the better, in case he was caught. She decided she was hopeless at all this intrigue.

He was smiling. 'Of course. Julie. What a lovely name. I remember it now. You've probably forgotten my name too. After all, why *should* you remember it! Anyway it's Richard. Richard Ashley.'

She nodded. 'Yes, I remember now.' She started down the stairs.

'Oh, and Julie.' His voice was very soft now.

She stopped, a strange feeling in her throat. It was the way he had spoken her name: so familiar, even intimate. She swallowed, 'Yes?'

'I *will* try to be good.' He sighed. 'But I'm not used to being cooped up. It's going to drive me quietly bonkers, I'm afraid. And not knowing what's happened to my ship doesn't help, either. For all I know they might have met an E-boat on the way out . . . Look – if I get bloody impossible or moan and gripe too much, just tell me I'm being tiresome, will you? Just be firm with me, and I'll behave. Honestly!'

She couldn't help smiling. 'Yes,' she laughed. 'I'll tell you.'

'Thanks! And,' he added solemnly, 'for my part, I promise to obey the rules. To the letter, ma'am!' He touched his forehead in a mock salute and then smiled, just a little sheepishly, an apologetic expression on his face.

He was making fun of her, she knew. But it was impossible to take offence: he had done it so amiably. And his eyes – they were so nice and friendly. She couldn't be angry with him.

Instead she smiled at him and, blushing slightly, went quickly down the stairs.

18

You could tell Americans anywhere, Vasson decided. They looked different in every way. There was the colouring – often blue-eyed and fair-haired, rather like the Germans themselves; the height – many of them were well over six feet tall; and, most telling of all, the well-fed look. Somehow people who ate lots of meat looked different from those who ate bread and starch: in fact, they looked rather like the fat cattle they ate. They sat differently, too, lounging on the train seats instead of sitting upright as the Europeans did. Some even had bright yellow nicotine stains on their fingers: something you never got from French and Belgian cigarettes. It was only because the Germans were so blind to anything but pieces of paper that these obviously alien creatures could travel on trains at all.

There were six of them, sitting in different places around the open carriage. All were airmen who'd ditched over Belgium and been found by 'friends'.

They were travelling to Paris, where they would be transferred to a south-bound train. Vasson was their courier. Eventually they would be led over the Pyrénées into Spain.

Or so they thought. Vasson viewed them with contempt: they were so naive, these people. They had no idea at all.

There was also a seventh man. The Americans thought he was

Czech and a pilot in the RAF. They were almost right about the first bit – in fact, he came from the Czech – German border. But they were quite wrong about the second bit. The man did not work for the RAF, he worked for Vasson. And he was going to tell Vasson every detail about the escape line, every courier and safe house all the way down to Spain.

It was a lot to ask of one man, but Vasson had spent four weeks briefing him. He had also arranged for his wife and child to be placed under arrest, just in case.

Vasson glanced round the carriage again. One of the flyers – a young, fresh-faced boy with an awful American haircut – winked at Vasson. Vasson stared back coldly. The boy had been a problem ever since Brussels, when Vasson had taken the group over. The boy had started chewing gum, quite oblivious to the stares of the other passengers. Then he'd started to whisper in English to his friend. Vasson had had to separate them.

Now, under Vasson's cold stare, the boy dropped his eyes and looked out of the window. There were no more winks.

They were approaching the Gare du Nord. Almost home. Vasson missed Paris very much; Brussels was dull by comparison. This was his fifth run to Paris, but he never got to stay for any length of time, and this visit would be the shortest yet. After seeing Kloffer he would catch the next train back. But for once he didn't mind too much: Brussels promised a great deal of excitement over the next two days.

The train ground to a halt. Vasson stood up. The airmen got to their feet, their eyes on Vasson.

Vasson joined the throng of people leaving the train and strolled down the platform towards the barrier. He could feel the others following him. At the barrier there were two French policemen checking papers and two *Feldgendarmen* examining people's faces. Vasson knew they would get through all right: he'd arranged it with Kloffer.

The gendarme looked at Vasson's papers and pushed them quickly back into his hand. Yes: he'd been briefed all right.

Vasson wandered slowly into the main concourse and glanced around, as if looking for someone. He glanced casually behind him and saw that all the airmen were through the barrier.

He waited until they had all found him again, then walked out of the station into the Rue de Dunkerque.

There were only two people at the bus stop. Vasson strolled up and stood behind them. The airmen followed suit. Vasson moved closer to the Americans' leader and muttered, 'I'm off now. Wait for a girl wearing a purple hat. Bye.'

276

Vasson went through his pantomime of looking at his watch, glancing up the street for a bus and then, after shaking his head, moving away. The other Americans looked around uncertainly, wondering whether they should follow Vasson, but, seeing that their leader did not, settled down to wait.

Vasson walked back to the station, went into the booking hall and, very casually, turned back until he could watch the bus stop from the darkness of the doorway.

The next courier was meant to pick up the passengers – or parcels, as they insisted on calling them – in five minutes. In fact she arrived in eight.

It was the same girl as before: a dark, rather plain girl with a permanent frown. She was wearing the purple hat. She stood patiently behind the group until a bus destination 'République – Bastille' came along. Then she moved forward to the front of the line and got into the bus. The airmen got in behind her.

It was the classic cut-out rendezvous. The two couriers never met, never saw each other and were incapable of identifying each other. Vasson smiled: doubtless the organisers were very proud of the method. After all, it worked very well – so long as everyone was on the same side.

As the bus drew away Vasson saw the Czech sitting in the back of the bus, staring calmly out of the window. He was going to be all right, that man. He'd deliver the goods.

But there was a back-up, just in case. It was only good for the first part of the journey, but if the Czech failed it would be better than nothing. He'd asked Kloffer to provide a tail.

He looked around for signs of one. There hadn't been anyone in the bus queue, he was sure of that. A car then. But there were no black Citroëns in sight. The only possibility was a battered old Peugeot which pulled out from the kerb and went off in the same direction as the bus. Yes, perhaps that was it. If so, Kloffer was definitely improving.

The concourse was crowded when Vasson got back into the station and it took him some time to get across to the other side. The plain unmarked door was behind the men's lavatories, next to the railway security office. But he didn't go straight there. Instead he went into the lavatories, glancing behind him as he went. No-one. He used the urinal and went out into the concourse again. This time he paused and took a good look round. Still no-one. He'd known there wouldn't be, but it was always best to make sure.

He strolled towards the unmarked door, took one last look, and slipped inside.

Kloffer was there, waiting.

They nodded at each other. Vasson sat down and said, 'You've done as I suggested?'

'Yes, we have several tails on them. They'll be followed as far as possible.'

'And the tails, they're not your usual gorillas, I trust?'

Kloffer looked annoyed. His men's appearance was an old bone of contention. He said testily, 'They will do their job well, don't worry.'

Vasson said, 'Good.'

'And your man, will he do *his* job? It's a lot to ask of one man – and not one of *my* men at that.'

'He's been properly briefed. As long as he can make contact all right, then nothing will go wrong.'

'Yes. As long as he *can* . . .'

'He will.'

'So!' Kloffer put his fingertips together. 'That takes care of that then . . .'

'Yes.' Vasson's only regret was that he wouldn't be in on all the arrests. He would have liked that.

Kloffer examined Vasson with his cold, hard eyes. 'Now, the Brussels end. Are you sure you have it under control?'

'Oh yes. I'll give you the lot within three days.'

'But the leader – have you identified him?'

'Yes. Finally.'

'And –?'

'Tomorrow. You'll have him by tomorrow.'

Kloffer nodded and stood up. 'After – when you've finished there – you'd better come back to Paris.'

'That was what I intended.'

Kloffer said deliberately, 'But not for too long. And you must stay away from your old haunts. You're no use to me if you're dead.' He smiled faintly. 'And you would be dead – very quickly.'

Vasson sighed, 'You're just saying that, Kloffer. Just to keep me in order. I'm beginning not to believe you any more.'

'Ah . . . but there's only one way to find out if I'm lying. And that might be fatal for you, might it not? Besides . . .,' Kloffer went on carefully, 'if you were dead you wouldn't be able to spend any of that money you're so carefully accumulating. That would be a pity, wouldn't it?'

Vasson suppressed his irritation. Kloffer thought he did it just for the money. He was a stupid man.

He decided that he couldn't be bothered to argue the point.

Anyway perhaps Kloffer was right – better to be out of Paris and alive than shot in the back.

'Okay. So I don't stay in Paris. So where do I go?'

Kloffer said, 'Ah! Where? Who knows? We'll see.' He smiled, enjoying what he imagined to be his little moment of power. Vasson thought: Screw you.

Kloffer stood up and put on his hat. 'But I promise you the job will be equally interesting and rewarding.'

First the stick, then the carrot. Kloffer was so predictable.

Kloffer paused at the door. 'Goodbye, and we look forward to some excellent results in Brussels.'

'And I look forward to some excellent results in the money department, Kloffer.'

'Don't be greedy. You earn enough.'

'But am I paid what I'm worth? That's the question.'

'You could be worth nothing. Remember that, *Marseillais!*'

Kloffer opened the door and chuckled to himself. 'Goodbye. That's what I always call you, you know – The *Marseillais!*' He watched Vasson's face, then, smiling still, went out.

The door closed and Vasson clenched his fists. He took a long, deep breath to calm himself.

The bastard must have taken his thumb print and had it sent round to every police station in the country. It was the only way he could have found out.

It all came back to that filthy foreign woman . . . If it hadn't been for her, he'd never have been on file . . .

It was her fault, the bitch.

Vasson shivered and stood up.

He hated Kloffer for knowing.

One day he'd get Kloffer. One day.

He looked at his watch. There was a train for Brussels in ten minutes.

As he walked angrily across the station he thought about the Brussels job. He saw the faces of the smug intellectuals running the operation, and imagined their expressions when they realised they'd been betrayed. It was the only thing that consoled him.

The train was late arriving. Vasson decided to go straight to the Café Mirabeau for dinner. The journey had made him hungry. Also Anne-Marie might be there and she would tell him the news. Or rather the lack of news. Even if there had been some early arrests south of Paris, no-one in Brussels could possibly have heard anything yet.

Anne-Marie. He'd be glad to be rid of her. She'd become a bore.

When he'd first met her, she'd been rather sweet and it had been quite enjoyable to win her over. It had taken time, of course, because she had been very cautious. She'd only just been released by Mueller and she was suspicious of everything. But he'd been patient. He'd led her on, slowly but surely. In the end she had come to trust him completely, just as he knew she would. When she'd introduced him to her friends they'd given him simple jobs at first: running messages and errands and that kind of thing. Then at last had come the courier's job: the real test. After that he was home and dry.

Anne-Marie. The trouble had started when she'd tricked him, that terrible evening. He'd quite liked her until then. He'd even imagined what it would be like to touch her, naked, and to hold her down, tight . . .

Then she spoilt it all. She tricked him by saying she loved him and that she just wanted to put her arms round him. *It was all her fault.* She'd flaunted herself, showing her knees, having those large breasts, smelling of sex . . . He'd found himself feeling her body and then she was naked and instead of staying still she *kept moving* – putting her arms round him, trying to kiss him on the lips. It had revolted him. In the end he'd put his arm across her neck and stopped her moving until he'd finished.

After that she disgusted him. He could hardly bear to look at her, particularly when she stared at him with those large reproachful eyes. Why couldn't she have left him alone? Why did she have to do *dirty* things?

But he still had to make the effort to see her, otherwise all his work would be for nothing. It almost killed him. Whenever she moved he could see those large breasts . . .

But it was just for one more day. That was all. He must remember that. He gritted his teeth and went into the café.

The bitch was there, sitting in a corner. He could tell she'd been waiting for him. She looked worried: she was probably going to be difficult.

As soon as he sat down she said, 'Everything all right?'

Vasson nodded. 'I think so.'

'Not sure?'

'I don't know. I always think I see shadows . . . You know.' It was important to sow a slight seed of doubt, just in case news of the Paris arrests reached Brussels before he'd finished the job.

She nodded. 'Probably nothing to worry about. But you –?' She looked at him with concern and touched his hand. It was all he could do not to snatch it away. 'Are *you* all right?'

'Sure. Why shouldn't I be?'

'It was just . . . you've been so . . . withdrawn and . . . well, cold,' she finished painfully.

'Oh? Well, it doesn't mean anything.'

She brightened a little and he realised crossly that she had misinterpreted his words.

She said, 'Oh, I'm so pleased. I thought – Well, quite honestly I didn't know what to think. After . . . you know. I've been very confused.'

'I've just been feeling the strain, that's all.'

'But – you seemed so angry! It's been torturing me. What did I do wrong? Why were you so cross? And – why, oh *why*, Paul, did you hurt me?'

He sighed impatiently. 'Did I?'

'Yes. *Yes.*' She spoke angrily, reproachfully.

'Well, it was just the strain, as I say. Let's just forget it, eh? You're really getting things out of proportion.'

She gave him an agonised look. 'Oh dear, I really don't know what to think . . .'

Vasson thought: Christ, she's going to go on and on unless I shut her up. He breathed deeply and said, 'Look, dear, I'm truly sorry for what happened. I was upset, you see. I had a girl once – I've never told you this before – but . . .' He made a face as if the memory gave him terrible pain. '. . . she died you see. And whenever . . . Well, whenever . . . I remember her I want to die too!' He looked away as if it was too much to bear. He couldn't help thinking what a good performance he was giving.

She said, 'Oh! Oh, I see. I had no idea . . .'

She was buying it. Good. Time to ease off the subject. 'Look, I'd rather not talk about it. D'you understand?' She still looked unhappy, but nodded gently.

He said quickly, 'How are things here, then? Quiet?'

She nodded.

He looked pleased – he *was* pleased. Then he put on a frown. 'Look, there are a couple of things I'm a bit worried about – to do with security and, well, other things. I'd like to discuss them with Guy. Can you arrange a meeting, here or somewhere near?'

'But – does it have to be Guy himself?'

'Yes, it does.' Of course it had to be Guy: he was the most important one of all. 'And Patrice, too. Any chance of arranging something for tomorrow morning at about eleven?'

'I don't know . . . It's a bit unusual. They don't like too many of us to meet at once. And, well, they'll want to know *why*.'

What a stupid woman, looking for problems. He was so irritated with her he could shake her by the throat. He said calmly, 'Look, I'm really worried and I do think it's important to talk the thing over with them. Really! Can't you just take my word for it? It's important. I have to have that meeting.'

She blinked. 'All right. I'll try.'

'Good.' He got up to leave. She frowned anxiously and said, 'Where are you going?'

'Mmm? Oh, home, I expect.'

'Don't you want to eat?'

The answer was yes but he didn't want to eat with her. It would spoil his appetite. He answered, 'No, I'm going straight to bed. I'll see you in the morning. You will arrange that meeting, won't you? It's important.'

She nodded, her face drawn and pale.

He realised she still wasn't convinced. Better make sure. He put his hands on the table. 'Look, after tomorrow, perhaps we'll go out for the day. Into the country. Would you like that? It would be nice to – well, relax a little. I have been feeling the strain, I can see that . . . Shall we do that? After the meeting?'

Her face was a mixture of relief and uncertainty. 'Yes. That would be nice.'

He forced himself to smile at her and then turned hurriedly away. Anything to keep the bitch happy. Anything to keep her quiet until after tomorrow. God! The things he had to do. But it would be worth it, he was sure of that.

It was a spectacular morning, the light as bright and clear as glass. Though it was still winter it was just warm enough to sit at a pavement table without feeling the cold. Vasson turned his face to the sun and thought that he'd never felt as good as he did today.

He ordered a second pastis and looked at his watch. Five minutes to go. His pulse quickened and he felt a delicious sense of anticipation.

It was almost the best part, the anticipation.

Anne-Marie was the first. She walked along the pavement towards him, her head down, her expression serious. She always looked serious. Well, today she really had something to worry about! The thought amused him and he had to lower his head to hide a smile.

She saw him and, giving a slight wave, weaved her way through the tables towards him.

As she sat down he asked, 'Everything fixed?'

She nodded.

He smiled brilliantly. 'Excellent! Now what would you like to drink? Pernod? Coffee? Yes? Then coffee it shall be!'

She was watching him, trying to gauge his mood. He smiled at her, elated. She said, 'You're very happy today.'

'Yes! Well, something's happened!'

'What?'

He held up his hand. 'All in good time! All in good time!'

She smiled thinly, but her eyes were serious, questioning. She was a bit wary, he decided. Nothing to worry about though, he could deal with her all right.

Stupid bitch. He smiled at her again. 'It's such a beautiful day, isn't it?'

'Yes.' She looked around nervously.

'What's the matter?'

She said quickly, 'Oh nothing. I'm just a bit jumpy today, I don't know why.'

Vasson eyed her sharply and wondered if she'd guessed something after all. She couldn't see Mueller and his men, of course: they were well hidden in a florist's shop across the street. And Vasson himself had given nothing away. He decided, finally, that she was just the nervous type.

Patrice, the number two in the organisation, was next. He was a doctor, one of the types who worked with the poor and the needy. His halo was so bright it was almost dazzling. Vasson watched him approach with satisfaction. Two down and one to go.

The doctor drew up a chair. Vasson said smoothly, 'My dear fellow, a glass of something? A Pernod?'

The doctor smiled kindly and said, 'No, thank you so much. Just a coffee.'

'Oh, but I did so want us to have a drink together!'

The doctor and Ann-Marie exchanged glances. Vasson realised he was pushing it. He said quickly, 'It's just that we hardly ever see each other and it's good to drink with one's friends.'

The doctor smiled. 'Another time, really.'

At last the leader, Guy, came. Vasson spotted him while he was still some distance away on the other side of the street. The man walked casually but with infinite caution, missing nothing. A wily man – a worthy opponent.

The leader arrived at the table and, taking a last look round, sat down.

Vasson beamed at him. 'Now I hope I have a customer for a drink! How about it? A pastis? A cognac?'

Guy eyed him and said quietly, 'No, let's have a drink after we have discussed our business. What, exactly, have you to tell us?'

A cool one, Vasson thought, a cool one. 'Ah!' He raised a finger and smiled. 'Good news, very good news.'

'But I thought there was something worrying you?'

'*Yes*, there is that too.' Vasson tried to look suitably serious. 'But to be precise it's something that should be worrying *you*.'

A nice little joke, that.

Out of the corner of his eye Vasson saw Mueller and his men coming out of the florist's shop. Only a minute left, then.

A look of concern had come into Guy's eyes and he said, 'What exactly is the problem? Spit it out!'

'The problem is that the Boches are on to you!'

The three of them froze, their eyes fastened on Vasson, waiting for him to go on. Vasson raised his eyebrows and shrugged mysteriously.

They exchanged glances, then stared back at Vasson, a mixture of uncertainty and cold horror growing on their faces.

Vasson looked past them to where Mueller and the men in black leather raincoats were making their way through the outer ring of tables. Then, just before the Germans arrived, Vasson smiled.

The two men realised almost simultaneously. They jumped to their feet and looked desperately around them. Anne-Marie was still staring stupidly across the table.

The men saw the black leather raincoats and froze like animals gauging the wind. Vasson wondered if they would try to run for it. He hoped not: it would draw attention.

The men turned and looked at each other, fear and terrible understanding written all over their faces. Vasson realised with satisfaction they were not going to run for it. Slowly, they sat down again and first one then the other stared at Vasson. The girl was still looking dully across the table, her mouth open.

Vasson said to the two men, 'Right. Now if you just tell me where to find the courier Francine, then we can be going.'

There was silence.

'If you don't tell me your wives and children will be arrested within the hour.'

'You bastard? . . .!' It was the girl. The dull look had gone and her eyes were blazing. 'You bastard! You filthy swine! You –!' Suddenly she screamed and, picking up an ashtray, raised it above her head. Before she could throw it one of Mueller's men swung at her. There was a *crack*! as his leather-gloved hand hit her cheekbone. The ashtray fell to the ground.

Shaking with anger, Vasson leant forward in his chair. 'That'll teach you, you bitch. Next time we'll make your face into pulp!'

Vasson leaned back in his chair and took a deep breath. 'Where do I find the courier Francine?'

The men were looking away now, their expressions grim. Only the girl was staring at him again.

They weren't going to talk. It didn't matter; he could send a false message to the courier and lure her out that way. Vasson said stiffly, 'Very well. If you wish to sacrifice your families . . .'

The girl had been quiet but now she let out a cry of agony and for a moment Vasson thought she'd reach across the table and try to scratch him. But she sank back in her seat, her face a picture of hate and self-loathing, and shouted, 'Oh God! Oh God!'

Vasson indicated to Mueller and one of his men yanked the girl out of her seat and took her away. She screamed as she was dragged across the pavement. Vasson wished she wouldn't make so much noise; people were staring.

Vasson said to Mueller, 'And the others!'

As the doctor was pulled to his feet he turned towards Vasson and said quietly, 'I feel very sorry for you. May God forgive you.'

Vasson forced a smile and said, 'Sod you too!'

He finished his drink and nodded to one of Mueller's men, who made a show of arresting Vasson. Vasson pretended to struggle a little, then walked quietly across the street to the waiting car.

In Room 900 of the War Office, Smithe-Webb of the French Section of MI9 was waiting for news.

There had been no news from Meteor for three days. Meteor, the largest of the evasion lines, had two wireless operators. Neither of them had made contact.

The major had to remind himself that this in itself meant nothing; wireless operators often had trouble getting through.

But then there was the silence from the Spanish end of the line. No airmen had come over the border for four days.

And then there were the rumours. They'd started coming in the previous day, from other evasion lines and from agents of the Special Operations Executive.

The rumours hinted at a disaster in the Meteor line.

All Smithe-Webb could do was to hope it wasn't true – and wait for news.

The news came at four that afternoon. From the Coding and Signals Section of MI9 headquarters at Beaconsfield, just outside London. The section had received a message. It was from Xavier, one of the Meteor wireless operators. The message was perfectly routine, asking for arms and money to be dropped in three days' time;

the code used was correct; and the 'touch', the operator's unique and personally identifiable Morse style, was definitely Xavier's.

But something was missing, something which made Smithe-Webb's heart sink. One of the security checks had been left out. One of the two intentional mistakes that operators were trained to put into their messages had been omitted.

That meant only one thing. It meant that Xavier was operating under German control.

Over the next three days more and more information filtered through and Smithe-Webb's worst fears were realised.

Meteor had been devastated. It was as if the line had never existed. Over a hundred and fifty arrests had been made: men and women, some in their seventies, others no more than eighteen.

It was a disaster.

When the news broke, the Head of MI9 shielded Room 900 from the worst of the flak which rained down on them from the Department's enemies in high places.

But Smithe-Webb didn't care either way. There was only one thing he cared about – finding out how it had happened so that it could never, ever happen again.

The next day his prayers were answered. A long signal arrived from the British Consulate in Lisbon. A man claiming to be a member of the Meteor line had reached Portugal by means of the Pyrénées and a Spanish jail. His code name was Gaston and he had operated in Brussels. Before escaping from the city, he had heard a whisper, passed from someone who had called up to the leader, Guy, in his prison cell. The whisper was that it was a traitor who had caused the disaster, a man who called himself Lebrun.

A traitor from within.

Smithe-Webb sighed. It was the one thing that was so very difficult to guard against.

All he could do was to help them prevent it happening again.

He would press for money to train agents, agents who could be sent over to start new evasion lines, people who, above all, would be skilled in *security* ...

He started planning straight away. It would be a mistake to set up another large-scale Belgium – Spain line too soon; the aftermath of the Meteor disaster would rumble on for a long time.

Instead he would reinforce the existing, smaller *réseaux*, particularly those well away from the Meteor route.

He looked at the north coast of Brittany. The recent upset there had been no more than a temporary hiccup. Most of the line was still intact. So too were the MGBs, though minus Ashley and his crew.

Yes, Brittany it must be. A new organiser, a new security system, and a much larger operation.

The line would need a new name.

He thought for a moment, then came up with a name which had been his mother's before she married. He would call the new *réseau* the Sheldon line.

19

Tante Marie took a last look into the front parlour, closed the door, and nodded to Julie. Julie picked up a plate of fish stew from the stove, a knife and fork from the table, and carried them quickly into her bedroom. Tante Marie closed the door behind her.

Julie walked through the room and started to climb the narrow stairs. Whispers and a small chuckle floated down from the room above. Her eyes reached floor level and she saw the two heads bent over some fascinating object on the floor.

They heard her and looked up. Richard grinned. For a moment she met his gaze and smiled back. Then she directed her eyes towards her son. Peter acknowledged her arrival with a matter-of-fact glance and said in his high-pitched monotone, 'Maman, look at this. It's nearly finished!'

Julie obediently inspected the rough model ship lying on the floor and said, 'It's lovely, darling. Really super!'

Richard got to his feet and reached out for the plate. 'Shall I relieve you of this? It looks too good to go cold.'

'Oh yes! Sorry!' Julie laughed and looked up into his face. He was still smiling, but there was something else, too: an enquiring, watchful look, as if he were trying to catch her out at some game they were playing.

She looked away and said to Peter, rather too quickly, 'Come on! Bed-time, young man.'

'But I'm not tired!'

'That's as may be, but it's still bed-time.'

'Oh, no! We were just going to stick the funnel on, weren't we, Richard?' He pronounced 'Richard' in the French way, softly and with no 'd', just as Julie had taught him. She was terrified that he would blurt the name out at school.

Richard put on a stern face. 'It can wait until tomorrow. Go on, *jeune homme*. Do as your mother says!'

Peter made a face, then nodded obediently and got up. Julie reached down to take his hand, but he said crossly, "No, I want to walk by myself!' Julie sighed. Such an independent little beast, her son, and hardly six. She shrugged, rolled her eyes at Richard, and followed Peter's stamping feet down the stairs.

She knew the bed-time stories so well that she could read them automatically while she thought of other things. Up until three weeks ago, she had thought about the shopping and the mending and Peter's clothes. But now . . . Now she thought about the evening ahead.

She was fascinated by Richard's view of the world.

Certain things – like politics – he found amusing; something the French would never do. He said that anything so serious which was so badly managed had to be funny. She wasn't sure she agreed with him, but the way he talked made her laugh – most things he said made her laugh. But then at other times he could be very serious, and those laughing eyes became as hard as stone, and she guessed he could be very determined when he chose to be. Particularly about things he cared about, like loyalty and integrity and duty. When he talked about things like that he reminded her of an earnest schoolboy – or perhaps a knight of old: chivalrous, honest and true.

And yet – whenever he was talking seriously he would add almost in the same breath something so irreverent that it made her gasp. At first his wickeder remarks had taken her aback and – well, shocked her. Then she'd started to find them rather funny and it dawned on her that he said them for that very reason: to make her laugh.

He made her talk too, about herself and what she believed in and what she cared about. She wasn't used to having long discussions. The conversations in the farmhouse kitchen were inclined to be short, almost monosyllabic. At first she found it difficult to express herself, but then, gradually, the words had come more easily.

'*Maman*, a kiss!'

She leant down and kissed the small round cheek. 'Good night, darling. I'll try not to wake you when I come to bed.'

'Night-night.' He was already half asleep.

Julie hurried to the mirror and peered into it. She brushed her hair a couple of times then examined herself critically. She really didn't look bad at all, she decided. She was doing her hair a new way – with a side parting – and it rather suited her.

She made her way to the stairs and went up, happy and confident.

He was sitting on the bed, finishing his meal. When he saw her he put the plate down and said, 'I'm putting on weight, you know. You'll have to stop feeding me like this!'

She sat down on the floor and smiled. 'Well, it's not exactly Cordon Bleu – and I wouldn't enquire about the vegetables you had in that stew. But we do our best!'

'It's wonderful!' And Julie had the feeling he wasn't referring to the food. She said quickly, 'Do you want to play crib tonight? It's about time you played an honest game and beat me!'

'Are you suggesting I cheat?' he asked.

'Yes!' Julie laughed.

He looked horrified. 'How did you guess?'

'Because I win so much.'

'Ah! I can't argue with that logic! I promise never to cheat again. Guide's honour.' Julie smiled because he didn't mean a word of it.

He looked at her more seriously and exclaimed, 'No, *don't* let's play cribbage. Let's talk instead! Come on . . .' He settled himself more comfortably. 'I want to hear the story of your life.'

She felt a stab of fear. She said quickly, 'No. There's nothing to tell.' There was an awkward pause. She looked for something else to say. 'I heard about your crew, by the way. Did I tell you? They're fine, apparently, but still very restless. D'you want another message sent over to them?'

Ashley shook his head absently. 'No. It'll wait a couple of days.'

He was watching her carefully. She went on quickly, 'But still no news from outside, I'm afraid. There's been a big clamp-down round Paris and the wireless operators have gone to ground. We still haven't managed to get a message through . . .'

He frowned. 'This Paris thing – is it connected with what happened here?'

'No . . . they don't think so. Our – incident – happened before the troubles up there. No, our problem was that leader of ours. We think he just talked too much and the wrong people heard . . .'

'But – will he have talked? To the Gestapo?'

Julie stared at him for a moment. 'No . . . Thank goodness, there's no possibility of that.'

'Why?'

'Ah. Well, he died, you see. On the way to St Brieuc, to Gestapo headquarters.'

'Oh . . . He –' Richard searched her face. 'He died immediately, did he?'

Julie thought: He's quick, he understands completely. She said quietly, 'Yes . . . The Germans found him dead on arrival. But then he would have died anyway –'

289

Richard nodded. 'Quite.'

Julie had been relieved to hear of the leader's death. It was amazing how hard and realistic you could be when it was your child and your family who were at stake.

Julie shook her head. 'But none of it need have happened. If we'd had our own people running it *their* way . . .'

Richard nodded sympathetically. 'Well, for what it's worth I'll put in a word with the powers-that-be when I get back.' He laughed. '*If* I get back!'

Julie said gently, 'I'm sorry there's no news.'

He leaned forward and touched her arm. 'Don't worry on my behalf. Actually, to be honest, I'm rather enjoying it in some ways. I've done a lot of thinking – much more than in the whole of the last few years. And I'm getting a lot of satisfaction out of making this model with your young man. Then, of course . . .' He paused and stared at her meaningfully. '. . . it's really rather nice to be locked up with you.'

Julie gave him a look of amused disbelief and said, 'You're just saying that!' But secretly she was pleased.

There was a pause. He said quietly, 'You very cleverly put me off just now, when I asked you about your life. But come on, Julie, don't be such a mystery woman. Tell me . . .'

Julie said softly, 'No, I'm really not ready to talk about it yet. I'm sorry.'

He gave her a questioning look. She was tempted to explain but instead she got up and fetched the upturned packing case they used for playing cards.

He gave a small laugh. 'All right. Cribbage then.'

He won the first game easily and Julie said, 'There, you see! When you concentrate you can beat me every time!'

He let her win the next game and the next, then she accused him of not trying.

He replied half-heartedly, 'Of course I'm trying.' But she knew he wasn't.

Julie looked at her watch and got to her feet. 'Well, work tomorrow as usual. About time I turned in.' She smoothed down her skirt and looked up with a smile. 'Good night, then!'

She turned to go but he stood up and touched her arm. 'Julie . . .' His voice was very soft. 'I wish you'd tell me . . .' He sighed. 'You know what I mean.' He held her by the arms and, moving closer, kissed her on the forehead, very gently, his lips barely brushing her skin. Then, for a single moment, he leant down and put his cheek against hers and Julie thought: I'm not going to survive this. He turned and whispered into her hair, 'Julie, I want you so much . . .'

Julie pulled away and looked unhappily at the floor. Then without a word she turned and made quickly for the stairs.

'Julie –?'

But she was hurrying down. As soon as she reached the bedroom she pulled off her skirt and top and quickly got into bed next to Peter. She closed her eyes tightly and thought: God, please help me to live through the next few minutes. She listened to the sounds upstairs. For several minutes he didn't move, then she heard him walk slowly across the room to the bed.

She stared into the darkness for a long time, full of longings, wretched with misery.

She wanted him too, of course she did. She wanted him with all her heart.

But there could be no question of that. He wouldn't care for her if he knew the truth. He wouldn't respect her. The humiliation would be terrible.

She closed her eyes tightly, thinking that sometimes life could be very unfair.

Richard eyed her critically. 'You look terrible!'

'Thanks!' Julie managed the ghost of a smile. She was feeling an awful lot better than she had first thing that morning. She'd woken with a thundering headache and it hadn't faded until the afternoon. Now, she was just feeling tired.

She put the plate down on the packing case and looked at him a little nervously. She hadn't seen him since the night before. She breathed deeply and said, 'If you don't mind, I think I'll go straight to bed tonight. I'm rather tired.'

He got up slowly, a frown on his face, and took her hand. 'Julie, if it's anything I said last night . . . If I offended you in any way . . . I'm terribly sorry . . .'

'No! Really.' She smiled and gripped his hand. 'No, I'm just tired that's all.'

'Well . . . if you're sure.' He looked uncertain. 'You promise that I didn't upset you . . .?'

Julie said, 'Honestly,' and wished he would let go of her hand. It was embarrassing her.

He said softly, 'If I did upset you, Julie, I assure you it was the last thing I intended . . . You know that, don't you?'

She nodded. 'I know that.'

Very gently he released her hand and said breezily, 'Well, how about a nightcap?'

'A nightcap?' she repeated dully.

'Yes, I did a little bit of bartering with your uncle. He ended up with three cigarettes and I got a bottle of wine. Rather a good deal, don't you think? Though who for, I couldn't say!' He laughed and leant down to pick up the bottle. 'Look, why don't you have a quick glass. It'll do you good! And make you sleep! Come on, keep me company! Just for a minute.'

Julie knew that if she didn't go to bed now she might stay all evening. She began, 'I really would, except . . .' Then she closed her eyes, and smiled faintly and said, 'All right.'

He grinned at her: he was pleased.

She sat on the floor and accepted a glass. He was right about the wine: it did make her feel better. After a while she felt beautifully calm and almost content again. Richard told some stupid stories about a pet goat his family had once owned and suddenly she found herself laughing again. It was as if nothing had changed . . .

Except that it had.

They talked about all the usual things and he looked at her with the same eyes, alive and sparkling with fun, but . . . it was all subtly different. The words from the previous night hung in the air.

She began to feel deliciously drowsy; she hardly ever drank wine. She said, 'I really must get some sleep now . . .'

'Of course.' He leaned forward and helped her up. 'But wait! Just for a second . . .'

He went to the candle and blew it out. She heard him move across the room and the next moment a square of light appeared where he had pulled the curtain back from the window. 'Come and see!'

She came up beside him and stared out. It was a brilliantly clear night. Myriads of stars carpeted the sky, like silver on black velvet.

He said, 'I used to sit on *Dancer* and watch the night sky for hours on end . . .'

She said, 'It *is* lovely.'

'It's even better when you're sitting on deck. Then you can see everything, all the constellations.'

They stared in silence.

He said pensively, 'After the war I'll take *Dancer* cruising again, to all the old places.'

'To the Scillies?'

He turned. 'How did you know that?'

'Well – you must have told me.'

'Not since I've been here. I wouldn't have.' He was very definite.

'You know, you must have remembered that from *before*. In Plymouth.' He laughed softly. 'And there you were, pretending you didn't even remember *me*! You quite hurt my feelings, you know!'

'Rubbish!' Julie said firmly. 'It did you good, not to be remembered. Otherwise you'd have got a big head.'

'But you *did* remember me, didn't you?'

Eventually she said, 'Yes, but I couldn't remember exactly where it was that I'd met you.'

'Well, I knew! I enjoyed that day we spent together, and I was rather disappointed when you announced – right at the last moment – that you were just about to go away!'

He touched her shoulder and, sitting on the bed, waited for her to sit down beside him in the darkness. He said, 'Tell me. About you.'

She murmured, 'I'd rather not.'

'But why? Do you think I won't try to understand? Whatever it is you don't want to talk about – well, it can't be that bad, Julie. It can't be so bad that I wouldn't –' There was a pause. '– that I wouldn't care for you any more. You know I care, don't you?'

Julie couldn't speak.

He moved closer and took her hand. 'Tell me at least . . . What happened to your husband?'

Julie stared into the darkness and thought: Whatever I say will be wrong. The past was like a terrible monster that kept rearing up in front of her, breathing shame and guilt and eternal damnation. However much he believed he would understand, he wouldn't. He would pity and despise her.

She sighed and looked up at the window. The sky seemed even darker now, the glittering stars like lights on a tree. Taking a deep breath, she said slowly, 'Peter never knew his father. And I – I haven't seen him since Peter was born.'

Richard gently squeezed her hand. 'More fool him. He must be mad. So then . . . he's not likely to show up again.'

'Hardly!' She couldn't keep the bitterness out of her voice. 'You see . . .' She bit her lip. 'We . . .' She spoke so softly that he leant closer to hear her. 'We were never married.'

For a moment he didn't speak and Julie thought that she had been right and that he wouldn't understand.

But then he put his arm round her shoulder and said, 'Bad luck!'

'For me, yes!'

He said quickly, 'But you mustn't think it matters any more.' He was stroking her hair, slowly, softly. 'You have a lovely boy. You have nothing to be ashamed of.'

'. . . Oh yes I do!' She pulled herself away from him and blew noisily into her hanky. 'I feel ashamed that it ever happened ... Except for Peter, that is. If only . . .' She sighed angrily.

'But Julie, lots of people have affairs, and . . . well, indiscretions, without being married. Society's incredibly hypocritical about all that kind of thing. They say it's forbidden – but they're doing it all the time. The secret is not to worry about it . . . about the past, I mean. It's not that important.'

'It's important to *me*. I mind! And Peter will mind when he grows up and finds out. No . . . I made a terrible mistake and, one way and another, I'm going to pay for it for the rest of my life!'

He said, 'But how are you going to pay for it? Nobody's going to make you pay, Julie! You'll only suffer for it if *you* let it bother you. Why should you ever *pay* for it?'

'You know what I mean,' she said miserably. 'People talk, people don't forgive.'

'Do they know round here?'

'Oh, they've guessed.'

'But they still accept you?'

'Well . . . yes.'

'There you are then! What's the problem? Julie, I can assure you of one thing – it doesn't matter a damn to me!' He squeezed her hand again.

She breathed in deeply. 'Well, thank you for saying so.'

'It was meant.' He leant down and she heard him pouring another glass of wine. He handed her the glass. 'Is that why you came to Brittany? To have Peter?'

'Yes, but please – don't ask any more!'

'All right.' He stroked her hair. 'But all I meant was, have you been here all this time? With your uncle and aunt?'

'Yes.'

'Not much fun.'

'At least I was welcome – which was more than I was at home.'

'Ah. Your parents didn't understand?'

'Just my mother. My father's dead. We're still not speaking, my mother and me.'

'After the war, though, you'll want to come back, won't you?'

'I don't know. The war . . .'

'It won't last for ever.'

'I suppose not.'

'And then –' he paused. 'you might come on *Dancer* again perhaps. For a cruise. Would you like that?'

'I'm a rotten sailor.'

'I'll teach you.'

'No, I meant –'

He laughed. 'I know what you meant.'

He put his arm round her shoulder and they sat for a long while, watching the night sky and talking quietly.

Eventually he stood up. 'Time you went to sleep. You still look terrible!'

She smiled faintly. 'Thanks!'

He took her face in his hands and kissed her on the mouth, warmly and for a long time.

As she went down the stairs he called softly, 'Julie, I'm glad you told me.'

A little later, when she lay in bed beside Peter, she thought: Perhaps, given time, everything might be all right after all.

'Be careful. The door's creaky.' The boy's whisper was loud in his ear.

'Right-o.'

Ashley turned the handle and felt the door open. He pulled at it gently, trying to lessen the squeak of the hinges. Finally the gap was large enough for him to squeeze through. He stepped out into the darkness of the farm yard.

He began to close the door behind him, but there was something in the way. He realised it was the boy. He whispered, 'Hey! What are you doing?'

'Coming with you!'

'Oh no you're not. Get back inside!' Ashley tried to push the boy back through the door, but the small body wriggled past him and shot off into the night. Ashley could hear the pad of his feet receding into the distance.

He swore under his breath and, closing the door, followed after him, stumbling slightly as his foot met an obstruction.

The boy was waiting at the gate which led into the pasture behind the house. He was jumping up and down with glee. 'Beat you!'

'Look, young man, your mother will kill you if she finds out!' He thought: She'll kill me too.

Peter sighed with the exasperation of dealing with an adult. 'But I often sneak out here on my own.' He clambered on to the top of the gate. 'Anyway she's not back from work yet. She won't know!'

'That's not the point,' said Ashley reasonably. 'We might get caught.'

'Oh no. The soldiers never come here. Come on! Let's go up the hill. Sometimes you can see the lighthouse from there.' He jumped to the ground and hopped impatiently up and down while Ashley climbed over the gate.

Then he was off again, running across the grass, a small black blur fading into the grey of the early winter evening. Ashley gave up the idea of chasing after him, and strode forward, stretching the muscles of his legs, breathing the cool fresh air, drinking in the delicious moments of freedom.

How he had needed this. He hated being cooped up. It drove him mad. He knew how animals felt now, doomed to stay in cages for ever. Slow death.

He pressed on, pushing harder, wanting to feel the sweat on his body and the ache of tiredness in his limbs.

He hated the thought of being locked up for much longer. The only compensation was Julie, of course. He had been intrigued by her from the beginning. She had an other-worldliness, a gentle serenity that appealed to him. At the same time she was quick to laugh, and he liked that too. Damn it, he liked a lot about her.

But the revelations of the previous evening had subtly changed things. It had cost her a lot to tell him the truth, he had seen that, and he admired her for it. But it made him feel – what? – a sort of responsibility towards her, and that rather frightened him.

Yet he knew he cared for her. Nothing had changed that.

And nothing had changed the fact that he wanted to make love to her. Quite apart from being lovely she had an earthiness, a suggestion of passion, that made her extremely attractive. What was more, he was sure that she wanted him too.

He tramped on, thinking that perhaps responsibility wasn't a bad thing. After all, it had to come at some point in one's life.

'Woo-hoo.' The soft cry came from a short way ahead. Ashley climbed the last few yards to a wall at the top of the hill and peered around. There was no sign of the boy. 'Come out, you rascal.'

There was a giggle. Ashley followed it and, reaching over the wall, lifted the boy up and into the air. 'Got you!'

Peter wriggled and tried to get free. Ashley held him high for a moment longer then let him fall into his arms. The boy dropped his head against Ashley's chest and lay there, panting slightly. Ashley hugged him and thought how much fun it would be to have a child of his own one day.

The giggling started again. Peter squirmed out of his arms and dropped to the ground. 'Come on. I'll show you the rabbit warren.'

They investigated the warren, although there wasn't much to see in the darkness. Then they looked for the beam of the lighthouse, but saw nothing and decided there were no convoys passing that night.

Ashley stared into the darkness, trying to make out the deeper shadows of the sea, and thought longingly of the MGB. Later they walked again, along the wall and round the other side of the hill.

It wasn't until Ashley saw the hooded headlights of a vehicle on the road that he realised they'd been gone a long time. He ran back to the top of the hill and looked down. The headlamps had stopped outside the farmhouse.

The boy came panting up behind him and saw the lights too. As they watched, the headlights went out.

The boy grasped Ashley's sleeve and cried, 'It's the Germans! The Germans!'

'Yes. I'm afraid you're right.' Ashley took the boy's hand and led him back to the darkness of the wall. 'I think we'd better wait here, don't you?'

Julie felt sick.

She looked at the clock again. Half past eight. And still no sign.

She sat absolutely still, her eyes on the wall, her hands tightly clasped in her lap. Tante Marie sat opposite, her face tortured with worry. Neither spoke: neither could begin to imagine what they would do if something dreadful had happened.

The familiar sound of scraping chairs came from the parlour. The two soldiers had finished their meal. The front door banged as they went out. Julie sprang to her feet and, going to the back door, opened it a crack. The soldiers had brought an armoured car with them tonight, she had no idea why. They had parked it in the yard. Now they were getting into it and slamming the doors. She prayed that, if Richard and Peter were out there, they wouldn't choose this moment to return.

The car started with a roar and two dull beams of light sprang out and illuminated a corner of the farm yard. Then the lights were swinging away and the sound of the engine faded into the distance.

Julie took a jacket off the back of the door and hurried out into the night. When her eyes were accustomed to the darkness she started up the yard, towards the back pasture. She couldn't be sure they had gone this way, but it seemed likely. They certainly wouldn't have gone on the road.

She opened the gate and went into the pasture. She let out a small gasp.

Two figures, one small, one tall, were running towards her.

She stood waiting for them, shuddering with relief, then stepped forward and scooped Peter up into her arms. Without a word she carried the child back through the yard, into the kitchen and straight to bed.

As she undressed him, Peter glanced nervously at her face. 'Sorry, mummy.'

Julie narrowed her lips and said at last, 'I'm going to say this once and only once. Don't ever, ever do that again. If you do, I'll hit you so hard you won't know what time of day it is. D'you understand?'

'Yes, Mummy.'

She tucked him up and, without another word, turned out the light.

She went into the kitchen and, ignoring Ashley, crossed to the mantelpiece and shook a cigarette out of a packet. Her hand was trembling as she lit it.

'Julie, I'm very sorry . . . I meant to go out just for a second or two, but . . .'

Julie inhaled deeply on the cigarette and, gritting her teeth, stared dumbly at the mantelpiece. She didn't trust herself to speak yet.

'Peter followed me. Of his own accord. That's not to say I shouldn't have dragged him back . . .' He put his hand on her shoulder. 'It won't happen again.'

Eventually she said stiffly, 'We've done our best, you know. To make it bearable for you. I know that going outside for a few minutes at midnight isn't as much fun as walking round the entire countryside . . .' She made a wheeling gesture with her hand. 'But it was safest. For you – and for us!' She spat out the last words, then exhaling, shook her head. 'If you knew what I'd been through in the last hour you'd . . . understand!' The unaccustomed cigarette was making her dizzy and she stubbed it out.

He sighed heavily. 'I'll go back to my room.' The way he said it, it might have been prison.

She realised it *was* a prison to him. She turned to say something softer, more understanding, but he was already gone.

After a moment she lit a candle and followed him. She climbed the narrow staircase and, through the banisters, saw him lying on the bed staring at the ceiling. She paused at the top and said matter-of-factly, 'I know it's awful for you, I do realise that. But it shouldn't be long now. Before you can get away.'

He stood up and came over to her. 'I *will* go mad if I have to stay much longer. You see that, don't you?'

She nodded and said briskly, 'And you must understand that I'll go mad if you take any more risks.'

He smiled ruefully. 'It's a bargain. Anything to avoid your wrath again.'

She said firmly, 'I was only angry because I was so worried.'

'Thank you.'

'Not at all.' She turned quickly and went down the stairs.

Most of the potatoes were half rotten. Methodically, Julie cut out the bad sections, peeled the remainder, however small, and chucked them into the pot. Nowadays you wasted nothing.

Tante Marie was tenderising a piece of beef, beating it with a large wooden mallet, until the meat was almost flat. They always had meat on Saturday evenings and, because they had their own chickens and cattle, often twice during the week as well. Most people were not so lucky.

Tante Marie put the meat into a pan on the stove, added dripping, garlic and herbs, and left it to cook.

Julie smelled the aroma of garlic and herbs and remembered that it was Sunday the next day and she could spend all day with him.

She smiled and realised she was staring into the pot, the potatoes forgotten. Tante Marie was watching her, a frown on her forehead. 'Juliette ... Your uncle will be a little late tonight. I think –' She lowered her voice. 'I think there's some news.'

Julie looked up sharply. 'Some news?'

'From – away. But I'm only guessing. I'm not sure. I just thought ... I might warn you.'

Julie tried to hold on to her thoughts, but they were shooting off at tangents. News. A boat? Coming soon, probably, then he would go away, she would be alone, he would be safe, she would be miserable ...

After she had put Peter to bed she went up to see him and they talked and she thought: It will never be better than this. I'll never feel closer or warmer towards anyone than I do now.

It was not until nine that Jean returned. Richard was just telling her about his sister who was married and lived in Sussex when Julie suddenly tensed. Somewhere in the house there was the sound of a door opening.

Richard looked at her. 'What is it?'

'Nothing. Just my uncle. I'll be back in a moment.' She left him and hurried down the stairs and found Jean already at the bedroom door, waiting for her.

She followed him into the kitchen. He whispered, 'We've heard! They're sending a boat on Wednesday. Unless the weather's bad. We'll know for sure on the night – the BBC will broadcast a message.'

'And the boat will take everyone – the sailors and the airmen?'

He nodded.

Julie blinked. 'Wednesday night, then.' She touched her uncle's arm in thanks and went back into her room. She closed the door and leant against it for a moment. It was only four days away.

She climbed the narrow stairs, slowly, and didn't turn her head until she reached the top. The moment Richard saw her face he stood up and frowned. He said, 'What is it?'

She made herself smile and said brightly, 'It looks as though you're going home!'

He came towards her and grasped her arms. 'When?'

'Wednesday night – unless the weather's bad.'

'Good Lord above!' he laughed. 'Marvellous! Marvellous!' He closed his eyes and clenched his fists and threw back his head and grinned with delight. 'Oh, marvellous!'

Julie smiled gently and tried to look glad, for his sake.

He took hold of her arms again. 'Julie, I'll miss you . . .'

She nodded silently.

'Wednesday – that's four days. Let's make it the best four days we've ever had! What do you say? Let's have a wonderful time! I'll take you out to the Ritz for dinner tomorrow night.' He smiled wrily. 'That means I'll buy another bottle of wine off your uncle and we'll eat off the packing case *together*, properly . . . Then the next night –!'

As he talked she watched him and thought: Only four days.

She reached out and touched his face. He stopped talking and smiled at her. Then, when he saw the expression in her eyes, he leaned towards her and kissed her on the mouth, gently at first, then, when he felt her mouth moving under his, much harder.

He said, 'I want you, Julie.'

She put her lips to his ear and whispered, 'I want you too!'

She cried. Afterwards.

He touched her cheek and felt the tears and said, 'Julie, Julie! What is it?'

She pressed her head against his shoulder and said, 'Nothing, nothing. I'm so happy, that's all.'

He turned towards her and stroked her back, following her spine with his fingers until he reached the curve of her bottom. Then he pulled her against him and kissed her again, very softly, murmuring, 'Julie, Julie . . . silly old thing, don't cry!'

'But it's only because . . . it was so lovely!'

'Yes!' He squeezed her against him. 'It was, wasn't it?'

And then she cried again, very softly, not only because it had been so lovely but because she could see the past six years for what they really were: barren and lonely. All the routines, Peter, meals, work, going through the motions of life . . . And all that time she had only dimly imagined what it would be like to have all this.

'No more tears?'

'No,' she laughed, 'I promise!'

'Julie, four days is a long, long time!'

'Yes, yes!' She kissed his mouth and his cheek, then his ear and his forehead . . .

'Julie, if you go on like that –'

She paused and pulled back, uncertain.

'No!' he laughed. 'What I meant was – go on! Please don't stop!'

But she did because she didn't know the rules and she still felt a little awkward about the order of things. She wanted him to tell her, to whisper to her . . .

And then it was starting all over again and he was touching her in a special way, and she felt the beginnings of that extraordinary warmth, that quite incredible pleasure.

Later, much later, she lay in the darkness and thought that, whatever happened – even after he'd gone – she'd never feel completely alone again.

20

It was a triumph.

Output had risen to fifty units a week – and fifty working units at that. David walked slowly round the despatch room and peered at the packing cases. Each was labelled 'Tested and passed', and each label had been stamped and counter-signed with the initials of the Technician-in-Charge. It was a new idea, to have one person testing and sealing each unit before despatch. David had introduced the system because it was one which had worked well before. He had asked for – and got – a German naval technician for the job because he'd wanted someone he could communicate with. He hadn't wanted a German for any other reason – and certainly not because he didn't trust the two Frenchmen who'd done the job before. It hadn't occurred to him not to trust them.

Another new idea had been introduced, too. It was Kapitanleutnant Geissler's idea this time, though David had endorsed it and put it into operation. Each device was now the responsibility of an individual on the assembly line. If a Metox was faulty it was returned to the man concerned. If the fault was not rectified within a day, then the man was summoned for an explanation. If the fault was still not cured, the man was fired and the special exemptions on his military papers removed. Everyone knew what that meant: you could be called up for forced labour.

In the six months that David had been with the company no-one had been fired. At the same time output and quality had shot up. Yes, it was a triumph. Kapitanleutnant Geissler was pleased. Presumably the Navy were also pleased. And doubtless the submarine commanders were grateful now that they had their Metox receivers to warn them of enemy planes.

A triumph. And, thought David, the worst thing I've ever done.

He paused in the doorway of the main workshop and stared at the line of men working at the bench. There was a gap in the line. David closed his eyes. Only yesterday a man had stood there, brave and alive. Today he was dead.

And it was David's fault. *David's*.

He had been too taken up by the challenge of the problem-solving, too intoxicated by the freedom of action to see what had been happening.

The workers had been sabotaging the Metox, from the very beginning.

There had been nothing obvious – no extra wires or smashed valves. Instead, for no apparent reason, small components had failed to function or valves had burnt out. David could see now that too much current must have been forced through them or reverse polarity applied.

He should have realised of course. It should have been obvious. But he hadn't *wanted* to see. When small suspicions had begun to enter his mind he'd dismissed them. No-one would dare to do such things, he had decided. The penalty, after all, was death.

Then David's new measures had come into operation. The subtle forms of sabotage which had been so successful were no longer effective. The men had been forced to use more open and dangerous methods. Yesterday one of them had been caught.

The penalty was death, and the man had died.

And, whichever way David looked at the event, he couldn't help feeling that it was his fault.

He stared blankly at the gap in the line of working men. One of the technicians glanced up and David looked quickly away. He couldn't meet the man's eyes; he couldn't look at any of them. They thought him as bad as the rest: just another Nazi. Him! A Nazi!

David turned away, full of shame.

In the passage he almost bumped into someone. It was Gallois, the French chief technician. Gallois nodded and, stepping aside, waited for David to pass. David almost spoke but changed his mind. It would be no use. Gallois must despise him. He must think David worse than a mere German – he must think him a traitor!

David walked quickly towards the front of the building, muttering angrily to himself. He went down the front steps and out into the road in full view of the guard. He had permission to do that, to walk the short distance to his quarters under the eye of the guard. Why? Because they trusted him. And why did they trust him? Because he had shown himself to be such a good German, that was why! He laughed bitterly. What an irony.

He should have died back there in the camp. It would have been better for everyone.

He walked rapidly along the road until he came to a compound surrounded by barbed wire. He walked in past the guard and along the side of a large warehouse. The warehouse served as a barracks for the East European labourers who worked on the U-boat pens. At one end of it was a long wooden hut where the guards lived. David had a cubicle to himself there. Geissler had arranged it. David had been very pleased with the cubicle. It was infinitely better than the solitary room in the naval barracks. Here, at least, he had company. He often chatted with the guards; he enjoyed talking German again. They baited him, of course, but for much of the time they overlooked his race because it was convenient to them – they sometimes needed a fourth at cards. He, in his turn, ignored the fact that they were soldiers and beat up Poles every day.

David went into the box-like cubicle and closed the door.

He lay down on the bed and, drawing himself into a ball, covered his eyes with his hands. He was a disgrace. A disgusting disgrace. A deeply selfish and despicable man without principles or integrity. All those scruples he had pretended to have back in the camp laboratory. All the concern for whether he was doing the right thing. And what had he done? He had done as he was told. As time had gone on he had even been happy to obey. He had worked with all his heart and soul. What had happened to him, that he could have forgotten? Where had he lost his way?

He could see now that it had happened slowly, so slowly. His greed for security had pushed all other thoughts out of his mind. He had thought only of himself, his health, his next meal, and of the vital need to survive and preserve his life at all costs.

I have betrayed everything and everyone. My race. My Cecile. Most of all I have betrayed myself. I am not a proud man.

After a while, when the self-pity had passed, he lay and thought about the future.

Then he had the idea. It came to him quite suddenly, but the moment it appeared he knew it was the answer.

He sat up and, dropping on to his knees, put his hand underneath the metal frame of the bed. He touched the familiar flat shape of the small package and, pulling it out, held it tightly in his hand.

They had travelled so far together, he and this package, that he had almost forgotten the real meaning of it. He'd tucked it away in the back of his mind as something for the future: his passport to Britain or America when the war was over, a sort of insurance policy for his old age.

But now . . .

He held it in his hand and remembered the pages of plans and specifications for the secret device.

Shortwave radar. Germany would never be able to develop it, not while her laboratories were closed and her research programmes at a standstill. And if she didn't have shortwave radar she couldn't defend herself against it.

Certainly the Metox would be useless against it. He smiled a little.

It would only be a question of getting the plans to the British. They should be able to develop it fairly quickly.

It would be the perfect act of sabotage. The U-boats would be defenceless against it and, in a single blow, David's work here would be undone.

He hugged the small package to him. Then he looked up and said gently, 'Dear God, you are looking now at a miserable worthless old man. But one who is going to try to do his best. Give me the strength to succeed. And, if You should also deign to give me positive assistance, I thank You. If not – then, dear God, I will have done my best!'

He lay down and thought to himself: What better thing can a man do than be brave just once in his life?

David often came into work early, at about six so that he could enjoy two hours of peace and quiet before everyone else arrived. In the calm of the early morning he could think more clearly than later in the day. This morning he had arrived well before six – and yet he still couldn't make up his mind what to do.

Gallois. He should try Gallois.

It was the obvious choice. David couldn't be sure that he was involved in the sabotage, of course, but he must *know*. Even if he himself was not involved, he must have *guessed*.

Yes, he would try Gallois.

He rose unsteadily from his chair and went next door to the drawing office where a young trainee was standing at a high desk. 'Go and ask Monsieur Gallois to come to my office, would you?' The young man nodded and went off in the direction of the main assembly shop.

David went back to his desk and sat down unhappily.

There were footsteps in the corridor. A bead of sweat trickled down David's forehead and he reached into his trouser pocket for a handkerchief. He mopped his brow and looked up. Gallois was already in the room, watching him. David started with surprise and, half rising, smiled a little and indicated a seat. 'Do sit down, please.'

The door was still open and David got up to close it. 'Well, well. Lovely weather we're having, aren't we?'

'Yes.'

David sat down again. 'It always makes life pleasanter, doesn't it, if the sun is shining?'

The Frenchman nodded, but David could see he wasn't in the least interested in the weather.

David drew breath and began again. 'I – wanted to talk to you about a rather delicate matter . . .'

The Frenchman stared back across the desk, his face blank and uninterested. He was not going to give David any help, that was obvious.

'It's . . . Well, it must seem to you that I have had every sympathy . . . every desire to make a success of this project . . . Indeed, I did at the beginning. I saw it as a wonderful opportunity to use my skills and to – give meaning to my life again. Do you understand that?'

Gallois made a gesture which seemed to indicate: If you say so.

David leant forward. 'Please – do you see that?'

'Yes –' He shrugged. 'I know you had no choice.'

'But I worked hard, didn't I? For success.' David frowned and looked down at his hands. 'I forgot, you see. I put my own satisfaction above . . . other considerations.' He looked up again. 'But now – I can see I was mistaken. I should not have done what I did – so wholeheartedly. I was wrong.'

Gallois was watching carefully now, studying David's face.

'The point is . . .' David went on, '. . . I want to help.'

There was silence. He was suspicious, and who could blame him? David leant forward urgently. 'Look, I am well aware of what was going on in this place when I arrived. Most of the devices were being

305

deliberately sabotaged. I know that now. But I have said nothing. So you see – despite what you may think – I *am* in sympathy with your cause.'

Gallois had not moved a muscle. He sat as still as stone.

David wished the Frenchman would give him a sign, some indication of encouragement. The sphinx-like silence was – difficult. 'Look, I realise it's hard for you to say anything . . . After all, why *should* you? I can only tell you that I do wish to help . . . and that I am in a position to do so in a very definite, a very concrete, way.'

Suddenly Gallois moved. He sat forward in his chair and cleared his throat. 'Monsieur Freymann, I cannot imagine where you have obtained these strange ideas. For one thing, there has never been any sabotage at this company. It is, if I may say so, an absurd idea! And second, I really cannot be involved with any activity against – the interests of this company. I don't know why you have approached me, monsieur, but I assure you I cannot help.'

He was getting to his feet. David sprang up and hurried round the desk. Gallois said, 'I think it is best if we do not continue this conversation. Really, monsieur, I cannot help you. Nor can anyone here. We are straightforward working men. We keep out of trouble.' He turned and reached for the door handle.

For a moment David was frozen with indecision. Then, just as Gallois was opening the door, he lunged forward and grabbed the Frenchman's sleeve. 'Please, you don't understand!' David looked nervously into the open passageway to see if anyone had heard, then stared imploringly at Gallois.

Very slowly, Gallois closed the door again. 'What exactly don't I understand?'

David thought miserably: I am going to have to tell him! In all this time he had never told a living soul.

As he stared up at Gallois, searching for the words, acid bit into his stomach and suddenly a piercing pain hit his abdomen. The room seemed to move in on him and he gasped for breath. He felt as if he was falling and reached out. A firm hand took hold of his arm and suddenly there was a chair under him and he was leaning forward with his head between his knees. 'My tablets . . . They're on the desk there . . .'

The bottle was thrust, open, into his hand. He took out three tablets and chewed them hard because they worked quicker that way.

Gallois' voice said from close by, 'Are you all right?'

David nodded. 'I'll be better in a minute. In just a minute . . . Don't go, please.' He reached out and gripped the other man's arm for a moment. After a while the pain eased a little and David leant his head on his hands and whispered, 'Don't judge me too harshly. I just ask you now, please, to listen to what I have to say . . .' He sat up slowly and leant back against the chair with his eyes closed. He felt very faint and his heart was thudding like a drum. 'I need *your* help . . .' He smiled gently. 'Not the other way round.'

He paused to take a few deep breaths. It often helped the pain. 'The thing is . . . before they made me leave my job in Germany – before the war – I stole something. A secret. A secret that could be very, very important – in the war. I am the only one who knows about it – it was my idea, you see.' He stopped to look at Gallois, to see that he had understood. He thought: Now is the moment of belief or disbelief. He pulled himself upright and grasped the Frenchman's arm again. 'I have always wanted to get the secret to the British, so they can use it. But . . . there was never the opportunity. And then, I came here and it seemed easier to carry on and do my job . . . You see, I was so happy just to be alive. This place, it seemed like heaven after . . . the camp.'

He sighed deeply. 'But now . . . Now I must do something about it, do you understand?' He shook his head. 'I just cannot do nothing – like before. If you knew what the camps were like! I must do something for *them*, do you see? I must in some way help *them*. And this is the one thing I can do.' He looked anxiously into Gallois' face. 'Tell me – do you understand what I am saying?'

Gallois looked down, as if making up his mind what to do. When he looked up again his expression was guarded, worried. He sighed and whispered firmly, 'Dear Monsieur Freymann, I am so sorry that you are unwell. I know you have been through a lot. I only wish there was something I could do to help but, really, there is nothing.'

'But I just want to take my secret to England . . .'

'I'm sorry.' The Frenchman's tone was cooler now. 'There is really nothing I can do.'

A terrible tiredness came over David and he slumped in his chair. It had all been for nothing.

Gallois looked over his shoulder and lowered his voice. 'Really, I think it is very dangerous to talk about this . . . Forgive me, but it really is unwise.' He moved towards the door. 'You're all right, are you? Do you want me to send someone along?'

David covered his face with his hands and shook his head. He heard the door close and got off his chair and lay on the floor. It often helped his stomach. But nothing, he knew, would remove the dull ache in his heart.

One week later a new project was announced. Goulvent, Pescard et

307

Cie was to build larger radar detection devices suitable for ships. The pioneering work had been done elsewhere; all that was required was to assemble components which would be sent from Germany.

For David, however, there was still a lot of work to be done, developing test programmes and equipment. He worked long hours but only because he couldn't bear to go back to his room any more. He had stopped playing cards with the guards. He had stopped talking to them – or indeed to anyone. He just wanted to be left alone. Whenever there was a discussion, he cut it short. He even barked at Geissler.

He didn't bother with meals; he hated having to go to the canteen to collect them. He knew it wasn't doing him any good – he felt awful – but he didn't care.

He hated his work. He hated his life. He hated himself.

Then Geissler summoned him to his office. 'It seems that they want you elsewhere, Herr Freymann.' The Kapitanleutnant picked up a letter from his desk and examined it. 'They don't say when ... However,' he smiled coolly, 'we need you more, so we are protesting at this proposed transfer. We have put in a request through the appropriate channels and expect to hear shortly.'

David was looking past Geissler to the window. Between a gap in the buildings it was just possible to glimpse the sea, misty today, but still beautiful. David said quietly, 'Where?'

'Excuse me?'

'Where do they want to send me?'

'Ah! Let me see ... It's not a naval project, that I do know.' He examined the letter again. 'All I have here is a code number and prefix. Perhaps ... Wait one minute ...' Geissler picked up the telephone and asked for HQ. He spoke for a few seconds then replaced the receiver. He coughed nervously. 'I cannot unfortunately tell you where exactly – we do not have details – but apparently the prefix denotes an SS establishment ...' He added unhappily, 'That is perhaps another reason why it would be best for you to stay here.'

Germany. Perhaps even a camp. Back into the pit.

'Herr Freymann, I will let you know the minute I myself hear the decision. In the meantime we must proceed with the preparation for the new project. Yes?'

'Yes.'

'I will do my best, Herr Freymann. I will try to persuade them to let you stay ...'

'Yes, thank you.' He was sincere, Geissler, but there would be nothing he could do. David stood up and, nodding briefly, walked out. The escort was waiting. David led the way down to the entrance and into the van. They began the short drive back to Goulvent, Pescard et Cie.

The van deposited him at the door. He went up to his office and finished his day's work. New component specifications, details of new testing equipment: work that could easily be done by someone less qualified. He would begin the business of handing over in the morning.

That night he slept badly for the first time in months. He dreamed he was back on a bare wooden bunk, crushed between two dying men. The *Prominente* came and made them get up and go to the quarry. It was still the middle of the night. The *Prominente* thought it was very funny, to make them get up in the night. Then they started beating people. David woke up.

For a while he couldn't get back to sleep and then, when he was tired again, there was pain in his stomach. In the end he hardly slept at all.

The next morning he went to the office early and began working out how best to delegate his work load. Feverishly, he started making lists of jobs and responsibilities, grouping them under different names and departments.

There was a knock at the door. David glanced at the clock on the desk. It was still only seven. 'Come in.'

It was Gallois. He took a seat. 'Good morning.'

David said, 'I'm glad you called in. I need to discuss this with you. It's a list of jobs that will need to be taken over by you and others when I go.'

Gallois said, 'You're going?'

'In all probability. Now, when this is typed, perhaps –'

'Where will they send you?'

David put down his pencil and said shortly, 'I don't know. Probably back to where I came from.'

'But you have done well . . . Surely they are pleased?'

David rubbed his eyes. He felt dreadfully tired. With effort he replied, 'Ah, but you don't understand the way they work. There are no rules, you see. You do badly, they send you back to a camp. You do well – the same thing happens. There are no rules.'

Gallois hesitated. 'You'll work on electronics, though. You'll have a skilled job?'

David shrugged. 'Perhaps. It's not really important.'

'Surely you want to work?'

'What I want isn't relevant. Anyway, I don't care. Not any more.'

Later there was a meeting about the new project. The atmosphere in the room was claustrophobic, hot and smoky. David felt enormously irritated with everyone. They were so slow to grasp the basics and he had to explain the simplest things to them. He couldn't believe how stupid they were. Someone – a junior technician – asked yet another idiotic question. David closed his eyes for a moment to stop himself from shouting, then he said between clenched teeth, 'Can't you understand *anything*? Why do you have to be so stupid? Are you *trying* to make things difficult? Really! It's impossible to deal with you people . . .'

They were all staring at him and he realised he had been shouting after all.

A second later his stomach ulcer ruptured. The pain hit him like a sledgehammer. It was incredibly sharp, like a fire burning inside. As soon as it started he knew it was different from anything he'd felt before. He also knew that in a few more seconds it would be so bad that he would have to scream. But then the room started to blur and he felt very cold and everything began to slip away. He was grateful. It was nice to slip away.

Peace and beauty always. A hundred years at least. Whenever the fire came back they pressed the black thing on his face and he was floating again . . .

He wanted to sleep for ever. The sleep was gentle, like clouds, floating . . . Flowers, there were flowers. Then whiteness again, soft and gentle . . . He wanted to sleep for ever.

They wouldn't let him. The *Prominente* were beating him, slapping his face. Someone was shouting at him. He moaned and tried to close his eyes again. But the voice was shouting again. It was a woman. She was speaking in French. 'Come on! Wake up now! Come on!'

He felt the pain again and moaned, 'No. No!'

Then they let him sleep again. He had won.

Someone slapped his face again. Why couldn't they leave him alone? The pain was more persistent now. It wouldn't let him sleep. He murmured, 'The pain. Please, can I have something?'

A woman's voice said, 'Not yet. When you're awake.'

He woke up only because the pain wouldn't let him sleep. Then at last they gave him something. It didn't help much. He discovered that nothing helped very much. The days blended into one another, he slept only when he was exhausted with the pain.

Then he woke up one day and realised that for once he had slept well. The pain was much less. He sat up and let them feed him with watery milk. He felt better. His only regret was having to face the world again.

310

Another day he woke up and found Gallois sitting beside the bed. The Frenchman smiled and said, 'How are you?'

David said what was expected of him. 'I'm all right.'

They exchanged more platitudes, then David was tired and the Frenchman left. As David fell asleep something nagged at his memory. He should have said something to the Frenchman, something important, but he couldn't remember what . . .

The next day he remembered and groaned because it was too late and the Frenchman was no longer there.

But it wasn't too late. Gallois returned. When he came into the room David stared at him in disbelief and, reaching out, grasped the Frenchman's hands.

Gallois smiled and asked again, 'How are you?'

David said, 'Never mind. Please listen. I have something to ask you. Something important.' He pulled himself up in the bed. 'Monsieur Gallois, when we had our conversation some weeks ago, you said you could not help me. That's as may be. But I'm sure you know of a way to get a small package to England. The information I told you about, it's all in a small package. I wanted to go with it, before. But since it's impossible now, then the information must go on its own.'

Gallois started to speak but David held up his hand. 'No, please don't bother with denials and so on. Whether or not you personally can find a way of getting this to its destination is irrelevant. Just come back, please, and tell me that you can get it to the right people! Please!' He leant back against the pillows, exhausted.

Gallois said firmly, 'I'll find out.'

David patted his hands; he felt sure that the Frenchman would find a way. He fell asleep happy.

Kapitanleutnant Geissler came to see him next. 'Well, are they taking care of you here? I am proud to say that we managed to bend the rules and get you put in here. It's rather a good hospital. I trust you like it here?'

'Oh yes. It's very good. Very good.'

Geissler looked awkward. David guessed he did not like sickness. Eventually he said, 'What I thought you might like to know is that you are to stay with us here in Brest. It's all been decided. Of course, that's as long as you manage to regain your fitness . . . You will, won't you, Herr Freymann?'

David nodded, dumbfounded.

'Good! Well, we look forward to seeing you back at your desk as soon as convenient then. In the meantime, I wish you good health!'

David stared at the door for a long time after Geissler had gone.

He was to stay . . . after all. He frowned; he had been so sure, so certain that they would send him away. It was most confusing. Another reprieve. Life was nothing but a series of reprieves. He didn't know what was worse: living in hope of life or in certainty of death.

He didn't feel glad, he didn't feel angry. If anything he felt a little annoyed. It was the constant chopping and changing that got him down . . .

The next day a nurse came in, a nurse he hadn't seen before. As she made a show of tucking in the bed clothes she started whispering to him. At first David didn't understand what she was saying. Then, suddenly, he realised. The nurse was saying, 'I have a message for you. Your friends will deliver both packages. They repeat: *Both* packages.'

He clasped his hands together and let the understanding slowly dawn on him. His prayers had been answered. He was to be allowed his small act of sabotage after all.

21

The bookshop windows looked blank and cold. Julie lowered her eyes and kept walking until she reached the shop door. She went straight in. A bell jangled loudly.

The proprietor was sitting behind the counter. He peered at her over his spectacles.

Julie said, 'I'd like a copy of *La Grande Chance*, please.'

'Is that by Maurik?'

'No, Lefarge.'

The shopkeeper looked quickly around. 'Follow me, I'll see if I have it in the back.' He led the way through some heavy curtains into the darkness of the store room behind. For a moment Julie couldn't see anything, then she realised there was a figure standing before her. A voice said, 'Thank you for coming.'

'That's all right.'

The figure came closer and Julie made out the features. It was the new man, Maurice. He had come from England with a wireless operator called Jacques.

Maurice led her towards the back of the store room. There was more light here. Maurice said, 'The same as before, if you don't mind. There are two of them.' His voice was quiet, calm and authoritative. It was like his face: trustworthy. The moment he'd started reorganising the line Julie had known he'd be all right. He'd discarded many of the helpers and reduced their numbers to a small tight group. Most important, he was very very careful.

He indicated a door which led to a small box room. 'The first's waiting in here.' He smiled. 'All right?'

'Oh yes!' It was easy now, not like the first time.

Julie walked in, sat down and faced the young man who sat at the small table. He certainly looked American, with his round face and his extraordinary haircut.

She smiled briefly. 'Where do you come from?'

'I'm from Milwaukee, ma'am.'

Julie regarded the airman as if she knew precisely where Milwaukee was. 'And which State is that in?'

'Wisconsin, ma'am.'

Julie tried to remember where Wisconsin was. Somewhere on the Great Lakes, she thought. Mid-West, anyway. She said, 'That's near New York, isn't it?'

The airman laughed drily. 'Goodness me, no, ma'am! Don't let nobody from Wisconsin hear you say that! Chicago – that's the nearest big city. New York! Why that's a thousand miles away.' He laughed again.

This one was genuine, no doubt about that. But best to make sure. 'You should be back in four weeks or so. Are you looking forward to that?'

The young man grinned. 'You bet. Haven't seen my family for over a year now.'

'Yes, let me see, it's late November now. You should be back in time for Thanksgiving then, shouldn't you?'

The airman frowned. 'Why, no, ma'am. We've just had Thanksgiving. Just four days ago!' He shook his head. 'No, no way I'll get Thanksgiving with my family till next year, ma'am.'

Julie smiled. 'No, of course not.' She stood up. 'You wait here. They'll come and collect you in a moment.'

The airman nodded and sank back in his seat. Julie went back into the store room. Maurice came forward. She nodded and said, 'That one's all right, I'm certain.'

Maurice looked pleased. 'Good.' He said over his shoulder, 'Get that one back into the cellar, Henri, and bring up the other one. Don't let them talk to each other.'

Julie leant against a bookshelf to wait. This was the third time they'd asked her to come to the bookshop. The first time had been difficult: she hadn't known what to ask and she'd found herself going through two generations of the Americans' family histories before she struck on the idea of asking questions about Thanksgiving. Now she could do an interview in as little as five minutes.

Stool-pigeons. *Mouchards*. She was pretty sure she hadn't let any through yet. *God forbid*.

She watched Maurice as he leant back against a bookshelf and lit a cigarette. He was about forty, stocky and she was pretty sure he was a Belgian – but one didn't ask. After the fiasco of the previous winter no-one asked anything any more.

He ran the line with a firm hand. No unnecessary contact, no unnecessary knowledge. That's why everyone trusted him.

Maurice came up to her. 'The other one's in there now. He's the one we're concerned about. He turned up near Rennes, saying he'd walked all the way from the north somewhere. That's a hell of a long walk without any help . . . Also he looks very nervous. We checked him out with London, of course. Everything all right there, but . . .!' He shrugged.

Julie nodded and went back into the box room.

The airman jumped when she came into the room: he was nervous all right. Julie took a good look at him. He was blond, blue-eyed and pale-skinned. He looked miserable. Julie began with the usual questions: name, rank, serial number, aircraft, squadron, where stationed. These facts had already been checked, but she asked the questions again so that she could watch him and listen to his voice.

There was a strange inflection in his voice: not quite an accent, more a hint of one.

She asked, 'Where are you from?'

'Omaha.'

'Have your family always lived there?'

'No.'

He was not very forthcoming. Julie tried again. 'Where did they come from originally?'

'Europe.'

'Where exactly?'

There was a silence. The boy narrowed his lips. Julie thought: Oh dear, this one's going to be difficult. On a hunch she asked, 'Was it from Germany?'

The young man was looking upset. 'Back to that again! You're going to be like the rest.'

'What do you mean?' Julie asked softly.

'They –' He was unable to speak and shook his head. Finally he said, 'They – hate me! They call me a Hun! And now I suppose you're going to accuse me of being a German spy!'

'Your family *were* German?'

He nodded slowly. 'But I'm an American! I'm as American as any of them! I suppose they've been telling you different?'

'No. No, they haven't. Really. But your name – Smith?'

'My family's name was Schmidt. They went to America a long, long time ago! We changed our name – oh, fifteen years ago.'

'That must have been about the time you went to school.' He didn't look much more than twenty.

He nodded.

'Where did you go to school?'

She took him through everything she could think of. School, summer camps, baseball, football, the movies he had seen, the girls he had known – not many, she guessed correctly – even the house his family lived in. She had no idea if his answers were right. She only knew that his eyes were honest and he never stopped to search for an answer and, when he spoke of home, his face lit up.

She asked him about his journey from Northern France. He had walked, he said, because he felt safer that way. He thought the local people might not be friendly so he'd avoided them and stolen food as he went along. He described the places he'd been to, how he'd narrowly escaped a patrol and had to hide in a tree. It all sounded plausible, Julie decided. She couldn't imagine anyone making up such a long and involved story.

Finally she said, 'Well, if everything goes smoothly you should be home soon – in about a month. That'll get you home at the end of December, won't it?'

He smiled and it transformed his face. 'Yes! Will it really be that soon?'

That makes a change, Julie thought. Most of them complained because they weren't being airlifted back in the morning. She said, 'If all goes well.' Then she smiled. 'But you might just miss Thanksgiving, I'm afraid.'

He shrugged. 'I don't care – just so long as I can see my folks.'

Julie thought: Blast, he hasn't risen to it. I'll have to keep going.

Suddenly the young man said, 'Hey! But we've just had Thanksgiving!'

'Of course!' Julie laughed. 'How silly of me.'

When she came out Maurice and the others were standing among the dusty book shelves, waiting for her expectantly. She said, 'I think he's genuine. But I can't guarantee it.' She hated giving them a woolly answer, but there was one awful possibility she could not rule out: his background might be everything he said it was, but he might have chosen to move back to Germany just before the war. He might be a superb liar. She said, 'He certainly lived in America as a child but whether or not he chose to stay there I cannot say. His family were German.'

Maurice touched her shoulder. 'Good enough. He stays with the others, then. But we keep an eye on him.' He turned to Julie. 'Thank you for your help. It's just what we need.'

Julie flushed with pleasure. 'I'm just sorry I couldn't be more certain –'

'No, no! Better to have doubts than pretend to be sure. Thank you again. We've kept you long enough. You should go now. Take care.'

Julie put her hand on his arm. 'One thing – you will call on me, won't you, for beach duty, when the boat comes?'

Maurice looked at her thoughtfully. 'If you wish. It would certainly be useful to have you there. But – it means more risk, you know that?'

'Yes, I know that.'

He nodded.

Julie waved briefly, then went to the thick curtain and waited behind it, listening. There was no sound and, tentatively, she pulled the curtain aside until she could see through into the shop. There were no customers: only the proprietor, standing behind the counter.

She stepped out briskly and went round the end of the counter. Near the shop door she paused, as if looking at one of the books on the shelf, then nodding to the proprietor, went casually out into the street.

She resisted the temptation to look over her shoulder. That would never do. Instead she looked at her watch. Her lunch hour was nearly over. She'd have to go straight back to the office. It wasn't far, only five minutes away.

She walked calmly, not too fast, not too slow. She kept her manner casual, glancing at the occasional shop window, or into the faces of passers-by. She had never realised it was so difficult to look natural. She wondered if she was fooling anyone. Her heart was beating wildly and she felt horribly conspicuous. She decided she'd never get used to this kind of thing.

When she arrived at the office it was quiet: her boss was away for the afternoon. She finished some accounts and typed three letters, then looked at the pile of copy invoices waiting to be filed. She hated filing: it could wait.

Instead she flicked through her diary, trying to work out when the next moonless night would be . . . That was when he would come . . .

It was seven months since she had seen him. She'd thought about him constantly, so much so that sometimes she couldn't remember what his voice sounded like or the exact shape of his nose. Not that those things mattered . . . But it did make him seem unreal and that frightened her. Sometimes she could even persuade herself that she'd never see him again.

He, his crew, and the stranded airmen had finally been collected in March. The boat had come back four times after that, on routine missions. It was then that she'd expected to see him. But he hadn't been on board. Instead there had been messages, usually relayed by the leader of the beach party.

Hoping to come soon. Please be careful.

Take care. Don't know when I'll be able to come.

In April the nights had got too short and the boats had not come any more. The summer seemed to last for ever – and not just for her but for the people hiding the growing number of airmen. Now it was autumn again and he still hadn't come. There were messages like the ones before, but no Richard.

Maybe he would never come again. But she'd go to the beach anyway, just in case.

That was why she was helping Maurice – to make sure she got to the beach. She was ashamed of her motives. Either one was committed or one wasn't. She had to make up her mind.

Immediately, she knew it was impossible. She couldn't choose between the safety of her son and seeing Richard again. She was greedy; she wanted *both*.

After. She'd make up her mind after she'd seen Richard. Yes: that was the answer.

She shivered slightly and got up to do the filing.

She left the office early. There was no more work to do and, by getting the five o'clock bus, she could have an extra hour with Peter before bed time.

It was only a five-minute walk to the bus stop, but she'd still have to hurry. She walked rapidly, head down and arms swinging. She looked at her watch again. There should be enough time . . . But she hated cutting things fine. She ran a little way until she was out of breath, then walked again. She arrived at the bus stop with four minutes to spare.

She flopped into a seat, breathless and rather hot. Why had she hurried? Because I'm a worrier, she thought with a sigh, and I'll never change now. She took the morning edition of *Ouest-France* out of her bag and, unfolding it, started to read. There wasn't very much of it – only two pages – and it was, she guessed, heavily censored, but some news was better than none at all and, like everyone else, she read what she could.

She was aware of someone sitting down in the seat beside her, then, with a lurch, the bus set off. After so many years Julie knew the route like the back of her hand. She didn't have to look up to know exactly where they were on the forty-minute journey.

The person next to her shifted in his seat. Suddenly there was a voice in her ear. 'You left work early!'

Julie started and looked round.

She sighed with relief and laid her hands over her heart. 'Michel! You gave me a terrible fright!'

He smiled briskly. 'My apologies.'

The bus drew to a halt at the checkpoint which marked the beginning of the Zone Interdite, the coastal zone restricted to all but those with the necessary permit. Julie got out her papers and glanced at the permit which had appeared in Michel's hand. She noticed that it was in a false name.

When the *Feldgendarmen* had glanced at the papers and the bus was on its way again, Julie stole a glance at Michel. 'Where have you been all this time?' How long had it been? Months.

'Morlaix. Mainly.'

'But I haven't seen you around. I thought you must have gone away!'

'No.' It was a statement.

'Anyway –' She took another look at him. 'What are you doing on this bus?'

'Going your way.'

'Ah.' She didn't ask why. With Michel; she never liked to enquire too closely. He was probably planning to blow up more Germans.

He read her mind and said quietly, 'I'll be behaving myself, don't worry.'

Julie glanced surreptitiously over her shoulder. Behind, there were two large country women sitting with baskets of vegetables on their laps. In front, there was a girl reading a book. No-one was listening.

Michel whispered, 'I hear that things have got a bit more organised around Tregasnou.'

Julie stiffened. How dare he! She said calmly, 'What do you mean, Michel?'

'There's a new set-up, isn't there? A new organisation to get people out?'

'If there is, I know nothing about it.'

Michel smiled. 'Of course. I must say your security's much better. Nobody's talking. That's very good.'

Julie said coldly, 'So how did you hear this story? If security is so good.'

'Ah. Small things . . . Guesswork mainly. And the silence.'

'The silence?'

'Yes. No-one's talking. That always means there's something going on!' He smiled at her.

Self-satisfied as ever, Julie thought. But he doesn't know as much as he pretends. That's the important thing. She said, 'If there *is* something going on, I really don't know. I keep well out of these things nowadays.'

'I hope so. Whatever they may think, they're still a bunch of amateurs.'

'I think not.'

Michel looked at her quizzically. 'You seem very definite.'

'I've just formed an opinion, that's all.'

He regarded her for a moment. 'You've changed, Julie –'

She frowned. 'Why do you say that?'

'You're more – self-confident. You never used to be.'

'You're making judgements again.'

'Yes. I think I'm quite good at them.'

Julie sighed with exasperation. 'But – you're so sure of yourself. And so intolerant of everyone else, Michel! It's really very trying.'

'You mean, like everyone else in your quiet neck of the woods, you think my politics stink! Well, I tell you – after the war you'll be sorry. You'll find you're living in a France run by fascists, just like it was before the Germans came!'

Julie shook her head. 'There, you see – you immediately turn everything into a political argument. All I meant was – you're very difficult to talk to!'

'Ah! But how very sure of yourself *you* have become, Julie. You're quite a different lady from the one I used to know. What *have* you been up to? I think you're busier than you'll admit to. Yes, a very busy lady!'

How she hated his games. She said impatiently, 'I am just the same person, Michel. Nothing's changed.'

He gave her a mocking glance. 'If you say so.'

The bus had stopped at a village. More people got on. With a loud roar the bus started again, juddering slowly up through the gears. Like most buses in Brittany, it had seen better days.

Michel leant closer. 'All right – no more discussions. I'll tell you. I caught this bus purposely – so that I could see you.'

Julie peered sideways at him. Again, she wasn't sure what he meant. She smiled and said archly, 'Oh really? I didn't know you cared so much, Michel. After all, you've managed to keep away from me for at least six months!'

He looked irritated. 'No ... Well, of course it's nice to see you – but actually it's about something else.'

'Yes?'

He said, 'Whether or not you know who's involved in ... local activities ... you must know someone who knows *someone*. Anyway, I have an important message for them.' He turned and looked at her. 'If I give it to you, will it get to its destination?'

'But why me? Why not send it more ... directly?'

'Directly? You're joking. There's undeclared war between your lot and mine. Or didn't you know? If your lot had their way we'd never touch so much as a hair of a German's head. Well, that's not our idea of how to fight.'

'But when you kill it means reprisals.'

'I thought we weren't going to argue ... Look, you're the best contact I have. Are you going to pass this message or not?'

Julie looked him straight in the eye. 'Well ... I can't promise anything, but ...' She shrugged and pretended to consider. '... if it's that important I'll do my best.'

'I thought you might be able to.'

Julie felt like strangling him.

He went on, 'The message is this: there's a scientist working in a factory in Brest who wants to get to England. The man's a German Jew. He used to be in a concentration camp until they dug him out to work on some electronic gadget at this factory. In theory he's a sort of prisoner, but he's hardly guarded. It would be easy to spring him. But the point is, he says he has a secret – an invention of some sort – which would be very useful to the British. He would bring all the details with him. Whether or not he *really* has a secret is another matter ... But they say he's very bright, so he might be of use anyway, secret or not.'

Julie frowned, trying to take it all in.

Michel thought for a moment. 'Ah, one more thing. He's not too well. He can't be shifted for another two weeks or so. They half killed him in the camp in Germany. Mind you, kinder than the way they treat most Jews. Usually they kill them straight away. Did you know that? They're killing them all, in their thousands. Women, children, babies ...'

Julie looked at him in horror. 'You don't mean it . . .'

'Oh yes. They're carting French Jews away now, by the train load. They'll never come back.'

Julie stared out of the window at the clean, honest countryside, thinking that it couldn't possibly be true.

'So –' Michel said '– do I take it the message has been received?'

'Yes. Yes. I think I've got it.'

'The point is, if we get him out, will you take him off our hands?'

'I . . . I'll ask.'

'Good.'

The bus stopped in another village, then started again, bumping slowly along the narrow lanes. Julie looked out of the window and wondered if Michel was holding anything back. Probably. He was a secretive man.

And this scientist – ill. How ill? she wondered. It might be difficult to get him down to the beach . . . She'd better send a message to Maurice straight away. He would know what to do. He would decide.

They were nearing Tregasnou. Michel nudged her. 'If you need to contact me I'll be at my old apartment during the week and at –' He paused and frowned. 'No, just at the apartment.'

She nodded. The bus shuddered to a halt in the centre of the village. The remaining passengers stood up and began to shuffle off.

Michel said suddenly, 'And another thing . . . If you ever need help – you yourself, I mean – come to me, won't you?' He was casual and offhand, as if he were asking her round for a meal, but Julie could tell that he was perfectly serious. He really was the most confusing person. She nodded vaguely and said, 'Yes . . . all right.'

'Good.' He got up and led the way out of the bus. Then, with a brief wave, he was gone.

Julie hurried up the hill to the farmhouse, feeling despondent. Whatever this thing involved – even if it was as straightforward as Michel had suggested – the idea of joining forces with his friends worried her.

She sighed. At least she wouldn't have to make the decision. That would be Maurice's problem.

'They say he's not to be trusted.' Maurice looked at each of them in turn.

There was silence apart from the crackling of wood burning in the stove. Someone said, 'Yes, but why should he want to plant someone on us? What would be his motive. Eh?'

Jean sighed deeply, took his pipe out of his mouth and said heavily,

'Who can tell? Michel has always had extreme views. To him, anything is justified if it furthers his cause.'

Julie could bear it no longer. She said to Maurice, 'But he would not betray us, I'm sure of that. After all, we *are* his family. He wouldn't betray us to the Germans, I'm sure . . .'

'Family –?'

'Yes!' Julie exclaimed. 'Cousins. He used to come here often . . .'

There was silence again. Finally Maurice said, 'It's what happens *before* we take delivery of this fellow that's the problem. There is no way we can be sure he's authentic. We're going to have to take *their* word for that. If they've been fooled . . . well, we'll have no defence . . . We'll get nabbed at the hand-over. When you think about it, it could be the perfect set-up.'

The others nodded slightly. Julie shook her head.

'But . . . Why would they make up this story about him being ill, if he's really a Gestapo agent? It sounds unlikely . . . Doesn't it?' Suddenly she was as uncertain as the other three. It was impossible to be sure.

Maurice grunted and passed a hand over his face. 'Looking on the black side, the Gestapo might need the extra time to train up their agent. Who knows?'

The fisherman, Gérard, said, 'But what if this scientist *is* genuine and he *does* have this secret, what then?'

Maurice suddenly slapped his hands on his knees and said, 'Well, I suggest we do this – we ask for as many details about this man as possible. We try to check him out with London. You never know, they might have some information on him – if he really is a top brain. Then . . . We take as many precautions as possible. We risk only one person at the pick-up, we blindfold this fellow, we guard him twenty-four hours a day . . .'

'So we go ahead?'

'Yes, I think we have to.' Maurice looked at Julie. 'Can you ask for more details about this man? And also ask if they guarantee his authenticity.'

Julie nodded. 'I'll ask.'

'Okay. That's it for the moment then.'

They all got up. Gérard said a quick good night and left immediately. Maurice paused and came up to Julie. He put a hand on her shoulder. 'May I speak with you one moment?'

'Of course.'

He led her to the other side of the table and they sat down. He said softly, 'Look, I'm concerned that you've become involved in all this when perhaps you didn't mean to. If – well, if you should decide to change your mind, that is understood. You only have to tell me. And there'll be no recriminations.'

He was asking her to choose. She thought of Peter asleep upstairs and instinctively looked upwards. There was no simple answer . . .

She said, 'I'll do what I can for the moment . . . I'll deliver the message and bring back the reply and all that. Perhaps when this scientist is delivered, perhaps then I might . . . want to be not quite so involved . . .' She trailed off, thinking what a half-baked person she was.

But Maurice was nodding. 'That's fine, then. We'll do that. But I do think we shouldn't be using your real name. I think we must find another for you. Would Marie-Claire suit you?'

The question took Julie by surprise. 'Er – yes.'

'Right, Marie-Claire you are then.'

A false name. Julie shivered slightly.

Maurice was getting up. 'Oh, and the boat. Sunday. It's coming on Sunday. You'll help bring parcels to the beach?'

Julie breathed, 'Oh yes! That'll be no problem!'

Sunday. It was three days away.

The darkness was made up of a million small dots which jumped and danced before your eyes. One moment you could see the outline of a rock against the sea, the next it had gone and there was nothing except the shimmering blackness. If you stared too long you began to see strange indistinct shapes that moved and faded and darted away. Then you had to look away and rest your eyes.

One thing at least, thought Julie, it was a perfect night for the gunboat. The sentries up on the headland wouldn't be able to see further than the cliff edge. Also, there was hardly any wind. That meant the boat would have a fast passage. They would come, she knew it. The BBC message had said so. It had come at eight. *Benedictine is a sweet liqueur*.

Whatever happened, it would be a great relief when all the parcels were gone. There were thirty-nine of them, there on the beach at that very moment. It was a terrifying number, but they had been accumulating fast in the last few weeks. Many had been diverted away, to Spain via Bordeaux, but those who had been sent down the line to Brittany – by train from Paris to St Brieuc – had all been hidden, some for as long as a month.

Now, miraculously, they were all on the beach. And restless. Julie could hear them muttering between themselves. She got up and, walking over to the voices, whispered, 'Please don't talk. The sound may carry.'

'But how long do we have to wait?'

'It's impossible to say. Just be patient. Please.'

They were quiet and Julie returned to her place. She felt very calm. She was sure everything would be all right. She had a feeling about it.

There was silence apart from the faint lapping of waves on sand.

She saw someone move, probably Gérard. Then another man. Then there was a sound, an infinitesimal, soft swishing . . .

They were here.

Her heart thudded. She made herself concentrate on what had to be done. She moved along the groups of airmen and said to each, 'You will see two small boats arriving soon. You must not move until you are told. Do you understand?' Then she crouched beside them and waited.

The surfboats seemed to take a long time. Then at last they were there, first one then the other gliding in to the beach, two solid dark shapes against the paler sea. Julie waited half a minute, then stood up and called softly, 'Groups One and Two?' The men – it should be fourteen in all – rose and followed her down towards the waiting boats. The surfboat crews came forward and Julie directed the two groups to different boats. The surfboat crews were in a hurry. They were already pushing their boats out and bundling their passengers in. Julie tried to get a look at their faces. But he wasn't there, she already knew it. Then they were gone.

Twenty minutes later the boats were back. Julie called two more groups of airmen forward. This time some of them didn't listen to her instructions and too many men peeled off in the direction of the first boat. Julie sorted them out and took the three extra men across to the second boat, which was already loaded and waiting. The three men waded into the water, rolled into the boat, and then it was gone.

Julie stared after it for a moment before turning away. One more journey, and they would be finished.

Someone was hurrying along the sand towards her. Gérard? No, too tall.

Then suddenly she knew exactly who it was.

She moved tentatively forward, laughing a little. Then he was hugging her, so tight she could hardly breathe. He put his cheek against hers and with a sudden shock she remembered the feel of his skin and the lovely animal scent of him. And she remembered his body, and how lovely it had felt against hers, and she murmured, 'Oh, how I've missed you.'

'Julie –'

He pulled away, trying to see her face in the darkness. He whispered, 'There's not much time and I must know – First, are you all right?'

'Yes, yes! *I'm* all right!'

'But is it safe? I bet it isn't!'

'It's fine, now. Really! Everyone's very careful. Really!' She laughed and pushed herself up on tiptoe and put her arms round his neck and kissed him. He kissed her back, hard. Then, after a while, he pulled away again. 'Julie, listen – I've had an idea. It's all been okayed. I've cleared it with everyone . . . Julie, you and Peter must come back to England. On the gunboat.'

Julie frowned in the darkness. 'What –? I –'

'Look, we can fix it for the next trip. You can just disappear. No-one will ever guess where you've gone. And then you'll be safe, *both* of you. Julie, say you will!'

'But . . . I don't know. I . . . I'll have to think about it.'

'But Julie, it *must* be the right thing to do! You're running terrible risks, don't you realise that? If you got caught, well – what *then*?'

'Yes, I . . . I suppose you're right.' She'd never thought about going herself. It had never occurred to her. But it wasn't that simple – and she couldn't explain.

He said urgently, 'Please, say you'll come!'

'I don't know – I don't know! I need time!'

'There may not *be* any time . . .'

She could hear the disappointment in his voice, and understood. He must have been planning this for ages, and now she was being reluctant and ungrateful. She said, 'Please – I love you with all my heart. But I must *think*. My family are here, and the others, and . . . It's all so sudden, Richard. Please, let me think and plan . . . And, next time you come, I'll tell you for sure, I promise. You *will* be coming again, won't you?'

'Yes. Yes . . .'

He was still disappointed, she could tell. She pulled at his arm and sat down on the sand. He sat beside her and put his arm round her. 'Julie – I thought you'd *want* to . . .'

'But I do! I do!'

'Then?'

Julie thought: He's right. I should go. I should get Peter to safety. I should be with him – I *want* to be with him. She said, 'Yes . . . perhaps you're right! I'll try. I promise!'

He squeezed her arm. 'Good! Good!' Then he chuckled. 'I thought for a moment your affections had been stolen by a tall, dark Frenchman!'

She laughed quietly. 'No, I ran after him, but he wouldn't have me!'

'He must have been mad!'

They grinned at each other in the darkness.

After a while there was the gentle sound of muffled oars and she stiffened. He pulled her to her feet. She suddenly realised she hadn't mustered the airmen. She said, 'I'd better get the passengers' and, before he could reply, ran quickly up the beach. When she got back the boats were ready and waiting and there was no more time.

She found him by the second boat. He said, 'We'll be back in a week or so. Come then, Julie! Please!'

'I'll try!'

He kissed her and ran quickly into the water to where the boat was waiting.

Then he was gone, vanished into the darkness that was the sea.

22

There was cloud at two thousand feet. The moon shed a soft silvery sheen over it as it appeared in a rapidly growing mantle beneath the cruising Wellington.

The pilot leant his head against the side cockpit window and looked down. The cloud was thickening all the time. He regarded it with satisfaction. The U-boats would think they were safely hidden under that lot.

The pilot peered at his watch and said into his mike, 'How long to turnaround, Wally?'

There was a crackle and the navigator's voice came through the ear-phones, 'Fifteen minutes, sir.'

'Right-ho.'

They were flying to the limit tonight, like they always did. Eight hundred miles west-south-west into the Atlantic, then a zigzag course east-south-east, across the Bay of Biscay to the French coast, then home. The pattern might yield up a U-boat or two. The only problem was, the U-boats usually knew they were coming.

It had all been so simple when they'd first got the ASV radar more than a year before. If the conditions were right you just turned the thing on and waited for the magic words, 'Radar to Skipper. Target thirteen miles to port. Angle twenty degrees.' Then you turned into the darkest part of the sky and approached up-moon, so that the U-boat was beautifully silhouetted against the moon-path. By the time the U-boat spotted you it was too late for them to dive – or even fight. The pilot had got a good tally in those days: two definite hits and a probable.

Of course, it hadn't been *that* easy. The radar was a bit temperamental and it was no good in rain, snow, sleet or heavy seas. But when the conditions *were* good, it could work quite well.

Then it all changed and the devilish U-boats kept disappearing before one's very eyes. You'd pick them up all right, but by the time you homed in on them they'd bloody disappeared. Of course, there was only one way they could do it so consistently – by countermeasure. A radar detector.

Bound to happen, of course, but still frustrating. Eventually Coastal Command worked out a counter-strategy. As soon as a target was picked up you ordered the radar scanner to be stopped and the radar aimed aft, where its waves couldn't be picked up. Then you manoeuvred slowly into position, asking for the radar to be turned through a full circle only once every minute or so, just to make sure you hadn't lost the U-boat. Only on the final run in did you leave the radar on continuously. At between one and two miles you turned on the two-million-candle-power Leigh light and, even if you didn't pick the U-boat up immediately, with a bit of luck the U-boat gunners wouldn't be able to resist the temptation of firing at it, thus, most obligingly, guiding you straight in to your target.

The strategy worked fairly well, but as often as not the U-boat sussed you out before you ever got near. Real cat and mouse stuff. Trouble was, the mouse got away with it far too often.

It would be nice to gain the upper hand again.

And, with a bit of luck, they might. There was a new box of tricks on board. An experimental device. He was rather proud of the fact that his old girl was the first in Coastal Command to be fitted with one.

H_2S, the boffins called it. Which, if he remembered his school chemistry correctly, was the chemical formula that stunk of rotten eggs. Some boffin somewhere had a sense of humour.

It was a new radar. They'd explained it to him. A completely new type, they said, which would give wonderful definition in *every* direction. Read the sea and the land like a map.

Certainly the radar operators were mad keen on it. The navigator, too – finding his way back to the coast was a piece of cake.

The new-fangled device had been fitted only three days before, so they were continuing to use the old ASV radar as well, to be on the safe side.

The pilot looked at his watch. Two minutes to the final turn and the start of the journey home. They were deep into the Bay now, only twenty miles from the French coast. They'd run parallel to the coast as far as Brest, then turn for home.

They turned. The engines droned on. An hour passed.

'Captain to Navigator. Position, Wally?'

'Fifty miles south-west of Lorient, skipper.'

Good hunting country, this. Close to both Lorient and St Nazaire. 'Captain to crew. Extra sharp look-out now – above *and* below.' Fighters weren't much of a problem in the Bay, but you never knew.

The acknowledgements from the nine-man crew came back through the ear-phones, one by one. The pilot leant his face against the side-screen and looked down at the thick cloud below. No chance of a visual. But somewhere down there was a U-boat, perhaps *several*.

Damn it, all he wanted was a stab at one. *Just a stab.*

The young officer watched the long nose of the submarine carve swathes of white foam through the dark sea and could hardly believe this great monster was really his.

Even now it seemed incredible that they had given him command. He was Just twenty-six and had been an Oberleutnant zur See for only a year.

He wished he felt completely confident – but it was impossible. Not when he'd looked up to the great U-boat commanders for so long: men like Gunther Prien who took U47 into Scapa Flow and sank the *Royal Oak*; or Karl Fischer, the commander with the greatest single tally of ships sunk. How could he think of himself on the same level? It was impossible.

He looked up. A thin veil of cloud was covering the moon. That would give them some cover at least. They needed it: the air patrols were heavy nowadays. He remembered the beginning of the war when he was a Leutnant zur See fresh from training. Then enemy aircraft had been rare and usually came in daylight.

It was five hours since they'd left St Nazaire. They'd left late, because of engine problems, and they'd left disorganised, because of last minute crew changes. Half the men on board had been transferred from another, crippled, boat and at least ten were fresh recruits who'd completed only half their proper training. It was unsatisfactory, to say the least. As soon as they were clear of the Bay he would put the men through their paces and do some intensive training sessions. It wouldn't make up for the lack of an experienced, well-trained crew, but it would have to do.

He looked at his watch. Seven hours of darkness left. Not enough to clear the Bay. He stamped his feet. The winter had come early this year and it was very cold.

The junior watch officer was at his shoulder. 'Radar bleep, Herr Oberleu.'

The young commander nodded. It was nothing to get excited about. The radar detector bleeped and whined and whistled all the time. Often the thing drove commanders so mad that they ordered it to be turned off. The device seemed to hear planes everywhere.

Still, better check it. After all, he was responsible now.

He stepped across to the other side of the bridge and looked at the aerial. It had been introduced as a temporary measure when the British first started using radar, and had quickly been dubbed the Biscay Cross. Now, a year later, they were still using it. This one had certainly seen better days. It looked as though it had been thrown hastily down the hatch and patched together dozens of times. Nevertheless the fragile wooden structure was correctly positioned and the wires properly connected. Nothing wrong there then.

He nodded to the second watch officer and went down the hatch to the control room. The Metox technician was bent over the set, fiddling with a knob. The set emitted a piercing shriek. The technician saw the young commander and said, 'Sorry, Herr Oberleu, it seems to be playing up. Shall I open it up and have a look? It would mean turning it off for a while . . .'

By habit the young officer almost referred the matter to the commander until he remembered with a slight shock that he *was* the commander. The eyes of several of the men were on him. Decision time.

He hesitated. The men's eyes hardened. He *must* decide. Suddenly he said, 'No! Don't dismantle it until we're clear of the Bay. Leave it on!'

The technician nodded. The young commander turned away and went to the chart table, to give himself time to recover. He'd almost made a fool of himself.

He turned on his heel and climbed purposely back up the conning tower.

On the bridge the men moved aside in deference. The young commander stepped forward and stared purposefully ahead. It was darker now. He looked up. The cloud cover was much thicker: both the moon and the stars had disappeared. Good! This darkness was safer and more cocoon-like.

Suddenly he began to feel more optimistic.

'Radar bleep, Herr Oberleu.'

The young commander nodded.

'Another radar bleep.'

Automatically he searched the sky, but there was nothing.

There was tension on the bridge now, as everyone waited for another bleep. If they came at regular intervals, then it might be an aircraft . . .

'Interference on Metox . . . Permanent signal.'

The young officer gripped the coaming. The cursed thing was really playing up. Useless. It was quite useless. It was said in the Officers' Mess that the device worked well only when the enemy were making their final run-in. That gave just enough time to alert the gunners and fire a few bursts on the 20 mm's. Not enough – but better than nothing at all.

'Metox functioning. No signal.'

He relaxed a little and looked out into the night.

Five minutes passed. There were no further reports from the control room.

There was no aircraft then.

The pilot was just beginning to think it wasn't going to be his night.

Then it came. 'Radar to Skipper. Target twenty miles to starboard. Angle ten degrees.'

The familiar excitement clutched at him. He gulped involuntarily and said, 'Stop scanner. Radar aft.' He switched the controls to manual and banked the aircraft to port, automatically beginning the manoeuvres that would bring them into position down-moon.

'Radar to Skipper. You don't want the H_2S scanner off too, do you, sir?'

'Is it picking up the target?'

'Loud and clear, sir. Only one that is. I had nothing on the old set at all.'

Of course. The range had been twenty miles: the old set had rarely managed that. He said, 'Leave it on then.'

They flew north-west until Radar gave the target bearing due east. Then they flew north-east until the target was bearing due south. Now the target would be in the path of any moonlight that might be filtering through the cloud. They turned for the final run-in.

So far so good. The U-boat, if it was one, hadn't dived.

'Captain to Radar. Keep it dead on the nose now.'

'Roger.'

'Still a good target, is it?'

'Oh, loud and clear, sir!'

It was too good to be true. Despite the cold, the pilot's hands were sweating as they gripped the stick.

'Radar to Captain. Range four miles. Dead on the nose.'

A minute and a half to go then. The pilot took her down to four hundred feet and they broke through the cloud base.

'Radar to Captain. Target three degrees to starboard.'

The pilot made the necessary course alteration. The target was moving west then: outward bound. The Wellington was down to three hundred feet.

'Radar to Captain. Target dead ahead. Range three miles.'

'Roger. Captain to Navigator. Bomb doors open.'

Normally they switched on the Leigh light at two miles. But with this much certainty the pilot decided to wait.

Hell, but it had better be a U-boat and not a bloody fisherman out after hours!

'Radar to Captain. Target dead ahead. Range two miles.'

'Roger. Call distances at every half mile now.'

'Will do.'

'Captain to Navigator. I want the Leigh light on at *one* mile, and, Co-pilot, keep shouting my height, will you? Yell if it gets too near a hundred feet.'

'Right-ho, sir.'

'Radar to Captain. One and a half miles, dead on the nose.'

The pilot peered into the murk ahead, but there was no moonpath. No sea, nothing. He was at a hundred and twenty feet now. He could feel the sweat running down his body and his heart hammering against his chest. God, but it had better be a U-boat!

'Radar to Captain. One mile and dead on the nose!'

Navigator to Captain. Leigh light *on*!'

The powerful beam sprang out from the starboard wing, carving a path of light far into the night ahead.

For a moment the pilot could see nothing.

Bloody hell! Where the devil – !

Suddenly there was a yell. 'There!'

And there she was.

Black. Sleek. Long.

A great big beautiful fat U-boat, a perfect target – just for them.

The pilot grunted with excitement. He knew, even before he released the depth charges, that nothing could save her. They had the beautiful black beast absolutely cold.

*

The young officer felt drained. He hadn't realised how tense he had been. Presumably it was something one got used to.

He rubbed his eyes.

When he opened them again he thought for a moment his sight had gone. He was almost blinded by light . . .

There was a scream from his right. 'Enemy starboard ninety!'

He spun round.

A massive light was blazing out of the sky, a great ball of white fire which dazzled the eyes. The entire submarine was covered in a bath of vicious cold light. The young officer wanted to order the light away so that they could slip back into the darkness and hide . . .

Simultaneously he heard the whine of approaching engines.

He began to scream, 'Fire! Fire! Fire all guns!' Even as he screamed the guns opened up, their staccato *rat-tat-tat* tearing into the eerie silence. The tracers wove their way up towards the blinding light.

But still the light came.

He yelled, 'Get the light! The light!' And then realised it was far too late for all that.

The light was so close, so dazzling, it filled the sky. The ominous drone of the engines grew to a higher pitch.

Behind the circle of light the dark shape of the plane was visible. Large. Like a bird of prey.

And still it came inexorably nearer. The young man was filled with blind rage.

He screamed, 'Fire! Fire! Fire!' as if his words would travel through the air and extinguish the terrible light.

Then the noise was a great roar, and the plane seemed to lift up and up, and suddenly its black belly was swooping over them and he raised his fists and cried, 'No-o-oooo!'

The plane was gone. There was an instant when the engine noise was receding and the darkness was descending round the U-boat like a protective blanket – an instant when he felt a flicker of hope.

Then, a brief moment later, he knew with awful certainty that there was to be no escape after all.

The boat gave a great shudder and the deck lurched under his feet.

There was a slow rumble which grew into a thunderous boom. The shock hit his ears and buffeted his body.

The young commander realised with astonishment that the deck was continuing to fall away under his feet. He looked up and saw the boat rolling slowly, almost leisurely, to port.

The deck lurched again, violently, and there was another roar, much closer. The blast threw him against the side of the bridge and he heard his head meet the metal with a dull thud. Then water was in his eyes, in his mouth, pouring down his face. He spluttered fiercely and gasped for breath.

He suddenly thought: I must tell them.

He got to his feet and, pulling himself up the slanting deck, gripped the coaming and shouted, 'Abandon ship!' But his voice was weak and there was too much noise. Men were running and screaming. Even if they heard, it would make no difference.

He almost shouted again, but his eye was caught by the astonishing sight of the bow, just visible in the darkness. It was out of the water.

As he watched he realised with amazement that it was rising slowly but remorselessly up into the sky.

There was another explosion, this time from deep within the boat. Then another. The boat staggered, then continued her terrible climb into the sky.

It was only when he saw the sea rising up towards the conning tower that he realised she wasn't climbing at all, but sliding . . . backwards, deeper and deeper, backwards . . .

There was frantic activity on the forward deck. Some men were trying to release the rafts. They were tearing at the hatch covers with their hands. The hatches would not open. A man began to scream . . .

The young commander felt water round his legs. He noticed in vague surprise that the sea was pouring into the conning tower. The sight made him desperately sad.

When the water reached his neck he swam for a while, thinking of his home and his parents and how much he loved and respected them, and crying because he had failed them so completely, and because he was so terribly afraid to die.

Then the waves were breaking over his head and he was swallowing water and it was incredibly cold and he knew it wouldn't be much longer.

It was twenty minutes, in fact. But he lost consciousness before he drowned and there are worse ways to die.

The streets of Berlin were dark and almost deserted. Rain and sleet were falling in a cold flurry, whipped sideways by the icy northerly wind. The roads were slippery from the long winter freeze and the staff car went slowly, the driver peering nervously through the windscreen at the unlit road ahead.

The weather had been bad for weeks. One storm after another, snow, Arctic temperatures. Doenitz reflected that even the elements seemed to be against them. Stalingrad was under siege, the Army was in retreat; at sea the U-boat crews were achieving remarkable results under terrible conditions. It seemed that the winter would go on for ever.

He could do nothing about the weather.

But he could and would fight against the other problems besetting the Navy. Like complete lack of air cover and reconnaissance for his U-boats. Like lack of steel for the building programme. Like the usual continental-minded attitudes of the leadership – Hitler still had not grasped the fact that he had to win the war at sea to win the war on land. Always the same problems.

Tomorrow Doenitz would get Hitler to approve the steel allocation. And he was slowly winning on the matter of air cover, too. Goering had actually been pleasant to him the last time they met at Fuehrer Headquarters, and Hitler had pressed Doenitz rather than Goering to stay to breakfast. Promising signs.

Doenitz fingered the gold bands on his arm. How much difference power made!

He had been Commander-in-Chief of the Navy for three weeks, ever since Raeder's sudden resignation. Raeder had resigned over Hitler's decision to lay up the battleships, which the leader dubbed 'useless'. Doenitz, on taking up his new post, had also fought the decision – and won. Since then Hitler had treated him with the greatest consideration and respect. Strange justice!

The trouble was, it might all be too late. The worst mistakes had been made and were difficult to put right.

Like the business of this radar.

Schmidt had requested an urgent meeting to discuss 'a radar problem'. Even Goering was going to be there. It must be something serious.

The car drew up outside the Chancellery. Doenitz got out and climbed briskly up the steps into the first of the vast halls, his two staff officers on his heels. The meeting was in one of the smaller conference rooms. Originally the meeting was to have been held in Goering's ostentatious Air Ministry building, but early the day before a bomb had fallen nearby and shattered all the windows. And it was Goering who'd promised that Allied bombers would never reach Berlin!

The others were already there. As Doenitz entered everyone except Goering got to his feet. Goering was sitting at the head of the table, his massive weight wedged into a large ornate gilt chair. He smiled benignly at Doenitz. Doenitz carefully sat at the opposite end of the table, in an equally grand chair. He nodded at Goering and noticed that the man's eyes looked rather odd. It was said that Goering took drugs: that would account for it.

The meeting began. Schmidt was sitting on Goering's right, looking unhappy, his eyes firmly on the papers on the table in front of him. Hesitantly he started to read from what Doenitz realised was a carefully prepared statement.

After a few seconds Doenitz felt his hackles begin to rise. Schmidt was saying, '... the enemy aircraft was shot down near Rotterdam on the night of February 12th 1943. Routine examination of the wreckage by Luftwaffe personnel revealed a box which was badly damaged and covered with blood. However the box was sufficiently intact for it to be confirmed that nothing similar had ever been seen before. Superior technicians were called in but were unable to guess at the function of the box. The only clue was the words "Experimental 6" written in pencil on the side.' Schmidt turned a page and went on, 'Luftwaffe Headquarters ordered the box to be dismantled and brought to Berlin for closer examination ... The Rotterdam Apparatus, as we decided to call it, was then examined by my staff in our laboratory. However ...' Schmidt paused and looked even more unhappy. '... two days ago, the RAF scored a direct hit on the laboratory, killing some of my staff and destroying parts of the apparatus. My staff climbed into the ruins of the laboratory and retrieved what they could. We are now trying to reconstruct the apparatus, using the parts which are left to us.'

'Herr Schmidt now has the use of the best possible laboratory,' Goering interrupted. 'It is properly fortified so that this cannot happen again.' The Luftwaffe staff officers nodded. Doenitz waited. He wanted to hear the rest.

Schmidt looked to see if Goering had finished then returned to his notes. 'With the components now in our possession it is impossible for us to reconstruct this apparatus to the point where we can make it function. We cannot therefore report on the performance, range or characteristics of the device – not unless we obtain another apparatus, more or less intact, from a crashed enemy bomber. However, it *is* possible to draw two basic conclusions: one, that it is a form of radar – a form that we have never seen before ...' Schmidt's voice was down almost to a whisper. He had his elbows on the table and his head in his hands, so that his face was hidden. 'And two, that it works on very short wave, possibly as little as ten centimetres.'

There was a long silence. Doenitz's staff eyed their commander nervously. Goering frowned and, staring out of the window, thoughtfully patted his large belly.

Doenitz stared at Schmidt, but didn't see him. His mind was in the Bay of Biscay, seeing the enemy bombers hunting, tracking, killing his U-boats with their magic new eyes; and on the convoy routes, in the wastes of the North Atlantic, seeing British destroyers lying in wait, ready to pounce, without warning . . .

'May we understand this more completely?' Doenitz spoke softly. Everyone looked at him. 'Are you saying that this radar is completely unknown to us?'

Schmidt licked his lips. 'Yes.'

'And – you believe it might be very effective?'

'We have no way of knowing, not yet . . .'

'And are you saying that, in the event of it becoming widely used by the British, we have no defensive measures against it?'

The Chief Scientist shifted uneasily in his chair. 'We do not have any way of detecting it at present . . .'

Doenitz leant forward. 'But *will* we?'

'It . . . would take time. We would have to understand exactly how this new apparatus worked. It is based on entirely different principles, you understand; *entirely different!*'

'Entirely different . . .' Doenitz echoed. 'I see. I will not enquire as to why we ourselves have never investigated these entirely different principles!'

Goering gave Doenitz a hard stare. 'May I remind you, Herr Admiral, that our radar has proved to be extremely effective in everything except this, er, field! We have led Britain, led the world, in early warning systems. Not a British bomber nears Germany without our knowing about it!'

Doenitz nodded and said testily, 'Yes, Herr Reichsmarschall, most effective when defending a land mass, but not very effective for protecting U-boats, wouldn't you agree?'

There was an awkward pause. Suddenly Goering slapped the table. 'Quite so! I assure you, my dear Admiral, that everything possible is being done! I have taken every possible measure to ensure that we crack this Rotterdam problem as soon as possible. First—' For emphasis the Reichsmarschall pushed his right fist into the open palm of his left hand. '—*First*, all firms in this field have been ordered to start research! Second, we are releasing all the necessary personnel from active service, *however* many people are needed!' He turned abruptly to Schmidt. 'How many, Schmidt, five thousand? Ten thousand?'

'Impossible to say yet, Herr Reichsmarschall. But maybe as many as ten thousand. Yes.'

Doenitz asked, 'Why so many?'

Schmidt frowned. 'We have to follow several avenues of research . . . We have to try lots of different approaches to make sure we find the right one.'

My God, thought Doenitz, they haven't a clue, not a clue. He said, 'But how long will it take to develop a warning device?'

'Ah, not too long, hopefully.'

'In the meantime . . .' Doenitz stared at Goering. 'In the meantime, we are defenceless.'

'Not entirely!' exclaimed Goering with a smile. 'Telefunken tell me they have not entirely stopped research into other wavelengths. They might be able to produce a detector quite quickly.'

'Might?'

'You will be kept fully in the picture, Herr Admiral, I assure you!'

'Yes,' Doenitz said tightly. Doubtless the picture would be the same as ever – the bare minimum imparted with the maximum reluctance. 'And shortwave radar itself. What would be its advantages?'

Schmidt said, 'It is small . . . compact. For the rest, as I say, we cannot be sure, not until we can actually get a Rotterdam Apparatus working.'

'And when could we have this radar ourselves?'

Schmidt breathed deeply. 'Eighteen months . . . Or two years.'

Forever. Doenitz looked at Schmidt with contempt. The man had sworn that shortwave radar was impossible. The man was incompetent. Doenitz said shortly, 'There is no more to be discussed, then, is there?'

Except, he thought, with the Fuehrer, in private. Then he would make quite sure Hitler knew who was to blame for this appalling catastrophe.

Everyone began shuffling papers. Suddenly a thought stirred in the back of Doenitz's mind. 'Schmidt!' he called sharply.

'Yes, Herr Grossadmiral.'

'A long time ago, on the *Welle*, when you first demonstrated radar to us . . .'

'Yes, Herr Grossadmiral.'

'. . . there was a scientist of yours, someone who'd worked on radar from the beginning. He talked to me about shortwave radar. He said it was possible.'

Schmidt looked pale. 'I – I don't remember exactly . . .'

'But I do! He was a round, jolly little man. One of *your* men, Herr Schmidt. I can have him looked up if you like. I'm sure I'll recognise the name when I see it. I remember speaking to him: he was quite definite, about shortwave radar. He said it could be done.' Doenitz shook his head. 'I'm surprised you don't remember. You seemed quite agitated about the matter at the time.'

There was an indefinable electricity around the table. There might be a fight, the staff sensed it.

'Ah . . .' Schmidt said, as if remembering for the first time. 'I think I know who you must mean. A fellow called Freymann.'

'Yes, that was the man. That was him.'

Schmidt said quickly, 'Herr Grossadmiral, we have already asked for this man! Of course we have! He was an obvious first choice! Yes indeed, he has been earmarked for the main team . . .'

'But his ideas were not worth investigating before?'

Schmidt looked injured. 'Why indeed they were! But they were unworkable, quite mad! Whatever this new device may be, I'm sure it can't be anything like Freymann's ideas!'

Doenitz was unconvinced. He said, 'I see. But he *is* about to join your staff?'

'Yes, indeed! We have made a request!'

'A request?'

'Yes. Of the SS.'

'Ah! He was detained?'

'He is a Jew.'

'Where is he detained?'

'Ah.' Schmidt smiled slightly. 'We have just been informed that he is working at a Naval establishment – at Brest in France!'

There was a short embarrassed silence. 'And a request has been made?'

'Through the appropriate channels.

Doenitz barked, 'I find it surprising, Herr Schmidt, that this request was not made immediately, direct to myself. I am sure that, addressed through the highest possible channels, Freymann would be with you by now!'

Schmidt looked as if he had indigestion. 'But until we realised the nature of the device we were not to know . . .'

'That this man was vital?'

Schmidt coughed. 'Indeed.'

'What about documents – research papers and so on. Surely something of his work remains?'

'Nothing. Apparently it was all mislaid.'

'Then I hope to hear that he is with you very shortly!' Doenitz stood up. 'And I look forward to hearing that the research programme is progressing with all speed. Until then, good day!'

There was a shuffling as people got to their feet. No-one bothered with Heil Hitlers nowadays.

Schmidt watched Doenitz stride angrily from the room and sighed. It was a nightmare, the whole thing. But not as bad as it would be if

Freymann didn't come up with the answer. When Doenitz had called Freymann 'vital' he'd hit the nail on the head.

Without Freymann it would take months, years.

It pained Schmidt to admit it, but that conceited little Jew was their only hope.

23

'You look wonderful today, madame!'

'Thank you, madame.' Julie smiled broadly at the shopkeeper and, picking up her basket from the counter, went out into the road. She walked briskly, waving and nodding to the people she met. Some of the villagers looked at her rather strangely. No woman had ever worn trousers in Tregasnou before. But then few women had ever been cowhands before. She grinned to herself. They would soon get used to it.

She'd given up her job before Christmas and it was the best thing she'd ever done. She now worked for Jean – which meant she worked from dawn until well after dusk for her keep and no money. But it was the best salary she'd ever had; she'd never been happier. The outdoor life suited her, the physical work made her feel better than she had in years, and, best of all, she saw much more of Peter. A pity she hadn't done it years ago.

It was the second big decision she'd taken.

The first had been even more important: she'd decided to escape to England.

At the right time. To disappear overnight would be to put her family at risk. She'd decided to do the thing properly. First, she'd left her job. Then she'd told people she was thinking of moving away – to Rennes, or another large city. Now all that remained was to leave, quite publicly, with farewells and luggage.

She'd even set her departure date: she'd told everyone she was going in two weeks.

Julie walked over the crossroads and down the road that led to the west of the village. Ahead, a front door opened and an old lady in Breton dress emerged from one of the smaller cottages. The old lady nodded at Julie, her tall white lace coiffe bobbing forward, and mumbled, 'You're away, I hear. Thought you'd be off sooner or later!'

Julie smiled and passed on. She thought: Silly old woman. But nothing could annoy her today: she was too happy. It wasn't just the thought of the actual journey and of being with Richard, it was the way everything had changed. For the first time she felt as if she was really in control of her own life. The decision to go had been hard – but once made, it was as if an enormous weight had been taken off her shoulders.

She'd seen Richard only three times the whole winter. The weather had been atrocious. Sometimes the boat didn't come at all; sometimes it was so late there was barely time to load any passengers; at other times she guessed he had had to stay on board because of the terrible conditions out at the anchorage. The last time she'd seen him he had urged her to leave straight away. But there were always so many passengers waiting to go, always more than there were places for, that she couldn't.

Also there was Maurice and the group. They still needed her and that was important to her. She'd never felt really useful before and, well, she liked it. She couldn't let them down. It would be disloyal and she wanted to be honourable and to do what was right. By staying this extra time, until the scientist was well enough to go, she would have done enough. After that she could leave with an easy mind.

She swung round a corner into a tiny lane that led between a number of small cottages. She knocked firmly on the front door of a cottage and, without waiting for a reply, walked straight in.

There was an old man beside the hearth.

'Good morning, Monsieur!'

The old man nodded and Julie went past him, through a door into a back room.

Maurice was already there.

'All right?' he asked.

She nodded happily. 'Yes. And you?'

'Fine.'

She sat down and, delving into the pocket of her trousers, handed him an envelope. He opened it and pulled out an identity card and a small box.

She said, pointing to the small box, 'I brought the ink pad. All it needs is the thumb print and the photograph, then give it back to me and I'll stamp it.' She had inserted the name – a totally fictitious one – and the details of birth and parentage. Maurice had already given her the age and colouring of the new owner.

340

She had only two cards left after this. But Maurice knew they were precious: he wouldn't have asked her for one unless it was important.

Maurice nodded. 'Right. We'll do the card in just a moment.'

Julie glanced up in surprise. That must mean that the new owner of the card was here, or nearby. She wondered who it could be. But she didn't ask: one had learnt not to.

Maurice began, 'First, the scientist. What's the news?'

Julie remembered the brief talk she'd had with Michel the day before. 'Everything's set for this week, but I don't know any more. They wouldn't give me any more details.'

'They wouldn't say exactly when?'

'No.'

'But the scientist's out of the hospital?'

'Yes.'

'And fit enough to travel?'

'So they say.'

Maurice made a wry face. 'I hope they're right.' He thought for a moment. 'We'd better aim to get him away in about ten days, then. I don't want him hanging about, but at the same time I do want to be sure he's everything he says he is . . . There's still something about the whole set-up that makes me uneasy . . .'

He looked hard at Julie. 'Will you help me to interrogate him? You have an instinct for it, you know.'

Julie smiled self-consciously. 'Thank you. Yes, of course I'll help if I can.'

'There'll be someone else, too. Helping us, I mean.'

'Oh?'

'Yes, a friend. From Paris. He's been with us for some time now, but further up the line.'

Julie frowned. A stranger. She had a dread of strangers. 'But – why's he come here?'

'He needs to lie low for a bit. He was spotted at Gare Montparnasse the other day and now the Boches are on the lookout for him. It was too dangerous.'

Julie looked down unhappily. Whatever the reasons, she wished the man hadn't come here.

Maurice watched her questioningly. 'This fellow will be useful to us, Marie-Claire. He was with Meteor. He's seen the sort of bogus airmen the Boches tried to pass down the line there. And he knew the traitor, Lebrun. He always suspected him, apparently. He's going to be very good on security.'

She asked. 'But how did he find us?'

'A mutual contact.'

'And he's . . .' She wondered how to put it. 'He's – definitely all right?'

Maurice nodded. 'I had him checked out very carefully. I had the mutual friend verify him personally. Face to face in the presence of one of our couriers. Then I had him checked with London. They know him well. He'd been with Meteor for some time.'

Julie nodded. 'Ah.'

'And since he's been with us, he's been doing very good work, I assure you.'

She smiled briefly. It must be all right. She was just worrying too much as usual.

Maurice stood up. 'You might as well meet him now. I'll call him in, shall I?'

She looked up in surprise. 'He's here?'

'Yes. In the next room.' Maurice went to a back door, opened it, and spoke quietly. He returned and sat down.

Julie waited expectantly. Slowly, almost imperceptibly, a shadow fell on the open door then, without a sound, a man appeared, silhouetted against the light. Julie had the strangest feeling he'd been there all the time, just behind the door, listening.

For a moment the man paused, his face in darkness. Then he came forward, and Julie saw that he was looking at her carefully, his eyes hard and searching.

Then he smiled, his lips curving into a friendly grin, the eyes warming a little. Julie automatically smiled back and put out her hand to shake his.

Maurice said, 'This is Roger. Roger, this is Marie-Claire.' Roger wouldn't be his real name, of course.

They sat down. 'Now,' Maurice began immediately, 'Let's look at security procedures. As a first defence I think we should aim for a new series of security checks further up the line . . .' As Julie listened she stole the occasional glance at the stranger. He had a thin face with rather sallow skin and straight black hair which flopped over his forehead in untidy straggles. He was dressed in rough clothes, but she noticed that on one hand he wore a thick gold ring. His eyes were so dark they were almost black and you had the feeling they didn't miss a thing. At one point they flicked up and looked straight into Julie's eyes. She glanced hurriedly away.

'. . . So Marie-Claire, you take the Americans and the British,' Maurice was saying, 'and Roger, you the other nationalities. All right so far?'

Julie nodded.

342

Roger said, his voice low and soft, 'Those already in hiding? Have they been checked?'

Maurice nodded. 'Pretty well.'

'No so-called Czechs or Poles?'

'No, none. But – there is one odd passenger we've been asked to take. A German by nationality, no less.'

Julie glanced at Roger. He remained impassive. 'A German?'

'Yes, but a reluctant one, apparently. A Jew who's doing forced labour for the Navy in Brest. He wants out with some vital documents.'

Roger said gently, 'What vital documents?'

'Ah, some scientific marvel that would be very valuable. We don't know the details.'

'And he's in a Navy establishment?'

'Yes.'

Roger asked softly, 'Which one?'

He was asking a lot of questions. Perhaps that was his way, Julie thought, perhaps that was how things were done in Paris.

Maurice shrugged. 'We don't know.'

Roger's eyes fell. 'And how is he to be removed?'

'Ah,' sighed Maurice, 'that's to be arranged by some – er, friends.'

Roger nodded very slowly. 'It does sound rather risky. I'd certainly like to interrogate him.'

'Of course. We all want to be certain about him!' Maurice sat forward in his chair. 'Right, let's call it a day. Unless you have any questions . . .?'

Julie looked at Roger. He was shaking his head. She looked back at Maurice and almost spoke – she wanted to confirm the arrangements for her and Peter. But she changed her mind; it didn't seem to be the right moment any more.

Maurice took the identity card from the table. 'Right, Roger. Here's your new identity. If we can bother you for a thumb print . . .?'

Julie watched as Roger rolled his right thumb on the ink pad and placed his print carefully on the card.

Maurice looked at Roger. 'And the photograph?'

'Of course!' He felt in his jacket pocket and brought out a small photograph.

Maurice handed the card and photograph to Julie. She pushed them into her trouser pocket and stood up. Roger sprang to his feet and bowed slightly.

On a whim she said, 'The Meteor thing . . . How did you escape?'

'A friend warned me, just before I walked into the trap.'

'But the others –?'

He looked down, sighed deeply and shook his head. 'Most of them gone . . .' He looked genuinely upset and Julie felt a little guilty for having asked. She said, 'Sorry – I . . .'

His eyes came up suddenly. 'No – please don't worry. That's the price we have to pay sometimes, isn't it? They knew that. They knew the risks. All one can do is learn the lessons.'

She nodded. 'Yes, of course . . .'

The distress had disappeared and now he was smiling slightly. She noticed, though, that his eyes were cold.

She muttered goodbye to Maurice and, turning back to Roger, said, 'I'll have your card ready in an hour.'

He bowed again. 'Thank you, madame.'

Julie went quietly through the house and out into the lane. Her happiness had evaporated. The presence of Roger troubled her, not just because he was a stranger, but because he was something new, and new elements made her nervous.

And there was something else. What? Yes – he frightened her. It was those cold watchful eyes.

A shiver went down her spine and, shoving her hands in her pockets, she walked quickly in the direction of home.

Vasson watched her go and wondered why she had been wary.

It was probably just native suspicion. She was like the rest of them: distrustful of anything from outside. There was nothing more to it than that. After all, she had no reason to be suspicious. No, she was an earnest, well-meaning type, but definitely not too bright.

He turned back to Maurice. 'A good girl, that.'

Maurice nodded. 'Yes, the best.'

Vasson sat down again. He waited for Maurice to speak: it would show the proper subservience.

Maurice said, 'Right. Now, I'll try to get the rest of your new papers by Thursday, but no promises. In the meantime, lie low –'

'But I've still got my own papers – I could use them.'

'No! You've been using them in Paris, haven't you? And you're known there.'

'Well –'yes.' He had to admit it: the owner of the papers, a man called Fougères, had indeed used them in Paris before he found his way into Kloffer's dungeon. Kloffer's office had then replaced the identity photographs with Vasson's – and a very professional job they'd made of it, too.

Maurice looked stern. 'Then it would be much too dangerous to use them! No, you stay here until your new papers are ready. If you *were* spotted at the Gare Montparnasse as you suspect, then they might be on to you! No! You must wait!'

Vasson nodded thoughtfully. 'Of course! Whatever you say!' It didn't make any difference: he had three other identities to choose from, any one of which would do perfectly well if he needed to slip away from the village. And the Gare Montparnasse thing was a nonsense, of course: he'd made it up.

'When your papers are fixed, then we'll send you to Morlaix or St Brieuc to interview parcels as soon as they come off the train.'

Morlaix was very convenient: it housed his local contact.

Vasson thought: Now for a little touch of finesse. He said softly, 'What about people *within* the *réseau*? Have they been checked recently?'

'No, but then there's hardly anyone who hasn't been with me from the beginning. Those who do join . . . Well, I check them very carefully.'

That was true enough. At the beginning Maurice had kept Vasson under close watch until his identity had been checked, first with London, who had okayed him straight away – they would, of course: Fougères was a long-standing member of the Meteor line – and then with the contact in Paris, the one who had got him the introduction to the Brittany *réseau*. The contact had, in fact, been under Kloffer's supervision for some two weeks. If Vasson remembered correctly, Kloffer had the man's wife in the basement at the Avenue Foch. Anyway, the man had done what was required and, in front of a witness, sworn to Vasson's identity as Paul Fougères. Vasson rather liked the name: it had an aristocratic ring to it.

Vasson stood up and walked to the window. 'So what can I do until Thursday?'

'Nothing.'

That suited Vasson very well. It would give him the time he needed.

But not if he was cooped up. He said with feeling, 'I'll go mad if I have to stay inside all the time. All right if I stretch my legs in the evenings?'

There was a pause. Maurice said reluctantly, 'If you have to. But stay in the village and keep out of sight of Germans.'

'Certainly. I'll be very careful.' Which was true: he would do his reconnaissance of the village very carefully indeed.

Maurice stood up. 'Right. I'm off now. Any problems, just leave a message at the café.'

They nodded to each other and Maurice left.

For a while Vasson sat quite still, thinking that it was all going quite well. There were, of course, a few minor problems; but then there always were.

He lit a cigarette and drew on it deeply. First, there was the security of the line. Unfortunately it was very good. Maurice had done an excellent job. It would be impossible to slip a bogus American or Britisher through, not with that girl interviewing them. And a Czech or Pole – well, everyone knew that was how Meteor had fallen. It would be tempting fate to try the same trick again. No a plant really wouldn't do.

So – what could he get on his own? The Bretons were close people, very suspicious of strangers. It would take ten years to get trusted around here. No hope of confidences then. No way of locating the safe houses easily. Nor of identifying more than two of the couriers: Maurice had made sure of that. So what did that leave him with?

Quite a lot, in fact.

He could get the organisers, no trouble there. Maurice, the girl and the people who actually went on beach operations, he could get them all right. And they, after all, were the real plums.

Then the Gestapo would have to do some of their own work for a change. They would have to extract the names of the small fry. It wouldn't do them any harm – he'd been handing them things on a plate for long enough.

It wouldn't be as clean and satisfying as Meteor had been. But what the hell? After this job he would be a very rich man. As long as he delivered most of the goods, what did it matter?

Anyway, he'd go mad if he stayed in this place too long. The silence was deafening, except for the racket of bleating sheep and the bloody wind howling the place down. And the cold! He'd never been so cold in his life. They'd never heard of heating in bedrooms, or bed-warmers. And the food – solid and inedible. It was the end of the bloody earth.

No: he'd just hit them hard and quick and then he'd be off, back to Paris. And Kloffer could threaten him all he wanted: Vasson would *stay* in Paris. This time he was going home.

He got up and went through into the messy, smelly back room he'd been given. It was like a rat-hole: disgusting.

There was a bottle of wine beside the bed. He picked it up and swigged at it. There was no point in going out until dark, but Christ! it seemed a long time away.

He lay and looked at the ceiling. He suddenly realised he'd forgotten something. Ah! Of course. There was the other matter: the scientist. What the hell was he going to do about that?

He could always do nothing, of course. But if the Jew really was important, then it might just be worth his while to organise something . . .

The main problem was to find out exactly who this fellow might be. It would be no good asking Baum, his Gestapo contact at Morlaix. The fool would probably blow it straight away by going to Brest and asking questions.

No, better to keep Baum out of it. That meant he'd have to handle it himself.

In the meantime there was nothing to do but wait.

He swigged at the wine again, gulping the liquid down in long draughts. It was the only way to drink the stuff: it was rough as hell. Then he lay back on the bed and slept fitfully through the afternoon.

At dusk he got up. He put an old cap on his head, a canvas working man's bag over his shoulder, and some identity papers in his pocket. Then, looking carefully out of the door, he slipped quietly into the night.

The dawn was pale and misty and very cold. Julie stepped into the yard, gulped the fresh, cold air and watched her breath floating away in long clouds, up into the white opalescent sky.

'Maman, are we *really* going in the van?' Peter ran up to her, skipping with excitement.

Julie smiled. 'Yes – well, I hope so! Uncle Jean got it going yesterday and it seems to be working. But we'll see.'

She opened the barn door and climbed into the ancient Peugeot van. Peter hovered next to the passenger door while she turned on the ignition, took out the starting handle and, coming round to the front of the vehicle, swung energetically on the handle. After four attempts, the engine fired a couple of times; at the fifth it started.

Peter squealed with excitement and, flinging open the door, jumped in.

'Got your school things?'

Peter nodded violently. Julie wiped her hands on her overalls, climbed in and slowly eased in the clutch. The van lurched out into the yard. Soon they were off, bumping down the lane and through the village. Julie tried to change into second gear. There was a loud grinding noise. She double de-clutched and tried again. Another rasping and clattering and then the engine settled on to a lower note: they were in second gear.

Julie sighed with relief then looked across at Peter. He was laughing uncontrollably, his little face creased with delight. She exclaimed, 'Well I never promised to be the world's best driver!' And then she was laughing too.

She concentrated on the road. It was a cross-country route to Kernibon, through narrow one-track lanes. Fortunately there was no traffic – few people had petrol nowadays – and it wasn't necessary to stop to let anyone pass. After ten minutes a stretch of misty water came into view: the Morlaix estuary. Julie looked into the distance, across the wide river to the village opposite, the one where she and Peter had landed after that terrible fishing boat journey. It all seemed a long time ago now.

Julie found the right farmhouse and drove into the yard. Eventually the farmer came out and grunted at her. She could see by his expression that he, too, had never seen a woman in trousers before. He waved her up to a shed, then opened the van doors and slid a plank of wood up into the back. He disappeared into the shed and emerged a moment later pulling an angry squealing sow on a length of rope. He pushed and shoved the pig into the van, then closed the doors. He grunted again. Julie smiled because he sounded just like his pig. Or rather, *their* pig, as it was now. Julie politely refused the customary invitation to coffee and, waving goodbye, restarted the van.

Peter said, 'Maman, couldn't we go down to the village for a minute?'

'Goodness, why?'

'I've never been there before!'

Julie stared at him, a little taken aback. Overcome with remorse, she said, 'Of course, darling! Though we can't be very long, otherwise we'll be late for school.'

Peter nodded happily and they set off down a slight hill, the pig snorting and squealing in the back. The village was nothing much, a few cottages built around a haven formed by a small peninsula which protruded into the estuary. There were half a dozen fishing boats moored in the centre of the inlet. It looked as if some had just come in: men were offloading baskets into small boats floating alongside.

Julie turned the van round and they got out. She said, 'There! Even smaller than Tregasnou!'

'Yes!' Peter exclaimed. He obviously thought smallness a great recommendation. 'Look at the boats! Do they go a long, long way?'

'No, darling. They're not allowed to go far.' She saw that all the boats had sails furled to their masts. With the lack of fuel fishing boats had to rely on the wind again, just as they had done a few years back, before the advent of engines.

Something caught Julie's eye. A figure had emerged from behind a stone barn on the far side of the inlet. She glanced away, then, curious, looked at the figure again. She stiffened: there was something about him that was familiar . . .

The man came nearer, then turned down between two cottages and disappeared. Julie frowned with disappointment.

A moment later he was back again, pushing a *vélo* which he must have collected from the alleyway. Julie frowned. It looked just like Michel.

The man got on the *vélo* and started pedalling towards her. Julie stared, trying to catch a proper sight of his face. After a moment the man looked up into her face, and wobbled.

He had recognised her too.

It *was* him!

But what was he doing here? Julie couldn't understand it.

He pedalled up to her and dismounted. His face was serious and unsmiling. He said sharply, 'What are you doing here?'

'I might ask the same of you.'

He sighed impatiently. 'Come on – what *are* you doing here?'

'Collecting a pig. I'm a farmhand now, you know!'

He glared at her. 'So I see!'

Peter was looking uneasy. Julie reached down and pulled him to her. 'We were just going anyway . . .'

She turned and, opening the door of the van, pushed Peter up into the seat.

'Julie –' He came up and held the door open for her. 'As a favour to me – don't tell anyone you've seen me here.'

Julie got into the van and turned to look at him. His face was even more severe than usual and she noticed that there were deep shadows under his eyes. He looked as though he hadn't slept for days.

She said, 'All right. If that's what you want. Though –' She looked away.

'Yes?'

She sighed. 'You're not creating trouble, are you, Michel?'

He dismissed the idea with a shake of the head. 'I promise.'

'In that case . . .' She picked up the starting handle and opened the door to get out again, but he took the handle from her and, going round to the front of the van, cranked the engine into life.

When he brought the handle back, she suddenly remembered the scientist. She said, 'By the way, no more news about the – delivery?'

He shook his head. 'No, nothing new. He'll be with you shortly, safe and sound.'

She put the van into gear. 'Goodbye then.'

He nodded, his face tight and angry, and turned quickly away.

Peter said, 'Mummy, why was he so cross?'

'What? Oh darling, I don't know. Really.' She smiled brightly. 'Come on, let's get you off to school!'

But all the way there, Julie kept thinking: He's up to something, I know he is! Oh Michel, what on earth is it now?

24

It was quite a farewell. Most of the senior staff had assembled. Geissler was there, of course, and Gallois.

Geissler held out his hand. 'So, Herr Freymann, I'm sorry we are to lose you after all, but I am sure that you will enjoy your new position. A great honour, a great honour!' On this occasion Geissler had not thought of questioning the order: it had come from the High Command itself, marked 'Most Urgent', and he was impressed. He smiled at David. 'I expect you will be most happy to see Berlin again.'

'Yes. Yes.'

Geissler inclined his head slightly in the German style. 'Are you sure, Herr Freymann, that you prefer to walk to your quarters?'

'Yes, thank you.' David nodded, then smiled in the general direction of the factory personnel. But he couldn't bring himself to look at Gallois in case guilt and conspiracy should show all over his face. He felt sick.

He turned and, grasping his briefcase tightly under his arm, walked slowly down the steps. The guard acknowledged him with a slight blink then glanced away.

David stepped on to the pavement and, his heart hammering in his ears, began the short walk down the road to the compound.

It would be any minute now. A car, probably; sweeping round the corner, opening its door, pulling him in, roaring off ... David imagined the guard watching curiously, trying to work out what the car was doing, slowly realising, pulling the rifle up to his shoulder, firing at David while he was still inches from the safety of the car ...

He felt his back itching and shivered. The urge to look round was almost compulsive. He resisted and kept walking, slowly, to give them time.

He came to the access road that led down the side of the factory.

He paused at the kerb, looked to left and right, stepped down and crossed the road.

Now, surely! He reached the opposite pavement and went even slower. But it was difficult walking slowly. He swayed and almost lost his balance. His legs were still weak.

The compound gates were getting closer now, the guards almost visible. David began to worry: it would be very risky to leave it any longer.

He paused and leant against the wire fence, as if he were resting. He listened carefully, but the road behind him was silent: no engine noises, no cars. Nothing stirred.

They weren't coming.

He moved away from the fence and began walking again. Almost immediately the guard post came into sight. The uniformed figures stared at him, their faces uninterested and bored. He turned in through the gates and walked past them, as he had a hundred times.

They hadn't come.

David went automatically towards the hut, opened the door and walked up the corridor to his cubicle at the end. He sat on the bed and stared at the wall, the briefcase still tucked under his arm.

The message had said they would come for him. He tried very hard to think how they would do it. Perhaps they'd come later. But *how*? Getting him out of here would be impossible.

Perhaps never, then. In which case he'd been deceived. He thought: I'm no good at this sort of thing. I don't understand.

He wasn't due to leave for Berlin until early morning, at seven. He'd wait until then, ready dressed, just in case. In the meantime he was tired; the walk, like any physical exertion nowadays, had tired him out. He lay down.

After a while he sat up and, opening his briefcase, took out a sandwich of bread and cheese which he'd kept specially for the journey. He ate it slowly, chewing each mouthful several times. He closed the briefcase carefully, lay down again, and dozed.

Much later he woke suddenly and pulled himself up. He guessed it was late, probably about one or two in the morning. Something had woken him. A sound. He got unsteadily to his feet and went to the window. There was a moon and the outlines of the buildings were just visible in the pale light. Nothing moved.

He was turning to go back to bed when he felt the floor shudder. He put his hand up to the wall to steady himself. A flash of light flickered against the walls of the cubicle. He turned back to the window, confused.

351

A low rumble sounded from far away, the window shook, another flash of light illuminated the night sky.

An air raid. They were common enough. Only this time the Germans hadn't had time to sound the siren.

There was another flash, much closer this time. Then orange and yellow lights flickered against the buildings: an incendiary. David frowned: there was something strange about all this. What was it? Yes – he'd heard no planes. Usually you could hear the drone of the bombers as they passed overhead. There were no searchlights either.

A siren sounded. It was from close by. Inside the hut there was a deafening noise of banging doors and running feet and shouting men. A moment later the guards streamed out of the hut, running in the direction of the flickering lights.

David opened the window and stuck his head out. There was another sound now, a drumming, as if people were beating sticks against a wall. Angry people. And there were voices, too, a thousand voices shouting and yelling while they beat the sticks against the walls.

It was the workers, the Poles. They were trying to break out.

David shook his head and cried, 'Oh no! Oh no!' and beat his fist against the wall. What *were* they trying to achieve? What did they hope to gain? It would mean death for many of them; death. In despair he murmured again, 'No! No!'

He froze. Something caught his eye: a movement away to the right, in the shadow of one of the buildings. A figure, running stealthily in a crouched position.

David pulled his head back inside the window and watched, motionless. The figure paused in the darkness of the nearest building, then ran again. He was coming straight for David. David felt a stab of fear and pulled himself back into the room.

The figure disappeared beneath his line of sight. Then, after a few seconds, a hand suddenly appeared over the sill. A head followed. David pressed himself against the wall.

A voice. 'Freymann?'

David stared at the silhouette of the head and whispered, 'Yes.'

'Quick! Climb out and follow me! *Quick!*'

David fumbled for his briefcase and, tucking it under his arm, approached the window. He said breathlessly, 'Are you – from . . .?'

'Shut up. No time for that. Come *now!*'

David looked at the height of the sill and said, 'I can't.'

The figure hissed, 'You *must!*'

David nodded and pushed the briefcase through the window. It disappeared rapidly. He got his left foot up onto the sill and pushed his leg out. It was impossible to get a second leg up: the frame was too narrow. He pulled his body up onto the sill and felt the window-catch dig into his thigh. He levered himself safely to one side of it and, sitting astride the sill, rested for a moment, breathing heavily.

'Come on!' the dark figure was pulling at his sleeve.

'All right! All right! I'm doing my best!' David looked down: it was a long drop, a man's height at least, and he only had one leg to land on. 'You'll have to catch me, otherwise I'll fall.' The figure seemed to nod and David levered himself out until he was hanging from the window, his right leg still over the sill. He tried to pull the leg out, but some of his weight was on it and it wouldn't come.

'Have you got me?'

'*Yes! Yes!*'

Only one thing to do, then. Let go.

He felt himself falling, body first, his left foot nowhere near the ground. A hand clutched at his arm and twisted him round. His right foot met the ground, followed shortly by his shoulder and his hip. He felt his head shoot back to hit the concrete.

He staggered to his feet, shaking slightly, and brushed himself down.

The man had hold of his arm and David found himself being pulled along behind. The man stopped at the end of the building and David bumped into him. Then the man was off again, running faster, his hand still grasping David's sleeve.

David ran as best he could, but he was already breathing hard. His legs felt like rubber and wouldn't do what was required of them. For some reason he couldn't swing his right arm either.

They approached the perimeter fence at the eastern side of the compound. With alarm David wondered why they were going that way. There was no way out here.

Normally the fence was brilliantly lit, but now it was in darkness. They stopped at the side of a small shed and waited. The man was listening, as tense as a cat. David put his head against the wall and tried to regain his breath.

Suddenly they were off again. The fence loomed up in front of them. The man looked up and down the length of the fence, pulled David a short way to the right, then dropped to his hands and knees. David saw that there was a gaping hole in the wire. The man hissed 'Down!' and David got on to his knees.

The man threw the briefcase through then put a hand behind David and pushed. David crawled through. The man came quickly after, picked up David's case and pulled him to his feet. He grabbed David's sleeve again and then they were running across open ground to the dark wall of a warehouse. They stopped, David gasped for breath.

Another pull. David said, 'Please! Please! Not so fast. I can't go so fast!' The man slowed down a little. They skirted three more buildings and came to another fence. This time there was no hole. David eyed it apprehensively. But then they reached a gate and the gate was open and they were through into a road.

A lorry was parked in the road. The man took David round to the tailgate. It was closed. David breathed, 'I can't ... I can't ...'

The man reached down and, grasping David's foot, heaved. David sprawled over the tailgate, unable to pull himself up. The man pushed again and David landed head first in the lorry's load, which smelt strongly of cabbage.

'Hide yourself!'

David panted, 'What?'

'Hide yourself under the vegetables!'

'... under?'

There was a thud as something landed beside David in the cabbages. 'Your case. Goodbye.'

There was silence. David took hold of the briefcase and crawled slowly over the vegetables to the far end of the lorry. How did one bury oneself in a load of cabbages? Painstakingly he began to remove the cabbages one by one until he had made a hollow in them, then he lay down, his case at his side, and pulled the vegetables back over himself.

It wasn't difficult to lie still – at that moment it was all he'd ever wanted.

Five minutes passed and the lorry hadn't moved. He wished they would hurry. He could hear the sounds of activity in the compound and the docks: trucks roaring back and forth, the distant sound of shouting and the occasional report of a rifle shot. It must be the Poles they were shooting at.

But why wasn't the lorry moving? Come on! Come on! If they didn't get going soon, they'd never get away!

But the lorry didn't move. After half an hour David realised it wasn't going to. Not for a long time. Perhaps not until daylight. He wished they'd told him.

Eventually he fell into an uneasy sleep, waking frequently. Finally he saw a tinge of grey light through the gaps in the cabbages above his head. He drifted off again.

Suddenly there was a loud crash from immediately behind David's head. He jumped, his heart racing. Someone started whistling and the next moment there was a loud whirring and the lorry's engine burst into life.

The whistler broke into song. 'I'm dreaming of you, my love, wherever you may be . . .'

The lorry stopped and started a few times. Once David heard the driver talking to someone, but then they were on their way again. The singer began to whistle once more, but softly, and the drone of the wheels fell to a steady hum.

There was silence. David realised that the lorry had stopped and the engine had been turned off. He waited, tense.

The driver was whistling loudly. The cab door slammed and footsteps came round to the back of the vehicle. The tailgate was lowered with a loud bang.

There was a moment's silence, then a voice called, 'Hello, friend. We've arrived.'

David wasn't sure what to do. He stayed still.

But the voice came again. 'You're safe, friend. Time to get out.'

David pushed the cabbages away from his face and tried to move, but he was very stiff. He reached up and, gripping the metal side of the lorry, hauled himself up into a sitting position. He blinked and, looking out, saw that the lorry was backed up against the doors of a wooden building. A man of about forty dressed in an old cap and working jacket was standing by the tailgate.

On seeing David, the man climbed up into the lorry and walked over the vegetables towards him. 'Here. I'll give you a hand.'

'Thank you. That's most kind.'

The man pulled David to his feet, picked up the briefcase, and helped him across the uneven surface of the cabbages to the open tailgate and down on to the ground.

David now saw that the building was a barn. The man led him quickly inside and into a corner behind a pile of sacks. 'Here! You're to wait here.'

'Thank you.' David looked around. The floor at this point was thick with straw and, gratefully, he sank down on to it.

The man had turned to leave.

David called, 'Wait! Please – tell me, what was the fire last night?'

The man paused and looked uncertain. Eventually he said, 'One of the fuel dumps.'

'But the Poles. Why did they try to break out?'

'They didn't.'

David looked blank. 'But the noise?'

'Noise. That's all it was.'

'But – why?'

'Because they were asked to. It was a favour.' The man turned again. 'Best not to know any more, friend.'

The barn door closed, the lorry's engine started up and slowly faded away. Then there was silence. David lay down on the straw. He tried to sleep, but it was impossible, so he lay still and rested instead.

Much later there was a sound. David opened his eyes. It was a creaking. A door opening. Someone was coming into the barn. He pushed himself up on one arm, but he couldn't see: his view of the door was obscured by the pile of sacks.

The person was advancing slowly up the barn: David could feel the movement rather than hear it. Finally, very slowly, the person came into view.

David's heart went to his mouth. It was a man. He was wearing a scarf over the lower part of his face. The man said gruffly, 'Turn around.' David turned and, almost immediately, something was placed round his eyes and tied behind his head.

The voice said, 'Don't move unless I tell you.' There was a rustling of straw as the man moved away, then silence.

The darkness was awful, like being in a pit. David tried to relax. They meant him no harm.

A long time passed. David's stomach began to ache with hunger.

Then there were low voices and footsteps. Someone walked up to him. The straw rustled as the person sat or knelt beside him.

'Hello.' It was the voice of a woman, rather breathless.

David cleared his throat. 'Good morning.'

'Are you all right?' The voice was warm, concerned.

He nodded. 'Oh yes! Yes! Very well, thank you. Yes, very well!'

'Good. We – er – heard you had been ill.'

'Ah. Yes, I was. But better now, thank you.'

There was a pause. 'Some others will be coming soon. To meet you. We have to ask you some questions.'

'Questions?'

'Yes . . . It's necessary. I'm sorry.'

David was disappointed. Questions? It sounded as if they were going to interrogate him. It had never occurred to him that they wouldn't trust him. He said half-heartedly, 'Yes. Of course.'

There was the sound of paper crackling. 'Here, I thought you might be hungry.'

'I am, thank you.' Something was placed in his hand. 'Thank you.' It was a roll. He bit into it. Cheese. He took another bite.

*

Julie watched him eat and felt sorry for him. He seemed so lost and bewildered. She'd be very surprised indeed if he were a German spy – he looked far too harmless for that. Certainly he was too frail to take anyone on; he wouldn't be able to hurt a fly. The hands were thin and veined and she noticed that when he brought the bread to his mouth they shook slightly. The face beneath the blindfold was lined and pouchy, rather like a dog's. She could see that he had been ill. Also, he was much older than she'd expected.

It was a pity to have to put him through an interrogation but there was no way round it. Maurice would allow no exceptions.

She peered at her wristwatch. The others were late. But she must wait. It would be wrong to start the questions without them.

Finally, there was a creaking. The barn door opened and two people slipped in. One was the unmistakable squat figure of Maurice, the other the taller, slimmer frame of Roger.

Maurice came up and looked questioningly at Julie. She nodded slightly to show all was well and, satisfied, Maurice turned to look at the old man sitting on the bed of straw. Julie glanced at Roger. He was approaching slowly, his eyes fixed on the corner of the sack pile. Suddenly he stopped in mid-step and Julie guessed he had caught his first sight of the old man. For a moment he stared, then he relaxed and leant casually against a wooden pillar.

His eyes darted up to Julie's. She looked hurriedly away. He was always catching her out that way.

Maurice was sitting on the straw, talking to the old man in a low voice. Julie went closer and sat down beside him. '. . . interrogation is necessary for our self-protection, do you understand?' The old man nodded briefly.

Maurice continued, 'Right, please tell us everything. First, your name and background.'

'Freymann, David Freymann. I lived most of my life just outside Berlin, in a suburb called Hennigsdorf . . .' Out of the corner of her eye Julie saw Roger come closer and crouch silently on the straw just behind Maurice.

'. . . mainly I worked on radio-wave development. Then just before the war started, it all got difficult. Because I was Jewish, you see. I was put in a camp . . .'

'Where?' Maurice interrupted.

'Near Munich. Called Dachau. I was there some time – two, maybe three years, I don't know. Time – is difficult to judge.' He spoke matter-of-factly.

'Then?'

'Then they sent me to Brest.'

'Why?'

'They needed me. There are very few scientists who are experienced in radar. They had to swallow their pride.'

Roger said, 'Explain, please. What is radar?'

The old man sighed deeply. 'I'll try to explain simply. It's . . . a way of using radio waves so that you can see with them. At night, in bad weather . . . it doesn't matter. You can see the echo of any large metallic object – a ship, an aeroplane, whatever . . . You can discover its range, and in the case of a plane its height. Nothing can hide from you . . .'

Maurice asked, 'And this is the information you're bringing with you?'

Freymann quickly shook his head. 'No, radar is already known. No . . .' He paused, as if debating something. His hands moved nervously. Finally he said, 'No . . . what I'm bringing is a refinement of it. A type which can see like a map, draw pictures almost. It will – create a great advantage.'

Maurice frowned. 'In what way?'

'For one thing, the Germans could not detect it as they do the existing radar. So they would have no warning of the enemy's approach. For another, well – it will, I believe, provide enormous detail so that for the bombers it will be like having a map of the country underneath.' He cocked his head slightly. 'Do you understand what I say?'

'Yes, I think so.'

Suddenly Freymann sat forward and felt for Maurice's arm. Maurice looked surprised. The old man said, 'Look, you cannot possibly know that what I'm telling you is the truth, can you?'

Julie looked quickly at Maurice. He dropped his eyes and smiled slightly. 'No, you're quite right. I can't.'

'Right. But you believe I am Jewish?'

'Well – yes.'

'Right. So I'm Jewish. Now what do you suppose would make a Jew want to help the Nazis?'

'Force? Coercion?'

'Yes. But I'm a free man now. That leaves coercion. But I have no family for them to threaten me with. My family disowned me a long time ago!'

'I can't be sure of that.'

Freymann started in surprise. 'Ah . . .!' He paused, taken aback, then nodded gently. 'Of course.' He seemed so downcast that Julie had the urge to lean forward and pat his shoulder.

'So – then, it is a simple question of whether you believe me or not.' He spoke quietly and with resignation. Julie wanted to say, I believe you.

Maurice looked at Julie then Roger. 'Any questions?'

Julie said, 'When you talk of your family, who do you mean?'

'My wife. My daughter.'

'And they've disowned you?'

'Yes. My wife was not Jewish, you see.'

'But your daughter?'

'She'll have forgotten me by now – and the best thing too!' His voice almost broke. 'She was pretty, you see. And clever. She had everything before her. It was *better*, you understand. *Better*.'

Roger leant forward and said sharply, 'What company did you work for in Brest?'

'Goulvent, Pescard et Cie.'

'Under what authority – what German authority?'

'The Navy. But I was on loan, so to speak, from the SS.'

'And when you were working in Germany, what company then?'

'Gema. The Gema Company.'

There was a short silence, then Maurice got to his feet. Julie and Roger followed him across the barn until they were out of earshot.

Maurice looked at Julie. 'Well?'

Julie said, 'I believe him. Everything about him seems – right.'

They both looked at Roger. He was glancing down, his eyes hooded and unreadable. Slowly, the eyes came up to Maurice's. 'Yes, he's genuine.'

Maurice nodded. 'I agree.'

Roger said, 'So he goes, does he?'

'Yes.'

'When?'

Maurice looked hard at Roger. 'Soon. The fewer who know the exact date the better. You'll be told in good time.'

Roger smiled. 'Of course.' But he was put out, Julie could tell.

Julie touched Maurice's arm. 'Can't we take the blindfold off? At least until we have to move him again.'

Maurice rubbed his lip thoughtfully.

Roger interrupted, 'No! It'll be much safer to leave him as he is!'

Julie gave Roger a hard look and said quickly to Maurice, 'Please. He's absolutely harmless. I'd stake my life on it. *Please*.'

Maurice smiled slightly. 'All right.'

Julie ran back. The old man shrank away at the sound of her steps. 'It's all right,' she said soothingly. 'I've come to take your blindfold off.'

'Thank you. How kind.' She leant over and untied the handkerchief from round his head. The old man blinked and put his hand up to his eyes. Then he smiled up at her. He had large, dark, sad eyes; again Julie was reminded of a rather mournful dog.

She smiled back at him. 'I'll bring you more food later. The guard has water when you want it.'

'Thank you. You really are very kind.'

Julie touched his hand quickly then went back to the others waiting by the door. Maurice exchanged smiles with her. Roger avoided her stare and put his face to the gap in the door.

'All clear?' Maurice asked.

Roger nodded and, opening the door, led the way out. As Julie stepped out into the daylight she looked up and found Roger staring at her. She almost gasped: there was rage and hatred in his eyes. For a moment she was bewildered. Why? The blindfold? Such a small incident – but what else could it be? She looked desperately at Maurice, but he had seen nothing.

God, Julie thought, the man's terrifying – and no-one knows it but me.

Vasson made himself smile to conceal his irritation.

The girl had outdone him, and he didn't like it.

It was time to get away. He said, 'I'll go now. Across the fields.'

Maurice looked up sharply. 'But do you know the way?'

'Oh, I'll find it, don't worry. Anyway, it's about time I found my way around. In case of trouble.'

'Careful not to speak to anyone.'

Vasson almost sighed with annoyance: Maurice must have told him a dozen times. 'Don't worry! I won't.'

'It's the accent. They'd know you were an outsider straight away.'

'But then they wouldn't tell, would they? Being good Bretons . . .'
Before Maurice could answer, Vasson turned and walked briskly away.

He went round the barn, over a wall and into a field. He spotted a gate on the far side and began to make his way across the field towards it. Almost immediately he regretted it: the field had just been ploughed. He pressed on, cursing under his breath as his feet slipped and stumbled over the hard, bumpy ground.

Finally he reached the gate, went through, and paused. He looked over his shoulder: nothing. The others were going back by the road. He looked ahead: nothing either. Away to the right he could hear the faint sound of surf and calling gulls: the sea.

He went on, across four smaller fields until the village came into view over a slight hill. There was a farmhouse immediately ahead and, he realised, a road beside it. He would have to cross the road then, to skirt the farmhouse and the village and reach the main Morlaix road.

He approached the wall which hid the road, peered over it and, climbing carefully up the rough stonework, jumped down. He crossed the road and prepared to climb the opposite wall. He stopped: there was someone walking down the road towards the village.

It was the girl.

She had seen him. He leant against the wall and waited. She approached, walking fast, her eyes down. When she was almost level with him she moved to the opposite side of the road. Then she was past, swinging on down the hill. He watched her for a moment. The trousers were ridiculous, he decided. They revealed and accentuated the movement of her bottom. She probably wore them on purpose. Bitch.

He shinned up the wall and dropped neatly over on to the other side. It was a pasture this time, with a few sheep pulling at the scant grass. The solitary farmhouse was nearby. He decided to skirt the buildings close, rather than risk being seen wandering across the fields.

He came up behind the barn and moved along until he could peer round the corner. There was a yard and, on the opposite side, the farmhouse itself. There were some iron railings with a gate which separated the yard from the pasture. He would have to walk along the railings in view of the farmhouse. He waited a moment, just to make sure that everything was quiet. Then, just as he was about to set off, he stopped.

Someone had entered the yard from the other end. It was the girl again. She was walking slowly, almost cautiously towards the farmhouse. She was looking around cautiously.

He ducked back behind the wall and wondered if she was looking for him.

He peered out again. She was at the back door of the farmhouse, pushing up the latch. She paused again and looked around.

He pulled back before she saw him.

There was the sound of voices. Hers, and a high-pitched voice: a child's. He put his eye back to the corner.

A small boy was jumping up and down beside the girl. She reached down and took his hand and, with one last look over her shoulder, pulled the child inside.

At last Vasson understood. The girl lived here!

She hadn't wanted him to know. He smiled to himself. It could be rather useful.

He looked at his watch: only fifteen minutes to go. There wasn't time to make the enormous detour which would keep him out of sight of the farmhouse.

He sauntered out from behind the wall and walked casually along the railings. He was being watched, he felt sure.

He walked past the house and then straight down the next field to a stile in the corner. He climbed over it and glanced back. He was out of sight of the farmhouse.

He went diagonally across the next field and the next so that he was skirting the village. Finally he reached the main Morlaix road and, after checking that it was empty, walked along it until he came to a small crossroads. Then he settled down to wait.

After half an hour he was still waiting. He wasn't surprised: everything in this bloody godforsaken place was always late.

Finally, the small battered bus came into view, its engine roaring. Vasson waved it down and jumped on board.

He settled himself in a seat and decided that the day might not turn out so badly after all: there was still time to get a decent lunch off Baum. There was only one thing still bothering him: the girl. She was suspicious of him. And he didn't like that, he didn't like it at all.

'Mummy, what are you staring at?'

Julie reached down and stroked Peter's head. 'Nothing, darling.' She moved away from the window and, going to the sink, started to peel some potatoes for the midday meal.

Jean came in through the parlour door and looked at Julie. 'I thought I just saw someone in the back pasture.'

Julie kept her eyes down. 'Oh?'

Jean reached onto the mantelpiece for his tobacco, then remembered he didn't have any. 'Yes, I'm sure I did. But . . . Probably just one of the lads. Eh?'

'Probably.'

It had been Roger; she had seen him.

He had been prowling around; he reminded her of a cat. She shuddered and thought: I don't like it any more. The sooner Peter and I are away the better. It wouldn't be long now. The moon was on the wane: the boat would come soon.

There was a rapping on the back door. Julie jumped and looked at her uncle. Jean shrugged and went to open it.

There was a short exclamation, then Michel strode into the room. His face was like thunder.

Julie gasped, 'What's the matter?'

Michel said bitterly, '*You* should be able to tell *me*!'

Julie pulled Peter up from the table. 'Go to your room.' The boy left, closing the door quietly behind him. Julie sat down. 'Now! Explain, please!'

Michel breathed in, then, pulling up a chair, began talking slowly, as if speaking to a disobedient child. 'Last night, in Brest ... The Germans were expecting us. At the fuel dumps. Three of my comrades died. Three! We were only able to fire one of the main tanks. The whole thing was a fiasco –'

'Wait!' Julie said sharply. 'These fuel dumps, what have they to do with us?'

'It was a diversion, of course!'

Julie was amazed. 'For the scientist? You did it especially for *him*?'

Michel dismissed the question with an arm movement. 'Yes ... No. Well, we were planning it anyway. But the point is, they were waiting for us! *They were waiting for us!* How did they know, Julie, *how*? My friends are asking questions! They –'

Julie stood up. 'I think it would be better if you didn't go on. To start with, nobody here ever knew *when* the operation was to be –'

'But I told you!'

'You said only that it would be the end of the week. Also we had no idea you were planning a diversion of that kind. And, Michel, the old scientist *did* get away. If they'd been warned, then they would hardly have let him escape!'

Michel stood up, his face hard and cruel, and hissed, 'But my comrades are *saying* this! They are saying, why is it that the first time we work with your lot, we get sold down the river! They are saying, we knew we should never trust that lot and look what happens! They are saying ugly things. They are talking of revenge. What am I to say to *them*?'

Julie felt the anger rising in her throat. She walked up to Michel until her face was close to his. 'You will tell them this! That they should look for a shark in their own ranks. Or bad planning! Or – something! Just don't look to us for a scapegoat! Because it was not one of *us*!'

Jean tapped Michel firmly on the arm with his pipe. 'Perhaps some of your own people used the opportunity, eh! Perhaps they wanted to get rid of some of their precious comrades, heh? And they wanted you to blame us!'

There was a silence. Michel looked unhappily from one to the other. Eventually he exclaimed, 'All right! I'll do my best to convince them! I just hope that –' He shook his head in frustration. '– that what you say is true! But, for God's sake, don't blame me if –'

Julie said coolly, 'If what?'

'If – emotions run high!'

She said, 'I think they already have!' She went to the back door and opened it wide. 'Goodbye, Michel. Please don't ever come here again.'

When he had gone she sat stunned, and thought: It's all falling apart again, just like before.

The pâté was very good but the steak was not as tender as it might have been. Vasson decided to leave the rest and, pushing the plate to one side, leant back in his chair.

Baum smiled across the desk. 'Better?'

'Much.'

'I'll send across for some of their *tarte maison*, if you like. It is really delicious.'

'Yes. And some decent cheese.'

'Of course!' Baum pressed the buzzer on his desk. Vasson noticed that he crooked his little finger as he did it. The man was probably a queer. Vasson wondered how he got his thrills.

Baum smiled again, his thick lips drawing back to reveal rather yellowing teeth. Vasson decided he would prefer to deal with Kloffer any day. Baum tapped the telephone and sighed. 'The Navy – not very efficient, you know. You would think they would have come back to us by now. When did we call? Yes, half an hour ago at least!' He picked up the piece of paper he'd written his notes on and peered at it. 'This – er – Freymann, he's a Jew, I suppose?'

Vasson nodded.

'Then I doubt he'll be of much consequence. Nevertheless –' He placed his fingers together in a neat arch. 'Nevertheless, it will be rather satisfying to sweep him up into our little net, won't it? Then we can deliver him back from whence he came. Yes?' He smiled sweetly across the table. A raving poof, Vasson decided.

Baum tapped his fingertips together impatiently. 'Now, now! Where *is* Schultz? You must have your dessert! *And* your cheese!' He leaned forward and pressed the button again. Vasson heard a buzzer sound in the office next door.

The door burst open. A young man, presumably Schultz, stood at the door. He looked as if he'd just seen a ghost. 'Herr Oberst! The telephone, it's Paris! General Oberg!'

For a moment Baum froze, then, swallowing hard, he reached for the telephone as if it were glass. He lifted the receiver carefully to his ear and said precisely, 'Ja? Ah, Herr General!'

In the next few moments Baum seemed to say 'Ja' rather a lot.

Then the German jerked his head and looked hard at Vasson, a look of amazement on his face.

Vasson tensed. It was something big. Concerning him. And Freymann. It must be Freymann!

There was a torrent of German from Baum and then he was replacing the receiver carefully in its holder.

Baum stared at Vasson for a moment, his lips quivering nervously. Finally he said, 'That was General Oberg. The head of the *entire* Gestapo in France.' He paused, as if to assimilate the information, then continued, 'It appears that this man – Freymann – is important to us. In fact, more than that! Vital!'

Vasson smiled slightly.

Baum leant forward, his pale eyes round with anxiety. 'We *must* get him back, do you understand? We must not fail! It is absolutely essential!'

Vasson looked away, already calculating how he could take all the credit.

He regarded Baum for a moment and said casually, 'Nothing is ever guaranteed.'

Baum nearly went purple. 'What do you mean by that! I thought you *had* the man!'

'Oh, I do! I do! But, when I am relying on your men to close the trap, then nothing can ever be guaranteed.' Vasson stood up. 'Now, it's about time we made a plan, isn't it?'

Baum nodded violently. 'Yes! Yes! Whatever you say!'

Part four
March 1943

Julie embraced Tante Marie very hard and said, 'Thank you again. For everything.'

Tante Marie sniffed and, flapping her hand with irritation, said harshly, 'Go on! Be off with you! Go on!'

Julie kissed the old woman quickly on the cheek, then, taking Peter's hand, followed Jean's dark figure out of the kitchen and across the yard. She leant down and whispered to Peter, 'All right, darling?'

'Yes, Mummy, I'm fine.'

Julie squeezed his hand and felt very proud of him. For the past few weeks she had been telling him the same story she told everyone else: that they were moving to Rennes. It was only the previous night, when she'd heard the boat was coming, that she had told Peter the truth. Bless him, he'd taken it like a lamb. He even pretended to be looking forward to it, though she could see he was very nervous.

She hitched the strap of the haversack further up her shoulder. It was light enough: she'd taken almost nothing. Peter had his own bag, too, with spare clothes, a food parcel from Tante Marie and some of his favourite things: a toy lorry, his coloured pencils and, of course, the carved ship.

They started briskly up the road. A faint drizzle was drifting down and a film of dampness formed on Julie's face. She pulled her beret further over her forehead and put a hand down to Peter's head. He had already raised the hood of his jacket. Julie had chosen practical clothes for both of them: warm trousers and windcheater jacket for him, and trousers and a cowjacket for herself.

As they climbed the long hill the dampness turned to a steady drizzle. The faint patter of the falling rain sounded a gentle rhythm in the stillness of the night. Julie had sudden doubts about Peter's jacket; perhaps it wouldn't be up to all this rain. She would check it later. She touched him again and almost smiled. He was doing well, her son, striding along as fast as his legs would carry him.

They reached the heathland and turned right, up a slight hill. After a while the outlines of a small building came into view. It was a shepherd's hut, made of stone with a slate roof, caved in at the far end. Jean crouched and entered. Tightly clutching Peter's hand, Julie followed.

It was dark inside, but Julie could hear the sounds of the waiting people: slight rustlings and the occasional muffled cough. She felt her way to the side of the hut and sat down in a space, pulling Peter down beside her. She put her arm round the small shoulders and hugged him. 'Won't be long now.' His hand felt for hers and grasped it tightly.

Julie moved her leg and bumped it against someone else's. 'Sorry.'

'No, no. My fault. So sorry.'

The voice was familiar. Julie leant across and whispered, 'Herr Freymann?'

'Yes.'

'It's me, from the barn. Are you all right? Have you been looked after?'

'Oh yes, yes. Thank you, thank you. *Most* kind.'

Julie smiled and thought what a nice man he was. She wondered vaguely how he'd manage the path to the beach.

Peter coughed slightly. She turned back and, squeezing him against her, settled down to wait. Her stomach was fluttering uneasily, but she forced herself to be calm. Whatever happened, she wasn't going to let herself think about all the things that could go wrong tonight.

She pressed her lips against Peter's hair and closed her eyes tightly and tried to imagine what life would be like in England after such a long time.

There was nowhere to shelter on the clifftop. Vasson was getting wet and he didn't like it. He pulled up the collar of his jacket and crouched down on his haunches.

The night was quiet: the only sound was the murmur of the sea far below and the steady splatter of the falling rain. It wasn't ideal for stalking – the air was too still – but it was good enough.

He took a look round. No sign of Baum. Thank God for that. The fool might not muck it up after all. Vasson worked out how long it would be before he could slip away and get to Baum's position. Half an hour maybe. After the passengers had gone down to the beach. Then he could sit on Baum – physically if necessary – until the right moment.

As always, it was a matter of timing.

He shivered and took another look round. What a good lookout he had become! Maurice *would* be impressed.

Clifftop lookout was his important new job. A promotion, no less. This was the first time Maurice had trusted him with beach duty. It was most ironic.

But the rain was a sod. Vasson cursed: the water was soaking right through his clothes to his skin. And bloody cold it was too.

Another look: still no sign of Baum. The man might stick to the plan yet.

He tried to guess what time it was. Eleven maybe. Not long before the first party would arrive.

Peering down into the darkness of the cove below, he thought what a very neat trap it made, and allowed himself a smile.

Someone came into the hut and said in accented English, 'First group now.'

A voice said, 'Hooray!' Someone laughed nervously.

There was the sound of people moving and then the silhouette of figures against the doorway.

The old man grasped Julie's arm. 'Is that us?'

'No. We go last, on our own.'

A few minutes later the second group moved out. Then the voice of Gérard, the fisherman, was saying, 'Ready?' Julie stood up and helped Peter to his feet. She leant down and said in Peter's ear, 'Do you want to do a wee, darling, before we go?'

'No. I'm all right, thank you.' The small, high-pitched voice sounded so faint and uncertain that Julie reached down to give him one last hug. Then it was time to go.

Gérard led the old man out and Julie followed, grasping Peter's hand tightly. It was raining more heavily now, coming in a steady downpour that seeped down one's neck and through one's clothes.

Jean was waiting. It was time to say goodbye. Julie said nothing, but flung her arms round his neck and hugged him. Jean patted her back, then pushing her gently away, reached down and took Peter up in his arms. 'Take care, young man,' he whispered. Then, putting Peter down, he turned abruptly away and disappeared in the direction of the village.

Julie wiped her eyes and, taking Peter's hand, hurried off in the direction of the path. When they reached the clifftop Gérard was stepping on to the path, turning with an outstretched hand to help the old man down. As Julie waited, a dark shape caught her eye. It was a man. He was crouching a few feet away. The clifftop lookout.

As she watched him he uncurled and came towards her. He towered over her, his face a featureless blur. 'Is that the last?'

She recognised the voice: the man Roger. 'Yes.'

He turned and seemed to see Peter for the first time. Julie began to move towards the path, but Roger stepped in front of her and said, 'Why's he here?'

'He's coming with me.'

'But why?'

371

'We're going, both of us.'

'On the boat?'

'Yes. Now – please – let us pass.'

There was a pause, then a slight chuckle. 'Of course.' Roger put out his hand and touched Peter's cheek.

Julie pulled Peter close in behind her, stepped round Roger and began to negotiate the path.

The rain had turned the path to mud. Julie went slowly because she didn't want Peter to slip and frighten himself, and because it was impossible to overtake Gérard and the scientist anyway. She could hear Gérard coaxing the old man past rocks and down the steeper slopes. The old man must be wondering what he'd let himself in for.

Julie slipped, grabbed for a handhold and missed. She landed on her hip. She breathed, 'Damn!' Peter's voice said anxiously, 'You all right, Mummy?'

She pulled herself up and, trembling a little, laughed nervously. 'Yes, darling. I'm fine. Are you all right?'

'Yes.'

Julie felt her way forward again, even more slowly, until at long last she realised they were near the beach. She heard Gérard saying, 'Just let go' and saw the old man poised on the top of the slide. Suddenly he was off and she saw him disappear towards the paleness of the beach.

She sat down and waited for Peter to sit down beside her. She whispered, 'It's the slide I told you about. We'll go together, shall we?' He nodded violently and, holding his hand, Julie pushed off. They shot down and landed safely on the shingle. With relief Julie realised it was the last time she would ever have to negotiate that path.

The other two were waiting for them. Julie picked herself up and wiped the worst of the mud off the back of Peter's jacket and trousers. Gérard moved off, with Freymann following. Julie looked at the thin, stooped figure of the scientist in his inadequate clothes, and then at Peter, his small figure huddled against the relentless rain, and thought: This is ridiculous. She moved forward to catch Gérard's arm. 'What's the earliest the boat will come?'

Gérard thought for a moment. 'Half an hour, I suppose.'

'Look, it's so wet and miserable, I'll take these two into the rocks over there.' She indicated the far side of the cove. 'It might be a bit dryer.'

Gérard hesitated. 'All right. I'll come and collect you when the time comes.'

372

Julie turned back to the two forlorn figures and said, 'Look, if we go further along we might find some shelter. We mightn't get quite so wet. All right? Just follow me.'

They moved to follow her. Julie grasped Peter's hand and led the way down to the water and along the sand. She tried to remember the layout of the rocks from the last time, all those months ago, but her memory wasn't very clear.

They came to the lower rocks and began to scramble over. Julie turned to Freymann. 'All right?'

'Oh yes. I can manage. Don't you worry about me!'

There were larger boulders now. It was somewhere near here, Julie felt sure. Suddenly she recognised the dim outlines of some larger rocks and, coming round the side of one, saw the neat crevice where she had hidden before. With Richard.

'In here!' she said triumphantly. Gently she pushed Peter forward. 'You first!'

When the old man and the boy had disappeared into the darkness of the crevice, she followed. It had been worth coming: the rocks curved in above their heads and formed a roof with only a slight gap in between. As long as one kept away from the drips that fell steadily from the bumps and lips of the overhangs, it was relatively dry. Julie said cheerfully, 'All right?'

Peter said plaintively, 'I am a bit wet, Mummy.' Julie felt his trousers and top, and said, 'Just a bit damp, that's all, darling. Really. You'll soon dry out. Think – sailors get wet all the time.'

'Yes,' Peter said thoughtfully. 'Mummy?'

'Mmmm?'

'Does Richard get wet all the time?'

'Oh, I think so. Yes! I'm sure he does.'

'Oh, that's all right then!' His voice sounded more cheerful now. Julie was glad. She guessed he was beginning to enjoy his adventure.

Julie tried to see Freymann's face. 'And you, Monsieur Freymann? Are you all right?'

Freymann's voice said, 'Thank you. Thank you. Much better. How kind.'

David sat back against the rock and closed his eyes. Already he felt tired and the night had hardly started. The worst – the boat trip – was yet to come. Still, he'd come a long way, a long way.

He patted the bag tied round his waist. Everything in it must be wet by now. He himself was soaked through. Never mind. It could be worse, much worse. And he mustn't complain. Not when these people were being so kind and brave.

Anyway what was discomfort when one was a free man? Ha! He was amused by the idea. A free man. It sounded so grand. Although he wasn't sure he knew what real freedom was. Was it being able to do as one wished? Or was it having the opportunity for fulfilment within a rigidly structured society? He'd been thinking about it a lot recently, while he'd been hidden in the barn. He still wasn't sure what the answer was. Perhaps he was about to find out. Perhaps freedom would be a tangible state, a conscious understanding. How nice that would be.

Something caught his eye. The small boy was fidgeting. Such was the way of small boys. Slowly he leant across and said deliberately, 'Waiting's not much fun, is it?'

Silence. He could feel the boy's eyes staring at him. David thought: The boy thinks I am about to eat him.

'When I was your age I used to play a little word game to pass the time.'

Still nothing.

'Would you perhaps like to give it a try?'

A pause then a cautious, 'Yes, please.'

'Excellent. Shall I begin then?'

Vasson lowered himself on to his belly and, holding the torch in his hand, pressed the button once, twice, three times. He waited, dropping his head behind a tussock of grass. There was a knot of fear in his stomach: this was where Baum and his friends might just do something stupid, like blast him out of the ground.

Come on, where the hell were they?

He wiped the rain off his face, lifted the torch up and flashed the signal again.

Suddenly a small pinprick of blue light appeared through the downpour: once, twice, three times.

Vasson got cautiously to his feet and, moving away to his left, approached in a slight semicircle. The hunched silhouettes of helmeted men appeared black in the greyness. One of them moved. Then another. They were putting rifles to their shoulders. Vasson thought: Christ! And dropped to the ground. Then someone was striding out towards him and a foot kicked him hard in the ribs. Baum's voice said furiously, 'What the hell are you doing?'

'Get those bloody rifles off me!'

Baum snorted, 'Even if they had thought of shooting you, my stupid friend, they are not going to shoot me too, are they!'

Vasson got angrily to his feet and hissed, 'Just keep them away from me, do you understand!'

'Don't be a fool. People can hear you.'

Vasson swallowed hard. 'Just keep your *animals* under control, d'you hear me!'

Baum ignored him and said, 'They're all on the beach, are they – the lot of them? We'll move in, then.'

'No! We wait!'

'What!'

'Because you want the lot, don't you?'

'Yes, but –'

Vasson put his face close to the German's and spat, '*We wait.*'

The MGB stole quietly in towards the coast on one muffled engine. Ashley peered through the darkness and thought: Some luck at last. The weather had been foul all winter but now, finally, they'd been blessed with a calm night. The rain was a nuisance, of course, because it reduced visibility, but it was clearing away now and, with a bit more luck, should be gone by the time they reached the beach. Anyway, rain was better than a crystal clear night. Once, Ashley had seen the glow of a German sentry's cigarette up on the point.

The voice of Tusker, the navigator, came floating up. 'Course 165 degrees.'

'Course 165 degrees,' the coxswain repeated and turned the wheel.

In a moment Tusker would start calling out the depth until, finally, at five fathoms, they would anchor.

Already Ashley could smell the strong scent of the land, an aromatic mixture of vegetable matter and earth.

His mouth was dry and he swallowed several times. The adrenalin was working overtime tonight. It was the thought of Julie and Peter waiting on the beach. After so long.

When she'd first told him that it would be at least a month, probably two, before she could get away it had exasperated him. He'd made all the necessary plans and he was surprised and a little hurt that she hadn't wanted to come straight away. But then he'd looked at it from her point of view and begun to admire her for it. After all, he would have done the same. Waited and seen the job through.

The waiting had been terrible. That was because no-one that he'd met in the last few months had been a patch on Julie. It had taken a long time for him to realise how much he loved her. And Peter. He loved them both, and now, at last, he would take them home.

Tusker's voice called softly, 'Seven . . . seven . . . six . . .

Ashley said, 'Stop engine.'

'All stopped, sir.'

There was a rock close by, Ashley could hear the water lapping against it. 'Port twenty.'

'Port twenty,' the coxswain whispered.

Ashley saw the dark shape of the rock slip past some five yards to starboard and recognised it. The best anchorage was a few yards further to the east. 'Steer 080 degrees.'

'. . . six . . . five fathoms . . . five . . . five . . .'

Ashley left it another minute then gave the order to lower the anchor. There was a slight plop then a swishing as the grass anchor rope unwound and raced out through the stemhead fairlead.

As he waited for the boat to settle to the anchor, Ashley stood listening to the night. Now that the rain had stopped, every sound was magnified by the stillness of the air. He could hear the gentle hissing of the surf in the cove, and the echo of the swell rumbling round partly submerged rocks.

They would have to be particularly quiet tonight; the slightest sound would carry for miles.

He waited impatiently for the men to launch the surfboats and stow the gear, then he dropped into the first boat and they were off, rowing softly towards the beach.

With each stroke of the muffled oars, Ashley thought of the woman and the boy waiting in the darkness, and realised with no surprise at all that he had been looking forward to this night for a long, long time.

It had to be well past midnight. The rain had eased off and Julie could see some way along the beach. She strained her eyes for sight of a boat. But there was nothing. She looked back into the darkness of the rock cave. The word game had finished some time ago. Peter was asleep, his head on his bag. The old man was silent, probably sleeping too.

She closed her eyes for a while to rest them, then looked out through the gap in the rocks again. If you stared too hard the blackness seemed to dance before your eyes.

And yet . . .

She stiffened: there *was* something. A black blur on the water. It was moving. And up on the shingle there were other movements: dark figures running down towards the water's edge.

The boat. It must be the surfboat.

She cried out and raised her fist to the sky in a gesture of delight. Peter woke up. 'Mummy?'

'Darling, it's come! The boat's here!'

'It's really Richard? He's really here?'

She laughed with excitement. 'Yes, darling!' She remembered the scientist. 'Monsieur? The boat. It's come!'

'Yes . . . yes . . .! I – I – It's wonderful. Yes!'

'Wait here, you two!' Julie went onto all fours and crawled out on to a flat rock. She stood up and peered into the night. The surfboat was there all right, just riding in towards the beach. A dark mass had appeared under the cliff – the first group of passengers being gathered together. It would take five minutes to load them and twenty minutes before the boat returned. Not long. *For ever*. She desperately wanted to run along the beach that very second – but there was Peter and she couldn't leave him.

She laughed with excitement. Richard. He was there, she knew he was. He would have come himself, just to make certain. She wanted to say, I'm here, darling, of course I'm here!

The boat flew on to the beach and figures jumped out. The dark mass of the passengers started down the beach.

They seemed to be going very slowly. She willed them to speed up.

At the water's edge there was some more movement – she guessed the crew were floating the surfboat off again, ready for the passengers.

Behind, another black shape slowly emerged from the darkness of the sea. That would be the second surfboat, coming in to the beach.

Julie watched with satisfaction. For once it was a perfect night. Everything was going smoothly. A marvellous piece of luck. She couldn't help thinking that it was *fate*; that, after all the storms of the winter, this calm night had been arranged, just for *her*.

The passengers had reached the water's edge at last. In a moment they would be in the surfboat and on their way.

She clenched her fists. *Hurry. Hurry up. This waiting is killing me*. And she laughed a little, because the anticipation was so sharp and warm.

Suddenly she gasped and froze, the last of the smile still on her lips.

Light.

There was light –!

The picture in front of her jumped from negative to positive, the blacks to whites.

She blinked and focused, disbelieving.

The surfboat and the figures around it were sharply illuminated, encircled with brilliant white.

Dear God –!

The brilliant whiteness was coming in a long shaft from the left –

from the sea. She jerked her head towards it. The beam was radiating from a single point out in the bay.

She let out a small cry.

The British boat must be mad. What were they doing? *What were they doing?* She hissed, 'Turn it off! *Turn it off!*'

Suddenly she jumped.

There was more light. This time from the clifftop. A great cone of dazzling brilliance which swung from side to side across the cove, searching, trying to trap the running figures.

Crack! Crack! Gunfire from the clifftop. Then, almost immediately, a deep low *Bang!* from the bay, where fingers of yellow-tongued light flashed across the darkness.

Suddenly she understood. It was a *German* boat out in the bay, shining the light. Just as there were *Germans* up on the clifftop.

A shot rang out, closer, much closer. Then more shots. Shouting. Men running or pausing to shoot back. Men falling.

Julie shrieked, '*No!*' and cried with rage. 'Please, dear God, No!'

A second great cone of light shone down from the clifftop, sweeping back and forth like the first, trapping running figures in its glare, figures which ran then fell, figures which froze, sometimes and raised their hands. The guns were rat-tat-tatting in a continuous stream of noise, from the beach, from the clifftop, enveloping the cove. In one sweep of the light she saw a group of figures crouched behind the surfboat, guns aimed upwards, towards the clifftop.

'Mummy! Mummy!' Peter was pulling at her jacket. 'Mummy! Come back! Come back! Come back in – please!'

For a moment Julie was frozen, unable to comprehend, then, slowly, she realised it was Peter calling her. She shuffled backwards until she felt the rock against her back. Then, her eyes on the beach, she pushed herself into the rock cave. 'Dear God . . . Dear God . . .' She buried her face in her hands and, rocking back and forth, cried with rage and despair, loudly, to shut out the terrible noise. Peter hugged her back, patting her ineffectually, crying too.

On the beach the rat-tat-tatting of machine-gun fire became more spasmodic.

Out to sea the low boom of the big guns had ceased and the faint roar of deep-throated engines was fading into the distance.

Suddenly, there was a deathly silence.

Julie looked up. Light was still reflecting from the beach. Sick with fear, she crawled forward on her stomach and looked down.

There were soldiers everywhere, encircling the beach, rifles at their shoulders. In the centre stood a ragged forlorn group, their hands above their heads.

Gérard . . . Maurice . . . Pierre . . . Many of the airmen, too.

But no oilskinned figure with a cap on his head –

Scattered around the beach were bodies lying inert on the pebbles. She stared at them in horror, terrified that she would spot some clue – a fleece-lined seaboot, a duffle coat . . .

Suddenly she realised she couldn't see the surfboat. She grabbed at the ray of hope. He must have got away. Yes, of course – he'd got away!

Then she remembered that the British boat had been chased away and that there was nowhere for him to escape to . . .

And she saw that some of the soldiers were down at the water's edge, raising their rifles to their shoulders, pointing out to sea, shouting . . . A light was shining from the sea again, but much closer.

Her heart sank. There were heads in the water, heads swimming around a waterlogged boat – the surfboat. For a moment the swimmers seemed undecided, then one tried to dive out of sight, surfacing some distance from the boat. But it was too calm. They spotted him the moment he came up. The sharp cracks of shots rang out.

Julie bit her knuckle and shook her head rapidly from side to side.

The lone swimmer held up a hand, as if in surrender, and began moving towards the shore. The others followed. There were four of them. They emerged slowly from the water and held up their hands.

She recognised him immediately. He walked through the other men and stood at the front. A soldier stepped forward and searched him roughly, then pushed him forward with his rifle butt.

Richard walked quickly to the group of prisoners and pushed his way through them. Julie realised he was looking for somebody – *her*.

She cried very softly, 'I'm here, *I'm here*.'

Shouts again, and some of the prisoners were pushed towards the dead and wounded. With difficulty they picked them up and rejoined the group. More shouts and the prisoners formed a ragged line and moved off towards the cliff path, the dead and wounded carried like sacks between them.

The last she saw of him was when he paused at the bottom of the path and took a quick glance over his shoulder.

Then the lights went out.

Only the weak beams of torches remained. She watched them weave their way slowly up the path to the clifftop. Then they, too, were gone and there was nothing but darkness.

Julie whispered, 'Dear God. I'm so sorry. I'm so sorry. Please forgive me. Please!'

Then she beat her hands against the hard rock until they hurt, because she couldn't *do* anything and because, *somehow*, she had the terrible feeling that it was all her fault.

David opened his eyes. A long time had passed. Through the opening in the rocks he could see a cold grey light. Dawn. How he hated it. He'd never understood how people could rapture over it. Dusk was more beautiful every time.

He peered along the rock cave. The young woman was finally asleep, poor thing. How he had felt for her – she had suffered so terribly. The people on the beach, they had been her friends, perhaps even her family.

And the child: so young to understand such terrible things. What a world for a child, what a world.

But what now? The woman had been almost hysterical with grief. What if she was still in a state? Who was to decide what they were to do? One thing was certain: David had no idea of how to get out of this place on his own.

He looked towards the patch of sky at the end of the crevice. At least it wasn't raining any more.

There was a sound. He turned. The woman was awake, her eyes open and staring. There was a hopeless look on her face. David recognised it: he'd seen it many times before. He whispered so as not to wake the boy, 'Good morning. How about some breakfast?'

She stared at him dully, her face blank. David smiled at her. 'I have – let me see –' He opened his bag and rummaged inside. 'Yes, cheese, *always* cheese. I think, one day I'll turn into a cheese! Then some bread. Yes, and an apple! I'm sure our young friend will like that won't he? We'll keep it for him. Just for him.'

She wasn't listening. She was looking into the distance. David could see that terrible thoughts were going through her head. She was remembering the night.

'Dear lady!' he said more firmly. 'I think we should begin our breakfast. *Then* we think! *No* thinking until then!' He wagged a finger at her.

She nodded vaguely and slowly sat up, trying not to disturb the boy on her lap. David broke off some cheese and handed it to her with a slice of bread. She stared at the remaining food lying in the paper on his knees. He realised she was checking to see how much was left. David said, 'It's all right. Plenty for me and the boy.'

She nodded and ate, slowly at first then hungrily. When she had finished she started to caress the boy's hair and he saw that she was crying again.

David pursed his lips. 'Well, now, let's make a plan! Let's be very practical!'

Her eyes focused and she blinked away the tears. 'Yes.'

'We need to decide what options are open to us. First . . .' He thought for a moment. 'First, can we just walk back up the beach?' Without waiting for her to reply he said, 'No. They'll have guards, won't they?'

'Up on the point. They have a post there. And . . . they've probably got extra guards at the top of the path.'

'Yes.' There was silence while they both thought. David ventured, 'Perhaps at night . . . Perhaps we can climb the cliff somewhere else?'

She shook her head. 'There's no other way that I know of. The cliff here is sheer. It's impossible to reach the next cove . . . This place is cut off.'

The silence was longer this time. David thought: I wish I could think of something else, for *her* sake. For myself I don't care any more. Enough is enough.

She gave a bitter laugh. 'Not much choice, is there?'

He waved his hand from side to side. 'Nonsense! We will think of something. Defeat is in the mind!'

The woman sighed. 'I suppose so, but . . .' She shook her head.

'What's your name?'

'Eh? Oh, Julie, it's Julie. Short for Juliette.'

'Well, Julie, there must be a way out of here. Mustn't there? Yes?' She shrugged hopelessly. 'Maybe . . .'

'For your boy's sake.'

She stared at him hard, her eyes round with anger and surprise. Then she softened and nodded gently. 'Yes. For his sake . . .'

David smiled. 'We'll think of something.'

'Yes, you're right.' She rubbed her forehead. 'We'll *have* to.' She looked at him again and David noticed that her eyes had lost their lifelessness and were alert again. She said softly, 'But *what*?'

Then her face took on a preoccupied look and he guessed she was going through the possibilities again.

He said, 'There's always *diversion*.'

'Diversion?'

'You know, make a noise somewhere to attract their attention. Then slip past.' He made a snaking movement with his hand. 'It can work very well. I *know*!'

'Really? Yes . . . Perhaps you're right. I –'

She paused and stiffened, her face suddenly sheet white. Then, moving the boy's head quickly off her lap, she scrambled towards the entrance. A moment later she was back, her eyes round with fear.

'Soldiers! Coming down the path!'

David looked at their rock cave: it was no good. Far too easy to find. He grasped her arm. 'Quick! We must hide!'

'Where!'

'Try to hide the boy . . . Right under a rock, in the sand . . .'

'Yes!' The boy was already awake, dazed and frightened.

David crawled through the crevice to the far side, away from the beach. The woman followed and overtook him. She looked wildly to right and left, grabbed the boy and, scrabbling feverishly, pulled him up over a rock and out of sight.

David knew he couldn't go climbing after them. He was too slow. He might give them away. Better to stay.

He looked back into the crevice and decided against it: they'd find him straight away. He crawled round a corner and almost immediately found a much smaller gap, under the overhang of a large rock. This would do. He thought wrily: It will have to.

There was nowhere!

Julie wanted to scream. Smooth rocks. Gaps in between. Nowhere to hide! God!

And she was losing the cover of the massive boulders behind. The back of her head felt as if it were ten feet square: the Germans were probably watching her even now.

Nowhere! She looked down towards the water.

Perhaps the water . . .

Pulling Peter behind her, she crouched low and ran down a gully towards the sea.

In the water? Yes! She hissed, 'Peter, we might have to get wet!'

He nodded. She climbed on to a rock and looked down. There was a gap in the rocks beneath, where the water sucked gently back and forth with a gentle lapping noise. It didn't seem too deep and it looked as though there was an overhang –

She removed her rucksack and Peter's shoulder bag and squeezed them into a narrow fissure in the rock above, where they couldn't be seen. Then she jumped down. She caught her breath. The water came up to her thighs: it was icy. She stumbled, found firm sand, and turned for Peter.

She reached up for him and he jumped into her arms. She tried to hold him above the water but he was so heavy that he slipped through and he was up to his waist before she got a grip on him and hauled him back into her arms. She heard him gasp as he met the water.

Julie looked quickly around and immediately saw an overhang where they'd be invisible from everywhere but the sea. Moving Peter round on to her hip, she pushed herself under the rock and pressed her back against it. She kissed him on the cheek. 'I love you, darling.'

'I love you too, Mummy.' He turned his face to her and kissed her on the lips. He was shivering already.

She thought: How long could they last in this water? And the tide! She'd completely forgotten about that! God! Perhaps it was coming up . . .

Time. It passed in fractions of moments that lasted for ever. The icy water got colder. The blood too. Peter shivered.

She held him closer.

She tried to guess how the time was passing. Five minutes? No, seven. Maybe eight.

A stone fell some way away. Julie gripped Peter tighter.

Another sound: someone walking over the rocks. Heavy boots. Nearer. *Much* nearer.

God!

Crunch! From just above. Just overhead.

Close your eyes. Believe.

Another crunch. Feet shuffling.

Moving away. *Away!*

Heavy boots stepping from rock to rock. Moving away!

But wait . . . *Wait.* Until you're sure they've gone. It might be a trap!

She felt a great shudder go through Peter's body. She put her lips to his ear and whispered, 'It's all right, darling!' He nodded, but she could hear his teeth chattering. His skin was deathly cold.

But wait . . . Wait.

So she waited. Twenty minutes – it felt longer. Perhaps it was thirty minutes. Peter was weighing her down, heavier and heavier. A brisk wind was blowing in from the water, scything through her clothes, making Peter's cold skin the temperature of ice. She whispered, 'A little longer, just a little longer . . .'

She looked down and realised with a shock that the water was higher than before – quite a bit higher. It had reached her waist. The tide was coming up.

They would have to go, like it or not.

She smiled into Peter's taut pale face. 'We're going now, darling.'

He nodded, his jaws clamped together to stop the chattering.

She moved out and looked up. Empty sky. No Germans.

There was only one way out: up a smooth rock face. She couldn't do it with Peter in her arms. She said, 'I'll have to put you in the water. Just until I'm up. I'm sorry, darling . . .'

He nodded and, without a word, slid out of her arms into the water.

383

It came up to his chest. He closed his eyes for a moment as the coldness hit him, then looked up to her.

'Right. I've got to get back up on to the rock. Give me a heave, will you?' She waited until he had moved out from under the rock then put her foot into a notch in the rock and pulled herself up. She felt Peter valiantly pushing from below. She paused, spreadeagled halfway up the smooth face, and took a long look round.

There was no-one in sight.

She looked for another handhold. She found one away to the right and hoisted herself up the last few feet. She looked again. No-one. She turned and lay down on the rock. Reaching down, she took Peter's hands and pulled. She raised him a few inches but could get him no further: she didn't have enough leverage. She lowered him back into the water. His lips quivered and silently he began to cry.

'Don't worry, darling, please!' She put her foot across on to another rock so that she was making a bridge across the gap and, reaching down, pulled. This time he came, desperately slowly, until he was halfway up the rock. 'Try and wedge yourself, darling!' He put out a foot to the rock opposite and locked himself against the rock face. Julie moved quickly across and, lying down on the rock again, pulled. Slowly Peter came up until he lay on the top, panting, in a pool of water.

Julie got to her feet and, taking the bags from the crack, pulled Peter to his feet. 'Come on, we'll get some dry clothes on!'

She led the way cautiously up the gully. No-one. Then they were on a plateau of rocks, hidden from the beach by the giant boulders. No-one.

Back to the crevice then. She crept forward, came round a large rock and they were facing the entrance.

Her heart was thudding in her ears. Perhaps they had got the dear old man . . . She stooped and looked inside.

'Hello, my dear!' Freymann's creased, smiling face peered out of the darkness at her. 'They've gone. I watched them go back up the cliff. There's no-one left.' He smiled again. 'How very delighted I am to see that you are safe!'

Julie smiled weakly. 'They've gone?'

'They've gone. They've given up! They think we have vanished into thin air! We're safe!'

Julie thought: But we're not, are we? It's only a reprieve.

Darkness again. Julie chewed on the bread and knew that she had to decide.

They had shared out the last of Peter's food parcel; most for Peter himself and the rest split between herself and the scientist. At first the old man had refused to take any, but she'd insisted. For drink they'd taken brackish rainwater from pools in the rocks.

Now there was no more food and the pools were drying out. Peter had put his one change of clothes on, but they weren't very warm and he'd been cold and shivery all day. He was probably catching a cold. Something would have to be done. But *what*? What could one do with a small boy and a sick old man?

The thought of having to take a decision made her feel slightly hysterical. She wanted to put it off. The longer they waited the better the chances might be . . . After a while the guards on the clifftop might go away. *Might* . . .

The decision was impossible. Perhaps if they waited another day . . .? Julie closed her eyes and started from the beginning again.

Freymann and she had been through it a dozen times since morning. The only thing they'd decided was to do nothing while it was light. Darkness offered the only hope. The old man favoured the diversionary tactic. He'd suggested that he should walk up the path and run, to lure the guard away while Julie and Peter escaped. Julie had pointed out that David would be shot instantly and bring the other guards from the headland within seconds.

After that, Freymann was silent for a long time. Julie asked him about his life and he told her about his childhood and the happy days in Berlin. He didn't tell her very much about what happened after that and she didn't press it.

She said, 'And what will you do in England?'

'Ah. Who knows? I've learnt not to think ahead.'

Then he'd been silent again, except to ask her to call him David.

'I'll try, monsieur.' Then she laughed. 'It's difficult not to call you monsieur . . . The only person of your age that I've ever called by his name is my uncle.'

'How old do you think I am then!'

'Well . . . Not *that* old. I – Oh dear, I've offended you.'

'No . . . No.'

'How old *are* you?'

'Fifty-two. Or fifty-three. I'm not sure.'

'Oh.' She was shocked. He looked well over sixty. 'Yes, of course. That's what I thought . . .'

He smiled at her because she'd lied to be kind. Then he settled down to sleep again and she was left to her own thoughts.

Now it was dark and the thinking still hadn't produced a solution.

It was Peter who gripped her arm and whispered, 'Mummy! There's something. A noise!'

Julie tensed and listened. The night was very still.

There was silence. Then, suddenly, a sound: a low whistle, long and low. A pause, then it came again. It was a man's whistle.

Silence. Then it came again, closer. Thoughts raced through Julie's mind: Friends? Germans! A clever trick? Oh yes: what a clever trick!

Now the sound was close. Panic began to grip her.

A voice called soft and low, '... Juliette ... Are you there? ... Julie ...'

Julie froze. It could be a trick, an elaborate trick ...

'... Julie, it's me ... Michel.'

Julie sighed audibly and squeezed Peter's arm. She got up and climbed out onto the rocks. 'Michel ...! Michel ...! Here! We're here!' A moment later a dark figure emerged out of the night. Julie grasped his arms and sobbed with gratitude and relief. 'Oh, bless you! Bless you!'

'Quick!' His voice was harsh and businesslike. 'How many are you?'

'Just me and Peter and the old man.'

'The old man?'

'Freymann. The scientist.'

'Oh.' He sounded cross.

'Why?'

'He'll be slow, that's all.'

'He'll do his best. I know he will.'

'Right. Come on then. We've got to be quick.'

'Yes. Yes. I'll get the others.' Julie scrambled back into the crevice. 'Come on, darlings. We're going! Don't forget anything, will you? Have you got your bag, Peter?'

'Yes, Mummy.'

Julie pulled on her haversack. 'Ready?' she called.

She led the way up on to the rocks again and waited while first Peter then Freymann climbed out and started down the fall of rocks to the beach. She heard someone grunt: Freymann. She found him lying against a rock trying to regain his feet. 'Here, let me give you a hand.' She pulled him up and, holding his hand, helped him down to the sand where Michel and Peter were waiting.

Michel said brusquely, 'Right, No talking. No noise at all. And stick in line. Freymann, behind me. Then Peter. Julie, you come last.' Julie saw for the first time that Michel had a machine gun slung over his shoulder.

Julie whispered, 'What about guards? On the cliff?'

'There's no guard. Not if we're quick!'

They set off at a cracking pace. Julie immediately worried that Peter and the old man wouldn't be able to keep up. But they strode out, the two of them, and in no time they had reached the bottom of the path.

But the path was a different matter. Even before they were a short way up she could hear Freymann panting. He'd never make the top without a rest. Nor would Peter.

Freymann slowed up then stopped altogether. She heard him apologising breathlessly to Michel. Julie leant forward and caressed Peter's cheek. There was a pause, then they were off again, but much more slowly. After that they stopped regularly. It took twenty minutes to reach the rim of the cliff. She could almost feel Michel's impatience.

Just below the clifftop Michel signalled them to wait and crawled on ahead. Julie found herself praying. Then Michel was back, waving them forward.

Julie came up onto the clifftop just behind Peter and, seeing Michel move rapidly off, grabbed Peter's hand and started to run. Almost immediately she tripped over something and, glancing down, almost screamed. It was a body. Wearing a helmet. Lying inert. The guard.

She ran on, pulling Peter behind her. Ahead Freymann was in trouble again. As soon as she drew level with him she slowed down and stayed with him.

David thought: I can't go on! It's not physically possible. I'll ask them to leave me behind. Then I'll make my own way.

He staggered and fell to his knees, gasping for breath. The girl stooped down beside him. 'Come on! You can do it. Not far now! Not far!'

There was fire in his lungs. He tried to speak but there was no breath to spare. Instead he shook his head.

Now the young man was back. 'Get up! Quick! We've got to get to the road! Come on!'

David rasped, 'Go . . . on . . . Don't . . . wait!'

The young man sighed impatiently. 'No! We can't leave you here. You'd be a bloody danger! Come on! You'd ruin it for *us*!'

David blinked. He hadn't thought of it like that. Right then. He got unsteadily to his feet and prepared to set off. Roughly, the young man thrust his shoulder under David's arm and half-carried, half-dragged him across the uneven ground.

It was downhill now. David tried to take more of his own weight: he could hear the young man panting with the effort of supporting him. But his legs were weak and, however hard he tried, he never seemed to be able to regain his breath.

Finally they came to a low wall. David disengaged himself and, determined to make an effort, climbed resolutely over. The others were over ahead of him and the young man led the way across what David realised to be a field. David followed unsteadily, wondering if he could ever keep up. The pace was slower now, the young man moving cautiously, like a cat. But even so, David knew he couldn't go on much longer.

Suddenly he realised that no one was paying any attention to him. He could hide here and no one would know. He wouldn't be a danger to them here.

Gradually he dropped back until the others vanished into the darkness ahead. Then, gently, gratefully, he dropped to his knees and lay down, one hand on the ground, one hand against his aching chest.

They were skirting the village, to the north. Where was Michel taking them? To Morlaix maybe . . . But where could they hide there? At his apartment? Terribly risky. It would be risky wherever they went.

She turned to look for David. No sign. She waited for him to loom up out of the darkness. He didn't. Michel came up. 'What the hell's the matter?'

'It's David – I can't see him. I'll have to go back.'

'We haven't time!'

'Well, I'm certainly not going to leave him there! Here – look after Peter while I go to look.' She turned and strode away into the darkness.

Almost back at the wall . . . He had to be somewhere near here.

Then she saw him. Lying on the ground. She ran up. 'David! David! Are you all right?'

For a moment she thought he was dead then he groaned slightly. 'Sorry . . . sorry . . . leave me here . . . Leave me.'

'Absolutely not! Come on! You're too important. Anyway, I need you! Where you go, I go.'

'Leave me. It's no good . . . Please . . .'

'But the Germans will find you!'

'So?' he rasped. 'All they can do is kill me.'

'No. No! They'll take you back to Germany and make you work. They'll get hold of your family and force you to work. Don't you see? Come on. *Come on*. David, make an effort, *please*.'

He didn't move and for a moment Julie thought he had given up completely. Then at last he groaned and, leaning on her, got unsteadily to his feet. Slowly, his arm over her shoulder, they set off down the hill.

Michel and Peter were waiting. Michel said impatiently, 'Hurry! We've really got to hurry!'

They left the village behind and struck out across the fields towards the south-west. After a while Julie realised they must be approaching the small road that led from Tregasnou to the estuary and Kernibon. Once they'd crossed the road, there was nothing but fields for miles. How far did Michel expect them to go? David was in a bad way, his breath coming in long shallow rasps. Peter was tired too, poor chap, dragging his feet, shoulders drooping.

A hedgerow loomed up. Then a gate leading onto the road. Michel disappeared into the darkness of the hedge. Perhaps they were to wait here for a while.

She followed Michel in towards the hedge, then stopped in alarm. Someone else was there, waiting in the shadows. She froze, but then recognised something familiar about the figure. Slowly she went forward. 'Jean!'

He took her arm. 'Quick! Into the van!'

'The van?'

Jean led her into the darkness of the tall hedge and there, parked close beside it, was the old Peugeot van.

Michel was opening the back door. He took Freymann's arm. 'In here. And you.' He helped Peter up into the back. 'Julie, you drive.'

'Me?'

'Yes, unless you want to take the Sten.'

For a moment she didn't understand what he meant, then she realised he meant the gun. It was an ugly great thing: she wouldn't have the first idea how to use it.

She grasped her uncle's arm. 'Jean, thank you! Thank you!'

'Don't thank me! It was Michel.'

'Take care of Tante Marie. And *please*, don't get caught! *Please!*'

He said gruffly, 'Off you go! Quick! There's no time to spare.'

She hugged him and, climbing in through the passenger door, eased herself across into the driver's seat.

Jean was opening the gate. He disappeared for a moment, then came back into view and waved them forward. Michel swung on the starting handle and the old engine burst into life with an ear-splitting roar. Michel jumped into the passenger seat. 'Out of the gate, turn right. Go!'

Her heart in her mouth, Julie threw the gear lever into first and the van jumped forward. She pulled the wheel hard over and they shot out of the gate into the lane. There was no chance to wave to Jean.

It was pitch black. 'I can't see anything!' she cried.

Michel reached down and flicked a switch. The lights came on but they had been well hooded: they cast only the faintest glow over the walls and hedgerows lining the road.

Julie peered forward, trying to keep the speed up. A sharp bend reared up and she almost missed it. She pulled the wheel over and the bumper crunched into the wall with a loud bang. 'Sorry.'

'Keep going!'

They shot through a tiny village and then down a hill towards some crossroads. Julie almost asked, 'Which way?' when Michel said, 'Straight over!'

She kept her foot down and the van shot across the crossroads. Michel looked rapidly right and left, then stuck his head out of the window to look behind. He pulled his head back in and said, 'Nothing!'

Another hill, leading down to the estuary. Júlie realised they were on the road to Kernibon. It was a dead end.

As they neared the village Michel leant over and turned off the ignition. The engine petered out and they coasted down the hill in eerie silence. 'Right at the harbour!'

As they approached the bottom of the hill Julie resisted the temptation to brake too much and the van was still travelling fast as she yanked the wheel across. They shot round the corner and along the road encircling the landward side of the cove.

Finally the van slowed right down and Julie pulled in towards the side. Michel jumped out, opened the rear doors and bundled the others out. Julie climbed out, trying to stop herself shaking.

Peter ran up and took her hand, then they were following Michel along the side of the tiny harbour. Suddenly he lowered himself over the sea wall and, climbing down, disappeared.

There was a slight clatter, some muffled movements, then Michel's voice floated up. 'The old man first!' Freymann lowered himself gingerly over the edge and hovered for a moment, searching for a foothold, then he moved on down the wall.

Julie peered over and saw that there was a metal ladder and, below, a small dinghy floating on the water. She sat Peter down and, turning him face to the wall, put his hands on the rungs of the ladder. 'Careful. Take it slowly.'

When he was safely in the boat beside Freymann and Michel, Julie lowered herself over. She hated heights almost as much as she hated boats. Finally her foot was in the boat and, wobbling violently, she threw herself into it. She fell awkwardly into the bottom, bruising her shin. She clenched her teeth and stayed silent.

The boat was moving away from the wall. Michel was weaving an oar from side to side over the back. Julie watched him, amazed: she'd never realised he could do this kind of thing.

Then she remembered when she and Peter had come to collect the sow, how they'd surprised him here at the harbour and how secretive he'd been.

They were approaching the fishing boats moored in the centre of the cove. Perhaps Michel was going to hide them here, on one of the boats.

The dinghy bumped alongside one of the smaller boats. Michel pushed the old man to his feet and helped him up the side. Julie went next and, reaching down, pulled Peter up beside her. Michel came last and tied the dinghy's rope to the fishing boat.

Julie looked around. It was a small boat, completely open and without so much as a wheelhouse. There was nowhere to hide.

Michel was beside her. She pulled his sleeve and said, 'Michel, we can't hide here!'

'No. But it'll take you across.'

'Across?'

'To England. That's where you want to go, isn't it?'

Julie gasped and stared at him in amazement. 'Yes but – in *this*?' It was much smaller than the fishing boat she and Peter had taken from Morlaix three years before. She saw that there was a small bit of decking at the front which came half way back to the mast. But otherwise it was entirely open. She could imagine the waves coming straight in.

Michel said, 'Right. Here are some waterproofs. Fresh water and so on are up in the bow. Not much, but it's all I could get hold of.'

He moved along the boat to the far end and Julie followed, a feeling of hopelessness creeping over her. 'Right.' Michel was saying, 'here's the tiller, for steering, and here, the compass. Now, I'll light the little oil lamp here, beside the compass, but keep it well masked until you're clear of the land. Now there *is* an engine but there's almost no fuel for it and anyway it's too noisy to use near the land so I think you'll be better off without it . . .'

'Michel! What do you mean?'

'The sails are quite straightforward. One large and one small. If the wind comes from ahead you'll need both, otherwise you could manage with just the large one . . .'

'*Michel! What are you saying!*'

He turned to her and said harshly, 'I'm sorry, I wish I could come with you, but I can't.' He shrugged. 'I *have* to stay. This is the best I can do for you, Julie –'

'*No! No!*' She grabbed his arms and tried to read his face in the darkness. 'I *can't*, Michel! I don't know what to do!'

'But I'll get the boat ready and rigged and I'll sail out with you into the bay. Then all you have to do is point north –'

'*Michel, I can't!*'

He took her by the shoulders and shook her slightly. 'You *must!* It's not ideal, I'll admit, but it's a damn sight better than getting caught by the Gestapo. And *that's* the only alternative!'

Julie stared at him in disbelief. She repeated desperately, 'But I don't know how to sail!'

'I told you, I'll get you going in the right direction. But we must go *now*! We're losing the tide!' He ran forward to the mast and started heaving on lines. Julie grasped the side of the boat and watched him, horrified.

Peter was at her elbow. 'Mummy, I can help . . . I think. Richard told me all about sailing . . . Mummy?'

Julie looked down at the small pale face and automatically touched his hair. 'Oh darling! I – wish I . . .' Then she remembered what the Gestapo did to children and, holding the small face in her hands, she made an effort to smile. 'We'll do our best then, shall we? We'll sail to England, shall we?' But even as she said it she was filled with despair.

Peter nodded and clutched at her hand. Up by the mast Michel was pulling on a rope. There was a great flapping and beating as a black sail rose slowly into the sky. Then Michel was leaning over the front of the boat, pulling hard on something. Suddenly he ran back, pulled another rope and dived for the tiller. Julie realised the land was moving sideways: the boat was free of its mooring. The beating noise diminished then stopped. She looked up at the sail. Its black curved shape soared up into the darkness, huge against the sky.

The mouth of the tiny harbour reared up ahead. Julie winced and drew back involuntarily. The high brick mole rushed past, an arm's length away, then they were through, slipping rapidly out into the vast blackness of the night.

Julie felt the boat move under her and grabbed at the side. She felt sick. It was a nightmare. She didn't understand the first thing about any of it – not the first!

Michel was calling, 'Come here!'

Lurching unsteadily across the deck she reached his side. 'Now, listen very carefully. We've only got a few minutes. So *listen*! There's a torch here just behind me in the bo'sun's box. There are the waterproofs I told you about. Here –' He placed her hand on the tiller, '– here is the tiller. You push it the opposite way to the one you want to go in. You'll get used to it . . .'

Julie stared into the darkness, her throat constricted and dry.

'And now listen *very* carefully. The course . . .'

After a while Julie realised he had stopped speaking and was moving away from the tiller, leaving it in her hand.

'Best of luck, Julie!'

'*But –*'

Then he was untying something – the rope holding the dinghy – and climbing over the side.

She almost screamed.

The next moment he was gone.

26

Vasson reached out and touched the painting. A tractor, bright red and crudely painted. Not bad, considering. Then it occurred to him – the mother probably gave the child some help with it. He imagined them sitting on the floor together, engrossed and happy in their task. The picture irritated him. He turned away.

There was a model plane hanging from the ceiling, a second picture and some posters of Paris. Angrily he yanked the cover off the bed; it was unmade, the blankets neatly folded, the calico bolster without a pillow case.

There was a wooden chest under the eaves. He pulled it out and, raising the lid, emptied the contents over the floor. Toys, clothes, old fabrics.

Rubbish.

As he moved towards the stairs his head brushed against the model plane. He pushed it impatiently aside. The fine thread holding it to the ceiling broke and it fell to the floor, one wing bent and broken. Vasson kicked it out of his way.

He went down the narrow stairs to the room below. The woman's room. It was clean and tidy, the bed neatly covered like the boy's.

She was expecting to be gone a long time, the bitch.

He pulled open the drawers of the dresser. The top one contained underwear, carefully folded. Scattered between the clothes were sachets which smelled of herbs. He pulled everything out on to the floor.

He leant down. In the next drawer were blouses, woollens – more rubbish. He threw them onto the floor as well. Impatiently he jerked open the bottom drawer. Papers. A ration card. Some letters. An old photograph.

He leafed through the letters. They were in English. They were signed 'Your Mother'. He stared at them, frowning. He didn't understand English. He threw them back in the drawer. The photograph showed two people sitting on a beach. One was the girl, much younger, maybe fourteen or fifteen. She was very slim, her angular body clad in an unbecoming, old-fashioned swimming costume. She was looking straight into the camera, her eyes screwed up against the sun. Beside her was a woman, much older, rather fat, dressed in a tight frock with a floral print on it. The mother.

Vasson flipped the photograph over and stared. There was some writing: English again. It said: Mummy and me. Cawsand. 1929.

Cawsand. It must be a place in England. The girl was not Breton at all then, but English. A worse thought – she was probably an agent, planted in France to spy. The thought made Vasson angry and uneasy. He had the unpleasant feeling that he'd been cleverly and ruthlessly deceived.

If Baum found out it would mean more stick and Vasson had had enough over the scientist. Vasson decided it would be best if Baum never found out.

He slid the photograph inside his jacket. It offered no clues as to where the bitch was now. And *that* was what he needed to know.

She had to be the key. She'd been with the scientist at the cliff. Now they were both missing. The girl must be hiding him.

Suddenly, he jumped.

A terrible cry came from the next room. Vasson shuddered and, bracing himself, stood up and went towards the door. He hesitated, half-revolted, half-fascinated by what he might see, then, his heart thudding, opened the door and walked through into the kitchen.

Baum was leaning against the mantelpiece, examining his nails. To the left, three of his men were huddled round a chair. Vasson moved across the room, his eyes on the backs of the men, until he could see between them into the chair. He swallowed hard and stared, fascinated. The figure lay inert. The face was a mess, the nose a pulp of blood and bones, and the eyes reduced to slits between the purple-red swellings of cheeks and eyelids. Apart from the hair, the old woman was unrecognisable.

Vasson glanced at Baum and raised his eyebrows. Baum made a face of disgust which indicated: Nothing.

Turning his eyes back to the monstrous sight in the chair, Vasson lowered himself on to a seat in the corner. One of Baum's men put his face down to the old woman's and chanted, 'Where is the girl?'

The old woman's mouth moved, as if to say something, then dropped open. With distaste Vasson saw that the gums were bare and devoid of teeth. She started to moan loudly.

The man standing directly in front of the chair turned to his companion and said something in German. The other nodded and, reaching into his pocket, pulled out some cord. It was in two sections. They took one piece each and tied the old woman's hands down to the arms of the chair. Vasson saw that they hadn't tied her by the wrists but across the width of the hands. Vasson moved his tongue around his mouth to remove the dryness.

The chant again. 'Where is the girl?'

The moan again.

They leant forward and each took a forefinger. Slowly they bent the forefingers backwards. The old woman's bloody eyes stared in disbelief, then she cried out, a loud shriek that filled the room. Suddenly she convulsed, her body arching upwards, straining against the cords, and she screamed, a long long, shrill, piercing scream. Vasson put his hands over his ears. The scream ceased. For a split second there was silence. Then there was an audible snap, quickly followed by another, and Vasson stared curiously at the two fingers. Though the men had moved away the fingers were still upright, at a strange angle to the hands.

The old woman's head had fallen back against the chair and she groaned, a long, low moan of despair.

'Where's the girl?'

The mouth dropped open again and tried to speak. Nothing happened. The old woman began to shake her head from side to side, first slowly then more rapidly until the movement became frenetic, like a mad animal's. Vasson felt uncomfortable and looked away. Suddenly the old woman's head dropped forward and he realised she was unconscious.

Baum shifted his weight and leant the other elbow on the mantelpiece. He said something in rapid German then turned to Vasson. 'We're getting nowhere.' The muscles in his jaw fluttered under the unnaturally pink skin. He said with irritation, 'What's so sickening is to think that this whole business need never have happened!'

Vasson snapped, 'But if your men had covered the beach properly, they would never have got away! *And* –' He stood up '– if the scientist had been properly guarded by the Navy, then he would never have escaped in the first place!'

Baum glared at Vasson and whispered, 'Don't get clever with me, you little pimp!' He raised a forefinger. 'And don't go spreading dirt behind my back. Just try, *just try* – and I'll carve you into little pieces, little pimp!'

Vasson smiled briefly. 'Don't get yourself in a state, my friend. We'll just have to find a way. What about the old man? The woman's husband?'

Baum rolled his eyes with exasperation. 'Yes! Yes! But *where* is he now? Eh? I do not see him here, do I?' He put a hand over his eyes and rubbed his forehead.

Baum was right. They had nothing. Personally Vasson didn't care a damn – he was fed up with the whole job – but there was bound to be a scapegoat and he had the unpleasant feeling that Baum would try to nail the whole mess on him.

Wearily, Vasson sat down and lit a cigarette, thinking: It's all that bitch's fault; it's she who's fouled the whole thing up.

The old woman groaned. Baum nibbled at one of his nails, roused himself, and nodded to his men. They moved in towards the chair.

Simultaneously, there was the sound of boots crossing the front room. The door opened and a soldier appeared. He saluted and spoke to Baum in rapid German. The men looked quickly at Baum, their faces worried. Baum turned pink and looked apoplectic. There was a long silence, then Baum said very slowly in French, 'I thought you had *caught* these people!'

Vasson shifted on his seat and said carefully, 'Most of them, yes.'

Baum almost choked. 'Why, then, are my men being murdered?'

Vasson said sharply, 'Where? Where were your men killed?'

'One man. On the clifftop. Those filthy murdering swine . . .!'

Vasson sat up and thought: Good God, why would they want to get down to the beach again . . .? What on earth? Then he closed his eyes and swore quietly. There could only be one reason. Oh hell. He said out loud, '*Merde!*'

Baum looked at him quickly. 'What is it?'

'They were there all the time. On the beach.'

'Impossible –'

'They were there!'

Baum looked at him sourly. 'I don't see how –'

'Shut up!' Vasson thought quickly. He tried to imagine where the girl's friends would have taken her. He said, 'If they've escaped from the beach that means they must have gone into hiding again, somewhere nearby . . .'

'Ha!' Baum exclaimed contemptuously. 'But *where!*' He shook his head. 'I tell you, there's only one way to find out. We take hostages and we shoot them tomorrow. Twenty. No! Thirty. The families of these murderers. That's the only way!'

As Baum began to give orders, but Vasson knew it would take too *long! Too long!* If only he'd got the old woman's husband. It was much more likely that *he* would know. Damn, damn. So *nearly* there. He clenched his fist and swore under his breath.

There was a shout outside and the back door opened. A soldier came in, pulling the figure of a short, stocky man behind him. The man was sixty-ish and dressed in peasant's clothes.

As soon as the man saw the bent, bloody figure in the chair he threw himself at it, crying, 'Marie! Marie!' The old woman moaned and the man cried out, 'No! No!'

Suddenly, Vasson realised who the man was and laughed out loud. His prayers had been answered. That's what came of being lucky.

The old man was sobbing violently. Vasson wished Baum would put a stop to it.

Baum jerked his head at his men and they hauled the old man to his feet. 'Please, please!' The old man was still sobbing. 'Please, leave my wife alone! Please! She knows nothing! Nothing!'

Baum leant against the mantelpiece and waited.

'Please – I am giving myself up because she knows nothing, nothing ... Please leave her alone!' The old man was panting shaking his head from side to side.

Baum said calmly, 'And you know something?'

The old man nodded slowly, his eyes tightly closed. Then he stopped moving, his body sagging between the two men. 'Yes – I will tell you what you want to know.'

'Excellent.' Baum looked at his fingernails again, smiling slightly. 'Is the girl with the scientist?'

'Yes.'

'Where are they?'

'On a fishing boat.'

There was a pause. The smile had vanished from Baum's face. 'Where is this fishing boat?'

'At sea. But I don't know where it's going.'

'You don't know where it's going.'

'No, they didn't tell me.'

'I see,' Baum said stiffly. 'You realise we will extract the information from you one way or the other.'

The old man nodded furiously. 'Yes, yes. Please, it's the truth, they didn't tell me. I suppose England, but I don't know where exactly . . .'

Vasson said, 'Of course England! Where else would they go!'

The old man looked at Vasson for the first time, trying to understand who he was.

Vasson said, 'The girl, she used to live there, didn't she?'

The old man nodded again.

'Of course England!' Vasson snorted. 'Who else was on the boat?'

'I'm not sure . . .'

'The scientist, Freymann?'

There was a pause. 'Yes.'

'And the boy?'

The old man whispered, 'Yes', and began to weep.

'No-one else?'

'I don't know. I only heard about those three. That's all I know. Please believe me. And please, leave my wife alone. Please!' He looked at Tante Marie and, sobbing bitterly, tried to reach her again, but they held him back.

Baum came up to Vasson. 'If it's not the truth I'll get it out of him.'

'But suppose it is.'

Baum clenched his teeth and said unhappily, 'I will have to notify High Command and alert the coastal units. They can't have got far!'

Vasson thought: I hope you're right.

Baum turned away but Vasson caught his sleeve. 'The old man. He'll be shot, won't he?'

Baum blinked. 'In the end.'

Vasson nodded. 'Make it soon. He's seen my face.'

The telephone jangled loudly. Doenitz woke up and blinked. The room was in darkness. He guessed it was about one. So much for catching up on some sleep. He sat up and reached for the receiver.

The voice of his staff man said, 'Berlin, Herr Grossadmiral. Reichsmarschall Goering calling.'

Doenitz turned on the light. There were voices on the line, then clicks. Absent-mindedly Doenitz smoothed down the blanket. Finally Goering's voice said, 'Ah! Admiral Doenitz?'

'Good evening, Herr Reichsmarschall.'

'Herr Admiral. And how is Paris? How I envy you your little trips there. So much beauty! And so quiet, so quiet!' Quiet, Doenitz supposed, must mean there was no bombing, which was true enough.

Goering went on, 'Yes, how I wish we could all take our command posts to Paris . . .' The words were slurred. Doenitz sighed under his breath: the Reichsmarschall was heavily drugged again.

'. . . Very soon, of course, life will be quieter in Berlin,' Goering continued, 'but we must get this radar business under way.' Doenitz wondered where the conversation was leading to. He murmured a noncommittal, 'Indeed.'

'. . . A scientist we need has been *lost* by Himmler's idiots. We must get him back. He's at sea –'

'At sea?' Doenitz asked incredulously. Goering began a long, rambling explanation. As it proceeded, Doenitz felt his blood run cold. He could see what was coming.

Goering said finally, 'So we must get this person back. A search will have to be mounted. How soon can you arrange it, dear fellow?'

'I cannot!' Doenitz retorted. 'It's out of the question! It would be like looking for a needle in a haystack! Even if I had any units available, it would be a complete waste of time –'

'But I don't think you understand, Herr Admiral – the Fuehrer himself has ordered the search. The matter is absolutely vital! You have S-boats, don't you? And your enormous fleet of U-boats. Something can be spared, surely, for what is after all a vital matter?'

Doenitz squeezed the receiver hard. He said tightly, 'I will consider what is appropriate when I receive the order direct from Fuehrer Headquarters.'

'Of course, dear fellow. The order will be sent directly, I'm sure.'

Goering had never called him dear fellow before. Doenitz realised that this must be really important to him. If that was the case . . . Doenitz said levelly, 'When – if – I receive this order, I will insist on air support. Several patrols will be needed to locate the fishing vessel. Then, and only then, might it be possible . . .'

The thick voice interrupted, 'My dear fellow, you know that this cannot be done. The Luftwaffe's resources are fully stretched. We have to defend Germany, first and foremost. And the English Channel . . . well, I cannot spare *anything* . . .'

Oh no, Doenitz thought, I'm not going to let you get away with it this time. He said briskly, 'Without air support I cannot hope to find this vessel. In fact, I would almost certainly fail! I *must* have air support!'

There was a short silence. 'A reconnaissance aircraft then . . .' The voice was grudging. 'I'll see what's available. After all, I wish to help as much as possible. The Fuehrer is most anxious, you see . . . most anxious . . .' The voice became brighter. 'You'll find this scientist for us, won't you, Doenitz?'

It was an impossible question. Doenitz said tightly, 'I'll see what can be done.'

'Good. Remember, we *need* him. Got to sort out this radar business, haven't we? Essential to get it right, essential. You do appreciate that, don't you?'

'Yes,' Doenitz sighed. Of course he appreciated it – how could he fail to? Two more U-boats had disappeared the day before. He added, 'This scientist – why is he so vital?'

Goering laughed. 'Ah! He worked on this new kind of radar, a long time ago. He understands it. He'll save us a lot of time!'

A suspicion flashed into Doenitz's mind. 'And his name? What's his name?'

'Ah . . . One moment.' There was a pause, then, 'Um, Freymann. Yes, Freymann. A Jew – but there we are!'

Doenitz closed the conversation and replaced the receiver. Freymann! So . . . He had escaped and Goering wanted him back. Or rather, it must be *Schmidt* who wanted him back. If the Chief Scientist was so anxious to have Freymann that he was prepared to put the matter to Hitler himself, then Freymann must be really vital. Schmidt must have realised that Freymann had been on the right track all along, from the beginning . . . Memories of a day long ago came into Doenitz's mind: the trials ship, the strange, tubby little man and the wild ideas tossed about like sparks from a firework.

Sighing, he got up and pulled his uniform jacket on over the shirt and trousers he already wore. He remembered that Freymann had been based at a naval establishment. God forbid that the Navy were responsible for letting him escape! He finished buttoning the jacket and went into the adjacent room. His staff officer jumped to his feet. Doenitz said, 'I am expecting an order from Fuehrer Headquarters. Bring it to me the moment it arrives. In the meantime please tell Admiral Kohl that I wish to meet him in the Plotting room in two minutes.' Protocol had to be observed. Admiral Kohl was C-in-C Gruppe West and this was his command post. Doenitz was a visitor here.

Doenitz waited one minute, then descended to the plotting room. He should wait for the Fuehrer-Command, but there was no harm in discussing the strategy. Anyway, he knew very well that the command would come. Goering had sounded very certain.

When he entered the plotting room there was a slight hush, then Admiral Kohl and his staff detached themselves from their work and followed him to the vast plotting tables. Doenitz stared at the array of wooden shapes that marked the positions of convoys and of each German vessel presently in the Atlantic. The black shapes representing U-boats were spread out far across the ocean, from the Mediterranean to the Caribbean, from the Cape Verde Islands to Iceland. Never before had there been so many U-boats at sea: a hundred and ten out of a total fleet of almost four hundred. The fleet was at last approaching the sort of size that Doenitz had always pressed for.

However there was not a single U-boat in the English Channel. The only vessels anywhere near were the *Schnellboote*, the fast torpedo boats with bases at Cherbourg and Guernsey.

The S-boats first then.

Admiral Kohl was waiting patiently. Doenitz said quietly, 'We are mounting a special operation. We are looking for a fishing boat which left this region, somewhere around the Morlaix River.' He took a pointer and placed it on the North Brittany coast. 'It left at some time this evening. We do not know the exact time. The craft is making for the English coast. Again, we do not know where exactly. But we must make every effort to find this vessel.'

There was silence. Doenitz could feel the officers exchanging glances behind his back. Eventually Kohl said, 'There are the S-boats. They would be our best bet.' He said over his shoulder, 'Werner, find out how many S-boats are operational at Cherbourg and Guernsey.'

Doenitz stared at the massive chart. 'I wish I could tell you course and speed, but apparently this is not available either . . .'

Kohl took the hint straight away. 'Well, I'm sure we can make an estimate. Is the fishing boat motor-powered, Herr Grossadmiral?'

'Unlikely . . . Unless they have managed to steal considerable amounts of fuel. And I believe the fishing fleet is searched regularly for excess supplies . . .' Doenitz looked questioningly at an intelligence officer, who nodded in confirmation. 'So,' Doenitz continued, 'I would imagine it's using sail.'

Kohl looked to one side. 'Braun! What's the weather situation?'

There was a rustle of paper. 'Channel area . . . Yes, north-easterly, Herr Admiral. Ten knots, increasing later, possibly veering to the north.'

Doenitz frowned. 'North-easterly . . .'

'Common in March, Herr Grossadmiral. The equinox.'

'Mmm. So – what speed?'

'Four knots?'

Doenitz nodded. 'Yes, I agree.'

Kohl went on, 'Course . . . it would have to be west of north. The best port to make for would be Falmouth. Otherwise . . . Well, there's nothing else west of there. No other major harbours. It would have to be Falmouth.'

Doenitz stared at the chart. The boat certainly couldn't hope to lay due north and reach Plymouth. So Kohl was right. The only major port on a north-westerly course was Falmouth. To the west of that was the Lizard, Land's End, then . . . He glanced further west to the Scillies, then brought his eyes back to Falmouth. He said, 'Yes, Falmouth. So – if the boat set out say at eleven, it should be somewhere around here by now.' He pointed at a point some six miles off the coast. He turned to Kohl. 'How long before it gets out of S-boat patrol range, would you think?'

Kohl frowned. 'Well, we don't usually operate S-boats beyond forty miles from the coast at this point . . . Enemy air patrols have been very heavy . . .'

'Forty miles . . . We have only until dawn, then. The escaper will be thirty to forty miles off by then . . .'

Kohl nodded slowly.

Doenitz said abruptly, 'So the S-boats won't be much use to us!'

Kohl blew out his cheeks. 'The Luftwaffe . . . I suppose there is no hope of an air patrol?'

Doenitz kept his eyes on the table. 'We have been promised air reconnaissance, yes.'

No-one spoke. They had been promised air support countless times before. It rarely turned up. And when it did the planes usually had very limited range.

'But even if we do receive air support, that will not be enough,' Doenitz said grimly. 'So we will have to deploy additional units . . .'

Doenitz waited for Kohl to suggest the only solution, but he did not. Eventually Doenitz said, 'We'll have to send a U-boat.'

Kohl sighed deeply and asked quietly, 'Is it really that vital, Herr Grossadmiral?'

Doenitz nodded. 'Yes, I'm afraid it is.'

There were no brass bands any more, no garlands either. Nowadays the boats arrived and left as quietly as possible, sliding in and out of their dark, dank pens like snakes from a hole. Nor did the men smile any more: many of the old guard had gone now, long buried in their tomb-ships. The fresh recruits had never learnt to smile: they were too frightened.

Except for Fischer's men. Fischer's men thought their commander was as close to God as anyone could get because he had kept them alive so long and because they believed that, after all this time, he would keep them alive for ever. Quite simply, they believed in him.

It was one of the reasons Fischer couldn't sleep any more, even when he was desperately tired. No-one could sleep with that kind of responsibility.

He felt tired now, and the patrol had only just begun.

They were heading south-west from Brest, beginning a long loop

402

out towards the North Atlantic. U-319 was travelling on the surface in company with two other submarines. The idea was that, in a group of three, the boats had a reasonable chance of fighting their way out of an air attack. In the event Fischer doubted that all three boats would actually escape a concerted attack – more like two. If that. The air patrols were efficient, heavy, and, if anything, getting worse.

He looked at the chart in front of him. Only sixty miles out. It should have been more but they'd left late: U-64 had been delayed with engine trouble. That meant they wouldn't be clear of the Bay by dawn . . .

The Bay. The Black Pit. Ever wider, ever deeper. Like everything else it got more difficult to face, more difficult to cross. The Happy Time was long gone.

Not that the kills weren't high – far from it. But Fischer sensed a desperation about the whole business that hadn't been there before: the satisfaction, the excitement, had gone.

'Herr Kaleu, Flotilla HQ are signalling.'

Fischer hurried over to the wireless area. The operator was typing a long signal into the Enigma cipher machine, his assistant copying down the deciphered letters as they appeared on the machine. Fischer peered over their shoulders, and his heart quickened. It was a personal signal from Doenitz. Fischer smiled. Just like the old days!

He began to read the body of the message and a small frown appeared on his face. When the staccato sound of the Morse ceased and the operator had typed in the last of the signal Fischer reached forward and picked up the sheet carrying the completed message. He read it again slowly, from the top.

It began in Doenitz's usual informal way: DOENITZ HERE. GOOD TO SPEAK TO YOU AGAIN, FISCHER. IT'S BEEN A LONG TIME.

Then came details of a special operation. *Imperative*, Doenitz called it. U-319 to abandon her patrol and proceed with all speed to search the following area – map references were given – to intercept a fishing boat believed to be at H17 P15 – another map reference – at 0100 hours, and now believed proceeding at 4 knots under sail on approximate course 330. Possible destination H24 P23. Occupants of boat to be captured but not harmed.

It was repeated that the orders were urgent and immediate. After acknowledgement U-319 was to maintain radio silence except in emergency. Doenitz signed off: IF ANYONE CAN DO IT, YOU CAN.

Fischer tried to absorb the information, to work out what it all meant. But however he looked at it, the whole thing was incredible.

He went to the chart table to check the map references, but he'd already worked out the rough position. The middle of the bloody English Channel.

If anyone but Doenitz had asked him he would have queried it, asked for confirmation, more information. But Doenitz had guessed all that – which was why he'd asked Fischer personally. *If anyone can do it, you can.* Fischer thought: I hope you're right.

Fischer went back to the wireless operator and dictated a reply: U-319 WILL PROCEED IMMEDIATELY. I WILL TRY MY BEST.

Back at the chart table he pulled out the large-scale chart of the English Channel and checked the map references again. The references were used by the Kriegsmarine for security reasons. Triton, the U-boat cypher, was, of course, secure and the Enigma machine itself invulnerable, but, where vital information on the positions of German vessels was concerned, the references were an additional safeguard.

Fischer thought again: Incredible. What a hell of a job!

The search area lay between thirty and forty miles south-south-east of the southernmost point of the English mainland – the headland known as the Lizard.

Fischer drew a line between the last estimated position of the – he almost called it 'target' then corrected himself – of the *prey*, and the given destination, the port of Falmouth, which lay to the north-east of the Lizard. Where the line intersected the search area he drew a cross.

He turned to the navigating officer, hovering at his shoulder, and said, 'A course, please, to *there*.'

The navigator bent over the chart. Fischer said to his first officer, '*Eins WO*, a signal please to U-64 and U-402. Tell them we have new orders and are leaving them directly.'

He returned to the chart. 'How far to the search point?'

'One hundred and ten miles exactly.'

Fischer calculated how long it would take to do the distance. On the surface, flat out at seventeen knots, seven hours. He looked at his watch: 0130. Dawn was at 0700 roughly. Not enough time. At dawn he'd have to submerge and he'd still be sixteen odd miles short of the search point. Still, he'd be in the right area and it wouldn't take long to complete the distance, even at the paltry seven knots they did under the surface. So, on target at about 0930.

Not bad. If this fishing craft was really doing four knots then they should be there well ahead of it. Even if it was doing six knots, they'd still be all right.

'Drop clear astern of U-64 and then turn to starboard on the course –?'

'008 degrees, Herr Kaleu, until abeam of Ushant.'

'Course 008.' The order was repeated by the first officer and the coxswain.

Fischer looked round for the Chief. He was standing in the after section of the control room. 'Chief, I'm going to need everything. Seventeen knots if you can manage it.'

The chief tried to frown, but Fischer could see that he was pleased. He liked a challenge. 'Right, Herr Kaleu. I'll see what I can do.' He disappeared in the direction of the engine room.

'Tell me when we're on course, *Eins WO*.'

After a few minutes the confirmation came. Fischer gave the order for full speed ahead.

The order was repeated through the control room. The whine of the diesels rose to a steady din and Fischer felt the vibration run through the boat. He ordered extra vigilance from the lookouts, then, with nothing further to be done, returned to the chart table to stare at the wide expanse of white paper that marked the English Channel.

It was a long time since he'd taken a U-boat into the Channel – it was a long time since anyone had. The British controlled it too effectively. He wondered what he'd find there – the lot probably: air patrols, motor torpedo boats, minesweepers . . .

Too much, far too much. There was only one point in U-319's favour: the British wouldn't be expecting anyone to take a U-boat into the waters where submarines had been proved so vulnerable. They wouldn't believe anyone could be so stupid.

It wasn't much of an advantage. But it was all he had.

From the outside the building looks solid and impenetrable – but not enormous. Certainly not large enough to house the operational headquarters of the British Admiralty. That is because most of the building is underground, a warren of subterranean rooms protected from bombing by concrete walls and roofs several feet thick. Not surprisingly, the building is called the Citadel. It lies in the heart of London, next to the main Admiralty buildings, to which it is connected by underground passages. Deep within it are two largish adjoining chambers which resemble billiard rooms. Both contain tables about nine feet square on which are enormous charts overhung by brilliant lights which shine day and night. In the first room is the Main Plot where Allied surface movements – both Allied and enemy – are plotted, as well as relevant air activity. Next door is the Submarine Tracking Room. Its sole purpose is to track enemy submarine movements in the Atlantic.

And, despite German beliefs to the contrary, it does it remarkably well.

On this occasion the night watch keeper was busy. Although the main interpretation of the data was carried out by the day staff, a lot of information came in during the night and it was his job to decide if there was anything requiring immediate attention, and to generally sort things out ready for analysis in the morning.

He had a staff of three. They were sifting information into groups according to the known facts. They had five sources of information: sightings, aircraft radar fixes, radio direction finding, Special Intelligence, and tracking using a combination of all available information. Radio direction finding was very efficient as long as the U-boat transmitted for long enough. Then the various stations around the country could take cross-bearings on the signal and obtain a fix.

But it was the euphemistically named Special Intelligence which really nailed the U-boats. Also known as Ultra, the information came from Bletchley Park, the Government Code and Cipher School. No-one outside Bletchley Park really knew how the boffins had cracked the German codes, but cracked them they had, though it usually took them a day – sometimes more – to decipher the signals. Once, some months before, the Germans had changed their codes and there had been a hiatus while the ciphers were broken, but then, after a while, the information had come filtering through again.

Sometimes the deciphered signals arrived in a matter of hours. Then the ex-lawyer who headed the department acted quickly, passing information to the naval and air commands and diverting convoys from the path of the waiting wolf packs – when the politicians allowed. Sometimes they did *not* allow, fearful that the Germans would awake to the fact that their codes had been broken.

More often than not it was twenty-four hours before information came through, a time when the Head of Department had to take decisions and make calculated guesses as to what the U-boats might be doing. When the information finally appeared it was amazing how often the Head's hunches proved correct. He was an astonishing man.

For the third time in an hour the watchkeeper leafed through the decoded Ultra signals that had come in at 0200. Nothing out of the ordinary. Routine signals from headquarters. Brief acknowledgements from the U-boats. He had checked the U-boats' call-signs against those known to be at sea. They all tallied.

A teleprincess – one of the girls from the telex and communications room – came in and put a telex in front of him. It was from Bletchley Park: a decoded message sent to U-boat headquarters by an escort vessel. At 2300 the escort had reported dropping three U-boats at

T3, the buoy which marked the end of the swept channel leading out of Brest. The U-boats concerned were U-64, U-402 and U-319.

The watchkeeper got up and, taking three tokens, marked them with the U-boats' numbers. He calculated the approximate distance the U-boats would have travelled since 2300 and placed the tokens on the plot, some fifty miles west of Brest.

U-319. He knew that number. Even before he looked it up on the list he remembered that it was Fischer's boat. Yes, there she was: U-319, Commander: Karl Fischer, Flotilla: Ninth, Base: Brest.

Fischer was well known. A very successful skipper, a German hero. He'd been around a long time.

The watchkeeper only wished he knew where the blighter was heading for. Sometimes one didn't find out until too late. Sometimes one never found out at all.

He returned to his desk. Almost immediately the telephone rang. It was Bletchley Park. He listened carefully, asked a couple of questions, and replaced the receiver. He stood up and stared thoughtfully at the plot.

U-boat headquarters had sent an unusually long message on the Atlantic U-boat frequency. The message had only just been intercepted and wouldn't be decoded for some hours yet, but it had had an urgent priority prefix. That was sufficiently unusual for Bletchley to call him.

Something was up then. The watchkeeper wondered what it could be. Perhaps German Intelligence had discovered the position of a convoy, perhaps a new strategy was being implemented . . .

He stared at the plot as if it could tell him the answer. But there was only one thing that could do that – the decode.

And that, as always, took time.

27

NxW. North by West . . . Where on earth was it! It had *disappeared* again.

Julie peered at the dimly-lit compass card and tried to read the letters. The boat lurched and she put up a hand to brace herself against the post that held the compass.

Come on! Which way? Which way?

Think. It was showing W – West. North was to the right. Therefore she wanted the card to swing – which way? She almost shouted with frustration: it was impossible to work out.

Frantically, she pulled the tiller towards her and watched the card. It hesitated then swung slowly towards North.

She breathed a sigh of relief, then made herself concentrate again. NxW. North by West.

NxW for one hour. Don't forget. NxW – North by West.

The problem was the compass. It wouldn't stay still. It kept swaying from side to side. And it moved in the opposite direction to the one you expected. The tiller did too!

NxW for one hour then you'll be safe.

Then you'll be safe . . . So there must be dangers either side, rocks, shoals, islands . . . She remembered on placid summer days seeing the rocks in the estuary and, further out, black towers marking hidden plateaus.

She gulped and gritted her teeth and concentrated again on the swinging card. However hard she tried it was absolutely impossible to keep it straight on NxW. The best she could do was to keep NxW in the centre of the swing. Even then, if she took her eyes away for a moment, it seemed to dive away.

She jerked the tiller towards her and realised the card was swinging the wrong way. 'Dear God!' She shoved the tiller away and the 'N' shot round towards the front of the compass. Too far! She yanked at the tiller again until NxW hovered for a moment on the marker before swinging inexorably away. She shouted out loud, 'Damn you!'

She closed her eyes tightly for a moment and made an effort to clear her mind.

She opened her eyes, breathed deeply and concentrated again. At last the compass evened out somewhere around NxW. She remembered something Richard had said, about boats having a feel to them, a balance . . . There was none that she could sense, none at all!

A sound floated back, a whimper . . . She peered towards the middle of the boat. 'Peter? Peter! Are you all right, darling?'

'Mummy!' The voice was tearful. 'Mummy, I'm awfully cold!'

'Yes, darling, I know. But –' Could she leave the tiller and get to him? No – it was too risky, even for a moment. She shouted, 'Darling, try to get under the deck at the front. And – look in your bag –'

'What?' His voice was faint, plaintive.

The course had veered again; Julie jerked at the tiller. 'Your bag, darling. Look inside it. There's another sweater somewhere!'

'What?'

Julie gripped the tiller and tried not to scream. She shouted angrily, 'Just do as I say and don't argue!'

There was a silence, then, 'I've got it.'

Julie calmed herself down. She said steadily, 'Take off your jacket and put on the sweater, then crawl up – No! Put the jacket back on *first, then* crawl up to the front. It'll be warmer there. Tell me when you get there.'

'All right.'

For an instant Julie wondered what had happened to the old man: he was very quiet. She thought of calling to him, then decided against it. Later. She had too much to think about now.

The boat moved suddenly and Julie reached for the post again, her heart lurching with fear. The waves – they were a little larger, she was sure of it. She shivered violently and looked quickly down at the compass. The boat was miles off course. She jerked at the tiller and thought: This is hopeless, *hopeless*! I can't *possibly* manage this on my own! God, why did Michel think I could!

If only there was someone else!

Richard . . . Best of all, *Richard* – why couldn't *he* be here? He would know exactly what to do. He must have been through lots of experiences like this. The thought encouraged her a little. She tried to remember other things he had told her about sailing, things that might help . . . But she could remember nothing very useful: he'd talked about compasses and courses – but he'd never explained how you actually held a course, far less how you managed the sails . . .

Peter's small voice floated back on the wind. 'Mummy, I'm here!' In the front, presumably.

Julie shouted, 'Try to go to sleep now, darling.'

'All right.'

She looked down at the compass. Good Lord: it actually read NxW. She giggled a little hysterically.

The night was so dark it was impossible to see anything clearly. The sky was slightly less dark than the sea – but that was all. Julie stared ahead, trying to make out shapes – something, anything. But there was no distance, no perspective and after a while the blackness seemed to rear up in front of her like a wall.

Quickly, she looked back at the compass. NW. She pulled the tiller towards her. NNW. Then, a sudden swing to N. She pushed the tiller away again. NxW – at last. *Stay there!*

She glanced up again, and shivered. It was eerie, the darkness. Unnerving. It made her feel utterly remote, like being on a hilltop, quite alone. And then there was the silence. Though it was broken by the whisper of the wind and the swishing of the water and the occasional slap of a wave on the boat's side, it was eerie too.

She shivered again, and couldn't stop. With faint surprise she realised she was terribly cold. No time to get more clothes on. Later. Later.

NxW for an hour – then you'll be safe.

How much time had passed? She had no idea. It felt like hours. She looked at her watch, but it was far too dark to read it. She put her wrist down to the compass and, leaning forward, tried to see the hands by the reflection of the compass light. The thing was a stupid woman's watch: it had a tiny face without numbers. Useless! She put her face closer. At last she thought she saw the hands. Midnight –?

An hour gone!

The compass had sheered violently off. She pulled on the tiller. Damn! Wrong way! Why did the blasted thing have to work *backwards*!

There: NxW. She put her wrist to the compass again and, steadying the boat, thrust her face down to the flickering light. It took half a minute to be sure, but yes: it was almost midnight. Nearly an hour gone! She'd wait another ten minutes to be on the safe side. Perhaps even more, to be absolutely sure. Then – ! She felt the beginnings of relief. Over the first hurdle. Something anyway, to have got this far.

Half-smiling, half-miserable, she thought: Richard would be proud of me!

Then she remembered where he was and the despair settled on her like a lead weight.

Don't . . . Don't think . . .

Mechanically she glanced at the compass.

It wasn't there.

Her heart went to her mouth. She gulped. It had gone – the *light*! The light had gone!

There wasn't a flicker. She said out loud, 'No! Dear God!' And, clamping her hand over her mouth, thought: What on earth do I do *now*!

Relight the oil? But she had no match.

Think. What had Michel said? He'd mentioned something . . . A torch. Yes! Where? In a box. That was it, he'd said it was in a box. She knelt down, one hand still on the tiller, and felt around. Nothing. The other side, then. Floorboards . . . a rope . . . Further behind . . .

Her hand came to an upright wooden surface. She felt up to a top lip and a lid. It was a box, full of things: rough ropes, a square metal box, then – a round metal object. She almost cried out in triumph.

Standing up again, she found the switch and a narrow beam of yellow light shot forward into the darkness. She was half-blinded. Fumbling she switched it off again. Far too bright.

She reached down into the box again and scrabbled around. At last she found a piece of cloth and, putting it over the torch, turned it on again, being careful to keep the beam pointing downwards. That was much better: the beam was reduced to a dull pool of light. She shone it at the compass. Not bad! Only NNW! She pulled the tiller towards her and the card swung back towards NxW. At last.

She switched off the torch. Mustn't waste the batteries.

She let her body sag. The boat leaned slightly and she stepped backwards to regain her balance. The back of her knees came up against something hard and, feeling with her hand, she realised it was a seat. Of course: a seat for the helmsman. She sank back on to it and wedged her foot up against the compass post. It was much more comfortable

She almost laughed.

She wondered if the full hour and a quarter had passed. Probably not: best to wait.

She tried to concentrate on the steering, to keep on course without having to shine the light too much. Sometimes it worked, sometimes not. Most of the time she just stared forward, trying not to see the darkness rearing up in front of her.

Finally she shone the torch on her watch. It was twenty past twelve. She clenched her fists and, looking up, said, 'Thank you, God!' She almost shouted the news to Peter, but decided not to: he was probably asleep by now.

What now? *Then anything between north-north-west and north-east . . . Or was it north-west and north-east?*

She couldn't remember.

. . . No, he'd definitely said between NNW and NE.

Julie felt into the box for some rope and, resting the tiller against her knee, unwound a coil. Her fingers were dreadfully stiff from the cold and from gripping the tiller so tight. Eventually she managed to tie a loop on to the tiller. She went to the side of the boat and felt along it for an anchor point. She found one on the top of the rail: a wooden thing with a point sticking out either end. She'd seen them used for tying up ropes before. She took the rope and wound it several times round the wooden thing, which had a name she couldn't remember.

Next she took the other end of the rope to the other side of the boat and tied it to another wooden anchor point. She shone the torch on the compass and watched. NNW moving towards NW. She let off one side of the rope and tightened the other, to move the tiller slightly across. The course held steady on NW. She loosened the right-hand rope a little more. The course came up to NNW and she tightened it again. The course was holding. More or less.

Taking the torch she quickly made her way along the left side of the boat towards the front. She knelt down under the small expanse of decking and shone the shaded torch on to the floor. In the reflected light she saw Peter, curled in a ball, sleeping peacefully. She felt his cheek: warm enough, but not as warm as she'd like.

She shone the torch around and saw, right in the point at the front, some dark material folded under a lobster pot. She crawled forward and pulled the material out. It was a sack. Under it was another. She went on pulling until she had four. She crawled back and put two over Peter.

Now the old man. He must be on the right-hand side somewhere. She was still blinded from using the torch and waited until her eyes readjusted to the darkness. Then she saw him: a dark shape huddled under the steep side of the boat. She went over and knelt down beside him.

He was very still. She asked tentatively, 'Are you all right?'

Silence. Julie reached out and touched his arm.

There was a slight moan. She thought: Thank goodness, at least he's alive! 'Are you all right?' she repeated.

'Eh? Oh . . .' The old man's voice was low, rough. 'Oh . . . Yes, yes . . . I'm all right.' He tried to laugh. 'I'm just not as young as I used to be, that's all!'

'I'm so sorry, I didn't mean to wake you. I'm so sorry!'

'No, no, dear girl. Please . . . please don't apologise. I only wish I could help you. I'm of no use at all, I'm afraid. Perhaps later . . .' His voice was weak now, and breathless.

'No, you just stay there and rest. Don't worry about me. Honestly, I can manage! Here –' She put the two sacks over him. 'Are you comfortable here, or would you like to go up to the front? It's a bit more sheltered there.'

'No, thank you so much. I'm all right . . . Thank you.'

There was a loud slap: a wave against the side. Julie said sharply, 'I must go now – back to the steering . . . Just shout if you need me.'

And then she was gone. David pulled the sacks more tightly round his legs and wished he didn't feel so ill. He closed his eyes and leant his head back against the side. Immediately, he felt disorientated and his head began to swim. He opened his eyes again. The boat was

412

rocking gently from side to side. If it went on rocking, he thought grimly, he would be sick.

He burped slightly and felt a pang of acid in his stomach. So he was to suffer that too! His stomach chose its moments very well.

He closed his eyes and tentatively let his head fall to one side. He decided he would be more comfortable lying down. Taking the bag from round his waist, he felt in it and found his tablets. He took one and, putting the bag on the deck, lay down with his head on it. Yes: that was better. He didn't feel so sick, lying down. He might even be able to sleep.

He would feel better later. Then he would give Julie a hand.

Julie untied the tiller and brought the boat back on course. Almost immediately she sighed with annoyance: she'd forgotten to get a sweater. But perhaps it wasn't necessary; it didn't seem quite so cold as before . . . Then she remembered that awful time on the fishing boat, and something Richard had said, about cold being the greatest danger of all, much more dangerous than the waves themselves, and she retied the tiller and set off towards the front.

Her bag was beside Peter, right up under the deck. She supposed Michel had put it there in case it rained. She undid the strap and felt around until she found the thick wool sweater. She took off the cowjacket, pulled the sweater on, and put the cowjacket back over the top. She felt warmer already. There was a scarf in the bag too; she rummaged around, found it, and tied it round her head.

Peter was sleeping peacefully. She went straight back to the tiller. When she shone the torch on the compass she almost laughed: the course had settled on NxW. She decided to leave the boat sailing by itself; the course was a good one and much steadier than anything she could achieve.

She sat on the helmsman's seat and tried to think. How far was it across the Channel? She had no idea. How long would it take to get across? She had no idea of that either.

Brilliant!

Try again. It must be at least a hundred miles across the Channel – perhaps even two hundred. Say a hundred and fifty. How fast were they going? Goodness only knew! It felt as if the boat was going quite fast – perhaps fifteen miles an hour. No: on second thoughts, that was quite a rate. What was walking speed? Five miles an hour, four? A bit faster than that, say six then.

Six miles an hour. A hundred and fifty miles. Mental arithmetic: always one of her worst subjects at school. Sixes into one hundred and fifty . . .

Eventually she got there: twenty-five. Of course. Six twenty-fives made a hundred and fifty.

Twenty-five hours then, call it twenty-four.

Immediately she felt depressed.

It was a dreadfully long time. A whole day out in the middle of the sea, a day when they would be exposed like a goldfish in a bowl. There were bound to be German patrols . . . aircraft . . .

If they survived the day, then there'd be most of the next night, a night when the land would be getting closer and closer, rushing towards them. How on earth would she know where it was, the land? And how would she know when the boat was about to crash into it?

I can't do this, she thought, I just can't do it!

Silently she began to cry, the tears hot on her cheeks. It was all such a mess, the whole dreadful thing. Everyone at the village caught and dead or more probably tortured. Richard a prisoner. And here – Peter and the old man relying on *her*, probably the most incompetent person in the world!

Angrily, she wiped the tears away. Whatever happened, crying wouldn't do any good.

Later, she realised a long time must have passed – several hours at least. Apart from shining the torch on the compass from time to time she stared ahead into the darkness, her mind half on what had happened at the beach, half on the nightmare she was living through now. One event seemed to lead on from the other, in a horrible dreamlike way.

For a while she dozed, perched uneasily on the seat, terrible pictures drifting in and out of her mind, the beach and the boat blending into a terrible fantasy of water and blazing lights and anger and suffering. The Germans were taking everyone away . . . Jean, Tante Marie, and Peter, *even Peter* –

Suddenly she was awake.

She looked blindly around, wondering what had woken her. The boat was still sailing along, the water hissing and gurgling past the hull. But the sky was different. It was clearer now: there were stars, thousands of them, carpeting the sky so that the sail stood out black against them. But there was something else and she couldn't place it. She shone the light at the compass. NW – North-West. The course had changed a little. But was that it? No.

Then she had it. The wind, it was much fresher. She felt it cold against her face, pulling at her scarf. A muted fluttering sound came from above, like a thousand birds beating their wings. Now and then there was the creaking of wood against wood.

Yes, there was more wind. She could feel it now, in the motion of the boat. The movements were much quicker than before and, instead of rocking gently from side to side, the craft was tilted stiffly over at a slight angle, its nose going down and up, down and up, like a rocking horse.

The bow hit a wave with a *crump*! and Julie realised that it was the sound which had woken her. A fine spray floated back on the air and drifted onto her face. Shaking slightly, she shone the light at the compass again. Still north-west, but tending to veer off towards the west. Not good enough. She untied the tiller and moved it until the compass read nearer to North.

Immediately the fluttering sound changed to a flapping and there was a fierce rattling as something close to Julie's head started to shake angrily.

She yanked the tiller back the other way. The flapping stopped, but when she looked at the compass the course was back west of north-west. Michel had specifically said she must steer between north-north-west and north-east. She was definitely *outside* that.

What should she do? She gripped the tiller, undecided. She could leave the boat on this course – but that *must* be wrong. The sails, then, she should stop them flapping. But how?

She tried bringing the boat back onto a northerly course once more, but the flapping started again, louder than ever. 'Damn!' She quickly pulled the tiller the other way. The flapping stopped. She breathed out sharply.

She stayed at the tiller steering north-west for a long time, frozen with indecision. She should do something to the sails – she knew *that* much – but what? And if she didn't – God, she'd probably miss England all together.

Impossible.

Because there was nothing else to do, she held the north-westerly course, thinking all the time: I'm failing! Miserably failing!

Perhaps if she held on, perhaps the wind would change . . .

A long time passed. Dimly she realised that she could see the side of the boat stretching away from her. When she looked again the bow itself was there, a faint black smudge against grey. Then the sea itself – waves; she could see waves like the ripples on an iced cake, but grey and murky. To the right, a thin line of pale white light appeared, stretching across the horizon from side to side; with a slight shock, Julie realised it *was* the horizon. The white light filtered gradually up into the sky, turning a delicate crystal yellow, the colour of pale primrose. One by one the stars disappeared until the sky became a clear unbroken dome over her head.

Dawn. It had come too soon.

Instinctively, Julie looked behind, but she could see nothing – it was still too dark. She looked again a few minutes later. It was difficult to tell: the grey area between the sea and the sky was too indistinct.

Half an hour later the southern horizon was visible, a grey line behind the boat. She looked carefully: there was no land in sight. They were clear of the coast, then. That was something at least.

Then, as she looked at the vast expanse of water appearing around her, stretching out barren and cold in every direction, she didn't feel so glad. It looked enormous.

Up in the front Peter's figure was clearly visible, curled up under the sacks. He was sleeping soundly. So was the old man, over on the right-hand side, against the side of the boat. Good. There was no point in everyone being tired.

Wearily, Julie looked at the compass, visible now in the grey light. Still North-West. Still the *wrong* course.

She should do something about it . . .

She stayed frozen at the tiller a moment longer then made herself stand up. *Time to get going.*

She said out loud, 'Right!' Gritting her teeth, she tied up the tiller and eyed the ropes that were coiled or fastened at various points round the boat. There were two sails. The first, a big sail, almost square, was fastened to the mast on its front edge, to a long wooden pole on its lower edge and to another, shorter, pole high up on its top edge. The fourth – back – edge wasn't fastened to anything. Up in front of the mast, there was another, smaller sail, triangular and attached to a sharp piece of wood that stuck out in front of the boat. She remembered: the piece of wood was called a bowsprit.

The big sail first. There was one rope which seemed to make the sail go in or out. The rope wound back and forth between wooden pulleys. She wasn't sure why – to make things easier perhaps.

The rope was tied off round a wooden anchor thing – was it called a *fastener*? Tentatively she reached forward and began to untie the rope. She paused, her heart hammering against her chest, then, very slowly, began to take off the last turn.

Suddenly there was an almighty jerk and the rope almost flew out of her hands. She cried out and, holding on grimly, tried to get a second turn of rope back onto the anchor-fastener. As she moved her hands the rope jerked out, pulling her knuckle sharply against the hard wood of the fastener. She gasped out in pain.

God, the pain!

She let go.

The rope whistled out from the coil, snaking up angrily towards the sail. The next moment there was a thunderous noise: the racket of beating canvas and rattling pulleys. Julie looked up. The sail had gone mad; it was beating itself about in a frenzy, girating back and forth until the whole boat vibrated.

Julie stared, aghast.

What now?

She put her hands over her ears, to cut out the dreadful noise, and looked round in desperation.

There was still some rope left in the coil; it hadn't all run out. Shaking like a leaf, she reached down and picked up the rope and, cautiously, began to pull in on it.

'Mummy!'

Julie spun round. Peter was standing beside her, rubbing his eyes, and looking curiously up at the sail. 'Mummy, shouldn't we pull it in?'

Julie stared at him and shook her head. Then, trying to smile, said wearily, 'Yes, Peter, we should.'

'I'll help you, then!' He was shouting to make himself heard over the thrashing of the sail.

'Don't you dare touch it!' Julie screamed. 'Just – leave it!'

There was no reply and, looking down, she saw that he was looking hurt and shame-faced. She sighed, 'Sorry, I'm just tired, sweetheart, that's all. I'll be all right in a moment.' She wiped her eyes on her sleeve and said ruefully, 'The trouble is, I don't know *how* to get the sail in.'

'You put the rope under the cleat.'

'The cleat?'

'Yes.' Peter pointed at the wooden anchor-fastener thing. 'That's what it's called – a cleat. Richard told me. And I know you put the ropes round it to take the strain. That's what he said . . .' He trailed off.

'Thank you, darling!' She almost kissed him. 'Let's have a go then!'

She picked up the rope and, with Peter tugging rather ineffectually behind, began to pull. Soon the rope was jerking in her hands. She leant down and slid the rope under the lower arm of the cleat. Alternately she pulled and rested, letting the cleat take the strain of the rope. The clattering of the sail lessened slightly.

Then she had the idea of standing on the other side of the deck, so that the rope was doubled back from the cleat. It was a great improvement: the rope seemed less inclined to jerk out of her hands.

The pull on the rope became much stronger and, though she put her full weight against it, she couldn't get it in any further. She rested for a moment, panting.

417

Suddenly the noise got much worse again. Julie looked up, bewildered, then realised the rope had gone almost limp in her hand. She pulled wildly, gathering in great lengths of it, until she could pull no more. Quickly, she tied the rope off round the cleat.

The noise stopped; the sail was full again. She waited. After a few moments the flapping started again. Quickly she pulled in on the rope.

She looked up at the sail: it was almost tight in!

Elated, she tied off the rope securely and looked at the compass. North by West – or thereabouts! And the sail full: a miracle.

How it had happened she had no idea. Then the flapping started again and she saw that the tiller had become untied. Perhaps that was something to do with it.

She took hold of the tiller, put the boat back on course, and grinned at Peter. What did it matter how it had happened? She'd got the sail in *and* the boat on course.

She went forward and hunted for the rope that controlled the other, smaller, sail at the front. She found it and, eyeing the sail with trepidation, undid the rope. It didn't have nearly so much pull on it and she was able to haul it in quite easily.

Returning to the tiller she undid the lines that tied it and said gaily to Peter, 'I'll make a sailor yet!'

The child smiled back and, coming to her side, put his hand in hers. 'Mummy, I'm hungry. Is there any breakfast?'

Julie's heart sank. Breakfast. She'd never thought of breakfast. Her smile vanished. Had Michel said anything about food? Water, yes, he'd definitely mentioned that. But food? No.

She sighed. How did one tell a six-year-old that there was nothing to eat? She said softly, 'There isn't any breakfast, darling. Sorry.' She took a deep breath. 'We're going to have to go without until we get to England. Sorry.' She squeezed his hand.

'Without – anything?' The voice was small and subdued.

Julie looked away and tried to sound brisk and matter-of-fact. 'Without anything. We finished all the food when we were on the beach, remember?'

'Perhaps there's some on the boat somewhere . . .'

She sighed. It was very unlikely. 'Perhaps. Why don't you go and have a look, eh?'

He nodded brightly and, dropping to his knees, started rooting around in the large box where Julie had found the torch.

It would, at least, keep him busy for a while.

A movement caught her eye: the old man was leaning over the side of the boat, his head down, as if staring at the water. For a moment

Julie couldn't think what he was doing then she heard a faint retching sound and looked quickly away.

She'd quite forgotten about being sick. Extraordinary. She couldn't understand why it hadn't happened to *her*.

There was a *crump*! from the bow and a thin veil of spray came flying back into her face. More wind: definitely more wind. The tiller felt different in her hand: it was moving of its own accord and she had to push harder to get the boat back on course. The boat was going faster, too, haring along like the wind. Perhaps her calculations had been wrong; perhaps they'd get to England before nightfall. The idea of more wind made her very nervous but it might be a blessing after all.

There was a whoop from the front. Julie tensed. Peter's face appeared round the mast, waving madly. She frowned. What on earth was he so excited about?

He emerged, holding a bag, and weaved his way back down the boat. He dumped the bag at her feet in triumph. 'Food!' he yelped.

Julie blinked. 'Food?'

'Yes, tins, Mummy! Cans of fish and beef and potatoes and *petit pois* and ...'

'Goodness gracious me!' She stared in astonishment as Peter opened the bag to reveal the cans, about ten of them, a little rusty but obviously quite usable. The whole thing was odd enough – Michel having this boat – but the food ... A thought came to Julie and suddenly she understood everything.

This boat was for *Michel's* escape. He'd planned it all – bought the boat, prepared it, put the food on board, even worked out the course for England. He'd planned it all – and then given the boat to her.

Crump! Spray flew into Julie's eyes and pattered against her jacket. 'Take the bag back to the bow, Peter, so it doesn't get wet. And you stay there too and have something to eat.'

'But it's awfully bumpy up there. Can't I stay here?' He was whining. Tiredness.

'Well – perhaps ... All right! We'll eat here together then. See if you can find an opener or a knife or something.'

He disappeared into the box behind her and rummaged around, then looked up at her dispiritedly. 'Nothing here, Mummy, only this.' He held up a metal spike.

'Try the front, then.'

'The bow, you mean. That's its *proper* name.'

Julie made the effort not to clip his ear. 'Don't argue with me!' she shouted. 'Just go and look.'

He wandered off down the deck. Instantly Julie regretted her anger: she was tired and hungry too.

The bow rose then dipped suddenly. There was more spray, heavier this time and icy cold: she could feel it seeping through her trousers. The wind seemed colder too; she shivered despite the extra sweater.

Peter came back along the deck, his hair dripping with water.

'Oh darling, you're all wet!'

'There was a big wave!' His lower lip trembled and he started to cry.

'Come on, let's get some food inside you!'

'There's no opener!' He was crying in earnest now, his face creased up in despair.

One thing after another. Julie took a deep breath and said calmly, 'Let's use the spike then. That'll have to do.'

Pushing her back against the tiller to hold it steady, she reached into the bag for a can and, holding it against her leg, tried to puncture it with the spike. On the third attempt the spike slid off and dug into her thigh. Hopeless.

God, she felt tired.

She put her hand into the bag to see if there was an easier can, perhaps a flat sardine-type with its own opener. She felt around and came out with a long metallic object – a can opener. She clapped her hand to her forehead and shook her head. It was, of course, where any intelligent person would have put it.

She opened a can of meat and one of pilchards. 'When you've eaten, go and see if Monsieur Freymann wants anything, will you, Peter?' He nodded, his mouth full of meat. Julie looked to the rail, but David wasn't there any more and she saw that he was lying on the deck again. His face was sheet white; he wouldn't want anything to eat. A drink, maybe . . .

Where was that water Michel had talked about? Heaven only knew.

She stuffed a pilchard into her mouth and was surprised to find how hungry she was. She ate ravenously, then opened a can of potatoes and ate most of that, too, before passing it to Peter.

Crump! The water was flying over the bow more frequently now. Did it matter, all this water? She remembered how wet it had been on that large fishing boat when she and Peter had tried to escape before, yet the crew hadn't been worried.

Peter got a face full of water and she made him move to the uphill side of the deck where there seemed to be less spray. She moved across to the same side and took the tiller in her other hand.

As soon as she moved across she realised just how much the boat was tilting over on to one side. The deck was at a considerable slant and the mast was leaning over at a distinct angle. Each gust of wind made the tilt worse. What was there to stop the boat going right over?

She had a sudden memory of another time ... With Richard all those years ago. The boat had tipped over then, quite far. She remembered clinging to the side, terrified. But *he* hadn't been worried, not in the slightest. She whispered, 'Oh Richard, why the hell aren't you here!'

There was a whoosh and a swishing sound. Water was racing along the downhill side of the deck. Julie felt a rush of fear. *Where had it come from?* Immediately she thought: We're sinking!

She clutched at Peter. 'Oh God, darling!'

'It's all right, Mummy, it'll go out through the scuppers.'

Julie stared at him in amazement. 'The scuppers?'

'Yes. Richard told me when we were carving the model. They're the holes in the sides, down there. For letting water out.'

'... for letting water out ...'

She watched, fascinated, as the water gurgled away through the small slits. A moment later the boat tipped again and the water came back, only to gurgle harmlessly away as before. She turned to Peter. 'What else did Richard tell you?'

The little face went blank. Julie realised it was the wrong way to ask. She tried again. 'Did he talk about what to do in strong winds?'

Peter made a face of concentration. 'Ummm, well I know what you do in *gales*.'

Julie gripped his shoulder. 'Yes, darling!'

'You shorten sail!'

'Yes ... and?'

'You reef! That's what you do!'

'Reef ... That's what he told you?'

'Yes.'

Julie thought desperately but she had no idea what that meant. She looked down at Peter. He was still thinking, she could tell by his face. Eventually he said slowly, 'You let the sail down a bit, then you tie up the loose bit with all those ropes hanging from the sail there. Richard drew me a picture.'

'I see.'

She couldn't imagine how it was actually done, but at least she might have a vague idea if the worst came to the worst. But when did a strong wind become a gale? How did you *know* when to reef?

Her head was aching violently: she couldn't think. Damn it. One thing at a time. Gales might never happen!

She settled back on the helmsman's seat and forced herself to stop worrying. After all, things could be a lot worse.

At that moment David Freymann cried out in agony and, from far away in the eastern sky, there came the low hum of an approaching plane.

28

The wind. It was coming from the north-east and freshening.

Fischer left the periscope and went to the chart table. The prey certainly wouldn't be trying for Plymouth – the course would put them hard on the wind. Too uncomfortable and too slow.

No: Falmouth it had to be.

But the speed estimate would have to be revised. Even a small boat would be doing more than four knots in this wind. Five, maybe more.

Fischer marked off two points along the prey's course line. The first point marked the prey's position if he were doing a steady six knots; the second, his position at four knots. These, then, marked the limits of speed probability. The gap between the two positions was twenty nautical miles.

Now, course. If this fellow strayed from his course, which way would he go? To the west almost certainly, because of this freshening wind. Fischer marked off a second course line ten degrees to the west of the first. He now had a long thin box of approximately a hundred square miles.

A hundred square miles . . . One hell of a lot of sea . . .

It would be impossible to search it all. No, the best thing would be to patrol back and forth across the probable track of the prey and wait for him to come to them. A waiting game.

The soonest that the prey could possibly be here was . . . right now. Unlikely, though, because he wouldn't have been doing six knots the whole time. At the other extreme, the latest he'd arrive was in five hours' time, at 1500 hours.

A waiting game.

In the meantime . . .

Fischer looked at the chart as a whole. Little danger of meeting enemy surface units here: U-319 was in the unofficial no-man's-land between Britain and France. But nearer Britain there would be a lot of shipping – minesweepers, coastal convoys – and guarding the shipping lane, maybe even some minefields. His chart showed one mined area just to the north of him. But Fischer was sceptical: in all likelihood the intelligence was out of date and probably not too accurate in the first place.

But overhead there was no such thing as a no-man's-land. The air was anybody's. Except that, around here, it was mainly British. That was one of the reasons U-boats didn't bother to operate in the Channel nowadays.

Fischer strolled thoughtfully back to the search periscope. A young seaman was manning it, circling slowly. Fischer watched him for a moment, his mind on what would happen if they did manage to find this fishing boat. To capture the occupants they'd have to surface. The operation would take a good fifteen to twenty minutes – if they were lucky. It was an awful long time to be on the surface in broad daylight.

Hell! What an operation!

The periscope stopped circling. The young seaman yelled, 'Aircraft bearing 045! Range – four to five miles!'

Fischer pushed the young man aside and took a look. A Catalina or something like it. Definitely one of the opposition's. Closing.

'Down periscope! Alter course forty-five degrees to starboard!'

Fifteen minutes: he'd give it fifteen minutes before he took another look.

After five minutes he said again, 'Alter course forty-five degrees to starboard.' The order was echoed twice.

They waited, as they'd waited so many times before, the crew automatically falling into Silent Routine, though no ship was tracking them. Everyone was still and the only sound was the quiet hum of the electric motors.

After a long while Fischer looked at his watch. Time to have a look. 'Up periscope.'

The periscope hissed up and, quickly lowering the folding handles, Fischer looked through the eyepiece. He made a quick circle: nothing. Then a slower one: nothing. The plane had gone.

It had been on a routine reconnaissance patrol, Fischer decided. It was unlikely it had seen them.

Another two circles to search the horizon. No fishing boat in sight.

'Resume course. Resume Patrol Routine.'

The men relaxed and started to move around again. Fischer made another circle of the horizon. The sea was definitely rougher. From one point of view that was a good thing: it meant there was less chance of the periscope being seen. On the other hand it would be more difficult to spot the prey.

If they ever got anywhere near it, that was . . .

'Wireless signal, Herr Kaleu.'

With the resumption of Patrol Routine the rod aerial – also periscopic – had gone up. Fischer went over to the wireless operator and watched him tap the signal into the Enigma machine. Fischer tore off the decoded message, said, 'Strictly *no* acknowledgement!' and strode over to the chart table.

He was jubilant: the target had been spotted! By one of their own reconnaissance planes – which meant the position wouldn't be terribly accurate, aerial fixes never were – but it was a darn sight better than nothing.

He measured the co-ordinates off the side and top of the chart and pencilled in a cross. There! Seen *there* at 0930 hours!

Slow. Going much slower than he'd thought. Almost at the lower edge of the box he'd drawn – and to the west, *well* to the west! He frowned. Where could they be making for?

And the slow speed, that was a surprise, too. They had averaged only four knots. Perhaps the fishing boat had set out later than first thought, perhaps that first position was wrong . . . All supposition.

The point was, he must get U-319 further over to the west, into the prey's path . . .

And then?

Then he'd wait. Nothing had changed. It was still a waiting game.

In the Submarine Tracking Room the Head went over the information that had come in during the night. He sifted through it slowly, measuring it against the probable speed and track of the various boats, and tried to calculate where wolf packs might be forming.

The job was getting increasingly difficult. The problem was one of scale. Never had there been so many U-boats – four hundred in existence, two hundred and fifty operational and probably well over a hundred actually at sea. It was almost impossible to keep track of them all, though he and his staff did their very best. Especially *now*.

He remembered the morning meeting and the appalling statistics – twenty-one ships lost from just two convoys. He remembered the words of the Vice-Chief of Staff. *We have reached a crisis in the battle of the Atlantic*. The crisis was simple – if the U-boats weren't driven off, then the convoys couldn't get through.

No-one needed to be told the consequences of that.

To fight the menace there was to be a new strategy: Ultra information was to be used to the full and convoys always diverted out of the path of waiting wolf packs; all convoys were to get full support group protection; and, finally, production of the new H₂S radar, which trials had proved to be successful was to be rapidly accelerated and units fitted to all bombers of Coastal Command.

It was make or break. The last ditch stand.

Doenitz knew that too.

Over the years the Head had learnt to understand the way Doenitz's mind worked. The U-boats' tactics reflected Doenitz's thinking, his favourite strategies, his master plan. A year before, when air patrols and radar had made things too difficult for the U-boats in the North Atlantic, the Grand Admiral had transferred the larger ones to the South Atlantic. And the Head had foreseen it. When that in turn got too hot for his boats Doenitz had sent them to the American coast. Again, the Head had guessed. Because he would have done the same himself.

Now Doenitz had put everything back into the North Atlantic.

This was Doenitz's last ditch stand too.

But for the Head it was hard work keeping the Plot up to date. The Head had a day staff of eleven track plotters and six DF plotters – not a lot to cover so many U-boats.

He re-examined the log entries made by the night watch, and the decodes.

Mainly routine. No specific evidence of a new wolf pack forming. The only unusual thing was the long message sent at 0115 hours and prefixed urgent,

A signal on the U-boat frequency – possibly an acknowledgement – had been sent ten minutes later. The signal was too short for the DF people to get a good fix on it, but a rough estimate had put the U-boat in the Bay of Biscay.

Just one acknowledgement . . . A single U-boat involved then. Curious. A change of orders perhaps? A new destination?

What he needed were the Ultra decodes.

An hour later he had them in an enormous pile.

Short messages, lots of them: acknowledgements, damage reports, notification of successful attacks (too many of them, always too many of them) . . . He passed them to his staff for routine processing.

He picked up the long signal and read the message with growing astonishment. Good Lord, what on earth did it all mean? A fishing boat, occupants to be captured but not harmed . . . Extraordinary.

He went to a side table. On it was a large chart marked with grid references. At the beginning of the war the Germans had made no attempt to disguise their grid references and, once a German chart had been obtained for the Tracking Room, it was a simple matter to read the references off. But now the references were disguised by a code which was changed every month and sometimes it took quite a while to crack it. At the moment they were still guessing. The code had only just been changed.

Grid references. The signal had dozens of the blasted things . . .

Some were familiar and did, he knew, lie somewhere in the Bay. Others were unfamiliar . . . H17 P15, for example. He knew the prefix 'H' and 'P', but he'd never seen them with those numbers and in that combination. Deduction – this boat was being sent somewhere different. Not into the Atlantic, nor to Greenland or Iceland.

Chasing a fishing boat . . . Biscay coast? Possibly. But there again the grid references didn't look right, certainly nothing like those used by U-boats close to the Biscay coast from where, after Allied air attacks, they sometimes had to call for assistance.

The North French coast then?

No U-boats had been into the Channel for a long time. Too dangerous and too few convoys to make it worthwhile.

He frowned, studying the signal again. The fishing boat was believed to be heading for another place with fairly similar co-ordinates – same prefixes, not too dissimilar numbers. So, somewhere fairly close to the first place? It would be easy to assume that the second place was a port or refuge – but it could just as easily be a point miles out to sea, a rendezvous . . .

The Head called across to one of his assistants and asked her to check with the various clandestine organisations, just in case they knew anything about a meeting with a fishing boat.

Back to the co-ordinates. Assuming the first of each pair of co-ordinates was the latitude, then the second position was at a higher latitude, assuming again that the code followed the normal practice and the numbers got higher the further from the equator you went . . .

An awful lot of assumptions.

But if the assumptions *were* right, then the second place was to the north of the first.

The fishing boat could conceivably be going north from somewhere like Bordeaux . . . But no, the co-ordinates would have been familiar. Also he felt that, instinctively, it didn't quite fit. They'd never send a U-boat if the fisherman was making a run for another part of Occupied France, or for neutral Spain, they'd send a coastal patrol boat or, even better, an E-boat.

That was it! Of course!

They had sent a U-boat.

Not anything else . . .'

Why?

The mission was important, of course, as Doenitz had stressed. But there must be more to it than that. This fishing boat had to be going somewhere where *other* craft couldn't go. Like towards enemy territory. Or *past* enemy territory, where Allied air patrols were likely to be heavy. Yes, *yes*.

The English Channel.

It had to be.

But where *exactly*? East Channel? No. However vital the operation was, Doenitz would never send one of his boats on a suicide mission. It was so shallow in the east Channel the U-boat wouldn't stand a chance.

So West Channel. Why not?

The Head looked at the clock on the wall. He must decide quickly – he still had an awful lot of work to do.

He went to the plot and, picking up U-319's token which the night staff had placed outside Brest, placed it in the middle of the English Channel, to the south of Plymouth.

Then, pulling his ear thoughtfully, he lifted the telephone and asked for Coastal Command.

He might be wildly wrong, of course, and be sending the lads of Coastal Command off on a wild goose chase. But he had one of his feelings about this one.

It was Doenitz's postscript. *If anyone can do it you can.*

There could be only one reason Doenitz had said that. Because he was asking his man to do the impossible. He was asking him to go into the jaws of the lion.

29

Julie slapped his face.

Awful, but it had to be done. 'Wake up! Please, wake up!'

He stirred slightly. 'Monsieur Freymann! David! David! Wake up!'

He was almost unconscious. In desperation she put her mouth to his ear and shouted, 'You've got to move!'

There was a *crump!* from the bow and, after a moment's pause, heavy spray came flying over the deck. Julie ducked her head but it was too late and the water trickled down her neck. The old man was getting soaked too: that's why he had to be moved.

His eyes had flickered open. The cold water must have woken him.

Julie shook him slightly. 'You've got to move. To the front, over *there*.' She indicated the bow. 'Otherwise you'll get soaked!'

He looked at her blankly then, closing his eyes with pain, nodded slightly. Taking his arm, Julie pushed him into a sitting position and began to pull him along the deck. At first she could feel him helping, shuffling sideways on his behind, but then he sagged and his weight fell against her leg. She saw that his face was white and contorted with pain.

She crouched down and, her arm round his shoulder, waited a while. The boat hit another wave and the inevitable deluge of heavy, cold spray rained down over them.

Julie blew the water off her lips, and standing up again, tried to drag the old man along, but he was terribly heavy and she couldn't keep her balance on the unsteady deck. Panting heavily, she knelt down and shouted desperately. 'Please *try*, David. Please *try*.'

There was the faintest nod. Julie started pulling and felt him helping again. This time they reached the shelter of the small decked area under the bow. The motion of the boat was much more violent up here – Julie felt her stomach take off a couple of times – but at least it was dry.

'Just a bit further, then you'll be comfortable!'

The old man made a final effort and, at last, Julie managed to pull him up against some coils of rope. He lay back and closed his eyes. Julie covered him with sacking and placed a rolled-up section of tarpaulin under his head.

She looked at him fondly and, very gently, stroked his head. 'Sorry I had to slap you.' But he didn't hear: he was unconscious again. She examined his face anxiously. It was deathly white, with an almost green tinge to it, and his breath was coming in short, shallow pants through a gaping mouth.

The pills: the old man had mentioned pills. She should try to get some more down him. He'd thrown the last lot up.

She looked in his bag and found a small bottle half full of white tablets. It had to be them: there were no others. The bottle had no label and no instructions. She guessed at two tablets and shook them into her hand.

Water. She'd need water.

She found a large, rope-clad bottle full of clear liquid, up by the lobster pot in the bow. She opened it and dipped a finger in. Water. But no mug or cup.

She placed the tablets on the old man's tongue then, raising his head slightly, put the bottle to his lips and tried to tip it up. It was too heavy. She wedged her body against the side of the boat and, resting the old man's head against her chest, used both hands to tip the bottle. Water poured everywhere. Some went into the old man's mouth. He moaned loudly, then spluttered and coughed.

Julie patted his shoulder and watched him carefully. The pills seemed to have disappeared. It was something at least.

A moment later the old man groaned and, clutching his stomach, turned his head to one side, and threw up over Julie's leg.

Julie stared in slight revulsion then realised with unhappy certainty that unless she moved away the same thing would happen to her. There was an uncomfortable feeling in her stomach and it was rising fast towards her throat. She got up and, lurching towards the rail, swallowed hard and gulped at the fresh salt air. She turned her face to the wind and looked out at the wide expanse of sea.

After a while she felt better. She looked back at David. He seemed peaceful enough. She couldn't face going back, not just yet. The smell . . .

She turned away and, holding tight to the rail, made her way cautiously along the tilting deck to the tiller. Peter was curled up against the side of the boat on the uphill side, right at the back, where it was dry. He was asleep, a slight frown on his pale face.

Julie looked at the compass. The course had changed a little – slightly more westerly than before. She altered the tiller lines and the course improved slightly, but she could already hear a slight fluttering from the sails. They'd start flapping if she moved the tiller any further. The sails would need adjusting again. It would have to wait: with a bit of luck it might not be necessary and, anyway, she couldn't face it at the moment.

She searched the sky. No sign of that plane. It was quite extraordinary: it had seen them, she was certain. It *must* have. It had changed its course slightly and flown almost directly overhead. Yet it hadn't come down to shoot at them, or even to look more closely.

Julie had taken Peter and dived under the bow and waited for the rat-tat-tat of bullets. But the sound had never come. Instead the plane had stayed high, the hum faint, and then the sound had faded slowly away into the distance.

She couldn't work it out at all.

But there was no sense in worrying about it. The point was, the plane hadn't come back, and that was all that mattered.

Time: almost noon. She felt dreadful. Her eyes were aching in their sockets and her head felt as if it were banded with iron. Sleep;

she would have to sleep some time. But at the moment she felt oddly light-headed and awake and in need of *doing* something – as if by keeping busy everything would turn out all right.

Chores: she would get the chores done. just like at home.

The compass light. It had to be repaired. She thought: But I don't have the first idea *how*.

She drew a deep breath. No harm in looking anyway.

To the side of the compass, mounted on the brass base, was a small flap fastened by a finger bolt. It undid quite easily. She looked. There was a wick. She touched it: quite dry. No fuel, then. Her heart lifted. It might be quite simple after all.

A filler cap: there had to be one. She peered into the small opening, then drew away sharply because it made her stomach feel queasy again. A moment for fresh air, then she took another look. Nothing.

Frowning, she looked all the way round the brass compass mount, and suddenly, there it was, on the forward side of the mount: a small brass cap which, when unscrewed, smelt of kerosene. She put a finger in. It came out dry.

All it needed was fuel. *All!*

She went to the box where she had found the torch. It was bound to be in there.

It wasn't.

She made her way up to the bow, choosing her moment between waves and flying spray. David seemed to be sleeping peacefully. She put a hand on his brow. He was warmer than before but his colour was still terrible. She wished there was something she could do for him.

Crouching, she went up into the point of the bow. Another rope-clad container. She opened it excitedly. More water.

She searched carefully under the lobster pots, ropes and the single tarpaulin. Nothing.

Where else?

She made her way back towards the tiller. Half way along the deck, in the centre, was a raised section built up from the deck in a large square. It had a sort of lid on it. The way into the hold, presumably, where the fish were usually stored.

Would the kerosene be in there? She'd have a look anyway.

There were fastenings around the lid: clips. They were stiff. She tried to prise one open and tore a finger nail. She bit off the nail and tried again. It needed leverage. The spike. The one Peter had found in the box.

It was still there. She brought it back to the hatch cover and, putting it under the clip, levered outwards. The clip sprang open. Triumph!

The other clips opened more easily. Now, the cover itself. It was heavy, but, standing on the uphill side, she managed to lift it slightly, then, using the slant of the boat, to slide it downhill.

She looked over the edge of the opening into the hold. Much of it was dark, but immediately below her was a large square brilliantly illuminated by the open hatch.

Julie stared in disbelief, but there was no mistake.

The hold was full of running water.

Spray pattered onto Julie's back, but she didn't notice; she was mesmerised by the water flowing in a great torrent through the boat. After a moment she realised the water was streaming first one way then the other, as the boat seesawed its way across the waves. At its fastest the water made a great rushing noise then, as the boat reached the crest of a wave, the entrapped water slowed down and paused before beginning its frantic return journey.

There was tons of it.

Julie wondered how long it had been there – and how fast it was coming in.

'Mummy!'

Peter was standing by the rail, well aft, out of the spray. 'Mummy!' he called again. He was looking unhappy. Julie got to her feet. The bow hit a wave and spray flew back over the deck and into the hold. She should cover the hold again – but then there was so much water in it anyway, a bit more wouldn't make any difference.

When she got to Peter he held out his arms and she hugged him. 'Mummy, I need to go to . . . I want to do a poo, Mummy.'

Julie sighed. 'Of course, sweetheart.'

'But where, Mummy?'

'Oh.' She hadn't thought of that. Up till now it had just been a question of standing him near the scuppers. A bucket: that would have to do. She looked around desperately. Knowing Peter, there wasn't much time.

'Wait here.'

She looked in the large wooden box beside the tiller, then up in the bow. There *had* to be a bucket somewhere.

No bucket. But there was a square tin box full of fishing tackle. She threw out the tackle and, grasping the tin box, ducked out from under the decking.

'Please . . . Please . . .' It was David. He was looking at her with pleading eyes.

Without waiting for an answer, she hurried down the deck. Just in time by the look on Peter's face. Without ceremony, she pulled down his trousers and sat him on the tin box.

'Ouch!'

'I can't help it! It's the best I could find!' She supported the child's weight, so he wouldn't have to sit on the sharp edges.

'Mummy, what about paper?'

Paper. Paper.

'Wait here.' The boy grabbed for the helmsman's seat as she let go of him.

Her brain was seizing up, she could feel it. She made an effort to think. Paper. On a boat? Never. Never! It'd be soaked in a moment. What then? A rag – yes, a rag.

The big wooden box let her down again: it was always letting her down. Back to the bow again. Only an oily black rag. It would have to do.

David was grasping her arm. 'Please, must talk ... It's very important ... *Please*.'

'Yes! Yes! In a minute. I promise!' She was begining to whine. She lowered her voice. 'Sorry ... I really *will* be back – but I've got to take this to my son. All right?'

As she made her way aft for what felt like the twentieth time, Julie thought: It's just a matter of keeping going, that's all.

David watched her go. She looked worried. Perhaps things weren't going so well.

He made an effort to keep his eyes open. Musn't let go. *Not yet*.

He had to tell her, had to get it to her ...

Before he couldn't any more.

He felt so weak. The pain was eating into him, gnawing away at his body, and it was impossible to fight it any more. He wanted to escape, to drift away so that there'd never be any pain again.

But first he *must* talk to the girl. After ... *then* he'd close his eyes and slip away. And there'd be no more pain, just peace.

But not yet. Mustn't let go ... Not yet.

When Julie got back David was asleep. Whatever he'd wanted to say would have to wait. She'd talk to him as soon as he woke up again.

In the meantime ...

She searched the deck carefully. There had to be a way of getting the water out. 'Manning the pumps', that's what they used to do in the stories she'd read. But was this boat big enough to have a pump? And if so what would it look like?

432

There was nothing on the deck that looked remotely like anything that might be a pump.

Nothing for it then . . .

She stared for a while at the gaping hold then, taking the torch, lowered herself over the edge and down into the darkness. She found a foothold and stepped down into the swirling water up to her calves. Immediately, she wished she's taken her shoes off and left them on deck. Too late now.

The torchlight revealed an empty shell. Julie stooped down and shone the light right into the bow. Nothing: just the timber frame and, half way down, the mast coming through the deck above. Behind, nothing either.

Crouching, she climbed forward and shone the torch into the bow again. The water was surging round something heaped on the floor – the anchor chain.

No sign of any kerosene. No sign of a pump.

The boat lurched and she grabbed for the mast. The nasty feeling began to rise in her throat again. She knew she must get out, and fast!

As she let go of the mast something cold touched her hand. *Must get up on deck* . . . Swallowing fast, she shone the torch back on the mast, to where her hand had been. A pipe. It ran parallel to the mast, down into the bottom of the boat where it was lost in the murky water.

She gulped hard and pointed the torch upwards. The pipe followed the mast until the spar disappeared through the deck, then it ran horizontally for a short distance until it stopped at a large metal object suspended from the deckhead.

I'm going to be sick.

She rushed for the open hatch and hoisted herself quickly over the edge of the coaming onto the deck.

She fell against the downhill rail and knew that nothing would stop it now. She heaved miserably for several minutes then began to feel better. She staggered back to the helmsman's seat and, resting her head against the compass, waited for the faintness to pass. It would be so easy to sleep now, to let go.

After a few minutes she stood up and, still shaky, made herself go forward to the mast. She looked to one side of it, to where the metal thing must be just under the deck, and there, set into the planking, was a short thick metal post. She'd thought it was some kind of bollard, but now she could see it was mechanical: it had a socket thing, and bits that obviously moved.

Spray shot through the air and struck her coldly on the cheek. She dropped on to her hands and knees and looked more closely at the mechanical post. The socket was clearly designed to take some sort of handle. Then it could be moved back and forth.

A handle. She was getting tired of looking for things . . .

She glanced around half-heartedly and saw, right beside her, attached by a clip to the mast, a long straight piece of pipe iron. A handle. It fitted the socket.

She pulled the cover across the open hatch so that no more water should get in from above, and sitting on the edge of the hatch, started to pump. At first the handle went back and forth quite easily then, suddenly, it became stiffer and she realised it was only now beginning to draw up water. She settled down into a rhythm and wondered how long it would take to empty the hold.

The pump was situated in what was probably the wettest part of the deck, where the spray was at its thickest. Water dribbled down her neck and into her clothing, which clung damp and sticky to her skin. But the action of the pumping was, at least, getting her nice and warm. She gave a small snort of amusement – you could make anything sound good if you tried.

After half an hour or so, she lifted the hatch cover and shone the torch down. Still tons of water. She'd half expected it. She settled back into the pumping, trying to clear her brain of everything but the necessity to pump. But her mind kept wandering; thoughts of home, and Jean, and Tante Marie, and *him* . . .

She made herself sing, and quite enjoyed it for a while, until she ran out of songs.

Her back began to ache. She took a rest, but it was a mistake: her back ached twice as much when she started pumping again.

After a while her hands blistered and she had to stop because of the pain. Wearily she lifted the corner of the hatch cover and shone the torch down. The water had almost gone. She nodded with satisfaction. Wrapping her hands in rags she pumped again, more quickly, desperately, until at long last there was a sucking noise and the pump was dry.

She put the handle back in its clip on the mast and slowly, shakily, made her way back to the tiller seat.

The course read North-West. *Too far west*. She rested her head against the glass bowl and closed her eyes.

'Mummy . . .' A small hand was placed on her arm. 'Mummy, are you all right?'

'Yes, darling, I feel fine.' It was about the last thing she felt.

'I opened another tin. I thought you might be hungry after all your pumping.'

434

She put her arms round his small waist and her head against his chest and said in a tight voice, 'Thank you, darling.'

A faint cry sounded from the bow. Julie looked round. It was David. His hand was raised as if to wave. She'd quite forgotten about him. He must want water.

Wearily, she got to her feet and began the long wet journey down the deck.

She was coming back at last!

David watched her fervently, willing her to complete her uncertain passage along the heaving deck. She paused halfway and for a moment he feared she'd changed her mind, but after waiting for a break between waves and ensuing spray, she came on, staggering slightly as the boat gave a sudden lurch forward.

As soon as she'd dropped on to her knees beside him, he grasped her hand. It was very hot. He was rather surprised because she looked so cold: her hair clung damply to her forehead and dropped in long wet strands around her shoulders. She looked worn out. Her face was very pale, apart from two bright patches of colour which burned on her cheeks, and her eyes were red and swollen, with dark smudges underneath.

David patted her hand. 'My dear, you must rest . . . Some time.'

She squeezed his hand and smiled. It quite transformed her face. 'Don't you worry about me. I'm fit and healthy. It's you who must take care. Would you like some water? You must be desperate for some by now.'

She reached over for the large glass bottle and, removing the stopper, held it to his lips. He drank greedily. It tasted good.

As she replaced the stopper he opened the bag he wore round his waist and, reaching in, took out the small package.

He took hold of her hand and, concentrating hard on the words, said, 'You remember . . . in the field. When you came back for me. I want to thank you.'

She smiled. 'Don't be silly. Of course I came back for you. I couldn't leave you, could I?'

'At the time . . . Well . . .' He coughed and breathed deeply to regain his breath. '. . . I wanted to give up. But I'm glad I didn't. You see –' He waited for a spasm of pain to pass.

She was patting his hand. 'Are you all right?'

'Yes, yes . . .' As soon as he could, he went on. 'You were right . . . about them making me work. They would've got hold of my Cecile . . . they would have threatened things. This way I'm *protecting* her. Just like I promised. Thank you for that, thank you.'

435

She almost spoke, but he interrupted quickly. 'Look . . . this package. It's got everything . . . about my ideas. The drawings. The specifications. Please, you must take care of it. In case anything happens to me –'

'It won't!'

He shook his head irritably. 'You will promise,' he went on slowly, 'that you'll take care of it . . . and hand it to the right people. It must be the right people . . . Do you understand?'

She still seemed unhappy about it, but nodded gently and, looking down at the small flat package, weighed it thoughtfully in her hand. She appeared to come to a decision and, turning slightly away, pushed the package down inside her jersey and buried it somewhere in her underwear.

David relaxed. He was free at last. It was like a weight off his shoulders. Now he could *really* sleep. He squeezed her hand. 'You're a good girl.'

She leaned forward and kissed him gently on the cheek. Then she stroked his forehead and asked, 'What about taking some of your pills?'

'Pain's not so bad now . . . Anyway, . . . Make me sick. Better not.' It was a lie about the pain, it was as bad as ever, but he didn't want to bother her with it.

She was regarding him thoughtfully. 'You know, I should thank you too. For snapping me out of it when we were hiding on the beach. If you hadn't – well, I would probably have stayed in a daze . . . I only wish I hadn't got you into *this* mess.' She sighed and looked away.

She didn't understand at all. She thought she was failing.

David said desperately, 'No . . . No, we're *trying*. And that's worth *everything*! *Everything*! You must realise that *trying* is the most important thing of all . . .!'

She nodded uncertainly. 'If you say so. Now rest. Please. Try to sleep.' She leaned forward once again and kissed him softly on the cheek.

'Remember,' he murmured. 'Trying is the most important thing.'

'Yes!' She gave a small laugh and, touching his hand, got to her feet and set off towards the stern.

David lay back and closed his eyes. His mind was at rest, he had done what had to be done; now, at last, he could sleep in peace.

Her body was seizing up like her mind. As she moved back along the deck she felt her whole body complaining. Her neck was almost unmovable and every time she turned her head a sharp pain shot through her temples.

Peter's face lit up at the sight of her. 'Mummy, here! You still haven't had any lunch. I've kept some for you!'

She sat down beside him, under the bulwark, and tried to eat. She didn't feel very hungry.

'Mummy, are you going to be better now?'

'I expect so. I'm . . . just tired, that's all.'

'Why don't you sleep and then I can keep watch?'

Sighing, she began, 'No, Peter, it –' Then she thought: Why not? The boat was sailing itself. Peter would probably keep a better look-out than she would. Yes: why not?

She finished her mouthful and looked at him. It was an awful responsibility for a six-year-old. But it would be night in a few hours. She'd have to be awake then and, without sleep – well, she'd never do it.

She said carefully, 'Darling . . . Would you promise to tell me the *moment* you saw anything?'

The small head nodded.

'Or the moment the weather changed . . . black clouds or more spray . . . or rain . . . ?'

'Yes, Mummy.'

'If you saw a ship or . . . anything floating, or a plane . . . You'd wake me then too, wouldn't you?'

'I promise, Mummy.'

'Anything at all . . .'

He nodded again. 'Don't worry, Mummy. I'll keep a really sharp look-out!' He smiled excitedly and pulled himself up onto the helmsman's seat.

Julie stood up and took a long look round. The sky was still clear, but now there was a slight haze around the horizon. The sea appeared as vast as ever – and as impossible to cross.

A sharp look-out . . . She lay down on the deck with her head on her arm and wondered if Peter had learnt that one from Richard too.

Richard. He must have been through this sort of thing countless times – the wet, the cold and the tiredness. The thought gave her comfort. Then she saw him in another setting – in a prison cell, hungry, cold, raging to be free, and hastily tried to shut the picture out of her mind before worse things appeared.

She closed her eyes and tried to sleep, but for a long time her body refused to relax. When she finally drifted into an uneasy doze a series of disconnected thoughts rampaged around her brain and several times made her wake with a terrible start. After a while her brain began to slow down. Only one thought remained. Something she should have done. What was it? As she drifted off into a deep sleep, she remembered at last. The course. It was still wrong. She hadn't reset the course.

30

A needle in a haystack.

And yet, and yet . . .

With his finger Fischer traced the fishing boat's course from Morlaix to the position the plane had reported, then followed the pencilled line on, in a straight projection. His finger arrived at a point midway between the Scillies and Land's End. It was the fifth time he'd checked the projection, but the result was always the same.

He still couldn't understand it. Where was the boat making for? Why go all the way round Land's End and then be faced with a long trek up the north coast of Cornwall, against the wind? The alternatives were – what? Wales or Ireland. Wales – again why bother? Ireland then. Now that *was* a possibility, particularly if the occupants of the fishing boat were seeking the safety of a neutral country. When one thought about it, the whole affair did smack of politics . . . Fischer decided that it was the most likely destination.

However there was still one thing that didn't make sense.

If the fishing boat was holding her course, why the devil hadn't they seen her yet?

U-319 was zigzagging four miles either side of the prey's projected track. The visibility was still good. Using the search periscope they should be able to spot even a small boat at four miles. She must have masts and sails which should be clearly visible against the skyline.

Even allowing for the worst: for U-319 speeding away from the approaching prey on the wrong leg of the zig-zag, and for the fishing boat being as much as four miles off course, they should still see her on the return leg because of their superior speed and because each leg of the zigzag took them very slightly forward along the fishing boat's track.

They should have seen her, but they hadn't.

Fischer sighed deeply and chucked the pencil down on to the chart. The control room was quiet except for the gentle hum of the electric motors. The men were at their positions, silent except for the occasional whisper, engrossed in their jobs. The man at the periscope was swivelling slowly, his eyes fixed to the lens.

Fischer wondered how long it had been since he slept. He thought for a moment and decided that his last proper sleep must have been over thirty hours ago. He'd tried to sleep early that morning, but had managed only a short doze.

He should try to snatch some rest now but he knew he wouldn't be able to. Not yet. Not while the hunt was on.

Once darkness fell – once they'd missed the boat for certain – then he'd sleep. During the night there was nothing they could do; they had no way of hunting a small boat under cover of darkness. All he could do would be to manoeuvre U-319 into a position ahead of the fishing boat and lie in wait for it at dawn. By then the margin for error would be enormous – the prey might have changed course a dozen times. The chances would be slim.

A needle in a haystack . . .

Men were moving around the control room, changing places, whispering in muted voices. The watch change. 1600 hours.

He was tempted to go to the periscope and take a look, but decided against it. A man from the new watch was just settling in. When the fellow finished his first trick at the periscope in about fifteen minutes, perhaps then he'd take a look. It was partly superstition: Fischer had the feeling that, by restraining himself from looking, the fishing boat was more likely to turn up. Ridiculous, of course . . .

Fischer wandered aft, towards the engine room. The Chief spotted him and, wiping his hands on an oily rag, made his way between the massive diesels to meet his commander.

Suddenly there was a muffled exclamation, the sound of voices from the direction of the control room. Fischer froze for a moment then, turning quickly, retraced his steps. Even as he turned he was thinking: No klaxon – not an aircraft. What then?

Eins WO – the first officer – was at the periscope. '. . . bearing 280!'

Fischer strode up and tapped him on the shoulder. The first officer stood aside. 'A small craft, Herr Kaleu!' Fischer put his eye to the lens.

For a moment he could see nothing, just seas, larger than before. He checked the bearing – 280 degrees – and waited. A wave rose in front of the horizon then fell again.

There!

Fischer felt the adrenalin leap into his veins.

'Raise attack periscope!'

There was a hiss of hydraulics as the much larger attack periscope rose from the bowels of the boat. The search periscope had a wide field of vision, covering large areas of the sky as well as the sea, but had limited powers of magnification; the attack periscope, on the other hand, had a small field of vision but much greater magnification. Fischer pulled down the handles and, swinging the periscope round, put his eye to it.

Greatly magnified waves obscured the horizon. He waited. They fell away.

There she was!

A small boat. Under sail.

The silhouette was unmistakable, even from this distance. He guessed the range to be over four miles. He could see almost nothing of the hull – it was hidden among the waves – but the mainsail showed black and distinct, a tiny curved shape against the brilliant yellow of the western sky.

The boat was sailing north.

He allowed himself a moment of satisfaction, then let his natural caution take charge. It might be a British fishing boat ... But unlikely in mid-Channel. It might be another escaped French fishing boat – equally unlikely. The coincidences of time and position were too great.

It *had* to be the prey.

Next – how to capture them. He'd have to approach submerged, then surface at the last minute. That way the occupants wouldn't have time to think about fighting. He wanted to avoid fighting, not only because he'd been told to bring back the occupants unharmed, but because the operation had to be completed in the shortest possible time, to avoid being caught on the surface.

He hated the idea of surfacing in broad daylight, particularly here. But it would have to be done.

Automatically he began to swing the periscope round, walking with it in a circle, sweeping the narrow band either side of the horizon. No ships. He couldn't see much of the sky, not with this periscope.

He stood back and let the first officer take a look.

It was time to close in. 'Alter course to –'

He broke off. Something was wrong: he identified it. The bloody stupid man on the search periscope wasn't swivelling it round, wasn't searching! Fischer felt a surge of anger.

'*Sweep!* Sweep the sky! Come on!'

The man glanced up, looked shaken, and rapidly spun the periscope.

Fischer clenched his fists. Bloody fool. That was the way to get caught. An aircraft could spot the wake of the two periscopes at a hell of a distance. But Fischer knew the sailor at the periscope: normally he was a good man. He decided to let the matter pass.

Now, the order to alter course.

A sharp cry, half-shout, half-scream, rent the air.

'*Enemy aircraft!*'

In reflex Fischer shouted, '*Down periscopes!*'

The two shafts began to hiss downwards.

'*Take her down! Alter course forty-five degrees to starboard!*'

The order was repeated.

Fischer had no idea whether the plane had been close, whether it was even making a bombing run, but he wasn't going to take any chances. He strode to the chart and looked at the depth of the water here. He barked, 'Take her down to thirty metres!'

After what seemed a long, long time but which was only a couple of seconds the submarine began to react to the re-angled hydroplanes and her nose tilted downwards. Slowly, peacefully, the boat slipped further and further down into the depths.

Everyone tensed and reached out for a handhold, waiting for the shock of the depth charges.

The silence lasted a long, long time.

The voice of the coxswain sounded calmly through the stillness. 'Depth fifteen metres . . . eighteen metres . . . twenty metres . . .'

'Alter course another forty-five degrees to starboard.'

'Altering course forty-five degrees starboard, Herr Kaleu.'

At last it came. 'Depth thirty metres.'

Fischer exhaled. The men shifted their weight and exchanged glances. No depth charges. They were safe.

'You!' Fischer barked at the sailor who'd been manning the search periscope.

The man approached, ashen white.

'Bearing and range of enemy plane?'

The man gulped. Fischer noticed that he was shaking like a leaf.

'*Bearing and range of enemy plane!*'

The man's mouth was gaping slightly and he glanced around like a frightened rabbit. Fischer raised his hand and quite deliberately slapped the sailor's face. The man fell back in surprise. For a moment Fischer thought he was going to cry.

Fischer repeated more quietly, 'Bearing and range of enemy plane.'

The man's eyes cleared. 'Behind us, Herr Kaleu,' he began breathlessly. 'No – slightly to starboard. Bearing about . . . I . . . I'm not sure.' He was shaking again.

Fischer said sharply, 'But a British plane?'

'Oh yes . . . A Catalina, I think.'

'Was he closing on us?'

The man nodded. 'Yes! Oh yes! Straight for us, it was coming straight for us.'

'Diving on us?'

'Yes – yes! Head on! About half a mile away. No – less. Less!'

Fischer nodded and said briskly, 'Stand down and pull yourself together!'

Fischer went to the chart table and leant over it, a wave of depression pressing in on him.

They might have been seen. It changed everything.

The enemy might send more aircraft, perhaps patrol boats . . .

They'd be hunted down.

Unless . . . unless they stayed submerged and slipped away. But the orders had been clear: he had no alternative but to close in and try to accomplish the task.

Damn! So near and yet so far.

He thought of the fishing boat sailing on, oblivious to everything, a victim ready for the taking, yet maddeningly beyond his reach.

He daren't surface now. He wasn't even sure if he dared go to periscope depth and have a look

Not yet anyway.

He'd take a look in half an hour, he decided. The plane might have given up by then. Even if it hadn't – well, he'd have to risk it, otherwise he'd lose the prey.

He passed the time bent over the chart, calculating and recalculating the course and speed necessary to stay on the fishing boat's tail. As before, the fishing boat had been slightly to the west of its projected track. Maybe the wind was backing. He redrew its course line and calculated the manoeuvres necessary to get the U-boat on to the new track.

At the end of an hour he checked with Sonar: there were no propeller noises. He gave the order to go to periscope depth. There was the muted hiss of blowing tanks.

'. . . Twenty-five metres . . . Twenty . . . Fifteen . . .' Then they were levelling off. Finally came the words, 'Periscope depth!'

Fischer pulled up the search periscope and, his heart in his mouth, put his eye to the lens. As he did so he thought: Please, dear God, let it still be there.

She was a long way away, in the country somewhere, lying in a barn, which accounted for the hard floor. Nearby was some soft straw which would be much better to lie on, but she couldn't get her limbs to move and carry her across to it. Her body was like stone, heavy and lifeless. For some unaccountable reason the barn was very noisy: there was a whistling and swishing and roaring which reverberated around the bare wooden walls. It was moving too, the barn, the floor tilting strangely . . . It was confusing, this place. Now something was shaking her. An animal – large, like a cow – was butting its head against her arm. The creature was getting more agitated . . .

'Mummy! Mummy! Wake up! Wake up!'

Julie opened her eyes. Instantly she closed them again: the light was blinding. Reality began to seep through into her consciousness: the awful awareness that a real nightmare was lying in wait for her, inescapable, ready to pounce on her if she awoke. She grasped at the image of the barn and tried to push her mind back towards it, back to the soft straw . . .

'Mummy, Mummy! *Please* wake up! There's a plane!'

Julie opened her eyes again and screwed them up against the light. A plane . . . She groaned slightly, and, rubbing her face with her hand, sat up. As she moved a sharp stabbing pain shot into her temples. Grasping the rail she pulled herself to her feet and the headache settled into a rhythm of dull throbbing blows that made her feel slightly sick.

'Plane . . . ? Where . . . ?' She looked around, her eyes refusing to focus properly.

'There! There!' Peter pointed away to the right. '*There!*'

Julie stared for several seconds before she saw it, a tiny black speck flying low just above the horizon. It looked a long way off. It was moving towards the north, rising now, gaining height. It seemed to hover for a moment, and Julie realised it was turning. She rubbed her eyes and looked again. It took a long curve away until it was hardly visible, then it was heading towards them, getting larger again. For a moment she thought it must have seen them, and was coming straight for them, but then she saw that the dot was banking and dropping down again, retracing its path along the far horizon, towards the south. It repeated the manoeuvre once more, and then again, going back and forth along its path several times.

The boat lurched and Julie clung to the rail to stop herself falling. Peter grasped at her jacket.

'Mummy, I'm hungry . . . and I want to go to sleep . . .'

The small face was pale and tired and a little frightened. He had done very well, considering. Julie tried to sound, if not cheerful, then reassuring. 'Of course, sweetheart. Let's open a can or two. Then you curl up down here.'

443

She bent down to search in the food bag and felt sick again. The boat was moving more jerkily now, its seesaws more violent. She fed Peter quickly and settled him down at the back of the boat under the high wooden side, out of the wind and spray.

She rubbed her aching temples and wished the headache would go away.

She looked for the plane again. It had gone.

She stared for a long time, but there was no sign. Maybe the plane had been German anyway.

She noticed that it had clouded over. High up, there was a solid ceiling of white; lower, there were angry black clouds scudding across the sky. The sea was grey and forbidding, the waves marching relentlessly towards the boat, their crests breaking with an audible hiss. Their onward procession was mesmerising, almost hypnotic.

She dragged her eyes away. *Must think* . . . David . . . She made her way slowly along the deck, trying unsuccessfully to dodge the spray and bumping sharply against the mast instead. The old man seemed all right. He was fairly warm and breathing normally. She lifted his head and put the water bottle to his lips. The motion of the boat was much worse up in the bows and it was a job to get any water into his mouth, but finally David nodded that he'd had enough and, falling back against the rope, closed his eyes.

The sickness was rising again. She hurried back to the tiller, shivering as water slopped over the side of the boat, splattered against her legs and seeped through her trousers.

Ignore the sickness. Wake up!

Course? WNW: West North-West. Still off-course – too far to the west. She frowned then grasped at an idea – perhaps it was a *good* thing. By heading too far west she'd probably miss the land altogether. Then she wouldn't have to worry about hitting it during the night. Once it was light again, *then* she could head the boat back towards the land.

It would solve a lot of problems.

Yes. She'd let the boat go where it wanted. Then – no land, no fighting with the sails, no worries. She felt a little more cheerful.

She looked at her watch. Five-thirty. God, was that all? She'd only slept for a couple of hours. No wonder she felt so terrible. Still, without any sleep at all she might have felt even worse.

She shivered again. So cold . . . And the headache, still hammering away . . .

She sat on the helmsman's seat and looked ahead into the greyness, watching the bow rise and fall against the pattern of the waves. It stopped her feeling sick. After a while she dozed, waking only when

444

the boat lurched and threatened to slide her off her seat. Then she came to with a jerk and, getting back onto the seat, stared forward again, concentrating on the grey smudge of the horizon, which seemed increasingly distant.

She should take a good look round and search for ships, but she couldn't be bothered.

She thought: I don't care any more, I really don't. I just want this to *end* ... To get somewhere, *anywhere* ... I just want it to *end*. That's all.

I don't care any more, I really don't.

Later she dozed again and woke with a jump when spray pattered against her face. The spray had never come this far back before.

Disorientated, she looked around. The boat was tilting further over, the downhill side of the deck awash with running water. The bow was digging deeper into the waves, pushing up solid sheets of water which, caught by the wind, flew diagonally back over the boat and fell down the deck in heavy cascades to the scuppers on the lower side. As the boat met each wave it gave a great shudder, pausing in its tracks for a second to throw off the weight of the water before picking itself up and leaping forward to meet the next wave rushing towards it. The mast was leaning over at a sharp angle, and the big sail bellied out, taut and strained, except for the back edge which vibrated violently. Suddenly, the boat rolled and almost dipped her rail in the rushing water. Julie gasped. The boat came back a little and the water receded.

The boat rolled again, then again. Julie watched with terrible fascination as the rail came ever closer to the rushing water. She thought: What's to stop us rolling right over? Perhaps she needed to do this reefing business, perhaps that would slow the boat down ...

Miserably, she regarded the enormous bulging sail and knew that it was hopeless: she wouldn't know where to start. It was impossible to do anything while the boat was like this, careering along like a mad thing.

The scene frightened her. After a while she realised what made it so terrifying.

The world was getting greyer, the outlines less distinct, the dark colours blacker.

The horizon was a blur, a featureless grey blending into the grey of the sea and the sky. The shape of the bows was beginning to fade ...

Julie thought: I *might* have done something, I really *might*.

But not in the dark, not *ever* in the dark ...

As night fell, and the greys faded into blackness, the fear gripped

445

her even tighter, until it held her firmly, mindlessly, on her seat by the tiller.

Two hundred miles out in the Atlantic the Liberator swept high over the darkening sea, searching.

The patrol had been going on for four hours now, with another three to go. The plane was flying one leg of a gentle zigzag designed to take it over the likely path of U-boats heading north to their hunting grounds.

Then, suddenly, the wireless operator received a signal.

A few minutes later the plane abandoned her search pattern and, banking steeply, headed east.

At first the plane headed for the position given in the signal – the last known position of the U-boat – which was thirty miles south-south-east of Land's End.

Then, later, when the pilot had done some thinking and the navigator some calculations, the course was changed to take the plane towards the English coast.

The U-boat must have been submerged all day, the pilot reckoned, which meant her speed would have been no more than seven knots. If, as he'd been told, she was heading north, then he would intercept her near the coast.

Where on the coast was another matter. The U-boat was shadowing a small fishing boat, apparently, but its destination was unknown. Falmouth? Ireland? Could be anywhere.

He would have to make a single sweep along the coast at a distance of five miles off. The channel between the Scillies and Land's End must be covered, also the Lizard, and the approaches to Falmouth.

He wouldn't have time for much more, not with the freshening headwind.

Only one thing was certain. At some point during the night the U-boat would have to surface, to get air and to recharge her batteries. And for quite a long time, at that.

There was just a chance they might catch her . . .

But where should they start from? How far west might the U-boat have gone?

He decided, and said to the navigator, 'Course to the Scillies, please. We're going to start from there and work our way eastwards.'

They lie at the end of the world, the isles of Scilly: far beyond the land; a nest of rocks and islets cut off from the mainstream of British life. On a chart they are mere pinpricks situated twenty-one nautical miles west-south-west of Land's End: a cluster of small dots on the wide immensity of the sea – the last fragment of land for three thousand miles. Being so remote and isolated, they remain, for the most part, unnoticed.

But sailors know and mark them well.

Sailing inward, towards the major European ports, ships must find their way into the beckoning but treacherous arms of the English Channel, between the rugged north coast of Brittany on the one hand, and the Scillies, harbinger of the English mainland, on the other. For many vessels this will be their first landfall for thousands of miles. Even in good conditions navigation can be the most uncertain of sciences, but after long periods of bad weather, or in fog or storm, the chances of error increase dramatically. When the weather is thick the navigator can do little but make his calculations, check the distance run – and then resort to hope, optimism and prayer.

He has reason to pray. The Scillies lie in wait for the unwary, eager to ensnare and reluctant to release.

The islands are unusually low – barely a hundred and sixty feet at their highest point – and therefore difficult to see from any real distance. In bad weather you can find yourself very close, even hear the surf on the rocks, before you realise you are on top of them.

Ships are led to their doom by the wind, which, for a greater part of the time, blows from the west, pushing ships speedily homeward, hastening the ship on her way, so that sailors have reason to be grateful to it. That is, unless the navigator is mistaken in his calculations. Then the wind blows the ship towards the crouching islands and the low teeth of the hidden reefs. A jagged grey mass of rocks is suddenly spotted close ahead, someone hears the thunder of surf on the ledges and the ship tries to turn, too late. All too late. Escape is impossible. The wind drives the vessel further and further onto the rocks, until she pounds heavily, and the teeth bite through, and the guts are torn out of her, and she is gone . . .

There are so many wrecks around the islands that even the inhabitants cannot count them. Hardly a year goes by without one, two – or in a bad year maybe a dozen – vessels meeting a lonely end on one of the outlying rocks.

The men who live here have a realistic, practical attitude towards shipwrecks. The Lord taketh away, the Lord giveth . . . There is money in salvage, there are sometimes rich pickings to be found on the long white beaches . . . Who would not take advantage of that which is given?

But they save the people first. Bravely, sometimes in gale-force winds, they set out in their open gigs and row to the dying ship to save whosoever they can . . .

Five islands are inhabited, four of them forming a circle round a shallow sound which was itself part of the land more than two thousand years ago. Most of the people live on St Mary's, the largest of the islands, which is just three miles wide. Across the sound to the north lie Bryher and Tresco, separated by an inlet which is the secret harbour of New Grimsby, where boats may hide . . .

Each of these islands has two distinct sides to it, like a coin. There is the windward side, bare and treeless, raked by the remorseless wind and salt spray, where only heather, hardy gorse, and a few stalwart flowers grow in the peaty soil. However, over the slight hills, in the lee of the land, it is possible to find shelter, and here, screened from the wind by tall hedges, of Pittosporum, Veronica and Tamarisk, there is a surprising fertility, with an abundance of early spring flowers, grain crops and grazing for domestic animals.

The fifth and smallest inhabited island, St Agnes, which lies to the south-west of St Mary's, is similar to the others – and yet somehow different. Lying outside the circle formed by the other four, it is surrounded by deep water, and has a feeling of isolation about it. Its western shore, craggy and strewn with massive red and silver granite boulders, marks what ancient men believed to be the end of the world.

Or very nearly . . . Because the land has not ended – not quite. Though few would call it land . . .

Strewn over the sea to the south-west for a distance of four nautical miles are numerous islets, rocks and half-hidden ledges. Some say that there are fifty islets around the main islands, some say a hundred. Many of them are here, to the south-west. No-one has tried to count the rocks.

Some of the larger rocks and islets support colonies of sea birds – puffins, shearwaters, petrels and gulls. Other rocks are coloured grey-green with lichen and coarse vegetation.

But many are quite bare. Washed by a hundred thousand Atlantic storms, the silver granite is unvisited, save for the seals who lie resting in the clefts before diving back into the restless rolling waves.

The most westerly of the rocks are so low that only the leaping, cascading surf reveals their position. In storms the angry white curtains of spray shoot high, high into the air – a terrible warning if you should be lucky enough to see it. The local people call these rocks ledges, though reefs might be a better name. They have ripped many a hull apart. Some vessels sank immediately; others pounded slowly and painfully to death, spilling cargo and people into the water for several days.

Once, a long time ago, the Royal Navy lost fifteen ships-of-the-line on the Western Rocks – the pride of the British fleet. Two thousand men drowned. Just over a hundred years ago during the height of the steamship era, a crack passenger ship died an agonised death on the Retarrier Ledges with the loss of three hundred lives.

The carnage had to be stopped. They decided to build a lighthouse. They chose the Bishop Rock, the last rock before the Atlantic, the final jagged point before the safe depths of the open sea. It is, unfortunately, a small rock, being only a few yards square. But they had no choice: there was nothing bigger.

They made three attempts. The first time the sea swept the structure away before the light was even lit. The second time the structure stayed up, but, pounded by winter storms, started to shake itself to death. Finally they built a third one around the second because it was easier that way – though nothing achieved in that wild, windswept desolation could ever be called easy. It took years of superhuman effort to build the third mighty tower – but it stayed up.

Now it stands proud and tall above the sea, unmoved even by the waves that sweep up and over its one hundred and sixty foot height – the tallest lighthouse in Britain. And the loneliest.

To navigators the light is a veritable godsend; in good conditions its powerful beam is visible eighteen nautical miles away. Even in poor conditions you are likely to see it before you are too close. In fog the loud blare of its foghorn will warn you away from the rocks. Sailors love the light: they have taken to asking how far out from the Bishop they have sailed, or how far back to the Bishop it might be, or how long it will take to reach the Bishop. To the sailor the Bishop means home.

The light is a veritable godsend.

. . . When it's lit, of course.

Tonight, like most nights during this war, it is not.

Only when a convoy is passing does the light flash twice every fifteen seconds, and then only dimly.

Tonight, like most nights, there is no convoy. The light is unlit, the revolving lens still.

The Western Rocks lie in total darkness, just as they always used to, before men dared to build the light.

31

Damn! Damn!

He'd missed her.

He still couldn't understand it. Had he misjudged the distance? Or, while U-319 was down deep, hiding from the plane, had the little boat changed course?

Whatever had gone wrong, when they'd returned to periscope depth there'd been no fishing boat in sight. Fischer had ordered All Ahead – full speed – towards the north-west, thinking the prey had got ahead.

But nothing. *Nothing.*

He had stayed at the periscope himself, sweeping the horizon until the waves seemed to dance in front of his eyes.

But nothing.

Then darkness had fallen.

It was infuriating. Fischer had gone back to the chart and recalculated the fishing boat's course. This time he allowed for a slightly more westerly drift, laid off the effects of the tide – also running to the west for the next few hours – and projected the line forward.

It led straight to the Isles of Scilly.

He sighed. He should have considered that possibility before. It seemed a curious destination – but on second thoughts, a very clever one. No-one would ever think of it.

Whoever was in this little boat had brains and nerve, he had to give them that.

But it wouldn't make any difference: he'd still chase them, up to the very rocks if necessary.

There was one problem though, one major chance of failure. The little boat would reach the islands before dawn and if the skipper knew the islands well he might try to enter during darkness and slip out of Fischer's reach. If, on the other hand, he didn't know the islands well enough, he would *have* to hold off till dawn or run a high risk of wrecking his boat . . .

Fischer was willing to gamble that the skipper was a stranger to the islands.

He'd catch him at dawn, then, trying to creep in. But he'd have to get in close, to be sure.

He looked up to where the young navigator hovered attentively nearby and asked him to find the largest possible chart of the islands.

Even before he saw it he knew it wouldn't be very detailed, but it would have to do.

In the meantime ... He had another problem. Recharging the batteries. He would have to surface to charge his batteries and compress some air for diving purposes. He had no choice. The power to the electric motors was already running low.

He called the Chief and together they calculated the minimum charging time they could get away with.

Six hours.

Full daylight at 0700. They'd have to get onto the surface by 0030 at the latest then.

Six hours. An awful long time. He shuddered involuntarily.

Then he had an idea.

It wouldn't eradicate the danger entirely, but it would reduce it considerably. It was risky: very.

But it was the only way.

The navigator brought the chart, the best he had. It covered the area from the Scillies to Falmouth. The islands were not shown as clearly as Fischer would have liked, but it would suffice.

The navigator said, 'There's also the pilot book, Herr Kaleu. I could make a larger sketch chart from that.'

'Very well.'

'Any particular features that you want me to study?'

Fischer stood back from the chart, 'Yes – rocks ... Or rather a lack of them. We need an area near the islands which is safe from rocks, yet close enough to make us *look* like a rock ... You see, we have to find somewhere to hide.'

The water came out of the darkness, flying across the deck in great sheets, drenching everything. Despite the waterproofs, Julie was soaked through. She could feel the icy water trickling down her neck, spreading slowly down, even into her crutch. Her eyes were sore, the eyelids sticky as if covered with glue, and her lips were swollen and tender from the salt. She didn't bother to duck when she felt the bow hit a wave. She didn't care any more.

She was hand-steering now, the tiller jerking and bucking in her hand. Since the wind had come up, the boat wouldn't sail by itself any more ... Not that she knew which way the boat was heading half the time. The compass was unreadable. She'd completely forgotten about the oil for the compass light. It was too late now. From time to time, when she remembered, she shone the torch on the compass, but its beam was getting dimmer all the time and the course more difficult to read.

451

The course, when she did manage to read it, was all over the place. God only knew where they were heading.

But it didn't seem very important any more.

She stared forward into the darkness, her body braced against the violent bucking motion of the boat. It was so tempting to just let your mind slip away into nothingness. The movements of the boat were hypnotic; so too the loud hissing and roaring of the wind and the waves. They rocked her into a state of mindless inertia. She saw the darkness as a friend now, a cocoon which encircled and protected . . .

Her eyes drooped, her head fell forward. She awoke with a jerk. God, her head ached . . .

She wondered if Peter was all right. And David. She hadn't heard from either of them for hours. She should go and see them, but she didn't. It was so much easier to stay here . . . and not to move, to let her mind drift . . .

She vaguely realised that the tiredness and the cold had paralysed her brain and frozen her will-power. It was weak and shameful to give in to it, she knew, but she was incapable of moving, of acting, of *doing* . . . She was in a sort of trance, half-believing that by staying still and ignoring things, the nightmare might somehow go away. She thought: I *would* pump the water out, I *would* go and see David and Peter . . . I *would* . . . But it's *safer* to stay here – and, oh God, *easier* too – And I've got to steer, haven't I? And, if the others had needed me, they would have shouted for me, wouldn't they? And I'm so tired, I can't do any more . . .

Her brain was so fuddled she couldn't sort the arguments out. They'd been scrambling in her mind for hours – though exactly how long she had no idea. Time seemed to spread out before her like a fan, wider and wider . . . until suddenly the fan closed and there was no time any more. She was confused . . . Sometimes she couldn't even remember how long she'd been at sea. One night? Four?

Once she saw grass growing out of the water . . . Another time she saw lights, sparkling . . .

Now, once again, she dozed.

Suddenly she was wide awake.

A noise. She could hear it, loud and distinct, above the persistent wail of the wind.

A *tearing* noise . . .

A second later there was a loud flogging.

The sails? – Or the mast . . .!

She murmured, 'God!' and stood up, feeling the first touches of panic. What to do? Christ, what to do?

'Mummy! Mummy!' Peter was almost screaming.

'It's all right! Just sit tight!' Julie shouted.

What to do?

The piece of rope was still fastened round the tiller. She took a loose end and tied it to the cleat on the uphill side of the boat. Then she made her way carefully across the deck and tied the other end to the lower cleat.

The flogging and rattling were deafening. Julie pocketed the torch and made her way forward along the uphill side of the deck. She lunged for the mast and found it. It was vibrating and shaking violently – but it was upright. Something at least.

An avalanche of spray poured down on her. She blew the water off her lips and wiped her eyes with her sleeve. She reached for the torch and shone it upwards at the sail.

Or what remained of it. She groaned. There was a tear right across the middle, from one side to the other. The tattered remnants of canvas were beating themselves to death, shaking the wooden spars like a dog shaking a rabbit.

They would have to come down . . . the lot: the sail, the long wooden pole at the bottom of the sail, the shorter pole at the top. She looked at the ends of the two poles: they were both held by ropes – ropes that must end here, at the bottom of the mast.

But which ones? There were a dozen ropes tied to cleats on a wooden frame at the base of the mast.

Trial and error. It was the only way. She undid one rope and, shining the torch upward, gently let the last turn slip off the cleat. Nothing: there was no tension on the rope. She tried the next. Ah! A lot of tension here. She searched the sail for signs of something coming down . . . Nothing. Without knowing why, she shone the torch forward. The little sail – it was half down! Blast!

She hoisted it up again as best she could and tried another rope. At last: the outer end of the lower pole was moving downwards. Right: mark that one and look for the ropes controlling the shorter, higher pole.

She found one finally and let it down until the outer end was almost in the water. Now the other inner end, the one joined to the mast. Triumphantly, she found that one too and lowered it.

Now, the two poles were lying almost parallel to each other, just a few feet above the water, but swung well out from the boat. She would have to get them in somehow . . .

She went back and hauled in on the rope near the tiller, the one she'd used to adjust the sail. There was much less pressure on it now and, to her surprise, the lower pole came in quite easily. She lowered it carefully on to the deck. Panting hard, she regarded the upper pole.

She couldn't see any way of getting it in: in the dim yellow light of the torch she could see no rope leading from its end towards the boat.

The boat lurched and the pole suddenly swung inwards, lunging over the deck. Aha! Julie thought. Nearly got you!

She waited for it to happen again. It swung in once, but not so far and she couldn't reach it. Then at last it swung right over, almost knocking her off her feet. She threw an arm round it and held on for dear life. The boat rolled back; she was jerked against the boat's side. She held on grimly and looked for something to tie round the pole. She felt around with her hand and touched a rope which was fastened to the pole. She took hold of it and held tight. The boat lurched and the pole tried to swing out again, dragging her towards the rail. She gripped the rope tighter until it ground into her flesh. Then the boat rolled back and the pole swung in again. She stepped quickly backwards and, fumbling around the base of the mast, felt for a cleat. The pole started to pull outwards again but she got one turn of the rope onto the cleat; waited, then got two more turns.

She went to the other side of the mast and, finding the right rope again, lowered the pole onto the deck.

Triumph! As she leant panting against the mast, she smiled to herself in the darkness. She'd actually tackled something! – And *succeeded*.

She said aloud, 'Well done!'

She unfastened the rope which held up the little sail in front and tightened it a bit more, then rubbed her hands. What next? Yes: the other jobs! She had the ridiculous feeling she could do anything now. Getting the big sail down had been only half as difficult as it had looked. Now everything else would be easy!

First – David . . . She went forward and shone the dim yellow light of the torch into the area under the deck. It was still fairly dry here, thank God. David was awake and bewildered, his eyes large and staring. He tried to smile but it was an effort. He seemed to be in constant pain. 'Sorry . . . not helping . . .' he whispered.

'Don't be silly. No need to worry!' She patted his arm. 'Just you rest!' She put the water bottle to his lips. As she put it down she noticed a dark stain on his sleeve. Vomit . . . And – she stared, horrified – something dark, blood. 'Are you all right, David? Oh, David!'

'I'm . . . all right.'

But he wasn't, she could see that. She shook her head miserably. 'Oh dear, I shouldn't have let you come!'

'No! No!' He gripped her arm. 'I'm glad, very glad . . . I always wanted to get to England. Are we almost there?'

Julie blinked. 'I don't know.'

He nodded slightly and closed his eyes. Julie watched him anxiously for a moment, then pulled the sacking up round his chin and made her way back to the stern.

Peter next. He was crouching in the corner of the deck, sobbing quietly. She hugged him and whispered to him until, at last, she managed to calm him. She adjusted his jacket so that it protected his head better from the spray, then went to the tiller and shone the torch on the compass.

North-west – or thereabouts. Not bad! Not bad at all!

Gradually she realised something had changed . . . It took her a moment to identify it. The boat was riding the waves much better now. There was less water coming over and the deck was not tipping so far. The tiller wasn't jerking about so much either, and the lines seemed to be holding the boat on course again. Yet the wind hadn't diminished. She realised dimly that it must be the loss of the sail that had made things easier. A blessing in disguise! She felt almost euphoric.

But the jobs now, the jobs! Pumping: that was essential. But before that, something she had been meaning to do for hours. She had noticed two life-rings on either side of the tiller, attached to the back of the boat. She found one and unhitched it and, leaning down, slipped it over Peter's head. She took the other one forward, to David and, waking him gently, made him put it on. There wasn't a third.

Then she went to the pump and, after inserting the handle in the socket, began to pump methodically, singing loudly as she rocked back and forward. Now and then she almost laughed. In the strangest way, she was ridiculously happy.

It took well over an hour this time. The sweat poured off her, and she felt hot and clammy inside her wet clothing. Her back ached terribly, but she ignored it, working herself harder and harder.

Once she paused in the eternal pumping and thought: I've discovered the secret of all this – perhaps it's the secret of everything! Never give in! Never give up! Richard wouldn't have. He would have enjoyed the challenge . . . Maurice too . . . Yes, the secret: Never give up!

Finally, when she could hardly pump any more, the handle went easy in her hand, the pipe sucking on empty air.

She staggered back to the stern and flopped down on to the helmsman's seat.

She made an effort to concentrate. There was one more thing . . . Yes, what David had said . . . About arriving . . . *When*, he had asked.

She had no idea. What had she worked out before? Twenty-four hours . . . That meant they should arrive *now*! God . . .!

But wait. They were going much slower now that the big sail was down. That would make a difference.

Also, they'd been west of their course for most of the time. She corrected herself: No, *all* the time . . . That meant they would miss the land altogether. It *must* do, otherwise –

She had a nasty thought. It had been in the back of her mind for some time. Perhaps Michel had given her a course to a *safe* part of the coast. Perhaps, by steering outside it, she was even now leading them straight for a dangerous, rocky part of the land . . .

Perhaps this north-westerly course *wasn't* safe after all . . .

She could think of only one thing to do. Steer even further west. To be absolutely sure.

Yes! *West* North-West. That would be the safe thing to do!

Until dawn at least. Then she would turn the boat towards the east again . . .

She decided to hand steer. But before she settled down, she reached into the oddments box and found another length of thin rope. She went to Peter and, kissing him, tied it round his waist. She tied the other round her own.

It was probably the wrong thing to do. If anything happened she would drag him down . . . She couldn't ever bear to think about it.

But whatever happened she wanted to be with him. She couldn't bear to think of him floating away from her . . . She murmured, 'Where you go, I go.' Then she untied the tiller and put the boat on to its new course.

'What you got, Radar?'

'The Scillies, bright and shining like a lot of little stars, Skipper!'

'Range?'

'Bishop Rock ten miles, bearing 030.'

'And how's the picture?'

'Good. There's a strong breeze blowing, about twenty five knots, but I'm not getting too much clutter. The waves can't be that big, probably because the wind's offshore now.'

'Right-ho. Taff?'

'Yes, Skipper?'

'When we get within five miles of Bishop Rock give me a course to a point five miles south of the Lizard, then we'll take another leg in towards Falmouth.'

'Roger, Skipper.'

'And Radar, shout when you see anything, however small.'

'Always do, Skipper. Eyes skinned like hard-boiled eggs.'

The pilot grimaced at the expression.

He looked down into the blackness and thought about the submarine and wondered what she was doing at this very moment. Racing for home? Creeping between the Scillies and Land's End? Hiding near the shore?

There might just be time for more than one run. If so, he'd try another further south, then perhaps a sweep to the north of the islands. He'd decide nearer the time.

The intercom crackled.

'Radar to Skipper. Contact ten miles to starboard, angle twenty degrees.'

The pilot licked his lips. 'Where is it in relation to the islands?'

'Five miles south of St Mary's. But it's a really small target, Skipper. I mean, it doesn't *look* like a U-boat. Though I can't be sure . . .'

'Keep an eye on it. Taff?'

'Yes, Skipper.'

'Give us a course to the target.'

'Roger.'

'Wireless?'

'Yes, Skipper.'

'Have we been notified of any friends at sea in this area?'

'No, sir. No convoys. No MTBs or MGBs . . .'

'Radar, could it be a mine?'

'Don't think so, sir. And we don't usually pick up anything that low in the water . . .'

'But it's definitely a target?'

'Oh yes. No doubt about that.'

If it had been the old radar the pilot might have doubted him, but it wasn't, it was the H$_2$S and he believed him.

'Wireless to Skipper.'

'Go ahead.'

'We *were* notified that the U-boat was meant to be pursuing a small craft, sir. Maybe this is the small craft –?'

That was exactly what the pilot had been thinking. If so, then where was the U-boat?

The navigator's voice came over the earphones. 'Taff to Skipper, course for target 055 degrees, range ten miles.'

The pilot switched to manual and took the plane onto her new course, reducing height at the same time.

He exchanged glances with Reid, the co-pilot, and said into the mike, 'Might as well go and have a look.'

'Definitely!'

But the pilot had a feeling about this one – a bad feeling. Something told him it wasn't a U-boat.

'Range five miles, Skipper.'

'Right ho.' As the pilot took the plane down to seven hundred feet he felt the familiar exhilaration, the thrill of the chase.

'Radar to Skipper. Look . . . I may be nuts, but . . .'

'Out with it!'

'I've got a moving rock. Just to the south of St Agnes. Quite close in . . . But it's *moving*, sir.'

The pilot stared unseeing into the night, his mind racing.

It couldn't be! But even as he thought it, he knew it could . . . just possibly . . .

He said into the mike, 'Size of contact?'

There was a slight pause. 'Larger than the first, though still small. Not a ship at any rate. *Could* be a U-boat.'

Jesus Christ! *Yes!*

The bastard was hiding!

'Taff, guide me in to this second contact. Reid, keep me above the rocks. How high are they, Navigator?'

'Navigator to Skipper. If we make a run from the south-east to the north-west, there's nothing above seventy-five feet . . .'

'Right! Guide me in!'

He would go straight in. Straight in and light her up at one mile. Then – *Bam!*

It was the U-boat, he *felt* it was the U-boat. And trying to hide, the bastard!

But there was no hiding place, not for U-boats. Not any more.

The sea was sluicing over the long, narrow bows, creating great swathes of phosphorescence which ran off in rivers of sparkling silver to the dark water beneath.

Normally Fischer would have worried about the phosphorescence, but U-319 was moving slowly so there was almost no wake to give them away. Besides, it was quite choppy and the luminescent path cut by the submarine would be indistinguishable from the multitude of breaking crests, flashing white and silver against the dark background of the night.

Fischer shivered: the north-east wind was cold. He pulled his scarf tighter round his neck and, moving over the hatch, shouted, 'Position?'

A voice came floating faintly up. 'Half a mile south of St Agnes Island.'

Fischer peered into the darkness. Nothing to be seen, but he couldn't help looking.

He hoped the navigator was right. After so long without a proper fix – visual or star – it was impossible to be positive about one's position. The navigator had got what he believed to be good bearings on radio beacons issuing from the French coast. Nevertheless Fischer had told the lookouts to keep a sharp watch for white water, just to be on the safe side . . .

These islands were the very devil. Lots of rocks and islets scattered around, especially here to the south-west. And the rocks rising steeply from the sea floor so that depth-soundings could give no warning.

The only warning they'd *ever* get would be white, breaking water . . .

U-319 was going at four knots, making tight circles in an area between a mile and half a mile to the south of St Agnes.

They'd been up on top for an hour now. Five to go. A hell of a time . . . Fischer hated being on the surface in a place like this, it made him nervous. But to enemy radar, U-319 would hopefully be just a tiny speck, another rock in the chaos of white blips that marked the Scillies.

He paced the small bridge then, on a whim, decided to go below to have another quick look at the chart. There was nothing to see up here anyway.

He half-slid, half-climbed down the ladder and, still in his wet-weather gear, went to the chart area. Just before dawn, at about six, he would take U-319 to the entrance to St Mary's Sound and wait for the prey. The little boat would have to go in that way: it seemed to be the only entrance into the islands – or at least the only *safe* entrance.

Then he'd grab the occupants – and quick. Once he was spotted all hell would break loose. He'd have five minutes – ten at the most. A slim chance. Was there any other way? He began to mull over the possibilities.

There was a muffled shout. Fischer tensed.

Then a cry. Fischer felt his blood run cold.

The klaxon shrieked through the silence, whooping obscenely. Twice.

'Dive! Dive! Dive!'

Fischer thought: *Oh God, no!*

There was a burst of noise.

Men were running forward to the bow to get the nose down; the watch were pouring down the tower from the bridge; the rest were busy in the control room, spinning stopcocks, handling levers, shouting as they completed each manoeuvre. There was a loud hissing noise as the main vents were opened, and Fischer stared at the depth-meter, waiting – *willing* – it to go down . . .

Christ! He remembered they were doing only four knots. At that speed it would take for ever. *Christ!*

Everything was happening with infinite slowness . . .

Fifteen seconds gone . . .

The last man fell down the tower and the hatch was clanged shut.

The depth-meter was just beginning to show something – *at last*. Come on. *Come on*. The water would barely be washing round the conning tower . . .

One metre! So slow . . .

Twenty seconds gone.

Fischer looked over the coxswain's shoulder. The stick was fully forward, the hydroplanes at maximum pitch, angling the nose down, down, down – but slowly, so slowly . . .

God, one could go mad in such a moment . . .

Thirty seconds gone.

They should have been down by now – safe!

Depth – four metres. Conning tower covered . . . Not deep enough!

She was going slightly faster now. Eight metres . . . Almost at periscope depth . . .

Forty seconds gone . . .

Perhaps they'd manage it after all.

Then time stood still. And U-319 took off.

Her port side shot up, up, up, twisting sideways and upwards by the bow. Fischer felt a momentary surprise as the floor rose up against his feet. Then the control room spun rapidly round and he realised he was falling.

Then came the noise, a vast long echoing boom which stunned the ears and reverberated in the brain.

There were shouts . . . Dull noises which dimly penetrated one's ringing ears . . . Men lying on the floor, reaching out . . .

Panting, Fischer pulled himself up. He tried to shout. But nothing came out. He tried again, 'Damage reports!'

The messages came back, slowly at first.

'Flooding in fore-ends. Watertight door closed!'

'Flooding in accommodation!'

The bow was settling down from its strange upward tilt, settling down – and falling.

He shouted, 'Blow forward tanks.' Christ, he had to get more buoyancy into her, otherwise she'd sink like a stone.

The bow was already beginning to tilt more steeply downwards.

'Depth twenty metres!'

Fischer gulped: she was falling too fast!

'Forward tanks blown!'

'Blow aft tanks!' It was risky, but even if they came up stern first it was better than falling this fast.

Men were pouring aft now, out of the accommodation. As the last man came through, the watertight door was slammed and bolted shut.

'Accommodation flooding rapidly, Herr Kaleu. We couldn't stop it.'

Fischer's eyes fastened on the depth gauge. It was falling steadily. 'Aft tanks blown!'

Thirty metres . . . thirty three . . . still falling.

And they had blown all the main ballast tanks.

The nose was tilting further and further down . . .

Fischer raced for the chart. How deep –?

Sixty-eight metres.

Christ, they were going to hit the bottom *hard*.

Forty metres . . . Fischer tried to think: What else, what else!

He looked at the men who had crowded in from the forward sections and yelled, 'All you to the after-ends!'

The frightened faces were blank and stunned, but they obeyed, grabbing handholds to start the uphill climb to the after sections.

But the nose was tilting further and further down . . .

Depth: Fifty metres and accelerating.

'Brace yourselves!'

Men flattened themselves against bulkheads or crouched against partitions. Then there was silence.

Those who could see the depth gauge watched it, their eyes round with horror.

Fifty five metres . . . Sixty . . .

She hit at sixty-one. The impact pushed in the first fifteen feet of her bow, opening up the already damaged forward compartment and completing the flooding process.

Fischer was aware of the breath being knocked out of his body, of his head meeting hard metal with a thud.

Then there was quiet, except for the hiss of leaking pressure pipes and the moans of men in pain.

U-319 was on the bottom.

Fischer pulled himself up against a partition. The floor was steeply tilted: the submarine was at an angle of about forty-five degrees, her stern high above the sea floor.

She was still moving though: twisting over, slowly and gently on to her port side.

Fischer brushed at the warm blood that was running into his eyes and looked round the control room. There was something wrong, something *else* . . .

He peered round the partition. Ahead was the bulkhead that separated the control room from the accommodation. The watertight door was still closed and locked tight. But to one side of it water was hissing out in a fan from the bulkhead itself. Fischer stumbled down the slope of the deck and fell against the bulkhead. He put his fingers to the metal. The water was spraying out from a wide fracture which ran from the deckhead almost to the floor.

He looked at it for a long time, then turned.

The men were watching him, their faces blank, patient, passive. Someone appeared from aft. 'Flooding in the engine room, Herr Kaleu. We're trying to patch it up now.'

They couldn't save her. They'd try of course, but Fischer knew it would be no good. Neither could they escape; no-one had ever made a free ascent from this depth and lived.

Fischer stared back at them. For the moment there was nothing he could say to them.

He would think of something later, something appropriate, something to prepare them for the end.

But all he could think of now was that they had put their faith in him and they had been wrong. Even now, they were waiting expectantly.

There is nothing I can do for you, my friends.

It might take them a day to die, maybe longer, depending on how long the air lasted.

Then he looked down at the gathering water and thought: No, it'll be quicker than that. We're going to drown first.

He shook his head and smiled at his brave uncomplaining men with affection.

He wanted to say: I never was a god. Why did you ever think I was?

But they already knew it. They could see it in his face and, one by one, they looked away.

Julie wished it wasn't so dark.

She wasn't so worried about the sailing now – the boat seemed to be dancing along quite happily – but she did wish she could see.

Still . . . there was only this night to survive, and then, some time in the morning, land would come into sight – or a plane – help of some kind at any rate. Then – she could almost imagine it now – the massive overwhelming *relief*. And the peace.

A picture floated in front of her eyes, as real as if she had seen it herself: it was a picture of a small cottage, standing alone on a hilltop, with a wonderful view of the distant sea which was pale and sparkling in the sunshine. The cottage was whitewashed and surrounded by a small garden with borders of softly coloured flowers. Sitting in the garden were two people: she was one of them. The other was Richard. They had been there some time, living in the small cottage. They were very happy.

Extraordinary how clear it all was. She tried to hold on to it but other pictures flashed into her mind: a small terraced house – her mother's – a clifftop, her uncle and aunt walking on it, a dance at Plymouth ... Then everything got jumbled up and people were laughing at her, and it was some kind of nightmare, and they were pointing at her ... Then she was drifting away, out to sea, in a strange boat without a tiller ...

She woke up. Reality.

She shone the dim torch at the compass and put the boat back on course. She looked around. Nothing had changed.

She peered down into the darkness by the stern. She could just make out the dark shape of Peter's body curled up in the corner.

Then she heard it.

A faint noise, so indistinct that at first she thought she was mistaken.

Wide awake now, she peered into the darkness ahead.

There it was again. A faint – something ...

A whispering? No, more of a swishing ...

She gulped and stood up.

Where was it coming from?

She looked around wildly. The sound seemed to be all around her. Or was it ahead, more?

It faded then died away. Perhaps she was imagining it ...

No! There it was again, like muffled thunder, a soft boom which rolled, then fell away ...

She stood still, frozen, gripped by fear.

Again, a low rumble. Closer. *Closer.*

She clamped her hand to her mouth.

Then she saw it and almost screamed. A flicker which grew into a long smudge of glimmering whiteness.

'*God! God!*'

It was water – white water, leaping, moving, rising, falling back, a great line that stretched across the sea in front of her.

She yanked the tiller towards her. Pulling, pulling until it would go no further.

'Turn! Turn! *Please* . . .' She pulled on the tiller until her hands hurt.

The boat turned on a wave and lurched over, throwing her sideways against the boat's side.

She grasped the rail and turned back to look.

White water . . . rising, thundering up against black walls, falling back . . .

She cried out, '*Oh God!*' And watched the terrible water, mesmerised, the fear gripping her like ice.

Then she remembered. The tiller: she had let it go. She reached out for it, found it, took hold of it, suddenly realised she had lost all sense of direction.

The white water was to her right now. Whimpering slightly she looked around her. Turn still more: she must turn still more.

Away, away, back to the open sea . . .

She pulled on the tiller, took another look at the white water . . . it was almost behind her . . . *behind* her . . . Yes, yes – behind her now . . . She shouted, 'Oh, go away! *Go away!*' For a moment it seemed that the white water was dragging her back, then she realised it was fading, turning grey again . . .

She collapsed, shaking and weak, on to the seat, murmuring, 'Oh, Oh . . .'

Something made her look up – a sound; a dull roar; falling water. Her blood froze.

Somebody screamed. She dimly realised it was herself. Ahead of the boat was a wall of brilliant silver and white cascading downwards and backwards, rushing out towards the little boat. Then a wave rose, higher and higher, and Julie was aware of the little boat rushing forward, hurtling headlong towards a black mass rising into the sky, blacker than the night.

She grabbed for the tiller and pulled desperately, but the wild forward motion of the boat was inexorable. The black mass rose higher and larger, rushing forward to meet the boat.

She screamed again and turned to reach out for Peter. A second later the breath was pushed from her body and she was thrown forward, flying headlong. *Peter! Peter!* She was twisting in the air; turning; then landing on something brutal and hard which dug deep into her back.

She looked wildly about and screamed, '*Peter!*'

Some way below her she saw the dim outline of the back of the boat, where Peter had been, but so dark that she couldn't see *inside*.

'Peter!'

Water came roaring towards her in a great deluge, flooding over the boat. She grabbed at something and, closing her eyes, held on tight. The water came thundering over her head, filling her eyes and ears and trying to drag her away. *Hold on, hold on.* She held on until her arms were breaking. Something jerked at her waist, pulling at her body.

The water subsided, sucking back in a great gasp, as if taking another breath.

She rasped for air and tried to move towards the stern, towards Peter, but the rope was tight around her waist, dragging her to the side.

'God, let me go! Let me go!'

She pulled on the rope, tried to yank it off, tried to tear it off, grappling wildly at the knot. *Get off!* Then she remembered – the rope! *The rope was Peter.* She screamed, *'P-e-t-e-r!'* and slid down the deck in the direction of the rope. Nothing. She groped around. She touched something soft and reached for it just as the next wave came thundering over the deck, knocking her sideways, roaring into her mouth. She reached out through the water – grabbed – found – clung – pulled him into her body . . .

She clung to him. She clung to him as the water carried them forward, bumping, crashing them along, forward, forward . . .

Something hit her head with a great bang. She swallowed water. Then they were up against something hard, and now the other way, now they were being dragged back, back, back.

And she clung to him. And in that fraction of a moment she would have died for him, *wanted* to die for him, the child of her body. She would have held the water back with her bare hands and clawed at the rock with her fists and killed any man or anything that stood in her way . . .

But now the water was carrying them forward again, faster this time and angrier, a great crested wave that carried them up, up, racing forwards to hurl itself on the unyielding granite, forward on to the mighty rock which waited to break the back of the impudent wave, as it had broken a hundred thousand before it.

Julie was aware that the deck had disappeared from under her feet. Instead there was only the water, spinning her round, trying to drag her down. She swallowed water, tried to breathe, choked, gasped for breath, found some precious air, gulped water again, felt the sea close over her head . . . flung out an arm and tried to fight her way up . . .

Still the wave raced forward.

And still she clung to him.

Then they were falling, falling in the great cataract of water. Julie braced herself. In that instant of time she saw a great panorama before her: a split second which covered all the happiness and joy of her life.

Something hit the back of her body with a sickening impact, it hit her so hard that her chin met her chest and her breath was exploded from her lungs. Then the water was clawing at her, dragging her over rough, sharp, hurtful things . . .

Everything began to slip away . . . She was drifting gently . . . the world was purple . . . white . . . black. She was drifting . . .

In a moment of lucidity she was aware of a terrible pain in her side, as if a great weight were pressing hard against it. One last time she murmured the child's name.

Then she was slipping away again . . . into a cloud where a soft gentle wave enveloped her, soothing her aching head, removing all pain, making everything right again . . .

David thought: How strange that I should die here, in the sea.

The boat lurched again, slipping further down, wood scraping loudly and unhappily against granite.

The rushing waves came higher into the raised bow, grabbing at David's legs, trying to pull him away.

David thought: I'll be ready for you when you come.

He'd already said his last prayers and made his peace with God. Now he concentrated his mind on the small house in Germany, as it used to be, in the days when they had been so happy.

He started from the time when Cecile was very small. He remembered her podgy little arms reaching out to touch his nose, he remembered the three of them in the park . . .

A wave washed up to his chest and covered his head with spray. He was almost swept away, but managed to cling on.

Was that the one God had intended for him?

No. When he could hold on no more, *that* would be the one.

He had got to Cecile's school days when the wave finally came. It was larger than the rest. It washed right up into the bow with a thunderous roar and as it receded his hands were torn away from the boat and he was travelling with the water . . .

Free at last. In a way.

Then he made himself go limp and waited, suspended by the lifebuoy. Water filled his mouth and nose and he choked and spluttered and fought for breath. He was vaguely disappointed. He'd thought it would be easy, just a matter of closing your eyes and waiting.

But finally the fight for breath became more difficult. He had no strength left. He felt himself ebbing away.

For one brief moment the soft air touched his face, then a wave hissed over him and filled his mouth and he knew he wouldn't struggle any more.

The lifebuoy slipped up over his shoulders and he was floating downwards, drifting gently. In the last few moments panic gripped him, but he calmed himself by remembering that he was a lucky man: his troubles were finally over.

32

Joe Treleaven sniffed the air. Cold. Cold for March and cold for the islands. The low dormer window was opaque with condensation. Puffing a little, he pulled a heavy oiled sweater over his head and, leaning down, rubbed the wetness from the glass and peered through.

It was almost sunrise. The dawn light was clear and hard as a diamond, the sky a yellow dome above the blackness of the sea. It would stay cold all day, Joe decided.

Easterlies. He shook his head and stomped down the cottage stairs into the kitchen. Easterlies were the only winds which could bring this kind of cold to St Agnes. Perhaps there was something to be said for turning the fields over to vegetables after all. Before the war he'd grown nothing but flowers and flowers didn't like too much sharpness in the air.

Mind you, the bulbs kept coming up: you couldn't stop them. And now that the transportation of flowers was forbidden there were fancy prices to be had on the black market, so he'd heard. Four pounds for a box of daffodils. By jove, that was enough to keep a man for a month.

He riddled the stove, opened the vent and poured more coal into the top. He picked up the kettle and, opening the latch, went out into the yard. He paused, as he always did, and looked out towards the Western Rocks. The wind of the previous night had dropped away and the air was still. It might be a good fishing day. Perhaps he'd take the boat and go lining for scad. But then perhaps he wouldn't; perhaps he'd go weed-gathering for pigfeed instead.

He filled the kettle from the water barrel and, returning to the kitchen, put it on the stove. He made himself a breakfast of porridge and tea, then pulled on his jacket to go and feed the animals. As he approached, the pigs snorted in wild agitation. He gave them their usual mixture of vegetables and kelp, then threw the chickens a handful of grain.

The sun was up now, illuminating the tall Tamarisk hedges a vibrant green. Beyond the fields, over the rugged shoreline, the far-away lines of jagged rocks were lit a dull pink-gold in a sea of palest yellow.

There was a distant buzzing sound in the sky. Joe screwed up his eyes and spotted the glint of a plane far away above the needle-like Bishop, heading south.

After it had gone he gazed a little longer, but more casually, eyeing the weather and getting the feel of the day. He decided he should really go weed-gathering rather than fishing, though he wouldn't enjoy it half as much.

He began to turn away, but something made him pause and look back. He stared at the distant rocks for a long time, a slight frown on his face. Then, slowly, thoughtfully, he walked back into the cottage and closed the door behind him.

He cleared the breakfast things from the table and piled them in the washing-up bowl. Then he went into the front room to the mantelpiece. The telescope was an old one which his family had come by many years before – probably from a wreck, though no-one would own to it.

He took the telescope through the kitchen and up the stairs to the bedroom. The small window hadn't been opened all winter and was warped with damp, but it finally yielded. He extended the telescope, rested it on the sill and peered through.

He stared for a long time before he was satisfied. He closed the window, compressed the telescope and went down to the kitchen again. From the back of the door he took a long oilskin coat, a sou'wester and a towelling scarf, and placed them on the table. He removed his stout farmer's boots and pulled on a pair of long seaman's boots. Then, picking up the oilskins, he left the cottage and made his way up the lane towards Lower Town, one of the four settlements on St Agnes.

When he reached the handful of dwellings he went straight to a cottage near the beach and knocked on the door. A man appeared. 'Mornin', Jeremiah,' Joe said.

468

'Mornin', Joe.' The man eyed the oilskins.

'Ther's somethin' out on the rocks.'

The man nodded and without further comment disappeared inside. After a while he returned with oilskins and together the two men made their way to the beach. A heavy boat was sitting at the top of a long concrete slipway, two pairs of oars lying across the thwarts.

Without a word the two men threw their oilskins into the boat and began to drag her down the slipway. Once she was afloat they gave a last push, hopped effortlessly in, fitted the oars into the rowlocks, and started to pull away.

From the cove they crossed the expanse of Smith Sound and passed between the low rocks of the Hellweathers out into the open sea. From here it was two miles to the main group of the Western Rocks.

They rowed silently, each man intent on the slow, steady swing of his stroke. There was a swell running, the last remains of the waves whipped up by the gale the night before. But the surface itself was unruffled by wind and the sharp bow of the boat cut cleanly through the glass-like water.

Joe sat on the forward thwart, the better position for piloting. He had noted the thrust of the tide as they passed through Hellweathers Neck and every now and then he glanced over his shoulder to get his bearings on the rocks ahead. They came abreast of Melledgan and the Muncoy Ledges to the south then, after another fifteen minutes, Joe saw the profile of Gorregan and the Rags out of the corner of his eye. Not so far now.

He paused in his stroke and, turning his head, took a good look at the rocks ahead. The other man paused also. 'Where d'ye reckon, Joe?'

Joe pursed his lips. 'I reckon Rosevean. Well, let's start there at any rate.' They began to row again.

The two men had searched the rocks many times before. Once, before the war, they had found the wreckage of a small boat and, on one of the higher rocks, the body of a man. He was on his knees, his hands clasped together as if in prayer, his body crouched, his head pointing towards the mighty Bishop Lighthouse as if in hope of rescue. When they got to him he was cold and stiff as a board and it had been the devil's own job to straighten him out.

Joe feathered his starboard oar to turn the boat to port and head her between the Rags and Rosevear. As Rosevear came up abeam he slowed the pace and examined the rocky surface of the islet with a critical eye. Nothing there. Only gulls, the occasional tuft of scurvy grass, and the jagged patterns of the rocks themselves.

The boat passed on, going due south now. They came to a scattering of small rocks, then, finally, the islet of Rosevean, a little taller than its sister, Rosevear, but smaller and utterly barren.

As they approached the islet they stopped rowing and let the boat drift under her own momentum. The only sound was the rumbling and swishing of the sea as the swell rose up the sides of the rock and rushed and tumbled in among the cracks and crevices, only to recede again, the water falling away from the granite walls in tumbling cascades.

The other man was pointing. Joe followed the direction of his finger. There was something in the white froth at the base of the rock face. It looked like wood.

The boat drifted on. They came abreast of the islet. There were more fragments in the water here. Again, they looked like wood.

The two men scanned the uneven surface of the rock but Joe saw it first. It was the object he'd seen from the land. A great blob of darkness against the pallor of the rock.

They came closer and saw that it was a ragged triangle of reddish-black material, caught on a spur of rock some fifteen feet above the sea. It looked to Joe like canvas.

Joe began to row the boat round in a circle away from the islet. Still the men stared at the rock.

There was something else: a touch of bright scarlet. This, too, was quite high up, half hidden behind a knoll. Joe pointed to it and the other man nodded. As they rowed away, more of the object came into view. It was familiar, something both men had seen before: the brightly painted transom of a small boat.

'Better take a look.'

They rowed back towards the rock, to a ledge they knew well: a ledge a man could jump on to.

'I'll go,' Joe said.

'Right-ho'.

Joe shipped his oars and, as the other man brought the boat in towards the rock, he stood up. He waited while the swell took the boat down then, as the boat rose again, he placed a foot on the thwart and, in the moment that they hovered at the top of the wave, he stepped across on to the ledge.

From here there was a gully which led to the top. There was only one point which was difficult to climb, but Joe knew the handholds.

When he reached the top he clambered across the rock to the side where he'd seen the blaze of scarlet. He peered down over the edge. It was wood all right, and, as he had thought, part of a boat. By the brightness of the paint, a fishing boat. By the gay designs, a French one.

470

He moved to where the triangle of reddish-black was spread across the rock. Yes: part of a sail. It was still attached to the gaff. The gaff was suspended by a halyard which had caught itself round the spur of rock.

But there was more.

Trapped by fingers of rock or marooned in rock pools and tiny plateaus there were all kinds of jetsam: rope, more pieces of tattered canvas, fragments of black-painted wood – even a lifebuoy.

The small boat had been smashed into a thousand pieces.

He climbed on, as close to the edge as he dared, peering down among the gullies and crevices.

He reached the northern side of the island and turned back. There was nothing worth risking his neck for.

Then he realised he'd missed something: a black sack-like object draped over a small outcrop. There was something else underneath it.

He went nearer until he could look directly down on the objects. He stared for a long moment then murmured, 'Poor devils.'

He clambered back to the other side of the islet until he could see the rowing boat. He whistled and indicated to the other man that he should row the boat round to the east side.

The other man nodded and Joe clambered back to the point directly above the sack-like object. With his face to the rock, he climbed carefully and slowly downwards. He paused to look down and get his bearings. Yes, at least one body and perhaps another.

The last few feet were difficult: almost vertical rock. He found a foothold and jumped the last few feet. He waited for the boat to appear round the corner and waved until he was sure that Jeremiah had seen him. Then he went over to the bodies.

He knelt down. One was a woman, her body arched backwards round a finger of rock, as if a wave had tried to pull her back into the sea and the rock had prevented it.

Beside her was a child of about seven or eight, his face white, his eyes closed.

The two were roped together.

Joe put his hand on the woman's forehead. Cold. He put his hand against her neck and felt for the artery. Nothing.

Then a flutter. A glimmer.

He moved quickly. He straightened the woman's body and laid her on her back. He saw that there was a nasty wound on her head.

He rubbed her hands vigorously then patted her cheeks. He felt her neck again. The fluttering was still very faint.

Something made him look up. He started with surprise.

The child's eyes were open, staring blankly.

Joe went to his side and took his hand. It was icy cold. The child was almost frozen to death. Joe rubbed his hands, roughly, almost angrily, then patted the sheet-white cheeks.

The child blinked.

'Now then, young fella, ye're goin' to be all right, you hear? I'm just goin' to get ye' something warm. Right?'

The child stared. Joe turned and shouted to Jeremiah, who threw a rope up. A few minutes later Joe had hoisted up the oilskins and an old piece of canvas they kept in the boat. He took off his own sweater and placed it over the child with an oilskin on top. Then he put the canvas and Jeremiah's oilskin over the woman.

He shouted down to Jeremiah. 'We'll need four more men, another boat, more warm clothes – oh, and a plank of wood to get them down on, Jeremiah.'

The other man called 'Right-ho', and rowed off in the direction of St Agnes.

Joe leant down beside the woman and went through his rubbing and patting treatment again. Warmth and blood-flow, that was what she needed. There was no response, but he kept going. It was probably the bump on the head that was doing the damage.

Then he returned to the child. This time the boy watched him as he approached.

'Hello, young lad.'

Fear came into the child's eyes and he looked desperately around, as if realising for the first time where he was. His lips moved but he couldn't speak, his teeth were chattering so much.

Joe smiled. 'Don't worry, we'll soon 'ave yer warm!'

Finally the child said, 'Mummy!' And tried to move nearer the woman.

Joe restrained him gently. 'She'll be all right, don' yer worry!'

'Mummy!' He was sobbing now.

Quickly Joe said, 'Look 'ere, who else was with yer? On the boat? Can yer tell me?'

The child was crying, rivers of tears falling from his cheeks, his face contorted with despair. 'M-M-ummy! P-p-lease let me g-go to M-M-Mummy!'

It was perplexing. Joe didn't know what to do. He'd never had dealings with children. He didn't know they could be so – strong-minded. 'Look 'ere, she's not too well. She's best left on 'er own, take my word for it!' He put a friendly but firm hand on the child. He didn't want the lad throwing himself around the place.

The child was sheet white now, his eyes staring. 'G-go away! Go away, you horrible man! L-leave us alone!'

Joe was taken aback. That was strong talk. He retreated a little and said uncertainly, 'Well . . . You won't touch 'er 'ead, will yer?'

'N-no!'

'Right, well . . .'

The child got to his knees and, crawling across to the woman, put his arms round her waist and pushed his head against her side. He murmured to her as if she were awake.

Joe shook his head. What a thing. He covered the boy with the clothing again and, when the child was calmer, asked him again, 'Was there no-one else with yer, lad?'

This time the child turned his head and nodded slightly.

'Yes? 'ow many?'

The boy looked away and Joe thought he wasn't going to answer. Finally the child said, 'D-David. D-David.'

'David, was it?'

The child closed his eyes and pushed closer to his mother.

'Was it just 'im?'

The child said something. Joe put his head closer. 'What did you say?'

'Just him,' the child whispered.

Joe patted his arm reassuringly. He should say something but it was difficult to think of anything. Eventually he murmured, 'Well, don' yer worry. We'll find 'im. We'll find 'im. One way or the other.'

And they did. Four days later. When his body, bloated with gases, floated to the surface again.

Part five
May 1943–June 1945

33

The car came to a halt. It wasn't difficult to see why. The road was blocked by fallen debris. A row of tall buildings had been almost totally destroyed. The ruins were smouldering in the dawn light, the heavy smoke in strange contrast to the pink blossom on the one surviving cherry tree.

Doenitz said suddenly, 'I'll walk from here.'

The driver leapt from his seat and opened the rear door. Doenitz stepped out and walked briskly away, picking his way round the piles of stone and mortar, his staff officer on his heels. The Hotel-am-Steinplatz was only just round the corner. Doenitz noted that the hotel was still standing: one of the few in central Berlin that still was.

He strode into the hotel and went down to the basement. But instead of going straight to the tracking room as usual, he turned into his office and closed the door behind him.

He needed time to think.

It was the day of decision.

The figures had been placed on his desk. He eyed them as he slowly and methodically pulled up the chair, sat down, and straightened his tunic. He picked up the sheet of statistics. It was now the twenty-third of May. In the first twenty-one days of the month the U-boat arm had managed to sink 200,000 tons of Allied shipping – a lot less than in any of the previous three months but still a commendable total, considering –

He brought his eyes down to the paragraph marked 'U-boat Losses'.

Thirty-one boats lost in just twenty-one days.

It was an unprecedented rate.

It was a disaster.

Thirty-one . . .

Boats had been disappearing everywhere – while hunting in the open Atlantic, off Iceland and, as ever, on passage across the Bay of Biscay.

Nowhere was safe any more.

Thirty-one . . .

He gritted his teeth and tried not to imagine how it had been for the men . . . And, in particular, for one of them, the special one so close to his heart . . .

With effort he turned his thoughts back to the problem. What was the answer to it all? No-one could tell him exactly what system or secret the Allies had hit upon. No-one had offered a countermeasure. Maybe the British had spies in the Kriegsmarine itself, maybe they had broken the German ciphers, maybe ...

Maybe that Rotterdam device which Schmidt and his scientists were still trying to rebuild held the key to it all ...

Doenitz had the feeling it did.

But nobody could tell him one way or the other. Not with certainty.

Meanwhile his men died.

The men had a name for what was happening. They called it the Thunderbolt. This month of May was becoming known as the Month of the Thunderbolt.

The question was, what could he do to prevent it? He had been asking himself that question all night. And most of the previous day. And the answer was always the same.

Nothing, not directly anyhow.

He looked up at the safe neutral walls of his underground office. Head of the German Navy and powerless to protect his men. He had done his best – but it had not been enough.

He sighed. He was left with only one possible decision and he must make it now.

He must withdraw all his wolf packs from the North Atlantic.

He had been brooding on it all night; now he was certain. He couldn't go on sending his men to their deaths. Nothing could be worth that.

The consequences of the withdrawal would be grave. It would give the Allies the freedom to plan their invasion of Europe. It would also give them the means of achieving it. Once their convoys could get through from North America unimpeded, they would quickly stockpile weapons and supplies. Then there would be no stopping them.

He had told Hitler this, he had explained it all. Doenitz wasn't sure whether the Fuehrer had understood the implications fully, but Hitler had been sufficiently worried to summon Goering and ask for a progress report on the Rotterdam device. Goering had brushed the matter aside, as he usually did, saying that radar probably wasn't at the root of the trouble anyway ...

In the meantime the disaster gathered momentum. He must withdraw the wolf packs.

There was no choice. Not for the moment.

Later perhaps there might be a chance ... There might be an opportunity to get the boats back into the North Atlantic when the scientists had discovered a countermeasure ... Yes, one never knew. There was always a chance.

He sat forward in his chair and picked up the telephone. 'A meeting

of senior staff in five minutes, Henker.' The staff officer acknowledged the order. Doenitz asked, 'What else must be attended to this
morning?'

'Special meeting with Herr Scheer at eleven. That's to discuss the
shortfall in the U-boat programme, Herr Grossadmiral. Then some
general correspondence. Oh, and some bereavement letters.'

'How many?'

'Five, Herr Grossadmiral.'

'Right.' He replaced the receiver.

Bereavement letters. Doenitz was in the habit of writing to the
families of missing U-boat commanders personally, even though his
present rank did not demand it. He'd always done it in the past, and
he liked to continue the practice.

Five. He'd already done ten this week. He would do them directly
after the staff meeting.

He must write another letter. To his wife. He'd written to her when
the news of his son's loss had first come through. Somehow it hadn't
been too bad then. But time was making it worse, not better, and it
was becoming increasingly difficult to find the right words.

He covered his face with his hands. In the past he had always
managed to avoid thinking about the boys. He had been careful to
close them out of his mind so as to show no favour. One could not
let emotion enter into one's judgement; one could not ask about a
particular U-boat just because it carried one's own flesh.

Now – now he wished he'd thought about them more often. He
wished he'd *seen* them more frequently.

Now one was lost.

He must write to his wife again. It would be impossible to find the
right words.

He sat upright and breathed in sharply. In a sense, all the crews
were his sons and now he must do his best to prevent any more of
them from dying.

There was a knock at the door. Doenitz started slightly. He
reached hastily into his pocket and, taking out a handkerchief,
rubbed his eyes where some dust seemed to have got into them. The
staff officer appeared in the doorway. 'The meeting is assembled,
Herr Grossadmiral.'

Doenitz nodded, got to his feet and, straightening his tunic, marched from the room.

'It's here in Paris, the job.'

'I thought Paris was too dangerous for me.'

Kloffer shrugged. 'You worry too much. Time has passed. People forget.'

Vasson thought: They never forget.

They were sitting in the back of Kloffer's Citroën, parked in a side street near the Etoile. Vasson viewed the scene with annoyance. It seemed to him that there was an atmosphere to the city which hadn't been there before. The people were more optimistic, more defiant. The sullen desperation had gone.

'Yes,' Kloffer went on, 'it's the students again. Communists, agitators . . . Usual stuff –'

'Look, before we talk about this,' Vasson interrupted firmly, 'there's the matter of payment. I haven't had the second payment for the Brittany job.'

Kloffer turned his head and stared hard at him, his eyes gleaming angrily. He said, 'You never give up, do you? You never learn!' He tutted and sighed heavily. 'The job was a mess, remember? And you were the one who messed it up. I strongly advise you not to mention the money again. Otherwise – even I will lose patience!'

Vasson was so angry that he couldn't speak for a moment. Eventually he said deliberately, 'I've told you before, it was nothing to do with me. It was that disgusting queer, Baum. *He* made the mistakes!'

Kloffer shrugged. 'So you say, Vasson, but in Berlin it's *your* name that's got the mud all over it. Nothing will change that.'

Vasson clenched his teeth. He hated Kloffer using his name. He said with difficulty, 'So am I to understand that I will never be paid?'

'That's correct.' Kloffer spoke matter-of-factly, but there was an edge of impatience in his voice.

Vasson said stiffly, 'I see.' He stared straight ahead, his face impassive. It was the one thing he couldn't forgive. Not being paid.

Kloffer gave a small sigh of relief. 'Good. Now, where were we?'

'One more thing,' Vasson interrupted. 'Am I to be paid for *this* job?'

There was an infinitesimal pause. 'Of course.'

He was hiding something, Vasson could tell. 'What are the terms?'

'The best available, given the circumstances.'

Vasson's pulse quickened. The bastard was going to try and screw him. 'Tell me.'

'No more gold. There's none available.'

Vasson said nothing.

'Also this is going to be a simple job for you. It shouldn't take more than a week. The payment will be a single payment of five thousand. On completion.'

It was chicken-feed. Vasson let his rage rise and subside again.

'Tell me,' he said carefully, 'is it that I'm worth less than before . . . Or that you now regard me as expendable?'

Kloffer considered for a moment. 'Your price has gone down.' He shrugged. 'That's all there is to it.'

'I see.'

'You'd be blind *not* to see, Marseillais. You have to realise that things have changed. You're not as – Well, we don't need you so much as before . . . We've got other methods. And other people – people as good or better than you.'

It was a lie about the other people, Vasson knew it. There wasn't anyone better. As for the other methods – they were cruder, that was all. And less effective.

There was a silence.

Kloffer glanced at him. 'Shall we get on, then?' He waited a moment, then began listing information and instructions.

Vasson pretended to listen, but his mind was already elsewhere, planning his moves, working out times and, most important of all, calculating how best to cover himself so that Kloffer would never find out the truth.

When Kloffer had finished, Vasson asked casually, 'Fougères. Is he dead?'

Kloffer said irritably, 'Fougères? Who's he?'

'The Meteor line. Based here. I used his identity in Brittany.'

'Ah . . .' He thought for a moment and shrugged. 'Dead. Yes, I'm almost certain.'

'And the other man? The one who swore to my identity?'

'Yes, yes! Dead too! Why do you worry about such things?'

Vasson managed the glimmer of a smile. 'I just like things neat and tidy, that's all.'

'You mean, you're frightened!' Kloffer looked amused.

'Not at all.'

'But you should be.'

Vasson smiled grimly. 'I thought you said it wasn't dangerous for me in Paris.'

'It's dangerous for you everywhere.' He removed a piece of fluff from his sleeve. 'But don't worry, we'll protect you.'

It was a lie. Vasson knew they would never protect him.

'All right? Are you clear about the job? Any questions?'

Vasson shook his head. 'No questions.'

'Oh? Well, well. Quite a change . . .' Suspicion flashed into Kloffer's eyes. 'You're not planning anything stupid, are you?'

'What?'

'Running for it.'

Vasson snorted with amusement. 'No, Kloffer. As you always tell me, there's nowhere to hide.'

Kloffer nodded slowly. 'Yes, and don't you forget it, Paul Vasson.'

Vasson smiled at him, and thought: Goodbye, you bastard. May you rot in hell.

As soon as he reached the apartment near the Porte d'Auteuil he set feverishly to work.

He took the three suitcases down from the top of the wardrobe and left them open, two on the bed and the third, which was rather shabby, on the floor.

From the wardrobe and the chest of drawers he took his best clothes and packed them hurriedly in one of the better cases. The cheaper working clothes which he'd used in Paris he placed in the second. The oldest clothes and the ones he'd worn in Brittany he threw into the third, shabby case.

Then he pulled out a drawer and, turning it over, tore off a small flat package which was stuck to the underside. Inside there were two sets of identity papers. He took one set of papers, which he'd never used before, and slid them into his wallet. The second set, which were in the name of Fougères, he placed in an ashtray. With a shaking hand he put a match to them. When they were burning nicely he added another set of papers – those he'd been using since his return to Paris – and watched them as they curled in the flames. When both sets of papers were burnt he tipped the ash into an empty cigarette packet and threw it into the bin.

He closed all the suitcases and, picking up two of the cases, carried them to the ground floor. He left them just inside the street door. He returned and, taking a last look round, picked up the third case and closed the apartment door behind him. When he reached the ground floor again he was slightly out of breath. He knocked on the *concierge*'s door.

When she appeared he said, 'I'm going. Urgent business. I won't be back. Are we up to date?'

The old woman shrugged. 'I suppose so!' Which meant they were up to date and he didn't owe her anything.

'Here. Take this.' He handed her the third suitcase. 'It's full of clothes I don't need. For a worthy cause.'

He picked up the two remaining cases and walked round the corner and across two streets until he came to the car.

He put the cases in the boot, got in and sat still for a moment until he felt calmer.

He started the car and took the familiar road to Sèvres and Number 22, Rue du Vieux Moulin.

He drove slowly past the house to take his customary look, then turned round and drove past again, just to be on the safe side. Then he parked two streets away and, leaving the cases in the boot, walked briskly back to the house.

The villa was deathly quiet, shrouded by its air of slow decay. Vasson hurried up the drive, his footsteps sounding horribly loud on the loose gravel. He ran the last few feet on tiptoe, then paused at the basement door and listened.

Nothing.

He let himself in and went to the bed-sitting room. From the underside of the shelf he took one of the two sets of papers that Kloffer didn't know about and slid them in his pocket. This particular set of papers was incomplete: no photographs, no thumb prints, only a name. The name belonged to a boy who'd been born and brought up in the French West Indies but had died just before the war, shortly after coming to France to work. The authorities didn't know he was dead. The identity was a marvellous one: it had taken a lot of research to find it.

He went along the passage to the store room and, moving the table, dug down until he found the waterproof bag he was looking for. It contained the only cash he had: sixty thousand francs. He put it in his inside pocket. The money would keep him for a year if necessary.

There was another bag lying at the bottom of the hole. He pulled it out and, opening it, looked at the contents thoughtfully. It was an Enfield No 2 revolver which he'd obtained from one of the Meteor line. With it were twelve bullets.

He'd never used the gun — nor *any* gun for that matter. But he knew he could if he had to. Should he take it now? A picture of Kloffer flashed into his mind and, without another thought, he loaded the revolver and thrust it into his pocket with the spare bullets.

He smoothed back the earth and, leaving some money and a note for the old lady, locked up and left.

Next, the car. He drove to the river and parked on the embankment. He waited a moment, thinking hard. How long would it take Kloffer to realise? A day? Two days? Maybe even longer.

Or was the German already suspicious?

He got out of the car, locked the door, removed the cases from the boot and threw the keys in the river.

He carried the cases to the side of the main boulevard and waited. It was soothing, standing anonymously by the road and he didn't mind having to wait. Finally, after half an hour, an empty taxi came along and he hailed it.

The *vélo* took him across the city to the Gare d'Orleans. He paid it off and, taking his cases, deposited them in the Left Luggage.

He looked at the station clock. Four. He might be lucky. He found a public telephone and, after referring to a slip of paper in his wallet, lifted the receiver and asked for a number.

His heart was hammering against his chest. He gripped the receiver more tightly and held his breath.

Someone answered. It was the person he wanted. He spoke haltingly. A time and place were agreed.

Vasson replaced the receiver. His hand was damp with sweat.

He had a quick pastis at the station bar, then walked to the Métro and took a train east. After changing trains he got off at the Place Gambetta and started walking through some of the unfashionable areas of the *vingtième*.

He looked at several rooming houses before finding the right one. It was the right one because the *concierge* was drunk and didn't bother to take him up to the room herself. She didn't even look into his face.

At one point he thought he was wrong and she was going to be nosy after all. When he came downstairs again she asked him what he did for a living. He replied 'Doorman' and she was satisfied. 'Just don't want anyone who's going to be trouble, that's all!'

'No trouble.'

He paid for the room and left quickly.

Four hours until the meeting.

He went and had a meal. He ate very little but drank a great deal. He wanted to be very drunk by ten. He drank a bottle of wine and several glasses of rough cognac. The owner of the restaurant looked disapproving.

At half past nine he paid for the meal and went in search of a *vélo-taxi*. The driver dropped him near the Porte de Pantin and then Vasson walked.

The cool night air cleared his head a little. He swore quietly. He should have had more to drink. He wasn't drunk enough by far. 'Christ!' he said out loud.

He followed the directions he'd been given. Past the cattle market, down to the canal, turn left and the warehouse was a few yards along on the left.

The area round the canal was very dark but there was a moon and eventually he found the warehouse. He didn't know whether he was glad.

The other person hadn't arrived.

He paced back and forth. He felt very light-headed.

For a while he tried to think seriously, about what he might have forgotten and what he might have left undone. Was there anything that would lead Kloffer to him?

He shook his head. No. No. He'd forgotten nothing. Kloffer would never find him, not in a million years.

Kloffer thought he was being so clever. Kloffer had been going to feed him to the wolves.

But not any more.

Not after tonight and *this*. The thought of what was to come made Vasson's stomach turn and he closed his eyes.

There was a sound. Vasson jumped. A man stepped forward from the shadows. He was large, his head almost square on his massive shoulders. In the faint moonlight Vasson could just make out his features. His face was puffy and his nose broken: he looked like a former boxer, which was exactly what he was.

'*Salut.*'

Vasson stared, mesmerised. '*Salut.*'

'You're sure about this?'

Vasson gave a high-pitched laugh. 'Of course!'

'What exactly do you want?'

'What are you offering?' It was such a ludicrous question that Vasson giggled softly. It was nerves, but he couldn't stop himself.

'How different do you want to look?'

Vasson made an expansive gesture. 'Completely.'

'The money?'

'Here.' Vasson reached in his pocket and threw some notes on the ground. 'One thing –!'

'Yes.'

'I don't want to feel any pain. Please.'

'All right.' The man stepped forward. The fear leapt into Vasson's throat and he felt his knees begin to buckle.

He made a conscious effort to close his eyes, thinking: Dear God, please let it be quick and not too painful.

He needn't have worried on either count.

A fraction of a second later the boxer's right fist smashed into his face.

After the first shock Vasson never felt a thing.

The big man put everything into his first blow. Backed by sixteen stone of still solid muscle, his fist sank deep into Vasson's left cheek and shattered the bone. The force of the blow sent Vasson flying backwards against the side of the building. As he fell to the ground his head hit a stone and he lost consciousness.

The big man finished the job in his own time. He sat Vasson up and smashed the nose a couple of times, just to make sure it was broken properly. He smashed the right cheekbone to match the left, which had been flattened. Then he paused for a few minutes while he examined the results. He decided a smaller jaw might improve things, so he broke that too.

The eyes were difficult, of course. Not much one could do to make them look different. But he did his best, cutting the eyebrows deeply in a couple of places and, hopefully, thickening up the bones underneath.

Finally he was satisfied that he couldn't do any more without risking internal bleeding. He left Vasson lying on his side so that he shouldn't inhale his own blood, and walked away.

When he arrived at the nightclub where he worked he phoned a priest he knew and, disguising his voice, told him there was a seriously injured man down by the canal who couldn't, for political reasons, go to a hospital.

It wasn't kindness. He just didn't want the customer to bleed to death by mistake. He'd never killed anyone in his life.

He promptly forgot all about the incident. Which was a mistake. Vasson never forgave him for calling the priest.

Three weeks later the big man was found dead in an alley, a neat nine-millimetre bullet hole in his back.

34

St Mary's post office was crowded, the people waiting patiently in a long line. The woman behind the counter seemed slower than ever. Finally it was Julie's turn. She stepped forward. 'Good afternoon. Do you have anything for me?'

'Name?'

The woman always asked her that. You'd think she'd know by now. Julie suppressed her irritation and said calmly, 'Lescaux. Madame Lescaux.' It was the way the major from MI9 had addressed her in the first letter.

The woman searched the rack but Julie knew, even before she turned round, that there would be no letter.

'Sorry, Mrs er – Lascoo.'

Julie managed a slight smile. 'Thank you.' She squeezed past the waiting people out into the main street, pausing to take a deep breath of the fresh May air. She crossed to the opposite pavement and began to walk, her eyes down, her face grim.

Every day it was the same: no letter. More doubts. Less hope. Every day it was more of an effort to be cheerful, to cope with life.

Some days it didn't seem worth bothering at all.

A voice said, 'Afternoon!'

Julie started slightly and looked up. It was a boatman, one of the men who ran ferries between St Mary's and the outlying islands.

She nodded and forced a smile.

The man shuffled his feet and asked kindly, 'Boy all right, is 'e then?'

'Yes, thank you. He's fine.'

'Amazin' 'ow they get over these things, these young people.'

'Yes.' Except, Julie thought, that he'll never get over it. He had seemed all right after the sinking, even when she'd told him about David. But later, when the letter had arrived, and she'd told him about Jean and the others, then he'd changed. He'd become quieter, more troubled. Not the Peter she used to know.

'You be stayin' with us awhile?'

She hesitated. 'Er – Yes, I think so.'

'Well, you always be welcome 'ere.' The boatman looked down, embarrassed.

'Thank you.'

'Bye for now, then!'

'Bye.' Julie smiled. 'And thank you again.'

She turned away with relief. They had all been very kind, the islanders, and they must think her ungrateful, the way she kept to herself and avoided their company. But she hated making conversation, particularly about the war. She just wanted to be left alone.

She walked briskly up the hill until she came to a place high above Hugh Town. She sat on the ground, her hands clasped round her knees, and looked out at the view. She often came here in the afternoons when she was waiting for Peter to come out of school. The scene was wonderful: you could see St Mary's Pool below and, away to the west, the glittering rock-strewn wastes that led to the open sea. To the north lay the Mediterranean-blue waters of St Mary's Road and the vivid green, yellow-fringed island of Tresco and, beyond, the starker, less brilliant Bryher.

There were rumours about these northern islands. It was said that fishing boats painted in French colours sometimes appeared from the open sea, crossed the sound, and disappeared between Tresco and Bryher towards New Grimsby Harbour. The craft were known locally as 'the mystery boats'.

Richard. He'd hinted at secret operations here in the islands. It would be just the sort of thing he'd have got involved with.

She thought of him all the time.

She thought of where he might be – in some hidden, secret place, perhaps. Or in a POW camp – it *was* just possible – or, when she was really depressed, she imagined him being cold and dead.

She thought of Jean, too. And Maurice. And the others.

She tried not to imagine what they had been through before they died.

That – *everything* – was a terrible torment.

But the thing that really hurt, now, was the suspicion that they – and she – had been forgotten.

Why, otherwise, had she had no more news?

She took the letter from her bag and looked at it for the hundredth time. She hated the very sight of it now: so efficient, so emotionless, so British: Dear Madame Lescaux . . . Thank you for letting me talk to you for so long . . . most useful . . . help prevent the loss of others . . . However I regret to inform you that news has now reached me from the other side . . . Your uncle, Jean Cornou, died in Rennes prison during the first week of April. So too did the agent known as Maurice, and at least ten others. Of your aunt I fear we have no news at present. If I receive any I will, of course, let you know . . . Deep regrets . . . You also enquired about Lieutenant Ashley. He has been posted missing. There is no record of him having entered a POW camp, nor of him being held by the German Security Forces. Indeed, there is no information about him at all. Enquiries have been instigated through the normal channels . . . Again, so sorry . . . If there is any news I will, of course, let you know. Some good news, however. The special parcel you delivered to me has been passed straight to the appropriate department and is receiving their immediate attention.

It was signed A. E. Smithe-Webb (Major).

She folded the letter and put it back in its envelope. She got up and paced along a narrow path that led to an old fort on the hill.

He'd said he would let her know . . . That had been four weeks ago. Since then, nothing. It was driving her mad. She couldn't believe there was no news at all. *Something* must have filtered through from the other side. If not about Tante Marie, then about the survivors of the *réseau*.

488

And about the traitor.

It must have been a traitor. It *had* to be.

And she knew who that traitor was.

There was no proof, of course, but she *knew*.

The cool, calm major hadn't believed her. He had listened patiently but he had been doubting, politely but firmly *doubting*. He had pointed out that 'Roger' – whose real name was Paul Fougères – had been vouched for and checked. Maurice had even had him personally identified. Perhaps, the major had suggested quietly, it had been someone else?

The hill steepened, but Julie kept her pace, pushing harder until the path levelled off again. She liked exerting herself: it made her tired and that helped her to sleep.

She sat on a rampart of the old fort and lifted her face to the warm sun. The islands were quite lovely now. Most of the heathland was covered in carpets of blooms – pink, yellow, white; flowers called sea pink, thrift, hottentot fig . . .

But no amount of loveliness could make things right again.

From the top of the hill it was possible to see some of the islands to the south-west. The tip of St Agnes and the beginnings of the Western Rocks. It was calm today. Hard to believe that they were the same rocks . . .

David was dead. They'd buried him in the quiet, shaded churchyard at Porth Hellick on the southern side of St Mary's, next to the dead from other shipwrecks of long ago. Every two days or so she walked there, picking a bunch of wild flowers from the hedgerows to place on his grave.

There was only one consolation for his death. His package had been delivered. It was something at least. It was the only thing that assuaged her guilt.

It was quarter to four. Time to go and meet Peter. She made her way down the path towards the town and, reaching the school, waited outside the gate with the other mothers.

Sharp at four a door opened and the children poured out, skipping and running and making a lot of noise. After a while Julie spotted Peter, slightly apart from the crowd, walking quietly on his own. Her heart went out to him. He looked so lonely.

When he saw her he gave a small wave and quickened his pace. She leant down to kiss him. 'How was it, then?'

'All right.'

They began to walk slowly down towards the town. 'What did you do today?'

'Oh spelling. And arithmetic . . .'

'Do you hate it terribly?'

'No,' he said matter-of-factly. 'It's all right.'

They walked on in silence.

Julie glanced down at him. He was frowning slightly. 'What is it, Peter?'

'Nothing.'

But she could see he was disturbed about something. 'Come on. Much better to tell me.'

There was a long pause, then he murmured, 'I had a bad dream.'

'Why didn't you tell me about it before? What was it about?'

He bent his head and she knew he wasn't going to reply.

They were almost into the town, only a few yards from the lodgings. Julie paused; she didn't want to go into the boarding house while they were talking like this. Her eye caught the gleam of water down an alleyway between two houses.

'Let's go and watch the water.' She led him across the road and down the alleyway to the sea. They sat on the harbour wall and Julie asked again, 'What was the dream about, Peter?'

Eventually he whispered, 'Uncle Jean. And Tante Marie.'

'And it was a bad dream?'

'There was –' The high voice faltered. '– the Germans took them away.'

Julie stared out across the harbour. She often had dreams like that herself.

Peter asked suddenly, 'Is that where Tante Marie is, Mummy, with the Germans?'

She replied quietly, 'I don't know. I wish I did.'

He was silent again, picking at the stone wall with his fingers.

Julie said impulsively, 'Peter, suppose I went to London, do you think you could manage on your own for a few days? Mrs Eldon would look after you.'

He froze. 'Mummy, don't go away. Please!'

She took his hand. 'It would only be for a few days. Promise. I – I'm going to find out about Tante Marie.' She added, 'And maybe Richard too. If there's any news.'

He nodded slowly.

'I won't be long, promise. It's just that . . . I've got to find out. You do see, don't you?'

He looked crestfallen.

She added brightly, 'And I tell you what, since you've finished *Swallows and Amazons*, I'll see if I can borrow another Arthur Ransome before I go in the morning. How about that?'

There was the faintest smile.

'But for now, how about helping me to send a telegram?'

He nodded again.

Julie jumped to her feet and, holding Peter's hand, made her way back to the post office. For the first time in a month, she almost felt cheerful.

Smithe-Webb looked at his watch and wondered when she'd arrive. The telegram hadn't been very specific.

She arrived, in fact, just ten minutes later.

As soon as she was announced, Smithe-Webb and his assistant, Forbes, went straight down to the main entrance.

She wasn't difficult to spot. She was waiting by the main door, a slim, nervous figure pacing back and forth over the stone floor. She was wearing a dress that was shabby and rather too large for her. Refugee issue, Smithe-Webb decided. It made her look particularly vulnerable.

'Mrs Lescaux?'

She spun round, as tense as a cat. Immediately Smithe-Webb noticed the wound on her head which, though almost healed, was still conspicuous.

He put out his hand. She shook it, her enormous dark eyes searching his face. He said straight away, 'No news, I'm afraid.'

She sagged visibly and looked down.

Smithe-Webb said quickly, 'Look, there's a flat we use not far from here. Shall we go and talk there?'

He led her by the elbow towards the door while Forbes went ahead and hailed a cab. During the ride she didn't speak but stared disconsolately out of the window. Smithe-Webb asked politely, 'How's the head? All healed up now?' She nodded vaguely and he didn't bother to speak again.

The flat was on the fourth floor of a mansion block in Victoria. Forbes unlocked the door and said cheerfully, 'What about some coffee, then?'

Smithe-Webb led the way into the sitting room and said, 'Do sit down. *Will* you have some coffee?'

She nodded. 'Thank you.'

She looked so thin and pale that he asked, 'How about something to eat?'

'Oh. Well, if you have anything . . .'

As he'd thought – she'd had no breakfast. He told Forbes to dig up a sandwich and said to her, 'Won't be a moment.'

She nodded. Smithe-Webb took out his pipe and tobacco pouch

491

and began the solemn ritual of lighting up. Through the clouds of smoke he took a good look at her.

She was in a bad way, obviously very depressed. When she smiled she was probably rather a looker – she had lovely eyes, a clear skin and a wide, sensuous mouth. But at the moment she was frowning grimly.

Her eyes darted up to him. 'No news at all?'

'Sorry. We've put out a request about your aunt but . . . with no-one on the spot, well, it takes time.'

She was nodding. 'Yes, I understand.' She looked at him again. 'And Richard Ashley?'

Smithe-Webb frowned and examined his pipe. 'I have to admit that . . . the lack of news is worrying. He still hasn't been registered as a POW.'

'The Gestapo have him then.'

'It's by no means certain. All sorts of things could have happened –'

'Yes.'

She was very pale, sitting motionless on the edge of her chair. Forbes came bouncing in with a plate of food and a mug of steaming liquid and put them on a side table.

She didn't move.

'You must eat!' Smithe-Webb got up and put the plate on her lap.

Mechanically, she picked up the sandwich and took a bite. The taste seemed to revive her and she began to chew. She said, 'Major?'

'Yes, Mrs Lescaux?'

Her eyes were suddenly hard and bright. 'What about Roger – the man Paul Fougères? Have you had any more news of him?'

'Apparently he was executed in Paris quite recently.'

She looked startled. 'You're sure?'

'Not absolutely . . . It's hard to be definite.'

She was shaking her head slowly from side to side.

'You still think it was him?' asked the major.

'Oh yes!'

Smithe-Webb raised his eyebrows and didn't reply.

'I *know* it was. As soon as you have contact with Brittany again, you'll hear it from there too, I'm sure! They'll know by now! They always find out . . .'

Smithe-Webb cleared his throat. 'I – er have heard from Rennes, through another organisation –'

She sat up.

'Apparently no-one has heard anything definite.'

'*Nothing*?'

'There's no certainty it was a traitor. Apparently.'

She stared at him, thunderstruck. 'But it *must* have been. Can't you find out more? Someone *must* know.'

The doorbell rang. As Forbes went to answer it, Smithe-Webb looked towards the door with relief. 'Look, there's a chap from the Scientific Intelligence Service who'd like to ask you a few more questions.'

'About the package?'

'I expect so.'

She nodded briefly. 'All right.'

The man from SIS was a round, balding man with pebble glasses – just what you'd expect.

He pumped the girl's hand warmly and sat down in a chair beside her. 'I'm a sort of intelligence officer – but on the scientific side,' he began. 'I just wanted to ask you a couple of things, Madame. I hope you don't mind –'

'Not at all. Please go ahead.'

The SIS man adjusted his glasses and began earnestly, 'When Freymann told you about the – er – device, what else did he tell you? Did he say *how* he got hold of the plans, for instance?'

She thought for a moment. 'Well, as I told the Major before, they were David's own plans. He'd been working on them. As I understood it, they were *his* alone.'

The SIS man nodded. 'But did he say if anyone *else* knew about them?'

'Well – he gave the *impression* that no-one else knew. But I couldn't be sure.'

'Did he mention destroying duplicate plans or anything like that?'

She shook her head, 'I don't remember. The Major – and the other people I talked to before – they asked me all these questions. And I'm afraid I still don't remember.'

The SIS man nodded. 'It was just that you'd had a big bump on the head then, and we thought that now you were fully recovered a few things might have come back to you.'

'No. Sorry. Is it really vital?'

'Yes. Very.'

She thought for a moment. 'I suppose you want to know if the Germans have got hold of the idea?'

'Yes, that's just what we'd like to know!'

'David's idea was a good one then?'

'Indeed.'

'Oh I'm so glad! I'm so glad!' She smiled a little, the first time Smithe-Webb had ever seen her smile. It transformed her face. She asked, 'It'll be really useful then – to Britain? To the war effort?'

The SIS man licked his lips nervously and looked at Smithe-Webb, as if for assistance. 'Well . . . er. In a way, yes. In a way.' He looked down awkwardly.

Smithe-Webb thought: My God, he's made a hash of it, bloody fool.

The girl was staring at the SIS man, confusion on her face. 'What do you mean – *in a way*?' She looked questioningly at Smithe-Webb, then back to the SIS man. 'Can't you use it after all? I thought you said –?'

'No, please forgive me,' the SIS man said unhappily, 'Of *course* we can use it –'

'You're not telling me the truth!'

Smithe-Webb breathed in deeply and said, 'What he hasn't actually mentioned, Mrs Lescaux, is that – we already have this type of radar.' He hurried on, 'Now that doesn't mean that what you did was any the less important. You stopped the Germans getting hold of Freymann and the secret, and that *was really vital*.'

She stared at Smithe-Webb, a look of blank incomprehension on her face.

He added quickly, 'You see, it was vital that Freymann be brought out of France. Otherwise the Germans could have tortured the information out of him. They could have held his family prisoner and *made* him work for them. So you see –'

She murmured something. Smithe-Webb missed it and hesitated. She said again, 'So it was all for nothing. All for nothing.'

'No, Mrs Lescaux. Really –' Rather exasperated, he turned to the scientist. 'You tell her, old chap.'

'Well . . .' The SIS man blinked nervously through his glasses. 'What Major Smithe-Webb says is absolutely right. The Germans don't have the radar and that gives us a tremendous edge . . . It means we can bomb their cities really accurately and . . . our planes can locate their submarines on the surface . . . But *they* don't have the same advantage. Do you see –?'

'But there were other ways, weren't there?' she cried bitterly. 'Like destroying his plans so they'd never be found, like hiding him and stopping him from being caught. Instead . . . he died, trying so hard –!' She put a hand over her face.

The SIS man was on his feet looking perplexed and mildly alarmed. Smithe-Webb said, 'Better go, old chap.'

The man nodded and left. Smithe-Webb pulled up a chair and patted the girl's arm. 'Now look, we wouldn't make this thing up, you know. What Freymann did really *was* important, you do believe that, don't you?'

She took a large breath and raised her head. Eventually she said wearily, 'Yes, I believe you. Yes . . . It was just that . . . I was so hoping that David's invention would be *useful*. In a positive way. I wanted it for him – I –' She sighed. 'I wanted him to have the *glory*.'

'Yes, I understand that. Yes, I do see. But what he did was very brave, you know. And very positive. I mean, he whisked the information away from under the German's noses, didn't he? They'll kick themselves when they find out.'

'Yes.'

Forbes brought in some fresh coffee and she sat drinking quietly, staring blankly at the opposite wall. Smithe-Webb could see that she was thinking hard.

Suddenly she put down her cup and looked hard at Smithe-Webb. 'Send me back. I want to go back.'

Here it was, Smithe-Webb thought. She was bound to ask. He sighed deeply. 'Mrs Lescaux, it would be most unwise. Think about it. You'll be on the Gestapo's list of most wanted people. They'll have your photograph, your description. You couldn't go anywhere *near* North Brittany. They'd have you in a second!'

She frowned. 'But –'

'What could you achieve there? Think about it. What would you *do*?'

'What would I do!' she exclaimed. 'I'd find the others! And regroup the line! And I'd –'

'Find the traitor –?'

'I –' She hesitated, almost spoke, then shut her mouth again. Finally she said firmly, 'If I could. Yes.'

Smithe-Webb sighed. 'Well, with all due respect, I really don't think it would be wise for you to go looking for him on your own. As for regrouping the line . . . Well, I'm afraid we wouldn't want that. We wouldn't want to inflict the risk on the same village again. In fact – well, I shouldn't tell you this – but we've already got plans to operate from another part of the coast. So you see, there really wouldn't have been a job for you to do. If there *had* been, well – you would have been the first person on our list . . .'

'So you won't send me.'

'No.'

'I could do special training. Wireless, guns –'

'No.'

'But I could work in another district. Away from Tregasnou. Away from North Brittany altogether!'

Smithe-Webb shook his head firmly. 'No, Mrs Lescaux. You don't understand. Anyone who's been compromised – agents, members of the Resistance, it doesn't matter *who* – does *not* go back. It's an absolute rule. It's too dangerous for *others* . . .'

She whispered tightly, 'I see.'

She stood up and walked over to the window and looked out for a long time.

Eventually she turned and said rather crossly, 'Don't think I've given up. I'll keep trying, you know. The Free French might send me.'

'Well, I can only tell you that no-one goes to France without the approval of my superiors. And I'm afraid to say that they won't give it.'

Her shoulders sagged. Smithe-Webb felt rather sorry for her, but it was for the best. She had to accept the situation.

'All right,' she said quietly. 'All right.' She turned to face him. 'But will you promise me one thing? Will you promise to get me back the moment it's possible, the moment the Germans have gone?'

He stood up and shook his head. 'Well – it's jolly difficult to promise something like that.'

She came close to him. '*Please*! Promise me you'll try. *Please*!'

'Well . . . All I can say is that I'll do my best. But I can guess how it'll be after an invasion. They'll be ferrying tons of equipment across the Channel, there won't be any room for passengers . . .'

'I'll get across *somehow*. Just promise you'll get me some papers – or whatever I need – *permission. Please*.'

She was standing very close to him, looking up at him with those beautiful dark eyes. Suddenly she smiled a little. The effect was quite lovely and rather touching. Smithe-Webb softened. She *had* been very brave and MI9 *did* owe her a debt. He thought: What the hell. He nodded. 'All right. I'll do my best. But no promises!'

She gripped his hands. 'Thank you! Thank you!'

'You may have to wait a long time, you know,' he said gently.

She stopped and nodded slowly. 'Yes, I know that . . . A year? People are saying we'll invade in a year.'

'It may well be longer.'

She sat down. 'I'll wait, then. For as long as I have to.'

35

It was September, The *next* year.

A whole year and four months later.

496

The Eighth Corps of Patton's Third Army had come and gone, sweeping the Germans before them, chasing them into the fortified west coast cities of Brest, St Nazaire, and Lorient where they rallied to fight again . . .

Behind them the Breton countryside seemed untouched. There was an occasional overturned jeep, a few cratered roads . . . But the fields themselves were gold with late crops and the rippling corn was largely undamaged by so much as a tyre track.

In the towns it was different; the towns didn't look the same at all. The marks of war were all too evident, in the ruins of the occasional house flattened by a shell; on the façades of the buildings riddled with bullet holes; in the empty shops, almost devoid of goods; and in the general air of decay. The townspeople were different too: thinner, harder and solemn with the knowledge that their troubles were far from over. It would be a long time before they'd have money in their pockets again.

And in the wake of the Germans' departure came the reopening of old wounds – public mourning for those who had been deported, tortured, killed . . . for the hostages, the innocents, the children . . . for the loss of pride and the deep humiliation of four years of occupation.

Among some of the people there was resentment, too, at the new occupation. At the small groups of cocky well-fed American troops who replaced the Germans at sentry duty and on street corners and in cafés. So brash, so *alien*, so lacking in understanding, these young men, none of them realising that all the French people wanted was to be left alone.

Left alone to their own lives and their own wars –

There were recriminations, often bitter. Against those who had done nothing . . . Against those who had helped, supported, *collaborated* . . . And not only against those who were *known* to have collaborated, but against those who *might* or *could* have collaborated . . . It was a time of innuendo, suggestion, rumour . . . It was a time to settle old scores. Men pointed fingers at their enemies and rivals, innocent or guilty. A few were ostracised: girls who'd been with Germans had their hair cut off; dead men appeared in alleys, summarily executed by their peers.

Of course, most rejoiced at the new freedom; most welcomed the new era with optimism. But for many the liberation brought fresh uncertainty, renewed bitterness, and in some, a hunger for revenge.

Amazingly the old bus was still running, though due to the shortage of fuel, it went only twice a day now.

As it progressed slowly through the country lanes, the shudderings and roarings were as bad as ever and, from the way the vehicle juddered and rabbit-hopped, it seemed that one of the gears had given up altogether.

Julie was rather glad. She didn't want anything to have changed, even the old bus. She sat by the window in a seat she'd occupied dozens of times before on the endless journeys to Morlaix and back. It made her feel at home.

As the bus ground up the slight hill towards Tregasnou she looked at the familiar countryside and felt a sense of unreality. Perhaps because she'd been dreaming about this moment for so long.

The bus stopped. Julie picked up her case and climbed out.

The bus roared off and Julie looked around. The village seemed untouched, the small grey cottages snuggling together as cosily and firmly as they had always done.

There was no-one about, not even nosy old Madame Gres who knew everyone's comings and goings. Julie strolled over to the café and paused at the door. She'd never been inside before. She walked straight in. The interior was dark and at first she couldn't see. Then, as she put down her case, she saw the *patron* standing behind the counter. He looked up and stared at her.

There was a moment's silence, then recognition spread over his face. 'Madame! Madame!' He said expansively. 'Welcome! Welcome!'

Julie nodded, smiled a little, and looked around. How extraordinary: this place wasn't frightening at all. There were two men drinking coffee at a table in the corner, otherwise the place was empty. She walked up to the bar and placed her hands on the counter.

'Madame – welcome, welcome!' the *patron* was repeating. 'Please! A little something – a glass of Pernod. Sadly we have no cognac . . .'

Julie said quietly, 'No, I won't. Thank you all the same.'

The *patron* nodded and waited expectantly.

Julie began, 'Monsieur, my aunt . . . Where is she, do you know?'

His face clouded and he dropped his eyes. He said carefully, 'Yes, madame. She's at Madame Boulet's . . .' He trailed off and looked away.

'How is she?'

The *patron* looked unhappy and shook his head. 'Not very well, madame. She – er . . . she's –' He dropped his voice and whispered confidentially. 'She's not of this world any more, if you understand me. But she's being well looked after, I assure you. Madame Boulet has nursed her like a saint, like a saint!'

It was just as the War Office had informed her. Over a year ago, in a letter. She asked, 'But does she know people? Does she recognise them?'

The *patron* pursed his lips. 'I believe . . . I believe not *usually*, no. But I'm sure she'd recognise *you*, madame!' He was only saying it to please her, Julie could tell.

She said, 'What about – the old group?' She saw that he knew exactly what she meant and went on, 'Is there anyone left? I want to . . . get in touch.'

'Ah.' He raised his eyebrows and said mournfully, 'Few left, madame. Most were taken, oh, more than a year ago now –'

'Yes, I know that,' she interrupted. 'But is there anyone left?'

He thought for a moment. 'There's old Rannou . . . up the hill . . . He ran a safe house . . . Then there's Doctor Le Page in Plougat . . . Lots of Americans stayed there . . . But –' he shrugged, '– that's about it really.'

Julie couldn't remember meeting either of the people he mentioned. That was because Maurice's security had been so good. 'But what about the group *here* – in the village?'

'No.' He whispered. 'No, madame . . . All gone. A sad day, that was . . . A sad day . . .'

'Did you ever hear what happened to the British crew, from the gun boat?'

'No . . . We never heard. No. We thought they must have been taken to Rennes with the others. No-one ever saw them again.'

She nodded. Nothing new, then.

Only Rennes. Everything seemed to have happened in Rennes. The Gestapo had killed Jean and Maurice and the others there. They might have taken Richard there. It would be the best place to start.

'Thank you,' she murmured. 'I'd better go and see my aunt now. Oh –' There was something else, '– the farm. My uncle's farm. What's happened to it?'

'The neighbours – they're looking after the animals and doing the harvesting. But the house . . . That's empty, madame.'

'Yes.' She could imagine the house, damp, deserted and cold.

She moved away from the bar. 'Well, I'll go and visit my aunt now.'

The *patron* nodded, 'Of course.' He came out from behind the bar. 'It must be a long time since you last saw her. A long time since you went away.'

'Eighteen months.'

'A long time.'

Yes, Julie thought bitterly, far, far too long.

She said, 'Goodbye then, And thank you.'

She walked towards the door and picked up her case. Footsteps sounded on the bare wooden floor and she was aware of the *patron* at her elbow. At first she thought he'd hurried over to help her with the case, but then he took hold of her arm and gripped it tightly.

She looked up into his face with surprise.

He was wildly excited, his eyes dancing.

'Yes?' she asked.

'I quite forgot to tell you! Good news! Good news!'

She frowned. 'Yes!'

'The traitor! The traitor!'

Her heart leapt. 'Yes! Yes – !'

'They've got him!'

Her mouth dropped open. She stared, dumbfounded. 'Got him . . .?'

'Yes, they charged him in Rennes a week ago. He was in Paris, about to make a run for it. Huh! But they were on his trail all right. No trouble! They brought him back to Rennes and now he'll pay the price!' He made a guillotine motion with his hand. 'Ha! He'll pay all right!'

Julie made the effort to speak. 'Who? *Who*?

'Ah!' The *patron* was smiling and formed his lips to speak. Then quite suddenly his face froze and he put his hand to his mouth. 'Madame, I quite forgot . . . Oh dear God, I'm so sorry. I quite forgot! Oh madame, prepare yourself for a shock!'

She put her face up to his and shouted, '*Who*?'

'It's . . . it's Michel, madame. The communist. Michel Le Goff. Your cousin.'

Neither of the massive doors would budge. The top hinge of the right-hand door had broken, so that the door had fallen and wedged itself firmly against the other one.

The count gave a last ineffectual pull then stood back, panting hard and feeling his age, which was seventy-two. In the old days the coachmen and grooms would have sprung forward and opened the doors for him. In the old days a hinge would never have been allowed to fall into disrepair.

It was hopeless. These doors hadn't been opened since the beginning of the war: they obviously weren't going to open now. The count decided to give up and get into the coach house by means of the side door.

He made his way slowly round the wall of the coach house, which, with the stables and gardeners' cottages, was screened from the château by a long hedge, once carefully trimmed but now grown wild.

Through a gap in the hedge the count noticed that another section of drain pipe had broken loose from a wall of the main house. Too bad. Like everything else it would have to wait. Repairs took money, and money was the one thing he didn't have.

As he opened the side door to the coach house he wondered, not for the first time, where all the money had gone.

He peered into the darkness and, fumbling in his pocket, lit a match. He would need an oil lamp. He went back to the château and searched the dusty, empty rooms until he found one. It took him another twenty minutes to get the lamp clean and the wick trimmed.

Back at the coach house he lit the lamp, turned up the wick and peered into the darkness. The giant tarpaulin, once green but now grey with dust, sat humped over the massive object in the centre of the floor.

It was a long time since the count had been in here. He'd rather forgotten about the coach house and its contents. He eyed the tarpaulin thoughtfully. Better get it off and start dusting and polishing straight away. Before the war he'd never dusted or polished anything in his life but, since the staff had gone, he'd got used to all sorts of things, even cooking and washing-up.

He put down the lamp, then tugged at the tarpaulin. It was snagged somewhere. He went round the other side, freed a corner rope, and pulled again. The tarpaulin slid smoothly to the floor.

The count stood back. Not bad, not bad at all. It looked much better than he'd dared to hope.

The car gleamed magically in the flicker of the dim lamplight, its paint a deep, almost black ruby-red which glowed warmly in the drab darkness of the coach house. The great sweep of its body reached from the wall almost to the very doors.

It was a soft-top D8/120 Delage. His last great indulgence before the war. He'd bought it in '37, the same year he'd set up Elfie, the glorious Elfie, in an apartment in the Avenue Foch.

He sighed. Perhaps he *had* been just a little extravagant.

He found a piece of rag and began to dust the wings and bonnet. When he'd finished, he eyed the car critically. The chromework could do with a good clean. There was a shelf littered with jars and tins and he searched through them for some chrome polish. Once the chrome was brightened up, he decided, the car would really look very good indeed. He might even ask a bit more for it. The chap had sounded very keen: perhaps he might go as high as seventy thousand.

He wetted his lips. That kind of money would tide him over very nicely.

From outside there was a loud hissing noise, and the crunching of wheels on gravel.

The count hastily wiped his hands and went out of the side door into the drive.

It was the taxi from the village, wheezing and snorting like a wild animal. Like many vehicles, it had been converted to run off gas extracted from a charcoal furnace strapped to one side. A well-dressed young man had stepped out and was speaking to the driver.

At the sound of the count's footsteps the young man turned.

The count's gaze faltered for a moment. What an extraordinary face! It looked as if it had been horribly injured at some time: the nose had obviously been broken and the cheek and jaw bones were lopsided, giving the whole face a curiously crooked look. Thick white scars ran through the dark eyebrows and there was a longer, more livid scar down the length of one cheek.

The count stretched out a hand and smiled. 'How d'you do? Monsieur Lelouche, I presume?'

'Yes.' The young man hesitated, then shook the proffered hand briefly. He said immediately, 'Where is the car?'

'In here.' The count indicated the coach house. 'Unfortunately I have not been able to get the doors open. No help, you understand. Would you care to come round the side for the moment?'

The young man said coldly, 'No, let's open the doors.' He beckoned to the taxi driver and together they lifted the right-hand door and swung it open. The count pulled open the other door, which moved quite easily.

The car glinted brightly in the morning light, its colour now revealed as rich gleaming wine-red.

The sunlight also revealed that the count's rag had missed some patches of dust and that he had been right about wanting to clean the chromework, which looked decidedly dull. The count wished he'd started work on the car the day before.

'When was she built?'

'1937. That was when I bought her. Brand new. Hardly been used.'

'How long's she been sitting in here?'

'Since the war.' That didn't sound too good and the count added hastily, 'She's been looked after, though. Always checked regularly, polished and so on . . .' A lie, but then one had to embroider a little.

'And the body's by Letournier and Marchand?'

'Oh yes, only the best.'

The young man went in and walked round the car, his eyes gleaming thoughtfully, his fingers running gently over the sleek lines. 'Is it in running order?'

'It *should* be . . .'

The young man raised his eyebrows. The count had a feeling that the fellow hadn't believed a word of what he'd said. The old man's confidence began to wane: perhaps the young man wouldn't offer such a good price as he'd thought.

The young man opened the driver's door and leaned inside. The count realised he was letting off the handbrake. The young man closed the door, went round to the front of the car and the next moment the Delage was rolling out into the sunshine.

The young man paused for breath and remarked, 'The battery's flat, I suppose?'

'Well . . . er, I don't know.'

The young man got into the car, found the crank handle and passed it to the taxi driver who took it to the front and started winding. Nothing happened, not even a rumble. The engine sounded very dead indeed.

After fifteen minutes the young man put his head out of the window and said to the taxi driver, 'Can you fetch a mechanic from the town?'

The driver nodded and went off to restoke his charcoal burner.

Lelouche came over to the count. 'Shall we talk about price? Assuming the engine *does* work . . . Eventually.' He sounded very doubtful.

'Yes, yes. A good idea!' The count did some quick mental arithmetic and decided that, in view of the dead engine, he'd settle for sixty thousand. He'd paid a hundred and twenty for it seven years ago. Since then prices had doubled, more or less. So in real terms he'd be getting about a quarter of what he'd paid for it. Yes: that seemed fair enough.

The taxi went hissing and snorting away down the drive. The two men began to walk slowly along the drive, towards the front of the château. The young man was considering. He said suddenly, 'I'll give you twenty. Twenty thousand.'

The count felt the blood drain from his face. He could hardly believe his ears. He said weakly, 'Twenty? But it's worth at least – *at least* fifty!'

'I don't think so.' The eyes were very certain, very calm.

The count averted his gaze and said bravely, 'I won't accept a *sou* less than forty-five!'

The young man stopped. 'That's a pity. A great pity.' There was

503

contempt in the hard black eyes. The count shuffled uneasily. 'I don't think you'll find many buyers around at the moment, even at a reasonable price,' the young man went on. 'And certainly none at that – unrealistic – price. There's no market for cars at the moment. None at all.'

He was right. The count knew he was right. It was infuriating.

Lelouche regarded the crumbling façade of the château with apparent indifference. 'If you want a sale you'll have to be a little more realistic.'

The count sighed. 'Very well. But twenty thousand is *ridiculous*, monsieur. Out of the question! What's your best offer?'

Lelouche shook his head. 'Twenty-five. And that's being very generous. It isn't worth any more. Twenty-five. And that's my final offer.'

The count swallowed hard. It was ludicrous, insulting! And yet without the money . . . It didn't bear thinking about. He couldn't go on living here in penury and squalor. He wanted to get back to Paris, to his friends, to the comfort of a smart apartment . . . He was too old to change now.

He'd advertised for two months in *L'Auto* and this had been the only enquiry.

He shook his head. 'Forty. Forty, monsieur. Not a *sou* less.'

The young man's eyes were hard now, like bullets. 'I said my final offer was twenty-five. I meant it.' He turned on his heel and strode away.

The count watched in dismay as the young man walked to the coach house and leant against the wall. The old man's heart sank. He was beaten and he knew it.

He left it a few minutes then walked over with as much dignity as he could muster. 'Thirty-five.'

The young man sighed heavily. 'I said twenty-five.'

'All right! *All right!*' The count could have wept. What a waste! His lovely car, worth nothing. Nothing! Tears of humiliation and anger pricked his eyes and he sniffed loudly. He made the effort to pull himself together. Because he was an aristocrat and breeding was everything, he forced himself to smile and say, 'Well, monsieur, you drive a hard bargain, I must say!'

'Do I?' The young man shrugged slightly.

For some minutes the count found it difficult to speak. He kept thinking of what one used to be able to buy with a hundred thousand francs – and how little one could get for twenty-five nowadays.

Lelouche was walking round the car again. He stopped and,

manipulating some clips, released the soft top and folded it back. He got into the car and sat at the wheel.

The count wandered over and leant unhappily against the door. After a while he found the silence embarrassing and, more out of politeness than interest, asked, 'You'll find enough petrol to run it, will you?'

The young man's lips narrowed. 'Yes, I've been saving my coupons.'

The count nodded. Out of a lifetime's habit of making conversation he eventually went on. 'There's so little of everything nowadays. Food. Necessities . . . It's been a long four years. Did you have a hard war, monsieur?'

The young man dropped his eyes. 'As hard as any.'

'You were in the fighting?'

A slight hesitation, as if not wanting to boast, then, 'Yes.'

'I thought so! By your face . . . If you'll excuse me saying so.'

There was a silence.

Despite the difficulty of the conversation, the count persevered. He wanted to show that he could rise above such petty considerations as resentment and hurt pride. 'Which service were you in?'

Again the slight pause. 'Airforce. I joined the British.'

'Ah.'

At that moment the taxi reappeared round the corner and the count was rather relieved.

It took an hour for the mechanic to clean the plugs and the points, change the oil and adjust the timing. Fortunately no actual parts were in need of replacement.

The mechanic closed the bonnet wiped his hands and, with some ceremony, cranked the handle. The Delage started first time, the engine purring smoothly like a large well-fed cat.

There hadn't been much wrong with her. The count began to feel rather sick.

The young man approached him and without a word counted twenty-five thousand francs off a roll that contained at least fifty.

The count took the money. 'We'll need a bill of sale . . .'

'I have one.' He went back towards the car and the count followed him. The young man took a document out of his pocket and, laying it on the car bonnet, wrote on it. Then he said, 'Sign here.'

The count looked at the document. It was a proper bill of sale. The young man's name, Lelouche, and an address in Paris were already entered, and the young man had apparently just added the car's details, the count's name and address, and the date. The young man was holding out a pen. The count took it and said, 'I'll need a copy of the details.'

The young man's eyes dropped. He looked cross. Eventually he said, 'All right.' And he tore a piece of paper out of a notebook, wrote down the details of the sale, and gave them to the count.

The count sighed. 'I'll get the car's papers,' he said. He went into the château, found the *Carnet de Route*, and handed it over.

The young man walked back to the car, got in and drove off.

It was only after the low throb of the exhaust had faded round the bend in the drive that the count realised that neither the taxi driver nor the mechanic had been paid.

Clenching his teeth, the old man took the roll of bills from his pocket and counted out some money.

As soon as he had turned the corner of the drive Vasson let out a great laugh of delight.

She was a beauty! Fantastic!

In need of some attention, of course. But it wasn't anything that a good mechanic, a little money and a bit of elbow grease couldn't cure.

He took the car carefully out on to the main road and concentrated on getting the feel of her. The steering was heavier than he was used to and the pedals stiffer. But it was only a question of familiarity. He pushed her gently up through the gears. Once in top he eased off the throttle and listened to the engine noise for signs of trouble. But she was going as sweetly as a bird. After a while he put his foot down a bit and heard the engine note change from a steady purr to a more urgent roar. The car surged forward.

The speedometer crept up. He felt the wind pulling at his hair and buffeting his cheeks. The tall poplars lining the road swished by, faster and faster. The long straight road stretched out ahead, empty of traffic, seductive, luring him onward.

He kept his foot down. The speedometer on the walnut dashboard read eighty . . . ninety . . . a hundred kilometres an hour.

He held his breath. His heart was almost bursting with joy and excitement . . .

Then he lost his nerve and slowed down for a while.

He found that he was shaking. He laughed to himself, and shook his head.

It had been worth all the effort. And all the waiting. He'd never been so happy in his life.

Then the slowness seemed rather tame. He wanted the intoxication

– the exhilaration – of the speed again. He pressed gently on the accelerator and felt a wave of delicious physical pleasure . . .

Yes! This was better than anything, *anything* . . .

He had to slow down for the villages, but on the straights he let her fly . . . On and on, with no end to it.

The suburbs of Paris came too soon.

He felt a vague disappointment until he saw how people stared at the car. Then he began to enjoy himself again, pretending that he hadn't noticed their glances, looking as if he'd owned the car all his life.

He smiled to himself. Oh yes! It had been worth all the waiting.

And the price – that made it even better. What a bargain it had been. Vasson couldn't believe his luck. The stupid old count was typical of his class. Useless with money. His type didn't deserve to have it in the first place.

Eventually he slowed the Delage right down and guided it carefully through a narrow archway, into a cobblestone yard and up to some garage doors. He jumped out, opened the doors and drove the car slowly in.

He turned off the engine and sat for a moment in the silence, reluctant to leave the soft luxury of the leather seat. When he did get out it was to touch the long lines of the bonnet, to admire the four external exhausts which led out of the right-hand side of the engine-casing and into the wing, and to feel the fine elegant sweep of the rear, which seemed to go on for ever.

Eventually he stepped out into the courtyard and closed and locked the doors. He hated to go, but it wouldn't be for long. He'd be coming back the next day with a mechanic, to get the dynamo and battery problems sorted out.

Automatically he looked around to see if anyone was watching him, but the dirty windows overlooking the courtyard were blank and anonymous. He'd been rather careless, he decided, driving through the Paris streets with the top down. In time it wouldn't matter who saw him, but at the moment it was just a bit too soon after the Occupation to be affluent . . . Rather, he corrected himself, to be *seen* to be affluent.

Once he'd got the club going it would be different.

He walked the short distance to his apartment. It was the fourth he'd rented that year. It was as dingy and cheap as the others. Soon – within the year – there'd be a decent apartment. But not quite yet. Again, it would be too soon.

But then, as he'd discovered with the car, the waiting would make it all the better.

He changed out of his best clothes and put on something cheaper and more casual.

Then he went out again.

It was a long journey to the *dix-huitième* by Métro; he had to change trains twice. Immediately he came out into the daylight and saw Pigalle and the familiar streets leading up to Montmartre he felt at home.

He walked a short way up a side street until he came to an almost derelict building. There were many buildings in Paris like this at the moment, their leases unsold, their owners vanished, their occupants bankrupt. It was a perfect time to make a good deal.

Vasson had bought a forty-year lease on this property for almost nothing – but then he'd paid in gold, and gold was worth more to a seller than any amount of paper money.

He ran down the steps to the basement, found the door open and went in. The builders were there, tearing out the partition walls of what had once been a series of store rooms.

Vasson wandered around, exchanging a few words with the men. He wanted to get on friendly terms with them so that they'd work harder and finish the job on time, and more important, on budget.

He'd worked the figures out very carefully. He should get his money back within eighteen months.

He stood back and examined the scene as a whole. Already one could get an idea of how large the room would be once the partition walls had gone.

Just right. There'd be a bar in the far corner, a small dance floor, and plenty of small tables. Then, the special touch . . . A girl, dancing all by herself, high up in a golden cage. Gold! He liked the irony of it.

That was what he was going to call it.

The Golden Cage.

An English name. Very smart. The sign would be gold on black. He'd helped to design it himself.

He smiled. It was happening at last. And what made it so satisfying was that he'd earned it all himself. Every single penny.

36

The police station was busy. People strode across the hall from one anonymous door to another, or from the main door to a sergeant sitting stoically at the front desk, and then back again. The waiting area was crowded, all the seats long taken. No-one looked at Julie. She sat very still, staring at the opposite wall, and, like everyone else, waited.

She'd been there for several hours, waiting at first, then giving her statement, and then waiting again. She would probably have to wait a while longer, but she didn't mind; she could stay for just as long as necessary.

It was almost midday. Her stomach was beginning to rumble. She ignored it for as long as possible then took a piece of bread out of her pocket and chewed on it. It would have to last until the evening: she could only afford one meal a day. She'd managed to save very little from the small pension the War Office had arranged for her, and most of that had gone on the train and ferry fare.

The sergeant at the desk was eyeing her with an expression of patience worn thin. He sighed heavily and beckoned to her. She put the bread back in her pocket and walked over.

'The commissaire's still tied up, madame. And probably will be all day. Look, we *have* all the details. Every single detail, every single word . . . It's all in your statement. The matter will be looked into by the appropriate department –'

'But I still want to see the commissaire.'

'He won't see you, madame! He's too busy.'

'Then I'll wait until he *is* able to see me. Thank you.'

The sergeant shook his head and rolled his eyes.

As she returned to her seat and her bread-chewing, she felt the sergeant's despairing gaze drilling into her back. She knew what he must think of her, but the statement wasn't enough. She had to be *sure*.

She closed her eyes and tried to sleep, but it was difficult: the chair was narrow and uncomfortable. Finally she managed to doze a little, dreaming strange, disturbing dreams which blended in with the sounds in the hall so that she couldn't tell what was real any more.

Then she sat and thought about Peter and how he was getting on without her. Later, she dozed again. The hours were interminable.

When she next looked at her watch it was nine in the evening. It had been a long day. To get to Rennes by nine that morning she had left Madame Boulet's before dawn. Now she had missed the last bus back to Morlaix.

A door opened. Laughter came drifting through. That's all they were probably doing, Julie thought angrily, telling jokes!

She got up and strode over to the desk. The sergeant looked up wearily. She said, 'Please – ask again! Please!'

The sergeant made a face. 'They already know you're here. There's no point. Anyway –' He looked at a clock '– the commissaire's hardly likely to see you now. He's had a long day.'

'But he's still here?'

The sergeant had been caught out and he didn't like it. He pressed his lips firmly together. Julie said, 'I'll wait then,' and went back towards the chair. It was a very hard chair indeed. She looked for other vacant chairs to pull together for a couch, but there were none. On an impulse she lay down on the floor, put her handbag under her head and closed her eyes. It was much more comfortable.

There was a hush. People paused in their journeys across the hall. Julie could hear their feet shuffling. She kept her eyes tightly closed and began to feel a little less comfortable.

Someone was approaching. 'Madame, get up please.' It was the sergeant's voice.

She didn't reply.

'Madame, do you want me to move you by force?'

She opened her eyes and said, 'No. But I must stay. I'm sorry.' Beyond the sergeant's legs she saw people staring and quickly closed her eyes again.

There was a pause then the footsteps receded. Julie relaxed a little and breathed deeply. She was beginning to regret her impulse. They'd probably throw her out.

After a while the footsteps came back. 'Madame, get up. Now, please.'

'No.' She could hardly believe she had said it.

He hissed. 'Come with me. *Please.*'

She held her breath.

The sergeant dropped his voice. 'To see the commissaire, madame. That's what you wanted, isn't it?'

Julie opened her eyes. He meant it. She got to her feet, triumphant. The sergeant was already walking towards one of the doors. She followed him hurriedly, her eyes on the floor to avoid the curious stares of the onlookers.

She was shown straight into an office marked 'Commissaire de Police'. Behind the desk sat a man in shirt sleeves, a cigarette in his mouth, a plump belly protruding towards the desk. For several moments he viewed Julie through heavy-lidded eyes. Julie stared back at him. Eventually the commissaire indicated that she should sit down. Then he said, 'Well, madame, I hear that you've been disrupting the entire police station. May I ask why?'

'I had to see you.'

'Yes?'

'It's about Michel Le Goff!'

The commissaire raised an eyebrow. 'What about him?'

'He's innocent. He was on our side. I can swear to that!'

'Indeed?' The tone was sardonic.

Julie paused, slightly nonplussed. She pressed on, 'He's not guilty of the crimes he's charged with. He must be freed!'

'Ah.' He glanced down at some papers on his desk. 'And this is the evidence you are presenting?'

She peered over the desk. 'Is that –'

'Your statement.'

So he had seen it after all. She had been certain it would get ignored or forgotten. She murmured, 'Yes. That's my evidence.'

'Would you like to go over it again? Now?'

She could hardly believe her luck. 'Yes!' She took a deep breath. 'I was a member of the *réseau* led by the agent known as Maurice, at Tregasnou. I interrogated the parcels – the airmen, I mean. And . . . I did beach duty . . . And, well, all kinds of jobs. I was with the group for over a year . . .'

The commissaire said solemnly, 'You were very patriotic, madame. And very courageous.'

Julie blinked at the unexpected compliment. 'Anyway, Michel Le Goff helped us. A lot. He got this very important scientist out of a factory in Brest and delivered him to us and . . . Then, when everything went wrong and the Boches closed in, then he helped us to escape –'

'Helped who exactly?'

'Me. And my son. And this scientist from the factory . . .'

'No-one else?'

'Well – no. The others had already been caught.'

'Go on.'

Julie stared at him. 'Well . . . That was it. I mean, he was on our side. He helped us. His actions prove it . . . He gave us his boat, he risked his life . . . I know him. I don't believe he betrayed us!'

The commissaire said gently, 'Why not?'

'I'm sorry?'

'Why couldn't he have betrayed you? Or rather, the others?'

Julie thought hard. 'Because – because he saved us. He risked his life . . .'

'He saved *you*, madame.' The slightly mocking tone was back in his voice. 'Tell me, what was your relationship with Michel Le Goff?'

'He was – *is* – my cousin. A distant cousin by marriage, in fact. But that means nothing. Half the people in the village are related.'

'Nothing more, madame?'

Julie felt herself blushing. 'Certainly not! Whatever you're implying it wasn't like that! Not at all!'

The commissaire looked at her dispassionately. 'If you say so, madame.'

There was a knowing look on his face. Julie glared back at him, hating herself for blushing, hating him for not believing her.

She made an effort and said calmly, 'My evidence will go before the examining magistrate, won't it?'

'Yes. But there is a great weight of evidence against Le Goff. He will go on trial, I can assure you.'

'What evidence?'

The commissaire raised his eyebrows. 'People – reliable people – heard him swear to get his revenge on your *réseau*. Apparently he believed that they were responsible for his comrades getting caught in Brest – on that evening, when the scientist was being removed from the factory.

Julie frowned. He knew it all.

'Also, he was seen in the company of informers from time to time. Believe me, madame, he was trouble. Always.'

Julie said quickly, 'But what about the others – in my *réseau*? There were plenty of others who might have betrayed us. Have you looked into them? Have you *interrogated* them?'

The commissaire shook his head. 'Madame, the Germans left only six weeks ago. We've had very little time. We have dozens of people coming in every day. You saw them out there! All of them have so-called 'information'. Most of it's sour grapes and make-believe! There are hundreds of cases under investigation . . .'

He raised a finger. 'However, we *have* done some work on this particular case and we *have* followed up the obvious leads. Many of your *réseau* died, as we know. Here in Rennes. Others, we know from the Gestapo records, were sent to Germany.' He threw out his hands in an expansive gesture and shrugged. 'Whether they are still alive or not we do not know. We *cannot* know until Germany is defeated.'

'What about Fougéres?' she demanded.

'Ah! The man you accuse.' He leant forward in his seat and said with emphasis, 'He died, madame. In Fresnes. Well over a year ago. We have confirmation from Paris.'

Julie stared in disbelief. 'There was no doubt it was him?'

Without a word the commissaire got up and went into an adjacent office. A few minutes later he came back with a file in his hand. He flicked through it. 'Fougères was seen by two other prisoners before he died. They were positive it was him.'

'When? When did the prisoners see him?'

The commissaire looked down the file. 'In approximately April last year.'

She frowned. It was about the time Jean and the others had died. It seemed to fit . . . 'But why was he taken to Paris when none of the others were?'

'Madame, I cannot say at this stage.' He started to shuffle the papers on his desk. The interview was clearly over. 'I'm sorry, madame. Now if you'll excuse me, I have a lot of work to do.'

She stood up. 'But wait! Please – there's more. I must know if you have information about the British crew! The men off the boat, the ones who were captured at the same time –'

'British –?' He sucked in his breath and shook his head. 'No. The Germans left a few records behind, but foreign sailors – they would have been prisoners of war . . . We don't deal with them. You should try the Americans. They might know.'

'But they were brought *here*, to Rennes. To the *prison*.'

'Sorry. Any records of foreign prisoners would be in the hands of the Americans. Really, you must go and see them.'

'I have.' And there had been nothing, no trace. It was as if Richard and his men had vanished.

'Ah.' The commissaire tapped his fingers on the desk. 'Well, I really must get on now. If you please, madame!'

'At least let me see my cousin!'

The policeman stood up, laughing. 'Quite impossible, madame! At least, not without permission from the examining magistrate. Applications take days and even then I doubt you'd be allowed to see him . . . People charged with treason don't get visitors! Goodbye, madame.'

She lingered, reluctant to leave.

The policeman was getting impatient. 'I'll have you shown to the main hall.' He called to someone in the next office then sat down and studied the papers on his desk.

Julie said quickly, 'Monsieur . . . Will you be interrogating him again?'

'What?' He looked up vacantly. 'Probably, yes.'

'Couldn't you face him with *me*? With someone from the group he is supposed to have betrayed? Wouldn't that be useful?'

The commissaire was way ahead of her. He shook his head. 'Madame, really –'

'But it might help your interrogation considerably!'

He looked at her quizzically. 'In what way?'

'He might talk freely!'

'You read too much fiction, madame!'

'But you have nothing to lose! *Please.*'

The commissaire shook his head and sighed deeply. 'Madame, I just cannot!'

But she nearly had him, she knew it. She leant over the desk and said passionately, 'He'll answer questions from me, I *know* he will!'

The commissaire regarded his hands, then shot a glance at her. He sighed and shook his head unhappily. 'You win. Be here at eight tomorrow morning.'

Julie clasped her hands together.

He added, 'But remember this! It's only because you were in the Resistance. No other reason! And whatever you do, don't tell anyone I let you see him. All right?'

'Yes, I promise!'

Julie closed the door behind her, pleased that she had achieved something at last.

Then she remembered it was a very small victory and there was still a long way to go.

The prison was large and sombre and forbidding, its high walls dotted with small barred windows from which escape was clearly impossible. Julie looked at it and felt sick at heart.

Inside it was worse. Dark and terrible, rank with the smell of humanity and suffering and untold horrors; yet hauntingly silent, as if empty of inhabitants.

A warder led the way down a series of long gloomy passages whose walls threw off a palpable cold. Julie shivered involuntarily.

'Not so good, eh?' remarked the commissaire. 'They haven't done much to it since the Germans left. But then most of the new inhabitants are collaborators and black marketeers . . . So –' He shrugged.

They came to a door. The warder unlocked it. The commissaire said, 'Wait here until you're called,' and disappeared.

Julie leant against the wall in despair. Her mind was full of terrible visions, of Jean and Maurice and Gérard and Jacques and the others. *Here.*

The Gestapo had brought them *here*. She closed her eyes. She

514

wanted to know nothing – no details. Not where their cells had been, nor the place where they'd been tortured, nor the courtyard somewhere just down *there* where they'd been taken to die.

The door was opening. 'Come in!'

She opened her eyes with relief. Then, hesitating slightly, stepped inside. The room was large and almost bare, and dimly lit by a single barred window. There was a table in the centre. Michel was sitting at the far side of it.

He looked up, startled. She thought: They didn't tell him I was here.

She smiled faintly. '*Salut*, Michel.'

He stared at her, confusion and amazement on his face.

The commissaire said abruptly, 'Madame, can you identify this man?'

'Yes, he is Michel Le Goff.'

'And do you affirm that he arranged the escape of the scientist, Freymann, from the factory of Goulrent, Pescard et Cie in Brest?'

Julie sharpened her wits. She hadn't realised it was going to be like this. She looked at Michel for help, but he was still staring at her. As she brought her eyes back to the commissaire's, Julie noticed that there was a young man in the corner, taking notes on a shorthand pad. She would have to be careful.

She replied slowly, 'He was the contact – between his group and ours. I don't know if he actually arranged the escape.'

'But as contact man, he knew certain facts about your group? The mode of operation, the people involved?'

Julie said firmly, 'No! He knew nothing. Maurice was very careful!'

'Your leader?'

'Yes.'

'But perhaps you told Le Goff certain things?'

'What things do you mean?'

'Things about the group.'

'No!'

'Consider very carefully, madame . . . I will ask you again. Perhaps Le Goff discovered certain facts about your group. Perhaps you mentioned certain things without realising –?'

'No!' Julie said angrily. 'I never told him anything! He knew nothing!'

'Then how did he know where to find you when you were hiding on the beach? How did he know *which* beach to go to?'

She hesitated. This was becoming a nightmare. 'It . . . must have been through my uncle. Jean must have asked Michel for help and then told him where to find us. That must have been it!'

There was a pause. Julie looked to Michel for confirmation, but he was still staring at her and she had the feeling that he wasn't really listening.

The commissaire asked, 'After he'd collected you from the beach, he took you to a fishing boat that he kept hidden in Kernibon?'

'Yes.'

'And you escaped on it?'

'Yes.'

'Did he say why he had a fishing boat?'

Julie blinked. 'No. But – I supposed it was to escape if the Boches got onto him.'

'But suddenly he felt no need of it and gave it to you. I wonder why he should do that?'

'Because – we were in desperate need. The Gestapo were looking for us . . . They would have killed us. He gave it to us because he was *kind*. He wanted to *help*.'

'Indeed . . . Or perhaps because he had just done the Boches a favour and felt safe. So safe he wouldn't be needing the boat any more and could afford to be generous to his – friend?'

Julie felt herself turning scarlet. She wanted to step up to the commissaire and slap his big, fat face. She made an effort and said quietly, 'That is not true. None of it is! He wasn't the traitor! I've told you who was – it was the man Fougéres.'

The commissaire ignored her remark. 'Is there any more evidence that you can offer?'

She wished there was. She said quietly, 'No.'

The commissaire looked at the warder. 'That will be all, thank you.'

Julie started in alarm. She caught hold of the commissaire's arm. 'Please,' she whispered, 'can I have a few words with him in private?'

The policeman's eyes were cold. 'No, madame.'

'Not in private, then. With *them* present.' She indicated the warder and the man with the pad.

The commissaire was considering. Eventually he said grudgingly, 'All right! But no more than five minutes.' He turned abruptly and the warder let him out of the door.

Quickly, Julie sat down at the table. 'How are you?'

Michel shook his head. 'You shouldn't have come.'

'But why not?'

'Because . . .' He shrugged. 'It won't do any good.'

'No! Don't say that! We'll –'

516

He interrupted, 'How's Tante Marie?'

Julie shook her head. 'Not – well. She hardly knew me.'

'And Peter?'

'Oh fine. I left him in the Scillies. But Michel we haven't much time. Please tell me how I can help you!'

'The boat. It got you to England all right then?'

'Not quite,' Julie said unhappily. 'It was wrecked.'

Michel nodded as if the news was to be expected.

She said, 'It was my fault.'

'You did well to get there at all.'

The time was slipping away. She said urgently, 'But what can I do to *help* you?'

'Help me? I think no-one can. They're out to get me, and they will. One way or the other.' He smiled but there was a hint of false bravado in it.

'But there must be evidence! Michel, who really did it, do you know?'

He laughed. 'You ask *me*?' He shook his head. 'How should I know? All I can say is it wasn't one of mine.'

She reached over and gripped his hand. 'I believe it was a man called Fougéres. A stranger in the line. He came from Paris and was meant to have survived the Meteor collapse. But I always distrusted him!'

'And what's happened to him, does anyone know?'

She paused and withdrew her hand. 'Well – they *say* he's dead. But –'

He nodded and gave a small shrug as if he'd expected it.

Julie said crossly, 'You've given up hope!'

'I'm a realist, that's all.'

She sighed deeply. 'Michel, what can I do for you when you won't give me any help!'

'Don't concern yourself, Julie. My friends are doing what they can. They're asking around . . .'

'Have they found out anything?'

'I'm not sure.'

'How do I find these friends?'

For a moment she thought he wasn't going to answer then he said, 'In Paris, a bar called Chez Alphonse. Ask for Pierre.'

She nodded. 'I'll do everything I can. Everything!'

There was a pause. He asked, 'Have you any money?'

Her face fell. 'Not much.'

'If you can get into my apartment you'll find some hidden under the bottom plate inside the oven. Just lever it up. All right?'

She nodded. 'I'll return any I don't need.'

He gave a bitter laugh. 'It's not important.' A strange look flashed into his eyes – a look of fear and despair. It sent a chill through Julie's heart.

The warder said, 'Time up!' and moved towards the door.

Hurriedly, she touched his hand. 'I've never really said thank you for what you did. The boat . . . and getting us from the beach . . .' She shook her head. 'You should have kept the boat and got away . . .'

'No, you needed it more.' He stood up and pushed the chair into the table. He smiled and his grave, lined face looked a little less severe. 'See you! Take care!'

'I'll do everything I can –'

'Sure.'

He turned quickly and walked to a door on the opposite side of the room. Though she waited an instant, he never looked back.

37

It was almost as if there had never been a war. The city lay pale and gleaming under the late September sun, its long boulevards and elegant buildings apparently unscarred by bombs and bullets. Julie was faintly surprised: it was so different from the devastation of London.

When one looked closer, however, one could see signs of the long occupation: years of stringency and neglect had left buildings in urgent need of repair; the streets were littered and uncleaned; and walls were daubed with slogans or, in some cases, with rough white crosses where people had died.

Nevertheless, the atmosphere was festive. Even the shabbiest buildings were draped with bright flags, many of them home made. More than a month after the city's liberation the bright colours of the Stars and Stripes and the Union Jack still hung from dozens of balconies. But, brighter, taller, prouder than these was the Tricolore, flying high above the rooftops of a hundred buildings, a symbol of many things, but to most Parisians a symbol, above all, of freedom.

Julie found a room at a small hotel in the *treizième*, then went in search of the place called Chez Alphonse. It wasn't listed in the telephone directory, but a shopkeeper knew it and gave her directions. It was a small bar, narrow and dim, its walls yellow with nicotine. When she asked for Pierre, the bartender told her Pierre might not be in for days, but it should be possible to send him a message. Julie composed a short message on the back of an envelope and left it with the bartender. He told her there was no point in coming back until much later, at about nine.

It was only five. Julie went to a brasserie and ordered a meal. It was difficult to make rabbit stew last four hours, but she managed it by ordering coffee afterwards, then water and then coffee again. The bread coupon she'd proffered entitled her to a full three-course meal, but she wanted to economise. She had money all right – she'd taken Michel's from the hiding place in the oven and there had been quite a bit – but she didn't want to squander it, not only because it might have to last a long time, but because it was Michel's.

To pass the time Julie watched the people in the street. The Parisian women looked incredibly well dressed, though how they managed it when materials were so short amazed her. They made Julie feel inadequate and inelegant; her frumpy, second-hand suit must look dowdy by comparison. She tried hard not to mind but failed.

At last it was almost nine and Julie headed back towards the bar. The streets were busy. Everyone seemed to be out for a stroll, talking in groups or wandering in and out of cafés.

When she reached Chez Alphonse it was crowded and noisy, and the atmosphere thick with smoke. The barman was busy serving and it was some minutes before she managed to catch his eye. He nodded and turned to speak to a man at the far end of the bar. The man stood up and came over to Julie.

He smiled and said, 'I'm Pierre.' He was about forty, fair and boyish and jolly-looking: not at all how Julie had imagined a hard-core communist to look. He took her elbow and said above the noise, 'Come. We can't talk here. Let's go for a stroll.'

He led the way out of the bar and waited for her to join him on the pavement. They began to walk slowly up the street. Pierre said, 'So! They're still trying to hang everything on Michel, are they?'

'I'm afraid so.'

'Ha! He always made enemies, Michel. Always attracted trouble, even in the old days.'

'The old days?'

'At university. I was his tutor.'

Julie looked sideways at him. She asked, 'Have you found out anything? That might help Michel?'

He shook his head. 'Not directly. I've asked around – my friends

519

in the police and so on. Nothing. No rumours, nothing. Mind you, they have a basinful at the moment, sorting out the black marketeers from the collaborators, and the collaborators from the informers.' He snorted. 'Most of the real villains will get clean away, of course!'

He made it sound hopeless. 'But why?' she asked.

'Oh, they'll have covered themselves well and in a little while they'll pop up as magistrates and bankers and swear they were never fascists . . .'

They came into a wide boulevard full of light and activity and crowded cafés.

Julie said, 'The traitor, the man I'm looking for, he came from Paris. At least I'm fairly sure he did. *Someone* must have known him . . . or seen him. His name was Fougères.'

'The name means nothing. He probably used a hundred different names. Do you have a photograph?'

Julie shook her head. She wished she had. But when she had prepared the identity cards she was always careful not to keep any spare photographs. It was maddening when she thought about it now.

'Never mind. Let's go and see what we can find.' He indicated with his head and quickened his pace.

'Find –? Where are we going?'

'I'm not promising *anything*, but there's someone you should see. Someone who might know something.' He emphasised, 'But I'm not promising a thing.'

Julie ran a little to keep up. 'Who? Who is this person?'

Suddenly Pierre gave a short laugh. 'Ah . . . Well, you see, we like to help the police out. In our own small way.'

She looked at him questioningly.

'We've caught ourselves someone. Someone who might otherwise have avoided the full force of justice.'

Julie tensed. 'Who –?'

'An informer.'

'And he might have known –'

Pierre said firmly, 'Not necessarily. But he knew the Gestapo well enough. He worked for them for at least two years. He might have heard something about your man, you never know. Anyway, let's go and see.'

Julie followed, trying to absorb the full meaning of what Pierre had said. This informer – would he have known about other informers? Would they have met? It seemed very unlikely. And would they have had the same contacts? Again, it seemed unlikely. She decided not to raise her hopes too high.

She found the idea of the captured informer rather disturbing; she

520

couldn't help wondering what they would do with him afterwards. She thought of asking more, but in the glow of the occasional light Pierre's face looked stern and un-boyish and she decided against it.

They walked in silence for ten minutes, into a darker quieter area with few cafés or restaurants. Julie had no idea where they were. Eventually they came to a tall, red-brick apartment building.

Pierre guided her into a narrow alleyway at the side and then to some steps which led down to a cellar. The alley was dark, filthy and oppressive. Julie hung back.

Pierre turned. 'It's all right. Just follow me.'

He led the way down the steps and knocked softly on a door at the bottom. There was a long pause. Finally the door opened slightly. Pierre put his head to the crack, murmured a few words, and the door swung open.

Pierre stepped forward. Julie followed, half-impatient, half-frightened of what she might see.

It was a bare cellar, cold and damp, its floor scattered with rubbish. There was a blinding electric light hanging on a wire from the ceiling. It cast a pool of white over the centre of the room, leaving the walls in deep shadow.

Immediately under the light was a chair. A man was sitting on it. He was bound to the chair by rope which had been passed several times round his chest, pinning his arms to his sides. The front of his shirt was covered with blood which seemed to have come from his face, though it was impossible to be sure because his head was lying forward on his chest. He seemed to be asleep.

Pierre strode across and, grasping the man's hair, raised his head. Julie gasped. The face was a mess, the nose bloody and the eyes blackened.

She stared hard for several moments.

Then she exhaled.

She had never seen the man before in her life.

She kept looking, just to be sure. But there was no doubt.

'You don't recognise him?' Pierre asked.

'No.'

Pierre nodded. 'No reason why you should.' He let the head fall again.

There were two other men in the room, the one who had opened the door and another who came up to Pierre and said under his breath, 'I think we've got the lot. Shall we –?'

Then they were whispering and Julie didn't hear any more. Eventually the conversation finished and Pierre came back to her.

Julie began, 'What exactly –?'

Suddenly, the man in the chair jerked up his head and moaned. Julie held her breath. Then he slumped forward again.

She asked again, 'What exactly did he do?'

'Oh, he was a little sneak, a tell-tale . . . He shopped people to the Gestapo. For money. Not much money, either! That's because he enjoyed doing it, you see.' He shouted, 'Didn't you, you *con*? Eh!'

The figure in the chair whimpered and began rocking his head from side to side.

'But he doesn't enjoy it so much now,' Pierre snorted contemptuously. 'His national socialist principles didn't last very long. In fact, he's prepared to swear to anything just at the moment.'

Suddenly the figure began to wail, a continuous whine that rose and fell like a dog howling in the night.

Pierre regarded the sight with distaste. 'Four of my comrades died because of him.'

'I'm sorry.'

'It's always the spineless little shits who do the damage. Look at him! He's frightened, the yellow-belly! Terrified of what we might do to him! Spineless little shits!'

She shook her head. 'Our traitor wasn't like that. He was clever . . . hard . . . and cunning. Not like that.'

'Ah. Well, let's find out what this creature knows.'

Pierre went up to the chair and pulled up the man's head again. There was a shriek and the man started sobbing and whimpering. 'No, no . . . please . . . please . . .'

'Your masters sent someone to Brittany. Do you know who? *Do you know who*?'

The man shook his head from side to side, his eyes wide and staring. 'No . . . No . . . Brittany . . . no!'

Julie stared, repulsed by the bloody face.

Pierre was getting impatient. He waved to one of the other men. 'Encourage him, Charles, will you?'

'No, please!' Julie exclaimed.

Pierre paused in surprise.

Finally he shrugged. 'All right. If you wish.' He said to the figure in the chair, 'The lady is kind. She doesn't want you to suffer. Tell her what she needs to know, eh? Otherwise we'll go back to the other way. Tell her! Who else did your masters use? Who was sent to Brittany? *Eh*?'

The wild eyes swivelled round and fastened on Julie's face. The mouth opened and closed, like a fish. Eventually the man whined to Julie, 'They're – going – to – kill me!' And started to cry. 'Please – stop them. *Please!*'

Julie looked to Pierre for help. He said roughly, '*Tell the lady what she wants to know.*'

The man's eyes were fastened on Julie. 'I know n-nothing! *Nothing!* I was innocent! The Gestapo blackmailed me. They forced me into it. Save me! *Please! Please!*'

She said quietly, 'If you could tell me what you know . . . I'd be grateful.'

The man gulped. '. . . I heard very little. They were *very* careful. They forced me to tell them things, then they made me go away. *Really.*' He was sobbing gently.

The sight was pathetic, cruel. Julie made herself remember that this man was a murderer, just like Fougères. She pressed, 'But gossip . . . rumours . . . there must have been *something.*'

He shook his head. 'I can't think . . . I can't think!'

Pierre said roughly, 'Who was in charge of informers?'

'Kloffer.'

Pierre said quickly, 'And did Kloffer ever talk about his – agents?'

'No! Kloffer was too grand for me. I never talked to Kloffer! Never! I wasn't important enough! I wasn't one of their informers. I only dealt with stockings, perfume – I was never an informer. Never!'

Pierre said to Julie, 'He's lying,' and made a sudden movement towards the chair. The man threw back his head in terror.

'Who *did* you deal with then?' Pierre demanded.

'There was a sergeant – and a junior officer. *Not* important people. They never told me *anything!*'

Pierre was getting impatient. '*Try harder!*'

The wretched man rocked his head slowly from side to side. 'Please . . . I was never told anything . . .'

'*Try harder.*'

'Oh please, oh *please!*' He was whining again. Suddenly he stopped. There was a long pause. He frowned with mental effort. Finally he gulped and said, 'The sergeant . . . he was in charge of false papers. I never had any, of course! I was only a black marketeer. I wasn't important enough. But . . . I know others did.'

Pierre urged, 'Others?'

'No names were ever mentioned. Never. But –' His bloodshot eyes fastened on Julie again and he spoke quickly through swollen lips. 'Once or twice I heard things. F-from the sergeant mainly. He'd talk about successes. Things they'd found out, groups they'd smashed, th-that sort of thing. There was one man I heard about, a t-top man, someone who w-worked for them all the time . . .'

Julie held her breath. '*Yes?*'

'. . . the tip of one of his fingers was m-missing! So the sergeant said . . .'

The man desperately searched Julie's face for a sign that he had said the right thing. She looked at Pierre and shook her head.

Pierre said coldly, 'No good, *con*.' He began to move away. 'That's it then.'

'*No-o-o!*' It was a great wail. 'Please, I *beg you*.' Then he was looking from her to Pierre and talking so fast that she missed the first few words. '. . . and there was another. Someone they gave false papers to all the time. He was important, I knew. He'd started as a dealer, like me. Usual things – petrol, stockings, perfume. Then he became an informer. The sergeant talked about him a couple of times. I never heard a name, never a *name*. But they called him the Marseillais. Or the Man from Marseilles. Something like that.' He looked desperately up into their faces. 'He was important, I know that – but nothing else. They never told me anything else! *Believe me.*'

A Marseillais. Julie tried to recall Fougères' voice. It had been an educated voice without, as far as she could tell, any regional accent. Not very likely, then.

She asked, nevertheless, 'Did this sergeant ever say what this Marseillais had done exactly? What sort of jobs?'

The prisoner's head fell to one side and she thought he was going to faint. But he mumbled, 'Infiltration. His s-speciality. Very s-successful . . .' The puffed eyes reopened. '*Réseaux* . . . he got inside an escape line . . . for airmen . . .'

Julie stiffened and put her face up to the prisoner's. 'Yes –?'

'That's all I know. He was very important!' The man grimaced as if in pain.

'But which line?' Julie took him by the shoulder and shook him slightly. 'Which line?'

'I don't know . . . I don't know!'

'Was it Meteor? Was it? Or ours in Brittany?'

The man threw his head from side to side and started to sob again. 'I don't know . . .'

Julie stood for a while, watching him. Pierre took her aside. 'It's not much.'

'No.' It was almost nothing. She asked, 'What about this Kloffer? Was he captured?'

Pierre shook his head. 'No! The Gestapo were the first people to disappear. He'll be holed up in Germany by now, planning his excuses.'

A cry came from the figure in the chair. '*Please, lady* . . . Please have mercy . . . Please don't let them kill me. Please!' He was wailing again.

Julie looked back. 'What about him?'

Pierre murmured, 'We'll decide.'

'Are you sure he did it?'

'We're sure.' He went to the door. 'Here, I'll see you back.' As she stepped out into the cool night air a howl came floating through the door. Julie clenched her fists and walked quickly up the steps towards the street.

Pierre caught up with her and they walked in silence for a while. Eventually he asked, 'What will you do now?'

'I don't know.'

'Will you go back to Brittany?'

She shook her head. 'There doesn't seem much point. Fougères wouldn't have gone back there.'

'So you'll stay in Paris?'

She sighed heavily. 'I suppose so.'

'Well, keep in touch. I might hear something. The police might come across your man, you never know. He probably shopped a lot of other people too. It's bound to catch up with him sooner or later. I'll leave messages at Chez Alphonse from time to time. Okay?'

'Yes.'

'I'm sorry there wasn't more. But one could hardly expect names.'

'No.'

'I'll ask about this Marseillais. Perhaps if he really *was* important he might be your man.'

'Yes –' She stopped and looked at him. 'The one back there. Couldn't you give him to the police? Couldn't you?'

Pierre's face was sad and cold. 'What would *you* do if he had killed *your* friends?'

Julie stared at him, then looked away. There was nothing to say.

They walked on and came to a street which she recognised. She said, 'I can find my way from here.'

They said brief goodbyes and separated. Julie walked back to the hotel, deeply depressed. She went straight to bed and lay awake most of the night, thinking.

The next day she returned to Chez Alphonse. There was no message.

She returned every evening for a week, after long days spent at police stations, military headquarters, and obscure departments of the new French government.

Nothing. No information on the Marseillais. No information on someone who might, at one time or another, have called himself Fougères.

The other branches of the Resistance could not help either. Fougères? No, he had been one of their own. He had never betrayed anyone. Had someone impersonated him then? They didn't know. Fougères had disappeared when the Gestapo made it too hot for him in Paris. He'd phoned a friend and said he was going to Brittany. Description – Yes, tall and dark. Yes, that was Fougères. He was long dead now, taken from Fresnes and shot at Mont Valérion.

But they would make more enquiries. No traitor would stay alive and unavenged while they still lived. If she ever heard a whisper about the true identity of the Brittany traitor, she had only to contact them –

On the eighth day there was a message at Chez Alphonse. It said, 'No trace of anyone known as the Marseillais. Nothing on any other informers. Sorry. Pierre.'

That night in bed she spent a long time thinking about the number of infiltrators the Gestapo might have used on a regular basis – was it a few? Or a dozen?

And what made one of those infiltrators really successful, so successful that he stood out from the rest?

By the morning she thought she knew, and then she made her decision.

The woman was leaning over him, her face leering and cruel. She laughed, loud and triumphant. He tried to move but she held him in a vice-like grip. He couldn't *believe* how strong she was.

It wasn't fair! He wanted to say it wasn't fair.

He tried to call out. But however hard he tried his lips wouldn't move. He couldn't believe it.

He made a superhuman effort to get free.

His limbs were heavy and useless. They wouldn't move either!

He begged, *move!* Please *move!*

She was killing him now, slowly but surely. Covering his face, squeezing his neck . . . He gasped for air, craved for breath . . . *sucked* for the precious air . . .

But she squeezed tighter.

He was panicking now. The blood was roaring and singing in his head.

He was *desperate* for air . . .

Death rushed up to him, nearer and nearer. He *sensed* it coming . . .

And all he could think was: It's not *fair*.

Then she was laughing again, the sound fading and swirling in the distance. Everything was fading . . .

With a terrible shock he realised he had slipped over the edge of a precipice and was falling down and down . . .

Oh Christ! I'm so frightened. Maman, help!

Maman!

He woke up sweating and murmured, '*Merde!*'

He looked up at the ceiling, then closed his eyes again and tried to calm himself.

What a stupid thing. He hadn't had a dream like that for a long time.

He wondered vaguely why it should come back now.

There must be a reason.

He rolled over and, taking a cigarette from a packet lying on the floor, lit it thoughtfully. He inhaled deeply and let the smoke take effect.

No, there was no reason for the dream.

It usually came when things were going badly. But nothing was going badly at the moment. In fact, everything was going rather well . . .

Perhaps he'd overlooked something. Quickly he went over everything in his mind: the club, the permits, the financial calculations, the details – always the details.

He'd forgotten nothing.

Stupid, stupid . . . that dream.

Still, it bothered him. He hated its power over him.

Angrily he stubbed out his cigarette. Immediately, he lit another one and inhaled deeply.

He closed his eyes and tried to think of all the good things that were happening, like the car and the new suit he had bought. Yes, there were *lots* of good things.

The dream meant nothing.

No-one would ever find him.

He was safe.

The dream belonged to the past. And the past was locked safely away.

The Man from Marseilles.

Julie looked at the people milling around the station and thought: But they're all from Marseilles!

She picked up her case and walked out of the station into the street. Though it was barely nine, the sun was blazing out of an empty sky.

527

She hadn't realised it would be so warm in October. Her woollen suit felt rather hot.

She was standing in a wide boulevard, busy with cars and the occasional horse-drawn vehicle. She was struck immediately by the noise – the hooting of the cars and the loud conversations – and by the colour: the people seemed brighter, more exotic. It was partly their clothes and partly the different races – Arab, Senegalese and Asian.

She looked around blankly. She wasn't sure where to start.

She crossed the boulevard and began to wander down what seemed to be a main street. After a while she paused. This sort of wandering would do no good; she had to do something positive.

The police first, then. She stopped and asked a shopkeeper for directions to the nearest police station.

It was not far – five minutes away – but it was the wrong police station. She needed the *Police Judiciare* – the criminal investigation branch. They redirected her. It was a long walk and her case began to feel heavy in her hand. She stopped and removed her jacket. She should have done it before: her blouse was damp with sweat.

It took half an hour to find a sufficiently senior officer and explain what she wanted.

Then they laughed at her as she had known they would. Not rudely or unkindly, but politely, with a shake of the head.

'A man called the Marseillais? Madame, have you any idea how many characters are called by that name?'

But they did let her look at the rogues' gallery. There were vast numbers of wanted men and ex-convicts. After three hours one face began to look much like another and Julie lost heart. Why should she find him there anyway? He probably had no criminal record. Nevertheless, before she left she arranged to come back the next day, just in case.

She ate a late lunch in a pavement café then, taking a slip of paper from her purse, made a telephone call. The number belonged to a friend of the Paris Resistance, a colleague of theirs, someone who might be able to help; a man called Alain.

The number rang. A woman's voice replied.

'I want to speak to Alain, please.'

'You mean Doctor Hubert? I'm afraid he is at the hospital at present. Please try later.'

Julie rang off. They hadn't told her he was a doctor. She decided to try again in the evening.

In the meantime she had the rest of the afternoon to spare. When the waiter brought coffee, she said, 'I'm a stranger to the city. Can you tell me where I am? In relation to the centre?'

'La Canebière is about five minutes away. Down there.' He indicated a direction with his hand.

'And that's the centre?'

'It's the main street.'

She nodded. 'And where would I find a reasonably-priced hotel. I mean – a cheap one?' She didn't want to waste money unnecessarily.

The waiter shrugged. 'All kinds of places. But try nearer the harbour. That's probably your best bet.'

'Where's that, please?'

'Turn right at La Canebière and you'll find it at the far end.'

She found La Canebière immediately, a wide street full of shops and restaurants. It looked a long way to the harbour and she hopped on a bus. After five minutes she glimpsed the water, got off and walked the last few yards, over the road ringing the harbour, to the quayside.

The harbour lay before her, its waters pale and tranquil, crowded with fishing boats and trading ships. To the left the city rose in an orderly jumble of multi-coloured buildings up the slope of a gentle hill to a magnificent church at the summit, the famous Notre-Dame de la Garde which Julie had seen in photographs.

To the right there was a quay . . . She frowned.

Then there was nothing. For quite a long way.

It looked like a giant demolition site.

Julie picked up her case and walked over, trying to imagine what could have happened to the place.

She climbed what had once been a narrow street of houses. Now there was little but a mass of masonry, splintered wood and the occasional door or window lying crushed and forlorn on its side. The place was disconcerting, like a graveyard. As she went further she saw that, here and there, there were makeshift stalls and shops constructed out of the ruins, where traders – Arabs mostly – were sitting waiting for business. There were shanties, too, with smoke coming from their roofs and washing hanging outside.

At the top of the street was a junction with a larger road. On the opposite side were buildings again, more people, and order.

She took a last look at the extraordinary derelict waste land and crossed the street to the normality of the other side.

She began looking for a hotel, and not a moment too soon. She was hot and very tired; she'd hardly slept at all on the train. The first hotel she came to was run-down and dirty, the second had a girl standing provocatively on the doorstep, and the third looked rather dark and uninviting. She decided on the third because she couldn't face going any further; her arm was at breaking point. She should have left her case at the station.

The room they gave her was clean and tidy and perfectly adequate. She lay down and rested her aching feet until six, when she went down in search of a phone.

The doctor still wasn't in. Would she like to leave a message?

Julie hesitated, instinctively reticent. Then she remembered that the war in France was over and there was no more need for secrecy. She said, 'Tell him a friend from the Resistance called.' She left her name and the number of the hotel.

The next morning there was a message. Doctor Hubert would come to the hotel at twelve.

She spent the morning with the *Police Judiciare*, looking at more pages of photographs. Still nothing. It got to the point where she wondered if she'd recognise him even if she saw him.

She got back to the hotel breathless and fifteen minutes late. An elderly man who had been sitting in a chair beside the reception desk rose to his feet with some difficulty.

She asked in surprise, 'Doctor Hubert?'

He bowed slightly. He was at least sixty, probably more, and was painfully thin with a marked stoop. He was leaning heavily on a stick.

She said hurriedly, 'I'm sorry I'm late.'

'Not at all,' he said softly. 'It is a pleasure to meet anyone – who is a friend.' He blinked at her over his spectacles. 'Are you here on a visit? Or –?'

'I need some help.'

'Ah. In that case, perhaps you would care for some lunch?'

They found a brasserie a few streets away and ordered what seemed to Julie to be a rather extravagant meal of soupe de poisson, veal – when had she last had veal? – and wine.

As they talked, Julie decided that Alain Hubert was a remarkable man. Gentle and self-effacing, he seemed an unlikely resistance hero. Perhaps that was why he'd never been caught.

When the food arrived, Julie ate heartily; she'd almost forgotten what good food tasted like.

'So this person might have come from Marseilles?' the doctor asked.

'Might, yes. It's not much to go on, is it?'

'Well, who can say? Maybe someone would recognise his description, you never know.'

'The police didn't.'

'Maybe he's not known to them.'

530

Julie sipped at the rich fruity Algerian wine. 'He's probably not known anywhere . . .'

'I'm sorry that I can't be of any help.'

She smiled. 'Not your fault.'

'The only thing I can suggest is the *milieu*.'

'Oh?'

'Most of the crime in Marseilles is highly controlled. There's an organisation which runs almost everything – black market, prostitution, and, of course, drugs. They must know a lot more about what goes on in this city than the police.'

He was describing a world that Julie didn't understand at all. She asked, 'It's possible they might know this man, then?'

'I really can't say. But if you have no luck with the police it's worth a try.'

'How do I find them?'

'Ahh, that I don't know.' He looked at her over his glasses, his eyes twinkling. 'I don't move in those circles actually.'

She grinned. 'No, of course not.'

'It would have been easier in the old days, before they demolished the Old Quarter. It was the centre of all that, it was the *bas-quartier*.'

'What happened to it? Why was it torn down?'

'The Germans decided it was undesirable and had it flattened. The real reason, I think, was that they couldn't control what went on inside.'

They finished their coffee and the doctor insisted on paying for lunch. 'It's my pleasure. Forgive me, but I have to go now.'

'Of course.'

He swivelled in his chair and reached for his stick. Julie got up to help him. He said, 'There is just one thing . . . There's an old friend of mine, a chap who's been in a little trouble from time to time. He might know how to contact the right people . . .'

'I thought you said you didn't mix with those sort of people,' Julie laughed.

'Ah, well, one's not so choosy about one's friends in prison.'

'In prison?'

He got slowly and painfully to his feet, falling slightly against the table as he did so. She held his arm until he had regained his balance. 'This leg . . . Slow to mend . . . An infernal nuisance . . . Yes, prison. We were lucky, he and I . . . We were lucky . . .'

So the mild manner had not deceived the Gestapo after all. It explained his frailty and the broken, badly-mended leg.

He was holding out his hand. 'It was a great pleasure, madame.

Goodbye. I'll make enquiries of my friend. I'll telephone. Goodbye.'
He made his way slowly down the street.

Six hours later there was a message. It read simply: Try Chez
Henri off the Rue Caisserie. Good luck.'

She had no trouble in finding Henri's Bar; the hotel proprietor
directed her straight to it. The place was narrow-fronted and dark.
She hesitated. Often bars were combined with cafés or restaurants
and a woman could go in quite happily. But this was a bar, a drinking
establishment pure and simple.

She drew a deep breath and marched straight in.

The interior was dimly lit and, seeing a vacant table beside the
door, she sank quickly into a chair. Then she changed her mind. She
might as well go the whole hog. Getting up, she perched on a stool at
the bar.

The place was, she imagined, typical. Dark polished wood, yellow
paint, and the odour of a thousand cigarettes. But there were exotic
smells, too, of spices and herbs and strange unfamiliar scents. A
handful of regular customers sat at the bar, well into café-cognac,
pastis and wine and cassis.

Behind the counter was a young man, busy serving customers, and
an older, plumper man, carefully adjusting the rows of bottles that
lined the back of the bar. The older man was surreptitiously watching
her in a mirror. She guessed he was the proprietor.

The young man came by and she ordered coffee. As he went to get
it she saw two oranges behind the bar and immediately wished she'd
ordered *orange pressé*. Oranges were virtually unobtainable in
England.

The coffee was put in front of her. A moment later the proprietor
drifted past.

'Excuse me –' Julie asked quickly.

The proprietor continued as if he hadn't heard her, took his time
putting a bottle on a shelf, then slowly returned. He said without
looking at her, 'Yes.'

'I want information.'

'Oh yes?' He gave her a hard look. 'What kind of information?'

'I'm looking for someone. Someone who might have lived around
here, or visited the Old Quarter . . .'

'His name?'

This was where it got difficult. But there was no way round it. She
said, 'That's the problem . . . I don't know it.' She sighed and smiled
a little. 'All I know is that he was called the Marseillais.'

The proprietor looked at her from under his eyebrows. 'The Marseillais?' He nodded slowly, as if humouring an idiot. 'The Marseillais?

Madame, can you imagine how many people are called that in the world? Eh? Every *mac* in Marseilles! And whenever a Marseillais goes away, guess what people call him! Why yes, madame!' He shook his head and sighed. 'They call him a Marseillais, that's what!'

Julie nodded. 'Yes, I know it sounds ridiculous but – he must have been known here. Before he went away. Known . . . in bars, around the place . . . He was the kind of person who might have been involved in – *le milieu* . . .'

'So –? Half the population of this place is involved in *something*!' He was glaring at her, hostile now.

Before Julie could say any more, he moved away and served another customer.

It was five minutes before he came her way again, hurrying past on the far side of the bar. She leaned over the counter and said, 'Please, another word –?'

He hesitated for a moment, poised to walk away again.

'Look . . . can you give me the name of someone who might know.'

'Who do you suggest?'

Julie began to get exasperated. 'Someone who can help. Look, this man – the one I'm looking for, he's wanted by –' She almost said the police, but realised it might count against her. 'By the Resistance. He was a traitor. He's responsible for people's deaths.'

She had him now: he was moving closer, his eyes curious. The rest of the bar was silent, too, and five pairs of eyes watched her intently.

Julie said, 'He worked for the Gestapo. He has to be found to save an injustice, an innocent man. And – for other reasons.'

The proprietor stared at her thoughtfully. 'Ahh. Well . . .' He nodded slowly. 'That's different. But – it won't exactly be easy.' He asked sceptically. 'What *do* you know about him? Did he have an accent? Did he speak like a Provençal? Like *me*?'

'No.'

'Mmm. An educated type, maybe?'

'Yes, very likely. I know it's not much to go on, but I could give you a description of what he looked like. And then – perhaps you could ask around? Perhaps you know someone –?'

He nodded. 'I'll ask the boys.' He used the slang word *malfrats* – good-for-nothings. Taking a pencil stub and an old till receipt, he painstakingly wrote down the details she gave him: dark hair, thin, about thirty, medium height, gold ring, no accent. It wasn't much. She made him add: clever, probably well educated, dislikes women.

He said, 'I'll do what I can, but –' He shrugged, 'I can't promise anything.'

She pressed him, 'How long before you might get news –?'

'Ah!' He shrugged. 'Two hours? Two days? You come back from time to time, then I'll tell you how long it'll take!'

Three days later Julie thought: I'm wasting my time.

The proprietor – Henri – was earnest and well-meaning but she was beginning to wonder if he had all the contacts he'd hinted at. He didn't seem to be getting anywhere at all.

But then, she thought unhappily, perhaps there wasn't anywhere to get to. There was no proof – not even a shred of a suggestion – that the Marseillais and Fougères were one and the same man.

And yet Fougères had been so very *good* at deceit and treachery that he *must* have been important to the Boches. She couldn't believe he was just a casual informer. No – he was *experienced*.

And yet, she had to face the possibility that the two men weren't the same. And if so, where did that leave her? In a dead end. There were no more leads to follow.

That was really why she had come to Marseilles – because it *was* the only lead.

After an aimless walk around the harbour she went back to the bar, utterly dispirited. It would be the third time she'd looked in that morning. Doubtless she would hear the same thing again: no news. Henri's shrugs and 'Don't worry' and 'Be patient' were getting on her nerves.

But when she went in, something was different. Henri was smiling slyly, his eyes gleaming. *News.*

He ducked under the flap and, coming out from behind the bar, beckoned her to one side. 'Someone wants to see you. He's been away, that's why there's been a delay. He'll see you this afternoon.'

'But who?'

'Ahh,' he whispered conspiratorially, 'he's what you might call the *Patron* – with a capital "P", you understand.'

Julie didn't completely, but she nodded anyway.

'You're very lucky. He's interested in your story. And if anyone can help – well, *he* can!'

'Where do I find him?'

'No problem, just be here at three. It's all arranged!'

She was there at two-thirty because she had nothing better to do. She drank coffee nervously and, though she'd hardly ever smoked in her life, accepted two cigarettes from Henri.

By three her eyes were fastened to the door. By ten past three she was looking desperately at Henri. He said, 'Don't worry. We keep Marseillais time here. Nice and slow.'

At a quarter past three a long black car drew up outside. Henri led her to the door. 'Good luck!'

The driver was standing beside the car. He had a broken nose, large shoulders and a surly expression. He looked just like a criminal. It suddenly dawned on Julie that he probably *was* a criminal. As she approached he slid into the car.

Henri ushered Julie into the back, closed the door, and the car moved away. Julie sat stiffly in her seat. The back of the driver's head didn't invite conversation.

The car eased gently through the narrow streets until they reached a wide boulevard. Then they accelerated past the harbour, across several junctions and onto the hill topped by the magnificent church. After five minutes or so, the driver braked and turned the car into a street full of small shops. They stopped. The driver turned and swivelled his eyes in the direction of the pavement. Julie guessed she was meant to get out.

As she opened the door the driver murmured, 'In there,' and indicated with his finger. Julie looked: it was a restaurant. The driver added something in slang that she didn't understand. Then he translated. 'The waiter,' he explained, 'ask the waiter.'

She crossed the pavement and pushed open the door. It was very dark inside. She paused, trying to get her bearings.

Someone appeared from the shadows. 'Come this way.'

She followed the man to the back of the room and saw the figures of four men dimly visible at a table. As she approached, one of them rose to his feet and extended a hand. The conversation at the table petered out.

Julie shook the man's hand and sat in the chair he offered her. As her eyes got accustomed to the light she took a good look at him. He was well dressed in a conventional but slightly flashy way. His suit was obviously expensive, and there was a gold chain visible across the waistcoat and another round his wrist. Several rings glinted dully on his fingers. As he sat back in his seat she caught the whiff of liberally applied cologne.

He smiled. His face was pleasant, his eyes twinkling under a high forehead and receding hair line.

He enquired, 'Would you like some wine? Or a coffee?'

'Nothing, thank you.'

He said, 'My friend Henri tells me you're looking for someone.' He had a strong Provençal accent, but the voice was soft and soothing.

'Yes. Someone who came from here. Probably a long time ago.'

He sipped some wine and smiled again. 'Tell me about him.'

'Everything?'

535

'As much as you know.'

She told him about Brittany and the escape line and the betrayal and how Michel had been accused; and she told him about the man from Paris, the outsider with the narrow face, the lanky hair, the dark almost black eyes, and the sallow skin. She finished, '. . . And he was cruel, that's what I remember most.'

The *Patron* frowned with concentration. 'And his manner?'

'Cold. Always – watchful. And underhand. Devious.'

'And – how did he speak?'

'He had no accent,' she admitted, 'not that one could catch anyway. Certainly nothing like –' She hesitated.

'Like mine?' He smiled again.

Julie nodded.

'And you said something about women. About him not liking women.'

'No . . . he hated them, I would say. And he was frightened of them – well, wary, anyway.'

The *Patron* sipped his wine again. 'No facial scars or anything like that?'

'No.'

There was the sound of the restaurant door opening and closing. The *Patron* looked up. 'Ah here we are!'

A man came up and put an envelope into the *Patron's* hand. He opened it and shook out the contents. 'Some pictures for you to look at. Just a few ideas.' He placed them in a pile on the table and turned to one of the others. 'Throw some light on the scene, will you, Isso?'

A lamp was switched on and the table was flooded with sudden light. Blinking, Julie picked up the first photograph. It was a snapshot of a family group. There were five people: a middle-aged couple and three young men, presumably their sons. The faces were blurred but she knew immediately that none of them was Fougères. She put the picture back on the table.

The second was in fact two photographs: a front and side view of an unsmiling man with frightened eyes. The pictures looked like the police shots she'd seen at the *Police Judiciaire*. She didn't recognise the face.

She picked up the third picture and, as she did so, she caught sight of the one now visible on the top of the pile. It was of a formal group, a dozen or so young men standing stiffly in a garden with, at either side, four black-robed men: priests. The picture was blurred and indistinct and had been taken in strong sunlight, so that the participants were frowning against the glare. But there was something – *familiar*.

For a second she didn't move then, with a trembling hand, she reached for it. Very slowly.

But even before she picked it up she knew.

It was him.

It was him.

She looked closely. Very young, perhaps only fourteen, but the hair, the narrow face . . . It was him all right. It was a moment before she could speak. Then she whispered, 'This one. This is the one.'

The *Patron* took the photograph gently from her hand and stared at it. He looked up at her. 'You're sure?'

'Yes. Positive!'

He shook his head and murmured, 'So! I knew the bastard would turn up again somewhere! Scum always do.'

'What's his name?' she demanded. 'Who is he?'

The *Patron* was staring at the photograph again. 'His name? Vasson. Paul Vasson.'

She said it over to herself. 'And what was he? Where did he come from?'

'He was the illegitimate son of a whore – a junkie whore at that. The authorities found him starving in a cupboard when he was about eight and handed him over to the Jesuits. The priests did what they could. They educated him well – Vasson was always a clever sod.' He paused. 'Later he became a small-time pimp with ambitions. He wanted to make the big time. He had expensive tastes . . .'

'And?'

'He disappeared in '35. No-one's seen him since. Not that we haven't been looking.' He laughed bitterly. 'We would love to find the cheap bastard again, believe me!'

She was gripped with excitement. 'But now we've got him, haven't we!'

He regarded her patiently. 'Got him? Listen, people have been looking for him for a long time . . . The police – *they* would like to find him. Me – *I've* had the word out for a long time now.' He shook his head. 'Nothing. Oh, once someone said they'd seen him in Toulon. But we never found him there. Another time someone saw him in Paris . . .' He shook his head. 'But never a real lead.'

He held up the photograph. 'Then I got hold of this. In about '40, it was. One of my men flogged it round. Thought I'd got the swine then. He'd been seen all right, in Paris, round the *dix-huitième*. Working in clubs, that kind of thing. Thought I'd got him. I put the word out. Then . . .'

'What happened?'

'He disappeared again. Vanished. Never a trace.'

Julie was crestfallen. 'Oh . . . I see.'

'We've tried, believe me. But he's a cunning little sod. He's kept out of sight.' He shrugged. 'He'll still be in a big city somewhere – Paris probably. With his liking for the big time he wouldn't be caught dead in a provincial town. But apart from that . . .'

Julie sighed heavily. 'Well . . . at least I know who he is, that Vasson was Fougères. That should be enough to free my cousin.'

'You don't seem very happy . . .'

She frowned and looked at her hands. 'I can't bear to think of Vasson not being caught.'

'Well . . .' he shrugged. 'Perhaps I'm wrong. Perhaps the *flics* will pick him up straight away . . .'

'Yes, but . . . suppose they don't?'

There was a silence.

'Where will you go now?' he asked.

She considered. 'To Rennes first to free my cousin, then – Paris.' She seemed to make up her mind. 'Yes. Paris.'

He watched her for a moment. 'And what are you going to do there?'

'See if I can help the police, identify him if necessary . . .

'You're going to look for him.'

She didn't know what to say. She wasn't sure what she was going to do herself. Eventually she murmured, 'If I have to.'

The *Patron* shook his head. 'He's a dangerous man – a lunatic!' He sighed and leant forward. 'Please, be very, very careful! Look – if you're really determined, then you'll need help. What about money?'

'I've got enough for the moment.'

'Well, if you need more, just phone this number in Paris.' He wrote it on one of the restaurant's cards. 'I'll tell them you're coming. They'll be able to help in other ways, too.'

'Other ways?'

'Manpower . . . That kind of thing.'

Julie nodded uncertainly.

The *Patron* tapped her hand. 'Look, if you *should* happen to find him, keep clear, won't you? And let my people know straight away – they'll be *neater* than the *flics*, you understand. Whatever you do, don't approach him yourself, will you? He'll kill you as soon as look at you. Just let my people know – they'll deal with him, eh?'

She had no doubt they would. She said, 'Thanks for your help. May I take the photograph?'

'I'd like it back when you've finished with it.' She nodded and put it carefully in her bag along with the telephone number. He got up and helped her to her feet. As they walked to the door she asked, 'What did he do? When he was in Marseilles, I mean?'

The *Patron* opened the door and the sounds of the street flooded in. He said quietly, 'He bought me three years inside, that's what he did.'

'Oh!' She didn't know what to say.

He looked thoughtfully out into the street. 'And . . .' His face clouded. '. . . he killed a woman.' There was a pause. 'My woman.'

Julie stared, aghast. Eventually she stammered, 'I'm sorry . . .'

He shrugged and said briskly, 'Now remember, if you *do* come across the bastard, whatever you do don't go anywhere near him. Just call that number and mention my name.'

She stretched out her hand. 'I don't know your name.'

'Jojo. Just say Jojo sent you.'

There was a midnight train to Paris. Julie packed her case, paid the outstanding money on the room, and, with plenty of time to spare, went to the bar to say goodbye to Henri.

He welcomed her effusively and pressed a drink on her. It was a cognac. She rather liked it. She liked it even more a few moments later when the alcohol sent a warm glow round her body. Suddenly she felt tremendously optimistic.

She knew almost everything about him, his name and his background. And most important of all, she had the photograph. What a bit of luck that was! Somebody somewhere must have seen him. Somebody somewhere would know where he was. The photograph *must* find him in the end. It would just be a question of looking hard enough and for long enough in the right places . . .

The telephone at the end of the bar rang. Henri answered it, put it down on the counter and came over to her. He indicated with his head. 'Telephone.'

'For me?'

He nodded. She went to the end of the bar and lifted the receiver cautiously. 'Yes?'

'Madame? It's me.' She recognised the *Patron*'s voice. 'I remembered something . . .'

Julie gripped the receiver. 'Yes?'

'It's not very much, but it might help?'

'Yes?'

'You remember I said he had expensive tastes? Well, he always longed for a fancy car. He was quite mad about it. Always had pictures of it in his room, even in his wallet . . . A Delage. He always wanted a Delage. Nothing else would do. You know the car I mean?'

Julie tried to hide her disappointment. 'Oh yes, I know.'

'Well, it's not much . . . But he really was mad about that car.'

'Thank you.'

'A Delage. Nothing else would do.'

'Thank you again.'

'Good luck.'

Julie put the receiver down.

A *car* . . . A Delage . . .

She shook her head. A long time had passed. Vasson had probably forgotten he had ever wanted a Delage – dreams didn't last. At sixteen she herself had wanted – what was it? – a fur coat. She never thought of having one now.

No, the car wouldn't lead her to Vasson.

But the photograph would. That was the key.

38

'Are there any further charges against Le Goff?' The examining magistrate peered at the commissaire.

'Not at the present time.'

'I order, then, that Le Goff be released forthwith.' The magistrate stood up and walked out. Julie got to her feet and stared blankly at the high ornate chair where the magistrate had been sitting. She should feel triumphant, or at least relieved. Instead she felt dissatisfied, almost cheated.

The commissaire was standing in the aisle, waiting for her. She made her way between the seats towards him. They walked towards the courtroom door.

'You were very certain in your identification of Vasson,' the commissaire said.

'Oh yes.'

'I wish all witnesses were as definite.'

They came out onto the front steps of the law-courts.

'You are a very determined woman, madame.'

'And what's wrong with that?' Julie demanded.

'Nothing – please don't misunderstand me!'

They began to walk down the steps. Julie asked. 'When will Michel be released?'

'Within the hour. One of my men can take you over there, if you like.'

'No, that won't be necessary, thank you.'

The commissaire looked surprised. 'You're not going to see him?'

She shook her head briefly.

'I thought –'

'You thought wrong, monsieur. I told you that before.'

'Ah. I stand corrected.'

They reached the pavement and paused. The commissaire said, 'We believe Vasson was involved in other crimes. We think he may have betrayed the Meteor line.'

Julie looked at him sharply. 'He was Lebrun?'

'Possibly. But it is difficult to find anyone who might identify him. They all died or got sent to Germany.' He added, 'Where can I contact you, madame – in case we have news?'

'England. I gave my address to your inspector. I'm going to Paris today, then on from there.' It was almost the truth. 'But – will there be any news?'

'In due course. His description will be everywhere by now. And his photograph. We'll find him.'

'But it's been two weeks.'

The commissaire threw up his hands. 'Two weeks. That's nothing, madame! He could be anywhere, hiding under an assumed name . . . It'll take time.'

'Yes.'

'We can only do our best.'

She stared thoughtfully at the sky, then said abruptly. 'Goodbye then, monsieur.'

'Goodbye, madame.'

The commissaire watched her slim figure walking briskly away and thought how deceptive appearances were. She may have soft, gentle looks, but she was like steel inside.

Julie sat in the train and read the letter again. It was from Peter, in his best rounded handwriting. He was very well, he said. He went to tea every day with John (his best friend) and on Saturday they had been fishing all day (this last part was underlined). He was glad about Michel. He sent her lots of love.

She put the letter away. He sounded happy enough. Julie had been away almost a month now. It was a long time to leave a child. But he was eight; quite old enough to look after himself.

She got out her purse and counted the money in it. Five hundred francs or thereabouts. A hundred of her own and four hundred which she had taken out of Michel's money. She had put the remainder of Michel's money in an envelope with a letter and left it with his *concierge*. In the letter she had explained how the money had been spent, wished him well and excused herself for not seeing him on his release.

She hadn't seen him, either, during the two weeks the police had been unravelling the Fougères identity. Instead she had gone to Tregasnou and arranged for the sale of the farm to provide money for the proper care of Tante Marie.

It was the end of her life at Tregasnou. Perhaps of her life in Brittany, too. Her debt to Michel had been repaid; she didn't want the embarrassment of his gratitude.

Five hundred francs . . .

She already had her train ticket back to England, so the cash should last three weeks. No, perhaps that was optimistic for Paris. Perhaps only two.

Two weeks, then. She would give herself two weeks.

She became a good walker. For eight days she walked all day – and a lot of the night, too. She tried a hundred places – cafés, restaurants, shops – in half a dozen different areas.

No-one had ever seen Vasson.

After the cafés, restaurants and shops she drew in her breath and tried the clubs. It took a lot to walk into a club, a woman alone, and ask for information. Sometimes she had to wait, standing conspicuously in a corner, while someone was fetched. Then people stared, wondering what a woman like her was doing in such a place. Even though she wore the darker and plainer of her two staid suits, she had to learn how to look unobtrusive and to turn down all kinds of propositions, some blunt and exotic. Once, a man actually stuffed a thousand francs into the neck of her blouse and started pulling her towards the door.

She hated everything about the clubs, the darkness, the stink of tobacco, the leering men. To keep sane, she forced herself to see the light side of it. It was there – if you looked hard enough.

But she didn't smile for long – the time was slipping away. Suddenly twelve days had passed, and no Vasson. No-one had seen him. No-one remembered him. It was as if he'd never been to Paris . . .

The clubs didn't open until nine-thirty or ten, so she spent the earlier part of the evening asking in restaurants and cafés. Then, once the doors of the clubs opened, she went in quickly, anxious to be away before too many customers arrived.

She completed the narrow streets of Montmartre, then started on the area around Pigalle.

One evening she managed three clubs before eleven. She came to a fourth club and, without bothering to examine the name on the neon light, went straight down the red-lit stairs. It was better going straight in – there wasn't so much time to hesitate.

There was no-one at the desk so, without slowing down, she walked across to the bar where a barman was polishing glasses. She pulled out the photograph, which she had masked with black paper to hide the other figures, and thrust it across the counter.

The barman looked at it then asked, 'So who's looking for him?' That was what they always asked. That, or, 'In trouble, is he?'

She replied, 'I'm looking for him. It's a personal matter.' It was the answer she always gave. It usually brought a knowing smile and a comment about all poor sods being on the run from some woman or another, and she wasn't going to give him a hard time when she found him, was she?

This time the barman said, 'You're looking for him, eh?' He eyed her thoughtfully. 'It doesn't seem very likely.'

Julie looked at him in surprise. 'No? Why not?'

'You don't look the sort to have mixed with him.'

Julie tensed. 'You know him?'

The barman took another look at the picture. 'Used to. Used to work here, the slob.'

'When? When was he here?'

'Ohhh. Must have been before the war. Yes, just before . . .'

'And since then?'

'He was around for a while at the beginning of the war, so I heard. Started dealing in specialities. You know stockings, cigarettes, fancy underwear, that kind of thing . . .'

'Then?'

The barman shrugged. 'Don't know. He wasn't seen again.'

'You've heard nothing since?'

He shook his head. 'Nothing. Not that I've asked, you understand. And he wouldn't exactly be welcome in this place. He half-killed the boss.' He rolled his eyes.

'What did he call himself then?'

'Ah . . .' The barman frowned. 'Can't remember exactly . . . Wait a minute. Ah yes . . . Biolet. That was it. Biolet.'

Yet another name. Julie asked, 'Where did he live, do you know?'

'No. Never knew. Never cared. Always changing rooms, I believe.'

Julie racked her brain for more questions. 'Did he have money in those days?'

The barman laughed. 'Money! Never. Always broke, he was. Tried to get into the big time, of course, but never made it. A real loser. Too clever-clever, see. No-one around here liked that, not one bit.'

And that was it. He knew nothing more.

Two days later Julie found another person who thought he recognised the photograph. A café proprietor up a steep hill above Pigalle. But he, too, hadn't seen Biolet for a long time. After some thought he remembered that the last time must have been '39 or '40 – before the Occupation. He, too, mentioned that Biolet had always been broke. But he couldn't remember any more.

After that – nothing.

She had been in Paris fifteen days. And she had nothing.

Wearily she went back to her cheap cheerless hotel in the *treizième* and fell on to the bed, exhausted.

Clubs, cafés, . . . Montmartre, Pigalle . . . He'd been there all right *before* the war.

But after –? Nothing!

Had he gone away? To another large city?

Perhaps . . .

Another area. Another name. Another job.

But would he *need* a job? The Germans must have paid him well; he was their most important informer. Yes, he *must* have money, and for the first time in his life!

She opened her eyes wide.

Of course. *That* was the difference. He had *money*.

The big time at last. All the things he'd ever dreamed about. She tried to imagine him with money . . . dressing well, wearing gold jewellery. Indulging those expensive tastes . . .

All the things he'd ever dreamed about.

She remembered what the *Patron* had said. Perhaps there had been something in it after all. It was worth a try –

Just one more day. She'd give it one more day.

Julie trudged along the Champs Elysées, looking for the right number. Most of the buildings didn't seem to have any numbers, but at last she spotted one in small figures high above a doorway; there was still quite a way to go. She eyed a passing bus longingly. It would be quicker and easier by bus, but they cost money and she was running dangerously short.

She was down to her last fifty francs and her train ticket home. In

Paris fifty francs would last two days, maybe three if she really spun it out and cut down on her food.

She walked on, watching the numbers. Nearly there. It must be on the next corner . . .

There was a smart shop selling handbags, a cinema . . . It must be the next one.

She walked faster. The shop front was clearly visible now. She stopped in front of it and stared.

It was empty. Most of the windows were boarded up. Only one window still had glass in it and that was whitewashed on the inside.

She went up to the window, found a tiny gap in the whitewash, and peered through. There was a large empty showroom, littered with rubbish and a few posters of cars.

She stepped back and looked up. The sign, made of letters fastened on to a marble facia, had largely fallen off. But the shadow of the letters remained. The name of the agents. Then, in small letters: Delage.

She went round to the side. There was a side door, again firmly closed.

Dead end.

She leant against the wall. She'd got this address from a garage. Obviously their information had been a little out of date.

She should try another Delage dealer – if there was one.

She tramped along until she found a post office. She looked up Delage in the telephone directory. Not listed.

Next idea.

None. She felt weak and tired. The thought of pressing on was terribly depressing. She decided to go back to the hotel for a rest. It was a real indulgence: she'd never allowed herself that luxury before. She saw a bus stop and, weakening, caught a bus in the direction of the *treizième*. She began to plan what she'd do when she got there: she'd go mad and buy cheese, fruit *and* bread and take them back to the hotel and eat the lot.

She had to change buses twice. At the second change she was overcome by guilt at her extravagance and decided to walk the last mile or so.

On the way she looked up and saw a garage. Without hesitating she walked straight in. A mechanic was working on a car. She asked, 'Where would I buy a Delage if I wanted one?'

'A new one, impossible. They haven't been making them recently, or hadn't you noticed?' he said with heavy irony. 'A second-hand one . . .' He shrugged. 'Wherever you could find one. There must be plenty about if you have the money.'

She thought: A real help. 'What about servicing one, then. Where would I go?'

'Juno's. Juno's garage. They're the only ones who do them nowadays.' He gave her an address. It was on the other side of the city, near the Bois de Boulogne, back the way she'd come.

She hesitated, thinking of the cheese, fruit and bread, and the nice soft bed, then marched firmly back towards the bus stop.

Juno's was a large garage full of smart cars in various stages of repair. There was a sporty racing-type car, a limousine, and a long, sleek open-top – all magnificently expensive.

A fierce-looking woman was perched inside a glass booth, guarding the working area. She raised a sliding window and asked sharply, 'Yes?'

'I'm looking for a Delage,' Julie asked.

'What do you mean *looking*?'

'I'm looking for someone who might have bought one recently.'

The woman looked Julie up and down and raised her eyebrows. 'We don't buy and sell.'

'I just wanted to ask if you knew of any Delages for sale – or recently sold, in the last few years'.

'We don't have records. Look, the answer's no, and that's all there is to it. She slammed the window shut.

Julie went past her into the garage. The woman spotted her and, pushing up the window again, started yelling. Julie walked briskly on.

She found a mechanic who was working on a long silver touring car. She said, 'Hello.'

He looked up and smiled appreciatively. 'Hell-o!'

She admired the car. 'Lovely. I didn't know people could still afford things like this.'

'Not many can! This one's been locked away all through the war. Now we're trying to get it going again. Anyway – what can I do for you?' He had a friendly grin.

'I want to find someone who owns a Delage.'

The mechanic made an extravagant gesture. 'For you, I'd buy one myself!'

Julie smiled. 'If I wanted to buy a Delage where would I look? A second-hand one, I mean.'

'You want to *buy* one!' Wiping his hands on a dirty rag, he gave a long low whistle. 'Well, well . . .!'

'No, not me exactly,' Julie said hastily. 'In fact I want to trace someone who *may* have bought one. In the last few years.'

He shook his head. 'You ask a lot ... My goodness, it would be difficult to know where to begin! And there aren't a lot about nowadays. Most of them are still off the road ...' He looked over Julie's shoulder and made a face. 'Ooops!' Julie followed his gaze and saw the fierce-looking woman waddling aggressively in their direction.

Julie said hurriedly, 'Any ideas?'

'What about the police? They have a register of all owners.'

'No – this person wouldn't be using his own name, you see.'

The mechanic laughed. 'More and more mysterious!' The fierce woman panted up to them, prepared for a speech. The mechanic took Julie's arm and led her quickly away, back towards the main doors. 'There *is* something called the Delage Society. Well, there *used* to be anyway. I've got the address somewhere. Would that be of any use?'

'Yes please. Anything.'

He opened the door of the glass booth and riffled through some papers on a shelf. He came out with a slim magazine in his hand. 'Here. They used to send out these things every few months. The address of the organiser will be in there somewhere.'

The fierce woman had followed them and was standing a few feet away, hands on hips, eyes blazing.

The mechanic shrugged apologetically. 'Better get back to work. Good luck!' He grinned at her, his expression full of many meanings, all of them nice.

Julie smiled back. He had cheered her up.

A few yards along the street she paused and opening the magazine, glanced through it. On the first inside page there was the name of the publisher and further down, the editor, with an address in Paris.

The editor's address was on the other side of the city.

She sighed and looked for a bus.

It was an apartment building. There were two long rows of bells with names on them. Some of the names were very faded and she had trouble in reading them, but then she found the editor's name. He still lived there; it was something at least. She pressed the bell.

There was a buzz. She pressed against the street door and it opened. The apartment was on the fourth floor. When she arrived, breathless, at the head of the stairs a man was standing on the landing, waiting.

The editor of *La Société des Proprietaires de Delage* was a man of about sixty, who wore shabby clothes and smelled strongly of garlic and old vegetables. He welcomed her warmly. 'I don't get many visitors. Please come in. Come in!'

The apartment was none too clean and rather shabby, like its owner.

The editor bounced around like a small boy, offering her a seat and a cup of coffee. Then he sat absolutely still, listening to what she had to say.

He nodded slowly and promised to help all he could. But there was a problem. 'We had to cease publishing at the beginning of the war,' he explained. 'And even before the war, only about half the owners belonged . . . As for finding out what's happened to the cars since then – new owner and so on . . .' He shook his head. '. . . it would be *difficult* . . .'

'This person *might* have been an owner before the war. It's just possible . . .'

He shot out of his seat like a jack-in-a-box. 'Say no more!' He disappeared into another room and a few minutes later returned in triumph with a dusty box full of yellowing papers. He pulled out the papers and looked at her expectantly. 'Name?'

'Vasson. Or Fougères. Or Biolet.' Even as she said them Julie realised it was hopeless: he wouldn't be using any of those names nowadays.

As the editor started to leaf through the papers she began to feel a deep despondency. This would never lead anywhere.

After half an hour the editor was satisfied: none of those people had ever been members of his club. 'I'm sorry,' he said.

Julie sighed and tried to think. 'What about buying a second-hand Delage?' she asked. 'How would one find one?'

'Ah! Ahhh!' The editor looked earnestly at the ceiling as if that could give him the answer. 'Mmmm. A newspaper. Yes, through a newspaper! That's about all that's been published, you see. Though there is *Auto* – I believe that's kept going after a fashion. Yes, there's *Auto* too. Here, I'll give you the address.' He scampered into the other room and came back with a piece of paper.

Julie got up to go and said wearily, 'Thank you. You've been most helpful.' At the door she asked, 'Did you have a Delage yourself once?'

'Me!' He laughed heartily, throwing back his head in a great guffaw. 'Goodness gracious no! I could never have afforded even a twentieth of one. I was only an enthusiast! I just loved being *near* the lovely things, you understand. The most beautiful cars ever made . . .' He chuckled again, 'No! I just loved being *near* them.'

*

The *Auto* office was quite near, only twenty minutes' walk away. Although it was late – almost five – and the place likely to be closing, she decided to try anyway.

In the end it was further than she thought, a good twenty-five minutes away. By the time she found the right doorway she was so tired she could hardly climb the four flights of stairs. No energy: she hadn't eaten since breakfast.

Finally she arrived, panting and shaking slightly, in front of a half-glazed door inscribed with the word *Auto* in scratched gold letters.

She knocked and someone called, 'Enter.'

The office was a single room with a large desk on which a lanky man of about thirty was sitting, speaking into a telephone. He waved her into a seat and continued his conversation, which mainly consisted of sighs and tuts and expressions of despondency.

Julie flopped down and closed her eyes for a moment. After a few minutes she opened them again and looked around her. She saw a copy of *Auto* on a side table and, picking it up, leafed through. Most of the magazine was made up of articles and photographs of racing cars, but at the back there were six pages of advertisements.

Julie scanned them quickly. There was a Delage for sale . . . and a second and third. It looked quite promising. She looked for the date at the top of the page and felt a pang of disappointment. March 1938. Years ago.

The telephone receiver was clanged down into its cradle and the lanky young man said with a frown, 'How can I help you?' He was, he explained, the editor, sub-editor, secretary and sole reporter of *Auto* magazine. 'We've had to cut down a bit. We haven't been able to publish very often. No paper, you see! No money! Nothing much to report – no new cars, hardly any races . . .' He sighed heavily. 'But you never know, we might be able to manage three editions this year.' He added morosely, 'Better than nothing, I suppose.

A really cheerful fellow.

She asked to see some of the recent editions. 'Oh *those*!' he said heavily. 'They're *awful*. I was only allowed four pages and an edition of five thousand. Hardly worth printing!' He looked up. 'When you say recent, how recent?'

'Since the beginning of the war.'

He gave her the editions for the last three years. There were a surprising number of advertisements. The editor commented sadly, 'It's everyone trying to sell cars they can't afford to run.' He pointed out the racing and sports types, the Bugattis, Maseratis, and Mercedes. Then there were the plush tourers, Delahayes, Bentleys – and Delages. Julie saw with relief that there weren't too many Delages

549

advertised. She started making a list. With only three editions per year for the last three years, the total number of Delages advertised, when she added it up, was only twenty-four. Some of those were duplicates of previous advertisements and when those were eliminated she ended up with sixteen.

Some Delages had been advertised under box numbers. 'May I have the names and addresses of the sellers?' Julie asked.

'I'm not meant to . . .' the editor sighed. 'But . . . seeing as the whole world's gone mad and I don't much care . . .' He pulled a number of files out of a cabinet and threw them on the desk. 'Here! They're all in there somewhere.'

And they were – scribbled in almost illegible pencil or heavy black ink with the words half smudged. After forty minutes she had them all. 'Thank you. If I need to look at some more back copies, may I come and see you again?'

'Why not!' he exclaimed with a look of deepest depression. 'I'll still be sitting here, most likely. No events to cover, no new cars . . . God, yes! Why not! Come and cheer me up!'

It was only when Julie got back to her room and was eating great mouthfuls of bread and cheese – the fruit had been too expensive – that she looked at the list properly.

Her heart sank again. The Delage owners were spread all over the country, some as far away as Nice. Contacting them would be impossible: letters would take too long and telephone calls would be too difficult and expensive.

There were telegrams, of course. But sixteen . . . They would cost more, much more, than she could afford.

She lay back on the bed and, shaking off her shoes, examined a blister on her heel. The entire thing was hopeless. Why *should* Vasson have bought a car at all? Perhaps he'd hidden all his money and was lying low. Perhaps he'd squandered it years ago . . .

The big time . . .

What did it mean to him now?

It was hopeless. She should go home. She barely had enough money to feed herself on the train. Her shoes were worn out. She was tired, so tired.

She should give up.

But then she remembered the hard black eyes and the *coldness* of him, and she muttered, '*Merde.*'

One more day. Just one more day.

She sat up and, reaching for her bag, searched in the zip compartment. The card was there, just where she'd put it all those weeks ago.

Jojo had offered help. Well she wasn't too shy to ask now. To use the language of the street, she needed the necessary. And the necessary was money.

The count heard the sound of crunching gravel on the drive and hid. He was quite an expert at hiding now; creditors and angry tradespeople arrived almost daily.

There were footsteps. The front bell jangling. The count peered through a crack in a shutter and saw a bicycle. It looked vaguely familiar. Of course – he had it now. It was the postman's.

Why should the postman be here in the afternoon? It must be bad news – a summons for a bad debt or something like that.

He chuckled. Only six more days and the château would be stripped of all its remaining valuables. Then he would disappear to Paris and they could send all the summonses they wanted.

The count watched the postman come into vision, mount his bicycle, and ride off down the drive. As soon as everything was quiet he hopped silently down the stairs to the main hall. He looked nervously towards the large double front doors. An envelope had been slipped underneath and lay invitingly on the stone floor.

Impatiently the count strode over, grabbed the envelope and tore it open.

'Good lord!' he exclaimed.

It was a telegram. It read: INTERESTED IN BUYING DELAGE. IS YOURS STILL AVAILABLE?

It was signed LESCAUX, followed by a post office box number in Paris.

At the bottom the post office had stamped: ANSWER PREPAID.

The count said, 'Damn! Damn and blast!' He'd known it! That deal had been a disaster. People were queuing up to buy the blasted car and he'd thrown it away. God, what a waste!

'Damn!' He repeated, and stamped off in the direction of the cellars to see if he could find a last bottle of claret.

Later, he considered whether to reply. He decided against it. He didn't see the point. He'd sold the damned car, hadn't he?

Another telegram came four days later. It read: IF CAR SOLD, STILL INTERESTED. URGENTLY NEED INFORMATION. PLEASE USE PREPAID REPLY. LESCAUX.

The count took more interest. Whatever this was about, he could smell money in it. He slipped down to the village and sent a reply, saying that he'd sold the car recently and adding that he'd be in residence for only two more days.

The following day there was the sound of an approaching car on the drive. The count took cover on the first floor. Through the shutters he saw the village taxi draw up. Out of it stepped a girl. Even from this distance he could see that she was rather a honey.

He straightened his tie, walked down the stairs, and flung open the front door.

The girl said, 'I sent the telegram.'

'Come in! Come in!' He gestured her inside to the main salon, which was the only room still with any furniture in it. He offered her a Louis XV chair and apologised for the rickety legs. When they were seated, he smiled at her charmingly. 'And to what do I owe this singular pleasure?'

'*Auto* magazine. I've been contacting everyone who's advertised a Delage for sale in the last few years. You advertised, so here I am.'

The count smiled again, though he had the feeling his charm was wasted on this rather serious young lady. 'But why come to me when I've already sold my car?'

'*Because* you've sold it. Your car was one of the few that did sell.'

The count frowned. 'Ah. Not many have sold, then?'

'No. Apparently there's no market for them.'

The count tried to feel mollified about his deal with the scar-faced young man, but he failed. He couldn't believe he hadn't been cheated.

'But continue,' said the count, 'Why are you looking for a car that's already sold?'

'I want to contact someone, someone who may well have bought one.'

The count's curiosity was pricked. 'You mean a *particular* person?'

'Yes.'

'Someone you wish to trace?'

'Precisely.'

What a businesslike young woman this was, the count observed. Normally he didn't like that in a woman, but in this case it would be an advantage. When they got to the nub of the matter – the money – she would be easy to deal with.

'So – you wish to have details of the person who purchased my car.'

'Please. Perhaps I could show you a photograph, to see if you recognise him . . .' She dug into her handbag and passed him a small rather indistinct photograph. It showed a young man, no more than twenty, with a thin face and dark lanky hair.

The count swore under his breath. This wasn't the man. And if it wasn't the man then there couldn't be any financial negotiations. How annoying!

552

The count pretended to muse. 'Mmmmm. It's hard to tell. This is a young man . . . The person I sold to was older, definitely older . . .'

'In his thirties?'

'Mmm. Maybe. Maybe.'

The girl leant forward and peered anxiously at the picture. 'What about the eyes? Do you look familiar?'

'Maybe. Maybe.' The count pretended to examine the face, then focused more sharply. Yes, now she mentioned it, there *was* something familiar about them. Good Lord. Maybe it *was* him after all! He said, 'Yes, it definitely *could* be him. But the man I sold the car to was heavily scarred. His face was terrible, quite *unpleasant* to look at. He'd obviously been horribly injured in some way. What he looked like before . . . well, it's difficult to be *sure*. It *could* have been this fellow, but I honestly couldn't swear to it.' Which was true enough and it should keep her sufficiently interested to come up with the lucre, which was the important thing.

The girl's eyes were blazing with excitement. 'Heavily scarred . . .?' She paused, deep in thought, then asked, 'But medium height, dark haired and thin?'

'Yes.'

'And his manner? Was it –?'

'Hard. Unfriendly. Not a very nice fellow. Not a very nice fellow at all.'

The girl's look was triumphant and full of hope. 'It just might be him!' she breathed.

'You're obviously very keen to make contact.'

'Oh yes!' she exclaimed. 'You *do* have an address don't you? And a name?'

So she didn't even know his name. Better and better. 'Will – *might* – this information be of value?' the count began.

For the first time she faltered. 'Of value?'

The count smiled sweetly and lowered his voice. 'Will this information be of material value to anyone?'

'Well . . .' She was confused now. 'If you mean, will it be of financial value, the answer's no.'

'I meant, rather, of sufficient value to someone to enable them to see me right. You know, recompense me for my trouble and the inconvenience of looking out the paperwork.'

Her expression had hardened. 'The person concerned has very limited means, very limited indeed. This is a matter of honour, of justice, not – money!'

The count was unimpressed. Honour, justice, it was no matter: the price would be just the same. He'd learnt his lesson from the scar-faced young man. When the market was all in your favour you named your price.

'I see, I see,' said the count soothingly. 'In that case I'm sure a very small fee will be sufficient. Shall we say four thousand?'

'Four *thousand*!' she gasped. 'Out of the question. I don't have a tenth of that!'

The count made tutting noises. 'What a pity! What a pity! There we are then.' He started to his feet.

She had gone quite pale, an expression of desperation on her face. She opened and closed her mouth a couple of times then whispered, 'One!'

'Three and a half!'

They settled on three. The girl looked as though she'd been hit over the head. She turned her back to take the money out of her purse and the count guessed her purse was rather full. He immediately regretted having let her beat him down. Why was it he always got cheated by people with lots of money?

He left her in the salon while he went to find the bill of sale. He copied the name and address of the young man on to some blank paper then put the bill of sale into his pocket. He took the piece of paper to the girl. 'There we are!'

She looked at the name and address as if she could devour it, 'Lelouche . . .'

He asked, 'Could I have your address – just in case I remember something . . .?'

She nodded and, reaching into her handbag, pulled out a scrap of paper and scribbled on it.

The count placed the paper carefully in his wallet. 'Did you keep your taxi?' he enquired.

'Oh . . . no. It's coming back in a few minutes.'

It couldn't be better. The count said gallantly, 'I'll go and see if it's on its way. Sometimes the fellow forgets.'

'That's not necessary.'

'No, I insist!'

Quickly he pulled on a coat, took his wallet and, leaving her pacing the hall, hurried down the drive.

He met the taxi a short distance down the main road. He flagged it down, told the driver that the visiting lady had already left, and asked to be taken to the station in her place.

A Paris train came in almost immediately. As the count got in he calculated that it would be a good two hours before the girl realised what had happened and walked to the station to find a train.

Two hours should give him plenty of time.

With a final lurch the cage rose to the ceiling. One of the workmen, balancing on a plank supported by scaffolding, leant across and guided the hook at the top of the cage into the massive eye which protruded from the ceiling.

'What I'd like to know,' one of the workmen mumbled, 'is how the girl's gonna get *in* there.'

'Rope ladder.'

At the sound of Vasson's voice the workmen fell back. Vasson stepped forward and eyed the cage critically. With the correct lighting it should look all right, he decided. The only disappointing thing was the height of the cage. He'd wanted it further away, more inaccessible. But the ceiling couldn't be raised any more, so this was it.

There was silence, the men waiting expectantly. Eventually Vasson said, 'Yes, that's fine.' He could almost hear the sigh of relief; this was one of the few jobs he hadn't asked them to re-do in some way.

But it had been worth it. Vasson looked around him. The group of store rooms had been completely transformed. There was now one large room, which, because of the lighting, managed to look pleasingly intimate. Around the sides there were booths with seating for between two and six people, while in the centre there were a dozen small tables. At one side there was a stage with room for a performer, an upright piano, drums and bass. On the other side of the room there was a bar.

The colour scheme was black, beige, and gold. Very striking. To soften the effect there were exotic plants everywhere, between the booths, hanging from the ceiling, around the light fittings. No-one had ever used plants before.

Vasson had overspent his budget, but it had been worth it.

Already everyone was talking about the place. At the opening the cage would be covered with a drape, then, accompanied by appropriate music, it was going to be unveiled to reveal a girl painted with gold. Her skin, that was. Apart from a G-string she'd be wearing nothing else at all. It would be a sensation.

He turned and hurried through the club into his office, a small room at the rear. There were still a thousand things to do before the opening, and there was only one day left.

Half an hour later there was a tap on the door.

'Yes.' Vasson barked impatiently.

The new barman poked his nose into the room. 'Someone to see you.'

'Who?'

'Wouldn't say. But something important.'

Vasson sighed. 'Very well.'

A minute later the barman showed someone in. Vasson looked up and stiffened.

It was the stupid old boy – the count.

Vasson swore to himself. He should never have put this address on the bill of sale; he had known it was a mistake when he did it. He said quietly, 'Whatever you want, forget it.'

The count smiled inanely. 'But I bring you good news.' He sat down in a brand new chair.

Vasson said quickly, 'I don't think so.' And, standing up, called for the barman again.

'I wouldn't be hasty if I were you. I bring you news from the past.'

Vasson suddenly felt cold. Slowly, he sat down again. 'The past?'

'Yes. I bring you information which I think you will be very happy to have.' The count grinned like a cat.

Vasson's mouth felt dry. Slowly, he licked his lips. 'Well? Go on.'

The count said triumphantly, 'Someone's looking for you!'

'Oh yes?'

'Someone who knew you some time ago.'

The fear clutched at Vasson's heart, but he kept his face impassive. He asked quietly, 'This person found me through the car?'

'Yes. Knew you'd bought it. Must have seen you at the wheel perhaps?'

'Perhaps. And who is this person?'

'Ahhh. That's the question, isn't it?'

The old bastard wanted money then. Vasson considered the alternatives. He could beat the information out of him, there was the gun of course, or . . .

'I don't think the information will be worth enough to pay for.'

'No?' enquired the count sweetly. 'But on the other hand, maybe it will.' Vasson picked at his fingers. 'If I *was* interested, then what would you be able to tell me?'

'Name. Address.'

'How do I know the name and address would be real?'

'No assurance. But I think they would be.'

'Is it just the one person?'

The count considered. 'I think I can say it's probably only the one.'

Vasson nodded slowly. 'Did the person say he'd definitely seen me in the car?'

'Ahh. Really I feel unable to answer . . .' The count looked supercilious, like a complacent schoolmaster.

Sickening old sybarite. Vasson observed him with distate. But the choices were limited. He *had* to know. 'I'll offer you five hundred.'

556

The count shook his head and laughed. 'Really! Really! Five thousand would be a little nearer, don't you think?'

It was more than the club would take in a good night. 'You're out of your mind!'

But he wasn't and Vasson knew it. Eventually they settled on four thousand.

Vasson handed over the cash and, his heart hammering, asked with difficulty, 'The information?'

'A girl. Named Lescaux. Dark hair. Mid to late twenties. Her address is Hotel Hortense. It's a cheap place in the *treizième*. She came to see me today. She had an old photograph of you. I didn't recognise you at first – the face was unmarked – but then I saw a similarity in the eyes and realised it must be you after all.' He paused, watching Vasson's reaction.

Eventually Vasson said, 'What . . . What led her to you?'

'The advertisement.'

'So she never saw me at all . . . in the car?'

'She didn't say.'

Vasson stood up stiffly and murmured, 'Get out and don't let me ever see your face in here again.'

The count needed no second invitation and disappeared rapidly out of the door.

Vasson thought carefully for five minutes, then, taking his coat from the peg, slipped out through the back door into the night.

39

The address was somewhere near Pigalle; Julie had realised that the moment she'd read it.

The street, when she found it, looked familiar and she remembered that she'd walked down it a week or so before. It was narrow and very dark, except for the occasional blaze of light from a small bistro. She went slowly, keeping close to the side and pausing now and then to look for the indistinct, sometimes invisible, street numbers on the shopfronts and door frames.

When she was almost there she stopped in a doorway and checked the numbers again. It was just two away now. Her heart beating in her ears, she looked out along the street. Next door was a shop, closed and shuttered. Then, beyond, a dull gold pool of light spilling out of a doorway on to the pavement.

That must be it. She peered into the darkness. There was a sign hanging over the door. It wasn't illuminated, but she could just make out some sort of painting on it. Above, there was a name. She wasn't sure, but it looked like The Golden Cage. A club then? How strange. She could have sworn the place hadn't been there before.

She drew a deep breath and, crossing the street, walked past on the opposite side. Without being too obvious, she took a good look. It was definitely a club. But not, apparently, open for business. The door was open but there was a plank straddling the entrance and, just inside, some kind of notice on a board.

She went on walking, resisting the temptation to look back over her shoulder. She saw a deep doorway ahead and slipped quickly inside. She moistened her lips and waited for her heart to stop hammering. Then she peered back round the corner.

Nothing. No-one had seen her. She relaxed a little.

What next? It would be madness to go in, in case Vasson was there. So she must wait; wait and watch.

Assuming this *was* the right address.

The count's behaviour had been so extraordinary she still didn't know what to make of it. At first, when he didn't return, she'd given him the benefit of the doubt, but after trudging wearily into the railway station at the end of a long walk from the château she had found the taxi driver waiting there, and slowly, the truth had come out. The count had done it on purpose. But *why?* What could have made him want to run away like that? Perhaps, she thought wearily, he was Vasson's friend and partner. Or perhaps she'd got this far only to be tricked and sent on a wild goose chase. This club might be nothing to do with Vasson at all.

It was very worrying.

She moved to a corner of the doorway where she could watch the club while keeping in shadow. The street was getting busier now as the evening trade began to pick up. A man spotted her and came into the doorway to proposition her. Julie got rid of him quickly enough – he was as nervous as a mouse – but she knew she'd got away lightly. Next time it might not be so easy. She remembered she still had a lot of money on her – over two thousand from the money the *Patron's* friends had given her. She wished now she'd left it at the hotel.

Someone was coming out of the club. Julie stared. It was a man dressed in baggy clothes with a beret on his head. He paused in the doorway, pulling on a jacket, then called over his shoulder. Another man appeared carrying a workman's bag, and the two of them walked off in the direction of Pigalle.

She relaxed again. Workmen. That would explain why the club wasn't open.

After that there was no-one for several hours. The time passed slowly. She was ravenously hungry; for once she'd forgotten to put any bread in her pockets.

By ten-thirty she was numb with cold. Then, just before eleven, there was a movement outside the club. She stiffened. Four or five people were coming out. She peered forward, trying to see their faces in the darkness.

Workmen again: most wore old clothes and carried tool bags. Another man appeared, well dressed and smoother looking than the others. He moved the plank, turned off the lights, closed the front door and locked up. He was very tall, with thick, rather bushy fair hair.

It wasn't Vasson. None of them was Vasson.

The men walked off. The club looked deserted; clearly, it was closed for the night.

She should go back to the hotel and get some sleep. There was no point in staying here.

She hesitated, then decided to take a quick look. It wouldn't take a minute and it couldn't possibly do any harm. She stepped out of the doorway and, looking quickly from left to right, crossed the street and walked up to the front of the club. She peered at the sign. Yes: The Golden Cage. Below, pasted on the door, was a notice. The club was opening on the 14th November. She realised with a slight shock that the 14th was the following night.

What a stroke of luck! If Vasson had any connection with the place, he was bound to be there . . . She could stand in the shadows and watch until he arrived. But would she recognise him at a distance? From the count's description he was terribly scarred.

She tensed and looked quickly over her shoulder. The street was darker now, full of deep shadows. Apart from the faint drone of traffic the only sound was the distant beat of music. She started to walk. Suddenly her hackles rose and she shivered slightly. She walked faster, an uncomfortable feeling in her spine, until she was safely into the brightness of Place Pigalle.

She took the Métro across the city, thinking hard.

An idea came into her mind. She should get one of the *Patron's* friends to take her to the opening. Yes! That would be perfect. She could imagine it all: arriving with all the other guests, looking into the scarred face, knowing immediately it was him, seeing the shock on his face . . .

In the next moment she knew it would never work. It would be madness to let Vasson see her.

No, the best thing would be to identify him from a position of safety, somewhere close enough but not too close. Then once she was certain that it *was* him she would tell – who? The *Patron's* friends. Yes, or the Resistance. Either group would kill him straight away.

The police would be too kind – or would they? No, perhaps it would be better to let him sweat through a long trial and the fruitless pleas for clemency before he was taken out and shot in cold blood. That way he would have more time to think about what he had done.

It was a fifteen-minute walk from the Métro to the hotel. Tonight it seemed longer because she was dog tired, but finally its dreary façade came into view. The Hotel Hortense was extremely modest, which was why she'd chosen it. It was so modest, in fact, that there was no night porter. The front door was locked at eleven, after which the guests were expected to let themselves in using a key for which they had to pay a generous deposit, in advance.

Julie trudged up to the door and fumbled in her bag. She swore quietly. The key wasn't in the bottom, nor in the side compartment. She looked nervously up and down the dark deserted street. Eventually she found the key wedged inside the pages of her pocket diary. She unlocked the door and went in, closing the door gratefully behind her.

The lobby was lit by a single white light, which cast a cold inhospitable glare over the floor and left the rest of the hall in shadow. Julie walked across to the stairs and started to climb. She'd taken a room on the fourth, topmost, floor because it was cheaper there. In the centre of the staircase there was an ancient cage lift in an open mesh shaft, but like most lifts in Paris at the moment it was usually out of order and she never bothered to try it any more.

The building was quiet. The only sound was the slight creaking of the boards under her feet. The hotel had very few guests – at least Julie hardly ever saw anybody.

She reached the first landing and paused. There was a sound; it was coming from the lobby. A gentle rattling. She realised that someone was trying to open the street door.

She went on, a little faster now, up towards the second floor.

From below there came a faint clang. Someone had closed the lift door. Julie reached the second landing and hurried on. Suddenly the lift machinery burst into action with a loud whine. Julie jumped. The lift wires started humming. The lift was coming up.

She reached the third floor and looked down the central well. The lift was rising steadily towards her, but the top was closed and it was impossible to see inside. She climbed on and, panting slightly, hurried across the top landing to her door. She opened her bag and started to look for the room key.

The lift mechanism whirred louder and louder. The key was nowhere to be found; Julie shook her bag impatiently.

There was a loud *Clunk!* and silence. The lift had stopped. There was a click as the gate was opened.

Julie thrust her hand into the outside compartment of her bag and at last her fingers closed over the large metal key tag. She raised the key to the lock but her hand was trembling slightly and she couldn't get it in.

A soft footstep fell on the thin carpet behind her.

She whirled round.

It was the tallest, blackest man she'd ever seen. Julie put her hand to her chest and laughed nervously. 'Oh, good evening! You startled me!'

The man was in French Army uniform. He was grinning from ear to ear, revealing an enormous row of white teeth which were in startling contrast to the blackness of his skin. Julie stared, fascinated. The soldier bowed low and straightened up again, swaying slightly. Julie realised he was rather drunk.

He said in a low booming voice, 'Mademoiselle, my sincere apologies!'

Julie nodded politely and quickly let herself into her room. As she closed the door, she saw he was still standing there, beaming happily. Drunk but quite harmless, she decided. She turned on the light and locked and bolted the door.

The room was quite simple: a bed, a rug on the floor, a chest of drawers and a narrow wardrobe. But it was clean and, most important, no-one in the hotel took any notice of her.

She threw herself straight on to the bed and lay there for a moment because it was so lovely to get her feet up. Then, reluctantly, she got up again and, opening the double windows, reached out to close the shutters. The window was a dormer, set into the roof behind a parapet. You couldn't see the street from there, but you could see an enormous amount of sky. It was very clear tonight and, above the faint glow of the city, Julie could see a thousand stars.

It had been a long time since she had seen a night sky.

For several moments she stood and watched and remembered Brittany a long time ago.

The night was cold. She fastened the shutters and closed the windows again.

Hastily slicing some cheese on to a slice of stale bread two days old, she ate ravenously. Then, gritting her teeth against the cold, she undressed as quickly as possible and pulled on her nightdress.

She didn't bother to wash, but hopped straight into bed, shivering violently. She spread her dressing gown over the thin blankets then pulled her coat off the chair and spread that over as well.

She wriggled down into the bed and curled herself up, wondering whether she'd ever feel warm again.

It was a bit of luck, the black soldier coming along like that. Vasson even helped him to find his key.

Vasson waited for the lift to disappear, then slipped quickly behind the reception desk and looked for the registration book. It wasn't there. He looked around. Immediately behind the desk was a door which probably led to an office. The registration book would be in there. He tried the door; it was locked. He cursed softly.

Then something caught his eye and he let out a small hiss of triumph. To the right of the door there was a notice board covered with yellowing fire regulations and taxi numbers – and a fresh white piece of paper with a list of room numbers and, where appropriate, names. He read it quickly. There weren't many guests – just six or so – and it took him only a second to find the name he wanted.

Lescaux. Room 25.

He took a swift look round the lobby, then tiptoed quickly across to the stairs. He ran lightly up to the first floor, checked the room numbers, and then continued up the building.

As he approached the fourth floor he slowed down and listened. Silence.

He climbed the last few steps and paused again. Softly, he padded across the landing until he could see the numbers on the doors.

Room 25 was in the left-hand corner, at the front of the building. Vasson crept up to the door and listened. He stiffened. Someone was moving about inside. There was a click as if a window was being closed.

He looked round the landing. There were several other bedrooms, then, on the opposite side, a door marked '*Salle de Bain*' and another marked 'W.C.'. Beyond was a plain painted metal door. He ran across and tried it, but it was locked. He looked up. Above was a sign: *Sortie de Secours*. Beside it was a key hanging on a nail.

He took the key and tried it in the lock. At first it wouldn't move but then he pulled on the handle and the key turned quite easily. He opened the door and put his head out. He looked both ways then, satisfied, pulled his head back in and closed the door again without locking it.

He walked lightly across to the bathroom, which was open, and went in. He flicked on the light, locked the door carefully, and turned the light off again. Then he sat down on the floor to wait.

He fingered the gun in his pocket and decided against it. Far too noisy. No, it would have to be done quietly – the other way.

Damn the woman. She'd been trouble all along.

What really upset him was that she'd found out about the car. But how? He couldn't imagine and it was driving him mad. He'd never told anyone about it, he was certain, at least not for years and years . . .

Damn her. Was she alone? Had she told anyone else? He'd have to risk it. If he didn't deal with her he'd be a dead man anyway.

Damn her.

He leant his head against the bath and, looking unseeing at the night sky, waited impatiently for the minutes to pass.

She couldn't sleep. She kept thinking about the day's events and what they meant. Every time she started to drift off she woke up with a start and began to go through it all over again.

There was another thing keeping her awake: she needed to go to the lavatory. She should have gone before, of course, but the bed had been too inviting. Now it couldn't be put off any longer. With an exclamation of irritation, she got out of bed into the cold air and pulled on her dressing gown.

She unlocked the door, walked quickly across the landing and went into the W.C.

When she came out, she went towards the bathroom to wash. She tried the door but it wouldn't budge. She glanced up at the fanlight; there was no light showing through. She tried again, pushing hard against the door, but it was firmly locked. She stood still for a moment, then gave up and went back to her room.

She threw her dressing gown back over the covers and dived into the still warm bed. This time she was determined to get to sleep. She closed her eyes and concentrated on relaxing each part of her body, limb by limb.

Eventually she began to doze off, but then she thought of Richard and was immediately awake again. She often thought of him, but tonight the memories were particularly vivid. It was that lovely night sky. She could almost see the little attic room. She missed him terribly.

She relaxed her body again and tried counting sheep.

Bump!

She was wide awake instantly.

A sound. *Something nearby.*

She stayed perfectly still, listening to the roar of the silence. But nothing.

Perhaps the sound had come from further away after all, from the street . . .

She stiffened.

A sound. This time a faint scratching. *Close.*

She sat upright, her heart hammering in her ears, and strained to locate the origin of the noise.

At first she couldn't hear anything, then it came again, a soft, barely audible scratching. An animal? It must be . . . She tried to see, but with the shutters closed it was very dark; the only light came from a small gap under the door, and then it was the faintest sliver.

Very slowly, she pulled on her dressing gown and did up the cord. Then she swung her legs out of bed and, careful to make no noise, stood up. She listened again.

The scratching had stopped.

She felt her way slowly past the bed and across the room until she reached the door. She put her ear against it. Nothing. Automatically, she checked the key and the bolt to make sure the door was securely locked. She put her hand up to the light switch, then changed her mind and moved slowly back to the centre of the room. She stood absolutely still, straining her ears.

This time the scratching, when it came, was louder.

Now she'd placed the sound. It was coming from near the window. She crept forward and, stooping down, listened again. A mouse, probably . . .

The sound was muffled now and very soft again. She crept right up to the window and waited, completely still.

Nothing.

There was silence again. It lasted a long time. She almost gave up.

Click!

Julie jumped and looked up. There was a sudden movement. A rectangle of light appeared in the window where the shutter had been.

Julie screamed.

The head and shoulders of a man were silhouetted against the light.

She cried, '*God!*' and staggered back against the bed.

The silhouette suddenly vanished. Julie stared in horror at the place where the man had been, the image of the crouching figure engraved on her mind. It was *him*, it had to be! *It was him*.

She couldn't move, she couldn't tear her eyes away from the window. *Was he still there?* She pressed the back of her knees against the bed and reached out for the bedpost.

Silence again.

She tried to gather her wits, but all she could think was: It's *him!* It's *him!*

The silence stretched on.

Suddenly, another movement.

She stifled a scream.

An arm. At the window. It had something in its hand. It was reaching for the latch.

She cried, '*No!*' and scrabbled around looking for something – *anything*. Desperately she lunged at the chest and pulled out a drawer. Raising it above her head, she ran to the window and rammed it against the frame.

She shouted, '*No-o-o!*' And pushed the drawer harder and harder against the window.

For a while she stayed there, her head against the drawer, murmuring 'God!' over and over again.

Then she moved her head away from the drawer and listened.

Not a sound.

She raised her head and looked. The arm had vanished.

She waited, frozen with indecision. He must have gone – *or had he?* For a moment she could have sworn he was still there, waiting under the window sill, poised to pop his head up like some ghastly jack-in-a-box . . . The next minute, she was sure he wasn't there at all.

But if he wasn't there, *where had he gone?*

She knew one thing: *she had to get away!* With an enormous effort of will, she dodged to one side of the window and, shaking violently, put the drawer down on top of the chest. Then, with her eyes fastened on the window, she retreated to the bed and slipped off her dressing gown. She reached down for her coat and pulled it on over her nightdress. She fumbled with two buttons and gave up the rest.

Shoes . . . God, where were her *shoes*? She felt around with her feet and touched one. She bent down and pulled it on. Crouching lower, she put a hand under the bed. Nothing. She almost cried out. She reached further. The second shoe was right under the bed. Panicking, she grabbed at it and pulled it hastily on.

All the time she watched the window. Nothing.

Slowly she stood upright and moved sideways towards the door.

Quietly she slid back the bolt and turned the key in the lock. She listened carefully. Silence.

She gripped the handle, turned it and opened the door a little. A beam of light darted in from the landing. She paused, suddenly full of doubt. Slowly she put her eye to the crack.

She could see the WC and the bathroom opposite, then the lift, and to the right, the beginnings of the stairs.

The landing – what she could see of it – was empty.

It was now or never.

She flung open the door, ran out and stopped dead.

A scream stuck in her throat.

He was standing against the wall at the top of the stairs, crouching slightly, poised like a cat.

She stared at him, horror-struck. The face was livid and ugly, the angry scars red against the pallor of his skin.

But it was Vasson all right. She recognised the eyes. Hard. Dark. Glittering in the dim light. Watching her carefully.

For a moment they were both still, staring at one another.

Then he moved.

She cried out and went rapidly backwards, past the door of her room, along the landing. She looked wildly over her shoulder. *Where was the black soldier?*

She drew a deep breath and tried to shout. The *Help!* came out as a gurgle. Vasson was coming faster now, poising himself to spring. A wall came up against her back. She screamed at last.

Vasson sprang forward. She dodged sideways but he caught her hair and pulled her head back with a snap. She cried out in pain. He clamped his hand over her mouth, digging his fingers into her cheek. She kicked out and pushed him away with her arms. But his other hand closed firmly round the back of her neck.

She lashed out again with her feet and felt her shoes fly off. She tried to claw at his face but he was keeping her at arm's length, gripping her head tightly between his hands.

He started to drag her across the floor. Panic clutched her. She struggled, throwing herself desperately from side to side, trying to tear the hand away from her face.

God, where was the black soldier! Surely he'd heard!

Vasson was pulling her faster now. She tried to dig her heels into the thin carpet, but he yanked her off balance and her feet went from under her. Her legs cartwheeled as she tried to regain her grip.

He gave a final heave, something hard bumped against her side and then it went dark. *They were in her room.*

She heard the door close and struggled harder. She kicked

viciously in all directions and heard him inhale sharply as her foot met his shin. Her next shot hit the bedpost and jarred her leg.

She aimed for his shin again but suddenly her head was being jerked sideways, fast. There was a moment of dizziness, then a sickening thud as her skull hit something solid. She saw stars and stopped struggling.

Still dazed, it took her a moment to realise what was happening. He had pushed her down on to the bed and had moved his hand away from her mouth. She opened her mouth uncertainly, gathering strength to scream, then froze. *There was something tight on her throat. His hands . . . round her neck. Getting tighter.*

Cold terror gripped her. Then she really started to fight.

She tore at his hands, digging her nails deep into the skin. She kicked with her feet, great wheeling kicks that circled the air. She felt him shift his body over hers, to stop the kicking. She pulled up her knees in a quick movement. She got him in the groin, not very hard, but he pulled back slightly. She arched her back and wriggled sideways on to the floor. His hands loosened slightly as he followed her, then he gripped again, much tighter.

She couldn't breathe. She tore at his hands again. His hands were the only things that mattered. *His hands.* Then she remembered she *must kick too.* She thrashed her body from side to side, striking out with her feet. She felt something in her stomach – something heavy, squashing her – *a knee.*

She couldn't breathe.

Air. She must have *air.* She panicked completely. She kicked out again, wildly, twisting her body round, pushing against something solid, wrenching her hips out from under his knee, lashing out again. *Kick! Kick!*

There was a loud *Crash!*

Then a splintering and breaking sound, followed by a muffled exclamation. The hands round her neck loosened. She opened her eyes. In the pale light she saw him pushing off a darker object – the wardrobe.

She scrabbled away like a crab and made for the window. She heard him get to his feet and start after her. She threw herself at the window and wrestled with the latch. He was almost on her.

She ducked and screamed, really loudly this time. She screamed until he got her firmly by the throat again. This time he squeezed very tight straight away.

This was it. She couldn't struggle any more.

Breath, no breath. *G-o-d. Agony.*

Her ears were roaring and singing, her body was screaming . . .
She felt as if her head would burst . . .

G-o-d. I'm going to die . . .

A fog spread over her in a claustrophobic blanket.

Blackness.

Then a vague perception.

Awareness again.

I don't understand.

A voice, a movement, the weight lifting off her body. The hands leaving her throat. She drew in great gulps of air, enormous greedy gasps of air, and felt the coolness shoot down into her lungs.

She opened her eyes, bewildered, dazed. There was light, a yellow light from the door. *Someone else. A voice.* A deep voice . . .

Everything faded for a second. She made an enormous effort and opened her eyes again. A large shape was filling the doorway. Voices. *The black soldier.* 'Hey . . . Hey,' he was saying. 'What's happening, little lady?'

Julie blinked and sat up. Giddiness hit her in a wave.

Vasson was crouched, watching the soldier like a hawk.

Julie's head cleared. She looked from Vasson to the figure in the doorway. Realisation came. *This was her only chance.* She got uncertainly to her feet, her head splitting with pain, and staggered towards the door. Vasson sprang up and grabbed her arm.

Julie shouted at the soldier, 'Help me! *Help me!*'

The soldier swayed forward a little. Vasson dropped Julie's arm. The soldier said, 'Hey! Hey! Let us all cool down now. Hey!' Julie dimly realised he was still very drunk.

She stumbled to the doorway and began to squeeze past the soldier. He swayed towards her and she caught the whiff of drink. He grasped her hand. 'Now, why don't we all relax, hey? What's the problem, little lady?'

She cried, '*Please! He's trying to kill me! Please* let me go, let me get away. *Please.*'

'Now, now . . . Why don't we all relax, hey?' He leered at her, his large face inches from hers.

She darted under his arm and staggered across the landing and down the stairs. She tried to run two steps at a time, but tripped and fell against the banisters. She took them singly then, her limbs shaking, her lungs gasping, *begging* for breath.

Faster, she had to go *faster*.

Third floor –

Above her she heard a voice raised in argument, then silence. Her leg gave way under her. She lurched to one side, grabbed the banister, . and pushed herself forward.

Second floor –

She ran on, her legs wobbling terribly, half-listening for other sounds. All she could hear was the hammering of her heart and the rasping of her lungs.

First floor. Just one more. As she raced across the landing and launched herself at the last flight of stairs something caught her eye and she glanced hastily upwards.

Legs. Running legs, beyond the wire mesh of the liftshaft. Above, but coming fast.

She gave a little cry and hurtled on. She jumped the last step into the lobby. The front door beckoned ahead. She ran for it.

She stopped dead.

No! He'd get her in the street.

She looked wildly about and darted sideways, past the desk and down a dark passage. On one side, she knew, was the dining room. *Not in there! Nowhere to hide.*

On the other side was the kitchen. *Kitchens had back doors.* Still running, she took a quick look over her shoulder. No-one in sight. She pushed at the kitchen door. It was a swing door and opened easily. She fell in and, panting wildly, spun round to grip the door and close it slowly so it wouldn't swing back the other way. The door had a circular window in it. She peered through. Nothing.

It was dark in the kitchen but there was a large window along one side and by its pale light she could just make out the lines of the room. There was a large table in the centre. She shuffled round. *There must be a door.* She reached the far corner. A door. She opened it. Cupboard. She closed it again and looked over her shoulder.

God. He'd be here any moment . . . God.

She felt her way forward. A recess here . . . Behind it – a passage-way! She stumbled down, the flagstones cold under her bare feet. Yes! A door! She gave a small sigh of relief.

She tried the door. It was locked. She found a key in the lock, turned it and tried again. Still locked. She gulped. *God, please let it open.*

Desperately, she felt the surface of the door with her hand. There must be a bolt. There was one at the bottom. She exhaled in triumph. It slid back quite easily. She tried the door again.

It still wouldn't move.

She imagined Vasson creeping along the passage towards the kitchen door. She muttered, 'Please, God, *please!*'

She felt the door again and guessed there must be another bolt right at the top out of her reach. She felt around for something to stand on. There was an object by the door. A fire extinguisher. She put her bare foot on it and, balancing precariously, reached up.

Her hand fell straight on to the top bolt and she tugged at it quickly. It wouldn't budge. She made another effort and tugged harder. At last it shifted, but slowly, the noise rasping loudly in the stillness. At the same time her foot slipped and she landed heavily on the flagstones. The fire extinguisher clattered over, rolling noisily along the passage.

She wanted to scream.

She held her breath and shivered violently. The extinguisher stopped its roll and there was a terrible silence.

She staggered to her feet, her hands shaking wildly.

She tried the door. This time it opened.

She closed it again and leant against it, trembling.

At the front door Vasson froze, his fingers on the handle.

It had sounded like something falling, a vague clattering. From the back of the hotel somewhere.

He listened for a moment, but apart from the panting of his own breath there was silence.

He decided to check the street anyway. If she'd gone that way he'd still be able to see her.

He threw open the door and darted out. Nothing. No running figure, no moving shadows. Just to be sure, he sprinted to the other side of the street and looked wildly up and down. But she wasn't there.

The hotel, then.

He ran softly back across the street and into the lobby, closing the door quietly behind him.

There were several doors off the lobby and two passages. Starting on the left he began trying the doors methodically, one by one.

Silence.

Where was he? When he came for her what would she do? Run? *God, he'd catch her just like that!*

She thought for a moment, then made herself creep back towards the kitchen and peer in. The room was empty and quite still. She looked towards the far door. Its round window, faintly lit by the distant lobby light, stared back at her, blank and expressionless.

She forced herself to go right into the kitchen. She crept towards the table and felt along its length. There must *be* a drawer! There wasn't.

The hackles on her neck began to rise. He was getting nearer, she felt it . . .

I can't stand this!

Along one wall was a dresser. Lots of drawers here. Hurrying now she tried one. Papers, all papers . . . The next drawer, *better* . . . Spoons, large ones . . . Forks . . . *But no knives.* She fumbled with the last drawer.

Open! Damn you, open!

At last! . . . Knives, neither large nor sharp, but *knives.* She picked one up and, looking hastily over her shoulder, started for the back passageway. Something caught her eye. The cooking range. Something *behind*. She stopped.

Knives, lots of them. Long kitchen knives . . .

She threw the small knife aside and picked up a long one. She touched it: very sharp.

She looked over her shoulder and darted down the passageway. Weak with relief, she fell against the door. She thought for a moment and deliberately turned the key in the lock – he might come at her from the *outside*.

Then she waited, her fingers round the key. *Ready.*

She leant her head against the door and breathed deeply. Her neck was hurting horribly and her head was stabbing with pain. Worse, her legs were like jelly. She wouldn't be able to run . . .

She bit her lip. *Must hold on.*

The silence crept on endlessly.

She couldn't believe how long it was –

She wanted to fling open the door and *run*. But no. He might be outside . . . Better to *wait*.

Her shaking fingers slipped off the key. She gripped the key again, more firmly.

The silence was appalling now, pressing in on her, *roaring*.

She jumped–

The sound of a lorry echoed from the distant street.

That was all . . .

Her heart thudded in her ears. She felt incredibly weak.

She rested her head on the door again.

She stiffened. Was there another sound?

Dear God! Her heart missed a beat.

Her fingers tightened over the key. She stared up the passageway into the kitchen, peering into the darkness, *listening* . . .

A faint sound.

From the kitchen.

Her heart leapt into her mouth. Hastily, she turned the key, then the handle and started to pull the door open.

Something caught her eye. A *dark shadow was racing across the kitchen.*

She gasped and leapt out of the door. She ran, bicycling her legs, pumping her arms, pushing her bare feet painfully against the rough surface. The nightdress flapped around her legs – it was *tight, too tight,* she couldn't stride out –

She was in an alleyway, very dark. It seemed to have no end –

Suddenly she heard the padding of feet behind her.

She gasped and raced on, faster and faster, pushing until her breath came in great pants.

The footsteps were closer.

Dear God, give me strength.

The alley – *where did it go?* It went on for ever, dark and endless!

She stumbled and almost fell. She righted herself and tried to accelerate again.

She could hear his breath now. G-o-d.

Light, a glimmering of light.

She raced for it, came to a corner, swerved round.

The street. Some way ahead. The ground was rougher now ... Suddenly she cried out. A terrible pain in her foot! Something sharp was in her foot! She tried to run on, but the thing was sticking *into* her foot!

She hobbled desperately for a couple of steps.

He was panting up behind her.

The panic was roaring in her ears. She gave a moan.

He was close now. *Close!*

She *wanted* to keep running, to run and run until her heart burst, to run and run – *for ever and ever.*

She let out an animal cry and spun round. She whirled round and faced him. She braced herself, the blood screaming in her ears. *Keep away, keep away from me!*

He was still running. He was trying to bring himself up short but his momentum was too great. He was cannoning into her.

She screamed, 'No!' And in the split second before he hit her she gripped the handle of the knife in both hands and, with a loud grunt, thrust it forward.

His body hit hers with a thud, carrying her backwards. She fought to keep her balance but staggered under his weight and fell. His body came down on top of her with enormous force, crushing the breath out of her.

His hand was on her neck and she felt an instant of blind terror.

Then his hand fell away and, by the light of the street lamp, she saw his mouth open in a ghastly grimace of pain. With a roar, he rolled off her and lay on his back. He clutched his belly and, raising his head, stared in blank amazement at the blood seeping out from beneath his hands.

His head fell back and he stared at Julie, pain and disbelief on the twisted scarred face.

Panting hard, Julie got unsteadily to her feet and looked down. The knife was still in her hand. Moaning quietly, she shook her head and walked backwards.

The sharpness stung into her foot. She cried out in pain and, dropping the knife, reached down. Glass. She got hold of it and pulled.

A *movement*.

She jumped.

He was getting up.

He had one hand on the ground, levering himself up, the other on his belly.

She growled, '*N-o-*!'

The knife! *Dear God, where was the knife?*

He was on his feet now, swaying slightly, his eyes piercing into her, dagger-like.

She caught a gleam. The knife. At her feet.

He moved forward.

She grabbed for the knife. He was still coming. Her fingers gripped the handle and she held the knife out in front of her. *Keep away from me, keep away!*

He paused, wary this time, keeping his distance, arms out, ready to spring.

He began circling, panting slightly. Occasionally he put a hand to the wound in his stomach.

She thought: I didn't hurt you enough, *not enough.*

Then she saw that one hand was in his pocket, searching. He was pulling at something. It got caught in the pocket lining, but then it was in his hand, reflecting dully in the street light. A gun.

A gun. I can't fight that. Can't –

There was a faint roaring from the street: a lorry. The sound grew louder until it filled the alleyway.

Vasson's eyes flicked away, towards the street, and then down to the gun. Suddenly she realised he was fiddling with the mechanism, trying to make it work . . .

Now. It's now or never. Dear God, I feel so weak . . .

Wobbling violently, she gathered all her strength and lunged forward. She saw his eyes dart up, his hands rise in defence –

She raised the knife high above her shoulder and with a loud gasp plunged it forward and *down*, hard, *hard* at his chest.

The knife travelled forwards then stopped.

Was it in? Had she hurt him at all? She kept pushing, straining to push the handle in, sobbing, '*Keep away, keep away. Leave me alone. A-l-o-n-e-!*'

At last she realised the knife was rigid, fixed in the man's body. She let go and fell back.

Vasson looked at the knife in amazement. It was sticking out of his chest. A sharp pain pierced through him, worse than anything he had ever imagined.

He couldn't believe it. She'd stabbed him again. *Hard.* She'd hurt him badly. *He couldn't believe it . . .*

He gasped for breath. There was a soft gurgling noise. His lungs drew in liquid.

Very slowly, he slid downwards, first to his knees, then on to his side.

Wet, black blood trickled from his chest on to the ground.

He lay still in the hope that the terrible pain would go away, the bleeding stop . . .

He felt very heavy now, his limbs like lead. Liquid was rising in his throat. He choked a little.

What did I do? Dear God, what did I do? It's not fair, it's not fair.

His lungs expanded but found only blood. He panicked, gasping for breath. He felt as if he were drowning.

At last the realisation came – this horror would be the very last, this final prison the smallest, darkest room of all . . .

He wanted to cry out but the darkness was already closing in.

Why did you abandon me? Why?

Why are you abandoning me now?

I don't understand.

For a moment his face was contorted with pain and rage, then a look of shock and terrible sadness came over it. His eyes opened wider and wider. Blood trickled out of his mouth. Suddenly he gasped. The eyes rolled once, then were still, glazed and unblinking.

She stood, sobbing quietly, watching him. She stared at his eyes, horrified in case they should move again.

She shook her head slowly from side to side, moaning, 'N-o-' over and over again.

There was a sound. A car in the distant street. She blinked and, looking hastily around her, hobbled back towards the darkness of the back alley. Her foot was still agony. She leant against a wall and felt the sole of her foot. There was still some glass in it. She pulled at it. A fragment came away. The foot was bleeding heavily; she was leaving a trail of blood. She tried to tear the bottom off her nightdress and make a bandage, but it wouldn't come. She found a handkerchief in her coat pocket and tied that round the foot instead.

She hopped and hobbled back round the corner and down the alley towards the hotel.

The door was still open. She closed and bolted it and hopped through the kitchen to the lobby. It was empty. She climbed the stairs as fast as she could, walking on the heel of her injured foot, and reached the top landing. She found her shoes lying on the floor where she'd kicked them, and picked them up. The door of her room was closed but not locked. She went in, switched on the light, and locked the door.

For a moment she stood perfectly still with her eyes closed, then methodically, she started to do what had to be done. She made a mental list: clothes, wash, change. She took off her coat and night-dress, which were both bloody, and wrapped them neatly in a bundle. Then she put on her dressing gown and picked up some day clothes. She went across to the bathroom and, trembling wildly, stripped completely and washed herself all over. She dressed and went back to her room.

The trembling had become a violent shaking. She ignored it and, taking out her writing pad, picked up a pen and began to write. At first she couldn't keep her hand still, but she gripped the pen tighter and forced herself to concentrate. She wrote carefully, in plain block capitals. The first attempt wasn't right and she tore it up and started again. Finally she was satisfied. The message was simple, but it would do the job.

It read:

PAUL VASSON. ALIAS LEBRUN, ALIAS FOUGÈRES, ALIAS THE MAN FROM MARSEILLES. TRAITOR, COLLABORATOR, MURDERER. BETRAYER OF METEOR AND TREGASNOU RESEAUX.

JUSTICE!

She read it several times.

The way she had worded it, it shouldn't lead to her. It could have been someone from Meteor, *anyone* in the Resistance.

It was two-thirty. Before she lost her momentum, she went quickly down the stairs to the kitchen, unlocked the back door and, after looking carefully up and down the alley, limped along to the corner.

She looked ahead. The distant street was deserted. The body was still there, lying heavy and inert like a sack of coal. She limped quickly up to it and, averting her gaze from the staring eyes, put the piece of paper beside it and weighted it down with a small stone.

She forced herself to look at the body. Swallowing hard, she leant down and gripped the knife handle protruding from Vasson's chest. She closed her eyes and pulled with all her might.

The knife shot out and she staggered slightly.

She looked over her shoulder and scurried back into the darkness, round the corner, and along the alley to the hotel.

She closed and locked the door, checked that she hadn't dripped blood on to the floor from her foot, and crept into the kitchen. Carefully, she washed the knife, dried it, and returned it to the rack where she'd found it. Then she climbed quickly back to the fourth floor.

As she reached for her door handle she heard loud snoring from the room next door. The black soldier. It had to be. Asleep. She listened to the steady rise and fall of the snores and felt a wave of despair. The black soldier could give her away.

She went into her room and locked the door behind her, then turned off the light and lay down on the bed, fully clothed.

She stared at the dark ceiling and it suddenly occurred to her that the black soldier would probably remember nothing of what had happened, nothing at all.

There was a glimmer of hope.

That left the blood-stained clothes – they would have to be disposed of. She would throw them in the river, weighted down with a stone.

Then there was the hotel register. Yet the body was some way away. There was no reason why they should look here.

Even if they did, who was Juliette Lescaux?

No! She was safe.

She closed her eyes.

Who was Juliette Lescaux? She didn't know any more.

She had been someone, a long time ago.

The shivering started again, first gently then violently until her teeth rattled.

She pulled the bedclothes over herself, and, curling up into a ball, closed her eyes tightly against the terror of the darkness, desperate for the oblivion of the sleep she knew would never come.

Epilogue

Summer, 1945.

There had been dancing and flag-waving on VE Day, cheering and hymn-singing on VJ Day, but for sheer uninhibited happiness there was nothing to beat the homecomings.

All over Britain there were joyous reunions, first in the privacy of homes and then outside in the streets and village lanes. People wept and laughed and hugged and shook hands, and realised that life would never be as sharp or intense again and weren't sure if they were sorry or glad that the war was over.

For those not welcoming sons, husbands and fathers it was still a good time because the festivities took their minds off the austerity and bleakness that seemed to have become a permanent part of British life.

In the main street of Hugh Town, St Mary's, a banner reading 'Welcome Home' was strung between two houses. The day before, no less than five men had returned: three soldiers, a sailor and a merchant seaman. It had been a day of great rejoicing.

Peter looked out of the window and giggled. 'Mummy, there's a soldier kissing Tommy Blair's sister! Mummy?'

Julie came in from the other room and went to a mirror on the wall. She patted her hair, put on some lipstick, and viewed herself critically. Older, of course. There were tiny lines at the corners of her eyes and the sides of her mouth. Less young in other ways, too. The look in the eyes, mainly. She frowned and turned away.

Peter was still giggling. 'Mummy, he's hugging another girl!' He turned to see if she had heard. He gasped. 'Hey, Mummy, you *do* look smart!'

'Not really,' she said briskly. 'It's just my old suit remade, that's all. Now, are you ready? Have you combed your hair?'

Peter came closer and peered at her blouse. 'You've got Tante Marie's brooch on!'

'Yes, it seems a pity not to wear it.' Tante Marie had died at Christmas – a welcome release under the circumstances.

'And Mummy!' He was jumping up and down now. 'That smell! Have you put on *perfume*?'

'Shush!' Julie said impatiently. 'We should go soon. Are you ready?'

'Mmm.' Peter shuffled off in search of something. A moment later he wandered back and asked, 'Mummy, d'you think he'll be different? You know . . .'

'What do you mean?'

'Will he *look* different?'

'Good Lord, how should I know? Now hurry up and comb your hair. It looks terrible.'

The letter had been waiting for her when she returned from France in November. It came from Major Smithe-Webb at the War Office. It was brief and factual. Notification had been received from the Red Cross that Lieutenant Ashley was being held in a POW camp near Stuttgart in Germany.

She couldn't believe it. Alive! She had been bracing herself for bad news for so long that it took her entirely by surprise.

Alive! Her first reaction was joy and relief. For *him*. Because he had always been so full of life and optimism and burning energy, and it seemed only right that he *should* be alive. For *him*. Because by staying alive he had cheated Vasson and that was a victory.

She was happy for herself too – at first. Then she had doubts. In Brittany, in the old days, everything had seemed so simple, a matter of right or wrong, and black or white. She had loved him with all her heart. She still did. And yet . . .

Nothing would ever be straightforward again. The events in France weighed heavily on her mind. She dreamed terrible dreams not only of Jean and Tante Marie and Maurice, but of blackness and running feet and blood . . . She often woke in the night, gasping for breath, crying out. At those moments she felt unbearably lonely.

Life with someone like Richard would offer love and security. Perhaps even peace of mind if –

If everything was the same. If he still loved her. If they both hadn't changed too much.

You couldn't stop people changing, she decided. It just happened. It was a long time since Brittany – two years. For him, two years in a camp. Now he was back home. With his family, his own people, the old way of life.

'Mummy, I'm ready. Come on!'

She led the way out of the house and along the street towards the harbour, her face solemn and pale.

The boy danced along at her side. 'It's so exciting, isn't it, Mummy? Will we go and have tea later, at the hotel, like we do on birthdays?'

'I don't know. I don't know what we'll be doing yet.'

'But I thought –'

'Quiet!' she snapped. A moment later she sighed, 'Sorry. I didn't get to bed till late.' She'd been finishing a dress for someone. It was her trade now, remaking clothes into new styles.

They walked in silence for a while.

'Mummy, you *are* glad he's back, aren't you?'

'Of course, darling! Of course! I'm – delighted.' And terrified, she thought, because in a way I'd rather remember everything – *him* – as it used to be.

They turned on to the mole that formed one arm of the shallow bay and walked past the inter-island boats waiting at the steps, towards the end, where the steamer berthed.

Halfway along she paused. 'Let's wait here.'

'But the ship stops up there!'

'I know, but – I'd rather we waited here.'

She wanted to avoid the group of people she saw gathering at the ship's berth.

She leant against the wall which ran the length of the mole and watched the boy standing on the edge of the quay throwing pebbles. She raised her face to the sun and tried to quell the fluttering in her stomach.

The *Scillonian* was late. She wandered slowly along the quay, back in the direction of the town. It was a balmy day, the breeze no more than a faint stir, and the light that strange translucent white which was peculiar to the islands. It was so very peaceful here, which was why she had grown to love it.

'Mummy! Here it is!'

She spun round. A trail of smoke showed above the high wall of the mole. A few minutes later the bow of the *Scillonian* appeared round the end of the wall, and the steamer began to manoeuvre slowly into her berth.

She walked back to Peter and took his hand.

After a while the lines were secured and the gangway lowered.

People started to come off in ones and twos. A couple of soldiers walked jauntily down the gangway, waving to some people on the quay.

Then Peter was pointing. 'There! Mummy, there he is! Look!'

She spotted him straight away. He was wearing naval uniform and carrying a bag. He looked taller than she remembered. As he came down the gangway he paused for a moment and she knew he was searching the knot of waiting people. He reached the quay and, looking round again, made his way clear of the onlookers.

She waved. He saw them almost immediately, and, waving back, started towards them.

Julie didn't move. The boy tugged at her hand. 'Come on, Mummy! Come on!'

'You go.'

The boy ran forward, a little shyly, and she heard him shout, 'Hello!'

Ashley stopped in front of him and, smiling, said, 'Hello, young man! How are you?' He reached out and towsled Peter's hair. 'You're a sight for sore eyes, I must say.'

He looked up to where Julie stood and came towards her.

'And you too.'

She smiled. He embraced her, gently, then bent and kissed her cheek and held her at arms' length, looking into her face. She stared up at him and was surprised. There were so many things she'd forgotten about him . . .

She said quickly, 'How marvellous that you're safe.'

'And you!' He was going to say more but changed his mind. She realised he was nervous too.

He tucked her arm in his and they began to walk slowly along the quay towards the town, Peter hopping up and down beside them.

She asked quickly, 'Will you be able to stay a while?'

'Several days, at least. Then I must go back and see my family for a while. Did you get my letters?'

'Yes. Thank you for writing. It was – lovely to hear so soon.'

He looked down at her for a long time. 'You look just the same.'

'Do I?' It wasn't true, but she smiled anyway. 'Well, it's very nice of you to say so.'

When he looked away she glanced up at him and noticed how thin he was and how pale his face. His eyes were the same, warm and caring, but she sensed a reserve behind them that hadn't been there before.

It was just as she'd thought. He'd changed.

A woman Julie knew slightly passed by and smiled. It was a knowing smile directed first at Julie then at Richard. It happened twice more and Julie quickly suggested they went and had some tea.

They chose the hotel on the harbour. Peter thought it was the best place in the world because it had scones and a sweet mixture that resembled jam. No cream, though; that was still unheard of.

Because of the boy, they talked lightly about school and home-comings and how difficult it was to find eggs and fruit and chocolate. Food, they decided, was not what it used to be.

Richard said, 'But it's a darn sight better than I've been used to, I can tell you.'

'Didn't you get anything to eat in the camp?' Peter asked. 'Was it awful?'

But Julie interrupted, 'Not now, Peter. Richard won't want to talk about that now.'

Richard nodded at the boy. 'Some other time, Peter.' He looked away and Julie saw that he was frowning.

Later they separated for a while, he to take a room in the hotel, she to put on her best dress and brush her hair and dab a little more perfume behind her ears.

'Can't I come too?' Peter asked hopefully.

'No, another time. You can come out to dinner another time, I promise. But not tonight.' She'd arranged for him to go next door to Mrs Trehearn's for the evening.

He stamped his feet a couple of times then accepted defeat gracefully and went off to find out what Mrs Trehearn was cooking for supper.

Julie was ready early and sat down by the window to wait. Her stomach was still fluttering. Excitement. He still had that power over her. Yet in many ways he was a stranger. And she was a stranger to him . . .

Finally he arrived, looking handsome in his formal dark uniform. And attractive. Very. She decided she was rather pleased about that.

They walked slowly towards the hotel and talked about the Scillies and the sort of war the islands had had.

Richard stopped and pointed to the far side of St Mary's Sound. 'In the early days we used to take Concarneau trawlers there, to New Grimsby, and repaint them in their proper colours.'

'Yes, I know. Everyone guessed what was happening.'

He laughed. 'I should have known. There isn't much you locals don't know.'

They walked on a little way. Suddenly he said, 'It all seems a long time ago, doesn't it?'

'Yes.'

The dinner was execrable, but then everyone was used to that. However it was made more palatable by a bottle of wine which the hotel proprietor had been keeping for a celebration. It was a celebration, wasn't it? Julie said that yes it was, and Richard smiled. The wine, when it came, was not much better than the food, but they drank it anyway.

'Not a touch on your uncle's stuff.'

'No.'

He smiled briefly and looked at her over his glass and she knew he was remembering the evenings in the attic room.

There was a silence. Eventually he said, 'Smithe-Webb told me everything, about what happened to the others. I never saw them, you know, after we were taken from the beach. Only my crew, and even then we got split up. I'm very, very sorry. And I'm sorry about your aunt.'

She nodded. 'It was a blessing. She wasn't very well . . .'

'But this traitor . . . Smithe-Webb told me you'd identified him and proved that someone else was innocent – your cousin, wasn't it? That was wonderful, Julie, a great achievement!'

She murmured, 'Thank you.'

'But how on earth did you do it? How did you find out who he really was?'

She hesitated. 'It's a long story . . . But it was the Resistance and other people – friends – who really found out who he was. Not me.'

'The major thinks you're something of a heroine all the same.' He smiled warmly at her. 'But I knew that anyway.'

She dropped her eyes.

He went on, 'But this fellow Vasson . . . I gather the Resistance got him and executed him, didn't they? That's something. It won't bring the others back and it sure as hell won't make up for my two lost years. But . . . well, it's something. And I bet they made him go through it before they finished him off.' He laughed briefly. 'I bet the devil suffered!'

She stared at him. 'Yes, I suppose so . . .' She opened her mouth to say more, but couldn't. She wanted to tell him, to share the dreadful weight of it . . . But what would he think? How would he look at her once he knew, once he realised she was capable of such a thing?

Better not to tell, much better.

Perhaps one day . . . perhaps never.

Instead she asked him about the camp. Haltingly and a little unwillingly, he sketched out the story. With relief she realised that there were whole areas of his life that he, too, didn't want to talk about.

Finally he said, 'It drove me mad, being locked up. There were thousands in the same boat, of course. But even now I can't talk about it without . . .' He shook his head.

She reached over and gripped his hand. 'Then don't!' He looked up in surprise.

She said, 'Let's talk about something else! Something . . . *nice*!'

He laughed. 'What a marvellous idea.' Julie noticed that the reserve had gone from his eyes.

They started to talk of less serious things and she felt more at ease. She even found herself laughing which she hadn't done for a long time. She'd forgotten how funny he was, how warm and vital. She began to remember other things, forgotten words, small incidents . . .

Perhaps, she thought, he hasn't changed so much after all.

They talked a little about the future, though not too much and not too deeply. He had lots of plans. She realised that, for Richard, the future was everything. She was glad, *thankful* – he made her feel optimistic again.

After a while he paused and asked, 'Do you remember the holiday we were going to have?'

'You mean . . .'

'Here, in the Scillies. On *Dancer*.'

'Yes, of course I remember. Perfectly.'

'Well? Would you like that?'

She smiled slowly. 'Very much. I'd like that very much indeed.'

Later, when the wine was finished and the meal cleared away she watched him and thought: There's something else I'd like very much too.

You.

In that respect nothing had changed at all.

And why not now, tonight?

Yes. Life was too short.

Yes, she would stay with him tonight, whatever . . .

Then, in time, maybe everything would be all right. Maybe there would be love and security and a new life. Perhaps the nightmares might eventually go away . . .

At least she'd be happy while she found out.

She smiled at him across the table.

'I'd love some fresh air. Shall we walk along the beach for a while, before we go home?'

Postscript

By the outbreak of war, Germany had developed several successful early-warning radar systems to guard herself against air attack. These systems were large and land-based and worked on medium to long waves. Thus convinced of Germany's security, Goering ordered a halt to all long-term research. The many Jewish scientists and technicians involved in the work were sent to concentration camps.

Later, when it was realised that the British actually possessed radar, there was panic and the armed services, industry, and finally even the concentration camps were combed for technicians.

An electronics research laboratory was set up by the SS in Dachau. Eventually over a hundred skilled prisoners were employed on dismantling captured enemy equipment.

Right up till the moment in August 1943 when the captured 'Rotterdam' device (the British H_2S shortwave radar) was finally pieced together and made to function – it revealed a perfect 'picture' of Berlin – the German experts were convinced that shortwave radar was both impossible and impractical.

14 May 1943, Fuehrer Conference Minutes.
Admiral Doenitz's Report:
> We are at present facing the greatest crisis in submarine warfare, since the enemy is for the first time making fighting impossible and causing us heavy losses, by means of new location devices.

Admiral Doenitz; Memoirs. January to March 1943, *Collapse Of The U-Boat War*:
> 'Radar, and particularly radar location by aircraft, had to all practical purposes robbed the U-boats of the power to fight on the surface. Wolf pack operations against convoys in the North Atlantic, the main theatre of operations . . . were no longer possible.
> '. . . I accordingly withdrew the boats from the North Atlantic.
> 'We had lost the Battle of the Atlantic . . .'

Many, many brave men and women risked their lives to help Allied servicemen escape from Occupied Europe. Occasionally, an airman shot down over Belgium would find himself back with his squadron in England in just two to three days. The record was nine *hours*. Usually it took a little longer . . .

There were numerous escape lines operating through Belgium and

France, most of them functioning on arms and money sent by MI9 in London.

One of the most successful lines was 'Comet' which ran from Belgium through Paris to the Pyrénées and Spain.

In 1943 the Brussels end of the line was hit hard by the Gestapo and over a hundred people were arrested, many dying by firing squad or in the horrors of the concentration camps.

For a while the Paris branch of Comet continued to function until that, too, was hit by a terrible blow. This time the traitor was identified. He was a new courier by the name of Jean Masson. It was an assumed name, as were all the names he used in his long and terrible career.

His real name was Jacques Desoubrie.

Later Desoubrie penetrated another escape line, further to the west. As a result of this treachery seventy British and sixty American evaders were caught and sent to Buchenwald concentration camp.

There is evidence that, on the orders of his masters, the Gestapo, Desoubrie penetrated at least two other lines . . .

The French Resistance was at its strongest in Brittany.

However, early attempts to establish an escape line through Brittany met with difficulties, mainly organisational. Later in the war properly trained agents were sent in, and the 'Shelburne' line was born. Motor gunboats, crewed with great bravery and daring by officers and men of the Royal Navy, made regular runs from Dartmouth across the Channel to rock-strewn beaches on the Brittany coast, right under the noses of the Germans. Knowing that coast as I do, I can only marvel at the incredible feats of navigation they displayed.

The Shelburne line was very successful; it transported 307 servicemen and agents to England in a single year.

Incidentally, when the Germans came sniffing round, the gunboats sometimes had to depart in rather a hurry. On more than one occasion some members of the gunboat's crew *did* get left on the beach.

The traitor Desoubrie continued his career of betrayal and treachery until the end of the war.

Then his luck ran out. He was, in fact, brought to justice and executed in Lille.

But it might have been different . . .

Red Crystal

For my parents

PART ONE
Spring 1968

One

Gabriele Schroeder chose her clothes thoughtfully.

What did one need for such an occasion?

Running-shoes certainly. Jeans. A top which wasn't so bulky that it would impede her arms. At the same time it would be cold waiting outside the hotel. She pulled on a sweater and took a scarf from the hook on the back of the door. With a leather jacket, that should be enough to keep her warm.

She made a half-hearted attempt to tidy the area around her bed, stuffing some clothes into a holdall, and then gave up.

A broken mirror sat on the mantelpiece. She looked at her reflection. Hair dark, shoulder-length, slightly wavy, parted severely in the middle; skin pale; eyes dark and hollow. She still wasn't used to herself without make-up – she'd worn it for years: the pale white foundation, the thick eye-liner and heavy mascara. A slave to fashion. But who needed make-up? That was for manufactured women who didn't know who they really were. She could see that now. But it had taken her long enough to realise. She was twenty-five.

Finally, the hat. It was a woollen one that came down over her forehead. After a moment's thought, she removed it, fastened her hair to the top of her head with a pin and replaced the hat. Better: now her hair wouldn't get in her eyes.

The complete political activist.

A small tremor of nervousness tugged at her. She'd never done anything like this before. Nor had the others. Nor had *anybody*. Demonstrations in Britain were usually orderly, good-humoured, well-behaved. *Passive*.

This was going to be different.

She ran downstairs to the kitchen.

The others were there. Eight in all, including Max and Stephie.

They were sitting round the room, drinking and smoking joints. No one looked worried. They seemed to think it was rather a lark. Gabriele relaxed a little.

Someone asked, 'Do we know who'll be there, Max?'

Max's thin, intense face was expressionless behind the wire-rimmed glasses. 'The American ambassador. A whole collection of dons—'

'A *disgust* of dons.' It was a boy with bright red hair. Gabriele recognised him from meetings on the campus at Essex. His name, she remembered, was Paul Reardon.

'– and maybe someone from the Foreign Office.'

'No cabinet ministers?'

Max shook his head. 'They didn't say so.'

Gabriele knew that Max's information came from his friends at Oxford, the organisers of the demonstration. The occasion was the Oxford Anglo-American Society Dinner.

Someone said, 'Pity.'

As they collected their banners and placards, Reardon came over to Gabriele. 'Linda, isn't it?'

She gave it a second to let her annoyance pass, then said firmly, 'No, it is not. The name is Gabriele, Gabriele Schroeder.'

He stared at her. 'Sure. Sure . . .'

To ease the moment along, she added, 'It's my *real* name. Linda was . . . Linda was just something I called myself for a while. Okay?'

'Okay.'

At five they set off in a single mini-van. It was rush hour and it took half an hour to get from Kentish Town to Paddington and on to the Westway. Gabriele began to worry about being late. But then the traffic improved and they were clear, bowling along the A40 towards Oxford.

There was plenty of time. She should have realised. Max, for all his apparent vagueness, was an efficient organiser. In their undergraduate days at Essex, it was Max who'd arranged transport to Ban the Bomb marches, who'd joined the International Socialists, and made the first demands for student rights. Now he and Stephie were two of the six permanent residents of the house in Kentish Town. It was more of a community than a shared house, really. There were always people coming and going. Every two weeks meetings of the Kentish Town Housing Action Group were held in the living-room, and sometimes homeless people stayed on mattresses on the floor. Victims of oppression, as Max called them. Gabriele was proud of helping the homeless; it showed that one really cared. It was the practical application of one's beliefs: praxis.

At twilight they came into the centre of Oxford, and turned north on to the Banbury Road. After half a mile, Max pointed to the right. There was a sign: The Linden House Hotel.

They looked in through the gates. Already there was a large

crowd outside, chanting loudly. There were also some blue uniforms.

They did a U-turn and parked. Everyone was silent. Gabriele got calmly out of the van and slid her placard out of the back. It read: US MURDERERS – OUT OF VIETNAM.

Max said, 'We'll give it till eight-thirty. Then they'll all be in the dining-room. And the pigs might have gone away.'

Someone giggled nervously. 'They won't even realise what's happening.'

The tension eased. There was a flutter of conversation, and they walked jauntily through the gates to join the crowd of shouting demonstrators. Gabriele hoisted her placard and took up the chant of the crowd – *Fascist killers*! and *Win, win, Ho Chi Minh*! She began to feel high, as if she'd been drinking, yet her mind was perfectly clear.

Although the crowd numbered at least two hundred, Gabriele counted only six policemen keeping the doorway to the hotel clear. As the dinner guests arrived, prominent in their evening clothes, the crowd waved their banners and roared abuse. But it was all very good-natured. No one tried to press against the police or jostle the guests.

After ten minutes a large limousine drew up. The American ambassador. A faint mask-like smile on his face, the ambassador walked quickly into the hotel, professionally oblivious to the screams of the crowd. The cool indifference was irritating.

The stream of guests trailed off. The demonstrators looked bored and started talking in groups. Gabriele saw Max slip away, towards the van.

She followed and found him sliding a long metal crowbar from under a seat. 'To get in with,' he murmured.

Gabriele viewed it with surprise. She hadn't thought anything like that would be necessary. The idea of using a weapon-like object made her feel uneasy.

As they walked back towards the hotel she decided not to say anything. After all, a new strategy required new tactics. She wasn't going to be the one member of the group to be faint-hearted.

Stephie, Reardon and the others were waiting, with about fifteen of the Oxford contingent. Silently, they slipped away from the other demonstrators in ones and twos until they were gathered at the side of the building. Gabriele took a quick look back. The police were hidden from view by the remains of the crowd; they

11

had seen nothing. But then they weren't really looking.

A high wall with a closed gate barred the way to the floodlit hotel garden beyond. However the gate was unlocked, and they filed straight through into the garden and hid behind some large shrubs. The dining-room looked out on to the lawn and the diners were clearly visible through the tall french windows. The top table, Gabriele noted, was to the right. She decided to make straight for it when the time came. She gripped the handle of her placard more tightly. She wanted to wave it right under the ambassador's nose.

Max ran forward, followed by Stephie and Reardon, and pressed himself against the wall to one side of the windows. He seemed to be examining the door locks. He reached out and tried a handle. Clearly it was locked.

He strode out in front of the windows. With a slight shock Gabriele realised what he was going to do. He was swinging the crowbar in a great arc. It came forward and hit the glass with a bang. A small hole appeared in the window with cracks running in several directions.

Max twisted his head to look questioningly at Stephie, as if he couldn't understand why the glass hadn't shattered. Then Stephie stepped in front of the window and lobbed something heavy from her shoulder. A brick-like object hit the window with a great crash. Max put his hand through the glass and the next moment the window was open.

The sound of protesting astonished voices swelled out from the dining-room. The next moment the rest of the group were running forward, whooping and yelling. Gabriele caught the exhilaration. She pulled her hat further down over her face and, letting out a great shriek, ran for the window.

Inside, Gabriele almost fell over a huddle of people bent over something on the floor. She side-stepped them neatly and made for the top table, passing behind a long line of angry, startled, bemused faces. A man rose up in front of her, shouted 'Outrageous!' and put out his arm. Fending him off, Gabriele dived past, rounded the corner of the room and, placing herself behind the ambassador, held up her placard and began to shout: *'US out! Hands off Vietnam!'*

There was uproar. She saw Reardon on top of a long table, stepping none too carefully across the china. Stephie was running round the far side of the room, waving her placard like a maniac. The others were parading up and down, shouting their slogans above the din. Some held chairs in front of them, herding startled guests into a corner. But most of the guests sat stunned, waiting in impeccable British style for somebody to do something.

The surprise was total. Gabriele almost laughed at the guests' incredulous outrage.

The noise rose to a crescendo. A table was turned over; there was the crash of breaking china and cries of alarm as the diners shot to their feet and examined their clothes, dripping with wine and hot greasy food.

Gabriele danced along behind the top table, enjoying the sight of the appalled faces. A shout rose above the din. Reardon, his hair flaming red under the lights, stood on a table, a wine bottle held high in his hand, and slowly, solemnly tipped the bottle until the red wine spilled in a long stream on to the table and splashed up at the diners, who hastily withdrew, wiping at their clothes with their napkins.

'*The blood of the Vietnamese!*' Reardon screamed. '*Murdered by the US aggressors!*'

Gabriele cheered loudly. She saw Stephie force her way past Reardon and approach the top table. Stephie raised her placard in front of the ambassador who was getting to his feet in an attempt to leave. Seeing her, the ambassador turned his back. With a yell of anger, Stephie raised the placard and, reaching across the table, brought it down on the ambassador's head.

Gabriele saw the ambassador clap a hand to his head, then a sudden movement to the right caught her eye. Uniforms had appeared: three of the policemen from the front door. They went for Reardon, pulling him down from the table head first. Another grabbed Stephie, but she swung at him and clipped him smartly in the eye. He fell back, his hand to his face, and Stephie sprinted away.

Gabriele hesitated: should she fight or run? Through the pandemonium she saw Stephie and Max moving across the back of the room towards the windows.

Time to retreat then. Gabriele turned to run, but stopped dead. A group of guests were standing in the aisle, blocking her way. They looked angry and obstructive, and she had the unpleasant feeling they would try to prevent her from passing. She felt a moment's fear, a clutching claustrophobia.

She fought it and, calming herself, gritted her teeth and rushed them.

All but one, an obese round-faced man, fell back. The man made an attempt to grab her, but she struck out, shooting an elbow sharply into the obscenely large stomach. She heard him gasp.

Now the way was clear and she raced to the end of the long table, rounded the corner and made for the open window. The huddle of people she had stepped over were still intent on whatever lay on the floor. She paused and glanced down. It was an elderly man, his eyes closed, his head cradled in a woman's lap. Gabriele had a vivid image of the woman's lap, bright red, a vast pool of wetness that was obscenely bright against the pallor of her dress.

She hesitated, but then people were bumping past her and Max was dragging her away, yelling. 'Come *on*!' Dropping her placard, she ran for the garden gate.

She arrived panting at the van to find the others clambering in. As the engine fired with a roar, Stephie reached out to pull her up into the front seat. The van shot off and swerved round a corner, the open passenger door swinging wildly on its hinges. Gabriele clung to Stephie, shaking slightly, not yet brave enough to reach out for the door and pull it closed, thinking only of the pale man with the closed eyes and the white dress covered in blood.

But then Stephie laughed, a wild hoot of triumph, and Gabriele realised that she was right to be exhilarated: the demonstration had achieved everything they had hoped for, and more. It was the end of passivity, the beginning of a new movement. *She – they –* were part of it.

But what really astonished Gabriele was that it had been so easy.

They rounded a corner, the door of the van swung shut. She was safe. Catching the mood, she hugged Stephie and began to laugh.

Nick Ryder frowned in concentration and read the passage again. 'Underneath the conservative popular base is the substratum of the outsiders, the exploited and persecuted of other races and other colours, the unemployed and the unemployable. They exist outside the democratic process . . . Thus their opposition is revolutionary even if their consciousness is not.'

Ryder wondered if he was really understanding all this correctly. Did Marcuse mean that the underprivileged could be revolutionary without *knowing* it? Seemed highly unlikely. Or did he mean that their opposition justified *other* people being revolutionary *for* them?

He put the book down and yawned. He was too tired to read this sort of stuff tonight. It was difficult enough at the best of times. Although he was finally beginning to understand some of it. He opened his eyes and looked at the line of books on the mantelpiece. Marx, Engels, Fanon, Guérin ... In two months he'd accumulated quite a library.

He marked his page and slid the copy of *One-dimensional Man* back among the other books.

Nine o'clock. It was the first time he'd been home before ten that week. It was a pity that nice girl Anne hadn't been free. She was a social worker and about the only one he'd ever met who didn't burst with good intentions or look like the back of a bus. In fact Anne was rather attractive. She'd said she had a meeting that night. He hoped that she wasn't feeding him a line.

He thought: What a suspicious mind you have. But then it went with being a policeman.

A nice hot bath was what he needed. He put on a record – *Traviata*, with Moffo and Tucker, and stood for a moment, letting the soft notes work their magic. Italian opera never failed to move him. His love of music had been the most amazing discovery of his life.

He never let on to the lads, though: they'd find it very curious.

He went into the bathroom and ran the hot water. The gas geyser hissed and roared and finally spat out a minute trickle of steaming water. From bitter experience he'd learnt that the hot water cooled off considerably during the twenty or so minutes the bath took to fill, so he added no cold.

The steam rose in wet curtains. It reminded him of the freezing bathroom at the back of the house in Barrow and his mam yelling at him to get the hell in before the water got cold. He hadn't been home in months, and probably wouldn't get round to it until summer. It was a bit of a chore now anyway. After four years the north seemed a lifetime away.

He went to the kitchen, which was so small you could reach everything while standing in one place, and poured himself a beer. He returned to the bathroom. It wasn't far. The flat consisted of a hall, bedsitting-room, kitchen and bathroom. For some time he'd been meaning to find himself something better. But, being in Lambeth, just across the river from Westminster, it was handy for the office. It was also very cheap.

Though the bath was only half full he was impatient and, undressing quickly, got in. Shivering, he lay back and felt the hot

15

water creep slowly up his body. In another five minutes, when the water covered his legs, it was going to be very pleasant indeed.

The phone rang.

Ryder breathed, 'I don't believe this.'

For a moment he lay still, considering whether to answer it. If it was the office they could go to hell. On the other hand, it might just be Anne . . .

He got out, grabbed a towel and padded wetly across the bedsitting-room to the phone.

A cheery, horribly familiar voice echoed down the earpiece. 'Hello, sport. Didn't disturb anything interesting, I trust?'

'Sod you, Conway. What is it?'

'Oxford. That Vietnam demo. A real fracas. Rampaged round the dining-room waving placards. About thirty or forty of them.'

Ryder sighed. 'The Oxford lads were warned, for Christsake. *Several* times . . .'

'I don't doubt it, mate, but the fact remains that it was a right cock-up. The *ambassador* got hit on the head. And there was an injury caused by a brick. Geezer's all right, but it could have been nasty. There's mutterings about bringing serious charges. Trouble is, they're short of customers—'

'Didn't they nab *any* of them?'

'Two, I think.'

'God, how many lads did they have on the job then?'

'They're not saying, but can't have been many, can it?'

Ryder was silent for a moment. 'I suppose they want some names tonight.'

'You got it.'

Wearily, Ryder went back to the bathroom and got dressed again. He should have known. This had happened before. It was the fault of the structure. There was no national police force, just a large number of county and borough forces, each, Ryder sometimes thought, more stubbornly independent than the next. You could give them all the information you liked, but you couldn't force them to act on it.

Names, they wanted, did they? Well, they were asking a lot. All the same, he was already turning some ideas over in his mind.

In 1968, as much as now, the work of Special Branch was deliberately unpublicised – not to say shrouded in secrecy – and the police liked to keep it that way.

It was generally believed that the three hundred or so officers of the Metropolitan Police Special Branch were merely the legmen for the Security Service – known to the public as MI5 – and indeed one of their main responsibilities was the arrest and charging of spies and subversives previously identified by the Security Service. But in fact Special Branch's brief went further, treading an uneasy line between pure police work and intelligence-gathering. Officially, the Branch had to keep an eye on undesirables – mainly foreign – entering and leaving the country, to help guard government ministers and foreign VIPs, and to investigate foreigners applying for naturalisation. But they were also expected to keep abreast of developments among the 'lunatic fringe' – the anarchists and the far-left and far-right extremists: those who were 'likely to threaten the country's security or to cause a breakdown of law and order'. Whereas MI5 dealt with foreign-linked plots and security leaks – counter-intelligence – the Special Branch kept tabs on home-grown trouble-makers.

Or tried to.

Ryder had transferred from Lancashire CID to Special Branch twelve months before and his speciality was Trotskyists.

He took a number 10 bus across the river and arrived at Scotland Yard shortly before ten. Special Branch was located on the seventh floor of the brand-new metal and glass tower block off Victoria Street that was the headquarters of the Metropolitan Police.

Ryder found Conway sitting in front of a heap of files.

'Oh *there* you are,' Conway said. 'The boss phoned. He wanted to know if this shemozzle was our fault.'

'You told him?'

'Yeah. He was somewhat relieved.'

Ryder took off his jacket. 'Any more news?'

'They've caught a few more. No names yet. But apparently they were local Oxford trouble-makers.'

'What about the two they nabbed?'

Conway handed him a file. 'Haven't got anything on one, name of Lampton, but there's a bit on the other, name of Reardon, Paul.'

Ryder took the file and remembered having seen it quite recently. Unlike other branches of the Criminal Investigation Department, Special Branch kept large numbers of files on people who had no form. In fact almost all the people the Branch were interested in had never been near a court of law, let alone a prison.

17

The file on Reardon was very thin. One four-line report on a slip of paper. It was no wonder Ryder had recognised it – he'd written it himself.

It read: Reardon, Paul. Date of birth: 17th April 1946. Student at LSE, 1964–67. Failed to sit finals. Feb 1968: Member of SSL Central Committee. Address: unknown as at February 1968.

Since Reardon had no passport, there were no further birth details or photographs, which Ryder would normally have obtained from the passport office.

Conway stared over Ryder's shoulder. 'There could have been less, I suppose.'

'Well, it's a damn sight more than there was before –' He almost said 'before I sorted it out' but didn't. Conway was well aware of the situation. Until recently there'd been quite a gap in the Branch's intelligence on the far left. Marxists, anarchists, and the Communist Party of Great Britain were covered by the relevant Branch sections, but the Trotskyist Section had got into a bit of a mess. The problem was that the Trots were increasingly difficult to keep track of. Some were still pro-Moscow, others vehemently anti-Moscow. The groups were continually splintering and merging, and almost impossible to categorise.

This Paul Reardon was on the committee of the SSL – the Socialist Students' League, a militant Trotskyist group, but violently anti-Moscow. It had been formed by a group of students at the London School of Economics – known in the Branch as the London School of Comics – an institution famous for its left-wing views. In the past LSE students had been revolutionary in an intellectual non-violent kind of way. But the Socialist Students' League was distinctly aggressive. That was why Ryder had opened a file on them.

Ryder examined the main file now and looked at the list of people suspected of membership of the SSL. It was impossible to be sure who the members were because the league was typically disorganised, charging no subscription and keeping no lists.

The list was very short, fifteen names, if that, and consisted of speakers at the two meetings that Ryder himself had attended. He tried another tack.

'What addresses have the two given?' he asked Conway.

'Home addresses. Reardon's in Birmingham. The other bloke – Lampton – in Cheshire.'

'What about occupations?'

'Market stallholders.'

That was a new one on Ryder. 'Oh, yes. What do they sell?'

'Second-hand books, apparently.'

'And they haven't given a London address?'

Conway looked at his notes and shook his head.

So, no lead to the other demonstrators that way. Ryder asked without optimism, 'Anything else to go on?'

Conway made a face. 'Well, the dinner guests did offer some descriptions. For what they're worth. You can imagine the sort of thing – student types, long hair, bearded, unkempt. *Really* helpful. But the assailant – the brick-lobber – was female, and the Oxford boys don't seem to have got her in custody. The description's a bit better.' Conway read from his notes. 'About twenty-five, long mousy hair, pale complexion, very thin, jeans, distinctive patchwork jacket covered in flowers.'

Ryder tried to fit the description to one of the names in the file, but couldn't.

Nothing for it then. It was time to go out and about.

Ten-thirty on a Saturday night was not the best time to find informants. As he left the Yard, Ryder resigned himself to the fact that he was unlikely to find any of his regular sources until late in the night, if then.

He began at the Carlton Arms, a pub off Gower Street, near one of the London School of Economics' halls of residence. Ryder had no trouble passing as a student. His fair wavy hair was down to his collar and he invariably wore jeans and an old denim jacket. He was twenty-six but could have been less. He had the classless anonymous look of a thousand other young men, which was just what he wanted.

The pub was crowded, mainly with students. But neither of the two men Ryder was hoping to see was there. He gave it ten minutes, until just before closing time, and hurried off to the Duchess of Teck nearby.

No one there either.

He didn't like pressurising his informants, and usually took care to make the whole process of giving information so casual that it was almost painless. But he needed those names.

Against his better judgement he went into a hall of residence off Endsleigh Place and asked for one of the men by name. Someone went to look for him. He was out. Ryder was almost relieved.

He found a callbox and phoned the flat where the second student lived. Also out.

It looked as though he'd have to wait until the next day.

Although there was always Nugent. He might be worth a try. Nugent had been at the LSE until he dropped out the previous year. He now lived on social security and, Ryder suspected, was heavily into drugs. Nugent lived in a flat in a rundown house in Upper Holloway and wasn't on the phone. It was a long way to go on the off-chance.

Ryder hesitated then, with a small sigh, set off for King's Cross to catch the Piccadilly Line north to Finsbury Park. It would probably be a wild good chase, but at least he would have left no stone unturned.

It was shortly before midnight by the time he got to the decrepit house where Nugent lived. The front door was open. The sound of loud beat music echoed across the street. Inside there was a party going on. About a dozen people were draped around a purple-lit room, in various stages of intoxication. There was a strong smell of grass.

Nugent was sitting on the floor, his lank Jesus-style hair falling forward over his face. He was smiling benignly. Ryder sat down beside him and raised his voice above the din. 'Hi.'

Grinning stupidly, Nugent made a valiant effort to focus. With a sinking heart, Ryder realised Nugent was more than well away, he was totally gone.

When Nugent finally spoke, it was to utter a stream of gibberish that was hard to make out over the noise, but seemed to involve a forthcoming Ying-Yang uprising and an Inner Space Adventure. Ryder nodded sagely. Then, without much hope, he shouted in Nugent's ear, 'D'you know Paul Reardon or someone called Lampton?'

Nugent made an effort to concentrate. 'Sure.'

'Where do they hang out?'

Nugent's eyes clouded over and took on a look that wasn't so much far away as out of sight.

'Who're their friends?' Ryder prompted.

'Friends, man? Who's got friends . . .?' Nugent giggled and nodded his head in time to the music.

Ryder repeated the question. For a moment Nugent ignored it, then turned abruptly and, his eyes suddenly hard and bright, said distinctly, 'Five smackers.'

20

Ryder thought: 'You're not so high as you seem, my friend. He said, 'Okay, but I'll want addresses.'

Nugent grinned. 'That's all I got, man. Try a house in Manor Road, Kentish Town. Can't remember the number . . . But the door's sort of purple.'

'Anything else?'

Nugent shook his head.

'What about a girl? Thin, tall, fair-haired. Wears a jacket covered in flowers.'

Someone passed Nugent a joint and he drew on it deeply. Ryder waited. Eventually Nugent mumbled with bad grace, 'Stephie. Same house, man.'

Ryder allowed himself a moment's satisfaction, then paid Nugent his five quid. If the information was good, it was cheap at the price.

Gabriele turned over and closed her eyes more tightly, but the morning light was bright and intrusive and she knew she wouldn't get back to sleep.

She had been dreaming of light, the light she had seen as a child: bright yellow summer light full of promise; the promise of fulfilments and pleasures and freedoms she could barely guess at, but which she knew with absolute certainty that she had to have. In the dream, however, the light was elusive, reduced to a few thin tantalising shafts that managed to find their way between the heavy oppressive curtains in the front room of the house where she had grown up.

Then, as in the dream now, every detail of the room was vivid in her mind. The curtains and the dark furniture pressed in on her, claustrophobic, devoid of life or hope, exuding blank despair. Tea was on the table: scones and heavy cream cakes, a pot of tea for her parents, milk for her. A pervasive deathly quiet, the clock sounding unnaturally loud on the mantelpiece. Her father reading, her mother bent over her embroidery. No one saying a word. Then for some reason Gabriele started to cry – she couldn't remember why – and her mother looked up in surprise. Gabriele asked for something – was it to go out and play? Or just to go for a walk? Or to be told a story? Or just to do something *different*? Whatever, the request was denied. With quiet and relentless patience her mother explained that the next day was a schoolday and she must rest.

And then the silence had closed in again, like a shroud.

Even now Gabriele tensed at the memory of her feelings: the intense frustration, the voiceless rage, the corrosive loneliness.

With an effort she pushed the memory out of her mind.

Opening an eye, she looked at her watch. Not even eight, and she hadn't got to sleep till three. She murmured 'Hell', and sat up naked on the edge of the bed. She reached for a towel and, wrapping it round herself, padded slowly out of the room.

Another memory nagged at her mind. Last night. The red-stained dress, the bleeding head. She still wasn't sure how she felt about that. Not happy anyway.

The kitchen was a mess. Glasses, bottles, saucers of ash lay everywhere. They'd talked for a long time last night. Then Stephie and Max had had a row – she couldn't even remember what it was about – and Max had stormed out. Gabriele wondered if he'd returned.

Her private supply of instant coffee was still behind the fridge where she'd hidden it. She looked in the cupboard for the muesli she'd bought the previous day. The packet was there. Empty. That was the trouble with living in a commune – people were apt to share things. The muesli wouldn't have been any good anyway – there was no milk. She settled for the coffee, strong and black.

Upstairs she tapped lightly on Stephie and Max's door and looked in. Stephie lay curled up in the bed alone. No Max. It must have been a big row.

Stephie was still fast asleep. Gabriele closed the door and went back to her own room. Tuning her transistor to Radio 4, she lay on the bed. The carefully enunciated voice of a BBC presenter talked about farming. An establishment voice. An audible reminder to the lower orders that the ruling class existed and was still firmly in control.

While she waited for the next news summary, she turned the radio down a little and, pulling a suitcase from under the bed, opened it and took out a book. She kept all her books in the case, otherwise they got borrowed and never returned.

She got back into bed and started to read. The book was entitled *The Revolutionary Society* and its author was an Italian philosopher named Petrini. She had already read the book twice. But there were still a number of passages she very much wanted to read again.

From the first reading, Petrini's ideas had impressed her deeply. He had taken the outworn ideas of the old left, discarded those that

22

were flawed or unworkable, and advanced those which were manifestly based in truth. His observations, his logic, his conclusions were faultless. He had made that great leap of the imagination which took his theories beyond the half-baked ideas of the past, to a series of brilliantly original truths that actually related to people's needs.

Society was structured, according to Petrini, to serve the capitalist system . . . The establishment controlled the people's very existence . . . People were not seeing the real world, but what they had been trained to see. They were encouraged to want material things, TV sets, cars and washing machines, because those things effectively subdued them. Their time was filled with empty repetitive pursuits to stop them from thinking . . .

This was all so true that Gabriele could only shake her head and wonder why she'd never realised it before.

The way forward was not to improve the present structure, but to replace it. People needed to rediscover the world as a physical sensual extension of themselves, and to realise they need not be cogs in the machinery of a harshly unnatural and alien world.

To achieve this, all institutions – schools, universities, factories – had to be subverted, so that people would question the existence of those institutions, and see the truth.

Gabriele marked her favourite ideas with a pencil and turned over the corners of the pages, so that she could find them more easily. There was one particular passage that she kept returning to.

It said: 'The way forward for the political activist is to sharpen and crystallise attitudes on the two sides of capitalist society. The social contradictions must be exaggerated, so that people are able to see them for the first time.'

Contradictions must be exaggerated.

Sharpen and crystallise.

Gabriele liked those phrases. It was what the demonstration had been about – hardening attitudes to Vietnam, getting some action. Yes: sharpen and crystallise. She underlined the words twice.

The voice on the radio had changed. She turned it up. The end of a programme. Finally, the news.

It was the third item. There had been a violent demonstration at a dinner in a hotel in Oxford. The US ambassador had been slightly injured . . . Another man still in hospital . . . Five people charged.

Gabriele's first feeling of elation at making the national news evaporated. They hadn't mentioned the *point* of the demonstration. Typical of the Establishment to conceal the facts. She thought bitterly: I should have known. She turned off the radio with an angry snap.

At least the man with the bleeding head hadn't been badly injured or they'd have said so. And as for Pete and Paul, they'd be okay. They'd get bail and be charged with causing a breach of the peace or whatever the quaint terminology was. There'd be a fine and a reprimand. And that would be that. No great deal. In fact, rather a feather in their caps. Neither of them would give away any names, of that she was sure. It was just bad luck – or good luck, depending on the way you looked at it – that they'd been the ones to get caught.

She heard a sound and looked up sharply.

A tall black man stood in the doorway. She relaxed. 'Hello, Tobago. Didn't know you were here.'

'Just short of a bed. So I helped myself to a mattress last night. Hope it was okay.'

She nodded, 'Sure.' Tobago was currently homeless and, when the pressures of the temporary accommodation the council had fixed up for him and his four-child family became too much, he grabbed a mattress on the floor somewhere. He knew where the spare key was hidden, underneath the dustbins round at the back.

'So, what's the news?' she asked.

Tobago came in and sat on the end of the bed and she settled back and half-listened to the long involved story of his struggle with the incomprehensible local authority system.

Suddenly a loud knock sounded on the front door below. Gabriele frowned. Who could it be at this hour on a Sunday?

She said, 'Go and see to it, would you, Tobago? And if it's anyone wanting help, tell them to come back later.'

He went out, pulling the door behind him. She heard him padding softly down the stairs and opening the door.

There were voices.

She sat up, very still, very tense.

A shout and the sound of feet . . .

Alarmed, she jumped out of bed and looked for something else to put on. There was no time. She could hear *dozens* of feet now, hammering up the stairs. Hastily she pulled the towel more tightly round her and tied the ends into a knot.

The door burst open and Tobago came in. 'It's the fuzz!'

She pushed past him and looked out of the door.

Men were streaming up the stairs, running purposefully. Already they were barging into the upper rooms.

Retreating into the bedroom, Gabriele slammed the door and stood there, panting with rage. She should do something. But *what?*

Tobago murmured, 'Shit, I don't need this—!'

The door opened with a bang and two tall figures stood in the doorway.

'Right,' said one, 'I have a warrant to search these premises . . .' He rattled rapidly through the technicalities.

Gabriele watched incredulously. She'd never seen a small-minded bureaucratic Hitlerite in action before. It was unbelievable.

The second man pointed at Tobago. 'You! Downstairs!'

Gabriele shouted, 'Leave him alone. He's done nothing!'

The first one turned in exaggerated surprise. 'Oh? And how do you know that, love?'

The outrage shot through Gabriele. 'Don't you *love* me!'

The policeman took a step forward and said condescendingly, 'Now, let's be a good girl and get dressed.'

'Not with you looking on, you dirty little man!'

'Believe it or not, I wasn't planning to watch,' he said with heavy sarcasm. 'Anyway, I didn't think you lot minded that sort of thing.'

'My God –! Go to hell!'

She went to the bed and, slowly and deliberately, got in.

The first policeman sighed. Gesturing to the other man, the two of them got either side of the bed and pulled her out. Their hands were firm and uncompromising on her arms. Gabriele thought: I can't take this.

She knew what she should do: stay *cool*. And for a moment she did manage to fight off the claustrophobia and stay passive. But then, as they pulled her to her feet, the panic rose in her, white hot and angry, and, catching them unawares, she pulled free and lashed out. There was a brief satisfying *ughh!* as her elbow hit soft flesh. She grabbed for her alarm clock, a heavy round metal one, and swung it through the air. It caught one man on the side of the head and his hand shot up to clutch the wound.

Then both men recovered from their surprise and their hands tightened like vices on her arms. She felt a new wave of panic and lashed out with her feet. But they were pushing her down and down, backwards. The bed came up against her back until she was lying helplessly on the mattress.

Suddenly a weight descended on her middle and with a shock she realised that one of them was *sitting* on her.

'*Get off!* You bastard, get *off!*'

'No chance,' came the reply. 'Not until you promise to come downstairs quietly.'

Gabriele felt the bitter taste of humiliation. She must look like a complete fool.

Four more people came into the room, including two women in plain clothes. One man started searching the room, but the others came over to the bed and regarded her coldly. She realised they were going to move her by force. One of the women asked, 'Well, are you going to come quietly then?'

Gabriele shook with anger. 'If you lay a hand on me, I'll kill you.'

'That's not very sensible, is it?' said the woman. Then, without another word, they went for her arms.

Ryder stood a little way up the street and waited impatiently. It was the right house, he was sure of that. Not only was it the only one with a purple door, but he'd checked on the place very carefully at six that morning, first with the newsagent on the corner, then with an early-rising neighbour. Both knew that the place was inhabited by hippy-type students. The *Ban the Bomb* and *US Out of Vietnam* posters in the windows had confirmed it.

Nevertheless the right address was no guarantee that the brick-lobbing Stephie would actually be there, and he watched the house impatiently.

He wondered what was taking so long. The raiding party – all Special Branch officers – should have got the inmates out by now.

Noise started coming from the house: shouts, some abusive language, and the crash of furniture. A moment's silence then a long agonised scream echoed across the street. Ryder shivered. What the hell was going on in there?

The front door opened and Ryder stood back so that he wouldn't be seen. First a black man was escorted down the steps and into a car. Ryder was surprised. There were no black activists in this group, neither had a black activist been seen at the demonstration. Next came a stream of ragged, jeans-clad individuals.

Ryder counted ten of them. Good God, how many lived in the place? Finally a thin girl with long mousy hair and a flowered jacket came sullenly down the steps. Ryder allowed himself a moment of self-congratulation. *Stephie*. Perhaps she was the one who had screamed.

They were driven away. Ryder ran up the steps and into the house. The remainder of the raiding party would be searching the place by now, and he wanted to see if they had found anything in the way of political tracts and pamphlets.

He pushed open the door and nodded to the officer in the hall. The officer, a constable of about twenty-three, made a face and indicated upstairs. Another scream reverberated through the house and Ryder looked upwards.

A group of four officers, two of them women, were at the top of the stairs, descending slowly, a thrashing figure in their midst. All Ryder could see were some long bare legs kicking out wildly from behind the leading policeman. Then he glimpsed a head twisting from side to side, the long dark hair obliterating the face. The unsteady group finally reached the bottom of the stairs and Ryder stood back. In the space of the hall the group opened up and Ryder saw that the girl was tall and slender and that she was covered by nothing but a towel.

The girl sobbed and writhed and all of a sudden the towel was on the floor. Ryder had a momentary impression of a slim lithe body and a pair of firm white breasts. Then he looked away.

A male voice shouted viciously, 'Leave that!'

Ryder looked back and saw that one of the women was reaching for the towel. The male voice snapped again, '*Leave that!* Just get her in the van!'

Ryder muttered 'For Christsake . . .' as the men half lifted the writhing body out of the door. The girl let out a long low moan, as if in pain, and then she was being carried down the steps and into the street in full view of the staring onlookers. At last she was bundled ignominiously into a police car, and handed back her towel. Ryder felt a spasm of shame.

The officer in the hall was nodding as if the whole thing was to be expected and Ryder realised that it hadn't occurred to him to look the other way. Ryder asked, 'Was that really necessary?'

The man regarded him with surprise. 'She was resisting arrest, sarge. What do you expect the lads to do?'

'I know, but . . .' He shook his head.

'Come on, sarge. She's not shy. I mean it's all free love for them, isn't it?' He lowered his voice. 'Besides, *she* was shacked up with the West Indian. I mean . . .' He gave a knowing wink.

Ryder sighed inwardly. Sometimes he thought he was in entirely the wrong job.

Two

The valley lay behind the downs, a rich pocket of verdant pasture and tranquil woodland tucked between the long ridges of the chalk hills. A narrow road, no more than a lane, ran from the main Salisbury road down into the valley, arriving, after many twists and turns, at Cherbourne St Mary, a pretty unspoilt village built of soft grey Wiltshire stone and boasting a particularly fine early Gothic church.

Victoria Danby drove slowly through the village, which appeared to be totally deserted. But then it was Saturday, and still early. She glanced at the estate agent's directions balanced on her knee. Another mile. At first she thought she'd missed the turning but then it appeared, a rough road off to the left with a large *For Sale* board on the corner.

The track was full of pot-holes and she had to weave the Mini from side to side to avoid the worst craters. She wondered if the estate agent would be there yet.

She angled the driving mirror towards her face and took a quick look. She grimaced in despair. Wild fair hair hopelessly frizzy, an undistinguished nose that she'd always disliked and far too many freckles. An angry spot on her right cheek glowed conspicuously through the cover-up stuff she'd applied that morning, and there were signs of another brewing on the other cheek. It was horribly unfair. Almost as unfair as eating nothing but one bowl of home-made muesli – no sugar, skimmed milk – twice a day and staying at a remorseless eleven stone.

The track ran between tantalisingly high hedgerows that hid the ploughed fields on either side, then threaded its way into the latticed shadows of a delicate woodland. Elms sprinkled with buds of palest green reached overhead in tall archways. As the end of the tunnel grew near Victoria caught a glimpse of sunlit meadows ahead, and then the Mini emerged into the open.

Victoria stopped the car and stared. She remembered the estate agent's details – two lower pastures fed by a stream, two fields of cereals, and some medium-quality grazing on the higher land. Twenty acres in all. Not a lot. In fact it was more of a smallholding than a farm.

But the house!

It lay at the end of a small valley, just above the stream, and was bound on two sides by rising ground. She loved it instantly. It was built of mellow grey stone with two dormer windows set into a slate roof. According to the agent it was a hundred and fifty years old, but it looked as though it had been there for ever, staring serenely across the tranquil valley.

Victoria just *knew* the others would love it too.

She drove on. The track dropped down into the valley through rich pastureland, passed over the stream at a narrow stone bridge, and rose up to the house. She parked in front of the house on rough gravel and, getting out, wandered round to the side where various sheds and outbuildings surrounded a concrete yard. Beyond were hen houses and a kitchen garden full of overgrown vegetables. She strode past the garden and up the hill, climbing higher and higher until she paused, panting, near the top. From here it was possible to see the whole property spread out below. Small, yes – but it had everything they would need to be self-sufficient. Well, *almost*.

High on the opposite side of the valley was the woodland through which she had driven. It had the effect of screening off the farm from the neighbouring property, making it somehow self-contained, almost *secret*. Victoria liked that.

In fact she liked everything about it.

At the same time she must be rational. It was a big decision. But if there was a catch, she couldn't see it. There was work to be done, obviously, things like painting and clearing up and general repairs, but that was part of the attraction, part of the challenge. Anyway, with eight people to do the work nothing would take very long.

She strolled along the side of the hill, picking at wild spring flowers, basking in a sense of contentment and home-coming. This was going to be the best thing that had ever happened to her, she just *knew* it.

The stillness was broken by the sound of a car bouncing down the track to the house.

The estate agent. Victoria ran down the hill and found an earnest young man getting out of his car.

He stared at her and blinked in surprise. 'Miss Danby?'

Victoria said a firm 'Yes', and realised he was taken aback by her age – or was it her clothes? Both probably. She looked younger than twenty-five and she was wearing one of her more psychedelic flower dresses. Doubtless he'd been expecting a farming type with brogues and a headscarf.

She said, 'It was nice of you to come on a weekend.' She offered him a spring violet. 'Have a flower.'

The young man took the flower awkwardly, then nodded in a knowing way, as if the tiny violet gave a clue to Victoria's appearance. News of the flower power movement had obviously reached this corner of Wiltshire.

They went into the house. The kitchen was dark and dirty, but Victoria was delighted to see that it had hardly been modernised at all. There was a coal-fired range, two stone sinks, a cool larder and, best of all, a large scrubbed kitchen table. The two living-rooms each had a ghastly thirties-style tiled fireplace, but these could soon be ripped out to reveal the originals underneath. Upstairs the four bedrooms had dark paint and gruesome wallpaper, but that could be stripped off in no time. Mentally she allotted the nicest bedroom to herself and Mel.

In the main hall was a door which led down some steep stone steps to a pair of large cellars, dark and cool, ideal for storing fruit and vegetables.

They went outside again. Victoria stood back and imagined the house in a year or so's time. Inside, everything would be bare wood and bright paint and Indian rugs. In the outhouses they'd have their craft workshops and storage for the farm implements. On the land they'd have goats and pigs, a few cows, a field of vegetables, an orchard of fruit. They'd work hard all day, and have discussions in the evenings, and music and singing . . .

It would be a real community.

'I'll take it.'

'Pardon?' said the agent. 'Er – you don't want a survey . . . or a look at the yields?'

'I'll take it, just as it is.' She smiled at her own rashness. Also at the pleasure in having surprised this rather straight-laced young man.

As she drove away she stopped and looked back.

Hunter's Wood. That was its name.

Hunter's Wood. Still and benign in the clear morning light.

She thought: I love it already.

Sir Henry Northcliff put down his pen and sighed. He wished that they weren't having to go out to lunch. He would have preferred to have had a light meal at home, gone for a walk on Hampstead Heath, and spent a quiet afternoon by the fire.

There was a soft knock and Caroline put her head round the door. 'We should leave in half an hour.'

He nodded. 'I'll have finished by then.' They smiled at each other. Whenever Henry looked at Caroline he was amazed by his good fortune. It seemed quite extraordinary that this lovely creature should be his wife.

He motioned her in and she came quickly over to the desk. They gripped hands. 'Six months tomorrow,' she smiled.

'And they said it wouldn't work.'

Their marriage had certainly been talked about. The wedding had been as quiet as possible and had taken place a good four months after Henry's divorce had come through, but it had made no difference. All the newspapers had carried the story, some with pictures. The gossips in Parliament and Lincoln's Inn had enjoyed a field day. It wasn't every day that the Attorney-General got married, and to a girl half his age. He knew what people were saying: that he was making a fool of himself. He knew equally well that it wasn't true.

'Will you have to work this evening?' Caroline asked.

There was a pile of legal gazettes which he should glance through, but he was loath to work that evening. With two dinners, a late meeting at Number Ten and a lot of paperwork to catch up on he'd been busy every evening that week. He replied, 'No.'

'Good! I didn't pursue you all these years never to see you at all.'

She touched his hand and left. He reflected on her 'pursuit' of him. It was utter rubbish, of course. Caroline was incapable of anything more forceful than calm resolve, and she had resolved to love him quietly and patiently from the time she was eighteen. He hadn't been aware of it then, of course. She was, after all, only a child, the daughter of a friend who had died long ago. But when his empty marriage had finally drawn to its long overdue conclusion, she had been there, quiet and understanding, the one person he felt at peace with. It was a year before he'd realised that she was right about the enormous age difference – that it didn't matter a bit. When they'd eventually married she had been twenty-five, he fifty. They had been exceptionally happy ever since.

The phone rang. It was David Garner, the Director of Public Prosecutions. David took many decisions with only the briefest reference to Henry, but anything with political overtones, anything that might 'develop', anything remotely sensitive, these things were brought straight to Henry as Attorney-General.

Henry had been so busy during the week, working on some proposed legislation the government wanted rushed through, that he and David had not been able to discuss all the outstanding business.

Henry guessed – correctly – that this call would involve the Oxford demonstration which had occurred several days before, on the previous Saturday. He pulled the file towards him and opened it.

'A total of thirty students have been charged now, all on breach of the peace charges,' the DPP began. 'But one has been positively identified with *both* assaults. A girl named Stephanie Kitson, who was seen to throw the brick which broke the window and injured the dinner guest. And also seen to whack the ambassador over the head.'

'And how *are* the victims?' asked Henry.

'The ambassador has a bruise on his forehead, but nothing more. Thank *goodness*. The other guest is recovering, apparently. No permanent damage, but several stitches in his head. There'll be a medical report, of course.'

'So, has this girl caused any trouble before?'

'No, but the police have successfully opposed bail – she's liable to disappear, so they think. She keeps announcing that she doesn't recognise their authority.'

Henry said, 'I see. Now, there were no other assaults. Is that right?'

'Correct. But some demonstrators held up chairs and waved them threateningly, others brandished banners, a table was overturned. So far only two people have been positively identified with these antics – names of Reardon and Lampton.'

'And neither has any previous form?' Henry asked.

'No, nothing at all.'

Henry thought for a moment. Violence during political demonstrations was a relatively recent phenomenon in Britain, one that was extremely distasteful to the average citizen, and he knew that the government were very keen to stamp on it hard. Particularly when an ambassador had been assaulted – and the US ambassador at that. It was politically extremely embarrassing and the press had been making a meal of it both in Britain and abroad.

And yet political considerations weren't really the overriding factor here. The point was, these demonstrators had to realise that they were subject to the law like everyone else, and that their political views did not excuse their actions in any way at all. Innocent dinner guests had a right to dine without being assaulted and abused. Besides, a man had been wounded. That on its own merited a serious charge.

'Right,' he said finally, 'if you're satisfied as to the evidence, let's go for actual bodily harm, assault and criminal damage for the brick-throwing lady. For the two who brandished chairs, affray. For the rest we'll have to leave it at breach of the peace. For the moment anyway.'

'Okay. Oh, and there's another girl out on bail, name of Linda Wilson' – the DPP laughed shortly – 'why are *women* getting so aggressive suddenly?'

Henry grunted in mystification.

'Anyway,' continued the DPP, 'they can't pin her to the demonstration. No positive identification at this stage. But they want to charge her anyway, with assaulting a police officer and resisting arrest.'

Henry asked, 'Where did they arrest her?'

'At a house in North London in the early hours of last Sunday, I think. The place where they found the Kitson girl.'

Henry could imagine it, the police rushing in, waking the occupants, giving them the fright of their lives. In his days at the Bar he'd defended enough people to know the outrage they felt at being hauled out of bed early in the morning, particularly if they were not habitual criminals.

'What sort of form did the assault take?'

There was the rustle of papers at the other end of the line. 'Er – an alarm clock to the head.'

Well, I'll have a look at that evidence in more detail, but my instinct is to forget about that one and concentrate on the offences at the demonstration itself. What do you think?'

They discussed it for a few minutes, and agreed the basic principles.

When the DPP had rung off, Henry considered the last matter of the Wilson girl. Yes, he was sure it was right to drop the charges. The student might have had a vindictive motive for assaulting a police officer but she could just as easily have been terrified out of her life. Besides in the eyes of the public and more particularly the media, dawn raids smacked of fascist tactics, and he didn't want to add fuel to that flame.

It was almost time to leave. He put the papers he'd been working on in his briefcase and tidied his desk. There was an hour and a half's drive ahead, just to go to a lunch with people he suspected he wasn't going to like very much. County types, rich. But they were distant cousins of Caroline's – second cousins by marriage, he seemed to remember – and she'd gone to stay there a lot when she was a schoolgirl. He must put a good face on it.

He went into the hall and found Caroline waiting with his coat. 'It's a lovely day,' she said. 'It'll be nice to get out into the country for a bit.' She shot an anxious look at him. 'I'm sorry if you're dreading it – I hope it won't be too boring.'

'I'm sure it won't.' He touched her cheek. 'Just give me a subtle kick in the shins when my eyes glaze over.'

It was either back to London or home to pick up her record player. Victoria decided on the record player. She could give Mel and the others the news by phone and tell them all the details when she got back to London.

Going home meant seeing her parents, of course. They wouldn't like her buying the farm, not at all. In fact, the thought of how intensely they wouldn't like it made Victoria feel a little nervous. But then she wouldn't tell them, not today anyway. She'd do it by letter during the week.

Cawsley Hall lay half an hour away on the edge of the Cotswolds, near the Wiltshire-Gloucestershire border, an imposing property situated at the end of a long drive in two hundred and fifty acres of park, paddock, and farmland. The house itself was a small but excellent example of early eighteenth-century Palladian architecture and, though the Danby family liked to think they'd lived there for ages, they had, in fact, only been in the house since 1890 when Alfred Danby, the son of a Bristol shopkeeper, made his first fortune from brewing.

As the house came into view Victoria winced. There were several strange cars parked in the front drive. She sighed. Weekend guests. She should have checked. She left the Mini out of sight at the side of the house near the walled garden and went in by a side door. She walked quickly through the gun-room, across the back hall and began to climb silently up the back stairs.

'Tor?'

Victoria spun round, then relaxed as she saw her sister in the hall below. 'God!' she exclaimed. 'I thought you were Mother.'

Diana giggled and shook her head. 'I saw your car. How *are* you? How's – *things?*'

'Are there many guests?'

'About four staying. But there'll be lots more for lunch.'

Victoria made a face and sat disconsolately on the stairs. 'Bother!' She hated parties, at least the sort her parents gave.

'It's all best behaviour stuff,' Diana went on. 'The county's coming – the Lord Lieutenant and Sir Harry Mortimer and the Gordons. *And* the Ranfurleighs! A coup for Mother.' She rolled her eyes. 'And of course there'll be Caroline and Henry—'

'Caro and Henry!'

'They're the *star* guests.'

Victoria was astonished. 'But Mother didn't *tell* me! *Honestly!*'

In the old days Victoria had often asked Caroline home for the summer holidays. Mother had tolerated the visits because Caroline was a distant relation, but there were other school friends she would have preferred Victoria to bring home. Now, ever since her marriage, Caroline was suddenly a bosom member of the family. Sometimes Victoria was amazed at her mother's transparency.

She said angrily, 'I mean, *honestly*, Di – Caro's *my* friend.'

Diana shrugged. 'Maybe. But Mother's been trying to get them down to lunch ever since the wedding . . .'

The sound of voices came echoing down a corridor. Victoria braced herself as Mrs Danby came into the hall carrying a vase of flowers.

'Ah, so you've decided to come after all! *Well* . . .' Mrs Danby looked at Victoria's clothes and made a visible effort to restrain herself.

Victoria said, 'I didn't know you were having a lunch party.'

'Oh yes you did. I told you. *Months* ago.'

Victoria vaguely remembered her mother mentioning it. 'But you didn't say Caro and Henry were coming.'

Immediately Mrs Danby was on the defensive. 'Well, darling, what if they *are*? We're very fond of them. Daddy and I have been trying to get them down for *ages*.'

'But—'

'Goodness gracious! I should have thought you'd be delighted. You haven't seen them in months, have you?'

Victoria dropped her eyes. How could she explain to Mother that it hadn't occurred to her to impose on Caroline's new life.

'Well, since you *are* here,' continued Mrs Danby. 'Daddy and I want to talk to you.'

Victoria had a sudden premonition of what was coming.

'Mr Rawlinson phoned me,' her mother said quietly and firmly, 'and he told me you had some funny ideas about Granny's trust.'

Victoria stared. She didn't think solicitors were allowed to tell tales. She protested mildly, 'But it's nothing to do with anyone else.'

Mrs Danby blinked at her. 'I beg your pardon.'

Victoria drew a deep breath and said with growing uncertainty, 'I can invest the capital in Granny's trust more or less as I like.'

'Well – !' Mrs Danby said with authority. 'I don't think that's true, Victoria—'

'Yes, it is.'

Her mother stiffened. There was a silence. Eventually she said coldly, 'I see. And what exactly are you planning to invest it in?'

'A farm.'

'A *farm*?' Mrs Danby exclaimed. 'Why a *farm* for goodness sake?'

Victoria said earnestly, 'Because I want to work on the land, to create things. To' – she searched for the right expression – 'to lead a meaningful life . . .'

'Ah!' Her mother pounced. 'Now, *wait* a minute. This isn't *you*, is it, Victoria? It's someone else who's been putting these ideas into your head. Am I right? A – *friend* – perhaps?'

'No.' Victoria lied. She'd never told Mother about Mel. Mel had hair down to his shoulders, wore embroidered clothes and had no job. She added defensively, 'Although certain friends *are* going to help me. It's going to be a co-operative.' The word sounded better than a commune.

Mrs Danby sighed long and loud, an expression of exasperation and exhausted tolerance. 'Well, I don't intend to discuss this any more *now*. I've got lunch to worry about. But I really think you're being exceedingly thoughtless, Victoria. *Exceedingly*.'

When she'd gone Diana said, 'Oh dear.'

'She can't stop me,' Victoria said unhappily. 'I can do it, Di. And I'm jolly well going to.'

A loud buzz of conversation was coming from the open door of the drawing-room. Going into rooms full of people had always filled Victoria with dread. She remembered all those agonising parties in her teens when, feeling huge and whale-like in some ghastly unsuitable dress, she'd clung to a wall, totally ignored, or been dragged across the middle of a room by the hostess, like a prize specimen across a show ring, to be introduced to someone who wasn't in the least interested in talking to her.

Some fears never faded. She drew a deep breath and went in. Her mother spotted her and, putting on her best hostess's face, came bustling over. 'Well!' she said tightly. 'Don't you look splendid, Victoria dear. Just like a Red Indian, with that' – she indicated the bright scarlet bandeau Victoria had tied round her head – 'thing! *Very* exotic!' She took Victoria's arm and cast round a little desperately.

At the far side of the room Victoria could see Caroline and Henry in a group of five or six people. Before she could move towards them her mother gripped her arm and, pushing her firmly sideways, said hastily, 'Come and talk to the brigadier for me, will you?'

The manoeuvre was too late; a brittle-faced woman was standing in front of them, waiting for an introduction. 'Ah, Lady Ranfurleigh,' Mrs Danby said with a nervous laugh, 'have you met my *other* daughter?' Then, retrieving the situation triumphantly: 'She's our *exotic* one, you know!'

Victoria thought: I'm going to scream.

Some drinks appeared. Victoria grabbed a gin and tonic and downed it in three. Lady Ranfurleigh was saying how colourful Victoria looked and how the young seemed to think they were the first young people ever to rebel, but of course that just wasn't true. She herself had been a bit wild in her time and worn rather a daring frock to the Savoy.

Spotting her father nearby, Victoria mumbled an excuse and backed away. She stood, uncertain, in front of him and said, 'Hello, Daddy.'

He smiled at her, blinking rapidly. 'Hello, old thing. What a surprise.'

In a surge of affection she reached out and hugged him awkwardly.

'I say, old girl. Well, well . . .' Embarrassed, he pulled gently but hastily back and patted her arm. 'You . . . er . . . keeping all right?'

'Daddy, I –' She looked into his face and grasped at the essential kindness behind it. 'Daddy, can I – *talk* to you later?'

A look of alarm came over his face, one she recognised well. She knew then that it was hopeless.

'A bit overdrawn, are you, old thing? Eh? Need some new clothes? Well, don't worry, I'll look after it . . .' He glanced away. Then, murmuring 'There's a good girl, there's a good girl', he was gone.

She stood still for a moment, working hard to make herself calm, then took another drink from a passing tray. It tasted good. She made her way round the edge of the room, head down to avoid strangers, and found herself in front of some canapés. She wolfed down half a dozen, then a few more, and felt better.

She found Caro and Henry still in a tight group. Someone was talking loudly about government policy on law and order and Henry was nodding vaguely, his eyes glazed with polite disinterest. Caroline was listening intently, her head inclined towards her neighbour. Victoria tugged at her sleeve.

Caroline turned and broke into a warm smile. 'Tor! How lovely to see you. I was wondering where you were. Gosh, it's been *so* long!'

As they talked Victoria was struck, as always, by Caroline's calm assurance. She had a rock-like core of honesty and serenity. Integrity: that was what she had. Victoria thought admiringly: She's everything I'm not.

Someone touched Victoria's arm. It was Henry. 'Well, well, how are *you*?' He kissed her warmly on the cheek. Victoria was pleased and flattered. She'd only met Henry three times, and she'd been a bit frightened of him. Yet here he was greeting her like an old friend. She smiled at him and wondered why she hadn't realised before how very nice he was.

He leant down and whispered conspiratorially, 'Good thing for everybody that you're here. You bring the average age in this room down at least thirty years.'

Victoria laughed and lurched to one side. She recovered, flushing with embarrassment. The gin had gone to her head. Henry looked politely away.

Lunch was interminable. On Victoria's right was the old brigadier. His breath smelled of whisky and stale tobacco. 'I say, rather like the garb!' he kept saying, as he eyed her dress. 'You a *flower* child, are you? Or a hippy? Never quite sure what the difference is meself. Tell me – d'you believe in all this make-love-not-war thing? I mean, it's all very well, but people will never stop being *aggressive*, y'know. Take it from me! I was a soldier.'

Victoria took a second, larger, helping of chocolate mousse and washed it down with more white wine. Her elbow slipped off the table and she realised she'd drunk a little too much.

In a moment of self-honesty of which she was rather proud she thought: No, not a *little* too much, a *lot* too much.

'What are you up to nowadays, Victoria?' It was a young man sitting opposite, the son of a local landowner.

'Setting up a collective farming project.' It sounded wonderful, put like that, except that she seemed to be having trouble getting the words out in a nice tidy row.

'Is that one of these *commune* things?' chortled the brigadier. 'Free love and all that? Gosh, all right if you can get it!' He leered at Victoria.

The young man said loudly, 'I knew a chap once who went potty and gave up everything to live in a sort of commune. Because the world had too many possessions or *something*. But really he wanted to opt out. Couldn't face responsibility. He was nutty as a fruit cake, of course. Quite mad.'

'Oh, I don't know,' hooted the brigadier. 'Got the *free love*, didn't he? Can't have been that potty!' He turned to Victoria and winked.

She stared, aghast. 'You think that's what it's all about! You think we – do it for *that*!' Her anger flowed out, white-hot and unsteady, a long passionate jumble of justification and explanation. Words mixed themselves up inexplicably, syllables jumped out of sequence, but she rushed on. 'We try to *care* about each other which is more than anyone usually does. *Society* – is so selfish an' *money*-centred. An' people pay *lip* service – about caring – but they *don't*. Not *really*. And peace. We care about *peace* and we make an *effort* to stop war. Which is more than any of the governments do. An' as for love – yes, sex if you like – it's open an' free an' *kind*.

Better than being hidden away an' joked 'bout an' *dirty* like *you* think it is . . .'

She suddenly became aware of her own voice unnaturally loud and ugly in her ears. Around her was an eerie silence.

At the far end of the long table there was a frozen, if blurred, tableau. Her mother's face, appalled and reproachful. Lady Ranfurleigh's, averted and embarrassed. And Henry, who was looking sympathetic and a little pained.

Victoria said under her breath, 'Oh shit!'

Conversations started to pick up again and Victoria stared hard at her plate, thinking: I don't care. And knowing perfectly well that she did.

After a few minutes she pushed back her chair and stumbled out of the room.

Caroline found her on her bed, crying miserably, and said quietly, 'Oh, *Tor.*'

'I'm sorry,' Victoria said, with all the dignity she could muster. 'I didn't mean to be an embrass –' she took another shot at it '– an embarr-*ass-ment* to you both.'

'Oh, never mind about *that*. What about you? Is there something the matter?'

'It's just – they were laughing at my farm. They think it's a joke. No one believes – or understands . . . No one's really *interested* . . .'

'But *I'm* interested, Tor. A *farm*? I'd love to hear about it. In fact' – she paused slightly, as if making up her mind – 'why don't you come over in the week and tell me about it?'

Victoria eyed her uncertainly, trying to suppress the dizziness. 'But – surely you're busy. I mean – aren't you?'

'I'm usually free for lunch. And sometimes in the evenings too. Henry often has to dine out. It'd be fun.' She patted Victoria's hand. 'Really.'

Victoria blinked and, gripping Caroline's hand, said, 'You know – you're very kind. Did you know that? Always have been. V-e-r-y kind.' She tried to bring Caroline back into focus, but without success. She shook her head and said in a small voice, 'Oh, Caro. Why's it all so difficult?'

Three

The British people had no idea how lucky they were.

Nick Ryder read the *Guardian*'s front page. He'd already gone through *The Times* and the *Telegraph*. There were serious riots in Paris, and the French had brought out the CRS riot police. The CRS weren't known for their gentleness and consideration – they went straight in with batons and tear gas and walloped you on the head. No British easy-easy tactics there.

But Nick wanted to understand the nature of this trouble. It had been started by the students – but why?

At eleven he went out and bought *Le Monde* from the newsstand at Victoria station. His French wasn't that good but he was able to get the gist of it. Three days ago, on the Friday, someone – either the Rector of Paris University or the Minister of Education – had called in the police to clear five hundred protesting students from a sit-in at the Sorbonne. By nightfall there were running battles all over the Latin Quarter. Hundreds had been wounded and almost six hundred arrested. The next day, Saturday, four students had been given two months in prison: unusually heavy sentences by any standards.

But what had caused the trouble in the first place? Nick ploughed through the editorials and after half an hour had the consensus of opinion. Gross overcrowding in the universities, childish old-fashioned rules, paternalistic overbearing university authorities . . . Yes, that would be enough to set most students off.

But was there more to it than that?

He called the DST in Paris, the French equivalent of a combined Special Branch and Security Service, and, after a long wait, spoke to the English-speaking liaison man, Claude Desport.

Nick began smoothly, 'Just wondered if there was any information you needed? Any way we could help?'

Desport replied wearily that he would appreciate a watch on the ports. 'We already have German, Italian and Dutch anarchists and Trotskyists,' he explained. 'You might as well let us know when your agitators are going to arrive.'

'We're keeping an eye out.' Nick knew from Conway, who'd been weekend duty officer, that the ports had been alerted to look for people on the political agitators list. Nick asked, 'D'you expect this trouble to go on for some time then?'

'Ah! Who can say? But I think – certainly.'

'Is it organised then, Claude? Who's behind it?'

Nick could almost see the Gallic shrug at the other end of the line. 'Impossible to say at the moment. But I think our trouble is our own.'

The moment he rang off, Nick got out the list of political agitators. It included members of anarchist groups, extremists of every political shade, and agitators who could be expected to turn up at whatever event was likely to cause the most trouble – rent-a-mob. There were pacifists who went on Ban the Bomb and anti-Vietnam marches – a lot of well-known faces here: actresses, churchmen, writers – as well as the purely political extremists.

The list was very long. The ports could never be expected to pick up so many names.

He went through the list carefully. Who out of all these people was most likely to cause the French real trouble?

He picked out twenty names from active far-left groups and, telexing them to Dover, Folkestone and Heathrow, asked for a special watch to be kept for them.

It was all he could do. With a bit of luck one or two of them might turn up.

But would it mean anything? He had the unpleasant feeling that there were many more figures in the shadows. Figures that had no names.

The train seemed to have reached the outskirts of Paris at last. Gabriele tapped her fingers impatiently against the window. It had taken a couple of days to scrounge enough money for the trip and now it was Thursday and she was quite certain they were going to be too late for all the excitement.

She turned to Max. 'Are we nearly there, d'you think?'

He didn't answer, but stared morosely at the opposite seat. He'd been in a deep depression ever since Stephie had been arrested two months before. Gabriele sighed, 'Come on, Max. This is *revolution*, for God's sake.'

She knew what was eating him: the thought of Stephie in that remand centre, and his own guilt at not having been caught. But the trial was coming up soon and then Stephie would be out with a suspended sentence and they could all forget about it.

Except that Gabriele couldn't forget. She still had terrifying nightmares. She dreamed that people came for her in the night and stripped off her clothes and took her into a brightly lit room full of cold watching eyes and left her there, naked and vulnerable . . . She woke from these dreams with an overwhelming sense of despair, as if she'd been defiled and raped. It was the kind of humiliation that never left you, even when your mind was occupied with other things; the kind of pain that made you shiver even after the memory of the incident itself had faded.

She'd only been held for two days, of course. And then they'd let her go. At the time she'd been relieved. Only later had she realised her mistake. It would have been much better to admit some part in the demonstration. Then they would have charged her. At her trial she could have defended herself, made a long impassioned speech, got publicity for the cause and shown her contempt for the judicial machinery.

It had been an incredible opportunity. And she had missed it.

Now everyone was talking about Stephie. Already there was a campaign to get her released. Already everyone knew her name . . .

At last the train crept into the Gare du Nord. In the main concourse Gabriele bought a copy of *Le Monde* and read it on the Métro. Thirty thousand people had marched up the Champs-Élysées the previous day in sympathy with the students and had brought Paris to a complete halt. Five Nobel prize winners had asked de Gaulle for an amnesty for the imprisoned students. And – Gabriele took special note – an opinion poll put four in five Parisians behind the students.

Gabriele had talked flippantly about revolution, but she realised with a slight shock that there was a good chance of it really happening. She wasn't sure that she was pleased; she wanted to be involved, to be an essential part of the movement and she vaguely resented the fact that she was not.

They got off at the Odéon and walked into the Latin Quarter. Police were everywhere – in large vans, in cars with screaming sirens, and manning the barriers leading to the Sorbonne, which had been sealed off since the weekend.

At the Students' Union in the Rue Soufflot, they were redirected to the Salle de la Mutualité, a large hall off the Boulevard St Germain.

They arrived to find crowds thronging the doorways. They

pushed their way through. Inside there must have been at least three thousand students, chanting, *'Libérez nos camarades! Libérez nos camarades!'*

Gabriele and Max made their way down the aisle to the platform, where forty or fifty of the organisers were gathered, standing in groups. Max led the way up on to the stage and Gabriele was relieved when he greeted several people by name, and introduced her. She had a fear of being left out.

A young man went to the front of the platform and raised his hand for silence. Everyone sat down.

Gabriele realised that it was Cohn-Bendit himself at the microphone. He began to give a dazzling display of the rhetoric and nerve which had made him leader of the *enragés*, the discontents who had started the protests against the university system. It was Cohn-Bendit who had stepped in front of the Minister of Youth and Sport at the Nanterre campus and asked him what he was going to do about the students' sexual problems – a reference to the strict segregation between girls' and boys' residential blocks. The Minister had replied that Cohn-Bendit should jump in a pool. 'That's what the Hitler Youth used to say,' retorted Cohn-Bendit. The conversation had been widely reported all over Europe and had become a part of student folk lore.

Now, as he talked about immediate reforms, Gabriele caught the electric atmosphere in the hall, the feeling that the changes he was urging would actually take place.

After long and enthusiastic applause a German went to the microphone, pledging solidarity from the students of West Germany. Then came a Belgian. Max whispered in her ear, 'Leader of the International Trotskyists.'

The next introduction was made, but it took a few moments for the name to sink in.

'Antonio Petrini.'

Gabriele tried to reconcile the figure standing at the microphone with the author of *The Revolutionary Society*. She had imagined him to be – well, more dynamic-looking. He was about fifty, and small, with a bald crown surrounded by a fringe of long straggly hair. His nose was large and he wore thick, black-rimmed glasses. Gabriele was disappointed.

But the audience had no doubts. They greeted him with loud applause, some rising to their feet and clapping their hands above their heads.

The moment Petrini began to speak, there was a hush. He spoke for less than five minutes in heavily accented French, pledging his support to the cause. He had a calm dignity and an impassive detachment that gave his words a tremendous authority. Gabriele thought: He isn't disappointing at all.

When he sat down again, she applauded loudly.

One of the organisers came over to Max and spoke in his ear. Max shook his head and, turning to Gabriele, said, '*You* speak.'

Gabriele stared, aghast. 'But I've nothing prepared!'

The organiser shrugged and started to move away.

Gabriele heard herself say, 'Wait – *je viens. Je parlerais.*'

She quelled the mounting panic and walked to the front of the stage, forcing herself to move with exaggerated confidence.

At the microphone she calmed herself and began in her best French: 'My friends, I bring you greetings from the students of Britain!' There was a small cheer. 'We too suffer from a repressive system.' She paused, aware that it sounded dull after Petrini's powerful words. Something different was needed. She licked her lips. 'You are an example to us all.' She raised her voice. 'Only two months ago I had a policeman astride me!' A roar of amusement and mock horror went up; she waited for it to fall away. '. . . The pig was pinning me to the ground, trying to make me see sense. *But*, my friends, all *I* could see was his great' – she searched for the appropriate word and hoped that '*cul*' was right for backside – '*son gros cul!*' They screamed with delight. 'Next time, I will follow your example, and give him a hail of bricks before he ever gets near me! You are our example. Long live the student movement. *Solidarité!*'

She raised a fist to the roof and walked away.

The applause rose in a great wave and roared over her. She grinned in pleasure. As she sat down Max patted her shoulder.

The next speaker went forward, and Gabriele tried to concentrate on what he was saying. After a time she became aware of being watched from the other side of the platform. It was a young man sitting immediately beside Petrini, a dark bearded man, lounging coolly in his chair. As she met his gaze he nodded at her and smiled. She was about to return the smile when she realised his admiration had more than a little suggestiveness to it. He was trying to attract her. She thought: What a nerve.

But she was in too good a mood to be angry. She gave him a brief dismissive smile and looked away.

It was only later, after the meeting had finished, that she realised the bearded man was with Petrini. That changed things considerably. The next time he looked at her, she held his gaze.

Two other men had particular reason to stare at Gabriele.

One was carefully dressed in casual clothes and held some text-books rather self-consciously in his lap. He was aged about twenty-five and had entered the meeting on a forged student identity card. He sat in the body of the hall and stared at Gabriele, trying hard to memorise her face so that he could pick her out from the central DST files back at headquarters. If he didn't find her there one of his informants would give her name and he would check with Special Branch in London to see if she was known there.

The man didn't worry about identifying the other speakers. He knew exactly who they were. Most of them had been on the DST files for some time. Cohn-Bendit, Petrini . . . The Italian had been involved with extremists for years, not just as mentor and guru to left-wing thinkers, but, it was suspected, in more concrete ways. He was known to visit Cuba frequently, also, more recently, Czechoslovakia.

The DST watcher had placed most of the others on the platform too, which pleased him. That was his job: to keep a track on the foreigners. France was a haven for deposed rulers and political refugees and had always been proud of it. Traditionally, these people had been welcome as long as they did not interfere in France's internal affairs. But appearing at this rally was interference of a serious kind, and most certainly would not be tolerated.

He stared at the girl again. Dark, very striking. Yes, he'd remember her face all right. Whether he'd ever manage to discover her name was a different matter. Many of his informants were difficult to track down at the moment.

The second man, also more observant than most, sat in the body of the hall, but further back and to one side. At fifty-four he was far too old to pass as a student, but then he didn't need to. Several of the people on the platform were acquainted with him and regarded him with great respect. He had dedicated his life to a cause of which they approved wholeheartedly. He was the champion of oppressed people, particularly in the Third World; the defender of those under the tyranny of imperialism and dictatorship; the protector of the poor and downtrodden.

He ran an organisation called Aide et Solidarité whose official function was purely humanitarian, helping refugees, exiles and those who were being persecuted for their political beliefs.

That was on the official level.

However, Aide et Solidarité had a second and distinctly unofficial function. It provided arms, papers, liaison, and every sort of logistical support for subversive groups in the free world.

The man, an Egyptian-born Jew named Duteil, was well known to the security services as an admitted communist who'd been involved in numerous liberation movements. He entered France clandestinely in 1953 and had actively backed the FLN, the Algerian nationalist liberation organisation, providing them with papers and arms. He had been imprisoned by the French until the general amnesty of 1962. Since then he had been deeply involved in national liberation movements in numerous countries – Angola, Mozambique, Haiti, Santo Domingo and Kurdistan.

In France itself, however, he had done nothing illegal, nor had he done anything to suggest he was interfering in the country's internal affairs. Thus he remained free to go about his business.

And now he watched. And listened. He knew Petrini well; they were old acquaintances. But he wondered which of these vociferous young people would in the years to come forget their anger and become model citizens, and which would never forget, but move forward to the point where they felt impelled to become active against capitalist society – which of them, in fact, he should get to know. The dazzling Cohn-Bendit? The next speaker, the earnest Belgian theorist? The funny, uncertain young English girl?

The only thing he knew from experience was that you could never tell.

It was four in the morning. Gabriele was in the young Italian's room.

She sat in a chair, regarding him with open interest. He was better looking than she had thought. The beard suited his distinctive features: the rich black hair, the long straight nose and dark hooded eyes. Very physical.

Yes, Gabriele decided, he would round the day off nicely.

His name was Giorgio.

He appeared to be Petrini's helper, his orderer of food and

fetcher of information, a role he played with the lazy amused feebleness of a child humouring a parent.

After the rally she and Max had met the student leaders – Cohn-Bendit, Sauvageot, Dutschke, the Germans, Belgians and Italians – over long discussions at the students' union.

Later Petrini had bought dinner for at least twenty of them. There was fillet steak and spring vegetables and plenty of good wine. Afterwards they went back to Petrini's room to talk again. In a series of brilliant submissions he had argued for the need to polarise the two halves of society and to demonstrate to people how empty and meaningless their lives really were. To do this dissidents had to be properly organised in active units. If necessary they must be prepared to use force to highlight the ruthless repression of the system . . .

Gabriele had followed his arguments carefully, grasping each thought and storing it carefully away in the back of her mind.

Afterwards she remembered one phrase in particular: '. . . people need to have the injustices of the world demonstrated to them, so that their own thoughts, which may be no more than suspicions, shall be crystallised in their minds . . .'

Crystallised . . . That word again.

But now it was four in the morning, and the talking had stopped. Everyone had gone to bed. Max had found a floor somewhere. And she was here, with Giorgio. She had already decided to sleep with him. She liked making these decisions in isolation, at her own whim. That way she kept control.

Now she glanced around the comfortable hotel room. 'This is very grand,' she remarked. 'Do you always live like this?'

'Petrini does,' Giorgio replied slowly. 'So when he pays, I live like this too.' He spoke English with a heavy Italian accent which she liked.

She wandered round the room to show that she hadn't made up her mind to stay. She was still high on the wine and the charge she'd got from the speech, and she wanted him to make a play for her, so that she could hold back and exasperate him a little. It would be more exciting that way.

'Do you work for Petrini?' she asked.

He seemed amused by the question. 'No. I work for myself.'

'Well? What is it you do?'

He shrugged, immediately bored by the question. 'I do what I want.'

'Are you . . .' She hesitated. The question she wanted to ask was difficult to put directly. 'Are you an *activist*?'

He gave her a long stare, as if considering whether or not to take her into his confidence. Then he raised his eyebrows and smiled suggestively. 'Of course.'

She realised he had purposely misunderstood her. She said impatiently, 'I mean, are you involved in a dissident group?'

He sighed. Deliberately ignoring the question he said, 'I'm tired. I'm going to bed.' He turned and walked into the bathroom.

Gabriele stood in the centre of the room feeling piqued. He was deliberately excluding her. Her vanity was hurt. She had almost made up her mind to leave when he reappeared in the bathroom doorway.

'Please,' he said reasonably. 'We've talked enough . . . All of us. Enough for a long long time.' Examining her face he added suddenly, 'But if you insist – *yes*, I am committed to direct action. Of course!'

She blinked, reluctantly impressed. 'I see.' She had a vision of him leading a charge of demonstrators into a line of police. Then she remembered that the Italians had probably gone much further than that and she allowed new images to develop in her mind. She pictured him hiding out at secret addresses; planning a campaign; perhaps even using a gun. The images were attractive and more than a little exciting.

'Okay?' he asked.

She smiled. 'Okay.'

'I am going to bed now,' he said. Then, matter-of-factly: 'Will you come with me?'

A few moments ago she would have kept the matter in doubt much longer, just to show that she had control of the situation, just to demonstrate that she despised his arrogance.

But now there was no need. He understood what she wanted from him: access to the right people, the means to learn. Now it was a straightforward arrangement of mutual convenience. The matter was decided.

The afternoon of the 10th May began quietly enough with a rally in the Place Denfert-Rochereau attended by students, school children, teachers, trade unionists and sympathisers of every age and sort. At six-thirty came news that at long last the government had made some conciliatory proposals. But *not* about the

49

imprisoned students – they were not to be freed.

A great roar went up: *Libérez nos camarades!*', and the crowds marched on the Santé Prison. A mass of police prevented them from reaching the prison walls and they turned away, heading for the Maison de la Radio, the government-controlled broadcasting centre on the Right Bank.

The government ordered all bridges across the Seine to be blocked and then they closed off the Boulevard St Germain – another ill-judged decision. Now the students were hemmed in on the Left Bank. They had nowhere to go: only back the way they'd come or into their own territory, the Latin Quarter.

The student leaders hurriedly conferred and announced their decision.

They would take the Latin Quarter and hold it at all costs.

It was the beginning of the worst violence Paris had seen for thirty years.

The news spread through the crowd like a bolt of electricity and the students ran for the Latin Quarter, fanning out through the maze of narrow streets around the Sorbonne.

Gabriele ran with Giorgio and it was only when she looked over her shoulder that she realised Max was no longer in sight, lost somewhere in the crowd.

They ran until they were short of breath, and found themselves in a small street to the south of the quarter among a group of about two dozen students. Already a car had been dragged into the middle of the street.

Then Giorgio had an iron bar in his hands and was hacking at the ancient cobblestones, trying to lever them off the road. Another car was pushed into the street and was rocked violently until it fell on its side with a loud grinding noise.

Gabriele searched desperately for materials, tugging ineffectually at gratings and street signs. Then she saw that Giorgio had got under the *pavés* and was levering them up fast. She joined the chain carrying stones to the rapidly growing barricade.

Later, when it grew dark, they were joined by more students, trade unionists and sympathisers, until there were over a hundred people in that one small street alone. Food and drink were brought by well-wishers and residents of the quarter. Everyone paused to eat. The atmosphere was warm with comradeship and the exhilaration of shared danger. Gabriele felt an overwhelming sense of achievement and well-being. Impulsively she put her arm through Giorgio's. She thought: I love it all.

A messenger roared up on a motorbike with information from the student leadership. Massive reinforcements of riot police were encircling the quarter.

The group set to work with fresh ingenuity, raiding building sites, tearing down scaffolding and barbed wire, until by midnight the barricade had grown into a formidable wall of cobblestones, cars, wire, and jagged metal. Gabriele armed herself with a metal bar torn from the frame of a shop's window-blind.

The CRS were sighted at two-ten. Gabriele felt her mouth go dry. Slowly, without urgency, the riot police formed themselves into ranks at the far end of the street. They made a sinister sight: the rows of long black coats, the invisible faces, the goggles and helmets, the shields which glinted darkly in the street lights. Someone shouted, '*Pigs! Fascists!*'

At two-fifteen a deathly silence fell, broken only by the sound of shuffling feet. The line of raised shields was moving towards them.

Gabriele took her position half-way up the barricade, adjusted the handkerchief round her mouth and gripped a cobblestone in her hand. She wasn't frightened any more; the adrenalin was making her light-headed, almost euphoric.

A shouted order, and the black line paused. Snub-nosed pistols were pointed in the air and fired. Missiles with long white tails sailed up and over the barricades. The air became thick with sharp pervasive gases . . . Gabriele pressed the handkerchief to her face, but the gas seeped through, stinging viciously at her eyes, stabbing at her throat until she choked.

A low rumble echoed along the dark street. The rumble grew to a clatter, a crescendo of batons beating on shields, and the black line was charging forward, unchecked by the hail of stones, *pavés* and missiles from the student lines. Gabriele stood up and hurled a cobblestone wildly into the darkness, then bent down to pick up another.

Suddenly she realised that the gleaming black figures were mounting the barricade. Dropping the cobblestone, Gabriele reached for the iron bar at her feet and grasped it tightly.

Quickly, so quickly it took her by surprise, a dark shape loomed up in front of her. The figure swung his arm up in a high arc, a baton clutched viciously in his hand.

She lashed at him with the iron bar. The metal made contact and swung back to hit again. The figure swayed as if off-balance. Then it was twisting to one side, the arm coiling back like a spring, and too late she saw the baton coming rapidly savagely down.

She raised an arm against the blow, but it caught her on the side of the head, a dull sickening jolt of pain. She fell back, the sounds of the battle ringing in her ears.

Another blow thudded on to her shoulder and with a cry she rolled down the mound of stones to the ground.

She covered her raging head, but there were no more blows. Through her dim agony she could hear the sounds of the fight: thuds, cries, shouts, boots scrabbling on the stone . . . Then the *whoomph!* of a small explosion and the crackle of fire. With an effort she crawled away, searching for the shelter of a wall, a doorway . . . Suddenly a foot in her side, a body falling over her and running off . . . Cries of pursuit growing fainter . . . Then quieter – just the crackle and spit of a fire nearby.

After some time she felt hands grasp her and started in alarm. But the hands were gentle, the voices soft. They pulled her to her feet and led her to a lighted interior. A cloth wiped her head, soothed her burning eyes . . . Rest, a soft pillow . . . Ah – peace.

She lay still for a long time until the pounding in her head dulled to a sullen throb. Outside, it was quieter. As much as an hour had passed. Dimly she concluded that the fight must be over. She dozed uneasily.

Suddenly there were sharp obtrusive noises: the sounds of heavy vehicles and shouted orders and doors opening.

Confused and alarmed, she opened her eyes and tried to understand.

Harsh voices, boots on the stairs.

What on earth—

The fear leapt into her throat. Through the door came black helmets, faces invisible . . .

She stared incredulously.

It was a bad dream relived, a second nightmare, except it was real again. She thought: *I'll die if they touch me.*

They grabbed her and she gasped. They pulled her to her feet. She yelled, '*Let go, you pigs!*' They were pawing her, searching her. A gloved hand came close to her mouth and she bit it hard, meeting flesh through the leather. There was a cry. She struggled and kicked out. They grabbed at her arm and, catching the wrist, twisted it harshly up her back.

She thought: *I'm going to go mad.*

She screamed and kicked out with her feet, finding a target. There was a shout of anger.

The next moment her head exploded and a wall of blackness closed in on her.

Through the blackness she heard someone groaning loudly and realised it was herself. Then, as if in a dream, she was being half-dragged, half-carried across a hall and down some stairs into the street. A veil of warm wetness covered her smarting eyes and there was a strange sweetness in her mouth. She was hauled roughly over stones and heaved backwards into a van, the metal floor cold and hard on her skin.

She mustered her strength to gasp, 'Fascist Nazi pigs! Fascist bastard pigs! Fascist—!'

Then the doors slammed shut and there was nobody to hear.

The night of the 10th May became known as the Night of the Barricades; over sixty makeshift barriers were thrown up in the streets of the Latin Quarter. From all over Paris thousands of young people, manual workers and professionals, rushed to the students' aid until the CRS riot police were faced with an enormous army of guerrillas. The fighting raged for four hours and was remarkable for its savagery and hatred.

But if the hand to hand fighting was bloody – beaten heads, broken limbs, four hundred seriously injured – it was the mopping up operations which were remembered with most bitterness. The injured dragged from stretchers to be beaten up for a second time; a Negro thrown into a van to emerge with a battered bloody face; girls stripped and taken naked into the street; innocent passers-by attacked. In many areas the police took their opportunities for revenge.

Local residents and onlookers were horrified. So too was most of France. The next day the government tried to mediate, but it was all too late. The workers and the students were united. Within two days there was a mass anti-government demonstration of over eight hundred thousand people. Three days later more than nine *million* workers were out on strike. A student soviet occupied the Sorbonne and several provincial universities were taken over. Even members of the most respected professions – the doctors, lawyers, scientists, musicians – rebelled, questioning the outdated structures in which they worked.

The revolution had arrived.

The hospital room was white and brilliantly lit and hurt her eyes. At least two days had passed, though she wasn't absolutely sure. At one point the police came and demanded her name. She closed her eyes and didn't answer.

They returned with her shoulder bag which she supposed they had found somewhere near the barricade.

They held out her passport.

Linda Wilson.

She smiled because it didn't matter if they knew that name.

Another night came – the third? – and a voice obtruded into her consciousness. It whispered urgently 'Gabriele! Gabriele!' Someone was shaking her.

She stared into the semi-darkness and saw two figures leaning over the bed. One of them was Giorgio. Already they were pulling her out of bed and wrapping a coat round her shoulders.

She said, 'I knew you'd come.'

Four

The weather was blustery but fine, and the coast of France was clearly visible across the straits. On the green, white-flecked sea beyond the breakwater a ferry turned in a stately arc to negotiate the eastern entrance to Dover harbour.

'She'll be docked in about seven minutes,' said the local Special Branch man. 'D'you want to come down to the desk or watch through the window?'

'The window,' Nick Ryder replied. He didn't want to be seen.

He picked up the batch of names and photographs, tapped his pocket to make sure he had a pen, and followed the officer down to the observation room.

The room was sited high in the wall of the immigration hall and had a large one-way window so that it was possible to look down on all six of the channels unobserved. Nick settled down in a chair and spread out the photographs on the shelf in front of him. Picking up a pair of binoculars, he practised focusing them. Below, the local Branch men were stationed behind the immigration booths.

The first passengers came into the hall at a rush, anxious to get to their trains and coaches. Then came the families and shoppers, hampered with children, large amounts of baggage, and trolley loads of French food. Orderly lines formed in front of the immigration booths.

Nick scanned the lines carefully, but there were no familiar faces. At the far end of the hall the slower passengers shuffled in: a group of older people; some young hikers with enormous back-packs . . .

He sat up. And some faces.

Yes. Several he recognised.

He took one at a time, matching each face to the list or, where he had a photograph, to that as well.

Ellis, Bishop, Wheatfield . . .

He tried to remember something about the first two although, as Marxists, they didn't strictly fall into his Section. Ellis: International Marxists and CND; Bishop: International Marxists and Vietnam United Front. The third was Wheatfield, Max. International Trotskyists and now Socialist Students' League. One of his.

Within ten minutes he had fifteen out of the seventeen names. He'd probably missed the other two in the crowd. He watched the last passengers pass through the channels, but there was no one else.

He made his way back to the immigration office and waited. The local man came in and announced, 'All accounted for.'

'I missed two,' Nick admitted.

They checked their lists and decided he'd missed the two who had passed through first.

'Well, that's nice and tidy for once, then,' said the inspector.

'As long as none of them sneak back into France,' Nick pointed out, 'or decide to start something similar here.'

The local man shrugged and put on a look that said don't let's worry about that now.

Nick made a call to Claude Desport at the DST in Paris and said, 'Can't say I'm grateful, but all seventeen have been received. Will there be more?'

'Another nine or ten tomorrow,' Desport replied, and gave him a list of names. 'If we find any more you'll have them within twenty-four hours.'

That's what Nick liked about the French system: any aggravation and it was immediate expulsion, with no chance of appeal.

'But there are – let me see – *three* we cannot send back to you,' Desport was saying. 'Two decided to go over the Belgian border, and a third decided to – er, stay.'

'Stay?'

'She got away. Her name is . . .' There was a pause. 'Wilson, Linda. If we pick her up again, we will let you know.'

Linda Wilson. The name rang a bell, but it took a moment for Nick to place it. Of course. The raid after the Linden House Hotel affair. The girl on the stairs. He had a fleeting vision of her body, long and beautiful, then, with an effort, closed his mind to it.

Three unaccounted for.

Nick reflected that the local men had been somewhat premature. Nothing was ever neat and tidy.

Gabriele forced herself to stand up. A moment later, when the dizziness had passed, she walked unsteadily from the bed to the window. She looked down into the street. It was quiet. There was nothing to suggest that, five days after the Night of the Barricades, the country was virtually at a standstill. Six million were on strike, so the radio said: train drivers, dustmen, car workers, lorry drivers, professional people; and the numbers were still increasing. The uprising had grown beyond the students' wildest dreams.

The street was quiet because the quarter was quiet: this apartment was a long way from the Latin Quarter. Gabriele was restless. She wanted to get back to the centre of things. She had already decided to leave the next day and go in search of Petrini and Giorgio.

Not that she hadn't been looked after. The apartment belonged to a young priest who brought her food and occasional news. A doctor came twice a day and shone a light into her eyes and gave her tablets to take away the pain in her head. Then there was a woman journalist who called every evening, to check on her. It was almost as if these people were part of a well-established organisation. But this was never confirmed and, after asking twice, Gabriele did not ask again.

Now she went back to bed and slept until evening. When the priest returned she told him she would be leaving the next day.

He frowned and suggested it would be unwise to be found on the streets without papers. After he left the room, Gabriele heard the slight ping of the telephone bell. Later, when the priest reappeared with some food, he said, 'You will be collected at three tomorrow afternoon. To make arrangements about your papers.'

Then Gabriele knew without any doubt: there was an organisation. She wondered what else it provided.

She was dressed and ready by three the next afternoon. She felt much better; the worst of the headache had gone.

At half past three the doorbell finally rang.

It was Giorgio.

She said, 'You're late.'

He shrugged good-naturedly and ignored the remark.

As they went down to the street Gabriele cast him a sidelong glance. He had come to visit her at the priest's apartment three days before, but only stayed ten minutes. He'd been restless and impatient, and she'd had the feeling that he was irritated by her incapacity. But now he was bright and attentive, and she was aware that he was trying to please her again.

'Your head is mended?' he asked as they got into his car.

'I'm all right.'

'Ah. That is good.' He seemed relieved.

He drove off fast, ignoring one set of lights that had just turned red, and shooting rapidly into the Avenue Leclerc. There were few cars about and no buses or traffic police. The city seemed half-abandoned.

Giorgio laughed. 'In the car, when we took you from the hospital, you moaned so much I thought you were dying.'

'My head was hurting. But it's all right now.' The memory of the pain was fading. She remembered feeling sick and feverish, but she could no longer conjure up the agony of the pain itself.

But she had forgotten nothing about the Night of the Barricades nor the way in which she had been injured. She had played the scenes of the two assaults over and over in her mind until each moment was etched vividly on her memory. She cherished the details; they were valuable.

Giorgio was driving steadily north towards the Latin Quarter.

She asked, 'Where exactly are we going?'

'I was given an address. A photographer's. I was told to take you there.'

'Who by?'

He shrugged. 'Friends of Petrini. But I don't know who *precisely.*'

She looked at him sharply. Was he telling the truth? If not, why

57

was he holding back? He must trust her now, surely.

'What happens after the photograph?'

'You will have papers. You'll be free to move around.' He paused. Looking across at her, he added, 'I am staying in the apartment of a friend, near the Sorbonne. There is room. If you like.'

Gabriele thought: He trusts me after all.

She considered. She wasn't sure she wanted to get too involved with this man. She sensed he was unpredictable, difficult even. On the other hand, his connections were too useful to give up. Particularly since he was in contact with this organisation.

She said, 'All right.' Then added, 'It'll be much more convenient.' She didn't want him to think she was moving in because of him.

They parked to the south of the Latin Quarter and picked their way on foot through narrow streets whose surfaces had been almost completely torn away, and whose sides were still littered with stones and burnt-out cars. Finally they entered a doorway beside a second-hand bookshop, and climbed some stairs. On the first floor was a small photographic studio. A man emerged from a back room and shook hands. He did not offer his name.

He sat Gabriele on a stool in front of a camera and rolled down a plain black background.

'Look straight at the camera.'

There was a flash and Gabriele blinked.

The photographer said, 'I'll need some details.'

She gave him her height and age. 'What languages do you speak?' he asked.

'English, French, a little Italian and German.'

The photographer scratched his head. 'At the moment I can only offer you Turkish, Dutch, or Argentinian. Perhaps Argentinian would be best. There are many people of English origin living there.'

Giorgio said, 'Take Dutch. It's safer. No one speaks Dutch.'

The photographer indicated that it was all the same to him. 'What about names?'

They went through some ideas, and decided Anneke van Duren because it was easy to pronounce. The photographer said, 'It'll be ready by tomorrow evening at six. Will you pick it up?'

As they emerged into the street, Gabriele looked for the house number. Eleven. And the name of the street: Rue Vauquelin. She filed it away in her memory. She still did not know the photographer's name.

They walked back towards the car.

Giorgio said, 'We'll go back to the priest's and pick up your things.'

'No,' she said carefully. 'I'll move tomorrow. When I have my papers.'

He shot her an angry look, and strode on ahead. He drove her back to the Porte d'Orléans in silence.

Outside the priest's she said soothingly, 'We'll have dinner tomorrow night.' She brushed his cheek with her hand. 'It'll be nice.'

He looked at her resentfully. It was his turn to be piqued. She was glad. It wouldn't do him any harm.

Eventually he gave a faint nod of resignation. 'Tomorrow.'

She got out of the car and watched him drive away. The moment he was out of sight she turned her back on the apartment and set off down the street. In the Avenue Leclerc she looked round uncertainly. She knew the buses were on strike, and probably the Métro too. She didn't have the money for a taxi. In the end she put out a thumb and a motorist stopped. He dropped her near the Latin Quarter.

She walked back through the narrow streets until she came to the Rue Vauquelin. She went to number eleven and looked at the name plates inside the front door. *Studio Vincenne – photos commerciales et portraits.*

She mounted the stairs, and listened outside the photographer's door. The sound of voices came from inside. She went down to the street and waited in the second-hand bookshop, browsing through the shelves near the window.

Half an hour later two men emerged from the side door into the street. One of them was the photographer. He shook hands with the second man and walked off.

Gabriele replaced the book she had been reading and went out into the street. The photographer had crossed the road and was walking unhurriedly away with his hands in his pockets.

Gabriele took a brief look over her shoulder and followed.

In the quiet embassy building on the Boulevard Lannes the Soviet Second Trade Secretary scanned the back copies of *Le Monde* for any last scraps of information that might flesh out his report. The report needed all the padding it could get. As the senior officer of the Paris Residency's Directorate K (First Chief Directorate, KGB) it was his job to know what was going on. Normally he liked to think he did. He had excellent contacts in the PCF (the French Communist Party), the FGDS socialist alliance, and the left-wing trade unions such as the communist-controlled CGT. But themselves taken by surprise, they had not been able to tell him very much. This uprising had sprung from small student groups about which there was little information. For one thing, they were newly formed; and for another, the groups were for the most part vehemently anti-Soviet. He had re-emphasised this in his report, both to explain his failure to predict events and to prepare the Centre for a continuing lack of information in the future. He hoped the message had sunk in.

Having said that, he had to try to discover what these students were all about. Over the last month *Le Monde* had carried interviews with most of the student leaders, who had talked of capitalist repression and reactionary forces and of the need for a socialist revolution in the Third World. This, he felt, was the key. This was the spot where they could be reached and their idealism turned further to advantage.

He fiddled with his pen, wondering whether to stick his neck out. Putting forward policy ideas was a risky business – it could earn you credit or a firm slap down and delayed promotion. He hesitated a moment then added a footnote: 'Despite the idealism and independence of the various new extremist groups in France and other West European countries, they are unlikely to be averse to logistical support when it is offered *indirectly*, through pro-Soviet Third World countries whose cause they champion, or by established organisations such as Aide et Solidarité. Help in the form of direct funding will be met with suspicion. It is suggested, therefore, that the support offered by Aide et Solidarité be stepped up to meet the requirements of these new groups.

'It is unlikely that we will be able to exert any influence over these groups either by infiltration or by threatening to control their logistical support. However, this need not be a major concern, since any acts of a disruptive or terrorist nature carried out in capitalist countries will, by their very nature, be destabilising.'

He laid down his pen. It was a fair assessment, though perhaps he had stuck his neck out a bit far on that last statement. Until now Aide et Solidarité had mainly provided support for Third World groups. Now he was suggesting that all other subversive groups, regardless almost of doctrine, should be encouraged. He just hoped it matched the current line of thought in Moscow. He switched a few words round to improve the flow, then sent it to be typed and encoded.

Later he made a telephone call across Paris, to a director of the Banque Commerciale de l'Europe du Nord (BCEN) in the Boulevard Haussmann. 'I have put in a few words for additional funds for your export friends,' the Second Trade Secretary said. 'I feel confident they will get all they need.'

The statement was acknowledged and the call terminated. The bank director wrote a brief note on a pad to remind himself to call the import–export company, which was a customer of the bank's, and speak to one of its directors. There was no point in calling just at that moment, as he knew the director would be out. And there was no secretary to answer the call. That was because the company did very little business.

The bank director knew a great deal about the import–export company because the bank covered the company's frequent over-drafts with loans. The loans were made without collateral and no interest was ever charged. Furthermore, all payments for goods and services imported or exported were made by draft through the bank. Not that any goods were actually transported. They existed solely on paper, and were merely a means of channelling funds into the import–export company. These funds – like the loans – originated from the country which owned and controlled the bank, which was the Soviet Union.

The two directors of the import–export company were both Frenchmen who also kept personal accounts at the bank. One of the few employees of the company was Bernard Duteil, known as Raymond, the head of Aide et Solidarité. In fact, his salary from the import–export company was his sole source of income, and Aide et Solidarité itself existed on funds provided by the import–export company.

On the memo pad the bank director made a further note to tell the director of the import–export company that a back-up request for additional funds had been made.

A board meeting of Aide et Solidarité was held that evening. There were more than twenty people on the board, including a Domi-nican priest, a Protestant pastor, a famous left-wing political philosopher, and various Paris intellectuals. It was fashionable to be a member of the Aide et Solidarité organisation. It showed that you cared about the worldwide anti-colonial struggle, the current cause beloved by the radical chic.

Many who sat round the table that evening chose not to think about how Aide et Solidarité was funded. For them it was enough that it existed at all. And although some of them knew that the organisation regularly produced false papers for those in need, only two of them were aware that arms, explosives, training and liaison were also provided. One of those people was, of course, Duteil, alias Raymond, and the other his deputy.

The meeting had originally been called to discuss two items: the accommodation of foreign refugees, and the next anti-Vietnam war demonstration.

However, not surprisingly, the discussion quickly turned to the revolt. Despite its rapid progress the final outcome was far from certain, everyone agreed. Admittedly the workers had latched on to the student movement very quickly and had been quick to come out on strike, but their motives were dubious. A great number of them, far from challenging the capitalist state, were perfectly happy with it. All they wanted was a larger slice of the cake. If the government dangled higher wages and the promise of greater representation in front of them the revolt might easily fall apart.

Horror was expressed at this possibility. The radical chic liked the idea of the workers sticking to their principles even if it meant turning down higher wages.

The discussion then turned to support for the revolt. It was pointed out that the organisation had many safe houses. Could they not be offered to students being sought by the police?

Duteil interrupted immediately. 'You all know that Aide et Solidarité cannot and must not help them. If we assist those who are fighting the French government, we will be closed down. We are only tolerated as long as we stay out of French affairs.' He offered a palliative. 'What you do as individuals, however, is your own affair.' Duteil shot a meaningful glance at the Dominican priest. The priest acknowledged it with a blink, unnoticed by the others.

The matter was dropped and the discussion moved on to other matters. Half an hour later Duteil brought the meeting to a close.

The priest stayed behind after the others had gone.

Duteil shook his head and said wryly, 'I have broken my own rules. I hope I'm not going to regret it.'

'The girl knows nothing.'

'I hope not.'

They walked the short distance from the luxurious offices which were lent to them for board meetings, to the offices of Aide et Solidarité, which were somewhat less well appointed. In accordance with its role as supporter of the poor and oppressed, Aide et Solidarité possessed three shabby rooms, two almost empty and the third with the bare minimum of furniture, including two battered desks, some chairs, two filing cabinets, and a couple of ancient typewriters.

The photographer was waiting for them. His role in the organisation was an important one. Quite apart from taking photographs, he was a master-forger. He could produce French identity papers and driving licences that were indistinguishable from the real thing. But for the most part his skills were used to produce passports. The organisation possessed a stock of well over four hundred blank passports stolen from various consulates around the world. The master-forger used his special talents to produce the embossing tools and stamps of authentication required. He enjoyed his job very much. Duteil saw to it that the job also paid well.

'What passport are you giving the English girl?' Duteil asked.

'Dutch.'

'You don't have a British one for her?'

'Not at the moment.'

Duteil thought for a moment. He didn't like the idea of the girl using the Dutch passport in France. She might well be arrested for a second time. The police would then discover she wasn't really Dutch. Worse still, they might match her face to that of the missing British girl. Either way, they would know the passport was a fake. And then they would want to know where it had come from.

Duteil decided his first duty was to cover himself. He had already broken his rules by helping someone who had been 'subverting' the French state. The only thing in his favour was that she was not a French citizen; that really would have been asking for it.

He didn't regret helping her. Her speech at the Mutualité, though rather flippant, had been different – funny, impressive. It had stayed in the mind. Just like the girl herself.

Also she was British. There were two reasons why this made a difference. The first was that there were no hardliners active in Britain at that time, and he rather liked the notion of encouraging one. The second – and more important – reason was that, though a Jew, he had been born and brought up in Egypt, and there were few educated Egyptians of his age who hadn't despised the British occupation of their country.

No: he didn't regret helping her. But his first duty was to himself.

'I think we must be careful,' he said. 'I think we must only provide her with the passport as she is about to leave the country.'

'I said she could have it tomorrow,' the photographer replied.

'Well, you'll have to say it is no longer possible.'

'If she stays in Paris she'll need papers of some sort,' the priest pointed out.

'We'll have to persuade her not to stay in Paris.'

There was a rapping at the outer door. Unhurriedly Duteil went to answer it. He wasn't expecting anyone, but there was nothing unusual about casual callers from among the many refugees living in the city under the organisation's wing.

Duteil turned the latch and swung open the outer door.

It was the girl.

He took a deep breath. 'Good evening,' he said eventually. 'What can I do for you?'

'The gentleman from the Studio Vincenne. Is he here?'

So that was how she had found the place. He stood back. 'You had better come in.'

He closed the door behind her and led the way down the passage into the main office. The girl entered the room and, seeing the priest, looked surprised. Then she smiled slightly as if his presence confirmed something.

'We were just talking about you,' Duteil began immediately. 'I'm afraid we think it unwise for you to remain in France.'

'Why?'

'Because the authorities know all about you. They have your passport. If they arrest you again, they will soon realise your new passport is not genuine. It would get us into a great deal of trouble. We – are reluctant to let that happen.'

She nodded. 'I understand.' She did not look too unhappy at the thought of leaving.

Duteil asked softly, 'Why did you follow us here?'

'I wanted to talk to you.'

'Yes?'

She chose her words carefully. 'I was hoping you could help me. In the long term.'

There was a silence.

'Ah.' Duteil nodded slowly. He turned to the other two men. 'We will meet another day.'

When the priest and the photographer had gone Duteil sat down opposite her and lit a cigarette. 'What sort of help did you have in mind?'

'Papers. Passports. Contacts . . . You see, I don't know how to go about – organising myself.'

'What exactly are you hoping to achieve?'

She gathered her thoughts. 'I want to – activate groups in England. Freedom groups. To operate against organised repression. To – *expose* the repressiveness of the Establishment. To show people what the system is *really* doing. The anger is there,' she added, 'the injustice, the repression. People just can't *see* it. The situation needs to be polarised – *crystallised*.'

'You follow Petrini.'

A flicker of surprise crossed her face.

Duteil smiled. 'Petrini is an old friend of mine.' He asked thoughtfully, 'You have no training?'

She stared at him. She obviously wasn't certain of what he meant. She said uncertainly, 'No.'

He considered for a moment. Her philosophy was raw and undigested. She had little idea of what was involved in being an activist. Yet she had qualities that impressed him: determination and straightforwardness.

'Then may I suggest something?' he said eventually. 'Why don't you join an existing group – a group who share your ideals – and learn from them?'

'There are none in England.'

'Quite so. I was thinking of Italy.'

'I speak hardly any Italian.'

He shrugged. 'That may be an advantage. You can always pass as a tourist.'

She blinked. 'What would they teach me?'

'A great deal, I think.'

'Who are these people?'

'Well . . . They have a name of sorts. Lotta – "struggle". But

65

the name is not important. What is important is that they have been active for some time – a year or more. They have experience.'

She thought hard. 'I have no money.'

'I will give you some travelling expenses.'

'Oh – and when I'm there?'

'The group will look after you. They have – er – benefactors.'

She nodded, slowly absorbing the idea. 'Then – when I come back – you'll help me?' she asked.

'As far as I can. But you must understand there'll be no money. You will have to do your own fund-raising.' He could see that she hadn't thought that far ahead.

Nodding briskly, she said, 'That's fine.'

It was a firm rule of Duteil's – one he never broke – that, apart from small amounts of cash handed out to refugees, he provided no money, and certainly not to hard political groups. He was happy to provide logistical support and training free of charge, and weapons at very reasonable prices. But large quantities of cash were out of the question. For one thing, there would be no end to the financial demands of the groups. For another, the money would be traced back to him sooner or later and eventually – God forbid – to its source. There would be an almighty international row. He would be closed down and considerable embarrassment would be caused to Moscow.

But as long as these new groups financed operations by robbing banks in their own countries, then he could not be accused of direct interference.

Indicating the poorly furnished room, he said, 'As you see, we are not a wealthy organisation. We rely on our friends for financial support.' It was true up to a point – voluntary subscriptions were always welcome. However they covered only a small amount of the running costs.

Duteil decided that further discussion was best avoided: the less the girl knew about Aide et Solidarité at this stage the better. He stood up. Catching the hint, she got to her feet and they shook hands.

She said, 'You won't help any other British group, will you? I mean, before me?'

Duteil shook his head.

They walked to the door. He said, 'You will get some travelling money, an air ticket and an address in Milan from the priest.'

At the door she turned and faced him. She was a very striking woman. She said, 'I want to do it properly, you understand that?'

'I understand. That's why I have agreed to help you. That's why I think you should go to Italy first.'

She paused. 'I don't know your name.'

'I'm known as Raymond.'

She shook his hand again. 'Goodbye, Raymond. I'll be back.'

He nodded. 'Yes, I have no doubt of that.'

When she had gone Duteil considered what he had promised, and was satisfied. He would not offer help to any other British activists because apart from a single group of unpredictable anarchists there *were* none. Even if a new group did spring up he doubted any leader would be quite as ambitious or determined as this girl. When she returned he would give her all the help he could.

She might not return, of course, but then she would not have been worth the trouble anyway.

But he had a feeling about her. She would return. He gave her six months.

Five

'You were injured in the fighting?'

Henry Northcliff said with emphasis, 'Only slightly.' He didn't want any false heroics creeping into the article.

'And where was that?'

'At Jarama, during the battle for Madrid. In February '36.'

'How old were you?'

'Just eighteen.'

The young journalist scribbled on the pad and referred to his list of questions. They were sitting outside, under the copper beech tree. Henry turned his face to the sun and thought how nice the garden was looking. Caroline had worked very hard on it. The borders were a bright mass of colour and the lawn had lost its patchy uneven look.

It was July. The summer recess was only a week away. Then at long last he and Caroline would have a holiday.

The journalist cleared his throat. 'What influenced you to go to Spain? Was it entirely your own idea, or were you one of a group?'

Henry made the effort to think back. It was such a long time ago that he could barely remember all the reasons for his decision. Eventually he replied, 'I came from a family who were very politically aware – *involved*. My parents felt very passionately about it.'

'For the Republicans?'

'Oh, yes!' Henry laughed. It was impossible to imagine his parents being for anyone but the people.

'So were you a communist at that time?'

'Now let's get this quite clear,' Henry said firmly. 'I was a fervent *socialist* at that time – as indeed I am now. The International Brigade included all sorts of people with all sorts of beliefs – including communists. But just because we fought together didn't mean we shared identical beliefs. So, let's not be confused about *that*.'

The journalist didn't like being talked down to, but he'd got the message, which was just what Henry intended.

The young man asked, 'So was it your family's idea for you to go?'

'Oh no, the idea was mine. I went entirely on my own initiative. Because I felt that one must follow things through and put one's beliefs into action.'

'Do you still believe that?'

Henry drew a deep breath. Journalists always tried to push you into a trite, quotable remark. He wasn't going to fall into that trap, he'd been in the game far too long. But at the same time he must produce a good reply and today it was rather an effort. It had been a long hard week.

'I believe you must do all you can to bring about the system that you believe is just—'

'Not by *any* means surely—'

'*No*. By political means.'

'But how do you define political means?'

He was fishing, Henry decided. Looking for a statement that he could apply to a specific issue. Henry wondered which one. He replied, 'Political means are the means of political expression which are permitted by the law of the land.'

The journalist came in quickly, 'Does that include demonstrations?'

Henry thought: Ah, so that's it. The Paris uprising. He hedged, 'Peaceful demonstrations are perfectly legal, therefore they are valid political means.'

'But demonstrators using violence are to be punished excessively?'

'I really cannot speak for what's been happening in France.'

'France? Oh no, I meant closer to home.'

Henry suddenly realised where all this had been leading. 'You are referring to the Linden House convictions, I take it?'

The journalist exclaimed, 'Of course. A three-year sentence for a first offence is excessive by anyone's standards. And you must admit that the convictions have been highly unpopular.'

He was right about that: the outcry had been considerable. There had been questions in the House, leading articles in most of the newspapers and hot debates in the correspondence columns of *The Times*. He remembered the final paragraph of one leader: 'These sentences are, presumably, designed to deter future demonstrators from the use of excessive violence. However, where the punishment is seen to exceed the crime, the effects may be quite the reverse, and serve to inflame the very young people whom it is intended to deter.'

Privately Henry thought the sentences were excessive too, but it was out of the question for him to say so.

'As you are aware,' he said firmly, 'I can only comment on the prosecution of the case, not on the sentences. But as the judge commented, it is immaterial whether violence stems from gang warfare or from political motives.'

'Do you agree with that?'

The aggressive young man was getting on Henry's nerves, but he said calmly, 'Yes, of course I do.'

'Although you yourself fought for your beliefs in an illegal manner?'

Full circle. And not a very subtle circle at that.

'If you want to be pedantic about this, wars usually *are* legal.' Suddenly he was impatient with this intense rather unlikeable young man. 'But *really* – is this worth debating?' He rose to his feet. Realising the interview was over, the journalist closed his notebook with a snap.

Caroline met them coming across the lawn and, grasping the atmosphere immediately, took charge of the journalist to show him out. Henry returned to the chair under the tree, annoyed with himself for agreeing to give an interview on a Saturday afternoon. He liked to keep his home as separate from his work as possible, and now the loveliness of the garden seemed a little spoilt by the aggressive young man.

Spain. The memories, sharp yet vague, echoed in his mind. He'd been desperate for action, he remembered. Burning with righteousness. And bitterly disappointed when he'd been wounded after a scant two weeks in the Brigade. It had all been very intense. He'd never felt quite so passionately about anything since.

He supposed the young people who'd terrified the diners at the Linden House Hotel felt passionate too. But their actions had been provocative and wantonly dangerous. And that was the difference.

Caroline re-emerged from the house and he got up to meet her. She said, 'The young man left looking less than happy with his interview.'

'Well, I was less than happy with it too. I'm used to getting stick in court and the House, but I object to smart-alec questions from a young man who's merely trying to prove a point.' He gave a short laugh. 'Actually, his principal mistake was to catch me on a Saturday when all I wanted to do was sit in the sun with you.' He squeezed her arm. 'Why don't we sit out here and have tea? Just us.'

'Ah . . .' Caroline looked a little sheepish. 'We've got a visitor.'

Henry groaned. He hated it when people dropped in. 'My God – *who*?' he asked peevishly.

'Victoria. She swears she's only staying a minute.'

It could have been worse, Henry decided. It could have been Victoria's mother.

They found Victoria in the kitchen. Henry blinked at her. The Indian outfit of a few months ago had been replaced by a floral yokel costume of quite astonishing design. There were enormous baggy trousers in vivid yellow, a loose top in white embroidered with large flowers whose colours took your breath away, and a battered old straw hat on top of the mass of fair hair. Just in case you failed to notice all that, she also had flowers painted on her cheeks.

'Cor,' said Henry. 'Don't you look rural.'

Victoria grinned and kissed him on the cheek. 'I'm only popping in because I *know* how busy you are – but I just had to bring you *this*.' She delved deep into her shoulder bag and brought out a jar which she waved triumphantly in the air. 'Honey!'

'Good Lord! Where did this come from?' Henry asked, already knowing the answer.

'From the farm! Isn't it wonderful?' She threw her head back and laughed and Henry was struck by the intensity of her happiness. He found himself smiling too.

'Don't tell me you got hold of some bees and persuaded them to produce in four weeks flat.'

'No. *silly*.' She creased up her nose, taking the teasing in good heart. 'We found them in an old hive at the far end of the upper meadow and the honey was already *there* . . . But we got it out! Isn't that amazing!'

Knowing the experience that Victoria and her friends had of farming and bee-keeping, Henry thought it probably was.

'And we've got two cows producing milk,' continued Victoria. 'And a goat. Oh *and* we've bought a pig. We've named her Bella. She's absolutely gorgeous!'

Henry guessed that the animals on the farm were going to live long and happy lives without fear of the slaughterhouse. 'How's all the work going?' he asked cautiously. 'The renovations and so on?'

'Oh, we're all working like mad,' breathed Victoria. 'From dawn till dusk. We've done two roofs and cleared out the yard and got the kitchen scrubbed and *planted* things and . . .' She shook her head. 'Honestly, it's *terrific*.'

Henry couldn't resist asking, 'And how's the communal decision-making going? Do you have solemn pow-wows at the end of each day?'

Caroline shot him a warning glance but he avoided her eye.

Victoria giggled. 'No-o-o. We just discuss things round the kitchen table. There are only six of us, after all.'

'I thought it was going to be ten.'

'Well, the others weren't really committed, so . . .' Suddenly she was kissing Caroline. 'Must fly. I only came up to see my stockbroker.'

To sell more shares, no doubt. Henry wondered how much the whole exercise was costing and if anyone else in the commune was chipping in. But he was afraid he knew the answer to that.

'By the way,' Victoria said on the doorstep, 'perhaps you'd better know . . . Mother's not best pleased, so I'm keeping clear of her for the moment.'

A wise move at the best of times, Henry wanted to say.

When the Mini had disappeared up the road, Caroline turned

and said, 'Oh dear, I do hope it's going to work out. She's so desperately keen to be happy.'

'If only that were enough.'

He closed the door and, leading Caroline through the house into the dappled sunlight of the garden, gratefully pushed all unwelcome thoughts from his mind.

The briefing meeting was already under way when Ryder arrived. An officer of the Security Service was speaking. The Security Service – known in the Met as Box 500 after its internal mailing address, and never by its more famous name of MI5 – regularly briefed Special Branch. The officer today was Reece-Jones from the 'F' Branch of Box 500, which covered extreme political parties on both right and left. Nick knew him well: Reece-Jones specialised in the Left. That didn't mean to say that the two men got on. On the contrary, Nick sometimes wondered if Reece-Jones didn't come from another planet. Or perhaps all Box 500 men were secretive and obscure.

'According to the latest reports,' Reece-Jones was saying, 'bar a few minor strikes, the workers have all returned to work. De Gaulle's government is firmly back in the driver's seat and the revolt has well and truly collapsed.'

The eight Special Branch men fidgeted in their seats. It was very hot and there was a fault in the air conditioning. Detective Chief Superintendent Straughan, Ryder's boss, sat sprawled in his chair, his shirt sleeves rolled up over his heavy forearms, beads of sweat running down his cheeks into the plump folds of his neck. The DCS roused himself and asked, 'So what's happened to all the French troublemakers? Any coming our way?'

'Not as far as we know,' replied Reece-Jones. 'But obviously we are interested in any political group who might try to start trouble of the same kind here. Specifically, it has now been decided that we would like you to keep a closer watch on certain Leftist groups. You're already familiar with these organisations, but now we've got to take an even closer look at them.' He handed out a duplicated list. 'We want to know about their leadership, about their links with known communists and subversives. It is quite a task, we realise.'

Nick read the list. All the organisations were well established, and some quite large. There were eight of them, ranging from the International Marxists to the Vietnam United Front and the

Campaign for Nuclear Disarmament. Nick raised his eyebrows. 'Why are the peace campaigners included?'

Reece-Jones replied in a tone that suggested the answer was obvious. 'They are communist based, and they've got strong links with the World Peace Council.' It was well known that the World Peace Council was Soviet-backed and had been manoeuvring behind the scenes for years. None the less, Nick felt that Box 500 were on the wrong track.

He said, 'Surely these people aren't about to start a revolt in the Paris style?'

'No, maybe not,' said Reece-Jones defensively. 'But their aims are still subversive, and it has been decided to keep a much firmer eye on potential troublemakers.'

Straughan gave Nick a look that suggested it might be best for him to shut up. But Nick continued, 'Well, if we're looking for real troublemakers shouldn't we be looking at the latest splinter groups?'

Reece-Jones took a deep breath. Nick sensed that the intelligence officer wished he was back among his colleagues in Box 500 where the atmosphere was more co-operative. Reece-Jones said patiently, 'Well, I think we have to concentrate on the main groups, the ones on this list, because they're the ones *known* to be communist-controlled. They're also the most *organised*.'

Nick frowned. Reece-Jones – and the rest of Box 500 for that matter – had tunnel vision when it came to looking for Soviet and orthodox communist links. That was virtually all they were trained for. Which was all very fine when there were spies and fully-fledged Soviet-trained subverters around. But the students weren't like that. Most of them had rejected conventional communism. But he was on to a loser here, he could see that. The policy had been decided somewhere in the Ministry of Defence and it wasn't going to be changed on his say-so. He decided to shut up.

Reece-Jones brought the briefing to a close with a resumé of the information Box 500 itself would be providing.

'We're putting taps and mail intercepts on all the leaders of these organisations who have communist contacts or sympathies. This information will be available to you as necessary.'

Nick thought: Like hell. Box 500 were notoriously mean with their intelligence. Their attitude was guarded and, if not actually obstructive, then distinctly unhelpful. Nick suspected this was partly because they were all public school and Oxford and stuck together, and partly because they regarded Special Branch as a force which existed solely for their convenience – to do all the dog's work and to make arrests for them.

Reece-Jones was summing up. 'So what we need is a record of these people's movements and who they associate with, the things they write and for which publications' – he smiled ingratiatingly – 'but then I don't have to tell you what we need, gentlemen. You've done it all before.'

Nick winced slightly. The flattery was unnecessary and more than a little patronising. He resented it. He glanced at Conway and saw that he did too, but then, like Ryder, Conway had spent some time out in the big wide world of regional CID. Which was more than ninety per cent of Special Branch ever had. In fact, Ryder and Conway were something of an experiment. Men with outside experience. And, Ryder sometimes thought, the only people used to getting things done.

When Reece-Jones had gone Straughan continued the meeting. 'Right, we're going to go into the mechanics of all this tomorrow, when the commander has okayed the deployments. In the meantime, let's tidy up some loose ends.'

He darted a look at Nick. 'Ryder, what about your lot? The students seem to have been reasonably quiet, thank God.'

'Well – maybe. But Paris has certainly given them ideas.'

The DCS looked displeased. 'Oh?'

'In Italy the disturbances are spreading like wildfire—'

'But *Italy* . . .' The DCS made it sound as if it were a faraway country reachable only by mule. 'What goes for Italy and France doesn't necessarily go for here. I mean, our students aren't as bolshie or as well organised, are they? *Also*,' the DCS added emphatically, 'the defeat of the French students is bound to make them think twice, isn't it?'

'On the contrary. I think it might *encourage* them.'

There was a heavy silence. The DCS frowned. Eventually he murmured, 'Well . . . We'll see, we'll see.'

Nick thought: I'm wasting my time.

'What about the students expelled from France?' asked Straughan. 'What news of them?'

The French had expelled twenty-four British students at the height of the troubles. Nick looked at his notes. 'Most of them have resurfaced in their usual haunts,' he reported. 'Two have made fairly inflammatory speeches, but that's nothing new for them. Oh, and three are still astray. Two went to Belgium and haven't chosen to return to the UK yet. The whereabouts of the third, a girl name of Wilson, aren't known. She was on the expulsion list but gave them the slip.'

'Any other loose ends?'

'Only a student leader who spoke at one of the big Paris rallies back in May. The DST report that her name was Schroeder and that she was British. But we can't find any trace of her, either in Passports or Naturalisation. Nor can French immigration – no one entered the country under that name. Bit of a mystery.'

Straughan grunted. Things like that were always happening. He looked at his agenda. 'Okay. So, what have we got coming up in the next few months?'

Nick went through the list of events being planned by Trotskyists and allied extremists, from a large anti-Vietnam rally in Trafalgar Square to recruitment drives in the universities. He brought up a final point. 'There's still a lot of aggravation over the sentences in the Linden House Hotel affair. There was another minor demonstration in Oxford only yesterday.'

The DCS said, 'Yes, well, that was bound to happen, wasn't it? Thought they were special, didn't they? Well, now they realise that they go to prison like everyone else. But the aggravation will die away in time,' he said with an air of absolute confidence. 'They're just letting off steam.'

He sat back in his chair. 'So, nothing to suggest that our Trots are up to anything in particular?'

Nick resisted the impulse to ask if the DCS wanted them to make a declaration in writing. Reluctantly he shook his head.

'Good,' said the DCS, 'let's get on to rent-a-crowd. I'll bet that's where the next bout of aggravation is going to come from.'

Nick sighed inwardly. It was back to the professional industrial agitators, Straughan's favourite bogey men.

Later, when they filed out of the meeting, Nick muttered to Conway, 'Should have saved my breath.'

As Nick threw the papers on his desk he reflected that the DCS's ideas were like the Ten Commandments: etched in granite.

The files on the expelled students lay on the desk. He glanced through them. Most of the information was painfully thin. Photocopies of passport applications and photographs. In ten cases a bit more: known membership of political parties or groups; an address. In two instances, arrests at demonstrations.

Not a lot.

He picked up the files on the three students who had failed to return to England and took another look. He wanted to be sure he had memorised the names. Cook, Appleyard, Wilson. He peered at the photographs one by one. They were typical passport pictures, that is, pretty awful. The one of the girl was particularly bad. Her face was a white blur with black dots for eyes, like a couple of currants in a rice pudding. She looked terribly young. The picture must have been taken when she was still at school. It was almost impossible to tell what she really looked like.

Roll on the day when the British had photographs on their identity cards or driving licences, then there'd be more to go on.

He had another fleeting memory of the Wilson girl's body at the house in Kentish Town, and reflected that if he'd been a better copper he would have paid some attention to her face.

As it was he had no decent picture. That was because someone had boobed. Though the girl had been held after the Linden House Hotel affair, no mug shots had found their way on to the file. When a charge against someone was dropped there was a strict rule that the negatives and prints were destroyed. That was, *officially*. But in practice Special Branch usually managed to 'acquire' a few copies on the quiet. However on this occasion someone somewhere had been excessively stupid – or stuck rigidly to the rules – and none had got on to the files.

He put the file into the tray to return to Records.

Cook. Appleyard. Wilson. At least he had the names. The ports had been posted. They'd turn up sooner or later.

It was late September, during the last hot gasp of summer.

The warmth of the day lingered in the stillness of the night. Gabriele could feel the heat rising from the dry dusty earth, drifting up through the pines towards the transparent blue-black sky. Beneath her, the hillside fell away in a series of slopes and ridges down to a wide valley. In the far distance another spur of hills, ink-black against the sky, reached away towards the higher ranges of the Apennines to the north.

It was very beautiful.

She raised the binoculars to her eyes and focused on the hills opposite. She watched for a long time, occasionally lowering the glasses to rest her eyes.

Then at last it came. A slight flicker of light.

She never heard the *woomph!* of the explosion itself; the distance was too great. Nor, unfortunately, was she near enough to see the brand new Mercedes enveloped in a ball of fire.

The tiny flutter of light died away, then rose up again, flickering gently. Suddenly a bright bolt of white flame leapt into the air, much higher than the first, and a distinct *crack!* floated across the valley.

Soft footsteps sounded behind her, and Giorgio laughed, 'An oil tank, eh? Or bottled gas.'

The new flame was voracious and spread steadily, forming an oblong block of fire that illuminated the surrounding hills. Soon the whole house was burning.

Gabriele watched impassively. It was no more than the owner of the house deserved. The man, an army general, was a fascist and a murderer. The fascist secret society of which he was a leading member extended into every branch of the Italian establishment, including the police and judiciary.

The general had ordered the bombing of a Bologna bank. Ten innocent men, women and children had died. With suspicious rapidity the authorities had arrested a group of harmless anarchists, and announced that the case was closed. The fascists looked after their own. The general would never be brought to justice.

The firing of his car and house was scant punishment. To Gabriele's mind he should have been executed.

She turned and led the way back through the woods. Suddenly there was a loud screech above their heads. Instantly Gabriele swung the Kalashnikov up into her hand, and sighted up the barrel.

'It's only an owl,' Giorgio murmured.

She slid the catch on to automatic and listened. The screech came again. She adjusted her aim and squeezed the trigger. The rifle rattled deafeningly at a hundred rounds a minute.

She stopped firing and listened. It was very quiet. 'I must have got it,' she said with pleasure.

They continued through the woods. Gabriele cradled the Kalashnikov under her arm. At over eleven pounds loaded weight the rifle was heavy for a woman – so she had been warned – which was one reason why she'd been determined to master it. It also had the disadvantage of being almost three feet long, which made it difficult to carry around unobtrusively. But she didn't care. The

77

Russian-made rifle was the king of weapons; she liked the weight and security of it in her hands.

She'd learnt to use other weapons too: the small ultra-light Skorpion automatic machine pistol, a short-range weapon, easily concealed and therefore ideal for urban missions, and the Makarov pistol, a handgun that each of the group used as a personal weapon.

But she liked the Kalashnikov the best. This one belonged to a leader of the Lotta; it was on loan for the evening. One day very soon she would have one of her own.

They came to the rough road where they had left the car. Leaning against the bonnet, Gabriele paused and lit a cigarette.

Giorgio hovered impatiently by the driver's door. 'We should go. Someone might have heard.'

She shook her head in the darkness. 'No, they couldn't have heard. We were too far away. We will wait here a while. It's safer.'

Giorgio acquiesced, as she knew he would, and settled down to wait. She had long since discovered the key to Giorgio's character. It was quite simple. He had a terror of being bored. And he got bored very easily. Indeed, left to his own devices, he was incapable of escaping it. He needed someone to take the initiative, to create the situations that stimulated him. As long as the promise of excitement was dangled in front of him, he would follow. And the person he followed was Gabriele. She enjoyed her power over him, just as she enjoyed the power of the rifle.

After half an hour they got into the car and drove towards Bologna and the Milan *autostrada*. Gabriele kept the Kalashnikov across her lap the whole way, but they saw only one police car, and it showed no interest in them.

They arrived in Milan at dawn. Giorgio was about to turn the car into the street where they lived when Gabriele gestured him to continue past and park some way beyond. Gabriele walked slowly back, turned into the street, and sauntered up to the apartment building. Making a show of searching for her keys, she took a good look round.

Nothing.

She went up to the apartment and checked it. When she was satisfied that everything was quiet, she went back to the car and unloaded the weapons into a large suitcase.

'You worry too much,' Giorgio said.

'It's impossible to worry too much.'

Once in the apartment Gabriele made some coffee and sat at the window, watching the street. It was unlikely that the police would suspect her or Giorgio directly – they'd been too careful for that – but suspicion could easily fall on them through the others. The others were often less than cautious. The man who had actually made the incendiary was known to the police. So were at least two of those who had planted the device. Yet they made little effort to be careful: like good Italians, they still visited their families and friends regularly. Also everyone in the group knew everyone else, if not by name, then by face. Security was appalling. No one thought of operating in small cells. They liked the camaraderie of large and frequent meetings.

Gabriele didn't want to be caught for someone else's carelessness. In Italy they put you in jail and threw away the key. You were lucky if your case came to trial within three years.

The more active the group became, the more nervous Gabriele felt. She had an intense dislike of being at the mercy of other people's decisions.

Eventually she left the window and joined Giorgio in bed, sleeping uneasily with the Kalashnikov beside her on the floor. She awoke at three in the afternoon and, still restless, went for a walk. She shopped for food and, for the first time in weeks, bought an English newspaper. She also went to the poste restante section of the main post office in Piazza Affari and, using her Dutch name of Anneke van Duren, asked for mail. Unusually, there was a letter. She recognised Max's handwriting.

Taking the envelope to a quiet corner of the post office, she opened it.

She reread the first part of the letter twice, to make sure she had understood.

Stephie's appeal had been refused.

The full three and a half years would have to be served.

Gabriele's first thought was: Thank God it wasn't me.

Three and a half years. She tried to imagine it. Holloway: dark, depressing. The other women: lesbian, ill-educated, cruel, scornful. The cell: cream-painted, tiny, *claustrophobic*. Three years. *God* – for *ever*.

She suppressed a shiver; she couldn't have taken it. Even though she might have become a famous martyr in the process.

She allowed herself a moment of satisfaction: avoiding that charge had been the smartest thing she'd ever done.

She read on. Max's scrawl was almost illegible. He must have been almost hysterical when he wrote it. The situation was desperate, he said. He had tried everything – he'd organised petitions and protest marches, written to MPs. It had done no good. He begged her to think of other tactics he might try. Did anyone over there have any ideas? He felt that everyone who'd been on the demo had a responsibility to Stephie, to help her, to get her free. Gabriele *must* help! The situation, he repeated, was desperate.

Gabriele thought: It's not my problem.

She owed Stephie nothing. They'd all run risks that day. The difference was that Stephie had been stupid enough to lob that brick. *And* get caught.

Gabriele tucked the letter into her bag and put it out of her mind.

On the way back to the apartment she stopped for a coffee and read through the British newspaper. The news reflected the usual preoccupations of a capitalist society: the bank rate, growing inflation, the number of strikes. The strikes, she noted, were not reported as a sign of workers' desperation, but as a bad omen for world trade and the profits of the fat capitalists.

And yet the stories interested her – very much, in fact. She discerned a strong current of pessimism. The newspaper seemed to think that everything was going to get much worse – strikes, inflation, trade. Reading between the lines, they seemed to be worried about a possible recession and widespread social unrest.

As she walked back to the apartment Gabriele reflected that social unrest would give rise to all sorts of opportunities – opportunities that shouldn't be missed. But how long would it take for the situation to deteriorate? She would have to study the British news regularly to make sure she kept in touch.

Giorgio was watching television when she got back. He was obviously morose and bad-tempered. He would be better later, when he'd had a few drinks. In the meantime she left him well alone.

At six a news bulletin was announced. With pleasant anticipation, Gabriele settled down to watch. She imagined the newscaster's opening words: *Last night the home of the distinguished soldier, Generale Fausto Lamberti, was gutted by fire* . . .

The newscaster appeared. He began to speak.

The smile vanished from Gabriele's face. She listened incredulously.

'. . . Generale Lamberti was shot in the knees as he left a restaurant in Milan last night . . .'

She stared at the screen, speechless.

It was nothing short of betrayal.

The others had kept their main plan a secret. They had purposely not told her. They had not trusted her. She had been excluded. It was a bitter humiliation.

Angrily she stood up and switched off the television.

She thought suddenly: This is the end.

'We'll leave tomorrow.'

Giorgio shot her an angry look. She touched his cheek. 'Will you come with me?'

'Where to?'

She said carefully, 'To Britain. Eventually.'

Giorgio asked resentfully, 'But what is there to do in Britain?'

'What there is to do,' Gabriele said, 'is to operate on our own. And to drive in the first splinter.'

PART TWO
October 1969

Six

Nick Ryder turned into the grim dark street near King's Cross and thought: It's places like this that make people give up hope.

The Barley Mow was half-way along, its tattered red and white façade the only splash of colour in the unremitting grey of the largely derelict buildings. Above the pub hung a sign depicting an incongruous sunlit harvest scene complete with joyful farmers.

Nick pushed open the ornate glass doors of the public bar and paused while his eyes adjusted to the darkness. It was already one-fifteen but Nugent wasn't there. He wasn't surprised; he'd been dealing with Nugent for eighteen months now, and the man was never on time. Buying himself half of bitter, he sat down in a place where he could watch the door.

The other occupants of the bar were students, railwaymen on their midday break, travellers who frequented the numerous cheap hotels in the area. Nick could only guess at their occupations, of course, but he was rarely wrong. He'd made a habit of watching people ever since he was a kid in Barrow, hanging around outside the Crown, waiting for his dad to come out.

It seemed a long time ago. It seemed a long time since he'd joined Special Branch. Almost three years in fact. It was eighteen months since the Paris uprising.

Nugent eventually turned up at two-fifteen, dirty, dishevelled, and jumpy as a rabbit. One look at his sunken eyes and white glistening skin and Nick knew that Nugent was in a bad way.

'Hi,' Nugent began in an urgent whisper, 'got things for you.' He reached awkwardly into a trouser pocket and, with a shaking hand, pulled out some much-folded papers. 'Latest stuff. Hasn't been around before.'

'Let's have a look then.'

Nugent held on to the papers, his eyes darting nervously up and down. 'It's good stuff. Er . . . Ten quid maybe?'

'Price of horse gone up, has it?'

Nugent exhaled through his teeth. 'Yeah. Prices are high – *high*.'

'I'll see what I can do. But I've got to look at the stuff.'

Nugent hesitated and Nick could see that he was reluctant to part with the papers before firming up on the deal. But defeated by his own desperation he suddenly handed them over. Nick glanced through the material. Three different broadsheets. Nothing amazing . . .

And a pamphlet.

He stared at the cover. This was different all right. Trying not to show too much interest, he flicked slowly through it and almost gasped.

Nugent leant forward in his seat. 'Something, isn't it?'

Nick thought: You can say that again. During his time in Special Branch he'd never seen anything like this.

Aware of Nugent watching him he made an effort to hide his excitement. 'It's *okay*,' he conceded. 'Though I've seen quite a bit of it before.'

'*Can't* have,' Nugent said sharply, 'It's new.'

'Maybe,' Nick admitted quickly. 'Where d'you find it?'

Nugent looked away and muttered evasively, 'Dunno . . .'

Nick handed him twenty pounds in fivers. 'Here. But I can't promise that much every time. It always depends on how good the stuff is. Understand?'

Nugent's hands clutched the money as if it were about to save his life. 'Gotta go now.'

Nick said quickly, 'If you find any more like this, you'll let me know?'

Nugent started to get up. Suddenly he paused, his face taut with indecision. 'There's something—'

'Yes?'

'A split.'

'Where?'

'In the SSL. And in other groups. Maybe.'

'What other groups?'

Nugent fidgeted nervously. 'Dunno. Not sure. Just know there's a group off on their own . . .'

He rose abruptly and was gone.

Nick followed in time to see Nugent disappearing in the direction of Camden Town. Within five minutes the twenty quid would be in the hands of a pusher and Nugent would be happy again. For a while.

Nick took the Tube back to Victoria, resisting the urge to look at the pamphlet tucked in his pocket.

He hurried into the office. The seventh floor was almost empty. There was a lot on at the moment: a top IRA man in the country and a visiting delegation from Bulgaria. Conway was in, however, lounging in his chair, looking half-heartedly at some papers. As Nick made for his desk, Conway looked up and brightened visibly. He was obviously in the mood for a chat.

'Blimey,' he said, eyeing Nick with amusement. 'You look more like a Trot every day.'

Nick sat down at his desk. 'Thanks.'

'Well, enjoy it while you can.'

Conway obviously had a gem of information to impart. Nick leafed through the pile of neglected paperwork in the in-tray until Conway could bear it no longer. 'We're on a big surveillance job next week, up in Neasden, you and me included.'

'Damn!' Nick said automatically. He loathed jobs like that at the best of times.

'Thought you'd be pleased. It's the strike at the photographic processing place.'

Conway finally achieved his reaction. Nick exclaimed, 'But that's purely *industrial*. Why aren't Munro's section handling it?'

'Rent-a-mob have been seen on the picket lines. They want us to have a look see. Also they're a bit overstretched.'

'So are we!'

'Trouble is, our students have been a bit quiet of late,' Conway pointed out. 'Whereas quiet is the last word for what's happening on the industrial front.'

It was true. On the surface anyway. Since Paris the students had been reasonably quiet. The last Vietnam rally, though large, had passed off without incident. Now, with galloping inflation and a wage freeze, all the trouble was on the workers' front.

Nick shook his head wearily and, putting an elbow on the desk, shielded his eyes with a hand to show that the conversation was over. Conway prattled on for a few minutes about duty allocations and finally gave up. 'You know, Ryder, sometimes I think Box 500 would be more your line. I've heard say they never even talk among *themselves* . . .'

Nick let the remark pass.

Conway wandered off and Nick pulled out the crumpled papers that Nugent had given him. With great self-control he looked at the broadsheets first. He had recognised two immediately and was certain he already had them on file. They were, he knew, printed by an extremist intellectual group called the Federation for Workers' Control. Their publications were always in the same vein

– workers must unite . . . form rank-and-file committees . . . take the offensive in every strike. The print style of the third sheet was different from the other two and it probably came off another press. He would try to find out which. He put the sheets on one side to look at again later.

The pamphlet.

He picked it up and began to read.

It was about twenty pages long and entitled *Strike Back!* The first few pages dealt with the basic philosophy of an urban guerrilla. It was strong reading. 'Kill as a matter of course – it is the guerrilla's sole reason for being. Do not kill in anger or haste. Kill carefully, coldly . . .' He recognised the ideas; they were very similar to those in the *Mini Handbook* written by the Brazilian revolutionary Marighella – a book which had just been openly published in Germany, Italy and Britain, although, to Nick's mind, such writings counted as blatant incitement, and should be banned.

But this pamphlet went further, much further. He read on grimly. There were detailed instructions on how to incite violence on picket lines and in demonstrations. Then half-way through there was a section headed 'Meet Violence With Violence!' One page was devoted to a drawing of a Molotov cocktail. The next to written instructions and a detailed recipe for what was called 'Easy Brew' – an explosive mixture of garden chemicals and diesel fuel – plus instructions on how to detonate it with a common wristwatch. There were specifications of incendiary devices, more sophisticated detonators, and letter bombs. Then at the end there was the really grown-up stuff. Plastics – the military RDX type was recommended 'if available' – and, in enormous detail, how to parcel and detonate the stuff, and where to place it in cars and buildings for maximum effect.

There was a final page of exhortations to ruthless direct action. 'Activate – Pulverise, Energise, Polarise! Fabricate crystal splinters!'

Nick stared at the explosives section for several minutes. He'd never seen anything so cool and detailed. A complete idiot's guide to killing.

It would have to be checked for accuracy. He phoned the Home Office Branch of the Royal Armament Research Establishment at Woolwich and asked them to check the copy he'd be sending over.

He made five photocopies of the pamphlet, collated and stapled them, and sent one by messenger to the armaments people. Then he went along to see the boss.

Straughan was in. He eyed Nick sharply, making an obvious effort to suppress his distrust of jeans and long hair. 'Yes, Ryder. What can I do for you?'

'I thought you might like to see this, sir.'

Straughan glanced through the pamphlet, frowning as he came to the explosives section. Eventually he murmured, 'Bloody hell – that's all we need. Everything in writing. Any ideas on this yet?'

'No. Only just got hold of it.'

'Source?'

'A student – or rather an ex-student. An addict.'

'And where did he get it?'

'Don't know. And he wouldn't say. But he used to be heavily involved with the left at the LSE – mainly the Socialist Students' League.'

The DCS pulled at his face as if it were india-rubber. 'This doesn't look like student stuff to me. It's far too – advanced. I'd have thought they picked this up from the Spanish Anarchists or the IRA or people like that. They're the only ones with this sort of knowledge—'

'*Lots* of people have this sort of knowledge,' Nick insisted.

The DCS looked unconvinced. 'Well—'

'We know that the IRA have connections with the Palestinians. And that there's a Swiss arms connection between the Basque Separatists and some of the Italian groups . . .'

The DCS stabbed a finger at him. 'Exactly! The professional terrorists. Not the *students*.'

'But I'm not saying the students *produced* this thing. I'm saying they might *use* it. We should find out exactly who's handing out these things and who's receiving them.'

'Look . . .' The DCS's voice assumed a tone of long-suffering tolerance. 'If any of the pros want to go on a bombing rampage they're going to use their own people, aren't they? I mean they're not going to use a bunch of wild kids, not unless they've gone out of their minds, are they?'

Nick tightened his lips and thought: Here we go again. 'Yes, but the students have their *own* causes, their own targets—'

'Such as?'

'Oh, unemployment, bad housing – the capitalist system in general.'

'But they're not organised,' the DCS said slowly and patiently, as if explaining something to a small child. 'Who's going to give them the explosives? Who's going to provide the back-up? Where's the money to come from? The foreign groups aren't going to help and the Soviets sure as hell won't be interested in the lunatic fringe—'

'But they're in contact with several groups who *are* Soviet backed. Indirectly.'

'No. No. I just don't see it. Students are all hot air and demos and shouting. Always have been. No, these kids have just picked up this pamphlet because they think it's smart. *Clever*. They picked it up abroad, no doubt.'

'But printed and produced here, or at least intended to be used here. The spelling's definitely English rather than American, and the grammar and style is – well, perfect.'

'It is, is it?'

Nick let the sarcasm diffuse into the air before saying, 'I'm sure I could find the source given time—'

'Well, let's try the Irish Section first. And Box 500. They'll probably know where it comes from straight away.'

Nick tried not to let his exasperation show. 'But – shouldn't we at least follow it up. I could ask around.'

Straughan nodded slowly. 'All right. But . . .' he paused thought-fully. 'Just be careful about your methods, I have the feeling that you've been getting perilously close to infiltration recently and we all know what that can lead to.' Some months before a Branch man had passed himself off as a docker at a union meeting and got half murdered. There'd been questions in high places. Everyone paid lip-service to the policy of non-infiltration, but if you wanted to get really good results you went your own way and shut up about it.

The DCS sat up in his chair. 'You'll get this circulated, will you? To the Irish and Anarchist Sections. And the original to Technical Support.'

'Look, I'm lined up for the Neasden surveillance. Could you square it for me?'

'Eh?' Straughan made a disapproving face, then looked at the pamphlet again. 'Well, *maybe* I'll see if I can get someone else to fill in for the first few days – but no promises.' He threw Nick a hard unforgiving stare. 'But just keep me informed, will you? No waltzing off on your own with no one knowing where the hell you've got to. Okay?'

*

As Nick opened the flat door a flood of warm light and safe domestic sounds swept towards him. He was glad to be home. Then the clatter of china in the kitchen reminded him – it'd been his turn to shop and cook, and he had forgotten. But Anne would forgive him – from the cooking sounds she already had. He realised he was extremely hungry and went hopefully into the kitchen.

'Hi,' she said sharply without looking up.

He stared, surprised. She was packing plates into a box.

'I'm leaving in case you're wondering.' She spoke harshly, her face taut and unyielding. Nick's heart sank. He leant back against the doorframe.

The silence stretched out. Eventually she said sadly, 'I wouldn't have thought you were capable of such a thing.'

Normally he'd do anything to avoid a row, especially on an empty stomach, but he parried, 'What does that mean?'

'All that gentle concern!'

'Oh—?'

She stared at him resentfully. 'Well, you're a sham, aren't you? A phoney!'

'Anne, what on earth is this about?'

'Your people came and spied on us!'

'*Spied?*'

'Came to our meeting and took notes.'

He asked incredulously, 'Your *social* workers' meeting?'

'Our Women Against Vietnam meeting!'

'I would have thought you'd be flattered.' Immediately he wished he'd left the words unsaid.

'My God!' she gasped.

'Anne, look – I knew nothing about it. Believe me.'

'Have you got a file on us? *Have you?*'

'I can't answer that.'

She shook her head. 'You leave me no choice.'

'If you're going it's because you want to.'

'Because I *have* to! I can't live with a' – she struggled to find the word – 'with a rotten *informer!*' She paused to find more ammunition. 'Besides, you're a chauvinist. It took a bit of time to come to the fore. But it's there, isn't it? *Who* ended up with all the chores, eh? Me! You're a sham, Nick!'

He thought: Ouch! and wondered why women always had to apportion blame, had to analyse and dissect until the last spasm of pain had been extracted. He shrugged and said evenly, 'Fine. Let's just call it a day then.'

Before she could make a retort he walked into the living-room and sat down with a magazine. There was a silence and he could almost feel the strength of her anger. Finally there were sounds of heavy suitcases being dragged into the hall.

She put her head round the door and, without looking him in the eye, said a stiff, 'Goodbye then.' A few moments later the front door slammed and she was gone.

Nick sat in silence, wondering what on earth had gone wrong. They'd lived together reasonably happily for – what was it? – eight months, and now suddenly she had gone. He'd never made a secret of the fact that he worked for Special Branch, and she'd known – or *guessed* – what it had involved. None the less it was unfortunate about the Vietnam meeting. He could have told her the truth – that many of the committee members were known communists – but she wouldn't have believed him. People only believed what they wanted to.

It was a pity she'd gone. They'd had good times, bed had been wonderful and he still thought her exceptionally pretty. But since getting involved in peace movements and women's rights her wonderful softness and vulnerability had given way to an increasingly strident and dogmatic harshness, and the magic had gone. As for the domestic front, he thought he'd behaved rather well there. Certainly he'd made an effort about cooking and going to the launderette – well, when he could. As for being a chauvinist, that was just unfair. He actually liked women which was more than a lot of men did. No, he couldn't see that he'd been unreasonable.

His stomach rumbled and he remembered that he was hungry. In the kitchen there was a stack of washing-up in the sink, a pile of dirty laundry on the floor and almost nothing in the fridge. So much for meeting each other half-way. Eventually he settled for a stale Ryvita and a tin of sardines. He looked for some beer but remembered that they'd run out some days ago.

He went to put on a record. He decided against opera – in his present mood it would make him maudlin – and chose Desmond Dekker instead. He flopped back in a chair to the soothing sounds of 'Oh-Oh-S-e-v-e-n . . .'

The problem with women like Anne, he finally decided, was that they were made to feel inadequate if they didn't take up causes and follow them through to the bitter end. In the early sixties

92

causes had been a mere fashion, now, in 1969, they were compulsory.

He thought immediately of the pamphlet. A cause taken to the limit. With relief he put Anne out of his mind and, finding the photocopy he'd brought home with him, began to study it. In the last year his library of political writings had grown considerably and, to simplify the impossible task of making sense of it all, he'd made detailed notes of all the various extremist philosophies and card-indexed them by doctrine, structure and actions.

Now he looked through the pamphlet for clues as to the writer's origins and affiliations. The philosophy *might* fall into one of several general categories – Marxist-Leninist, Trotskyist, anarchist, nationalist. Then again it might just as easily *not*. Each category consisted of dozens of splinter groups, each preaching the true and only philosophy. Furthermore, the New Left were inclined to pinch ideas from all over the place, regardless of origin, and stick them together in whichever way suited them, so that you couldn't categorise their ideas in the old way at all. They were an elusive bunch, constantly merging and splitting and reforming.

If it was an organised group at all . . .

Then he looked at the jargon they had used. Most of it, as he'd thought, was borrowed from the urban guerrilla leader, Marighella. Then there was this sign-off, about pulverising and polarising and fabricating crystal splinters, whatever that may mean.

No: he couldn't narrow the field at all.

Where would they have got the explosives info? Cuba? North Korea? The IRA? But the IRA weren't in need of education on the making of bombs nor so philanthropic as to be printing pamphlets for the benefit of other people.

Suddenly he realised he was looking at the problem from entirely the wrong angle.

He should be looking at the *why*.

Why would anyone want to produce such a document?

Only people dedicated to spreading the word.

It had to be a group with missionary zeal, prepared to spend the money on what was undoubtedly an expensive piece of printing, happy to hand it out to whoever might use it, and not at all fussy about which cause the information was put to.

Anarchists? Unlikely. As one might expect, they were usually very disorganised.

A subversive group with funds behind it, then.

He sighed. It was pointing to a Soviet-backed organisation. And that was most definitely Box 500's sphere of interest.

Perhaps Straughan had been right after all.

By midnight he was feeling thoroughly discouraged and decided to pack it in for the night.

Before going to bed he checked his diary. According to *Red Notes*, the periodic guide to revolutionary meetings published by the New Left, there was to be a major meeting of the Socialist Students' League at the LSE next week. Nugent had mentioned a possible split. It might be worth going along, just to see if any of the usual faces were missing.

Another splinter group, another faction, another entry on the card index.

He switched off the living-room lights and stood in the hall, absorbing the quiet calmness of the little flat. In some ways it would be enjoyable to be on his own for a while. But not for too long. He'd got used to having someone else around. He'd enjoyed the domesticity and the companionship.

Yes. He would find someone else. Quite soon.

Six days later, on the dot of seven, Nick turned off the Aldwych into Houghton Street, a narrow lane overshadowed by the numerous grey buildings of the London School of Economics. He automatically assumed the preoccupied, tense look of a student, his eyes down, a frown on his forehead. He walked briskly up the steps of the main building and into the Old Theatre, pausing only to read the notice-board.

The audience was smaller than he'd expected for such an important meeting – there were no more than eighty. Perhaps the Socialist Students' League was going out of fashion. He slid into a seat and pretended to read the latest issue of the Red Mole, a student publication of impeccable Marxist dogma. Only when the meeting finally started ten minutes late did he begin to study the group of young men and women on the platform: the Central Committee of the Socialist Students' League.

He recognised three of them immediately – postgraduates who'd been in the league since it was founded in '67. Their names came to him from the files which he'd examined earlier in the afternoon. Another two were familiar; he memorised their faces so that when he went back to the office he could identify them from photographs taken at marches and demonstrations.

94

There were a couple of others. They looked pretty young – probably new recruits. He studied their faces too so that he would know them again.

Who was missing?

The red-haired one called Reardon. He'd got two months for the Linden House Hotel affair. He'd always been an angry one, just the type to walk out in disgust at any lack of action.

And there was someone else missing, another who'd been heavily involved since '67. An undergraduate with a sullen intense look. One of those who'd been booted out of France. What *was* his name?

The meeting was starting to warm up. There was some disagreement about joining yet another protest march to the American Embassy. Someone from the floor was arguing that the march would be a complete waste of time because they wouldn't be allowed near Grosvenor Square. Too right, thought Nick: there'd be no repetition of that first large demo when a breakaway group had got within yards of the Embassy.

In patronising terms one of the comrades on the platform started lecturing the floor about the importance of attracting media attention. The floor replied that the media was capitalist-controlled trivia and wasn't worth attracting in the first place.

Nick wondered if he could slip away. The thought of sitting through another hour of this stuff bored him rigid.

But he decided against leaving – it would attract attention. Instead he tried to think of the name that went with that missing face ... It was earthy, he remembered ... Rural? No, agricultural. Mower, reaper, farmer ... Suddenly he had it. Wheat. *Wheatfield*. First name Max. *Max Wheatfield*.

He sat through the meeting for another half an hour until a couple of nearby students got up to leave and he was able to slip out behind them. He went back to his office and found the files marked Wheatfield, M. and Reardon, A. In both he pencilled the comment: 'Not present at 15th March meeting of SSL at the London School of Economics. Possibly forming splinter group?'

It was almost nine. Time to go home. Then with a sigh he remembered that he hadn't filled in his daily diary for almost a week. He loathed the bureaucratic side of police work, but if anyone like Straughan chose to notice the incomplete diary, it could get him into trouble. He went back to his desk and half-heartedly began to write.

Seven

Once an outlying hamlet, the village had long since become a suburb of the ancient walled city of Chester. None the less it retained its identity in a comfortable almost complacent way. The houses were well maintained, the gardens tidy, unemployment was low. The local industries – Morgan's, the brewery, and Bradbury's, a plant assembling electrical appliances – were busy. There were rumours that, even allowing for the traditional caution of the management and the gloomy economic outlook, both would soon be taking on more workers.

Fridays were always difficult for parking in the centre of town, and Mrs Ackroyd peered anxiously through the windscreen as she manoeuvred the Morris into the car park. But it was all right. There was a space and quite near the entrance too. She turned off the ignition and looked at the time. One minute to ten. Perfect. She did like to be punctual on these occasions.

There were butterflies in her stomach. But she was quite used to that. Her boss, Mr Wilson, the financial director of Bradbury's, always apologised for asking her to make these trips, but in truth she rather enjoyed them. It gave her a thrill to carry so much money. And it wasn't as if she had to do it every week. Four of them, all trusted employees, took it in turns. They also tried to vary the timing as much as possible, but with two hundred wage packets to prepare – and a hundred and twenty of those before the end of the day shift at four – one couldn't leave it too late.

She patted the grey curls to her head and, picking up a voluminous shopping bag, got out of the car. The bank was only just across the High Street. As she went in Mr Chesil, the assistant manager, looked up and nodded to her. He met her at the last window and they exchanged greetings through the glass screen. She handed over the withdrawal cheque. As always, the bank had been notified of the exact amount by telephone the previous day, so the money would already be prepared in tidy parcels.

As she folded up the shopping bag and pushed it under the screen, Mrs Ackroyd said, 'How's the football going, Mr Chesil?' She knew that the assistant manager was very keen on the game and played for the bank's regional team.

'Very well, thank you,' he replied. 'We won last Saturday.' He disappeared into an inner sanctum where he always put the money into the bag.

Five minutes later he reappeared and, taking a cursory glance around the bank, went to the door which connected the banking and public sections. He emerged and handed the bag to Mrs Ackroyd, saying, 'Yes, we're playing Barclays tomorrow. Should be a good match.'

'Hope you win,' she said cheerily. 'According to the weather people you should have a good day for it.' She waited expectantly for a suitably light response that would mark the end of the conversation.

But the poor man suddenly looked quite ill. His face had gone deathly white and his eyes seemed to be popping out of their sockets.

His gaze was fixed on something over her shoulder. Feeling the first flutter of anxiety Mrs Ackroyd began to turn.

She cried out in alarm.

Something cold and hard was jabbing into her neck, preventing her from looking round.

She cried out. Another jab and she found herself staggering sideways.

Shocked, she turned at last, and gasped.

A figure stood before her, dressed entirely in black. A devil-mask hid the face, except for the eyes which glinted darkly through the slits. The figure moved, and Mrs Ackroyd suddenly realised what had jabbed her. An enormous great gun.

Her knees went weak and she had to lean against the wall. As she told the policeman later, everything after that was a complete blur. Although she *did* remember to grasp the shopping bag.

The assistant manager knew what he should do. He should get to the alarm button. But the black figure was advancing on him and he froze. The long thin neck of the gun met his ribs and he gave a small cry.

The figure was holding up something in front of his eyes. A message. He blinked rapidly and read it. Nodding, he stepped slowly into the banking section and, with the black figure a short pace behind him, went into the manager's office. A few moments later, he and the manager were standing helplessly beside the safe.

Out of the corner of his eye Chesil saw that all four of the tellers were in their seats. He felt a glimmer of hope. By now one of them was bound to have pressed a foot alarm. Almost immediately he realised he was mistaken. The tellers were sitting well back from the tills, out of reach of the alarms. He saw why. The barrel of a second gun was visible above the glass screen, pointing down at them. Even as he watched, the tellers were leaving their seats to lie face down on the floor. Only one remained in her seat. Keeping a cautious eye on the gun, she began to open the tills and stack the cash neatly on to the counter.

The manager showed no hesitation in opening the safe which, everyone later agreed, was the most sensible thing to do. As the manager piled the money into a large sack the assistant manager made an unhappy mental calculation. Fifteen thousand-odd in the safe plus seven in the tills: twenty-two thousand. Then he remembered Mrs Ackroyd's bagful and thanked God they hadn't got hold of that. It contained over ten thousand pounds.

But a minute later he realised that this hope, like the first, was premature. He heard Mrs Ackroyd's voice crying hysterically, 'Take it! Take it!'

The first gunman appeared with the shopping bag and threw it on the floor next to the two sacks of money beside the safe.

Suddenly there was a commotion and, almost sick with fright, Chesil craned his neck to see what was happening. Framed in the main doorway was a customer whom he recognised as a cantankerous ex-colonel. The old man was haranguing the second gunman, shouting, 'Put that thing down *immediately*!'

Dear God, thought the assistant manager, this is no time for British heroics.

Suddenly a voice rang out. 'Shut up or I kill you!'

There was a dull thud and a shower of glass. The assistant manager jumped with fright. He looked up, terrified, but the colonel was still standing there, alive but shocked. The old man lay down on the floor beside the other customers.

The first gunman, hovering nervously at the connecting door, spun back to face the manager. He held up another written message. The manager nodded furiously. With a thud of fear, Chesil realised the gunman was motioning to *him*. He was to pick up the money and take it towards the back of the bank. They knew about the rear door then. Of course.

With shaking fingers he unlocked the heavily secured back door and carried the sacks out into the alleyway. There was a delivery van waiting there. He got a brief glimpse of someone in the driver's seat before the gunmen hurried him round to the rear doors, which were ready open.

Just before he was forced to climb into the back of the van he made a mental note of the registration number. But it didn't do any good. The van was found abandoned two hours later, not half a mile from the lay-by where the assistant manager himself was discovered, trussed hand and foot, his trousers unceremoniously tied round his ankles.

Gabriele pushed her foot down and watched the speed of the Vitesse climb to over a hundred. But there was no exhilaration in it and, with an effort, she reconciled herself to a long boring drive to London. She felt unexpectedly depressed. The tension of the last few hours had vanished, leaving her drained and strangely dissatisfied.

Max sat silently beside her, shaking his head now and then at some confusing inner thoughts. In the back Giorgio was cleaning the Skorpion, clicking the magazine in and out, whistling contentedly.

Gabriele tried to concentrate her thoughts. She was feeling a letdown after the action, certainly, but there were other, more concrete doubts nagging at the back of her mind. Had they made any mistakes? She went through the raid, detail by detail, looking for deviations from the plan.

There was the shot Giorgio had fired. But no one had been hurt.

And – what?

Giorgio had said something.

She looked at him in the driving mirror. 'What did you say – in the bank?' she demanded.

'What – to the old man?' He laughed. 'I don't remember.'

'Try.'

He sighed loudly and there was a long pause. Eventually he replied, 'I said, "Shut up or I kill you".'

Gabriele thought: I *knew* there was something. She tried to control her anger. '*Exactly* like that?'

She saw Giorgio shrug. He said heavily, 'Yes, like that. So?'

'You could have spoken proper English. You sound – like an Italian waiter!'

Giorgio let out an exclamation of disgust and lay back. Max shifted uneasily in his seat.

Gabriele turned the problem of the words over and over in her mind. One moment they seemed like a horrendous mistake, the next she convinced herself they meant nothing. In all the confusion, no one would have noticed the precise words. Anyway, what if they had? Where would it lead? No, she was worrying too much.

All things considered, her meticulous planning had paid off. She allowed herself some satisfaction. It was the first raid. There would be many more, and each would be just as successful.

They hit the M1 at last, and she accelerated again. She smiled, her optimism returning, and said, 'We'll go out and have a good meal tonight.'

Max eyed her uncertainly. Good food was wasted on him. Not that she'd planned to include him anyway. 'You'll go back to your new place,' she said. 'I'll give you some money. We'll speak on the phone in a few days.'

Max nodded. Ever since her return he had been dog-like in his devotion. He was riddled with guilt about Stephie and pathetically grateful for any opportunity to do something to strike back.

Giorgio was a different matter. He was more difficult to please. But money would make him happy. For a while. Then she would dangle the plan of the next action in front of him, and he too would follow her unquestioningly.

She glanced in the mirror and stiffened. There was a white Rover some distance behind, approaching fast. She slowed down until the Vitesse was doing a safe seventy and moved into the middle lane.

The police car approached and slowly overtook. The men inside did not even glance at her.

'All right,' said Inspector Morrow wearily, 'let's go through it again, shall we?'

The bank manager and his assistant shifted in their seats and waited obediently.

The inspector tapped his fingers on the interview-room table. 'An exceptional amount of cash in the bank. The accounts lady from Bradbury's with ten thousand in a shopping bag. And no security guards.'

There was a silence. Put like that it didn't reflect too well on anyone, especially the bank.

'Tell me,' the inspector continued, 'do Bradbury's always get little grey-haired ladies to carry large amounts of cash for them?'

'They have always used their staff,' said the manager defensively.

Morrow shook his head. He'd been in Cheshire CID for fifteen years and it never failed to amaze him how stupid people were with their money. He said, 'Bradbury's tell me they use four different people and vary the times when they collect. Is that true?'

The manager nodded.

'You didn't actually *see* the gunman take the bag from Mrs Ackroyd?'

'No,' the manager said firmly. 'We were by the safe. The customers lying on the floor had the best view . . .'

'Quite. Now – this is very important. Mr Chesil—' The assistant manager sat up. 'When you handed the bag of money to Mrs Ackroyd were the gunmen already in the bank?'

The assistant manager thought desperately. 'I don't know. One moment everything was normal then . . . I'm afraid I didn't see them until they were *there*.'

'What I'm trying to discover,' said the inspector patiently, 'is whether the villains *spotted* you handing the cash to Mrs Ackroyd. D'you see what I mean?'

They saw, but couldn't help. Morrow drew a deep breath and moved on. 'Right. Now what about the guns? You've had a chance to look through our little gallery of photographs, but I gather you're not quite agreed about the type.'

'Well, *I'm* quite sure,' declared the manager. 'I pointed the gun out to your sergeant. I'm positive it was the one.'

The assistant manager shook his head. 'I'm afraid – I don't think the gun was there in your collection. There were *similar* ones, but . . .' He trailed off and shrugged.

The inspector wondered what else the numerous witnesses could disagree about. He supposed he should be grateful for what he'd got: that the two weapons appeared to be sub-machine-guns, and probably identical. Although the thought of sub-machine-guns did not make him happy, not at all. No one had used those kind of weapons on his manor before. The local villains and the ones from Liverpool and Manchester who did him the honour of committing armed robbery on his patch used sawn-off shotguns.

Ballistics had not been as helpful as he'd hoped. The bullet fired at the wall of the bank had spread, and it was impossible to establish the calibre. Neither could the interim report establish *why* the bullet had spread: it might have been a consequence of using a silencer – all the witnesses were agreed on the lack of a loud explosion – or it could have been a result of using a soft-nosed bullet. Or both.

Inspector Morrow drew a deep breath. 'Any more thoughts on the gunman's voice?'

Both men shook their heads. The manager said firmly, 'I only remember his words. "Shut up or I'll kill you!" he said.'

'And what about the van driver, Mr Chesil. You've no more to offer us in the way of a description?'

The assistant manager shook his head. 'It was only the briefest glimpse. Like I said, he had dark hair. And a white face. But as to what he *looked* like, well, it was all rather a *blur*.'

There was a pause. The inspector reflected that you couldn't get blood out of a stone. He tried to end on an optimistic note. 'But we do have some serial numbers, I gather.'

The manager looked pleased. 'We do indeed. We had an unusual amount of new notes in the bank. We have numbers for notes totalling almost six thousand pounds.'

Almost a fifth of the money. Better than nothing.

The inspector then interviewed Mrs Ackroyd. The sergeant had told him what to expect: an earful. And that was what he got. Mrs Ackroyd had decided she was in some way to blame for what had happened and was determined to share the burden.

The inspector interrupted her, 'Mrs Ackroyd, I need to establish one fact. But it's very important.'

She blinked. 'Yes?'

'Did the gunman come *straight* up to you and take the bag of money?'

'What do you mean?'

'Did he seem to *know* you had it?'

'Oh . . . I see what you're getting at. Well, yes, I *think* so. But – I can't be sure.'

'No?'

'Well, you see, I was lying down like the others. And – I didn't *see* a lot. In fact,' she said miserably, 'I had my eyes shut.'

When she'd gone, the inspector pondered. This one had more than a whiff of inside knowledge. And yet there was nothing *conclusive* . . .

He was wondering if he'd ever know for sure when his assistant, a particularly bright WPC, came in and said that in her opinion one of the witnesses – another bank customer – would most definitely be worth talking to.

The witness, Miss Izzard, was about twenty-five and very precise. She answered questions with a calm composure. The inspector wished that more witnesses were like her.

'So Miss Izzard. You are positive about the gun.'

'Yes, I looked at it very carefully to be sure I would be able to identify it when the time came.'

He looked at the sheet the WPC had put in front of him. *Skorpion VZ 61 machine pistol; .32 cartridge; 840 rounds a minute automatic, 40 rounds a minute single shot; made in Czechoslovakia . . .* He ran down the specifications and noticed that a silencer was among the optional extras. His eye fixed on one of the notes at the bottom. *Use of the silencer has the effect of spreading the shot.*

He looked warmly at Miss Izzard. 'And did you notice if both guns were of the same type?'

She nodded. 'Definitely.'

'Did you see the gunmen enter the bank?'

'Yes. I was standing waiting my turn and I saw them come in. They already had their masks on. One jumped on to the counter, the other went straight to where Mr Chesil and the woman – Mrs Ackroyd – were talking.'

'Talking?'

'Yes, I saw Mr Chesil hand her the shopping bag and then start ·talking.'

'*Before* the gunmen came in.'

She nodded.

'So the gunmen couldn't have seen the money change hands?'

'No, but they knew it was there.'

The inspector started slightly. 'How's that, Miss Izzard?'

'After they'd got everyone lying down and quiet they went straight to the bag and took it out of her hand. They didn't search her – or *anyone*. They obviously knew.'

He could have kissed her. 'Yes, Miss Izzard. That's what I think too.' It was too much to hope that there'd be more, but he asked, 'Anything else you think I should know?'

She thought for a moment. 'Yes, two things.'

The inspector felt a stab of excitement. 'Yes—?'

'The one who spoke . . . Well, he talked like a *gangster*. He said, "Shut up or I kill you." Not I'll kill you but *I* kill you. Like in a gangster film.'

He tried to hide his disappointment. 'I see . . .'

'And the other thing,' Miss Izzard continued. 'The gunman who went into the banking section . . . was, I am absolutely certain, a woman.'

103

'A *woman*!'

'Yes. I only saw her for a moment when she walked through the bank, and then again briefly when she grabbed the money from Mrs Ackroyd. But I'm sure.'

He shook his head in amazement. No one else had spotted this, there hadn't been so much as a *suggestion* . . . He asked incredulously. 'Why are you so sure?'

'The way she moved. She was wearing very loose clothing – a sort of boiler suit. In black. She was tall and at first sight she could've passed as a man. But she moved like a woman. In the hips, you understand.' She added hastily, 'Oh, and she had small hands and feet. Far too small for a man.'

A few days later the inspector found himself wishing Miss Izzard hadn't been quite such a wonderful witness. The information about the shopping bag had been first class – it pointed firmly to someone having inside information or, at least, a great deal of local knowledge.

But the rest . . .

There had been no fingerprints. Neither had Scotland Yard been able to match the *modus operandi* – and particularly the machine pistol – to any known criminals.

For a while he'd pinned his hopes on an Irish connection. But Special Branch in Liverpool were doubtful. The IRA used a variety of arms – their favourite was the Armalite sub-machine-gun – but they weren't fond of Skorpions which were essentially close-range weapons. Also they preferred to rob banks on their home ground in the Republic where they stood the best chance of going to earth and evading capture.

It didn't leave him with very much: a local job which had none of the hallmarks of the local talent; and two villains, one of whom appeared to be a gangster film enthusiast, and the other a woman.

He would just have to hope that some of the numbered notes turned up soon.

All in all the case had a bad feel to it. And the more he went into it the more he suspected it was going to drag on to a less than satisfactory conclusion.

The flat was on the third floor, overlooking Montagu Square. It fulfilled all the requirements: it was in a block of fifteen similarly anonymous flats, it was just the right size, and it came fully furnished. But there was one problem: Gabriele hated it on sight.

The furniture was appalling: a brown Dralon three-piece suite with black screw-on legs and brass feet, miniature chandeliers and too much gilt. In itself the overblown look wouldn't have mattered if it hadn't reminded her so forcefully of her childhood.

She said to the agent, 'No. It won't do. Haven't you anything else?'

'Nothing similar in this area,' said the young man. 'Although if you were prepared to change your mind about having a *flat*, I do have a lovely mews house. Just behind here.'

She hesitated. A mews would be too quiet and one's movements too easily observed. Also the neighbours were likely to be nosy. She shouldn't even consider it. At the same time she was getting tired of looking. She agreed to go and see it.

Montagu Mews was even worse than quiet: it was a dead end. Number 42 was half-way down on the right. It had been fully converted into a house, the old stables on the ground floor having been replaced by a gaily painted brick façade with large windows. Two small fir trees in wooden tubs stood either side of the front door.

Full of misgivings, Gabriele followed the agent inside. She had to admit that the place was rather nice. The house was a snug arrangement of small rooms, each brightly decorated in sun colours and floral prints. The living-room, which ran the depth of the house, had a sitting area at one end and a small dining table at the other. A plant had been trained up the wrought-iron banisters of the spiral staircase which rose from one corner. In the bathroom the loo had been painted bright yellow with a ring of green and red flowers inside the bowl.

She looked thoughtfully out of the window. There was parking immediately outside which would be handy ... And perhaps the quietness would be an advantage.

It was much too expensive, of course, and she quibbled with the agent. But she could see that he wasn't going to budge on the price; she looked too well dressed.

Eventually she said grudgingly, 'I'll take it.'

In the agent's office she gave her name as Gabriella Carelli and produced an Italian passport as proof of identity. She stated her occupation as freelance photo-journalist, and gave the magazine *La Posta* of Milan as a reference. She paid a deposit and two months' rent in advance.

Gabriele drove straight to another house agent behind Marble

Arch. This time there was no problem about getting exactly the right thing: the agency specialised in service flats for visiting foreigners. She was shown several in the area north of Oxford Street, and settled on a fifth floor three-roomed flat in a block on Weymouth Street. It was furnished in a modern characterless style and had a well-equipped kitchen. She took it for four weeks in the name of Mr and Mrs L. C. Hoerst of Bern, Switzerland. She paid the deposit and rent in cash on the spot. The agent looked pleased.

On her way back she drove past the end of Montagu Mews and noted that it was only two minutes away from Weymouth Street, which would be most convenient. Then she headed the car down Park Lane towards Knightsbridge and Chelsea. The Vitesse had gone back to the rental firm three days ago, and she was now driving a small Fiat which she had bought through *Exchange and Mart*. The Fiat was better suited to her new occupation.

She parked off the King's Road and, going into a couple of the better boutiques, bought a pair of high boots and a trouser suit in white cotton. In the last three weeks she'd spent over two hundred pounds on clothes. The camera equipment had cost even more – there were two Olympus OM1 camera bodies, three lenses from 28mm to 50mm, a zoom, and a powerful telephoto.

She took her purchases back to the flat in Chelsea Manor Street, where she and Giorgio had been living since their arrival nearly four weeks before.

Giorgio was not at home. Systematically, she began to sort everything out, ready for the move to the mews house. She would keep this flat on, but only as a safe house to be used in the last resort. Certain things would need to be left here: a little money well hidden, a change of clothes, a list of telephone numbers, a passport.

She took a briefcase containing the money from under the bed. There had been just over thirty-two thousand when they'd first counted it. Now there was twenty-four. It seemed to go surprisingly quickly. And she would need a great deal to pay for supplies from Paris. Nevertheless it should last some weeks. Although there was one complication.

The money was divided into two piles, carefully separated. On the left, the slightly dog-eared used notes which they had been using for their expenses. On the right, the clean crisp new notes, virgin and untouched: six thousand-odd, sequentially numbered. She eyed the wads of notes uneasily.

It was far too risky to use the new stuff, either here or in Paris, and yet without it they'd be short.

Something would have to be done about those notes. And at the moment she couldn't think what.

She removed two thousand pounds from the pile of old notes and put it on one side. From her old clothes she selected a pair of trousers, a blouse, a jacket, and some flat shoes, which she put with the two thousand.

Taking a list of numbers from the lining of her handbag, she copied the numbers on to another slip of paper, replaced the original, and tucked the copy into an Argentinian passport, which she slipped into the pile of clothes.

Finally, she took a copy of *Strike Back!* from her bag of books and papers and put in on top of the clothes. She couldn't think why she should need it if she was on the run, but one never knew.

Now to find a hiding place. The kitchen units were built in, the base units raised above the floor by a recessed plinth. The cooker, however, was free standing. She pulled it out and, kneeling down, tried to lever out the plinth that ran alongside the cooker. She broke two knives before she thought of going down to the car and getting the wheel-changing kit. The small wrench used to remove the hub caps was strong enough to lever the plinth out and, wrapping the clothes, papers and money in a bag, she slid the bundle under the unit, knocked home the plinth and replaced the cooker.

She peered down. Apart from a slight splintering of the wood on the corner of the plinth, there wasn't a sign.

Now to pack. She put her considerable number of new clothes into a couple of holdalls, and put them by the front door. Closing the case of money, she placed this too in the hall.

There was one last job to be done.

Going to the fridge, she removed a thick plastic container, the size of a large shoebox, from the bottom shelf. Opening the lid very carefully, she peered at the contents. Then, slowly, she put her nose to them and sniffed.

Satisfied, she closed the container again and placed it in one of the holdalls, well protected by clothes.

There was nothing to do now but wait for Giorgio.

Whenever she was on her own and had a free moment she liked to look at her list. With anticipation she sat in a chair and pulled the slip of paper out of the handbag lining again. The telephone numbers which she had copied were on one side, numbers which she had jumbled slightly to hide their true sequence. On the other side was a list of abbreviations of names.

The chief targets. The capitalist oppressors.

The list of names was not complete. But she was working on it.

Eight

Victoria braked hard and spun the wheel. In a hail of loose stones the Mini careered off the road and, skidding sideways, shot on to the farm track, missing the ditch by a whisker.

The car ground to a halt. The radio was blaring '. . . the age of Aquarius, A-quar-ius . . .' Victoria sat shivering in a hot sweat. It had been a near thing, that ditch. The tiredness had ruined her judgement. She just wasn't used to staying up late, not after all this time. But then it wasn't every day your sister had a party in London. She shouldn't have gone, though. She hadn't enjoyed it.

Shakily she started off again. The bottom of the car hit the lip of a pot-hole with a loud grinding noise. The holes needed fixing – like everything else.

Ahead the chestnuts arched upwards, their summer magnificence quickly fading in a flurry of dry yellow leaves. Soon she would get her first glimpse of the house. During the early months at Hunter's Wood she'd always looked forward to this moment, even if she'd been away a short time. But today . . . Today she remembered the work list, and how very long it was and how behind they were.

She drove on and pulled up in front of the house. The camper van, the only other vehicle in sight, was parked carelessly in the middle of the yard. Victoria looked at the house and frowned. Although it was noon and the day fine the living-room windows were tightly shut and the curtains drawn.

She stiffened, listening hard. Away past the tractor shed Bella, the sow, was grunting, not in her familiar snuffly contented way, but in long sorrowful snorts. And the chickens – there was no sound from them at all.

Apprehensive, Victoria hurried round the corner of the house and across the yard. The door of the tractor shed was open and the engine of the ancient Massey Ferguson lay strewn in small pieces over the floor. She sighed inwardly; there would be no ploughing today then.

In the sty a distressed Bella pushed an anxious snout over the wall. Her trough was quite empty. Victoria realised with growing despair that it had probably been so for some time. She gave the wildly grunting pig some water then went to the reed store. That too was empty. She exclaimed aloud, 'God! It isn't much to ask. Not *much*!' Who was it – yes, Martin – who was meant to have picked up the monthly supplies? How *could* he have forgotten?

Angry now, she marched across to the chicken shed. She stopped short and caught her breath. The door was wide open and there wasn't a bird to be seen. Only feathers and remains scattered widely over the ground. Foxes' leftovers.

Muttering bitterly to herself, she strode into the farmhouse kitchen. The remains of a meal were spread over the table and draining board. Victoria went straight to the slop pail, topped up the sparse plate-scrapings with porridge oats and stale muesli, pulled up a whole fresh cabbage from the vegetable patch, and gave the mixture to a grateful Bella.

Crying now, she returned to the kitchen and stared dejectedly at the mess. A note was propped conspicuously against a bowl on the dresser. She recognised Ned's tidy handwriting. Victoria reached out hesitantly, uncomfortably sure of what it would say. She unfolded it. 'We hereby resign. We feel that the original spirit and intentions of the commune have been lost. We have taken a few vegetables, but nothing else. Ned and Kate.' There was a forwarding address.

She leant hard against the dresser, thinking: They're right, the heart has gone out of this place. She felt a black despair.

She went into the hall, the slap of her sandals echoing loudly across the stone floor. The living-room was empty and dark, the air close and stale. The other ground-floor rooms were lifeless too. She climbed wearily up the stairs and stopped outside Martin and Janey's room. Gentle snores were audible through the closed door. She thought bitterly: How *could* they? She opened the door and looked in. The room was dark but she could see the two figures sprawled across the mattress. Martin muttered angrily in his sleep. Janey was very still. Victoria went up to the mattress and touched her hand, then shook her firmly and shouted her name a couple of times. Janey responded with a loud moan and turned over.

On the floor beside the mattress were the leftovers of the party: home-made elderberry wine, a couple of half-smoked joints, some pink tablets – speed – and a plate.

Victoria stared at the plate and her heart moved painfully. On it were the remains of a brashly coloured cake, marbled with veins of vivid yellow and green and purple. Crouching, she picked up a piece and, lifting it to her nose, sniffed it.

She should have known. Mel had joked about it often enough. Rainbow cake – psychedelic and mind-blowing. Full of junk.

In the passage she took a long deep breath and started towards the room she shared with Mel. Even as she approached, she caught the whiff of booze and grass and overflowing ashtrays.

Suddenly she had a horrible yet tantalising thought: that there'd be someone else in the bed with him. Another girl – the blonde art student, the one who often arrived uninvited and walked naked in the back meadow; the one he sometimes disappeared with. She hesitated at the door, miserable in case her suspicions were correct, yet desperate to know.

She walked in. He was alone. She exhaled, half with relief, half with a curious sense of disappointment.

He was lying on the bed, face up, his mouth wide open. He was out cold, like Janey. The room was a mess and the smell unpleasant. With despair she realised that at one point Mel must have been sick.

She screwed up her face and muttered, '*Honestly . . .*'

After a few moments she went closer, drawn by a need to see the full extent of his dissipation.

Suddenly she held perfectly still, her senses reaching out like an animal scenting the wind.

With disbelief yet perfect certainty, she knew.

He was dead.

She remained still, as if the moment could be frozen or undone. But gradually she became aware of her own breathing, of infinitesimal fractions of time flickering past. Slowly she began to absorb the details of the sight before her: the eyelids which were not quite shut, the whites of the eyes which gleamed dully through the lashes, the bluish, almost transparent skin. Slowly she reached forward and touched his arm. It was cold. Cold and dead.

She felt nothing. Not then. The day took on a curious dreamlike quality. It wasn't until much later when a policeman asked her what her relationship had been to the dead man that her detachment peeled away like a bandage from a wound.

And then she cried, not just for Mel but for herself. He'd never loved her very much, she realised that; but he was the only man who'd ever accepted her just as she was; the only man who'd made her feel at all desirable. Now he was dead and she felt ugly and fat again.

It was dawn the next day before the police drove them back to the farm. Martin and Janey, drowsy and shocked, went to bed. Victoria climbed slowly up to the top meadow and sat in the dewy stillness, watching the thin light creep into the secret valley.

She thought: This is the last time I'll sit in this meadow.

There was no point in going on. It was the end. And she didn't even understand why . . .

The sun rose. The valley filled with a strong yellow light which illuminated the lush fullness of the dying summer. It was still the most beautiful place she had ever seen.

Defeated, she walked down the hill and wandered round the farm buildings, seeing as if for the first time the dilapidated fences, the rusty gutters, the patchy repairs, the roofs that had started leaking again.

Eventually she slept for a few hours. At ten she woke the others and by midday most of the arrangements had been made. A neighbouring farmer agreed to buy Bella and arranged to fetch her at two. The three cows and one heifer were going to be collected for market on Tuesday. That left only the goats grazing up in the meadow and the fruit and vegetables unpicked in the field. Martin and Janey could deal with all that. They were staying on, for a while at least.

Victoria packed her belongings. She left Mel's things – she couldn't bring herself to touch them – except for the embroidered Tibetan jacket and collar of bells she'd bought him last Christmas. These she put in her bag.

At some point arrangements would have to be made to sell the few modest pieces of furniture, the farm equipment, the vehicles – the tractor – such as it was – and the camper. Finally the farm itself. But she couldn't face that just yet.

She left without saying goodbye to Martin and Janey who

were meditating in the living-room, softly chanting their mantras. As she drove away up the hill towards the vaulted chestnuts she didn't look back.

A week later Henry Northcliff sat in his study at home, holding the telephone slightly away from his ear, and wishing the conversation would end.

But Mrs Danby's voice continued to travel relentlessly down the wire. 'It's just so *dreadful*, the whole thing. *Drugs* – I mean, I had no idea Victoria was mixed up in such things – all those drop-outs and drug-addicts. Honestly, Henry, I'm really *hurt* . . .'

He made a few pacifying noises then pointed out, 'She's not actually being charged with any offence, Mrs – er – Elizabeth.' She had insisted on the use of her first name.

'Maybe not. But the *inquest*. It's all going to come out. It's going to be dreadful – for *Victoria*.' A distinct whine had come into Mrs Danby's voice and Henry found himself thinking that her concern didn't extend to Victoria at all.

'And what's even worse,' Mrs Danby continued, 'is that she should drag *you* into this! I'm so embarrassed I don't know what to say.

'She didn't drag me into anything,' Henry corrected her. 'She phoned me and asked me for the name of a good solicitor, which I was delighted to give her. She didn't ask anything more.'

'No? She hasn't come round to see you then?'

'No,' Henry lied.

'Oh . . . well. That's *something* at least . . .'

She rang off at last and Henry sat at his desk for a moment, wondering if he was wise to get embroiled in all this. He was doing it partly for Caroline, of course, but also because there was a vulnerability and innocence in Victoria which appealed to the protective side of his nature. At the same time he would have to be careful not to let things get out of hand. Unhappy people could be leech-like in their consumption of other people's time.

He found the women sitting either side of the kitchen table, Caroline composedly in her chair, Victoria slumped over a cup of coffee.

The moment Victoria saw him she jumped to her feet. 'I must go. I only meant to stay a minute—'

'No, don't go yet,' Henry found himself saying, and hoped he wouldn't regret it. When she was back in her seat he added, 'That was your mother on the phone. I didn't tell her you were here.'

Victoria closed her eyes and shook her head as if the news were the final straw in an already heavy burden.

Henry sat down and said patiently, 'Now – let's look at the positive side of things. Everything's been sorted out on the legal front. There's absolutely nothing more to be done about what happened last week. What you must consider now is your future.'

Victoria looked at him blankly. 'I – haven't a clue. The commune was what I wanted .. Or what I thought I wanted.'

'Isn't there anything else you could do?'

She shook her head miserably. 'That's the trouble. I'm not *trained* to do anything. I was brought up to be jolly company at hunt balls and make a terrific quiche lorraine and avoid serious subjects. And I'm not very successful at *that*!'

Henry couldn't help smiling. 'Well, there's nothing wrong with tackling serious subjects.'

'Oh! You wouldn't say that if you'd met my county friends!' she exclaimed passionately. 'They think it's bad form to discuss politics or Vietnam or the Third World. And if anyone *does* mention anything like that, they just make a ghastly *joke* of it.'

'The British disease,' said Caroline. 'Making jokes.'

Henry watched Victoria and realised what else he liked about her. She had a delightful ingenuousness. She was incapable of guile or subterfuge. Everything came spilling out, straight from the heart.

He said gently, 'Look at it another way. Can you afford to go without a job for a while?' She nodded. 'Well then,' he went on, 'why don't you do voluntary work? For some charity or another. Something you really care about.'

She thought for a moment. 'Well – I do feel strongly about poverty. And bad housing. And Vietnam. And the Third World. And oppression. And injustice—'

'That should do for a start.'

She caught the gentle mockery in his tone and shot him a self-deprecating smile. 'Well, perhaps I'd choose *one* thing to start with ... Perhaps Vietnam. I do feel very strongly about that.'

'And how exactly would you serve this cause?'

Her round freckled face puckered into a frown of concentration. 'I think – by helping raise awareness of the atrocities committed against the people ... And collecting money to help the victims of American bombing ... And combating American imperialism generally – that sort of thing.'

The speech had more than a hint of propaganda to it, but Henry let it pass.

She said abruptly, 'I suppose you don't approve? The British government always supports US imperialism, whether it's Labour or Tory.'

Henry didn't want to argue the point. Remembering his own commitment to Spain when he was young, he said, 'If that's what you really believe, far be it from me ...' He got to his feet and, taking her cue, Victoria picked up her bag and followed Henry and Caroline towards the door.

'Thank you *both*,' Victoria said. 'And I'll think very hard about what you've said.'

Henry paused thoughtfully. 'Only one thing, Victoria. I'm all for the free expression of opinion, whatever that opinion might be. But if you do get involved in any of these movements, take care, won't you?'

'What do you mean?'

'Well' – he tried not to sound like an old woman – 'keep a sense of proportion. There's always an element who like to take things too far, to – use an issue to provoke discontent rather than to make a point.'

'Oh, you mean at demos and things? Don't worry, I wouldn't get involved in any of *that*. It frightens me rigid.'

'Was I too pompous?'

'No,' said Caroline. 'I thought you were – just right.'

'She probably won't take a blind bit of notice of what I said anyway.'

They walked slowly towards his study. 'I've still got a pile of work to do. I'm sorry.'

Sensing that he still wanted to talk she followed him in and sat on the edge of the desk.

She said, 'You're tired.'

He sat down and ran a hand across his forehead. 'No more than usual. It's just that' – he thought for a moment, trying to analyse his mood – 'I've lost my optimism, I suppose.'

'Any particular reason?'

He exhaled slowly, a long pensive sigh. 'For the first time I feel that, as a government, we've failed – in a number of important areas. We've been evading some vital issues and now we're paying the price – the highest strike record of any government, wages out of control, prices going mad. And it's going to get worse. I feel it.'

'Why do you think so?'

'There's a new discontent – a real anger. People are in a militant mood . . .' He looked up at her. 'It'll lose us the election, you realise that?'

'I see.'

He patted her hand thoughtfully. 'For myself, I won't be that sorry.' He examined her face. 'In fact, I thought of stepping down anyway. Even as Shadow Attorney-General. I've been meaning to talk to you about it—'

'Whatever you think is best—'

'Would you mind very much?'

She laughed a little. 'Mind? No, of course not. You work too hard and if it's what you *want* . . .'

Having voiced his decision, Henry knew it was the right one, and felt the beginnings of an immeasurable relief.

Nine

The rain beat furiously against the showroom windows, cascading down the glass and blurring the outlines of the buildings opposite. Manchester at its wettest. Not a good afternoon for selling cars, even the expensive ones that filled the showroom. In monsoon conditions, well-heeled people liked to stay at home just like everyone else. Bisley, the joint proprietor, sales director, chief – and only – salesman, got out his paper and had another look at the clue for twenty-five across. 'Illegitimate form of history (7).'

Bastard something? he wondered. No, that didn't sound right. What else were illegitimate children called . . .? Another word was just easing its way into his mind when the showroom door opened with a bang. He looked up and saw a young woman shaking out an umbrella.

She was well dressed in a modern casual sort of way. Comfortable middle class, he decided, with artistic tendencies. Not the buying type – Bisley could tell these things at a glance – but very striking. Worth a pleasant chat anyway.

He put on a smile and went to meet her. 'Good afternoon,' he began warmly, running an admiring look over her. 'And what can I do for you on this *lovely* day?'

She looked at him as if he were slightly mad. 'I want the blue Aston Martin, please. Assuming there's nothing wrong with it, of course.'

Knock me down with a feather, thought Bisley. You never can tell.

'Ah, now that's a very fine car – one owner, regularly serviced. And of course, less than a year old. I think you'll—'

'Let's cut all the talk, shall we?' she said briskly. 'Just tell me what you're prepared to offer?'

'Offer? Do you want a part-exchange?'

'No, no,' she said with a touch of impatience. 'I want a price reduction for cash – and I mean notes, not a cheque.'

The car was an expensive model – a DBS – and was priced at five thousand four hundred. Bisley thought quickly. The cash would certainly be useful; he could easily falsify the books. At the same time he was a little annoyed at this young woman's peremptory tone. He wasn't sure he was prepared to play her game.

'It's already a fair price,' he said firmly. 'In fact, we price *all* our cars fairly. There really isn't a lot of room for manoeuvre.'

She gave him a hard stare and he could see the anger behind the dark eyes. 'I was offering you a straightforward deal,' she said sharply. 'And all *you* want to do is go through the boring old rituals just to satisfy your ego. Don't you think it's rather a juvenile waste of time?'

Bisley blinked. For northern bluntness she beat any Mancunian into the shade. Although, from her accent, he'd bet she was a southerner.

Trying to recover the advantage, he joked weakly, 'My ego's perfectly satisfied. I have it serviced regularly. How's yours?'

They settled on five thousand one hundred – a drop of three hundred on the asking price. It was much further than he would normally have gone, but he'd bought the car at a good price and the sight of the tax-free wads of crisp new notes was too much to resist.

She produced an insurance cover note and announced she was going to take the car with her.

'For yourself, is it?' asked Bisley, wondering where she'd got the money for such an expensive machine.

'No. For my employer. He's a wealthy businessman.'

That explained a lot. When she'd gone Bisléy wondered if she wasn't *more* than just a rich businessman's employee. She was very – *animal*, that one. Definitely one of the permissive Society.

It was 4.00 p.m. and Friday. He would take the money home for the weekend and bank a small part of it in his business account on Monday – some, after all, had to go through the books. The rest he would keep in cash. He might even buy a new lawn mower tomorrow, and a bicycle for his daughter.

Flush with well-being, he went back to the crossword. A moment later he grinned with satisfaction. He had it at last: illegitimate form of history – *natural* history.

He decided that, despite the rain, it had turned out to be a most satisfactory day.

Gabriele chose Hendon to dispose of the car because it was a prosperous area of London and the garage forecourts were already thick with used Jaguars and Mercedes. The first garage offered her a cheque, which she turned down, but the second promised cash by 11.00 a.m. on Monday. She decided it was safe to accept. There was no way that the hot money could be spotted in the Manchester banking system, traced back to the car and every garage in the country alerted in that time. Even assuming the police were bright enough to realise the point of the whole exercise.

Nevertheless when she returned on the Monday morning she watched the garage for an hour before driving on to the forecourt. By noon she was back in the mews house with four thousand seven hundred pounds in used notes. Enough to pay rents, bills and major expenses for some months.

That left only nine hundred of the difficult money to dispose of. It should be safe to use it for small transactions, as long as it was spent in crowded places well away from the area of the mews house.

Things were beginning to look a little tidier.

She had several more jobs to do that day. First she went to a small printer's nearby and picked up some business cards. These gave her name as Gabriella Carelli and her occupation as photo-journalist accredited to *La Posta*. The address and phone number of the mews house were printed at the bottom.

Next she telephoned several photographic processing laboratories, and went to visit one in Covent Garden which specialised in fast developing and machine duplication. It was run by three energetic young men who were perfectly happy at the idea of doing rush jobs at odd hours. She left them one of her new cards.

At three she went to a firm called Inter-News, off Fleet Street. This was a photo-news agency which, for a modest fee of fifteen to twenty per cent, took freelancers' pictures and tried to sell them to newspapers and magazines worldwide. The firm had a staff of five, including the tea boy, and was headed by Stan Geddes, a former picture editor on a national newspaper. Like most newspapermen, he liked to think he'd seen it all.

Putting his head out of his office door he spotted the girl waiting. Quite a looker. He decided to see her personally.

He glanced at her card. '*La Posta* – but we can't handle their stuff.'

'No, no. I'm freelance,' she said firmly. '*La Posta* commissions me to do occasional jobs. Otherwise I'm on my own. Will you handle my pictures?'

'I'd have to see some of your work. We don't take on people just like that.' He thought: Even when they're as tasty as you.

She eyed him firmly. 'Look – if I walked in here with some hot news pictures, what would you do with them?'

Ah, he thought, a smart dolly, this one. He gave in gracefully. 'We'd flog 'em.'

'Quite.' She got to her feet and shook his hand. 'You'll be hearing from me then.'

After she'd gone, Stan Geddes smiled to himself. Then, taking her card, asked Beryl, his secretary, to enter her name and address on the file.

On her way home, Gabriele made a detour to the Marylebone Public Library and spent an hour in the reference section, taking notes from such diverse publications as *Who's Who, Encyclopaedia Britannica,* the *Legal Gazette* and the London Telephone Directory. It was amazingly easy to discover who did what in Britain, and, more important, their private addresses.

It was six when she finally got back to the mews. Giorgio and Max were already waiting. She didn't like Max coming to the house, but since they were going to meet so rarely in the future the risk was really quite small.

'Well, what have we got then?' she asked Max.

He fished a copy of *Red Notes* out of his pocket and, opening it at the right page, passed it to her.

The item was listed under Forthcoming Events for October, and was printed in bold type and capital letters, to give it emphasis. The item read: '25th: DEMONSTRATION AGAINST NATIONAL FRONT. Meet 12 p.m. Speakers' Corner. March to Russell Square. All welcome. Organisers: Third World Liberation Council.'

Max also passed her a leaflet, giving the objectives of the march:

– To show our abhorrence of the racist, fascist National Front and all they stand for.
– To demonstrate to these fascists that the people of this country will NOT tolerate anything to do with their vile aims. The stated aims of the National Front are 1) to protest against the presence of *all* coloured people in Britain, 2) to demand repatriation of all coloured people to their country of origin and 3), as an immediate aim, to ban all further immigration by coloured people to Britain.

These aims are obnoxious and abhorrent to all free thinking people!

On 25th October the National Front are holding a rally in Holford Hall, Russell Square. We must counter-demonstrate to show our repugnance.

COME AND JOIN US! DEMONSTRATE AGAINST FASCISM!

Gabriele read it a second time. Yes, it would do very well. The National Front always provoked strong feelings. This counter-march should produce an explosive situation. A popular journalistic phrase came into her mind: emotions are likely to run high.

She said, 'It looks as though it'll be quite an event. How many people are likely to turn up, Max?'

'Several thousand.'

'I think we'd better find out exactly who's going to be there. We need to be sure that the crowd will be – the right sort.' She added, 'What about your group. How many people can we rely on?'

'Twelve or so. Including Reardon, of course.'

Gabriele pondered. It would mean depending to a certain extent on people over whom she had no direct control. Her instincts were against it. And yet an opportunity like this might not turn up again for months.

She looked sharply at Max. 'And you're prepared to' – she didn't know quite how to put it – 'to be the *star*?'

Max looked at the floor, frowning. 'Yeah. It's okay. I don't mind.'

Gabriele guessed that he was thinking of Stephie, and how the event would cheer her up. She warned, 'We're going to keep a low profile on this, you know. There can't be a communiqué.'

'No, I understand.'

Giorgio roused himself from his silence. 'But some time?'

'Maybe. When it's necessary.'

'Then we should have a name,' Giorgio said. 'The Fifteenth of May Group!'

'Too – complicated,' Gabriele said. And, though she didn't voice it aloud, far too similar to the names of other groups in Europe. It was important to have their own quite separate identity. She suggested quietly, 'The Crystal Faction. I prefer that.'

Giorgio frowned. 'What does that *mean*?'

Gabriele sighed inwardly. Sometimes Giorgio could be very awkward. 'Crystal, as in clarify – *harden* – and faction, as in *splinter group*.'

She fetched her bag and took out the notes she had made in the library. 'Now, I've been making a list. A sort of strategy. It's only provisional. But I think it'll make a good start.'

It takes four hours in an unheated warehouse early on a cold October morning to seize up one's bones, Ryder discovered. It takes less than an hour to become bored rigid.

The gates of the factory opposite were deserted. Very sensibly, the pickets were having a nice warm breakfast elsewhere. He thought: What a waste of bloody time.

Conway turned up late, at ten past eight, muttering, 'Don't complain, mate. You've only done *one* morning of this. We've done *four*.'

Nick went straight to the office, shuffled through the pile of bumf on his desk for an hour, then joined the rest of the squad in the briefing-room.

'Okay, let's get going then,' said Straughan. 'The National Front march and counter-demonstration. One, A8 has given permission for both marches. You'll find details of the planned routes and stops on the operation order. Two, there are going to be about fifteen hundred on the National Front side. No surprises likely there – all the usual faces. Three, the leftist march is being organised by the Third World Liberation Council. Now, this lot have always been reasonably peaceable in the past. Mainly lobbying and propaganda. *However* –' he paused to add weight to his remark '– this time they're obviously out to provoke. Choosing to rally in Russell Square at the same time as the Front.'

Straughan clasped his hands together to make a precise arch. 'Now, what I want is the following – I want to know who's in with this Third World Liberation lot. Normally they've only a few dozen members at the most. Now, all of a sudden, they're expecting a thousand supporters. Where do they come from? My bet is that they've been busy phoning round their friends.'

The DCS looked at Nick. 'I want to know exactly who those friends are, Ryder. Then we'll know who to be looking out for on the day. Right? Any questions?'

The room was silent. Nick scribbled on the information sheet: *CPGB, IMG, IS, VUF.* They'd all be there, he'd bet his life on it – the Communist Party of Great Britain, the International Marxist Group, the International Socialists, the Vietnam United Front.

He thought for a moment then added *SSL* – The Socialist Students' League.

The briefing turned to other matters. The DCS held up a copy of the *Strike Back!* pamphlet. 'We're still on the look-out for this, all right? If you see something like it, I want to know where it came from and how it got there.' The DCS shot a glance at Nick. 'Although I gather we do have something from Technical Branch, Ryder?'

'They seem to think it might have been printed on the Continent.'

'Right!' Straughan's eyes gleamed triumphantly. 'Probably a foreign group then. As we thought. Still, we've got to keep a sharp look-out. In the wrong hands this could be dynamite.'

The pun was awful. Nick gave a short derisory laugh. Straughan shot him a hard look and Nick realised the joke had been strictly unintentional.

As soon as the meeting broke up, Nick went to Records to see what they had on the Third World Liberation Council.

The Council appeared to have a staff of one, a part-time secretary who worked in a borrowed office in Camden Town. Originally it had been formed by the 'broad left', including some members of the Labour Party and the Communist Party of Great Britain. It still had a Labour peer as its president. The organisation was run on a shoe-string and had at one point almost faded into obscurity.

Recently, however, it had come to life again, becoming increasingly vocal on the subject of immigration and the rights of millions of citizens in former British colonies to full British citizenship.

Nick wondered how best to tackle this one. Sometimes there was nothing like the direct approach. He closed the office door and dialled the number of the one-roomed headquarters in Camden Town. It seemed to be permanently engaged but finally he got through on the sixth try.

A crisp female voice answered. 'Yes?'

'I'd like to know about the march . . .'

'Twelve noon. Meet at Speakers' Corner.'

'What about banners. Are we co-ordinating?'

There was a slight pause and the voice asked cautiously, 'Who is this calling?'

'Manchester branch of the SSL. The name's Randall.' The name was perfectly accurate. He just hoped the secretary didn't know Randall.

'Oh, nice to talk to you.' The voice was trusting, friendly. 'We've been lent a place, in fact. Belonging to the Vietnam United Front. 2a Berners Road, off the Holloway Road. We're getting together there most evenings. Bring some materials, won't you? We don't have much money. Paint and stuff. You know. Are you in London now?'

'Er, not yet. On the Thursday, I hope.'

'Right. Well, we look forward to seeing you. You'll be bringing a group down, will you?'

'Yes.'

'Oh, good. How many?'

'Not sure yet. But at least fifty. We *hope*. Look forward to seeing you.' He cut the conversation short. He didn't want it to get too detailed.

He picked up the jottings he'd made in the inspector's office and ticked off the Vietnam United Front. No prizes for getting that one – the Vietnam protesters were into everything.

2a Berners Road. That was new. He checked his pocket notebook which he used for quick reference. The Vietnam people had been using a place in Tufnell Park up till now. He went back to the main files. Yes: just the Tufnell Park address.

He made a call to his friend Barbara at the GPO and within five minutes had three phone numbers in use at 2a Berners Road. One he immediately discounted: a tailor's on the ground floor. The other two, on the first floor, were in the name of the Holloway Workers' Council.

Another name, another organisation. It was like a jigsaw puzzle which was impossible to complete because the pieces were constantly changing shape. Yet the connections would be there, in the people. The same faces turned up time and time again.

The direct approach had got him this far. He decided to keep going, and dialled first one then the other number serving the first floor of 2a Berners Road.

No reply.

What next? It might be worth trying Nugent. If he could find him.

He phoned the flat where Nugent sometimes stayed. Eventually a sleepy masculine voice answered and told him that Nugent had 'split, man'. The voice had no idea where he'd gone and, no, they didn't know when he'd be back, if at all.

Nick wasn't surprised. Nor was he disappointed. Nugent had more or less dropped out and, apart from the pamphlets, the information he'd been passing recently hadn't been worth very much.

There were two other possibilities; good contacts Nick had built up in the previous year. But he wouldn't be able to find either of them until the evening, and he was impatient.

It had to be 2a Berners Road then.

He took the Tube to Islington and walked up the Holloway Road, not yet certain of what he was going to do. Number 2a was at the beginning of Berners Road, an undistinguished two-storey building, its façade once painted but now streaked in grime. The tailor's window was covered in heavy reinforced grilles. Those of the upper floor were blank and uncurtained. There was no access to the first floor from the front of the building; however there was an alleyway running down the side.

It was two in the afternoon. The sensible thing would be to come back later and watch for the evening arrivals – the organisers and banner painters. But to do it properly he'd need the van and the full camera set-up. Too much aggravation.

Besides, he was feeling lucky.

He walked purposefully into the alley. It led to a courtyard and an unexpectedly large two-storey storehouse which abutted the main building. There were two doors. On one of them was a sign: *Holloway Workers' Council*, and beside it in chalk: *Vietnam United Front*.

The door was unlocked. At the top of the stairs were two doors, one of them open. The open door led to a large airy room which was empty except for four trestle tables, several piles of boxes and, spread over the floor, wooden poles and sections of white fabric.

On the nearest table was a pile of broadsheets; on the next posters. Mostly Vietnam United Front, but some for the Third World Liberation Council, advertising the march.

'Hello.'

The voice startled him, but he made the effort to turn slowly.

It was a girl in her mid to late twenties. Plump. Long frizzy fair hair decorated with beads. Ethnic clothes. Sandals. No make-up. Freckles. Nice smile.

He replied, 'Hi,' and waited.

She came forward, looking friendly. '*Sorry*. I just popped out . . . Can I help? Did you want some literature? There's quite a bit here. And more in the office . . .' She indicated the closed door across the landing. 'Gosh, I've been here all morning and the moment I pop out somebody *comes*. Honestly, *typical*!' She laughed awkwardly, waiting for him to respond and ease the moment along.

'Just wanted some details of the march on the 25th.'

She brightened visibly. 'Oh, right! *No* problem. Gosh – do you want a poster or would a broadsheet be okay? And, let's see – what *else* do we have? Mustn't let you go away without *everything*, must I!'

Nick thought: God, what *have* we here. The accent – straight out of Cheltenham Ladies' College. Upper-class Belgravia gone native.

She handed him a broadsheet and a leaflet. 'That's all there is, actually. Sorry. Will that be enough? We're only helping out on this one. It's not really a Vietnam Front thing, although of course we all support it. God, wouldn't *anyone*? I mean, really, when you see the blatant racism it' – she shook her head as if it were impossible to find the right words – 'it makes you *sick*, doesn't it?'

'Ya. Makes you sick.' Nick agreed. He strolled towards the closed office and paused by the door. She got the hint and, opening it, let him in. He wandered casually around. There were two desks, two telephones, and a clutter of papers piled haphazardly on the floor.

She came up behind him and asked, 'Who are you with?' The question was conversational rather than probing.

'Oh. Er – various groups. But mainly the SSL.'

'Ah.' A moment of complete blankness, then she nodded doubtfully.

She obviously hadn't a clue. Nick almost smiled. With growing confidence he asked, 'Er ... D'you know what the order of marching is ... You know, who's going to be there and who'll be leading the thing up ... That sort of thing?'

She frowned. 'Oooh. Got me there. You see, I'm a bit new and, well, I man the desk and do what I can. To be honest, I'm just a volunteer and ...'

He amended his opinion: naïve upper-class Belgravia do-gooder with a social conscience – perfect left-wing fodder. He nodded understandingly. 'Know where I can find out?'

'Oh yes! Tomorrow evening. There's a meeting here at seven. I expect they'll be discussing all that ...'

Nick thought: As simple as that. He said easily, 'Thanks. You've been really helpful.'

Her face lit up at the compliment. 'Not at all! That's what I'm here for!'

He paused at the top of the stairs. 'Bye. Er – sorry, what was your name?'

'Oh, Victoria. Victoria Danby.'

The moment he'd gone Victoria realised she'd forgotten the name of his organisation – SOL, was it? And she hadn't even asked for his name. She *should* have – the committee were very keen on that.

She muttered 'Blast!' and made a mental note to get everyone's name in future.

Still, it was only her second day here and, all things considered, she wasn't doing too badly. She'd read all the information sheets, articles and pamphlets issued by the VUF, and quickly realised how little she really knew about the Vietnam conflict. It made her ashamed to think how ignorant and ostrich-like she'd been in the past.

All that was going to change now. She was determined to be useful, and that meant knowing her stuff.

Taking a doughnut out of the desk drawer, she began to read a pile of news clippings. The doughnut disappeared very quickly and she found herself eating another. Weak and sinful. But she was *definitely* starting a new diet next week.

The telephone rang a couple of times. One caller wanted to join the VUF, the other wanted details of the anti-Front march. At first she'd been confused at the VUF's involvement in the march. But as one of the committee had pointed out to her, the coloured immigration issue and the Vietnam anti-colonial struggle were two sides of the same coin. She'd never thought of it like that, but of course it was absolutely true. Blindingly obvious, in fact.

The Workers' Council phone rang on the other desk and she took a message. There'd be someone in later. People were always coming and going.

The time began to pass more slowly; she had nothing more to read and by three she'd finished sticking down the last batch of envelopes she'd been given. By four she was wishing she'd brought a book with her.

There was a sound. She gave a slight start and looked up.

A man was standing in the doorway. She smiled. 'Hello, can I help you?'

He came in. He was very dark, with rich black hair that came down to his collar, and a thick but well-trimmed beard. He wore jeans – good ones, she noticed – and the sweater was pale blue cashmere.

He looked slowly round the room then fixed his eyes on her. They were dark brown and penetrating.

Victoria thought: Absolutely gorgeous. The kind you could die for.

She reminded herself that dozens of women probably had.

She laughed nervously. 'Did you want some information?'

He gave her a small rather mechanical smile. 'I want information about the march . . .'

An accent. Very attractive. Latin? She replied, 'Yes, of course. I've got a leaflet or a poster or—'

'Yes . . . But we wanted details –' He came up to the edge of the desk and looked down at her. He was even better close up. She caught a scent of eau de cologne.

He went on: 'We want to know who will be there, and how many . . . We want to bring many, many friends, but we want to know what is happening . . . You understand?'

'Yes, of course. There's a meeting. Tomorrow at seven. For all the organisers.' She looked away hurriedly, aware that she had spoken in a silly girlish voice, and thought: Get a grip. This one is *way* out of reach.

She suddenly remembered to ask, 'Who are you? Which organisation do you come from?'

For a moment she thought he wasn't going to answer, but then he replied a little grudgingly, 'We are foreign students. We want to show our solidarity against fascism.' He pronounced 'fascism' in a totally foreign way – Italian or Spanish, she decided.

He was wandering back towards the door. 'Thank you,' he said, looking back at her with a sudden warm smile. 'You have been most kind.'

She smiled to herself until long after he'd gone.

Then she remembered that she was large and whale-like and unattractive, and he wouldn't have smiled so much if he'd seen her standing up.

Completely beyond her reach. But there was no harm in imagining.

Ten

At six it would be twilight. Nick took a look through the lens of the Nikon and focused on the alleyway. On the other side of the van, Wicker, a young detective constable who specialised in photography, was tightening the clamp on one of his two Canons, which were loaded with high-speed 400 ASA film. Nick checked that the spare film and battery cartridges were to hand, so that he'd be able to pass them to Wicker when necessary.

They settled back to wait. They had managed to park in a good position, a few yards beyond the alleyway, so that people coming from the Holloway Road were facing the van's one-way back windows.

Nick said, 'You just keep firing the shutter until I tell you to stop, okay? Even if it's a housewife with shopping bags.'

'Okay.'

It was only ten to six. Plenty of time.

Then, suddenly, there were two of them. The first arrivals.

Looking at street numbers, searching for the alleyway.

Nick urged, 'Go!' and heard the Canon's motor-drive fire off half a dozen shots. He took a couple of frames himself, just in case. But it wasn't vital because he knew the faces anyway. He scribbled their names in his notebook.

After ten minutes there were more. Committee members of the Third World Liberation Council. He knew their names too.

By six-forty they were coming thick and fast, and, with only seconds to spare, Wicker had to switch from camera to camera while Nick hastily loaded new film.

Then it grew dark and the dim streetlights cast deep shadows. Nick put his camera aside and left the photography to Wicker.

At seven-ten there were a couple of latecomers, and five minutes after, one more. Then nobody for a long time. Nick began to relax. There'd been a few he hadn't recognised, but those would soon be identified from Wicker's shots. There were no surprises: all the usual trendy-lefties – the smooth articulate revolutionaries loved by the media; the university lecturers living in intellectual cuckoo land; the well-paid actors assuaging some deep-rooted personal guilt by assuming it for the world as a whole; the self-important clerics with their messages for mankind; and the proud self educated worker activists.

Nick didn't hate them or anything like that. In a curious sort of way he actually admired them – the clever ones at least – for the way they stuck at it. The problem was, they weren't to be trusted. They advocated lunatic policies and, like all zealots, turned a blind eye to the means. Not that they themselves cared to get involved in any dirty tricks. They left that to the followers, the ones who worshipped at the shrines of wealth-for-all and revenge-on-the-rich; people so eaten up by envy that they were incapable of clear thinking; the ones whose anger, having no rational outlet, became bottled-up and explosive. They were the really dangerous ones. And they had to be stopped.

That was why Nick did the job – because they had to be stopped and he was the best person to do it.

Nearly eight. Suddenly Nick sat up. Two men. Nearly an hour late. He said 'Go!' to Wicker, and peered at the fast-approaching figures.

He exclaimed softly, a gentle 'Hah!' of satisfaction. One of the men was Wheatfield. Max. Late of the Socialist Students' League.

But the other—?

His satisfaction evaporated. The head was down, the features hard to distinguish. But foreign-looking. Black hair, beard, dark complexion - or was that a trick of the light?

Damn it, put your head up. How can I get a good shot if you don't show me your *face*?

But even as the man came into the dim glow of a streetlight he turned his head away, looking back towards the Holloway Road, as if checking on his retreat.

Then they were gone, disappearing into the darkness of the alley, and Nick sat back with a sigh of exasperation. 'Dammit!'

Wicker decided to state the obvious. 'Impossible to get a full face on that one.' After a moment he added unhelpfully, 'Was he important?'

Nick gave a wry laugh and murmured sarcastically, 'Sure. Very important. Wasn't it obvious from the back of his head?'

Victoria sat by the door and counted thirty-five people crowded into the storeroom. They sat on the trestle tables and the available chairs or leant against the walls. She had managed to account for almost all of them by name or by organisation. Athena, one of the VUF committee, was very keen on security. Because of the bloody spies in Special Branch, she had explained, though sometimes she suspected it was MI5. Victoria had laughed until she'd realised that no one else thought it a joke. Somewhat chastened she had then kept quiet.

Now Victoria tried to concentrate on the meeting, but it seemed to have developed into a rather woolly discussion about long-term objectives.

Suddenly there were footsteps on the stairs and Victoria quickly got up to open the door. Two men appeared: the first a thin, intense-looking man with long straggly hair and wire-rimmed glasses; the second, she suddenly realised, was the gorgeous foreign man from yesterday. She brightened. Then, remembering her task for the evening, politely asked which organisation they came from. The first man glared at her with sudden and vicious hostility and, without answering, pushed rudely past.

Victoria stared after him, feeling well and truly snubbed. The foreigner was still by the door, leaning unconcernedly against the frame, casting his eyes slowly round the room, looking bored. She said a little peevishly, 'Anyone would think I'd asked him how often he kicked his *dog*.'

His eyes swivelled round to her, deeply puzzled. 'Kicked his *dog*?'

She laughed nervously. 'Er – old English expression.' She regarded him hopefully. 'Don't suppose there's any chance of knowing your name—'

'My name?' For a moment he didn't answer, then a flicker of amusement passed over his face, and he gave a slight shrug. 'Vespucci. "A" for Amerigo.'

The name was vaguely familiar but she couldn't quite place it. Definitely Italian though, just as she'd thought. She added the name to the list.

She looked up to find him smiling, and she noticed how white his teeth were against the darkness of his beard and skin. He leaned down and put his lips to her ear. 'You like it?'

'I – what?'

'You like my name?'

She stared at him. 'Yes. Yes, very nice.' She suddenly realised he was making fun of her. Looking as businesslike as possible, she went back to her seat and sat down again. She thought a little resentfully: This is the last time I do *this* job.

The meeting droned on, with a lot of talk about support and press coverage.

At the mention of the press the Italian stood up a little straighter. She stole a look at him. A small frown of concentration had appeared on his forehead.

She wondered why he was interested. Then she wondered all sorts of other things about him, none of them to do with the meeting ... Like the sort of women he went for – beautiful, inevitably. And how many he knew – without doubt, a depressingly large number. She could imagine him with a woman, sensual, confident in his approach, very practised, yet caring, wanting to give a woman pleasure.

Lucky women.

Unlucky *her*.

She sighed inwardly. Thinking about unobtainable men wasn't any help when there was an empty flat to be faced again tonight. A place of her own had seemed a good idea, but she hadn't allowed for the loneliness. The decision to break with Mel's crowd had been right, she was sure of that. Yet she had no wish to see her county friends from the old days either. And, though the people in the VUF were friendly in a brisk no-nonsense sort of way, they weren't likely to become real chums. It was all very difficult.

The meeting was coming to an end. People were standing up and talking in groups. The Italian went to join his companion. Because she couldn't think of anything else to do, Victoria took her list across to Athena who was busy talking. Athena stared at it vaguely and was about to tuck it under her arm when she took another look and gave a short laugh. 'What on earth is *this*!' she exclaimed, pointing at the Italian's name. 'A joke? Amerigo Vespucci – *really*!'

Cold fingers of embarrassment crept up Victoria's spine. It came to her now that, according to the history books she had paid such scant attention to at school, Amerigo Vespucci had at some time or another been associated with the discovery of America.

The committee woman demanded, 'Who gave you this name?'

Victoria indicated the Italian. The woman seemed mollified. 'He came in with Max Wheatfield. He should be all right then . . .' She gave Victoria a hard look. 'Still, it was hardly worth writing it down, was it?'

Victoria turned away. As she made her way back towards the door she eyed the Italian resentfully and thought: You aren't very nice at all.

Suddenly, on a whim, she veered across and tapped him on the back. Smiling pleasantly, she said, 'It's remarkable. You don't look a day over three hundred.'

His face flashed with suspicion then, suddenly understanding the joke, he said. 'Thank you. Nor do you.' His tone was friendly and she softened a little.

She explained, 'I was only doing as the organisers asked, you know.'

'Sure.' With deliberate effect, he fixed his eyes on her and, putting his hand lightly on her shoulder, moved his fingers across it in a soft caress. 'It was their mistake then, to ask it of you.'

Ah, the treatment, Victoria thought. She tried to show that it wasn't going to work on her, and almost succeeded.

'What *is* your name?' she asked, for something to say.

He gave a slight bow. 'Emilio.'

'Nicer than Amerigo,' she replied. 'Not so continental.' She giggled slightly at the joke.

The thin straggly-haired man called Max came up and glared at her again. She said a fleeting goodbye to Emilio and retreated.

As she made her way down to the street, she reflected that

Emilio was the type of man that good girls were warned against. Yet she had a sneaking suspicion that it was merely sour grapes; that people only said that because they were jealous of the fun and excitement that surrounded people like him.

If she ever had the choice she knew what she'd go for. The fun and excitement.

That she should be so lucky . . .

When she got outside she paused for a moment and breathed in the cool autumn air and wished that, instead of heading back to an empty flat, she was looking at the vast dome of glittering stars above the calm stillness of Hunter's Wood.

Nick watched the girl staring at the sky and recognised the Belgravia-type volunteer from the previous day. While Wicker took a couple of snaps he wrote in his notebook: Victoria Danby, VUF.

Then she was on her way, walking rather listlessly towards the Holloway Road.

He barely had time to look back towards the alleyway when they were there: Wheatfield and his foreign friend. He said sharply to Wicker, 'Quick, those two!'

The camera motor whirred away, firing the shutter at staccato speed. Nick squirmed with frustration. Although Wheatfield's profile was visible for a brief moment, the dark-haired man kept his back firmly to the camera and was even now disappearing briskly down the street.

'Damn,' Nick said simply.

He left it a moment then, stretching his arms wearily, said, 'Okay, let's call it a day.'

'Already?' asked Wicker. 'There're still quite a few to come out.'

In the dim light Nick gave him the benefit of a hard stare. 'Yes – *already*. You may want to sit through another performance, but I've seen enough of the actors, thanks very much, and I'd like to get home.'

Only eight days to the demonstration.

Gabriele beckoned to Giorgio and, taking out a large sheet of plain paper, spread it out on the floor of the mews house. Using a thick pen she drew a large square in the centre, and marked all four sides with small counter-strokes. 'Railings,' she explained. In the middle of the square she drew a few trees. With one eye on the street plan of London, she added an outer square, with approach roads at all four corners.

'Russell Square.'

Using a red pen she drew a dotted line down the northern approach road to Woburn Place, into the square at the north-eastern corner, and along the northern side. 'Is this right for the National Front?' she demanded.

Max indicated a point about half-way along the northern side. 'The hall's about there.'

She brought the dotted line up to the approximate position of the hall. Then, starting from the opposite south-western approach road of Montague Street she traced another line up into the square, along the south side and out again towards the south, like an inverted U.

'That's the route of our march, right? Now, we can be absolutely sure that the police won't want us anywhere near the fascists on the northern side. So, to keep us firmly to the south side, they'll have to seal off the right- and left-hand sides of the square.' She drew two lines where she imagined the police would be.

'Now, after the column has entered the square, we've got to get it to slow down. Jam up a bit. That's where your friends come in, Max. Right?'

He nodded thoughtfully. 'Yeah. They'll just make some noise or something . . .'

'Then – you and Giorgio and Reardon and the other three, you must end up here.' She marked a cross on the demonstrators' side of the first police line.

'And I'll be just behind the police . . . Here.' She added a red blob in the no-man's land between the two demonstrations.

Giorgio said, 'But they will not let you arrive with a car . . .'

I'm going to park it there on Friday night. There's no reason for them to move it.' She looked up at Max. 'Reardon – how much have you told him?'

Max shrugged slightly. 'He had to know everything, otherwise he'd be no good. Don't worry. Reardon's okay.'

She nodded. She'd have to believe him.

They went through the whole operation again, trying to foresee the snags. Then she destroyed the map.

When Max had gone Gabriele made some calls. First she phoned

Stan Geddes at the Inter-News Agency and told him she'd be covering the demonstration. His tone was polite, but uninterested. He confirmed that the office would be staffed until at least five on the Saturday afternoon.

Then she called the processing laboratory and told them she'd need some rolls printed up very quickly the same day.

That covered the picture side of the operation. Except for the quality of the photographs themselves. That was up to her. She'd taken several test rolls of people walking in Hyde Park, to get familiar with the Olympus equipment. The results had been reasonably good.

There was nothing else left to do so far as the demonstration was concerned. She turned her mind to the longer term.

She needed supplies.

Taking the slip of paper from her handbag lining, she checked the dialling code for Paris and then called the third number on her list. The connection took some moments but eventually it rang. Gabriele was aware of being nervous and gripped the receiver more tightly.

A woman answered. Gabriele asked for Acheme. There was a pause and a male voice asked for her name. When she had given it, he told her, 'Your consignment will be ready for Wednesday, the 29th. When you get to Paris telephone between ten and noon. You will be told where to go. You will need to bring the money.' He added, 'The consignment will be bulky. You understand?'

'All right for a car, though?'

'All right for a car.'

Gabriele put down the receiver and immediately considered the problems. Only twelve days away and a bare four days after the demonstration. She would have to get organised. She would have to find a suitable vehicle, something in which the consignment could be safely hidden. None the less, passing through Customs would be very risky. Perhaps they should use a circuitous route?

No, there had to be a better way, one which involved less risk. Or best of all, one which involved no risk at all.

Eleven

Ryder wondered if he was in the right place. The groups of marchers had got fairly muddled, but as far as he could see the bunch around him was Vietnam United Front. They were young, most of them, and noisy, their chants echoing loudly across Great Russell Street towards the dark dignified mass of the British Museum. Nick kept step with them, mouthing the chants, merging into the group.

Futher back were the Marxists, the International Socialists and various other factions; ahead the organisers – the Third World people – with whom he'd mingled at Speakers' Corner. A few known agitators in each group. But no indication as to which lot – if any – were planning trouble.

Ahead was Montague Street which led directly into Russell Square. Somewhere in a building on the corner was Conway with an array of cameras hidden behind a curtained window. There would be other Branch members in the square itself, some behind the uniformed police lines, others on rooftops.

As the procession turned into Montague Street Nick decided to move up towards the leaders who were in clear view about twenty yards ahead. He made up ground gradually, picking up the chant of the forward group, swinging his legs and pumping his arms to the rhythm of 'Fascists *out*, fascists *out*'.

Trees became visible over the sea of heads – the square. And ahead, a line of helmets – the mass of uniformed men blocking the marchers from the western perimeter.

He followed the leaders into the square, and made the swing right, past the cordon and along the south side. The crowd was bunching up now as the leaders slowed down and the back-markers, anxious to get into the square, pushed forward. Movement slowed to a shuffle. The chants became louder, the waving of the banners more agitated as the leaders shouted their message in the general direction of the National Front somewhere on the far side of the square and, more particularly, Nick guessed, to the inevitable band of mediamen, hungry for some colourful pictures.

He took a quick look round. No pushing or shoving nearby.

Craning his neck, he gazed back over the mass of heads towards the entrance to the square. The middle of the column seemed to have come to a halt and a thick concentration of demonstrators was pressing up against the police line.

A nasty feeling crept into Nick's stomach; he suddenly had the suspicion that he was in the wrong place.

He took a last look at the head of the column, and then, turning against the tide, tried to make his way back. It was hard work. The crowd was closing in tighter. Why the hell weren't the uniformed boys keeping the front of the column moving? People panicked when they got claustrophobic.

Almost on cue a banner jerked into the air ahead, somewhere near the police line, then jerked rapidly down again, as if being dragged to the ground. Anxiously Nick stood on tiptoe and peered over the throng.

A person turned. A quarter-profile. Tantalisingly familiar. Long straggly hair . . .

Wheatfield.

Where on earth had *he* sprung from?

And beside him – dark hair, beard. Wheatfield's foreign friend. The one who was camera-shy.

And then another, with bright red hair. Reardon.

Suddenly Nick was certain of where the trouble was going to be and with a hard shove, forced his shoulder into the crush of bodies and began to fight his way through.

The police line was thick, about five men deep. Gabriele hadn't bargained on that. From her vantage point on the car bonnet she could hardly see over them.

Clutching her cameras, she scrabbled up on to the car roof, and hastily reset the tripod.

That was better. She could now see the demonstrators well bunched up against the rows of uniforms. Almost immediately she spotted Giorgio, his dark head clearly distinguishable in the crowd. Max would be close by. They were right in position.

She braced her legs well apart and, focusing the camera, took a couple of shots.

Just in time. A roar came up from the crowd, there was a surge, and the middle of the police line began to sag.

Any moment now . . .

A voice yelled from close by, '*You! Down!*'

She ignored it. A hand grabbed her by the ankle. She looked down angrily. A senior policeman in a peaked cap was motioning her off the car. 'Come on! We're moving everyone back!'

She shrugged as if she didn't understand, and pointed to the press pass strung around her neck.

'I don't care,' he yelled. '*Everyone* back!'

Gabriele looked desperately towards the crowd. It would be any moment now! She stalled again, shrugging her shoulders.

Another roar went up and the crowd surged. The police line showed signs of breaking completely.

The senior officer hesitated, then, abandoning his attempt to move Gabriele, ran towards the straining line.

The roar died down, the line held and for an awful moment Gabriele thought the momentum of the demonstrators had been lost.

Then from behind her came a clattering sound and a drumming of heavy boots on the roads. She spun round and saw a stream of reinforcements running from a side street. They ran towards the bulging line and, at a shouted order, the line opened up to let them through.

Immediately a bitter throaty howl of anger went up from the demonstrators. Gabriele saw Max jostling for position, Giorgio beside him.

It was going to happen. Tense with excitement, Gabriele settled back behind the camera and, carefully framing the picture, placed her finger on the shutter.

Victoria yelped as someone stood on her foot. She turned, intending to smile and show she didn't take it personally, but an elbow came out of nowhere and hit her on the side of the head.

'Oh, please mind out. *Please.*'

She began to feel uneasy. Everything was changing. The unified, friendly, chanting faces had gone. The voices were ugly now, the shouts and cries jarring in her ears. Tall bodies were pushing in on her, jostling roughly.

It wouldn't last, she felt sure. Everyone was bound to sort themselves out in a minute.

Suddenly voices rose angrily and the crowd surged. The movement pushed Victoria sideways. She cried, 'I say!'

But the mass moved on, crushing in on her, carrying her relentlessly forward. Victoria was appalled at her own helplessness. She stifled the urge to panic.

A leaden weight came down on her foot. Stumbling, she fought to regain her balance, but couldn't disentangle her foot from the weight. With terrible certainty she suddenly realised what was happening, and panic shot through her like a wedge of ice. Everything moved into slow motion. She was being dragged down, slowly, inexorably. The bodies were closing in over her and the patch of light that had been the sky slowly receded . . .

She shrieked and grabbed at whatever she could find – hands, clothes, legs . . .

A kick, a foot in her back, a sharp pain. Her head hit the ground and she flung up her arms to protect it. But the feet kept coming – hard, brutal, kicking, stumbling, crushing.

They'd realise in a minute, then they'd stop. *Surely* . . .

But they didn't stop and through her pain, all Victoria could feel was an immense and profound surprise.

Nick ducked as an arm swung wildly over his head. He came up, trying to get his bearings. He knew Wheatfield and company must be very close, but they were maddeningly invisible due to a large belligerent bull of a man who was bellowing and roaring in front of him.

All of a sudden the crowd heaved to one side, throwing some people to their knees, and a gap opened up. Nick forced his way through.

He was close to the police line now. Dimly he took in the fact that the line had been reinforced by the Special Patrol Group. And then, right in front of him, almost at the front of the crowd, he spotted Wheatfield. Next to him was red-haired Reardon carrying a banner pole and yelling a chant that sounded like 'Go! go! go!' Even as Nick struggled to reach them, he saw Reardon lower the pole and thrust it forward, stabbing viciously into the mass of police.

Immediately all hell broke loose and the crowd became a fighting screaming mass.

Wheatfield was close. Nick went for his arms but withdrew with a yelp of pain as the full force of a truncheon landed on his elbow. Fleetingly he thought: Christ, that's all I need. He regained his balance and in the maelstrom reached for Wheatfield again, a Wheatfield who was jabbing and kicking furiously at a sack on the ground, except it wasn't a sack it was a policeman. Nick thought: You bastard. He almost had him, but one of the SPG was already there, yanking Wheatfield out of the crowd, raining blows on his head.

138

Nick elbowed through to the front and, fending off the shoves and pushes of the crowd, saw the SPG man deliver a couple more blows to a strangely apathetic Wheatfield, inert on the ground. Nick wished the stupid idiot of an SPG man would stop. This sort of thing looked bloody bad.

At last the SPG man reached for Wheatfield's arm and, bending it up his back, pulled him to his feet, ready to haul him off into custody. Nick thought: One safely out of the way at least.

Even as he was thinking it, five or six people pushed out of the crowd and closed around the two men. The next moment they retreated and Nick felt a small tremor of shock. The SPG man was on his knees looking dazed.

And Wheatfield had disappeared.

It had all happened so *quickly*.

Nick thought: *Oh no you don't*! and cast quickly around.

Got you! There was Wheatfield. Back in the crowd, just away to the left. Black Beard and red-haired Reardon on either side of him.

Nick went for him again, but fell foul of two sprawled bodies on the ground. He got clear, then let out a sudden yelp of surprise as someone grabbed his arm and tried to wrench it out of its socket. He yanked his head round and glimpsed a black uniform.

Nick yelled, 'No you great . . .' but no one was listening and the truncheon was whistling down through the air and Nick reacted in the only way he knew. He dodged the blow and, with only passing regret, flung a hand up and simultaneously twisted and shoved at the face under the helmet. The SPG man staggered back, clasping a bloody nose, and Nick dived away.

Damn it, where are you, Wheatfield?

He craned his neck.

Black Beard. Reardon. Very close but in the thick of the crowd.

They were leaning over something.

Nick ducked down to see. It was Wheatfield lying on the ground.

Injured? Not *that* badly. Then *why*?

Nick gasped. Something black thudded into Wheatfield's head and snapped it viciously to one side.

What the hell?

A *kick*?

But who from?

The foot appeared again, coming in with a vengeance, landing full in Wheatfield's face.

The foot belonged to Black Beard.

Fighting among *themselves*? No. *No*.

This was something else, something that stank to high heaven.

Curious, Nick held back and watched.

Black Beard and Reardon were lifting a slumped Wheatfield to his feet and, supporting him by the arms, beginning to elbow their way through the crowd. They were heading towards the remains of the police line.

A flicker of a suspicion lodged itself in Nick's mind.

And then, suddenly, he knew.

He exclaimed, '*Shit!*' and rushed forward.

Almost immediately he realised he was too late. The wounded man and his two bearers had already passed between the groups of uniformed men, and through the line of mounted men now advancing on the crowd. The strange group was out into the open. Already, a photographer on a car top had her camera trained on them.

Nick followed, dodging through the line. He was stopped by a mounted man but, having identified himself, managed to squeeze between two horses without getting a truncheon on his head.

He was far, far too late.

Ahead, Black Beard and Reardon were setting Wheatfield down on the pavement and leaning him back against the railings, revealing a face bright scarlet with blood. The girl photographer had come down from the car and was taking shots from a variety of angles.

Nick groaned. He couldn't possibly grab Wheatfield now: it would look even worse than it undoubtedly looked already. Also, he would get his face in the paper, and that would be horribly public.

But the others were a different matter. However he would need help. Panting, he ran up to a group of three coppers and, showing his warrant card, led them back to where Wheatfield lay.

As they approached, Nick felt his heart sink. Reardon and Black Beard had disappeared. He looked everywhere, but there was no sign of them.

As for Wheatfield, he was the centre of a veritable circus of attention. Five or six photographers and a TV news crew were all vying for the best shot of the blood pouring down Wheatfield's smashed and agonised face.

Terrific theatre. Wonderful television.

Bitterly, Nick watched as the newsmen carefully recorded Wheatfield being lifted gently on to a stretcher, Wheatfield moaning loudly, Wheatfield being attended by a doctor who looked sufficiently worried to suggest that Wheatfield was somewhere between the critical list and death.

Someone should have provided hankies.

As Wheatfield's stretcher disappeared into an ambulance, Nick cast around again desperately. Where *had* the other two gone?

Suddenly he had a glimpse. A head of red hair in the distance, down a side street, walking jauntily past a police van.

Reardon.

Nick yelled to the coppers, 'There! The red hair!' And they pounded off at the run.

Nick ran up the steps of a house and, hoisting himself up on the railings, searched the crowd.

The police line had dissolved into a series of violent skirmishes, with horses pressing hard into the remains of the crowd. At the rear, many of the demonstrators were trying to escape down Montague Street, back the way they had come.

No sign of Black Beard . . . And yet he *must* have gone that way.

Nick dropped to the ground and loped towards the police line. A gap opened up and he dived through it. Dodging past a group of fighting police and students, he forced himself back through the crowd until he came to the beginning of Montague Street.

He paused on the corner of the street and hoisted himself up on the railings again. He watched the demonstrators leaving the square. Nothing. He examined the last few groups still facing the police. No sign.

He'd lost him.

What a hell of a day.

Out of habit, he kept an eye on the crowd, looking for other faces, but saw none he recognised.

The crowd was quietening down at last, the police were pressing forward and forcing more and more demonstrators out of the square.

Across the street there were groups of demonstrators who had retreated into doorways or, like Nick, had climbed up on railings and steps to watch the action. Nick cast his eyes over them for perhaps the fifth time. And nearly fell off his perch.

He stared in disbelief.

Black Beard.

Moving out of a doorway.

He must have been there all the time, but hidden from view.

Right, thought Nick. This time I've got you.

He jumped to the ground and pushed his way through the crowd, tense with excitement, keeping his bearings, working out the right angle to cut Black Beard off . . .

He caught a glimpse of the black hair. Further ahead than he'd thought.

He quickened his pace to close the distance. A last group of people were in his way. He pushed violently past them.

Almost there.

A couple more strides.

Yes! *Got you now.*

Triumphantly, he reached for Black Beard's arm.

Then, in a split second of incredulity, Nick realised everything was going dreadfully wrong.

An enormous weight was driving into him from behind and crashing him to the ground. He kicked out and, wriggling violently, managed to stagger to his knees. But his arm was suddenly forced half-way up his back in a text book arm lock. Nick twisted his head and dimly took in the sight of an SPG man with a bloody nose . . .

Nick began to yell 'Special Branch –' when something with the solidity of a sledge-hammer smashed into his head and sent his cheek grinding into the road.

As the world faded in a nauseating storm of blinding lights, Nick thought hazily: What a bloody shambles.

Victoria sat on the doorstep and had a good cry. After a while she felt better and dried her eyes on her sleeve. Still trembling she lifted her skirt to examine the red blotches and grazes that covered her legs. Some patches were swollen and very tender. She moved her shoulder and winced – something strained. A bruise on the ribs, too. And then her eye – a bump above and a big swelling below.

It could have been worse. She might have broken something. She could have been dead. She gave a laugh half-way between a giggle and a sob, then, realising she was getting mildly hysterical, forced herself to calm down.

Someone – she didn't know who – had brought her to this side street. In the midst of the terrible crush the feet had suddenly stopped bumping and kicking, and somehow a space had opened up and some kind people had reached down to pull her to her feet. A man – she hadn't even seen his face – had got an arm round her waist and led her clear. He'd left her here in this doorway, when – ten minutes ago? She'd lost all track of time.

'You okay? Do you need an ambulance or something?'

She looked up. Curious faces stared at her, standing a little back, concerned but distant.

She said quickly, 'I'm fine, I'm fine,' and they left, hurrying on. Many people were walking quickly past, escaping the pandemonium in the square. Perhaps she should get away too.

Shakily she gathered herself together. She brushed some of the dirt off her skirt and tried unsuccessfully to tie up a broken strap on her sandal.

Then she put her hand to her waist.

Her bag. It had gone. It had been tied round her waist.

Not much money. Two pounds. But her *keys*. Then she remembered that the caretaker would probably be able to let her into the flat.

Just no money then. No way of getting anywhere.

A taxi and write an IOU? Hardly: no cabbie would trust her looking like this. Her sister? No, Diana was away for the weekend.

She got to her feet, almost in tears again.

People were still streaming past, moving fast, talking angrily, not looking her way. She moved tentatively forward, plucking up courage to ask someone for a lift, when she stopped dead, unable to believe her luck.

'Emilio!'

He was quite close, walking purposefully down the centre of the street with his head down. She called again, louder, but he didn't hear. She was sure it was him.

She went after him, running painfully, almost tripping over her loose sandal. Eventually she caught up with him and touched his shoulder. 'Emilio!'

He spun round, looking defensive and angry.

She said quickly, 'It's me. From the meeting. Please – I've lost my money. I was wondering – could you lend me some . . .' She trailed off under the blank incomprehension of his gaze.

His eyes flicked past her, back towards the square, and then he seemed to focus on her for the first time and, seeing the state of her, raised his eyebrows. He started to walk on, simultaneously reaching into his pocket, and handed her a five-pound note. She limped along beside him, and exclaimed, 'This is too much. Really. Two pounds – one – would be plenty.'

He didn't reply. Putting in a couple of extra steps to keep up, she gasped, 'How can I repay you? Is there somewhere I can find you?'

He gave a minute shake of the head and strode on. After a few moments he stopped abruptly. 'I must go now. Sorry.' He repeated, *'Sorry,'* in a tone somewhere between impatience and regret.

She insisted, 'Please – I must repay you. If I can't contact you, then will *you* find me, Victoria Danby, 53 Moscow Road.'

'Danby. Moscow Road,' he repeated vaguely, then turned on his heel and was gone.

Victoria walked slowly away. The effects of the shock were beginning to wear off, leaving her exhausted and horribly empty.

The young man in the processing lab was very quick and Gabriele had the contacts in front of her in forty minutes. She spread them out on the viewing table and peered at them with a magnifying glass. Occasionally she marked the promising shots with the Chinagraph pencil. Then she went over them again.

The shots of Max sitting on the pavement had come out well – lots of blood and agony and tragedy. But good as they were, these shots weren't vital – there had been enough photographers around to ensure that similar pictures would appear in every newspaper.

It was the earlier shots from the car roof that were essential. The picture had to contain a policeman with his baton raised over a clearly identifiable Max. She had got one of a raised baton all right, the policeman in a wonderfully aggressive stance over a cowering Max. But maddeningly, Max's face was blurred. Obviously the shutter speed had been too slow.

She drew a ring round the face and, taking the contacts through to the young technician, asked him to blow up all the pictures she had marked and to see if he could get more out of the ringed face.

It was four. The Sundays would be setting up their front pages. Time to get things moving. She telephoned Stan Geddes at the photo-news agency. Someone offered to take a message, but she insisted on talking to Stan. When he eventually came to the phone he sounded harassed.

She said briefly, 'I got some good shots of the demonstration this afternoon. I think a lot of people will be interested—'

'Love, there's only one problem,' interjected Stan's voice, 'the whole of Fleet Street was there and I think you'll find they're all running their own pics.'

'But they don't have what I have,' said Gabriele confidently. 'There was a demonstrator seriously injured, and I've got a picture of him being beaten up by the police.'

'Actually being beaten?' Stan's voice was suddenly loaded with interest. 'Where are you?' She gave him the name of the photo lab and he promised to call right back.

The young technician came out of the darkroom with the first batch of eight-by-tens. 'Just to be going on with,' he explained. Gabriele looked rapidly through them. *Much* better now they were blown up. She spread them out in sequence: Max being pulled from the crowd, Max falling to the ground, Max with the raised baton high above his head, and finally a terrific shot of the riot policeman bringing the baton down on to either Max's back or head – it was difficult to tell just which. And Max's face, though blurred, was clearly identifiable.

Gabriele clenched her fists in a small gesture of triumph. The young technician smiled.

A door opened and she glanced round to see Giorgio coming in. '*There* you are!' she exclaimed angrily. 'God, I could –' Aware of the young technician, she prevented herself from saying what was on her mind. Instead she asked harshly, 'Have you got the car right outside? We'll have to get these over to the papers right now.'

Giorgio regarded her sullenly and didn't reply. She was about to demand an answer when she was called to the phone. It was Geddes. 'The *Sunday Times* is interested in an exclusive,' he began.

'No exclusives.'

'Why the hell not!' Geddes exclaimed. 'It's worth *money*, for Christ's sake.'

'No exclusive,' Gabriele insisted. 'I want you to offer the pictures to everyone.'

Geddes sighed. 'Blimey. If you insist. Though the total fees won't add up to an exclusive . . . But anyway, the *Sunday Times is* interested, although it may not be front-page stuff.'

A *frisson* of anger shot up Gabriele's spine. 'Why not?'

'Well, they've got to see the pics, of course.'

She relaxed. 'They'll put them on the front page, don't worry.'

She put the phone down, and seeing that the young man had gone back into the darkroom, advanced on Giorgio. She could hardly contain her anger. 'You nearly *killed* Max, you bloody idiot! What did you think you were doing? What came over you? All that was necessary was a little *blood*. And you go and mangle his face up! You—'

'He is not badly hurt.'

'Did you *see* him? He was badly hurt all right! You must have really hit him hard. No control. You've got no *control*, you bastard!'

Almost immediately she realised she had gone too far. Giorgio's face had gone pale with rage. He said very quietly, 'You cannot have it both ways.'

Then, abruptly, he turned on his heel and was gone. Thinking fleetingly of the car and the importance of getting the pictures to the agency quickly, she nearly called him back. But she was damned if she was going to chase after him and apologise. She would rather take a cab.

Victoria knocked back another whisky and felt much better. Slowly and rather stiffly she stripped off her clothes and examined her body. She was going to have some terrific bruises. Who needed body paint when your body was a work of art?

She wrapped herself in a bathrobe and went into the bathroom which led directly off the bedroom. Carefully avoiding her reflection in the mirror – she didn't want to make herself cry – she turned on the hot tap. The gas geyser hissed and popped and refused to light. She bashed it with her hand to no effect and realised the pilot light had gone out. She went in search of a match and, while passing the bottle, took another small nip of whisky. Marvellously warming.

The doorbell rang and she jumped.

The caretaker?

She wrapped the robe more tightly round her waist and cautiously opened the door.

She blinked in disbelief.

Emilio.

She began ineffectually, 'I – er – gosh, come in, won't you?'

He entered and wandered through the flat, peering into the rooms, picking up a couple of her Indian ornaments. 'Nice.'

She recovered slightly. 'Well, it's small, but it suits me.'

He wandered up to her and regarded her gravely. She was

suddenly aware of how very dreadful she must look.

He remarked, 'You're shivering.'

'Yes, I feel very cold. I was about to have a bath.'

'Please . . .' He gestured to show that she should go ahead.

'But you've come for your money. I'll give you a cheque.'

He shrugged. 'No, I didn't come for the money.' His eyes slid away. 'I come to see if you are okay.'

'Oh –' It was such a simple kindness that she was overwhelmed. She stood stupidly, trying to think of something to say.

He insisted, 'Please – take your bath.'

'I can't light the geyser.'

It took him only a moment to relight the pilot with a match. As the bath began to fill, she followed him back to the main room.

He remarked matter-of-factly, 'Your eye – it will be very black tomorrow.'

'Oh dear, will it? Oh dear!' Victoria ran exploratory fingers round the eye and suddenly felt very ugly and dispirited. 'You're right,' she sighed. 'I've never had a black eye before.'

He stood by the window, looking out, restless, she sensed; thinking of other things. In an effort to pull back his attention she said brightly, 'Would you like some whisky, Emilio? or wine? I have some in the fridge.'

His eyes slid round to hers. 'Giorgio. My name. Not Emilio. And wine, please.'

'Oh.' So *that* name hadn't been true either. But she was so glad to have his company that she took it in good heart and smiled. 'Giorgio then. A nice name. I'll get the wine.'

She went into the kitchen and, taking out the wine, made a fumbling attempt to open it and broke the cork. She took the corkscrew and the bottle in to him and shrugged apologetically. 'Not very good at this, I'm afraid.'

He leant over the bottle, drew out the cork first time and looked up at her, smiling a little. Chameleon-like, the indifference and remoteness had vanished from his face. Instead, the eyes were focused, interested, amused.

She looked away, only too aware of her dirty face and swollen eye. 'I think I'll go and have that bath then . . .'

'Leave the door open,' he said, 'then we can talk.'

'Er – yes.' Another kind thought. Victoria was pleased and rather flattered. Perhaps she had misjudged him: he seemed very considerate. She just wished she felt more relaxed in his company.

She went into the bathroom and closed the door almost to the jamb, so that only a small crack remained.

The water was so hot it made her shiver as she got in. But the heat was glorious, like a balm, soothing her, creeping slowly through her body, easing the pain. She shouted, 'This is wonderful!'

He muttered a vague response. She guessed that for the moment he was preoccupied.

When the delicious warmth had penetrated every inch of her blood, she dropped her head back into the water and wet her hair. Sitting up, she let the water drain off her head, and reached for the shampoo.

There was a movement in front of her.

She jumped and let out an involuntary cry.

It was Giorgio. Sitting on the closed loo, leaning forward, offering her a glass of wine. 'I thought you would like your wine, so – I brought it. You don't mind?'

He said it as if only someone exceptionally stupid and unworldly would mind. She gaped, horribly aware of her beastly unattractive white body billowing massively out of the water. He must be horrified.

She thought: I'm not going to show a thing. Not a *thing*.

Trying to look calm and sophisticated she drew her knees carefully up in front of her and managed a thin smile. 'You gave me a bit of a shock.' She took the wine and drank a great gulp of it.

Completely unembarrassed, Giorgio inspected her colourful legs and asked her how she'd got the bruises. When she had told him, he remarked, 'These things – they happen. It is a necessary part of the struggle against oppression. Always, people will be hurt when fascists try to exercise their power.'

She had half a mind to point out that it had been the crowd who had crushed her. 'You feel very strongly about it?' she ventured.

'In Italy it is part of our lives, always a danger. Fascism did not die with Mussolini. In Italy the rich are very rich, the poor very poor. The rich exploit the poor completely. You understand? Completely. Politically, economically ... In every way. And, to stay rich, they use force. The police. The law.'

He sounded very sure, very knowledgeable. Discussing such things with him made her feel very responsible and wise. She asked, 'Do you think there's a danger of it happening *here*, though?'

He gave an infinitesimal shrug and she sensed he was suddenly bored with the conversation. 'Of course.'

He reached down and, picking the bottle up from the floor, poured himself some more wine. Victoria sat still, feeling awkward. She wished she was liberated enough to sink back into the bath and finish washing her hair.

She stole a look at him. He was watching her again, his eyes sharp and gleaming. She averted her gaze and pretended to soap her feet.

'Why do you hide your breasts?'

She almost choked. 'What?'

'You shouldn't. They are very beautiful.'

'No. No, they're . . .' She reached wildly for the shampoo and poured some into her hand.

'Here, let me help you.' He knelt beside the bath and lathered her hair. Then he pushed her firmly back until her head was in the water and her hair rinsed. As he guided her up again he caressed her shoulder, then her arm, and finally her breast, murmuring, 'Very beautiful.'

Victoria sat quite motionless, unable to speak.

He got up and, taking a towel, waited beside the bath. Reluctantly she half stood up and reached for the towel.

'No, stand up. Let me see you.'

'No!' She remained crouched sideways, horribly aware of what gravity did to her body.

'You don't like it? You don't like being as you are?' He laughed. 'You must learn to be proud of your body. It is *important* to love your own body. In Italy we like many kinds of woman. And many men, they *prefer* women like you. Here.' He wrapped the towel round her and pulled her upright. 'You must love your body,' he repeated and, leaning forward, kissed her slowly on the lips.

His hand reached under her towel. She froze, not daring to move, in case the moment should somehow evaporate. She gulped as he found her breast again, and, taking it firmly in his hand, kneaded it gently. The towel dropped away and then he was kissing her body, infinitely slowly, travelling each inch as if it were precious and beautiful. She closed her eyes and decided that she didn't care what he really thought as long as he didn't under any circumstances stop.

Abruptly he moved away from her and she opened her eyes in alarm. But everything was going to be all right – he was holding his

149

hand out, motioning her to take hold of it and follow him. He led her to the bed and, as she lay down, began to take off his clothes with a deliberate almost teasing slowness.

As last he bent down and began to kiss her again, going over every part of her body with his mouth until she pulled him to her, desperate for him, wanting him with such a powerful longing that even after his weight had sunk, motionless and spent, on top of her she kept him inside her, hugging him, covering his head with kisses, weeping gently, wondering what on earth she had done to deserve a man like this.

Twelve

The doors opened and a stream of Sunday visitors entered the ward bearing flowers, bags of fruit, and children. The noise level rose to a babble.

Nick turned his head and winced.

'Serves you right for not taking your pills,' said the nurse mercilessly as she straightened his bedclothes.

Nick had already got the message: taking your own decisions was a criminal offence in this hospital. For what must have been the tenth time, he explained, 'I'd rather have a headache than feel half alive.'

The nurse retreated, shaking her head. Nick closed his eyes for a few moments only to reopen them and find Chief Superintendent Straughan standing beside the bed.

'They say you're going to live,' said Straughan, without enthusiasm. 'No thanks to what went on in that mob yesterday.' He sat down on a chair by the bed and, glancing at the nearest visitors, lowered his voice. 'Assuming you're feeling up to it, I'd rather like to have your version of events, if you don't mind.'

'My version of the whole demonstration?'

Indicating Nick's bandaged head, Straughan said angrily, 'Your version of this bloody fracas.'

From the sound of it, the DCS already knew quite a bit about it. Nick prompted, 'You've been hearing about it, have you, sir?'

The DCS gave him a hard stare. 'Yes, of course I have! The Special Patrol Group have an officer who says you mashed his face up, then ran off into the crowd without identifying yourself.'

'And what did he have to say about crushing my head in?'

'He says he was only trying to arrest you but you put up a fight.'

Nick rubbed a hand over his aching eyes. 'The first bit's true, except he was walloping me hard with a truncheon when I twisted his nose. The second bit isn't true. He got me from behind and I never raised a finger. Wish I had.' There was no love lost between the elitist Special Patrol Group and the other branches of the Met.

'God save me from small boys who belong in playgrounds,' Straughan remarked heavily. 'I won't even ask what the hell you were doing in the middle of the crowd when you were meant to be observing from the sidelines.' He sighed. 'As if it wasn't enough of a fiasco.'

Nick felt a ripple of alarm. 'Oh?'

The inspector's mouth was a thin line of disgust. 'It could have been worse, but I can't imagine how.' He chucked a newspaper on to the bed. On the front page were two large photographs, one of a person being beaten by a member of the Special Patrol Group, the second of the same person propped against some railings, covered in blood and looking half dead.

Wheatfield.

On page three there was more: a sequence of six pictures, obviously taken with a motor-drive camera, which showed Wheatfield being hauled out of the crowd and cowering under a hail of blows from a truncheon.

The photographs were excellent; the point of the story inescapable. And the journalists had made the most of it. Nick knew that he had been thoroughly outmanoeuvred. It made him feel slightly sick.

'All the other papers have got at least one picture,' said Straughan wearily. 'On the front page, of course.'

Nick tapped the pictures. 'This is why I asked to see you.'

'Yes, so they told me.'

'It was a put-up job. They set it up. This bloke – Wheatfield – was beaten by his friends, *in* the crowd, and *after* the SPG man had hauled him out. I saw them doing it. They kicked him in the face . . .'

151

Straughan exhaled slowly. 'Let me understand this – you are telling me that this customer was injured by his friends to make things look bad for us?'

'Right.'

The DCS paused, then shook his head. 'Well, they've bloody succeeded, haven't they? I mean in making things look bad.'

Nick argued. 'But I *saw* them do it.'

'Yes, so you did.' He didn't look happy about it.

A suspicion began to harden in Nick's mind. He asked, 'This is going to be taken further, isn't it?'

'Of course.'

'But?'

'But it's your word against these pictures,' said Straughan briskly. 'You'll be believed in the Force – that goes without saying. But outside – they'll think we're making up stories to cover our thuggery, won't they? And they'll argue that the kick you claim to have seen was in all likelihood accidental, won't they? They'll say you were seeing what you wanted to see. Get my point?'

Nick settled his pounding head back on the pillow. He got the point all right, and it was the one he'd suspected he would have to accept all along.

'Well, at least this sod Wheatfield's not going to die on us,' said Straughan, getting to his feet. 'Apart from a broken nose and an ugly face he's not badly hurt. They say he'll be out in three or four days. That's something at least.'

Nick said a little too quickly, 'Where is he?'

The DCS gave him a sidelong glance. 'Never mind that. The best thing you can do is to forget about the whole business for the moment, okay? I don't want to see you back until you're fully recovered. Two weeks, three weeks – whatever. You're no use to me with a sore head. Right?'

As soon as he'd gone Nick rang for a nurse. Eventually the disapproving girl arrived. He asked, 'Is there someone called Max Wheatfield here?'

She replied waspishly, 'Did you bring me all the way here just to ask me *that*?'

He gave her what he hoped was an open and appealing look. 'Yes.'

'You've got a nerve,' she said with half-hearted annoyance. 'Well – the answer's yes. He's in a room up the corridor. Your colleagues have been in there most of the morning.'

Absorbing the information greedily, Nick muttered vaguely, 'My colleagues?'

'You *are* a policeman, aren't you?'

He asked suddenly, 'Does everyone know that?'

She shrugged. 'I wouldn't think so. I've only just found out this minute.'

'Well, keep it a secret, will you, love? There's a good girl.'

She winked at him. 'Mum's the word, eh?'

After she'd gone, Nick thought for a long time, until, irritatingly, his eyelids began to droop. But even as he fell asleep, the image of Wheatfield remained tantalisingly in his mind.

Gabriele cut out the front page of the *Sunday Times* and taped it to the kitchen wall beside the other cuttings. The collection was impressive. Altogether, four newspapers had featured one or more of her pictures, and a fifth had published their own less spectacular pictures, showing Max against the railings. One far-right paper had published hardly anything, but then that was to be expected.

Later there would be more, in weeklies, monthlies, and political publications. Inter-News expected good foreign sales. Stan Geddes had even mentioned the possibility of *Newsweek* and *Time*.

It had gone remarkably well.

But, best of all, there might be *more*.

Max's injuries had been awful, certainly. When she'd seen his face she'd almost forgotten to take any more pictures. But then, later, she'd begun to see the possibilities . . .

With Max seriously hurt, the affair could become a major issue, a focus for student discontent, a *cause célèbre*. All it needed was a long stay in hospital, some uncertainty about whether he would ever fully recover, a lost memory, an inability to concentrate. A ruined life. That should be easy enough to arrange. He could fake most of it.

She regarded the cuttings again with satisfaction.

The phone rang.

She jumped slightly then relaxed. It would be Giorgio, of course. Announcing his intention of coming home.

Pips sounded down the line. She waited for him to get the money in, then said a very cool 'Hello'.

The reply came back and she gulped. *Max*.

She listened, gripping the receiver in disbelief. 'It's just a broken nose . . . And my face looks pretty bad. But there's nothing serious. I'm going to discharge myself tomorrow. Can't stand this place . . .'

She said, 'Can't you stay in for a while?'

'No . . . They're driving me mad. And the filth are here, giving me aggravation . . .'

'They're not going to charge you with anything, are they?'

'Haven't said so.'

She sighed heavily. 'Well, sit tight for the moment. I'll be in touch.' She rang off quickly.

The vision of Max the martyr evaporated before her eyes. Now the media would print a couple more articles, letters would appear in the correspondence columns, there'd be a question in the House – and then nothing. The story would die a death.

She sighed heavily and said, 'Shit!'

She strode into the kitchen and searched for a cigarette. At last she found one and lit it angrily. She felt cheated.

What was she going to do now?

It would have been a help to discuss it with someone, but without Giorgio . . .

Damn him, where had he got to? He'd been off before, of course. In Italy he'd disappeared quite often, usually on one-night stands. But she'd always ignored it for the simple reason that she didn't care. That, of course, was why he always came back. Because she never gave him any hassle.

But this time was different. She didn't want to be alone.

She paced restlessly around the house. Then, suddenly, she stopped. There was still a way . . . Still a possibility of getting more out of Max's situation. It wasn't much, but it was better than sitting around doing nothing. There was an element of risk, of course, but she rather liked that. Besides, it would give her someone to talk to.

She scribbled a note in case Giorgio returned.

Grabbing her camera bag, she checked that she had enough film, and hurried out into the mews. As she turned the corner the phone began to ring inside the empty house.

Victoria forced a piece of bread and marmalade into her mouth and realised it was the first food she'd had for nearly twenty-four hours. She didn't feel a bit hungry.

She wrapped the dressing-gown more tightly round her waist and peered at her face in the bathroom mirror. Not a pretty sight.

The black eye was a stunner, covering the whole of her eye and half her cheek. It was psychedelic purple and black, with tinges of dark green and red.

The bruises on her arms and legs had also developed well. In an odd way, she felt rather proud of these scars of war, as if they gave her an entry into the exclusive group to which Giorgio belonged, a group, she vaguely realised, in which action was everything.

In the long night hours he had told her more about Italy and the corruption and injustice of the system there, and of the need to fight fascism and the repression of the poor. She was very impressed by his commitment. She was also flattered and pleased that he should have taken the trouble to explain it to her.

Then they'd made love again.

She brushed her hair and ran her hands thoughtfully over her body. She still found it extraordinary that someone should like her just as she was.

The door opened and Giorgio stood there.

'Did you manage to get through?' Victoria asked with a smile.

He shook his head briefly, with irritation. She saw that his mood had become dark and ominous. She felt a twinge of alarm. 'Why not try again in a few minutes?' she suggested.

There was a long pause, then he sighed angrily. 'I have to go away. Abroad. And I must organise . . .'

Her heart sank. She should have known. It had been too good to last. She said lightly. 'Perhaps I can help . . . with the arrangements.' She thought: What a brave face I'm putting on it.

He was hardly listening. Instead he sighed again and murmured petulantly, 'Idiotic arrangements . . . It is left to me to do it all.' Suddenly he shot her a glance. 'Have you any wine?'

'No, but I can go and get some.'

'And food. And newspapers, all of them.'

'Yes, of course.'

Hurriedly she got dressed. At the door she called, 'I'll be about fifteen minutes,' but there was no reply.

The newspapers were easy, but it took her twenty minutes to find a food shop that was open on a Sunday and, because she couldn't remember where the nearest off-licence was, she had to go into a pub to buy the wine. The landlord stared at her black eye with frank curiosity.

When she returned she had an appalling suspicion that he would be gone. She fumbled nervously with the key.

155

The living-room was empty. She felt sick. She called, 'Giorgio?'
'Mmmm?'

She let out a sigh of relief. The sound came from the bathroom.

She took a glass of wine to him in the bath and kissed his head and touched his cheek.

His mood had not improved. 'The newspapers,' he demanded impatiently.

'Sorry!' She hurried to get them.

'Hah!' He flicked the *Sunday Times* with his fingers. 'Hah!' It was a small cry of triumph.

She looked over his shoulder at the front page. There were two photographs, one of a battered demonstrator. She stared more closely. Underneath the blood the face looked familiar. She gasped, 'Oh – *oh!* Isn't that – isn't that your *friend*?'

He didn't reply but opened the paper to the next page and laughed out loud.

It was hard to see anything funny in the appalling sequence of pictures. She was shocked by the viciousness with which the policeman had obviously struck his victim. The man looked as though he was in agony.

Then Giorgio exclaimed, 'This shows what *really* happened, yes?' and she finally understood. He was pleased because the police had been caught in the act, red-handed. It had never occurred to her to look at it from that point of view.

The newspapers and the wine seemed to have improved Giorgio's mood, and he began to talk with animation about his days in Paris during the student uprising, about the viciousness of the police there, and the way the students had fought back.

As she sat on the closed loo watching him, she thought: It's no good, I love you already, and it's going to break my heart.

'They were good days,' he said finally.

'It sounds very exciting.'

He sat up suddenly, sending water slopping over the edge of the bath. His face had clouded and she could see he was irritated again. He sighed peevishly, 'Tomorrow I have to find a van to go to Paris. How can I know how to rent a van in London?' He asked the question rhetorically, gesturing with upturned hands.

'But I can arrange that for you,' she replied quickly. 'First thing in the morning.'

He stared at her then, coming to a decision, nodded slowly. She felt a surge of happiness.

'What kind of a van?' she asked.

His eyes slid away. 'Something – where it is possible to conceal things. I want to return with certain' – he thought for a moment – '*publications* that must not be discovered.'

It took a moment for everything to sink in – that he was returning. She couldn't help visions of the future leaping into her mind: visions of the two of them together, loving each other . . .

'Publications,' she repeated vaguely, to keep the conversation going. Then the meaning of the other words became clear. He was talking about an important, perhaps even dangerous, journey. Yet he had not hesitated to trust her, to confide in her. She felt very proud. She thought: He won't regret it.

In a businesslike way she repeated, 'A van. Where things can be hidden. It'll take a while to find one, but I'll start first thing in the morning.'

He nodded briefly, obviously relieved at having handed the job over to her. She could see that his mind was already on other things. He said pointedly, 'I'm very hungry.'

'I'm *so* sorry! What *was* I thinking of.' She hurried into the kitchen and started peeling potatoes, wondering feverishly how she was going to find precisely the right van. Suddenly she stopped dead.

Of course.

When she got back, he was standing naked beside the bath, drying himself. She panted, 'Stupid of me, but I've *got* a van! A camper van, in fact. It's got cupboards and bunks and plenty of places to hide things!'

He threw the towel over the edge of the bath and was silent. His body was very beautiful. With an effort she continued, 'You could borrow it for as long as you want.'

He went to the mirror and began to brush his hair. She murmured, 'Well, why don't you think about it,' and returned to the kitchen.

She tried to make the meal a success. She laid the table with care and, though it was the middle of the day, placed candles on it. She put out a fresh bottle of wine and crisp French bread and served thick steaks with sauté potatoes, and tomato and olive salad. Later, she produced Brie and fruit and freshly ground coffee.

While they ate she tried to be light and amusing but he hardly spoke except to ask her about her family. She showed him a couple of photographs, one of the family having a formal tea on the lawn.

He remarked on the house and how large it was. But then he fell silent again and the conversation trailed off. Dejected, she thought: He's not interested in me at all. I was a fool to think he was.

Then without warning he focused on her and smiled a small intimate smile. 'This – er – van, it will get to Paris all right?'

Surprised, she stumbled, 'Yes . . . *Yes*. Some friends have been using it, so it should be working okay. When did you want it?'

'Tuesday.'

Only two days away. She thought rapidly. 'I'll have to go and fetch it. Tomorrow. It's in the country, you see. I'll have to get someone to drive me down there. It's a bit out of the way . . .'

He eyed her thoughtfully, weighing her up. Eventually he said, 'If I had business in Paris, could you bring the van back for me – into England?'

'Of course!' she exclaimed, laughing.

Paris. With him. She could hardly believe it.

'Even though the – publications – would be inside?'

She met his gaze and shrugged, as if such a risk was something she dealt with every day. 'It's no problem.'

'Good.' He was smiling, obviously pleased with her. She grinned back at him, and, in a burst of bravado, said, 'You'll stay tonight, won't you? And then we could drive down to the country together! In the morning. To collect the van.'

His expression changed subtly, and a thin but impenetrable barrier dropped over his eyes. She could have kicked herself. She'd obviously pushed him too far. In an attempt to retrieve the situation, she said mildly, 'Well, think about it.'

She cleared the table and did the washing-up. When the last dish had been put away she stood uncertainly by the sink. How could she persuade him to stay? How could she make it as wonderful as it had been the night before? What on earth was the *right* approach? Discretion? Indifference? Blatant interest?

She took a large gulp of wine and considered the options. Eventually she decided that, whatever the situation called for, it probably wasn't discretion.

After swigging more wine direct from the bottle, she walked into the living-room. Shaking slightly, she went straight up to Giorgio and knelt in front of him. With what she hoped appeared like calm confidence she began to undo his shirt. His expression was impassive. She had a moment's doubt. But it was too late now.

158

She pulled the shirt off his shoulders and, kissing his arm, worked her way slowly across his body, just as he had done to her the previous night. Then she pulled him gently to his feet and began all over again.

Still he stared at her, his face emotionless.

Then, finally, he moved. His fingers grasped her hair and she looked up to see the glint of desire in his eyes, and she knew that she had won him. For the moment at least.

Despite all his years of legal training, Henry Northcliff was a great believer in instinct. One still had to keep one's mind open to new possibilities, of course, to different interpretations of the evidence, to shifts of emphasis. But, having studied all the facts and heard the various arguments, that first intuitive conclusion – what the Americans called gut-feeling – was, in Henry's experience, rarely wrong.

He'd got a very strong feeling about this one an hour ago and since then the other two had said nothing to make him change his mind.

They were sitting in Henry's office at the House. The Sunday stillness, devoid of traffic noise and secretaries' chatter, clung to the room, creating an air of unreality.

Opposite Henry sat the Commissioner of Police, Peter McCabe, looking slightly uncomfortable in golfing clothes, and David Garner, the DPP, immaculate in blazer and flannels.

'The fact remains,' said Peter McCabe, 'that if no prosecution is brought against this Wheatfield they'll háve made monkeys of us. And that'll be bad for morale.'

'But we *will* be prosecuting – what – about thirty, people,' pointed out David Garner. 'In fact, nearly all those arrested. I'd have thought that would keep morale high enough.'

The Commissioner indicated the Sunday newspapers. 'But not the person responsible for *this*. I realise that we're not blameless and that the officer in the photograph went a little too far perhaps. But, according to the Special Branch evidence, we were set up. The lads know that and they want to see justice done. So do *I*, for that matter.'

Henry sat up in his chair. They were repeating themselves. It was time to bring the discussion to an end. 'Let's just be clear about the facts,' he began. 'There is absolutely no doubt that this Wheatfield *was* assaulted by a police officer. The newspaper

159

pictures are, I'm afraid, irrefutable. Now, whether that officer used reasonable or *excessive* force can never be established. Neither can we ever know how many of Wheatfield's injuries were sustained at the hands of the police officer and how many as the result of the attack by his companions.'

He chose his next words carefully. 'There is also the problem of pinning the whole case on the evidence of one man, albeit a Special Branch officer, who was in the centre of a heaving, jostling crowd, where, as I understand it, there were a large number of skirmishes going on. Can he be certain of what he saw? Can we establish that the kicks Wheatfield received to the face were delivered *deliberately*? For all we know the men who kicked Wheatfield might have been perfect strangers to him, or, if we believe that they were indeed friends of Wheatfield, then there is nothing to say they didn't kick him for some purely personal motives, without the slightest intention of conspiring to prevent the course of justice.'

There was a silence. The Commissioner looked unhappily out of the window. Henry thought: He knows he's lost.

Time for the concluding shot. Henry added, 'As David has said, it would be best to go for what we can be reasonably sure of getting – affray. Even then – well, we might have trouble getting good witnesses. As for assaulting a police officer . . .' He shook his head. 'In view of the rather damning evidence of the newspaper photographs, that may be difficult to prove, particularly if it goes to a jury. In which case Wheatfield could become something of a martyr and the image of the police suffer accordingly.'

The Commissioner shook his head. 'So they get away with it almost scot-free?'

Henry sympathised with the Commissioner's point of view. To his own mind there had undoubtedly been a plot to make the police look like bully-boys, but his instinct told him that no case of conspiracy could ever be won on the existing evidence.

He offered a few crumbs of hope. 'But I think it's certainly worth proceeding against this fellow Reardon on assault charges. He was seen carrying the sharpened banner pole and he was seen wielding it against a police officer. I know it's not as much as one would have hoped for. However : . .' He paused, hoping he was not about to make a rash promise. 'I'm sure the Home Secretary will examine the facts of the apparent conspiracy very carefully. He may even choose to make a statement . . .' Henry left it at that, hoping that he had judged the situation correctly.

160

Later he spoke to the Home Secretary. It was their third conversation that day. Predictably, the Home Secretary was worried about the risk of martyrdom inherent in bringing the charges, but finally accepted Henry's recommendation to proceed.

Remembering the Commissioner's concern, Henry mentioned that, to his own mind, a conspiracy *had* almost certainly taken place, although it was impossible to prove. The Home Secretary agreed. 'In fact, I was thinking of making a statement in the house to that effect . . . But it would have to be suitably vague.'

'Even so, it would be very effective in improving police morale,' Henry suggested gently.

It was impossible to keep everyone happy, but as Henry got into his car to drive back to Hampstead and a late and probably ruined lunch, he felt he had done his best.

Nick waited until the ward was quiet, then slowly sat up in bed. Not a pleasant experience. A hammer tried to pound its way out of his head. He felt a moment's hatred for the truncheon-happy SPG man, then concentrated on exerting mind over matter.

After a minute, he felt better and got gingerly to his feet. Yes: not too bad at all. It just went to show how over-protective these hospitals were. The doctor had talked about a week in bed. He had to be joking.

The hospital-issue dressing-gown was not exactly what he would have chosen – faded plaid with a pink collar which had been washed almost to destruction – and the slippers were fluffy and rather feminine, but he put them on all the same, to make it look as though he had permission to be wandering around.

He padded up to the doors at the end of the ward and peered through the windows. No fierce nurses in sight. He went out into the corridor and, going in what he hoped was the right direction, started reading the labels on the various doors.

No private rooms that way. He retraced his steps past the ward and along the opposite corridor.

It was the third door along. Wheatfield.

The window was blocked by a curtain on the other side.

A nurse appeared at the far end of the corridor. Without any further hesitation, Nick pushed the door and went in.

He had a brief impression of a figure with a heavily bandaged face lying on the bed before he realised with a slight shock that there was someone else in the room.

161

A girl. Back to the window. Dark hair lit by the sunlight. Attractive face. Camera in hand.

Strangely familiar.

Then he had it.

Of course – the *photographer*. Standing on the car. *The taker of those damned pictures.*

'Hi,' he murmured.

She regarded him coolly. 'Hello.'

'I came to see my – er friend.' He indicated Wheatfield whose bleary eyes gazed black and bruised from beneath the stark whiteness of his turban of bandages.

'Your friend?' she asked, tilting her head to one side.

'Well, in a way.' He went up to the bedside and said to Wheatfield. 'I heard you were bashed around yesterday, like me. A truncheon, was it?'

Wheatfield was silent. Nick gave a short ironical laugh. 'They came for me when my back was turned. Bloody marvellous.'

'Going the opposite way, were you?' There was a hint of scorn in the girl's voice and Nick looked at her sharply, thinking: Charming!

He said, 'Just getting my breath back. Ready to go for another.'

'Another?'

'Cop. I'd already got one. Mashed nose. Bled like a pig.'

She dropped her gaze. 'I see.' When she met his eyes again her expression was softer, less critical. 'Pity I didn't get pictures of that.'

'You were there?'

'Yes. I'm a freelance journalist.' Briskly, she moved to the bedside. 'Well, Mr Wheatfield, thanks for the pictures. I hope they didn't tire you too much. Get well soon. Goodbye.'

She moved towards the door.

Nick said, 'Did you take those pictures in the paper?'

She paused beside him, so close that he could see the flecks of gold in her eyes, and the slight break in the line of one eyebrow. 'It depends which paper. But yes, most of them had my pictures.'

'Congratulations. They were very good.'

Something seemed to amuse her and she smiled suddenly. It transformed her face and Nick couldn't help noticing that she was rather attractive. Pity she was a journalist.

Wheatfield or no Wheatfield, he suddenly wanted to provoke this self-confident lady who'd caused all the trouble. He repeated his thoughts out loud: 'Pity you're a journalist.'

'Why?'

He wanted to say, because you're biased as hell and only show one side of things. Instead he said drily, 'Journalists are the most promiscuous people I know.'

She stared at him, uncertain and defensive.

He said, 'They're only faithful to a cause or a story as long as it gives them what they want. Then they abandon it. They're anybody's for a night.'

She scoffed, 'At least we give satisfaction while we're around. I'd rather do some good for a short while than stand on the sidelines and do fuck all. Anyway – I haven't abandoned *him*, have I?' She indicated Wheatfield.

'You will when you've finished with him.'

'But he'll have had all the publicity he needs by that time, won't he?'

Nick conceded the point with a shrug of the shoulders. 'What about me though?'

'You?'

'I get a bash on the head and no publicity at all.'

She hesitated and he was aware that she wanted to end the conversation. She said vaguely, 'I didn't get any pictures of you . . . It's different.'

'Always the bridesmaid.'

'Tough.'

Suddenly everything went a bit strange. Nick leant back against the wall, feeling very ill. The girl looked at him curiously. 'You okay?'

He didn't reply. A hot sweat was spreading over his body and his legs had gone weak. He sat down on a chair and put his head in his hands.

He was aware of the door opening and closing then the bossy nurse stormed in and demanded to know what on earth he thought he was doing. As they put him in a wheelchair to take him back to the ward he caught sight of Wheatfield staring at him impassively from the bed.

The girl, however, had gone.

Thirteen

The wind swept down from the hills, gusting against the blank farmhouse windows, sending an army of dry leaves scritch-scratching across the drive. The place looked desolate and neglected, as if nobody had ever cared for it.

Saddened, Victoria led the way round the corner into the yard. At least the camper was there, as Janey had promised. It sat in front of the tractor shed which still contained the shell and entrails of the Massey Ferguson, now brown with rust. She noticed that the fencing round the kitchen garden, which they had repaired during the early days of the commune, was down again, and that the garden itself had already become a wild tangle of weeds and overgrown vegetables. She was surprised at how detached she felt. It was as if her time here belonged to a dream long in the past.

But Giorgio. He belonged to the present. And she didn't want him to see her depressed. Indicating the house, she said brightly, 'I'll have to go in and find the keys to the van.'

She unlocked the back door and he followed her into the kitchen. The auctioneers had taken away some of the better furniture – the scrubbed table and a pine dresser – and the room was bare and cold. 'It used to be lovely . . .' she said wistfully.

The keys of the camper were in their place on the mantelpiece. She picked them up and, having no desire to prolong the visit, turned to go. There was no sign of Giorgio. She found him wandering through the living-rooms, glancing incuriously at the faded curtains and brightly-painted walls that now seemed garish and out of place.

Giorgio stooped to pick up a leaflet from a window-sill. Victoria recognised the estate agent's brochure. He flicked through it and, pausing at one page, shot her a glance.

'A lot of money . . .' he said.

'What?' She looked over his shoulder. He was pointing at the estimated price for the forthcoming auction. 'It's the land that makes the price so high,' she explained. 'But I'll be lucky to get it. Quite honestly, I'll be very happy just to get my money back. The place is a bit run down, you see . . .'

They strolled back into the hall. Idly, Giorgio opened the door to the cellar and peered down the steps. He turned back and said casually, 'So you're rich.'

Was he mocking her? She said a little defensively, 'No, not really. I don't have money to *burn*, if that's what you mean.' Then, because she wanted him to enjoy her company, she made a little joke of it. 'Anyway, I wouldn't complain. If you're good I'll buy you an outrageously expensive dinner in Paris.' She grinned up at him, with a look that she hoped was full of fun and the promise of good times to come.

He accepted the remark with a slight nod. She turned away to hide her pleasure.

'Is this working?' He was indicating the telephone.

'I think so. I paid the bill.'

He put the phone to his ear to check. Satisfied, he held the receiver against his chest and stared at her. She realised he was waiting for her to leave.

She smiled. 'I'll go and try to get the camper started. See you outside!'

She closed the back door loudly behind her, so that he would hear it and know that she respected his privacy. There was a very secret side to him, she had to admit, and it took some getting used to. But she was determined not to resent it. This phone call, for instance: it would be very easy to imagine that he was calling another woman. But that would be childish. It was much more likely that he had a meeting to arrange or important matters to discuss with some of his friends. In which case he was merely being discreet and trustworthy, which was admirable.

She jumped into the van, full of optimism. She was certain that this was the start of a wonderful new phase in her life, and that the key to making it a success was to think positive. Even when the starter produced a low strangulated moan and lapsed into deathly silence, she wasn't disheartened.

Whistling cheerfully, she went in search of some jump leads which, if she remembered correctly, should be under a pile of junk in the tractor shed.

Gabriele could hardly believe her ears. 'Who *is* this girl?'

There was a pause and Gabriele could almost feel Giorgio making a face at the other end of the line. 'Don't worry,' he said, 'she's fat, stupid and rich.'

'So? What the hell are you doing there?'

'I tell you. She has a van.'

'But I told you to hire one.'

He sighed heavily. 'But this way there is no connection. She drives the van – a nice little English girl – *innocent*, you understand? And she is not stopped by the Customs. I go through later. More safe, more simple.'

Gabriele thought for a moment. She hated to admit it, but he was right. 'Maybe it's a good idea,' she conceded reluctantly. 'But for God's sake be careful. She mustn't know anything.' She added coldly, 'And when she's done the job, drop her completely.'

'Yes, no problem,' he said immediately, and she could hear the scorn in his voice. He was bored then. He didn't like this girl. She was glad.

When he'd rung off, she thought for a while. She hated the idea of having someone new involved. Especially this kind of girl. She could imagine the type only too well. British upper class. Not a brain in her head, not a seriously-considered thought in her repertoire of upper-class trivia, effortlessly patronising to the rather quaint but not to be mixed with lower classes. How on earth had Giorgio got involved with her?

Yet it was worth the risk of using her. Giorgio was right.

Going into the kitchen she turned on the radio for the one o'clock news in case there was anything more about the demonstration. The newsreader began to drone through the first item about a wildcat strike at Ford's. She put on the kettle for some coffee and paused to admire the latest additions to her cuttings display. Two newspapers had printed shots of the heavily bandaged Max swaddled in the hospital bed, and three had sent reporters to get a story.

Not great, but a lot more mileage than she'd expected.

Suddenly she stiffened.

The newsreader's voice was saying, 'In a statement to the House of Commons this morning, the Home Secretary said that Saturday's demonstration in Russell Square had been the scene of unprecedented violence in which the police were subjected to deliberate and vicious provocation. The Home Secretary went on to state that there was some evidence of a conspiracy to blacken the reputation and good name of the Metropolitan Police. He added that such attempts to undermine public order would not be tolerated, and those responsible would be dealt with most severely.'

Gabriele went cold. She thought: They *know*.

166

Then she decided it was impossible. They *couldn't*. It was just a suspicion. It *must* be.

Suddenly she listened again.

'In answer to a question the Attorney-General, Sir Henry Northcliff, stated that, as a result of the Russell Square demonstration, a total of thirty-five people had been charged. He confirmed that the most serious charge brought so far was that of causing an affray.'

She turned off the radio and sat, thinking rapidly. They *couldn't* be sure about the conspiracy – they didn't even know about Giorgio. And they hadn't charged Max.

Or had they?

Uneasy, she went out and bought an early edition of the *Evening Standard*. She leafed quickly through it.

'The following appeared at Bow Street Magistrates' Court this morning charged with causing a breach of the peace ...' There was a long list, then: 'Paul John Reardon of no fixed abode was remanded in custody on a charge of causing an affray.'

She walked thoughtfully up the mews.

They must have spotted Reardon stirring up trouble, that was all. There could be no proof of a conspiracy. Reardon knew nothing damaging. So even if he talked, no real harm would be done.

No. These accusations in Parliament were a great big guess. A shot in the dark to make up for the Establishment's humiliation. What else could they be?

There was no need to worry. It was going to be all right.

All the same, it was time to move on to the next event. Time to let this one go.

As she let herself into the house, the feeling of unease persisted and, before stepping inside, she looked over her shoulder.

Nick wondered if conversations with Wheatfield were always onesided. Probably.

Ignoring the other man's silence, he continued with the story of his life. 'I went to work in the foundry, like my father,' Nick said. 'Then I organised a stoppage and got fired. Of course, the bastards were out to get me from the beginning. The union didn't protect me either. Just as bad as the bloody employers.'

None of the facts was true, except for Nick's father working in the foundry. But they *could* have been.

Wheatfield said nothing. Most of the bandages had come off to reveal a bloated purple face. Beneath the bruises his expression was impenetrable.

Nick said, 'Now I'm a mature student.' And then he thought: That's a mistake. Wheatfield would have contacts at all the universities and polytechnics and could check. He thought rapidly. 'I mean, I'm *meant* to have started at Newcastle this term. But I want to transfer down here, to the North London Poly.' Nick added, 'There's more happening down here, isn't there? By way of action, I mean.'

Wheatfield murmured something like, 'Sure', and seemed preoccupied.

'Something the matter?'

Wheatfield seemed to be struggling with a decision. Finally he said, 'They've charged a friend of mine with affray. D'you know if that's serious?'

Nick frowned, as if thinking hard. 'Wait, let me think . . . Um, there was a mate of mine who – what *was* it? Yes, yes . . . It *was* that charge. It's serious, I think. Goes before a Crown Court rather than a magistrate. Could carry a couple of years.'

A look of bitter hatred crossed Wheatfield's face. He hissed, 'God, the bloody bastards.'

Nick said casually, 'Mind you, they've still got to prove it, haven't they? And it's a difficult one to prove.'

Wheatfield shot him a suspicious glance from his bloodshot eyes. 'How d'you know?'

Nick decided to go the whole hog and paint himself black. 'Oh, I'm – well acquainted with the ways of the law. From *this* side, you understand.'

Wheatfield waited for him to continue.

Nick shrugged. 'I took a car once. No – twice, I suppose. But the owners were rich. They didn't miss them. And then there was a bit of trouble about going into a house uninvited. I only wanted to stay the night.' Nick hoped he'd got it right. He didn't want to appear like a common criminal, but as someone who considered himself above the law.

Wheatfield nodded slowly. 'And you think he might get two years?'

'Or he might get off altogether. You never can tell.'

Wheatfield got out of bed and taking off his pyjama top, pulled on a shirt.

With alarm, Nick realised he was planning to leave. 'You off?' he asked.

There was a slight nod.

It was now or never. Nick said smoothly, 'I'm running a bit short . . . You don't know where I could doss down for a while, do you?' He paused. 'I mean, you wouldn't have a few feet of floor to spare?'

Wheatfield was reaching into the bedside cupboard and taking out a sweater. Eventually he replied, 'I've no room.'

'Oh.'

A pause. 'There are places . . . Try 43 Tulip Street. In North Kensington.'

'Thanks.'

Wheatfield was pulling on the sweater.

'They're letting you out, are they?' asked Nick.

Wheatfield snorted, 'How should I know? Who cares. I'm off anyway.'

'Yeah. Not a bad idea.' Nick got to his feet. 'Well, see you again some time. These are friends of yours in Tulip Street?'

Wheatfield nodded briefly.

'See you around then.'

Nick sauntered back to his bed, then hurriedly threw on his clothes. Sister came pounding up to him. 'Where do you think you're going?' she demanded. 'You've got a fractured skull!'

'Home, Sister. And it's only a hairline fracture.'

'Now, don't be ridiculous!'

He didn't have time to argue and pushed firmly past her. When he got to the corridor he saw a nurse come striding purposefully out of Wheatfield's room. He intercepted her. 'Is he there, nurse?'

'No!' she exclaimed indignantly. 'I think he's just walked out!'

Nick ran along the corridor and pounded down the stairs. A sharp pain shot through his head and he felt a moment of nausea.

He came to the last flight. The main hall of the hospital was visible below. He ground to a halt.

Wheatfield was emerging from the lift.

Nick stayed still, ready to dart back out of sight if Wheatfield should look round. But Wheatfield walked straight towards the main doors and went out.

As Nick emerged into the street and picked up Wheatfield twenty yards ahead, he wondered if the man would be watcher-conscious. If so, he hadn't a hope in hell of keeping on his tail. Not on his own, not without any back-up. But Wheatfield was no professional. With a bit of luck he'd never know.

Wheatfield turned into Tottenham Court Road. Nick guessed he was heading for Warren Street Tube station. In which case he would have to close the gap. Risky.

He quickened his step a little. So far so good. Wheatfield hadn't looked back once.

But now Wheatfield was stopping at a crossing and glancing back. Nick looked into a shop window.

Suddenly a small warning bell sounded in his mind. A nasty nagging little feeling that made him uneasy.

He looked behind him.

There.

On the other side of the road.

He groaned inwardly and thought: I should have known.

A watcher.

He looked back. There was another, further behind, walking faster, coming up to overtake. Nick recognised him. The man was from his own section.

Nick thought furiously. But he knew it was no good. There'd be a hornets' nest if he went on.

He stopped and leant against the shop window. The one on his side was coming up fast. As he approached he gave Nick a long look and, passing close to him, said out of the corner of his mouth, 'Conway wants a word with you.'

Nick thought: I bet he does.

Wheatfield had reached the station and disappeared into the darkness of the ticket hall followed by the first watcher and then the second.

Nick waited. After a few moments an unmarked car slid to a halt by the kerb. Nick went over.

Conway wound down the window. 'Why aren't you in bed like a good boy?'

'Couldn't sleep. Look, do me a favour. Don't tell Straughan.'

Conway looked doubtful. 'Well, all right. But piss off home, will you? I can do without the extra aggravation.'

'How long's the watch on for?' Nick asked quickly.

'Until we know where our friend lives.'

'That's all?'

'Yeah, for the moment.'

'Another favour. Give me the info when you've got it. I'll phone later.'

170

Conway groaned, 'Now what would you want to know that for?'

'Come *on*.'

'All right,' Conway agreed reluctantly. 'But don't go and get into trouble, for Pete's sake. Oh, and as far as I'm concerned, we never even saw each other, right?'

The headache was a stinker, the sort that makes you feel heavy, bad-tempered and sick. Nick regarded his bed longingly. It looked very tempting. But it would be a mistake to lie down. He'd only sleep for hours. Instead he found some aspirin in the kitchen and washed three tablets down with a cup of bitter strong coffee.

He put on a record of *Carmen* and, massaging his temples, wished the aspirins would take effect. He felt so damned *fuzzy* . . .

He risked sitting down for a moment. He wondered if Conway had found Wheatfield's abode yet. Even if he had, it wouldn't achieve very much. It wouldn't establish who his friends were . . . Only a proper surveillance would do that . . .

Nick considered phoning the boss and making a request for a proper observation, but immediately discounted it. He'd only get bawled out for not taking sick leave. Of course, if he was really stupid he could watch Wheatfield on his own, but it would be impossible to do a good job.

What else was there?

His eyes were trying their best to close. He fought them open and, turning up the music, walked backwards and forwards across the floor.

Photographs.

Damn. He'd forgotten to ask Conway what 'makes' – positive identifications – he'd got from his shots at the demo. Perhaps there was something on Black Beard.

He suddenly remembered the pictures taken by the girl journalist. They had been very good. He wondered if any of the lads had checked the rest of her shots, the ones that hadn't actually been published.

He thought for a moment. It would give him something to do . . .

He called the *Sunday Times* and asked for the picture editor. He got an assistant who gave him the information he wanted without even asking for his name.

Miss Gabriella Carelli. Care of Inter-News.

An Italian? He was puzzled. She'd had no accent that he'd noticed.

A brisk woman answered the Inter-News number. She said firmly that all enquiries for Miss Carelli could be channelled through her and that, no, it was impossible to give him Miss Carelli's private number. She'd specifically asked them not to give it out.

Nick thought of saying it was a police matter, but decided against it. If it got back to Miss Carelli she would refuse to see him. Being an avid left-wing journalist, she would be no lover of the police.

He hung up and called his friend Barbara at the exchange. He chatted her up for a minute, then asked for a fix on any telephone number in the name of Carelli, Gabriella.

There was a long pause. Nick began to feel pessimistic. Barbara usually prided herself on producing numbers in two minutes flat.

Then she was back.

727 8674. 42 Montagu Mews, W1. A new number. Ex-directory. Hence the delay.

After Nick rang off, he thought for a while. Strange for a journalist to be ex-directory. Perhaps she had an ex-boyfriend who'd been bothering her. Perhaps she just liked her privacy.

It created a problem though. How was he to explain finding her address and number?

Through Wheatfield? No.

Then he had it. Not perfect, but good enough. However it would be best to go straight round without phoning first.

The headache was showing no signs of responding to the aspirin so, on his way out, he took another two tablets and, after a moment's thought, thrust the packet into the pocket of his jeans.

It was five by the time he walked up Montagu Mews. Number 42 was a typical mews house, expensively converted, though in need of a fresh coat of paint. The miniature firs on either side of the front door were looking neglected and some flowers hung brown and shrivelled over the edges of the tubs and hanging baskets.

He pushed the bell. The sound echoed inside the house. He had the feeling the place was empty. If so, he would come back later.

There was a tiny sound from inside. He waited patiently. A moment later a latch turned and the door swung open.

It was the girl.

He smiled. 'Hi.'

She glared at him. 'What on earth?'

172

Not at all friendly. Nick dropped the smile; he wasn't going to beg for anything from this lady. He said coolly, 'Look, I was wondering if I could see all the pictures you took at the demo. Just in case there was one of me being bashed. The civil liberties people are interested in my case, you see. But we're a bit short of evidence . . .'

She demanded, 'How did you get my address?'

'Well . . .' He hesitated, as if not wanting to betray a confidence. 'There's a journalist on one of the Sundays who's helping me out a bit. He got it from – would it be your agent?'

She exhaled loudly to show her annoyance, then paused, eyeing him thoughtfully. Eventually she murmured with ill grace, 'All right. But you'll have to be quick. I haven't got a lot of time.' She stepped back to allow him in.

He went into the centre of the living-room and took a quick look round. 'You're busy then?'

'Busy enough.' She walked quickly to the far end of the room and bent down to pick up a large brown envelope from a pile of magazines and papers on the floor. Returning, she said abruptly, 'What was your name?'

'Nick. Nick Riley.' Close enough.

'And which group were you marching with?'

'Well, I suppose with the VUF mainly.'

'Mainly?'

She was interrogating him. Typical journalist. He replied a little impatiently, 'I'm involved in several groups. The VUF, the IMG, the SSL . . . I couldn't march with them all.'

'You're a student?'

'Yeah.'

'Where?'

'Look, is this an interview?' Nick demanded. 'If so, then I'd like to know how and when you're going to use it.' The last thing he wanted was to have Nick 'Riley' spread across the newspapers like Wheatfield.

'No . . . it's not an interview,' she said, retreating slightly. 'I just wanted to know who I was dealing with.'

But I bet it gets stored away for future use, thought Nick. Nevertheless, she would have to be given something.

He told her the same story he'd told Wheatfield, about being accepted for Newcastle but wanting to get into the North London Polytechnic. She appeared satisfied.

She turned on some lights then, kneeling on the carpet, took some enlargements out of the envelope and sorted through them.

She passed him a batch. 'Might be something there . . .'

There was one in which Nick himself was clearly identifiable in the crowd. He pretended to show an interest, then searched quickly for Wheatfield. Yes, *there*. But half hidden.

He went on to another and another print. Several showed Wheatfield, but not, unfortunately, doing anything provocative.

Ah, but even more interesting . . .

Black Beard.

Hiding his excitement, Nick examined each shot, looking for a full face. He checked them all again.

Maddening. *Strange*. There wasn't a single one.

He laid the enlargements out in sequence and realised there was a large time gap between the first batch of pictures, taken well before the trouble started, and the second batch which showed Wheatfield being dragged from the crowd by the SPG man. There was nothing of Reardon thrusting the lance into the police or of Wheatfield kicking the copper when he was down. He supposed those events might have been hidden from the camera. But, just as disappointing, there was nothing of Wheatfield being dragged back into the crowd by his friends.

It was odd. He asked, 'Is this it?'

She nodded.

'No contact prints?'

Her eyes hardened. 'No, they're with Inter-News. Anyway, I got everything blown up. It's all here.' She scooped them up and put them back in the envelope. 'How do you know about things like contact prints?'

Damn her, Nick thought, why the hell's she so suspicious? 'The newspaper guy,' he explained. 'He let me look through all the stuff their photographer took.'

He threw the last picture back on the pile, and regarded her thoughtfully. 'Carelli. An Italian name.'

'I'm half and half. Italian father.' She raised her eyebrows. 'Am *I* being interviewed now?'

He nodded. 'Where were you brought up?'

'In both countries.' She was more relaxed now. She seemed to want to talk about herself. 'I went to school in Italy, then came here as a student, then went back to Italy to train as a journalist.

My father's dead. He was a war hero. He fought with the communists.' She said it with pride.

'And your mother?'

'She was English. But she was never interested in coming back. She hated Britain.'

'You've hardly any accent.'

'I spoke nothing but English until I was five. Then my father started to take me everywhere with him, and I became a real Italian and forgot all my English for a while. Then my father died.' She looked wistful. 'And I came here to relearn my English.'

They stood up. He made a mental note to check up on this lady, just as a matter of routine. He asked, 'So are you going to stay in this country for a while?' She was standing close to him. He was aware of those eyes again, extraordinarily clear and steady. And the lovely dark hair. And the arched eyebrows against the pale skin.

She shrugged in an exaggerated way, making the movement unexpectedly sensual. 'For a year or so, I expect. It depends on how interesting it is.'

'The work?'

'Yes. *And* all the rest.'

He examined her face, looking for her meaning. 'The rest?'

'Life in general.'

'Quite.'

'The British are cold and dull.'

'You're probably right.'

'Which is a great pity.'

Had he misunderstood her again? But there was no doubt about it. There was a slight but unmistakably provocative smile on her lips.

'Well, I trust that you'll get a pleasant surprise.'

She was enjoying the tease. 'I doubt it.'

'Really? Well, you've obviously been mixing with the wrong people.'

'Yes.' She held his gaze. It was an open expression of interest.

He should leave, of course; go home and rest his head, call Conway . . .

Yet there was something about this lady.

He heard himself saying, 'I have exactly five quid in the world. How about fish and chips?'

*

It had started to rain heavily. Gabriele ran round the Fiat to the driver's side and got in. She unlocked the passenger door and watched Nick Riley ease himself into the opposite seat. He was very attractive. A nice body, strong face. And amazingly self-assured, sophisticated even. She liked that. That and the fact that he'd stood up to her.

Besides, she was bored with being alone.

She enjoyed playing the part of the sophisticated Italian photo-journalist. She felt the role suited her very well. It was much closer to the real her than Linda Wilson had ever been. Anyway, the story of her parents hadn't been that far from the truth.

She drove towards Chelsea. She noticed Nick tearing at a packet and putting some tablets in his mouth. 'Aspirins,' he explained. 'For my thundering head.'

'I'm surprised they let you out.'

'They didn't. I discharged myself. Like Wheatfield.'

Her foot slipped on the throttle and the car lurched. He looked at her sharply. 'You didn't know?'

She gripped the wheel and thought: Damn bloody Max. Why the *hell* did he do that. After a moment she said easily, 'No, I didn't know. But I'm surprised, I must say. I thought he was meant to be seriously hurt.'

'Only skin deep,' Nick murmured.

Realising what he had said, she made an effort to recover herself. 'What do you mean?'

There was a short silence. 'Nothing. The nurse just told me that his head looked worse than it was.' He added in an undertone, 'Unlike mine.'

'Is yours bad?'

'Split up the back apparently. Mind you, it might be an improvement.'

They drove up the King's Road and Gabriele pointed to a restaurant she'd never been to. 'Let's try that one.'

'My fiver should buy the first course and the wine.'

'I'll stand the coffee,' she said archly, 'and we'll negotiate over the main course.'

The rain was coming down in a solid wall, drumming against the car windows and bouncing noisily off the roof. Eventually they found a parking place some way beyond the restaurant. Passing cars were sending up sheets of spray. Gabriele locked her door and slid across to the passenger side. She got out on to the pavement, locked the door and slammed it. Nick offered her a newspaper to put over her head. The gallantry of the gesture took her by surprise. She thought: What a strange man you are.

Suddenly she groaned, 'Oh *shit!*'

'What is it?'

'I've left the bloody *keys* inside.' She could have kicked herself. God, what a thing to do. She *hated* making stupid mistakes. She searched through her bag, but she knew she didn't have any spares. 'Shit!' she repeated.

There was no sound from Nick and she looked round.

He was leaning over the door handle as if trying the lock.

'It's no good,' she sighed. 'I damn well locked it.'

He took no notice, intent on his task.

'Come on. Let's get out of the rain at least,' she said irritably. 'I'm getting soaked.'

The next moment she stared in amazement.

The door of the car was open. Leaning down, Nick disappeared inside. The next moment he was holding the keys in his fingers.

'How on earth did you do that?'

He took her elbow and hurried her along the street. 'Old Indian trick.'

She stared at him, wondered what other talents this man possessed.

She was good, Nick had to admit. As one would expect, she knew her stuff about the Italian student and communist movements, but she also had a good understanding of the philosophies of the New Left throughout Western Europe.

He found himself thinking that she might be quite useful. If handled with care. There was no doubt where her personal politics lay – well over to the left.

Nevertheless, she would have good contacts. Yes, useful – as long as she never discovered who he was.

The aspirins had clouded his mind, and he was feeling horribly tired again, but he made the effort to keep the conversation going and to draw her out as much as possible.

While discussing politics she was reserved, almost formal. But when he asked her about Italy, she became animated and relaxed. She described the many places she knew in Piedmont and Tuscany, and talked knowledgeably about the cultural life of Milan. She added, 'The Italian way of life beats Britain hands down. And the Italians themselves – well, they are culturally far less inhibited. That's why I like them.'

'They're certainly less inhibited. But I wouldn't know about the cultural side.'

She raised her eyebows. 'I suppose like all the British you disapprove of Latin emotion?'

'Not at all. I think it's great. It's good and wholesome and refreshing.'

She pulled at the tablecloth. 'But your family weren't open with their emotions, were they?'

He remembered his mam. She clouted him when he was cheeky and looked surprised if he was good. She hadn't been open exactly, but he'd always known she was on his side. His father – that was different. There had been a lot of affection there, shown as often as possible, but, being northerners, expressed by nothing more than a pat on the shoulder.

He answered, 'Not open by Italian standards, no wild hugs and tears, but it was pretty good really. And you?'

Her eyes dropped and he felt her withdraw slightly. 'Great on the Italian side, rotten on the British.'

'I'm sorry.'

She looked at him sharply, as if she wasn't certain of his sincerity. 'It wasn't that bad.'

A touchy point. He tried to smooth it over. 'But the Italian part of you has come to the fore. I mean, you're obviously more Italian than British. So . . . it's all right.'

She was pleased. 'Yes. It feels good to know what you are and where you're going.' She smiled. It made her face look quite different.

They talked about the problems of choosing the right path in life, and whether you should stick to it, and the importance of commitment. He was aware that some barrier had been passed. The reserve, the careful choice of words, had gone. He had the feeling that she was being direct, even trusting, for the first time.

Eventually she said, 'You know, I was wrong about you.'

'Yes?'

'I thought you were one of those sheep – the blind followers of the nearest tame philosophy, the ones who *call* themselves political thinkers but actually haven't an idea.'

'But?'

'You're all right.'

'Thanks.'

He had a sudden feeling that there was a purpose behind the appraisal, as if she had something serious in mind for him, some involvement.

It suddenly occurred to him that the involvement she might have in mind was an affair. He hoped not. He didn't mind the idea itself – on the contrary, now she'd decided to be open and friendly, he found her extremely attractive in a dark, brittle sort of way. What worried him was his ability to deliver the goods, tonight at least. The wine had made him dizzy and tired, and he knew he was slurring his words, which was unusual for him. Something to do with all those aspirins or the head or both. Whatever, it didn't bode well for a night of passion. He drew a deep breath. Better to get these things sorted out sooner rather than later. He said, 'Look, I'm not feeling too well. It's something to do with this head . . .'

A spark of disappointment – or was it annoyance – passed across her face; she'd got his meaning all right. But then her face cleared and she was nodding understandingly. 'That's all right. I'll get the bill and drive you home.'

He said with relief, 'The complete liberated woman.'

'God, you're not a goddam reactionary, are you?'

'No. I like independent women.'

She tapped his hand. 'Good. Because you've certainly found one here.' She laughed, suddenly gay and happy.

God, he was feeling really awful now. He glanced at his watch. Ten. With a jolt he suddenly remembered Conway.

Getting to his feet he said, 'Completely forgot to make a call. It's' – he tried to think, to be consistent in his new story 'about some floor space at a friend's.'

There was a phone by the kitchens. Reaching it, he had to lean hard against the wall. A cold sweat hit him. When the worst had passed he called Conway.

Conway didn't sound glad to hear him.

Nick said, 'Well where does Wheatfield hang out then?'

'Wish we knew.'

Nick's stomach did a nasty turn. 'You bloody *lost* him?'

'Showed no signs of having spotted us, not one. Then he did a disappearing act as neat as any I've seen. Into a shop and straight out an emergency exit.'

'Bloody marvellous.'

'You would have done better on your own, I suppose?'

Nick let it pass. 'All right. What about "makes" on Wheatfield's friends?'

'Only Reardon, who's up for assault anyway. Nothing on your bearded friend. No good snaps, I'm afraid.'

Nick put the phone down in disgust and leaned his head against the wall. To hell with Conway, to hell with Wheatfield. The only thing he cared about now was getting his head down on a nice warm pillow.

The mews house was dark. No Giorgio then.

She said, 'You can stay here.'

He didn't argue. His head was resting on the back of the seat, his face ashen.

She opened up the house and led him upstairs.

Before she could decide where to put him he had stumbled into the main bedroom and sunk on to the bed. She began, 'Why don't you get *into* bed?'

But he didn't reply. He had the look of someone who wasn't going to move again that night.

Gabriele regarded him critically. Even if she wanted to share a bed with a half-conscious man, which she didn't, it would be very uncomfortable with him on top of the bed and her inside it.

She went to the linen cupboard, got out an eiderdown, and placed it over him. Then she found some sheets and took them into the spare bedroom.

PART THREE

Fourteen

The lights changed and the four lanes of traffic roared away up the wide boulevard, like racing cars from a starting grid. Victoria gripped the wheel and accelerated. Driving in Paris was certainly different.

'Here!' Giorgio pointed sharp right, up a side street.

They were almost past it. Victoria flicked on the indicator and braked hard. There was an angry blaring of horns and a car wove violently past, the driver gesticulating rudely.

'*Excusez* – so sorry,' Victoria muttered, and, hoping there wasn't something coming up behind, turned right across the traffic.

Safely into the side street, she stopped and put her hand to her chest. 'Well, French drivers certainly have something,' she said breathlessly. 'If only a short fuse.'

Giorgio was already getting out. He said, 'You wait here.' He walked off and, half-way up the street, disappeared into a doorway.

A horn sounded: the camper was blocking the road. She drove on a little and, where the street widened, pulled up on to the kerb and turned off the engine.

She looked across the road. It was somewhere near here that Giorgio had disappeared. There was a linen shop, a boutique selling mini-skirts and jeans, an antique shop, and, in between, doors leading to the upper floors.

But what did it matter where he had gone? The important thing was, everything was going well.

The journey had gone very smoothly. She'd left London at seven that morning, caught the ten o'clock ferry and been at Orly to pick up Giorgio by three. She hadn't got lost once. Well – just for a moment, coming into the city, when she'd misunderstood Giorgio's directions.

She wasn't sure where they were now – she didn't know Paris that well – but the Seine was close by, and Giorgio had mentioned the Left Bank.

She closed her eyes for a while, then checked her face in the mirror. The black eye was fading fast and she'd managed to cover the greeny-blue shadow with make-up so that it barely noticed. Her skin was much clearer, too, and she had lost quite a bit of weight in the last few days. Definitely an improvement. It was Giorgio's doing. When he was around she forgot all about food. She forgot about everything. She sighed deeply. That was the problem. She was in love with him. And not just a little, either. She could hardly think about anything else. His presence obsessed her; she related everything she did to him. The thought of displeasing him was agony. She vaguely realised that the relationship was unbalanced, that there was too much pain with the pleasure. But it merely made her more determined to please him, to become indispensable to him, so that he would get used to having her around, and maybe even come to care for her.

She thought: It's all right for beautiful women. They can pick and choose. But for people like her – well, one had to grab at whatever one could. Better to feel alive for a short time than to drift along waiting – *imagining* – for ever.

It was getting dark. She looked at her watch. He'd been gone nearly an hour.

A movement caught her eye.

At last. There he was. Coming from beside the antique shop. Striding across the street.

He jumped in and said immediately, 'We must go to one more place.' He motioned her to drive off.

As she negotiated the streets she noticed that he was agitated and restless. She kept quiet.

They turned into a wide tree-lined street. At some lights Victoria managed to read a sign: Boulevard St Germain. Then they were into another network of narrow streets. Using gestures and the occasional word Giorgio directed her to the next address. Again, he left her waiting in the van. This time she watched to see where he went. It was a doorway beside a newsagent's. She examined the windows above. Nothing to indicate what went on there. But she'd noticed the street name: Rue St Médard.

It was six now. She wondered what sort of an evening they would have. A meal on the Left Bank, a stroll along a boulevard, a coffee in a pavement café? Yes, she'd wear that long black midi-length skirt and pull her hair back in a knot and look smart.

Five minutes later he was back. 'Okay, we go and find a hotel now. Then we eat.'

She smiled and started the van.

'But I have not much time,' he added. 'I have a meeting later.'

Count to five. 'When?'

'At nine. It will last until late.'

'I thought we'd have the evening together at least.' She could hear the peevishness in her voice and hated it.

He gave her a sharp look. 'I have to do my business,' he replied. 'That is why we are here.'

With an effort, she said quietly, 'Of course.' And, doing her best to drive smoothly, negotiated the camper into the thick of the rush-hour traffic.

As the van moved away, its registration number was noted.

The DST man was sitting in a car a few doors away from the newsagent's. He sat in this spot quite often, sometimes several days running, at other times not for several weeks, watching the doorway to the right of the bookshop, noting who came and left. It was rather a farce really. The people at Aide et Solidarité knew he was there, and he knew that they knew.

But the purpose of the surveillance was merely to let them know that they *were* being watched. A reminder that they and the numerous other political organisations encamped in Paris were tolerated but not condoned.

The number of the van would be logged in the central records and that would be that.

It was getting on. He'd been there four hours. Quite long enough to ensure that his presence had been noted. Starting the engine, he drove quickly away.

Nick had seen worse places than 43 Tulip Street. It was on the border of Kensal Green and North Kensington, off the Harrow Road. The house was shabby on the outside, but reasonably neat and well kept on the inside, with ethnic rugs thrown over the ancient furniture and posters on the white-painted walls.

'There's a mattress somewhere,' the girl said. She looked half-heartedly round the living-room and then gave up. She drew heavily on her cigarette. 'Or there's the settee . . .'

'Don't worry. Anything'll be great.'

Her name was Bet – short for Elizabeth presumably, though he hadn't asked. She appeared to be one of the permanent residents of the house, which, as far as he could tell, was occupied by six people. She was about twenty-five, he guessed, and fashionably dressed in a trendy off-beat way.

She asked abruptly, 'Where's Max living, d'you know?'

It was exactly what he'd been hoping to find out himself. 'Not sure,' he replied. 'He split.'

She nodded, unsurprised.

'You've got no gear?' she asked.

'No. Travelling light.'

'Going to stay long?'

'Dunno.'

'That's okay,' she said. 'A friend of Max's . . . But it might be difficult after a week. I mean, staying without contributing.'

'I understand.'

They strolled into the hall. She said, 'I'm going to the pub to meet some friends. Want to come?'

What he really wanted was to go home to bed. He'd slept until eight that morning, when Gabriella had woken him and offered him a hasty breakfast, but he had got up dog-tired and stayed that way all day. He decided the sleep would have to wait a while longer. The Bet connection might be tenuous, but it was all he had.

He said, 'Yeah, that'd be great.'

The Red Lion was crowded. Bet's friends, five of them, were at the bar. Two of them were teachers, Nick gathered, and one worked for a big charity. The remaining two were not forthcoming about their occupations.

He was disappointed. Neither the names nor the faces were familiar. If they were on file, it must be as ordinary members of relatively harmless organisations. Not likely to be bosom pals of Wheatfield.

Nevertheless he asked casually, 'I'm trying to get hold of Max. Know where he might be?'

One of them answered, 'He's got a new place, but nobody knows where. You might find him at the Duchess of Teck. Up in Camden Town. He used to go there a lot . . .'

Nick wondered if he could face going straight away, tonight. It was a good half-hour away and he was still feeling pretty rough. He put off the decision by having another beer.

Fifteen minutes later two girls joined the group. He recognised neither. Then he realised there was a third arrival, standing at his shoulder just outside the circle. A man.

Nick's interest quickened.

This one he knew.

It took him half a minute to place him, working backwards from the face to the organisation, then to the occasion and the year, and finally to the name.

London School of Economics. SSL. Linden House Hotel affair, 1968. Wally Bishop.

Definitely a friend of Wheatfield.

He left it for twenty minutes then, just as he was wondering how to introduce the subject, Bet did it for him.

She said to Bishop, 'Nick wants to find Max.'

Bishop nodded, a flicker of defensiveness in his eyes. 'He's around . . .'

'It was about the demo on Saturday,' Nick said easily. 'We both got walloped. I'm trying to get the civil liberties people interested in my case, and I wondered if Max was taking the matter further . . .'

'You got beaten up, did you?' Bishop asked, looking at the slight graze on Nick's cheek.

'Fractured skull.' Nick drew an imaginary line from the back of his collar upwards. 'Right up the back.' He laughed and took another swig of beer.

Bishop looked impressed. While the others were talking he said, 'Tell you what. Max'll probably be around later. Up the Portobello, in the Castle.'

Nick asked doubtfully, 'Er – much later?'

'Ten.'

Nick pursed his lips. 'Well, to tell the truth, I'm dead beat. I'll have to give it a miss. But give him the message, will you? And tell him I'll catch him later. Okay?'

It was eight when Nick left the pub. It was raining again and there was a cold wind blowing. Pulling up the collar on his jacket, he walked briskly to keep warm. He bought some fish and chips on the corner, and ate them as he walked down Ladbroke Grove to the Portobello Road. The Castle was a small pub sandwiched into a terrace of shops at the northern end of the road, on the unfashionable side of the elevated motorway, and well away from the tourists and the antique markets.

There was no obvious place to wait. He chose a doorway with a deep recess, diagonally opposite the pub. His head was aching again.

At quarter to ten he recognised Bishop coming along the street and turning into the pub.

Ten came and went. No Wheatfield. Ten-fifteen. Ten-thirty. For some reason he was unbelievably cold. He shivered violently and stamped his feet in an effort to keep warm.

Only half an hour until closing time.

Then at ten-forty, suddenly, there he was.

There was no mistaking the long hair, the black donkey jacket he always wore, and, as he came into a patch of light, the narrow bruised face with the wire-rimmed glasses.

Nick felt a surge of triumph. Then calmed himself. *Don't count on anything. Not yet.*

At chucking-out time Bishop and Wheatfield emerged together. They paused on the pavement, exchanged a few words, and left separately, Bishop heading north, Wheatfield south.

Nick gave Wheatfield thirty yards then followed, staying on the opposite side of the road.

Wheatfield walked under the Westway elevated motorway then, pausing to look over his shoulder, crossed the street and headed down Lancaster Road, parallel to the Westway. The glance had been cursory, checking for traffic. Wheatfield was not worried about being watched.

That made all the difference. Nick relaxed a little.

Wheatfield paused at the next junction and turned left into a small residential street, quiet except for the drone of the traffic on the elevated road.

Wheatfield paused outside the front door of a house and, reaching into his pocket, produced a key and let himself in. Half a minute later a light went on in a top second-floor window.

Number eleven. And the street was called St Mark's Villas.

Nick allowed himself a moment of satisfaction. Nailed Wheatfield all on his own. Wait until he told Conway.

But now it was decision time. He could stay for a while and see if anyone else went in. Or he could go home and return early in the morning in the hope of tailing Wheatfield to his friends – specifically to Black Beard. But he was feeling horribly tired again – the head seemed to make him permanently sleepy – and to make matters worse he seemed to be getting a cold. The sensible thing would be to go home.

He started back along the street, but hesitated on the corner.

Damn it, he couldn't bear to let Wheatfield slip through his fingers again.

There was a telephone box in the next street. Out of order. He swore vehemently. Eventually he found a working box in Westbourne Grove.

Conway wasn't at home. He tried the office. He wasn't there either.

He returned to St Mark's Villas and waited for over an hour.

When he tried Conway's number again, he was in. He was not happy to be disturbed. 'What the hell, Nick. It's one in the bloody morning!'

Nick said, 'You won't be so cross with me in a moment, Conway. I have something for you. But it's going to cost you, old lad.'

Victoria didn't need to ask Giorgio how he felt: it was only too obvious. He had all the signs of a terrible hangover. She'd heard him stumble in at four that morning, the smell of drink on his breath. The meeting must have gone on a long time. She conjured up the scene in her mind: the political discussions, the bottle of brandy, the smoky room. Men together, sharing ideas, scornful of outsiders. She was envious.

Now it was eleven and she was driving south-east out of the city, towards the suburbs. Giorgio sat beside her, his head against the seat, his eyes closed. Victoria resolved not to say anything unless it was absolutely necessary.

When they reached Ivry she finally stopped and, dreading the moment, whispered, 'We're here. Do you have directions?'

He groaned slightly and, pulling a screwed-up paper from his pocket, handed it to her. It was a street name and number in Ivry, but she had no idea where. She showed the paper to a passer-by who gave her directions and, after a couple of false turns, she found herself in a small backstreet. It was a poor area, near a main railway line. The houses, which fronted straight on to the street, were shabby and colourless. Half-way along there was a car repair works, but otherwise there were few signs of life.

The house numbers were difficult to read but finally she identified the address on the paper, and stopped outside. It was a house, shuttered and quiet. She turned off the engine. Giorgio opened an eye and frowned. He said, 'Down the side.'

She started up again and, after reversing, began to manoeuvre the van forwards into the gap between the house and its neighbour.

'No, backwards!' Giorgio hissed impatiently.

Victoria gripped the wheel and stopped. She backed out, did a three-point turn, and slowly reversed the van down the alley to a courtyard at the end.

Giorgio said, 'You go for a walk now, for one hour.'

She opened her mouth to object, but he added impatiently, 'I should not have brought you at all. I was not meant to – you understand?'

As she walked away she made the effort to accept the snub. But it was difficult. They were only leaflets, after all. Why she couldn't be trusted to see them being loaded was beyond her.

She sat on a wall and watched the trains thundering past on the main line. She thought the matter through again. Perhaps she was being ungenerous; perhaps Giorgio was only trying to protect her.

She returned in a more cheerful frame of mind to find Giorgio waiting by the van. As she approached he got in and they drove off in silence. 'Everything all right?' she asked.

He nodded matter-of-factly. 'Yes. Okay.' But she noticed that he was wide awake now, his eyes gleaming, his manner restless.

When they reached the main road Victoria couldn't at first identify what was different about the van. Then she realised that it was slower, more sluggish. There must be a lot of leaflets. She said, 'You managed to get everything in?'

He gave her a black look, but she went on, 'The load's very heavy. I can feel it.' Suddenly she wasn't in the mood to be put off. She demanded, 'Tell me, what are the leaflets for? You never told me exactly.'

He was silent for a moment and she could feel his eyes on her. Eventually he said, 'They are to be sent out, given away . . . To working people. To' – he was searching for the English words – 'to make them realise they are being exploited.'

'I see. Can I have a look at one?'

'No, not possible.'

'Why not?'

'They are in boxes, hidden away . . .'

He was looking at her differently now, appraising her. He slid his hand across the back of the seat and began to stroke her neck. 'Don't worry. It is just better that you do not see them.'

She kept silent, but she wasn't happy and she let it show on her face.

Giorgio said pleasantly, 'We will have a good lunch – do you like seafood?'

'Yes.'

'Then – later, perhaps dinner too. Would you like that?'

'Will you be going to another meeting afterwards?'

He shook his head.

She softened a little. 'What about getting back?'

'The morning will be all right. If you leave early.'

'And you?'

'I will fly tomorrow afternoon. You can meet me at the airport.'

She pictured the evening: a long leisurely dinner, candles, no rush, no meetings. And then back to the hotel to make love. One perfect evening. An opportunity that might never come again.

Her resistance vanished. One had to grab these moments – why not? Everyone else did.

Suddenly gay she said cheerfully, 'I promised to take you out for a meal in Paris, remember? Well, dinner will be *my* treat! We'll go somewhere really good. Do you accept?'

He shrugged. 'If you wish.'

She glanced across at him, but he had turned to stare out of the window and she could not see his face.

Nick dreamed that he was in the wreckage of a road accident, sitting in a car which had been crushed by a lorry. Something heavy was pressing on his head. Helpers were trying to cut him out. Faces bent over him, discussing his condition. 'It's no good,' someone said. 'He's had it.'

Then his mother was leaning over him, saying, 'I told you this would happen.' It wasn't a car that he'd crashed now, but his go-cart which he'd built out of plywood and old pram wheels, his pride and joy and the envy of all his schoolmates. There was only one good slope in the area, at an old tip, and he'd raced down it for a bet, and hit a ridge and crashed into a metal refrigerator. His mam had said, 'I told you so, but you wouldn't listen.' Which was true enough, because he never did listen. And now his head was hurting like hell and the ambulance bell was ringing loudly in his ears.

It jangled on and on. He woke resentfully and reached out for the alarm clock. He opened his eyes and screwed up his face. The cracking headache wasn't a dream, nor was the raging sore throat and stuffed up nose. He thought: Terrific.

Before he had second thoughts about getting up, he swung his legs to the floor and sat up. He may have felt worse in his life, but he couldn't remember when.

Ten-thirty. He'd had three hours' sleep. And now he must hurry. He'd promised to relieve Conway at eleven.

Finding a piece of stale bread in the kitchen, he covered it with jam and made his way out. He saw a cruising cab and, taking it as divine intervention, hailed it and sank gratefully back against the seat. Extravagant, but today he didn't care a damn.

He left the cab in a road adjacent to St Mark's Villas and wondered if he'd find Conway on station or not. By now Wheatfield – and therefore Conway – could be anywhere in the Greater London area, which made it difficult for Nick to relieve him – a point Nick had carefully glossed over, both on the phone the previous night, and at seven that morning, when Conway had stood in for him.

But when he turned into St Mark's Villas Conway was still there, sitting in his car, looking fed up. 'Not a dicky bird,' he reported as Nick climbed in. 'No one remotely like Wheatfield.' He gave Nick a hard stare. 'Now look, me old mate, this is lunatic. You can't stake this place on your own. Why don't I go back and persuade the boss to do it properly, eh?'

Nick shrugged. 'If he agrees, great. But I doubt he will.' A full-scale surveillance was costly in men and resources, and was mounted far less often than people imagined. Nick added, 'Just don't mention my name, that's all. He'll go bananas.' He hunted through his pockets for a handkerchief and sneezed.

'And I'm to say I got this address from a snout, am I?'

'Well, don't complain, for God's sake,' Nick retorted. 'It'll be a gold star for you, won't it?'

'I'm not *complaining*. I'm just trying to get it right.' He eyed Nick harshly. 'You look bloody terrible, did you know that?'

'Piss off. And without the car, if you don't mind.'

When Conway had gone, Nick slid across to the driver's side and, sinking deeper into the seat, settled down to wait. A heavy sneeze shook him. An aspirin would have been a good idea, but it was too late now.

He closed his eyes and dozed off for a second. Waking, he sat upright with a guilty start and turned on the radio. He listened to the news, then retuned the station. There was a symphony on Radio 3. He tried to identify it. Brahms? No, more like Mahler. Yes . . . lovely.

It was nice and warm in the car. The sun streamed in through the windscreen. His head fell forward. He dozed.

Wonderful dreams. On a warm beach. The sound of people in the distance. The whole afternoon ahead of him. But no. There was something wrong. The dream was disturbed. There was some reason why he mustn't sleep and he couldn't remember what it was . . .

Waking with a jolt, he rubbed his eyes and peered at his watch. Hell! How long had he been asleep?

He really *must* make an effort.

He looked up.

Christ!

Wheatfield.

Crossing the road. Heading this way. Coming towards the car.

Quickly, Nick opened the driver's door and, sticking his feet out, spread his body across the front seats and pushed his head under the dashboard. He made a show of hunting for some imaginary electrical trouble.

Count to ten. *Slowly*.

He looked up tentatively. No Wheatfield in front.

He swivelled round. There! Behind – and disappearing fast round the corner.

The car would be a nuisance. He abandoned it and followed on foot.

Wheatfield was moving more cautiously today. Like a cat. Glancing from side to side. *Much* more alert.

Nick felt a twinge of excitement. *Whatever you're up to, Wheatfield, I'll get you.*

Twenty minutes later Nick was trying hard not to feel disappointed. After visiting a chemist, Wheatfield had gone into a stationery shop in the Bishop's Bridge Road and emerged with a small parcel.

Now he was in an old-fashioned hardware store. It was all horribly domestic. Nick looked through a newsagent's rack in disgust.

Wheatfield remained in the store for some time. Nick waited impatiently. Eventually Wheatfield emerged with a large packet of some product or another under his arm: a white packet brashly printed with what looked like a manufacturer's name in bright red; with a gaudy green picture underneath. It was impossible to see exactly what it was.

Next Wheatfield went into an electrical shop. Then a small supermarket. Nick took the risk of peering in through the numerous cut-price posters stuck on the window. He spotted Wheatfield at the far end of an aisle, putting a large packet of washing powder into his basket. At the next aisle he appeared to have trouble finding what he was after, but after much searching finally picked up several packets of what could have been either sugar or flour, and came towards the check-out.

Nick moved away and waited up the street.

Wheatfield came out and, despite the obvious weight of the

various packages, moved off fast, away from home, in the direction of Paddington. After a while the weight of the shopping slowed him down and, pausing to redistribute the bags, he carried on at a slower pace.

Suddenly Wheatfield stopped and took a long look round. Nick side-stepped into a doorway and peered out cautiously.

He swore under his breath.

Wheatfield had hailed a taxi and was climbing in.

Not another in sight. As Wheatfield's cab drew away Nick ran to the next corner. Still no cabs. Only one, cruising round a corner two streets to the south. Nick put two fingers in his mouth and whistled hard. The cab braked and he sprinted towards it.

His lungs aching, he jumped in and shouted, 'U-turn, right at the top and then go like hell. I'm trying to catch someone.'

The cabby held his tongue with difficulty and, executing the turn, went for the lights, which were red.

'Jump them. I'm a police officer.'

Muttering hard, the cabby found a gap in the cross-traffic and swerved right into the Bishop's Bridge Road. He shouted over his shoulder, 'I've been waiting for this for twenty years.'

They roared across the next two lights, which were green, and came to the roundabout under the Westway. There was only one other cab in sight, heading east out of the roundabout towards Marylebone.

Nick realised that in his panic he'd forgotten to take the number of Wheatfield's cab. Now he couldn't be sure he had the right one.

They closed on the cab ahead. A single passenger was visible through the back window. They followed past the Planetarium and Madame Tussaud's, then the cab slowed and turned right into Marylebone High Street. Half-way down it turned left into Weymouth Street and came to a halt in front of a small block of flats.

Nick told the cabby to stop a little further on. He looked back. It was Wheatfield all right. Paying off the cab.

Exhaling with relief, Nick reached in his pocket for some money. 'You're joking, mate,' said the cabby, gesturing his refusal. 'Worth a guinea a minute. I wouldn't have missed it for the world.'

Wheatfield was going up the steps, taking a good look round before disappearing into the building. There appeared to be only the one entrance. It looked the sort of place to have a porter.

Nick gave it three mintues, then approached cautiously. The main doors were open, revealing an empty entrance hall. Nick strode in purposefully, looked around as if searching for someone, and said to the porter, 'Just saw a friend of mine come in. Does he live here?'

The porter stared at him blankly and shrugged.

Nick demanded, 'D'you know which flat he went to?'

'Probably fifth floor, I would say. That's where the lift stopped at any rate.'

'You don't know which number?'

The porter put on the air of having to deal with an idiot. 'These are service flats. People come and go all the time. Always changing. How should *I* know?'

Nick found a phone box and called the office. He told Conway to get hold of the letting agent and discover who'd rented the flats on the fifth floor. Conway cut him short, quietly triumphant. 'The boss has agreed to a proper job. Didn't I say he would? Give me ten minutes and someone'll be over.'

As he waited, Nick made an effort to keep a watch on the front entrance. He tried to memorise the description of each person passing in or out of the block. There were ten people in five minutes. By the time his relief arrived he couldn't remember anything about the first eight.

He briefed the new man then set off wearily for home. For some reason he began to feel very hot. Within minutes was sweating like a pig. It must be the flu. The thirty-minute Tube journey with a longish walk and nothing but an empty cold flat at the end suddenly seemed very unattractive.

He paused. Montagu Mews wasn't far away. Ten minutes at the most. Would she mind? Surely not. They'd made a tentative arrangement to meet that evening. So he'd be a bit early. She wouldn't turn him away; most women had some maternal instinct tucked away somewhere. He could do with a bit of tender loving care.

He was feeling distinctly shivery now. The walk was longer than he thought. By the time he reached the mews he was ready to drop.

He rang the bell. She wasn't in. He considered going home after all, but the prospect was very depressing.

He checked the wall of the house for an alarm. No sign. The door had a single Yale lock: a fifteen-second job. He reached into his wallet and took out one of the four 'loids' – strips of celluloid – he kept there.

As the door yielded he listened for a hidden alarm, but there was

195

none. He went in. Pausing only long enough to find a scrap of paper and leave a note on the stairs, he went straight up to the bedroom and undressed. Vastly weary, he climbed into the double bed and was instantly asleep.

Fifteen

Considering what she was about to do, Gabriele felt very calm.

She checked the contents of the parcels which Max had spread out on the table. Six batteries, two lengths of thin single-strand electrical wire – one in red, one in black – a pair of cutters, a soldering iron, a stick of solder, electrical tape, Sellotape, a roll of corrugated cardboard, six sheets of stiff white card, brown paper, small white plastic bags, string, six padded envelopes measuring ten by seven, a packet of wooden clothes pegs and a box of drawing-pins. Also a quantity of common garden weedkiller containing a high proportion of sodium chlorate, five bags of sugar, and one large packet of Surf soap powder. She rearranged everything in the right order, so that she could put her hands on the items as she needed them.

She said, 'Go and empty the Surf packet.'

While Max was gone she went to a holdall and removed the plastic container which she had been keeping in the fridge at the mews house. She opened it and took out six detonators. These she laid on the table.

With care she then removed the contents of a second box: two tubes, about ten inches long, each marked 'Nitramite 19C' and stamped with the French manufacturer's date and identification codes. The mixture consisted of TNT and ammonium nitrate, extremely powerful when detonated, but safe to handle under normal conditions.

She put the sticks of explosive on the far side of the table, next to the batteries and wires, but well away from the detonators.

Almost ready now. As a final preparation she tore two pages out of *Strike Back!* and taped them to the table where she could read them easily.

Max returned with the empty Surf packet which Gabriele placed on the floor. Handing Max the sugar and weedkiller, she motioned him towards the kitchen. She followed with a piece of paper and taped it on to the wall just above the work surface. On the paper were written the quantities of weedkiller and sugar to be weighed and mixed together in five separate batches, four small and one large. She pushed five plastic mixing bowls and the kitchen scales towards him. 'Take your time, mix the stuff well, and leave it in the bowls. And when you come in, don't speak to me or disturb me in any way.'

She returned to the main room and began work.

The important thing was not to rush it. With five devices to make it would be tempting to cut corners. That was the way to blast herself to pieces.

She decided to start with the simplest job. The four small packets.

First she made the initiators – the triggers that would fire the explosive. She took a wooden clothes peg and cut two lengths of red wire ten inches long. She made a small hole in each of the two jaws of the clothes peg, and pushed a wire through the hole from the outside. She stripped the end of each wire and wrapped it round the pin of a drawing-pin which she pushed firmly into the wood. When the clothes peg was clamped shut the two drawing-pins touched and contact was made between the two lengths of wire. She sprang the peg open and shut several times to make sure the drawing-pins always made good contact.

She made three more of these devices, then slid each inside a padded envelope and fixed them firmly in place with strong tape. Next she cut four rectangles of heavy card to fit inside the envelopes. As she put each card into the envelope she slid it between the jaws of the clothes peg. In this way, the card prevented contact between the two wires.

She got up and went into the kitchen. She found Max bent over the scales, spooning minute amounts of sugar back into a packet. She was pleased to see that he was doing the job with care.

He had completed three batches of the sugar-weedkiller mixture and these she took back to the table. She poured each batch into a white plastic bag and thrust a detonator into the centre of the crystals. With the wires from the detonator trailing out, she then sealed the bag with Sellotape, and slid it into the padded envelope on top of the card, being careful to keep the wires to one side.

Now, all that remained was to connect the various components to a battery.

She paused. She'd watched one of the Lotta make a similar letter bomb in Turin, and she'd practised it without explosives, but this was the first time she had done it for real.

She wired up the device until, if it weren't for the card, she would have a complete electrical circuit: one wire of the detonator to positive terminal on battery; negative terminal to clothes peg via red wire; clothes peg (second red wire) to second wire of detonator.

Max brought the last batch of sugar and weedkiller and she completed the last envelope.

There were now four small bombs in front of her, consisting of trigger, detonator and explosive. She sealed the envelopes.

When an envelope was opened and the card pulled out the circuit would be completed, the charge from the battery would fire the detonator – which would make a suitably frightening *bang*! – and the sugar mixture would go up in a sheet of flame complete with smoke.

Under normal circumstances it shouldn't kill anyone, but then it wasn't designed to.

She put the completed envelopes into the holdall, along with the things she no longer needed – the spare envelopes, cards and clothes pegs. The empty mixing bowls went back to the kitchen.

She relaxed for a moment.

So far so good.

Now the large parcel. This was different. This would very definitely kill.

She moved some of the items on the table nearer to her. Then after reading the instructions carefully, she began work.

First she taped the two HP2 batteries together and wired them together in series. Next she soldered a short length of red wire to the spare positive terminal, and a longer length of black wire to the negative.

Using insulating tape she strapped the two sticks of Nitramite together, and then strapped the batteries on to the sticks. From now on it was essential that the two wires leading from the batteries never touched one another, so she taped them on to the explosive, but as far apart as possible, the red running up to the top of one stick, the black to the bottom of the other.

So far it had been easy. Now the tricky part. She took a detonator and connected one of its wires to the red wire leading from the battery.

She now had half a circuit. The two loose wires must on no account come into contact with each other, otherwise the electrical charge from the batteries would fire the detonator, and that would be that.

She stretched the wires well apart and, to be doubly safe, wrapped some insulating tape round the one from the detonator which she would remove only at the last moment.

She paused. The operation had become oddly unreal. She had imagined having to make an enormous effort to create something like this. But it was incredibly easy. Apart from an odd feeling in the pit of her stomach, she had no fear. Instead she felt a curious detachment, as if this device would have come to exist anyway, without her help.

Max appeared from the kitchen, carrying a large bowl of the weedkiller and sugar crystals.

At that moment the telephone rang. Max gave a visible start. The bowl jerked in his hand and some of the mixture spilled on to the carpet.

Gabriele hissed, 'For Christ's sake!' and, getting up, took the bowl from his hands. She said impatiently, 'Answer the phone!'

Max picked it up. He turned to her. 'It's Giorgio.'

Gabriele let out a sigh of irritation. She had spoken to him the previous night and again that morning. He'd told her everything was going to plan. So why the hell was he calling again? And *now*.

Putting the bowl carefully on the table, she took the receiver from Max and snapped, 'Do you realise what you nearly *did*!'

'You told me to call if there was a change of plan.'

'But not *now*!' She forced her anger back. 'So what is it?'

'The girl. I can't do things too fast.'

'What do you mean?'

With obvious irritation Giorgio explained. 'She wants to take me out to dinner. She expects it. I have to go.'

Gabriele tried to think calmly. The girl had to be played along. She said harshly, 'Okay. But make her start for England first thing in the morning.'

'It's arranged. And I will fly at midday. I'll call you—'

'Don't call me *here* again!'

'The number's on the list,' Giorgio replied angrily. 'How was I to know?'

She put the phone down and spent several minutes sitting at the table, composing herself again. Then she went back to work.

Pouring most of the weedkiller–sugar mixture into the bottom of the empty Surf packet, she bedded first the detonator, then the

Nitramite sticks well down into it, and poured more of the sugar mixture on top, until it was flowing over the sides. Leaving the two loose wires trailing out of the top of the packet – one from each side – she taped the hinged lid of the Surf packet well down.

Now the trigger. She used a spring-loaded mechanism, rather like a mousetrap. It had to be rigged so that it would be activated by the opening of the parcel.

She took some corrugated cardboard and, wrapping it round the Surf box, cut it to size and taped it very tightly around the box. Then she took the mousetrap device and, without attaching it to the wires, cocked it and slipped it under the corrugated cardboard at the side of the box. She chose the side of the box because the pressure of the outer wrapping was greater there and would keep the trigger firmly cocked, and because people generally lay parcels flat when opening them, so leaving the side unimpeded and the mechanism free to operate.

She took a careful look at the trigger. There was no way it could operate accidentally while the corrugated cardboard was in place. But as soon as it was removed . . .

To test it, she tore the cardboard away, as if opening the parcel, and heard the mechanism give a satisfying snap.

She took another section of corrugated cardboard and fastened it tightly round the box.

Her mouth was dry. Fear at last. She was aware of Max close by, breathing down her neck. To get rid of him she said, 'Get me a coffee, would you?'

While he was in the kitchen, she took the red wire, removed the safety tape, and soldered the exposed end to the contact on the mousetrap mechanism. Next she pulled back the spring and pushed the mechanism between the layers of cardboard until it was held firmly in place, properly cocked, but with the base of the trigger still visible.

Now. The worst moment. The black wire had to be soldered to the terminal on the base of the fuse itself. Her heart thumped in her ears. She swallowed hard. It was one thing to know that the two contacts couldn't meet, and quite another to be aware of them being so close, separated by only a few inches.

Shaking slightly, she put the wire on the terminal and, holding the stick of solder, put the hot iron against it. The solder dripped on to the wire and cooled.

The bomb was now live.

Gently, she pushed the trigger mechanism further down the side of the box until it was out of sight. She exhaled deeply and sat back.

Max brought the coffee. She allowed herself a moment of satisfaction. A workman-like job. And a good explosive chain. The electrical circuit would heat the hot wire inside the detonator which would explode the extremely volatile fulminate of mercury. This in turn would explode the sugar–sodium chlorate mixture, which would finally explode the more stable TNT and ammonium nitrate of the main charge.

For a moment she imagined the explosion, the man being blown apart and plastered over the walls and ceiling in the split second before the house collapsed around him.

When she had finished her coffee she wrapped the parcel in brown paper and string, and then addressed it in bold block lettering, using a thick black felt-tip pen. Finally she placed it carefully in the holdall.

'What now?' asked Max.

'Keep the cutters and the spare wire. Put everything else into a rubbish bag and put it downstairs, in one of the communal dustbins.' They weren't coming back here, but she disliked the idea of leaving even the smallest amount of evidence behind.

As Max collected the empty containers, the wrapping, the off-cuts of red and black wire, Gabriele wiped the table, hoovered the weedkiller and sugar from the carpet and checked the kitchen. Max had been rather messy here too, and it took her a good ten minutes to clean the work surface and the floor. But she found the cleaning therapeutic; it seemed to tidy her mind. When she'd finished she was in high spirits.

Max was waiting at the flat door with the rubbish. She said, 'You've got the communiqués?'

He nodded.

'Remember to give the cabbies plenty of money, so they don't hesitate to take them. If you argue about it they'll remember your face.' She opened the door. 'You go first. I'll follow in a minute.'

In fact it was ten minutes before she was ready to leave. She put on a long blonde dolly-bird wig, some dark glasses, and a nondescript coat, which she normally wouldn't have been seen dead in. She was rather amused by her disguise, and stood in front of the mirror for a couple of minutes. It was really very simple to look completely different.

Down in the street she loaded the holdall and the large parcel into the boot of her car. **Then,** like dozens of young office girls all over London that afternoon, she took her batch of envelopes to the nearest post office to catch the last post of the day.

There was no one to see her go. The watchers had spotted Wheatfield leaving ten minutes earlier and, pleased to have identified him safely, were tailing him westwards, back towards North Kensington.

Gabriele parked outside the mews house and went to the boot. She decided to leave the parcel in there overnight – the car wasn't worth stealing, and there was no reason why anyone should be interested in it. However, she removed the spare detonators, to be on the safe side. There must be no accidents.

The holdall itself could stay in the boot until she found another service flat some time the following week.

She locked the boot. Letting herself into the house, she went to the kitchen and put the detonator into the fridge. Then she removed the wig and sunglasses and shook out her hair.

Now what?

Restlessly, she paced the kitchen. She was still exhilarated from the bomb-making. She wanted company. She wanted to talk. But now Giorgio wouldn't be back until the next day. And it wouldn't be wise to go calling on Max.

There was Nick Riley, of course. In fact if she was being honest he was the first person she'd thought of. But he hadn't phoned since he'd left the previous morning. And she didn't know where to find him. *Damn.*

Coffee mug in hand, she wandered into the living-room.

She stopped in her tracks.

A white blob of paper stared up at her from the staircase.

Her stomach twisted unpleasantly. *Who?*

She grabbed the paper and read fast.

Nick Riley.

For a second she went very cold, thinking of what he might have discovered.

Then she calmed herself. There was nothing in the house, nothing to suggest she was anything but a journalist. *Even* if he'd been snooping around, which he probably hadn't.

But how the hell had he got in?

She thought: How *dare* he!

But mingling with her annoyance was a tinge of grudging

admiration: he certainly had a nerve. As she climbed the stairs she rehearsed what she'd say to him.

The door of the bedroom was ajar. She pushed it wide open. Clothes were littered over the floor.

He was in her bed, breathing quietly, fast asleep. His top was bare. She suspected he was naked.

She shook him by the shoulder. 'Hey, wake up, you!'

He turned over and, opening half an eye, groaned, 'Hello.' He stretched and rubbed his hand mercilessly over his face. 'What time is it?' His voice was a thin croak.

She retreated slightly and said accusingly, 'You've got a cold.'

He opened the other eye and pulled himself up on to one elbow. 'I didn't actually *ask* to have it . . .'

'It was uninvited, was it – like *you*?'

'Quite.' His tone was unrepentant.

She demanded, 'May I ask how the hell you got in?'

'Ah.' For a long moment he looked at her through half-closed eyes, and she thought he wasn't going to answer. But eventually he said, 'There was a window open.'

She thought: Ah no, you don't get me that easily. She said firmly, 'Oh no, there wasn't.'

He made a face to show he'd been caught out. 'Well, you remember the car door? I used a trick like that.'

'Show me what you used. To get in.'

He looked at her for a few moments then slowly reached down to his jacket on the floor. From a packet he brought out what was known in the trade as a jiggler, a thin dagger-like steel spike. He said, 'What I used for the car. Nothing to it.'

'That wouldn't do it.'

He stared at her, suddenly wary. 'No?'

'You can't open locks like Yales with *that*.'

There was a silence. Suddenly he grinned. 'Well, you're absolutely right. Now how did you know that?'

She'd learnt a few basics from a former housebreaker in the Lotta. She persisted, 'So how did you get in?'

His smile vanished. Taking out his wallet, he removed a strip of celluloid and held it in the air. 'Takes fifteen seconds.'

'But only when you know how.'

He slipped the plastic and the spike back into his jacket. 'I can see that you're thinking bad things about me.'

She decided to go on giving him a hard time. She got a curious pleasure from it; also she wanted to know more. She said, 'Yes, I am.'

He reached out and, without a word, took the cup of coffee from her hand and began to drink from it. The bedcovers moved and she saw the side of his hip. Naked.

She said, 'You're a thief.'

He looked at her over the cup. 'No.' It was a bald statement.

'Then you break and enter for amusement?'

'Useful for getting into friends' flats. It's just a trick I learnt in my misspent youth and – I like to keep it up.' He shrugged, draining the last of the coffee. 'Strange though it sounds, it's the truth.'

She didn't believe a word of it. He was a thief, no doubt about it. But she wasn't angry. On the contrary, she was seeing Nick Riley in a new and very interesting light.

But she decided not to pursue the subject for the moment. All in good time. Instead she said caustically, 'So – do you usually sleep in the afternoons?'

'Only when I'm feeling bloody awful.'

'The cold? Or is it still the head?'

'Both. And lack of care and attention.'

'Well, well, that won't do, will it?' she replied archly. 'Can I get you something – apart from *my* coffee, that is?'

'Aspirin and hot lemon.' He added a hasty 'Please', and gave her a big smile.

'I'll get some from the chemist.' It was a long time since she'd gone on an errand for a man. But this was different.

As she moved to the door, he said, 'Any chance of a bath?'

'I should think so. The bathroom's next door.' She added facetiously, 'You're sure you'll be able to manage the lock?'

He grinned appreciatively, his expression warm and unguarded. Very attractive. For a common thief.

On the way back from the chemist, she began to realise that her snap judgement was probably mistaken. If he was just an ordinary thief then he was an extremely bad one – he had nothing to show for it in the way of a car or a place to live – and she couldn't believe that he was bad at anything he did.

No, going by his part in the demonstration and their conversation at dinner, he was undoubtedly committed politically and therefore above such things as common thieving. As such, he would keep his housebreaking and car stealing talents for special occasions: *political* occasions. The chances were he was *already* an activist.

If so, what a stroke of luck. It couldn't have worked out better if she'd planned it.

Back at the house she made a hot lemon drink and took it up the stairs. Sounds of splashing came from the bathroom. She paused and, leaving the drink on a shelf, looked into the empty bedroom. Most of his clothes had disappeared, but his jacket was still there, hanging up on a chair.

Silently she crossed the floor and, feeling through the pockets, pulled out the wallet. Money. The piece of plastic – no, *three* pieces of plastic. A train ticket. In the pockets, a comb, the steel spike, some paper handkerchiefs.

And a full set of keys. Skeleton keys.

But nothing else.

She frowned. Strange. No bus pass or student union card. Nothing to identify him.

His voice said: 'I hope it's interesting enough.'

She spun round.

He was standing in the doorway, wrapped in a towel. He walked casually up to her and, feeling through the jacket, pulled out the comb. He met her gaze and said mildly. 'If you want to know more about me you only have to ask.'

'Just checking. After all, it's not every day I find a housebreaker in my bed.' She asked lightly, 'What's your real name?'

'Nick Riley. Just like I said.'

She stared up into his face. Even if it wasn't his real name, did it really matter?

This man was exactly what she wanted. In every way.

The trouble with telling a lie, Nick thought unhappily, was that it led you into deeper and deeper water. The original lie – pretending to be a student – had been harmless enough, but now he'd had to tell a dozen more to cover himself.

Of course he could always tell her the truth, but that would be the end of that. Once she realised he was one of what she so charmingly called the filth, she'd never give him any information. In fact she'd chuck him straight out.

Also – and by no means least – there was the lady herself. Today she was radiating a nervous energy, an excitement that was overtly sexual. There was the firm promise of an affair, he was certain. And why not? Besides, the cold was making him feel sorry for himself and he wanted to be spoilt a little.

She handed him the hot lemon, asking, 'Would you like something to eat as well?'

He'd forgotten when he'd last had a meal. 'Yes, I'm starving.'

'Chicken, pasta, salad okay?'

'That's very good of you.'

She gave a little smile of triumph. 'Not of *me*. But of the Italian restaurant on the corner. I'll ask them to send it over.'

He thought: No chinks in her armour.

He went back to the bathroom and, finding a razor in the wall cabinet had a shave. It was a woman's razor. It may have been great for legs but it was blunt as hell on his face.

He examined the other contents of the cabinet. A stick deodorant. A bottle of eau de cologne. Brand: Rocco. Made in Italy, purchased in Italy. Packaging: masculine. Wording: *per uomini*. For men.

Ah. Masculine tastes.

Or a lover.

Back in the bedroom he looked in the wardrobe. Male clothing. Definitely a lover, then. Some of the shirts had Italian labels. He had a quick look through a jacket and some jeans. Nothing.

Presumably this lover was away. He wondered how long for. She didn't seem worried about an imminent return.

Feeling better for the bath, he got dressed and checked that his ID was safely tucked into the lining of his shoe. Gabriella had been quick off the mark searching his jacket. But then she was a journalist and they were always nosy.

As he went downstairs he thought of phoning Conway. It was seven: there might be something on the Wheatfield observation by now. But Gabriella was already putting plates of food on the table and he realised he was ravenous. The meal was delicious and he wolfed it down. His headache had disappeared. She produced a bottle of Chianti and he drank several glasses. They talked quietly, reflectively. The atmosphere was mellow, almost dreamlike.

Gabriella turned on Radio 3. There was a symphony. He recognised Brahms' Fourth. They listened for a while in silence. The music worked its usual spell on Nick. Everything became accentuated: the warmth and comfort of the room, the taste of the wine, the loveliness and desirability of Gabriella.

She met his eyes and smiled. There was still a reserve there, he noticed, a guard she was determined not to let down. He said quietly, 'Thanks for looking after me.'

She bristled immediately. 'Don't start being polite. That's

bourgeois crap.' She hesitated. 'Besides I wanted someone around. I didn't want to be on my own tonight.'

'I wouldn't have thought you'd be on your own very often.'

She regarded him over the rim of her glass. 'I hope you make love better than you talk, otherwise we're in for a disappointing night.'

The directness of the approach gave him a slight shock. Then he laughed, 'Well, there's only one way to find out, isn't there?'

He's just another man, she told herself. Another man like any other. To be enjoyed on her own terms.

And yet . . . Even now, he still had his arms round her, was still caressing her gently, making small sounds of pleasure. Unafraid of affection.

She wasn't sure she understood men like this.

He murmured, 'Your skin is incredibly soft.'

She turned her head, trying to examine his face in the darkness. He began to cover her cheeks with small kisses. Then, aware of her reserve, he pulled back. 'Was it all right for you?' His voice was soft, concerned.

'Yes.' It should have been – he had been very generous, over-whelmingly so – and yet she had felt nervous, unrelaxed.

'I – had the feeling – that it wasn't.'

'No. It was – great.'

He sank back on the pillow, drawing back from her. She wanted to explain. She said awkwardly, 'I've just got a lot on my mind, that's all.'

He said wryly, 'Thanks.'

'I meant . . .' What had she meant? That he made her feel vulnerable, and she didn't like that. 'I meant that I'm very bound up in my work at the moment.'

'Tell me about it.'

She hesitated. 'I'm working towards an important goal. Some-thing I feel very strongly about. And – it takes all my energy.'

He was silent for a moment. 'What is this goal?'

'I'm trying to – make people see the world for what it is. A twisted, rotten place. I'm trying to make them see how meaningless and empty their lives are. Living in boxes, working like ants – and for nothing. For crap like television sets and washing machines – things that they *think* will make them happy. They don't realise that they're just being bought off, made to live the roles that society has allotted to them . . .' She paused. 'I want to change all that.'

'Why? I mean, why d'you feel so strongly?'

'Because nobody counts for anything. Not in the system as it is now. The system crushes you if it can. It doesn't care a shit about the individual. I know. I've *been* there.'

Nick could feel the shudder of rage pass through her. Her vehemence vaguely worried him, nagging at an idea in the back of his mind. But then he remembered the early life in Italy, the dead father and the cold mother, and he saw that there was a lot of the hurt child in her; a child full of anger and resentment who still didn't understand why things had gone wrong for her.

He pulled her gently towards him. 'It's all right, it's all right . . .'

She was still fretting and he could feel the tension in her body. But finally she calmed down and her body relaxed against his. She turned her face to him and he could feel the warmth of her breath. Raising her head off the pillow, she stared at him in the darkness and seemed to come to a decision. She lowered her mouth on to his and kissed him, slowly at first, and then hungrily. This time there was no reserve.

Much later, after the last sigh of pleasure had come from deep within her, she held him close to her for a long time.

Sixteen

Henry Northcliff glanced at his watch. Seven fifty-five. His driver was already outside the house. He should leave in five minutes if he wasn't to be late for his early meeting.

He finished his coffee and went into the hall. He wondered why Caroline hadn't appeared yet. Then saw her, just coming down-stairs. He noticed she was still in her dressing-gown, which was unusual for her. As they met at the foot of the stairs the telephone rang.

Caroline said, 'I'll take it,' and went across the hall into the study.

Henry picked up his coat and briefcase, checked that he hadn't forgotten anything and stuck his head round the study door. Caroline was perched on the desk, listening hard, muttering the occasional 'No, I'm afraid not.' She saw Henry and beckoned him over. Henry was about to shake his head and point at his watch, when she beckoned again, more urgently. He put down his things and, going to the desk, looked at her questioningly. She thrust the receiver into his hand and panted, 'Elizabeth Danby.'

The horror showed in his face.

Caroline shook her head briefly. 'Sorry! Got to go – sorry!' She rushed past him and out of the room. Henry thought: What on earth?

Crossly, he put the receiver to his ear. Interrupting Mrs Danby's abject apologies, he managed to establish that she had heard some disquieting news about Victoria; a rumour that she had been injured.

'Injured?' he asked.

'In this awful demonstration, apparently. I mean, *really* – I thought I'd better check up on her, but her phone doesn't answer. For all I know she might be in some *hospital* . . . I just wondered if you'd *heard*.'

He cut her short with assurances that they hadn't heard anything, but would let her know the moment they did.

The instant he'd got rid of the woman, he went in search of Caroline. He called out but there was no reply. He was about to look upstairs when he heard a sound from the downstairs cloakroom. He strode across the hall and pushed open the door.

Caroline was draped over the basin, swilling out her mouth with water. He suddenly realised that she had been sick.

She looked at him sheepishly. 'I was going to tell you, but I wasn't really sure until today.'

He stared at her, shocked, trying to take it in.

She said unhappily, 'I know we hadn't exactly planned a baby . . . And it's a bit of a surprise for me too . . .' She caught the expression on his face and trailed off.

Henry's first reaction was one of sharp disappointment and – yes – resentment. The two of them had been perfectly happy. He'd been looking forward to their having time together, to travel and explore Florence and Venice . . . To enjoy *each other*. And now *this* . . .

A baby would intrude into their relationship, steal from it, diminish it. The extra dimension their happiness had possessed would be suffocated by the sheer weight of dreary day-to-day trivia; nappies, feeds and sleepless nights. And by the time they were free again – God, he would be an old man . . .

In a wave of self-pity he looked at her and thought: All I ever needed was *you*.

She dropped her eyes and turned away to pat her face with a towel. She was putting a brave front on it, but he could see that she was upset. He realised he was being very selfish. He should look at it from her point of view. She would enjoy being a mother. He mustn't deny her that.

He grasped her shoulders and leant his head against hers.

She said in a low voice, 'You're not happy about it.'

He stroked her hair and said finally, 'Of course I'm happy about it. It was rather a shock, that's all. Really.' He managed a thin smile. 'It's wonderful.'

For all its faults the British postal service is more efficient than most. In 1969, in the days before it was split into a two-tier system of first- and second-class mail, eighty-seven per cent of all letters were delivered the next day, a figure which rose to well over ninety per cent for letters sent within the London area or to other large cities such as Manchester or Birmingham.

The first padded envelope was delivered at seven-fifteen to an address in Bradford. It was not opened immediately for the simple reason that there was no one there. The place was the one-roomed office of an organisation called the Anglo-Asian Society, one of the many groups and societies that had sprung up in the area since the large influx of Asians in the fifties and sixties. Although the organisation's title suggested that it embraced all Asian immigrants, in practice the membership did not include Pakistanis, who as Muslims liked to keep themselves to themselves, but consisted almost entirely of Indian Hindus.

The organisation was a peaceful one which prided itself on furthering understanding between the British and Indian communities. This was not always easy because, like most immigrants, the Indians liked to stick together and Bradford's Asian population had now got to the point where, in many streets, it was rare to see a white face. To the consternation of the society's president and secretary, Mr Binodh Gopalji, this fact was somewhat resented by the shrinking white community. However, he worked hard to smooth out what he called 'the minor little hiccups' that interrupted the smoothness of his community's absorption into the British way of life. It was a source of some satisfaction to him that, by and large, his modest efforts appeared to be successful.

The next envelope was delivered at seven thirty-nine, to an address in the North 8 district of London. This was the location of the West Indian Action Group, which, as its name suggested, was fairly forceful in pursuing the interests of its West Indian members, though even its critics could hardly describe it as militant. The members, who were mainly younger second-generation black immigrants from the islands of the Caribbean, were vociferous, educated, and angry. They wanted jobs, houses, and an end to discrimination. Despite the provocative suggestions of certain right-wing politicians that they should be encouraged to return to Trinidad or Barbados, they regarded Britain as their home, which was not surprising since most of them had spent the greater part of their lives there.

For much of the time the office was run by a slim twenty-two-year-old law student called Leonie Brown, whose family had emigrated from the island of Antigua in 1949. But, being a girl who liked to go out dancing almost as much as she liked going to bed with her lusty new boyfriend, she didn't often get to sleep before two, and was rarely in the office before nine-thirty.

This envelope, too, remained unopened on the floor.

The third envelope was delivered later, at eight-twenty. Here, at an office in the City, there was someone to receive it. David Levene often arrived early. He found he got a lot of work done in the quiet time between eight and eight-thirty. Although he was a journalist and it wasn't really his job to do so, he picked up the mail and sifted through it.

He noticed the buff-coloured padded envelope straight away. The six staff at the *Red Star* kept a wary eye open for unusual packages. As an official publication of the Communist Party they were used to receiving the occasional hate mail. People had been known to send dog turds, bad eggs, and other such subtle indications of resentment.

But *was* this package unusual?

No clue to who the sender might be. Post mark: W1.

He flexed it in his fingers. A hard object half-way down. The rest crunchy – as if it contained granules of some kind. He sniffed at the flap. Slightly acrid. Could be a chemical that let off a bad smell.

He thought for a moment. Always better to be on the safe side. He put the envelope in his desk. As soon as the others got in he'd discuss it with them.

At two minutes to nine Binodh Gopalji unlocked the door of the

211

Anglo-Asian Society's office in Bradford and, as was his habit, carefully hung his coat and hat on the hook behind the door. Then he stopped to pick up the mail off the mat. He recognised an electricity bill, which was not at all welcome since the society was always short of funds; two circulars; a batch of Indian publications; fifteen letters and a padded envelope.

He sat down at his desk and looked out of the window for a moment. A nice day, and getting better. The sun was making an effort to break through. It didn't happen very often in the British winters. But he didn't mind that. He loved Britain: it was tolerant, ordered, and comfortable. He thought with pride: Simply the best country in the world.

He began to open the mail, carefully and methodically, as was his way. Leaving the bills and circulars until last, he began with the letters. Requests for news of relatives, requests from India for an introduction to a possible bride – the only quick way of getting into Britain nowadays – requests for help. Requests, always requests, which was just how it should be.

He came to the padded envelope. It was taped down at one end. By opening it carefully, it could be reused. Since this type of envelope was expensive, it was a consideration not to be sniffed at.

Patiently, he stripped off the Sellotape and was pleased to see it had not brought away any of the paper.

Then, angling the envelope so that he could see inside it, he unfolded the end. A piece of card. He pulled it out.

Although he remembered nothing about that afterwards.

The force of the explosion, though relatively small, was sufficient to knock him backwards off his chair on to the floor, leaving him stunned. However, it was the sheet of flame that blasted outwards in a three-foot arc that did the damage. It scorched away all the hair and much of the skin from his face and hands. And, though the eyelids can close faster than the shutter of a camera, Binodh Gopalji's reacted a fraction of a second too late, and the blast hit his eyes.

He was found almost immediately, by another tenant, and fifteen minutes later was in the emergency room of the nearest hospital. His condition was not critical, but severe enough – skin grafts would be required to repair the burnt skin; and his eyes would never quite recover from their blasting. However, for Binodh Gopalji the blast to his body was nothing compared to the shock to his moral sensibilities. Life could never ever be viewed in quite the same way again. The exploding envelope had blasted more than his face; it had destroyed the tolerant comfortable Britain he had loved like a true son. Moreover, he was totally mystified as to the reason why.

The fourth envelope was delivered at nine-ten to the Council for Civil Liberties, a fiercely independent organisation which fought for and defended individual rights. Although it examined all manner of threats against personal liberty, it had inevitably concentrated its efforts on protecting the interests of the underprivileged, and was regarded as firmly left-wing.

The envelope was opened by the secretary-receptionist, a girl of twenty-three. She was extremely lucky. For one thing, she was standing up when she opened it on the desk, so that it was some distance from her face. For another, she was talking to someone else at the time, so that her chin was up and her face at an obtuse angle to the blast. Finally – and luckiest of all – the weedkiller – sugar mixture did not ignite properly. As a result, she was stunned but not seriously hurt.

Leonie Brown was not so lucky. She arrived at the office of the West Indian Action Group at nine-forty, having had far too little sleep. She made some coffee, took a couple of phone calls, and yawned. At ten she looked at the mail, such as it was. Nothing very interesting. Except for the padded envelope. Sitting at her desk, she ripped off the Sellotape and pulled out the card inside.

The blast itself would not have hurt her seriously, but for the fragment of metal from the detonator case which, sharp as a knife, flew into her chest and pierced a lung. Unfortunately there was no one about and it was some ten minutes before she was discovered, choking on her own blood and hardly breathing. She was taken to hospital where they poured ten pints of blood into her and, against all the odds, just managed to save her. It was four weeks before she left hospital.

In the offices of the *Red Star* David Levene was working hard on an article which had to be finished by that afternoon, and completely forgot the envelope in his desk. Then at noon a fellow journalist, coming in late, mentioned the news story he had just heard on the radio.

Then, with something of a shock, David Levene remembered the envelope. Very quietly he locked his desk, and told the others not under any circumstances to approach it. Then he telephoned Scotland Yard.

At about the same time a communiqué was delivered to *The Times* and the *Daily Express*. It was titled: 'Britain for the British', and contained a vitriolic tirade against immigration and subversives. It purported to come from an organisation called the National Coalition.

'Who the hell are the National Coalition?' demanded Chief Superintendent Straughan.

Everyone stared at Mason, the Branch man who covered right-wing organisations. He shook his head. 'Nothing on file, sir. Never been heard of before.'

Ryder sneezed and blew his nose. He'd just arrived, having phoned in earlier and heard the news. He was rather glad he wasn't in Mason's shoes, having to admit he knew nothing.

'Right,' said Straughan, 'Commander Kershaw, late of the Serious Crime Squad, is in charge of the investigation. Mason and Smith are being seconded to assist. For the rest of you – I want ears to the ground. I want to be reassured that no one on the left is going to get agitated and start thinking about reprisals.'

As they got up to leave Straughan frowned at Nick. 'No one told me you were back with us, Nick. Got clearance from the CMO, I trust?'

'Sir. Should come through tomorrow.'

As they returned to the office Conway murmured, 'Careful, he'll check up on it.'

With bad grace, Nick phoned the Central Medical Officer's office and made an appointment for later that afternoon.

Then he went down to the incident room, which had the air of frenetic activity that marked the early stages of a new case.

Nick found a face he vaguely recognised, a sergeant he'd worked with a few months back, and reintroduced himself. After chatting for a bit, Nick let it be known that he'd like to hear when any info came back from the explosives people at Woolwich. There was no reason why the sergeant should keep him in touch, except it was asked as a favour, and a lot of business around Scotland Yard was done by favours.

Nick went back to his office and, tempting some hot water out of the coffee machine, made himself an aspirin and hot lemon drink from a sachet that he had taken from Gabriella's supply.

He thought back to the morning. What a strange lady she was. On waking she'd been cool and distant, almost resentful. She'd watched him covertly, as if assessing him afresh. Then, abruptly, she seemed

214

to break out of whatever constrained her, and to regain a little of her confidence. Some of the previous evening's mood had returned, and she became sharp and funny again.

He wondered if there was any future in the affair. Probably not. And in some ways he was sorry. She was good company when she made up her mind to it. He liked her smartness, her clever mind, the tough exterior which hid the vulnerability underneath. But at the same time she was uncertain, evasive, and volatile, as if, underlying all the toughness, there was a deep lack of self-confidence. She didn't seem to know who she was, and that was a pity.

In the end she'd be trouble, he sensed it. And yet – there was something about her that intrigued him.

Also – he couldn't help remembering – she might be useful.

The sergeant from downstairs phoned up with the preliminary report from Woolwich – the Home Office Branch of the Royal Armament Research and Development Establishment. The device found at the offices of the *Red Star* consisted of a continental-style detonator, a home-made initiator and a mixture consisting of a weedkiller containing sodium chlorate, and sugar.

'No trace on the source of the explosive?' Nick asked.

'Dunno. Nothing reported anyway.'

Nick rang off, wondering how a right-wing group had suddenly got so proficient in the making of explosives. One somehow expected trouble of this sort to come from the Left, who had a traditional fondness for drawing attention to their cause with violence and loud bangs. He remembered *Strike Back!*

God! He had a sudden thought. Perhaps, by a perverse stroke of chance this National Coalition or whoever they were had got hold of a copy. That would be an ironical twist: the Left hoist by its own petard.

He took a copy of *Strike Back!* out of the drawer and looked through the explosives section. Here it was . . . under the heading 'Easy Brew'. Sugar and weedkiller. Flashes up with searing, yellow flame. Not most powerful explosive . . . but ingredients easy to buy and easy to make. *Required*: sugar – any type; and sodium chlorate – principal ingredient of certain weedkillers (it listed the best brands).

The detonation – it went on to explain – could be effected in any number of ways. But, if limited to easily available means, then the methods on page 12 or 13 were recommended.

Nick looked at page 12. Glowing element of a broken light bulb powered by battery. Page 13. Drip acid on to a contraceptive, until it leaked through on to the mixture and explodes it.

But the letter bomb had contained a proper detonator. Things hardly available from a mundane shopping expedition. No. These right-wingers had contacts, sources, *sophistication*.

And yet – it was no good: something about all this bothered him deeply. It just didn't ring true. The right-wingers were stirrers, agitators. They liked to march in black uniforms through immigrant neighbourhoods shouting loud slogans. And they were young, ill-educated and unsophisticated for the most part. Somehow these letter bombs just didn't *fit*.

He would have believed it of Wheatfield's sort. Every time. If the recipients of the letter bombs had been *right*-wing he'd have put Wheatfield near the top of his list straight away.

It was ironical that Wheatfield, of all people, *had* been on quite a shopping expedition the previous day.

Somewhere in the back of Nick's mind a small alarm sounded.

That large bag bought from the hardware shop. It had looked just like a garden product. And the purchases in the supermarket – he had thought he had seen Wheatfield buy flour. But it could just as well have been *sugar*.

It was ridiculous of course. There was no motive.

It didn't make sense.

And *yet*.

He racked his brains to remember the name of the shop in Westbourne Grove. His mind was a blank. He called the local Notting Hill nick.

After a long wait while someone asked around, he finally got it.

Westbury's.

He called them.

Yes, said the sleepy assistant, they stocked all sorts of weedkiller. Nick sat a little more upright in his chair.

Containing sodium chlorate? the assistant repeated back to him. He hadn't a clue, he'd have to ask the boss. After a long time the boss came to the phone. Weedkiller with sodium chlorate? Well – he'd have a look. There was a long pause. He came back to the phone and, obviously reading off the packaging, listed various chemical-sounding names. Then Nick realised that they probably *were* only names: manufacturers' registered names for the concoction of chemicals in that particular product.

'Is there a brand in a white bag with red lettering on it?' Nick asked.

The shopkeeper answered without hesitation. He named a well-known brand. He described the red lettering, and said it had a picture of a garden underneath. And, yes, the picture of the garden *was* mainly green. Nick could almost hear him thinking, well, it would be, wouldn't it, being a garden.

'How big is this bag?' Nick asked.

'We've got it in bags of five, ten or twenty pounds.'

'And the manufacturer – what's their address?'

The shopkeeper gave it to him. Nick rang off, his mind racing.

Conway wandered into the office and opened his mouth to speak. Nick waved him to shut up and got on to the telephone exchange to find the number of the weedkiller manufacturer. Within five minutes he was talking to their chief chemist. Two minutes later he was replacing the phone, shaking his head with disbelief.

Mainly sodium chlorate.

Conway, who'd been listening avidly, demanded, 'You on to something, Ryder?'

'God only knows.' He jumped up and grabbed his jacket. 'Where's Wheatfield, Conway?'

'*Wheatfield?* Why?' Then, catching the full implication of the question, he exclaimed, 'But he's left of *Marx*, for Christsake!'

'Where *is* he?'

Conway suddenly looked crestfallen. 'At this precise moment no one knows. The watch was called off an hour ago.'

Nick tried to contain his disbelief. '*Why in hell?*'

'Because we *know* where he lives. And because a lot of people were needed for *this*.'

Nick closed his eyes and said, 'Oh shit.'

It took half an hour to get hold of Commander Kershaw, to stop briefly at the shop in Westbourne Grove and pick up a packet of the weedkiller, and meet him at St Mark's Villas with a raiding party. Even before they had stationed two men at the back, obtained confirmation that a search warrant had been granted, and run panting up the stairs to the room on the second floor, Nick knew what they would find.

Nothing.

Wheatfield had done a bunk. They spent ten minutes establishing that no trace of the shopping expedition remained, and sped across town to the service flat in Weymouth Street, where they met up with Conway. Faced by five policemen the porter was suddenly more forthcoming about the occupants of the fifth floor. He thought that flat number 502 was most likely to be the one they were after. Conway referred to the list of residents he'd obtained from the letting agents. Four of the flats on the fifth floor were let, either to companies or American visitors. However, flat 502 had been let to a Mr and Mrs Hoerst of Switzerland.

They knocked on the door of the flat. There was no reply. The porter let them in with a pass key.

It was quite empty. There were no signs of a hurried departure. Conway phoned the letting agents again. The rent was paid up for another two weeks. No, references had not been requested because the tenants had paid the rent in advance and left a £150 deposit. And no, the deposit had not been reclaimed.

Everything was very neat and tidy. The porter explained that the maid would have been in that morning. She would have cleared out the wastepaper baskets and the kitchen rubbish.

Nick walked round the flat with an empty feeling in the pit of his stomach.

An expensive service flat, money to burn, smooth organisation. The letter bombs were Wheatfield, all right, but *this* set-up? No. Not on his *own* anyway. This sort of lifestyle was quite out of his league.

He sat disconsolately in an armchair, ignoring the angry glare of one of the two forensic men who were bent over tables and carpets, busy with small brushes and scrapers, like a couple of fastidious housewives.

Kershaw came in and sat in the opposite chair. He was a tall, thoughtful, softly-spoken man, although Nick had the feeling the calm manner was deceptive. 'Okay, Ryder,' he said. 'Tell me about Wheatfield.'

Making an effort to remember all the details on the file, Nick listed the catalogue of Wheatfield's political activities.

Kershaw drew a deep breath. 'Any ideas as to why a well-known left-wing activist might be trying to score against his own side?'

Nick drew a deep breath. 'Trying to stir it up. That's all I can think of.'

'Well – I'm not saying you're wrong, but according to the surveillance reports, Wheatfield did not go near a post box yesterday.'

'No. But then there were others involved. I'm sure of it.'

'An organisation?'

'A group. Trained, possibly abroad.'

Kershaw stroked his chin thoughtfully. 'Okay, Ryder. I'll buy that. But I can't say I'm happy with the motive. If you can come up with some more answers, that would be appreciated.'

'Excuse me –' It was one of the forensic men. He was holding a number of small plastic bags. 'I think you might find this interesting . . .' The bags all contained granules of what looked like sugar. 'I found these crystals down several cracks on the kitchen work surface. Also on the kitchen floor. And quite a quantity in the carpet, just here. Also a few were caught in the bristles of the floor brush. They'll have to be analysed, of course. But taking a preliminary look, there appear to be two types of crystal here. At least one is granular, like sugar, the other more powdery, like salt . . .'

At that moment the telephone rang.

Giorgio held the telephone to his ear and counted the rings with growing impatience.

Suddenly it answered.

There was a pause, then a man's voice said, 'Hello?'

Giorgio hesitated then slowly replaced the receiver. It wasn't Max's voice. Gabriele must have given up the flat. Why hadn't she told him? And would it be relet already? He sighed with annoyance. How could he be expected to understand the British way of doing things?

He looked at the last number on his list. He'd already tried the mews house. There was only the flat in Chelsea. It was strictly for emergency use, so it was unlikely she'd be there, but he tried the number anyway.

As he'd expected, no reply.

He stared out of the window of Victoria's flat until a movement distracted him. She was offering him a glass of wine. She had already laid the table for a meal. Her efforts to please were almost painful.

He sipped the wine and regarded her. She was pliable, naïve, impressionable. And of course she was madly in love with him to the point where she would do anything for him. It was rather amusing to see how far he could make her go. Sometimes her submissiveness annoyed him, sometimes it pleased him. At this moment it was just about tolerable.

'Do you want to unload the van?' she asked.

Immediately his good humour evaporated. Women were unbelievable. They could never leave you alone; they always had to try to manipulate you, to try to make you as small-minded and obsessed with trivia as they were. He was overwhelmed with irritation and didn't answer.

'Well then,' she was saying. 'I'll start to get the meal, shall I?'

Suddenly he felt bored. And resentful. This girl had nothing to say. He rather missed Gabriele. She was tough on him, but she knew what he wanted.

He drained the glass of wine and decided that, as soon as the van was unloaded, he would drop this girl. She had served her purpose. He had put up with her for quite long enough.

The telephone rang and Victoria answered. From her manner it was obviously a good friend. He wasn't in the slightest interested; her friends would be dull and unimportant.

He flicked idly through a magazine, only half-listening.

'. . . Oh, I just got caught up in the crowd . . . No, no, honestly, I'm fine now . . . Just a little bruised . . . Promise . . . Yes, I *will* call mother. Yes . . . Yes, Caro, I *promise* . . .'

Giorgio fidgeted and wished she would get off the phone. Her high-pitched chatter was annoying.

'. . . How's Henry? . . . Really? But I've got it here. Hang on . . .'

Victoria pulled one of the newspapers up off the floor and spread it out. 'Got it . . . Yes, *what* a good picture.'

Giorgio let the magazine fall to his lap and stared out of the window.

'. . . Is he very busy? . . . Yes, I'm sure . . . No, I quite understand. Perhaps in the next holidays – what do you call them? Yes, the *recess* . . .'

Giorgio picked up the magazine again. Finally Victoria rang off and said brightly, 'Sorry about that. Family – sort of.'

She disappeared into the kitchen. After a moment Giorgio reached out and slowly slid the newspaper towards him. The paper was open at the centre page. There were two news pictures, one of some visiting foreign politicians, and one of a man in a preposterous white wig.

The caption under the man with the wig read: The Attorney-General, Sir Henry Northcliff.

Henry. The name on the telephone.

He refolded the newspaper and, getting up, wandered into the kitchen and leaned against the door frame. Victoria was at the stove, adjusting the gas under a pan.

She turned and jumped. 'Oh! You gave me a fright.'

He was still for a moment then, reaching out, he caressed her cheek. She looked at him uncertainly, not sure of what he wanted.

220

He smiled to show that he was pleased with her. She stepped forward and, putting her arms around him, leant her head against his chest.

He said gently, 'Tell me about your friends.'

Gabriele found the address and, driving on a little, turned a corner and parked the Fiat on a double yellow line. She looked at herself in the driver's mirror. The blonde wig was uncomfortable. She readjusted it and checked her make-up, which was heavy, with thick black eyeliner and several layers of mascara. She added a preposterously large pair of sunglasses. A real dolly bird.

She got out and went round to the boot.

The parcel sat lodged against the side of the car where she had positioned it the previous day. She picked it up and put it on the pavement while she slammed the boot shut.

Picking it up again, she crossed the pavement and went into the office of Cardinal Couriers Limited, a company who specialised in fast reliable deliveries.

She put the parcel down on the front desk.

A young man in overalls appeared. 'Where's it to go to?'

'Putney.'

'When do you want it delivered?' He looked at the clock on the wall. 'It's a bit late for today—'

'First thing tomorrow morning would be ideal.'

Taking the address from the top of the parcel, he made out the chit, asked her for two pounds ten shillings, and began to make out a receipt. 'What company?'

She hesitated for a moment. 'Crystal Designs. 3 Margaret Street.'

He entered the details on the receipt, and passed it to her.

'We do collect, you know. You only have to ring.'

She nodded. 'I know, but I was passing. I thought it might be easier.'

She returned to the car. No warden, no ticket. Her luck was good today.

She turned the ignition and, revving hard, let the clutch in with a jerk. The Fiat shot off down the street, barely missing a slow-moving pedestrian.

Gabriele hardly noticed. She was thinking: Wait until they read about this one in Italy.

Seventeen

Helen McCabe stared at herself in the bathroom mirror and sighed. There seemed to be a dozen more wrinkles on her face since she had last looked. She was getting old, and she couldn't think where all the years had gone.

The house was lovely, of course. Four bedrooms, double garage, standing in a third of an acre in a very pleasant part of Putney; quiet yet only five minutes from the river and twenty minutes from Peter's office. For years all she had ever wanted was a nice home. Now she'd got it and . . . And she felt empty and dissatisfied and she didn't understand why.

She walked through into the bedroom and thought vaguely about what to wear. It was eleven and time she got out of her dressing-gown.

The doorbell rang. She muttered, 'Oh dear!' Pulling on a sweater she hastily stepped into a skirt and, still shoeless, went breathlessly down the stairs to the front door.

A rather startling figure stood in the porch. He was dressed entirely in black leather with a shiny black crash helmet on his head. He looked like one of those Hell's Angels she'd read about. Then she saw that he was holding a parcel. Of course: a delivery boy. What else would he have been. Silly of her.

She signed for the parcel and took it into the kitchen. It was addressed to Peter. She wondered what it could be. Had he ordered anything? Unlikely. He usually left all the household purchases to her. Something to do with the garden perhaps. Even then, he would have told her.

She went back upstairs to find some shoes. She brushed her hair and half-heartedly patted a little powder on her nose.

Back in the kitchen, she made herself a cup of coffee and, sitting at the table, considered what to do with her day. She should write a note to her daughter.

She got up to put the cup in the sink and noticed the parcel again. Quite large – something interesting, certainly. A present? She wondered if Peter had got her a surprise. But it wasn't her birthday and – well, he wasn't that sort of husband. He was considerate, but not *imaginative*. That was because he was so busy and didn't have time to think about domestic things. She was pleased at his success,

222

of course, and didn't resent the long hours he worked. At the same time she felt left out, excluded. *Useless.*

She found a scrap of paper and tried to start a shopping list for the weekend. She should make the effort to find a new dress as well. There was an official dinner coming up in two weeks and she had nothing suitable. She dreaded occasions like that. She didn't feel at home among crowds of important people. And she had never got used to being Lady McCabe, although it was four years now since Peter had become Commissioner and been knighted.

She watched a pigeon pecking at the lawn, then, aware that her list was still blank, wandered over to the fridge to see what was needed. On the way she fingered the parcel, and picked it up again. Quite heavy and solid. What *could* it be?

Suddenly it seemed rather a treat, this parcel. Something unexpected and exciting in what was otherwise a dreary day. It *would* be nice to open it.

She mustn't, of course. It was addressed to Peter. She looked at her watch. Twelve. Perhaps she might just give him a ring . . . She didn't often, so he wouldn't mind. Yes, why not? It would be nice to hear his voice, if only for a minute.

She dialled and waited a little nervously. The line went direct to his secretary, who answered immediately. They exchanged greetings, then the secretary said she wasn't sure if he was free, but she'd just find out.

A few seconds later Peter came on the line. Helen's heart sank. She could tell from his tone that he was busy. Although she already knew the answer because he'd told her that morning, she asked what time he expected to be home. He was abrupt; she'd obviously chosen a really bad time. Quickly she mentioned the parcel. Was he expecting anything? Did he want her to open it? There was silence for a moment. No, he wasn't expecting anything. Unless it was something to do with his wine club. Or maybe it was that golfing book Harry Sidley had promised to send him. Yes, why didn't she open it. He asked after her, as he always did, and rang off.

He was a good husband, Helen decided. She really mustn't complain.

With a sense of pleasant anticipation, she got the kitchen scissors out of the drawer and approached the parcel.

What a treat. Not a book. Too big. Wine perhaps.

She snipped the string and pulled at the Sellotape fastening one end. She removed the brown paper with care so that it could be reused. The parcel was certainly well wrapped. There was a thick layer of corrugated cardboard and under that another piece of brown paper.

Wine, almost certainly.

Impatient now, she cut quickly into the corrugated cardboad.

Alison Miller shouted at her son, Matthew, to come back immediately. But the three-year-old had no intention of being denied a run and scampered off across the lawn. Alison put her load of shopping down by the front door and ran after him. She caught him and, unlocking the door, carried him into the kitchen. She popped him down beside the sink while she undid his windcheater.

As she pulled off one arm of the jacket, there was an enormously loud noise.

She felt herself lifted up and thrown backwards through the air. She opened her mouth to cry out, but the wind had been knocked out of her.

She found herself lying on the floor with a small weight against her chest. Matthew. *Safe*. She thought: Thank God! She grasped him to her.

Panting, she regained her breath. Matthew started to scream and, sitting up, she saw that the back of his head was bleeding. She had a moment of utter panic, then saw that the cuts to his head were superficial. Glass. It was everywhere.

Still holding the child, she stood up and staggered uncertainly to the window, which had been completely shattered. Finding a tea-towel she put it to Matthew's head. Then, realising the towel would be covered in glass, she looked for another in the cupboard.

As she wrapped it round the child's head she looked out of the shattered window. She stared blankly at the McCabes' next door, trying to comprehend what she was seeing. There was a great empty space in the side of the house where the kitchen had been.

For a moment she gaped. Then she reached for the wall phone and, shaking so much she could hardly get her finger in the dial, called 999.

She tried to speak slowly and clearly, and she managed very well until she happened to look back towards the McCabes' garden and saw a piece of meat-red flesh with a hand attached to it hanging from a tree.

Then she screamed.

Two minutes later the first police car arrived.

224

By chance the newsmen got their first whiff of the story almost immediately and before Scotland Yard could even think of putting an embargo on it, an item went out on the radio news at one o'clock, saying that there had been an explosion at a house in Putney.

Half an hour after that a taxi drew up outside the offices of *The Times* in Gray's Inn Road, and the cabby delivered a letter to the reception desk.

There was a stunned hush in the incident room. Nobody could think of the appropriate thing to say. Kershaw and his team had rushed off to Putney and those who remained were manning the telephones.

Nick paused only long enough to discover that there was no fresh news before dashing up to his own office. Conway was already there, looking ashen-faced.

'Christ,' he said. '*Who?*'

Nick shook his head. But he had a feeling. It was Wheatfield's friends. It had to be.

He went to Records and, collecting the files on all Wheatfield's known associates, took them down to the incident room.

The phone call from *The Times* came through five minutes later. A sergeant took the message down in longhand. Then the room burst into activity. A car was sent to *The Times* for the original communiqué, a message was transmitted to Kershaw in Putney, and the sergeant's handwritten jottings were photocopied.

Everyone read the communiqué. Then they looked at Nick. They were expecting him to have an answer.

He read it fast, then again more slowly:

THE PSEUDO CHIEF OF PIGS WAS SENTENCED TO DEATH BY THE REVOLUTIONARY TRIBUNAL FOR:

1. THE CRIME OF ENCOURAGING AND PROTECTING THE FASCIST BOMBERS.

2. THE CRIME OF GROSS OPPRESSION AGAINST THOSE WHO OPPOSE THE CAPITALIST SYSTEM WHICH HE AND HIS KIND SUPPORT.

SIGNED: THE CRYSTAL FACTION.

The Crystal Faction. Nick had never heard the name before, he was sure of that. He shook his head so that those watching would realise that he didn't have any quick and easy answers.

Then he sat with his head in his hands, thinking his way through it.

Faction equalled dissenting group equalled splinter group – equalled *new* group? New group.

Crystal. Glass? Yes, but . . . what did the word actually *mean*. A substance that was hard and clear. Clear. This group was seeking to clarify things? Or to harden existing attitudes.

It all added up to – nothing. A new revolutionary group.

Crystal . . . Crystal . . .

It rang no bells.

Start again.

He thought for a long time, jotting words down as they came into his head. He put the word crystal in the centre of the page with a sunburst of connecting words round it. Crystal – hard – clear – transparent – glass – crystalline – sweet – crystallise . . .

He paused. A tiny memory nagged at his mind.

But which word had prompted it?

He went through them again. Crystalline . . . *crystallise* . . .

He closed his eyes, trying to see the word in his memory.

Then at long last he had it. Yes.

Jumping up, he raced back to his office and grabbed the facsimile *Strike Back!* pamphlet from his tray. On the last page: 'Pulverise, Energise, Polarise! Fabricate crystal splinters!'

He walked back down to the incident room, trying to work out what if anything he'd gained. A connection.

Between a single word and a bomb-making guide.

A connection. Which led nowhere.

It was possible that the authors of the pamphlet had direct connections with the makers of the bomb; it was possible that the authors were themselves the bomb-makers.

But it was equally possible that Wheatfield's friends had no direct connection with the people behind the pamphlet. Influenced by the call to action, they might simply have set themselves up in isolation.

The incident room was busy now. Someone had seen a motor-cyclist call at the Commissioner's house about an hour before the explosion. The witness thought it might have been a delivery boy. All the phones were manned as every delivery firm in London was checked.

Half an hour later, just as Commander Kershaw returned from Putney, they got the lead. A company by the name of Cardinal Couriers had delivered a parcel to the McCabe address that morning. The receipt had the sender's name: Crystal Designs, 3 Margaret Street. It took only fifteen minutes to establish that there was no company of that name in Margaret Street nor at any other address. Companies with similar names were checked but, not surprisingly, had no knowledge of any parcel. Two men were sent round to the courier company to get a description of the person who had left the parcel.

Apparently it was a woman. Long blonde hair. Dark glasses. Tallish. Attractive. But the description of the woman's face was vague, due to the dark glasses.

A grim-faced Kershaw summoned Nick. Straughan was there, looking grey and worried.

'Well?' Kershaw said in his quiet voice. 'Do we have anything?'

'Nothing concrete,' Nick said truthfully. 'Only a possible link between the communiqué and this *Strike Back!* pamphlet.' He explained the crystal connection. 'But I think we could waste a lot of time and energy trying to go into that link, sir. We've a better chance if we go straight for the motive.'

'Yes?'

'Now, this first "crime" mentioned in the communiqué – the crime of "encouraging and protecting the fascist bombers" – it suggests that the bomb this morning was in direct retaliation for the letter bombs yesterday. Well – that's rubbish, sir. First, we know that the supposed "fascists" who sent the letter bombs were in fact Far-Lefters trying to stir it up. Second, it's highly unlikely that any group would have had time to hear about the letter bombs, get hold of the explosives, make the bomb and leave it with the delivery firm, all in the space of a few hours.'

'So?'

'So it was all pre-planned.'

'By the one group?'

'Yes. Wheatfield's friends.'

Kershaw nodded and said slowly, 'Yes, that's the way I see it too.' He picked up the communiqué again. 'What about the second "crime"? Of gross oppression against the opponents of capitalism?'

'That's what they're really about. Bringing the system down. Revenge.'

'For what?'

Nick drew a deep breath. 'There could be a link back to the Linden House Hotel affair. Through Reardon – the one charged with assault at the Russell Square demonstration. Now he did six months last year for the Linden House affair. He was probably a friend of Stephie Kitson, who's still serving time for assault and actual bodily. Now *both* of them were – *are* – friends of Wheatfield.'

Kershaw rubbed a hand over his face. 'So we're saying Wheatfield's behind all this?'

'No . . . I think there must be others who . . .' He paused, trying to clarify the suspicions in his mind. 'Who are trained, *practised*.'

'Good God!' exclaimed Kershaw, glancing at Straughan. 'Are you suggesting a red *plot*?'

Nick shook his head. 'Not exactly. Just that . . . They're so *good*, so *polished*, they must have had experience elsewhere.'

Looking unhappy, Kershaw nodded his agreement. There was a strained silence.

Eventually Straughan said, 'Have we got anything else, Ryder?' But he knew the answer even before Nick shook his head.

Kershaw said grimly, 'So, where do we go from here? The explosives report is still to come, of course. But – what we don't have is a lead on Wheatfield, and *that*'s what we want.'

Straughan looked as if he could shoot himself. It was he who had called the watch off Wheatfield.

Kershaw mused, 'We *could* issue a warrant and plaster his face all over the papers . . . But it might just send him to earth. At the moment he probably doesn't realise we're on to him. That might be the only advantage we have.'

'Give me a few days,' Nick said.

The two men looked at him with sudden interest.

'It may lead absolutely nowhere,' Nick added hastily. He didn't want false hopes raised. 'But it's just possible I might be able to find him again.'

Kershaw said immediately, 'Do it.'

'I might not be in touch for some time.'

'Agreed.'

'I might have to go right under cover.'

'Agreed.'

'It'll only work if Wheatfield has no idea we're looking for him.'

Kershaw nodded. 'Agreed. Do whatever you have to do. I don't care what it is. Just *do* it.'

Henry Northcliff had thirty seconds to get from the House of Commons to Number Ten for a meeting with the Prime Minister. It was impossible, of course, but with a bit of luck he would be no more than three minutes late.

Picking up his briefcase, he went into the outer office with the idea of rushing straight through and downstairs to his car. But his secretary had a look on her face that suggested he wasn't going to get away that easily. She said, 'Sir Henry, there's an officer from Special Branch here . . .'

The officer, who looked quite senior, stood waiting with that air of stubborn patience that all policemen seemed to possess. Henry could see there would be no escape. He said, 'Join me in the car, would you, and we'll talk there.'

Henry's car was waiting at the Members' Entrance and they got in. As the driver nosed into the traffic around Parliament Square the officer identified himself as Inspector Smith of Special Branch Protection Group. Henry knew this group: they guarded the Prime Minister.

The inspector said, 'Following the tragic bombing of the Commissioner's home today, sir, we are extending police protection to all those members of the government directly concerned with law and order.'

'Oh?' Henry had a nasty suspicion of what was coming.

'That will include yourself, of course, sir, as well as the Home Secretary and certain other Cabinet Ministers.'

Henry frowned. 'This protection – will it be full-time?'

'Most certainly, sir. Round the clock.'

Henry considered the implications. It would be comforting to have a policeman outside the house at night, he had to admit, but the thought of having someone hanging around the whole time – on Sundays and on private evenings out – was rather odious.

'It's absolutely necessary, is it?' he asked.

'We think so, sir,' said the inspector with an air of finality.

Henry thought: Well, there's no arguing with *that*.

The car completed the near-circuit of Parliament Square and turned into Whitehall. The entrance to Downing Street was just ahead.

Henry said, 'Very well, inspector. I'll try to make your men's job as easy as possible. When do they start?'

'Immediately, sir. You'll find a Constable Hunter waiting for you after your meeting. He will be with you until midnight.'

The car drew up outside Number Ten and they both got out. Henry shook hands with the inspector and went in through the famous black door. The protection would be a temporary measure, he was certain. After all, violence had never been a part of the British way of life. He couldn't see why it should suddenly become so now.

Gabriele pushed the curtain aside and looked out into the night. The mews was empty. No one. Nothing.

229

Restless, she turned away. The newspaper stared up at her from the sofa. She turned it over, so that the screeching words of the headline were hidden face down.

Stupid woman. Why had she opened the parcel? What sort of a marriage was it when the wife opened something addressed to the husband? Extraordinary.

Stupid woman. It was all her own fault.

But the bomb had worked. Very well. Gabriele permitted herself some satisfaction. It was a professional job. That was the way to think of it. Professional.

She must close her mind to negative thoughts, close her mind to thoughts of the woman. Already one part of her mind was becoming separated and frozen, the part that thought of the woman, blown to pieces. The suppression of the mind must be complete, just as her training had taught her. It was a matter of determination, that was all.

There was a sound and Gabriele stiffened. A key turned in the front door. Giorgio and Max came in at last.

She said immediately, 'Were you followed? Did you check?'

Max replied, 'There's no one. It's all right.'

'And where are you living? Is it safe?'

He nodded. 'A bedsitter in Paddington. People come and go. They don't notice me.'

They sat down. Max picked up the newspaper and stared doggedly at the front page. Gabriele could see that he was unhappy.

To pre-empt any discussion she demanded, 'Well, Max? Did you find out about Reardon?'

'He's coming up at Bow Street on Monday. For remand.'

'That's it, then. That's what we'll go for.' She turned to Giorgio. 'Where's the stuff?'

'In the van.' He indicated that it was outside in the mews.

The van mustn't stay there. She probably shouldn't have let Giorgio bring it at all. But events were moving so fast and she hadn't had time to find another service flat.

'We'll take out what we need now,' she said. 'And keep the rest in the van. Until we find another place. Then we'll empty the van and get rid of it.' She gave Giorgio a sharp look. 'And then you can finish with that girl.'

Giorgio picked at his fingers with deliberate indifference. Then he grinned, 'Maybe. But she has special friends, this girl.'

Gabriele didn't like guessing games. She said impatiently, 'Yes?'

'She is a special friend of a government minister. His name is Northcliff. He is the Attorney, the Attorney of the government.'

Gabriele frowned. 'What do you mean she's a *special* friend?'

'A family friend. She speaks to the wife on the telephone.'

Gabriele absorbed the information greedily. Northcliff. Attorney. The Attorney-General. He was on her list. He was one of the names. The one directly responsible for Stephie's prosecution. The information was bound to be useful, though she wasn't yet sure how.

She smiled at Giorgio. 'Well, aren't you a clever one?' She went across and sat beside him. She stroked his hair, aware that she felt nothing for him but a dull worn-out familiarity. 'That's different, then, isn't it? You must stay with the girl.'

Giorgio sighed. 'It's hard. She is boring. And not pretty.'

Gabriele thought: But I bet that didn't stop you. She prompted, 'But you can keep her interested.'

He shrugged.

'You must. Just for a while longer. Just for a while.'

He looked doubtful, but she knew he would do it, because she had asked him to and because he knew it was important.

She stood up. 'I have some more money for you.' She picked up two piles of notes off a side table and handed the men one each.

'But there're some new notes here,' Max said.

'This time, yes.'

'I won't use them—'

'It'll be perfectly safe as long as you use them in different places, where nobody knows you.'

He stared at the money for a while then, shaking his head, repeated, 'I won't use them.'

Gabriele suppressed the urge to argue with him and said calmly, 'Okay. But hang on to it, just in case.'

He nodded and, separating the money, slipped the old notes into his wallet and the new ones into an inner pocket.

They went to the van and, prising up the floor with a crowbar, removed a number of containers and took them into the house. Then Gabriele settled down to make the device. It took an hour. She used an acid delay fuse. The timing was not as accurate as a clock and battery, but it was simpler. Sulphuric acid was placed in a small serum bottle and a contraceptive stretched over its neck. When the bottle was upturned the acid burnt through the rubber on to a mixture of sugar and potassium permanganate, which exploded with a sheet of hot flame. The hot flame then ignited the detonator and thence the main explosive.

The nice thing about using an acid fuse was that there was less chance of it going off accidentally. Even if you were stupid enough to upturn the bottle of acid at the wrong moment there was plenty of time to reverse it. To keep the finished bomb inactive you merely kept it the right way up and upturned it once you arrived at the target, knowing you had plenty of time to get away – roughly forty minutes per contraceptive.

When she was finished, she put the bomb in a holdall, packed plenty of newspaper round it, then gave it to Max to take back to his room in Paddington.

'Now, there's one last thing,' Gabriele said. 'We need a car. In time for Sunday night.'

'We could hire one,' said Max.

Gabriele shook her head. 'Too much trouble. And too risky. No – there's a much better way. And it won't involve any risk at all.'

Eighteen

Nick woke early, cold and stiff. He tried to stretch his legs, but his feet came up against a chair arm. Then he remembered where he was: on a lumpy sofa at the house in Tulip Street. He listened hard, but the house was silent. Nobody was up yet. But then it was a Saturday morning and people would sleep in.

He had arrived at eight the previous night. Bet had been out, but another girl living at the house had let him in. He'd gone to the Castle in the Portobello Road and waited until ten-thirty, but Wheatfield hadn't been there. He wasn't entirely surprised: it would have been too much to hope for.

At eleven he'd returned to the house and waited for the others to drift in. He'd chatted to those in the mood to talk – only two – then he'd gone to bed. If Bet had returned he hadn't heard her.

Now he got up and, pulling on a sweater, padded through into the kitchen and made himself a cup of coffee. There was still no sound from upstairs. Time for a quick look round. He started in the hall where various coats and bags were slung over an old table, and went swiftly through them. Nothing. The living-room was full of books, magazines and piles of papers and looked more promising, but after half an hour it too had yielded nothing apart from a few copies of *Time Out* and *Black Dwarf*, a library of political writings, and some Ban the Bomb literature.

Later, if he had the chance, he might try some of the bedrooms. But it would be more out of habit than expectation. The lead to Wheatfield would not come from the house itself but from Bet or one of her friends. And that lead was flimsy enough, God only knew. It could be a complete dead end – he might hang around this place for weeks without hearing a whisper of Wheatfield. The thought was exceedingly depressing.

In the meantime he could search. He'd scooped up a few of the more fashionable New Left books from his flat the previous evening. Now he picked one up and, lying on the sofa, began to read. What was he looking for? He wasn't sure. But a clue, anyway, something to do with crystal perhaps. It was all very tenuous. But it was *something* at least.

Half an hour later he heard a door opening upstairs, then another. One by one the occupants of the house began to clatter downstairs. Nick strolled into the kitchen and chatted with them over coffee. Two hours later he had drunk a lot of coffee and discovered that Bet was at her boyfriend's and wouldn't be back until Sunday. At one point he mentioned that he was looking for Max Wheatfield. One of the girls knew him all right, but hadn't a clue where he was living. Nick didn't dare force it, and the conversation moved on. Gradually the occupants drifted off on various errands until he was alone in the house.

Keeping an ear open for the front door, he went quickly through the bedrooms. The search revealed nothing.

At midday he went off to visit a few pubs in the area. He returned at two-thirty to find the house empty. He thought: This is a complete waste of time.

He had two options: to wait and hope something would turn up, or to make the rounds of his contacts. But would people like Nugent know anything? He doubted it, or they'd have told him before now. No: this place was still his best bet.

Depressed, he settled down to read some Vaneigem. But he couldn't concentrate on the obtuse and convoluted thinking, and found he had read the same page three times without understanding it. He put the book down. Was there a better way than ploughing through books? Who might be able to throw light on the crystal connection? Conway was already trying a tame professor at the LSE, and inquiries were being made abroad through the intelligence services.

Part of the conversation floated into his mind. He tried to remember the circumstances.

Of course.

Gabriella. Yes. He should have thought of her before. She certainly knew her theory. It would definitely be worth a try. But *when*, that was the question. He couldn't spend a whole evening, let alone a night, away from Tulip Street. Perhaps he could meet her for a drink. Yes: he would phone her a little later and suggest it.

The afternoon dragged on. At five Nick was so restless that he went for a short walk. He made a plan for the evening. If Bet's friends couldn't suggest where he might find Wheatfield, then he would make one more round of the pubs which Wheatfield was known to visit. At some point he would meet Gabriella if she was free.

At five-thirty he let himself back into the house. He called out, 'Hi!' in case anyone had returned.

There was silence.

He went into the kitchen and put on a kettle. Taking a spoon out of a drawer, he scooped some coffee into a mug. There was a battered transistor radio standing on the side and he turned it on. It was dead. He picked it up and fiddled with the knobs.

Suddenly a floorboard creaked.

There was someone else in the room.

Surprised, he turned, ready to say a casual hello.

He stared, unbelieving.

Wheatfield.

Nick recovered as best he could, keeping his face in a mask of indifference. 'Well, hi. How goes it?'

Wheatfield's expression was unreadable under the still-bruised face. He advanced into the room and leaned against a cupboard.

With an effort, Nick turned back to the boiling kettle and poured his coffee. He asked, 'Want one?'

Wheatfield gave the briefest of nods.

'Well, how's the face?' Nick continued, pouring another cup.

'Okay.' He shrugged as if it were totally unimportant.

Nick handed him the coffee. 'My head's mended,' he said

conversationally. 'At least it doesn't ache any more.'

Wheatfield grunted a response. Nick thought rapidly. Wheatfield wasn't exactly the warm outgoing type, yet Nick had to establish some sort of friendship with him. But *how*?

He sat on a chair and said, 'You're–er–not being hassled by the cops any more?'

Wheatfield shot him a sharp glance and for a moment Nick thought: That was a mistake.

Then Wheatfield relaxed. 'No. After those pictures in all the papers, they wouldn't dare.'

'That girl photographer certainly did you a favour.'

'Ya, lucky she was there.'

There was a silence. Wheatfield was certainly heavy going. Nick racked his brains for something to say.

'A pity she didn't get a shot of *me* being bashed. Still . . .'

He was aware of Wheatfield watching him critically, and thought: He suspects something. But then Wheatfield was pulling out a chair and sitting down at the table beside him and saying, 'Look, I was wondering if you could do me a favour . . .'

Nick gave it a second. He mustn't seem too keen. 'Ya?'

'I need a car – er – borrowed.'

'Mmm.' He looked a little doubtful.

Wheatfield responded, 'For Sunday night. Something ordinary, a Ford or Vauxhall or something.'

Nick pretended to consider the idea. 'What's it for?'

'A demonstration. A big one. Against the fascists.'

'Ah. So a good cause?

'Absolutely.'

As if making up his mind, Nick nodded. 'Sure. Be glad to do it.'

'It'll be easy, will it? I mean, there won't be a problem?'

Nick remembered what he'd told Wheatfield in the hospital, about having got into trouble for pinching cars. He said quickly, 'No, no. It only takes a minute. I've done it many times before. There's never a problem.'

Wheatfield was getting up to go.

'You off?' Nick asked in surprise. 'What about a drink?'

'No. Gotta go.'

Nick followed him towards the door. 'Tomorrow then? I was going to go to the Castle at one.'

'No.'

Nick gave up. He'd already pushed as hard as he dared.

235

'What about the car? When d'you want it?'

'Tomorrow night. By ten.'

'Where shall I take it?'

'Here. I'll meet you here.'

Wheatfield opened the front door and, with a brief wave, was gone. Nick went to the kitchen window and watched him stride up the street. His instinct was to follow, but it would be too risky. Wheatfield would see him and realise immediately, and then there'd be no hope of finding his friends.

Nick watched Wheatfield disappear round the corner and hoped he wasn't making a terrible mistake.

After ten minutes he left the house and went to the nearest phone box. He called Kershaw and spoke to him personally. They arranged to meet half an hour later in Notting Hill.

Nick left the booth and paused. Gabriella. Was it worth calling her now? The crystal information could surely wait.

But no, it was best to leave no stone unturned. He went back into the booth and dialled her number. She answered straight away. He suggested meeting for a drink at ten that night.

There was a pause. She said, 'Can't you make it earlier, for dinner?' There was a hint of resentment in her voice.

'I'm tied up at the moment.'

'Tied up?'

'Trying to fix up a new place to stay,' he lied.

'All right then,' she conceded. 'But come over here, will you? We'll have a late dinner. I don't want to go out.'

He thought: Damn it, she's trapping me. He said evenly, 'I don't know if I'll have time for more than a drink . . .'

There was a deathly pause. 'I see.' Her voice was like ice.

He suddenly gave in. She had outmanoeuvred him. 'Okay, we'll have dinner. I'll try to make it before ten. But I could be late.'

He put down the phone, angry with himself. Damn. He should never have phoned. She was bound to expect him to stay the night.

The door closed behind Giorgio, and Victoria burst into tears. He was gone again, and as usual she had no idea when he'd be back. She could take almost everything else – the sudden changes of mood, the caustic remarks – but not this terrible uncertainty. She never knew where she was with him, and it was eating away at her.

And she'd been so good until now. When he'd disappeared on Thursday she'd put a brave face on it. When he'd come back again yesterday to collect the van, she'd been calm and smiling. But when he'd returned this morning and settled down to a meal and read the papers and treated the place like his own, she'd been silly enough to let her hopes rise. That had been her mistake. To think he'd stay. What a *fool*.

And now he was gone and she felt very empty and it was Saturday night and she was on her own.

She dried her tears. She must look on the bright side. He hadn't actually *said* he wouldn't be coming back. And then there was the van – he needed it some time in the week, so he'd said.

The van.

She went to the window and peered down into the dark street. It was there; he hadn't taken it. But it was parked very untidily on a corner with two wheels on the pavement. Typical. She found the spare keys and, putting on a coat, went down the two flights of stairs to the street.

As she approached the van she saw that a number of parking tickets were tucked under the windscreen wipers. She removed them and got into the van to repark it. She drove round the block and finally found a space.

She looked into the back. It was a bit of a mess. Putting on the interior light, she climbed over the driving seat and half-heartedly began to pick up bits of paper and cellophane off the ancient carpeting. As she walked over the floor, she noticed it was uneven, as if there was something between the metal floor and the carpet. She stooped down and, lifting a corner of the carpeting, examined the metal floor.

Of course. It was the lid of the spare wheel compartment; it wasn't quite closed.

She got out of the van by the front door and, going round to the back, opened the rear doors. She tried to force the lid of the wheel compartment down, but it wouldn't close. She rolled the carpet back and pushed up the hinged lid.

She saw immediately why it wouldn't close. Arranged around and inside the spare tyre were six or seven bundles wrapped in heavy cloth.

She hesitated for a moment then slowly picked up one of the bundles and unwrapped it. Inside the cloth were six tubes about ten inches long and an inch or so across, covered in a heavy oiled paper. Each tube had a printed label on it. She squinted at one of them. It read: Nitramite 19C, *Explosif Rocher, Société Française des*

Explosifs, Usine de Cugny. Underneath was a date: 20th March 1968.

She stared at the tubes for some time, thoughts chasing through her mind, clashing, failing to connect.

Then the realisation of what she was holding hit her like a punch in the stomach.

A moment later came the related thoughts, equally terrible; how had they *got* here? How *long* had they been here?

Slowly a dreadful scenario came into her mind: that she herself had brought this terrible load from France, brought it through Customs, that Giorgio had lied to her, that the leaflets had never existed.

Feeling sick, she replaced the tube in the bundle, wrapped the cloth round it, and put it inside the wheel. She rearranged the bundles so that the lid would close properly and unrolled the carpet over the top. She closed and locked the doors.

She went up to the flat and let herself in. She went into the living-room and sat in the darkness, trying to make sense of the thoughts ricocheting around her brain.

Whichever way she looked at it, the conclusions she reached were appalling. It was impossible to find a reasonable explanation. And yet – it was just possible there *might* be.

She must give Giorgio the chance to explain.

Just one chance.

Drawing her legs under her, she curled up in the chair and, sick at heart, settled down to wait.

Nick lay in the bed and thought: I should never have stayed.

He'd hardly slept at all. Neither had Gabriella – she'd tossed and turned all night. And the evening had not been a success. During the meal Gabriella had been brittle and tense. He'd tried to bring the conversation around to extremist groups, but she'd wanted to talk about other things. Then, when he'd got up to go, she'd snapped out of her mood and turned on that animal sexuality of hers. He had weakened. But for all her passion there had been something mechanical and heartless about their love-making. There was no sign of the warmth and vulnerability she'd shown a few days earlier. She was like two different people – and he didn't like this one at all. He'd been left feeling empty and cold.

The trouble was, he didn't really *know* her. He thought: I should never have stayed.

He heard Gabriella moving around downstairs and, getting up, went into the bathroom. He noticed that the male toiletries had gone. Perhaps she'd chucked the lover out. It might explain her mood.

He dressed and went down to find Gabriella sitting on the sofa reading the Sunday papers, a frown of concentration on her face.

Nick glanced at the headlines. Not surprisingly they were all about the bombing of the Commissioner's house and the death of Helen McCabe. He made himself a coffee and, sitting down beside Gabriella, said, 'Who d'you think did it?'

Without looking up, she said, 'Could be anyone, couldn't it?'

'Why d'you say that?'

'Well, there are so many people who've had a raw deal at the hands of the filth, aren't there?'

'But not many who can hit them with explosives.'

She shrugged. 'Explosives are easy enough to get.'

'But what political group is it? I mean, if it *is* political.'

She turned to him. 'Oh, of course it's political!' she exclaimed. 'This is a statement. A warning.'

'But who by? I mean, Trotskyists or what?'

'No, *no*,' she said impatiently. 'These people are way beyond that.'

He tried not to let his interest show.

'What philosophy do they follow then? Situationism?'

'Possibly.' She paused. 'But that's a bit general. Things have moved on since Paris, you know. These people will be way ahead, past Vaneigem and Debord and old stuff like that. They're probably into Petrini.'

He tried to remember. Petrini. Italian. Philosopher.

'Tell me, what's different about Petrini then?'

'Ah.' She began to talk with the fervour of a teacher lecturing a new pupil. 'He believes in the necessity of *action* to accentuate and polarise the divisions in society so that people *see* and *understand* the exploitation that's happening right in front of them. He says it's necessary to clarify things on their behalf; to crystallise their thinking.'

Crystallise.

She talked on but Nick was hardly listening. *Crystallise.* There it was! Good God, why hadn't he got on to this Petrini before? Why hadn't he realised that this new philosophy had been taken up by the young activists? *She* knew all about it. He'd obviously slipped up somewhere in his research. He could have kicked himself.

He asked, 'Are they a big group, these – what do you call them?'

She shrugged and said very carefully, 'They have no name, as far as I know. But they won't be a large group. The whole idea is to work in small cells, in isolation.'

'I see.' He did, only too clearly. He saw that the answer had been there all the time and he'd missed it. Thank God for Gabriella. He forgot his coldness towards her and smiled encouragingly.

She continued, her eyes gleaming. 'They're the beginning of a big movement, though. They'll succeed where all the others will fail. In a few years the movement will have spread all over Europe.'

He stared at her. 'How do you *know* about this?'

'I just know. I keep my ear to the ground.'

'Do you . . .' He hesitated. It was a difficult question. 'Do you have any idea of who these people are? Where they might come from?'

Immediately her face became a mask, and she said deliberately, 'No. Why do you ask?'

He shrugged. 'I just wondered, that was all. What sort of people they were.'

'You're interested? In their ideas?'

He must step carefully here. She was probing. 'Yes,' he said vaguely. 'It seems a good way to get things done.'

She said, 'Perhaps the *only* way.'

There was an awkward pause. The baldness of the statement had taken him by surprise. He said, 'If you believe in the Petrini philosophy that strongly, yes, I suppose it *is*.' He thought: She's no better than the rest. An intellectual revolutionary without the courage of her convictions. Spouting precious theory without the nasty consequences. All talk and dangerous hot air – from a safe distance.

'So what do you think of direct action?' she asked.

He had a good mind to tell her what he really thought of her half-baked ideas, but he didn't want to alienate her. The information had been pure gold, and there might be a lot more to come.

She was waiting for his reply; he sensed his answer was going to be important. 'I certainly believe strongly in changing the system,' he began. 'And I suppose I'd do almost anything that was necessary . . .'

She looked pleased. 'Of course you would.'

He stood up. 'Well, I've got to go now.'

To his surprise she didn't argue. It was almost as if she was expecting it.

'Will you come back later?' she asked.

'No. I've got a favour to do for a friend and I won't be finished till late.'

She nodded and led the way to the door. She turned abruptly and, putting her arms round his neck, kissed him for a long time. 'I'll miss you.'

Now she was all warmth and softness. A very confusing lady. He said, 'I'll see you again very soon.'

'Can I contact you? At your new place?'

'What?'

'You said you were moving.'

'Oh yes, but I don't know where to yet.'

'It was just that – there were some people I thought you might like to meet. People you'd find very – *useful.*'

What *did* she mean? Whatever, the opportunity was too good to miss. Without a word he wrote his Lambeth number on a piece of paper.

'Give me the address too, in case I'm passing.'

He hesitated. Normally he liked to keep a distance from informants. But this was different. He added his address. 'It's the flat of a friend,' he explained. 'He's letting me borrow it while he's away.'

Gabriele closed the door behind him and thought: He's going to be all right. At one point she'd had her doubts. But then he'd said he would do almost anything that was necessary. And that was just after they'd been talking about the bombing. Yes: he was going to be all right.

Stealing the car would be a start. If he made a good job of that then she would give him another more demanding task – driving on a robbery perhaps. Finally, when she was sure she could trust him she would bring him right into the group.

There would be problems, of course. With Giorgio. She hadn't worked out what she was going to do about that. She only knew that her relationship with Giorgio was going to have to change. He would have to find someone else.

She wanted Nick. The truth was, he had got under her skin. She shouldn't have let it happen, of course. Even more important, she shouldn't have let it show. She shuddered to remember how she had clung to him that first night . . .

It was a weakness, to show feelings like that, and he would only despise her for it. But it had been all right last night – she'd got herself under control. She would never let her feelings show again.

Everything was going to work out very well. Nick would come and live with her here and be a member of the cell. He was clever and cool and decisive; he would be a great help with the planning. Someone to share the load. She needed that. It was hard taking decisions on her own.

It was lonely at night too. She had nightmares all the time. They were often the same. A group of people sat in a circle and talked about her as if she wasn't there. 'She's *always* been difficult . . . Ungrateful and inconsiderate . . . We've done all we can . . . A strong will, of course. Uncontrollable.' Then someone took the decision to punish her, and she was locked up in her bedroom without books. The time crept by so slowly that she could have screamed. She felt her life slipping away, unfulfilled and hollow.

Then, instead of her bedroom, she was in a prison cell. She looked for Stephie, but there was no one else there, and she realised that she was on her own. And always would be.

Last night it had been worse. She had been making a bomb. Everything had gone fine until she connected the timing device. It started ticking and wouldn't stop. She tried to get out of the room, but the door was locked. She tore at the parcel, but she'd wrapped it too well and couldn't find the wires. In horror she'd watched the contacts closing on each other.

Then she'd woken, gasping for breath.

With a vast relief she'd realised that Nick was there beside her, breathing quietly. Gratefully, she'd moved over until her body lay close to his, and she was at peace.

The car was a two-year-old Ford Capri with thirty thousand miles on the clock. It was pale blue with wire wheels and a slight dent on the rear near-side wing. It was perfectly unremarkable.

'It was used in a robbery in March,' explained Kershaw. 'Mechanically sound. Oh, and we've put on some new plates, just in case someone somewhere thinks of checking against the stolen list.'

Nick went round the car and peered inside the wheel arches. Opening a door, he leant in and checked the interior.

'You won't find anything,' said Kershaw. 'It's all too well hidden.'

Nick nodded. Wherever they were, the listening devices and radio bleepers had been properly concealed.

'I might as well go then.'

He got in and Kershaw slammed the door.

Kershaw said through the open window, 'Well, we've done all we can.'

'Let's just hope he shows.'

Kershaw said a heartfelt, 'Yes.'

Nick could imagine the pressure Kershaw was under. The man must have everyone from his immediate boss to the Assistant Commissioner breathing down his neck.

The first car picked him up the moment he left the garage. It was a green Vauxhall Victor. As he came to Hyde Park Corner it peeled off and a white Morris took up station behind. A third car took over north of the park. They were using this trip to test the radio tracking device.

As he made the final turn into Tulip Street the last car, a dark blue Mini, left him and sped straight on. He parked immediately outside the house. The street was very quiet. One resident had the bonnet of his car open and was tinkering with the engine. Another was up a ladder repairing a window. It was a typical Sunday afternoon.

As Nick got out of the car he glanced up and down the street. Wherever the watchers were, he couldn't see them. Unless the man under the bonnet was part of the team. Or the one on the ladder.

Nick let himself into the house. Bet and a group of her friends were in the smoke-filled living-room, stuck into some red wine. He gave Bet ten pounds for rent and use of hot water and explained that he'd be moving out, probably that night. She said he was welcome any time.

The party went on into the evening. Nick managed to nurse a single glass of the rough red wine for two hours, then took it into the kitchen and poured it down the sink. Whatever happened he must keep a clear head. He remembered that he hadn't eaten since morning and, finding some cheese and bread, ate it hungrily.

At ten he listened for the front door and tried to suppress the awful suspicion that Wheatfield wasn't going to turn up.

At ten-thirty the party broke up and one by one the guests left the house. At eleven Bet and the other residents drifted upstairs to bed.

Nick sat on his own, feeling sick at heart. Wheatfield wasn't going to come. *Oh God.*

He tried to read but the words skipped in front of his eyes. Finally he lay on the sofa, staring at the ceiling, thinking of what other leads he had if this one failed. Gabriella, that was all. Gabriella and her friends, whoever they might be. It wasn't much. It was *damn all*.

Twenty to twelve.

Damn all.

A key sounded in a lock. Nick lay motionless.

A door was opening. The front door.

A floorboard creaked in the hall. A movement from the doorway. Someone was coming into the room.

Nick put his head up over the sofa. 'Hi,' he said casually.

It was Wheatfield. He could have shouted with relief.

Wheatfield came round the sofa and stared down at him.

'I got it,' Nick said calmly. 'It's just outside. A Ford Capri.'

'Okay.' Wheatfield looked relaxed, unworried. He obviously had no suspicions. 'It works all right, does it?'

'Should do. It's not very old.' Nick swung his feet to the floor and stood up. 'I'll show you how to start it.'

Wheatfield followed him out. Nick showed him how to start the car without an ignition key. Wheatfield practised connecting and disconnecting the necessary wires, which Nick had extended and led through from the bonnet to the interior.

Wheatfield was ready to go. 'Thanks. It's appreciated.'

'No problem. Can I ask what it's for? I mean, I wouldn't mind being in on the fun. You know.'

Wheatfield paused and looked at him thoughtfully. 'Perhaps next time. It's a bit late now, for this time . . . But you'll hear about what we're doing okay.'

'Great. Soon?'

'Yeah. Tomorrow.'

Wheatfield slammed the door shut. The engine fired. He fumbled with the switches on the dashboard and found the lights. The car moved forward and out into the street. Wheatfield did not look back.

Nick gave it a few seconds then, going into the house for his bag, let himself out again and ran to the corner of the street where Conway was waiting with the engine running.

Nineteen

The traffic was unexpectedly light for a Monday morning and Gabriele found herself driving north up Bow Street earlier than she'd intended, at a quarter to ten. On the left was the tall neo-classical façade of the Royal Opera House, incongruously grand for such a minor street. Opposite was Bow Street police station and just beyond it, the magistrates' court.

She took a careful look at the entrance to the court. There were no police in sight and no cars parked outside.

She drove on across Long Acre into Endell Street. She parked a few yards up, on the left-hand side, so that the Fiat was pointing north towards New Oxford Street.

She waited impatiently, her eye on the rear-view mirror. At five to ten a delivery van came bumping up the street and parked immediately behind her, blocking her view. She cursed and, looking at her watch, tried to work out if she had enough time to do a circuit and find a better parking place. The decision was made for her by the sight of an approaching traffic warden. She started the car and, turning right, drove round the block into Drury Lane and Long Acre. Coming to the junction with Bow Street she glanced sideways and gripped the wheel more tightly.

There he was.

A car was parked in front of the court. A Ford Capri. The unmistakable figure of Max was just getting out.

Right on time. Good dependable Max.

In a few minutes he would come looking for her.

To the right the delivery van was still parked at the beginning of Endell Street. It would be too awkward to stop behind it; she didn't like the idea of being boxed in. She continued down Long Acre for a few yards and stopped behind a row of cars parked on meters. The position was good. When Max came round the corner he would only have to look up the street to spot the Fiat.

She waited, keeping a careful watch in both directions.

She imagined Max putting the note on the windscreen – saying the car was broken down – opening the boot, turning the parcel upside down, walking away.

A horn sounded. A lorry was blocking the road near the junction with Bow Street. The traffic was slowing down to a crawl. She glanced at the cars slowly approaching from the opposite direction. One was indicating a left turn into Endell Street.

She stared.

No, it wasn't possible.

For one amazing moment—

She shook her head. She obviously had him on her mind. She was imagining things.

But for that one instant the front-seat passenger *had* looked amazingly like Nick. Ridiculous. The man, whoever he was, was in shadow now, bending his head down, holding something to his mouth. He looked as if he were eating.

Ridiculous, she repeated. She just had him on her mind.

She took a quick look in the mirror. No Max.

Then she glanced back at the traffic.

The car was almost opposite her now, moving very slowly. The passenger looked up and the light fell full on his face.

His face.

Gabriele gaped. The car passed by.

She twisted violently round in her seat. The car drew up beyond Endell Street and reversed back round the corner out of sight.

Nick. *What the hell?*

Nick. What was he *doing?*

She gaped.

Whatever was happening, something was wrong, appallingly wrong.

An idea shot into her mind and she grabbed at it. The pigs. It was the pigs. They'd got him! They'd forced him to tell. She said out loud, '*Oh Christ!*'

But then in her mind's eye she saw his face again, sitting in the passenger seat, looking composed, the hand held to his mouth, holding something.

Something with a wire hanging from it.

Then she knew.

The shock hit her like a punch in the stomach.

For a split second her mind was frozen. Then she looked in the mirror. Max. He had just appeared round the corner. Max, whose every move was being watched. Max, who had spotted her in the Fiat and was even now quickening his pace.

With a shaking hand she turned on the ignition. She slipped the car into gear and, using her indicator, pulled firmly out into the road. A car braked suddenly to avoid her, but luckily did not sound its horn. She accelerated rapidly down Long Acre.

No car pulled out behind. No one followed.

Nothing.

Only Max standing stock still on the pavement, staring at her.

Nick said, 'Something's up.'

Wheatfield had paused, like an animal scenting the wind. Nick couldn't work it out. What had changed? One minute Wheatfield had been quite happy, now he obviously had the wind up. For an awful moment he thought Wheatfield might have spotted him, but he'd been very careful to keep his distance and Wheatfield had never once looked this way.

'I think he's going to bolt for it.'

Conway whispered, 'Yeah.'

Wheatfield was looking wildly about him. He was badly frightened. Suddenly he began to move. Fast.

Nick spoke into the mike and told Kershaw, 'He's off. West down Long Acre.'

The acknowledgement came back. Nick watched two of Kershaw's men fall in a safe distance behind Wheatfield; then, a few seconds later, Kershaw's car went by.

Simultaneously Kershaw's voice came over the radio. 'He's obviously abandoned the Capri. There could be a bomb in it. Proceed with bomb clearance procedure *now*. Get everyone away from that damned car!'

Nick nudged Conway. 'Come on, let's go.' Conway fired the engine and they shot forward into Long Acre. As they turned west to follow Kershaw, Nick saw the beginnings of all hell breaking loose in Bow Street as they cleared the area around the Capri.

Ahead, Kershaw's car had slowed right down so as not to overtake the men on foot. Nick could see Wheatfield in the distance. He was half walking, half running, and looking frequently over his shoulder.

Nick sighed heavily. He couldn't think what the hell had gone wrong.

Wheatfield reached the junction with St Martin's Lane and stopped, waiting for a break in the traffic. He turned and took a long look behind him. The two followers did their best to look inconspicuous as they closed on him.

Suddenly Wheatfield seemed to panic. One moment he was poised in a loose crouch, the next he was off, sprinting across the street, his long hair flying behind him. Nick gripped the seat. There was a loud hooting and a car braked as Wheatfield shot in front of it and ran for his life towards Leicester Square.

Nick said, 'Oh shit!' He could have wept. All that planning for nothing.

Kershaw's voice came over the air. 'Take him!'

With a screech of tyres Kershaw's car accelerated across the junction. Conway stepped on it and, hand on horn, jumped the lights. Ahead, Kershaw's car swerved on to the pavement beside two other squad cars. Men were already pouring down into the Underground.

Conway pulled in behind Kershaw's car and turned off the ignition.

There was a heavy silence, then Nick said wearily, 'What happened, Conway? What the hell went wrong?'

Conway shook his head. 'He just sussed us, that's all.'

'Balls. There was a bloody *reason*, I *know* there was. Something *happened*—'

'Or maybe didn't happen!' ventured Conway.

Nick looked at him and blinked. 'Yes. Maybe that was it.'

They brought Wheatfield out of the station ten minutes later, his face bloody, his arm twisted half-way up his back. Nick watched with mixed feelings. They may have caught themselves an Indian, but they'd probably lost all hope of finding the chiefs.

Victoria hoisted the shopping on to her left arm and pushed the key into the lock. As she opened the door she heard a sound from inside the flat. Giorgio was back.

Whatever happened she must stay calm. She went straight to the kitchen and, sorting through the shopping, put the milk and yogurt in the fridge. He came in as she was emptying the fruit into a bowl.

'Where were you?' she asked.

'I had to see a friend. It was easier to stay the night.'

She examined his face. He'd been drinking, she could tell; his eyes were red and his skin was pale and slightly mottled around the cheeks. He looked defenceless and lost, like a child who'd been sick from eating too many sweets. She suppressed the old urge to protect him, to make everything better for him.

'I was not clever,' he said. 'I drank too much and . . .' He looked at her ruefully and touched her arm. 'I would have been clever to come home. Yes?'

Her heart went out to him. When he was like this she could forgive him anything. *Almost*.

She pulled herself together. 'I have to talk to you.'

He dropped his eyes. 'Yes?'

'I went down to park the van last night and – I tidied it up.'

His eyes met hers, bright and wary.

'I found some – *things* – in the spare wheel.'

A flash of what could have been fear leapt across his face. There was a long pause. Then he nodded slowly. 'Ah. Yes, we must talk. Come . . .'

She followed him into the living-room and they sat down on the sofa. He took her hand and stroked it gently. 'You must believe me when I say I did not know these things were there – *before*.'

'Before?'

'When we were in France. The leaflets I put in the van myself. But that stuff – someone *else* put it in. I did not know. Not until yesterday. Believe me, Vittoria, it was terrible, *terrible*, to discover these things. Who could have *done* this to me? I am so upset. That is why I am out late last night. To try to discover who has done this terrible thing to me. Also, I must decide what to do.'

'What to do?'

'How to get *rid* of these things. Where to *leave* them. It is not easy.'

Victoria rubbed her forehead. It was so hard to make sense of it. She exclaimed, 'But Giorgio, those sticks are explosives. Whoever put them there must have – had a very good *reason*. They—'

'Yes. They were *using* us, Vittoria. They used us to carry this terrible stuff.'

'But who's *they*?'

'Extremists, Vittoria.' There was a pained expression on his face. 'We are both innocent *vittime*. You understand – victims. I have been used. You too. But I must tell you that they will try to collect the stuff, and this we must not let them do. We must stay hidden. They do not know you. They do not know where you live. As long as we stay here together, they will not find us.'

'But we must hand the stuff to the authorities. It's *far* too dangerous to have around.'

'Vittoria' – he gripped her hand – 'they will arrest us. They will never believe we did not *know* about it. They will think that *we* are terrorists. You understand?'

'Can't we just leave it somewhere? At a police station or something.'

'It's too dangerous,' he said quickly.

'Then what are we going to do with it?'

He made a wide gesture of despair. 'I am not sure. I am thinking all the time. Perhaps we take it somewhere and bury it. But we must be careful. We must think *very* hard before we do anything.' He looked at her fondly and took her face in his hands. 'I must tell you, I am glad that you know. It makes me feel better to share this knowledge. You make me feel strong. You make me feel we can escape from this thing. Will you be strong? For *me*?'

Her stomach twisted with pleasure. She thought: How I misjudged him. No wonder he'd been tense and difficult. No *wonder* he'd looked so worried. She breathed a long thankful sigh of relief. 'Oh, my love,' she whispered. 'You poor thing. Don't worry. Of course I'll help. We'll work it out together.'

She hugged him, and felt his arms close around her, warm and strong. And she was glad that this dreadful thing had happened, because it had brought them together. From now on she would be able to share in the other, secret, part of his life, and everything would be all right.

The phone rang. For a second Victoria ignored it. Then, kissing Giorgio hard on the lips, she got up to answer it.

A woman's voice said, 'I want to speak to Giorgio.'

Victoria felt a moment's surprise then without a word she handed Giorgio the receiver. She stayed to listen. Somehow she felt she had the right.

Giorgio grunted 'Yes' several times. Then his expression suddenly hardened. He closed his eyes and clenched his jaw, as if containing some deep fury. Victoria held her breath. It was obviously very bad news. Finally he said, 'I come . . . Yes. Right now.' And rang off.

For a moment he stared at the phone, deep in thought. Then he came and took her by the shoulders. She had never seen him look so grim.

He said, 'A friend, she' – he paused as if searching for the right words – 'she needs help. The extremists are coming for her. They have a crazy idea that *she* knows where to find the explosives. It is terrible. She must leave her house—'

'Who is this person?'

'Someone who is innocent, like us,' he said smoothly. 'I must help her. You understand?'

'I'll come too.'

'No! You stay here. It is better. We will talk later. About what we must do.'

Doubts fluttered about in Victoria's mind, doubts she couldn't put her finger on. All she knew was that she hated the thought of him going without her. But then she looked up into his eyes, and saw tenderness and concern. And she realised that he must have more than a little kindness to help his friends in this way.

It was some time after he'd gone that she began to wonder about the woman on the phone, and how she'd known where Giorgio would be.

Kershaw came out of the interview room at Cannon Row Police Station, looking grim. 'His mouth's shut tighter than a clam.'

Nick wasn't in the least surprised. Wheatfield was never going to be a great talker.

Kershaw said heavily, 'The only time he showed any interest was when I told him we'd defused the bomb. Then he raised his eyebrows.'

'If he'd spoken he'd only have said he was disappointed.'

'Quite.' Kershaw started off along the corridor. 'I'm just going to have another look at his belongings.'

Nick followed to the charge room. Spread out on the table were some keys, a battered old wallet, a ragged student union card, various scraps of paper, a wad of money and some coins. The scraps of paper looked interesting, but proved on closer examination to be nothing but bus tickets, receipts and other printed matter. There was only one piece of handwriting: an address in North London.

'We've checked that,' said Kershaw. 'It's Reardon's place. We went over it a week ago. We're taking it apart again now. Also the place in St Mark's Villas.'

Nick picked up the wad of notes and flicked through it. There was over three hundred pounds. 'A lot of money for a poor student.'

'And some of it brand new,' Kershaw pointed out. 'Just drawn. We're checking the banks and building societies to see if he had an account.'

'I doubt it. Wheatfield's not the sort. Banks are capitalist institutions.'

Kershaw rubbed his chin. 'Where did he get it from then?'

'It was given to him, I would think.'

'By the others in the group.'

'I would imagine so.'

'Then *they* must get their money fresh from the bank.'

Both men thought for a moment, then Kershaw said, 'We might

be able to trace the bank, but never the account against which the money was issued.' He sighed and shot Nick a glance. 'Any ideas, Ryder?'

'Only that this proves what we'd thought – that there's a high degree of organisation. That the Crystal Faction has backing.'

Kershaw said sharply, 'Yes. But where does that actually *get* us?'

It was a good question. Nick made a face to show he didn't have an answer. 'I'll see what I can dig up.'

He accepted a lift in Kershaw's car and the two men returned to the Yard in silence. Avoiding the incident room Nick went straight up to his office. He needed time to think. Kershaw's team would follow up the direct leads. What Nick must do was find the link between the crystal philosophy and Wheatfield. Somewhere in the middle might be a clue to the identity of Wheatfield's friends.

Conway was on the phone. He beckoned Nick over and, covering the mouthpiece, said, 'I've got the info on Petrini.'

Nick picked up Conway's notes and read: Antonio Petrini. Born 5th Aug 1929, Milan. Wealthy landowning family. Private schools, Milan and Switzerland. Graduated Rome University, philosophy 1952. Post-grad course Milan. Lecturer in philosophy and politics, Turin 1956–63. Publications inc. *The Revolutionary Society*, 1963; *The Tyranny of Modern Capitalism*, 1966; both pub. Gritti. Joined Italian Communist Party, 1956. Resigned 1963. Close links Far Left. Known associate of extremists.

Beneath, Conway had scribbled various notes about the Red Brigades, the Italian Communist Party, as well as some dates and places. At the bottom in a corner were the words: Gritti – *La Bandiera Rossa, La Posta*.

Nick stared. *La Posta*.

Gabriella's magazine.

Conway had rung off. Nick asked, 'What's this? The Gritti bit here?'

Conway peered at his notes. 'Ah, he's Petrini's publisher. Those are two of the magazines he owns. Leftist, of course.'

It figured. Gabriella would hardly work for a right-wing publication. It also explained why she knew so much about Petrini and his philosophy. Both she and Petrini had doubtless been part of the fashionable left in Milan – the radical chic who attended smart publishing parties and talked about revolution.

He remembered that he'd never got round to checking up on Gabriella. There just hadn't been time. As soon as he had a second he'd do it. But for the moment it would have to wait.

He brought his mind back to the immediate problem. Petrini's followers. 'Is there any more to come on Petrini?' he asked Conway.

'The SID in Rome are coming back to us. I also contacted the DST in Paris. Petrini was certainly there at the time of the troubles. Claude is digging out what he has. Oh, and Box 500 and the SIS are suddenly taking quite an interest.'

'Why?'

'Covering themselves, I expect. In case there's a KGB connection. Anyway, they're looking into Petrini too.'

Nick shook his head. It was all going to take too long, far too long. And they didn't have the time.

There was a call from the incident room: Nick was wanted downstairs. The lift was floors away so Nick ran down the four flights of stairs. One of Kershaw's team briefed him. The Bow Street bomb had been completely dismantled at Woolwich. The explosive was French. Manufactured by Explosif Rocher, Cugny, on 20th March 1968. Type: Nitramite 19C, a mixture of TNT and ammonium nitrate. Inquiries were being made through Interpol.

The stuff was bound to be stolen, of course. That would be no surprise. But it would be interesting to know if the French had unearthed any other explosives from the same batch and if so, where. It would be even more interesting if it had turned up in terrorist hands. It would be useful to talk to Desport. Nick picked up a phone and dialled the DST in Paris.

As the number began to ring Nick became aware of a hush in the incident room. Something was up. The senior detectives were getting to their feet and moving towards the door. Kershaw was standing there. Catching Nick's eye, he beckoned him over.

Abandoning the call, Nick hurried into Kershaw's office.

Kershaw waited until everyone had settled.

'The money found on Wheatfield is hot,' he said. 'It was stolen from a bank on the outskirts of Chester a month ago.'

Kershaw continued, 'This is not the first of the money to have shown up. They laundered several thousand by buying and selling an expensive car. Bought it in Manchester, sold it in London three days later. Small amounts have been surfacing regularly since then, and always in the London area. We have a list of shopkeepers and publicans who've inadvertently handled it. They've not been able to provide descriptions though. Not *yet*. But four of you will attempt to jog their memories.'

A thankless task if there ever was one, Nick thought. The witnesses would already have been interviewed and their statements taken; they wouldn't take kindly to a whole new round of questioning.

'There were two people involved in the robbery itself,' Kershaw went on. 'Both were masked. Both carried Skorpion machine pistols. A third drove the getaway car. Beyond that – not a lot. Cheshire CID have made no significant progress with the investigation, and have no suspects to date. Two of you will go up there and get a full briefing.' He named two officers.

'A couple more things,' Kershaw said. 'There's no firm evidence, just a *suspicion*, that it was an inside job.' He looked doubtful. 'But we'll see about that. And the other thing' – he paused for effect – 'it seems that one of the robbers might have been a woman.'

There was silence in the room. Nick shivered slightly. A *woman*. Like the one who had left the parcel bomb at Cardinal Couriers. He had several women agitators on file – it seemed that women were making up for their centuries of political inactivity with a bang. But bank robbery? That was a very different story.

Suddenly he made up his mind. Conway could stay on the end of the phone in the office and follow up all the leads from abroad. He wanted to take a few hours off and go to Chester.

Gabriele sat in the Fiat for a long time and watched the entrance to the block of flats in Chelsea Manor Street. Finally she was satisfied. She said to Giorgio, 'I'll be fifteen minutes.'

She took a bag from the luggage on the back seat and got out. She carried the bag up to the flat and let herself in. The place seemed to be just as she had left it. She went from room to room until she was satisfied that nothing had been disturbed. In the kitchen she moved the cooker slightly and examined the plinth. The wood showed no signs of having been forced.

She brought in the heavy bag and, opening it, pulled out five magazines of ammunition for the Kalashnikov and placed them on the floor. She wrapped them in a towel. The bundle was bulky. There was no hope of hiding it under the kitchen unit with the other things. Besides, secrecy didn't seem so important now. No one could possibly know about this place and she would only be coming back here if everything went wrong. And if everything went wrong she'd be fighting her way out.

She would love to use the Kalashnikov on Nick Riley. For the

254

twentieth time she imagined killing him. In her mind's eye she saw herself creeping up on him and bursting in with the rifle in her hand. He would stand up and stare in horror. He would raise his hands and look at her imploringly. He would stammer, 'Please don't.' Then she would smile and step forward. He would stumble backwards and start to shake with fear. The sweat would show on his forehead and he would beg her not to shoot. She would let him sweat a little longer, perhaps even make him kneel, then she would tell him what she thought of him. Finally, when he was so scared that he couldn't speak, she would pull the trigger.

She licked her lips. What she would give to make the scene a reality. Anything to obliterate the other vision that kept coming into her mind, the vision of him on top of her, pretending to love her, laughing secretly as he made love to her. She bit back the acid taste of humiliation, and thought: I'll get him one day.

She examined all the possible hiding places in the kitchen and settled on the gap between the wall and the back of the fridge. The bundle sat neatly on the condenser, and could be reached easily by sliding a hand down the wall.

She picked up the empty bag and, locking the flat, went down to the street. She looked carefully around before walking across to the car.

As she got in, Giorgio started the car and asked, 'Where now?'

'To eat. Then to visit your little friend.'

He gave her a curious glance. Pulling out into the King's Road, he laughed, 'She's not little.'

'Maybe not. But she's useful.'

'Oh?'

'Yes. She going to get Max back for us.'

Twenty

It was late afternoon by the time they left London and it took an hour to get on to the motorway. It was raining heavily and very dark, making the road treacherous. The driver, a young detective constable, was silent with concentration. The other man, an inspector with fifteen years' service, made the occasional attempt at conversation, then gave up.

Nick sat in the back, feeling tired and depressed. It had seemed a good idea to make this trip but now he wasn't so sure. What would he find? Proof that Wheatfield had been involved in the robbery? That would be nice, but it wouldn't necessarily get him anywhere. What he really needed was the identity of the others – and that would be a lot to hope for. Cheshire CID hadn't found any evidence, and they'd been working on the case for weeks.

In fact, the trip could well be a complete waste of time. And yet he was intrigued by the hint of inside knowledge. That, and the reason Wheatfield and his friends had chosen such an out of the way place as Chester: somewhere a long way from London, with banks presumably no easier to rob than those elsewhere. There might just be a good reason.

At the same time he was impatient to get back to London, to follow up the explosives lead and the Petrini connection. He decided he would stay in Chester for the night and perhaps two hours of the morning, but no longer.

As the car sped on, he brooded. He had made so many mistakes with this case. Not grabbing Wheatfield at the demonstration. Not getting Black Beard. Finding Wheatfield at St Mark's Villas and then *watching* him buy the ingredients for his bombs. Then losing him again – not strictly his fault, that one, but something he should have prevented. And now a nice comfortable unsuspecting woman who'd had the reasonable expectation of living out her life in peace and fulfilment was dead, blown to pieces in her own kitchen, her only crime to be the wife of the Commissioner.

There mustn't be any more mistakes.

Wheatfield was safely locked up. But Nick wanted to get his friends. Very badly.

They arrived in Chester at eight-thirty. Inspector Morrow had the case file ready for them. He also had the assistant manager of the bank, Mr Chesil, waiting in an interview room.

Nick started with the assistant manager. 'Now, Mr Chesil, I understand you got a glimpse of the driver of the getaway van.'

'Only the *briefest* glimpse.'

'I see. But I'd still like you to look at some photographs for me.' He placed the mug shots of Wheatfield on the table. 'Is this the man?'

The assistant manager stared hard at the pictures and shook his head. 'It *might* be. But I couldn't be sure. It happened so quickly, you see. I hardly had a chance.'

Nick nodded. 'Okay, now I'm going to show you some more photographs and some names. I want you to tell me if any of them are familiar. I mean in any context at all.'

He pulled out a sheaf of photographs of Wheatfield's known associates, a list of their names, and of the organisations that Wheatfield had been involved with.

Chesil went through them slowly, then shook his head.

Kershaw's detectives took over, and Nick returned to the inspector's office.

Inspector Morrow said, 'Some of the other witnesses are coming in during the evening.' He explained who the various people were, and Nick chose to interview Miss Izzard, who was waiting in another room.

She told him about the guns and how she'd identified them as Skorpions. She also described how the first gunman had gone straight to the shopping bag full of money.

'That gunman was a woman?'

'Oh yes,' said Miss Izzard definitely.

Inspector Morrow prompted, 'And the other acted like a gangster.'

Nick asked Miss Izzard, 'Oh? How was that?'

She explained about the 'Shut up or I kill you.' She paused, then added thoughtfully, 'You know, in hindsight I could have been wrong. Maybe I've seen too many films. Now I've had time to think about it, well – perhaps I was *too* certain.'

Nick sighed inwardly. Inspector Morrow had described this lady as a perfect witness and now she was back-pedalling.

'You see,' continued Miss Izzard, 'in actual fact when you come to think about it all he did was to speak like a *foreigner*. Not just a gangster. *Any* sort of foreigner.'

Immediately, Nick thought of Black Beard. Nevertheless, he showed Miss Izzard the photographs and the list of names that he did have. After fifteen minutes she admitted defeat, saying firmly, 'I know none of these people.'

There were no more witnesses to interview for the moment so Nick spent the next hour in Morrow's office going carefully through all the statements in the case file. He kept thinking: There's nothing here. I was wrong to come. After a while his mind wandered. He imagined the remainder of the terrorist cell – perhaps three or four of them – hiding out in London. Would they be lying low? Or would they be busy planning more bombs? He tried to picture them. They would be arrogant, like Wheatfield. And cruel. One failure wouldn't put them off: it would probably encourage them. Even now they were probably planning their revenge.

Uneasy, he phoned Conway in London. Conway told him the explosives had been traced to a batch stolen from the French explosives factory at Cugny the previous June. Ten sticks of Nitramite 19C from the same batch had been discovered in Bilbao, northern Spain, in January, in a raid on the hide-out of some Basque Separatists.

What did it prove? Only what he'd known before; that the terrorists co-operated with each other.

There was no other news.

He rang off and returned to the pile of statements. At ten-thirty Morrow put his head round the door.

'The financial director of Bradbury's has come in. Would you like a word?'

It was Bradbury's payroll which had been in the shopping bag, Nick remembered. Picking up his batch of photographs, he said, 'Yes, why not?'

Morrow led the way down the corridor. 'Well, don't expect too much. He's a taciturn bugger, this fellow. And he says he can only stay ten minutes.'

Kershaw's detectives were already interviewing the man. Nick sat down and listened. The man's name was Leonard Wilson. He was about sixty, thin-faced with grey hair receding at the temples. He was neatly dressed in a grey suit, and sat stiffly in the chair with his hands folded precisely on the table in front of him. It was soon apparent that Mr Wilson was not best pleased at being questioned again. He was quietly but firmly dismissive, and answered the questions as briefly as possible. He obviously didn't suffer fools gladly.

No, he was saying, he had nothing new to add to his statement. He certainly had no idea why some terrorists should have chosen to rob the bank at the precise moment the payroll was being passed over.

After a few minutes he looked at his watch in an obvious way.

Nick stepped forward. 'Would you mind very much looking at these photographs, sir?'

Mr Wilson gave a small but unmistakable sigh of annoyance. 'If you insist.'

He looked at pictures of Wheatfield and raised his eyebrows in vague distaste. 'I've never seen this person before.'

258

He barely glanced at the other photographs before shaking his head.

'And just a list of names and organisations, if you wouldn't mind.'

The list was quite long, but within ten seconds Leonard Wilson had passed it back across the table.

Nick thought: Oh no, you don't. Pushing the paper back, he said firmly, 'If you wouldn't mind, sir, taking another look. It *is* very important.'

A momentary flash of irritation crossed Leonard Wilson's face, then, pulling the list towards him, he began to read again. Nick watched his eyes travel down the list, flicking from side to side as he read each name.

Half-way down he seemed to pause. Then he started again, reading more slowly, taking more care.

Finally he looked up. 'I'm sorry. I don't think I know any of the people or organisations on this list.'

It was the longest reply he had given that evening.

He stood up to go. Morrow caught Nick's eye and raised his eyebrows as if to say: What did I tell you.

Wilson picked up his coat from a chair. Standing up, he looked unexpectedly thin and frail. As he unfolded the coat a pair of gloves and a scarf fell to the floor. Nick picked them up and handed them to him. He noticed that Wilson's hand was trembling. Well, he was sixty or so; that was old age for you.

Nick helped him on with his coat.

Wilson said, 'Thank you.'

Nick looked up sharply. There was something different about the voice: a warm tremulous quality. Almost as if he were relieved. Or nervous.

The tiniest suspicion crept into Nick's mind.

He opened the door for the older man and walked with him down the corridor. He said, 'The people who robbed the bank are terrorists. Did Inspector Morrow tell you that?'

Wilson nodded. 'Yes.'

'Former students who think they can change the world.' Nick glanced across at him. 'Do you have any children yourself, Mr Wilson?'

'Not any more.' The answer came very quickly.

A child had died, obviously. 'I'm sorry.'

They reached the main entrance of the police station. Nick stopped so that Wilson was forced to pause for a moment.

'It was very good of you to come over. Do you have transport?'

'Thank you. I have a car.' He turned and, pushing rapidly through the doors, was gone.

Nick stared after him. He could swear something wasn't quite right there, although he couldn't put his finger on it.

He went back to the interview room and looked thoughtfully at his list. There was no Wilson on it. And *yet*.

He racked his brains. The name rang a very distinct bell. It was maddening, but he couldn't quite place it. He tried matching it with a dozen Christian names but nothing clicked.

Records would turn it up. He got one of the detectives to phone Conway in London to start the hunt through the files, then he went in search of Morrow.

'Who else can I talk to?'

The inspector thought for a moment. 'Well – there's always our friend Mrs Ackroyd. The lady who carried the payroll. She's worked at Bradbury's for twenty years. But I thought I'd save you an ear-bashing by not asking her in—'

'Would you mind telling her that I'd like to come round?'

Mabel Ackroyd dropped the receiver on to its cradle and raced upstairs in panic. Reaching the bathroom she tore off her hairnet and, grabbing a tissue, rubbed the cold cream mercilessly off her face.

It was important to look her best. Scotland Yard indeed! In the last few weeks it had gone very quiet on the robbery front. She'd told everyone her story, and some of them had been interested enough to hear it several times. But more recently people had started to drift away when she'd mentioned the subject. It was most disappointing. If only Harry, her husband, were still alive. He would have listened. She missed having someone to talk to.

But now! Scotland Yard indeed!

She fluffed out her grey curls and wondered whether to get dressed. No, it was better to stay in her dressing-gown. It would sound more *dramatic* when she told everyone in the morning.

She went back downstairs, turned some lights on, and put on the kettle for some tea. She had butterflies in her stomach.

The doorbell rang and she clasped her hands together in pleasure.

She opened the door with a warm smile. There were two of them. She recognised the nice Inspector Morrow immediately. 'Good evening, inspector,' she said graciously.

She turned to examine the second man and suppressed a deep disappointment. This couldn't be the Scotland Yard detective. This person was frightfully young, with longish hair and blue jeans.

They came in and Inspector Morrow said, 'This is Sergeant Ryder from Scotland Yard.'

So, he *was* from the Yard. But only a *sergeant*.

Never mind. She determined to make the best of it. She led the way into the lounge and asked them to sit down. She noticed that the sergeant was rather good-looking. She smiled, 'How can I help you?'

The inspector began, 'Er, it's a delicate subject, Mrs Ackroyd. It's about Bradbury's. We wanted to know a few personal details about some of the people who work there. About Mr Wilson, for example.'

'Mr Wilson?' she repeated curiously. 'Oh-h-h.'

'Yes. We wondered if you could tell us if he had any children?'

She blinked in surprise. What on earth had this to do with the robbery? 'Well,' she said eventually, 'there was a daughter, I believe.'

'What was her name?' the sergeant asked.

'Her name? Now let me see . . . Yes, Linda. Linda.'

The sergeant put a hand to his eyes and inhaled sharply as if something had just come back to him. Then he exchanged glances with the inspector, and gave him a firm nod.

Mabel Ackroyd felt a small twinge of alarm. 'May I ask *why* you are asking me these questions?'

The young man replied, 'It's very important that we know about Linda Wilson, Mrs Ackroyd. Is she – er – *dead*?'

'Dead? Well, not as far as I *know*. I mean – one would have *heard* if she was. Goodness . . .' She put a hand to her bosom. 'Is she meant to be dead?'

'Can you tell us anything more about her, Mrs Ackroyd?'

The sergeant hadn't actually answered her question. She felt rather put out. 'Well, I don't know the Wilsons well, you understand. They keep themselves to themselves. But I do remember Linda. I used to see her quite often. She was my own daughter's age, you see. Although they weren't friends, as such. She was clever, you see, Linda. She went to a grammar school, and then to university. She was very clever.'

'Anything else about her? What was she like?'

'Oh, quiet. A bit withdrawn, really. She – was very protected,

261

you know. An only child, of course. Always neatly dressed. Always well behaved. Until she was about fifteen.'

'What happened then?'

'She went wild.'

Mrs Ackroyd enjoyed the effect of her words. The two police officers were positively drinking them up.

'Wild? Do you mean with boys?'

'Yes. And in every other way. Her clothes – well, once I saw her wearing the shortest skirt you've *ever* seen. And make-up! Well, you could have scraped it off her face.'

'What sort of friends did she have?'

'Oh, arty types. Layabouts. Not what her parents wanted, not at all.'

'Have you seen her recently?'

'Oh no. She's never been back. Her parents washed their hands of her, you see. When she went away to university. They never forgave her. Never.'

'What for?' the sergeant asked.

'For being so wild. And outrageous. She was very outspoken. They never forgave her for being so – *ungrateful*, I think.'

The young sergeant stood up. 'Thank you, Mrs Ackroyd.'

'But aren't you going to *tell* me what this is all about? I mean, is it about the robbery? Was *Linda* involved in some way?'

The inspector said quickly, 'Something like that.'

She jumped up. 'But you haven't had any tea.'

The sergeant said, 'Another time.' He fixed his gaze on her. 'Can I ask you a favour, Mrs Ackroyd?'

He was giving her such a charming look that she revised her opinion of him. He was obviously very bright and clever as well as being good-looking. It suddenly occurred to her that, despite being a sergeant, he might be important after all. She swelled with pride.

'Of course.'

'May I ask you not to say anything about the – *nature* of our conversation?'

'Oh,' she exclaimed. That was going to be very difficult. She'd already planned how she was going to announce it in the office.

'Just for a day or so. Until we've completed our inquiries. It's important.'

Ah, *now* she understood. It was hush-hush. He was an undercover man. That explained the jeans. She breathed, 'Of *course*.'

It was only after she'd closed the door behind them that she remembered something else. Good Lord, how could she have forgotten? She threw open the door and called down the path, 'Hello? Hello? Are you still there?'

The young sergeant re-emerged from the darkness. 'Yes?'

'I completely forgot – she once told me that she was *adopted*, Linda did. But it can't have been true. I mean, one would have *heard*. Probably one of her little fancies.'

The young man blinked. 'Thank you, Mrs Ackroyd.'

After they'd gone she made herself a cup of tea and sat up for a while thinking how exciting it had all been.

Then she thought about poor Mr and Mrs Wilson, and how awful it was going to be for them, and felt rather sad.

The house was situated in a quiet residential street, set back from the road behind a tall hedge. It was a house with, Nick guessed, about four bedrooms. There was a light shining in the porch, but otherwise the place was in darkness. A path led from the gate to the front door through a neat ordered garden, the rose beds well dug and covered with manure, ready for the winter.

As they rang the bell Nick noticed a sliver of light showing through a chink in the heavily curtained windows. Someone was still up.

It was a good minute before they heard someone approach the door. Finally a bolt was pulled back, and the door was opened a short way. The face of a woman appeared, but standing well back out of the harsh light from the porch. The woman was small and grey-haired.

Inspector Morrow went through the formalities of identifying himself, then asked if they might come in.

The woman did not reply, but stared at them as if in shock. Nick realised that she had been crying.

She retreated further into the shadow of the hall, and glanced to one side. Suddenly the door was pulled wide open, and Leonard Wilson stepped into the light. He did not look surprised to see them.

He said stiffly, 'You'll want to come in, I suppose.'

They were shown into the living-room, a vaguely oppressive room densely furnished with a brown Dralon three-piece suite, numerous side tables and occasional chairs, lamps with deep fringes, and heavy velvet curtains. Every surface was covered in china ornaments and bric-a-brac. The walls were decorated with a busy beige and tan wallpaper.

The four of them sat down.

Morrow began, 'I believe you have a daughter, Mr and Mrs Wilson. By the name of Linda?'

Leonard Wilson replied, 'Yes.'

'And she's not dead, is she?'

'She is to us.' He closed his eyes for an instant, as if reinforcing an inner resolve.

Morrow paused. 'When did you last see her?'

'Four years ago.'

'And you've had no communication with her since then?'

'None.'

'She – hasn't visited the neighbourhood recently?'

'No. Not that we are aware of.'

Nick said, 'Mr Wilson, you recognised some names on that list that I showed you. Which were they?'

Wilson stared at him. With an effort he replied, 'There were a couple that she might have mentioned . . . Friends of hers at Essex University. Members of that political group – the Socialist League or whatever it was. She brought one of them home once.' His mouth curled up with distaste.

'What was his name?'

For the first time Leonard Wilson's face showed some emotion. He dropped his eyes. 'Wheatfield.'

There was a long silence. Nick asked, 'When was this?'

He shook his head. 'I'm not sure. Probably four or five years ago.'

Mrs Wilson spoke for the first time. 'It was four and a half years ago exactly.' Her voice was thin and tired and defeated. 'In May.'

Nick glanced around the room, searching the tables and mantelpiece for photographs. There were only two, and they were faded pictures of the young Mr and Mrs Wilson taken, he guessed, during the war.

'Do you have any photographs of your daughter, Mrs Wilson?'

She had buried her head in her hand and he realised that she was weeping.

Nick said, 'I'm sorry, but – if you *could* find something . . .'

She dabbed at her eyes and got up. 'I'll go and look. '

'Shall I come with you?'

She nodded her assent, and Nick followed her upstairs into a spare room which seemed to be used as both study and store room. She knelt on the floor and, unlocking one of the desk drawers, pulled out a box.

She started to open it then paused. Her head fell on to her chest and Nick realised she was crying again.

'You'll use this to find her, won't you?' she whispered.

Nick sighed. He could only tell her the truth. 'Yes.'

'And – she'll be locked away.'

'Yes, eventually.'

She shook her head from side to side. 'Nothing but pain. Always. Always the same. Nothing but pain.'

Eventually she blew her nose and taking a deep breath, opened the box.

Nick looked over her shoulder. Baby pictures. A toddler firmly gripping an adult hand. A small girl in a gymslip. The family on a beach somewhere. Then older, about twelve.

Nick stared.

He felt a twinge of alarm.

There was something vaguely *familiar*—

He frowned and very slowly reached out for the photograph.

'The more recent ones are at the bottom,' Mrs Wilson murmured.

Nick's mouth had gone very dry. He stared, horrified yet transfixed, as Mrs Wilson pulled a large black and white portrait from the bottom of the box.

Everything stood still.

Then he heard himself cry, '*Oh Christ. Oh God.*'

For a moment he was incredulous.

Then the shock came to him like a pain, a small ache which grew and grew until it was vast and ugly.

'*Oh God, Oh God.*'

He tried to find another answer, but he knew there was none. And then the realisations came thick and fast, each more ghastly than the one before, each tearing away a new layer of horror like so many layers of skin torn from a wound.

He felt physically ill. He wanted to be sick.

Mrs Wilson's voice came from far away, shrill and frightened. 'What's the matter? *What's the matter?*' He heard her get up and hurriedly leave the room.

He put a fist to his mouth and bit into it until it hurt.

Henry Northcliff dreamed that he was standing at the dispatch box in the House of Commons. He opened his mouth to speak but couldn't think of anything to say. Something ghastly had happened: he'd been caught out in some way, and the members were shouting,

265

'Resign! Resign!' A member of the Cabinet was shaking him by the shoulder, trying to get him to sit down.

He awoke with a start, and realised he was in bed at home. Caroline was shaking him gently by the shoulder.

He twisted round. 'What is it?'

'I heard a sound. A sort of scraping noise. From downstairs . . .'

Henry listened, but apart from the humming of the wind the night was silent.

Caroline said, 'It's probably nothing. I'm sorry.'

Henry roused himself and, throwing back the covers, swung his legs to the floor.

Caroline said ruefully, 'Oh darling, don't bother. Honestly.'

'I'm up now.'

He pulled on a dressing-gown and went out to the landing. He listened for a moment, then, turning on the light, went downstairs. He noticed it was just after one o'clock. He made the rounds of each room, checking the doors and windows.

Finally he went to the front door and peered through the peep-hole. In the dim street lighting he could just make out the figure of the policeman at the front gate, pacing slowly back and forth.

He turned back and listened again. Nothing.

He switched off the lights and started to climb the stairs again.

There was a sound. He paused to listen.

From the distance, beyond the kitchen, there was a definite noise, a faint screech.

He retraced his steps and went into the kitchen. He crossed the room and looked out of the window into the garden. The night was very dark. It was impossible to distinguish much apart from the outline of the trees, which were swaying frantically back and forth, pulled by the wind.

The sound came again, more like a wail than a screech. He went to the back door which opened on to the side of the house, and unlocked it.

He put his head out. The wind came whistling down the side of the building and blew at his hair. He peered towards the boundary fence and the dim silhouette of his neighbour's house.

Suddenly it came again. A high screech.

He stood listening.

Suddenly he gave a small snort of amusement.

He closed and relocked the door then hurried back upstairs.

Caroline was sitting up in bed waiting.

'Oh poor darling,' she said. 'It wasn't anything, I suppose.'

'A branch. Rubbing against the Collins' greenhouse. It's the wind.'

He got back into bed and she snuggled against him.

'Poor darling. What an idiot I am.'

'Not at all. I'm glad you woke me. Otherwise you might have stayed awake worrying. You weren't awake long, were you?'

'No. Well – only a few minutes.'

'You should have woken me sooner.'

They lay for a while in the darkness, listening to the wind.

Henry said, 'You don't worry, do you, about these bombers?'

'What? Oh no. Anyway they've caught one of them, haven't they? I mean, very quickly. So they're bound to find the rest, aren't they? Thank God. That poor woman.' She shuddered. 'So dreadful.'

Henry hugged her to him. He suddenly felt exceptionally happy. Here he was in this warm bed with a woman he loved more than anything in the world, secure in a nice comfortable house, with no money worries, and a job that, even if it was causing him worry at present, was on balance most satisfying and rewarding.

'I do love you,' he murmured.

She kissed his neck.

'And you know, I *am* pleased about the baby. *Really*. They always say that late parenthood is an unexpected joy. And I *know* it will be for me too. In fact, I'm very much looking forward to it.'

'We'll still be able to go to Venice. We'll just leave him behind.'

'Yes,' he said. 'That's right. We'll still be able to go.'

A few minutes later, as Caroline's breathing became deep and steady beside him, Henry thought about the baby again and discovered that he had meant every word he'd said. Now that he had got used to the idea, he was most definitely looking forward to it.

Twenty-one

Victoria dreamed that Bella was in the farmhouse kitchen, eating rotten vegetables out of the fridge. The floor was covered in mud and dirt; the creature had obviously been there a long time without food. She walked into the hall. Her footsteps echoed through the cold empty

267

house. The curtains were drawn in the ground floor rooms. She climbed the stairs. The door of Pete and Janey's room was ajar. She pushed it open and looked in. The room was empty. She started up the passage towards her own room. The door was wide open. She hesitated, suddenly sickened. The air was thick with flies. She didn't want to go in alone. But there was no one else in the house.

She woke up, holding her breath. She exhaled with a long sigh. The bedside clock read one. She'd been asleep for less than half an hour. The other side of the bed was empty.

She lay still, trying to shut out the dull ache of the loneliness and the knowledge that he was probably with someone else.

She thought: It's my own fault. I should have known. A man like that was never going to be easy. But the constant uncertainty was hard to bear. It was so wearing. Never knowing when he would be back. If at *all*.

And then there was the awful business of the bundles in the van. If only he could be more definite about what he planned to do with them. He couldn't just *leave* them there. Doubtless he was hoping they would just disappear. But life wasn't like that. He had to *do* something about it. She would make another effort to persuade him. When she saw him. *If* she saw him. She sighed unhappily. What a mess.

There was a sound. She lay tense and still, listening. A window rattled. The wind.

Another sound. *In* the flat.

She got out of bed, her heart pounding.

Giorgio. It must be.

She padded into the living-room. It took a moment for her eyes to adjust to the light spilling in from the hall beyond, and at first she thought the room was empty.

Then she saw something move.

'Giorgio!'

He was standing in the shadows, staring at her, his eyes glinting in the darkness.

She went to him and, reaching up, kissed him. The smell of drink was strong on his breath.

She said, 'You're late. I was worried . . . Is your friend all right?'

He frowned mockingly. 'All right?'

'You said . . .' She trailed off. She could see he was in one of those moods. He was going to pretend he'd never said anything about visiting the friend in trouble. It was one of his favourite tricks, pretending not to remember.

He reached out and, lifting her shift, began to caress her thigh. 'You missed me?' he murmured thickly. 'You want me? Mmm?'

She looked into his face. She sensed he was taunting her. And yet . . .

Closing her eyes, she leant her body against his, and put her arms round him. It was impossible. She just couldn't turn him away. It didn't matter what he thought of her. He brought out strong feelings in her that she'd never realised she had. He made her feel brazen and shameless. He made her feel *alive*.

She laughed, warm and low, and started to unbutton his shirt.

He breathed, 'You want me very badly? Do you? Do you?'

'Oh yes, oh *yes*. *Now*. Every part of you . . . Every *inch* of you.'

'You've been waiting for me, have you?'

'Yes. *Yes*.'

He laughed triumphantly and pulled away. 'Such passion.'

She took his hand to pull him gently towards the bedroom, but he held back.

He was looking at something on the other side of the room.

She followed his gaze.

At first she saw nothing.

Then she jumped back, uttering a small cry.

Somebody was there.

She stared, aghast.

The person moved, coming further into the light. It was a woman, tall and dark.

The memory of what she'd just been saying hit Victoria first, and she flushed with embarrassment. Then came the sickening realisation that Giorgio had staged the whole thing. He had *known* the woman would hear. He had set up the scene just to humiliate her.

She turned on him. 'My *God*!'

Ignoring her anger, Giorgio said smoothly, 'Oh, I forgot. This is my friend Gabriele. She needs a place to stay. I said she could come here.'

Victoria gaped at him. What *was* he trying to do to her? She spluttered, 'Really . . . *Really*! How *could* you?'

Giorgio spread his hands in a wide gesture of surprise. 'She only wants the sofa. I thought you wouldn't mind. She is in need of a bed, that's all.'

Victoria hardly trusted herself to speak. 'You might have told me.'

'I didn't know.'

'That she was *here*, I mean.'

He shrugged. 'She didn't mind. Did you, Gabriele?'

The woman sat calmly down on the sofa. 'No, I didn't mind.'

Victoria thought: This is a nightmare.

The woman lit a cigarette. She said, 'This sofa'll be okay.' She was very composed. She stared at Victoria with cold assurance, her gaze steady and unblinking. But there was no warmth in the gaze, nothing that invited further contact.

She was very good-looking, Victoria noticed, the face dramatically pale against the dark hair, the features strong and well formed; a woman who could be attractive to men.

Immediately, a nasty suspicion sprang into Victoria's mind. She looked from Giorgio to the woman. There was no reason for believing it, nothing she could put her finger on. And *yet* . . .

Giorgio said, 'She'll need some blankets.'

Sick at heart, Victoria went into the bedroom and dug out a spare eiderdown and pillow from a box under the bed. She could be wrong, of course, about the woman. But she knew she wasn't. One got a feeling about these things.

She took the bedding back to the other room and dropped it on the floor by the sofa.

The woman said, 'Thanks.'

For an instant Victoria thought there was some warmth in the tone, then she looked into the woman's face and knew she was mistaken.

Victoria went into the bedroom and closed the door. There was a pause then she heard the low murmur of voices. They were talking about her, she knew they were. She wanted to scream. What a fool she'd been.

A door opened and closed: the bathroom.

Victoria climbed quickly into bed. A moment later Giorgio came in and turned on the light. She closed her eyes. She heard him undress. Then the light went off and he got into bed.

After a few seconds his hand came across and stroked her leg.

She hissed, 'Don't touch me.'

He took no notice, and rolled his body next to hers.

'Don't *touch* me!'

He pulled her over on to her back and, pushing her shift up round her neck, began to kiss her body.

'You're *foul*. You humiliated me. On *purpose*!'

270

He paused. 'Vittoria. No. I was proud of you. Proud. Otherwise why would I have kissed you in front of her?'

She didn't believe him. It was a complete lie. She should have said so, but she couldn't. Instead, she let him continue, hating herself for being so weak, loathing herself for what he must think of her, yet wanting him terribly.

It might be the last time. It *would* be the last time.

And if she was never going to see him again, what the hell did it matter anyway?

The night seemed to have lasted for ever. It was only two-thirty. Nick made himself a cup of coffee and, leaning back against the work top, looked dully around him. The kitchen was old-fashioned: the wooden cupboards of a type popular thirty years ago, the wallpaper old and over-fussy. The paintwork was an oppressive mid-blue, the overhead light inadequate, the effect dim and depressing.

Yet once she had been a child here; once she had eaten her breakfast at the table under the window in the brightness of the early morning. Once she must have run in and asked for sweets, and been given a kind word, and run out again to play. Surely it can't have been so terrible. *Surely*.

The telephone rang in the hall.

He drained the coffee and went to answer it.

It was Conway.

'Cleaned out. Not a sign of life. The forensic people are going over the place now.'

Nick rubbed his forehead. It would have been too simple to find her at the mews house.

'What about the Fiat?' he asked.

'Parked outside. Nothing in it.'

'What about Records? Anything in the passport details?'

'No. Nothing to say she was adopted anyway. Usually they put a special note on the form, don't they? When it's checked.'

'Yes. Let me know if you find anything.'

He rang off, feeling very low. She'd done a bunk. It shouldn't surprise him. It was becoming increasingly obvious that she was a real pro. That was what hurt the most, the way she'd completely fooled him on a professional level. He'd never had a flicker of suspicion. And yet all the pointers had been there if only he'd chosen to see. It made him cringe to think of the things she'd been doing under his very nose – things he could have *prevented*. The bombings. He thought of Mrs McCabe and felt bitterly ashamed.

He'd never *checked* on Gabriella.

He'd meant to. He'd intended to.

He'd just never bloody well *done* it.

There was a footfall on the stairs above. It was Mr Wilson.

Nick met him at the bottom. 'Is Mrs Wilson better?'

'Yes, but she's resting. I'd really rather she wasn't disturbed until morning.'

'Would it be convenient to have those few words now?'

Wilson nodded. He looked tired, but the stiffness, the unrelenting formality, was still in place. Nick sensed that Wilson was not a man who ever let go.

They went into the living-room and sat down.

'She was always wilful,' Wilson began slowly. 'She never wanted to be told what to do. She never listened.'

'When did she first become involved in politics?'

'What? Oh, at university. She picked up all sorts of – *rubbish*. She couldn't stop talking about it. She got very aggressive. Used to shout at us when we didn't listen. It was all complete nonsense, of course. Half-baked theories about this and that . . .'

'About what exactly?'

He made an impatient gesture. 'Oh good God, I can't remember now. I don't think I listened much. It was all about' – he sighed heavily – 'changing the order of things, or something like that. Complete nonsense.'

'Mr Wilson, apparently Linda was under the impression she was adopted. Is that true?'

Wilson hesitated slightly, then said vehemently, 'No! Another of her fantasies. She was always romanticising everything.'

Nick eyed him thoughtfully.

'Was there any particular reason for this fantasy?'

'No, no. She was just over-imaginative. She could never come down to earth. Always felt that the world owed her something. She was – selfish, demanding, difficult. We could never do anything with her.'

'Can you think why she should choose the name Gabriella?'

The slight hesitation again. 'No.' He dropped his eyes and stared at the empty grate.

'Or Schroeder? Or Carelli?' pressed Nick.

'No.'

The denials were being delivered more confidently now, as if he were getting used to a lie.

Nick rubbed a hand over his face. 'Mr Wilson, I don't have much time. Please tell me – is there anything more I should know?'

A woman's voice said, 'Tell him, Leonard.'

The two men turned. Mrs Wilson was standing in the doorway. She said awkwardly, 'I couldn't sleep—'

She came and sat down. Folding her hands in her lap, she said again to her husband, 'Tell him.'

Leonard Wilson stared at her and shook his head briefly and violently.

Marie Wilson raised her eyes to Nick's. Taking a deep breath she said coldly, 'She's not our child.'

'Marie—'

She raised a hand to her husband. 'No, Leonard, it doesn't make any difference now. And I don't want people to think she's our daughter any more. Not when she *isn't* . . .' She looked at Nick again, and continued in a firm voice, 'She's not our child at all. She was my sister's. My sister was what you might call – *wild*. Just like Linda. Very impressionable. She had a boyfriend, just before the war. A German called Schroeder.' She spoke the word 'German' as if it were distasteful. 'He was a writer, an intellectual. Rose, my sister, was quite bowled over by him. She had . . . a strange fascination for those sort of people. Always hanging about them, making a fool of herself. She went to Germany with – this person. But then, in '38, I think it was, there was trouble – he was almost arrested.'

'Why?'

'Why? Oh, I'm not sure—'

'For being a damned communist!' interrupted Wilson.

Mrs Wilson folded and refolded her hands. 'Anyway, he came here as a refugee. When war broke out he was interned. Rose – well, she never stopped making scenes about it. Trying to get him freed. Hysterical, she was. She took a job near the camp in Scotland. He was allowed out in the day to work on a farm. She'd sneak out to – see him. Then – she became pregnant.' She shook her head. 'It was out of the question for her to keep the baby. I mean, she was quite hopeless as a person. Irresponsible. She would never have looked after it. Besides, she didn't *want* the child. She was frightened that the German would drop her. And of course he *did*. After the war . . .' She bristled with righteous indignation.

'Go on,' prompted Nick.

'Well. We decided to – take the child. We couldn't have children of our own, you see.'

'But you never actually adopted Linda?'

Mrs Wilson assumed a look of high moral standing. 'No . . . We didn't want there to be the slightest stain against her name. If anyone had discovered that she was – born out of marriage. Well, we felt it would be terrible for her.'

Or for *you*, Nick thought.

'We decided to make her ours immediately. Rose had the baby in Scotland, in the cottage where she was living. The doctor didn't know Rose at all. It was wartime. People were moving all over the place . . . When we told him her name was Marie Wilson and the baby was to be called Linda, well . . . He took us at our word. And so – *we* brought Linda up. *Properly.* Much better than Rose could ever have done. Anyway – Rose died a few years later.'

Wilson said firmly, 'But the wildness was in her blood. She was just like her mother.' He shook his head. 'Nothing we could do.'

There was a long silence. Nick felt empty and hollow.

Wilson said in an icy voice, 'I suppose this will mean prosecution.'

For a moment Nick couldn't think what he meant. 'For what?'

'For the false birth registration.'

Nick sighed. 'Quite honestly, I have no idea. It was a long time ago.' These people were incredible, he reflected. All they could think about was protecting themselves from something which happened more than twenty-five years before.

'Just tell me,' Nick said heavily, 'how did Linda find out? About her parents?'

Mrs Wilson wrung her hands. 'She discovered a letter. From this – Schroeder man. He'd – written to me, asking about her. I thought he was *dead.* It had been so long . . . And I've no idea how he *found* us. It was awful.'

'When was this?'

'Oh . . . In 1962. Thereabouts. From then on she could think of nothing else. She romanticised him. Saw him as a knight in armour, fighting for freedom . . . A martyr. She became *obsessed* by the story. And as for *us* – well, *we* became monsters. And after all we'd done for her!'

'One last question. Why would she call herself Gabriella?'

Mrs Wilson's mouth pulled back in a grimace of pain. 'That's

274

what the Schroeder man called her. At least, *Gabriele*. In the letter. He seemed to think it was her name. Rose had promised him. That she would call the child by that name. But then Rose always made promises she could never keep.'

Nick stood up to go. Automatically Wilson began to get out of his seat, but, changing his mind, paused and sank back into the cushions. Nick left them sitting in the dark oppressive room, staring at the walls.

Victoria sat up in bed, feeling awful. She'd slept very badly. She remembered waking several times in the night and being unable to get back to sleep. Now, astonishingly, it was ten.

The other side of the bed was empty.

She pulled on a dressing-gown and went to the door. She opened it. There were voices in the living-room. As she went in they ceased.

Giorgio and the woman sat there, looking at her.

Immediately Giorgio rose to his feet and came towards her. He put his arm round her. 'Did you sleep all right?'

She blinked at him. 'No, as a matter of fact . . . I didn't.'

'Ah,' he said without interest. Then, more warmly: 'I make you some coffee.'

He disappeared into the kitchen. Victoria was left with the woman. She was not quite as beautiful as Victoria had thought. There were dark circles under her eyes and in the light of day her skin looked rather sallow. At the same time, there was something magnetic about her, a forceful energy that made it difficult to take your eyes off her.

Victoria immediately felt inadequate.

The woman said, 'We were just talking about you.'

'Oh?'

She uncurled herself from the sofa. Her movements were cat-like. 'You see,' the woman said smoothly, 'you're the only one who can help.'

Victoria sat down in a chair. 'Me? In what way?'

'This awful business with the van. And those people who slipped in the explosives—'

Victoria closed her eyes. Just the mention of those dreadful bundles made her depressed.

'You see, Giorgio knew nothing about them. You realise that, don't you?'

Victoria nodded.

The woman reached down to the floor and took a cigarette from a packet. She lit it slowly and deliberately. She had what Victoria's mother used to call poise.

'These people have used Giorgio. And of course *you*,' she continued. 'And now they want the stuff. We have to decide whether to give it to them.'

It was like a nightmare. Victoria shook her head. 'No, no. That must be wrong.'

'I agree.'

Victoria smiled with relief. 'Thank goodness. We'll give the stuff to the police, won't we? And explain.'

'Well, I don't think it'll be quite as simple as that.' The woman's gaze was very penetrating. 'They'll almost undoubtedly arrest us.'

'Oh God!'

Victoria couldn't even imagine what it must be like to be arrested on a serious charge. After the business with Mel and the farm, and the violence at the demonstration, it seemed that her life was staggering from one horror to another, each worse than the one before.

Giorgio came in with the coffee and put it down beside her. He sat on the arm of the chair and stroked her hair.

'Can't we *go* to someone?' Victoria asked plaintively.

The woman shot a glance at Giorgio, then smiled. 'Why, yes. That was exactly what we thought—'

'Oh good!' Victoria felt the first glimmerings of hope.

'But it must be someone who can put our case – *properly*,' the woman said. 'Someone with legal knowledge that we can trust absolutely. And someone with *influence*. You know how it is – the old-boy network and all that. It's *who* you know that's important . . .'

'There's my solicitor.'

There was a slight pause. 'No, Vittoria, my love,' Giorgio said softly. 'Not important enough. We need someone who can give the best advice. Someone like your friend.'

Victoria felt a small twinge of alarm. 'Who do you mean?'

'Your friend . . . Sir Henry. Now he would *really* know how to handle it.'

Victoria shook her head vehemently. 'Absolutely not. I couldn't possibly. He's been so kind. I couldn't *involve* him—'

'But you wouldn't be involving him,' the woman said in a soft persuasive tone. 'Just *asking* him. That's all. Surely he wouldn't mind giving a bit of advice. And it would make all the difference. Then at least we'd know we were going the right way about things. After all, we're talking about the rest of our lives. We don't want to make any mistakes.'

Victoria stared at her. Suddenly, for no particular reason, she noticed that the woman's hands were shaking.

She looked up at Giorgio. He squeezed her shoulder. 'Please, Vittoria. It would mean a lot. To you and me. And to Gabriele.'

Gabriele leant forward. 'If you just phone and ask if you can see him. We wouldn't come in at all. Just wait outside—'

'Go and *see* him?'

'Of course.'

Victoria felt weighed down with responsibility. Whatever she did would be wrong. She tried to put herself in Henry's place. Would he mind terribly? He was bound to be busy. The last thing he needed was to hear more about her troubles.

And yet – he was understanding, kind. And, as Gabriele had said, they *were* talking about the rest of their lives.

She sighed and heard herself say, 'All right, but – I must go and see him on my own. When he's got a moment. I don't want to *embarrass* him in any way at all.'

Gabriele's eyes flashed. 'Then it'd be best to see him at home, wouldn't it? Quietly. So no one will know.'

Victoria looked at her. Perhaps she'd misjudged her: she was obviously a considerate person. She breathed, 'Yes.'

In a burst of shaky optimism, Victoria thought: Everything'll be all right. It *had* to be.

'Oh yes, that's her all right.'

The car dealer stared at the photograph. His name was Bisley and he looked rather flash, befitting someone who dealt in the more expensive sort of car.

'Rather a sexy sort of number.'

'Yes?' asked Nick painfully.

'In a cool businesslike sort of way, that is. Knew exactly what she wanted. No mucking about.' He whistled through his teeth. 'Boy, did she take me for a ride!'

Nick thought: I know the feeling.

'And all that cash. Thought it was my lucky day.'

Nick gave him a knowing look. Doubtless none of it was destined to go through the books.

They walked towards the door. The rain was pouring down the showroom windows.

'It was a day just like this,' said Bisley. 'She rather brightened it up, I thought.' He shook his head. 'Boy, was I taken for a ride.'

Nick paused at the door. 'Anything more you can add to your statement?'

'To be quite honest, I can hardly remember what I told your colleagues at the time.'

Nick nodded. He hadn't expected anything else really. It was just another bit of the jigsaw that had to be checked. And Manchester was only a few miles on from Chester.

He said, 'Thanks,' and went into the downpour. He got into the car and shook his head at the others. They weren't surprised either.

Without a word, the sergeant started the car and headed for London.

PART FOUR

Twenty-two

Henry put down the phone and went thoughtfully into the hall.

'Jenkins?' he called.

A chair scraped in the kitchen and the Special Branch man appeared in the doorway. 'Sir?'

'I'm expecting a caller. At about seven. A Miss Danby.'

'Right, sir, I'll answer the door, shall I?'

'Oh, thank you. That'd be most kind. Lady Northcliff won't be back till eight or so.'

Henry returned to his study and closed the door. He sat at his desk and wondered what on earth it was that Victoria wanted this time. It was a bit unreasonable of her, asking to see him like this. Surely nothing could be so urgent that it couldn't wait until a more convenient moment. He felt a little resentful. Particularly since, from the sound of it, the problem was serious. Not that she'd said a great deal. But if she couldn't even go to her own solicitor . . . He dreaded to think.

A boyfriend in trouble? Drugs again? Some people were doomed to attract disaster, and she was obviously one of them. Yet in a way he was rather curious to find out what it was. During his many years at the Bar he had never failed to be both amazed and fascinated by the difficulties people managed to create for themselves.

In Victoria's case he must try to be charitable. She was still finding her way in life. It was all too easy for him to mix with successful confident people all the time, and to forget that, for many others like Victoria, life was treacherous and riddled with false turns.

Still, this couldn't go on. She really had to learn to manage on her own.

He would see her. But this, he firmly decided, would be the last time.

Detective Constable Jenkins returned to the kitchen. He wondered whether to make himself another cup of coffee but decided against it. He'd already had five cups that day and they said it did terrible things to your blood pressure. But then the problem was really his weight. He was rather fond of his food.

He sat down at the table and picked up the *Financial Times*. It wasn't something he normally read, but he'd already digested his own copy of the *Mirror* from cover to cover, and Lady Northcliff had kindly left the *FT* and some of the other more serious newspapers out for him in case he got bored. She was a very thoughtful lady. Charming and kind too. And obviously very happy in her marriage. Mind you, what a nice man *he* was. He was everything Jenkins thought an upholder of the law should be: fair-minded, extremely learned, and very hard-working. Jenkins was proud to have been assigned to him.

Not everyone liked this sort of job, of course. That's why one had to volunteer to join the Protection Group. Other coppers liked to be where the action was and were horrified at the thought of guarding one individual for months on end. But Jenkins rather liked it. He was fond of routine and familiar surroundings.

Not that the job was entirely cosy, of course. There *was* a heavy responsibility. This bombing business was terrible. Killing the Commissioner's *wife* – you wondered what the devils would think of next. Nothing like this had ever happened in Britain before. It was appalling to think that these terrorists could get away with it. Well, of course, they *hadn't*. One of them had been caught, and now the identity of a second was known. A woman. He'd seen a rough facsimile of her photograph that morning at the briefing. A woman. Whatever next? It had been the Swinging Sixties that had done it. All that permissive society bit. Moral back-sliding, if you asked him.

Later, when the squad car would be coming to pick him up at the end of his shift, he would have a chance to look at a better print. They were bound to have a batch of posters available by then. As soon as the posters were distributed this lunatic woman wouldn't have a chance. Every copper in the entire country would be on the lookout.

Jenkins settled down to read the *Financial Times*. After a while he felt a bit peckish and reached into his pocket for a Mars bar.

Unwrapping the bar he bit into it, and tasting the thick gooey toffee, immediately felt comforted.

Gabriele rammed the van into second gear and turned into the tree-lined street. Ahead, the tail lights of the Mini slowed a little and she guessed they were almost there.

Beside her Giorgio pulled the holdall up from the floor on to his knee.

The Mini's indicator flashed and the car turned across the road and parked by the opposite verge in front of a large detached house set some forty feet back from the road. A double driveway led up to the house. Gabriele noticed it was particularly well lit.

She drove past and parked in front of the neighbouring house where it was much darker.

Victoria was already walking towards them. Gabriele got out and said, 'We think it would be best if we came with you.'

'But you said . . . *Why*?'

'If he meets us, then he's much more likely to believe us.'

Victoria looked indecisive.

Gabriele waited impatiently. She was tired of nursing this girl along.

Trying to sound reasonable, she pressed, 'We could wait in the hall. While you talk to him. We just thought it would make a difference if he could meet us, just for a second.'

Victoria sighed heavily, 'Oh, dear, I don't know. I really don't. It seems a bit . . .' She suddenly shook her head in defeat. 'Oh, all *right*.'

Giorgio appeared from the other side of the van. Automatically Gabriele glanced down to make sure he was carrying the holdall.

The three of them walked up the driveway to the front door.

Victoria put her finger on the bell.

After a moment clipped footsteps approached across a hard floor. They halted by the door and there was a pause. Gabriele guessed someone was looking through the peephole. She looked away towards the road.

A lock was turned and the door opened.

A voice said, 'Miss Danby?'

'Yes.'

'Come in.' A plumpish young man in an ill-fitting grey suit stood in the doorway.

Gabriele exchanged glances with Giorgio. She had guessed there would be some sort of bodyguard.

They went into the house. The young man closed the door behind them. Gabriele took another look at him. His hair was short, cut in an almost military style. She decided he was definitely a policeman. They moved into the centre of the spacious hall. Giorgio came up beside Gabriele. Keeping her eyes on the policeman she slowly reached down into the holdall and ran her hand over the two Skorpions to be sure they were the right way round.

The policeman was saying, 'I expect Sir Henry will be out in a minute.'

At that moment a door opened and a man appeared.

Sir Henry Northcliff.

Gabriele felt a small surge of excitement.

Sir Henry looked surprised at finding so many people in the hall. With a tense smile, he said, 'Hello, Victoria,' and came forward to kiss her cheek. The policeman watched from a distance.

The moment had come.

Gabriele took a deep breath and reached into the bag. Then, out of the corner of her eye, she felt the policeman looking at her.

She froze, her hand in the bag.

He was staring at her.

Something was wrong.

Shit!

She smiled at him.

He stared back, a look of horror slowly growing on his face.

With a sudden shock, she thought: *He knows who I am*.

In a strange way it rather added to the excitement. She remained perfectly still, her hand in the bag, and smiled at him.

She saw him gulp and wet his lips. Then he began to move slowly towards her.

She felt Giorgio stiffen. His free hand came across his body and slid into the holdall. She felt him grasp the other weapon. The policeman didn't seem to notice: he was still advancing, staring at Gabriele. Victoria and Sir Henry were still talking.

Slowly and deliberately, Gabriele pulled out her gun.

She saw the policeman's eyes drop in astonishment.

Then she yelled, a loud piercing whoop, and jumped backwards to give herself room. Almost simultaneously Giorgio pulled out his Skorpion and shouted, 'Don't move!'

Gabriele went straight into a firing stance, slightly crouched, the machine pistol lodged firmly against her ribs, her thumb against the safety lever, to ensure it was set on automatic. She aimed straight at the policeman's stomach.

Giorgio had retreated until he was covering the other two.

For a split second there was a deathly silence, the five of them frozen in a strange tableau.

Then Gabriele saw the rich-bitch opening her mouth and shrieking, 'What are you *doing*! What are you *doing! Stop it!*'

Giorgio shouted, '*Shut up!*'

The screaming seemed to have snapped the policeman out of

his trance. He began to move forward again, his face twisted with anger and fear.

Gabriele hissed, '*Don't!*'

The policeman said in a low voice, 'Drop that weapon!'

Gabriele clutched the Skorpion more tightly. The policeman hesitated for a moment, looking at the gun, then, making up his mind, stepped deliberately forward and reached out for it.

Gabriele felt the familiar panic surge up in her. She cried out: '*No!*'

He kept coming.

She squeezed the trigger.

It was just the same as in training: the strong feel of the gun in her hands, the juddering as the bullets left the silenced barrel, the soft *thwack! thwack*! as they hit their target. Except it wasn't a dummy now, it was a person.

The policeman staggered backwards, a look of amazement on his face, his hands clutching his stomach.

Then he fell slowly on to one knee, one hand on the floor, the other on his stomach. Blood spurted out all over the place.

Gabriele thought bitterly: That'll teach you.

The girl screamed, an ear-piercing screech that filled the room. She seemed to be able to scream for a long time without drawing breath.

The sound was getting on Gabriele's nerves. She strode up to the girl and thrust the pistol into her belly. The girl stopped in mid-scream.

'Shut up.'

The girl gaped.

Beside her the Attorney-General was very still and very white.

He understood perfectly.

There was a gurgling sound. It was the policeman dying. Gabriele glanced at him and, for a fleeting moment, felt a twinge of doubt. Then she remembered that she'd *had* to do it. She was a trained fighter, and the man had been attacking her. It was no different from a soldier defending himself against the enemy. Soldiers killed all the time.

Now they must hurry. She nodded to Giorgio. He reached into the fallen holdall and took out a roll of strong electrical tape. Putting the Skorpion down, he pulled Sir Henry's arms roughly behind his back and bound them together. He put another strip across his mouth.

Apart from briefly closing his eyes the man showed no emotion.

The girl, on the other hand, was a disaster.

She was gaping, her eyes starting from her head, and wailing loudly. Giorgio looked at Gabriele questioningly. She thought quickly, and said, 'No, bring her.'

Giorgio took hold of the girl's wrists and pulled them behind her back. Immediately she became hysterical.

Gabriele began to regret her decision; this girl was being a pain. Gabriele stepped forward and hit her hard on the side of the head with her hand.

The girl yelped and started sobbing more quietly. Gabriele said, 'Next time I'll use the gun.'

Giorgio grasped hold of the girl's chin and stuck a large piece of tape over her mouth. There was silence at last.

Gabriele went to the door and looked through the peephole. The driveway was clear. She tested the light switches beside the door. One worked the light in the hall, the other the outside lights.

She paused to think. She mustn't forget a single detail.

Going up to the Attorney-General she demanded, 'Is there anyone else in the house?'

He shook his head.

'Your wife's out?'

He nodded.

What else? The girl's shoulder bag. She picked it up and searched through until she found the keys to the Mini. She put the bag over her shoulder.

She had one last thought. She went up to the dead policeman. He was lying on his side in a pool of blood. She pulled open his jacket and searched the pocket. No radio transmitter that she could see. There was, however, a small notebook. She pulled it out and examined it. It was a sort of log. There were entries for each day, saying where the attorney-man had been, and, when at home, what visitors had called.

She looked at the last entry. It was for six-thirty when the attorney-man had arrived home. There was no mention of Victoria Danby.

She dropped the notebook on the floor.

She looked at Giorgio to see if he was ready. He nodded.

While he hustled the prisoners up to the door, she turned off all the lights and took a last look through the peephole.

The road was visible in the faint street lighting.

A car passed. Then nothing.

Opening the door, she listened and, satisfied, stepped back to let the others pass. She closed the door and ran on ahead to make sure there was no one coming along the road.

Behind her there was a slight sound. The stupid girl had stumbled and fallen, but Giorgio was dragging her back to her feet. Gabriele waved them forward to the van and, opening the doors, helped Giorgio to push the girl and the Attorney-General inside.

She ran to the Mini and got it started. As soon as the van moved off she followed. No car passed. No person walked the quiet road.

They had got away unseen.

Caroline Northcliff was tired, and sitting in a traffic jam didn't help. It was solid all the way from Westminster to Regent's Park, and by the time she got on to the Finchley Road the journey had already taken half an hour longer than usual. She couldn't imagine why: it was well past rush hour.

One way and another it had been a trying day. Normally she rather enjoyed going to do's at the House. On this occasion it had been a cocktail party given by the Parliamentary Wives Against Persecution. She'd had to go because she was on the committee. But she'd been feeling distinctly under the weather, and the noise and inevitably intense political conversations had been rather a strain.

Also, these occasions were meant to coincide with evenings when the House was sitting, so that the wives might dine with their husbands afterwards. But Henry had spent all day at his chambers and had then gone straight home to do some urgent work, so he'd not been able to come to the party. Somehow Caroline always felt incomplete and a little lonely when he wasn't around.

And now she was having to deal with all this beastly traffic.

Finally as she approached Hampstead the traffic thinned, and she realised she would be home very soon. What a relief. It was quarter to eight. With a bit of luck Henry would have finished his work, and they could enjoy a quiet evening. She wondered what to make for supper. Something light. There was some cold meat in the fridge, she remembered, and she could throw together a quick salad.

And then she usually offered the officer on duty a snack of some sort. She always felt sorry for the young men who were sent to guard them. It was such a rotten job, having to hang around all the time, knowing you were in the way, yet trying to be as unobtrusive as possible. Today Jenkins was on duty, and he never turned any food down. She smiled to herself.

She turned into the road and felt the tension of the day begin to ease. It was good to be home.

The road ahead seemed strangely dark. She couldn't work it out. Then she realised it was the area in front of her own house which was unlit. Yet she had carefully switched on the lights before going out. Had there been a power cut? No . . . there were lights in all the other houses. Perhaps the house lights had fused. Yet it was unlike Henry not to have fixed them.

She drove straight into the open garage and turned off the engine. As she got out it occurred to her that Henry might have been delayed at work and might not be home after all.

She closed the garage door and looked down the side of the house. The study light was on. Henry *must* be here then. How strange.

In the darkness it took her a moment to fit the key into the front door, but then the lock turned and she was in. She called, 'Hello?'

Light came from the open doors of both the kitchen and the study. She put a hand to the light switch and turned on the outside light. It worked perfectly. Then she tried the hall light.

For a second the light dazzled her.

Then she saw an object on the floor.

A person.

Jenkins.

For a moment she couldn't take it in. There was no reality to the blood, the ghastly open mouth, the silence of death.

Then she had a single appalling thought: *Henry!*

She stumbled to the study door and, terrified of what she might find, looked in. Then she ran across to the kitchen. When she had searched all the ground floor rooms, she ran upstairs.

Nothing.

She called out, 'Henry!' But the silence was final: there would be no answer.

Finally she sank on to the bed and, trying to control her shaking hands, called the police.

Victoria thought: Let me die.

It would be better for everyone.

I'm vermin, I'm evil, I'm sick, I'm hateful, I'm a pathetic *murderess* . . .

There was no limit to her evil.

It was her fault the policeman had been killed, her fault Henry had been captured, her fault that Caroline would be crucified with unhappiness.

It would be better for everyone if she were to die.

The van went over a bump. Her head banged against the floor.

Good. She wanted to suffer. Let there be pain.

She cried again until the tears dried up.

Something nudged her leg. *Henry.* Trying to make contact with her. She was lying on the floor, facing away from him. She was glad. She couldn't possibly look him in the eye. She was glad, too, that the tape was over their mouths so they couldn't speak. The nudge came again. Hurriedly she moved her leg away. She couldn't bear it. He was trying to establish communication. But he wouldn't want to have any contact with her once he knew the truth.

She wanted to cry again, but couldn't. She was too disgusted with herself.

Much later, after the van had been going for a long time, a sound made her open her eyes. Someone was singing.

Giorgio.

She imagined him, sitting in the driver's seat, the same person who had touched her, made love to her . . . She had never *tried* to see him as he really was. She had been far too selfish.

Selfish, self-centred, *hateful.*

At one point the van stopped and there was a flood of light. The front door opened and shut again. There were the unmistakable sounds of petrol being put into the tank. Then they were off again, the van droning on endlessly.

She wondered vaguely where they were going. But what did it matter. It changed nothing.

She just wanted to die.

After a long time the van started twisting and turning and Victoria was thrown against the side of the seat, then back against Henry. Instantly she recoiled and tried to jam herself against the seat. A few minutes later there was a great lurch, then a bump and the back of the van did a violent leap. Victoria's head crashed into the floor. Another lurch and bump. The violent movements continued until Victoria was forced to hold her head clear of the floor.

The engine note changed to a lower pitch and they seemed to be going down a hill. There were several more lurches and the van climbed. Suddenly it ground to a halt.

The engine was turned off. The silence was abrupt and complete.

Then it was broken by a familiar sound: the distinctive high-pitched whine of the Mini. This came nearer, then stopped.

Doors were opened and closed. There were voices.

The rear doors of the van were unlatched and swung open with a loud squeak.

She felt Henry being pulled out from beside her. Then a hand grabbed her foot and pulled her roughly across the floor. She was twisted over on to her face so that, when she was half out, her feet fell to the ground.

'Stand up!' It was the woman's voice.

A hard object stabbed at her back, then a hand took her shoulder and pulled her upright.

Reluctantly she made the effort to stand.

Suddenly she tensed.

It was the sounds she recognised first: the murmuring of branches, the rustling of dead leaves, the crunch of the gravel underfoot. The unmistakable scent of damp fertile earth hung on the air.

She jerked her head up.

The shape of the farmhouse loomed black against the night, silhouetted against the pale light of a million stars.

Twenty-three

The road was jammed with parked cars. Nick drove past the brightly lit house and found a space further along. As he walked back an ambulance pulled out of the driveway and came towards him. The driver was in no hurry; they never were when it was a body.

Nick watched it pass and thought: Poor bastard.

At the entrance to the driveway a group of uniformed men were standing guard. As Nick approached, a TV crew came screaming up in a van and wound down their window. The sergeant in charge shook his head firmly. 'Complete embargo on this one, lads. Off you go.'

The newsmen nodded as if a story had been too much to hope for anyway, and drove off.

Nick showed his warrant card and walked up to the house.

He showed it again at the door and went in. The spacious hall was buzzing with men, standing in groups talking or walking desultorily around the sides. No one went near the centre of the room. Here an enormous patch of dried blood sat obscenely on the beautifully polished floor and, to one side of it, an outline of a body had been drawn in chalk.

Nick dragged his eyes away and looked around for one of Kershaw's team. A door opened and a group of men came out of an adjoining room. The first was Straughan, the second the head of Special Branch, Deputy Assistant Commissioner Norris, the third Kershaw, and then some very senior men indeed: the Assistant Commissioner Crime, and finally the Commissioner himself, Sir Peter McCabe. The Commissioner looked very grim. It was hardly surprising: he had buried his wife that afternoon.

Nick was overwhelmed by a sense of despair. He already felt a crushing guilt. This bloody mess got worse and worse. And all because he'd *never checked on her*. Even now he could hardly believe his own stupidity. The blow to his personal pride was bad enough; the way he'd been taken in by her. But pride didn't actually matter. What mattered was his professional failure – and that was unforgivable.

He leaned back against a wall and waited unhappily for the crowd of senior officers to break up so he could talk to Kershaw.

But Straughan spotted him first and glared. After a few minutes the DCS left the group and came over.

'Well, Ryder, what an almighty cock-up this is.'

'Sir.'

'I gather you not only *knew* this Wilson woman, but saw her as recently as *Sunday*. She must have been making bombs under your very nose!'

Nick winced. Salt in the wound. He said unhappily, 'She was a contact, sir – I mean, I *thought* she was.'

'*Thought* she was. Jesus Christ, Ryder, she'd already blown up the Commissioner's wife and injured two other people – and you thought she was a *contact*.' He put his face closer and hissed,

'You're off this job and I don't want to see your face around until I call for you. Understand?' The DSC was shaking with rage. Nick kept silent. It wasn't the moment to argue.

But Straughan hadn't finished. He pointed to the room he and the senior officers had just emerged from. 'Lady Northcliff is in there. Waiting, hoping to hear that her husband is going to be allowed to live. Shall I tell you something? I found it difficult to face her, knowing I had such a blindingly incompetent – *idiot* – on my staff. I found it –'

He broke off as someone cleared his throat. It was Commander Kershaw. He said to Straughan, 'May I have a word?'

Nick moved out of earshot and waited. The two men talked for several minutes then, with a last backward glance of disgust aimed in his direction, Straughan walked off. Kershaw came over.

He said quietly, 'I've said I want to keep you on my team, Ryder.'

'Thank you, sir.'

'It's simply that we've got to find these people.'

Nick nodded. He hadn't thought Kershaw was doing it out of the kindness of his heart.

Kershaw rubbed his eyes. 'It *is* the same bastards, isn't it, Ryder?'

Nick had never heard this soft-spoken man use even the mildest swear word before. He said, 'Yes. It must be.'

'What's going to happen next, then? Presumably there'll be some kind of demand. But what will they want? Money?'

Instinctively, Nick answered, 'No.' He thought of Gabriella and her half-baked philosophies and the intensity with which she believed them. 'Well, not *just* money. They'll want *more*. I think they'll want to humiliate us as much as possible. Publicly.' Nick voiced an idea he'd had when he'd first heard about the kidnapping. 'And I think they'll want their friends back.'

'Wheatfield?'

'And Reardon. And perhaps the woman, Stephanie Kitson, too.'

Kershaw nodded. 'Anything else, I wonder. What about getting out of the country? They can hardly expect to move around freely after all this.'

'I don't know ...' Nick ventured. 'They've got excellent backup. The Wilson woman had an Italian passport, didn't she?' The agent who'd let Nick the mews house had been positive that she'd shown him an Italian passport in the name of Carelli. 'If they've got one false passport, they've probably got several.'

'But we've got her photograph.'

'We also know she uses disguises.'

'The woman at the delivery firm,' he agreed reluctantly.

Suddenly Kershaw closed the subject. 'Well, all this is conjecture. Let's get back to the office and plan the campaign. By the way' – he paused awkwardly – 'the ACC is taking personal charge of the case. So when we get back it might be wise for you to – er – stay upstairs in your own office. I'll call you when I need you.'

Kershaw turned to go but hesitated. 'I told your boss that I wanted you because you were the only person who understood these madmen. I also said you were a good officer. We all make mistakes at one time or another, Ryder. It's just a pity . . .'

Nick almost finished it for him: a pity that your mistake was so appalling. Nick said quickly, 'Thank you, sir. I appreciate it.'

Kershaw hurried off. Nick stared after him, both cheered and depressed by his words. A good officer . . . Just a pity . . . God, he didn't know whether to laugh or cry.

The least he could do for Kershaw was to give him maximum support. And at this precise moment that meant keeping a low profile.

He walked back towards the door and stopped for a moment to take another look at the brown stain on the floor.

He thought: Here an innocent man died. And I won't ever forget.

He turned to go, then noticed another chalk mark on the floor beside the outline of the body. One of Kershaw's team was standing nearby. Indicating the mark, Nick asked, 'What was that?'

'Jenkins' pocket book.'

'Was there any entry in it?'

The officer shook his head. 'Nothing after six-thirty.'

Nick thought for a moment and said, half to himself, 'I wonder why it fell on the floor?'

The officer shrugged. 'Search me.'

'*Could* it have fallen out of his pocket?'

There was no answer. The officer was giving him a cold look. Nick thought: Ah, I'm overstepping the mark – trespassing on detectives' territory. Then he realised that this alone wouldn't account for the cool attitude.

293

Of course: everyone knew. Everyone knew that it was Ryder who had ballsed it up.

Dropping his eyes, he nodded his thanks and left.

He didn't care what they thought. All he cared about was getting that woman.

It was eleven. He would go back to the office and work. All night if necessary. He would work until he found something.

Victoria jumped out of an uneasy doze. She was immediately aware of the cold, which had slowly penetrated her body and chilled her into a state of half-sleep from which it was difficult to wake. The earth floor was hard and rough against her cheek. She moved slightly and felt the tape that bound her wrists chafe her skin.

She opened her eyes. A faint grey light was filtering in from the main cellar, giving shadowy outline to the deep recesses of the brick chamber. She and Henry were in a second, smaller cellar, which consisted of two arches supported by wide pillars. The thin grey light emanated from a ventilation brick high up in the wall of the main cellar. Somewhere outside, it was day.

A loud noise: a door opening. Through the archway she saw a block of light. A figure stood silhouètted in the open doorway at the top of the cellar steps.

Giorgio.

Her first instinct was to curl up tighter and make the whole scene go away. But the next moment a bright electric light sprang on and footsteps sounded on the stone stairs. Screwing up her eyes against the glare, she saw Giorgio walking straight towards her. He bent over and reached for her face. She jerked her head away but he grasped the tape covering her mouth and yanked it off. She bit back a cry. He moved off towards the other corner where Henry lay. She made an effort to sit up. She rolled over on to her back and used her elbows to manoeuvre herself upright. Her over-full bladder ached for relief.

There was the sound of tape being ripped away. Victoria forced herself to look at Henry. He sat propped against the wall six feet away. He was blinking rapidly, his eyes smarting from the removal of the tape. His clothes were dishevelled, his hair awry, his face smeared with dirt. He seemed older and somehow smaller.

Suddenly he looked across at Victoria and narrowed his eyes in an unspoken gesture of mutual support.

Victoria's stomach lurched and she looked away.

294

Giorgio stood back and said to them both, 'The mouth tapes – they go on again if you make any noise.'

Victoria stared at him. She realised without surprise that he was *exactly* the same as before. He hadn't changed a bit. The only difference was in herself: she was seeing him for what he was.

Giorgio repeated, 'No noise. Understand?' He walked back into the main cellar, heading for the steps. He was going to leave them again. In the dark and cold.

Finding her courage, Victoria said, 'Please!' Her voice came out as a high-pitched whine. She controlled it. 'We need water. Please let us have water. And some blankets. And a lavatory.'

Giorgio paused deliberately on the first step and swung slowly round. He said heavily, 'I said no noise.'

She hesitated. '*Please*. Water. And a bucket. Something . . .'

He turned and walked deliberately up the stairs. Through the archway she saw him pause with his hand on the light switch.

She called out, 'And leave the light on. *Please*.'

He made a face of annoyance and, turning abruptly, went out and closed the door. The light was still on.

There was a long silence.

Eventually Henry said, 'Well done. We've got some light at least.' His voice sounded strangely matter-of-fact. He was trying to reassure her.

Victoria couldn't meet his eyes. 'I . . . I don't know what to say to you. It's all my fault. The whole thing. I . . .' She swallowed hard and forced herself to go on: she couldn't bear him to think that she was innocent. 'I – thought they were – *we* were – in trouble. They persuaded me to come and see you. I – had no idea that – they had guns or anything. I – was a complete fool. I—'

'Please stop.' The voice was firm and final.

'I just can't bear to think of what I've done to you.'

Henry said tensely. 'There's just no point in wasting energy on – talking.' He added less sternly, 'We may be here for a long time. We must – husband our resources. We must concentrate on dealing with these people in the only way they understand, which is to be businesslike. I suggest we speak only when we are spoken to, and without aggravating them in any way. We must be co-operative, but without earning their contempt. If we do have to make requests, we should make them politely and firmly. Then – at least we will have done all we can.'

He was right, of course. She could see that. He was being

everything she was not: cool and rational and dignified. He was refusing to be defeated by these people, and raising himself above their ghastliness. The least she could do was to support him. She thought: I mustn't let him down.

'Yes,' she said quietly, 'I agree.'

After a while he asked, 'Any idea where we are?'

She braced herself to speak the words. 'Yes. At – my farm.'

He looked at her sharply. 'Then – someone will find us, surely. Someone will call in, won't they?'

'Only people hoping to buy the place . . . But there haven't been many, so the agent said . . .' She trailed off.

'But people will realise you're missing. So they're *bound* to come here.' There was a note of optimism to his voice.

Victoria shook her head slowly. 'I'm afraid not . . . I don't think anyone will miss me.' She thought: What a thing to be able to say.

'But –' He broke off. Finally he said in quiet resignation, 'I was thinking that, once they realised you'd come to my house, they would work it out from there.'

'Yes?'

'But no one knew. Except Jenkins.'

There was a heavy pause and they did not speak for a long time.

Victoria thought about her life and how different it would be in the future. If she ever got out of this she would be utterly changed. Unselfish and caring. She would spend her life serving other people. She would never be the same again. Never.

The cellar door opened.

The woman came down the steps. A gun was slung over her shoulder, the gun she had used before.

She peered at them, then disappeared, leaving the door open. When she reappeared she was walking backwards, carrying something large and heavy. It was a long wooden box with handles. Giorgio was carrying the other end.

Victoria blinked. She recognised the box: it belonged to the tractor. It contained all the spare parts – the couplings, the tools, the wheel braces. But *why* were they bringing it down here?

They moved with a relentless purpose that filled her with foreboding.

They brought the box into the brick chamber and dumped it on the floor. The woman opened the lid. Victoria saw that the hinged lid had been sawn into two sections, and the interior partitions removed.

Giorgio went up to Henry and pulled him to his feet. Reaching behind, he cut the tapes from Henry's wrists. Henry stretched his arms and let out a long gasp of relief and pain.

The woman stood back a little way. She had the gun at her hip, aimed at Henry.

Victoria watched, stiff with dread.

The woman said, 'Get in.'

There was a ghastly silence. No one moved.

'Get in!'

Victoria stared in horror. She meant into the *box*.

Henry drew a long and deep breath. He looked very white. He took a step forward and stared at the box. He whispered, 'I don't think I'll fit.'

'*Get in!*'

Henry swayed slightly, then leant down to take off his shoes.

Victoria said, 'No!'

The woman turned the barrel of the gun on her. 'Shut ... up ...'

Henry stood at the side of the box, staring down into it, disbelief on his face. He looked up at the woman questioningly.

She hissed, 'This is the last time. *Get in!*'

Slowly he climbed in and attempted to lie down. The box was too short by at least a foot and he could not straighten his knees. The woman stepped forward and, pushing his knees over to one side, forced the main section of the hinged lid shut. The smaller lid section was left open, so that only Henry's face remained visible.

The woman said, 'That'll do.'

She went back up the steps and disappeared. Giorgio stood back, apparently waiting for the woman to return.

Victoria climbed to her feet and staggered over to him. 'You can't do this! It's appalling and cruel! You can't do it!'

He regarded her calmly. 'Why not? Tell me.'

'Because – it's *inhuman*.'

He shrugged. 'The whole world is inhuman. Especially humans. They are the worst of all. Didn't you realise that?'

'But *he's* not inhuman. He's – a *good* man!'

He was contemptuous. 'You don't know *anything*. You're a spoilt child, Victoria. You're rich and stupid. Yet people like you rule the world. Why should that be? It must be wrong. And you tell me that *I* am inhuman.' He shook his head. 'You try being poor and having nothing, Vittoria, and being shut up in jail by people like *him*!' He shot a glance at Henry. 'Your little world would not be so happy.' He spoke with exasperation and contempt.

She whispered bitterly, 'You're *sick*! You should be *put down*! You—'

The cellar door opened. The woman was returning.

Giorgio said under his breath. 'Get away or she'll kill you.'

Victoria knew it was true. She retreated into the main cellar and shrank back against the wall.

The woman ran down the steps, carrying a holdall. She glared at Victoria, and went past her into the small cellar. She barked at Giorgio, 'Keep the gun on him. In case he moves.' Giorgio aimed it at Henry's head.

Then the woman set to work. Victoria watched through the archway. At first she couldn't understand what the woman was doing. Then Gabriele reached into the holdall and Victoria caught sight of the contents, and felt very sick.

The sticks. The explosives that had been hidden in the van.

Victoria cried softly, 'Oh no . . . Oh no . . .'

The woman worked inexorably on. She taped a bundle of the explosives together and placed them on Henry's chest.

Victoria moved forward. 'Let it be *me*. Please,' she begged. 'Let it be *me* instead. Oh *please*. Let him go. Oh *please*.'

The woman bent down to replace something carefully on the ground. Then she whirled round. The first thing Victoria saw was the gun butt coming through the air, then there was an explosion in her head and she was falling rapidly backwards.

She fell heavily and for a moment lay stunned. She regained her breath and slowly, painfully, pulled herself upright. The woman was working on. She was strapping the explosives to Henry's body. Then she sat down on the floor and remained bent over some intricate task for a long time. Finally she knelt over Henry and, moving very carefully, appeared to complete her work. She gestured to Giorgio to close the lid of the box very slowly. Just before it closed, she peered under it and nodded.

Giorgio put down his gun and, taking some nails and a hammer from the holdall, nailed down the lid of the box. Finally the woman bent down beside the box and pulled at something.

The woman stood up, a length of thread in her hand. She looked rather pleased with the job. She said, 'Right. This thing is booby-trapped. If anyone tries to open it, it'll go sky high. I'm the only one who knows how to defuse it. Understand?'

Then she bent over Henry's face and whispered, 'How does it feel, attorney-man? How does it feel to be locked up like all those kids in prison? Like being in a coffin, isn't it? Soon you'll be lying in your own dirt, in your own coffin. *Then you'll know.*'

Victoria thought: *This is a nightmare.*

The woman tidied away her tools. She was very neat.

Giorgio came towards Victoria. He had a knife in his hand. Victoria held her breath. He reached behind her. The next moment her hands were free. He said, 'You are to keep him alive. I'll bring water and food later.'

Then he and the woman were leaving, climbing the stairs, switching off the light, closing the door.

Victoria crawled slowly back into the small cellar, feeling for the box with her hands in case she should bump into it. Finally she came to it. Kneeling close beside it, she put her head near to Henry's and cried softly, 'Henry . . .'

She paused. There *were* no words. She breathed, 'Oh, Henry, I'm so – desperately – sorry.'

There was no reply.

She began to cry silently. 'If there's anything I can do – I will. I *will.*'

Finally, after a long while, there came a whisper.

'Leave me alone. Leave me – alone.'

Gabriele zipped up the holdall and put it in the kitchen. She glanced at her watch. Eleven. Time was getting on. In Paris it was already twelve.

She took the slip of paper out of her handbag and, going to the phone that stood on the window-sill in the hall, she dialled the number of the dingy offices in the Latin Quarter. She'd already called the number once that morning, but much earlier.

It answered.

'Raymond? Any news?'

'Far, far too soon,' came the reply. 'It will take me many more hours. It is not something that can be arranged quickly.'

'I thought there would be no problem—'

'I am sure there will not, but it is still something that cannot be rushed.'

'When shall I call back?'

'Tonight.'

Gabriele hung up. She hated the uncertainty. She wanted all the arrangements to be made and her retreat secure. But she would have to press on.

She took a sheet of paper from her handbag and unfolded it. Earlier she had spent some time composing a communiqué. She had rewritten it several times until she was satisfied. However she had been forced to leave a blank after the words 'Guarantee free passage to'. Now, reluctantly, she wrote in: 'the country of our choice.'

Then, on the stroke of twelve, she lifted the telephone and dialled a number in London.

Nick's mind felt like a thick soup. It was twelve noon. He'd been at it since midnight and had come up with precisely nothing.

He'd begun with listing everything he could remember about Gabriella. Everything she'd said or done. Everything she'd worn, down to her jewellery, which was one gold chain around her neck. Details of her life history, year by year. Conway and two other Branch men had helped there; they'd been on the task all the previous day, finding out about the missing years between university and the present time. At first there'd been several large gaps in her history, but one by one they had been accounted for. She'd been issued with a permit for a stall at Camden market and had sold second-hand books there; she'd worked briefly at a small publishing company; she'd been involved in a housing action group; she'd spoken at minor anti-Vietnam meetings, she'd applied for unemployment benefit. Gradually the picture had built up.

There was only one large gap remaining, and that was for the time between her escape from the hospital in Paris and her reappearance in London as Gabriella Carelli. The gap was sixteen months. Where had she been in that time? There was no clue.

The French couldn't help. They had no trace of her in the chaos after the student uprising. The Italians? They had never heard of her. The British Intelligence Service, MI6, could offer no suggestions.

It was a mystery.

But wherever she had been, she had learnt to make bombs and kill people.

Next Nick turned to Black Beard.

Wheatfield's friend – and Gabriella's lover?

He had to be. Who else had the clothes in the mews house

300

wardrobe belonged to? And the masculine toiletries in the bathroom?

It was another realisation that made Nick sick with remorse. Black Beard had been close by all the time. A simple check, a surveillance, would almost certainly have led straight to him.

The immigration files had been combed for any likely Italians who fitted Black Beard's description, but thousands and thousands of Italians visited Britain every year. It was like looking for a needle in a haystack.

The Italian authorities had promised to look at their own lists of undesirables to see if they had any who fitted the sketchy description Nick had sent them, but it was pretty hopeless. The situation in Italy was what one might call confused. The authorities didn't really know the nature – let alone the names – of the new left-wingers they were up against.

So much for Black Beard.

Then there were Wheatfield and Reardon. Both had their lips sealed as tight as clams. Barring torture – which was unfortunately banned under the British system – there was no way of getting them to talk.

Dead end. Nothing.

And now his mind was like soup: turgid and thick and utterly useless.

He thought: Damn and hell!

At twelve-twenty a call came up from the incident room.

It was Kershaw. The ultimatum had arrived.

As Nick sprinted downstairs he reflected on Kershaw's choice of word. Ultimatum. He shivered: it didn't bode well.

The message had been phoned to *The Times* fifteen minutes before. It read:

You can dream up all the law and order you like, but you shall be subject to our justice. The attorney-man has been sentenced to death for gross crimes against the people. However, if our terms are met we shall consider leniency. Free Max Wheatfield, Paul Reardon and Stephanie Kitson. Guarantee us free passage to the country of our choice. You have until noon tomorrow or he dies. There will be no negotiation. Print your acceptance in *The Times* tomorrow. We will then contact you. Remember – twenty-four hours and he is dead. It is the people's justice. Signed: The Crystal Faction.

301

Kershaw went straight off for a top level conference in the Commissioner's office, leaving Nick, Conway and a group of detectives in the incident room. Everyone read the ultimatum several times. Conway murmured, 'We'll give in. We have no choice.'

Nick hoped not, but he could see the attraction for the government. Sir Henry would be returned alive and the terrorists would be out of the country. The only sensible solution ... But *humiliating*. It was total surrender. He thought of the way Gabriella and her friends would laugh. The way they'd be encouraged to do it all over again somewhere else.

Nick rubbed his hand over his face. He was too tired to think any more. He'd had two nights without sleep. He wasn't going to be any use to anyone in his present state. He stood up wearily and said to Conway, 'I've got to go and get some kip. If anyone wants me I'll be back in a few hours.'

On his way out he stared at the story board Kershaw's team had drawn up. On a large sheet of paper that spanned almost an entire wall they had written the sum total of their knowledge, along with various suppositions and possibilities. Thus Linda Wilson's name was prominent in black on the left-hand side, while the words *Soviet-backed? Self-motivated? Allied to foreign group?* were written in blue just underneath.

In the centre was a series of questions with answers, such as: *Why the Attorney-General? Because senior law officer. Motive for kidnap? Ransom or political demands (assumed).*

On the right-hand side there was a scenario: Doorbell rings, Jenkins/Sir Henry opens door, three shots fired, Jenkins falls, hall and outside lights extinguished, Sir Henry abducted. Then there were various unknowns: vehicles used by abductors, route taken, destination.

God, if they knew the *destination*.

Then there were a list of facts: the approximate time the crimes took place, the ballistics details, the wounds suffered by D. C. Jenkins, the location of the pocket book. At the bottom someone had added: *N.B. Blood on underneath of Jenkins' pocket book.*

Nick stared, trying to comprehend the meaning of the cryptic note.

Under? Then the book had been placed on the floor *after* the blood had spread.

What else did it mean? He tried to progress the idea, but his mind wouldn't function. He gave up.

He went back to his office to pick up his coat and took the lift down to the street. It was a blustery day, with heavy black clouds scudding across the sky. London looked very grey.

He walked to the nearest bus stop, intending to take a number 10 over the river. There was a long queue at the stop and no buses in sight. He stood in line and wondered if it wouldn't be better to walk.

Funnelled between the tall buildings the wind came roaring down the street in great gusts. People clutched at their coats. A man left the queue to shelter in a shop doorway. He reached into his breast pocket and pulled out a small map, which he examined and then replaced in his pocket.

Nick stared at him.

Jenkins would have kept his book in his breast pocket. Could it have slipped out after he had fallen bleeding to the floor? Unlikely. In which case someone must have taken it out of his breast pocket and placed it on the floor afterwards.

But *why*?

A half-formed idea flew into Nick's mind, and he grasped at it furiously. Maddeningly, it evaded him and in a desperate attempt to recapture it, he went through each thought one by one.

Why would they want to look at the book? To see what it had in it. So what would it have in it?

Information. Sir Henry's movements that day.

It didn't make sense. Why would they want to know that? Curiosity. *No*. They were in a hurry, they didn't have time to be curious . . .

Come on. *Come on*.

A bus drew up noisily and the queue moved forward. Nick remained still, staring into space. People overtook him and clambered on to the bus.

Then he had it.

The idea came winging back into his mind and he cornered it.

They'd left the book *behind*. So everything had all been all *right*. They'd checked the book. They had checked the book to make sure there was nothing in it.

Therefore it was what *wasn't* there that was important.

Since coming on duty Jenkins had kept a record of Sir Henry's movements, or had appeared to. Except for . . .

The last appointment.

Nick turned and ran back to the office.

As he went up in the lift, another thought fell into place, like a piece in a jigsaw.

Jenkins *must* have opened the door. He would never have stood on one side and let Sir Henry do it. What was more, *Jenkins had opened the door and let the people all the way into the centre of the hall.*

He wouldn't have done that if they had been strangers. He would have challenged them on the doorstep.

Nick pounded into Kershaw's office, but the commander was still in his meeting. Nick spotted Conway sitting in the incident room drinking a cup of coffee, and beckoned him over. Conway caught the mood immediately and hastily followed him into Kershaw's office. Nick scribbled a note and left it on Kershaw's desk.

'What's up?' asked Conway.

'We're going to see Lady Northcliff.'

The room looked over the garden. She sat on the window seat, looking tired and pale in the grey light. Nick hadn't realised how young she would be.

'I'm very sorry to bother you,' Nick began, aware of the disapproving gaze of the other occupants of the room: a chief inspector from Special Branch Protection Group, a senior member of the Attorney-General's staff, and a woman of about Lady Northcliff's age, presumably a friend.

'No, please – I *want* to help,' Lady Northcliff said immediately. 'I'm glad ... I don't care how many questions you ask me.' She shrugged apologetically. 'If I looked disappointed it was only because I thought it might be news. When I heard the doorbell.'

Nick was silent. He hadn't told her about the ultimatum. That was someone else's job – someone very senior – and, on an entirely practical level, he didn't want her distracted with worry until he'd had a chance to put his questions.

'Lady Northcliff, what I'm about to ask may seem rather strange . . .'

The chief inspector looked even more threatening. The only reason Nick had got in for the interview was by saying Kershaw had sent him.

'The thing is, are you or your husband acquainted with anyone with extreme political views? I mean, even *slightly* acquainted?'

You could have heard a pin drop. Everyone in the room looked vaguely horrified. Lady Northcliff frowned in concentration. 'It's so difficult to say,' she began. 'We meet so *many* people. At receptions and so on. It's very hard to know exactly what their views are. I mean quite a few members of the Labour Party used to be well, *more* left-wing than they are now.'

'Yes, of course.' Nick paused and wondered quite how to phrase the next question. 'What about people you know well enough to see here, in your house?'

There was an awkward silence.

She gulped slightly. 'Oh, you mean . . .' Nick could almost see her thought processes working their way to the inevitable conclusion. 'You mean – the people – last night – might have been known to us.'

The chief inspector frowned at Nick and narrowed his lips.

Nick ignored him. 'Yes, don't misunderstand me. I'm not suggesting that one of your closest friends is involved. I'm just asking if – by any chance – someone's name was used to gain access to the house. Or an appointment was made. Or . . .'

She nodded. 'No, you don't have to explain . . . I understand.' She put a hand over her eyes and thought for a long time. Finally she shook her head and sighed deeply. 'No. I'm sorry—'

'What about left-wing journalists?'

'Well, journalists *sometimes* come here. And it depends what you mean by left-wing . . . Besides, they always make appointments a long time ahead. And Henry wouldn't see one here during a weekday evening. He just wouldn't. Not without telling me.'

'Someone else then? One of these new activists. You know, the sort that go on anti-Vietnam marches?'

'Well, I met that actress once. You know, the one who's always making speeches . . .' She trailed off. It wasn't the sort of information Nick wanted and she knew it.

Nick tried one last stab. 'What about an acquaintance, a friend, the son or daughter of a friend. Anyone who's involved in fringe politics, or pressure groups, or anti-war campaigns. *Anything*.'

A shadow of a smile crossed her face. 'Oh, well, there's dear old Victoria of course.'

Nick waited.

Lady Northcliff suddenly realised he wanted to hear more and continued, 'She's a sort of cousin of mine, and – she dabbles in anti-Vietnam things. But very half-heartedly. She's a bit of a lost soul, one way or another.'

'But she comes here from time to time?'

'Very occasionally. When she needs advice, generally.'

305

'What's her name, Lady Northcliff?'

'Her name? Oh, Victoria Danby. But really, she's perfectly harmless . . .'

Nick managed to keep his face completely impassive. 'Well – perhaps we'd better just talk to her. Routine, you understand. Could you give me her address?'

'Oh . . .?' Then she shook her head as if bringing herself to her senses. 'Yes, of *course*.' She searched in her handbag and found an address book. 'It's Moscow Road, W2. Number 53.'

He rose to his feet. 'Thank you, Lady Northcliff. Again, I'm sorry to have bothered you.'

Her eyes filled with disappointment at the realisation that the interview was over and that she could be of no more help. She nodded a brief goodbye then turned to stare out into the wind-swept garden.

Twenty-four

It was four-thirty and already dark. Gabriele drove into the airport tunnel and glanced in the mirror. There was no reason to suppose anyone would be looking for her, but it was an automatic reflex now to examine other cars.

The Mini whined its way up the incline at the other end. The sooner she was rid of the car the better. It belonged to the girl and she didn't like the idea of using it any longer. More to the point, it was old and not very fast and probably unreliable. It had to go.

Also it had been essential to get away from the farmhouse. The place got on her nerves. There was nothing to do there. Except wait. And she was incapable of just sitting and waiting. She had an insatiable need to attend to each detail, to cover each possibility. Everything must be neat and tidy.

Taking a ticket at the barrier, she drove into the car park beside Terminal 2, and parked in a dark corner of an upper storey. She scraped back her hair and twisted it into a knot on the back of her head. As an after-thought she pulled a scarf out of her bag and tied it round her head. She pulled out a deep tote bag and hitched it over her shoulder. In it was the Skorpion: she took it everywhere now. She liked the idea of carrying it into crowded places, as if it were a harmless piece of luggage. The Kalashnikov was far too bulky for this sort of work, and she had left it at the farmhouse.

As a back-up she had a handgun, a Walther 38, in her coat pocket.

She locked the car and dropped the keys in a waste bin some distance away. As she walked across the bridge to the terminal building, she slipped on a pair of dark glasses.

The arrivals floor was thronged with people. There was a long queue at the Hertz desk, so she moved on to the Avis desk. There were three people ahead of her. They seemed to be taking a long time. She glanced around.

A pair of uniformed policemen were walking slowly through the crowd towards her, examining the faces of the people hurrying by. One looked straight at Gabriele. He hesitated in his stride, then continued his professional swagger. But his eyes stayed on her and, inclining his head to his partner, he muttered a few words.

Hastily Gabriele thought: It means nothing. It's just the dark glasses. Or they like eyeing girls.

It means nothing.

The two policemen halted a few yards away. One reached into his pocket and pulled out a sheet of paper. His partner peered over his shoulder to look at it.

Gabriele felt the first flutterings of excitement and fear.

The two men looked at her again, as if comparing her to something on the sheet of paper. She stared back at them through the dark glasses.

They were coming towards her now. Casually she turned her head away and changed her attitude, moving her weight to the other leg, and putting her hand in her pocket. Her hand closed over the grip of the Walther.

'Excuse me, madam.'

She turned slowly. 'Yes.'

'What is your name, please?'

She raised her eyebrows in surprise. 'My name? It is Anneke van Duren.' She put on the slightest accent.

'Your nationality?'

'I am Dutch.'

'Could we see your passport, please?'

She took her hand out of her pocket, and reached into the

shoulder bag. Opening the inner zip compartment, she brought out the Dutch passport.

They examined it, looking carefully at the picture.

'Could we ask you to remove your sunglasses, please?'

Slowly, Gabriele took them off and put them in her coat pocket. She grasped the Walther again.

The two men compared her face with the passport photograph and the information on the sheet of paper. Gabriele craned her neck and took a quick look over the top of the piece of paper. There was a photograph on it.

Her stomach lurched.

She said, laughing, 'Is that someone who looks like me?'

They both stared at her. One said, 'Whereabouts in Holland do you live?'

'Amsterdam.'

'Do you have any other form of identification?'

She shrugged happily. 'Sure.' She reached into the same compartment of her handbag and pulled out a driving licence.

One took it and asked, 'What's the address on this?'

Treating it like some great joke, Gabriele gave them the correct address in a suitably guttural Dutch accent.

The two men glanced at each other. It was obvious that they were uncertain about what to do. Feeling more confident, Gabriele said brightly, 'I'm sorry if I'm not the right person.'

One nodded at her and handed back the passport and driving licence.

Gabriele smiled, 'Thank you. I hope you find the person you are looking for.'

The two men pulled back and stood some distance away, talking between themselves. Gabriele turned her attention to the Avis desk. A second girl was just coming on duty and waved Gabriele forward. Gabriele forced herself not to look at the policemen again until all the paperwork had been done. Then, gathering up the keys of the hire car, she turned to go.

The policemen were nowhere in sight.

Nevertheless she was exceptionally careful. She went to the ladies' washroom and spent several minutes there. Coming out, she took another look round. Then she went by a circuitous route to the hire car pick-up point, going downstairs, through the departure hall, then back along the outside of the building, as if she were slightly lost.

When the Avis bus arrived, she took a seat near the back so she could keep watch on the road behind. By the time the bus dropped her at the Avis depot she was certain there was no one following her.

But it had been a close thing.

Once safely in the hire car – a Ford Escort – she took stock.

The photograph. She had recognised it immediately. It had been taken when she was eighteen.

Linda Wilson.

They knew all about her then.

How? Not through Max. *Never* Max.

How?

She went through all the possibilities – but there was really only one.

Nick Riley. It had to be.

Just the thought of him made her wince.

He must have gone to the mews house, and guessed she had done a bunk. He must have combed his records, just like the filthy little spy he was, and finally linked her to Linda Wilson.

He must be gloating at his success.

Or was he?

Suddenly she saw the other side of it. He'd had a terrorist right under his nose, *in bed* . . . And never realised. What a humiliation for him. What a fool he must look to his colleagues. He must be sick at having been taken for such a ride.

The thought took some of the edge off her anger and made her feel slightly better.

And as for the police having her identity – in a way she was rather pleased. Now they knew who they were dealing with. No one would ever take her lightly again. They would broadcast her name on television. Petrini would hear about it, and the Lotta in Milan, and Raymond in Paris. From now on her name would be synonymous with active struggle . . . And that pleased her.

She drove on to the A4, heading west towards the farmhouse.

A new worry nagged at her mind.

It was a potentially serious one. It would be unwise to use the Dutch identity again. Which left just one passport – the Argentinian one hidden in Chelsea – to get her out of the country. A single passport. And no margin for error.

It was all a matter of control.

Dear God.

The longing to move was so powerful that Henry had to grit his teeth to stop himself from trying to break out of the box. His mind had accepted the necessity to stay still, but his body hadn't. The muscles in his legs were burning with a terrible energy that was independent of his brain. He had the awful feeling that, if he stopped concentrating for a moment, his legs would spring out from his body and force open the lid of the box.

After a while he tried moving his toes in the hope that this would alleviate the pressure on his legs. But it only encouraged his leg muscles to scream out for action, and the burning sensation was almost more than he could bear.

Control. He must *not* lose control.

In the wild rangings of his imagination the loathsome package on his stomach seemed, at one moment, to be benign and incapable of causing the slightest harm, and the next moment, to be so evil that he could almost feel it burning a hole in his stomach, like a ball of virulent acid.

Reaching for lifelines, he tried concentrating on work, on a new bill the PM wanted ready for the next session. He made himself go through the proposed clauses one by one.

On the fourth clause his mind wandered to Caroline . . .

With an effort he brought his thoughts back to the bill, but her image floated into his mind again.

Yielding, he indulged himself for a moment, and thought of her sweet face and her lovely smile and how much he loved her.

But thinking about Caroline was a slippery slope. He imagined her now, worried to death and having to face the full horror of the situation without him, and he felt so angry at the savage inhumanity of these people that he wanted to assault them physically.

But that of course was exactly what they wanted: to provoke him. Whatever happened, he must never give them that satisfaction.

Control.

Oh, but it was hard . . .

Thinking about Caroline gave him a desperate appetite for life. It was impossible to face the idea of death with any equanimity at all. Death would be an outrage, an appalling waste. The thought was so painful that he had to clench his fists to force the emotion out of his mind.

The voice, when it came, seemed to float on the air. 'Henry – would you like some water?'

Victoria.

He opened his eyes. The light was on. She was kneeling beside him. He said, 'Yes, a little . . .'

She held the water cupped in her hands and dripped it into his mouth. She said, 'They left the water in a bowl. I didn't want to risk spilling it all over you.'

'Thank you.' He took a little more, then shook his head. He didn't want to take too much liquid. He had already had to relieve himself where he lay. A singularly unpleasant experience, but a necessary one which was surprisingly easy when one had no choice in the matter. Since then he had deliberately ignored the uncomfortable wetness of his clothing; as a matter of principle he refused to let it bother him. None the less, it was something he would rather not have to repeat too often.

'Have you managed to sleep?' Victoria asked.

'Not really.'

'I left you – in case.'

She offered him food, but he refused.

She said, 'Do you want to talk?'

He looked at her. She was much more composed now, as if she had made an enormous effort to suppress her feelings. The expression on her round freckled face was cool and concerned. He remembered his own word: businesslike.

He said, 'Yes, let's talk.' Talking would be useful; it would help take his mind off the object on his stomach.

She looked relieved. She asked rather formally, 'Is there anything in particular that you would like to talk about?'

He could think of a dozen things he *didn't* want to discuss. He sighed deeply. It was all too much.

She said immediately, 'What about talking about all the things the police are doing at this very moment to find us?'

The place was in darkness but they took no chances.

First ultra-sensitive listening devices were put against the walls. Then marksmen with Enfields were positioned on the roofs opposite. When they finally went in, the first men through the broken door carried Smith and Wesson .38s.

They had taken no chances. But they need not have bothered. The flat was empty.

Nick went in behind Kershaw and Conway. As soon as the armed men had withdrawn, Kershaw's detectives got silently down to work.

Nick went quickly from room to room. Everything was neat and tidy. There were no signs of hurried departure. Nor had Victoria Danby been away for very long. The milk in the fridge was fresh, the soft fruit on the small dining table was not overripe. There was only one letter lying on the mat inside the front door, and that had been posted the day before.

The flat looked so normal that Nick had the dreadful feeling he'd got it all wrong again and that Victoria Danby bore no connection to anything at all.

He wandered around the living-room. Behind the sofa a pillow and eiderdown lay carefully folded in a neat pile on the floor.

An extra guest.

In the bedroom the bed was made and the coverlet smoothed over without a crease. In the bathroom the towels were folded over the hot rail and some women's underwear was drying on a rack in the bath.

All horrendously normal.

Back in the living-room Kershaw was on the phone, a letter in his hand. He gestured Nick towards an expandable cardboard file which someone had put on the table. Covering the mouthpiece, Kershaw said, 'Go through the rest of this lot, will you, Ryder?'

The concertina-type file had twenty compartments. The Danby girl was very orderly. Each was carefully marked with a category. Nick began with cars. There were two registration documents: one for a camper van, one for a Mini. He waved them in front of Kershaw just as Kershaw said into the telephone, 'Is this Mrs Danby? My name is Commander Kershaw of the Serious Crimes Squad at Scotland Yard . . .'

Nick placed the papers in various piles. There was a passport – the details matched those obtained half an hour ago from the passport office; three sterling travellers' cheques for ten pounds each; an outer folder showing that two cheques had been cashed only a week before, in Paris. Some French money. A ferry booking – again for only the week before.

Kershaw was saying, 'So you have no idea where your daughter might be, Mrs Danby? We wouldn't find her at work somewhere?'

Another compartment contained bills, marked 'Paid' with a date scribbled underneath. Another, bank statements. There was certainly no shortage of money. Nick wondered where it all came from.

Kershaw was asking patiently, 'May I ask, Mrs Danby, does your daughter still have two vehicles, a Mini and a – VW camper van?'

Nick went to the next compartment marked: Hunter's Wood. In it were more bills for a property somewhere in Wiltshire. There were also letters from a firm of solicitors called Makepiece & Makepiece, concerning the purchase of the property in May of 1968. Then another series of letters, which were much more recent, relating to a sale.

As Kershaw said, 'It is vital we find your daughter, Mrs Danby, to eliminate her from our inquiries,' Nick put one of the solicitor's letters in front of him and pointed to the Wiltshire address.

Kershaw said, 'Mrs Danby, does your daughter have any connection with a property in Wiltshire, a place called Hunter's Wood?'

Nick went quickly through the last few papers: letters from someone who might be a sister; an old diary; some invitations to weddings and parties – all very grand, he noticed.

Kershaw was bringing his conversation to a close, murmuring the appropriate thanks and apologies. He put the phone down.

'Nothing much,' he said, 'She doesn't work. Money of her own. The mother has no idea where she is. Oh, and that place, the farm, has been sold. The girl hasn't lived there for some time.'

Nick had a sinking feeling in the pit of his stomach. This was getting nowhere. He couldn't believe it. The Danby girl had been at the pre-demo meeting that Wheatfield and Black Beard had attended. And she knew the Attorney-General. There had to be a connection. *Surely*.

He wandered round, watching the team of men at their work. They were taking the place apart, ripping the bottoms out of the sofa and chairs, pulling up the floorboards, emptying all the food out of containers ... Kershaw's orders had been simple: he wanted information at any cost, even if it meant losing fingerprints.

In the bathroom a man was bent over the bath removing hairs from the surface enamel with a tweezer. He said, 'Straight black hair here. Isn't the Danby girl fair?'

Nick nodded. So she had a friend with dark hair ...

Another man was emptying tins of talcum powder on to a sheet of polythene. Three tubes of toothpaste lay waiting to be given the same treatment. In the bathroom cabinet a few items remained: a woman's shaving kit, some medicines and ointments, suntan lotion. On top of the cabinet were bottles of half-used shampoo.

A sponge bag in a bright floral pattern lay on top of some boxed-in pipework beneath the sink. He unzipped it: nothing special.

A rubbish bin. He poked through it with one finger. Dirty face tissues, pieces of cotton wool, a razor blade, and –

His heart stopped with a thud.

He whispered, '*Jesus!*'

He reached slowly down and picked out an empty bottle.

The bottle had contained eau de cologne. Brand: Rocco. Made in Italy. Legend: *Per uomini*.

Nick thought: Don't get excited. But he did.

It *couldn't* be coincidence.

Holding the empty bottle by the neck he took it into the living-room and, catching Kershaw's eye, held it up.

Giorgio brought food again in the evening. He put it next to the cheese and bread that remained untouched from the afternoon.

Victoria ignored him. She wasn't going to give him the satisfaction of begging. That was all in the past. She sat stolidly beside Henry and waited for Giorgio to leave.

But he lingered, standing by the archway, watching her.

She realised he wanted to talk.

'Poor little Vittoria,' he murmured. 'Life is not so beautiful . . . But soon you will be home in your big rich house.'

She said unbelievingly, 'I will?'

'Of course. The pigs will give in. Completely. They have no choice.'

She'd imagined that the motive for capturing Henry was something to do with revenge. The idea of bargaining was unexpected. Glancing at Henry, she got to her feet and beckoned Giorgio into the main cellar.

'What are you asking for?' she whispered.

'The release of our comrades. Free passage.'

Victoria felt a spark of hope. They weren't asking much. The government was bound to give in.

'And Henry? You'll let him go free, won't you? And you'll let him out of that thing as soon as your people are free. *Won't* you?'

Giorgio shrugged. 'If the pigs do as we say . . . And in time.'

'In time?'

'They have twenty-four hours.'

'And then?'

'Then –' He gestured a sudden explosion with his hands.

Victoria had a desperate need to know precisely what he meant. 'Then *what*? What do you *mean*?'

Giorgio gave a small secretive smile. 'The box will go bang. He will be dead.'

She gaped at him. Finally she breathed, 'When?'

'When we choose. Midday. Maybe before.'

A timer. A remote switch. Midday. Tomorrow. It wasn't very far away.

She said, 'You can't – please say you *can't*.'

Giorgio gave a short contemptuous laugh, as if such a question was unworthy of a reply, and, turning on his heel, climbed the steps and was gone.

Sick at heart. Victoria went back into the small cellar and resumed her seat next to Henry.

She felt him watching her.

'What exactly did he say?' he asked painfully.

It was impossible to tell him the truth. Already he was visibly more distressed than before. For the first time she saw fear and despair in his face. She smiled at him confidently. 'They've made their demands – the release of their friends and safe passage. The government are *bound* to give in. It's only a matter of a few hours, I'm sure.'

Henry frowned in concentration then closed his eyes as if a great weight of responsibility were descending on him.

Victoria repeated quickly. 'They're *bound* to give in.'

Henry whispered. 'They shouldn't. It would be quite wrong to do so.'

'But – they *must*.'

Henry made a last effort to speak. 'There's no *must* about it . . .' He trailed off and turned his head away.

Victoria sat back unhappily. He obviously wanted to be left alone. She had the awful suspicion that he might have overheard what Giorgio had said. In which case he knew about the twenty-four hour deadline. And the dreadful appalling timer on the bomb.

The knowledge brought Victoria to a decision. That she would stay with Henry. Whatever happened. She would not leave him alone.

It was a surprisingly easy decision to make. She thought: It'll be the first decent thing I've done.

She sat close by the box, in case he should need her. After a while he dozed a little and muttered in his sleep. She kept a hand close to his shoulder to wake him in case he had a nightmare and started struggling to get out of the box. But finally the mutterings ceased and he slept.

She left her hand on his shoulder, for the slight reassurance it might give him, and because it made her feel closer to him. She was very calm, now that she had come to her decision.

At one point she stared at her watch. Eight in the evening.

Time was passing. Fast. The night would slip away, then it would be morning . . .

And here she was, totally helpless. Someone cleverer would think of something. But she wasn't clever. No brains, no sense, never did have.

She made an effort to think everything through, calmly.

Removing her hand from Henry's shoulder she got up and went into the main cellar. She looked up the steps to the door.

Think. *Think.*

He must be alone. Otherwise why had he come to chat? And why had he been so relaxed. He was never relaxed when the woman was around.

But was he *still* alone?

She climbed the steps and put her ear to the door. Nothing.

She tried the handle, just in case. It turned, but the door wouldn't open.

Think. *Think.*

She would only have one chance. She mustn't foul it up. At the worst the woman *would* be there after all, and would shoot her. At the best, she might escape and save Henry. Eiher way, it was better than sitting and waiting. *Anything* was better than that.

But when she tried to work out exactly how she was going to escape, her determination faltered. There *had* to be a way, but she couldn't think what. The phrase 'play it by ear' came into her mind, and she clung to it as a temporary prop.

She listened again. Still nothing.

Then there was a sound. But it was only Henry, moaning softly. She heard him inhale deeply and guessed he was waking. She

316

suddenly realised that she would have to tell him something.

She hurried back into the small brick cellar and knelt beside the box. He was awake, staring upwards, a look of faint horror on his face as if he'd just woken from a nightmare.

'Henry?' she whispered. He focused on her, the nightmare still in his eyes. She said, 'I'm going to try to get out. Now, you mustn't worry.'

He looked horrified. 'Victoria, don't do *anything*. I forbid it.'

'I must, I'm sorry.'

'But *what* are you going to do?'

'Er. Well, I don't quite know . . .'

He sighed with exasperation. 'Victoria, these people will *kill* you. Without a second thought. I forbid it. It can only make things *worse*.'

She touched his shoulder. 'I'm sorry, Henry . . .'

Before he could speak again she got up and, taking the water bowl, emptied the last of the contents into a corner.

'Victoria?' Henry's voice was urgent, pleading.

She took a last look at him, the pale haggard face showing in the window of the obscene coffin-box, and her stomach lurched. She cried, 'I'm sorry, Henry. For everything. I really am . . . so sorry.'

She turned quickly and, holding the empty bowl in her hand, climbed to the top of the steps again. Taking a deep breath, she beat on the door.

Twenty-five

Nick shouted into the phone, 'It's very urgent!' then held the receiver away from his ear. The babble of voices boomed down the wire. He waited impatiently. This was the fourth restaurant he had tried. The flatmate hadn't been certain which one Diana Danby had gone to and had named five or six possibilities. Each restaurant appeared to be staffed by Italians who took a maddening delight in failing to comprehend straightforward English.

But it was worth trying. This girl, Victoria Danby's sister, might have some idea of where she was.

He waited for what seemed like a long time, but which was

actually four minutes. Around him was the clatter and buzz of the incident room where a team – now more than fifty strong – was based. Someone at the next desk shouted across the room. Nick flinched; all noise seemed unnaturally harsh. It was the tiredness. He didn't think he'd ever felt so tired in his life.

He pressed the receiver back to his ear. Finally he heard a clunk as someone picked up the phone at the far end.

'Hello?' It was a female voice.

'Miss Diana Danby?'

'Speaking.'

With relief Nick introducèd himself. 'I need to find your sister, Miss Danby. She's not at her flat. Have you any idea where she might be?'

'Oh gosh! She's not in trouble again, is she?'

'Miss Danby, *please*. Do you know where she might be?'

There was a pause and the clatter of the diners echoed down the wire. 'Oh dear, I can't *think* . . . Quite honestly, I haven't seen her for a while . . . I mean, I only know about her *flat* . . .'

'What about boyfriends?'

'She didn't tell me about any. Not new ones, anyway.'

'Relatives. Friends. Anybody—'

'She used to be involved with a whole lot of people in a commune. Did you know that? Well, ever since then she's been a bit on her own really. It all broke up, you know. *Maybe* she still sees some of them – the commune people, I mean. Have you tried them?'

'No. What were their names?'

'Oh. There were a couple called Martin and Janey, I think. But I never knew their *other* names . . . And as for the rest – no, I haven't a clue, I'm afraid.'

Nick rubbed a hand over his face. This was getting nowhere.

'But they might still be living at the farmhouse,' she continued. 'Though I'm not sure.'

Remembering Kershaw's conversation with the mother, Nick said, 'But I thought the farmhouse was sold?'

'Oh no. Not yet. For some reason it didn't sell. So it's going to auction. Next month, I think.'

'But your mother – she seemed very definite.'

'Oh, she knows *nothing* about it.' Her tone was scornful. 'Don't take any notice of what *she* says. It isn't sold yet. I know it isn't.' There was a pause. 'Hello? Are you still there?'

Nick had been miles away, thinking of the unoccupied farmhouse.

He gave Diana Danby the number of the incident room, in case she heard from her sister, and rang off.

He went straight to Kershaw and gave him the news.

The brief look of excitement that passed over the commander's face was quickly replaced by one of anxiety. Momentarily, he plunged his face into his hands. He came up looking very tired. 'It's definitely worth a look, of course. We can mount a discreet watch on the place – but we can't search it.'

'What do you mean, sir?'

'I mean, I've had a directive from upstairs – and it comes from Downing Street itself. There's to be a hands-off until negotiations have been successfully concluded and the Attorney-General safely returned.'

Nick sat down and tried to absorb the implications.

'Surely we can approach with caution?' he asked.

Kershaw looked uncomfortable. 'Apparently we must do nothing that might jeopardise the situation . . .'

Nick sensed that the commander didn't like the directive any more than he did. He shook his head. 'Seems crazy to me, sir.'

Kershaw raised his eyebrows in silent agreement, and said heavily, 'The argument is that if we go nosing around and the terrorists get wind of it then – the feeling is that they are perfectly capable of murdering Sir Henry. And that mustn't happen.'

'But if the terrorists *are* there, then it would be a real chance for us to get the upper hand. Show ourselves. Surround the place so that they realise there's no point in killing anyone. In fact, it would be Sir Henry's best chance of staying *alive*.'

'Maybe. But would you like to be the person responsible for putting that argument to the test?'

Nick hesitated. The image of Lady Northcliff came into his mind. He saw her at the window, staring out into the garden, despair behind the pale composed face . . .

He nodded slowly. 'Yes, I see what you mean.'

'This is a new type of criminal, Ryder. And we don't know how to deal with them yet. We can't go blundering around finding out.'

'But giving in entirely? Pandering to them? It'll just encourage them! They're not going to go away.'

Kershaw sighed, 'I know, I know.' He stood up and made for

319

the door. 'But don't let's get excited about anything yet. Let's find out if there *is* anyone at that farmhouse first.'

Nick got hastily to his feet. 'What sort of party were you thinking of sending, sir?'

Kershaw pondered. 'Very small. Six men.'

'And an indirect approach, sir. On foot over the fields. I'll get an ordnance survey map right now. We can be ready to go in five minutes.'

For a moment Kershaw eyed him quizzically then, giving in gracefully, nodded his agreement. 'Okay, Ryder, you're on. But' – he raised a forefinger – 'you're to keep your distance. Look for signs of life – lights showing and vehicles parked outside – no more, no less. And if you *do* find anything, report straight back to me.'

'Do we tool up?'

Kershaw shook his head. 'I daren't, Ryder. Not in the present climate.'

Nick wasn't surprised. The Met, like the county forces, was proud of its long tradition of not carrying firearms. It was considered a virtue to approach dangerous armed criminals with no more than a truncheon in your hand. Nick was one of many younger officers who believed the policy to be ridiculously out of date.

It took fifteen minutes to muster the rest of the party – Conway and four of Kershaw's top men – to draw walkie-talkies, binoculars, cameras, maps and extra-warm gear, and to get down to the cars.

They set off with eighty miles and well over two hours' driving ahead of them. At first Nick was unnaturally alert and jumpy, a dozen thoughts ricocheting around his head, thoughts which, maddeningly, refused to connect in any sensible pattern. He realised that his mind was increasingly muddled. He'd be no good to anyone if he didn't get some sleep.

It wasn't until the car sped into Middlesex that a deep aching weariness finally overtook him and, resting his head against the seat, he was instantly asleep.

Victoria pounded on the door again. There was no sound. Where was he? Perhaps he'd gone away. Perhaps she and Henry were alone in the house. In which case it was just a matter of getting *out*. She rattled the handle and pulled violently at the door, but it wouldn't budge. It was a heavy door, made of thick wooden planks with solid crossbeams.

Defeated, she leaned back against the wall. The plan probably wouldn't have worked anyway.

Suddenly there was a sound. She put her ear to the door and listened.

A door closing. Footsteps in the distance . . .

She pounded on the door.

More sounds, closer. Footsteps coming across the hall.

Victoria retreated quickly to the foot of the steps and waited, trembling.

A key turned. The door swung open. It was Giorgio. 'Yes?' he demanded.

She held up the empty bowl. 'We need more water.'

Giorgio looked irritated. 'You use too much.'

'I need a wash.' She indicated Henry in the far cellar. 'And now he's thirsty.'

With visible annoyance, Giorgio came half-way down the steps and reached out for the bowl. He went out again, locking the door behind him.

Her heart thumping wildly, Victoria ran up the steps and pressed herself against the wall. When he returned she would be hidden behind the open door. Or would she? There wasn't much room. If he flung the door open it would probably bounce off her body. He was *bound* to realise that there was someone there.

She thought: Dear Lord, why couldn't I have been *thin*?

And her *feet*. She suddenly realised that, standing as she was two steps below the threshold, her feet would be visible beneath the open door. But she couldn't *get* any higher.

It was hopeless. Why had she ever thought any different?

Footsteps sounded in the hall.

She hesitated, torn with indecision.

The footsteps shuffled to a halt.

Too late.

She turned her feet sideways, pulled herself in and held her breath.

A key sounded in the lock. The handle turned. The door swung open fast. It swung towards her face. It came up against her body. She sucked in the last of her breath.

The door was bouncing back off her body.

She grabbed the door knob and pulled the door hard against her. She almost cried out. *He must realise!*

There was an agonising pause.

Then, unbelievably, Giorgio appeared. Walking slowly down the steps, the bowl in his hands, peering curiously towards the far cellar, wondering where she was.

He hadn't realised.

For a moment she was frozen with amazement.

Then she knew she had to move. Now – while his back was turned. Before he reached the bottom of the steps. Before he turned to walk across the cellar and spotted her out of the corner of his eye. Before he discovered she was not in the far cellar after all.

She began to move her weight down on to a lower step, to manoeuvre herself round the open door.

He was almost at the bottom.

She hesitated. Had she left it too late?

She eased herself round the door.

He had reached the foot of the steps. He turned towards the far cellar.

She moved clear of the door.

Then his face flicked round.

He saw her.

The fear leapt into her throat.

For a moment he was motionless, a look of black rage on his face.

Then, throwing the bowl of water aside, he coiled himself and sprang up the steps.

She let out an involuntary cry and pulled herself up the last two steps. She reached out for the door handle. He was half-way up and coming fast. She pulled the door shut. He was almost there. She grasped the handle tight and held it fast. She fumbled at the large metal key that protruded from the lock. Suddenly the handle twisted violently under her hand and, with a desperate gasp, she gripped it with all her strength to prevent it from turning.

She jerked at the key and almost screamed.

It wouldn't turn!

Finally there was a firm click.

It was locked. She fell back with relief.

The knob twisted violently from side to side. Victoria stared at it, mesmerised.

The next moment, there was a crash and the whole door shook.

God!

Another crash. The door vibrated but held firm.

She retreated fast across the hall, watching the door.

She looked longingly at the telephone and hesitated. There was a momentary silence from inside the cellar. She reached for the phone.

Suddenly there was a deafening *bang*!

She sprang back with a gasp.

It came again: *bang*! A gun. The door was splintering around the lock.

And then she realised there was no time. *He was almost out.*

Scrabbling at the front door, she pulled it open and ran out into the night.

The darkness was impenetrable, a mantle of black that enveloped itself around her. She ran blindly forward, away from the house in the direction of the drive.

She stumbled once but regained her footing. Then she hit a bump and felt herself pitching forward. She threw out a hand and caught her fall.

And kept running.

Gradually her eyes became accustomed to the darkness; she could make out the pale surface of the road and the shadows cast by the ridges and pot-holes. But the soles of her boots were hopelessly slippery, and the slight heel made her ankles keep twisting over.

She cried inwardly with frustration and ran on, glancing over her shoulder, looking for him. She felt the blind fear of the pursued, the panic of a thousand nightmares.

Her lungs were hurting, her legs maddeningly heavy.

God, give me strength!

She stole another look behind.

Nothing – or *was* there?

She pushed desperately on, half running, half walking. The road was curving upwards, steepening between the open fields. Ahead she could make out the deeper blackness of the woods and the archway of chestnuts on the brow of the hill.

Soon there'd be somewhere to hide.

She staggered forward, her heart crashing in her ears, her legs like lead. She pulled at the air, trying to breathe, but her lungs wouldn't *draw*.

The trees – if only she could get to the trees.

Then she heard it.

The sound of an engine. Coming from behind. Roaring into motion; followed by the grating and squeaking of a van being driven hard over a rough road.

She looked wildly about her.

There was no cover here. Only the woods ahead – but they were too *far*. Or the woods away to the left. Yes, *nearer*. Her only chance.

Then she saw the beam of the headlights, swinging slowly round, reaching out towards the woods, illuminating the trees, arcing towards her . . . And she realised the lights would catch her, pin her fluttering to the darkness behind.

To the right, then. There was nowhere else to go.

She dived for the barbed-wire fence and forced herself between the middle and upper strands. Her sweater caught on a barb. She pushed her body through the wire and yanked furiously on the sweater. The headlights were swinging round, almost upon her.

She screamed, *'Come on.'*

With a final wrench the sweater gave way and she was free.

She ran desperately. It was downhill, a little easier now, down into the valley. *Back* into the valley – the wrong direction. Almost back towards the farmhouse. Yet she *had* to get away from the road.

Her legs were weak now, wobbling violently over every tussock and undulation.

Behind her the vehicle was roaring up the hill. The reflection of the approaching headlights illuminated the ground around her. She could almost feel Giorgio's eyes boring into her back. She ran at a crouch, looking for cover.

There was a slight rise in the ground. She threw herself behind it and lay flat, gasping for breath.

The engine noise rose to a crescendo then faded as the van passed by on the road above. She thought: Perhaps he didn't see me after all. She pulled in great gulps of air then lay still, the grass cool and soothing against her cheek. She wanted to stay there, lying against the damp ground, for ever.

She stiffened.

The engine note had changed. She raised her head slightly, listening hard. The engine was idling, the van stationary . . .

Suddenly the engine spluttered to a stop. There was an unearthly silence, broken only by the pounding of her heart.

She craned her head. The headlights had been extinguished. There was only darkness, a great expanse of black where the light had been.

Where was he?

She peered forward. The deep shadows merged one into another until they formed an elusive mosaic of shimmering dots. The patchwork shifted constantly until there was an illusion of movement in every fragment of grey, a dark racing figure in every shadow.

She *must* move.

With an enormous effort, she raised herself into a crouch, her senses reaching out into the stillness.

Distant sounds ... An owl's hoot ... The faint whispered undertones of the wood.

Where was he?

She began to creep away crabwise, down the hill, away from the road, further into the valley.

A sound.

The crunch of feet on pebble. Up on the road.

She accelerated down the hill, down on to the flat meadowland.

Ahead was the stream, gurgling faintly. She reached the bank and, pausing for an instant, looked back.

Darkness. Nothing. *Where was he?*

She gasped.

There.

A dark shadow up by the road, detaching itself from the surrounding grey.

Running.

Running straight down the hill. *Towards her.*

She leapt into the stream, dragging her feet through the clutching water, and stumbled up on to the bank. She ran up the slight incline, her stride ragged, her ankle turning on a hump.

Ahead, the rolling pastureland climbed towards the steep valley side and the distant ridge. To the left, fields, open and exposed. *Nowhere to hide.*

She swerved to the right, towards the black familiar mass of the farm buildings. There, at least, there would be somewhere to hide.

She willed herself on but her body wouldn't respond: it was a sluggish weight, pulling her back, dragging her down. Her lungs ached with pain, the breath coming in long whooping gasps. She was incapable of running any more. She staggered forward at an untidy lope, forcing one foot in front of the other, her arms swinging uselessly at her sides. She couldn't bring herself to look behind. Then, suddenly, she didn't need to. She *heard* him.

She heard the pounding of his feet on the turf, the scrape of his shoe against a stone. The sound of panting, faint at first, growing louder, coming up behind her.

The panic gave her a last burst of strength. She pumped her arms, forced her legs into a run, pushed herself forward over the ground. The sheds loomed up ahead. *Not so far.* The sheds . . . The house beyond . . .

But what was this ahead?

The *gate*.

She'd forgotten. The gate. Barring her way.

She heard a short pant, the rasp of his breath, close behind.

Then she knew: this was the end. Nothing would save her now. She could almost feel his hands on her back, dragging her down. She screamed inwardly.

The gate was coming up fast. As she reached out for the latch, she suddenly realised – *the gate was slightly open.*

She reached out a hand and swung herself round the end of it and half fell through the gap, pulling the gate closed in an instinctive attempt to delay him.

She gave a violent start. To the right a dark shape was vaulting the fence. Jumping high, a hand on the gate post. She veered to the left, across the yard. The solid blackness of the tractor shed loomed close ahead.

Behind her there was a thud and a muffled shout.

She reached the shed and ran blindly along the side until she came to the back wall. She stopped, gasping for breath, and listened. She could hear nothing but the hammering of her own heart. She put her head round the corner and looked back down the side. The eaves cast deep inky shadows on the narrow pathway between the shed and the rising ground. Was he there? It was so difficult to be sure.

What had the thud meant? The cry? He must have caught a foot on some wire and fallen.

She took another careful look.

Nothing..

Then she remembered the *other* side. The house side.

He might be creeping up *there* . . .

Go and look! But suppose she met him at the corner?

Oh God!

She forced herself to creep along the back of the shed to the opposite corner. Bracing herself, she thrust her head out.

Nothing.

326

What now?

Should she wait here – or go back to the other corner?

No: stay still. Wait for him to make a sound. *Wait.*

She kept as still as she could, her senses reaching out into the darkness, listening for him, watching for him. She had a desperate need to know *exactly* where he was.

The silence grew, punctuated only by her own breathing and the rustle of the grass in the wind. Somewhere far away a night creature called.

She thought: Perhaps he's gone. Perhaps he's hurt himself. But how was she to know? He might be waiting at the far end of the shed, waiting for her to reappear, or he might be circling in a wide loop, expecting her to make a run for it across the kitchen garden. Or he might have returned to the house. He might be – anywhere.

Perhaps she should move. Perhaps she should try to reach the house and find a gun. Immediately she thought: Hopeless. There wouldn't be guns lying about. Not just like that.

No: she *had* to know where he was.

She had a terrible urge to run into the middle of the yard and shout, so as to end the appalling uncertainty.

She stiffened.

A faint snap.

Where from?

She took another look down the side of the shed facing the house. Definitely not there.

Infinitely slowly, she moved herself round the corner.

Again.

A footfall.

Where?

From the *other* side.

The fear leapt into her throat. She moved quickly away, down the side of the shed nearest the house, until she was back in the yard.

Where now?

The interior of the shed, gaping blackly, beckoned to her: a place to hide. She slipped inside. The tractor sat hugely in the centre. She went deeper into the darkness, feeling her way quickly round the bulk of the vehicle, taking small anxious footsteps in case of obstacles.

At the back of the tractor she paused, listening hard. Almost immediately, she heard him. Through the side of the shed, the faint crunch of feet on earth, moving slowly, following her route, heading for the yard.

The footsteps faded then halted altogether. And restarted.

And then he appeared, a black figure silhouetted in the wide doorway.

He was coming in.

Very slowly, she began to move, keeping the bulk of the tractor between her and the slowly advancing figure. The footsteps halted again. She pressed herself against one of the massive rear wheels.

There was a long silence which seemed to whine and jangle in her ears.

Another footstep, but very faint. He was treading more carefully.

She put out a foot to move further round and began to transfer her weight. Her heel pushed against something – something *loose* – something she had inadvertently shifted slightly. She began to withdraw her foot. *Too late*. The object rocked back, making a minute sound. She froze. The sound seemed to hang for ever in the roar of the silence.

She clenched her teeth.

She heard him coming round the back of the tractor. She ducked down behind the immense wheel, retreating under the body of the machine. In the faint light from the doorway she became vaguely aware of what her foot had touched – a heap of objects on the floor beside her: metal, abandoned tools, cog wheels.

The outline of a long metal bar showed grey in the darkness. She reached for it, grasped it, and felt a tiny spark of confidence. Yes – he wouldn't get her without a fight!

A sudden wild courage made her pick it up and back quickly under the tractor until she was standing on the other side. Her footsteps echoed loudly. There was a moment of electrified silence, then he moved.

He moved quickly, darting towards the doorway to cut her off. But she sprang round to the back of the tractor again. And waited.

He came more confidently this time. He called softly, 'Vittoria, I have a gun – come out or I must kill you.'

She thought: He still thinks I'm a fool.

She waited for him behind one of the large rear wheels. As he approached, she braced herself, then, with a small cry, she leapt out at him, swinging the metal bar wildly from side to side, viciously, violently, advancing on him, wanting only to hurt him, hating him. She caught him off-balance and he retreated slightly, his arm up to deflect the blows. Then, finding his feet, he brought a hand up, pointing something at her. A weapon.

She thought: *No! No, you bloody don't.*

She swung again with all her strength. She felt the bar glance off his arm. There was a clatter as something hard hit the ground. He gasped and his hand went up to clutch his head. Exhilarated now, she swung again, scenting the possibility of another hit. But she missed. He grabbed for the bar. She spun it downwards, out of his reach and up again the other way, up until it was raised high above her head. With all her might, she brought it down again. He reached for it, ducking at the same time, but she pulled sideways, so that the downwards motion became an arcing sideways loop. His hand snatched at the bar and missed. In the split second before the bar hit him, she realised with a raging triumph that he had not ducked far enough.

The bar hit him. He fell back.

Then she swung the bar with cold calculation, going for his arm, and then his back, and then a part of his head that he wasn't covering with his hands. Recovering, he lunged for her, but she sprang out of his reach. She felt all-powerful now, as if the bar in her hand was a mighty weapon quite independent of her. She swung wildly, back and forth, back and forth. Suddenly there was a soft thud. She'd got him again! She could have laughed. It was a satisfying feeling, hitting him. She wanted to do it again.

He was on one knee now, moaning loudly.

She danced behind him and, with one last massive effort, she raised the bar and brought it winging down on to the top of his head. He toppled over and fell to the ground. She swung the bar back and forth in the air, waiting for him to come up, longing for him to try to catch her again, so that she could *hit him harder*. Massively hard.

'Come on, come on!' She hovered impatiently. *'Come on!'*

It was only after several minutes that the wild elation left her and she realised that he was not going to move. She felt a sharp disappointment.

Eventually she became aware of the silence and the passing of time. She looked down at the hunched outline on the floor. He was utterly still. She blinked, not understanding . . .

It took several more moments for her to realise that she was free, and there was nothing to stop her leaving. But something nagged at her mind, something that she had to do. What was it?

Henry.

She staggered out of the shed towards the back door of the house. She heard a clacking sound and realised it was her teeth chattering. She was suddenly very cold.

The door was open and she lurched into the kitchen. She was shaking like a leaf. She felt very disorientated. She leant against the dresser. No – that was wrong. She must get on. She realised she still had the metal bar in her hand. Putting it on the kitchen table, she went through into the hall. The door to the cellar was open, the light still on.

She must tell Henry. No – *first* she must telephone. That was by far the most important thing.

Leaning heavily against the wall, she picked up the receiver and listened. A comforting buzz sounded in her ear. She put a shaking finger in the nine and began to dial.

She dialed the final nine and allowed herself a small glimmer of hope. In some extraordinary way everything was going to be all right after all. She sighed shakily, half-way between tears and laughter.

A split second later she knew nothing was ever going to be right again.

Her hair was being wrenched backwards off her skull. It must surely come *off*. She screamed out in pain and fell heavily backwards, falling aginst the doorframe.

As she fought for breath she heard the receiver being dropped firmly back into its cradle.

Twenty-six

Gabriele took hold of the girl's hair and pulled hard. 'Where's Giorgio?'

'I don't know.'

Gabriele let the girl see the short grey barrel of the Skorpion and repeated in a low voice, *'Where is Giorgio?'*

'He went away.'

'How do you know?'

'He said so.'

'Did he give a reason?'

'No. He just said he wanted to go away. He didn't say why.'

Gabriele thought furiously. *Why* would he have gone away? It didn't make sense. She asked through tight lips, 'But why would he bother to tell *you* that he was going?'

The girl shook her head violently. 'I don't know, I don't know. He just *did*.'

'How did you get out?'

There was a whimper. 'I – I just did.'

Gabriele pulled the hair harder, jerking the girl's head from side to side. The girl yelped with pain. 'I – used a wrench.'

The girl was lying. There had been no wrench. She gripped the hair more tightly. 'Try again. This is your last chance.'

The girl's mouth moved, but no sound came out. Gabriele loosened her grip. Eventually the girl gasped, 'There *was* a wrench. I found it in a corner – when we first came. I hid it – and then when Giorgio left I levered the lock off. I *did*.'

Letting go of the girl, Gabriele considered. It was just possible, about the wrench: the lock was dented and pulled at an obtuse angle to the wood. It was *possible* . . . 'Where is it now?' she demanded.

'I – left it in the kitchen.'

Gabriele went into the kitchen, dragging the girl behind her. A metal bar lay on the table. The food Giorgio had bought earlier in the day sat on the draining board, along with the whisky and cigarettes. Most of the weapons were still there – her own Kalashnikov, as well as Giorgio's. However there was no sign of either Giorgio's Skorpion or his handgun, a Makarov. He must have taken them when he went out.

If he had gone out.

She desperately tried to think. Nothing made *sense*.

The van . . .

What was the van doing abandoned at the top of the hill?

Something must have happened. He must have been on his way somewhere when the van broke down. But where had he been going? There were plenty of booze and cigarettes. And why, when the van broke down, did he set off on foot? This bloody place was miles from anywhere: he couldn't have gone far without transport.

None of it made sense.

Unless –

There was a pub in the village. Brightly lit, inviting. But she immediately dismissed the thought. Not even Giorgio would go wandering off to a pub at a time like this. Going back into the hall, she turned off the lights and, pulling open the front door, stared into the darkness.

The night was silent. She looked up towards the woods where the road passed through the avenue of trees. She had left the car up there beside the van. When she'd first seen the van she'd thought something really dreadful had happened: that the police had discovered them and Giorgio had been trying to escape. But there had been no signs of life, no other cars, nothing else to suggest that something had gone wrong. So she had run silently down the drive, the gun in her hand. As she'd neared the house she'd heard a sound – a door closing – and thought it must be Giorgio. But then she'd looked through the window and seen the girl at the telephone and realised something *had* gone very wrong after all.

But *how* wrong, that was the question?

She snapped on the hall light and put the barrel of the gun to the girl's forehead. 'How long have you been out? Did you make any other calls?' She pushed the barrel hard into the girl's head. The girl shrank against the wall and closed her eyes.

'I was only out for a minute,' she blabbed. 'I didn't make any other calls, I swear it. I swear it . . .'

Gabriele prodded with the gun once more. 'The truth!'

'It is, *it is*. It's the truth, *honestly*.' She started to cry, sobbing quietly, her face contorted like a small child's. She was pathetic, Gabriele decided. And probably telling the truth.

But even if there was no immediate danger Gabriele was filled with a deep instinctive unease.

She came to a decision: she had to get out. It was too risky to stay here. She would go to Chelsea. And Giorgio would meet her there, sooner or later.

This place would have to be tidied up then, made secure. Gabriele eyed the girl. She was a nuisance. Gabriele had never wanted to bring her; it had been Giorgio's idea. Now the girl was a threat as well as a nuisance. She might break out again. She would have to be dealt with.

Gabriele considered the alternatives but there were none. The knowledge reassured her. She was only doing what any commander would do when covering his retreat. A matter of logistical necessity.

It would have to be done in the cellar, so as to be out of the way. Just in case a casual caller came to the house.

She hesitated; she hadn't thought *that* possibility through. What *would* happen if someone came? The risk was slight, and yet – if someone did come they might find the attorney-man. Then the disposal people might dismantle the explosive before the deadline ran out and then she'd have nothing to negotiate with. That mustn't happen. No one must discover what was in the cellar.

Turning on the cellar light, she examined the door again. Apart from the lock there was nothing wrong with it. It must be possible to seal it in some way. She'd look into it when she'd dealt with the girl.

Yes: first things first.

'Get up!'

The girl looked at her in terror. Gabriele thought: She knows.

She repeated furiously, 'Get up!'

The girl got unsteadily to her feet, her face very white.

'Get in there.' Gabriele waved the gun towards the cellar.

The girl walked slowly across the hall and started down the steps. Gabriele followed. A sudden spasm of nervousness hit her. She wished Giorgio or Max were here. Yet it shouldn't be hard. Everyone had told her it wasn't. Provided you didn't look them in the eye when you did it. She would turn her head as she squeezed the trigger. And then, once it was done, she would close her mind to it and everything would be all right again. A logistical necessity.

She reached the foot of the steps and ran her tongue across her lips. The girl was staring at her again. Gabriele blinked and, raising the gun, took a step forward.

Something caught her eye. A movement from the far cellar. It was the attorney-man, lifting his head out of the box.

Then, suddenly, the germ of an idea came.

Gabriele gave it a moment, letting it develop. She looked up to the cellar door and then the idea crystallised.

Of course. Simple. She smiled a wild ragged smile. The girl's jaw dropped open.

Gabriele turned on her heel and ran up the steps. She called down to the girl, 'Stay right there or I'll blow your head off!'

The holdall was still in the kitchen. She scooped it up and went back to the cellar door. Putting the Skorpion down, she sat on the top step and thought for a while. Then she removed some plastic explosive from the bag, cut off a small section and placed it in an empty fuse box – a small container of hard plastic. Burying a detonator in the centre of the putty-like explosive, she wired it to a small 1.5-volt battery and, keeping the positive and negative separate, led the wires out through a hole which she made in the lid of the container. She put in a safety device: the usual clothes peg with a stiff piece of card in between the contacts, and a length of strong thread attached to the card.

She was rather enjoing herself. She had never made anything quite like this before.

Now to set the whole thing up.

She chuckled with excitement. Better and better.

She looked down at Victoria and beckoned. 'Come here.'

The girl advanced uncertainly up the steps.

'Arms in front of you.' Gabriele tied her wrists together with wire, then passed the wire round her waist, so that her hands were held firmly in front of her. Then she taped the plastic box with the wires hanging from it on to Victoria's back. The girl staggered slightly. Gabriele snapped: 'Don't move!'

Now for the interesting bit.

Gabriele fixed the wires to a simple pressure release switch. Now only the card caught in the clothes peg prevented the device from being live. She passed the thread from the card loosely under the half-closed door.

Leaving just enough room to squeeze through the door, she turned the girl round and pulled her down on to the edge of the top step. She taped the pressure release switch on to the stone step, facing upwards.

She squeezed through the gap in the door, out into the hall and pulled the door closed, leaving Victoria on the other side.

She called. 'Sit right back against the door!' Through the crack under the door she saw the girl's shadow move as she obeyed.

'Can you feel something on the step? Are you sitting right on it?'

There was a silence, then the faintest, 'Yes.'

'Well, you'd better be, otherwise you'll go up with a bang in a minute. Understand?'

The girl groaned.

The adrenalin shot into Gabriele's veins. This was it then.

Paying the thread out through her fingers she moved away from the door and sheltered round a corner. Very carefully she pulled on the thread. She felt it tauten. She increased the pressure. The card was resisting. She jerked it slightly and felt it give a little. She swallowed nervously, then pulled again. Suddenly the cord was free. She pulled it until the card appeared under the door.

She allowed herself a moment of satisfaction. Very neat. Now only madam's weight was keeping the pressure switch down. If anyone tried to get in, or if the girl tried to move, her back would be blown off.

Of course they might still get in *through* the door. She'd forgotten that. Her mind searched for a solution – she imagined herself in *their* place, imagined someone like Nick Riley looking for a way in.

Then she had it. Going into the kitchen she tore up a grocery bag and, using a pen from the holdall, wrote a message on it. She put the message in front of the cellar door.

Gabriele glanced at her watch. It was nine. Late. She must go. This place was a trap. Coming here had been a mistake, right from the beginning. Giorgio's idea.

Giorgio – where the hell *was* he?

She hurriedly repacked the holdall and took it with the Skorpion to the front door. The telephone sat silently on the window ledge. She snatched it up, and referring to the slip of paper in her bag, dialled the number in Paris.

Eventually it connected and the number rang. She waited tensely. It didn't answer. She dialled again. This time the call did not connect. Impatiently, she dialled a third time. It rang once more. There was no reply.

Angrily she reached down and pulled the cable out of the wall. She turned off the hall light. The house fell into darkness apart from a sliver of light gleaming under the cellar door. That light should have been turned off. She swore under her breath. There was nothing she could do about it now.

Taking the spare explosives and her Kalashnikov, as well as the Skorpion, she stepped out into the darkness and listened for a moment before closing the door quietly behind her. The atmosphere was eerie and still. She thought: How I loathe this place.

She set off up the drive, a cold dread pulling at her mind. High on the hill a breeze sighed softly in the trees. She quickened her pace.

Finally the van came into view and, beyond it, the hired Ford.

She put the holdall and the gun into the car, and then approached the van. Apprehensive, she hesitated for a moment then, opening the back doors, climbed in. She felt around with her hand. Then, impatient, she risked the interior light. Everything was there still: sleeping-bags, clothes, ammunition clips, spare explosive. Giorgio had not taken anything. *Strange*. She gathered some of her own gear.

She glanced over the back of the driver's seat into the front.

She stiffened.

Giorgio's Skorpion lay on the front seat. She stared at it for a long time.

Picking up her gear she turned off the light and went round to the front. The keys were in the ignition. She sat in the seat and tentatively turned the key. The starter whirred noisily, shattering the silence. The engine burst into life.

There was nothing wrong with the engine at all then. She put it into gear to make sure. The van leapt forward.

She turned off the engine and looked at the machine pistol again. Its presence worried her deeply. *He would never have gone anywhere without it.*

What should she do with it? Leave it in case he returned?

She couldn't think. Part of her was filled with a deep foreboding. She had the feeling Giorgio would never return.

Picking it up, she got out of the van and stood quite still for a moment. The echo of the engine still rang in her ears and she strained to hear. Slowly the sounds of the night returned: the whisper of the woodland, the murmur of the wind. The faint hum of a car sounded in the distance, somewhere on the main road.

Making up her mind, she threw the Skorpion back on to the front seat and hid it under a sleeping-bag. Just in case. It would be terrible if he did come back, only to find it gone.

She ran to the Ford and drove quickly to the main road. It wasn't until she was through the village that she began to relax her grip on the wheel.

As she neared the A4 the traffic gradually increased. She barely noticed the two Rovers that swished rapidly past her, one behind the other, going fast in the direction from which she had come.

'Wake up.'

Conway's voice. Nick opened his eyes and for a moment couldn't remember where he was. He rubbed his aching temples.

The sleep might have been a mistake. He wasn't sure he felt any better at all.

The car was travelling fast through country lanes. They rounded a bend and, coming into a small village, slowed down.

'We're about half a mile off,' said Conway, shining a penlight at the map on his knee.

A few minutes later the car slowed to a crawl and turned left into the gateway of a field. The second car followed. They parked them both well back from the road, in the shadow of a hedge. When they had sorted out their gear they split up into three groups of two men each: one, including Conway, to stay with the cars and form the radio link with the nearest police HQ at Swindon; the second to go along the road and keep watch on the lane leading to the farm-house; the third – Nick and a man called Williams – to go across the fields and do the recce.

Before setting off, Nick took a good look at the map, mem-orising the layout of the farm and, as far as he could decipher it, the topography.

The sky was overcast and it was very dark. Nevertheless they made fast time across the fields and soon came to a belt of wood-land which had been clearly marked on the map. Presumably Hunter's Wood. Not far to the right was the lane that led to the farmhouse, but Nick wanted to stay well away from that. They looked for a path through the woods and found a small trail which started well but soon evaporated into a tangle of undergrowth.

They fought their way through with difficulty, then, reaching an area of more mature trees, the undergrowth thinned and they were able to press on. Through the pitch darkness Nick caught the glimmer of open sky ahead and, after negotiating one more dense patch of brambles and a barbed-wire fence, they were through into an open field. They now kept to the edge of the field, following the line of the trees. To the left the ground sloped down into a valley. Nick reckoned the farmhouse must be only a short distance away, a little further up the valley.

The outline of some fencing came up ahead, and beyond it a road: the driveway to the house. Nick whispered to Williams, 'Better head off down into the valley and round.' The other man nodded and they altered direction, going straight downhill. They crossed a narrow stream and climbed half-way up the other hillside before changing direction again to continue their journey along the valley.

Suddenly Nick put out a hand and they halted. Immediately below them, only fifty yards away, were the dark shapes of several buildings. The farm. But they had got rather close. Nick waved to Williams to retreat a little. Once safely out of earshot they took a long look through binoculars. There was no light showing, not even a glimmer. They had a hurried conference and decided to make a large circuit of the property, to examine it from different angles. Climbing higher up the valley side they passed behind the house and made a wide detour until they had reached the woodland immediately above the drive and overlooking the front of the house.

Nick took a long look through the binoculars and felt a deep disappointment.

There was nothing, not even a suggestion of life. No light, and as far as he could see in the darkness, no vehicles parked outside. There might be something parked in one of the outbuildings, of course. But somehow he doubted it: the whole place looked utterly lifeless.

His heart sank. Another dead end.

He took one more look, then made a large sweep with the binoculars from one end of the silent valley to the other. He examined the track in its long traverse from the farmhouse across the field immediately beneath him to the dark woods two hundred yards to his left, where the track disappeared into the trees.

He paused, took the binoculars away from his eyes and stared. There seemed to be something on the track at the point where it disappeared into the trees. A gleam ... The suggestion of shape ...

He nudged Williams and they walked cautiously along the tree-line, keeping to the shadows. As they got closer they approached at a crouch.

It was a van.

They halted and watched it for a while.

A van. The Danby girl had owned – *still* owned – a van.

What was it doing here, Nick wondered. Abandoned perhaps? It was a funny place to park ...

He remembered his orders not to approach the house. Well, this wasn't the house, was it? This was a vehicle and it was clearly unoccupied. There was no risk of putting the wind up any terrorists just by taking a little tiny look.

He indicated to Williams to stay put, and crept forward. The van was parked at an odd angle, as if it had been left in a hurry. Nick felt a small spark of hope.

He listened hard, then climbed through the barbed-wire fence and went up to the van. He peered in through the windows, then tried the passenger door. It was not locked and the handle gave easily. He began to open it. There was a loud creak. He winced. Trying not to open it any further, he put his head in.

There was something lying on the seat. He couldn't quite make out what it was and ran a hand over it. A bulky padded fabric. Something hard beneath. He slipped his hand under and grasped metal.

He shivered with excitement.

He pulled the object out and held it up until it was silhouetted against the windscreen. A machine pistol. With silencer.

He replaced it carefully on the seat. He felt around the floor. Nothing. Closing the door as quietly as possible, he went round to the back of the van and pulled open one of the rear doors. He thrust a hand in and felt clothing, shoes, a polythene bag.

He decided to risk a little light. Taking a penlight from his pocket he shone it over the floor. A sleeping-bag, pillows, clothing . . . And in the polythene bag five magazines of ammunition.

And a stick of explosive.

He flicked off the light and closed the rear door.

Returning to Williams, they retreated a short distance into the trees and radioed back to Conway.

Less than fifteen minutes later there was a reply from London. No one was to move until further notice. Under no circumstances was the house to be approached. Nick found a tree trunk with a good view of the house and drive and, pulling his collar up, settled himself against it. He might as well make himself as comfortable as possible. It was going to be a long cold night.

Gabriele lay on the bed in the darkness, knowing she would never sleep. Once or twice she almost dozed off, only to be woken by the distant hum and click of the nearby lift. She kept thinking about Giorgio, wondering if he was caught, wondering if he was even now in some pig-hole. If so, she would get him out, with the others. She would demand it.

As the long night drew on she finally dropped into a fitful sleep, and saw Giorgio in her dream, a Giorgio who was very distant and strangely uninterested in what was happening. She called out to him, but he was separated from her and somehow couldn't hear . . .

She awoke, troubled, and heard the sounds of early traffic rising from the street outside and realised it was almost morning.

At seven she got up and tried the Paris number again. It rang for a long time without reply: the loneliest sound in the world. Gabriele suppressed a feeling of despair.

Going to the window, she watched the street for several minutes. The first glimmerings of dawn delineating the grey outlines of the small but expensive Chelsea houses. The Ford was just opposite, parked under a street lamp. Apart from the occasional passing car, nothing stirred.

She kept thinking about the Paris number. Why didn't it answer? Raymond knew how urgent it was. There were only a few hours to the deadline. When had she first phoned him? Yesterday morning. So he'd had twenty-four hours to contact people. It *must* be long enough.

Eventually she went to the kitchen and, searching the cupboards, found some coffee. There was no food. As she waited for the kettle to boil, she unwrapped the bundle she had left behind the fridge so many days before. She had already brought all the weapons up from the car. The Kalashnikov gleamed at her, sleek and deadly.

She levered open the plinth beside the cooker and pulled out the parcel she had hidden there. She opened it, pleased with her own resourcefulness. Her planning had paid off.

She examined the Argentinian passport, checked the money, and laid out the change of clothes, ready to put on.

Still time to kill. There was no radio to listen to. She sat drinking coffee as the minutes dragged by. At last it was seven-thirty; in Paris eight-thirty: all the offices would be open by now.

Trembling, she dialled the number yet again.

It answered straight away. She felt a warm flood of relief. It was a man's voice.

'Raymond?' she breathed.

Raymond was not there, the voice replied, but he was expected in at any moment. Did she want to leave a message?

It was vital to speak to him direct, she told the voice. Could he call her?

'What is your name and your number?' the voice asked.

She told him and rang off, bitterly disappointed.

340

Then she remembered that she *had* to go out and buy *The Times*. Supposing he rang back while she was out? Would he give up and never call back again? Stay calm. *Stay calm.*

Giorgio would have helped her to think. *Giorgio* . . .

She suddenly felt very alone.

She pulled on her jacket and hurried out into the street. There was no one about; she looked over her shoulder a couple of times to make sure. She found a newsagent in the King's Road and, picking up a copy of *The Times*, leafed quickly through it.

Where would they have put it?

She tried the Personal Column. She felt a shiver of excitement. It jumped out at her: the first item, prominent in block capitals.

It read: 'CRYSTAL. OFFER ACCEPTED. PLEASE CONTACT SOONEST. 01-875 2289.'

Henry's body was icy cold, but nothing could ever feel so cold as the chill in his heart. The minutes passed ruthlessly, and with each moment he became more bitterly aware that in all probability he would die quite soon.

He had until midday. He knew that. He had heard the man telling Victoria.

And now Victoria would probably die too.

As long as he had believed that only the lid could trigger the explosives he had been able to cope; there was a strange security in being locked in the box with the means of one's own destruction. But then had come the bolt from the blue: the realisation that he had a finite amount of time; and then he had discovered a fresh and more incisive fear. Though he tried not to, he couldn't stop himself from imagining the final moments. Though he might be unaware of exactly how long remained, there was the ghastly possibility that he might know – *sense* – the final moment approaching. He would probably be overcome by panic of the most debasing and loathsome kind, he would probably sweat or – even worse – call out. And he couldn't bear the idea of any of that. Better to go quickly, thinking of Caroline . . .

She would be all right in time. She was so young. And she would have the child. What a blessing that would be. What a consolation. And, though she would find it hard to believe at first, she would find someone else in time, someone to take care of her.

The thought was reassuring. Though not half as reassuring as being able to tell her himself. That would be his great regret. Not having the opportunity of a final word or a last message.

He thought about Victoria. He must tell her that he bore her no grudge: that he forgave her. It wasn't quite the truth. He didn't think he could ever completely forgive her. But he must make his peace with her; and he must tell her soon before it was too late. It was the right thing to do, and he very much wanted to do the right thing.

There were no other sections of his life that he could tidy up. It would have been marvellous to tell Caroline how much she had meant to him, but then she knew that already. He had said it often enough. So many people went through life *without* saying these things, but he had never been embarrassed by emotion. Quite the contrary. How very glad he was of that now.

The thought brought him a transitory peace and for a few moments he lingered in the memories of that warm and simple love.

Nick drifted out of a dream. He was dimly aware that he had slept for an unusually long time. A sound disturbed him, something scratched at his face. He sprang awake. There was a branch against his face. He pushed it away and thrust his watch up to his face. Nine. *Christ!* He sat upright and looked wildly about him.

But it was all right. The three officers who had relieved him and Williams in the early hours were just moving away, and a new team were taking over, crouching in the undergrowth, their rifles across their knees.

Kershaw had put men everywhere: behind the ridge, throughout the woods and hidden beside all the access roads to the village. The place was sealed tight. But what were they waiting for? As far as Nick could tell, they were waiting simply to watch helplessly as the terrorists left the farmhouse and got clean away.

If they were there at all. There still hadn't been a sign of life.

Nick wondered whether to head back towards Kershaw's base, which had been set up at a neighbouring farmhouse. Quite apart from anything else he was wolfishly hungry.

He went to tell one of the men that he was leaving and began to retreat through the woodland. But a sound came from behind and he stopped. One of the officers was speaking into a walkie-talkie. Nick retraced his steps. The officer turned to him and whispered, 'Car approaching.'

They waited silently, watching the track where it emerged from the avenue of trees. But they heard it long before they saw it, the innocent sound of a car being driven along at a moderate speed.

The engine note slowed a little, then it appeared: a red Morris 1300. It carefully negotiated the stationary van, then progressed down the drive towards the farmhouse. Nick followed it with the binoculars. There was a single occupant: male, youngish, collar and tie. A picture of respectability.

The car drew up in front of the farmhouse. After a moment, the driver's door swung open and the young man got out. He slammed the door shut and stood still for a moment. Then he sauntered about. He turned his back to the farmhouse and stared back up the hill.

Looking at the van.

After a moment he turned away and leaned against the car bonnet.

Waiting. Very relaxed. Who on earth?

Then Nick shook his head. He called up Kershaw on the walkie-talkie and reported: 'I think we've got ourselves one estate agent.'

Twenty-seven

Archie Pinker looked at his watch. Five past nine. He always gave clients a reasonable time before giving up on them – at least twenty minutes, sometimes longer if he was in a good mood.

It was a lovely morning. He would give this one until nine-thirty. Probably too generous. Some people could leave you waiting for hours without feeling a moment's remorse.

It occurred to him that he should open the house up. It had been empty for quite a time and probably smelled musty inside. Women were always on about throwing windows open and airing rooms. Maybe they had a point.

He sorted through the bunch of keys in his hand and selected the one that looked most promising for the front door. He tried it in the lock but it wouldn't turn. He was a little put out: he usually prided himself on matching keys to locks.

From hard-gained experience of the perversity of people who fitted locks to doors, he twisted the key the other way.

To his surprise it turned. He tried the knob. The door wouldn't budge. Finally he realised: he had just *locked* the door. When he had first tried the key, it had been *open*.

Perhaps that mad hippy girl who owned the place had been down here. Or her equally mad friends. That would account for the open door and the van parked half-way up the track.

He went in and walked through the hall into the kitchen. He tutted. Just as he'd thought: food and drink on the draining board. How one could be expected to sell a place when there were hippies coming and going, he didn't know.

On his way to the living-room he passed through the hall again, and noticed a scrap of paper on the floor. Typical, he thought. Litter all over the place. He scooped it up. It had writing on it. KEEP AWAY. FROM BOTH DOOR AND GIRL. THE SLIGHTEST VIBRATION AND BANG! THE CRYSTAL FACTION.

Some weird game they'd been playing, no doubt. Quite mad. He screwed the paper into a neat ball and threw it in a waste bin in the living-room. He drew back the curtains and opened a window. The room certainly needed the air: it smelled of spilled drink and old cigarettes.

He wandered back into the hall, humming softly to himself.

A sound startled him. A muffled female voice.

'Hello?' he called cautiously.

The voice came again. This time he heard the words quite distinctly: 'Who is it?'

Archie Pinker advanced slowly towards the door which, he remembered from the details, led down to the cellars.

'Hello?' he said again.

'Whatever you do, don't open this door!'

Archie blinked. The voice sounded – *awful*. And what on earth was someone doing in the *cellar*? 'Um – is there anything the matter?' he asked uncertainly.

'Yes! Please phone for the police. Straight away. *Please*. It's desperate. *Please*. Tell them it's a matter of life and death and that they must come *immediately*.'

There was a pause.

Archie was a bit taken aback. What *was* going on? Good God – of course. It must be another drug orgy, like the one in which the chap had died. Lord. What a nasty thought. And now *he* was being dragged into it. It really was most unreasonable. At the same time, it would be quite a thing to inform the police. A good story to tell in the pub.

The voice was saying, 'Please, please, are you still there?'

'Yes.'

'Are you from the estate agents?'

'Yes. Archie Pinker.'

'Well, please tell the police it's to do with the Attorney-General. *Please*. They'll understand. You will tell them, *won't* you?'

'Oh . . . Yes . . .' Archie felt a pang of disappointment. The girl was obviously nuts. The Attorney-General indeed. And as for the police understanding, he was beginning to be uncomfortably certain that they wouldn't.

Nevertheless he looked around for the phone. Seeing one by the front door, he picked it up to dial 999. The phone was dead. He looked at it crossly. Silly girl hadn't paid the bill.

Blast. What a nuisance this all was.

'Hello?' he called through the door. 'Your phone's been cut off. I'll have to go into the village or something.'

'Ohh.' The voice sounded very distressed. Archie was not very fond of emotion, especially in women. He said briskly, 'Right. Well, I'll be off now.'

'Please – make sure they realise. They mustn't – absolutely mustn't – open the door!'

'Right ho.' Archie retreated fast. He got straight into the car and tried to decide what to do. It was nine-fifteen. No client in sight. If he left now he'd probably miss him. Really, this was too much.

Finally he decided to whizz quickly up the road to the nearest phone box and then whizz straight back. He drove quickly up the drive, or as quickly as it was possible to go on the dreadful road surface, and three minutes later arrived in the village.

He was looking for a phone box – there was always at least *one* in these small villages – when a car appeared from nowhere and forced him to brake sharply to a halt. Brimming with righteous indignation he wound down the window, ready to give the driver a piece of his mind, when he saw four men getting out of the car and approaching in what he quickly appreciated was a serious manner.

'Mr Pinker?' the first man asked.

'Yes,' he replied, wondering nervously how they knew his name.

'Could you tell us, please, what you saw at Hunter's Wood just now.'

Archie looked at the card the man was holding in his hand and realised that, due to some strange stroke of providence that he didn't quite understand, the police were already here.

How long would it take? Victoria imagined the estate agent driving up to the village, finding the phone box, having to wait while someone else finished a call, then getting through to the local police station. They wouldn't believe everything he told them, of course . . . But they would send someone anyway, just to check. A local man. In a slow car . . .

How long?

At least half an hour, she decided.

She must be patient. Another half-hour was not very long. Not after a whole night of biting pain from the wire on her wrists, and the nightmare of trying to prevent herself from falling asleep.

She called down to Henry again. 'Another half-hour, I should think. Then they'll be here!'

A faint 'Yes' came up. His voice sounded flat and uninterested, as if he didn't quite believe what she had told him.

She couldn't quite believe it herself. Everything had gone wrong for so long. She was still kicking herself for not having picked up Giorgio's gun. It must have dropped on to the floor of the shed, but she'd never even stopped to look for it. If only she *had*, then she might have been able to stop the woman. Shot her if necessary. It couldn't be that hard to aim and fire a gun. She could have done it, she *knew* she could.

After all, she'd stopped Giorgio.

For most of the night she'd been in terror of him returning, injured and viciously angry, and barging in through the cellar door. But as the long cold hours had dragged by she'd realised he would not return. Instead he had come to her in vivid appalling dreams which leapt into her mind as soon as she dozed. The nightmare always ended in the same way – with her falling forward, off the step. Then she awoke with a terrible start, her heart thumping, her mouth dry.

Now, as she waited, the memory of what had happened in the tractor shed had become just another vague half-realised horror that jostled with all the others in her tired mind. If she had hurt him badly she felt no remorse at all.

There was a sound. She was instantly alert.

The creak of a hinge. A footfall in the hall.

346

She gasped, 'Hello?'

A slight pause, then a voice close to the door. 'I'm a police officer. My name is Nick Ryder. Is that Victoria Danby?'

'*Yes.*'

'Is there anyone else in the house, Victoria?'

'Just us – me and Henry.'

'Sir Henry Northcliff?'

'*Yes.*' Victoria felt a wonderful relief: he *knew*. She wouldn't have to explain. She shouted the news down to Henry and he acknowledged it briefly.

The voice continued, 'Why mustn't we open the door, Victoria?'

'Because – there's a bomb. And another on Henry. And' – she whispered, putting her mouth close to the crack in the door – 'it's going to explode at midday. That's what they said. You will – be able to stop it, won't you. *Won't* you?'

'I'll have to get help, Victoria. Straight away. Can you hang on a minute?'

'You're not going?' She couldn't bear the thought of being alone again. He had such a reassuring voice.

'No,' he said quickly, 'I've just got to speak into my radio, that's all. I'll be straight back.'

She heard his voice, muted and efficient, and the tinny sound of amplified voices coming back in reply. While he was busy she called to Henry again. He replied in a voice that was stronger, more certain. He, too, was allowing himself to hope.

'Victoria?' It was the calm voice at the door again.

'Yes.'

'The bomb disposal people are on their way right now. They'll be here as soon as possible.'

'Thank you. Thank you.'

'Victoria, listen – what can you tell me about the people responsible for this? Where have they gone to – have you any idea?'

'There were two of them. A woman, Gabriele – I don't know where she's gone. She left last night.' She paused. 'Then there was a man. Giorgio. I think – I'm not sure – that he may be in the shed.'

There was an electric silence. 'In the shed!'

'I hit him,' she said calmly. 'I think he's still there.'

He was still there all right. Stone cold. Nick touched a hand. He'd been dead for some time. A Walther pistol lay on the floor some yards away. And the girl had killed him. Extraordinary.

He had known it would be Black Beard. There was no one else it could have been. Giorgio: he turned the name over in his mind. Italian then. He still didn't know his second name. He shook his head: there should have been a way of finding out before now.

In the yard behind him more cars were drawing up and men appearing from their stake-out positions.

A breathless Kershaw came up beside him and stared down at the body. 'One of *them*?' he asked.

'Yes. Our friend from the demo. Wheatfield's mate. The user of that Italian cologne.'

'How many does that leave then?'

Nick ventured, 'Just one. Just the Wilson woman. Unless –'

'Yes?'

'Unless she's got more friends.'

Kershaw grunted sharply. Waving a couple of his men forward he barked, 'Right, no pauses for snaps. Give him a good going over.'

They rolled the body on its back, and went through the clothing. As the contents of the pockets came out, Kershaw examined them and passed them to Nick.

Wallet . . . Money . . . Door keys . . . An Italian passport in the name of Riccardo Enrico. Crumpled receipts, a restaurant card, small change. And, folded in a back compartment of the wallet, a small slip of paper.

It had a list of five numbers on it, four of them with seven digits, the last with eight.

'Phone numbers?' Kershaw suggested. 'Right, let's go and try them.'

As the detectives cut the jacket off the body and tore the lining out, Nick followed Kershaw back towards the house. 'There's an army bomb disposal unit in Salisbury,' Kershaw said. 'They're on their way by road.'

'We only have till noon, so the girl says.'

'Ask her how she knows. Ask her *everything*. It'll be good for her to keep talking anyway. Meantime we'll get going on these numbers.'

Nick returned to the cellar door where another detective was crouching, his ear to the crack, talking softly.

Taking over, Nick said, 'Hello, Victoria. It's me again. Nick.'

'Hello.' She sounded pleased in a breathless panicky sort of way.

'Victoria, I'd like to have a long chat with you. About

everything. About how you got involved in this. Everything that might help us. Just until the bomb disposal people get here. Will that be all right?'

'They won't be long, will they?'

'Not too long. They're coming as fast as they can.'

'It's just – there's so little time.'

Nick looked at his watch. It was ten to ten. God!

In what he hoped was a comforting voice he said, 'Don't worry. If you could just—'

'But tell me,' she interruped firmly, 'did you find him in the shed?'

Nick hesitated for a moment. He didn't want to upset her – or did she already *know*? He said, 'He was there all right—'

'Tell me.'

Her tone was insistent. Hoping he was doing the right thing, Nick said, 'He was dead.'

There was only the slightest pause. 'Good,' she said matter-of-factly. 'I'm glad. He was a terrible person.'

'Yes.' So she had known. 'Now, Victoria. Please tell me what you know, about these people's contacts, their friends—'

'You want to find that woman—'

'Yes.'

'She was a terrible person too.'

Her words turned in his stomach; a knife-like memory that had lost none of its sharpness. He said, 'Yes, I know.'

She talked for a long time, first in great bursts, then more slowly, with greater effort. He could hear the tiredness in her voice as she dredged her memory for any small detail that might be useful.

He pressed her for more and more facts about the trip to Paris. She tried hard to remember the address where the van had been loaded, and the two streets where she had waited while Giorgio went to his appointments.

'He went into a door beside a newsagent's . . . There was an antique shop on the other side of the doorway. And then at the other place not far away – he came out of a second-hand bookshop – I *think*. Oh *dear*. I memorised the name of one of the streets. I really did. It was *Rue* something . . . But I can't remember!'

He could hear the exasperation in her voice. They had talked for thirty minutes. He guessed she was near her limits.

Some men in army uniforms were coming into the hall. Nick

said, 'Look, don't worry now. 'We'll try again later. The bomb disposal people are here. And they'll want to talk to you. I've got to go and make a phone call—'

'I was no use, was I? I'm *sorry*.'

'You were! You are! Really. And I wouldn't just say that.'

She started to speak, but her voice quavered, and he sensed that she was on the point of tears.

He said, 'Please don't – *worry*. You've been doing so well.'

There was a sniff and she said in a deliberately calm voice, 'You'll come back again, won't you?'

'Yes, of course.'

'I – feel so . . .' The voice trailed off and her silence hung painfully in the air.

'I'll be back,' Nick repeated softly. 'I promise.'

The bomb disposal men moved in to talk to her and Nick went to the phone, which a uniformed man with a screwdriver had just succeeded in reconnecting. Nick called Desport at the DST in Paris and gave him the details, such as they were, of the places the girl had visited. He also gave him the name of the girl, the name on the Italian's passport, details of the van, and the dates when they had been in Paris. It might not find Gabriele for them, but it could lead to the people responsible for helping her. And he wanted to know who they were, very badly.

He found Kershaw in his car, speaking into the radio mike. The commander clicked it back into its cradle. 'Nothing on those numbers. I've given them to a cypher bloke but . . .' His voice was heavy with pessimism.

Getting out of the car he added, 'We've heard nothing from the remaining terrorists, either. No contact at all. And only an hour and a half to go. If that bomb *is* on a timer, it doesn't leave much leeway.'

They walked towards the house. The head of the bomb disposal unit, a Major Phipps, came up. He was a typical army type, Nick observed. Short schoolboy haircut, crisp no-nonsense manner. 'We're going through the door,' he announced. 'Cutting a hole in it. Then we can get men inside and start work on both devices simultaneously.'

'It's safe, is it? To go through the door?' Nick asked.

'Should be. I've had a long talk to the girl. The device is strapped to her back. And the initiator is underneath her behind, so it is reasonably safe to assume that her weight is the critical factor.'

Nick gave an involuntary shudder. He remembered the jolly,

350

plump girl at the Vietnam United Front offices. Naïve, unworldly, pathetically enthusiastic. He had been scornful of her then. But, looking back, she hadn't been guilty of anything more than gullibility. She had trusted the first man who'd given her a good time. She wasn't the first to have fallen into that trap. She certainly didn't deserve this.

He looked into the hall and, seeing there was no one at the cellar door, he ducked under the tape that the army had slung across the front doorway and hurried across.

An army sergeant intercepted him. 'We're sealing this place off. Could you keep clear now, please.'

Nick waved him impatiently away and put his mouth to the door.

'Hello, Victoria.'

'Nick, is that you?' She sounded hopeful. Dangerously so. 'They're coming through the door, they said.'

'Yes. Any moment now. Be brave a while longer. You *have* been very brave, you know.'

'No. No. I haven't. I've made a complete mess of everything.' Her voice was full of anguish. 'I can't believe how *stupid* I've been.'

'Well, no point in brooding. It's in the past now.'

'I never realised, you know, who they were. Not until I found those sticks in the van.'

'I know.'

'The trouble was' – there was a pause – 'he made me happy. I never *thought* about – I just wanted to be happy. For a while. He was so – *different*. I'd never known anyone like him before. I didn't think about what or who he was or what he was doing. I just – wanted to be happy.'

'I understand.' There wasn't much else he could say.

'Everything's my fault—'

'You must stop thinking about it. You must think about helping the lads when they get through to you.'

'Yes. So sorry. Of *course*.' She added, 'I'm glad you're here. You – make me feel it's all going to be all right. You'll be staying, won't you?'

'Yes, of course.' He hated himself for being so definite; it was a promise he wasn't sure he would be able to keep.

'I – I feel – you'll think this is silly' – she gave a nervous high-pitched laugh – 'but I feel that you really *understand*.'

He thought: Better than you'll ever know. He said, ruefully,

'Yes. I – got involved with people like this myself once. Without realising it. So – I know how easy it is.'

'Oh.' She sounded surprised. Then, taking comfort from what he had said, she added, 'Thank you for telling me. Thank you.' Then, a tinge of worry returning to her voice: 'Are they coming soon?'

The army team were even then unrolling cable and preparing cutting tools.

'Any moment.'

She sighed softly.

Nick had a sudden thought. 'Victoria, we have met before, so don't be surprised when you see me.'

'We have?'

'Yes . . . Off the Holloway Road, at the VUF offices. I came in one day to ask for information.'

'Oh.' She sounded bewildered.

'It was in the line of duty,' he added apologetically.

'D'you know, I had the feeling I knew you. Isn't that odd?'

They made him move away then, out into the drive. He went to join Kershaw by the cars.

Suddenly there was a shout from inside the house. He spun round. He'd thought he was the last of the team to leave, but he could see Conway in the hall, talking urgently with Major Phipps. The next moment Conway hurried out into the yard, his face very grave. He was holding a piece of crumpled paper in his hand.

Nick took it from him and read the faintly written message.

KEEP AWAY. FROM BOTH DOOR AND GIRL. THE SLIGHTEST VIBRATION AND BANG! THE CRYSTAL FACTION.

A bewildered Archie Pinker confirmed he had found the paper in front of the cellar door and thrown it away. Which meant that the message was intended to be found straight away. It could be a bluff, of course. Everyone realised that.

Major Phipps questioned the girl again, to ask if she had seen anything attached to the door. She didn't remember. And she couldn't see very well without moving . . .

Then she did remember something. There had been a string . . . something the woman had led under the door.

Major Phipps withdrew his team from the door. The string might mean nothing. On the other hand it might have been used to arm an initiator attached to the door itself. It was too risky to

352

go in that way. For the moment at least. They would have to try something else.

And someone would have to tell the people in the cellar.

It was ten forty-five.

Gabriele stared at the telephone, hating the very sight of it.

She'd called Paris again, half an hour before, but the impersonal voice had reported that there was no news. They had not yet called back.

Now she couldn't delay any longer. If all the arrangements were to be made by noon, she must communicate them to the pigs.

She pulled *The Times* towards her and prepared to dial the number in the ad. She imagined a circle of men, sitting by a telephone somewhere in Whitehall, waiting for her to call. They must be in a sweat. Running around like chickens with their heads cut off. Perhaps the whole British government was waiting for her call. It was an intoxicating thought.

She dialled the number and aware of her thumping heart, picked up the piece of paper on which she had prepared her message.

The number connected and began to ring. It was answered immediately.

'Hello?' A clipped male voice.

She began to read: 'A plane is to be prepared at Heathrow airport for immediate departure. It is to have maximum fuel and a full flight-deck crew. Wheatfield, Reardon, Kitson and the Italian known as Giorgio are to be taken to the airport straight away and put on the aircraft. If these terms are not met, you know the consequences. You are to have a radio link set up between the plane and this number so that we can speak to our comrades.'

'But how do we know –' the voice began to protest.

She quickly broke the connection. She knew their tricks. Trying to get you to talk so they could trace the call. Well, they wouldn't catch her that way.

She went into the kitchen and made herself another coffee. She'd already drunk several cups. Her hands were shaking and she was as jumpy as a cat. She should go out and get something to eat, but she wasn't hungry any more.

She went to the window and stared down into the street. She wondered if they really did have Giorgio. Well, if so, she'd get him on to the plane with the others, and Nick Riley and his friends wouldn't be able to do a thing about it.

But her optimism was shaky and she didn't dare examine it too closely. Somewhere in the depths of her mind there was a nagging sense of abandonment. She had the feeling she would never see Giorgio again; already she was distancing herself from the memory of him.

Ever restless, she picked up the Kalashnikov and, unclipping the magazine, checked the mechanism.

Nick tried to make light of it. 'They just think it would be safer to go through the ceiling, that's all.'

'But it's so thick. It'll take hours.' Her voice was high and fearful.

'Well, they're going to *try*. They just think it would be safer,' he repeated.

'But – I don't understand. It would have been so *easy*.'

'I know. But, give them a while. If it doesn't work, they'll come back and try the door again. Okay?'

There was silence. After a while he realised she was not going to reply. He said, 'Chin up, there's a brave girl,' and then wished he'd kept quiet. He felt, instinctively, that it had been the wrong thing to say.

He stood up, heavy-hearted, and watched the army moving equipment into the dining-room which was situated above the cellar.

Conway appeared in the front doorway and beckoned him over.

'I've got an idea about those numbers, the ones our Eyetie had on him.'

They went and sat in the back of a car. Conway indicated the fourth number. 'See this one? It's got all the same numbers as the Danby girl's phone number. They're just in a slightly different order, right?' He pointed at a combination he had written alongside and Nick saw that the numbers were the same, but with the first four in reverse order.

'Now the third one has the same numbers as the service flat in Weymouth Street, but again in a different order. The *same* different order, if you see what I mean.'

Nick felt a shiver of excitement.

'And the others? What about the mews house?' he asked.

'I was going to ask you for the number. To save me getting it from London.'

Nick reached into his pocket and pulled out his address book. Looking under 'C' for Carelli, he read it out.

'Bingo,' said Conway quietly. 'It's the first number.'

Nick grasped Conway by the shoulder and gave him a rough shake of delight. 'You clever sod!' he exclaimed.

'Now, now, don't say things you might regret later,' said Conway. 'Right, let's get a make on this second number then, shall we? Must be a London number like the rest. Seven digits. But this last number – somehow I doubt we'll get much on that. Eight digits. An odd number of numbers, if you see what I mean.' Conway got out and, climbing into the front seat, called up Wilts HQ on the radio.

Nick went in search of Kershaw and found him talking rapidly to some of his men. Kershaw caught sight of him. Even before he spoke, Nick knew that something was up. 'Ah, Ryder, there you are. The terrorists have made contact. And a decision has been taken.' He sighed. 'They're to be allowed to leave. Unimpeded. From Heathrow, I want you to come with me in the airport party. We leave in five minutes.'

Nick stared in dismay. The government seemed to be caving in without a fight. And without a single guarantee for the safety of the two in the cellar. What a fiasco.

A minute later Conway had an address for the second phone number: a flat in Chelsea Manor Street. Kershaw hurried off to the phone to organise an immediate raid.

Nick waited for Kershaw to finish. Before leaving for the airport he must call Desport back. And the office. And then – then he would have to have one last talk with the girl, to tell her that, despite his promise, he couldn't stay after all.

Twenty-eight

It was five to eleven. Gabriele began to get ready. She put the Kalashnikov, the ammunition clips and a few personal items into the large holdall along with fifty pounds of the money. She placed the holdall by the door. She washed briefly, splashing water over

355

her face, then brushed her hair. It was important to look good. She eyed herself critically in the mirror. She changed her clothes and jammed the Makarov into her jacket pocket. The rest of the cash and the precious Argentinian passport also went into the jacket, in an inner zip-up pocket.

That left the Skorpion. She wanted to keep it handy. In the past she'd always carried it in the tote bag, but another bag would be cumbersome. Best to abandon the tote bag altogether. She put the Skorpion in the top of the holdall, where she could grab it easily.

But she wasn't sure if she had done the right thing. It was the nervousness. She must calm down. And make some more decisions.

Eleven. The airport was half an hour away. She would leave at quarter past eleven and arrive just before noon. Whether or not Raymond phoned. It was impossible to leave it any longer.

Somewhere near the airport she would stop and phone and talk to Max on the radio link to make sure everything was going all right.

Once at the airport she would take a hostage and walk on to the plane. For perhaps the twentieth time that morning she conjured up the scene in her mind: the plane waiting on the tarmac, the others already inside, the pig-police watching but helpless to do anything about it. Then she imagined herself, walking out on to the tarmac, a slim dramatic figure holding the Kalashnikov at someone's back.

She had a sudden doubt. Would it be wise to do it that way?

There might be marksmen on the rooftops. They might pick her off.

And yet – they wouldn't dare, would they? She would still hold the trump card: the attorney-man, and where he was, and how to de-rig him. They daren't touch her until she'd given them the information.

In her imagination she resumed the scenario on the airport tarmac. She would walk slowly, confidently . . . All those watching would notice her poise, her command of the situation. Perhaps there would be TV cameras and pressmen. Yes: there were bound to be. They would record the whole thing. Perhaps she would turn at the top of the steps, so they could get a good view of her. They would love that. They would call her the beautiful gunwoman, or something similar – they always called a woman beautiful if she was half decent-looking and if it would add to the drama of the story. Her picture would be on the front page of every newspaper in the world. The headlines would express outrage at this unthinkable event: blatant terrorism in Western Europe, the stronghold of law and order. And, most galling of all for them, they would have to report that one person – and a woman at that – had outmanoeuvred the entire British police force (not difficult, admittedly) and the might of the British government.

A real coup.

She reminded herself: When it happened.

If only Raymond would phone. She loathed hanging around.

She attempted to read *The Times*, but her eyes skimmed the words without taking anything in. There was, of course, nothing about the disappearance of the Attorney-General. She wasn't surprised: they were bound to hush it up if only to save face. But they wouldn't be able to hush it up much longer.

She walked to the window. The street scene was becoming irritatingly familiar.

The silence was split by the jangling of the telephone.

She jumped violently, and stared at it as if it had struck her. Tentatively she walked over and picked it up.

'Yes?'

'This is Raymond.'

She felt a surge of relief. '*Oh*, Thank God—'

'That special friend of yours,' he interrupted, 'the one you're hoping to see. He's in Damascus. I'm sure he'll be very happy to see you there. But why don't you surprise him? Don't tell anyone you're going – just drop in. Do you understand what I mean?'

Gabriele thought rapidly. She must get this right.

'Yes. You mean – make it a total surprise.'

'Absolutely. In fact, if he knew you were coming he might put you off – you know how it is. So many commitments and pressures. But if you just arrive, I'm fairly sure he won't turn you away. So my friends tell me.'

'I understand.'

'Goodbye then.'

She put down the phone, elated. She'd known he would fix something. She'd known that he would move heaven and earth. There was a bond of commitment and loyalty between them: a bond that was strong and pure and enduring; something the money-grabbing materialists could never understand.

The thought lifted her, and she felt a new optimism.

It was only five past eleven. *Think*. Should she go yet? She didn't want to hang around the airport. They'd be looking for her there.

Wait then? She didn't like that either.

She decided to call *The Times* number again, to make sure everything was going to plan. She would drive to a phone box some distance away and make it from there. That would use up the time nicely.

She checked the flat to make sure she hadn't left anything behind, then went to the window to take a last look out.

The Ford was parked in its usual place. Another car was manoeuvring into a space just in front of it. She watched it park. A girl in a very brief mini-skirt got out and, locking the door, walked jauntily off along the pavement. A youth coming towards her gazed openly at her legs and, passing by, stopped to watch the rear view wiggling ridiculously away.

A delivery van roared along the road and turned into an adjacent street.

Nothing. Nothing to worry about at all.

She was about to turn away when another vehicle caught her eye. It was stopping some way up the street to the left, almost on a corner. She watched it park and waited for the driver to emerge. A minute later the door still hadn't opened.

She glanced impatiently at her watch. It really *was* time to go now. She looked back at the car. She was worrying too much. It was just someone waiting.

She went to the door, put on her jacket and lifted the holdall. It was heavy. Perhaps she should have abandoned one of the weapons. But it was too late now.

Checking that she had the car keys handy in her pocket, she went out into the communal hall. Everything was quiet. She slipped down the stairs to the street and paused in the doorway. She eased her head out and looked up the road. That car was still there. It was hard to see if there was anyone in it. Maybe the driver had got out while she was on her way down.

She looked the other way, to the right. A Harrod's van was growling up the street towards her. She waited for it to pass. Some distance behind, a car was approaching normally.

She glanced back to the left. Nothing to worry about. She walked across the pavement and paused between two parked cars to look for traffic. The approaching car was fifty yards away and braking suddenly. She kept perfectly still, watching. It swerved violently into the opposite kerb and stopped.

Unusual. Swerving suddenly into the kerb. Not many people drove like that.

She pulled back a step. No one was getting out of the car.

That made two cars that no one had got out of.

It meant nothing. *Surely*.

She waited motionless, staring at the second car, dark blue and ominous, gleaming darkly. She caught a glimpse of movement inside. The driver. And someone else. Perhaps even a *third*.

Her stomach turned. She looked across the road to the Ford. So near. The width of the street. All she had to do was walk over. Yet a warning bell screamed in the back of her mind. If she moved it would invite disaster . . .

Better to stay still and uncommitted . . .

The faint chug of a diesel engine sounded in the distance. Beyond the second car, a taxi was approaching. The cab came parallel with the car. It was moving between her and the mysterious watching figures.

She had only a split second.

She reached into the holdall and, pulling the Skorpion out, thrust it under her jacket.

Not enough free hands.

The cab roared past. She followed it with her eyes as if checking that the absence of a For Hire light had told the truth and that it was indeed occupied. Then, as if searching for another cab, she looked back.

Behind the windscreen of the dark car something caught the light and gleamed.

Binoculars?

She looked again at the Ford. It would seem odd if she suddenly walked across to it and got in. Or would it? She could easily have given up the idea of taking a cab and decided on a car instead . . .

But a *car*. A car was something which could be followed and stopped. A car was a trap.

Before she could change her mind, she turned and stepped back on to the pavement. She made herself walk casually along the pavement, away from the second car and towards the street that ran down the side of the block of flats. Diagonally ahead of her was the first car. She could see two people in it.

Keeping her elbow tight against the Skorpion, she reached the corner and turned left down the side street. Out of the corner of her eye she saw the door of the first car start to open.

This was it then.

She quickened her pace and examined the street ahead. On the right, there was an estate of council flats whose blocks were connected by a honeycomb of courtyards and archways.

She crossed the street and risked a quick glance behind. A man wearing a raincoat had appeared at the corner, hovering, eyeing her uncertainly, as if he wasn't absolutely sure.

Ignoring the archway leading into the estate, she hurried on, walking fast. Ahead was another street. If she turned right, it would take her along a second side of the council estate. She came to a decision. Making a supreme effort not to look behind, she walked on. She reached the corner, rounded it—

Now.

She burst into a sprint.

It was difficult to run with both hands encumbered. The holdall bumped maddeningly against her leg. She held it up, clear of her leg, and felt her arm complain. The other arm she kept firmly jammed against the Skorpion under her jacket. She pushed on, running wildly, her eyes on another archway ahead. She could almost feel the man behind her, rounding the corner, his eyes burning into her back.

She came to the archway and, diving in, stopped. She put her head out and took a quick look back.

He was just appearing at the corner, looking round in alarm, beginning to run with no clear idea of where he was going.

He hadn't seen her.

Immediately she darted off into the courtyard. Ahead was another achway, leading to a second courtyard. She sped towards it, trying to work out how long it would take the raincoat man to reach the archway and see her.

Once through, she wheeled to the left. Ahead was an archway which would bring her out on the third side of the estate. She approached it cautiously. She put her eye to the corner and looked both ways.

Nothing.

Rapidly, she pulled off her jacket, draped it over the Skorpion and walked out into the street. Her jacket was black, her sweater green. If she was seen, the difference might just be enough to confuse them.

360

She turned left, heading back towards the street where she had last seen raincoat man.

This was the tricky bit. The fear rose in her throat.

If she'd got it right he would be chasing through the network of yards and passages inside the estate. If she'd got it wrong, he would even now be loping along the street and they would meet face to face on the corner . . .

She grasped the butt of the pistol. *God, but she felt so much better with a gun in her hand* . . .

The corner came up. She slowed and inched forward.

Nothing! Exultant, she hurried away, heading for the King's Road. She could see it ahead, busy with traffic and shoppers. Once there she could lose herself in the crowds and find a cab to take her out to the airport . . .

No more than a hundred yards now. She looked behind. Clear. She hurried on, almost sick with apprehension.

Coming to a junction, she glanced automatically down the side street. And froze.

God.

The dark car. Right at the far end, *coming.*

She forced herself to continue her journey across the street to the next corner. She heard the car accelerate suddenly. *They had seen her.*

Time to stop running.

Dropping the holdall on the pavement and throwing the jacket aside, she grasped the Skorpion in both hands and, flicking the change lever on to automatic, crouched behind a parked car.

The engine roared up noisily, then slowed as it braked for the corner. The car shot into view. She stood up. The surprised faces stared out of the car windows at her. She gave it a short burst. The driver's hands fought the wheel, the car shot on across the junction. There was a loud crash of colliding tearing metal, and the dark car was at a halt against a parked car.

Gabriele reached for the holdall, ready to run, but hesitated. A man, completely unhurt, was getting out of the back of the police car, poising himself to run at her. Bracing herself again, she aimed slightly to the right and squeezed the trigger, intending to fire the burst across his body.

The pistol vibrated in her hands, spitting its muted cough.

Then silence.

She squeezed the trigger harder.

Nothing.

A jam!

She looked wildly from the gun to the man. The man was staggering and falling, grasping his side. She'd got him then, after all.

She paused, scenting the wind. Sirens sounded in the distance, coming closer. Far down the street she saw a running figure coming rapidly towards her, raincoat man. She felt a flutter of panic. Impossible to shoot it out, even with the Kalashnikov. Take a hostage? Run?

She threw the Skorpion down and, picking up the holdall, started to run. Crossing the road she darted into a small side street. She kept running, glancing over her shoulder. She rounded another corner into another street of small Chelsea houses, zig-zagging her way gradually towards the King's Road. The wail of the sirens grew steadily closer. She began to tire.

She glanced over her shoulder. Nothing. *Yet.* But a siren was coming closer all the time. From behind.

Ahead, the King's Road, tantalisingly close. Yet too *far*.

Gabriele thought: I can't bear it.

Two yards ahead, a woman was standing outside the front doorway of her home, looking out into the street, irritated at all the noise in her quiet expensive neighbourhood.

Without slowing her pace, Gabriele swerved in through the metal gate, up the steps to the door and, before the surprised woman could utter a word, had yanked her inside the house and slammed the door.

The siren wailed to a crescendo, hovering in a high-pitched scream which filled the air, then slowly faded.

Gabriele leant against the door for a moment, panting hard, letting the relief flow through her, before turning her attention to the woman. The woman was making a lot of noise. She was sixty-ish, with tightly curled hair rinsed a pale shade of blue, and several rows of pearls over a massive bosom. She was squawking indignantly, her bosom swelling like a set of massive bellows. She reminded Gabriele of a ludicrous turkey, gobbling and parading.

Gabriele said, 'Shut up.'

The woman gaped and said, 'Well *really*! I'm going to phone the police!'

Gabriele saved her breath. The wobbling gobbling mouth would clam shut once it saw the Makarov.

She reached down to her pocket.

The jacket.

In the holdall. *It must be.*

But even as she bent down and thrust a hand into the bag she *remembered.*

Throwing the jacket on to the pavement.

Leaving it.

She cried out, 'Oh *no*! Oh G-o-d!'

The Makarov.

Then she froze in disbelief as the realisation dawned that it was much, much worse.

The money. The passport.

She had nothing but fifty pounds. And the Kalashnikov.

They'd said it was urgent. Nick sat in the car, waiting impatiently to be connected through the radio link-up. He might as well be calling Mongolia as Paris for the time it was taking. And he only had a few minutes before the last car left for the airport; minutes which he needed to make a brief explanation to the girl.

He was just about to give the call up when the number finally rang and he was through to Desport.

Nick listened to the DST man with growing incredulity.

'What do you mean the camper van was *seen* outside this organisation?'

'It was logged by our man.'

'Then this Aid and Solidarity place is well known to you?'

'Yes.'

'Why weren't we *told* – about the van, I mean.'

'You were,' replied Desport. 'The information was passed on in the normal way, to our liaison man who would have passed it on to your Security Service.'

Bloody Box 500. Bloody Reece-Jones. Doubtless the information was filed away in some dust-coated archive and no one had thought it worth disseminating to Special Branch. Secretive and incompetent to the bloody end. Nick thought: Sod them all.

'So tell me, Claude,' Nick asked bitterly. 'Who are these people, Aide et Solidarité?'

'They help political refugees, particularly Third World people. With accommodation, contacts, that sort of thing.'

'So what would our Italian be doing there?'

'Well, there's a possibility they provide other services.'

'Like?'

'Papers, false passports . . .'

'And?'

'And maybe even more.' He was sounding a little defensive. 'But – that is not certain.'

Nick ventured, 'Arms and training?'

There was a pause. 'It's possible.'

Nick thought: Marvellous. A subversive organisation operating under the noses of the French. 'And did these people realise they were helping terrorists to operate in Britain?' he asked.

'Ah, yes. I was getting round to that. We have already notified your headquarters that there was a telephone call made from Aide et Solidarité just a short time ago which could be of interest. It was to England. A veiled conversation. But there was a mention of Damascus. It is possible this is the destination that has been arranged for your terrorists.'

Nick absorbed the information. So they'd been tapping the organisation's phone for some time. Pity nothing of 'interest' had come up before. Nick said coldly, 'Thanks. You'll keep us informed?'

'Of course. We don't like these people any more than you do, you know.'

Nick rang off and thought: I wonder.

Now – Victoria.

He hurried across the drive and into the house. The loud whine of an electric saw sounded from the dining-room. Major Phipps was crouching by the cellar door, talking urgently. He was not looking happy with the conversation. As Nick approached, the major flung him an imploring glance.

'It's very difficult to be certain,' he was saying. 'I'd have to know how much explosive there was. But if it's a tiny quantity like you say, then it's *very* unlikely.' He added hastily. 'Look, I've got to dash now. But Sergeant Ryder's here. I know he wants to have a word with you.'

He stood up and whispered to Nick, 'She's asking all sorts of questions about the devices. Seems to be worried about one setting off the other. Anyway – I've reassured her as best I can.' He indicated the dining-room. 'Got to get back. That floor's made of ship's timbers with enormous cross-beams. It's taking longer than I thought to get through.' He strode off, looking immensely relieved to be returning to the job in hand.

Nick sat down and put his mouth to the door. 'Hello, Victoria.'

'Hello. I'm glad you're here.' Her tone was brisk. 'There's something I want to ask you.'

'Yes?'

'Promise to tell me the truth?'

Nick hesitated. He didn't want to be put in an awkward corner. He murmured reluctantly, 'I'll try.'

'Tell me why they're not coming through the door.'

So that was it. He couldn't see any reason why she shouldn't know. It couldn't make things any worse, and the uncertainty was obviously bothering her.

'A note was found. Saying the door was booby-trapped.'

'But it *isn't*. I would have seen.'

'Well – it isn't that we don't believe you. It's just – we don't want to take any chances with your safety.'

There was a silence.

'They'll be through the ceiling in no time. It's safer this way. You *do* see?'

'Yes.'

'How's Sir Henry?'

'He's all right. I spoke to him a moment ago.'

Now for the awkward bit. 'Victoria, something's come up. The terrorists have asked for a plane to be laid on at the airport. And – I have to go.'

A pause. 'I understand.' Her voice was so low he could barely hear it.

'Believe me, I would stay if I could. I'm sorry.'

He could imagine her, sitting there on the step, feeling alone. He had promised to stay, and now he was breaking his word.

'I'll come back and see you just as soon as I can. The minute the airport business is over. And that's a definite promise. You'll be out of here by then.' He struggled on, wishing she would reply and ease the moment along. 'And then I'll make sure you're looked after. I promise.'

'That's all right.' Her voice was ragged and uneven. 'I'll see you later. When you get back.'

He sighed. He felt a bit of a heel.

'Goodbye then, Victoria. Remember, I'll be thinking of you.'

'Tell me, have you got fair wavy hair? Longish?'

Her question took him by surprise. 'Yes.'

'I remember you then. I remember what you look like.'

He laughed, 'You'll know who to be angry with then.' Looking at his watch, he said a last goodbye and hurried away.

Henry wondered if it wasn't better to be without hope. Then at least you knew where you were. But he dismissed the thought almost immediately: better to live with the uncertainties of hope than to die alone and in despair.

The hum of the saws was getting louder by the minute. They should be through very soon now. Then—

Then, he reminded himself, it could still end in disaster. The only difference was that other people would die with him. That worried him. It was unnecessary.

At the same time, the hope that everything would end well had grown steadily in his mind. He had resisted it at first, but now he let it lift and sustain him. It could do no harm. It took his mind off the fact that he was exceedingly thirsty and that the pins and needles which had plagued his right leg for some hours had given way to a dull aching numbness. No: hope could do no harm . . . Better to pass the time thinking of a future with Caroline than to brood about having no future at all.

He imagined himself and Caroline sitting on a beach. The baby was playing in the sand nearby. He noted that the beach was nowhere near Venice. Venice didn't seem important any more.'

The three of them were bathed in a glow of warm yellow light. The light of happiness. He had always doubted that people's hearts could swell with love, but he felt it happen to him now.

He pulled himself up. He was getting dangerously sentimental. It wouldn't do to be in an emotional state.

There was an especially loud noise.

Were they through?

If only he could see into the main cellar. But he must be patient.

'*Henry*?' Victoria's voice was hardly audible above the noise.

He drew breath to reply but the sound grew louder and the effort was too great.

The next moment there was a crumbling sound and the patter of falling plaster.

Suddenly the patter grew to a deep rumble and a great whoosh of air blew across the box, bringing a dense cloud of fine white dust in its wake.

366

Henry coughed and tried to turn his head away, but the dust was everywhere, filling his nose and lungs.

He coughed more violently, but with each gasp he sucked in more of the dense, choking dust. He couldn't *breathe*. As he fought desperately for the air that wasn't there he felt the beginnings of a cold remorseless panic.

Victoria raised her head from her chest. The fine white dust hung suspended in the air like a cloud. Coughing violently, she peered down into the cellar. It was almost impossible to see.

'Henry? *Henry?*'

She called until she was hoarse but there was no reply. In exasperation she turned to the door and shouted for help. Why wasn't anybody *there*?

At last someone replied. She recognised the voice of the army man.

She cried, 'Quick – *quick* – you must help.' She could hear herself babbling. 'Henry – I think something's happened to him. Please – *help*.'

'We're not quite through yet.' The man was using the tone that adults use to placate small children. 'In fact, I'm afraid there may be a lot more dust. We can't quite see – but it looks as though the entire ceiling may come down. It's obviously a bit dicky. Can you hold on in there?'

She coughed harshly, trying to clear her lungs. Regaining her breath, she begged, '*Please* – why don't you come in through the door?'

'Er – well, we might end up doing that. But we're going to press on with the ceiling. Just for the moment.' He spoke with finality.

She shook her head. It was a nightmare. A sort of Mad Hatter's tea party where, for no apparent reason, everyone did the opposite of what they should. Through the depths of her tiredness she couldn't work out why.

She called to Henry again. *Nothing.*

The hearty voice was still there. 'Just hold on, won't you!' it said, full of forced optimism. 'All right?'

'What time is it?' she asked.

'Ah. Don't you worry yourself about that. Plenty of time yet. Got to go and see how the lads are doing. Back in a mo.'

Victoria knew then. *Of course.* He hadn't dared tell her. That there wasn't much time at all. How long? Half an hour. Ten minutes. *Less?*

There was still no sound from Henry. She couldn't bear it. He *had* to be all right. That was the whole *point* of everything ... The reason for making all this effort: this keeping going for hour after hour, this good behaviour, this talking through the door as if everything was normal. She couldn't *bear* it if all that had been for nothing. Henry *had* to be all right. Without him, nothing would ever be the slightest bit right again.

Her own future tightened round her like a band. She could feel it encircling her head. In time it would crush her. There would be no escape from what she had done. No forgiveness. People would always remember: she didn't blame them. The shame would be with her always. Unbearable. And lonely. And she *would* be alone. Alone and lonely. She was fat and ugly, she could see that now. Men might be kind, like that police sergeant, but no one would ever want her. Not really. No. She could see that now.

She felt ashamed to think about such things. What mattered was the poor young policeman lying in the pool of blood, appallingly dead because of her, and Henry suffocating in that dreadful box.

A sudden vision of Giorgio came into her mind. She saw herself swinging the metal bar like a mad animal, the blows crushing his head. Then in some extraordinary way he was all right again and getting up and coming towards her, smiling secretly, knowing he could make her do it all over *again*.

The thought was loathsome because it was *true*. Or was it? What was true? She couldn't think. It was all getting very strange. Nothing was quite real any more. A deep weariness pulled at her, confusing her thoughts. And yet one idea remained vividly clear.

Someone *must* get to Henry. If anything happened, she would never forgive herself.

Tears slipped down her round cheeks. She knew what she must do.

It should be safe, the army man had said so. The small brick cellar was far enough away ...

She gave herself a moment to let the intolerable pressure of thoughts subside. Then she grasped at two simple, comforting ideas. That she would soon be released from the burden of what she had done. And that Henry would be all right.

Then it was easy.

She screwed up her eyes and, uttering a loud cry, stood up.

Nick cried, '*Pull over!*'

The driver beside him didn't need any encouragement. He was white as a sheet. Finding a lay-by, he swerved in and braked to a halt.

The four of them sat in silence, listening to the flat monotonal voice on the radio.

'. . . The second subject is okay. The army is through and working on him now. Over.'

The mike lay forgotten in Nick's hand. The driver took it from him and acknowledged.

Nick put his head in his hands.

One of the detectives in the back said, 'Thank God for that. Only the girl. I thought for a moment—'

'Yeah,' said another. 'Lucky they didn't both go up. At least there's a chance now. For *him*.'

'I wonder what happened,' murmured the driver. 'Think it was on a timer?'

'No. She probably panicked and thought she could run away from it.'

Nick flung open the door and, walking a few yards away, drew in some deep draughts of cool fresh air.

Twenty-nine

'Thank you, sir. That seems to give me the picture.' Captain Edwin Harris, Royal Engineers, specialist in bomb disposal for more than twenty years, spoke cheerfully, not only because he wanted to reassure the pale tense figure lying in the box, but because he *was* quite cheerful. This was going to be a challenge, and if one didn't like the idea of meeting challenges then one had no business being in bomb disposal.

He sat in thought for a moment, going over what Sir Henry had told him, trying to picture the form that the infernal device – as it was known in the trade – might take. Possibly a time–delay fuse, if Sir Henry had overheard the terrorists correctly. Four or five sticks of explosive, nine or ten inches long. Possibly this mixture of TNT and ammonium nitrate called Nitramite 19C, if the terrorists were using the same stuff as before. Not that the exact make was vital. All explosives went bang.

The exact make and type of detonator didn't matter that much either. What really counted was the initiator. If it was a delayed-action fuse, as the terrorists had suggested, then the delaying mechanism might be electrical or chemical. If electrical, there must be a timing device, and a sophisticated one at that – not an ordinary clock and certainly not an egg-timer – since it had been set over twelve hours before. A chemical delay was unlikely but not impossible. The method favoured by anarchists involved filling a rubber contraceptive with acid which slowly burnt its way through on to a highly combustible substance. But it was unreliable, since one could never be sure how long the process would take.

No. If it was a delayed-action fuse, then he was pretty sure it must be electrical. First thing, then, was to have a good listen. From his box of tricks he took out a device not unlike a doctor's stethoscope, except it was powered by batteries which amplified sounds up to five times. He listened for a good three minutes, moving the sensor from place to place on the surface of the box. He was listening for any sort of ticking, or the click of an electrical timer. Around the stomach area, where the device was apparently located, all he could hear was Sir Henry's laboured breathing. It was possible that a faint sound could be lost behind it.

So – it could still be anything. At this stage it was important not to rule anything out. He must keep his mind open to every possibility.

One possibility – and quite a strong one, he believed – was that it wasn't a delayed-action fuse at all, but a mechanical initiator that would be triggered by the opening of the box or the handling of the device itself.

One thing was for sure: it wasn't vibration activated. Otherwise the blast five minutes ago would have set it off and blown up not only Sir Henry, but a lot of the house as well.

'All right then,' he said brightly. 'We'll get going. Anything you want to ask before I start, sir?'

Sir Henry coughed violently. He wasn't sounding at all well. His breathing was heavy and laboured. The shock of the explosion can't have helped. The poor bloke had probably thought he was going up too. Lucky he didn't.

The coughing ceased. He was trying to say something. 'She died instantly, did she?'

Captain Harris said gravely, 'Yes. Instantly.' In fact she had lived for a minute, but only in a technical sense; her heart had kept beating, pumping blood out through the massive hole in her back. But she had been unconscious, so it had hardly counted. The body was still here. No point in removing it and endangering more lives. Harris had thrown a coat over it.

Now there was just Sir Henry and himself. Harris wondered how long Sir Henry could withstand the strain. At the moment he was still calm and composed. It was vital that he didn't panic.

Although he generally preferred to work in silence, Harris said, 'Look, if at any time you're worried, feel uneasy, or just want to talk, do so, won't you? And of course you will tell me if you feel anything move or click or whirr or anything like that. Are you with me?'

'Yes, I understand. The only thing is, I may not be able to stop myself coughing.'

'That's all right. But perhaps you could give me some warning.'

'I'll try.' Sir Henry managed a weak smile. Harris smiled back. They were going to get on fine.

Harris began by taking a good look at the box. He crawled round it, minutely examining the wood for signs of holes or fittings. He stopped on the right side, where Sir Henry had said the girl had been sitting while setting up the device. There was a small hole. Of course it might have been there before. On the other hand it could have been used to remove a safety device and arm the bomb.

The lid itself was fixed down with nails. There might easily be a spring mechanism jammed underneath; the lid was definitely *not* the way to approach the problem, then.

He shone a torch down past Sir Henry's shoulder and had a look with a mirror. However, the poor man's body was jammed so tight up against the lid of the box it was hard to see beyond his chest.

Sir Henry was lying with his knees pushed over to the right, so he had said. The obvious approach was from that side. However, it would be wisest to start from the end of the box, as far away from the device as possible, and see what he could discover from there.

After asking Sir Henry exactly where his feet were located, he cut a small hole in the end, well away from the lid and hopefully from Sir Henry's feet, and removed the offcut. Nothing untoward in sight. Cautiously he slipped a finger into the hole and felt gently around. When he was satisfied, he made the hole a little larger. Eventually, the hole was large enough to take a really good look.

As far as he could tell there was nothing in this end of the box at all. Unfortunately, however, Sir Henry's thighs were twisted across to the right and, apart from the area by the knee, jammed up against the lid, so that he could not see beyond to the stomach area.

But what was that by the knee? Something screwed on to the side of the box, just under the lid.

And a wire leading from it.

Ah.

He cut a hole in the side of the box below the knee, where he knew it was clear, and had another look. Ah yes, more and more interesting. A pressure release switch, which would be activated by the opening of the lid. Two wires led from it but were lost to view between the clothing and the lid.

Part one of the puzzle.

He asked, 'As far as you remember the entire device is on your stomach?'

'Yes.'

'Nothing on your sides?'

'Only the tape she fastened it on with.'

'And where is your right hand, sir?' he asked.

'Against my right leg.'

'And your arm is pressed hard against the side of the box?'

'Yes.'

'I'm going to take a section of the side away in that area. You may feel the saw but hopefully not the cutting edge.'

'Right.'

Harris cut into the side of the box half-way along, where he judged Sir Henry's stomach to be, and made a six-inch hole near the bottom so as to keep well away from the lid and from the small hole which might or might not be significant. He removed the offcut. Nothing but clothing in sight. He slipped his fingers inside the edge of the hole and felt around. No wires. He pushed his entire hand in. Nothing. He listened. No unusual sounds.

He enlarged the hole to within four inches of the lid. Ah, that was more like it. He could see over Sir Henry's arm to the area of his stomach. He shone a torch in. *There*. The side of the device: two sticks of explosive visible. Plus . . .

Bother, he reflected mildly. He couldn't quite see.

He pressed gently down on Sir Henry's sleeve so that he could aim the torch beam higher up into the box.

There.

Wires.

Right. The wires could belong to a simple electrical circuit connecting the charge to the pressure release switch. In which case a simple cut of the wire would deactivate it. On the other hand, the wires may be part of a collapsing circuit which, if cut, would complete a second circuit and fire the device. A sophisticated booby-trap. The firm rule was: do nothing until all the components of the device have been identified.

Often easier said than done.

Cautiously, he pushed his hand in through the hole and felt up the side of the box. This was fairly safe, since Sir Henry had, according to his story, wriggled his arm on several occasions.

Nothing so far. He pushed his hand further up the side until the tips of his fingers came to the join with the lid. He ran his fingers along the join. Nothing.

Checking with his hands to make sure it was safe he enlarged the hole still further, the whine of the jigsaw shattering the eerie silence. He peered in.

Ah. More of the wires were visible. They ran away from the infernal device along the underside of the lid towards Sir Henry's hip. One of them was hidden between the lid and the hip, the other dipped back down towards the floor. To the very thing he had been looking for.

A clothes peg. The wires connecting across two drawing-pins. On the floor beside it a piece of card attached to a strong thread. The safety device.

From the clothes peg the wire ran straight back up to the area where he had seen the pressure release switch.

Harris ran his fingers further along the join where the lid met the side. Yes, there it was. He barely touched it with the tip of his fingers. Two wires, one to a metal washer, the other to the plunger.

He felt a small satisfaction.

Two parts of the puzzle in place.

Now he must check that the second wire, which was caught up against the lid, did indeed run straight to the explosive charge. Very gently he pulled on the wire until it was free.

It did run straight to the charge.

He took a breather.

Then he cut into the other side of the box. He examined the explosive charge. No more wires in sight.

He'd got almost all the information he needed. There was only one unpleasant possibility. That there was more to the device than met the eye – a second circuit hidden *under* the explosive itself, next to Sir Henry's chest, which he couldn't see.

But that would be pretty sophisticated stuff. From what Sir Henry had said they had made this device fairly rapidly. Also, each bomb-maker had a style, a *modus operandi*, and this girl had done nothing before to suggest she was into clever booby-traps. Careful, *yes*. But sophisticated, *no*.

Sometimes one had to make a judgement. He made it now.

Taking some small wire cutters he reached in. At that moment Sir Henry made a sound and, drawing in a rasping involuntary breath, coughed loudly. Harris held still. The coughing fit lasted for a good thirty seconds. He gave it another minute to make sure Sir Henry was over it. The man was looking agitated now. Yes: this business would be over none too soon. Giving Sir Henry a comforting smile, he reached back into the box and felt for one of the wires.

He snipped it.

And blinked.

The great thing about getting it wrong was that, though something happened all right – and how – you would know nothing about it.

Next, he carefully capped off the two severed ends of wire with plastic tape. You could never be too careful.

Time for another breather. Sitting back on his heels, he said cryptically, 'Well, I think we've made progress. But still a few more things to check.'

'Well done.'

'You okay?'

'Oh yes,' he whispered. 'Don't – consider me. I've been here so long that . . .'

In his mind Harris finished the sentence for him: A little longer won't make any difference.

He turned his mind back to the job in hand.

He cut another hole in the left side of the box, near the feet. Nothing. He tried the other side, looking into the triangle formed by Sir Henry's bent knees.

Nothing.

Eventually he had cut enough away to have examined the entire lid where it met the wall of the box. No more pressure release switches anywhere.

It was still possible that there was some kind of initiator sitting directly on top of the charge. Very carefully he reached in and felt the device itself. He tried to slip his fingers over the top, but it was pressed up very close to the lid. However, by squeezing the device downward into Sir Henry's stomach, he eventually managed it.

There was nothing. He came to a decision. It was time to open the box. He took a wrench and began to lever open the lid. At each stage he checked the rim. Then, as soon as he could get to it, he taped back the plunger on the pressure release switch, just to be doubly sure. When he was satisfied, he prised the lid completely free of its nails. And swung it open.

There was a small gasp from Sir Henry, but Harris was too busy taking a good look to pay attention. No horrid surprises in sight.

Sir Henry's face was contorted with pain.

'Best stay as you are, sir,' Harris said. 'I've still got some checking to do.'

He thought: Very much so. He had to check the tape that bound the device to Sir Henry. This he did very carefully, looking for wires and triggers. Once satisfied, he cut it, keeping a steadying hand on the device itself.

A nasty mind would have put another pressure release switch underneath the device, next to Sir Henry's body. With exceptional care he examined the device from every angle then probed very gently underneath.

Two minutes later he lifted the device off Sir Henry's chest.

It still wasn't over.

'You sure nothing was put underneath you, sir?'

Sir Henry was obviously in a bad way, but he managed: 'Pretty sure.'

Harris checked anyway.

Five minutes later he called in his team to take the remains of the device away, and the stretcher party came down soon after. Then it really *was* over.

Harris shook Sir Henry's hand. He was a brave man. Strangely, the fellow didn't look very relieved, just dazed. Probably hadn't hoisted it in yet. And then there was the delayed shock. Harris guessed it would take him a long time to recover from his experience.

For Harris it was a lot easier. He was trained for it. Nevertheless, it did sometimes cross his mind that one day, for no good reason, the grand lottery in the sky might throw up his number. As usual he was rather pleased that today had not been the day.

Gabriele paid off the taxi at a phone box on the airport perimeter.

It was a quarter to twelve.

There was a petrol station further along the road. A good place to take a car-driving hostage. And she could still get into the airport by twelve.

She pulled *The Times* out of the holdall and propped it up in front of her. Her hand was shaking. She felt hot and feverish.

She put the money in and dialled, preparing her speech.

The number rang three times.

It answered. The same clipped voice. 'Hello?'

She pressed the button. The money dropped. She began, 'We will arrive at noon. You have fifteen minutes to complete the arrangements. Once we are safely in the air I will give you directions on how to locate the hostage and defuse the explosive. Now let me speak to my comrades.'

'I'm afraid it hasn't been possible to fix up the link—'

'*You have two seconds to get them on the line.*'

'Er – can you give us a little longer?' The voice was confident and strangely unperturbed.

She thought: They're just stalling. 'You don't *have* any longer!' she snapped. 'The attorney-man dies in half an hour. And I'm going to take more hostages! And if you haven't got that line open when I call back again the first hostage dies. *Understand*?'

There was a pause. Gabriele felt a burning impatience. Even now they must be tracing the call. She was about to slam the phone down when the voice came smoothly back.

'In that case the deal's off.'

Gabriele's heart gave a great lurch. The voice was very cool. Something was dreadfully wrong.

The voice continued, 'Sir Henry is safe and sound. The bombs are all defused. The deal's off. Although we are prepared to discuss surrender—'

'*Give me proof.*'

Another pause, as if the voice was conferring. Back it came, calm and controlled. 'Hunter's Wood Farm. In the cellar.'

Gabriele slammed down the phone, raging with anger. For a moment she couldn't grasp the enormity of the disaster.

Max, Stephie, Reardon. *Success.*

All gone. All gone.

Failure hit her like a punch in the stomach. She had been massively outrageously cheated, and the bitterness rose like bile in her throat.

Then she realised: they would be coming for her. Trying to catch her, trying to put her away.

Grabbing her belongings, she stumbled out of the box and walked rapidly away, looking over her shoulder. She crossed the A4, went past the petrol station, until she came to a residential road. She cut down it and lost herself in the network of roads beyond.

She came to another phone box. Someone was in it, a large homely woman who looked as though she was going to chat for hours. Gabriele paced up and down outside then beat on the glass. The woman gave her a withering look. Gabriele flung open the door. 'It's urgent!' Using all her strength she pulled the woman out.

'How dare you! Who do you think you are!'

Another squawker, like the woman in Chelsea. Gabriele had left that one tied up in the bath. To this one she merely snapped, '*Fuck off*!' The woman retreated, looking outraged.

Gabriele pulled the door shut behind her. Fumbling, she found her list of numbers and getting through to the international operator, asked for a transfer charge call to Paris, person to person.

Asking for the number restored some of her confidence. Raymond would know what to do. He would send her papers and money. He would get her out of the counry.

At last she heard the number ring and answer and the operator cut in, asking if they would accept the charge. With vast relief Gabriele heard Raymond's voice.

In the fraction of a second before she spoke two dull clicks sounded on the line.

*

Nick got back to the office in a mood of rage and disbelief. They had missed her at the hideout in Chelsea and now they had missed her at the airport.

Unbelievable.

The airport had been the perfect place for a trap. She could have been lured in under the pretence that all was well, and then been caught. Somehow. But the plan had been vetoed. Too dangerous. Innocent people might have died.

Now the intention was to seek her out in the normal way: plaster her picture over every air and seaport, watch for her on the streets, offer a reward for information. But it wasn't enough, not by a *long* way. They knew of two false passports she had used. She probably had others stashed away.

The more he thought about it the more convinced he was that she *would* escape. The idea filled him with bitter anger.

In a side room off the main incident room the items found near the scene of the shooting in Chelsea had been laid out. He recognised the jacket immediately. She'd worn it the evening they'd gone to dinner in Chelsea. It was strange to see it again now, familiar and harmless, beside the two chilling weapons. A machine pistol and a handgun. He didn't recognise the types and looked at the tags tied to the butts. Skorpion. Makarov. Russian or Czech presumably.

Then there was money. New notes in sequence: the bank job.

Finally, there was a passport. Argentinian. He picked it up and flicked through the pages. A very good fake. He paused at the photograph. The sight of her still had the power to unsettle him. That look – so intense, so antagonistic; the small angry abandoned child.

He snapped the passport shut and put it back on the table.

Conway put his head in. 'We're wanted.'

'The DST have been in touch,' Kershaw said as soon as they reached his office. 'They've just telexed a transcript of a phone conversation which took place half an hour ago.'

Nick grabbed the telex. Attached to it was an English translation. it read:

Call logged at 12.55 French time. Reverse charge from England to premises of Aide et Solidarité, Rue St Médard, 5th Arrondissement. Person to person: Gabriele to Raymond:

Female voice: Raymond? I need help. I – things have gone wrong. I've got to get out—

Male voice: I'm so sorry, this is not in fact Raymond. He's out at present. Could I ask you to call him later on the other number?

F: What? But I . . . (*Pause.*)

M: He'll be on the other number in about one hour's time. You have the other number?

F: Er . . . Yes, I have it. Yes, I understand. I'll call then. In one hour. He will be there won't he? It's very urgent.

M: Yes, he'll be there. Goodbye.

F: Goodbye.

(*Conversation ends.*)

'Have they got a tap on this other number?' Nick asked excitedly.

'How *can* they when they don't know what the number is?' Kershaw demanded shortly. He looked tired and irritable. He said more reasonably, 'They *have* got a tap on this Raymond's private number, so they say. But apparently he knows perfectly well that it's tapped, so . . .'

So, Nick thought, there wasn't a cat in hell's chance of them using it. His excitement evaporated.

He asked, 'Don't the DST have any contacts inside this Aid and Solidarity place?'

Kershaw raised his eyebrows slightly. 'We've requested all possible assistance. That's all we can do—'

'We might ask bloody Box 500 and the other lot what else they've been sitting on,' Nick exclaimed hotly. 'If the van incident is anything to go by, they've known about these people in Paris all along.'

Kershaw rubbed a hand over his face. 'I've got their report in front of me, Ryder. It doesn't add a great deal to what we already know.' He regarded Nick thoughtfully. 'Why don't you go home and get some rest? You look as though you need it.'

Nick opened his mouth to speak but something in the commander's face made him shut up.

He went up to his office and sat at his desk for a while. There was no question of his going home. Not while Gabriele was out there. Free. He couldn't bear to think of her getting away. The idea made him so angry that he had to get up and move around.

There must be *something* he could do. Even if it was only to go out and search the streets.

Ridiculous. *Think.*

He sat up again and eyed the telephone, deep in thought. An idea came to him. He turned it over in his mind. It was worth a try. *Anything* was worth a try.

Picking up the receiver he dialled Paris and, after some discussion with Claude Desport's office, not all of it amicable, managed to get Desport called away from his lunch.

'Sorry to ruin your meal, Claude. Nothing special, I trust?'

'Hah! With the time available? A sandwich, my friend.'

'Do you owe me any favours, Claude?'

'Well, I like to think we come out even, Nick. Fifty-fifty. Eh?'

'I want to use them up all at once.'

'Ah.'

'We've asked the DST for assistance in the matter of this girl. Right? Where do you think that's going to get us, Claude?'

'We will of course do all we . . .' There was a silence. 'Not so very far perhaps. Not directly.'

'Quite. That's why I'm asking you. To do what you can. It means a lot to me. Maybe even my job, Claude.' Nick mentioned the job as a weapon of persuasion, instinctively trying to add a touch of drama, but even as he said it he realised it was probably true. 'I was thinking,' he continued. 'There must be something you could pressurise them with. Something you've got on them. They've been operating for quite some time. Surely —'

There was a sharp intake of breath. 'Nick, these people are not just – *anything*. They're not just a political group. They have contacts. Links. Perhaps all the way to Moscow. You ask more than I can give.'

'All we want is a lead to the girl, Claude.'

'You ask too much.' But there was a thoughtfulness in his voice. 'But your job . . . You mean it?'

'I mean it.' Nick made a feeble attempt at humour. 'I got everything ever so slightly disastrously wrong.' He gave it a moment then pressed: 'It will mean more than I can say.'

There was a deep sigh. 'I promise nothing. You hear? Absolutely nothing.'

From the closed door of the darkroom in the Studio Vincenne came the occasional sound as the photographer worked at his task. He had promised to produce two passports in one hour. There really couldn't be anyone better, not only for speed but for quality.

From stolen blanks the man could produce a finished passport complete with personal details, photograph, embossing, and stamps so near perfect that only a real expert could tell the difference. He was the organisation's greatest asset.

Bernard Duteil waited, thoughtfully smoking his cigarette, and wondered which courier he should send to England. There were several young people who were glad to do little jobs for him in exchange for trips abroad. He never asked them to carry anything really compromising. No arms. Only money, papers – things that would never get them into serious trouble. Most of them enjoyed doing their little errands.

This time, however, he must choose carefully. There was quite a risk involved. It was possible he might be sending someone straight into the arms of the British police. When Gabriele had made her second call – to the priest's number – she'd sworn that she'd take care not to be followed. But she was sounding nervous and frightened. Capable of error.

He had known she was in deep trouble. He had heard the radio news. The kidnapping idea had been quite clever, but she had obviously made some very basic mistakes. Two of her group dead. And the hostage discovered before she'd got away.

It could have been bad luck, of course, but he was beginning to believe otherwise. She had failed in both her tasks: in subverting British society and in forming a group capable of continuing the work. It had turned into a fiasco.

And after all his hard work arranging the welcome in Damascus. He felt justified in being irritated. He had used a few favours there.

But if the Damascus business was annoying, the interest in Gabriele's telephone calls was worrying. The phone taps were back in full swing and, by the number of clicks on the line, they didn't mind letting him know. It was a not-so-subtle warning. And yet he owed some sort of loyalty to the girl, if only to get her out and away before she did any damage. And, more importantly, to cheat the British government of total victory. He didn't want them to gloat. If the entire group were imprisoned it would be a bad example to those who might one day follow in Gabriele's footsteps.

So he would send her the passports and some money, with the suggestion that a ferry to the Irish Republic and a plane from Dublin to Stockholm might be the safest route out of the country.

He had already told Gabriele where to meet the courier and how to recognise him. Now he must choose the right person.

He finally decided on a bright young art student who, though very new to the organisation, had a way with him: an apparent naïvety and endearing loquacity which could fool anyone into believing he knew nothing about the contents of the envelope.

As soon as the passports were ready, he would send a message to the student asking him if he wanted a trip to London. Duteil was confident he would agree. The only important thing was that he should wear a red scarf. A rather ridiculous device as a means of recognition, but serviceable enough.

Finally the photographer emerged. He was not a man to boast about his skills, but Duteil could see that he was satisfied with the results of his hour in the darkroom. Duteil did not need to inspect the finished products.

He made his way back to the Rue St Médard. It was necessary to get the details tidied up as soon as possible. The student had to be on the ten o'clock plane to London the next morning.

As he approached the door beside the newsagent's shop a car door opened and a man emerged.

'Monsieur Duteil?'

Duteil knew immediately. The man had authority written all over him. DST? Yes, he decided: DST.

He gave a small nod.

The man said, 'There is something of interest I would like to bring to your notice. May we talk? In the car?'

Duteil considered. These people had absolutely nothing on him, nothing they could ever make stick. He could refuse point blank to talk either in the car, at the station or anywhere else. At the same time the man's opening remark suggested there might be something in it for him.

'Not in the car. In the café.' He indicated a small place up the street. He preferred neutral territory.

They settled at a corner table.

'Monsieur Duteil,' the officer began carefully, 'you have managed to live quietly in this country for some time. A visitor who has respected the laws of France and up until this moment has given us no reason to believe you will not continue to do so.'

Duteil stayed silent. He could guess where this was leading to.

'However, we have reason to suspect that – *inadvertently* – you are about to transgress one of the more important rules. Which would be a great pity, as I'm sure you would agree.'

Duteil continued to stare. There was really no need for him to speak.

'The thing is, we are quite *generous* about many things. But we do lose our – what should I say, ability to overlook matters? – when we are dealing with a person wanted on a serious charge. I refer to a certain foreigner who was active in the Troubles. We have been looking for her for some time.'

Duteil narrowed his eyes at the mention of a serious charge. It seemed unlikely. She had only done what all the other students had done. Lobbed a few cobblestones.

The DST man saw his doubt. 'She is wanted for subversion against the state,' he elaborated. 'There was also another matter – she tried to kill a police officer. Took a knife to him. He was stabbed in the shoulder. This cannot be overlooked.'

Ah, now he was beginning to understand. Gabriele was perfectly capable of having stabbed someone. And yet why hadn't he heard about it? Why hadn't she told him?

'The thing is,' the officer continued smoothly. 'We have good reason to believe you aided and abetted this person at that time. And may indeed be considering doing so again. As a peaceful organisation dedicated to a worthwhile cause' – he said it with only the faintest sarcasm – 'you will not want to commit an offence which will have serious consequences for you.'

'What exactly are you asking?'

'Help us find the girl. We want her. The British want her. If you lead us to her you will be left in peace. On this matter at least.'

'Are there *other* matters?'

'Not at present.'

Duteil tapped his fingers thoughtfully against his mouth. 'A man's reputation is everything in life, wouldn't you agree?' he murmured. 'Suppose I knew someone who could help you – which I'm not saying for a moment that I could – what would happen to that man's reputation? Particularly if he was known for assisting refugees and victims of oppression. Would this man be trusted any more? I think not.' He laughed ironically. 'What would a man's friends think?'

The DST man whispered, 'Ah, but no one would ever know. This man could complete the arrangements and merely let slip a small detail. The meeting would go ahead in the normal way.'

'And the messenger?'

'Would be untouched. You have my guarantee.'

Duteil thought very carefully. He wondered how serious this threat to the organisation really was. He didn't believe this story

383

about the stabbing. If it was true he would *definitely* have heard about it at the time. But he realised that the truth was irrelevant. If he did not respond to the pressure they would merely find another way of making his life difficult.

He sighed inwardly. This would teach him to break his own rules. He should never have helped the girl in the first place.

At the same time he strongly resented this pressure being exerted on him.

He commented, 'Blackmail is not a very pleasant development.'

'I would call it a mutually convenient arrangement.' The DST man leant forward. 'And be certain that this is a very important matter.'

The whole thing could be a great big bluff, Duteil realised. There was no guarantee that they would keep to their promise.

The DST man pressed home his argument. 'The government is being pressurised by the British. They are looking to *us* for an explanation of how aid to a terrorist group could be emanating from Paris. Either we must produce culprits or we must produce information. It is one or the other. There can be no compromise. Do you follow me?'

Duteil followed all right. He had also made up his mind.

The girl had failed. She was unlikely to be of much use in the future.

Regrettable. But it was the way of the world. One had to be prepared for sacrifices in the service of the greater cause.

Thirty

Darkness was going to fall early, even for November. Yet it had been a long time coming. Gabriele had spent the afternoon freezing in a dreary place called Gunnersbury Park, a meagre patch of green in the western suburbs, half-way between the airport and central London. She detested killing time in this way, but the empty park was the safest place she could think of. For a while she had dozed on a bench, which had made her feel better: the jittery nausea left her stomach, and her hands became steadier. But then cold and lethargy crept over her and she realised she must force herself to move.

The meeting was still many hours away, hours that stretched out before her, fraught with difficulties. Somehow she had to find shelter for the night. And food. And a place to hide until noon the next day.

The meeting was set for two the next afternoon, on the bridge in the centre of St James's Park. Thank God for Raymond. She had known he wouldn't let her down. He was the one constant factor in the appalling run of uncertainty and bad luck.

The moment she had the papers and the money she would be as good as free. She would go to Paris first, of course; then to Milan to see Petrini; and then . . .

Back here. In time.

A grey cheerless twilight enveloped the monotonous rows of suburban houses; it was time to move. She went down to the main road and caught a 27 bus to Hammersmith and Notting Hill. She sat next to a window, examining fellow passengers in the reflection of the glass. For a while she was convinced the conductor was staring at her and gripped the edge of her seat, ready to run. But then he chatted to another passenger and, without a second glance, climbed up the stairs to the top deck.

She left the bus at Notting Hill Gate and went into a large chemist shop. The lighting was very bright. She kept her head down. There was a great craze for synthetic wigs and a large stand of them stood in the centre of the shop. She chose one in auburn with a deep fringe. She also bought sunglasses and make-up. She kept an eye on the shop assistant but the girl didn't give her a second glance.

In a nearby side street Gabriele pulled the wig hastily over her dark hair and put on some lipstick. She re-emerged into the brightly lit street with more confidence.

Now food. She'd had nothing since the previous day. It had got to the point where she didn't feel hungry any more. But it was essential to force something down. There was a Wimpy Bar further along the road on the other side of the Tube station. She set off, keeping her head down as she approached the Tube exit. It was almost five: the rush hour. People streamed out of the station.

Someone bumped into her. She veered away, stepping into the street to circle the crowd. As she stepped back on to the pavement she halted, face to face with her own picture. Duplicated dozens of times. All over a newsstand.

The headline screamed: WANTED!

She felt a sudden thrill, an extraordinary burst of exhilaration.

She turned away, then, changing her mind, reached into her pocket for some coins and bought an *Evening Standard*.

Tucking the newspaper under her arm she approached the Wimpy Bar and looked in through the window. It was fairly crowded but she spotted a seat in the far corner. No one took any notice of her as she walked in. She ordered a double cheeseburger and chips then, unfolding the paper, started to read.

She gave a small snort of disgust and amusement. They'd decided to call her the 'glamorous gunwoman'. How transparent and cliché-ridden. But worse, the story bore no relation to the truth. They talked of 'fanatical extremists'. What rubbish: the fanatical extremists were closer to home – the people who owned newspapers that printed distortions like this.

She flicked on through the story.

Then stopped.

And read the section again. Two deaths at a remote farmhouse. Both believed to be members of the terrorist gang. A girl killed in an explosion. A man found dead in an outbuilding. *A man*.

Giorgio.

He had been there all the time. Dead.

She felt no sadness, only a chilling sense of aloneness. And a strong sense of betrayal, as if he had somehow died on purpose in order to make life more difficult for her.

God! How could he have been so *stupid*. And *how* had he managed to get himself killed? By the *girl*?

But her mind soon veered back to the present.

She was really alone now. Everything would be harder. She would have to be doubly careful. She would have to find somewhere safe to hide.

The food arrived. As the waitress put it in front of her she noticed a man looking at her. Her heart gave an unpleasant lurch. She stared back. He dropped his eyes.

Keeping an eye on him she stuffed the food into her mouth and discovered that she was ravenously hungry after all. She picked up the newspaper again and read on: A watch was being kept on the ports . . . Linda Wilson believed armed and dangerous . . . On no account were the public to approach . . .

386

Distortion again: they made her sound like a madwoman who'd shoot anyone on sight. *Definitely* not true. She only had one target: the oppressors. These filthy lies were making her sick.

Then she almost choked. In the centre of the paper there was a double-page spread headed: Attorney-General Freed at Eleventh Hour. Brilliant detective work – it read – had led to the location of the remote farmhouse a bare two hours before the terrorists' dead-line ran out . . . Army disposal rushed in . . .

Brilliant detective work. The phrase rankled. It suggested Nick Riley and his friends had outmanoeuvred her. Well, they may think they had, for the *moment*. But the war wasn't over, not by a long way.

The thought of Nick Riley still had the power to fill her with an uncontrollable rage. What she would give to get him face to face. The memory of his cold cynical manipulation of her was like a knife turning in a wound; it gave her no peace.

The man at the other table was looking at her again. She wrapped the second burger in a napkin and stuffed it in the holdall. She went to the cash desk, paid, and hurried out. She went down a side street and doubled back into the main road. The man did not follow her.

She headed north up Ladbroke Grove. Her route took her past a police station. She hesitated, but it was completely dark and there was no one outside. She walked on.

The holdall was getting very heavy. She felt stupidly weak but forced herself on. The rise of Notting Hill seemed endless until finally she reached the top and headed down the gentle slope towards North Kensington.

Beyond the Westway she found the road she was looking for, the street where Max's friend Bet lived: Tulip Street. Through Bet she should be able to pick up some old contacts – someone like Wally Bishop, who'd been on the Linden House demo and was a close friend of Reardon's. He was sure to be okay. He would have a place to go.

She approached the house cautiously, watching it for a good five minutes before climbing the steps and ringing the doorbell. A man opened the door. She asked for Bet and waited outside while the man shouted upstairs.

Eventually a girl came crossly down the stairs to the door, wrapping a towel round her dripping hair. 'Yes?' she demanded.

Gabriele kept back from the door, away from the pool of light. 'I was looking for Wally Bishop. Can you tell me where to find him?'

'Sure,' Bet began. Then she paused and peered more closely at Gabriele. She stiffened.

There was a nasty silence. Gabriele could almost feel the other woman's animosity. Bet looked back over her shoulder, then scanned the street.

She whispered, '*Go away*! They came asking about you this morning. And they've been to *Wally's*. And they're coming back, they said they were. *We* can't help you. You *must* go away!' The girl swallowed nervously. 'Look, I won't say a word about you having been here. Not a word. Honest. Just go. *Please*.'

Wordlessly, Gabriele turned and walked away into the darkness.

Back in Ladbroke Grove she headed south. After a while she hailed a taxi. 'Where to?' the cabby asked.

'Earl's Court.'

Gabriele hardly knew the Earl's Court area. Which was the whole point of going there. No old haunts, no friends, no way of tracing her. Just the anonymity of street after street of rooming houses used by thousands of visiting Australians – the area was commonly known as Kangaroo Valley.

The cab dropped her in the Earl's Court Road. She set off down a side street and came to the first of a long row of rooming houses and cheap hotels. She hesitated outside a place with a 'Room to Let' notice in the window, suddenly wary. Something about this idea was making her deeply uneasy. It was the prospect of sitting in a box-like room, with no means of escape, not knowing who might have recognised her, not knowing if the police were closing in. A rat in a trap.

But she forced her doubts aside for a moment and, going in, knocked on a door marked 'Enquiries'.

A smiling Pakistani emerged. The terms were two pounds a week and the room was on the third floor at the back. He offered to show it to her and went back into his room to fetch a key.

Gabriele moved forward until she could see him through the open door. She watched him pick a key off a hook. He was not suspicious. It was going to be all right. She looked down. There was a low table in front of an easy chair. Evidently he had been reading the evening paper. Upside down and at a slight distance her picture seemed to fill the whole of the front page.

He was turning, the key in his hand. She pulled her eyes quickly away from the newspaper.

She tried to smile. 'I'm sorry – I've decided it wouldn't be suitable.'

The Pakistani looked surprised. 'But you haven't *seen* it!'

'It's the stairs. Too far up. Thanks anyway.'

He gave her a long hard stare. She turned hurriedly and went out into the street.

She could have kicked herself. That had been very stupid. There must be no more mistakes.

She walked rapidly away from the area, heading south. She racked her brains for somewhere to go. There *had* to be somewhere. It was just a case of thinking it through. She just wished she wasn't feeling so tired.

She plodded on into Chelsea. A chill hung over the misty river. Battersea Bridge loomed up ahead. There was a park on the other side where it might be possible to stop for a while; but it was another cold, damp, desolate, godforsaken place. She felt a bitter resentment. She couldn't believe it had come to this. She'd had nothing but bad luck. Then the *others* had let her down so badly – Giorgio. And Max . . . And then of course *him* – the spy.

Suddenly she had an idea and grabbed at it. She stopped in her tracks and gave a small exclamation of triumph. Of course. It was so perfect she couldn't imagine why she hadn't thought of it before.

A man could give his soul for this, Nick decided, no trouble at all. A warm flat – at least it would be in a moment, when the electric fires had done their job – fish and chips from down the road, and a hot bath within half an hour. Already the geyser was hissing and roaring, spitting its thin jet of steaming water into the tub below.

But most important of all – *vital* – the prospect of catching Gabriele. By this time tomorrow it should all be over. And, though it never paid to count one's chickens, there was reasonable hope for optimism.

Two. At the bridge in St James's Park. A man wearing a red scarf. With a bit of luck they'd pick him up at the airport and tail him all the way there, just to be sure. In his mind he gave Desport another pat on the back. It was quite a coup. And, since Desport had passed the information direct to Nick, some of the credit would undoubtedly rub off on him.

If all went well.

One thing was certain: once in the trap Gabriele would never escape. The place was going to be crawling with men – and marksmen. Would she try to shoot it out? If so, she'd be dead in an instant. All things considered, it might be for the best. He caught himself thinking: What's one more death?

Yes. They would get her. One way or another.

God, he was going to sleep like a baby tonight. The tension that had gripped him for days had eased, leaving him pleasantly languorously weary. He dug into the grocery bag and found himself a beer. The phone rang.

It was Conway. 'A possible sighting in Earl's Court, at a cheap rooming house. Had second thoughts about a room and scarpered. But the ident is far from certain. The geezer thought the face was right but the hair was the wrong colour. Could have been a wig of course. Anyway, Kershaw's put ten cars in the area and started a house-to-house.'

Nick considered. It *could* have been Gabriella. Although a cheap rooming house in Earl's Court was hardly her style. Which might have been the reason she tried it. Perhaps she had nowhere else to go.

'Keep me posted, will you?' he asked Conway, and rang off.

He wandered across to the record player, deep in thought. Eventually he selected *Norma* with Callas and Corelli, and listened to the familiar melody of the overture. He turned up the volume – to hell with the neighbours for once. He placed the next disc – which went to the end of Act II – on the spindle, ready to drop, so that he would have a good hour's listening while he was in the bath.

He took the beer into the bathroom and stripped off. The water was only about eight inches deep. Good enough.

He stepped in and uttered a sigh of bliss. He lay back and felt the water creep up his body. It was so deliciously hot it was almost unbearable. He knew what was going to happen; he was going to fall asleep. But he didn't care. It was irresistible.

'*Sediziose voci, voci di guerra . . .*' Norma's entrance. Callas's raw sensual voice filled the flat, rising effortlessly above the belches of the geyser. He shivered. He couldn't begin to imagine how it must feel to sing like that.

At last the water covered his body. He turned off the geyser and slipped into a doze that glowed with warmth and peace. He reflected that this was the closest to heaven he was ever likely to get.

Yet a deep unease nagged at him. It was the stake-out, of course. He would worry about it until the very last moment, until he actually saw her walk into the trap.

There was a lull in the music. A sound intruded. Reluctantly he opened his eyes and tried to identify it. It came from downstairs somewhere. Then he had it. Someone was at the street door buzzing the flat below. That was the trouble with these houses. You could hear everything.

He woke once, briefly, when side one came to an end, but then the next disc dropped and the rich music swelled into the room and resonated through his mind, expunging all thought, and he slept again.

Gabriele stood on the front steps. She took another look at the names by the door. Flat 3: Ryder.

Riley. Ryder.

It *had* to be him.

She went down the steps and examined the house from the street. Lights were burning on the second floor and she could hear the faint sound of opera music. It *had* to be him. Right there. And not expecting her. *Hardly*. He'd probably forgotten that she had this address. The knowledge gave her a curious thrill.

Now, to get in. She'd tried ringing the bells of the other three flats, but there was no one in. She purposely hadn't rung his bell: he might call out of the window. Or there might be a scene at the door. People might notice.

Besides, she wanted to surprise him.

There was no obvious way up the front of the house, which was anyway too public. The narrow street was residential, with rows of small working-class houses on either side: the sort of street where people were nosy.

Even at that moment there was the sound of voices and a noisy group emerged from a house two doors away. As they passed they gave her a curious glance.

It would have to be the back then.

The house was on a corner. She went down the side and had a good look. Rows of back yards stretched out behind the houses. Easy. She hoisted the holdall over the wall and, gritting her teeth, let it drop. There was a dull thud. With an effort she pulled herself up and over the wall. The holdall was lying on concrete. Taking the rifle out of the holdall, she strapped it over her back.

As an after-thought she tore off the hot uncomfortable wig and jammed it in the holdall with everything else.

She examined the back of the house. There was a door. She tried it. Locked. She looked up. At the first floor level there was an open window and, just to the left, a drainpipe. She hid the holdall behind some abandoned sheets of wood in the yard and, with only the rifle against her back, pulled a dustbin across to the drainpipe and climbed on top of it. The window wasn't far. She gripped the drainpipe and slowly began to pull herself up.

Suddenly a door opened and she froze. It was next door. There was the sound of scurrying paws and a dog started yapping noisily. A shaft of light sprang out into the darkness. A voice called, 'Bisky? Bisky? Come here! Good girl!'

The dog stopped yapping. Gabriele twisted her head round and looked down. The dog had its nose up, sniffing the air, trying to catch her scent. It growled threateningly, then thought better of it and scampered inside. The door closed. Gabriele took a couple of deep breaths and continued her climb.

She pulled herself up level with the window and reached a foot across to the sill. So far so good. Now she had to find a handhold. She put her arm out and grasped the rough brick corner of the reveal. Not good enough. Still holding on to the drainpipe with her left hand she shifted her weight as far as possible across to the sill and stretched her hand out further. At last she managed to get two fingers over the top of the open window. It wasn't much. With her heart in her mouth, she pushed away from the drainpipe and pulled herself across. For one moment she swung outwards, her left foot scrabbling for the sill, her weight hanging over the yard below. But then she managed to get her left hand over the window and pull herself in. She stood on the sill, shaking and hot with fear.

She gave herself a moment, then pushed the sash window fully down and climbed in. As she descended into the dark room her foot upset an object which fell with a great thud to the floor. She remained still, listening, but there were no lights showing and no one came.

She dropped to the floor and found her way across the room and into a tiny hall. She listened at the front door and, satisfied, turned the lock and opened the door a fraction. Light streamed in from the stairs and communal landing. There was no one about.

Putting the door on the latch she stepped out and pulled the door to behind her. She ran lightly up the stairs. There was only the one door on the top landing. Flat 3. The music was very loud.

She examined the door. Strong, with a Yale lock. She felt along the top of the door frame, in case there was a key hidden there. There wasn't.

She padded back downstairs and into the empty flat, closing the door. There was two options: force her way into the flat by shooting open the door – which was out of the question because the whole street would hear – or simply knock and wait for him to come to the door. But it *wasn't* the way she wanted to do it.

She gritted her teeth. There had to be a way.

She went back to the window and, climbing on to the inner sill, stuck her head out.

Ah. The *next* window.

She dropped down again and, going quickly into the next room, pulled open the window.

A back extension – traditional in many mid-Victorian terraces – abutted the wall just inches from the window. As usual, the extension was only two storeys high. The roof was just inches away. The roof pitched up to a ridge – a ridge which ran very close to a second-floor window. She examined it carefully. The only problem might be the window itself.

She went back into the flat and, risking a light, rummaged through the tiny kitchenette. Thrusting a collection of knives, tin-openers and skewers into her back pocket, she killed the light and went back to the window.

Getting across to the roof was the tricky bit. She had to put a foot on the open window frame, lever herself up, and scrabble across to the roof, trusting her weight to some ancient guttering.

Once safely on the roof, the worst was over. She waited for her heart to stop pounding before climbing upwards to the ridge and the waiting window.

She pushed the handle of a tin opener under the window frame and levered it downwards.

The window gave a fraction. She pushed the lever further in and got her fingers underneath the frame.

There was no resistance. The window slid up several inches.

The exhilaration pounded in her chest. Carefully, she pushed it completely open and climbed in.

The dream had been going so well. He was somewhere nice, somewhere warm and cosy. There was a fleeting image of Conis-

393

ton, in the Lake District, where his parents had once taken him on a rare holiday. They were sitting in some tea-rooms which they had reached after a long tiring walk in the hills. He remembered the strangeness of those rugged hills and his feeling of puzzlement at the sight of all that wilderness. Nothing in his life had ever suggested that such places existed.

But then the memory was slipping and the mood changed. There was a coldness around him, and a deep worrying silence. He was back at the farmhouse. The army chap was announcing that more bombs had been discovered: it wasn't over yet, he said in his rather pompous voice, not by a long chalk. This time there were many more hostages. Nick discovered more and more of them in the bedrooms upstairs, each attached to some even more ghastly device. Time was running out but there appeared to be no way of helping them. It was extraordinary, but no one seemed to be concerned. All they were interested in was getting organised. More and more equipment kept arriving. Nick shouted out: For God's sake can't we save *anybody*? And the army chap replied: Shouldn't think so. Better get clear.

The feeling of impotence was infuriating. He wanted to *make* these stupid people do something, to shake them until their teeth rattled, to scream at them.

Suddenly something made him wake. He opened his eyes for a moment.

He took a deep breath. It was only a dream . . .

The water had gone cold. The music had stopped. In a moment he would get out. He dozed again, trying to channel his thoughts away from the morass of the nightmare.

Christ – !

Something jabbed into his head, cold and uncomfortable.

For a split-second he convinced himself it was part of the nightmare.

But then he woke with a violent start that sent his body arcing out of the water.

Christ!

He didn't need to look round.

He *knew*.

His heart pounded in his ears. His mouth hung open. One thought leapt burning in his mind.

It was *her*.

And she was going to kill him. In cold blood.

394

He stayed completely still, his mind racing.

She spoke. He gave another involuntary start.

'*Frightened*, are you?'

He forced himself to speak. 'Yes. Of course.' The gun was pressed hard against his head. He couldn't see her: she was to one side and slightly behind.

'Think I'm going to kill you?' The voice was low and ragged.

He whispered, 'Probably.'

'Too right. Nasty little gigolo. Sell yourself for anything, wouldn't you! Cheap bastard.'

He licked his lips and said carefully, 'I didn't know who you were when . . .'

There was a nasty silence. '*When you screwed me.*'

'I never looked on it like that.'

'*Like what?*'

'Like just a screw.'

'No? Well, *I* did! *I did!* It was just a screw!'

He blinked agreement. She had to be humoured, but not too obviously.

'*Well?*' she demanded.

He thought desperately, trying to guess what she wanted him to say. But it could be *anything*. He stayed silent.

The voice came from close by his ear; he could feel her breath. 'Don't you want to know how long you've got?'

Thoughts flashed through his mind: a yes and she might say five seconds in which case he'd rather not know; a no and she'd tell him anyway. Better to say nothing.

She prodded the gun barrel further into his temple. He cringed, his eyes tightly shut.

She said, '*Now!* Yes, why not! How's it feel, you bastard, to be on the point of having your brains splattered over the wall?'

Nick felt sick. His stomach turned to water. He began to tremble violently.

Christ – he couldn't cope with this.

She was still speaking. 'You were my unfinished business, you cheap bastard. I didn't want to go without attending to you. Just so you couldn't screw anyone ever again.'

The gun was pulled away from his head. Out of the corner of his eye he saw the barrel travelling down over his stomach. *Down.*

He stared in horror.

Dear God, she was going to kill him in stages. The pain. And it would take a long time to die.

She was putting the gun barrel into the water. On to his flesh.

He closed his eyes, trying to shut out the wall of fear. Then, through the panic, a part of his mind rallied. *Say something! Something to distract her!*

What was it *she'd* said. Some words echoed in the back of his mind. He clutched at them. *I didn't want to go without attending to you.*

Sure that even now it was too late, he babbled, '*You can't go!*'

'What do you mean!' She gave a nervous contemptuous laugh. 'I'll go just as soon as I've finished with *you*, bastard!'

He took a few deep breaths. He had her attention. He said more steadily, 'They know all about it.'

There was an electric silence.

'Know – *what?*' Her voice was high-pitched and unsteady.

'You're meeting a courier. Tomorrow at two. In St James's Park.'

Nick gave it a moment, then risked a slight turn of his head.

She was staring through him, grey with disbelief. She looked very different: ravaged, drawn, older. She stood back, letting the gun barrel fall slightly.

She hissed, '*How?*'

He made his voice more relaxed. 'A tip-off. From Paris.'

'*Paris?*'

She seemed to dissolve before his eyes, swaying slightly, her shoulders falling forward.

'*Who in Paris?*'

He must be careful here; she mustn't know the truth or his instincts told him she'd kill everyone in sight including herself. He said, 'I don't know.'

The gun came up and jammed into his temple again. '*You do! Tell me!*'

'The courier! The courier was a traitor!'

She breathed, 'The *courier!* I don't understand . . .'

He said quickly, 'I'll offer you a deal. I'll get you out of the country in return for my life.'

The gun was pulled away from his temple. He turned and looked straight at her. He had to make her believe him. He repeated, 'I'll get you out.'

At last she seemed to absorb what he had said. She shook her head. 'I could never trust you!'

'Why not? It's a fair deal. I've only got my job to lose and I've lost that already.'

'Your job?' she asked vaguely.

'Of course. Because of you.'

She was hardly listening. She was clutching her forehead, a deep frown of concentration on her face. Her mouth opened and closed, but no words came.

Suddenly she exclaimed, 'No! You bloody bastard! You'll try to trick me! You're a pig, just another pig!' Her mouth was screwed down at the corners in an ugly grimace. 'You're out to kill me. Just like the rest! You think you have the right to persecute and rape and *humiliate* people.'

He thought: She's mad.

What should he say next? He wasn't sure any more.

He ventured, 'I know ways of getting out of the country. Places where they don't check too closely—'

'*Where?*'

'The Liverpool–Belfast Ferry. Once in Northern Ireland it's easy to get into the Republic. From Dublin you can fly to lots of places.'

She glared at him with an expression of deep uncertainty. He wished she would believe him: it was undoubtedly the safest route.

She whispered, 'What about papers? A passport?'

'Surely your friends can get you one. Send it to Dublin?'

'And money?'

'I can get some. Take a chequebook anyway.'

'Transport?'

'There's a friend's car that I often borrow.'

'How do I know it isn't a police car?'

'There's no radio in it.'

She nodded slowly, the fear beginning to recede from her eyes. She appeared to be coming round to the idea.

'Why do *you* need to come along? Why shouldn't I go *alone*?'

Nick thought: Because if you leave me here, you'll leave me dead. But aloud he said, 'You'll need someone to drive you on to the ferry in Liverpool. They'll be watching it. And again, possibly, at the Irish border.'

'But they'll have missed you by then!' she accused. 'They'll be looking for you too!'

'Not if I phone and say I've got flu.'

Suddenly she laughed nervously. 'I like the idea of you getting me out. It seems *right* somehow. After all, you got me into this mess. *Bastard!*'

He tried to make light of it. 'It was my job—'

'That's what the SS used to say when they sent the Jews to the gas chambers.'

'I never meant to harm anyone . . .' It was a nonsensical remark. But anything to keep the conversation going.

There was a shrill jangling.

They both jumped.

The telephone rang again.

It would be Conway.

Gabriele was pointing the gun at him again.

He said quickly, 'If I don't answer they'll know there's something wrong. *They know I'm here!* And it would be a good time to tell them I've got flu!'

She seemed to be thinking frantically, her eyes darting from side to side. Finally she shouted, 'All right! *All right!* But one – *one* – wrong word and I'll blow your head off!'

The phone kept jangling.

Nick climbed slowly out of the bath. Gabriele retreated a little, both hands on the rifle. His flesh crawling, Nick walked carefully out of the room. He felt Gabriele taking up station behind. He advanced to the phone and stood dripping in front of it. She nodded. He picked it up. As he put the receiver to his ear the gun jabbed into his temple.

Conway's cheery voice said, 'What were you doing – getting well-earned rest or something?'

'Having a bath.'

'About time too. Anyway, here's the latest. The ID in Earl's Court looks a little more positive. She had a holdall which tallies with the one she was carrying when she left the flat in Chelsea Manor Street. I'm going up there now. Wanna come along?'

'No, I'm too tired, old boy. In fact I'm not feeling too well. Flu or something. I think I might have to crash.'

'What's with this "old boy" business? You gone posh or something?'

Nick said coldly, 'No. Er – when are we due back on duty?'

'God – don't ask me!' Conway exclaimed. 'Since when did we ever work *hours*.'

'Oh. Seven o'clock, was it?' Nick nodded gravely.

'What on earth? You're not making any sense, old mate. Don't tell me,' Conway exclaimed conspiratorially, 'you're otherwise engaged! Why didn't you *say* so?' He chuckled, already losing interest. 'Don't know how you find the energy.'

Nick's heart sank. The gun jabbed into his head. She was signalling angrily. He had a last attempt. 'Look – can you get Andrews to fill in for me tomorrow?'

There was a short silence. Nick could almost hear Conway working things out. Nick thought: Come *on*. Come *on*.

'Who the hell's Andrews?' Suddenly Conway got on to the right track. 'Is everything all right?'

'No, not in the slightest,' Nick said casually. 'Bye. Got to go now.'

Nick put the phone down. He noticed his hand was shaking. For something to say, he murmured, 'I got rid of him as quickly as I could.'

'Who was it?' she demanded.

'A colleague.'

'How do I know you haven't warned him?'

'You heard what I said—'

'Get dressed! We're going this minute!'

Nick thought: Conway, dear plodding Conway. Please understand. May God beam down a great shaft of illumination upon your brain.

Thirty-one

Old boy, indeed. Conway thought: Huh!

But then it had been a strange conversation all round. Ryder was obviously overtired. What *had* he meant with that seven o'clock business? There was no chance that Conway was going to be around at seven the next morning. He was going to be in his bed, snoring loudly, and nothing but nothing was going to get him up any earlier.

Besides, like he'd said, when did they ever have fixed hours? And Andrews? Who the hell was he? Perhaps there was someone of that name in Kershaw's team. Because there certainly wasn't in Special Branch. Or was there?

Conway couldn't think straight any more. No sleep. Bad food. Small brain. He left his office and went to the nearest coffee machine. Blasted coffee. Never knew if it was going to do you any good. He sipped at it. It tasted like old cardboard. Or maybe that was the cup.

He went back to his desk and started sifting through some papers.

After a moment he gave up. It was no good. That conversation kept coming back into his mind. It worried him.

Why would the presence of a woman make Ryder sound so strange? Even allowing for the astonishing possibility that, after a week without sleep, Ryder was capable of a romantic evening?

And that proper tone. The 'old boy'. It wasn't in character. Normally, he would have expected Ryder to give him a polite 'Sod off' or something similar. After all, they were good friends.

And why, in their earlier phone call, had Ryder asked Conway to call back if he knew he was going to be busy?

Finding a piece of plain paper, Conway jotted down what he remembered of the conversation. Then he underlined the remarks that had seemed strange. Particularly that one when he'd asked: Everything all right? And Ryder had answered: No, not at all. Or was it: No, not in the slightest.

That damned seven o'clock.

What *could* he have meant?

He looked at his watch. It was seven. In the evening.

Now.

He should ring back.

He reached for the phone then hesitated.

Extremely nasty thoughts had whistled into his mind. And if they were in the slightest bit right, then the last thing he must do was call back.

Getting hastily to his feet, he grabbed the piece of paper and made for the stairs at a run.

He could be making a fool of himself, of course. This might be the largest dose of egg that he'd ever got splattered on his face. But better that than—

Anyway, he had a feeling about this one.

It took a moment for him to identify what it was that made him so sure. Then he had it.

It wasn't just the oddness of the answers, nor even that dreadful 'old boy'. It was that appalling *politeness*.

Not Ryder, not Ryder at *all*.

Nick dressed as slowly as possible, but even then he couldn't draw it out for longer than five minutes. She watched his every move, getting increasingly impatient. He tried making conversation but she silenced him with a motion of the gun.

As he picked up his wallet she demanded, 'How much is there?'

He counted the notes. 'Fifteen pounds.'

'*God*! That's not going to get us very far, is it!'

'I *told* you, I've got a chequebook.' Immediately he realised he'd used the wrong words and the wrong tone. She wouldn't like remonstrations. He braced himself.

'I *know* you've got a bloody chequebook!' she said furiously. 'But is it going to *work*? What happens when we try to get cash? They'll phone your *bank*, and then they'll know *exactly* where we are!' She paused for breath. 'Give me a jacket!'

He found an old denim one and threw it across the floor to her. Picking it up, she draped it over the rifle. 'Now where's this car?'

'It's usually parked further up the road, outside the friend's house.'

'Will it *be* there?'

'He only uses it at weekends.'

'What about keys?'

'I have some. They're in the hall drawer.'

She gestured him into the hall. She said, 'Pull the drawer out slowly and empty the contents on to the floor.'

He did so and the keys fell out, followed by a flurry of papers and library tickets.

Slowly he bent down and picked up the keys.

'Have you got a gun?' she demanded suddenly.

He shook his head.

She gave a short laugh. 'What, not even to use against dangerous terrorists?'

'There's a firearms squad. They're specially trained . . .'

'Okay. Let's go.' She waved the gun in the direction of the door, and stepped back. She was no fool. She always kept her distance when he was about to move. Not that he felt like being brave. Not yet anyway.

As he opened the front door he tried to think of a reason to delay her.

He said, 'I might have some more money in the bedroom. I'm not sure . . .'

She was instantly suspicious. 'Get out!'

He almost argued, but sensed it wouldn't be wise.

As he stepped into the hall the gun jabbed into his back.

He tried to work out how long it would take to reach the car. No more than three minutes. Even if there *was* a team on the way they'd never get here in time.

Hopeless.

They began down the stairs. There was a sound from below. They both stopped dead. There were noises of doors opening and closing, then silence. The occupant of the ground-floor flat. They started down again, passing the first-floor landing, down to the ground floor. The beat of rock music suddenly bellowed from the ground-floor flat. As they passed the door Nick willed it to open, but it didn't.

At the street door, she hissed, 'Stop!'

She came up close behind him, holding the gun to his ribs. 'Can we get out to the back from here?'

'The back?'

'The *yard*!'

'No. It belongs to the guy in there.' He indicated the door of the ground-floor flat.

She prodded him forward. 'Okay. Open it slowly.'

He turned the latch and swung the door open. She made him halt in the doorway. He guessed she was looking up and down the street.

She wasn't the only one. He searched desperately for signs of life. But it was quiet as the grave.

Even now Conway was probably packing up his desk and heading for Earl's Court, blissfully unaware, imagining merely that Nick had flu and had gone appropriately strange in the head.

The thought filled him with quiet despair.

'Move!'

They set off down the steps. He was about to turn left, towards the car, when she pulled him the other way. 'I've got to collect something first!'

Nick felt a small flutter of hope. It was a delay. More time. And time was what he wanted.

*

Gabriele pushed him forward. She hated the delay. But she *had* to get the holdall. There was the spare ammunition. The wig. The make-up. The sunglasses. And the tote bag with her few remaining belongings. She'd feel naked without them.

At the corner she prodded him to the right then made him stop by the wall.

This was the hard bit. She hadn't allowed for this – having to retrieve the holdall with *him* around. She looked up and down the side street. A car approached, slowed at the junction, turned left and drove off. Another car passed in the road they had just left then another. At last there was nothing. She pulled the jacket off the Kalashnikov and let it fall to the pavement.

She said, 'Give me a leg-up.'

He looked surprised but obediently cupped his hand. She put a foot in it, careful to keep the rifle at his head, then said, 'Push me up!' She added harshly, 'If you try to drop me, I'll kill you! So don't even think about it!'

Grunting with effort, he pushed her up. With her spare hand, she gripped the top of the wall. 'Higher!'

He gave a last heave and she levered herself on to the top. She swung a leg over until she was sitting astride.

'Now you!'

He took a deep breath then scrambled up until he too was on top of the wall.

'Go down and find my bag. It's in that corner.' She pointed in the approximate direction.

He dropped down and searched for it. She watched him, thinking hard. He might even now be planning something. But if he imagined she was relaxing her guard for one moment he was making a big mistake. No chance. In fact she was feeling much better now: more alert, more in control. The shock of discovering they knew about the courier, that had been appalling. Like being hit in the face. It had taken a bit of getting over.

But she'd still get out all right. She knew she would. The pigs were stupid. One had to bear that in mind all the time. It was simply a question of keeping one's nerve.

He was standing up. He had the holdall in his hand.

Another car passed along the adjacent road. She reached down and took the holdall. She gestured him to climb back on top of the wall. He pulled himself up and sat astride, facing her. She was about to tell him to drop down into the street again when she caught a movement out of the corner of her eye.

Someone was walking along the street towards them. An old man wearing a cap. Doubtless a nosy old man. He was even now looking up. He couldn't fail to see them sitting up on the wall.

She could kill him, of course. But the *noise*.

The passer-by had almost reached them. He was slowing, inclining his head to peer up at them.

Gabriele wavered. She should do something . . .

Then it came to her. Jabbing the rifle into Nick's ribs, she leaned forward and, putting an arm around his neck, drew his head towards her. He pulled back in alarm, but she kept the pressure on until she felt his cheek come up against hers.

She squinted down at the passer-by. He was gawking up at them. He muttered a vague, 'Blimey . . .' Then shouted, 'There are safer places, yer know!' Muttering to himself, he finally began to move off.

She gave it a moment. In the silence she was aware of Nick's breathing, the touch of his flesh, warm against hers. The contact sent startling echoes reverberating through her mind: memories of friends, of feeling a warm sense of belonging; of good times in Italy; of the weeks when Giorgio and Max had been there to support her; of times when she hadn't been so horribly alone.

Times when—

She pulled away angrily. The touch of him almost made her choke. She said with difficulty, 'You make me sick! Now – get down!'

'Gabriele.' His voice was soft. 'I *did* care.'

She hissed, 'How *dare* you think it matters to me one way or the other. I don't care a damn!'

He looked away.

A ghastly loathsome self-pity overwhelmed her and, with disgust, she heard her voice break. 'Well, if you care so much,' she managed bitterly, '*why the hell aren't you getting off this wall and getting me out of here!*'

With satisfaction, she saw him draw back. Silently, he manoeuvred both legs over the wall and dropped to the pavement.

'Move away from the wall.' She wiped a hand angrily across her eyes, then, letting the holdall fall, followed it to the ground. She threw the jacket back over the Kalashnikov and picked up the holdall.

In the distance a siren sounded. She glared in horror at Nick. A flicker of excitement seemed to pass across his face. She thought: *He was hoping for this! He's just been playing for time! The speech on the wall – just for time!* Jerking the rifle up to her hip, she trained it on him. 'If that's anything, you're *dead*!'

'It's just the local police.'

Was he telling the truth? *God!*

They waited tensely. Slowly the siren faded into the distance.

She breathed again. Throwing him the holdall, she gestured him forward. He moved cautiously. She prodded him roughly to make him go faster.

Retracing their steps, they turned the corner and passed in front of the house again. She looked around nervously.

Nothing. No cars.

Nothing.

She felt jumpy again.

His fault. He had unnerved her. She wouldn't let him do it again. There'd be no more talking.

The shadows seemed darker, longer. Up towards the end of the street she thought she saw black shapes. *Moving.*

Shit!

She'd just got the jitters. That was all.

Suddenly she realised why. It was so goddam *quiet*.

Nick drew in an involuntary breath. Hardly even a gasp. Yet for an awful moment he thought she'd heard it.

He waited in an agony of suspense.

But there was no sound from her. They walked on. It was all right.

He breathed again. Then took another look at the van parked some way up the street. Between two pools of lamplight. A darkish van. But it was so hard to see – *damn* it! He squirmed with frustration. It *looked* very like it but—

Suddenly he caught a glint.

The glint of metal. A whip aerial.

Yes!

His heart almost burst through his ribs.

A whip aerial. It *must* be.

Some of his exhilaration evaporated.

What *now*, for Christ's sake? The training manual didn't cover this. Desperately, he tried to think.

Suddenly she spoke and he jumped.

'Where's the car?' she snapped.

The car. He looked. Not far. He recognised the shape of the Vauxhall Viva just ahead. They were almost there. *Too near*.

Gulping, he lied, 'It must be further on. I can't see it yet.'

'Well, find it!'

'I think I can see it, just up there.' He indicated vaguely towards the end of the street.

His mind raced: now he was committed to a lie he had to find a way out of it. He looked for the next street lamp. It was about fifteen yards ahead.

Not far from the van.

As they approached the lamp, he could feel himself trembling.

'Just over there.' He pointed across the road to a Hillman Minx which he'd never seen before in his life. He thought: Dear God, let me be right about this. Otherwise when he failed to open the car she would realise that he had tried to trick her. And then he knew what she would do. She would kill him.

He stepped off the kerb between two parked cars and automatically looked for traffic.

Then it suddenly struck him – and then he *knew*.

There *was* no traffic. There had been none for some minutes.

It seemed to have stopped everywhere. Only the faintest hum rose into the night air high above the city. Somewhere nearby there was the muffled beat of music.

But the street itself was silent. Their own footsteps echoed large in the stillness.

Suddenly there was a sound. From up the street. Like metal against metal, the *clonk!* exaggerated in the silence.

He was jerked to a halt by his collar.

'*What was that?*' She was sounding frightened. There was a quaver in her voice.

He kept still, pretending to listen. Eventually he whispered, 'Nothing. A cat perhaps.'

He could hear her panting, her breath coming in short uneven gasps. Then she thrust him forward again, into the road.

He eyed the Hillman Minx, gleaming innocently. And stepped out.

He crossed diagonally, keeping as close as he dared to the pool of light around the lamp-post.

Surely something would happen now. *Surely*.

She wasn't too close. There was at least a foot between the two of them. She *must* make a good target. *Surely*.

They reached the centre of the road. He braced himself for the crack of a rifle shot.

Surely . . .

The Minx was getting close. He couldn't believe it.

He reached the car door.

Nothing happened.

Didn't they realise!

Fumbling in his pocket, he reached for the keys.

She came up close behind him.

Christ. Now it was too late.

He pulled the keys out and started sorting through them. His hand was shaking. The keys fell with a loud jangle on to the road.

'*You stupid bastard!*' She was spluttering with rage, all the arrogance back in her voice. 'Pick them up!'

'Sorry,' he murmured.

Then he knew what he had to do.

As he bent down and grasped the keys, he braced himself, and thought fleetingly: Dear God, let me have it right!

In the split second before he moved he glanced sideways. Her attention was distracted; she was looking nervously up the street. He tried to judge the distance.

Her eyes were coming back to him.

Then he sprang, twisting round, uncoiling himself from the ground.

He caught the rifle barrel with the first swing of his arm. It jerked out of his vision. He saw the surprise leap into her face.

Then he raised his foot, pulling his knee high up to his chest, and gave an almighty kick in the general direction of her stomach. It went home: he heard her suck in a great rasping breath as his shoe went punching into her body. He fell back against the car. Gabriele shot backwards, wheeling one arm, trying desperately to regain her balance. She tottered for a moment then fell in the middle of the road.

But she was rolling over, pulling herself quickly up on to one knee.

She was coming up again.

Then he saw – *she still had the rifle in her right hand.*

Her eyes were blazing at him, vicious with shock and hatred. She was regaining her balance, bringing the barrel up.

He should have moved. He felt the car hard against his back.
It was too late.

She was pulling the rifle back against her hip.

He caught a glint of cold determination in her expression, and felt a moment of total disbelief.

Then it came.

A loud booming amplified voice that split the silence.

'Drop your weapon! You are surrounded! Do not attempt to fire!'

Gabriele gave a violent start and dropped her weight forward as if poising herself to run. But then she hesitated, her eyes swivelling wildly, suddenly aware that she had nowhere to run to.

She was in the centre of the road. She hadn't got a chance.

He could see that she knew it.

She remained frozen like an animal, her eyes on Nick, but filled with a huge unimaginable terror.

The voice echoed between the houses.

Drop your gun! You are surrounded! Drop your weapon immediately! We are police officers! We have orders to fire!

There was a silence.

Nick urged, 'Do it! Gabriella – *just do it!*'

She blinked at him questioningly, a look of bewilderment on her face. Then her expression sank into bitterness and despair.

'Do it!' he whispered. 'Just drop the gun!'

She gave a small cry of anguish and shook her head. Very deliberately, she tightened her grip on the rifle.

He cried, *'Don't!'*

But she was already dropping. Quickly, so quickly. Down into a crouch, hunched over the rifle. For a moment he thought she was going to aim at him, but she swung the rifle away. The air filled with noise, a staccato of loud cracks as she sprayed the street, ranging the rifle back and forth across the width of the road.

She made no attempt to run.

Then it happened. In the noise, he never heard the other shots. He just saw her. Hit by some powerful force.

The rifle jerked. The force plucked her upwards and back. For a moment she seemed to hover, twisting round in the air. Then she crumpled. Neatly. Going at the knees first, then sinking gracefully to the ground. Her head falling back on to the road. The mass of dark hair falling ... Her face a pale oval, deathly white in the lamplight.

There was a silence.

Nick walked slowly forward. He knelt beside her.

She was already dead, her eyes sightless and half-closed.

He knelt there for some moments.

She'd made the decision, when she'd raised the rifle. She'd made the decision to die.

Yet she hadn't tried to kill him. Perhaps she hadn't hated him so much after all.

There was the sound of running feet. Soon a circle of men stood staring down at her.

A voice said, 'Thank God.'

He knew what they were thinking: That she was dead and it was right that she was dead because she had got to enjoy killing, and there was nothing worse than that.

They were right, of course. That was the only way to look at it.

And he tried to lock the confusing blend of bitterness and guilt and pity out of his mind.

Thirty-two

The drizzle fell in unremitting grey curtains, cloaking the car park in a mantle of gloom. The group of pressmen – well over twenty of them – huddled under the porch of the crematorium, stamping their feet, chatting desultorily, their breath hanging in white clouds on the damp air. The local newsmen wore a slightly pained expression, the consequence of being heavily outnumbered by the national boys, and having a correspondingly slim chance of getting anything of their own into the dailies. Two television crews, enveloped in voluminous waterproofs, adjusted and fussed over their equipment. While sustaining necessary journalistic appearances of boredom and disinterest, everyone maintained a firm eye on the long drive that snaked down between bare lawns to the gates at the bottom of the hill.

It was almost ten to two, but no mourners had yet arrived. It was going to be a quiet funeral.

Suddenly there was a subtle change in the atmosphere, a buzz of interest. The photographers started manoeuvring for position,

409

tucking their cameras inside their raincoats and trotting out into the wet.

A black car had appeared and was slowly climbing the hill. The TV cameramen raised their cameras to their shoulders; the soundmen dusted their cans. There was silence as each man peered forward, trying to identify the occupants.

The car rose over the brow of the hill and swung in a slow arc into the covered area in front of the doors, its dripping black metal momentarily glistening in the flash of the camera lights.

The car halted. The newsmen pressed in closer. Someone whispered. 'The parents!'

The driver got out and opened the passenger door. There was a pause then a woman in a black hat with a heavy veil emerged. The light danced with the blinding flicker of flashbulbs. She lowered her head and put a hand up to shade her eyes. The photographers jostled in front of her, crouching to get shots of her face.

She swerved, but they pressed in on her. She gave a small cry of rage or anguish and ran forward into the sanctuary of the chapel.

The father came next, an upright figure in a military tie, his face set in an expression of British impassivity. He did not attempt to hide his face, but took the bombardment of lights with a series of fierce blinks and a firm set of the jaw.

Finally a girl in her mid-twenties. The sister. The hacks had all her details: name Diana, age twenty-four, Sloane Square address, seen around London with the minor aristocracy. She too wore a veil, but not a thick one, and the boys knew that, by getting up really close to the face, they'd get a good shot through the thin gauze. As she stepped forward someone called, 'Were you close to your sister, Diana?'

The girl gulped, and her face completely crumpled. The photographers fired off a cacophony of shots and silently thanked the guy who had shouted the question. An anguished face was always good front-page stuff.

As the sister stumbled in through the doors of the chapel, the journalists scribbled away happily on their pads. They'd have no trouble building their notes up into something substantial. This was a gift of a story – had been ever since it had broken five days before. There were so many punchy phrases that sprang to mind.

Heiress to fortune. County set. Wealthy land-owning family. Hints of connections in high places. Educated at top school. Turned hippy. Despair of her parents. Country commune. Drug orgies. Sex orgies (not established, that, but a good hint added a lot of spice). Italian terrorist boyfriend. Trips to France. Gunrunning. Putty in his hands. Leads gang to victim's home.

Poor little rich girl.

The story had all the ingredients you could ever hope for: sex, drugs, murder, intrigue, lost innocence. And of course, the best of all, a sudden and violent end. In the pubs of Fleet Street it was being said that a severed foot had been found days later, stuck in a corner of the cellar. Couldn't print that, of course. None the less they wished they got stories like this every day.

Another car appeared in the gateway at the bottom of the drive. It didn't look very promising. A dark blue saloon. Nothing special. There was cautious lack of interest among the watchers.

The car did not drive up to the doors, but parked beside a grass verge some distance away. Two men got out, one with fair collar-length hair, snappily dressed in casual dark slacks and jacket, and an open-necked shirt.

Immediately there was a rekindling of interest. Looked the type who might be a friend of the dead girl.

One of the experienced newsmen, a hack of twenty years' standing and now a feature-writer with one of the tabloids, inched his way forward. He knew exactly who these two men were.

As they approached he stepped forward and introduced himself to the fair-haired young man. 'You talked to the Danby girl through the door, I believe, sergeant. Can you tell me what she said?'

'No comment.'

'And I believe that you were the police officer taken hostage by the Wilson woman. Is that correct?'

The young policeman spun round angrily. 'We're not allowed to give interviews, as you well know. And you can't publish my identity either.'

The photographers, who had been snapping away, came out from behind their cameras. They were getting the gist of the conversation.

The second police officer shouted, 'Forget the pictures, boys! I'm a Special Branch officer and you're not permitted to publish pictures of me or my colleague here.'

The fair-haired officer gave the hack a last angry look and turned on his heel.

They all muttered amongst themselves. The trendily dressed

one was the undercover man of course. They pretended that they'd known who he was all the time. Pity they couldn't use him. But at least they were all in the same boat.

An electricity suddenly gripped the crowd.

Their eyes were riveted on the end of the drive.

Was it too much to hope for? It *looked* promising. My God, if it *was* . . .

There'd been rumours, of course. But none of the official government sources would confirm or deny it. And unofficial sources were apologetic, but equally unhelpful. A purely personal decision, the sources said, so not something they were likely to hear about.

But, oh boy, if it *was* . . . What a complexion *that* would cast on the story! Victim comes to mourn girl-terrorist. Terrific. It suggested that he had kept some sort of affection for the girl.

It also suggested he had been deeply affected by what had happened, that he had lost his detachment . . .

There might even be a resignation.

The group stood, for once completely silent, their eyes locked on the black chauffeur-driven car rolling up the drive.

Caroline gripped Henry's hand. 'Oh *darling*! There are thousands of them.'

'Yes. I knew there would be.'

'Why couldn't they—'

Henry shook his head briefly. 'Inevitable, I'm afraid. Just remember – keep your face impassive, even if they tread on your toes. And stay close to me. Anderson will force a way through, won't you, Anderson?'

The Special Branch man nodded firmly. 'Yes, sir.'

The car climbed inexorably up the hill. Even as they swung in towards the covered porch the cameras were up against the car windows. Henry gripped Caroline's hand. They exchanged fleeting smiles of encouragement.

The car pulled up. Anderson leapt out and fought his way round to help the driver, who was trying to clear some space by the passenger door.

The door opened. Henry got out first, then turned to help Caroline. There was a babble of voices. 'Sir Henry! Can you tell us why you're here?'

'Sir Henry – what is your attitude to terrorism?'

'Sir Henry! Sir Henry! How do you *feel* at this moment?'

He ignored all the questions, especially the last one. They weren't enquiring after his health. They just wanted some raw emotion for the front page.

Tucking Caroline's arm firmly into his, he walked slowly forward into the space cleared by Anderson. The pressmen fell back. They knew better than to badger a politician if he wasn't in the mood to talk. Politicians and newsmen knew the game too well.

Henry led Caroline into the sudden calm of the chapel's anteroom.

Caroline breathed, 'My goodness. What hyenas.' She gave him a sudden, anxious look. 'Are you all right, darling?'

He nodded and they walked into the body of the chapel.

It contained just five people. The large black hat, he rightly guessed, belonged to Mrs Danby. A brief greeting would have to be endured at some point; he might as well get it over with straight away.

He and Caroline approached and stood by the pew.

Mrs Danby looked up. An expression of horror crossed her face and she gasped audibly. Then it all seemed to become too much for her, and she buried her head in her hand.

A wave of sympathy overcame Henry and, bending down, he murmured, 'You know, she was a fine girl. I really believe that. And I'm sorry that . . .' Henry broke off. Mrs Danby had raised her head. Her mouth was open, her expression aghast. She whispered fiercely, 'After what she did to *you*? Well, *I* can never forgive her! *Never!*'

Henry stared, taken aback. 'But you must understand – she did try to make amends. And you know, she was very brave, right to the end.'

Mrs Danby shook her head vehemently and looked away.

Caroline tugged at Henry's sleeve. She was right; there was no point in discussing it. Not here and now. He nodded briefly to the sister and the father, and turned away.

He didn't know the others. Two young men. Their eyes met, established a fleeting contact, then slid away.

Henry and Caroline chose a pew and sat down. Almost immediately Henry began to wonder about the two young men. He examined their profiles, his curiosity roused. The furthest one was dark and soberly dressed in a suit, the nearest one was fair, wearing dark but casual clothes. He thought he knew who they might be. He would find out later, after the service.

The chapel was cold and bare. There were no flowers. Some trestles stood in front of the altar, ready for the coffin. On one side of the altar was a long rectangular stand on which the coffin would eventually be placed. At one end of this was an opening covered by black curtains: the road to the cremation chamber. Henry suppressed a shiver. It was all so depressingly sinister.

There was a mild commotion outside, the sound of doors swinging open. Recorded organ music suddenly filled the chapel. The meagre congregation stood up.

Henry turned. A parson was walking slowly up the aisle in front of a plain wooden coffin borne by professional pallbearers, their faces grave with superficial and well-polished solemnity.

The coffin came level. Henry's heart gave a small lurch. He was always hopelessly sentimental on these occasions. He tried to control the surge of emotion, but all he could see in his mind's eye was the cellar and the pathetic heap under the hastily arranged coat and the blood, the appalling scarlet blood, splattered everywhere like a slaughter room in a ghastly abattoir . . .

He closed his eyes. When he opened them again he found himself looking at the fair-haired young man. His face was turned to the coffin, his expression serious. Or perhaps it was closer to remorse: it was difficult to tell.

He thought: At least someone else cared enough to come.

The coffin was placed on its stand. The service began. It was obviously going to be brief and to the point. The parson announced a hymn – 'The Lord is My Shepherd' – normally one of Henry's favourites, but with the pre-recorded music, so few voices and those raised half-heartedly the hymn sounded thin and joyless.

They knelt to pray. Tears came to Henry's eyes. He couldn't help it. He was still deeply tired. And the memories of the long hours in the cellar were still clear in his mind. Moreover, since the rescue, he'd been feeling strangely depressed, guilty almost, as if the suffering that had been visited on Caroline and everyone around him was somehow his fault. It was all nonsense of course, he realised that. The doctors talked knowledgeably about shock and reaction, but he was still finding this period of adjustment difficult and confusing. Time, everyone kept telling him; time would heal . . .

Caroline touched his hand. He nodded to show that he was all right, and took her hand in his. It had been hardest of all for her.

414

She still couldn't believe he was safe. Nor, sometimes, could he. Each day was a miracle.

He put his mouth to Caroline's ear and whispered, 'Bless you . . .' Then: 'I'm glad we came.'

She smiled her agreement, and then they rose to listen to the address. It was brief in the extreme. A few platitudes. The parson obviously hadn't known Victoria.

The pallbearers moved forward and, lifting the coffin, slid it on to the rollers. Almost immediately the curtains opened, the music swelled – to cover the whirring of the electrically operated rollers, Henry realised – and the coffin trembled and rocked its way into the black void.

Henry stared blankly. His emotion was spent.

He was only sorry that it had been such a poor, sad, lonely funeral. Somehow *shameful*. And no one deserved that.

He thought again: I'm glad we came.

The service was over. The family went out first. Henry and Caroline followed.

Henry paused in the ante-room and waited for the two young men.

He approached the fair-haired one with his hand outstretched. 'Henry Northcliff.'

The young man shook his hand and replied, 'Sergeant Ryder, Special Branch. This is my colleague, Sergeant Conway.'

Henry shook Conway's hand then turned back to Ryder. 'I thought it must be you. The Commissioner kindly sent me some of the reports.'

Ryder dropped his eyes. 'I'm sorry I couldn't do more to prevent what happened.'

'No, no.' Henry gestured to show that he had no wish to discuss it. The two men strolled to one side of the ante-room. Henry paused. There was something he wanted to ask this man, but the question wouldn't form clearly in his mind.

'I wondered – at the farmhouse, when you talked to her through the door – did she seem . . .' He trailed off. He didn't know how to phrase it.

'She was surprisingly calm, really,' Ryder volunteered.

'Yes, but ' Henry knew what he must ask. But he hesitated for a moment, to prepare himself for the answer. 'Was she worried – about time running out? About the explosives going off at a certain time?'

Ryder shot him a look of sudden comprehension. There was a long pause. He said reluctantly. 'She was aware of it. Yes . . .'

Henry nodded slightly. It was as he had thought all along.

'It was a pity she never realised,' he said softly. 'I mean . . . That there was plenty of time after all.'

The two men exchanged glances, then looked away. There was not a lot to say.

They strolled back towards Caroline who was waiting by the doors.

Henry shook Ryder's hand. 'Well, at least we know. How brave she was. That's something, I suppose.'

Tucking Caroline's arm in his, he took a deep breath and facing the doors, prepared himself for the barrage of pressmen who, he knew from experience, would still be waiting patiently outside.

Lynda La Plante
Special limited edition
The Legacy/The Talisman £4.99
Two bestsellers for the price of one!

A breathtaking saga of love, desire and destiny from the
award-winning creator of *Prime Suspect*.

From the early 1900s to the 1980s, from an era of innocence to an era
of corporate power, Lynda La Plante's epic two-part saga unveils the
lives and fortunes of a family held to ransom by a proud gypsy's
curse. Available in one volume in paperback for the first time. *The
Legacy* and *The Talisman* bring gripping drama from the hottest TV
writer around.

Raised among the poverty of a Welsh pit village at the turn of the
century, prize fighting is the last chance of glory for Hugh, two-fisted
lion of the valleys, and his loyal daughter Evelyne. But *The Legacy* is a
curse no generation will ever escape . . . Sixty years later, their
hard-won fortune powers a business empire stretching halfway
across the world. Yet *The Talisman* still marks them; the curse that
made their name . . .

'A torrid tale of love, intrigue and passion . . . packed with glamour,
big business and big, big money' *Daily Express*

Tom Sharpe
Special limited edition
Wilt/Wilt on High £4.99
Two bestsellers for the price of one!

The complete *Wilt* now in one outrageous volume!

With the feckless yet all-too-mortal Wilt, Tom Sharpe created one of English literature's most enduring – and endearing – comic characters. A martyr to the sins of the flesh and a rebel against all known causes, Wilt's adventures spanned two bestselling novels and inspired a classic film.

Now available in one low-price anthology, Tom Sharpe's immortal *Wilt* and *Wilt on High* will guarantee a bellyful of wicked, riotous laughs for all lovers of satire and brainteasing literary humour.

'The loudest laughs in literary comedy' *Mail on Sunday*

'A major craftsman in the art of farce' *Evening Standard*

Colin Forbes
Special limited edition
The Stockholm Syndicate/The Stone Leopard
£4.99
Two bestsellers for the price of one!

The struggle for power, global conspiracy and the deadly workings of
international terrorism are just some of the hallmarks of Colin
Forbes's classic adventure thrillers – bestsellers in over thirty
countries around the world.

. . . thrill to blackmail, bribery and calculated murder in *The Stockholm
Syndicate* as a devastating secret strike force seeks out an enemy
attempting to control the West's economy, by any means at its
disposal . . .

. . . follow the hunt for a Resistance hero turned international
conspirator in *The Stone Leopard*, the gripping thriller which
introduced fictional hero Marc Grelle, Prefect of the Paris Police.

COLIN FORBES
'Has no equal' – *Sunday Mirror*

All Pan Books are available at your local bookshop or newsagent, or can be ordered direct from the publisher. Indicate the number of copies required and fill in the form below.

Send to: Pan C. S. Dept
              Macmillan Distribution Ltd
              Houndmills Basingstoke RG21 2XS

or phone: 0256 29242, quoting title, author and Credit Card number.

Please enclose a remittance* to the value of the cover price plus £1.00 for the first book plus 50p per copy for each additional book ordered.

*Payment may be made in sterling by UK personal cheque, postal order, sterling draft or international money order, made payable to Pan Books Ltd.

Alternatively by Barclaycard/Access/Amex/Diners

Card No.

Expiry Date

Signature

Applicable only in the UK and BFPO addresses.

While every effort is made to keep prices low, it is sometimes necessary to increase prices at short notice. Pan Books reserve the right to show on covers and charge new retail prices which may differ from those advertised in the text or elsewhere.

NAME AND ADDRESS IN BLOCK LETTERS PLEASE

. . . .

Name _____

Address _____

_____

_____

_____

6/92